kiss me slow

TIJAN • CORINNE MICHAELS
WILLOW WINTERS • LOUISE BAY

Kiss Me Slow
Copyright 2019

Ryan's Bed by Tijan
Copyright © 2018 Tijan

All rights reserved. No part of this book may be reproduced or transmitted in any form without written permission of the author, except by a reviewer who may quote brief passages for review purposes only. This book is a work of fiction and any resemblance to any person, living or dead, or any events or occurrences, is purely coincidental. The characters and story lines are created by the author's imagination and are used fictitiously.

Edited: Jessica Royer Ocken
Proofread: Paige Smith, Kara Hildebrand, Chris O'Neil Parece, AW Editing
Formatting: Elaine York, Allusion Graphics, LLC (http://www.allusiongraphics.com)

We Own Tonight by Corinne Michaels
Copyright © 2017 Corinne Michaels

All rights reserved.

No part of this publication may be reproduced, distributed, or transmitted in any form or by any means including electronic, mechanical, photocopying, recording, or otherwise without the prior written consent of the author. This book is a work of fiction. Names, characters, places, and incidents either are products of the author's imagination or are used fictitiously. Any resemblance to actual events or locales or persons, living or dead, is entirely coincidental and beyond the intent of the author or publisher.

Editor:: Ashley Williams, AW Editing
Proofreading: Kara Hildebrand, Janice Owen

Irresistible Attraction by Willow Winters
Copyright © 2019 by Willow Winters All Rights Reserved.

No part of this publication may be reproduced, stored in a retrieval system, or transmitted in any form or by any means, electronic, mechanical, photocopying, recording, scanning, or otherwise, without the prior written permission of the publisher, except in the case of brief quotations within critical reviews and otherwise as permitted by copyright law.

NOTE: This is a work of fiction.
Names, characters, places, and incidents are a product of the author's imagination.
Any resemblance to real life is purely coincidental. All characters in this story are 18 or older.
Copyright © 2019, Willow Winters Publishing. All rights reserved. willowwinterswrites.com

King of Wall Street by Louise Bay
Copyright © 2019 by Louise Bay

ryan's bed

TIJAN

This is for all those hurting from pain so deep and so dark that you don't think you'll ever be rid of it. This is for those who suffer while watching their loved ones suffer and feel helpless to take that pain away.

A note to reader that all towns and locations are fictional.

chapter one

THE FIRST TIME I SNUCK INTO RYAN JENSEN'S BED WAS AN ACCIDENT.

I'd been lying in bed next to this girl I'd been introduced to twelve hours earlier at a company picnic. My family had just moved to Portside, Oregon, from Schilling, Arizona, because of my dad's promotion, so the whole picnic had been new faces, new names, and that feeling of being the newbie on the scene. Portside wasn't huge, but it wasn't small either—maybe around twenty thousand people lived in this suburb outside of Merridell.

Robbie would know. My brother could spit out statistics because he was the family genius. Willow was the family artist. She excelled at almost everything creative, or it seemed that way. Piano. Dance. Painting. Once, she made a six-foot papier-mâché dragon that won a state competition.

Trust me. That was a big deal. She was on the local news.

Maybe that was when it started. Maybe she felt as if she had to compete with Robbie.

I'd found empty bottles of laxatives in our shared bathroom, smelled the dried puke in the toilet, and a couple of times, I'd woken up to find her exercising in the middle of the night. We were the only two sisters, so it made sense we shared a bathroom. We'd shared the bedroom too until our pre-teen years, and then we got *freeeee-dom!* (I'm saying that in the best *Braveheart* yell I can muster.)

I didn't know why she felt she had to compete with Robbie.

No one could compete with that kid. He was a walking, talking, and eating computer. Robbie wasn't ever going to be normal, but Willow and me—we were. Or I was.

I wasn't the best at anything.

Willow had been popular in Arizona. I hadn't.

Well, I hadn't *not* been popular. I wasn't in the top tier of the social hierarchy, but I was liked. Everyone knew me. Everyone was nice to me, though, thinking back, that might've been because of Willow. If someone came at me, they came at her. And she was *not* one to be messed with.

Same thing with grades. I did okay. My B+ average made me beam with pride. Not Willow. It was A+ or the end of the world. There'd been talk at our old school about raising our GPA from a 4.0 to a 4.2 scale. Willow was all for it.

Not me. That meant I'd have to try harder. No way.

Maybe that was my role in the family. I was the slacker.

Yes. I liked that. I'd been the slacker in the family—or maybe I was the lazy one. There was a difference between being a slacker and being lazy. One slacks, and the other excels at slacking. That seemed to fit better.

Yes, that was me, and I had been once again fulfilling my role when I missed Peach's door and tiptoed into the wrong room. I went in search of a glass of water and got lost trying to find her room again. It was easy to do. The place was a mansion.

I didn't realize it at the time. Both bedrooms were cool, with fans forming a breeze, and large, comfortable beds. These people were rich.

Wait, not rich.

They were wealthy. According to my sister, there was a difference.

I'd met Ryan and Peach at the company picnic—or, rather, I met Peach. I assumed she was nicknamed for her fuzzy red hair. Freckles all over her face. Blue eyes. Blending. That was what she did, just like me. I blended into the crowd, whereas Willow never did. It was the same with Peach and Ryan. She blended, and her brother didn't.

I wasn't actually introduced to Ryan, but he didn't need it. I noticed him anyway. He was that kind of guy. People noticed him, even adults.

Golden brown hair long enough that it flipped over his face and still looked adorably rumpled, hazel eyes, a square jaw, and a dimple in his right cheek—Ryan had a face girls sighed over. Even with him sitting at a picnic table, it had been apparent he was tall with a lean build and wide shoulders. Since his shirt had flattened against his arm, it was also obvious that there was good muscle definition underneath.

The guy worked out.

And judging by the look on his face, he'd been bored out of his mind.

He'd been sitting on a picnic table with two friends, not doing anything. He wasn't talking or shouting or waving his arms around. He was literally just sitting with his feet resting where people would normally sit, and he'd drawn attention. His elbows had been braced on his legs, and there was an air around him. He'd exuded a nonchalant charisma.

I wasn't the type of girl to notice a guy and stalk him from afar. No, no, I was the type to notice a guy and then notice the hot dog stand beyond him. Willow would go for the guy, and I would go for the hot dog.

Priorities, right?

But even though I hadn't talked to Ryan earlier, I knew he was popular. A person just knew, and my hunch was confirmed when two girls walked past him. They'd paused, hands in front of their faces, and whispered to each other. One of Ryan's friends had tapped his leg and gestured to the girls. He'd looked, and the girls had erupted in giggles before running away, their faces flaming red.

Meanwhile, Willow refused to come so I was on my own, sitting at my own table, feeling like a loser while I stared at all the other kids there.

They'd all seemed beautiful or remarkable in some way. And they'd all managed to find each other, like with my little brother. He'd been at a table with two other boys and a girl. All were focused on their iPads. I was pretty sure they were speaking nerd language, and if I'd walked over, the conversation between the eleven-year-olds would've gone over my head.

Again, I was the slacker of the family. I should be able to communicate with an eleven-year-old, but no. I'd been to other outings with Robbie. I knew the routine. He'd found his crowd, and I could tell he was happy.

Then again, Robbie never endured what another genius eleven-year-old might.

He was never bullied because he was smart. He was almost worshiped. People thought he was going to be the next Steve Jobs, and his classmates had caught on, already sucking up to him. Yeah, maybe there was a jealous kid every once in a while, but Robbie never talked about it. If he was picked on, I wondered if he was even aware of it.

I wondered how things would be for him . . . after. Robbie had always seemed happy. Would some of that be gone? I hoped not—stop.

Mind, back up here. Mental reverse, and back to Ryan again.

I should've known something was different from the minute my head hit the pillow in his room. I felt warm, at ease, and my body relaxed. It shouldn't have. I should've remained awake like I had been while I was in Peach's bed. They said I'd be 'better off' not being alone that night so I'd been in a stranger's bed. I was tense and gripping the sheet with white-knuckled hands, replaying in my head what had happened at my new house earlier over and over and over.

But not in Ryan's bed.

He was as surprised as I was when we woke the next morning.

He jerked upright. "What?" he asked, his mouth gaping open at me.

I grabbed for the covers, made sure they were pulled tightly over me, and I gawked back at him. That was it, really. My body was still relaxed. Only my mind was alarmed, but then my mind lost the battle. There was other shit up there that I didn't want to stir and think about, so I gave in and let my eyelids droop again.

"I must've gotten lost," I murmured.

Ryan and I hadn't talked—not at the picnic earlier when our parents greeted each other, and not when Robbie and I were ushered into their home that night. Everything was hush-hush when we got there. Mrs. Jensen had whispered something to Peach, and she gasped, her hand covering her mouth as her eyes filled with tears.

I looked away at that point. My chin had started to tremble, and I didn't want to start. If I started, I didn't know if I could stop.

So there in the darkness was the first time Ryan and I talked, and it wasn't really a conversation. He looked to the door like he should tell someone, but I said, "Please don't. I couldn't sleep until I came in here. I don't know why, but I can now. I just want to sleep."

His eyebrows pinched together. His dimple disappeared, and slowly he lay back down. He didn't say anything. A minute passed, and I realized he wasn't going to. He was going to let me sleep, and thankfully, that was exactly what happened.

I slept.

"I don't know, Mom. I woke up and she was there."

I could hear Ryan on the other side of the door.

"Well, I don't get it."

"I don't either," he grumbled.

"I thought it was weird when she didn't come back last night."

A sigh.

I recognized Peach's voice, but I couldn't place where it came from. Then it didn't matter. I was asleep again.

The bed shifted under me, and I heard a whispered, "Mackenzie." A hand touched my arm and shook. "Hey. Are you awake?"

It was Robbie. I rolled over and opened one eye. "What?"

He'd been crying. The tears were dried on his face, and I could see two fresh ones clinging to his eyelashes.

He wiped at one, embarrassed. "Are you going to sleep all day?"

"If I'm lucky."

He frowned and then glanced to the door. "I don't want to be out there alone. I don't know these people."

I scooted back until I felt the wall, flipped back the bedcover, and patted the place next to me. "Scootch in."

He looked to the door again, indecision on his face, and then let out a small breath. His tiny shoulders slumped as if he'd lost what little fight he had. He sank into the bed, clasping the covers tight over his shoulder, and looked at me, lying on his side. I moved closer, mirroring him so our foreheads almost touched.

We didn't talk, but a fresh tear welled, pooling on the bridge of his nose. I reached over and smoothed it away.

"Mom and Dad are going to be gone all day today. I checked their phone calendar."

How Robbie could do that, I had no idea, but I wasn't surprised.

"Why aren't you crying?" he whispered.

"I can't."

He nodded as if this made perfect sense. "I wish I were like you sometimes. You're the strong one, Kenz."

Strong? Was that my role in the family?

I tried to muster a smile, but I knew I failed. I probably looked like the Joker instead. "Can you sleep?"

"I'll try. Can we stay here all day?"

"I'm going to try."

That seemed okay with him. He closed his eyes and a settled look came over him, one that resembled peace. But I knew it was a lie. There was no peace. Not anymore.

"Hey, Kenz," he whispered a minute later.

"Yeah?"

"Happy birthday."

※

It was dark when I woke again, and Robbie was gone. The door was open, and I could hear the sound of silverware scraping against plates. The smell of food must've woken me, and for a moment, I was cross.

They could've closed the door. But then the fog left my brain, and I realized it was probably Robbie who'd left it open. He had a habit of doing that, and it always annoyed Willow.

Willow . . .

The small grin that had tugged at the corner of my mouth fell away.

God.

I drew in a rasping breath, and this time, I knew I couldn't keep the thoughts at bay.

※

It had been a weird smell. A rich, rusty smell, like wet metal. It made my stomach cramp, and I'd been biting my lip even before I opened the bathroom door. Willow's arm had gotten scraped earlier when we were moving boxes around the house. If she'd opened her bandage and dumped it onto the counter, I was going to be pissed. She was always yelling at me for leaving my toothbrush and paste on the counter. Everything had a place in her world, and for the life of her, she couldn't understand why I didn't remember that.

My answer was always the same: because I wasn't an anal, obsessive control freak. That usually angered her, but this time, I was going to be the one to explode. Willow wouldn't know what was coming her way. I was going to wave my arms in the air, stomp my feet, and yell like I just didn't care.

She knew how much I hated blood.

But then I was there, pushing the door open.

I don't remember when I realized what I was seeing. I suppose I felt something, because they told me later that I went into shock. My body shut down, and I left it. They said this could happen when a person experienced a traumatic event, but all I knew was that I watched from the doorway as my body fell to its knees.

My hand covered my mouth, and my shoulders jerked like I was throwing up. I learned later I'd been screaming.

Then I was shaking her, sliding on the blood on the floor, because it was everywhere. Thinking about it, I could feel it on my hands again. *Warm.* Liquids were supposed to be refreshing and cool. This was heavy. It felt no different from my own body temperature. I didn't like that. It should've felt different. Because it was Willow's, it should've felt perfect.

I stood in the doorway as I watched myself. And I kept screaming, until suddenly, I stopped. I choked on a sob, and like that, I was back in my body.

My face: dark eyes, golden blonde hair, heart-shaped chin.

My body: slender arms, long legs, and petite frame.

My heart: beautiful, broken, bleeding.

All of it on the bathroom floor in a bloodied pile.

Feeling a weird serenity, I gasped on a breath and moved next to Willow. I sat on the tile the blood hadn't touched yet. But it would. It was seeping out of her.

I knew she was already gone. Her eyes were vacant, but I wanted one more moment. My sister and me.

I lay down, just like her.

On my stomach.

My face turned toward hers.

My hand on the floor, palm up, mirroring her.

I watched over my sister one last time before we were discovered.

There was a flash of light. Someone was coming in through my bedroom—Mom. I didn't look up at her. I couldn't hear much. A dense cloud came over me, dulling my senses, but I heard her screaming, as if she were far away.

She was shaking Willow.

Time sped ahead. Time slowed to a crawl. Time was all over the place, in patches.

When I noticed the sirens, the flash of red and white outside my bedroom window, I reached over and held Willow's hand.

My face. My body. My heart—it all went with her, because she was me.

My twin sister killed herself on June twenty-ninth.

We would've been eighteen the next day.

chapter two

"Uh. Hey."

It was nearing eleven the next night. Robbie and I had been there almost twenty-four hours. I hadn't left Ryan's room except to visit the bathroom, and I was currently sitting on his bed, book in hand. He edged into the room, his hands in his pockets and his shoulders hunched forward.

I should've felt all sorts of weirdness, but I was at the point where I'd sit on the roof and not give a flying fuck what anyone had to say. Keeping my finger between the pages, I closed the book and waited.

"Um . . ." He paused, staring right at me.

He had no idea what to say. I could see the floundering on his face, but he shook it clear and a small smile showed. His dimple winked at me. He raked a hand through his hair, leaving it as rumpled as it was yesterday. I knew why those two girls had squealed. He was all sorts of dreaminess.

I waited for the spark to flicker in me. I should blush? Giggle? Sigh?

No. Nothing.

I felt nothing, and then I remembered how it felt to lay in his bed, and I knew that wasn't true. I felt some peace around him for some reason.

He scooted farther inside, glancing back at the door before leaning against his closet. "The whole my-bed thing . . ." He motioned to where I was sitting. "Did you want the bed again tonight?"

I looked down. I didn't want to see his eyes when I asked this question. "Are my parents coming back?"

There was silence, and it stretched past the point of not having an answer. He had one. He just didn't want to say it.

I shook my head, letting the book fall to the bed. Wrapping my arms around myself, I turned away. "Never mind."

He cleared his throat. "For the record, I'm not supposed to know about your folks."

I looked back. "But you do?"

The hesitancy and fear I'd seen on his face melted away to reveal the sorrow, and he nodded. "Yeah. I eavesdropped on the call. They're at a hotel. I guess your grandparents are coming tomorrow."

"Oh. Okay." I cleared my throat. "Thank you."

"Yeah." He sighed. "You don't have to thank me for anything, but I do have to know about the bed. I was trying to tell my mom maybe it was me—like, you could sleep when you were around me because of my teenage pheromones or something."

I cracked a grin. "That's a new theory."

"Hey, not all of us are child Einsteins like your brother."

"Touché, and neither am I. I'm the only normal one in my family."

But I wasn't normal anymore.

"Yeah."

Maybe he thought the same thing because another silence descended over us. It felt like a sullen quiet too, as if maybe we'd both realized the true travesty of this situation. My remark-able quality had gone from being the slacker to the surviving twin.

"Well, fuck." I breathed.

He'd been picking at his jeans but looked up. "What?"

"Nothing. Yes, I'd like to sleep in your bed, if that's okay with you."

"It's fine with me." He grinned. "It was kinda nice, waking up to find a hot chick in bed with me. My friends will get a kick out of that—"

"You aren't going to tell them!"

His eyes widened. "No. I know, I wouldn't, I mean—I'm not that kind of guy, but my sister has a crush on one of my friends. She already told him. I overheard that phone call too."

"What are you? A male Veronica Mars?"

He scoffed, but that dimple was flirting with me.

"I get bored easily," he said. "I shoot hoops to keep busy. You know, like restless leg syndrome? I have that, but it's my entire body and brain. It doesn't turn off sometimes."

"Oh."

"Anyway, Mom said I couldn't play today. She was worried some of my friends would show up, and she didn't want anything to get out." He snorted, rolling his eyes. "I'll get blamed for it, but it's always Peach who tells. She never gets in trouble."

Robbie was beloved. Willow was perfect. And I guess I was the one who got in trouble, like him.

"It's the same for me," I offered faintly.

I got blamed for the laxatives. I was the one they thought had an eating disorder. They ignored the bowl of Cheetos in front of me during the "intervention" talk.

"Mackenzie, your father and I want you to know that we love you a great deal. Looks do not define our self-worth . . ."

There'd been other times, like when Willow wanted me to ask for a treadmill. They didn't see her on it during the day, only me. She ran in the park during the day and then used the treadmill at night. I did the normal thirty minutes Coach Ellerson required from us during the off-season for soccer. I should've done more, but Cheetos and being lazy were a lot more fun.

"So . . ." Ryan pulled me from my thoughts.

I almost sagged with relief. No more memories.

He tugged at one of his sleeves. "Do you, uh, want me to stay with you? Or, I mean, do you want to sleep alone?" He rushed out, "I can do either, that's cool. You just let me know."

"What?" Someone knocked on the door. One quick, hard tap.

He groaned. "My mom said it's fine, but she's going to put the nanny cam on us. So, you know, no messing around." His head shot up. "Not that that's what I have in mind. I mean, you're hot, but you're grieving. You lost your sister, so . . . you know . . ." He flinched, cursing under his breath. "Sorry. I shouldn't have said that last part. I—sorry. I'm shutting up before I say any more shit."

"What?" I asked, hoping the upward curl of my lips resembled a grin, or better yet, something cool and maybe even seductive. "You mean you've never been asked to pretend you're a grief counselor?"

He barked out a laugh. Then his eyes darkened. "I lost a friend almost two years ago, so I kinda know what you're going through. Kinda. Not really. I mean, he wasn't my brother or my twin or anything, so it isn't the same. But . . ." He stopped himself, closing his eyes for a moment.

Loss was loss, as far as I was concerned. Yeah, there could be different degrees of it, but it was the same emotion. The only thing that differentiated was whether it came suddenly or slowly. But I kept that to myself because honestly, who the hell wanted to talk about that?

I pointed to his television and video console. "You have Warcraft?"

"Yeah." He brightened up. "You play?"

"Got a sudden urge to learn."

"All right." He grabbed a controller from his desk, found the other next to the bed, then climbed up next to me. Leaning back against the wall, his leg next to mine, he taught me how to play. His arm and hand brushed against mine randomly, and every time they did, I felt a small but warm tingle.

We played Warcraft most of the night. Robbie played with us too, until I convinced him to go to bed. Ryan and I only turned out the light when his mom stuck her head around the door.

"It's after two," she told us. "Time to sleep." She gave me a soft smile. "I hope you can sleep okay, Mackenzie."

Me too.

She gave Ryan a pointed look, jerking her eyes to a stuffed rhino on his desk. A red light blinked in its nose.

He ran a hand through his hair. "Yeah, yeah, Mom."

"Good night, both of you."

The next morning, I ventured to the kitchen for the first time and found it filled with an uncomfortable tension. They could have been sitting in silence *before* I showed up, but I doubted it. I didn't need Robbie to decipher who'd been the subject of conversation two seconds before my arrival. It was one of those scenes where you walk in and know they were talking about you.

Mrs. Jensen was at the counter, making coffee. Peach sat at the table, and a middle-aged lady—I assumed their maid or something—placed Cheerios in front of her. I had to stop and take that in. A maid. And she was wearing a blue dress with a white apron over the top of it.

These people didn't just have house staff; they had house staff in uniform. That was, like, a whole other level. *Wealthy* rich. That was what Willow would've said, and she was right. She was always right.

"Mackenzie." Mrs. Jensen sounded breathless. Her cheeks flushed a little, and she smoothed a hand down her hair. "How are you? You slept well?"

I had, and I glanced over at Ryan, who was coming in from outside. A warm breeze came with him. Seeing me, he paused with his hand still on the door's handle. His mouth formed an O, and he gripped a basketball in his other hand.

"Hey!"

Peach made a sound. I registered it in the back of my mind, but I ignored it. I could hear the disapproval in her voice, and I already knew who Peach's friends would be at school. She'd run with the snooty girls—mean, catty, and looking down their noses at peeps beneath them. Those types of girls. And in other words, most definitely *not* my type.

"Hey." I gave a brief wave, glancing to the side.

Robbie sat next to Peach, and he lifted his hand to wave before it dropped back to his lap. I noticed the toast in front of him, how it was untouched. My gaze skirted away. I didn't want to see the sadness or bags under my little brother's eyes. I didn't want to remember why.

"Uh, how about a seat, Mackenzie?" Mrs. Jensen extended an arm to a chair across from Peach.

I took the chair next to that, across from my brother instead.

She cleared her throat, holding a cup of coffee tightly right in front of her chest as if it were protecting her. "Toast, Mackenzie? Rose could get you some."

In the next moment, I had a piece of buttered toast in front of me, but I couldn't touch it. Peach circled her spoon in her bowl of Cheerios. She was glaring at me with a hint of confusion.

I lifted an eyebrow. "Yes?"

She dropped her gaze but still circled her spoon around her bowl.

Ryan dropped into the chair at the end of the table between my brother and me so he was facing the kitchen.

Both Mrs. Jensen and Rose fussed over him. What kind of cereal did he want? Oh, he didn't want cereal. Toast? Bacon? Wait, Rose could whip up some pancakes. Not pancakes? French toast, then? After the fifth question, Ryan got up and poured his own bowl of cereal, rolling his eyes as he started back to his chair.

"Mil—" His mom started to suggest, but he'd already grabbed it and poured a hefty glug into his bowl.

"Knock it off, Mom," he grumbled, hunching over his bowl. "Fuss over Peach. She actually likes it."

"I do not."

He shot her a look, his spoon poised in front of him. "You do too. The whole spoiled thing works for you. You love it."

She transferred her glare to him, giving me a respite. "You're such a jerk sometimes."

A cocky grin spread over his face. "Sometimes? I heard you on the phone with Erin. I thought it was *always*?"

Her eyes got big, and she slammed a hand down on the table. "Stop listening to my calls!" Her head whipped around. "Mom!"

Ryan shrugged. "Not my fault your voice carries through the entire house. Close your door next time." He rolled his eyes. "Might help, genius."

"Okay, you two. Stop it." Their mother decided to wade in, sitting at the head of the table. Her coffee remained gripped with both hands. A frozen yet polite smile appeared as she turned to me. "Mackenzie, you and Ryan are in the same grade. You're a senior, right?"

Miracles did happen, after all.

I nodded.

Peach's eyes were narrowed on me, watching for a reaction. I kept my face straight, but I was doing somersaults inside.

Mrs. Jensen cleared her throat. "Your grandparents are going to arrive today. They'll be picking you and your brother up and taking you back to the house . . . or . . . a hotel. I'm not sure where you're going, actually, but I know they're eager to see you."

"Grams is coming?" Robbie's head popped up.

I shot him a look. "Didn't see that on the calendar, huh?"

He rolled his eyes, but one corner of his mouth lifted. He leaned back against his seat. "I can't check everything."

"What?" I teased him. "How is that possible?"

He shrugged, but anything he would've said was cut short.

Mrs. Jensen exuded a relieved and forced laugh. "Brian told me one of Phillip's children was brilliant. That must be you, Robert."

Robert. I almost scoffed at the name no one called him except Grams.

Mrs. Jensen kept going, leaning forward to beam at Robbie. "Portside has an advanced program for gifted children like yourself. I think you'll really like it. I know sometimes the exceptional children can be outcast by their peers in other places, but rest assured—" Her voice was so cheery. "That isn't the case in Portside."

She paused, waiting for Robbie to say something.

He looked at her and then to me. His little hand fisted around a fork, and a tear welled up in his eyes. He looked away.

"Oh." The corner of her mouth turned down. "Dear."

Shit. It was time to do my big-sisterly duty. I coughed and scooted back my chair. "Thank you for breakfast, Mrs. Jensen."

She had paled, but she tried to muster another smile for me. "Yes, well, you should thank Rose. She does most of our meals. We wouldn't know what to do without her." She turned toward Rose, who paused at the sink. "Right, Rose? The entire household would fall apart if it weren't for you."

"Yes, Mrs. Jensen. Yes."

Mrs. Jensen laughed, and I tried not to wince at how fake it sounded. Her hand came to rest on her chest. "Well, I brought up school before because Peach is having a few of her friends over at the end of the week. If you wanted—"

Ryan groaned.

She showed no sign of hearing him. "—to come and meet some of them. Her friends are so well-behaved, and they're good girls. They're the type you'd want to be friends with. Right, Peach? You and your friends seem like the popular girls in your class, even though Mackenzie is a grade above you."

"Mom!" She was horrified too. "Shut up."

"Mom," Ryan drawled. "She doesn't want to hang out with strangers right now."

"Mmmm?"

I could only sit there and watch this unfold in front of me. Mrs. Jensen seemed oblivious, sipping at her coffee as if it were an IV filled with morphine. I frowned, scanning the back of the kitchen for a hint that maybe she put something else in there besides coffee. Then I felt Robbie's foot pressing into the top of my knee. He was pushed right up against the table, holding on as he stretched his leg all the way to me.

I thought I'd done my sisterly duty before, getting the attention off him, and I lifted an eyebrow at him.

He mouthed the word *bathroom*.

I nodded. "Can we be excused from the table?"

"We?" Mrs. Jensen looked from me to my brother. "Oh. Yes. Of course." Her eyes fell to our plates. "Neither of you has eaten. Okay, Rose? Can we make sure there's food left out in case they want to grab a bite later? We could order bagels if we don't have any on hand."

God. Bagels. I felt whiplash at that word.

"Willow, you aren't hungry?"

My mom never knew. Right? It wasn't that she didn't *want* to know. Right?

"Well, we have bagels, Willow. Make sure to grab one, okay? You need to start the morning off right. Snack on it during the day if you need to."

Tears threatened to spill, but nope, I would not cry. No way.

Robbie's chair scraped against the floor. He pushed it back and stood there, a look of surprise on his face, as if he didn't realize what he'd done. "Um . . ." His mouth opened— nothing. It closed. Then opened. Still nothing.

I said softly, "Bathroom."

"Oh yeah." He darted around the table, around Ryan, and hurried up the stairs.

Another uncomfortable silence descended.

I looked down at my lap because, honestly, why would I want to see their pity? I'd had to remind my little brother why he stood from the table. That wasn't normal, and nothing about our visit was. We weren't friends with these people. We barely knew them. We had no other friends or family here. I mean, I was pretty sure I was sort of friends with Ryan, but we weren't there for a fun visit.

I could feel their attention. I hated it.

Willow had wanted attention. She and Robbie. But it was on me, and not in the way I'd always gotten it before. I was the laid-back one. The one who could joke. The one in the background. The one who everyone always forgot about. I was the steady one. That kind of attention—or lack of attention—was what I liked. This attention, I loathed.

It wasn't mine to have. It had been forced on me.

Clearing my throat, I had to get out of there. I turned to Ryan. "Warcraft till my grandparents show up?"

He stood right away. "Hell yes."

He was as happy as I was to leave that kitchen. I should've wondered why, but I didn't.

We spent the rest of the day in his room, Robbie too, until the doorbell rang around seven that night.

chapter three

Shit got real once Grams and Grandpa Bill arrived.

There were tears. Hugs. Patting on the back, a lot of it. And that was between the adults.

"Have they met each other before?" Robbie asked me in a whisper. Once they turned to us, he stuck to my side. Still, he was almost mauled by Grams.

Ryan, who was leaning against the wall next to me, snorted but coughed to cover it when his sister shot him a dark look. It transferred to me before she seemed to remember why I was there. Her head hung, and she kicked at the floor. I couldn't really blame Peach. I suppose I wasn't like the other girls she knew. I mean, I wasn't crying. I'd left her bed and had stuck like glue to her brother, and the few times she'd talked to me, I hadn't been the most receptive. I wasn't rude. But I didn't respond to her the way she was clearly used to. That was Willow's role. She'd been the social one, the engaging one.

The perfect one.

I folded my arms over Robbie, pulling him back against me, and rested my chin on top of his head. "No. I think Grandma needs to cry. That's all."

Robbie found my hands and held tight. "Grandpa looks like he wants to cry too."

Standing off to the side, Grandpa Bill clutched a white cloth handkerchief in his hand. He always had one in his pocket, Grams insisted on it, but I'd never seen him use it before today. As Grams talked with Mr. and Mrs. Jensen, Grandpa Bill scrunched his nose, blinked a few times, and turned to the side. His hand came up before he turned back, and he blinked his eyes a couple more times. At the end he lifted his shoulders and rolled them back, as if he had to keep reminding himself to stand tall.

The conversation started to dwindle, and that was my cue to get ready.

I knew Grams's questions for me would start soon.

Had I known? Did Willow say anything before it happened? Could anyone have done something to stop it? Did something happen that day? I sucked in my breath, already feeling the slap of each inquiry.

"Ouch, Kenz." Robbie wiggled out of my hold. "You're hurting my hands."

I released him immediately, seeing white imprints where I'd been holding on to him. A wave of disgust rolled over me, and I replicated Grandpa Bill. Blink. Blink. Turn. *I will not cry. I will not cry.* Blink. Blink. *I'm okay.*

Lift your head.

Stand tall.

I can do this.

Robbie touched my hand, and his sympathy almost undid everything I'd shoved back. I was the strong one, that was what he said.

Head high.

I couldn't cry. Not yet.

I gave Robbie a little smile, pretending to hit his shoulder. "Ready for the adult melodramatics?"

"Mackenzie!"

Grams had heard me.

"How crass and insensitive of you! Your sister died two days ago. Melodramatic? That's what you call a grieving grandmother?"

I cleared my throat. "You're right, Grams. How insensitive of me." Willow hadn't been her twin sister, her other half, her partner from the womb. How thoughtless I was.

"Mom?" Ryan straightened. "Are you guys going to talk for a while more?"

"Uh . . ." Mrs. Jensen glanced to Grams, the question in her eyes.

"Charlotte and Phillip were hoping we could talk about the children before we went to the hotel," Grams said.

"Of course." Mrs. Jensen touched Grams's arm, and both couples turned down the hallway.

When they were out of earshot, Ryan said, "They're heading for the formal dining room. That's where Mom takes all our guests, unless she really wants to impress them. They'd go to the formal living room then. We can go back to the kitchen if you wanted to eat something."

I hadn't eaten all day.

That was odd. Was I trying to be like Willow? Was I trying to be close to her, or had I lost my appetite?

Robbie's stomach grumbled, and I squeezed his shoulders gently. "Looks like we have an answer."

Rose was in there, and it was as if she'd read Robbie's mind. A packet of pizza rolls appeared, and it wasn't long before my brother was stuffing them into his mouth. I lifted an eyebrow. "Didn't you eat today?"

He paused mid-stuff and shrugged as he swallowed a bunch of them all at once. "You didn't. I wasn't sure if I should or not."

Definitely not like Willow. I knew then. "You can eat any time you want. I didn't have an appetite today."

"Ryan, why are you acting like this?"

Peach's question came from left field. She was almost glowering in her seat at the kitchen table. She'd followed us in and locked her gaze on her brother.

He frowned. "What do you mean?"

"You never act like this." She gestured to us with a brisk motion. "All hostess and stuff. You usually can't wait to get away from guests. You're acting like she's your girlfriend or something. She isn't."

"Shut up, P. Seriously. I'm being nice, and the reason I usually leave when we have guests is because I don't like the guests."

"You didn't care when Erin came over on Sunday."

He lifted his eyebrow. "I ate a pizza at the same table with you two, and then I left. Don't make it something it isn't."

Her face got red, and if possible, her glower went up a notch. "Whatever. You're being weird."

"What does it matter?"

Robbie was on his second handful of pizza rolls. He was nearly through them all, and Rose must've noticed because she pulled out a second package. Once they were cooked, they all went on a single plate. Just for him.

"It doesn't. It's . . ." Peach cast me a look, chewing on her bottom lip. "It doesn't. Never mind."

Ryan looked as confused as I felt when he met my gaze. He shook his head, and for a moment, it was just the two of us. I knew the others were there, but they all melted away and an invisible, unbearable weight lifted from my chest. It was over as soon as it happened, but I was already yearning for the next time.

"Okay." Mr. Jensen came into the room, rubbing his hands together. He swept a look over all of us, lingering on Robbie before falling to me. "Your grandparents are going to take you with them. I guess your mother packed some bags for you two. It's all waiting at the suite."

"Are my mom and dad going to be there?"

My throat burned, and I was glad Robbie had asked the question. I couldn't bring myself to voice the words.

"Uh . . ."

And like his son the night before, Mr. Jensen gave me the answer without saying a word.

Shoving back my seat, I avoided his gaze and said to Robbie, "Come on. We gotta be strong for Grams now."

"I don't want to be."

I whipped around to face him. "Robbie! Just . . . come on."

His lip started to tremble, and I experienced instant self-hate. Taking his hand, I pulled him with me. "If you're still hungry, we can make Grandpa stop at a drive-thru somewhere."

I wanted to stay.

I didn't want to have to be strong for Grams either. I didn't want to see Grandpa struggle to keep from crying, because he too had to be strong for Grams, and I really didn't want to think about how the last time I'd seen my mother, she'd seemed all too relieved to see me go.

I held tight to Robbie's hand until I heard him hiss. I relaxed my hold. "Sorry."

"It's okay."

But it wasn't. Nothing was okay anymore.

We were halfway to the car when Ryan called my name. I looked back, stopping as Robbie kept going. Ryan was coming down the sidewalk, the house door closed behind him. Everyone else had stayed inside. Glancing over my shoulder, I could see Robbie settling into the car. Grams was already seated, and Grandpa headed to the driver's side. He'd left the back door open for me.

"Hey," I said.

Ryan stopped, and a flurry of expressions flashed over his face. Doubt. Confusion. Then wariness. He started to rake his hand through his hair, but he realized what he was doing and stopped.

He laughed shortly. "I do that all the time. My hair's always a mess."

"It suits you. You look cute."

His eyes widened. "Oh. Thanks."

I shrugged. It was the truth. Well, it made him hot, not cute. But I kept that to myself.

He looked back at his house, like he was deciding whether to say whatever he'd come out to say. He slid his hands into his pockets. "Are you going to be able to sleep okay?"

Ah. The bed. "Are you going to miss me?"

His dimple winked at me, teasing. "Maybe." The other side of his mouth curved up, and I realized he had a second dimple. "For real, though. Are you going to be okay? Your Grams doesn't seem the most soothing type, you know?"

"Oh boy. I know." I tried to grin but failed. Ignoring his question, I said, "Thank you."

"For sleeping with you?"

"That too. Thanks for spending time with me. I know I'm . . . not really myself."

"With reason."

"Yeah." I had to get going. I probably had three more seconds before Grams would be lowering her window to call for me. "Look—"

"My sister isn't that bad," he said.

"What?"

"My sister." He pointed over his shoulder toward his house. "I could tell you thought she was a spoiled bitch, and yeah, she can be that. But she isn't always. I think she wanted to be friends with you."

"Why?"

Ryan looked as if he was trying not to laugh. "You're kidding, right?"

I wasn't. I didn't know what he meant. Two seconds. I was already bracing to hear Grams's voice. "I should go."

"Nolesrock at gmail. You can email me if you want. It goes right to my phone, and I'll get an alert. I can call you if you want."

I opened my mouth, but I heard the car window coming down and swallowed my thanks. Before Grams could say anything, I remembered I didn't have my phone. I'd dropped it when I saw Willow.

Willow . . .

"I'll email you," I said quickly before hurrying into the car.

I wanted to look back to see if Ryan had stayed to watch us go. But I didn't. I didn't know why. And as soon as we got one block away, I regretted it. I wished I had looked, but again, I couldn't explain why. I just did.

Then Robbie said what I was thinking. "Ryan's cool."

Yes. Yes, he was.

COUNSELING SESSION ONE

"Hello, Mackenzie. My name is Naomi. Your parents thought it was a good idea if you had someone to talk to during this time, but I want to help you in any way you need. So, why don't you tell me where you'd like to start?"
"I want to leave."
And I did.

chapter four

One month later

"Counseling isn't working," my father said. "She won't go to most of the sessions, and it's been a month. What about Arizona? Should she go back home?"

I shouldn't have been eavesdropping, but the temptation was too great. They'd been in the kitchen talking about what to do with me for the last twenty minutes, and I finally gave in, moving from my room to sit at the top of the stairs.

And no shit, Sherlock.

The whole push for counseling had started right away. It was Grams's idea, and everyone except me agreed with it. I'd fought hard, but nothing I said made a difference. So, I resorted to some stupid-shit tricks. And I say stupid shit, because it was as basic as I could get. I didn't go. Literally. If they dropped me off, I went in and left once the car moved ahead. If they parked and waited the whole hour, I went out through a back door.

The only way I would've stayed the entire hour was if one of my parents went in with me, and I knew that wasn't happening. Deep down, they were about as fond of counseling as I was. So, no, it wasn't working. After a few missed appointments, the counselor called my parents, and I don't know what they discussed, but something shifted. I bargained down to one session every other month. That was the most I'd agree to, and anyone who thought it wasn't enough could suck it. It wasn't their twin who died.

"Nan Jensen was telling me about the Portside Country Club," my mom replied. "They have programs that Mackenzie could attend. Her daughter goes to them with her friends. She says they're very beneficial for her daughter, teaches her respect and how to act like a lady."

My dad's snort told me his thoughts on that suggestion. "What about back home? That'd be more beneficial, wouldn't it?"

"You want to fly her back and forth the rest of summer? I don't think that would be helpful. Besides, you can't push her Arizona friends like that. I talked to Emily and Amanda."

"Who are Emily and Amanda?"

"You know, Emily Christopherson and Amanda Green. Their daughters are Mackenzie's friends in Arizona—"

"The ladies you had your wine walks with?"

I almost smiled as I imagined Mom bristling. Dad thought the wine walks were stupid. Mom thought they were the next best thing to going to church.

"Yes. Those ladies." Her voice dipped low, almost a growl. "But I talked to them about Zoe and Gianna. They said they want to be there for Mackenzie, but you know how it is. Teenagers don't know what to say, so they hold off."

"Isn't that the same with adults?" Dad griped. "We haven't heard from Tony and Danielle since the funeral."

Silence.

A sniffle. "Well, we're talking about Mackenzie's friends right now—"

"If they don't want to support their friend, then that's on them. We have to deal with the here and now, and getting her into some form of activity is the best idea. She needs to be busy. She needs to be . . ."

I leaned forward, my hand wrapping tight around one of the stair posts. What was he about to say?

"What?" More sniffling, but she sniped back. "She needs to be gone? Away from us?"

"Tell me who Nan is again." He was resigned.

This was fight number I'd-lost-count. This was what they did. They thought Robbie and I were sleeping, so the checkered flag dropped, and off they raced. They couldn't get to fighting fast enough.

They assumed too much.

While they made sure Robbie was tucked in bed with his lights off, I got only a gentle tap on the door and a "You in bed, honey?" The term of endearment was on a rotating schedule. Every fifth night was *honey*. Others were *sweetheart, baby girl, my sweet daughter,* and *Kenzilicious,* and to answer their question, I never was. My light was always on, but they left after I replied with a loud and clear yes.

I shouldn't complain. We'd spent a week with Grams and Grandpa, and it was a week too long. Our parents had been busy while we were away.

I didn't know the specifics, but they got a new house. Then there was the funeral. It was in Portland because they'd buried Willow where we could visit her. We flew back to Arizona for a memorial service, though. It was more for everyone there—Willow's friends, my friends, our parents' friends, and relatives.

When we came back, we'd gone straight to the new house. I called it the new-new house since it was the second one we'd had in this town. Everything was already there for us, which was weird. In the new-new house, I didn't share a bathroom with anyone. There were four bedrooms. My and Robbie's were upstairs, and we each had our own bathroom. Our parents' room was on the main floor, and we had a guest room in the basement.

There was no room for Willow.

She'd been the only one who'd already decorated her room in the first new house. No one else had completely unpacked.

Willow . . .

An image of Willow in her casket flashed in my head—no, I wasn't going there.

My phone beeped.

I grabbed for it, silencing it so my parents didn't know I was eavesdropping. Again.

Unlocking the screen, I saw the text was from Ryan. A warm fluttery feeling spread in my chest.

Ryan: **Going to the movies with friends tonight. Want to come?**

Movies? I checked the time. It was after nine. I typed back.

Me: **Late movie?**

Ryan: **Yes.**

Me: **What movie?**

Ryan: **It's the new superhero one. You in?**

I didn't care about the movie.

Me: **Yes.**

I wanted to see Ryan, even if I had to sneak out.

We'd emailed at first. That had progressed to him calling our hotel room. Once I got a new phone, we texted daily.

He mostly asked how Robbie was. I asked how Warcraft was. He'd asked twice if I could sleep okay. I never answered. The answer was always no, but that was depressing. I didn't want my conversations with Ryan to be sad. Everything else was steeped in sadness, but I didn't want it to touch him. Not anything to do with him. We'd seen him and Peach once. They came to the hotel to go swimming, but that'd been it. Robbie and I had been holed up in the new-new house for weeks.

Ryan: **Sweet. Pick you up in ten minutes.**

Ten minutes? Wait.

Me: **You know where I live?**

Ryan: **Yeah. My friend lives next door. Be there in ten.**

For the first time in a month and one day, I hoped my parents would keep fighting. I sneaked back to my room and dressed. My light was off, but to be safe, I did the whole pillow-acting-like-a-human-body under my covers.

Slipping out, I didn't need to worry about going to the back door. The fight was still fully engaged. My parents never saw me on the stairs, and I headed out the front door. I was waiting on the curb when a car pulled up in front of me.

"Hey!" Ryan rolled the passenger window down and gestured to the back seat.

Another guy was driving, bobbing his head up and down in rhythm with the bass blaring from the radio. He watched me where I stood, faint curiosity in his eyes.

"We gotta pick up one more. Then we're good to go," Ryan told me as I got in.

Once I'd settled, the driver started off, and Ryan twisted around. He pointed to the guy next to me, who held up a hand. "This is Tom Sanderson and Nick Lumoz."

Nick was the driver, and he held up a hand but didn't look back. "Yo."

Tom nodded again, a friendly smile on his face. Both guys looked gangly. Each had their hair spiked like Ryan's and wore Portside High School shirts.

"Is this the chick who—"

Ryan cut Tom off. "Yeah, so shut up."

I caught the regret and sympathy that flashed in Tom's eyes. They knew about my sister.

"Tom's the guy Peach likes," Ryan explained.

"Ah, man." Tom groaned, slinking down in his seat. He'd been tapping his hands on his legs but moved to cross his arms. "It isn't something that's supposed to be acknowledged. It's the thing no one talks about, you know? Why'd you have to say something?"

"Because it's wrong. All sorts of wrong."

Nick snorted. "You didn't think that way when my sister liked you last year."

Ryan turned sideways, facing the driver. "Because that was last year, and your sister's hot." His eyes flicked to mine, and he amended, "Not that I was interested in her."

Tom snorted. "Right. Because that's why." He turned to me. "Nick's parents split, and his sister went with her mom. He stayed with their dad because of basketball, and us." He patted Nick's seat. "Right? You couldn't leave us. That's why you didn't go with your mom."

Nick scowled in the rearview mirror. "Thanks for blasting my personal shit. No offense," he added, looking at me.

Tom guffawed. "Whatever, man. And I said my thing because we know something personal about her. I felt it was fair."

"Fine." Nick leveled him with another look. "Then I'll tell her how you'd really like to date Peach, but you don't because of Ryan. You're too worried about losing him as a friend. How's that feel, buddy?"

"You do?" Ryan turned fully around.

Tom closed his eyes and heaved a deep sigh. "Oh God. This sucks."

Ryan frowned. "You actually want to date my sister? Since when?"

"Since never now," Tom grumbled under his breath.

"Since May," Nick said. "Since Parker's party where they kissed."

"You kissed my sister?"

"Shut up, Nick! You made your point. I'll never share another thing about you unless I have your written approval."

"Good. Glad we're clear."

"Crystal," Tom snapped.

Ryan sat back, waiting for the exchange to conclude and then turned to me. "My friends are idiots. They aren't usually like this."

"Yeah, we are," Nick and Tom interjected at the same time.

Ryan nodded. "Okay. They are. But . . ." He raised his voice, giving both a meaningful look. "Maybe *they* can simmer down? At least for the night or until after the movie?"

I shook my head. "Please. Keep going. I'm enjoying this."

Tom held up a hand, and Ryan narrowed his eyes. "Don't think I'll forget hearing about you and my sister. I know you talk on the phone, but kissing her is a whole other thing."

"They kissed twice."

"Shut up, Nick!" Tom yelled.

"Okay." A satisfied smile stretched over Nick's face. "Now I'm done."

"You're such an asshole."

Nick lifted a shoulder as if to say *meh* before slowing the car and pulling into a driveway. I assumed another guy was coming out, so I was surprised when a girl came out the front door instead. Long, beautiful brown hair bounced behind her as she hurried down the sidewalk. Ryan stepped out as she approached.

"You got shotgun," he told her. "I'll sit in the back."

"What?" Then she got in and saw me. Understanding dawned as Ryan sat next to me. "Oh."

"Cora, this is Mackenzie." Ryan gestured between us. "Mackenzie, Cora."

"Hi." I waited, tensing slightly. You never knew what would happen if you encroached on another girl's territory. I was the new girl, and I was ready for the bitchy comment, but nothing came.

Only a tiny bit of hurt flashed in her very aqua eyes before she tucked her hair behind her ear and looked down. "Hey." The word was a soft mumble.

I felt bad. I didn't need to be Robbie to know what that look meant. She liked Ryan.

And judging by the way Ryan shut his door and said, "Ready to go!" he had no clue about her feelings.

The other two were quiet, watching Cora.

They cared about her, and she cared about Ryan.

I'd stepped into something. I let out a soft sigh.

"You okay?" Ryan asked, lowering his voice.

Nick had pulled out of the driveway and turned the music up louder. Cora looked over and mouthed *thank you*.

We drove with the music surrounding us for a while. Nick wasn't talking. Cora wasn't either, and Tom had settled back, looking out his window.

I turned to Ryan, unsure of my place. "Are you meeting any other friends at the theater?"

He shook his head. "Nah. Just us." He gave me a thoughtful look. "I wasn't sure if I should ask you about the movie. Tom said the lights have been shutting off early. Since you guys hadn't come over again, I thought maybe you were on lockdown."

The knot in my stomach—the one that was always sitting there—loosened a small bit. I'd forgotten. This is how it had been with him before. And he wasn't going to ask about the memorial service. He wasn't going to ask how awful it had been to sit with my friends, who suddenly didn't know what to say to me. I wouldn't have to explain how they'd either stop crying or cry even harder when I walked into a room. He wasn't going to ask about Willow's boyfriend and how Duke couldn't look at me, how *no one* could look at me.

I was there—the face they wanted but not the person they wanted.

With Ryan, in this car, I wasn't Willow's surviving sister. I was just Mackenzie.

I nodded. "Kind of. I think my mom wants me to get out of the house and do more stuff."

"That's perfect. We're doing shit all the time. You can hang with us."

As Ryan said that, I caught Cora watching us from the corner of her eye. Her lips tightened a bit at his suggestion.

"Uh, yeah. Maybe."

"We're hitting up a party later tonight, if you want to come to that."

The invite came from Tom.

I lifted a shoulder. Old Mackenzie wouldn't have gone—that was more of a Willow thing to do—but everything was different.

A party sounded like the best thing ever. "I would, actually."

Cora lifted her head, giving Ryan a wolfish grin. "Erin's going to freak."

The other two guys started laughing.

I frowned. "Peach's friend Erin?"

Ryan hardened. "Yeah, but she's kind of an ex of mine too." He leaned forward, raising his voice, "And I can do whatever I want."

Peach's friend who was also Ryan's ex, and she was going to freak because I was going to a party with him. This was the second situation I'd stepped into.

Lovely.

Cora glanced back at us. "She even has a hard time with me, and Ryan and I have been friends since second grade."

My lips thinned. "Let me guess. She's popular at school?"

Cora's eyebrows lowered. "She's one of the most popular girls in school, even though she's a junior this year. Stephanie Witts is the one from our grade."

I raised an eyebrow. "Is she coming tonight too?"

Cora shook her head. "No, just Erin."

Nick spoke up. "Erin's included because of Peach and . . ." His eyes darted to Ryan, and he shut his mouth.

Coughing, Tom said quickly, "But she isn't the hottest." He was smiling at me like he wanted to reassure me. "Don't worry. You're way hotter than she is."

Cora squeaked.

My knot tightened back up.

"Tom." Ryan glared at him. "Shut the fuck up."

"What?" Tom gazed around, blinking. "What'd I say?"

Cora shook her head, trying not to laugh. "You honestly need to get a clue one of these days."

Tom looked mystified. "Huh?"

Nick pulled into the movie theater's parking lot. We all piled out of the car, and the guys headed in first. Cora fell back to walk next to me. She looked up, tucked some hair behind her ear again, and dropped her gaze to the cement.

Her hand touched the back of mine lightly. "Can you hold back a second?"

I stopped.

Ryan and the guys were going inside, and he glanced toward us. Holding the door open, he stood there, waiting.

I saw the question in his eyes and had to pull my gaze away. Cora was saying something. It seemed like something I needed to pay attention to, but all I wanted was to be next to Ryan. I didn't care about this Erin girl. I probably should've. My brain was telling me to be smart. I was entering high school drama. Ryan was wanted, but I wasn't surprised. He had *that* look—dark molten eyes, broad shoulders, trim waist. Both of those dimples. Lean, but muscled. His shirt rode up once, and I saw the six-pack there.

I'd noticed all this on day one.

He was going to have girls after him. Of course.

Willow would've been after him.

I blinked a few times, shocked at that thought. Yes. She would've. And I would've done nothing. After seeing that she'd claimed him, I would've melted into the background, found my own group of friends, and I would've had no problem in school. All these issues—Cora and the ex—these would've been Willow's battles.

Was I taking her stuff on?

"So, you know." Cora had finished whatever she was saying.

I cringed, but I had to ask. "Sorry. I spaced for a bit there."

"Oh." She frowned. "You lost your sister, right?"

I nodded.

"Look, maybe it isn't my place, and I know we just met, but people have been talking about you. They don't know about your sister. I mean, I haven't heard any of that. Ryan made us all promise not to say anything, and I'm guessing he threatened Peach too. She has a big mouth, so if it got out, it would be from her. But anyway, she told Erin you slept in Ryan's bed when you were there, and Erin freaked." She rolled her eyes. "Erin could be inside, which is why I'm saying all this to you now. Ryan doesn't think things through sometimes. He doesn't think Erin's as bad as she is, but she's evil incarnate. I swear."

"Does she come at you sideways or straight on?"

"What?"

I wasn't a fighter, but an eerie calm settled over me. "I need to know how to fight her, so how does she fight? Usual catty-bitch way? You know, saying shit behind my back and verbal jabs. Or is she a face-on bully kind of girl? There are all different sorts now."

"Um . . ." Cora looked at the sky, her hands sliding inside her back pockets. "She has bleached blonde hair, and she'll be surrounded by a whole bunch of girls. They all look the same. Glitter on their face, something pink. If she sees you inside, don't go to the bathroom. She has a gang. They'll come at you and try to hurt you but make it look like it was an accident."

She was the type to sic her friends on me. I nodded. "Got it."

"Wait."

I had turned to go but looked back.

Cora seemed surprised. "Aren't you scared?"

An image of Willow lying on the floor, her blood pooling around her, flashed in my head. "Not a goddamn bit."

I started off. I was looking forward to this.

chapter five

I KNEW INSTANTLY WHICH ONE WAS ERIN.

She was the tall drink of water trying to cling to Ryan as they waited in line for tickets. She kept putting her hand on his arm, and he'd move it out of the way, shrugging off her touch.

It wasn't working.

He was irritated, and he wanted her away, but his scowl and the way he kept messing his hair up were having the opposite effect on her. The blonde could-be-a-model only stood closer each time he rebuffed her.

Nick and Tom were already in line for snacks, along with a group of girls. I didn't need two guesses to know they were Erin's friends. Cora was right. They all looked the same—with tight jeans and different shades of pink sweaters, glitter all over their faces and necks.

Cora came up next to me. "That's her."

There was a mix of envy, fear, and caution in her voice. It hit me in the chest. This girl was reacting to the ex the same way she would've reacted to Willow. Willow *was* Erin. I couldn't believe it, but it was true. The way she was standing, the way she whispered in Ryan's ear—that was how Willow had been with her last boyfriend, and how she'd intimidated his previous girlfriend. She'd been scared of Willow the same way Cora feared Erin.

For some reason, that pissed me off.

Then Ryan saw me, and with his wave, the beast saw me too.

Her demeanor changed. Gone was the seductress. Her eyes grew cold, and her lips formed a sneer.

Hello, cold-hearted bully.

I fought against grinning. This girl was trying to intimidate me.

It was working on Cora, who shied away from her place beside me. She actually took two steps away, and I looked at her, meeting her gaze so she knew I knew.

I grunted. Well, screw it. I'd take Erin on alone.

I turned back to regard the ex again.

She was smug under a layer of frostiness. She assumed I would be afraid of her.

Her mistake.

Something came over me. It'd been itching at me since I heard about this Erin girl, but right then, it was like a blanket wrapped around me. It wasn't a supporting or warm blanket. I wasn't being enveloped like that. It was eagerness. It was anticipation. It was . . . I had a target.

This girl wanted to make *me* the target, but no, honey. It wasn't going to work that way. Even if she knew about my sister, I wouldn't have cared. I was fast feeling the first peak of adrenaline.

I had an outlet, and I went straight at her. No hesitation. No lagging. I wanted this fight, consequences be damned. I had nothing left to lose.

Surprise flared in her eyes, but then the authoritative look returned to her face. She expected me to bow down to her.

My lip curled. She had another thing coming.

"Hey."

Even Ryan was cautious around this girl. I was beginning to wonder what powers she had tucked away for this reaction.

"I got you a ticket," he added. He glanced at Erin before handing it to me. "Here you go. I wasn't sure if you had money or not."

I gestured behind me. "Give it to Cora."

If he was scared of this bitch, then fine. I'd buy my own ticket. He hadn't asked me on a date. He'd asked if I wanted to go to the movies. But instead of pulling out some cash, I continued staring at Erin.

She narrowed her eyes. "Do you have a staring problem?"

"Move." I loved that simple command, and I stepped even closer. I was almost in her personal space. "You're in my way."

My voice was strong and clear. No break. No trembling. No softness. And I wasn't being aggressive. I wasn't tense. She *was* in the way. The ticket guy was right behind her.

"Oh." She moved aside, but only barely. Folding her arms over her chest, she was still in the way. There was enough space for me to move forward, but I'd have to hunch to the side, stand awkwardly, and feel her breathing down my neck to get the ticket.

Fuck that.

I stepped right up to the counter, my arm jabbing into her.

She cried out.

I turned to look her right in the eye, our faces inches apart. "Then *fucking* move."

She gasped, but I ignored her and bought my movie ticket.

After I pocketed my ticket, I turned to her. I was an inch taller, but I had to give her credit. Cora said Erin could've been a model, and she was right. The funny thing was—so could I and so could have Willow.

I'd never cared for our height. Sometimes I hated it during soccer, but I almost reveled in it while I stood toe to toe with Erin.

There were other people behind us, waiting to get their tickets, but I wasn't going to be the first to move. No way. I couldn't. She'd made this a pissing contest, and I wasn't going to be the one to falter.

So there we were, standing ridiculously close, staring at each other. Her eyes were heated, her sneer reinforced, and I was dead inside. I had no problem showing her that.

You can't battle someone who's lost everything.

Erin broke first. She whipped around and left, her hair flicking over her shoulder.

As soon as she did, I moved to the side so the next person could get a ticket. Her friends flanked her immediately, and she paused to glare at me. I stared back. I couldn't look away first. She had to do that too. This was her home turf. Not mine. I had to win both battles to have even footing.

Cora moved beside me. Ryan was off to the side, frowning.

"That was unexpected," Cora said, moving closer. "No one's been able to out-Erin Erin before."

She was impressed. I felt nothing inside.

Tom and Nick headed our way, their hands full of soda and popcorn.

"What'd we miss?" Tom sounded damn chipper.

Ryan studied me a moment before glancing to where Erin had disappeared, but all he said was, "Are we ready for the movie?"

"Let me take one of those." Cora took a soda, leaving with Tom for the theater.

Nick held back, giving Ryan and me a look before turning, popping a kernel of popcorn in his mouth, and following at a more sedate pace.

Ryan stayed with me. As soon as they were out of earshot he said, "I'm sorry about Erin." I felt him move a little closer, his arm brushing against mine.

I waved that off. I didn't even care about his ex-girlfriend. "It isn't a problem," I assured him. "Really."

"I knew she could be a bitch, but I haven't seen it like that in a long while. I can talk to her—"

"No!" I grabbed his shirt, and my hand formed a fist in it. "Don't."

He frowned. "She can't be a bitch. It isn't right."

Was he clueless about how girls worked? I shook my head. "Let it go. I can handle myself, but word to the wise." I nodded in the direction his friends had gone. "I've got a feeling she's been a bitch behind your back to Cora."

His head moved back a centimeter. "You serious?" His mouth pressed in a hard, flat line.

Good. I liked that he cared about his friend.

It was good that he cared, and that look told me so much.

He'd do something about it.

He was like Willow in that regard. If she saw an injustice, she did something. Unless *she* was the injustice.

My stomach twisted.

I had been that friend, the one who wouldn't do anything. I never had to. Willow fought our fights for us.

I felt nauseated thinking about that, and I suddenly, didn't want to think about it. I didn't want to think at all anymore. I didn't want to have memories in my head, making me feel things I couldn't handle.

I was ashamed. I should've been this person before . . .

No. Stop thinking. Stop feeling. "Let's go watch the movie."

Ryan gazed at me a moment longer and then nodded. "Okay."

Once we sat, once the lights turned off, once the move started, I let the first tear fall.

chapter six

I PASSED ON THE PARTY AFTER THE MOVIE. NO ONE PROTESTED WHEN NICK TOOK ME BACK TO my house, and I suppose it was partly because they all had the same survival instinct as I did. No shock there. Heads would roll if I went to that party, and I wasn't sure if it'd be mine or Erin's first.

Ryan crawled out right behind me, and I turned around. "Wha—"

He ignored me, shutting the door, and tapped twice on top of the car.

Nick rolled his window down, but before he said anything, Ryan leaned close and smirked. "Don't be reckless, kids. Use safe drinking protocols. You know, lick the salt *before* you shoot the tequila. And no backwashing."

Nick flashed us two fingers. "Peace." His eyes slid me up and down. "Use a condom, children."

Tom started laughing, and the car shot forward.

Cora was in the back, her face resembling a sad owl's as she watched us until they turned onto the next street.

"That one is Tom's house." Ryan pointed to the house to the left of mine. A lamp was still on inside. "We were all out at Nick's, and Tom told me about his new neighbor, asked if you were the same girl who'd crawled in my bed." His hands slid into his pockets, and he hunched his shoulders forward. His shirt strained against his form, showing off those muscles again. "I'm glad you came to the movie. I thought it was a shot in the dark."

I was glad he'd texted too. And I was surprised at that, but I was. Even dealing with the ex was a good distraction.

I tilted my head to the side. "Did you really not know how mean your ex is? She seems like the resident bully."

He hesitated before letting loose a long sigh. "Guys don't see that stuff. I'm not using that as an excuse, but we usually focus on the good stuff about chicks. Boobs, you know. Other stuff." He gave me a half-grin. "I've heard rumors, and Peach told me a few things, but seeing how she was with you tonight—and how you handled it—that was eye opening." He chuckled softly. "It's the same with girls, you know. You don't see the shit guys do to each other."

"Is that supposed to make it better?"

He shrugged. "No. Just the way it is. And for what it's worth, I feel like an asshole for not knowing how bad Erin is."

A brief flicker of anger had sparked, but it fanned out, and I shrugged. "I think I was spoiling for a fight. I can't take it out on my parents like a normal teenager. They're in this thing called mourning."

I bit back a grin, but Ryan saw it. His right dimple showed.

"Did you want to come in?" I gestured to my house. It was completely silent and dark.

The other dimple winked at me. "I was hoping. If you don't want to go in right away, we could sneak into Tom's house. His parents are in San Diego, and he's staying at Nick's tonight."

I eyed Tom's house. "He's okay with you sneaking in there?"

"Yeah. We've done it before, use someone's house if it's empty, you know."

I suddenly didn't want to know any more. "You know how to get in there?"

He nodded, watching me. He was waiting.

The thought of going somewhere that was not my home had my mouth watering. And that place was empty. No parents. No Peach to stare at me weirdly. No crazy ex girlfriend. No little brother in the room where my sister wasn't. No worrying if he'd hear me crying when I couldn't sleep at night.

"Let's go." Decision made.

"Yeah?" he asked.

I nodded.

"Sounds good. We should go to the back. It's easier not to set off the alarm there."

Ryan led me to the backyard and pulled the hidden key from under a plant. Unlocking the door, he keyed in the code and returned the key a second later. I slipped inside, and he turned the system back on.

I rolled my eyes. "Tom's parents must be geniuses."

"Eh. They're no Robbie Malcolm, but I'm sure they do okay." He gestured to a picture where a couple stood with one of the older living former presidents. "They go golfing with that guy."

And I was reminded that Portside was not Schilling, Arizona. Cripe's sakes. They knew one of the presidents.

Yeah. *So* not Schilling, Arizona.

Ryan chuckled. "We aren't any better. We use the fake frog, though the alarm system is the real backup."

"Yeah." I joked. "Remind me tomorrow to tell my parents to install infrared security system. I'm thinking we could use a handprint machine. Fuck the fake frog."

He laughed, leading the way inside.

As we walked toward the kitchen, a different feeling settled over me. We were alone. I'd wanted to get away, but maybe I hadn't thought this through.

I hadn't been thinking anything through, not for a whole month.

Ryan nodded toward the kitchen. "You want a drink? I know where they keep the good stuff."

My stomach rumbled.

He heard and flashed me a grin. "Or something to eat?"

"You know where they keep that stuff too?" I teased.

"I can make an educated guess."

I ended up sitting on a stool by the island while Ryan scored leftover pizza. He popped the pieces into the microwave and pulled out two glasses.

I lifted an eyebrow. "You and Tom must be close." He acted as if this were his house.

"Since second grade." He ducked down to pull out a bottle of whiskey. "He won't care. Trust me."

"You bring girls to his house often?"

He laughed, pouring some lemonade to mix with it. He took a sip before pushing it my way. "No, but he brought a girl to my place once. More than once. My family was on vacation, and he asked, so since then, it's a given. If one of us has an empty house, it's an open invitation if we want to use it."

"You've done that before?"

"I haven't, no." He looked at me, his eyes darkening.

Our gazes caught and held, and I felt a tickle at the bottom of my stomach. It was a good feeling, a thrilling one, and I held my breath for a moment because I didn't want it to go away. The knot next to it relaxed, and maybe this was what I'd wanted since Ryan texted. I wanted to be around him. I could sleep.

I could feel normal, just for a while.

He took his glass and gestured to mine, the pizza in his other hand. "Let's head downstairs. Feels weird going anywhere else."

I followed him down to a large sectional couch that formed half a square. It looked like one large bed, and Ryan crawled onto it, scooting to the rear. He placed his glass on the back of the couch, which looked like it had been made for that purpose. I hesitated, but he patted the spot next to him, picking up the remote.

"I can grab us blankets and pillows too, in case."

It felt so weird, but it also felt so right, and that made it even more jarring. For whatever reason, I was becoming addicted to this boy.

When I still hesitated, he lowered the remote. "What's wrong?"

"This."

"Us?"

I shrugged. Yes, but I felt stupid saying it. "I don't know."

He frowned and tilted his head to the side. "We're hanging out."

Okay. I nodded. I could do that. Hanging out. "You're right."

"That's it."

I nodded again. "Yeah."

"So." He looked at the spot next to him, and I climbed onto the couch, scooting to sit beside him.

After that, no words were needed.

It wasn't that I didn't want to talk, but Ryan put on a movie and seemed content to eat his pizza, watch the show, and sip his drink. When mine was emptied, he went upstairs for refills, but the same thing happened. He returned to the couch, scooted back, and started the movie again.

It was my second movie of the night, but I couldn't remember either of them. The only thing I remembered was relaxing. That was it. Willow, my family—they were all pushed to the back of my mind, and I felt everything start to unravel inside me.

I fell asleep during the movie, scooting down to lay next to Ryan. And at some point, I felt him get up, but he came back. He placed a blanket over me, and I curled into it, once again falling asleep.

When I woke, he was on his back beside me, one of his hands on my side.

He had fallen asleep like that, like he was protecting me.

chapter seven

"Mackenzie."

I woke to Ryan saying my name and gently shaking my shoulder. "Wake up. We gotta go."

"What's wrong?" My eyelids were freaking heavy, but I sat up. A big ass yawn on my lips.

"Tom's parents are home."

"What?"

"We gotta go. Quick." He scrambled off the couch, and I could hear footsteps above us.

"Was Tom here last night?" a woman's voice asked. "I thought he was at Nick's."

More footsteps, and a man's voice rumbled, a murmur through the ceiling.

I hurried after Ryan. He led me up some back stairs and then circled through the garage and to a side door. A door was open between the main floor and garage, and I heard the woman ask, "Was he drinking?"

The male voice grew louder. He was coming toward us. That was when I saw the car doors still open. They were unpacking.

"He had the pizza. The whiskey's out, but I can't tell if he drank any of it."

"We'll definitely have a talk with him," the man replied.

He was right there, almost to the doorway.

Ryan slipped out the side door, and I pushed him the rest of the way. We clicked the door shut moments before we heard heavy footsteps from the garage.

Ryan shot me a look, letting out a deep breath. "That was close."

"Too close."

"I'll call Tom. He'll cover for us."

"We'll owe him one."

"No." Ryan shook his head. "I'll owe him one."

I didn't agree with that, but he looked determined.

We moved out of the yard and headed up the driveway to my house. I couldn't hear or see movement inside, but I knew my parents were probably having coffee. That was what they liked to do since Willow. Before, they would've been rushing through the kitchen, yelling at us. We all would've been rushing around, whether it was a weekend, weekday, or summer day. There were always activities to go to.

The quiet creeped me out.

"Are you going in?" Ryan asked.

I twisted around. I'd been standing on the front steps, staring at the door. I must've looked whacked out, like some space cadet who couldn't sleep by herself, couldn't handle being around her family, and couldn't even bring myself to walk up to the porch.

"You're too nice to me."

"What?" Ryan stepped closer.

I saw that he had his phone in hand. "Are you going to call Tom?"

"Yeah. I'll let him know what happened last night so he's prepared in case they call when they're done unpacking the car."

I nodded. Yes, that would be soon. It didn't look like they had much more to do. "I suppose you should call now."

"Yeah."

But he wasn't. And I wasn't leaving.

We stood there. I watched my front door. He watched me. We sounded normal. We probably even looked normal, but one of us was very much not normal.

"Why are you doing this?" I asked.

An irritated huff came from him. "Is this the same thing as last night? You and me?"

"You and me, you being nice to me, doing this. Are you going to get in trouble?"

"The only one who might get in trouble is you. Tom will cover, say he stopped by earlier for food and that's it. Trust me. This isn't our first rodeo."

But why was he being nice to me? Why was he going out of his way to help me? We didn't even kiss, so he wasn't doing it for an easy hookup. He was just sleeping next to me.

"Stop. Okay? Stop." He touched both of my arms, coming to stand in front of me. "I can see the wheels going in there. Stop."

"But why—"

He cut me off, his hands squeezing once before falling away. He stepped back. "Because I want to."

"But why do—"

"I don't know, okay? I don't know either. I . . . I don't know either. It is what it is. I don't want to think about it any more than that."

And that was the end of it. The questions plaguing me went away as if he'd silenced them. We didn't have a formal goodbye. I nodded and slipped inside my house. The door was unlocked and the alarm off, so one of my parents had already been outside this morning. Once I was inside, I went to the living room window and watched. Ryan continued to stand in our driveway a moment longer before heading back down the road.

"Good morning, honey." My mom sailed past me on her way to the kitchen.

No, "Oh, you're up," or "Where were you last night?" or "When did you get home?" Just "Good morning, honey."

I followed her to the kitchen and stared. She never looked at me—not while she filled her coffee cup, not while she put a piece of bread in the toaster, not while she poured some orange juice in a glass. Her head remained down as she buttered the toast.

"Would you like some breakfast?" she asked. "I'm making some for Robbie. I can put more bread in the machine for you."

My stomach had rumbled last night, so I said, "Sure. Yeah."

And she did, putting two pieces in before pushing the lever down. Then she picked up the plate with Robbie's toast and the orange juice.

"Be right back for my coffee," she said over her shoulder as she left.

She took him *his* food. She was coming back for *her* coffee, and me? I buttered my own toast.

"I know you snuck out last night. I saw you."

My door was open an inch, and Robbie was there. I would've teased him about being a creeper except for the sadness, yearning, and caution that filled his eyes.

"Hey, kiddo." I was at my desk and slid the chair over enough to toe open the door. "You come around these parts often?"

A soft giggle was my reward, and he came in, bouncing to a seat on the bed. His eyes calmed.

"So you caught me, huh?" I smiled, leaning back in my chair. "What do I owe you? You didn't rat me out to Mom and Dad."

He rested his hands next to his legs and lifted his shoulders. "You were with Ryan. I knew you were safe."

"Yeah?"

His cheeks pinked, and he looked down at his lap. "Ryan's cool."

"I agree."

"Did you sleep together again?"

For a moment, I had no words. It sounded wrong, that sentence coming from my eleven-year-old brother.

"Uh . . . what?"

"Sleeping next to him helps you sleep. I overheard at the Jensens' house, and I assumed there was a reason you were in his bed." He lifted his hands, folding them in his lap. "Is that why you left last night? So you could sleep?"

He thought I left to sleep. Then again, maybe he was right. It wasn't about seeing Ryan or sneaking out and giving a silent middle finger to my parents. I sighed. Robbie was too young to deal with any of this—with Willow's decisions or mine.

"Forget about me. How're you doing?"

He'd been kicking his feet back and forth, but he paused at my question. He looked away. "I'm fine."

"Hey." I scooted my chair closer and tapped on his knee. "I mean it. How are you?"

He looked back, and my heart was almost ripped out. Unshed tears hung on his lashes. "I'm fine." His voice trembled.

We'd been there for each other before the funeral, during the funeral, and I'd like to say afterward, but I couldn't. Since we'd come back to Portside, I'd shut down. Literally. Going to see Ryan last night had been almost the first thing I'd done besides going from my bedroom to the kitchen or bathroom. Seeing his tears made me want to curse myself.

"Hey." I gentled my voice even more. "If you need anything, you can come to me. You know that, right?"

"Where'd you go?"

"We went to the movies."

"Where'd you sleep? At Ryan's?"

"I . . ." The words were stuck in my mouth. He looked at me, completely innocent and vulnerable, and I contemplated lying to him. That was what it was. Not telling the truth was a lie.

I shook my head. "We came home. I was going to come in, but we snuck into his friend's house. He lives next door to us."

"And you slept there?"

I nodded.

"Good. You look better today. And I didn't hear you crying last night."

"I didn't know you could hear me."

He bobbed his head and jumped up from my bed. I could see his mind whirling. He was already thinking about whatever he would do next in his room, and he headed for the door.

"You cry every night. I'm glad you didn't last night." He pulled open my door. "You should do that every night." And then he was gone.

I could've looked down to see my beating heart at my feet. He'd ripped me open. Again.

COUNSELING SESSION TWO

"Hello, Mackenzie. It's been a while since our last meeting. Would you like to talk today?"
"No."

chapter eight

It was almost another month before I saw Ryan again.

He traveled with his family and then went to New York to see his grandparents. He was all over, including a wilderness camp. We texted back and forth, but when he was finally home, my parents shipped me off to Arizona. It was supposed to be four days where I'd heal with my friends, but some major miscommunication happened somewhere between the parents. They set it up, but the friends I used to cry with, laugh with, and who I thought had my back didn't show up. Strangers did.

Zoe and Gianna spent most of the time talking to each other, laughing over someone's tweet, and they forgot I was there. No joke. I was watching television in Gianna's basement when I heard the door shut upstairs, and the house was quiet. They'd gone. I checked on social media and saw they were at the community pool, but I wasn't going to get mad. I mean, seriously. Fighting with Erin was fun. She was someone I hadn't known since second grade. She was someone I hadn't shared chain letters with or plotted with on how to get even with Mia Gillespie in fourth grade when she stole Zoe's boyfriend.

Erin was easy. There was nothing emotional there, but my two old best friends—too much history.

Instead, I booked my own flight back home and ordered a car.

It was close to midnight when I texted Ryan, telling him I was outside his house. The driver's taillights were disappearing when he came out the front door.

"Hey." Dressed in lounge pants and a soft shirt, he folded his arms over his chest, tucking his hands under his arms. He eyed my small suitcase. "You really came straight from the airport?"

"Was this stupid?" A normal girl might've had that thought in her head. But my head? There wasn't enough room for second thoughts in there. I gestured to his house. "Should I go home?"

"No." He'd hunched over a little but straightened and shook his head. "No. It's fine. Seriously." He went back to eyeing my luggage. "I thought you were joking about the airport. I could've picked you up."

"Oh." That meant a lot. "No, this is fine. Simple. No fuss. That's how I roll these days."

He fought back a grin. "Except when we break into my buddy's house to spend the night, right?"

I laughed. "Except for that."

"Come on." He jerked his head toward the house before reaching for my suitcase. "My mom has book club tonight, which is aka wine night, and Peach is at Erin's house."

"Your dad?" I had to admit it felt nice as I stepped inside, warm and cozy. I hadn't known how cold I was until then.

Ryan closed the door behind me, locking it. "He's downstairs watching the baseball game. He DVR-ed it, and trust me, by the time it's done, he'll be a full case in. He'll either sleep down there or head straight to bed. I've had friends over before when it's a baseball night for him, and he had no clue." He stepped around me, moving quietly. "You want something before heading up?"

I fought back the smile this time. "Going right to it, huh?"

He glanced back, and his eyes darkened. "You know what I mean."

"I do." I shook my head. "And I'm good." My stomach rumbled, which makes Ryan's eyebrows rise. "You sure? Your stomach says otherwise."

Thinking about it, I didn't know when I'd last eaten.

I ate breakfast Thursday morning. My mom drove me to the airport two hours later. There was a meal offered on the plane, but I didn't eat it. Gianna's mom picked me up, and we went to a pizza place. I picked at a slice, but I couldn't bring myself to chew it and digest it.

Zoe and Gianna had eaten popcorn that night while we watched movies. They'd laughed. I'd curled in a blanket and tried to sleep.

Then this morning, I had orange juice and coffee. That was right. Zoe and Gianna went to the coffee shop and brought back bagels and lattes. I had one of the lattes. Lunch was licorice for them, which Gianna's mom didn't approve of. She made a big salad, and the other two nibbled on it, but they were too full from licorice.

And this afternoon they'd left me.

I hadn't eaten on the plane again, so it had been almost two days.

I shrugged. "Maybe a drink?"

He clipped his head in a nod. "Got it." We went upstairs first, and he stowed my luggage in his room before returning to the kitchen. I went into his bathroom, grateful it was attached to his room, and by the time I'd cleaned up and felt a little refreshed, he was back, carrying a glass in each hand and a bag of chips in his mouth.

"Here." I started to take the bag, but he shook his head and held up one of the glasses. I took that instead, and as soon as I did, he opened his mouth.

The bag of chips fell to the bed and he took a sip from his own glass. "Mmmm . . ." He winked. "Rum and Coke. Good stuff, right?" He clinked his glass to mine and then settled on his bed, moving back to rest against the wall. The chips went on the stand next to him, along with his drink after a second good sip.

He had a loveseat against the other wall in his room, and I perched there. Fuck. This drink was good. I craned my head back, staring at it. "I could down this whole thing in two seconds."

"So do it." He opened the chips and popped a couple in his mouth. Grinning at me, he added, "Not to tread where you might not want me, but I'd think you'd want to pass this year in a drunken haze. I would."

Yeah. I drank a third of it before leaning back against the couch. "It isn't my style."

It would've been Willow's, though. She would've drank, partied, and become a nympho if I'd been the one . . .

My throat burned, and I took another long drink. Shit. This really was good. Two more sips, and I'd need a refill.

I eyed Ryan over the top. "You aren't the type to take advantage of me, are you?"

He chuckled. "Nah." He winked. "But I might graze the side of your boob when we're sleeping later."

I laughed and stopped immediately.

Shit. The last time I'd laughed, the last time I'd smiled, had been with him—not my old friends—or ex friends—and not anyone else. Just Ryan.

"Does it get better?" The question was out before I could take it back.

Ryan was quiet, holding my gaze across the room, and then he sighed. "I think it has to, at some point."

God. I hoped so.

Pain I didn't want to feel or acknowledge rose in my throat. It threatened to choke me, but I sat there. I waited, and it passed. I could breathe again a second later.

I finished my drink.

Ryan scooted forward, handing his glass over. "Here, take mine."

"It's yours."

He shrugged, eating more chips. "I'll down a beer later, maybe. Trust me. It's fine."

I took the glass, feeling his fingers on mine for a moment, and a warm and cozy sensation settled over me. It was the same tingle I'd felt when I had stepped into his home. Everything else was flat, black and white, gray, dull, cold, and then I went to him, and it felt like color was turned on.

I could feel hunger again, thirst again. I remembered it was normal to feel warmth.

Feeling the choking come back up my throat, I turned off my thoughts. Life was easier that way.

"You're staying here tonight, right?" Ryan asked.

"Hmmm?" My shoulders sagged in relief. Thank you, Distraction.

He gazed around his room. "You're sleeping here. That's why you came, right?"

I nodded. "If that's okay with you?"

A slow and wicked grin spread over his face. His eyes darkened, falling to my lips. "I'm a nice guy and all, but I'm not *that* nice, and especially lately, so trust me when I say this. You can sleep here any time you want." His head leaned forward, his eyes almost digging into me. "That offer doesn't go to anyone except you."

The back of my neck warmed. I almost felt tongue-tied. "Thank you, and yes, that's the plan."

"But what about your folks? Won't your friends or their parents say something when they realize you skipped town?"

I shook my head, feeling the booze loosening me up. "I left a note for Gi's parents, but that was it. I doubt they'll even notice till tomorrow morning."

"You serious?"

I nodded. I should've felt sad about that. I felt relief.

"Gi and Zoe didn't want me there. I knew it. They knew it. The parents didn't care, but my friends have moved on. They have new lives."

"That's bullshit."

Maybe. I drank half of Ryan's drink instead of caring. "They loved Willow too. They were my best friends, but Willow and I were a package deal. I was friends with her friends." I gestured to my face. "You weren't at the funeral. It's easier to forget Willow than to mourn her." I remembered the disgust I saw on Duke's face. "Her boyfriend couldn't get out of there fast enough. He had his hands all over Serena, Willow's best friend."

"Yeah. Well . . ." Ryan balled up the bag of chips and tossed it across the room. It landed on the desk next to me. "People suck. Trust me. I get it." He stood, pointing to my glass. "I'll bring the ingredients. We can mix drinks till we pass out, huh?"

He left, so he didn't see my response.

I was smiling so damn hard, and I wasn't even sure why. All I knew was that I was happy when he came back. I could relax in this room with him, and I laughed until we did exactly what he said.

We passed out around three in the morning, after I drank myself into oblivion.

It was the best night I'd had in a long while.

chapter nine

I WOKE THE NEXT MORNING AROUND EIGHT.

I would've freaked, but Ryan rolled over, put his arm over me, and tugged me in for a side-hug. "No one's here," he murmured. "Trust me. We're good."

He was right. Even two hours later, the latest I allowed us to sleep, no one was around.

"My dad golfs on Saturdays."

"What about your mom? Peach?"

He yawned, raking a hand through his hair as he padded to the bathroom. "Mom's probably sleeping. Her book club doesn't mess around. When they drink, they drink." I heard the shower turn on, and he yelled over it, "And gossip. They wine hard and gossip hard."

I stood, edging to the opened door. I almost gulped, but he didn't seem to care. This was a different level of intimacy. Then again, maybe it was because we'd slept together. Yeah. That was it. Either way, I was feeling nerves and flutters in my stomach that I didn't recognize. I'd never felt like that. Ever.

"What about your sister?" I asked, not moving inside the bathroom.

Ryan looked over, his hair getting mashed down from the water, and he gave me a side-grin.

God. A whole new level of flutters exploded in my gut at that sight.

The shower doors were frosted, so I couldn't see anything from his chest down. But I could see the silhouette of his body, and I think that was enough. My whole neck and face were getting warm now.

"She won't be back till this afternoon, or even tonight," he drawled. "She might stay till tomorrow too. We could hang out all day, if you wanted."

I perked up at that suggestion—no home, no angry or absent parents. But also no brother who I knew needed me.

I shook my head. "I can't." But wait—I remembered a conversation. Robbie was going somewhere today. "Wait. Maybe I can."

"Yeah?" He was shampooing his hair, and I tried not to watch as the suds fell down his body, his nice lean body, the body that felt so strong when he held me.

I tore my gaze away. Was I becoming like Willow? Was that what was going on? I couldn't see her, talk to her, be with her, and so I was starting to *become* her?

I grabbed my phone and sent a text.

The shower turned off, and I kept my head down as Ryan stepped out and began toweling off. He came back to the bedroom, going to his closet as my phone pinged a response.

Robbie: **Mom and Dad are taking me to a school. I thought you knew? Where are you?**

"What?" I typed back a response.

Me: **What school? I'm coming back early.**

"What's wrong?" Ryan came to sit next to me. He had jeans on and bent over to pull on socks and shoes. He was close enough that I felt the brush of his shirt before he sat up and leaned backward on his bed.

"Robbie's going to some school today."

"Oh." Ryan snapped his fingers, pointing at my phone. "There's a private place not far from here. All sorts of gifted and smart kids go there."

I twisted around to face him square. "You're joking." My stomach took a nosedive. I wanted him to be joking. This school was made up, a figment of his imagination.

"What?"

He wasn't. This had become my new nightmare. My phone pinged another response from Robbie, but it almost fell from my hands.

They were taking him away. I knew it. I could feel it.

Willow had left, and they were taking away Robbie.

Who was next?

"What's wrong?" Ryan leaned forward again, his voice soft. He took the phone from me, reading Robbie's message aloud. "It's fine. I want to go. I'll see you tonight. Love you, sis."

He handed my phone back, but I almost didn't want it. And seeing that, he put the phone on the bed, tossing it by his pillow.

His shoulder nudged mine gently. "You okay?"

No. I was *so* not fine. I didn't know if I ever would be again.

But all I said was, "I'm down to hang out today."

Sometime between grabbing an early lunch—where Ryan ordered food for me and didn't give me a say in the matter—and returning to the house, our plans changed.

We walked in and heard shouts and laughter coming from the backyard.

"What?" Ryan frowned, tossing our bag of food onto the counter and going to the back door.

Peach ran in, opening and shutting the door behind her. She didn't see me but greeted Ryan with a wide smile. "I call pool party today!"

"What? No."

"What?" She mocked him, fluttering her eyelashes. "Yes. And get ready, douchebag. Your friends are coming over. I called 'em. And some people from your grade. Stephanie Witts and her friends are already here."

"Mom and Dad okay this?"

Peach didn't answer. She'd spotted me, and I watched the life drain out of her. "Oh. You."

I rolled my eyes, but Ryan beat me, saying, "She's a friend. Back the fuck off, Peach."

Her mouth snapped shut. His growl worked wonders.

The doorbell rang, and the door opened. "Yo, Ryan!"

Tom, Nick, and another guy barreled in. They stopped short when they saw me. They didn't give Peach a second look. It shouldn't have pleased me, but it did.

Tom's eyes went wide. "Hey, Mackenzie. I didn't know you'd be here."

Nick added, "Yeah, long time no see. You ditched us after movie night."

The third guy pointed to me. "This her?"

The back of my neck got hot. "Are you asking about my sister?"

"Sister?" the guy echoed.

"No. Erin, man," Tom told me. "You took her down. You're infamous."

Nick rolled his eyes. "He means you're a big deal in our group. At least among the girls." His eyes went to Peach then, who still stood watching the exchange. "Hey, Ryan's little sister." He tossed a smirk at Tom, who seemed flustered.

Tom went into the kitchen, and Nick lounged back against the wall, his eyes sliding from Peach to the rest of us.

Ryan ignored all of it, asking around a clenched jaw, "You guys knew about this?" He nodded to the backyard, and I turned to inspect what was happening.

A bunch of girls stood around the pool, clad in bikinis, and there were a few other guys with them. I recognized Erin and assumed those were her friends, but there was a separation out there. Some girls were in the pool and playing a game with a bunch of guys while Erin and her friends stood on the sidelines.

"Yeah. Your sis put the word out. Pool party at the Jensen household. Everyone's coming." Nick was still salivating over Peach's uncomfortableness.

She looked down at her fingers, picking a nail.

I felt Ryan's gaze and looked over, meeting his eyes. I saw the apology there and knew our hangout had been replaced with a party with a bunch of his friends. I shrugged, trying to give him a small smile to let him know I was okay.

I didn't want to be there with them, but I wanted to be there with him. I'd take it how I could get it. This was better than an empty house, and I wasn't going to turn my phone on. An hour ago, Gianna had sent me a text asking why I left, but she was almost twenty-four hours too late for me to respond.

"So," Nick said. His grin was wicked. "Peach. Do anything fun last night?"

She turned and fled.

As soon as she closed the patio door, Tom was across the room and punching Nick in the arm. "You're such an ass!"

"What?" Nick laughed, rubbing at his arm as he moved down the wall, closer to where Ryan and I stood. "It isn't my fault you were texting with your buddy's little sister."

Ryan's eyes clamped shut, and his hands moved through his hair. He pulled them out, leaving his hair sticking up in an adorable mess. Swinging stormy eyes over his friends, he grabbed Tom and shoved him against the wall. "You're into my sister?"

"No!"

Nick snorted. Even I knew that protest was too much.

Tom's shoulders slumped down. "I don't know. We were texting last night. She asked where you were, if you were hanging with us, and it kept going from there."

"He texted with her for three hours. I heard the damn phone beeping the whole fucking game."

Tom shot Nick a glare. "There's no way you could hear my phone. We went to the summer league basketball game. The entire gym was loud as hell."

Nick shrugged, his wicked grin still there. "I stand by what I say." His eyes were hard. "It's wrong, and you know it."

Ryan rolled his eyes. "Whatever." He pushed Tom back against the wall again, but there wasn't much heat in the action. "Don't fuck with Peach unless you're going to marry her. Got it?" He tapped Tom's cheek and then swung his gaze my way.

The third friend grunted, his hand in the air. "Uh . . ." He cleared his throat. "You're insanely hot."

Tom and Nick grinned, and the tense moment was gone.

"Hands off. Ryan laid claim long ago," Nick said.

Ryan pointed between the newcomer and me. "Pete, Mackenzie. Mackenzie, Pete." He added, "Pete's Nick's cousin. He visits when he wants to get high."

"Yeah," Nick drawled, throwing his arm around his cousin's shoulder. "He comes to the cool table then."

Pete shrugged off his arm. "Hate to break it to you, cousin, but Ryan's the cool table. He's the basketball star. Not you. You aren't good enough"—he began edging backward, his arms already in the air as if to ward off a hit—"at anything!"

"Shut it." Nick went after him, delivering two quick punches to Pete's side. The two wrestled before Nick ended up pinning Pete. Only then he flicked him the forehead and got up. "Loser."

"Asshole." But Pete was grinning.

They were both grinning, and when both were on their feet, I waved to Pete.

"Nice to meet you."

"You too, and I go to Frisberg. It's a few hours away, so I'm not around that much, but if I do show up, it isn't just to get high, Ryan."

Ryan only grunted in response. He didn't seem to care too much.

Nick added, "We call him Peepee sometimes. Feel free."

"Hey!"

Peepee rounded on Nick, and soon insults were flying back and forth. But Nick eased up on the jabs at Tom.

After everyone raided Ryan's kitchen, we headed upstairs, drinks and snacks in our arms. I was thankful we'd made the bed before leaving, and I was doubly glad I hadn't left anything behind, putting my suitcase in Ryan's truck, where it still was. No questions, just the way I liked it. And finally, I was glad the guys continued giving each other shit as they sat to play Warcraft.

They weren't watching me because of Willow, and unlike the movie night, as I sat in Ryan's room and listened to his friends joke, I felt normal. It was small. And I knew it'd be gone soon, but I felt it, and I savored it.

"Hey! Fuck no, man!"

"Ah!"

Tom and Nick had the video controllers, and as Tom bent to the side, trying to get his car to turn all the way left, Nick jumped up and down. He bit his lip. His eyebrows were furrowed in concentration, and I knew at any moment the room would explode in cheers or curses—probably both.

I glanced to the door and saw Ryan watching me. He gestured with his head to follow him out, and I scooted off the bed as Nick won the race.

He dropped the controller and thrust his arms in the air in victory. "YES!"

"NO!" Tom shook his head.

Pete stuffed a handful of chips in his mouth and reached for Tom's controller. He mumbled around a mouthful, "My turn."

I slipped out of the room.

Ryan waited at the end of the hallway, nodding for me to keep following him.

I trailed behind. He led me down a back way to the basement. We could hear footsteps above, along with giggling.

I arched an eyebrow. "Let me guess, the female brigade is above us?"

Ryan ducked his head as he opened a refrigerator. "We're out of drinks in the room, and I know my parents keep more booze down here. The guys will want more to drink. Peach and her friends can have the main floor."

I gazed around, noting the more casual-looking décor. It was one large room with a living area on one side and a kitchen on the other. There was a pool table in the back, along with a basketball game, two couches, and three super-sized beanbags in front of a large television screen. Two wooden tables sat in the kitchen area.

It looked like every teenager's dream apartment. The only things missing were a movie projector, a popcorn machine, and maybe a stage for karaoke.

Willow would've salivated over the room.

Ryan pulled out some more rum, and I slid onto one of the barstools.

"Is this where you guys really hang out?"

He nodded. "Tom's too." He looked at me. "Well, you know that."

"Is Cora coming over?"

Ryan was done with the drinks. He moved to the cupboard and pulled out bags of chips and cookies. Then he slid some Cheetos toward me.

"That's a negative on Cora."

My eyebrows went up. "What do you mean?"

"She tends to avoid anywhere Erin might be." He paused and amended, "Usually."

Ah. I nodded. "Doesn't want to get thrown to the wolves, huh?"

He pressed his lips together, closing the cupboard and leaning against the counter. He seemed to be choosing his words carefully. "Cora's never liked to go anywhere Erin is. We didn't know why. I knew it had to do with Erin, but Cora never explained it. I did shoot her a text, though." He pulled out his phone from his pocket and showed me her response.

Cora: **If Erin is there, hell no.**

"She's never said it so clearly like that before." His eyes seemed to soften. "I think it's because of what you did. I would've listened to her before. She just never thought I would."

"You seemed oblivious to Erin's bullying, so I don't blame Cora."

"I know." His hands gripped the counter. "Erin and I didn't really have a relationship. We just fooled around during a time last year, but it's on me. I should've paid more attention."

Well, that made me feel bad. I shrugged. "Give yourself a break."

His hands relaxed.

"Most guys are idiots," I added. "They don't see past the boobs and smile."

He groaned, his eyes sparking. "Thanks for that." He began to gather the drinks and snacks.

I took what was left and slid off the stool. "No problem. I believe in realism. I like to keep my friends grounded. The more realistic they are, the more humble they seem to be."

"You mean you squash their egos into the floor."

"That too."

As we headed back, Ryan turned around to use his back to open the door. Our eyes met and held, and I felt an instant sensation. It was us. No sister problems. No exes. No bullying. Nothing. Just him and me, and I let out a soft sigh before I realized it.

His eyes warmed.

I'd had this feeling before, but it was stronger this time.

I coughed, lifting my foot. "You caught me at a disadvantage today. I like to really grind my friends' egos into the ground with heels. The sharper the better."

He grinned, shifting back a step. "Thanks for that. I needed it."

"Always here for you. Call me Ego Crusher."

He barked out a laugh, and his hand touched the small of my back.

It was a tiny gesture, a silent touch, but it wiped away my amusement. I'd started to laugh, and then it was gone, transformed into something else. My body warmed like it had last night, and the feeling intensified, as if it were supposed to be the two of us, as if everyone else was the outsider and not wanted.

I suddenly didn't want to leave that basement, didn't want to deal with everything that lay beyond these walls. My breath caught in my throat, and my eyes watered. I blinked rapidly. A surge of grief rose up, but I stuffed it down. It was too strong, too threatening. I couldn't handle it.

"You okay?"

No.

I never would be again. Didn't he know?

I sighed. "You're having a pool party. You ready to par-tay?"

He shook his head. "That's right."

chapter ten

THE GUYS DECIDED THEY SHOULD BE "SOCIAL" AFTER ANOTHER HOUR OF PLAYING VIDEO games. Should be. Yes. Because they wanted to be polite not because they wanted to drool over girls in bikinis. It had nothing to do with all the bare skin running around Ryan's backyard.

I joined, but I was the non-social one. I was fine to pop in my music and hang on my own. The booze had simmered me out. Ryan checked on me a few times, but I reassured him I was good, and he finally went over to his friends, laughing and doing what was expected of him. Erin was there too, her friends in tow. They all basked before her, as if they were trying to catch whatever sunglow she had in excess. Peach kept shooting her nervous looks.

From my vantage point—on a lounge chair in the corner—I saw again what I'd noticed earlier. There were two groups of girls—Erin's group and another clique. I assumed they belonged to the infamous Stephanie Witts. A couple of them were in the water with some other guys, playing a new game of dunk basketball.

As I watched, one of the girls caught the basketball but turned and glared at Erin.

One of the girls from that group walked by me, and I asked her, "What grade are you?"

She stopped, seeming surprised by my question. "Senior." Then her lip curved up and she sneered at me.

Silly me. She was a popular senior. Who was I to talk to her?

I ignored my desire to flick her my middle finger and lay back down. With my sunglasses in place, I resumed the antisocial role.

I plugged my earbuds back in and "Glory" from Dermot Kennedy filled my ears. I filled my lungs. Sitting there, with all these strangers around me, in a social scene I didn't care about, I was having a come-to-Willow moment.

What was I doing there?

This wasn't my scene, not even if Willow had been with me.

I would've been home. I would've been with my soccer friends, and if they'd wanted to go and scrimmage, I would've tried to talk them out of it. Seriously. Netflix and junk food were way more appealing.

This was Willow's scene.

She cared about popular girls, about popular guys. She would've already scoped out who to maim, who to kill, whose ass to kiss, and who to fuck.

Her world whirled around me.

Their laughter sounded like kids playing on a playground as it filtered through the music. I was in a self-assigned tornado, and everyone else seemed fine.

Why couldn't I be normal?

Why didn't I even want to try?

I felt tears fall from my eyes, trickling down behind my sunglasses, and I didn't care. I never moved. I didn't wipe my eyes. I wasn't going to stop them, but I also wasn't going to keel over in sobbing hiccups. That wasn't me either.

I didn't even remember the last time I'd cried before Willow.

She was the sobbing, melodramatic twin. Everything was ending if she got dumped, if she did the dumping. If a friend betrayed her, God forbid, her life was over . . .

Bad choice of words there.

I thumbed over to the music, hitting the next one. I needed a change of tempo if I was going to stick with socially appropriate behavior.

"I Need My Girl" by The National was next.

Oh, for fuck's sake.

I hit forward again.

"Sleep Baby Sleep" by Broods.

Shit.

I should hit it again, and my thumb lingered over the button, but I couldn't.

The words made me remember that night.

She had been on the floor. Her eyes had been vacant, open. The blood had pooled around her.

I had laid down, my head next to hers, my hands in the same position. Her blood surrounded me, and it had felt like mine.

We would lay together. She would tell me a secret. I would pretend to be excited to hear it.

That's what we did before, and I pretended that's what was happening that night as I had lain there.

God.

Fuck.

Shit.

My tears had tripled into a steady flow, and though I hadn't moved, I knew people would eventually notice.

Letting my music blast, I got up and went inside.

The world was better this way. Having tunes in my ears, I could handle the looks, the questions, the vibes people sent my way. The music protected me. I was in my own world. I didn't have to feel their shit, whatever it was. It was me and the music—and somehow Willow.

I felt her everywhere.

I'd planned to go upstairs to Ryan's room, but I glanced back.

He and his friends were in the pool playing with the others. That same girl who'd sneered at me was hanging on Ryan, attempting to dislodge the ball from his hand. Erin's group watched from the lounge chairs I'd vacated. Their heads were bent together as they glared at the other girls. Still others were tanning and or laughing on the sidelines.

They were all normal.

I was not.

And I felt her with me.

Suddenly, like she had pulled me there, a blast of anger rose in me.

I wasn't going to take on her life. That wasn't my role.

"Fuck you, Willow," I whispered under my breath as I turned my back on them. I hurried upstairs.

I wanted to grab anything I'd left up there and leave because that *was* me.

"Hey."

I turned to find Ryan standing in his doorway, his hair wet and water dripping down his chest. He frowned. "You're leaving?"

Another round of *fuck, shit, damn* ran through my head. Let's say it again, folks.

I scowled, flicking away a tear. "Yeah." I wanted to say more, but my throat wasn't working.

"Why?"

Let's go for broke. All the religious swear words flared in my mind before I could speak. "It's, uh . . ." I gestured behind me, in the direction of the pool. "I shouldn't be here."

He repeated, "Why?" His frown turned to a scowl.

"Why do you think?"

He blinked, and his face changed. A sheepish look came over him, and his shoulders hunched forward. "I wasn't thinking."

"Hanging with you is different from taking on the full social scene down there." Another pointless hand gesture. "I thought I was fine, and I like your close friends, but this is too much." I looked out the window. "I think I'm just going to go home."

"Let's go."

"What?"

His hand was in his hair as if he'd spoken before thinking. He blinked a couple of times and nodded. "Yeah." His shoulders lifted. "I'll go with you. Your suitcase is in my truck anyway."

"Ryan—"

"Look, you don't really say much, and I've got a feeling I'm the only one you *are* talking to, but I know things at your house are sad. And that's reasonable, but when you feel like shutting the world out, you don't have to do that to me. I'm not everyone else."

My heart had been ripped out of my chest, and he was putting it back together.

I laughed but felt my chest growing tight. "Willow would've been all over you."

I hadn't meant to say that.

His eyes grew keen. "Yeah?"

God. What was I saying? I wasn't Miss Talky-Shary, but this guy? I shook my head. "Why do you affect me so much?"

"I affect you in a good way, right?"

I bobbed my head. He already knew he did.

"I'll sneak in."

I lifted my head. "What?"

"So you can sleep." He nodded to himself again. "I know where you live, and your room's on the west side? I'll sneak in, every night if you want me to."

"Second floor."

"I can climb up. You have that big tree by your window."

"You won't get in trouble?" He could sneak in and stay until I fell asleep. "If you get caught?"

He shrugged that off, a cocky smirk tugging at his lips. He tucked a hand in his swimming shorts' pocket. "We can improvise, but my mom never checks my room after midnight. I'll come over after, climb in, sleep. I can set an alarm and slip out before anyone knows. As long as I'm back in my room by seven, I'm good."

A few hours would be nice.

"Okay." I was still unsure, but I needed sleep. If I became a zombie, the world was in trouble.

There was a stampede up the stairs.

"Dude!" Tom, Nick, and Pete rushed in, breathless. "Man! We—oh."

They saw me, and it was like they'd hit an invisible wall.

Tom gave me a nod. "Hey, Mackenzie. How's it going?"

Pete rubbed his forehead.

Nick rolled his eyes to the ceiling.

Tom frowned, glancing at them. "What?"

Ryan took two steps toward him and punched him in the shoulder. "You're being weird. Don't be weird."

"Ouch!" Tom rubbed where he'd gotten hit. "What was that for?"

"We were talking." Ryan wasn't messing around. He glared at Tom. "What do you want?"

Nick and Pete began snickering.

Tom shot them a look, his hand falling away from his shoulder. "We got a text. Mullaly is having a party, and the girls are going over there." His eyes lit up again, and he turned toward me. "You want to go, Mackenzie?"

But before I could answer, he was looking back at Ryan. "We were rushing up here because Nick's brother said he'd get us booze, but we gotta go now. He's heading to Lakeville for a college party—"

"Let's go to the college party." I winced. The words were out of my mouth before I realized what I was saying. What the hell was going on with me?

This was not me. I didn't care about college parties. If I'd been to one before, it was because someone forced me or tricked me into going. I would've needed to be promised Taco Bell on the way home, and maybe I would've tried to go in my pajamas. A good fluffy robe was hella sexy.

Ryan's eyes snapped to mine.

Tom's eyes went round. "What?"

Ryan studied me a moment, as if he were looking for something I wasn't sure was there. I don't know whether he found it or not, but he turned to Nick. "Would that be okay with Ben, if we went with them?"

"Um . . ." Nick's lip twisted.

"Let me ask him," I suggested. *Okay, then.* I was throwing all caution to the wind.

The guys glanced at each other, and another round of: *what the fuck am I doing?* circulated my head.

I didn't even think Willow would've done this, or maybe she would have. Maybe she wouldn't have been happy with tackling the seniors. She might've moved on to college guys. I knew she'd started talking to one before we moved. Duke didn't know it, but he'd been about to be dumped. *Sorry, Duke.*

I wanted . . . something different.

Apparently, a college party was it for me.

"Nah. Um . . ." Nick frowned. "I'll text him quick." He glanced at Ryan before adding more quietly, "I can tell him you're coming."

Ryan's jaw clenched, and he jerked up a shoulder. "That's fine."

I glanced between the two, noticing how quiet everyone else got. "Uh, what's going on?"

They all looked at Ryan, who shook his head briefly. "It's nothing. Ben's a big b-ball fan. He'll want to shoot the shit with me for a bit."

"Oh." There was more. I could tell, but after a quick scan, I could tell no one would speak on it. Some unspoken situation had just materialized, and I wasn't in on it.

Nick's phone beeped a second later.

"Yeah." He looked around the room. "He said we could go, but we gotta move now."

The guys flew around, preparing to change from their trunks to their regular clothes. They forgot I was in the room until Ryan snapped at them. Tom and Nick's hands were pushing their swim shorts down, and they froze.

I threw up a hand and looked at the floor. "I'm good. I'll grab some clothes and get ready downstairs."

"Hey." Ryan followed me into the hallway, making sure his door was shut. "You sure about this?"

I jerked up a shoulder. "I think it's safe to say I'm up for anything right about now."

Robbie was going to his new school this week. I'd be going to mine.

Who the fuck cared? Right?

"Mackenzie . . ."

I clipped my head to the side. "I'll be ready in a few minutes."

"If you're sure." His eyes were heavy with concern, and the look warmed me, but he was talking to me like I was normal.

Normal died in my twin sister's puddle of blood.

I slipped away, grabbing some clothes from my suitcase in his truck. I'd planned on using a random downstairs bathroom, but the entire first floor was crowded. The guys were still in Ryan's room, so I looked around, seeing Peach's door open.

Sorry, Peach, but I'm about to use your shit.

I ducked in. After dressing, I went to her bathroom. She could sue me; I didn't give a rat's ass. I used some of her stuff, putting product in my hair, and I went through her makeup too.

We were going to a college party. I had to look the part.

When I finished, I'd aged five years. Heavy eyeliner and eye shadow helped the image.

I pulled on a pair of jean shorts, and I undid one button to shimmy them down an inch on my hips. There. That completed the look.

Ryan and his friends were at the front door, and when Ryan caught sight of me, his eyes rounded, darkening.

"Whoa." Pete actually took a step toward me. "You're fucking hot, Mackenzie."

Nick snorted and hit him in the arm. "Real smooth, Peepee."

"Shut up—and what?" Pete gestured to me. "She is."

"You have to say it in a nice way, a way that doesn't make us think you're creeping on Ryan's girl."

Pete looked from Ryan to me, his brows furrowing. "Um . . ."

Ryan only raised an eyebrow; his lips remained shut.

Pete's face reddened, and he coughed. "Mackenzie, you are—"

I snorted, waving at him. "Please stop. We all look good. Let's leave it at that."

A satisfied smile settled on his face.

I looked at Nick and narrowed my eyes. "You, on the other hand . . ." He called me Ryan's girl. I should correct him, but after a quick glance at Ryan, I didn't want to. He was staring steadily at me, his eyes heated.

Yep. He was totally affecting me, and I coughed. "Are we ready?"

The guys took off out the front door.

Ryan held back till they were gone. Without saying a word, he took my hand. He threaded our fingers together as we headed after them, and I tried to ignore the little flutter in my chest.

chapter eleven

RED SOLO CUP IN HAND, RAP MUSIC BLARING, SLIGHT BUZZ STARTED—I WAS THERE. AND we'd been embraced as if none of us were losers. Hell yeah. We'd turned down a high school party to be at a college one.

I was damn right succeeding in life.

Willow would've been fucking green with jealousy.

A mean streak raced through my insides, causing my stomach to twist around. I raised my cup, looking at the sky from where I stood in some college dumbass' backyard.

You up there, Wills? Or are you right next to me?

I hated her. She wasn't supposed to be either of those places. She was supposed to be there, not me. She was supposed to be yelling at our parents, telling them they couldn't send Robbie away. She was supposed to be stressing about school, making sure I got my locker number, and only she knew what else. I had no fucking clue.

It was Saturday night. I had one more day, and then I was going to the new school—just me. It wasn't supposed to be just me.

She was my partner in crime. No matter how much she pissed me off, made my blood boil, annoyed the crap out of me, she was my other half.

"You okay?"

I didn't know the girl who spoke to me, and maybe that was why I was honest. "I'm going crazy."

She'd been passing by, empty cup in hand, but did a double take.

I waved her on, a nice fake smile on my face. "I'm good. You?"

"Oh." Her head tilted to the side. I could've been a green alien, and she would've looked at me the same way. "Okay. Good then." She edged away.

Run, little girl. Run from the crazy, pissed-off psycho drunk.

No, scratch that. I was the crazy, pissed-off psycho buzzed chick. The little buzz I'd had before faded on the drive there. I was playing catch-up. Two more beers, and I'd be in the drunk stage. And that was something I needed to address.

I swung around, looking to follow that girl, but Ryan was there. He grabbed my arms as I walked into him, and he took away my cup.

"No." He tossed it to the side, turned me around, and began walking me away from the beer.

I pointed behind us. "I have to go that way."

He shook his head, still walking behind me. "We're going this way, away from the keg."

I pointed again. "But the keg is that way."

"Exactly."

"I want to go toward the keg."

"I don't."

I dug in my feet and crossed my arms over my chest. We were about to have a difference of opinion, but Ryan didn't care. He kept pushing me ahead, and when I locked my legs in place, his arm wrapped around my waist, and he lifted me.

"Oooh!" I squeaked. I hadn't been expecting that.

Two points for him.

He carried me until we were far away from everyone with some trees to our right, lawn to the left, and a creek crossing both. I ignored the full moon above us. I'd already looked up as I talked to Willow. The sky and anything else up there were cut off from my attention. She didn't deserve it anymore.

"Sit."

Ryan's hand went to my shoulders as if he were going to push me down, but I shrugged off his touch and moved farther away. Wrapping my arms around myself, I warded off a chill that wasn't in the air.

"Mac."

I waved a hand at him. "I'm good. I won't drink anymore."

"That isn't why I stopped you."

I looked up, frowning. "Why did you?"

He shrugged, cocking his head to the side. "You looked upset. Okay, and yeah"—his eyes flicked upwards—"maybe it was to stop you from drinking. Getting drunk when it's just me is one thing. Getting drunk around strangers . . . I don't know." He looked back at where we'd come from. The bass thumped softly in the background. A few laughing shrieks rang out. "I didn't like how some of the guys were looking at you," Ryan confessed.

"Oh." I'd already forgotten how Nick's older brother had gaped at me. I'd gotten that a lot since Willow. I blocked it out. "Don't worry." I shot him a grin. "I won't sleep with any of them. I think the magical sleeping aid exists only with you." And remembering how Nick's brother and then his other friends had fawned over Ryan when we arrived, I nudged him with my elbow. "I'm not sure if I liked how they were looking at you either."

He smiled and seemed to relax. "Sit with me?"

I nodded. It was stupid, but I liked that he asked. This time I wasn't told where to go. I wasn't taken somewhere. I wasn't given a rule.

As I folded down next to him, he asked, "What?"

"What?" I looked over.

"You sighed. You okay?"

I frowned for a second. "It's weird. My parents don't really watch me, but in some ways, that's all they do."

"What do you mean?"

"I don't know." And I didn't.

I didn't know a lot lately, but maybe, that was to be expected. A person's always trying to make sense of things, and probably more so in a time like this.

I let out a breath. "Everything's fucked up."

His knees came up, and he put his arms around them, resting his chin atop. "Yeah. I can imagine."

I looked at him, hearing the knowing tone from him. "Your friend died."

"It isn't the same as a sister."

"You still know a little."

"Yeah." His eyes found mine, warming and holding mine captive. "I know a little."

"Is that why you're being so nice?"

He groaned, his head tipping back. His arms moved behind him, and he stretched out his legs. "We've been over this."

"You said you didn't know. You just were.'" I used his words.

He laughed under his breath. "You know, most girls would jump at the chance to sleep in my bed."

"Yeah?" I hid a grin as my eyebrows went up.

"Yeah. I'm hot stuff. If you weren't in mourning, I'd think you were blind. Check me out." He waved a hand over his chest. "Hot shit. I'm a basketball star too, if you didn't notice my greeting tonight."

"Oh, I noticed." He'd been heralded like a celebrity, but I also knew he didn't want to talk about it. He was polite to them, but after a bit, his friends stepped in and had been shielding him the rest of the night. And he was hiding with me. I laughed. Maybe I was hiding with him. I needed this banter. An invisible weight on my chest lifted a little. "Thank you." I raised my knees and rested my cheek on them, turning to peer at him. "And you *are* super duper cute."

"Super duper?" He sat up, wincing. "Are you serious? You couldn't go with something more manly?"

"You're still a boy. We're only in high school."

He shook his head. "See? That's where you're wrong. We're on the edge of adulthood. One more year for us, and that's it. Off we go."

"Like a little bird kept protected," I teased. "They're letting you fly."

"Exactly." He flinched. "I think. Or an eagle. Not a little bird. I'm an eagle. I'm lethal."

I laughed. "Go for a vulture. I think they're bigger."

"But they're ugly." He winked at me. "They aren't beautiful like eagles."

"You're beautiful?"

"Fuck yeah." He puffed his chest out again. "I could be in magazines, I'm so pretty."

He wasn't lying. Give him some high-fashion runway threads, and the guy could go to Paris.

As if sensing my thoughts, his eyes grew serious—or maybe he was reading from me. Was this . . .

He leaned toward me.

I was almost tipping because my arms were still wrapped around my knees, and like all the other times, it was like he knew exactly what was happening with me. He touched my shoulder, steadying me, and I closed my eyes.

No guy should make me feel like I needed his touch to be anchored in place, but it had happened. Somehow, whether he wanted it or not, Ryan had become that anchor. I was starting to wonder if I could go on without his presence. I was spinning, but then his hand switched, moving toward my head, and his thumb came to rest against my cheek.

He was so close, his eyes lingering on my lips.

Were we going to do this?

And then, his lips were on mine.

They felt like home, as if I'd been kissing him forever already.

I let out a sigh, and my mouth opened. He moved forward, his mouth answering mine, and I felt his tongue slip against mine.

I wasn't going to think. I was feeling, and I felt him pull me closer.

I'd kissed a few guys back home. And I'd had one boyfriend, but it wasn't serious. Some heavy petting—that'd been it—and it hadn't felt like this. Somehow, I wasn't surprised one bit.

We lay back in the grass, his mouth still fused with mine. He was tasting, kissing, nipping, teasing me. Someone moaned, and I could feel his hands around my face, as if he were cradling me literally in the palm of his hand. I suddenly tasted salt.

They were tears. My tears.

I was kissing Ryan and crying at the same time.

He paused, lifting his head. "Are you—"

"Oh God." I rolled away, curling in on myself. What was I doing? Seriously? Fucking crying as I was making out with a guy?

"Um . . ."

"I'm so sorry, Ryan." I couldn't look at him. The tears wouldn't stop. I brushed at them, and they kept rolling. "I have no idea—" Nope. We both knew. Everyone knew.

I was mortified.

Then, instead of leaving awkward silence, he laughed.

Laughed.

I looked up, and his head hung between his knees. His shoulders were shaking.

"What . . ."

"I'm sorry." He shook his head but more chuckles rang out. "I'm—this is every guy's worst nightmare, to make a chick start bawling when you're putting the moves on her."

Oh. "You know why I'm crying," I said gently. "It has nothing to do with you. You know that, right?"

"Yeah. Yeah, but still." He gazed at me again. "Telling someone this story?"

He had a point.

My mouth twitched. "I'm so sorry."

"I can hear the jokes. You kissed her so bad, she broke out into sobs. You kiss so sad, you literally made the girl cry." He shook his head, his laughter subsiding. "No one can hear about this. No one."

"Got it."

"No one, Mac. I have a reputation to uphold."

It was the second time he'd called me Mac. A rush of pleasure went through me. I liked hearing that nickname from him.

But he was still waiting, and I nodded. "Got it. Not a word that I broke down in tears."

"You can be crying. That's fine, but I was out here consoling you—not putting the moves on you. That's key."

He seemed so serious, but like before, I could see dark humor lurking behind his eyes. I nodded. "Got it. I'm a crybaby, not a whore."

"Well . . ."

I laughed, shaking my head. "I'm kidding." And because I couldn't help myself, I leaned forward and whispered, "But you have no worries. You're a damn good kisser." My lips met his again as I closed my eyes.

Someone groaned—maybe both of us—and he pulled me on top of him this time. He fell back, cradling me in his arms. And we kissed. Then we kissed some more.

chapter twelve

I WAS A HUSSY.

It had been almost dawn when Ryan and his friends dropped me off after the party.

I snuck in, but if I'd been expecting any big confrontation with my folks, I would've been disappointed. They hadn't started moving around the house until around nine this morning, and when I got up, there was a note on the kitchen table for me. Robbie had liked the school yesterday—so much so that they were taking him back. For good.

That was that.

I got no say in the matter.

Ryan came over in the afternoon, and we hung out in my room most of the time. There was kissing, but also video games, cookie dough, pizza, and sneaking some wine. Okay, lots of wine and lots of kissing, and I ended up putting a note on my door telling my folks I was sleeping before I snuggled up with Ryan the rest of the night.

And kissing. There was still more of that, but there wasn't anything heavy.

When I woke Monday morning, I glanced at the clock. Six AM.

Ryan was already on the edge of the bed, bent over. His shirt was on, but it wasn't pulled all the way down. He was fixing his shoes.

I sat up, tugging his shirt into place and letting my fingers skim his back as I did.

He glanced at me, his eyes darkening, the look of lust there that I'd started to recognize from Saturday night and yesterday.

"Morning," he murmured. Leaning over, he kissed me.

"Hmmm." I pulled back, scrunching my nose. "I have morning breath."

He laughed, grabbing my arm and tugging me back to him. "You're fine." And he showed me, his lips finding mine again and not letting me move away.

I was panting in a second, feeling all sorts of tingles in my chest when he groaned, pulling away.

He rested his forehead on mine. "I gotta head home to change and get ready." He sat up again, his eyes holding mine. "First day of school. You want a ride?"

I opened my mouth, figuring my parents would take me, and then I remembered they were probably headed to work already.

"Yeah."

"Okay." He nodded, opening my window. "I'll be back around seven thirty."

"Okay."

His lips curved in a crooked grin before he was out the window and down the tree. I heard his truck start up a moment later. As it turned down the street, I lay back in bed and stared upward. I wasn't looking at the ceiling. I wasn't really looking at anything.

I was . . . I didn't know.

We didn't have sex last night, but our shirts had come off and jeans were unsnapped. I got up halfway through the night to put on pajama pants and a sleeping tank top. Shortly after that, the top was pulled off and pants pushed down a bit. Ryan had shucked his jeans off, but he kept his boxer briefs on. He held me, chest to chest, and I slept.

He was gone, and my limbs felt heavy, my lips swollen. I could easily sleep the rest of the day away. I felt content until I heard the floor creak outside my door. There was a knock, and I sat up.

"Honey?" My mom.

Whoa. I reached for my sleeping tank and tugged it on. "I thought you were gone already?"

"We're leaving in a few, but are you going to be okay to get to school? Do you need a ride?"

"No. I'll be fine."

She didn't ask if I wanted to talk about Robbie. I shouldn't have been surprised. My biggest battle had been the counseling sessions. After that, it was like they'd learned not to even give me a chance to voice my opinion.

I listened to them move around the house.

I'd been with them for eighteen years. I knew their routine. My dad made the coffee. My mom made the toast. My dad would eat that and a yogurt, and then they'd finish getting dressed. They'd take the coffee with them. I heard keys jingling while they discussed who would come to say goodbye.

My mom must've won because my dad's heavy footsteps came up the stairs.

A slight knock. His voice was muffled through the door. "We're heading out. You'll call if you need anything."

It wasn't a question. He wasn't asking, and he didn't wait for a reply.

Again, no word about Robbie. Did they not think I'd be affected by that? Then again, I didn't know what was going on in my dad's head anymore.

Did he leave feeling as if he'd fulfilled his good-father role? Or did he go off not thinking about me at all? As if checking on me were another part of their routine for the morning? Because it was. They'd always checked on Robbie and Willow . . . and there was usually something happening there that kept their attention. A few times they'd gotten to me, but the focus was usually with Willow.

My phone sprang to life, and I scooted to the edge of my bed. Bracing my elbows on my legs, I cradled my head in my hands for two seconds.

The ringing didn't stop, so with a groan, I grabbed for it. "Hello?"

A soft and tentative voice. "Is this Mackenzie?"

I stood. "Who is this?"

"Cora."

Ryan's friend. No, correct that, the girl who had a crush on Ryan—the guy I kissed last night.

I bit my lip. What was my role?

"Uh, hey. Yeah. It's Mackenzie."

"Oh, thank God." She laughed. "I swiped your number from Ryan's phone. There's another Mackenzie in our class who likes him, so I wasn't sure if I got the right one or not."

Another one? I frowned. "No, this is me. That other girl, does she text him too?"

"What?" She sounded distracted. "No, no. Well, yes. She texts him, but I don't think he responds."

Relief. Phew.

Seriously, how many girls were after him?

"Okay."

And then silence.

I waited a beat. She called me.

"Um, so okay, I called to see if you needed a ride to school, or if, like, you wanted to meet me somewhere in school? I could be your guide through classes, you know?"

Well, fuck.

She was going the friend route, which meant I'd have to adhere to the friend code. So hands off Ryan, but I'd already violated that rule. And because I didn't have the energy to worry about this, I blurted out, "Look, I have to tell you . . ."

I paused for a breath. She started to break in, but nope, I *was* doing this. She probably knew what I was going to say and wanted to put up a roadblock. But I had to say this because I didn't know her when I met Ryan. But I'd begun to depend on him since June twenty-ninth.

I spoke over her. "Ryan and I are something."

"What?"

I groaned inwardly. She sounded like she wanted to cry.

"I'm sorry, I—"

"Oh, that's okay. Just don't do it again, you know?"

"No. You aren't listening to me. I'm sorry you're hurting, but I can't step back. I wanted you to know this before we even think about becoming friends." I took a breath. "And if you don't want to anymore, I understand."

Ryan wasn't into her. I knew that, and she knew it too. She also knew he was into me.

Maybe if Willow were still alive, I wouldn't need Ryan and I'd really like Cora. Maybe then, I would have been able to step back, but I wasn't in that place.

I gentled my tone. "I'm sorry, Cora. I know you like him."

She sniffled on her end. "Then why are you pursuing him?"

It wasn't like that, but . . .

"Because I need him right now."

More sniffling. I heard her blow her nose.

"I always thought maybe, you know?" she finally said, her voice resigned. "He seemed disgusted with Erin the last time we saw her, and I had hope. Like I had a chance, finally."

Sadness weighed in my chest, but my need to get through this shitstorm outweighed that. Call me a bitch. Call me a whore. Call me whatever negative thing you want, but in that moment, I was just a survivor.

My phone beeped again.

Ryan: **Leaving in thirty. You want coffee?**

Crap. I had to get dressed.

"Cora," I said into the phone. "I gotta get going, but I'll see you at school."

I hung up, typed out a quick "yes" to Ryan, tossed my phone onto the bed, and hurried into the shower. I didn't have time to wait for her answer.

chapter thirteen

TWO THINGS DIDN'T HAPPEN LATER THAT MORNING:
I didn't tell Ryan about Cora's phone call. If she wanted to mention any part of the conversation to him, that would be her decision.

And my arrival at school in Ryan's truck did not go unnoticed.

Heads turned and people were starting over to him when I got out. Their mouths dropped, and everything erupted in chaos.

That was an exaggeration, but with my fragile sense of reality lately, it seemed like chaos. The girls who had been walking toward him turned and hightailed it back to their friends. I could hear the whispers.

It didn't get any better when we got inside. Someone tripped as she tried to veer around us to get to her gossiping friends, squeaking as she fell. When she scrambled to her feet, her face was flaming red. She pushed all the way into her group of friends for cover.

Ryan's eyebrows went up at that one, and when he turned to me, I saw the apology in his eyes before he said anything.

I shook my head. "Trust me. In the grand scheme of my life, this doesn't factor at all. I don't care."

He gave me a small smile, but I knew he didn't believe me.

He should've. I'd rather have this attention than the other kind. The Willow's sister kind. Then again, they didn't know Willow. She was only that girl who'd killed herself.

If they even knew that. Common sense told me the news had to have gotten out, but Ryan was adamant that he and his friends didn't talk. I was still waiting for it to come out of Erin's mouth one day, and when that happened, I was prepared for my first jail time.

It wasn't that I was hoping or planning for it, but I had to be realistic. I was probably going to punch the girl.

Pure agony tore through my chest as I missed Willow more than I thought possible in that instant. I faltered a moment. I felt suspended in hell. I forced myself to exhale and then fill my lungs and bring my head up. My neck felt as if it was lifting cement, and I had to break concrete to resume walking.

One step. Two. Three.

The agony was still there, but it wasn't bone crushing.

Four, five, six, and I didn't feel like I was going blind.

"You okay?" Ryan looked toward me as we walked.

He'd noticed. Of course he had.

I forced a nod—God, that hurt—and cleared my throat. "I'm going to the office, get my schedule and everything."

"You sure you're okay?"

There was no appropriate answer to that. I didn't know when there would be, so I ignored it. "I'll check in with you later."

"Okay." I felt him watching me as I continued down the hallway. I didn't stop feeling his eyes until I turned the corner and found the school's office.

The interest in me waned once I hit the second hallway, which meant the school gossip train must not have traveled as fast as I'd thought. Nearing the office door, I saw Cora lingering outside of it. As I approached, she pushed off from the wall, adjusting her hold on a textbook and notebook.

Her eyes slid to the floor, but then she straightened and her little chin firmed in determination as she looked at me again.

She reminded me of a wounded bird. I was the eagle who'd torn her wing, but for some idiotic reason, she wanted to befriend the eagle. No, wait—Ryan was the eagle. I'd be the vulture in our little scenario.

"Hey."

I paused, nodding to her in greeting.

She picked at some imaginary threads on her shirt before rushing out, "IknowRyanlikesyouandI'msorryforwhatIdidbutIwanttobefriendsifthat'scool withyou?" Her cheeks pinked so she had to stop. Smoothing out her shirt, she asked, "Would you?"

"Yeah." There were no hard feelings. She should be the one pissed at me anyway. "I'd like that. Thank you."

The office door opened, and I stepped back, clearing the way for some students headed out. I stepped inside, and Cora followed. The office was full of activity—teachers going in and out and three ladies working behind the desk. One waved me over with a harried expression on her face.

"Name?"

I gave her my info and slid over the papers my mom had left on the counter for me this morning.

"People are already talking about you," Cora murmured.

The lady interrupted, asking, "Mackenzie Malcolm?"

"Yes."

She went back to typing at her computer.

I glanced at Cora, who edged closer, looking over her shoulder. I saw the two girls standing in line behind us, both watching as they talked to each other. I only hoped the gossip was Ryan-centered. I could handle that.

They looked vaguely familiar. One had auburn hair grazing the top of her shoulders. The other had darker hair that was styled the same. Pink sweaters. Blue jeans. And glitter. They all seemed to wear glitter.

"They popular?" I asked Cora.

"They're friends of Erin's."

Aha. So they would've been at the Jensens' on Saturday. "Gotcha."

"Okay, Miss Malcolm." The lady reached for the printer behind her and then extended the papers to me. "Here's your class schedule, locker number, and combination, and you'll have to stop in the nurse's office. She'll have a form to give to your parents to sign, giving us permission to give you pain pills or Band-Aids, things like that." She plastered a nice smile on her face, one she'd probably used twenty other times this morning already. "Is your sister coming in?"

Cora gasped.

She didn't know . . .

The lady froze, noting my reaction and Cora's. She was thinking, but I could tell she couldn't figure it out. She cleared her throat, and when she spoke again, there was an authoritative and slightly condescending tone to her voice, as if we were wasting her time.

"Your sister, Willow Malcolm? If she's absent today, she'll need a note. I only received the information for you, my dear."

I couldn't say it. The words were stuck in my throat, and I hushed Cora before she could explain.

My fingers were clumsy as I grabbed a pen and piece of paper off the lady's desk.

She died June 29th, I wrote. **Not coming.**

I folded the paper over and then folded it again.

Sliding it to her, I grabbed my stuff and hurried out of there. I didn't want to be anywhere near her when she read it.

I failed.

I heard her gasp as the office door closed behind me.

"The records must not be updated. Or the records at your old school weren't updated. I don't know." Cora was right next to me, holding her books close to her chest.

I was walking blind, no idea where I was going, and it took a moment before I regrouped.

Locker. I needed to find my locker.

Glancing down at the number, I realized I was in the wrong hallway. I'd have to walk back in front of the office again, and there was no way I wanted to do that.

I read my first class and showed Cora the classroom number. "Where is this?"

She bit her lip, tugging at her shirtsleeve. "It's down the hallway."

That was welcome news, and I nodded. "I'm going to class."

"We still have twenty minutes—"

I was already off. I called over my shoulder, "That's fine with me."

I'd find my locker later.

When I got to the room, the teacher wasn't in, so I couldn't ask if there would be assigned seating. I slid into the seat in the back row and farthest from the door. I still had my book bag with me, but I didn't care. I pulled out a notebook and pencil, and I put my phone in my lap, making sure it was on silent. Then I looked out the window as everyone came in.

Conversations slowed as people filled in around where I was sitting.

I felt them watching me. I didn't look. I couldn't. A few tears slipped down, and I willed them to stop. I was doing a great impersonation of a statue.

Perhaps that was what I'd be for Halloween.

"Okay, everyone." The teacher paused when the door opened.

I finally looked around, surprised at who sat beside me. Before I could process that, a student darted into the classroom and handed a note to the teacher.

As he stopped and read it, a weird déjà vu came over me.

I knew. I knew what he was going to do next.

The teacher stiffened, looking up. His eyes moved over the students, landing on me.

Remorse flared in his eyes before he coughed, handed the student back the note, and murmured, "Maybe let the next teacher know as well. All of them, in fact." He said it quietly, but I heard him in the back of the room.

The school didn't want teachers to make the same mistake as the office lady, so news of my sister's death was circulating, room to room. No teacher would read the attendance sheet and ask for Willow Malcolm. No one would ask if we were sisters and where she was.

It was a nice gesture, but I felt stripped raw anyway.

I had a strong feeling the teacher wouldn't call my name during attendance, and I was right. He named every other student in the room.

When he called on Ryan's friends—Nick and Tom—they replied "Here" from the seats around me, and I was grateful. I wasn't sure if this was where they normally would've sat, but I'd take it.

Their presence shielded me.

chapter fourteen

I WAS BRAVE ENOUGH TO SNEAK PAST THE OFFICE AFTER MY SECOND CLASS. IT WAS RIDICULOUS. I was sandwiched inside a group of students, but I swear I felt the office lady watching me. I knew it couldn't be true.

Ryan came over as I was closing my locker to go to my fourth period. We had one more class before lunch, one more hour before goddamn freedom.

"How's it going?"

And cue the other form of attention. I rested against my locker, looking down, but I could see from under my eyelashes. Oh yes, everyone was dying to know about Ryan and the mystery girl.

"What are you? The Greek god of dating?"

He smirked. "Hot shit. Did you already forget?"

"Right. Eagle of hotness."

"Um, yeah." His grin turned wicked, and he glanced around and saw all the attention too. Leaning closer, he dropped his voice. "For real. How are you? Cora told me about Margaret."

I took a leap and figured Margaret was the front desk lady. "I don't really want to talk about it."

"Okay." He gestured to the hallway. "What's your next class?"

"*Espanol. Y tu?*"

"*Si, si.*" He nodded. "Come on. You can be my table partner."

I shot him a dry look, which he returned.

Once we got there, I realized it wasn't a seniors-only class. Erin and Peach were in one corner, and I couldn't stop my groan. Ryan snorted. His hand came to the small of my back, and he urged me forward. We walked to the back of the class and the very last table in the room. A guy after my own heart. We both slid in, and as if they dropped out of midair, Tom and Nick came to occupy the table in front of us.

"Hey, man." Tom leaned over after the class started and worksheets were handed out. He did a fist-bumping thing with Ryan. Nick followed suit. Both looked at me, saw my face, and waved instead.

"You made it out of first period unscathed," Nick noted.

"I did. Thanks for sitting by me."

He shrugged. "It's cool. That's where we sit anyway. Seemed fitting you were there already."

That was true.

They began talking to Ryan about classes, a party already in the works, and girls. I felt their glances, but I tuned them out.

I wished I cared. I really did, but I didn't.

I felt her everywhere.

Sitting next to me.

Standing with me.

Walking beside me.

She was me, but I wasn't her anymore.

I glanced at Ryan from the corner of my eye.

I'd latched on to him. He was a bandage over my wounds—covering them but not really healing them. They were still raw and open, but I was hoping to move fast enough that my insides wouldn't spill out everywhere.

I was no longer a part of any of this, any of these people. I was on the outside, and I was the only one who really understood that.

No one else around me could claim to be a twinless twin. But that was my new identity.

I could almost hear Willow yelling at me, *Those girls need to be taught a lesson. They aren't the queens anymore. We rule now. You and me, Mac. The Willow Mac Attack. That's you and me.*

"Mac?"

I drew in a ragged breath. I could fucking hear her.

Her hand touched my arm. "Mac?"

I screamed, lurching out of my chair. Scrambling backward, my back hit the wall, and I gaped at where I'd been sitting.

Everyone was watching me.

Ryan's hand stretched out toward where I'd been sitting. He slowly closed it into a fist and turned around in his chair toward me. He bent forward, resting his hands on his legs. "Mackenzie?"

God. It wasn't her. Ryan had touched me. Ryan had only used her nickname for me.

"I . . ."

"What's wrong with her?" Tom whispered.

Nick threw him a disgusted look, slamming his elbow into his chest.

"Ouch."

As the teacher rounded the tables, heading toward me, Ryan stood and got between us. He blocked me from the rest of the class at the same time.

"What's the problem?" the teacher asked.

I heard chairs scrape against the floor, and soon Tom and Nick were standing in front of me as well. All three of them shielded me. The gesture was so sweet, so kind, that I almost lost it again.

I reached out, grabbing Ryan's shirt, and he sucked in his breath at the touch.

His voice came out a little strained. "She, uh—she needs a minute."

I bent my head forward, my forehead resting against Ryan's back.

"Well, take her outside," the teacher added softly. "I know about—"

"Will do," Ryan cut him off.

He swept his arm backward, sliding it around my waist, and pulled me with him. Twisting against his chest, I walked with him toward the door.

"My stuff," I mumbled.

"Tom and Nick will grab it for us."

Then we were out in the hallway, but Ryan didn't pause. He let go of my waist and threaded our fingers together. Tugging me behind him, he stopped at his locker, grabbed his bag and keys, and took me to mine.

"Combo." He pointed to it.

I didn't want to let go of his hand, but I did, unlocking my locker.

Grabbing my backpack and some of my books, he paused. "You have your phone?"

I nodded before reaching to get it.

Then he shut my door.

Slinging both backpacks over his shoulder, he threaded our fingers again, and we walked to the parking lot. We were skipping school. Only a few students were in the hallway, but all of them watched us go, their eyes on our hands. No one stopped us.

We were pushing out the doors as a guy in a black bomber jacket came in the opposite way. He had long black hair, dark eyes, and a sneer that turned into a frown when he saw Ryan.

"Hey, man." He stopped, his hand catching the door as Ryan let it go. "Where are you going?"

Ryan's hand tightened over mine. His jaw clenched. "The fuck? You're back here now?"

They knew each other; that was obvious. But there was something else there.

Cousins, maybe? Maybe they were family?

The guy ignored Ryan's question, his dark eyes sliding over me. He'd been chewing on the end of a pen, and he took it out, pointing at me. "You're skipping with a chick? Am I in an alternate universe? Did we switch roles?" He looked at Ryan. "Are you the badass rebel and I'm the basketball star?"

"Fuck off, Kirk." But Ryan seemed to lose his heat. He started grinning and rolled his eyes. "You're a pain in my ass."

Kirk cocked his head to the side, popping that pen back in his mouth. "Tell me something different. You've been a pain in my ass since we were kids."

Ryan laughed, and as Kirk held up a fist, Ryan met it with his free one.

They gave each other a sideways hug, and then Kirk nodded at me again. "Who's the chick? I thought I was the only bad influence on you."

Ryan lifted our linked hands, nodding toward me. "Mackenzie."

I waited for more of an explanation. Apparently, so did Kirk. We both looked at Ryan, but his mouth was set in a firm line. That was all he had to say.

Good.

I hid a grin. There she was—my twin speaking in my head like she was with me.

Kirk nodded slowly. "Nice." He held his hand up, his grin becoming wicked. "Nice to meet you, Mackenzie. I'm Ryan's real best friend. The others are just posers."

"Nice try." Ryan rolled his eyes again, knocking Kirk's hand down. "What are you doing here for real? You're coming back?"

The rebel-smooth-Casanova look faded. "Yeah. My folks are divorcing. I'm surprised Nan didn't tell you. I'm back with my dad."

"Emily?"

"My little sister stayed with Mom. They're down in Los Angeles."

Ryan winced. "I'm sorry, man."

"Yeah, well . . ." Kirk's eyes found mine again. A mischievous spark lit there. "Looks like you've been busy."

"It isn't like that," Ryan replied. His words seemed defensive, but his tone wasn't. He spoke as if they were discussing the weather. "We're taking off for the day."

Kirk nodded. "Don't worry. I'll watch over the posers."

"Be nice to Tom!" Ryan yelled as his friend headed inside.

A hand in the air was Kirk's response.

Ryan sighed, still watching his buddy.

"I'll be fine."

He looked at me, frowning slightly. "Hmm?"

I waved in the direction Kirk had gone. "If you want to go talk to him more, I can head out on my own."

"I gave you a ride here."

I shrugged. "I can call a car. That's no problem."

He shook his head. "No way. Kirk's crazy. I'm not this golden boy who doesn't do anything wrong. You're my *excuse* to skip today. I'm actually using *you*."

"Are you sure?"

He still seemed worried about his friend, but he nodded with a soft smile. Letting go of my hand, he threw his arm around my shoulders and pulled me into his side. "Let's go before the bell rings and the guys run out here."

We didn't quite make it.

The bell rang as we were getting into Ryan's truck. Students were heading out for lunch as we left the parking lot.

"So." Ryan glanced over. "Where we headed?"

I couldn't figure this guy out.

He'd wanted to skip school. I really *was* his excuse, but then his friend had shown up. The other guys he hung out with seemed like normal, loyal friends. Kirk seemed more dangerous.

Willow would've been all about Ryan until she learned that, until she got a glimpse that he wasn't the pretty boy/good guy she'd made him out to be.

Looking at Ryan, another small thrill coursed through me.

Maybe he *was* the guy I would've gone after in the first place. Willow could step aside.

"I don't care," I told him. "Anywhere is good."

chapter fifteen

WE WENT TO MY HOUSE.

It wasn't original, but it made sense. My parents were both in the city at their jobs. They'd be gone till seven or even eight in the evening, and there was no Robbie during the week anymore.

Ryan didn't have the same emptiness at his place with his mom in and out, Peach coming home after school, and the staff.

So my house it was.

Going into the kitchen, I dropped my bag onto the counter and picked up a delivery menu. "We could order food since it's technically lunchtime."

Ryan smirked, jumping up to sit on the counter next to my bag. His feet almost touched the floor. "Whatever you want. You guys have food here?"

I opened the fridge.

Lettuce. Milk. Cheese. Two cartons of yogurt and some apples. The freezer wasn't any better: some diet ice cream bars for Mom.

I closed both doors and picked up the menu again. "Ordering it is."

He nodded. "Sounds good to me. Order whatever. I'll pay."

I grinned over the top of the menu, reaching for the landline phone. "Are we on a skip date?"

"We're on a skip day, and you can pay next time if you want."

I laughed, the sound a little hollow. "Deal."

After ordering pizza, we grabbed some drinks and headed into the theater room. I kept the door open and my phone close by so I could hear when the food arrived.

Ryan followed me in, lying on one of the couches and resting his arm up over the back. He kicked his legs up on the chair in front of him. I started to perch next to him, but he grunted and reached for me, hauling me almost onto his lap.

"What are you doing?" he grumbled. "After last night, you're shy?"

I felt the back of my neck heating up and looked at my hands in my lap. "Yeah, actually."

"What?" He pulled back so he could better see my face. "Really?"

I looked up. "I don't really know what I'm doing day to day," I admitted. "Hell, even hour to hour."

I kept to myself how I could almost see Willow sitting on the far end of the couch. She was everywhere.

"I'm going a little nuts."

He shrugged, taking the remote from me. His hand brushed against mine, leaving a tingle in its wake.

"I think if you weren't, something would be wrong."

I leaned my head back, watching him as he turned on the large screen and began scrolling through the channels.

"You think?"

His eyes found mine again, holding them a moment before softening. "Yeah. My friend died, and I wanted to rail at everyone. They acted like I was supposed to be over it and done by the time school started again. I got a four-day weekend to mourn. My parents didn't understand why I wasn't so interested in doing things afterward."

"What do you mean?" I sat up next to him, but he grabbed my legs and pulled them onto his lap. His thumb rubbed the inside of my calf.

He leaned back, turning toward the screen again, but he wasn't watching it. A mask settled over his face, one I was starting to recognize—it fell into place any time he talked to someone who wasn't one of his friends or me. Even his sister got the mask.

"I don't know." His chest rose silently and then fell again. "He died during the winter, at the end of our holiday break, so football was done by then. But I probably would've quit that. I played basketball, kinda had to. The whole town would have erupted if I hadn't, but I quit everything else. Baseball. Anything extra I was supposed to do. My parents were having a crisis. They didn't know what was going on with me. I stopped giving a shit about anything they did." He laughed quietly. "I smoked a lot of pot that year with Kirk. Drank a lot too."

"How old were you?"

"It was two years ago."

My chest ached. I looked over, and Willow seemed to have moved closer to us, but she was fading. I almost couldn't see her. I tuned her out and tuned into Ryan.

"I'm sorry."

His hand began to move again, caressing my leg, moving a little farther down the inside and back up.

My throat felt like it was closing in. "You and Kirk partied together that year?" I rasped.

"No. Well, yes, but that isn't why we became friends. Derek was Kirk's cousin. He was as messed up as I was. He says I was worse. I say he was worse, but yeah, we did a lot of stupid shit together that year."

"And he's been gone?"

"Yeah. He moved to L.A. last winter. His mom got transferred or something, but I guess he's back."

"You didn't know?"

He didn't answer. A few beats passed before he looked at me again, his eyes haunted. "He called the last couple weeks, but I didn't call back. I was distracted."

Me. I happened.

"Maybe he can come over later?"

Ryan laughed quietly, moving to face me more fully. Letting go of my hand, he slid his hands up the outside of my legs, grabbed my waist, and pulled me onto his lap.

I gasped and then moaned as his hands slid around to my ass. His mouth hovered over mine, his eyes darting from my lips to my eyes as he murmured, "I don't think so."

He dipped down, and I closed my eyes, already lifting to meet him halfway.

His lips touched mine at the same time the doorbell rang.

"Fuck." He pulled back, panting a little.

He deposited me gently onto the couch and then headed for the door.

I heard it open, and a second later, "Thanks."

The door slammed shut, and Ryan hurried back downstairs. He strode into the room, deposited the pizza on one of the other chairs, and lifted me once again. He sat and pulled me to straddle him. I smiled, feeling lazy and sensual as I looped my arms around his neck. My hands slid into his hair, grabbing fistfuls as I bent down to him. He tugged me the last inch separating us.

A thrill burned in me as I felt him plastered against every part of me.

God.

We'd kissed for the first time Saturday night. That was two days ago. He'd come over, and we'd fooled around more on Sunday and again that night, but those times were nothing compared to how this made me feel.

I was breathless as his mouth opened over mine, as I felt his tongue slide inside. His hand went to my waist and slid underneath my shirt. He paused there, waiting for me to let him know what was okay and what was not. It'd been the same way Sunday night. He'd asked before touching me then, and he was asking again. And like that night, I answered by touching him the way I wanted to be touched. My hand went under his shirt and slid up his torso, over his stomach muscles and chest as I pushed his shirt the rest of the way.

I began inching up my own shirt.

He pulled back. "Are you sure?"

I nodded, my mouth finding his again. I couldn't stop touching him, kissing him, tasting him. My shirt went up, and his hands were on my bare stomach, smoothing to my back, then down to my ass as he anchored me more firmly against him. I couldn't get enough.

I wanted more of him, more of this.

I wanted anything that helped me forget I was starting to feel like a ghost.

We kept kissing long past when the pizza had gone cold.

※

The sound of the garage woke me up.

The room was dark. The big screen was off, and an arm curled around me.

Ryan had fallen asleep behind me. We were tangled up together on the couch in the theater room.

I bolted upright. "Shit!" I shook Ryan's shoulder, but his eyes had opened as soon as I moved.

"Wha—"

We both heard the garage door going back down.

He repeated my sentiment, "Shit."

Groaning, he swung around from behind me, pulling his shirt on. I grabbed for my shirt and then looked down. Yes, my pants were fine. I glanced at his; they weren't. He was searching around, his hand raking through his hair.

I pointed. "Crotch."

"Huh?" He looked down, another curse leaving him. He quickly buttoned his jeans.

We hadn't had sex, but we went a little further than last night. Grinding 101. I'd definitely felt him against me, and I'd definitely strained to get closer to him, which was a reality that was hitting me like a sledgehammer, I was glad that was all we'd done.

"What if the school called them already?"

He grabbed for his phone, scrolling through his messages. "Tell them the truth. You thought you could handle it, and then you couldn't. You lost your sister, Mac. Your parents should be sympathetic to that."

He was right. I felt a little better, the old Mackenzie's guilt lessening over skipping half a day.

They would come inside. I could hear my parents talking to each other.

They would call my name.

When I didn't answer, they would go in search of me.

I wouldn't be in my room, so they'd call again.

They would come down because this was the obvious place I'd be. If I wasn't in my room or in the living room, then check the theater room.

So, I waited, my heart pounding against my chest, listening . . .

The fridge opened. I heard glasses clinking. My dad walked to his office.

The microwave started in the kitchen.

Plates clanked as someone pulled them out of the cabinet.

And then . . . nothing.

They never called for me. They never went up to my room to see if I was in there. My mom went down the hallway to their bedroom. The microwave beeped and then the oven. My dad walked from his office back to the kitchen.

"Food's done," he called.

My mom's soft tread came back to the kitchen.

Chairs were pulled out, moving against the floor.

I heard utensils hitting the plates, scraping.

I couldn't move.

Ryan's phone was flashing as texts came in, but he silenced it. Wait—I grabbed for my phone. I'd put it on silent too. There'd be a text from my parents, something to check in with me. They would've asked where I was, how school was, told me they were eating without me. They probably thought I was with friends. But when I looked?

The screen was blank. No calls. No texts. Nothing.

My parents weren't going to look for me.

Ryan scooted over and showed me his phone. He typed out: **Want to sneak over to my place? Rose made spaghetti.**

Did I?

A numb cold settled in. I saw the pizza we'd ordered and had never eaten. It was still on the chair, but I had no appetite. I ran through the scenarios in my head: go upstairs and pretend my parents hadn't forgotten me or go to Ryan's place. Peach would be there, but so would other people.

I nodded, suddenly desperate to be anywhere else.

chapter sixteen

We didn't have to sneak.

As we were going up the stairs, my parents finished eating. I heard them put their dishes in the sink, and as we came to the top of the stairs, they moved past us. My dad went into his office. My mom went to their bedroom. I saw each of their backs disappear into the different rooms, and then Ryan and I headed out the door.

I locked it behind me.

Holding my phone as we drove, I was sure it'd buzz any second. My parents would remember me. They'd want to know where I was.

It hadn't moved by the time Ryan parked in his driveway, and with a sigh, I slipped it into my book bag.

Ryan eyed me as he rounded the front, waiting for me. "I'll give the guys a call and find out if we already have homework for tomorrow."

I nodded. There was a storm battling the icy cold numbness inside me, and I would've jumped at anything to quiet my mind. "That sounds like a good idea."

But turns out, he didn't have to do that.

When Ryan opened the door, yelling, techno music, and laughter assaulted us.

A blur streaked from the living room, past the entryway, and into the kitchen, then backtracked.

Peach gaped at us and hollered, "RYAN'S HOME!"

Footsteps stampeded toward us, coming from all angles. I stepped back instinctively. It was jarring going from my empty and almost haunted house to this. Ryan's was full of life.

Erin and two other girls ran from the direction Peach had come. Tom and Nick came down the stairs. Cora and Kirk busted up from the basement. As they skidded to a stop, most were red in the face and more than a little sweaty.

"What the fuck?" Ryan dropped his bag with a thud to the floor.

Kirk grinned at us, lopsided. He rested a hand against the wall next to him, his chin lifting in a cocky posture. "Your parents are at some banquet event overnight in the city—"

"And Rose cooked a bunch of food for us and then left. It's all in the fridge," Peach cut in, her chest heaving.

Ryan looked from her to Kirk. "So you thought you'd have a party here?"

Kirk lifted a shoulder. "Seemed the best option, especially since your ass skipped out today." There was an added heat to his words, and everyone's eyes moved to me.

You're going to take that? I could hear Willow hiss.

No, I answered in my head. *No, I'm not.*

I looked right at him. "You didn't seem to have any problem when you ran into us leaving."

"That was before I realized he'd be gone all day." He switched to Ryan. "Seriously, man—"

I interrupted, "Why the change of heart?" I flicked a look at the girls, who were following the back and forth like a volleyball game. "Have you been listening to my *fans*?"

Erin's eyebrows shot up. Her friends gasped, giving her nervous looks.

Peach got redder in the face.

Ryan looked from me to Kirk, his mouth curving down in a frown.

"According to them, you've been all over my man since you arrived on the scene. You're like a leech, taking him away from his friends, and I think it's bullshit." He raked me over, sneering. "I thought Ryan was taking you for a literal ride over the lunch period. Then I hear it's been like that all summer long."

This asshole.

I growled, jerking forward a step. "Are you kidding me?"

A twinge of wariness stirred in his eyes. The sneer dropped, but his glare was still there.

"Let's run down the timeline. My family moves to Portside in June. I see Ryan at our parents' company picnic June twenty-ninth. I didn't even talk to him. Eight hours later, my sister kills herself."

The glare faded.

"Four hours later, I'm at the Jensens' house. Fast forward another month, I go to the movies with Ryan and his friends. Fast forward almost *another* month, I saw him this past weekend and yeah, we skipped today. Want to know why?"

I didn't know when I'd advanced on him, but I didn't think anyone could hold me back. I was seeing red. "Because I couldn't fucking deal with not having my twin *motherfucking* sister with me today."

I felt Ryan behind me. His hand on my back acted like a coolant. I felt some calm seep in, but I could still feel everyone in that room—their attention, their derision, their judgment.

Willow would've creamed them in minutes.

Feeling a bit more in control, I said, "You lost a cousin. I lost my other half. Save your judgment for the bitches who got in your head today."

Silence.

If you're going to get away with clocking one of those bitches, I'd do it now.

Willow was in my ear again. I could imagine her snide looks at Erin. I suppressed a laugh, knowing I couldn't do either, but she *so* would have.

Ryan's hand found mine. Softly, as if he were crooning to a cornered wild animal, he said, "Come on. Let's go upstairs."

Another surge of rage was coming, so I let him pull me upstairs. Nick and Tom moved aside. Ryan said something to them, but it was so low I couldn't make it out. He led me upstairs to his room, and once inside, I waved him away. "Go. I know you want to talk to them. I'll be fine."

He hesitated at his door. "You sure?"

I nodded, not looking at him. "Yeah. I have to chill out. I know."

"Kirk isn't usually that wrong on things. He'll correct himself."

I wasn't holding my breath.

I was embarrassed.

Those girls wanted a reaction, and they got one. I'd lost it in front of them. They got the win. They'd used Ryan's best friend to get it out of me.

Point one for the rich bitches.

I sat at Ryan's desk, grinning slightly at Willow's words. She would've been impressed with them too.

You were cool as tight back there. Proud of you, little sis.

Cool as tight? I had no idea what that meant, but it was something my twin would've said, in a moment when she was "cool as tight" too.

There you go, thinking you're funny. And look at you, getting it on with Ryan like you're rabbits. Watch the sexual activity, twin sister. You don't want to pop out little babies for Mom and Dad to ignore too.

I was full-on smiling. *Fuck you, you dead bitch.*

She would've laughed, and I swear, I almost heard it.

God.

Her presence was so strong.

Head's up. Your Willow-replacement's little sis is approaching. In three, two . . .

"Mackenzie?" Peach knocked on the door.

I froze for a second and then looked around. Was Willow actually there?

No.

I was going insane. That seemed more logical.

Ryan's sister poked her head in. Seeing me, she pushed farther inside, shutting the door behind her with a gentle *click*. Her back kept to the door, and she looked down at her linked hands in front of her. "Um . . ."

She was there for something. I waited for whatever it was.

"I'm sorry."

She stopped after that, and I frowned. "For what?"

"For?" Her chest lifted. She took a deep breath and looked up. Shame hung heavy, like bags under her eyes. "I didn't really think about what you went through." She held her hands up. "*Are* going through, and I'm sorry."

Okay. She apologized. I had no clue why. "I don't understand you. What'd I ever do to you?"

Her face closed in on itself as if she were in pain. "You're going to think I'm an idiot."

I already did, so I kept quiet.

She sighed. "I was jealous of you, and worried because of you."

"Huh?"

"It's so completely stupid. I—Ryan doesn't like anyone."

I snorted. "Besides Tom, Nick, Cora, and Kirk?"

"Yeah, but they've only recently come back in the picture, and he doesn't talk to anyone in the family. I'm his sister, and after Derek died, Ryan only hung out with Kirk. Then Kirk left, and . . ." She didn't finish.

"What are you talking about?"

"Derek died during Ryan's sophomore year. Except for ball, he stopped doing everything for an entire year, and then Kirk left, and it was—he was like you until a few months before you moved here. When that happened with your sister, and you came here, I hated you. I saw how you attached yourself to him, but Ryan wasn't pushing you away. He pushed everyone away until you showed up." She faltered, glancing down for a moment. "I didn't want to lose my brother again."

"You thought I would do that?"

She jerked her head up. "I was scared he'd slip back into whatever had him before."

It made more sense. Ryan's response to me, why maybe I was pulled to him, even her attitude.

"I'm sorry for that."

"No." She shook her head, smoothing back some of her hair. "I'm sorry."

I saw the tears that lined her eyes.

She wiped them away. "Anyway, I wanted to say that."

She slipped out again before I could respond.

I sat there, feeling . . . nothing. Again. Or maybe still?

Another quick knock, and Kirk's head came around the door this time.

I read the apology on his face before he started to speak, and I held up a hand. "Please. Don't."

"What?"

"You're here to apologize?"

His head lowered. He grabbed the back of his neck, kneading it. "Uh. Yeah. I am."

I shook my head. "I honestly don't need it. I didn't go off on you and then come sit up here, expecting you to come to me with your tail between your legs."

"Well." He looked down, the beginning of a playful grin tugging at his mouth. "It's there." He moved his hips from side to side. "I can let my hair grow longer, if you want, so there'd be a real tail."

"No." I laughed a little at that. "Ryan's letting everyone have it down there?"

His hips stopped moving, and he nodded. "Yeah. I feel like a dumbass. Erin never told me any of that stuff. She just said that Ryan had changed since you came into the picture. I'm protective of him, and it isn't just because of my cousin. If you hadn't noticed, Ryan's loved. By *a lot* of people."

I was getting that.

I shook my head. "It's fine. Don't jump down my throat again, okay?" I laughed. "I think I've reached my quota of confrontations. There've been more the past few months than ever in all my life."

"Yeah?"

"Yeah."

I could imagine Willow standing next to me, her arms crossed over her chest as she rolled her eyes. *Yeah, because that was my job. You're stepping into my shoes, sis.*

Kirk rubbed his hand over his face. "Look. I might be overstepping, but I get what you're going through. I thought I was going crazy. After Derek died, I saw my cousin everywhere—or, I thought I did."

I didn't know what to say. "Did he go away?" I finally asked.

He didn't reply at first. A second passed, and a hollow look entered his eyes. He was staring at me, but he wasn't seeing me.

"Not really, no," he replied softly.

Great. I should just go ahead and reserve my room in the mental hospital.

"But I don't want him to." He nodded to me. "You won't either, if it's the same for you."

I sighed. "I'm sorry for going off on you."

"I'm sorry for being the asshole you had to go off on. And for the record, I deserved it. You don't have to apologize for anything."

Willow grunted next to me. *Damn straight.*

Kirk motioned for the door, grabbing the doorknob again. "Ryan sent me up here to grovel and see if you wanted the spaghetti he promised. He's heating some downstairs. Guess pizza got shot down."

I thought of the forgotten one at my house. I hadn't been hungry then, but my stomach rumbled. Spaghetti sounded good.

I motioned for the door. "Lead the way."

He paused before opening the door. "We're good, right? I can tell him we're good? He won't kick my ass then."

"He said that?"

"His exact words were, 'Get up there, apologize, and mean it, asswipe, or I'll kick your ass.'"

That made me smile.

chapter seventeen

Ryan glanced my way when I returned with Kirk, a question in his eyes as to whether I was okay. I nodded and moved to sit in a chair behind the table. I was the new girl to this group. I'd fought for my place twice—and I would continue if needed—but as I observed everyone, I saw there was no more resistance. The only one unhappy with me was Erin, but everyone ignored her, including her friends. They seemed more eager to flirt with the guys, Kirk most of all.

When the food was heated, everyone got up and filled a plate before returning to the table. Someone pulled out drinks and passed them.

Ryan made sure everyone had food before grabbing his own plate.

He headed for the empty chair by Kirk, but before he could sit, the guys all moved down a spot, emptying the chair to my left. So Ryan took that one. Cora sat to my right, and no one paused their conversation as all of this happened.

I got it then.

All the resistance against me from the girls, from Peach, from Kirk—it was because they depended on Ryan. No one started eating until Ryan sat. And no one said a word about it. It was an unspoken rule. Once he touched his fork, so did everyone else.

Whether he knew it or not, Ryan was the core of this group. He was the glue.

A different emotion filled me. Warmth. It combatted that cold and almost-dead sensation, making me feel something I wasn't sure I wanted to feel.

"You okay?" Ryan asked quietly.

I nodded. "Yeah. I'm okay."

I felt proud of him, but I didn't know why. He wasn't my boyfriend. Yet, I'd laid claim to him somehow, and he'd reciprocated. I knew he'd had a choice, but in some ways, he hadn't—I'd crawled into his bed that night and woven a spell over him, never letting him go. The sane part of my mind knew that wasn't the case. He would've kicked me out, rejected me if he didn't want anything to do with me, and he hadn't.

I'd thought he was a nice guy who fell for the damsel in distress. He'd wanted to save me, but that wasn't the case.

He did what he wanted. He was turned off for a year. He smoked pot. He drank. He stopped caring about sports. He rebelled from his life and what was expected of him—in that way, we weren't the same.

No one had expectations of me.

Robbie does, I heard Willow remind me.

I sucked in some air, feeling moisture pooling at my eyes. Robbie. I hadn't texted him all day.

He's fine—stupidly happy at that school, but he's worried about you. Send him a text. Let him know you're fine, and then call him later.

I almost rolled my eyes, like I was going to take advice from a voice in my head. But I stood from the table. "I'm going to call Robbie."

Ryan nodded. "Okay."

I didn't go far, just sat on the front step and pulled my phone from my pocket.

Texting Robbie, I waited for a response. There was none. I didn't know his room number, so I called the school's main number.

"This is Haerimitch Academy. How may we help you?"

It didn't take long to be transferred to Robbie's room, and a second later, I heard his voice.

"Hello?"

"I'm a horrible sister."

He laughed. I could hear him brightening up. "Hey, terrible sister. I'm your terrible brother here."

I snorted. "Why are you terrible? I'm the one who didn't call to check in last night."

"I'm terrible because I didn't call to check in with you today."

"You didn't have to."

"But I didn't think about it."

"Let's cancel each other out so neither of us is terrible."

He sounded happy, and I relaxed a little. Maybe the voice in my head was all-knowing somehow?

He's happy to be away from the memories. Willow was sitting next to me.

Yeah, maybe. I spoke to her, but it wasn't aloud. I kept that last safeguard from slipping further toward my insane side. I wasn't talking to her as if she were a real person. She was a voice in my head.

Willow laughed. *You're such a dope. I'm not made up. You're too chickenshit to admit it.*

I ignored that, clearing my throat into the phone. "Tell me everything. I want to feel like I was there."

Robbie laughed. He sounded like a kid there, like a young genius, eager to be challenged for once.

Good.

Maybe my parents got one thing right after all.

As long as Robbie was okay, I'd be okay.

I listened to him for the next hour, hearing about his roommate, his classes, his teachers. They were talking about testing him for college courses already, and I wasn't surprised. My brother was damn brilliant.

He's going to be fine there. He's more worried about you. I ignored Willow again, but I could feel her smile as she added, *Don't give him reason, sis. He'll blossom there.*

As he should. Finally.

Toward the end of the call, he said, "Keep calling, Mac."

He used her nickname too. My cheeks were starting to hurt from the smiling and the beaming and the whole trying-not-to-cry thing. Damn. That was work.

My throat was hoarse because of all the happiness. "I will."

"You tell me how you are next time. Deal?"

"Deal." I stuffed it down. He didn't need to hear me being emotional. "When?"

"Um . . ." He was quiet a second. "Maybe Thursday? I talked to Mom and Dad. I'm going to stay here this weekend."

"What?" I went rigid.

"There are a lot of others who stay, and they have weekend programs." He sounded so sorry.

He'll come home when he wants to. Trust the little Einstein. He knows what he's doing. Don't make him take on your shit. He's eleven, not seventy.

I ignored her again, but Willow had a point.

"That sounds awesome. Maybe I should try to get in," I teased. "Think they have a placement for older students? You could be my mentor."

Robbie started giggling. Once he started, he couldn't stop. "That's silly, Mac."

There. There was my little brother.

"Okay." I felt like I could hang up. He *was* okay. "I'll call on Thursday."

"No. Let me call you. Some of us are going to create a video game, so I'll call you when I get finished."

My little brother: future creator, inventor, and computer hacker. I was so proud.

"Love you," I told him.

He said the same, and after ending the call, I sat for a minute.

I had to get up. Someone would come looking for me, probably Ryan. The guy was taking me on as if he were my mentor instead of Robbie. He didn't need to. I wasn't like him. He had slipped away, and Peach feared she'd lose him again.

It made sense, but I wasn't going to do that.

Right?

Or maybe I should pull away? Try giving him space, make him seek me out. Then it wouldn't be me affecting him. It'd be him, his decision. I could do that, except . . . I couldn't. Even thinking about it had a hard weight slamming into my chest.

I wouldn't be able to do it.

Somehow, some way, Ryan had become necessary to me. He shielded me, protected me. My head was above water with him. Without him, I would sink.

I would drown alone.

I heard the door opening and wasn't surprised when he sat next to me. His arm brushed against mine.

"You sleeping here tonight?" he asked.

Did I have any other choice?

Water pressed down on me. I felt the air slipping from my lungs. I almost felt myself thrashing, trying to get to the surface.

"I'll hide in your closet till your mom goes to bed."

His grin turned rakish, and mine matched.

He nodded. "Deal."

COUNSELING SESSION THREE

"You didn't leave during our last session. I think you're making great strides, and thank you again for coming back. I know you've been missing the other appointments, but I feel I need to remind you that the school and your parents both agreed these sessions are a necessity for you. It's been a few months since your sister died. I was hoping today you could talk to me about her?"

A heavy silence. "No."

She sighed. "I don't know your sister. I can't comprehend what it's like to lose a twin or to be the one who finds her. Please, Mackenzie. I really would like to know more about your sister. Tell me about her."

Another heavy silence. "Her name was Willow, and she left me."

chapter eighteen

One month later

WE WERE AT A DANCE. Black, silver, and pink balloons hung from the walls and pooled all over the floor. There was a pink banner at the back of the gymnasium—we were at our old school.

A sad song was playing, and our friends were dancing, their arms wrapped around each other. It was Homecoming.

Willow stood on the stage, her Junior Queen crown on her head and her pink dress shimmering. She looked like part of the it, as if they'd specifically designed the theme around what she was wearing.

If I hadn't known better, I would've believed that wholeheartedly.

Willow and I both had light brown hair and sometimes golden blonde hair. It ranged in shades—it all depended on the season or whether Willow had been to the hair stylist lately. She'd spent more time in the sun over the summer, and her hair was almost a normal blonde. It hung in curls down past her shoulders, extensions adding another six inches, and it looked good. She was like some sort of Greek goddess, owning the attention of everyone around her.

No, it was the way she wore it, the way she stood—as if she owned the entire gym. That was what drew everyone's eyes.

Only a few might've realized it, but we were all living in Willow's world.

She turned to look at me, her eyes haunted. "Don't ask me."

I stepped up next to her and looked down; I was wearing the same dress. I hated pink. I felt the crown on my head. I hated crowns. And I looked over my shoulder—my hair had grown and was a lighter shade than normal.

I was her.

I looked over the gym again. We were no longer at our old school. I didn't recognize this one. It was new to me, like the question burning in my throat.

"Don't. Please." She began to whimper.

I looked at her. I mirrored her body posture—chin raised, shoulders back.

"Why did you do it?" I asked.

Black tears rolled down her face, her makeup smudging. "I can't answer that."

I tried a different question, the one I almost hated her for. "Why did you leave me?"

I bolted upright in bed screaming.

A hand clamped over my mouth and pulled me back down. Arms wrapped around me, and Ryan pushed me into the bed. He braced himself over me, and I could barely make out his eyes in the dark.

"Ssshh!" he whispered.

Fuck.

Reality flooded back. I was in Ryan's room, Ryan's bed, and this was my fourth week of sneaking over.

A door flew open down the hallway.

"Shit!" Ryan jumped over me, running to his door.

Feet pounded down the hallway.

"What are you doing?"

"Hide!" he whispered. Then he was out the door and running to meet his parents.

"Ryan!" his dad bellowed. "That sounded like your room."

"It was Peach!" Ryan yelled back.

"It was Peach?" Their mom's voice hitched up in worry. "That didn't sound like one of her screams."

Three sets of feet ran down the hallway and then another door opened and a light went on.

He'd said to hide, but I had to be quiet. Stealth. They couldn't find me or this was over. Panic began clogging my throat. I pushed past it and started to slide from the bed.

"Peach? Honey?"

"Uh . . .what?" Peach's voice was groggy.

"You screamed," Ryan said.

"I did?"

"Honey, did you have a nightmare?"

"Uh . . . maybe? I must've."

"Oh, honey."

Their mother turned nurturing, and someone's footsteps crossed the floor as another two sounded closer in the hallway, as if they were leaving the room.

"You acted quick," Ryan's dad said.

I almost squeaked. It sounded like he was walking Ryan back to his room.

Moving like a ninja, I lowered myself to the ground and rolled under the bed. This had been my move to hide from Willow if she decided she wanted to talk late at night.

Two shadows stood at the door.

"How are you doing? I know you and that Malcolm girl have become close."

"What?" Ryan's voice matched the slight hysteria I felt.

Shit, shit, shit. If they found out about me, if they told my parents, if this, if that—so many ifs ran in my mind. But they couldn't. None of that could happen because then my parents would start watching me again. I wouldn't be able to sneak out, and Ryan wouldn't be able to sneak in, which was our pattern. We traded off unless we knew one of us absolutely couldn't get away.

"I talk to Phillip every now and then at work. He's struggling. I'd assume they all are. How's the girl?"

"Uh, she's dealing. I think."

"Peach said you were close. Rose said she's been over a bunch."

"Oh! Yeah. I mean, yeah. She's dealing. I mean, that's all I can say."

His dad sighed. "I suppose. Phillip said the littlest is at the gifted academy. He seems to be liking it a lot. They go down there four times a week to see him."

They do? That was news to me.

"What about her?" Ryan asked. "Are they checking in with her enough?"

I almost cursed. What was he doing?

"I suppose. It was her twin. I'd imagine they worry about her the most." A second later, he added, "Why? Are they not?"

"No. I don't know."

"You're friends, aren't you? You're acting weird, Ryan. What's going on with you?"

"No. I know. I mean, I'm not. Yeah, we're friends. She's in our group with all of us."

"She and Cora are friends then?"

"Uh." Ryan sounded so stiff, like he had a stick up his ass. "They're both the girls in our group. It'd be weird if they weren't."

"You're still being weird."

"It's in the middle of the night. What do you expect? Peach woke us up with a blood-curdling scream."

"Yeah." His dad sighed. "You're right. All right. Listen, go to bed. Maybe I'll ask Phillip if they want to come over for dinner sometime. Would you like that? Have your friend over for a meal with the 'rents?"

"Sure. Yeah. Sounds good."

Again, I wanted to smack him. He could've discouraged that in two seconds.

"Okay, son." A thump on his back. "Try to get some sleep. I love you, Ry."

"Love you, Dad."

One shadow entered the room, the door clicked shut, and soft footfalls moved back down the hallway. I waited for Ryan to come back to the bed, but he didn't move.

"Mackenzie?" he whispered, half-hissing. "You here?"

I could stay under the bed. He'd assume I slipped out, went home, and I could haunt him the way Willow continued to haunt me. But that wasn't nice, and he wasn't the person I wanted to get back at.

I crawled back out from under his bed. "You were having a nice chat with your pops there." I stood, sliding back into the bed.

He came over and reached for the covers. "What could I do? If I acted weird, he might've thought something was off."

"He *did* think you were acting weird."

He shrugged. "Normal is easier said than done. I kept thinking, *Whoa shit! I got a hot chick in my room somewhere, and they can't find out, and whoa shit, whoa shit, whoa shit!*"

I laughed, lying back down in his bed. "I got it. I'd be weird too."

He gazed down at me. "You aren't normally pissy with me. You mad about something else?" Waiting a beat, he added, "He brought up your family."

My throat burned, his words echoing in my head. "I didn't know they'd been going to see Robbie four times a week."

"They didn't tell you?"

I shook my head.

"Your brother didn't say anything?"

Another head shake.

I was barely home, and if I was, it wasn't for long or I wasn't alone. I had no clue they were driving to see Robbie. A part of me was glad, thankful they checked in on him, but another part of me ached with jealousy.

I was there. I was in their house, and I struggled every day to say something.

My parents weren't evil. They didn't mean to forget about me because they didn't love me, but I fully believed they didn't want to see me.

They saw her when they saw me.

So, I stayed away. Hell, I didn't even enjoy looking in the mirror myself.

My eyes were hers. My hair. My body. I'd lost weight, losing the healthy weight I held with those Cheetos. The more I dreamed about her, the more she talked to me, the more she haunted me—I was becoming Willow.

If I took her place, would they mourn Mackenzie? Maybe that would be easier for them.

"If they do the dinner, we can have everyone crash it."

I laughed lightly, my body curving toward Ryan's. "They'd love that, actually."

"Your parents?"

"No, the guys." The guys included me and Cora.

After the night of apologies a month or so ago, I'd gone to school the next day, and they'd all walked next to me like I was one of them. That was how it had become. I considered Tom, Nick, Kirk, and Cora friends as well.

A hand touched my cheek, and I started as Ryan brushed away one of my tears.

God. I brushed at it, and then the rest. My whole face was like a waterfall.

I groaned, turning and pressing my face into his pillow.

"Hey." His voice was so soothing, so kind, it almost broke me again. He straightened some of my hair and then smoothed his hand down my back. He shifted, lying on his side. He continued rubbing my back, and his voice came from above my head. "You never actually talk about her, you know?"

I shook my head, rotating from side to side.

I couldn't talk about her. I just couldn't.

"What was your sister like?"

He cared and thought he was doing the right thing. At least, that was what I told myself.

It *so* wasn't the right thing though.

I turned, not caring about anything except avoiding talking about her, and grabbed him. I pulled him down on top of me, finding his mouth with mine.

I was desperate for it.

I was desperate for hi—no. I had to be honest, at least with myself. I was using him. There. I admitted it. I did care for Ryan, and maybe there were real emotions underneath all the craziness inside me, but I wasn't in touch with them right at the moment.

He could chase her away; he was the only thing that worked.

"Ryan," I breathed, opening my mouth under his, coaxing.

"Mac?"

God.

I normally loved hearing her nickname from him, but not tonight.

I sat up, still kissing him, and feeling something rising in me—something reckless, something wild, something intoxicating—I took my shirt off. I didn't sleep with a bra on, so as soon as my shirt was off, his hand was on my breast.

Yes.

That helped.

She was fading. I could feel her go.

"Are you—"

I shook my head, my mouth finding his again. I didn't care if I was coming across frenzied and desperate. It was how I felt, but the throbbing for him had started too. I . . . I stopped thinking. That was the only way she'd completely leave, and tonight, I didn't care how far we had to go for that to happen.

I wanted him, and that ache grew more and more fervent.

I gasped.

"Shit, Mackenzie," he growled, pushing me back down and looming over me. He was panting, but he fitted himself between my legs.

I could feel him through his boxer briefs, through my pajama shorts. I reached down, grabbed his hips, and jerked him close.

Right there.

I felt him where I needed him, and I began grinding against him. He moved with me, his hands growing more sure, more demanding, more rough. My frenzied need stirred the same emotion in him, and he was crushing me, getting as close as he could.

I could feel him press into me.

Move his briefs aside, my shorts aside, and we'd be one.

My mind had stopped working.

I no longer knew why he wasn't in me already.

My mouth opened beneath his, and reaching down, I touched him.

He cursed, shoving against my hand. He broke his mouth from mine. "You sure?" he rasped next to my ear and then lifted to peer at me through the darkness.

I nodded.

I had a small window of sanity, but I was ready. We were going there anyway. Willow was making me crazy, but yes. I was sure.

"I'm on the pill."

He reached up, brushed some of my hair away from my forehead. "You are?"

Another searing pain in my chest. "Willow had sex last year with Duke. We both went on the pill once our mom found out."

Good old Wills. My mouth turned down, and his thumb fell to my lip, rubbing it out.

"I have condoms," he whispered. "We'll be safe."

I nodded.

Take a goddamn breath, Mac. Fuck's sakes. Think about this. This is major. S-E-X, the big sex here. He's the guy you want?

I almost cried out, hearing her concern, and why the *fuck* was my mind working again? My mind wasn't supposed to be on her, but I listened to her question and focused on him.

I focused on Ryan.

I was a virgin. Was he the guy? And suddenly, I felt Willow leaving again. She was fading and taking all the pain, all the anger with her until it was only me lying in his arms.

The answer bloomed in my chest, and I nodded.

I was ready. I did want this, and with no one else except him.

"Yes," I almost whispered the word.

I wanted nothing more, and it wasn't tainted by the pain of my sister. It was pure, rooted in the feelings I did have for Ryan.

"Please."

His eyes darkened, and that was all he needed. He bent down, his mouth finding mine again.

Yes.

chapter nineteen

I HAD SEX.

I did it. That particular first in my life was done, and I was happy about who it was with. Under the seven layers of my emotional shit, there were real feelings for Ryan. I mean, I knew myself. I wasn't so damaged by WWD (what Willow did) that I was completely screwed up and would lose my virginity to some asshole.

Ryan was the right guy. I didn't know what was in the future—I could barely function with the today—but there it was.

Done.

I was no longer a virgin, and I was supposed to be different. Right?

I was supposed to look different?

No?

Gazing at myself in the mirror after showering, and knowing Ryan was waiting in bed for some post-coital cuddles, I searched those two eyes where a soul is supposed to be.

I saw nothing. For real.

There was the usual iris, eyeball, and such. Eyelashes. The literal round hole, but that wasn't me.

I winced and averted my eyes.

Fuck. I didn't even want to look myself in the eyes. Me. *I* didn't want to see what everyone else must be seeing.

There was nothing there. Emptiness. Dead. Dull.

I was gone.

There was nothing lively in there. No happiness, elation, a big fat nada.

I'd lost my virginity, and I was half-considering going in there and doing it again just so I could feel something.

Morbid much?

Oh, lovely. Time for my usual haunting.

Hey, Wills.

She leaned against the sink and crossed her arms. *You know, Mac, if you're actually crazy, you wouldn't be thinking of me only when you can handle it. I'd be popping in all the time and really haunting you. I'd be telling you to kill someone or something. Isn't that what voices do? Tell you to do bad shit?*

I wouldn't know. I'm not schizo. I'm mourning.

Willow snorted. *You're a head case, that's for sure. And yeah, maybe you're mourning, but honestly, aren't you prolonging the inevitable?*

I shut her out.

I felt what she was going to say, and I stopped her, literally imagining her out of my head, out of the bathroom, out of the house, and far, far away. I could almost feel her flying backward.

Then I opened my eyes.

Still here, dumbass.

She hadn't moved an inch.

Bitch.

She laughed. *Finally. Some sass. You're so fucking depressing. What happened to you? I mean, I know.* She indicated herself, her hands moving up and down her body. *But you know what I mean. You should've had your shit together a long time ago, but you're sucking at it. Come on, Soccer Superstar.*

I wasn't the soccer superstar.

Yes, you were. You were the superstar in everything. You just didn't know.

I was lazy, and I ate junk food, and I—

You were normal, but you were the best on your soccer team.

But—

You were normal, Mac. Her voice was so soft. *And that was a good thing. You got to be the normal one of us, even if you really weren't. You were what we needed. You were our anchor, still are.*

"You're the strong one, Kenz." I heard Robbie's voice, and I could see him all over again, looking at me from the doorway to Ryan's room that day. I'd flipped the cover back and let my little brother hide in there with me.

If only we hadn't ever left that shelter.

I expected a smart comment from Willow, but none came. Then I looked, and I almost gasped. Tears glistened in her eyes, and her hands were balled as if she were trying not to cry.

I'm so sorry, Mac.

What? A searing and burning sensation began to build in my chest. I started for her, my hand reaching out.

If I could take it back . . .

And poof. She was gone.

"No!"

She was right there. She was real. I could see her, speak to her, and she was gone.

Footsteps pounded on the floor behind me. The bathroom door flung open, and Ryan's eyes were wild.

"Mackenzie? What?" He saw I was staring at nothing and turned in a circle, looking around the bathroom. "Mackenzie? What . . ."

The same words, but such a different meaning.

No. Nope. I wasn't—I couldn't say it aloud.

She wasn't real.

She wasn't there.

She *was* gone.

"She was supposed to be here for this." The words wrung from me.

He turned around and sighed. "Oh, Mac."

Tears rolled down my face. I felt them falling, but I couldn't move, and I couldn't stop them.

"Mackenzie." He said it quietly, tenderly, and he pulled me into his arms. "I'm so sorry."

He cradled the back of my head and held me.

chapter twenty

"I KNOW WHAT YOU AND RYAN DID LAST NIGHT."

I jerked back, my hand hitting the locker and slamming it shut. I turned to face Peach, who seemed pissed. Her eyes were angry, her mouth a firm line. Her arms crossed over her chest.

She didn't seem it. She *was* angry.

And she was tapping her foot.

I eyed that foot. Who tapped their foot like that? Seriously?

"Say that again."

She couldn't be talking about what I thought she was talking about because then . . . ew. How the hell would she know that?

Her arms uncrossed, and her hands formed fists, pressing into her legs. "You screamed last night. I was dreaming about taking a puppy to a fair. Ryan put it on me, but it was you. I know what you two are doing. He's either sneaking over to your place or you're at ours. It was you who screamed last night."

Prove it.

I sooo wanted to say Willow's words to her, but the truth was, Peach could. Easily.

Open the fucking bedroom door at three in the morning, and the proof is there. So I kept my mouth shut.

Ugh!

I ignored Willow. I was still mad at her for disappearing last night.

Fuck you.

I ignored that too.

"What do you want?" I asked Peach.

Fine. She wanted to play ball with me? Well, there were consequences. I was going to call her on it.

She frowned, her head lowering an inch as she moved back a step. "What do you mean?"

"What do you want? If I screamed, what are you going to do about it?"

"Nothing." Her frown deepened.

"Then why'd you come over all heated like this?"

She shrugged, crossing her arms again. "I don't know. I wanted you and Ryan to know that I know. And why'd you scream?"

It wasn't something nightmare-worthy, at least not to others.

"I dreamed my sister and I were at Homecoming."

"Oh." She tilted her head. "That sounds kinda nice."

I snorted. "I knew you'd think that."

"It wasn't?"

I gave her a dark look. "It was my sister. Me. Homecoming. I'll never be able to go to another dance with her. You do the math." I turned toward my locker again.

I left out the part where I was becoming Willow. The creep meter was off the charts there.

"I'm sorry, Mackenzie."

Her quiet voice drew my eyes up to her again.

"I'm sorry your puppy dream got interrupted," I offered.

A giggle left her and then another. She shook her head. "Sorry. Just . . .puppy dream. Sounds funny when you say that."

I grunted. "I'd take a puppy dream over the weird shit in my head any day."

She sobered. "Yeah. I'm sure you would." A new softness emanated from her, and she murmured, "I'm really sorry about your sister."

I couldn't remember if she'd told me before, but the ring of sincerity told me she meant it this time.

Feeling choked up again, I nodded.

The warning bell rang.

I was standing in the hallway, getting all emotional with Ryan's sister four minutes before the next class.

Fuck this.

"I'll see you later," I told her.

I didn't wait for her response. Everyone else had started for their classes, and I merged with the stream to veer toward my classroom.

Ryan and I had sex.

Yes, I was on repeat, but I was giving myself a break. I had to process things while I was refusing to process something else, and that something enjoyed haunting me.

Aaand back to processing what I could: I was no longer a virgin.

It hurt at first, but then it felt good. Then it felt really good.

I was there for Willow after she had done the deed. I sat on her bed and listened to every detail.

I hadn't been crying last night because I couldn't share that experience with her. I cried because I wouldn't have.

Willow was supposed to know. She would've cried, begged me for the 411, and I wouldn't have said a thing because Ryan would've been important to me. Willow would've been jealous. She would've wanted him for herself, but I had him, and I got him because I crawled into his bed that night.

Willow was supposed to know . . .

Get over yourself. I'm so here, but you won't admit it. Right, Mac? When did you start talking to yourself? Yes. Yes. You're crazy. You're so nuts, they'll ship you to a hospital so you don't do what I did. That's your real worry, isn't it?

"Enough!" I roared, and like that, I was staring at my classroom, and Willow was gone.

Every person in the room—including the teacher—was looking at me.

I was smack dab in front of the door as the last bell rang.

Mr. Breckley cleared his throat. "I quite agree. Enough. It's time for some learning." He ignored the light smattering of laughter and motioned to me. "Now, if you'll close the door, Miss Malcolm, we'll get to today's lesson."

My neck felt warm.

I kicked the doorstopper out and went to my seat, ignoring the questioning looks from Tom, Nick, and Cora.

chapter twenty-one

"Hey." Ryan's greeting shouldn't have stood out with all the noise in the hallway, but it was as if I'd become attuned to his voice, his body, him. The rest of school, all of it melted into the background, and I turned, knowing he'd be standing there, watching me with the quiet concern maybe he shouldn't have had. The tension eased from my body.

This was wrong.

I shouldn't be depending on him this much, but I moved toward him. My body was already betraying me.

"Your sister knows." I meant to say more, explain, but the need to get Willow from my mind made me forget.

I stepped toward him, and he mirrored me. It was as if we moved as one unit. My back went against the lockers, and he stood in front of me, his hand resting against the locker beside me. I couldn't stop myself. I leaned into his hand and reached for the loop on his jeans. He reacted to my touch, sucking in his breath, and I saw him go rigid, but I didn't pull him against me. I held on to that loop. It was an attachment to him.

"What?" His eyebrows went up.

"About me sneaking over," I clarified. "That I screamed last night, not her."

"Oh." His shoulders slumped. "Not about the other thing, right?"

"No. Not that."

"Fuck, Mac." He gave me a crooked grin. "You gave me a slight heart attack."

I smiled. "Yeah. Not that."

"We didn't talk after . . . well, after us and after your bathroom thing," he said.

Right.

I glanced down, feeling all sorts of awkward again.

He'd held me until we had both fallen asleep. His first alarm woke me, and I told him I could hurry to my house alone. I'd started bringing clothes to his place and vice versa, but it was never the same as getting ready at your own house. I needed some space this morning, and when he'd picked me up an hour later, I'd been the Avoidance Girl.

Avoid the sex talk. Avoid the bathroom meltdown. Avoid. Avoid. Avoid.

I felt the walls closing in on me, and I knew I couldn't keep avoiding forever, but I was going to do my best. Call me the Superstar of Avoidance. I'd wear that pin proudly, if I got around to it.

I shook my head, a small signal that I still didn't want to talk about it, and my finger moved against his stomach.

His eyes warmed, and an invisible rope tightened between us, pulling us toward each other. He leaned closer, and I felt myself moving away from the locker door.

The next bell was going to ring. We'd have to go into our class, but I didn't want to pull back. I didn't want to be with other people. I wanted to stay here, stay with him, or go somewhere else and just be alone with Ryan.

I wanted to skip.

I hadn't skipped since that first day, and a part of me didn't want to do it again. If I did, I didn't know whether I could stop myself later. Already I could barely manage the temptation to disappear with only him. I could shut everyone else out, shut out the world, and yes, shut out Willow. She was the main one I wanted to shut out.

Love you too, asshole.

That was all I needed.

"Let's get out of here."

"Yeah?"

I nodded, scanning up and down the hallway. The others were starting to head to class. If we were going to go—I saw Kirk and Nick headed our way. Their eyes were right on us like we were targets and they'd locked in.

"Never mind."

Ryan looked around and cursed under his breath before he moved, half blocking me from their gazes. "Hey, guys."

Nick's eyes narrowed suspiciously, but he hung back as Kirk stopped in front of us.

"Let's skip," he said.

Ryan and I both straightened in surprise.

"What?" Ryan asked.

It was only then that I noticed how Kirk's eyes were blazing. A scowl was firmly in place, and everything about him radiated anger. He shoved his hands into the pockets of his black bomber jacket, pulling it tight around his form.

"I gotta bounce from here. Let's skip." He looked around at all of us. "You game?"

Nick wasn't saying anything, but Ryan looked at me.

"I'm in," I said.

Ryan studied me a moment.

"Are you going?" I asked Nick.

Kirk shifted, throwing his arm around Nick's shoulders. "Hell yes, he is." He thumped him on the arm twice. "He's coming."

"Yeah. Sure."

His tone didn't suggest he was eager.

Then Ryan pulled me away from my locker, opened it, and put away his books. Grabbing my hand, he shut the door and nodded. "Lead the way, Kirkus. You got point on this one."

"Sweet. Let's go."

A few others saw us go, but Kirk ducked out through a side door, and we jogged across the lawn, heading for the parking lot. Nick and Kirk went for his truck, but Ryan grabbed my arm and pulled me a different way.

"We'll follow in mine," he called.

Nick looked like he was going to say something, but Kirk raised his arm. He didn't look back, and if anything, his pace picked up. After a couple of beats, Nick turned and hurried after him.

Ryan and I wove through a few rows of vehicles, closing on where he'd parked. Without speaking to each other, we broke apart, going to our doors. I waited until he unlocked the truck, and then I was in and grabbing the seatbelt.

He climbed in, and a moment later we were easing out of the slot, waiting for Kirk's truck, which didn't take long. A black SUV sped past us, only pausing for a second at the exit before it took off.

Ryan wasn't as fast, but he caught up after a block.

"Where are we going?"

"I don't know; Kirk will choose a place."

I remembered the almost-crazed look in his eyes. "Did something happen? Do you know?"

"Who knows. Kirk gets like this. He needs space or has to get his mind off something."

"What do you guys do when that happens?"

Ryan shrugged, flicking on his turn signal and pausing at an intersection. "Honestly, this isn't that normal. I mean, it is for Kirk and me, but since he's come back, he's been with the others more than he was before. It used to be him and me."

I read between the lines there. "And you're with me most of the time now."

"Yeah." He started through the intersection, glancing at me as we moved in behind Kirk's SUV.

"You okay?" he asked moments later when we pulled into a driveway.

We parked behind Kirk's truck, but I didn't see anyone still inside.

"Where are we?"

"Kirk's place."

"Won't his parents—"

Ryan laughed. "His dad works in the city like yours, and the staff won't say a thing. Kirk skipping *is* normal."

Great. Another abnormality that was becoming normal. I was on the fast track to becoming a juvenile delinquent.

"Okay."

Ryan laughed a little and then sighed. "We didn't talk about last night."

He'd brought this up earlier. I wanted to evade it then, and I still wanted to.

Normal life, normal Mackenzie would've been freaking. I would've called or texted Willow from the bathroom. I would've lain awake the rest of the night, wondering if I'd done everything right. If I should've showered or was I clean enough? How was I supposed to lay with him? Any move he made, I would've analyzed. Or, who knew? Maybe I was channeling Willow again, because that was what she would've been doing.

Willow told me all about her first time. She freaked out, but she never showed it. Not in front of her boyfriend, not in front of the guy she'd been dating at that time, not even in front of her friends. I saw the freak-outs. They were behind closed doors. Always behind closed doors.

Goddamn. Duke's abs were like a seven-layer cake I could lick all day, but he was as dumb as the barbells he used in the gym.

I almost sighed and thought to her, *Thank you, Wills, for reminding me.*

Happy to help. You're going on this whole memory-lane journey. I want to clean it up, make sure you're using my language and not yours.

Yes. Thank you. I was not serious.

Willow snorted.

"Mac?"

A rush of heat swept through me. Ryan had been staring at me the whole time I talked to Willow in my head.

"Sorry. What?"

"You okay?"

I was going insane. "Totally fine. Let's go." Opening my door and jumping out, I took in Kirk's house.

The driveway curved up and around a hill and there was a Spanish-style fence outlining a large yard. The house looked Spanish, too, and it had with brightly colored tiles and a veranda in front. Large, neatly trimmed bushes ran up and down the length of the yard.

Kirk's house was huge, but I wasn't surprised. They had a cleaning lady and a butler, and as Ryan predicted, neither seemed surprised nor disapproving as we all traipsed in.

"Thanks, Mitchell." Kirk clapped the butler on the shoulder.

His dark blue suit didn't seem to move under the touch, and he barely blinked an eye. He had one of those faces that might've been warm and friendly if he smiled. He didn't. His face seemed encased in plastic, like if he smiled it would break the whole thing. I placed him around sixty, with silvery graying hair, perfectly combed in place.

"Will your guests be staying for dinner?" he asked.

Ryan opened his mouth, but Kirk said, "Yes, and we'd like to have a full-course meal from Joann's delivered."

That got a reaction.

Mitchell blinked a few times. The muscle near his mouth twitched and then . . . nothing. The mask was back in place, like he'd magically gotten a dose of Botox.

"Very well." He disappeared down a hallway.

I watched him go. I saw his shoes touch the tiled floor, but heard not a sound. How was that even possible? Willow could take haunting lessons from him.

She snorted. *The stiff has nothing on me.*

Kirk led the way to the back. He hit a button and two walls on the end slid open, revealing the pool. Parts of the backyard were outside, but parts were indoors with glass walls separating them. There were benches made out of blue and white tiles, but there were also couches and lounge chairs with cushions on them. Two different grills sat on opposite ends of the deck, and the whole thing was covered in cobblestones.

The backyard was massive.

Kirk went to a refrigerator and hollered over his shoulder, "Who wants a beer?"

Nick moved past me, grunting. "If we're going to skip, let's do it the proper way."

Kirk threw him an almost evil grin, and I was surprised to see Nick's eyes darken, matching it.

Putting the beer away, Kirk pulled out a tequila bottle instead. Grabbing five shot glasses, he held it in the air. "Tequila it is."

Ryan groaned. "This is not a good idea."

"Come on, lover boy." Kirk's eyes narrowed, passing to me before moving back to his best friend. "What? You think you're the only one who can be the bad boy? Move aside, buddy. I was your partner in crime before. I'm claiming my place again."

Ryan laughed. He was close enough that I could feel the tension ease from his body. "Fair enough." He moved ahead, his arm brushing mine. "All right. Let's do this the proper way, hmmm?"

Nick frowned. "What's the proper way to take a tequila shot?"

Kirk and Ryan shared a grin as Kirk bent, bringing out salt and limes from the fridge.

Ryan narrated as Kirk poured tequila into all five glasses.

"Salt that hand."

Kirk salted.

"Lick it."

Kirk licked.

"Down the shot."

Kirk drank it in one gulp.

"And suck on the lime."

Kirk sucked.

"Holy shit!" Kirk spat out the lime, wincing and shaking his head. "Now that's the right way to do a shot." He pushed all the ingredients toward Nick. "You're next."

Nick eyed everything warily. "We're going to be hurting by tonight, aren't we?"

Ryan laughed. "Did you really see any other ending for one of Kirk's skip days?"

Nick groaned as he reached for the salt. "You're right. God. This is going to hurt." He poured it over his hand and eyed Ryan at the same time. "You aren't on the football team, but I am. I was supposed to have practice today."

"Convert. Join the basketball team with me."

Kirk started laughing.

Nick grumbled before licking his hand. "I'm on that too." He made a face as he grabbed the shot, downed in, and planted a lime in his mouth. "Goddamn! That burns."

He moved back, still grimacing, and then it was Ryan's turn.

There were no words or pauses. He took the shot like a pro and had no reaction afterward. It was as if he drank water. I couldn't decide if that was alarming or if it turned me on. Either way, it was my turn.

Three sets of male eyes settled on me.

This was what I wanted: another way to escape my life.

I reached for the salt, and the world melted away.

This scene should've made me nervous, right? Drinking tequila in the middle of the day with three guys I barely knew? This never would've happened a year ago. I would've been in school, talking with friends, and griping about soccer practice.

But that was then, and things had changed.

I wanted to do this.

I felt Willow at my side. *Come on, Mac. This is stupid. Getting drunk? Really? You already had sex. I mean, how many more cliché ways can you rebel against—*

I blocked her out, pouring the salt. I licked it and then took the shot. Ryan held out a lime, but I ignored it. I reached for him instead and fused my mouth to his.

Yes! There was the burn I wanted, and after a thorough kiss, I reached for the salt again.

I heard the guys saying something, and I felt Ryan's surprise, but he was behind me. His hand fell to my waist and tightened there. I could sense him thinking of saying something to stop me, but I shook my head, and his grip softened.

I took a second shot, ignoring the lime once again and fully turning into Ryan's arms.

He was waiting for me this time, and as his mouth opened over mine, I was aware of him pulling me away from the others. He kept kissing me, licking, tasting, teasing until suddenly the sounds of the water, of Kirk and Nick, all fell away. Darkness surrounded us. We were in a building, and when Ryan reached for the light switch, I stopped him.

"No." I grabbed him, pulling him back, and he pressed me into a wall.

His mouth became more urgent, more demanding.

My body grew heated, and as my head fell back, gasping for breath, I knew this was what I had hoped to be doing today instead of sitting in class.

I wanted to get lost with the feel of him, and I wanted more tequila.

I didn't want Kirk and Nick there. I wanted to be alone with Ryan, and as his mouth fell to my throat, I could tell he felt the same way. His hips pressed into mine, and I could feel him wanting me.

With a growl, his hands caught my hips, and he ground into me.

chapter twenty-two

A KNOCK CAME ON THE DOOR. "HORNY LOVEBIRDS!"
Kirk stood outside the door, and he gave two more knocks before Ryan pulled away.

Growling, he jerked the door open an inch. "What?"

A smug snicker came from the other side. "You two can get it on later. Today's my day."

Ryan wasn't amused. "Your skip days are usually about getting high, drunk, and/or laid."

"Not today."

I caught a quick flicker of a grin on Ryan's face before he masked it and moved farther away from me. His hand still rested on my waist, but once my hot flashes had subsided, I enjoyed watching this exchange play out on Ryan's face.

He loved Kirk. That was obvious, but he was wary of him. Still, he was becoming more open to whatever Kirk was going to say. His hand had relaxed on my waist, and since we were at his friend's house, I thought maybe the right thing was to cool our lust jets a bit. But once we were alone again? Hell yes, I'd be jumping Ryan.

And you still think you aren't trying to be me?

I stiffened, hearing Willow's mocking tone. I ignored her.

I'm you, Mac. You can't ignore me, and you know it. That's like you ignoring yourself.

I gritted my teeth and caught Ryan glancing at me.

I can ignore myself all I want, I shot back and shoved toward the door—and out of Ryan's hold.

"Wha—" Ryan watched me stalk past Kirk, who shifted quickly out of the way.

I went back to the tequila bottle, saw a shot already poured, and downed it. Salt be damned. I still didn't need the lime either.

And goddamn—that burned. I felt it this time, and that meant I needed another one. I was reaching for my fourth shot when I felt another presence beside me.

Goddamn Willow. She was never going to leave me alone.

"So, not to be blunt in an offensive way, but . . ."

Not Willow.

I looked up. Nick was staring at the shot in my hands like he could see a worm in it. His eyes flicked up to mine. "But your damage is your sister, right?"

It took a second for his question to penetrate. The booze was starting to fog everything. I blinked at him. "What?"

"I mean . . ." He coughed, turning around to rest against the table. He gestured over his shoulder to Ryan and Kirk, still talking outside the pool shed. "Kirk's damage is his parents' divorce, and his dad is hardly ever around. Ryan's damage is losing his best friend close to two years ago, and yours is your sister, right?"

My hand felt like punching him.

I scowled. "Yeah. That. No big deal." My tone was biting.

He paused, and then a crooked grin formed. "Oh. Sorry." He straightened from the table, his hand running through his hair. "I'm not trying to be a jerk—"

"Too late."

He didn't blink. "I wanted to ask because I didn't want to assume anything. My sister says I do both. I'm a jerk, and I assume too much."

"I might love your sister."

He laughed, easing back to rest against the table again. "I know we've all been hanging out for a while, but since you and Ryan are obviously more than fooling around, I figured I should try to get to know you a bit. You know, one on one."

I took the shot, dropped the glass on the table, and moved away from him. Without breaking stride, I said, "That's weird."

Four shots. Dear Tequila Lord, please work more. I don't want to feel *anything* anymore.

He followed me toward the pool. "My sister says I'm that too."

Nick mostly stuck to conversation with Kirk and Ryan. If he wasn't talking to them, chances were high he was ragging on Tom. He rarely talked to me, and I could see why. I was on edge, and I knew he had a mean streak in him, so I was thinking this combination wasn't a smart one.

I called to Kirk, "You have bathing suits around here?"

Kirk pointed inside the pool shed. "In here. Marie keeps everything washed, so if it's on the floor, just leave it. It hasn't been cleaned yet." He hit Ryan's shoulder and jerked his head backward. "Come on. Let's take another shot."

He stepped aside as I came over to them. His words were for Ryan, but he was watching me. "I don't want to lose you in there with your girlfriend again. Who knows when the two of you will come back out."

I stopped right between the two. I could feel Ryan behind me, and I knew he was going to touch me. And in three, two, one, his hand came to rest on the small of my back.

I suppressed one of the good shivers and forced myself not to lean back against him. It would've been so easy.

Instead, I fixed Kirk with a glare. "Tsk, tsk. You're coming across as jealous."

Kirk's smug grin vanished. His eyes widened, and he straightened. "That isn't what I meant."

"Still." God forbid we didn't play by Kirk's rules for how he wanted the skip day to happen. I winced inwardly at the amount of anger I felt.

I didn't like being chastised by Kirk, but I also didn't like the way I was acting.

I could feel Ryan's gaze on me as I shut the door with him outside. He was saying something to Kirk, and I recognized reproach in his tone. I leaned back and let out a deep breath.

Good God, what was I doing?

Skipping. Taking four shots of tequila. Making out with Ryan and smarting back at his best friend? Being snide to his other friend?

Reaching behind me, I locked the door and slid down, my head hanging between my legs. One moment. I needed one goddamn moment for everything to settle.

Willow sat next to me. *It's only going to get worse, twin sister.*

Go away.

I have nothing better to do. I check in with Robbie, and he's sad, but he's at least grieving me in the right way.

Was I going to indulge in this? Yes. Apparently, I was. *What are you talking about?*

He cries, but then he goes and plays with his friends. When he feels the grief, he stops and feels it. He doesn't deny it like you do.

I couldn't. She didn't understand. If I let it come—I shook my head and pushed myself back to my feet. I couldn't have this conversation, real or not. If I let any of it in, I'd be crushed. It was a mountain of raw, blistering pain, and I wouldn't come out intact.

She didn't know. She didn't understand. No one did.

Swimsuit, Mackenzie, I told myself. *Find one and stop thinking. It's fucking simple.*

I felt Willow's presence as I found a suit and put it on. She was always there, but I was getting better at pretending she wasn't. And feeling the tequila really begin to kick in, I knew she'd be gone real soon.

Completely gone.

Grabbing a towel, I threw open the door. *You can stay in here.*

After that, I walked right to the pool and dove in. Once I was in there, I didn't stop. I couldn't. The tequila was fast starting to dull my senses, but it'd wear off. I had to keep going. I started doing laps. I'd tire myself out.

And it worked. I don't know how long I went, but I just kept going until the others jumped in with me.

I felt the splashing before a pair of arms slid around my stomach, and then I was airborne.

Shrieking, I saw Ryan grinning at me a second before I crashed into the water again. I rose back to the surface in time to see Kirk lunge at Ryan, and then the wrestling was on. Nick cannonballed over them, letting out a yell as he joined the fray. The three dunked each other a few more times until Ryan noticed me watching. He grabbed my ankle, yanking me to him. I felt the slide of his body against mine before he threw me in the air once again.

After that, it was war.

Kirk, Nick, Ryan, and I spent the next hour trying to dunk each other. I was mostly the loser, but every once in a while, I pulled out a surprise and got one of them.

I'd gone from feeling crazy, to wanting to jump Ryan, to almost fighting with Kirk and Nick, to crying, to laughing and playing in the pool.

As skip days go, it was one of the better ones.

After another hour, I pulled myself out. My body was tired, my mind lethargic, and the booze still securing me in a warm fog. That was all I cared about. I padded barefoot to one of the lounge chairs. Two towels were on the end of the chair and I settled back, pulling both on top of me like blankets. I settled in, curling as much into a ball as I could, and watched the guys roughhouse.

At some point a shadow blocked the sun. It was enough to wake me, and I opened my eyes to find Cora frowning down at me.

"You were sleeping?"

I sat up, rubbing a hand over my face. There was a small pounding behind my temples—goddamn tequila. I looked over, but the guys weren't in the pool anymore. They'd moved to the couches, tossing a basketball back and forth.

"Yeah. I guess." I skimmed over her, noting her backpack still on and her shirt untucked from her jeans. "What time is it?"

"Almost four."

"You came over right after school?"

She nodded, studying the guys before letting out a sigh and dropping her backpack to the ground. She sat on the lounge chair beside me but didn't move to lie down. She stayed on the edge, turned toward me, and kept her eyes on the guys.

I saw the worry lines around her mouth and sat farther up, pulling the towels with me to keep warm. I was a little chilled.

"What's wrong?" I asked. "They in trouble for skipping?"

Her narrowed eyes met mine briefly. "I doubt it. Kirk never gets in trouble for skipping. He never did. Nick's mom will probably get a call, but she doesn't really care. If he says it's because one of the guys had a hard day, she'll be okay with that. And Ryan . . ." Her bottom lip stuck out farther, and she trailed off.

Aha. I got it. She was worried about Ryan.

"I thought you were okay with me and Ryan?"

Her eyes jerked back to mine, widening slightly. "What?"

"You're concerned about him."

"No." She tugged at her shirtsleeve and then smoothed the ends of her shirt over her pants. "I mean, he skipped the first day because of you, and now he skipped because of Kirk. He went downhill the other year because of him."

"His friend died."

"I know, but . . ." She stopped talking, her teeth sinking into her bottom lip.

She didn't get it. It didn't make sense to her how grief could be overwhelming. It made more sense to blame Kirk's influence than Ryan losing a friend.

Fuck. What did she think my problem was?

"It must be nice," I murmured, resting my head back against the chair.

Her eyes flickered. "What?"

"Not to have lost anyone."

Her head lowered. "My hamster died when I was twelve."

Pets could be family members too, but I didn't assume hers was. She didn't sound too broken up over it.

Real and genuine jealousy slammed through me. It hit my chest, my heart, my stomach, every single cell in my body—all the way from my toes to my hair. I wanted her life. I wanted it so badly I was almost crying.

I would've given up Ryan to have what she had.

"Everyone knows the four of you cut today."

I was still envisioning life without that pain, so it took a second for those words to register.

It was my turn to frown. "So?"

"So." She reached up to tighten her ponytail. "Everyone knows you guys skipped."

I wasn't following her. "Is that a problem? Or what? I'm not getting what you're saying."

"No." She went back to chewing her bottom lip before shrugging. "Stephanie Witts knows. All the girls, and guys. They wanted me to call them when I found out where everyone was."

Oh. Shit.

"Tell me you didn't call. Right?" I leaned forward, pulling my legs in and tucking the towels under my arms. "You didn't call those girls."

She didn't answer, and I could see she was chewing the inside of her cheek.

Fuck! She did. I groaned, letting my head fall forward to smack my palm. "How long until they all descend?"

She jerked up a shoulder, sitting silent.

"Hey!" I waved my hand in the air. She was staring at the guys and barely answering me. "When did you call them?"

"Oh." She glanced at her phone. "Like ten minutes ago."

More voices came from around the side of the house. Tom rounded the corner of the house first and the rest of the guys followed. I saw Peach and Erin with them. There were more shadows behind her, and as Tom reached over a fence and opened the door, they filtered in. Erin's friends had come with her.

The line didn't end.

I recognized some guys from my grade coming in.

Cora muttered almost to herself, "Those are the basketball players. The football team isn't here. They had practice." She watched as Nick pounded a few of the guys on the arm. "Nick's going to get in trouble for missing today."

More people came in, flooding the entire backyard.

I stopped watching, but I heard what she said.

His coach would get upset, but not his parents.

Erin called Cora's name, and I jumped up from the lounge chair.

"Where are you going?" she asked.

I didn't answer. As Erin headed over, I zipped back into the pool shed and locked the door behind me.

I couldn't do this. Not all these people.

My insides felt pulled apart and put together wrong. Nothing felt right anymore. I couldn't sit on a lounge chair with Cora, hearing whatever Erin had to say—whether she was going to take digs at me or kiss my ass. She'd resorted to the latter over the last few weeks, and I didn't get it. Whether she wanted to be friends or not, it wasn't happening.

My only real friend was Ryan.

And that's the problem.

God, not now! I snapped at my ghost.

Willow rolled her eyes. *You haven't made it right with Zoe and Gianna at home, and you aren't making friends here. I get that Cora's a little weird, but Mac, you're fast becoming weirder. You're almost a leech on Ryan.*

Shut up. I paused a beat. *And Zoe and Gianna, that's on them. They wanted me gone, not the other way around.*

She snorted. *So yell at them. Curse them out. Get mad. Don't just disappear. I mean, I know.* She changed the subject. *I get it, Mac. A part of you wants to go grab your boy and pull him away from his friends, but you can't. Let the guy have a fun day for once. Don't make yourself his problem. If you're together or not, it isn't going to last if you keep going on like this.*

I said shut up.

This is tough love. I get that you're falling apart because of me, but don't mess up the one thing you've gotten right. Give him some space.

She was right, but I didn't want to be lectured anymore. Surging to my feet, I changed back into my clothes and grabbed my bag. I had no clue where Kirk's house was, but I figured I was safe. Everyone was talking or laughing when I slipped out of the pool shed. Some were in the pool, but I didn't see Ryan anywhere. Guessing he was inside, I moved around the backyard and left through the same gate everyone else had come in through.

I'm not running away, I told myself firmly. But I was lying.

I was totally running away.

Not wanting to be a clinger, as Willow claimed I was becoming, I sent Ryan a text.

Me: I'm heading home. I forgot I was supposed to go see Robbie with my folks. I'll give you a call when I get back.

My phone vibrated almost right away.

Ryan: **Are you sure? How are you getting home?**

I was walking, but I pulled up the car service app. After ordering one to pick me up, I relayed that to Ryan.

It took a moment before my phone buzzed back.

Ryan: **Okay. Call me later then.**

I thumbed back, right as the car pulled up next to me.

Me: **Totally. Have fun!**

Then I climbed in, and the car took me away.

chapter
twenty-three

I EXPECTED THE HOUSE TO BE EMPTY WHEN I GOT HOME.
It wasn't.
I walked inside, dropped my bag onto the counter, and looked up to see my mom at the kitchen table, her laptop in front of her. A coffee mug sat to her right and there was a bowl of fruit to her left. She wore her headphones, and she bit her lip before she looked up.

Seeing me, her eyes widened, and we stared at each other.

"What are you doing here?" I asked.

She took off her headphones. "What are *you* doing here?"

I frowned. "It's after school."

"Yeah, but you never come home anymore."

I pointed to her computer. "You're working?"

She turned to look down at her laptop as if she'd forgotten it was there. "Oh. Oh yes. I decided to take a day at home." She stood, her chair sliding back, and she paused there. It was as if she wasn't sure why she'd stood. "Do you want something to eat? An after-school snack?"

I didn't want to, but I felt myself grinning. It was like I was in third grade again. "What? You're going to cut up apples for me?"

"No. I would . . ." She stopped and continued to frown at me.

I heard her in the mornings, moving around, getting ready for work. My parents used to check in every night, and I stayed in my room until that was done, but they'd stopped last week. I stared at my mother, trying to remember the last time I'd seen her, the last time I had really talked to her.

I couldn't remember.

But I did see how she flinched when she met my eyes, how she looked back down, how her hands gripped the table, and how she swayed in place as if she were about to collapse.

A silent storm built inside me. I felt a scream in the back of my throat, and as I stared at her—not moving, not looking away—I could feel that scream ripping at my insides.

I was wailing. I was crying. I was pleading for her to look at me again—because what mother doesn't want to see her child's face? But no sound came out.

I stood there for another minute. She didn't look up. It was a reverse staring contest. I was demanding her attention in a passive and peaceful way, and she wasn't budging.

"I'm still your fucking child."

Her head snapped back. She was already pale, but her lips seemed to turn blue, and she swallowed.

"I know." It came out as a whisper.

I moved forward a step and then stopped. She wasn't saying anything else.

She should've been saying something else.

I waited, my heart pounding, and I heard her sniffle.

Her hand brushed over her cheek, and I saw her tears. She was crying so soundlessly, I wouldn't have known it if she hadn't moved.

She looked away before she began to speak. "I lost a child, and I have continued to fuck up being the right parent ever since. I work too hard every day to keep my mind straight. I don't sleep at night because I know you aren't in bed, but I'm so scared to make demands of you. I know you can make demands on me in return. Your father and I barely talk, except when we go see Robbie, and we haven't once told you about those visits." She heaved a deep and shuddering breath. "You don't sleep at home, but then some nights you are here, and I have no idea how I'm supposed to feel about anything anymore."

I couldn't—what did she say? "You know where I am at night?"

She laughed bitterly. "I've not been the best mother, but I'm still a mom. You're goddamn right I have a tracker on your phone." She stared at me hard. "Are you having sex with him?"

My mind raced, but my stampeding pulse stopped completely. I felt it fall with a thud to my stomach.

"You know?"

Her lips barely lifted in a smile. It was more of a grimace. "Of course. I've known, and so do they, Ryan's parents."

"I . . ." I had no words.

"Nan called the other day, said you'd screamed in the middle of the night. Ryan put it off on their daughter, but they guessed it was you later on. She didn't know if I knew or not."

I felt lightheaded. "How long have you known?"

She took a breath and sat back down. "The first night you didn't come home. You were with him?"

"You knew then?"

"We didn't. We guessed."

"Oh."

I reached for the chair in front of me and pulled it out. My butt hit it with a hard *thud*.

My mother laughed again, the sound hollow. "It started that first night, didn't it? Nan told us how Ryan helped you sleep, and then it continued."

God.

I gulped.

My throat hurt so much.

Her voice grew thick. "We have never stopped watching out for you, loving you, or thinking of you. But we've been selfish, selfish people lately."

She still wasn't looking at me. Her eyes remained fixed on her computer.

"I'm supposed to be at the office today, and your father and I were going to go see Robbie, but I couldn't bring myself to go in. I got ready. I sat in the car, and when your father began to back out, I told him to stop."

Tears traced down the sides of her face.

"I've been working all day here."

"What about Robbie?" I winced. My voice sounded gruff and hoarse.

"Maybe I'll go tomorrow." Her eyes found mine, and they seemed clearer for a moment. It was like seeing the moonlight on a clouded night—one second it was there, and the next second, the clouds closed over it. "Would you like to come?"

A lump the size of the Titanic settled in the back of my throat.

I started to nod, and then I couldn't stop myself. I kept nodding and nodding. "Yes. I'd like that."

She stared at my bag on the floor. "Do you have homework to do?"

"I skipped today."

Her eyes flicked back to mine, and she swallowed. "Really?" She coughed once and frowned. "What did you do today?"

"We went to Ryan's friend's house."

Her head shook once. It was swift, an abrupt movement. "Was there drinking?"

"Yes."

We'd had almost no communication for weeks, and it was as if the dam had opened, and I wanted to tell her everything. I wanted to get in trouble. I wanted . . . I wanted to be normal again.

"Sex?"

Okay. That wasn't one of the things I wanted to share. "No."

"No as in ever, or no as in today?"

Her eyes were beady and staring hard.

Damn. She had me.

"No as in today."

Her eyes closed, and her chest lifted in a silent breath. "Okay. That answers the question you avoided. You and Ryan have had sex?"

My tongue felt heavy. "Yes."

"When?"

"Last night."

She looked up, her eyes wet. "Was last night the first?"

I nodded as my throat closed.

"Ever?" That word was hoarse.

I nodded.

"So you're no longer a virgin?"

I felt my tears then. They rolled down my cheeks and somehow, I felt a piece of me fit back in the right place.

"Yes."

Her shoulders began to shake. She lifted balled-up fists to her mouth and hunched over, shoving her chair back. Her head rested on the table as she cried.

I couldn't hear a sound. Still.

chapter twenty-four

"SHE KNOWS EVERYTHING?" RYAN ASKED.

I lay on my bed later that night, my phone to my ear. "They've known about it the whole time."

"Shit."

"Yeah." I rolled to my back.

I could hear music blaring in his background and assumed he was still at Kirk's. He'd texted a few times since I'd gone, so after the meltdown with my mom, I called him. He needed to be warned about what was coming. I'd also had to fess up about not going to see Robbie.

"You lied?" he'd asked, his voice sounding off.

"I didn't want to be a clinger and make you hate me for being all fucked up in the head."

He laughed. "I've never told you, but I think the reason I let you stay in my bed that first night was because of how fucked you are in the head."

I sat up. "No way."

"The more fucked up they are, the more I like them."

I rolled my eyes, hearing the teasing in his voice. "You're messing with me."

He laughed again, a short bark. "Yeah, I am. You aren't that messed up, and if I'd met you without everything that happened, I still would've wanted you. I can tell you that much. You don't have to worry about me."

You hear that, Willow?

I imagined her response: *Bite me.*

But we moved our conversation on to the fact that I was going to see Robbie tomorrow.

"Are you going during school or after school?"

I frowned. "I imagine after school? My mom wasn't too thrilled to hear that I'd skipped today."

The two pieces that had molded together earlier seemed to reach out and fit with another. That was three pieces of me put back together right. I could feel an almost calm emanating from them.

I could only smile, knowing I looked like an idiot, if anyone were to see me. They would've assumed I was glowing because I was on the phone with Ryan, but nope—just me, my messed-up self, and three little pieces.

It would've made sense only to Willow.

Hearing the shout of voices from his end, I asked, "You're still at Kirk's?"

"Yeah." He sighed and then barked at them, "Leave me alone! I'm on the phone!"

Something slammed, and the sound was suddenly muffled. He came back to the phone, clearer. "Everyone's drunk. Kirk's shut himself in a room with two chicks. Cora is crying, and she won't tell me why." He sounded so tired. "I made Peach go home, but I'm pretty sure she hates me now."

He was being a good brother. "Come over here."

He didn't reply at first. "Are you sure?" he finally asked. "I mean, with your mom knowing . . ."

"I'll sneak you in." I suddenly wanted to see him so badly. "Can you drive?"

"Yeah. I only drank when you were here, and it was those two shots of tequila. I've been holding the same beer bottle since then so everyone stays off my back."

My heart sped up.

He was coming over.

"Okay. Park around the corner. I don't know if my mom is back to being a mom or if she was on a break from her mourning this afternoon, so it's better to be safe than sorry."

He chuckled, sounding tired. "Okay. I'm sneaking out of here. Be there in a bit."

After we hung up, I went to my door and opened it an inch. I listened, but there were no sounds coming from anywhere in the house. I knew my mom was home. And it was around eleven, so if my dad wasn't home, he'd be coming soon.

Tiptoeing down the hallway, I felt wrong—like I was breaking and entering on my own property, but I wanted to know. If my mom was up and about, that'd make things difficult for sneaking Ryan in.

The main living room was empty.

So was the study.

Her office.

The kitchen.

No longer caring about sound, I ran upstairs. My heart pounded again.

It was still somewhat early for us. Usually, my mom would be in her office or in the living room, but I never checked their bedroom.

It should've been the first place I looked, and once there, I flung open the door.

I expected . . . something. Snoring, the blankets bunched up where my mom should've been.

But there was nothing. Absolutely nada.

No one in her bedroom, her bed, her bathroom, her closet. I even looked under the goddamn bed, because you never knew. I was hoping.

I raced down to the basement. Nothing.

I still turned on every light in every room, even in the freaking closets.

The same. Nothing.

The back patio. Some nights she would sit out there with her laptop and a glass of wine, and I held my breath as I climbed the stairs. But to no avail. Even before I opened the back door, I knew no one was out there.

I felt the dread stirring in my gut.

I had one last place to look, and going to the garage, I stood a moment in the doorway before I comprehended what I was seeing.

There were no cars.

My dad had the main one, but . . . our Tahoe was gone, too—the vehicle my mom used if she had to go somewhere on her own.

They were both gone.

She had left me.

After the whole no-more-virginity talk and everything . . . well, there hadn't been a talk. She'd sat and cried until I got uncomfortable and started to slip away. She asked if I wanted something to eat. I told her no and changed my mind later.

I went back down to the kitchen, but she wasn't there. I'd heated up some food—who knows how long it had been in there—but nothing else looked good to me.

It made me wonder if she been gone this whole time. Had she already gone then?

I was walking back to my room to get my phone when I saw the answering machine blinking. I usually ignored the messages. They were always for my parents, but what did I have to lose? Maybe she'd called and left me a message?

Hitting the button, I heard, "You have one new message, sent from Charlotte Malcolm."

I moved closer.

"Hey, honey. Your cell isn't working for me, for some reason. I went to the store to get some food. We only have old pizza in the fridge, but your father called. Something came up. I'm heading into the city tonight. Be a good teenage daughter. No sex. I'm sure Ryan will sneak over, and that's fine as long as you guys sleep. Only sleep. You got that, right? And go to school tomorrow. I'll leave work early to pick you up before going to Robbie's. I love you, and—" The message clicked off.

I hit the next button, skipping to the message after hers, but it was someone for my dad.

I don't know how long I stood there.

She hadn't left me. She'd called. She remembered me.

She was gone for the night because things came up. That made sense.

The three little pieces, which had started to splinter apart again, started to settle back into place. They were still intact.

I took a calming breath.

My hands were sweating. I rubbed them down my lounge pants.

They still cared.

She still cared.

A soft knock came from the door, and I looked through the window.

Ryan had arrived.

chapter
twenty-five

I WAS BARELY SLEEPING WHEN I HEARD A SOFT THUD.

Sitting up, I felt Ryan's arm tighten around my waist, and I paused. His breathing was still even. I hadn't woken him. Gingerly slipping out from underneath his arm, I crept out of bed.

There were two nightlights set up in the hallway, one at each end, so I could walk toward my parents' bedroom without needing to turn a light on.

Shivers moved down my spine as I padded away from my room.

Thud!

"Shit."

I paused. That was my father. Frowning, I moved closer. Their door wasn't closed. It was open two inches. One of the lamps was on, and as I peered inside, my dad walked past me, heading for the bathroom.

The bed was made. No one was sleeping. Instead, piles of clothes were all over it with a bunch of boxes set around the room. Some were open, and some were already closed. They had been moved closer to the door, as if ready for pick-up.

My dad came back out of their bathroom, his arms full of toiletries. He dumped them into one of the boxes and tossed some of his shirts on top before closing it.

"What are you doing?" I moved inside, opening the door wider.

My dad cursed, whirling around. He ran a hand over his face. "Holy shit, Mackenzie. Warn a dad next time, would you?"

I ignored him, focused on the boxes. "What are you doing?"

Were we moving?

I knew we weren't.

That wouldn't have made sense.

"Oh, honey." A whole new voice came from him—the one I'd heard when he told me we were moving to Portside.

I started shaking my head.

"Where's Mom?" I asked.

"She's . . ." He took a breath, looking around, and his hand went to his hair. "I can see how this looks, but—"

"It isn't that? You aren't moving out?"

My eyes met his, and I knew it was happening.

I could feel Willow behind me, but she was quiet. For once.

"No." His shoulders slumped suddenly. His hand fell to his side. A look of sadness flashed in his eyes.

I didn't feel sorry for him.

A foreboding dread sat at the bottom of my sternum. It wouldn't move so I could breathe easier. It was blocking everything, and I felt like I was going to throw up.

"What are you doing? No bullshit, Dad."

He gazed around the room once more and gave me the strangest look, like he was seeing into me.

"I'm moving out."

I didn't know if I should be relieved or sad. I was neither. I just was. I nodded, looking away.

This made sense.

Grief tore families apart. Didn't a brochure tell me that one time?

I hugged myself, half turning away. "Are you leaving Mom or are you leaving us?"

He didn't respond at first, and I knew the answer.

I wanted to turn completely away, give him my back, but I couldn't bring myself to do it. I could feel his gaze.

"I'm moving closer to Robbie."

So he was just leaving Mom and me.

I knew Robbie was at a school and that he seemed to be enjoying it. I knew it was probably good for him not to be living in this dead house, but that was all wrong too. He should be at home. My mom should be there too. My dad shouldn't be leaving.

I shouldn't be left alone.

"Mac?"

And the award for best timing ever went to Ryan.

The floor creaked from down the hallway.

"Who is that?" my dad demanded gruffly. "Is that a boy?"

I wanted to roll my eyes. I refrained. Barely. "You're leaving us. What do you care?"

His mouth closed with a snap, and his Adam's apple bobbed. I could see him thinking about it, and that was when I noticed the graying hair at his temples. There was more around his ears. The bags under his eyes were epic, and I could've sworn his wrinkles had doubled since this summer.

My dad wasn't an old man, but he was close to resembling one.

"Mac?" Ryan's whisper was a lot louder. He was right outside the door.

"Who are you?" my dad demanded.

Ryan opened the door and looked at him but had no other reaction. He knew what he was walking into.

"Ryan Jensen, sir. You work with my father." His shoulders were firm, and he didn't slouch as he spoke. He wasn't going anywhere.

That was when I knew for sure. He had come for me, no matter what happened after this.

"Oh." My dad lost all of his fight. "That's right. Your father talked to me, mentioned you and my daughter were friends." He looked between the two of us, lingering on my tank top and shorts before going to the lounge pants Ryan wore. He had pulled on a T-shirt.

My dad rubbed at one of his eyebrows. "You're sleeping here, Ryan?"

"Yes, sir."

"He's sleeping with you, Mackenzie?"

I nodded. "You know he is."

"No. No, I didn't." His tone was quiet. "Your mother's been in touch with Nan. I'm assuming that's what you're talking about? Your mother knows?"

I nodded again. Why did it feel like I couldn't swallow anymore?

Silence filled the room, and Ryan moved closer to me. "Are you okay?"

My dad started laughing and turned toward one of his boxes.

I shook my head, my gaze holding Ryan's, but I said, "My dad is moving closer to Robbie."

Ryan didn't respond. He wasn't there for the details. He was still waiting for my cue, if I needed him to stay or if he could go.

I hadn't made up my mind, so I didn't answer.

My dad resumed packing, his shoulders tight, and he flung a hand up, knocking his tie over his shoulder.

He was still dressed for the office. I hadn't registered that before. It seemed pertinent for some reason.

"It's almost three in the morning," I murmured, half-asking myself. "Why haven't you changed clothes?"

Had he gone somewhere after work? Was he going in to work early?

Willow snorted behind me. *I doubt he's even going to work, sis. You aren't paying attention. Smell, Mac.*

Smell what?

Him. You aren't wearing vanilla perfume, and I don't think your honey is either.

I felt choked, like someone had reached around and tightened their hold on my throat. She was right.

There was a distinct smell, but it wasn't vanilla. It was lavender. He smelled like flowers.

I turned to Ryan.

My mom wore a citrus perfume. She hated lavender.

"Mom said you wanted to meet up in the city. Was she wearing perfume when you saw her?" Somehow, I doubted that was hers. My mind was putting two and two together faster than my emotions could, and I felt myself weaving on my feet.

Ryan moved closer, resting his hand behind my hip. His touch steadied me enough to keep me from falling.

"You're seeing someone else."

My dad whirled back to us. The blood drained from his face, and then his eyes found Ryan's hand.

"Get your hand off her."

I ignored him and surged forward. "Who is it? Who are you leaving us for?"

"Honey." He flinched as if I'd slapped him across the face.

"Does Mom know?"

His shoulders slouched, and his head hung down. He balled up the shirt in his hand, holding it against his chest. "She knows."

He couldn't look at me.

He wasn't just leaving us; he was going to someone else.

A new family.

Willow and I thought the same thing at the same time.

My stomach twisted, and I could feel the bile rising.

"Who?"

"You won't know her, honey."

He was speaking in whispers. I wasn't. My voice grew firmer with each question I asked.

"Who?" I might not know her, but maybe Ryan did. "Is it someone you work with?"

It had to be.

He'd only worked since Willow. And he went to see Robbie, but that was with my mom. Right? They went together?

"Mackenzie, we can talk about this late—"

"WHO?"

I didn't need Ryan to help hold me up. Rage was doing fine all on its own.

"Mackenzie, honey . . ."

My nostrils flared. "I said who. I want to know who!"

His mouth clamped shut. His hands went to his hips, the shirt too, and he regarded me. It was as if the air had turned solid between us, and my question was like trying to cut through it with my bare hands.

So be it. I wasn't afraid of blood. Anymore.

I took a step closer. "Who, Dad?"

"This isn't the time to talk about this."

"You tell me or I will make your goddamn life hell."

Our eyes locked, and he seemed to be weighing whether I meant my threat. I did. I *so* did.

He let out a sigh. "Her name is Mallory Lockhart. And yes, she works with me."

I didn't look back, but I sensed Ryan's surprise.

"You're moving in with her?"

"I . . . yes. At least for a while. Your mother and I talked about everything earlier tonight."

I couldn't fathom any of this. My mind went blank, and I pushed forward. I needed to get as much information as I could.

"Where's Mom right now?"

"She's at a hotel near Robbie."

That was three hours away. I wouldn't be going anywhere except to school tomorrow.

"And that was a lie? You saying you were going to move closer to him?"

"No. Well, yes. Mallory's home is closer to the city and closer to Robbie." He coughed. "I don't think your mother is going to be home tomorrow. Are you, I mean . . ."

I looked up. He was watching Ryan with a hard expression.

"What?"

"You'll be okay to fend for yourself? At least for a few days?"

I laughed then.

I knew everything I needed to know.

No Robbie tomorrow.

No Mom tomorrow.

No Dad until who knew when.

I didn't answer my dad. I turned, my hands brushing against Ryan's as I did. It was as if I were watching us from outside my body. It was the three of us again.

I left.

Ryan went behind me.

And Willow brought up the rear.

COUNSELING SESSION FOUR

"You told me a bit about Willow last time. How about you today?"

Naomi's smile was nice and bright, and I wanted to scratch it off her face. She folded her arms over her lap and gestured toward me, her smile trying to make me feel like we were friends.

"Your mother called. She said you're seeing a boy. What's his name?"

A heavy silence. I was becoming so used to them; they were my real friends in this room. I smiled and leaned forward. "We fucked."

That nice smile-that-was-not-really-my-friend vanished. "What?"

chapter
twenty-six

Mallory Lockhart was thirty-seven. Her relationship was complicated, and she was an ads manager at West Coarse Technology. She had brown hair, a heart-shaped face, hazel eyes set a little too close together behind wire-rimmed glasses, perfectly trimmed and arched eyebrows, and a petite and compact body.

Her bachelor's degree was from West Scottridge University.

She'd shared five puppy memes over the last day, three sarcastic quote memes over the last week, and she had more than two thousand social media friends.

She'd recently gotten a golden retriever named Bugsy, and she was "excited to have her new pup for a new chapter in her life."

I leaned forward to see the timestamp on that last post. It was four days ago, posted at 7:03 in the evening. I scrolled through the comments.

"Love you!! So proud of you."

"Big hugs, babe xoxo"

"Can't wait to meet Bugsy!"

"Adorable! Yay!" (insert a gif of a puppy tearing up a pillow and then falling backward off of a couch.)

Heart emoticon heart emoticon heart emoticon heart emoticon

"Wonderful to hear. So happy for you."

I stopped reading them. Apparently, all her friends were ecstatic for her. I wanted to piss on each one of them.

Fuck them. Fuck her. Fuck my dad. Fuck them all.

That "new chapter" wasn't just about a dog. I bet they didn't know that. Maybe I should educate each one.

"Are you still cyberstalking her?" Cora asked as she dropped into the seat next to me in our school library.

Still. I almost laughed at that, but rage had been a firm friend since last night.

I hadn't slept after Ryan and I went back to my room. He had, but I couldn't. I went right to the computer and got all the information on my dad's mistress. I knew her mailing address and her birthday. I had figured out her family members. I knew where she had gone to high school and college. And Google had helped me guess at her annual income.

But none of that told me why.

Why my dad? Did she pursue him? Did he seek her out? How did they meet in the first place? A joint project? Did she work with him on projects? Had they started flirting at the water fountain? Coffee hut, maybe?

I hated her.

I didn't know her, but I hated her.

I looked over at Cora. I'd given Ryan the task of questioning his parents about Mallory Homewrecker Lockhart, but I needed someone as crazy as I was with the stalking skills.

"I want to drive to her house and slice her tires," I told her. "No, no, I want to drive to her house, ring the doorbell, and make her as uncomfortable as she's made my family hell." Which would be a lot.

I didn't need Willow to call me out. I was projecting everything onto this mistress, and I knew it.

I didn't care.

My dad was grieving. He was supposed to go to my mom for that.

Pot meet kettle.

Okay. I heard Willow there. Our family sucked all around at comforting each other, except that my mom had actually decided to be a mother. She went above and beyond. I got a text saying the visit to Robbie had been postponed and she knew I'd talked to my father. She promised to speak to me later because she knew I would have questions. And if all that wasn't enough, she'd called Ryan's mom.

I was supposed to stay at the Jensens' for the rest of the week and weekend, but not in Ryan's bed. I was to go home after school, pack a bag, and Ryan would drive me to his house.

I rolled my eyes when I read that last text. Such a silly (or delusional) mother, acting like I was in third grade and she'd arranged a weeklong sleepover. I'd go over to Ryan's, but probably not in time for after-school snacks. I'd go when I wanted to go. Sometimes she forgot I'd actually turned eighteen.

I rolled my eyes and clicked on the mad icon under one of Mallory's posts.

Cora leaned forward and laughed under her breath. "You're in your sister's Facebook account. That's creepy and hilarious at the same time."

I felt Willow's pride and shrugged. "She'd think it was awesome."

Cora looked at me, her gaze lingering, but I ignored it. I kept scrolling through more of Mallory's posts to put the mad icon on all of them.

"She'll know it's you. You know that, right?"

She would, and I grinned. "She can prove it."

Cora shifted back. "Dude. You look evil right now."

If she only knew what went on in your head.

I ignored Willow and clicked the mad icon under another post.

"That's a Pinterest meme on DIY Halloween decorations."

I kept scrolling. "My dad hates Halloween. She should know that."

Cora laughed again, but the sound was becoming less amused and more cautious.

I couldn't be bothered with any of it. I was a madwoman on a mission. If my mom wasn't going to rage about this whole situation, I was. Willow would've been going nuts. She would've screamed, demanding answers. She would've been on the phone, calling the mistress and our mom at the same time.

She would've burned our house down—figuratively . . . I think?

I waited to see if Willow had anything to say, but she was quiet. Come to think of it, she'd been quiet more and more lately.

I'm taking on her personality.

That was why. Willow was living through me, so she didn't need to—and the bell rang.

Thank the gods. That stopped me from having a whole conversation in my head about why my dead sister wasn't talking to me anymore . . . in my head.

Cora grabbed her bag and stood. She hugged it against her chest as I clicked out of everything on my computer. "Everyone is going to Patty's for lunch. Are you going too?"

I grabbed my bag and began walking out of the library. "Who's everyone?" I asked as we got to the door.

She ducked out behind me. "The guys. Ryan, I think. Erin. Her group." She shrugged. "I don't know. The popular people."

Ah. Popularity.

The stuff normal teenagers cared about.

I glanced over at her, but she wasn't looking at me. "I'm not popular."

"Yeah, you are."

"No." I shook my head. "I'm not."

"Yes, you are. Trust me. You are, even if you don't know it. You're with Ryan, and the other girls are scared of you."

They should be. There were two of me, and one of us could haunt their asses. I snickered at that but didn't reply. I wasn't popular, and I didn't care. I hadn't cared in Arizona, and that hadn't changed. Ryan was the only benefit of moving.

I stopped in the middle of the hallway. Some students protested behind us. I ignored them.

Cora had taken a step forward, but she stopped and looked back.

"Is that why you wanted to be with him?" I asked.

Her eyes enlarged, and her mouth made a popping sound. "Uh, what?" She adjusted the bag in front of her, hugging it tighter.

"You want to be popular?" I shook my head. "But aren't you? You're friends with those guys. Shouldn't that make you popular too?"

A strangled squeak left her throat. "This is so embarrassing."

"Why?"

People were trying to press around us. One guy cursed at us, then saw me and coughed to cover it up. "Sorry. Hey, Mackenzie." He was gone before I could say anything, but I could see the back of his neck turning red.

"See? DJ Reynolds has no idea who I am. That would not have happened with me." She pointed in the direction he went.

"No, I'm not. I'm . . ." *Damaged. Broken. Half-dead. Having sex*—make that I *had* sex. Once. I was sexually experienced, kind of. "This is not normal me. Trust me. Normal me is not popular. Normal me . . ." I hesitated, but normal me was like Cora. Somewhat.

Everyone likes you, Mac. Get over yourself. You never have to try for anything.

Willow had said to me the day we found out we were moving. I flinched when I remembered.

She had been so wrong. She was the one everyone liked. Even my two best friends had dropped me because they missed her so much. Didn't she get that? Had she really not gotten that? She was the star.

I looked away. "Normal me was invisible. Trust me."

I was wrong. I hadn't been like Cora. She cared the way Willow cared, but Willow had succeeded. She'd thrived with the social hierarchy stuff.

I needed to stop thinking about Willow.

I felt her snort and thought to her, *Sorry, but you make me slightly deranged.*

Only slightly?

Cora and I needed to get moving. The next bell would ring soon, and I clamped on to her arm. She was watching me with her head tilted to the side, but I wanted to make sure she heard me.

"I lost my sister. My brother moved to a different school, and I found out last night that my dad is leaving our family. If I could switch places with you, I would. I'm not saying you don't have problems or struggles. Everyone does, but I'm saying rethink what you want. If you want to be popular so much, forget it. It isn't worth it."

She looked down, but I heard her say, "It isn't worth it to you."

"It isn't worth it to anyone."

That would be utopia. If everyone was kind, if everyone was worthy. If there were no hatred, pain, or suffering. If people couldn't see someone's skin color, quality of their clothes, where they lived. If nothing mattered except the heart and mind.

I wanted to live in a world like that. I could almost taste it, I wanted it so bad.

I gentled my tone, "If I'm popular, then trust me. I'm miserable. You aren't. I've seen you with the guys."

The second bell rang.

I was late, but as I turned down the empty hallway, which was thankfully empty, I looked back. Cora hadn't moved, her back toward me.

Hope fluttered in my chest. It was small, but it was there.

A fourth piece inside me found the other three. They fit the right way.

chapter twenty-seven

Cora acted differently the rest of the day. I don't know why it made me feel good, but it did. We went to lunch with everyone else, taking seats in the booth next to the guys. When Erin and her friends came over, Cora didn't react like she normally did. She didn't get all nervous. She didn't start fidgeting. She didn't jump when Erin said hello.

She was cool. There was a confidence radiating from her, and I knew the guys took note. Erin too, with a slight frown as she went back to her table of friends. The guys kept sneaking looks at Cora on the way back, and for the rest of the day.

I wasn't sure if Ryan noticed anything. He was more perceptive than people realized. He just hid it better.

Kirk nudged my shoulder in our seventh period.

"What?"

He pointed his pencil at Cora, who was filling out the worksheet we'd all gotten. "What's going on with her?"

As if hearing him—and she might've—she straightened, holding her head high. If she'd been wearing a crown, it would have remained firmly in place, not like the other times when she'd duck her head or hunch her shoulders.

I almost smiled with pride, but I shrugged instead. "I don't know. She looks sexier than normal, doesn't she?"

Ryan glanced at me, a strange look on his face.

But Kirk was studying Cora, and he nodded. "Yeah. She does." A mystified expression flitted over his face. He nodded again. "Yeah."

He grabbed his worksheet and bag and left our table. Sliding into the seat next to Cora, he nudged her arm.

I felt Ryan's gaze on me, but I bent over to finish my worksheet.

His foot went to the book rest underneath my seat, and he pulled my chair toward his. He drew me close enough that our legs pressed against each other's. "What happened there?"

I shrugged. "Beats me." But I was grinning. I almost felt silly.

Something felt right. For once.

Ryan didn't push it. I knew he'd ask later, and I'd tell him. Cora was his friend. He'd be happy.

After a few more minutes, I stopped trying to fill out my worksheet. My concentration was useless, so I sat back and studied the way Cora and Kirk were half-flirting/half-studying each other. They both knew something new was happening, but neither fully understood what it was.

Ryan gave me the answers for the few problems I didn't have done, and after class, I hurried to catch up with Cora.

I bumped into her arm, grinning.

She looked over and ducked her head, but I saw her smile.

"So." I jerked a thumb toward Kirk, who was headed toward his locker. "What was that about?"

"You know." She weaved over, deliberately bumping back into me. "I took your advice to heart."

"That you aren't miserable?"

She laughed, shaking her head. "No. Well, yes." We veered toward her locker.

I went with her and Ryan passed us, moving toward his. But he looked back with the same questioning expression on his face.

Later, I mouthed, and he nodded, stopping at Kirk's locker first.

"Do you like Kirk?"

She'd never talked about him, just about Ryan.

"I don't know." She opened her locker and began to put her books into her bag. "Maybe. I mean . . ." She paused, looking at him as he joked with Ryan. "After Ryan, he's the hottest guy in school."

She stared at him, really stared at him, and let out a sigh. "What am I doing? He made out with the Bellini twins last night. He'd never be interested in me."

I frowned as I really looked at Cora.

She was a little smaller than me. Her brown hair was pulled back into a messy bun with some fraying ends framing her face. Aqua eyes. A fair complexion under a smattering of freckles. She wasn't beautiful in the heavy-makeup kind of way. She was pretty in a natural way.

She was kind, shy, and loyal. I never heard her say anything negative about her friends. The only person she'd been negative about was Erin, but that made sense. She was terrified of the girl.

There was no reason Kirk wouldn't want to be with her.

"He'd be nuts not to want you," I told her.

She fixed me with a dark look. "Come on."

"I'm serious. I mean, I'm taking inventory. If he doesn't want to date you, the only reason would be because he wants to keep fooling around with people who aren't girlfriend material. Sorry, Cora, but you're dating material. And he was interested. He asked me what was different with you today."

"What'd you say?" She was so still.

I leaned against her neighbor's locker. "I told him I didn't know, but you seemed sexier to me. He agreed."

Her mouth almost fell open and color splashed across her cheeks. "He did?"

"Yeah. He did."

She ducked her head again, sneaking a look at him.

Ryan and Kirk were both watching us.

Kirk was staring at Cora like he'd never seen her before. Ryan watched me with the same expression. It took me a second to place it, because it was different. His eyes were locked on me, his mystified expression from before mixing with a look of approval. Then it hit me, and I almost fell back against the locker behind me.

I was the old me.

This was something I would've done.

I would've helped a friend who needed a pep talk. There might've been a guy I helped steer in the right direction, and I would've been at that friend's locker talking to her about the guy. This was the real me. It felt good. I mean, it felt weird, but it felt right.

Ryan was seeing this side of me for the first time.

I pulled my gaze away and glanced down.

Willow was with me. I felt her, and I waited, expecting her to say something. She didn't. She remained quiet, and I couldn't help myself.

Really? I shot at her. *You don't say anything this time?* And like she was really standing there, I heard a huff right before she turned and walked away.

She left me. I was struck speechless a second.

"You okay?"

Cora had shut her locker and had her bag over one shoulder. She was waiting for my response.

"Oh yeah." I stood straight. "I'm good."

My ghost of a sister left me, and I didn't want her to go.

I'd gotten used to her haunting me.

chapter twenty-eight

"What was up with you and Cora today?"

I knew this question was coming, and I looked over to Ryan in the driver's seat. He'd asked me where we were heading after school, and he hadn't flinched one bit when I said, "My dad's mistress's house." He hadn't questioned how I knew her address.

I rested my head back against the headrest and smiled. I hadn't needed a PowerPoint presentation to get him to be a stalker with me.

But I did need to answer his question. I gazed at him as we drove down the highway, the wind whipping his hair back.

How could I explain that I'd only said a few words to Cora, but it seemed to have helped? Or how much that meant to me for some stupid reason?

How could I tell him Willow had left me today, and I ached at her absence?

How could I—*Dude, stop. Talk to him.*

I almost grinned, hearing my sister's voice again. It settled me.

"I don't really know," I said aloud.

Ryan frowned as he rolled up his window. The wind noise faded, and it seemed intimate in his truck. "What'd you say?"

I cleared my throat, sitting straighter in my seat. "I don't really know. That's what I said."

"What does that mean?"

I shook my head a little. "She was telling me that I'm popular, and I told her to go jump off a cliff." *Same sentiment. Different words.* I shrugged. "I'm miserable—" Ryan turned to look at me for a second. "Being popular isn't worth it."

He was still frowning, but he nodded as he went back to watching the road. Flicking on the turn signal, he merged into the passing lane, and we moved smoothly, seamlessly around a white car.

"Kirk thinks she's hot," he said. "Was that your doing?"

I turned to sit almost sideways, as much as my seatbelt allowed. "Cora used to like you until I came along. Is there a part of you that wishes she still did?"

I stared at him hard.

He threw me an annoyed look. "That's what you got out of that?"

"You're annoyed with me."

"Annoyed?" He flashed me a cocky grin. "No, never annoyed. I've started to be able to read you and figure out where you're going, but this thing with Cora threw me. That's all. I'm not worried about Cora or Kirk. If Cora's new confidence is attractive to him, I hope she keeps it up, and I hope he doesn't hurt her. I'm more worried about you."

"Why? I'm fine."

I was. Totally sane.

I was fine that my mom wasn't home again. I was fine that I wasn't driving to see Robbie today. I was fine that I'd lost another member of my family.

Yes. It was all copacetic with me.

There were no slightly psychotic tendencies at all.

My nails sank into my arm. I didn't pull them out, even when I felt a trickle of blood. It felt good, refreshing.

Thirty minutes later, we turned off the interstate and Ryan glanced down. "Holy shit! Mac!" He reached for my arm, and I pulled my nails away. Five indented pockets had formed, and blood flowed from all of them.

He cursed under his breath and hit the turn signal, veering into a gas station parking lot. "What the fuck just happened?" Slamming to a stop in front of the building, he threw open his door. "Get out. We're getting that fixed."

He held my arm, locking the door with his free hand and pocketing the keys. With a firm hold, he led me inside and asked for the first aid kit. The gas attendant eyed me warily but handed over the kit and said the bathroom was in the back.

We started down an aisle, and he barked at us, "I meant outside."

Ryan glared at him. "Thanks. Your sensitivity is commendable."

The attendant shrugged and grabbed some smokes for another customer.

Ryan's back hit the door hard, and he continued to pull me with him, glaring over my head.

There was a metal picnic table around the corner near the hose. Ryan went there instead, patting the top. "Hop up."

He placed the kit beside me, and as I sat, that numb feeling came back. It was like a blanket encasing me, shielding me from the real pain going on. The nail cuts weren't even a blip on my radar.

One of the four pieces loosened. It was going to fall away.

I frowned. "I was getting better."

Ryan was hunched over, cleaning out my cuts. He paused, straightening to meet my gaze. "What?"

"I was getting better." My head felt so heavy suddenly.

I was sleepy. I bent forward, my forehead resting on Ryan's shoulder.

"She went away today, and there were four pieces," I mumbled against his shirt. "They all fit. I was getting better."

Ryan went rigid and slowly, agonizingly slowly, reached up to cradle the back of my head. "Who went away?"

"Willow."

But that wasn't completely right. She'd spoken to me, hadn't she? That had been her in the car. Right?

He was like a statue. "Willow's been with you?" His voice sounded rough.

I nodded, straightening. It hurt to look at him. The sun behind him was so bright that it made me tear up. "She left me earlier, but she talked to me in the car."

"She talked to you?"

"Once."

That had been her? The question was still bugging me.

"She's been talking to you?"

His hand moved to my neck. He traced some of my hair, smoothing it over my shoulder. Bending forward so only a few inches separated us, his eyes found mine.

I looked away. I couldn't look him in the eyes. I didn't know why, but I had messed up. I wasn't able to think clearly. What did I say wrong?

Willow, what did I do?

I felt a tear slide down my face. "She won't answer me."

"Willow won't?"

Willow . . .

I shook my head. "She's gone."

I wanted her back. My heart clenched. I wanted her back. I wanted to talk to her again, feel her again.

More tears slid down my face. "Ryan, where did she go?"

He stared at me, his pupils dilated.

Willow. I wasn't supposed to talk about her. But she was gone again.

I crumpled inside. I felt myself curling into a ball, and Ryan cradled me to his shoulder once again.

I cried while my arm bled.

chapter twenty-nine

THE SANITY SHIP SAILED. I'D OFFICIALLY SNAPPED.

I was talking to dead people, seeing dead people—and I wasn't psychic.

Ryan drove me to Mallory the Homewrecker's house. He'd cleaned up my arm after I got myself back together, but I kept using my arm to clean my tears. So the bandage was soggy, and blackened from my makeup.

Going up to the door, Ryan knocked. His other hand laced through mine.

I considered lifting my bag and saying, "Trick or treat," but the door opened, and nothing came out of me.

The woman gasped, seeing me.

"Is Mr. Malcolm here?" Ryan asked.

Her hands shot up to cover her mouth. She matched her pictures on Facebook, but she was even prettier in person.

I hated her.

My hostility helped push away some of my craziness, and I was able to stop some of the tears—some of them. I was still sniffling like a crack head.

She eyed me for a moment and leaned forward. Comprehension flared, and she stepped backward. "Phillip!" she yelled over her shoulder before turning back to me. "You're Mackenzie."

I didn't answer. I summoned all my energy into a glare. I wanted to give her the full force of Willow and me. It was only right, since she was missing out on the more wrathful one of us.

She sucked in her breath, her mouth twitching down.

Footsteps came from behind her, and she moved back. My dad filled the doorway, frowning at her and then us. "Wha—Mackenzie?"

His gaze switched to Ryan, whose hand tightened around mine. "Can we, uh . . . can we come in?"

I don't know why Ryan brought me there—if it was closer than a mental hospital, if he didn't want to deal with me, if he wanted to pawn me off on my dad. It could've been any of those reasons. When I'd realized where he was taking me, I had tried to pull my hand from his in the truck.

"No, Ryan. Take me where I need to be to get the right help. Going to see her won't do it. I was wrong."

He hadn't let me go, and he'd pulled our hands from the console between us into his lap. "We're going to see him." His voice was gentle but firm, and his eyes were tender as he looked at me. "And that is where you'll get help. Trust me."

His gaze almost sent me off on another crying escapade, not that I had really stopped. But as he kept holding my hand, a fifth piece had melded with the others. I didn't know why, or how, but it had happened. I was coming together even as I was falling apart.

Go figure that one out.

"Yes. Come in, come in." My dad ushered us in, his hand falling to my shoulder. I heard him murmur to Mallory, "Can we use the screened-in porch?"

"Yes. Sure, sure. Anything you need."

"I'm sorry."

I stiffened and whipped around. "Yes." My tone was scathing. "Please, Dad. Keep apologizing. Tell your whore you're sorry we showed up here because I'm losing it over my dead sister. So goddamn sorry to inconvenience you."

"Wha—"

She turned to my dad, but he coughed, interrupting her. "We'll be outside if you need me."

"Phillip."

His hand tightened on my shoulder, but Ryan tugged me out from beneath my dad's hold and led me toward the back patio. He opened the glass door and shut it behind us, leaving my dad behind.

I took the seat farthest away, and Ryan sat beside me.

He didn't reach for my hand again, and I didn't know if I wanted him to. He watched my dad and Mallory talk just on the other side of the door.

His hand went to her arm, but she pulled away. She looked out at us with angry eyes as she said something else to my dad. His shoulders drooped, and she crossed her arms over her chest, disappearing down a set of stairs.

"I might be crazy, but I don't think your dad is with her like that."

I grunted. "Trust me. No one will be calling *you* crazy."

He grinned at me, leaning back in his chair. "You know what I mean."

"Still no. You're amazing. Not crazy."

Raking a hand over his head, my dad regarded us through the glass doors. I noticed his clothes. Sweatpants and a thermal long-sleeved shirt—he paused just outside the door to slip his feet into a pair of black slippers.

A low growl started in my throat.

"Where's your robe, cigar, and newspaper?" I asked as he opened the door. "You look more at home than you ever did at the new-new house."

He stiffened and then stepped out and shut the door behind him. I looked for the bags under his eyes that I saw last night, but they were gone. The bastard looked almost refreshed.

"You're angry." He sat across from Ryan.

I snorted. "What gave it away?"

Fuck him.

He got the new job.

He wanted to take it.

He made the decision to move.

He was the one who brought us to this town.

I leaned forward and hissed, "You promised us a better life."

He looked at the floor.

Ryan coughed, sitting forward too. "Uh, Mr. Malcolm?"

He was a lot nicer than I was.

My dad looked up, and I saw the anguish on his face. It was real and genuine. He mirrored everything I was feeling inside. Torn and twisted.

The bags under his eyes might've disappeared, but a grayish tint had settled under his skin, making him look almost half-dead.

He tried for a kind smile. "Yes, Ryan?" The smile faded fast. It'd been only a small blip.

"I don't know my place here, but I feel like I should speak up about something."

This was it. My heart started to press into my chest. He was going to tell him about Willow. I was slipping to the mental side.

Ryan folded his hands together on the table, and looked at them. "I've been spending a lot of time with your daughter—enough to know I shouldn't have been."

What?

He looked up then, staring right at my dad and not looking away. "I'm aware of the hell your whole family has been put through, but if you were still doing your job, your daughter wouldn't have been in my bed half those nights she was."

Good Lord. What in all the Willows was he doing?

My dad's face went flat. "You think so, huh?"

"I know so, sir."

"You think you know how I should've been parenting more than I do?"

Ryan didn't flinch, grimace, cringe, or look away. His tone was soft but strong. "When it comes to Mac, yes."

My dad was the one who twitched. My nickname acted like a repellant. I could almost see my dad shriveling, and I knew he was going to make an excuse, stand, and ask us to leave.

It was coming . . .

He sighed, leaning back in his chair. "Maybe you're right."

Uh, what?

I sat straighter in my seat. I hadn't heard that right. I should've been halfway to the door by that point.

"I *have* been messing up this whole time, and it takes a seventeen-year-old to set me straight." He laughed, the sound bitter and weak.

"I'm eighteen." Ryan grinned, shaking his head. "Not that it matters."

"Oh. Well." My dad tried to grin back, humoring him. "That one year makes me less pathetic, I'd say."

I didn't know if I should laugh, make an inappropriate joke, or what? Dissolve into tears again? What would Willow do?

I'd attack, sweet cheeks. I could hear her again, and I relaxed.

"Willow talks to me," I announced.

They both looked at me.

I kept on, needing to do this. "She's around me all the time. I have conversations with her. I dream of her. And I hated it at first. I didn't want to think of her, feel her, hear her, but she wouldn't go away. She haunted me, until today." My voice broke and I let my eyes drop. "She went away today, and I fell apart." *Keep going.* "I hate her, and I love her, and I need her. But Dad . . ." A break. My throat ceased to work, just for a moment. "You're the one alive. I need you more, and you left." I wasn't talking about just the night he moved out. "You stopped checking on me. You stopped knowing where I was." I faltered again.

I heard sniffling and my dad clearing his throat over and over again.

"Mackenzie."

His chair scraped against the floor. I couldn't look up. I didn't have the heart, and then I felt his arms around me. He knelt beside me, holding my head to his chest, and he took a deep breath.

"Mackenzie, I am so sorry." His arms tightened around me.

I could've fallen apart then. I could've stopped, contented myself with the confessions I'd given, but that wasn't all the truth inside me.

"I couldn't bear to see myself, so how could I make you look at me?" I whispered.

I missed her.

I wanted her.

I didn't want my dad's arms around me.

I wanted *hers* around me.

"I don't want her to be a ghost, Dad."

"I know." He patted my head and pushed back some of my hair like my mom used to, like Willow did at times. "I know. Trust me." His voice grew thick and hoarse. "I miss your sister so much that I can't bear it some days."

It was right to be crying to my dad. But he wasn't the one I needed. I thought it was him. I thought it was my mom. It wasn't Robbie either.

There was one person I needed to hold me, and she couldn't.

I pulled away from my dad, and he framed my face with his hands. "I'm sorry, honey. I'm so sorry." His hands fell from my face to my shoulders, and he pulled me back to his chest, wrapping his arms tight around me.

I looked at Ryan from within my dad's hold, and he must've seen something in my eyes because he leaned forward in his seat again. "Uh, Mr. Malcolm?"

My dad eased back. "Yeah?"

Ryan watched me, and I nodded to him, smoothing out my shirt. There were stains everywhere.

"What's really going on with you and . . ." He gestured inside.

"Oh."

My dad looked at me, and I tried to smile. "I'm fine."

He still paused.

"Really," I added.

"Okay." He sat in the chair closest to me and ran a hand over his face. "I'm not cheating on your mother. Mallory is a work colleague, and I came here because we have a project that needs to be finished as soon as possible. We've been working at it all day and had to call in more people to help. We have to work around the clock, and—" He looked up and found the clock on the wall. "We might get interrupted shortly. More of our colleagues are supposed to be coming here. They're coming straight from the office."

"You told me you were leaving us. You said you were leaving us for her."

"I did, but I'm not." He didn't seem flustered by the accusation in my voice. "I mean, I said I was moving closer to Robbie, and that's the truth. Your mother is with Robbie today, and I'll be going tomorrow. Coming here wasn't planned until my boss called me last night while I was on the highway. I thought I was cleared for the day off. That didn't happen."

I shook my head. "Why did you tell me you were leaving us for another woman?"

"Because it made sense. That's what you thought, so I just let you." He took a breath, started to say something, and took a second breath. "I was working yesterday with Mallory, but that's all it was. Work. And your mother and I *are* separating, but I'm not leaving her for anyone. I'm here for work, only for work. And I *am* moving closer to Robbie, at least until your mother and I work things through."

I could feel Willow railing inside me, but I had enough clarity to know it wasn't really her. It was me. It was the part of me that was still connected to her.

"None of this makes sense," I snarled. "You aren't making sense. You or Mom." I leaned forward. "I get it. I'm not talking, but neither are you. Why is no one talking?"

I was yelling.

"Fucking start talking! Talk TO MOM! TALK TO ME! TALK TO—I DON'T CARE! TALK TO A FUCKING COUNSELOR!"

No one told me to lower my voice. No one hushed me.

And if they had, I would've turned on them.

This was my anger. It was deep and unhealthy, and I had it in excess.

Calm down, Mackenzie, I told myself.

A beat of silence passed on that porch.

We heard the doorbell ring. Mallory came up the stairs, glancing to us before moving toward the door.

More people were arriving. They flowed in, wearing work suits and business skirts. My dad hadn't lied. They looked like they'd come straight from the office.

He hadn't lied.

He hadn't lied.

Shoving my chair back, I pulled my feet up and hugged my knees to my chest. I rested my head against them and breathed.

He hadn't lied.

When I didn't say anything more, Ryan said, "Maybe we should go?"

I nodded, moving my head against the tops of my legs.

"Are you going to be okay, Mac?"

God. He used her nickname—but that wasn't fair. Everyone in my family had called me that. It'd become *her* nickname for me since—I felt the anger and hysteria rising up.

"You want to go?" Ryan leaned closer to me.

I lifted my head, feeling raw and stripped bare. I nodded again. "Yes."

Ryan took my hand and led me back through the house. My dad followed us, saying something to Mallory as he passed. All of their people had gone downstairs where she'd been earlier.

"I'll be right there," he told her. "Give me a moment with my daughter."

He stepped outside to the front steps with us, closing the door firmly behind him. "They ordered food from the office, so we might get interrupted again." His eyes fell to me.

It was hard not to see my dad's suffering. He looked closer to sixty than forty.

"If you need me, I'm here," he said. "I will drop everything and come to get you. I mean it."

I'd needed him when Willow died. I'd needed him all the months in between, and I would need him until I was an adult. But how could I say that when he was choosing work today? Could I even say that?

Yes, you can.

Fuck it. "I need you at home, with Mom, with Robbie. I need my family back together."

He winced, but he didn't look away.

I waited, staring at him.

Then he nodded. "Okay. I'll call your mother. We'll make it happen."

I looked down and saw how white Ryan's hand was. I'd been squeezing too tightly. Relaxing my hold, I gave him an apologetic look. He shook his head. He didn't care.

"You're okay to head back to the house?"

I turned back to my dad, and I felt that fifth piece.

"Yeah. I'm okay." And like that, a sixth tagged along.

We were starting to go when my dad asked one last question, "Did you troll Mallory's Facebook account?"

chapter thirty

RYAN DROVE US BACK TO MY HOUSE. It was dark, but I knew my mom would still come back tonight. Ryan asked if I wanted company till then, and I told him no. It felt right—the most it had in so long—for me to go inside, do my homework, and hope to get in trouble for still being up whenever my mom came home.

I kissed him and said, "I'll be okay." And I meant it. I gave him a smile before heading inside.

The house was cold when I got in, so I kicked up the heat and ordered a pizza. After that, I did what I would've done last year.

I did my homework at the kitchen table, paid for the pizza when it came, and I had half of it eaten by the time the garage door started to open. I was getting up, intending to pour a glass of wine to further mess with my mom, but as I reached for the bottle, I heard his voice.

My heart stopped.

"Mackenzie!"

I whipped around, my feet moving before I realized it.

I was halfway to the garage when the door flung open. Robbie threw himself at me.

I caught him and held him up. It'd only been a month and a half, but I swore he'd gotten bigger.

"Robbie!"

"Heya, sis," he mumbled into my neck, his arms wrapped tight. One last squeeze, and then he pulled back.

I didn't want to let him go, but I had to. I kept my hands on his arms and set him to stand on his own feet. "You look so big. You're tall too."

He was an inch shorter than I was. I looked at our mom. "Is that normal? How tall is he now?"

She laughed, coming inside with a pizza box and two other bags hanging from her arms. "Well, he shot up half an inch, but I don't think he's the one who changed."

I frowned at her, eyes lingering on the pizza box.

"You lost weight!" Robbie nearly shouted. "I got taller, but you got smaller." He could wrap his fingers around my arm, or the bottom of my arm. My bicep still had some muscle to it.

I shrugged, grinning stupidly. "That's probably going to change." I pointed to the pizza I'd ordered.

Our mom started laughing. "I got confused for a second." She held up the one she was carrying. "Robbie insisted on stopping and getting you food. He was worried." She gazed at him, her eyes softening. Everything about her softened. "I told you, you didn't have to worry."

He smiled. "I'll always worry." Then he tightened his hold around me again, hugging me. "I've missed you, Mac."

I hugged him back, closing my eyes. "Me too."

If I could've held him all night, I would've. It was as if he wasn't just my brother anymore, but half me, half my son, half my responsibility. Or that might've been Willow's influence. She was gone, and I didn't want to lose anyone else, ever again.

"Okay." Mom clapped her hands, pushing her sleeve back to peer at her watch. "It's close to midnight. Robbie, you don't have school tomorrow, but you need to go to bed. And Mackenzie . . ."

I waited for her order, my arm resting around Robbie's shoulder.

She paused, staring at us and rubbing away a tear. "We have lots to talk about, but you do have school, and you aren't allowed any more skip days. Off to bed, and no boys sneaking in. Got it?"

She was pretending to be the stern parent. Robbie and I both saw right through the act, though.

We nodded, and Robbie went first, hugging her before running upstairs.

"Take your bag!" she called after him.

His footsteps pounded back down the stairs. He grabbed a bag and gave us a huge smile. His cheeks were flushed. "I forgot." Then he was off again, pounding the stairs as if he had never been gone in the first place.

I felt her hands first, a soft touch as she pulled me in for a hug. "Are you okay, honey?"

I didn't know for sure, but I felt a seventh piece attach to the others. Fitting right.

I hugged her back and whispered, "Please bring Dad home too."

"Oh, Mackenzie."

I wasn't the only one who'd lost weight. Her almost-frail form shook in my arms. She smoothed a hand down my back, brushing some of my hair.

"I will. I will." She coughed and leaned back, holding me like I'd held Robbie moments before. Her eyes traced all over my face. "Please be okay. Please."

My throat swelled, and I blinked a bit at that. Shocked.

I nodded. "I'm trying."

"Okay." She tugged me back for another hug. "And I mean it; no Ryan tonight."

I nodded again, and with a soft smile and flutter in my stomach, I went upstairs after my brother.

∽

I was getting ready for bed, or at least curling into bed with my Kindle, when there was a soft tapping sound.

I almost went to the window, thinking it was Ryan, but my door creaked open.

Robbie poked his head around the corner, his hand still hanging onto the doorknob. "Hi."

He might've been eleven, but he was three in my mind. He was still my little brother.

Feeling everything melting inside, I patted the bed next to me. "Come on."

A big, wide smile appeared, and he hurled himself onto my bed. Scooting under the covers, he laid his head on my second pillow and gave me his toothy smile.

This guy—he owned me. I balled up a fist and pretended to punch him in the stomach. "How's it knocking, little brother?" Instead of hitting him, I began tickling.

He laughed, shrieked, and twisted around, but he looked over his shoulder when I stopped. I started tickling his side, and cue the shrieks and laughter again.

"Hey! What are you two doing?"

Robbie was breathless, panting as we heard Mom yelling from downstairs.

I chuckled and then yelled back, "Robbie won't get out of my bed! Mom, come make him."

His mouth dropped and he sat upright. "She's tickling me, MOM! It isn't true!"

We could hear her laugh, and I closed my eyes for a moment. This was what I had needed all summer long.

My mom was laughing.

Robbie was laughing.

I was smiling.

And Dad was coming home.

We're going to be okay, Wills.

She didn't answer, but I knew she wouldn't, and I didn't need her response. I already knew she was happy for us.

The tickling continued until Robbie yawned, and I started to feel bad that he was still awake. It was long past his bedtime. Hell, they came home after his bedtime. After a minute he curled up with my blanket. Without asking, I brought up one of his favorite books and began reading to him.

Five minutes later, he was sleeping soundly.

He had the entire blanket wrapped around him. I didn't have it in me to wake him or carry him to his own bed.

Sneaking around my room, I checked my phone. There were a couple of texts from Ryan:

Ryan: **How's it going?**

Thirty minutes later.

Ryan: **Finished my homework. Want to talk for a bit?**

An hour after that.

Ryan: **I'm hoping everything's good on your end. I'm heading for bed.**

And ten minutes ago.

Ryan: **I think I'm in love with you.**

Ten seconds ago.

Ryan: **Goodnight.**

I almost dropped my phone, but with my heart pounding its way to my eardrums, I texted back.

Me: **Goodnight. I think I—**

"Robbie's sleeping?"

I jumped. The phone flew in the air. Stifling a curse, I caught it, and my hand hit the send button.

Oh no!

Shit, shit, shit.

My mom stood in the doorway, frowning as she watched me.

"I—hold on." I glanced over, but Robbie was still sleeping. I moved closer to the door. She moved back, and I followed her out. She closed the door with a soft click, and I checked my phone as she did.

Oh my God.

Oh my God.

That text had gone through. I hadn't answered, and—I couldn't think.

"What's wrong?" Mom looked from me to the phone.

"Nothing." I held it behind my back. "I didn't have the heart to take Robbie to his room, and I've missed him. A lot."

She nodded, resting against the wall. Her arms crossed over her chest, and a tear slipped down her face. "We worried whether seeing you was good for him or not." She gazed at my door. "I think we did more harm than anything. I'm sorry we kept you guys apart."

They'd done this on purpose? I had wondered that, but to hear it confirmed . . .

"I thought he wanted to stay there?" I was gutted and reeling. How could they do that?

"He wanted to stay, but he wanted to see you too. I don't think he wanted to come back here."

It was a new house. Willow didn't have a room there, but her things were still with us. My mom had hung her pictures on the walls. As if feeling her presence coming from them, we both looked over.

Willow smiled back at us from her junior-year school picture. She'd straightened and brightened her hair so it was almost platinum blonde. She had it pulled over one shoulder, her head tilted to the side as she flirted with the camera. A coy smile on her face, she looked on the verge of bursting out laughing.

"Oh, honey." My mom reached out, wiping a tear from my face.

She was still crying, and I realized I couldn't be angry with them. We all tried to cope in our own way, whether wrong or right, healthy or unhealthy.

"I'm going to go back in to sleep."

She nodded, pressing a kiss to my forehead. She rested her cheek there. "Be safe and be smart. Okay, Mac?"

I nodded, looking up at her. "Don't take him away again. I mean it, Mom."

She pulled back. She started to nod, but then she did a double take. Mine was not an idle threat. She'd find out what would happen if she did.

I moved back into my room and texted Ryan back.

Me: I want to say things to you, but not till tomorrow. Let's talk in the morning?

Then I checked to make sure my alarm was set, put my phone on silent, and grabbed a second blanket. Curling up next to my brother, I closed my eyes.

Ryan said he loved me . . .

chapter thirty-one

Ryan was waiting for me in the front of the school the next morning. He had texted earlier to see if I needed a ride, but I'd said no.

"Okay, honey." My mom put the car in park. Her eyes looked past me to where Ryan was waiting, and she sighed. "That's Ryan?"

"Yeah."

"He's handsome, isn't he?"

"Mom!" The back of my neck got hot.

She grinned, ducking her head. "What? I have eyes. I'm not blind." She bit her lip and narrowed her eyes. "Have you guys been sexually active since that first time?"

Yep. My neck was definitely burning up. "You're killing me here."

She rolled her eyes, tsking me under her breath. "You're so dramatic." Her grin softened. "Keep it up. I know Willow would be ecstatic for you."

"Mom." I looked down at my lap, tugging at my backpack's strap.

Why'd she have to bring Willow up? All it brought was different feelings, the twisty and angsty ones.

"But I mean it, no more sex."

She was trying to be stern, and she was serious about the sex, but I could tell part of her was trying to move on. There was no real oomph behind her words. I'd still been awake when my dad got home last night, and I heard them talking for hours after that. When Robbie had started tossing back and forth, I'd shut my bedroom door and turned on my fan to drown out the last murmurings. I was able to sleep after that, and I was pretty sure my mom had been sporting a little glow this morning at breakfast.

There was a bit of a spark in her, but she couldn't entirely mask the big hole that was still there. I saw it, because I felt it too. We all did. Robbie had it in his eyes.

"Mackenzie."

She'd been waiting for a reply from me.

I blinked a couple times. "What?"

"Tell me you aren't going to have sex again."

"Ever?" I reached for the door handle.

"Ever."

I began to edge out of the vehicle. "Come on, Mom. You know I can't promise that."

She frowned. "Mackenzie! Don't you shut that door before—"

I shut it, bent, and waved at her with a bright smile plastered on my face. "Love you, Mom. Be safe. Have fun with Robbie."

"Mackenzie!" she shouted again, but I was hurrying across the sidewalk and lawn toward Ryan.

He grinned as I joined him to walk toward the doors. A bunch of students were lingering out front. Most seemed to be talking, but a few were riding skateboards up and down the main sidewalk in front of the school.

I didn't usually enter the school this way. The parking lot was in the back, so I knew that side would be three times as busy, but this still seemed too busy for the conversation I knew Ryan was waiting to have.

This conversation was the real reason I'd stayed awake as long as I did.

Ryan stopped to lean against the building and nodded at my mom as she pulled away from the curb. "Your mom isn't working?"

"Robbie's home, so she took time off. She asked this morning if she could drive me in."

He nodded. "You need a ride home then?" He shifted, turning to face me and resting his shoulder against the school's brick exterior.

This felt weird, and I frowned.

"What?" He straightened, but the movement drew him even closer.

My backpack hung behind me, and I fiddled with the strap like I had been in the car. I fingered the shredded ends and, without thinking about it, began shredding more of it.

"I got your text last night."

He grunted. "Which one? I sent you four."

"All of them."

He was silent a moment. "I see."

No. No, he didn't. He was guarded, and I could only guess as to the reason, but I knew he had no clue what was going on with me.

I took a breath because I needed some extra air. "You don't know. You don't see everything. I got your text, and I . . ." How could I explain this? I didn't even know if there were words. I had to try. "I'm reserving the right to respond."

His eyebrows went up. "Say what?"

I flushed, feeling the heat scorch my cheeks. "You told me the L word, and I was ecstatic to read that, but it wasn't fair. I'm . . . I'm behind you."

His hand rested on the wall, and he moved forward, leaning over me, and I moved so my back was against the brick. I gulped, my throat and mouth suddenly dry. His hazel eyes locked on mine, starting to smolder.

God.

I'd forgotten how tall he was.

"Have you gotten taller?" I asked breathlessly.

A smirk pulled at his lips, and he shifted again. His hips were almost touching mine, but he still braced himself with a hand above my head.

I was fast forgetting what I was going to say, and I wet my lips. "Ryan."

"Mmm?" His eyes were on my mouth.

I touched his chest but pushed him back an inch. "You're making me not be able to think."

His free hand went to my waist. "Is that a bad thing?" He didn't move back. I could feel his chest moving up and down with shallow breaths and his muscles shifting under my touch.

He was as affected as I was.

"You're reserving the right to respond to my text."

"Yes." I nodded again, trying to clear my head. I was remembering the first time he'd kissed me at the college party, when we'd kissed again in my theater room, and how he'd felt sliding inside me. "I'm a mess."

He chuckled, and good gracious, even *that* was a caress.

"Ryan," I murmured.

"Yes?" He dipped closer.

I closed my eyes because I could feel him, his breath on my face. I felt him straining under my hand, holding himself back, and I couldn't help myself. I moved my thumb side to side over his chest. It was a small touch, but it elicited a groan from him.

"You want to take this somewhere else?"

Yes! But I groaned. "I promised my mom I wouldn't skip."

"And that's important."

It was. Wait, he was agreeing with me?

I opened my eyes, and he was right there. If I tilted my head a fraction, he'd be kissing me.

What had I been saying before? It felt important, too important to go a day without saying.

I was a mess. Yes. That was it.

I began again, clearing my throat first. "Things are just getting to be a little normal at my house. I don't know if it's going to last or what's going to happen, but I've been a mess." I still was. The hole was still there. She was still gone. I kept going before a different ache had me sobbing in his arms. "I'm trying to tell you that—" I flattened myself back, giving me an inch, and I looked up to his eyes. "When I return your text, I don't want it to be because you said it. I want to feel it, and I want to mean it, and I want . . ."

Some of the smoldering dampened. "You don't feel it?"

I pressed my hand against his stomach. "It isn't that I don't feel it; it's that I have too much other stuff going on inside me. My parents are home today. Robbie is back today. Willow . . ."

My stomach knotted, but it was too important that he understood what I was saying for me to stop. "I've been trying to ignore that she was gone." I've been trying to ignore a lot of things. "I used you to do that. I skipped school to run away. I tried tequila." *Deep breath, Mackenzie.* My heart beat in a rapid staccato. My hand wrapped around his shirt and tugged. "There are layers of pain inside me. Pain that I can't put into words, and underneath it all is hell. It's raw and bloody. Agony. Suffering. Torture."

And denial. That lined the bottom of me. It was a dark, black hole.

His hand curved around my waist, but the touch took on a different feeling. It was more soothing than sensual.

"I can't text you that back because it isn't fair to you, or me. I want to say it when I'm feeling that and only that. Willow's gone, and I'll always feel as if half of me has been ripped away, but I know someday those wounds might heal over. I'm not saying I'll completely be right one day, but I'm saying that until most of those layers of pain have gone away, I can't say it back. There isn't enough room inside to say it back. Not yet."

I pulled him against me, feeling his surprise before he caught himself so he wasn't crushing me against the building. He put an inch of space between us, but that was too far in my mind. I wanted all of him against me, his whole body plastered against mine.

That soothed me, but I wanted more than soothing.

Ryan's hand cradled the back of my head. His thumb brushed over my cheek. "I know what you're saying, and I'm not mad."

"You aren't?"

He shook his head, his eyes firmly attached to my lips. "When I texted you that, I knew you couldn't say it back. That isn't why I sent it. I pressed send because it felt right to tell you. I wanted you to know, but I get it. I really do." He groaned again and dipped down. His lips finding mine for a brief second before he pulled away.

I went with him, arching on my toes, not wanting to break the kiss.

He rested his forehead to mine, his gaze boring into my eyes. "You say it when you can, and I'll still be here."

An eighth piece fit with the other seven.

Five hundred ninety two to go, but it was good. So much good.

I tugged him back to me.

chapter thirty-two

Two months later

COUNSELING SESSION FIVE

I sat on Naomi's couch, and she took the seat across from me.

To say I'd been a participant—willing or otherwise—in the first four would've been an outright lie. I'd walked out of the first one. I'd refused to talk the second one. The third session lasted a few minutes longer as I recited obvious facts, like that Willow had died. And I'd dropped the bombshell about Ryan and me in the fourth one.

Naomi smiled at me. I saw the caution there and felt a little remorse.

She was in her mid-thirties with a medium complexion. Her black ringlets framed her face today as she'd let it hang loose. Some days they were slicked down with product, but today they were a little frizzy and free.

I liked how they looked. They seemed to match all the freckles on her face—almost like they didn't want to be tamed. They wanted to be themselves.

I could relate. Somewhat. Okay, not at all. The counseling sessions had been the only limitation put on me by my parents since WWD, except lately. They had given me too much freedom in the beginning, but after everything blew up, it was starting to be the other way around.

"How are things going at home?"

I'd been waiting for Naomi to speak, and I looked up. I was somewhat surprised. She usually came at me friendly, but with a determination to get me to talk. That wasn't what I heard today.

She sounded curious.

Some of the tension left me, and I found myself answering. "Better."

Her mouth dropped open, but she coughed and smoothed out her shirt, sitting more upright in her seat. "What do you mean by better?"

I told her.

I didn't see why I shouldn't start being honest, at least a little. I still didn't want to talk about Willow, but a conversation about my family was something else.

When I was done, I glanced at the clock. That had taken me twenty minutes. She'd sat in silence the entire time.

"In my work, I've learned that families either come together in times of severe grief, or they fall apart. The fact that your father was leaving doesn't strike me as uncommon. The fact that you stepped forward, you said something, and everyone listened to you is *not* common." She stared at me. "You changed the narrative. Do you realize what you did?"

I frowned. I didn't know what she was talking about, and I was starting to wish I hadn't said anything.

"You helped your family, Mackenzie."

"What?"

"You spoke up, and your parents listened to you. I've had other children in here because of grief. In some cases, they didn't speak up, or if they did, no one listened. I can only speculate as to the reasons your parents were going to separate, but you said your father moved back home?"

I nodded. "He's been home since the day I talked to him. My mom too."

"Is your little brother at his school again?"

"He's there during the week, but he comes home on the weekends."

We had movie dates every Saturday afternoon.

Her hands rested on her knee, one on top of the other, and she leaned even closer. "I don't know your sister. I never met her, but I can tell you this one thing: she would be proud of what you did."

The session turned awkward after that, at least for me.

Naomi said a bunch of nice things about me, and I tried to change the topic every time. A joke. A debate. I asked her ridiculous questions about why she didn't have more plants in her office. I even tried to piss her off. I told her if she didn't stop praising me, I'd feel like I was being propositioned and could report her. She only grinned and went right back to telling me all the good things I'd done since Willow died.

She was wrong.

Everyone was wrong. I knew my parents looked at me a little differently since the whole Mallory-stalking/yelling-at-my-dad event. It was like they were seeing someone new.

I didn't understand it, and I didn't like it.

And there was one other topic I didn't want to talk about, and so far, Naomi hadn't brought it up.

She did when I was leaving this time.

"Mackenzie."

I was at the door and I paused, looking back. "What?"

"We have to talk about your sister's suicide note before I'll sign off on these sessions."

Yeah. That.

chapter thirty-three

"How was your session yesterday?"

I jumped, and my hand hit my locker as I whirled around, but I shouldn't have been surprised.

Ryan and I had talked a little last night on the phone, and I knew he would seek me out today. This was the new normal. Things were returning to a more regular schedule at home, which meant my mom stayed home twice a week. She reserved the right to drive me to school those mornings, and this was one of them.

Cursing, I waved my hand around.

"Shit." Ryan touched my arm and leaned forward to inspect my fingers. "I didn't mean to scare you."

I tried for a smile, but it felt like a twisted clown grimace. My fingers really hurt. "Oh. No problem. It was my bad. I was zoning out."

He ran his thumb over my knuckles. "You jammed two of your fingers. I can reset them, if you want. This happens all the time with basketball."

Oh God.

My knees wanted to crumble because it hurt so bad. I jerked my head in a nod, bracing my other hand against his shoulder. "Okay. Do it."

"Yeah?"

"Yea—"

He pulled, and I screamed.

"AH!" I did crumple this time. Grabbing his arm, I caught myself.

People were watching us, and I was being a bit overdramatic, but I was happy. I could be dramatic about this. *This* pain would go away.

"You okay?" He ran his finger over mine and murmured, "All better now?"

I tensed, waiting for the pain, but none came. I moved my fingers around, bending and wiggling them. "No. It's fixed. Thank you."

A cocky smirk came over him. "I found my calling. I'm going to be a doctor. I like fixing girls and having them swoon over me."

I hit his shoulder with my other hand. "So hilarious."

He chuckled, his eyes darkening.

I straightened, responding to him. That throbbing need began to build, and I leaned toward him.

"Yo."

Kirk, Nick, and Tom sauntered over to us.

Kirk held his fist up, and Ryan met it with his, turning to rest against the locker behind me. His hand moved to my waist as he nodded to the others. "What's up?"

"We're having a party after your first game, right?" Kirk was the spokesman. He glanced to Tom and Nick, who both nodded.

Ryan's hand flexed on my hip, but his tone remained casual. "Yeah, sure. Your place?"

"I can throw it. That's no problem." Kirk looked at me. "You coming, Mackenzie?"

I looked at Ryan before speaking. "I think so."

"I gotta ask because you've gone all goody-student lately. No skipping. No drinking.

You haven't partaken in our parties, and we haven't had to interrupt you and Romeo here during any PDA. What happened?"

I'd started healing. "Things got better at home."

Things weren't a hundred percent. That wouldn't happen. But they were definitely over the fifty percent mark. One day, I figured I'd have to claw my way higher. It would suck. There were layers in me even I didn't want to share, but I'd have to deal if I wanted to get up there.

I was okay where I was for the moment.

I settled back, moving to lean fully against Ryan as he talked over my shoulder with his friends. His hand on my waist moved behind me, and I felt it slide under my shirt, rubbing up and down.

It felt good, calming.

We stayed like that until the warning bell rang and everyone dispersed. It was nice to have just the guys at my locker. That wasn't a normal thing anymore—there were almost always girls around too. If it was Kirk standing with us, sometimes Cora would come over. Kirk would throw an arm around her shoulder and talk to Ryan while flirting with her. Sometimes, Erin approached, and if she came, her friends followed behind. Things were still tense between us, but she'd been giving me a stiff smile or hello lately, and sometimes I gave it back. She didn't deserve my friendliness, in my opinion, and it'd be a long day in hell before she and I became anything other than civil to each other.

After seventh period ended, Ryan caught up to me at my locker. "Are you sticking around during practice?"

I switched out my books, putting the ones I needed for homework into my bag. "Yeah. My mom and dad are going to a counseling session tonight."

"So we can hang out afterward?" He moved in as I closed my locker, tugging me close so I was almost resting against him. I felt him through my jeans. He was already hard, and I knew what else he was asking.

Feeling my body warm, I grinned at him. "Oh yes."

"Yeah?" His eyes were teasing, a twinkle in them. He tugged me closer, closer, closer until every inch of my body was plastered against every inch of his.

I could feel his breath against me, and I murmured back, "Hell yes."

I felt him smiling before he kissed me.

A loud slam sounded right next to us, and Ryan's head jerked up. His hands tightened on my waist as he growled, "What the fuck, man?"

The guy grinned at us as he bounced a basketball. He threw it at the locker on our other side, moving down the hallway. "Want to make sure you're coming to practice," he called over his shoulder.

"Now I might not."

The guy caught his basketball and stopped in his tracks. "You serious, man?" His fingers tapped on the ball.

I didn't know who the guy was, but it wasn't a stretch to guess he was a senior. No junior would've talked to Ryan like that.

"I'll come when I come." Ryan pushed away from my locker, standing in front of me. His shoulders were rigid, and he kept a tight grip on my hand.

Kirk and Nick materialized from behind us, moving in to flank Ryan.

Kirk's hands shoved into his pockets. "What's the deal, Wachowitz?"

"My deal is Jensen. He's more interested in getting laid than getting to practice."

A low growl came from Ryan, and he started forward.

Nick held his hand up, halting Ryan, but he was speaking to Wachowitz. "You might want to watch your words. Ryan hasn't missed one practice this week, and he's already captain. You know he has a say in who gets nominated."

"Team nominates the co-captain."

Nick's grin went wide, and his head cocked to the side. "But Ryan gets final say. If he doesn't like you, he isn't going to pick you."

Wachowitz's stance grew less intimidating. His head lowered, and he stuffed one of his hands into his pocket. "You serious?"

Ryan released my hand. He passed both his friends, moving purposefully. He went up to Wachowitz and shoved him against the locker. "I don't give a rat's ass if I'm captain or not. You come at me like that again, and I'll get your ass kicked off the team."

Kirk and Nick pushed forward, standing close behind Ryan.

Wachowitz swallowed, his Adam's apple bobbing up and down, and he moved his head in the same motion.

"Yeah, man. I apologize." He held his fist up, but Ryan ignored him.

Meeting my eyes, Ryan spoke to Wachowitz, "Do it again, and we'll have more than fucking words. Got it?"

Wachowitz's gaze jumped to mine, and he swallowed again. He didn't say anything else, only turned and disappeared down the hallway. He didn't bounce the basketball against any more lockers.

"Well, that was fun," Kirk said as Ryan came back.

Ryan was still holding my gaze. I had darkness in me, but so did he. There'd been a few glimpses over the last couple months, but this was the first time I'd really experienced it. It was a window into how he'd been before I showed up.

A shiver went down my spine as Ryan bent to kiss me.

"I'll see you later?" he said softly.

I nodded, feeling all sorts of flutters in my chest.

He stepped back and clapped Nick on the shoulder. "Let's go. Wachowitz is going to have a hard practice today."

Nick's grin was almost evil. "Hell yes, he is."

They took off, but Kirk lingered behind.

"Basketball isn't your thing?" I asked him.

He laughed, shaking his head. "Sports in general are not my thing. I love to watch, bet on the game, hit on chicks in the bleachers, but that's it. You?"

Me?

Come on, Soccer Superstar.

I heard Willow calling me that again and found myself saying, "Soccer, actually."

"Really? It's a spring sport here for us. You going to play?"

I heard myself saying, "Yeah. I think I am."

I wasn't sure who was shocked more, him or me. Then again, I hadn't thought about sports since June twenty-eighth.

chapter
thirty-four

BOUNCING BASKETBALLS SOUNDED LIKE A THUNDERSTORM—WITH WHISTLES SHRIEKING, tennis shoes squeaking against the gym floor, and a whole ton of yelling. The smell of sweat filled the room, but someone had propped open the double doors so fresh air circulated through, along with the sound of dance music being played somewhere down the hall.

I'd gone to the bathroom and saw some of the dance team practicing a routine near my locker.

There were a lot of students out and about in the school, but I was one of the only audience members for basketball practice. The coach came in, saw me, and started to protest. I saw how his shoulders tensed, and he scowled, but Ryan ran over, with Nick and another guy hot on his heels. They talked to their coach and after a bit, his shoulders relaxed and the scowl flattened to a firm line of disapproval. He said something to Ryan, who nodded and ran back to his place for drills.

I went back to my homework, not making a peep, and finally practice ended.

The guys stayed around for a scrimmage game, and I sat and marveled at how damn good Ryan was. He'd been the first to finish the drills. He'd given the calls.

I mean, I could be biased, but he seemed to be the best at shooting, and he worked the hardest.

Wachowitz, on the other hand, was dragging. He'd been lagging behind half the team since the middle of practice. He missed a pass, and after he missed another, one of his teammates yelled for him to tag out.

He did just that, and the game kept going.

"Can I sit?"

I turned, surprised that I hadn't noticed anyone coming up the bleachers, and saw Cora pointing to the seat beneath me.

I nodded. "Sure." I moved down a little, giving her some space.

She sat, straddling the bench so one foot was next to mine and the other was below her. She watched the court. "I always forget how good Ryan is until I see him."

"Really?"

She nodded, her gaze solemn.

We watched the game for a moment. Ryan's teammates cut across the gym, and he passed to one of them. The toss was so fast that the ball was in his teammate's hands before he blinked.

She sighed. "Just get ready. It's about to be insane, especially with you being Ryan's girlfriend."

"What do you mean?"

She looked to me, almost reluctantly pulling her gaze from the court. "Ryan's nice and humble, not arrogant. People forget how good he is until the season starts. But they remember real quick. Friday night, after our first game, it's going to be insane. Girls will be throwing themselves at him nonstop."

Lovely. Willow had slowly stopped talking to me over the last two months, but I might have to pull out some of my inner Willow for this. Bitches might have to go down.

And as soon as I thought that, I was tired.

I was tired of the fighting, tired of the cattiness, tired of the way some girls seemed to hate each other just because.

"Don't you get sick of it all?"

"What?" Cora frowned at me.

I glanced over and saw that she wasn't the only one who'd come into the gymnasium once practice ended. A whole bunch of others had congregated beside the bleachers. Erin, her friends, Peach, some of the popular senior girls. There were guys with them too—half were talking to the girls, and the others shouldered past the group to sit on the first row of the bleachers.

I gestured to the group forming. "What you were saying—all the girls, all the fighting."

She stared at them and raised a shoulder. "I don't know. I don't really get an option, you know?" She turned back. "I feel like I have to fight just to have my friends notice me."

"Not Kirk."

She threw me a look, half rolling her eyes. "He noticed me because you told me not to give a shit. I didn't, and he came right over, but it hasn't been like that since. I give a shit. I don't know how not to. I'm not at the top of the food chain. I mean, look at him." She gestured to Kirk, who had his arm around Erin. His face was bent toward her neck, like he was nuzzling her, and she laughed. "He flirts with everyone, makes out with everyone—"

"Not when you're around."

She gave me another one of those "are you serious" looks. "I'm around right now."

"Bet he hasn't seen you yet." I flashed her a grin and hollered, "Kirk! Up here."

"Mackenzie!" she hissed under her breath.

Too late.

Kirk lifted his head, saw us, and a broad smile lit up his face. His arm dropped from Erin's shoulders. She shot me a scathing look as Kirk left her side and came darting up the bleachers to where we sat.

He dropped down next to Cora, straddling the bench like she was. She could've leaned back into him, and he eyed her backside like that was what he wanted.

"I didn't see you guys up here," he drawled. "What are you doing?"

Cora stiffened, pointing to me. "She's waiting for Rya—"

"I'm talking to you. I know what Malcolm's doing here." His eyes were steady on her.

I saw her blush; it traveled up her neck to her cheeks.

"I'm talking to Mackenzie," she said quietly.

"Interested in going somewhere and talking to me?"

Cora's eyes were glued to mine, and they widened. I watched as she sucked in her breath.

"What?" It came out as a strangled squeak.

Kirk snorted, moving up behind her so there was no point in her not leaning against him. If she didn't want to be touching him, she would have to move forward. She didn't.

He ducked his head so his lips could find her shoulder. "You heard me."

Another strangled sound came from her. She still didn't look at him, but she wasn't moving.

Kirk's eyes flicked up to mine in confusion.

The buzzer sounded, ending the scrimmage game. I nodded to Ryan, who was walking over to his bench. "I'll be taking off with him in a minute," I told them. "Go. Hang out. Have fun."

Kirk's grin widened. "Yeah. What she said. Let's hang out and have fun."

Cora was so stiff that when she nodded, it came out looking like a robot. "Yeah. Okay. Let's hang out."

"Great." Kirk was up on his feet, pulling her with him. "Tell your boy I'll call him later," he told me. He tugged Cora behind him, though she couldn't seem to stop looking at me. Her mouth hung open.

I waved at her, and when Kirk turned around, I gave her two thumbs-up instead. *Have fun*, I mouthed.

She flipped me the bird, but she was grinning.

I chuckled to myself.

The bleachers moved underneath me, and I looked up again. Ryan was loping up the seats, but he stopped and turned in the direction Kirk and Cora had disappeared.

"Did I see what I think I saw?" he asked.

"You think he'll hurt her?"

He looked at me, his eyebrows shooting up. "They leaving to mess around or something?"

I frowned. Was he clueless? "They're holding hands."

"Kirk holds hands with every girl." He thought about that and growled, "Except you. He better never touch you."

That made me feel good. "If she likes him, you think that's a bad thing?"

He sat next to me, straddling so one knee was touching mine and his other knee was behind me. He was sweaty and smelly, but neither mattered. I felt myself calming, just having him this close, and I was startled to realize I hadn't even known I wasn't calm until he touched me.

I relaxed into him, and he pulled me close. "I don't know. Kirk always had a thing for Cora growing up."

"He did? When did that stop?"

He didn't answer right away, and I turned to look at him more fully. He was suppressing a grin.

"When she started liking me."

I swatted his knee. "And you pretended to play dumb, didn't you?"

He shrugged, pressing a kiss to my shoulder. "I never liked Cora like that, but she never said anything. I would have been an asshole if I'd told her straight up not to like me."

"There were little ways you could've set her straight."

"I did. I dated other girls. I emphasized that she and I were friends, but that's all over." He hugged me close. His chin rested on my shoulder, and I felt his voice through his chest to me as he spoke, "Who knows? Maybe that'll be a good thing. I think Kirk actually does like her."

I was starting not to care, being in his arms.

"Ryan!"

And I was back to caring.

I looked down. Erin was waving at us—at him—wildly enough that her shirt rode up, showing off her midriff. I felt a growl forming, and Ryan bit back a laugh.

He nipped my shoulder. "Easy now."

"Right." I locked eyes with him. "Imagine me saying that to you about Wachowitz two hours ago."

He winced. "Sorry." Lifting his head, he called out, "What, Erin?"

She stiffened. That hadn't been the inviting tone she wanted, but she pushed out her chest anyway. "A bunch of us are going for pizza. You want to come?"

I waited to be included in the invite, but it didn't happen.

A full growl erupted, and I surged to my feet. "You did not do that, did you?"

I wasn't waiting. I started down where she was, and Erin squeaked, backing up.

I didn't know what I was going to do, but I wasn't going to let the insult stand.

"Hey." One of her friends backed up in front of her like she was going to block me. She waved her hands in the air. "Come on, Mackenzie."

I ignored her. I ignored everyone watching us, and I really ignored how I knew I was overreacting. But this was a personal affront.

How could I *not* react?

I went right up to Erin, and I kept going until she was backed against the gym wall. I slammed my hands against the wall beside her, trapping her.

My eyes were dead. I couldn't see myself, but I knew they were. I was channeling all the anger, grief, and sadness inside me, everything I'd started to suppress. I let it all up to the surface and turned every ounce of it on her.

"What do you think you're doing?"

She gulped, not daring to look away. "I was going to ask you the same thing."

"You ask your ex out for pizza while he's sitting right next to his girlfriend? When I'm right in front of you. What'd you think I was going to do?"

I felt Willow snort beside me. *It's because you've been nice. She's forgetting the crazy in you.*

Fine. I'd let her see how crazy I was, and I pulled back the last remaining wall. I let her see the girl who cyberstalked her dad's mistress (well, who I thought was his mistress) and showed up at her house. I let her see the girl who'd been talking, seeing, feeling, smelling her dead sister, and I let her see the girl who had yet to talk about what it was like to find her sister in her own pile of blood. That girl had never been let out, yet.

I let her see the darkness in me.

Erin had almost shrunk in half, starting to ball up, but I wasn't letting her go.

This was an insane scene. I was causing it, and I knew people were recording it on their phones. They'd talk about what a lunatic I was, probably talk about how Ryan deserved better, but I didn't give a shit. I meant what I'd said to Cora—you couldn't care. Once you did, they had you.

Are you really fighting them? It wasn't only Willow's voice in my head. It was Robbie's. It was my dad's. It was my mom's. It was mine.

Maybe not. Maybe I was fighting myself.

Maybe I was fighting something else entirely.

"I don't know, okay?" Erin yelled, throwing her hands wide and shoving me back.

I gave a step, but I didn't flinch. I didn't even feel it. I knew it happened because I heard the crowd gasp behind me.

"I don't know. All right?" She was heaving, her hands in the air, and she stormed at me.

I didn't move.

Not one goddamn inch.

She could've hit me, but she backed up at the last second.

I smiled. "You're a fucking liar. You know exactly why you did that, and you're lying about it right now."

"What? Are you going to hit me?"

I contemplated her question, my head moving to the side. "No, but if you hit *me* again, yes."

She paled at my words. I didn't think she knew she'd hit me.

"What do you want, Mackenzie?" She shoved some of her hair from her face.

"I want you not to hit on my boyfriend in front of me, or at all. I want you to stop thinking I'll take it. It isn't even him. You come after anyone I care about, I'm going to say something." I narrowed my eyes, moving a step closer to her. "I'm going to fight you, whether it's physical or verbal or mental. I've been through hell, so I have no problem reaching up and pulling you down with me. If you're looking for a girl to bully or intimidate, it isn't me."

She should've known this, but apparently she really had forgotten. It'd been months since our last real exchange. Or maybe she forgot in the rush of basketball? Cora had warned me, and maybe I was setting the precedent. Go after Ryan and expect a fight. No. That wasn't me. Girls would hit on him. If he indulged, that was his decision. I'd walk then. I wouldn't fight that, but this was a different situation.

"Was it even about him?" I asked her.

"What?"

"Just now. Did you really want Ryan to go for pizza with you? Or was it about me?"

She rolled her eyes. "Of course, it was about you." Her eyes moved past me, and I saw the group of senior girls standing there. "They dared me to ask Ryan for pizza and not include you."

They were testing me.

I kept my eyes narrowed and took a step toward them. "You'll have to excuse me," I called. "I've been preoccupied since coming to Portside. I have no clue who the 'leader' is here."

The girls were shocked, their mouths hanging open, except for one.

She pushed forward and pushed her hair over her shoulder. "I guess that's me."

"You have a problem with me?"

"Yes."

"Why?"

"Because of Kirk."

I was dumbfounded. "What?"

She exchanged looks with her friends before turning back to me. "He was talking to us."

"His arm was around her." I gestured to Erin.

She huffed and then shrugged. "But I was the one he was talking to."

"You're pissed at me because I called him over."

No. As she was talking to me, she kept looking at Ryan. This fight wasn't about Kirk. This fight was about Ryan. Cora's warning might've been more realistic than I realized.

"You are what's wrong," I said.

"Say again?" I saw the storm building in her eyes.

"You're what's wrong. You're saying this is about Kirk, but I think you're full of bullshit. You're going at me, and you're sending Ryan looks this whole time. This is about him, and why? Your ego is bruised because he isn't with you? Is that the problem?"

She shook her head. "You are unreal. You have no clue who—"

I stepped right into her face. There was an inch between us, and she stopped talking. I waited, watching as she struggled against moving back, but she didn't. She knew how this game went.

I was in her space. I could feel Willow riling up next to me. She used to live for this stuff, and a bleak part of me thought to her, *You've been silent for almost two months, and now you're back?*

I'm here because you need me here.

"You think you're going to win?" snapped this girl, smirking. She'd been at the pool party at Ryan's house, and later at Kirk's after we skipped. "I have friends. We can make your life miserable—"

"Do it." I included her friends, sweeping a look over all of them. "Cyberbully me. Text me *whore*, *skank*, whatever other fucking stupid words you can find that are beneath you. Do it. Send it to me. Call my house. Whisper to my mom about how she should wish her second twin would kill herself too."

I felt their surprise at those words. But I'd said it before. I knew it was out. They knew about Willow.

"Send me the emails about how I should die. Slice my tires. Slice my mom's tires. Write *loser* on my locker. Do all of it. I will fucking eat everything up. I will record your calls. I will screenshot your tweets. I will save every fucking email and forward it to our principal. I will turn every goddamn thing you do to me back on you threefold. I will make it so you bury yourselves until you're the ones getting called to the principal's office, where you'll hope the *best* thing that happens is being expelled. Do it."

I hated them in that second.

I hated what they stood for.

I hated what they did.

But it wasn't really them I hated, not even a tiny bit.

Erin wouldn't step up to the plate. Cora backed down right away. Even Peach had expressed her sympathy, but these girls—they were worth the fight.

I wanted this fight. I could breathe it in. It could be my purpose for living. But none of them replied, and I glimpsed Ryan in the back corner. I locked eyes with him, and just like that, the rage drained from me.

It left me weak, and shame bloomed in my chest.

I felt tears coming to my eyes, and I turned away.

It wasn't them I wanted to fight.

chapter thirty-five

"Mom?" My phone began ringing not long after my standoff with whatever-her-name-was, so I didn't have much time to dwell on how embarrassed I should be. Grabbing it, I moved out to the hallway and huddled against a locker with my finger in my ear so I could hear her.

"Yeah! Hey, honey. How was your day at school?" She didn't wait for my answer. "Listen, something's come up. Nothing bad, but your father and I are staying in the city tonight. We'll go to work like normal tomorrow, and then pick Robbie up for the weekend. We'll be home tomorrow afternoon."

Oh.

I felt someone standing behind me, and I knew it was Ryan before I looked. I was attuned to his presence.

I turned to face him, still leaning against the locker, and put my other finger in my ear. "You aren't coming home at all tonight?"

His eyes lit up.

I rolled mine, knowing what he had on his mind.

"Yes. I mean, no, and Mackenzie, please be good. Please, please, please, no Ryan in your bed tonight."

Wait—what was she saying? I leaned forward. "But he can stay over?"

I heard a long sigh from her end. "I really wish you'd make some female friends, but yes. Ryan can stay over as long as he doesn't sleep with you and there's no sex. Got it?"

I gave him a thumbs-up. "Yes. We got it. No sex, and he won't sleep in my bed."

Ryan was grinning when I hung up. "We're sleeping in the basement then?"

"Hell yeah."

He tugged me in for a kiss.

I let myself get lost for a few seconds before pulling away. My anger was still raw from the gym confrontation, but his touch helped calm the edges. I didn't feel so much like a combustible balloon—one prick and I'd explode.

"Thanks."

"For what?"

For making me feel sane again. "For not looking at me like I have two heads." I started to pull away, not wanting to see his response, but he tugged me back.

A fierce look filled his eyes. "Hey," he said softly. "I get it. Okay? You've only had words with a few girls. Kirk and I trolled for actual fights some weekends. It was stupid, and bad—really bad."

A slice of fear went through me at the thought of Ryan in a fight. "Were you hurt?"

His grin turned lopsided. "That was kinda the point."

"Did your parents know?"

He nodded. "I couldn't hide the evidence, but I stopped. Peach looked traumatized every time she saw me afterward. I couldn't do it after a while."

I was shaken by the thought, but I remembered how it had felt to square off against the girls in the gym. Flames started flickering, warming me. It was almost addictive, and so simple. Hurt or be hurt. Those were the options, and both were an escape from what I didn't want to feel.

I shuddered, feeling it starting to burn again. "Let's go." *Before I go in search of another fight.*

I didn't feel Willow beside me, but I heard her. *And you always thought I was stupid for fighting. You get the appeal now? You can forget yourself . . .*

They were her parting words as I walked away.

◦∽◦

We went through a drive-thru for a couple of burgers. Ryan pulled up to the window and started fishing for his wallet to pay, but an older guy replaced the food attendant at the window. He shook his head, holding out the bag of food. "Not for you. Your food is always free during basketball season."

Ryan grimaced. "No. Thank you, but I'd rather pay, sir."

"I won't hear of it." He held the bag out and shook it a little. "I know you're going to take us to the championships again. This is an easy payoff. Take the food, Jensen."

I could tell Ryan was reluctant, but he took the bag. "Thank you."

The man nodded before pulling his arm back inside and letting the window close behind him.

Ryan didn't move forward, not at first. His head bent forward, the bag in one hand and his money in his other. "Fuck it," he growled.

There was a donation box for a children's hospital past the window, and Ryan stuffed the entire wad of cash inside before heading out.

I didn't say anything, only took the food from him so he didn't keep squeezing the bag. I understood—Willow was the artistic star, and Robbie is a genius. I understood the special favors that came their way because they were that: special.

"I know it may seem stupid, but—"

I cut him off. "I get it. I've seen it happen time after time with Willow and Robbie."

People like people who are deemed gifted, which was a good thing, but there were consequences to that too.

"It's starting. I like getting free shit, but after a while, there are hooks inside you, and you never know when someone's going to pull one." He paused at a stoplight and looked over. "Does that make sense?"

"Yeah." I said it lightly, but I knew how he felt. I saw it tear Willow apart some days. "People give you things and are nice to you, and it's wonderful at first, but there can be strings attached."

"Exactly." He rubbed at his chest. "You start to owe so many people that you lose yourself. It's a weird feeling, and I feel like a dumbass bitching about it. There's a reason I'm getting the free shit. I shouldn't be complaining too much."

"No." I turned toward the window, lost in thought. "I get it. I do."

Was that what Willow had been feeling?

Did she feel pulled in too many directions? Did she feel like she owed too many people? Or did that add to the problem?

"You okay?" Ryan asked.

"What?"

We had started to drive again, but Ryan was skirting looks at me. "Did I lose you just now?"

"Sorry. I . . ."

I needed to talk about her. I knew I did, but the words weren't there. I could think them. I could feel them, but the idea of saying them aloud filled me with dread.

I shook my head, turning back to the window. "No. I was thinking about something else. I hear you, though. Too many people wanting something from you can make you lose yourself."

chapter
thirty-six

RYAN AND I PULLED THE QUEEN-SIZED MATTRESS FROM ONE OF THE GUEST ROOMS OUT TO the theater room. We'd fallen asleep watching a movie, but the credits had already rolled through and the screen shut itself off, so I didn't know what woke me.

I didn't need to go to the bathroom.

There was no chill in the room, but I sat up, the sheet falling to my waist. The mattress was on the carpet so I crawled to the floor before standing. Ryan was still sleeping. He was turned toward me, his arms curled under his pillow, and I watched the way his shoulders and chest moved with each deep breath.

I didn't want to be one of those girls who devalued themselves, but I didn't get why he cared. I really didn't. I was a mess, and yes, he said he understood. He said he'd been there, but I had baggage up to my neck, and I'd only dealt with the tipping point of it. There was so much buried deep inside me, buried so far down that I was half wondering if Willow's ghost had woken me. That made sense.

Willow and I had shared a Jack-and-Jill bathroom at the old, new house, and there was one of those in this basement. The two guest rooms shared it, but no one had used either of the rooms so far. This was the first night we'd even touched the room, pulling the mattress from the frame.

Maybe that was what had woken me. Awareness had tugged at my subconscious all night. Maybe it had finally rose to the surface. I left the theater room and went to stand in the doorway.

I could smell her.

She'd liked vanilla-scented perfume, and she'd mixed it with a lotion called Pink Promises. It always reminded me of a vanilla rose. I could smell it. The early morning sun wasn't up yet, so I didn't know what time it was. My guess was around four or five, maybe even earlier. The moon was still out.

I shouldn't go into that bathroom. I knew I shouldn't, but my legs weren't listening to me.

I was pulled there.

My stomach churned in its place.

I could hear her laughing. It was a whisper on the wind—but there was no wind, and I knew there was no whisper. It was only an empty room and me.

There was light coming from inside the bathroom and spilling out into the guest room.

The laughter faded, and a song took its place. Willow's favorite song.

I shook my head. Recognizing the song, I knew it wasn't Willow's favorite. It had only recently come out, and I'd heard it for the first time this morning. "Barbies" by Pink.

I heard the rest of the song play out in my head.

"Ow!"

I almost fell. That was Willow's voice, but it wasn't in my head. It sounded real. It sounded from the bathroom.

My knees were shaking as I stepped inside.

Willow was bent over, shaving her leg, her hair pulled up into a messy bun. She wore a tight top over cut-off jean shorts, and the radio on the counter was blasting that song.

I rubbed my eyes.

I was seeing things. I had stepped into a full-on hallucination, and my next stop would be the hospital.

Pinch yourself. You'll wake up then.

But as I reached over and pinched myself, I felt the pang. I wasn't dreaming.

Willow danced in place, that razor sliding up her leg in rhythm with the bass.

"Willow?" My voice cracked.

She looked up, a bright smile on her face. "Took you long enough. Jeez. Do you know how many times I've shaved my legs, hoping to get you down here? Too many, my sister, too many." She touched her leg where there was no shaving cream and rubbed it. "Feel it. Totally smooth. I don't even need to shave, but what do you do, I guess."

"This isn't real."

She straightened, putting the razor in the sink and cleaning it off. "That's what you think. It feels real to me."

"You're a ghost then?"

She tilted her head to the side, her messy bun tipping too. "No, I don't think so. I don't feel like a ghost."

"But I can see you. I can hear you." I could talk to her. I could smell her. If I reached for her, would I be able to touch her too?

Could I hug her, one last time?

She finished rinsing her razor and put it in the drawer. "You've been talking to me for months, but you keep thinking I'm a voice in your head."

She was. Wasn't she?

I rubbed my forehead, starting to feel some pressure there. "You're saying this is real?"

She held her hands up in a helpless gesture. "I'm saying why do you have to classify it? Maybe you're supposed to see me tonight? Maybe you're supposed to hear me at times? Maybe you're supposed to let me help you when I can, and maybe this is all your baggage trying to wake you up. Who knows? Who cares? You shouldn't. You aren't getting more messed up by talking about me. Trust me. You'll only get more fucked up by *not* talking about me."

I couldn't handle this.

Grief rose in me, sharp and hungry as it threatened to eat me alive. I felt it taking over me, taking little bites.

What was happening to me?

But then Willow was in front of me. She had crossed the room. A light came from behind her, and I felt its warmth on me. Her vanilla-scented rose infused my nostrils, and she was so real. Tears slid down my face.

I wanted her to be real.

I wanted to see my sister one more time.

"Ssshh." She touched my cheek, and all the pain was gone.

It was swept away, replaced with a warmth like sun touching my skin.

"Willow," I choked out.

"I know. I know." She traced her hand down the side of my face, tucking some of my hair behind my ear. "I know, Mac. I really do, and I am here. I am real. I'll always be here."

I was still crying. "You aren't really here. I can't laugh with you, grow with you. I can't—I'm alone, and you know it."

I didn't know when I'd be able to touch her again.

"Why'd you go?"

I couldn't bring myself to say the actual word for what she did, but I could see it all again.

My face: dark eyes, golden blonde hair, heart-shaped chin

My body: slender arms, long legs, and a petite frame

My heart: beautiful, broken, bleeding

All of it on the bathroom floor in a bloodied pile.

I was down there. I lay beside her, my palm in her blood, and my face turned toward hers.

"Don't. Don't, Mac." She tried to soothe me, pull me back. Her hands kept tracing down my face, trying to shake my memories. "Don't go there. Don't remember me that way. I was sick. I was sad. I was hurting, and I didn't ask for help. I was sick, Mackenzie. I was sick. You can't understand because I never told you."

There were warnings. I knew there had been.

Her dried puke on the toilet.

Her exercising at midnight.

How she cried when she got an A- on a test. Her spending whole weekends in bed.

"You shut yourself off from us."

"Yes." She made sure I maintained eye contact with her. If I stared at her, I couldn't see her the way she'd been the last time I saw her. "I was sick, Mackenzie. That's the best I can tell you. It was horrible what I did. I can't go back. I can't make things right. I can't . . ." She broke off, and I saw her crying.

Could ghosts tear up? Could she do that, whatever she was?

She sniffled, shaking her head briskly to clear the tears. "I never talked. I never said what was going on with me, but you have to. You have to talk. You *have to* talk about me. You can't keep yourself bottled up and suppressed. Nothing good will happen then. I know you don't want to feel the grief. I know you don't want to let me go, but you have to. You will make yourself sick like I was. I don't want you here. You got it? I don't want you with me. Not you. This is mine to carry. Not yours. I want to watch you live a long life. I want to see you married. I want to see my little nephews and nieces. I want to see what my children would've looked like—"

I gripped her arms and squeezed.

"Please. Please, stop. I don't want this," I whimpered.

She wasn't letting me pull away. She wasn't letting me fall back. The more she said, the more my grief rose and bubbled inside me.

I didn't want to feel what she wanted me to. I wanted to stay like this, with her. She was happy. She was dancing. She was alive. I felt her sunshine against my face, and I only wanted that. I didn't want to think about her gone.

If I started, that darkness might open again. I shoved it down. I'd gotten better the last two months. Things were better.

"No," she snapped. Her eyes blazed with determination. "You aren't better. You're faking. I can't let you do that. Feel me. Mourn me. Say goodbye to me. Then . . ." She was fading.

The warmth chilled. The room's coldness returned.

The light was leaving. The shadows were returning.

I couldn't smell her perfume anymore.

The song fell away, leaving the ticking of a clock from the hallway.

"Willow," I cried out.

Her legs disappeared.

Her arms.

Her face—I clung to her eyes. I clung to the feel of her hands on my face, and then she said, "You have to tell them, Mac. You have to tell them."

Her hands were gone.

So were her eyes.

I was alone.

But I heard her last words, "Remember me, and cherish me. That's the last step, Mac. I love you . . ."

I collapsed, sobbing. My chest heaved. Salt filled my mouth, and not knowing what else to do, I crawled to where I remembered her lying as if we were back there, as if this was that same bathroom.

I lay there, my palm down, my face turned toward where she'd been.

And I stayed like that until I fell asleep.

Two more pieces fit. They fit right.

―――

A bunch of things happened later that day.

I woke up before Ryan did, and I crawled back into the bed with him.

We went to school.

Robbie came home.

My mom and dad smiled at each other.

I didn't know if Willow was real in that bathroom, though, I did know I wasn't going to torture myself trying to explain it. I'd always thought I was going crazy, but when I woke that morning in Ryan's arms, I felt a little less crazy.

I felt a little bit better.

And I felt a little more whole.

chapter thirty-seven

THE STANDS WERE FULL. ALMOST LITERALLY. People couldn't line up against the court's walls—it was a safety hazard—so at any given moment, ten people were huddled in the doorway. Their necks craned as they tried to watch the game. A few students hung out on the side of the bleachers, but every few minutes, someone acting all official would go and wave them away.

Basketball had been popular in Arizona, but not like this.

When I saw a woman wearing a basketball jersey with Jensen on the back, I assumed there was another Jensen on the team. She wasn't his mother, and he hadn't mentioned any other family coming to the game. But there wasn't. There was no other Jensen on the team, and when the players came out to start warming up, the second Ryan was visible, a roar took over the gym. Both sides of the bleachers.

It was insane.

Cora saw my look and started laughing. She patted my knee. "Yeah. Get ready. Ryan isn't like any other player on the team, on any team in the state." She leaned across me, pointing to a bunch of guys sitting in the back who were all wearing baseball caps pulled low and writing on clipboards. A few other guys, wearing Portside apparel, sat with them. "Those guys aren't college recruiters."

I nodded, remembering the ceremony. "He already committed."

"Those are professional guys."

I knew Ryan was good, but I hadn't thought he was *that* good. I sat up straighter, feeling proud of him, and as if he could feel me watching, he sank a three-pointer and glanced up to me.

My mouth watered for him; his hair was messily rumpled like I always loved. Some guys had shirts under their jerseys, but Ryan didn't. I could see the definition in his shoulders and upper arms. As he caught the ball and jumped for another shot, his shirt bounced up. A nice glimpse of his stomach showed me what I already knew. He was tightly muscled, and it hit me. All the warnings I'd gotten about him—how intense basketball season was, how much he was loved by his friends and family—hit me like cement bricks.

He wasn't just the top of the chain within his group of friends. He was literally the top over everyone. That time we went for food and got it free? That wasn't the only time. That'd been the first of many times.

I was starting to understand why.

Cora nudged me again, nodding below us on the bleachers. "Stephanie Witts is planning on making a pass at Ryan tonight. Just warning you."

That was the girl I'd had the confrontation with yesterday, and she was sitting with a bunch of her friends. Erin and Peach were at the end, but whispering on their own. Tom was in the row behind Peach, along with a few other guys I didn't recognize.

"Where are the other guys?"

As if hearing my question, Kirk and Nick showed up, walking in from the hallway. Two other guys were with them, but I only recognized Pete.

"That's Nick's cousin, right?" I asked Cora. "And why isn't Nick playing?"

"He got in trouble. I don't know why he's not on the bench with them. And yeah, that's his cousin."

She stood, waving with a smile stretching over her face. "Hey! Pete! Up here."

He looked around and saw us.

Kirk and the other two lingered behind, talking to Stephanie and her friends, while Pete came toward us. There was an opening by Peach, so he started his climb there, ruffling her hair in greeting and pausing to knock fists with Tom before coming the rest of the way.

"Hey, Cora." He grabbed her in a big hug before smiling politely at me. "Mackenzie, right?"

I nodded. "Peepee, right?"

He barked out a laugh. "Man. That's right." He sat right behind us, his knees behind Cora, and she leaned back, draping her arms over his legs. He was a human backrest. He jiggled her a bit. "Not that I'm not excited to see you, but please, please let me flirt with you. Kirk's already warned me off. I could die happy if I could shake him up a bit tonight."

Cora stilled at his words, watching me.

Pete just laughed again, moving his knees to jostle her. "Hmm? Cora?"

She was watching me.

I just shrugged. "I'm fine."

She nodded, only needing that before turning and punching Pete in the leg.

"Ow! What was that for?"

He was clueless. "You're an idiot sometimes," she told him.

"An idiot like my cousin and your new beau?" He tapped her shoulder, pointing to where we'd just been watching.

Kirk was watching us, a keen look on his face. He narrowed his eyes, focusing on Cora before turning to respond to something Stephanie said. She leaned forward, her hand touching his arm, before falling back as if she'd made a joke. Her friends began laughing. Nick swept an easy grin over Kirk's face before sensing his focus on us. He looked up then too, his eyes narrowing at Pete.

I glanced over, seeing that Pete had leaned forward to drape one of his arms around Cora's shoulders. He was wiggling his eyebrows in suggestion.

Cora shook her head. "You're going to get beat up." But she wasn't moving away from the touch either.

Kirk lifted a finger and waved it side to side.

His message was clear, but Pete only laughed harder. "The fucker can sweat a little." He pretended to rub his cheek next to Cora's.

She shrieked, pushing him away, and sat forward.

I looked down, noticing that almost their entire section was watching the display. Stephanie's eyes locked with mine and darkened with anger. Her friends whispered to each other, looking from her to me.

"Whoa," Pete said. "What's going on? I'm totally egging Kirk on, and no one's caring . . . except him." He laughed to himself.

Cora rested an elbow on his knee again. "Stephanie Witts and Mackenzie got into it yesterday."

"Got into it?" Nick asked as some people left behind us. He and Kirk had decided to join us, and Nick sat behind me, adding, "More like Mackenzie decided to get in some practice of her own, with Stephanie's head as the ball." He nudged my shoulder with his fist. "Hmm? Hmm? Am I right?"

"Yeah?" Pete grinned. "I remember hearing you wiped the floor with an ex of Ryan's too." He tipped his chin to me. "You the next badass of Portside High?"

I laughed at that. "Badass?"

"She holds her own," Kirk said as he dropped down beside Cora. He nodded to me before turning and shoving Pete off his seat. "Touch what's mine again, and we'll have real words."

"Oh yeah?" Pete was unfazed, scrambling back and pushing his face close to Kirk's. "So Cora's yours now? You claiming her?" It was small, but I caught the smallest wink in Cora's direction.

I studied my friend, and I didn't miss the small smile on her face or the way her head suddenly ducked down. I was starting to wonder if this hadn't been set up by Cora herself. Maybe Pete was doing a little friendly favor for one or both of them.

"I . . ." Kirk was unsure, glancing to Cora. "Well?" He frowned, softening his tone. "Do you—do you want to go out sometime?"

Her head popped up. "Sometime?"

"Tonight."

Nick made a noise.

Kirk corrected, "Tomorrow night?" He winced. "There's a party tonight I already said I'd go to."

Her face was almost bright red. "Oh! Um. Y-yes. Yes."

She beamed, and Kirk nodded. "Cool."

The two continued to stare at each other, having a small moment before Nick punched his cousin in the shoulder.

"Ow!" Pete clamped a hand over his arm and glared. "Honestly. What is up with the physical violence?"

"From what I remember, you hit him the first time I met you." I pointed at Pete and then Nick.

Both cousins froze and then Nick cracked up. "Ha! She got you there." But he swung back and tried to punch his cousin again, only Pete was ready this time. He leaned back, and Nick's arm went in front of his chest, and he grabbed it. Nick retaliated, and the two started brawling right there in the stands.

Kirk grabbed Cora and me, pulling us down a seat, but most of the others around them scrambled out of the way. A few little kids started crying.

"Ah! Stop it!" A middle-aged lady took her purse and began batting at Nick and Pete's backs. "You two. Stop it at once."

It worked, and it didn't.

They stopped wrestling and returned to their seats, but they started shoving instead.

"You guys." Tom had run up the side of the bleachers, using the actual stairs, and he paused at the end of our row. "Kirk." He gestured to the court where some of the basketball players had stopped to watch the scuffle. "They're going to call security."

Kirk groaned, but he started to wade in between the cousins. "I can't take these two anywhere, I swear."

The purse lady gave up and passed her weapon to her husband, who was the only one who didn't seem perturbed by Pete and Nick. He remained almost in the middle of it, sitting calmly and watching the court. I followed his eyes and found his attention fixed on where the cheerleaders were stretching. One had her back to the bleachers, bent over so she could still talk to her friend. Her ass was right there. I didn't think she cared.

Then—*smack*! I reeled backward, feeling blinding pain on the side of my face.

"Hey!" Kirk yelled, but I couldn't see. I just knew I was falling—falling—until hands caught me, more than one pair of hands.

"Oh, dear." A lady gasped from beneath me, and then an arm came around the back of my waist and lifted me back upright.

"HEY!"

I recognized that chest pressed against mine and started to protest even as I relaxed. "No, no. You're supposed to be warming up."

Ryan's arm tightened around me. His whole body tensed, and he barked again, "Knock it off! NOW!"

He kept me cradled against him with one arm, his other moving around.

The pain started to recede, and I opened one eye enough to see Nick and Pete staring at me.

"Oh no." Nick started forward.

Tom had waded in too, and he made a gurgling sound. If it was meant to stop Nick, it worked because his shoulders dropped dramatically. "That wasn't Pete I hit with my shoulder, I'm betting."

Pete pushed forward. "I'm sorry, Mackenzie. He's sorry too."

Nick hit his shoulder. "I was about to say that. I'm sorry too, Mackenzie."

"Yeah." Pete's head bobbed up and down. "We're both sorry." They looked at Ryan, and if they could've taken a step backward, I was sure they would've. Pete gulped before adding, "Sorry, Ryan."

"Fucker," Ryan grit out, flinging a hand toward the court. "You hit her, and you're causing a scene. Security was coming in before I told 'em I'd stop it." His entire body was rigid, and hearing a threat of violence in his tone, I looked up a little more intently.

I wasn't the only one.

Kirk met my gaze, and I could tell he was also slightly concerned.

I frowned, placing a hand over Ryan's chest to calm him. "I'm okay. Honestly." I blinked my eye open a few times, testing it out. "I can still see."

Ryan didn't respond as he wrapped his arms around me for a hug. He pulled me in tight, dipping his head down a moment. His lips grazed my neck, and then he released me.

He pointed at Nick and Pete. "Sit your asses down, and shut the fuck up." Pointing at Tom, he said, "You. Sit." He pointed on my left side. "Stop hitting on my sister, and if these assholes start fighting, use your face to protect Mackenzie next time."

Ryan glanced at me for a second before leaving for the court. As he went, a few people patted him on the back. One guy pumped his fist in the air. "Bring home the win, Jensen!"

Kirk chuckled once Ryan got back to the floor and turned to Tom, adding, "Or next time just get your ass in here to help out."

Tom sat, but he leaned around us to give Kirk a menacing look. "It isn't my fault these two revert to being nine year olds when they're around each other."

"Hey."

"Hey?"

Everyone ignored Pete and Nick, and Kirk rolled his eyes as we all took our seats again. "You should rethink dating Peach, and you know it. It's going to cause problems with your friendship."

Tom glowered at him but didn't respond, and as if everyone had decided the excitement was done, we all turned back to the court.

A loud alarm sounded, and the players stopped warming up.

It was time to play.

chapter thirty-eight

RYAN SCORED THIRTY-TWO POINTS.
Twelve rebounds.
Six assists.
Three steals.

I was starstruck—and ashamed I didn't have a Jensen jersey to wear myself. As the last buzzer signaled the end of the game, I was tempted to ask that lady where she'd gotten hers made.

"Fun, huh?" Cora's eyes were invigorated, but it could've had something to do with her spending the last two hours holding Kirk's hand.

I nodded. "Yeah. Is it always like that?"

She saw the jersey lady going past us down the bleachers and shook her head. "That's a bit much, but it's the first game too. This is nothing compared to state. It's insane then."

Kirk rested his arm around Cora's shoulders. "You need a ride to the party? Are you going?"

I nodded, laughing. "I think I have to."

I'd heard the warnings. I saw some of the excitement leading up to this game, but being there—my eyes were open wide as fuck. Cora's whole heads-up about Stephanie Witts had a new seriousness to it.

"But I know Ryan will drive me."

"I figured, but I still wanted to ask. He and I haven't talked about the party."

Tom had returned to Peach's side after halftime. He'd left for snacks and never came back, slipping in with their crew below. Nick and Pete had stayed with us, but they were down there, talking with some of Stephanie Witts' friends.

"They're just flirting. You and Cora are taken."

Kirk must've seen where I watched.

"No, I know," I told him. But I'd never felt this emotion before, at least with these guys. It felt a little like betrayal, which was stupid. I knew that wasn't what it was.

Maybe . . .

Ryan's friends are guys. They want to get it on. I could hear Willow rolling her eyes. *Just because they didn't sit the whole time with you doesn't mean they're losing interest in your friendship, and no, Ryan definitely will not. The guy is gaga over you. I'd die from boredom from how cute you two are if I weren't already dead.*

I stiffened. *Willow . . .*

Yeah. Yeah. I can feel your disapproval, but guess what? I'm dead. I can joke all I want. She snorted. *What are you going to do about it? Kil—*

Enough!

I suddenly had to get out of there, and fast. "I'm, huh, I'm going to wait for Ryan down by his locker." I didn't know if they understood me, I spoke in such a rush. But I couldn't take the dead jokes. It was too fresh, too raw.

She told me to remember her, to cherish her, and then let her go. But she was making that difficult. I could still feel her around me. Maybe she wanted to comfort me, apologize . . . I didn't know, but I did not want to hear it. Not right then. It was Ryan's night.

"Mackenzie!"

I heard Nick yell my name, but I pushed past them.

Fuck.

He was standing between Erin and Stephanie Witts, both girls I knew would love to be with Ryan. And there I was, literally running away from a ghost that was in my own head. This wasn't *Supernatural*. I wasn't a medium. Willow didn't exist.

There, Willow! I half-shouted to her in my head, but half-whispered because I still didn't want to hear her response. *You don't exist. I've analyzed myself and decided—you are dead. Make all the fucking jokes you want.* I didn't want to actually hear them.

Going through the doors and into the emptied hallway, I curled my hands into tight fists, waiting for her response. It never came, and slowly, as I approached Ryan's locker, I unclenched my fingers.

I didn't feel her either. She had gone away once more.

Feeling lighter, since she wasn't sitting on my shoulders, I slid down to the floor. My back was to Ryan's locker, and I pulled my knees up, hugging them to my chest.

I clasped my eyes tight, pressing my forehead to the back of my knees.

Even then, I wanted her gone. I wanted all of this out of my head, but I also didn't. I felt less crazy than a few days ago, but I was still halfway crazy. Or one-third crazy. Once that healed, would she really be gone then?

"Planning world domination?"

I started to laugh, lifting my head. My laughter died when I saw Erin standing over me. "You."

She laughed, shaking her head before holding her hands up. "Look. I've given up. I'm laying my flag down, and I think I've done that a few times. You don't have to keep with the hostility."

I sighed. I was already so tired of this conversation. "What do you want, Erin?" Because there was an agenda. She was just one of *those* people.

"Okay. Fair enough." Her hands went back to her side and then she crossed them over her chest. "Look, I never went after your sister, and we both know I could've. You mentioned her twice, and Peach explained." Her head inclined. "She explained better how you and Ryan got to be so close. I get it. I honestly do. He understands your pain, like you understand his." Her top lip curled in a small sneer. She kept going, sounding bitter. "Grief is a great foundation for a relationship, but whatever. I'm not the one fuckin—"

"Get to the point."

If she didn't, I was getting to my point where I'd get to my feet and we'd have a confrontation of a different sort. Maybe. Most likely. Probably not. I'd throw insults at her and leave once I thought I'd given her my best zinger.

Since my physical visit from Willow, the fight in me had dwindled. It might take a bit more to tap into it, but I knew it was there. A good well of craziness.

"—tonight at the party, okay?"

I had tuned her out.

Oh yes, I was such an ace fighter. I got so bored, I only *thought* I might want to fight her.

"What'd you say?"

"Were you listening at all?"

"No."

"Nice. I'm trying to do you a solid, and you aren't even listening."

A second sigh from me, and I leaned my head back against the locker. "I'll listen now. What were you saying before?"

She looked at the floor. "That friend of Ryan's who died?"

"Yeah?" My gut twisted in a knot. I didn't think I was going to like what I was about to hear . . .

She looked up, flicking away a solitary tear. "He was my boyfriend."

"Wait." So that meant—

She was already there. "That's why Ryan and I dated briefly. It wasn't long, and to be honest, it was more just messing around because we both missed him so much. I'd been with Derek for two years when it happened."

It made sense, why Erin was around so much.

"I couldn't figure out why they let you hang out with them," I mused to myself. "I thought it was only because of Peach, but you guys were at the house when Kirk came back."

"Yeah. Derek's cousin. All of us were friends. Then Derek died, and I messed around with Ryan afterward, like a few months afterward." She grimaced, her whole body shuddering. "Want some more honesty? No. I'm not even asking." She plunged ahead. "I don't regret sleeping with Ryan. I just regret the timing of it."

She understood. Somewhat.

"I'm not with Ryan because of my grief."

Yes, I had used him in the beginning, which was something Ryan knew about. Something he understood since he'd used Erin in the same way.

That was why he understood.

"Thanks for telling me." I meant it.

She nodded. "That's the reason I never went after you about your sister, but that's why I'm here. You need to watch Stephanie. She isn't going to understand."

"Yeah." I meant everything I said to her and her friends, but that was before my coming-to-Willow moment. "I heard she's going to make a pass at him tonight."

"She is, and she can be ruthless sometimes. Just watch your back with her. Okay?"

I studied her a moment. Trust her or not?

Erin was the popular girl in her class. Even though she was a grade younger, I knew she didn't need to hang out with Stephanie and her friends. There'd been a divide between them earlier in the year. I hadn't been noticing much at that time, but I had noticed that at Peach's pool party.

"Why are you hanging out with her?"

A fleeting smile was my answer. She started to leave but said over her shoulder, "Because sometimes it's smart to keep your friends close, and your enemies closer." She winked at me. "It's a classic for a reason."

She was leaving as Ryan headed toward me, his gym bag hanging from one shoulder. He glanced at her as she passed him.

"What was that about?" he asked as he drew close to me.

I beamed, feeling the same way I always did.

He pushed back the darkness, sometimes literally.

"Stephanie Witts is going to make a pass at you tonight, and I'm supposed to watch my back," I said, almost upbeat about it. I winked at him. "I heard she's ruthless."

He matched my grin, but didn't respond as he let his bag drop to the ground and then slid down to the floor with me. "You know you have nothing to worry about, right?"

I nodded. "I know." But there were knots in my stomach. I couldn't deny them. "Just . . ." I leaned my head back and turned toward him so we were inches apart. "I don't trust them."

"Yeah. I get that." He dipped down, his lips touching mine and resting there a moment before he whispered, "But I don't want Stephanie Witts. I don't want anyone else." His eyes were hard on me.

My body warmed. A tingle shot through me.

I grinned, my lips curving against his. "You're all I want too."

He pulled back, an uncharacteristic seriousness on his face. No smile. No grin. No smirk. No amusement in his gaze. He was suddenly so serious. "I just want you. I just love you."

My tongue felt heavy.

I should say it back, but I was still hearing Willow.

Pain sliced through me, and I turned away—I started to turn away.

He caught me, his hand touching my chin, and he moved me back to look at him. His thumb caressed my jawline, and his eyes dipped to my mouth. "I couldn't have said this a year ago. I couldn't have said this six months ago, but I can now. It took me that long, Mac. Derek's death fucked me up, so when I say I get it—I get it. But I want to say it."

I needed it.

It was like air to me.

I turned my body, my head holding still, and slowly, I crawled until I was straddling him in the darkened hallway. It was empty, but people were probably lingering just around the corner or by the gym. Two steps—that would be all it would take for someone to round the corner and find us there.

I so wasn't caring at that moment.

I settled down on top of him, feeling him beneath me, and his hands moved to my hips.

I leaned forward, my lips nipping his, and I whispered, "I want to show you what I can't say, not yet."

"Oh yeah?" A small grin pulled at his lips, and he watched me with dark amusement.

"Yeah." I shifted, pushing down with my hips. He was hard for me. His gym pants didn't obstruct him much, and my jeans were a little baggy.

God.

I glanced left and right, but no one was there.

Biting my lip, feeling all the right tingles and pleasure filling me, I knew I should get up. We should take this somewhere else, but I was not caring.

This was reckless.

This was stupid.

This was dangerously intoxicating, and with that last thought—I stopped thinking. My hips pressed against his, and he pulled me in, holding me against him and lifting his hips a little to grind against me.

"Fuck, Mac." He pulled back, his eyes so damned dark I wanted to get lost in them. His left hand slid up my waist, up my arm, around to my front, and lingered between my breasts. They were straining for him, but he didn't go any farther. He just stayed there, feeling my heartbeat and watching me all the while.

He groaned. "You make me feel things I thought were gone."

He seemed tormented by that, and I shifted back a little and slid my hand through his hair. It was half-dry, so there was a tiny little bit of a messy curl to it. I loved how it was chaotic.

"What do you mean?" I asked.

His hand went back to my hip, and he cupped me there, jerking me back in place. He fit right, perfect.

I was having a hard time not moving my hips again, rocking on top of him.

He rested his head back against the locker, watching me. "Derek was my best friend, not Kirk."

"I thought . . ."

He shook his head, his eyes still so dark. "Kirk became my best friend after Derek died, but it was him and me. Even the others—Tom, Nick, and Pete—they knew that. It was me and Derek. Then he died, and God—" He let out an anguished breath, closing his eyes as lines of tension formed around his mouth. "I used to think no one got it. No one understood."

I shifted back even farther.

My gut was sinking. My chest was starting to tear open.

I had a feeling I knew exactly what he was going to say.

He looked at me. "I thought no one would understand what it felt like to hurt so badly that you just wanted to go with that person." His hand smoothed down my hip, stopping on top of my leg, and he looked down at it. "Until you."

He lifted his gaze again. The torment was so real, so haunting, that it hurt me to be there. Every bone in my body started to ache, but not from him. Not because of him. Not in a way that made me want to run from this.

It was an ache because someone else understood.

It was almost as if, for a split second, I got her back. Ryan took Willow's spot. I took Derek's spot, and we were the other's mourned loss for a moment.

Then I gasped, and the feeling left me.

It was back to us. Ryan and me. The ghosts had gone again.

"I didn't know."

He shrugged and went back to watching his hand. He traced it up and down the inside of my leg. "He died before basketball season that year. Some told me I didn't have to participate, if it might be too much for me, but I wanted to. All the others who kept quiet, I knew they were relieved. They wanted me to play. They didn't care about Derek, but it was him and me. We were co-captains on the JV team. I played varsity too, but I don't know . . ."

His eyes met mine. The anguish was back. He whispered, "All I did right away was play ball. It was like I was half-trying to forget him, and half-trying to kill myself. You know?"

I nodded. My heart was in my throat. "Yes."

"But everyone wanted something from me. They wanted me to win. They wanted me to keep going, get faster, learn more drills, learn more tricks. The coaches. The teachers. My friends. My parents—it was all of them. I never got a fucking break. All they wanted was to fucking win. All I wanted was to fucking die."

"Ryan," I whispered, moving back to him. I hurt, but this time, the pain wasn't mine. It was his. I put my hand where his had been, right in the middle of his chest. I felt his heart pounding. It was so fast, almost skipping a beat before going even faster to try to make up for it.

I wanted to say something to calm him, slow his heartbeat, but there were no words.

There was only grief and the silence that accompanied it.

He bent and took my hand, kissing it and holding it tightly. "I gave everything that year, and I was empty after it. I had nothing when the season ended."

"That was when you stopped caring."

"Yeah." He squeezed my hand, resting it against his chest. His other hand went to my hipbone and burrowed under my jeans, his thumb rubbing over my skin. "Kirk and I, we didn't give a damn. Drugs. Drinking. Fights. Fucking." He grimaced. "None of it worked." His hand started up my back, sliding under my shirt. "It took a year and a half, but all of that went away." He stopped, his hand right next to my ribcage. He held me in a gentle embrace, as if I were a delicate treasure. "I get what you feel. I get you talking to Willow. I get you sitting in a dark and empty hallway. I get you leaving the bed to cry in your guest bathroom. I get it. You don't think I do sometimes, but I do."

"Ryan." Tears slid down my face. I reached up, cupping his cheek. "I . . ."

I wanted to say it.

I was feeling it. I was feeling more than just that word, but . . . the words wouldn't form.

His eyes flickered, shuddering a second, and then the agony was gone. He had closed up, returned to being the old Ryan again, and my heart sank because I realized this had been him the whole time.

He had been shut down this whole time too.

"Don't." I leaned forward, catching his face with my hands. I moved so close, my eyes jumping back and forth between his, my lips almost touching his. "Don't do that. Not to me."

"Don't what?"

But he knew. He so knew, and I shook my head.

"Don't shut me out. I'm not them."

His eyes shut again, resting a second, and his chest rose as he took in a deep breath. Then they opened, and I was seeing the real him. He just opened up for me again.

"There." I raised my hands, cupping the sides of his temples, right next to his eyes. My forehead rested against his. "There you are."

More pieces fit together.

Both his hands went to my hips, and he gripped me, just holding me in place.

And then, because it was the right time and a gate had shattered inside me, I said, "I love you, and I love you for loving me."

His eyes closed again, as did mine, and we stayed there, just holding each other.

chapter thirty-nine

My first warning should've been Erin. She was standing on the curb in front of Stephanie Witts' house when we pulled in. Peach was next to her, and Tom right behind her, but for some reason, their welcoming party didn't sound the alarms in my head.

It might've been the feeling I was basking in at that moment—telling Ryan I loved him and genuinely feeling it, not feeling all the other baggage inside that had kept pushing it down so I couldn't say it. It felt like a weight off my shoulders.

Or maybe it was because I had a strong feeling I couldn't hold up my promise not to have sex with Ryan again. Though, it wouldn't be sex. It'd be making love.

I suddenly wanted to know what that felt like so bad it was almost worth risking my mom's anger.

Or maybe it was that Ryan hadn't let go of my hand. The only time was when we separated to get into his truck, and he was still holding it as he pulled up to the curb and threw his truck into park.

Of all people to greet us, it shouldn't have been those three.

Peach? Maybe. Tom? Maybe. Both of them together? Terrible idea but still plausible. But Erin? There might've been a temporary truce or a tentative peace between us, whatever we had, but we weren't friends. So yeah, all three of them should've been sounding my alarms at full blast.

We got out. Ryan came around the front and still the trio said nothing.

Tom wore an uneasy grin. As Ryan came to my side, he stepped away from Peach and dipped his head. "Ryan. Mackenzie."

Peach shared his uneasiness, biting her lip and looking as if she wanted to reach for his hand. She didn't. She tucked it under her other arm, almost holding herself back, and her head hanging a tiny bit.

It hit me then. Those two were backup for—and my gaze found the girl who'd been my first enemy at Portside: Ryan's ex-girlfriend/fuck buddy.

Then the alarms sounded, tightening my gut. "Erin."

She didn't even look at Ryan. Her eyes were only for me, and I saw the sorrow. It flickered there, but it was strong. It was evident. Her eyes clouded, her eyebrows pinched together, and she frowned, tucking a strand of her hair behind her ear.

"I had no idea," she said.

"No idea about what?"

Ryan moved forward a little, as if he wanted to shield me. "What are you talking about, Erin?"

She still didn't look at him, but his sister did. Peach went to Erin's other side, standing in front of her brother. She held her hand out, saying softly, "Ryan . . ."

He ignored her, barking out, "Erin!"

The door opened behind them. Music, light, and people spilled out.

"Ryan!"

"Mackenzie!"

Kirk, Cora, Nick, and Pete darted down the front lawn.

Cora was unnaturally pale, and her face was streaked with tears. Once her eyes hit mine, she jerked to a stop, and I watched as she sucked in her breath. Kirk stopped too, looking toward her. He frowned and reached for her hand, but like Erin, she only had eyes for me.

She and Erin were both terrified—for me.

The guys were sending nervous looks at me, but they were more wary of Ryan.

Because . . .

Because why?

Why were they concerned about him when the girls were so scared for me?

Me.

Because of . . .

Because Ryan was protective of me, but Erin and Cora . . . the way they were looking at me, as if they pitied me and were horrified at the same time.

It's me.

I jerked backward, hearing Willow's voice like she was standing in front of me.

I swayed, clasping my eyes shut.

No . . .

Yes, Willow sighed. *They're going to use me to get at you.*

I looked again, past everyone in front of me, and I saw her.

She was faint, like a mere reflection in the wind, wavering all around, but I saw her.

Willow was looking right at me, wearing the same dress she had on in the dream. A pink, shimmering dress, but there was no crown on her head. This time, her hair was pulled up into a braid and wrapped around her head, looking like a crown in and of itself.

But she looked alive, so alive that I heard myself exhale a ragged breath.

I blinked a few times, but she was still there.

There were no more words. She didn't come toward me. She didn't point inside, but I knew she was leading the way.

She wanted me to go in, and feeling her courage join mine, I grew calm. I felt ready, and I started forward.

Everyone turned then, and I heard Cora gasp.

"Holy sh—" Kirk exclaimed.

They saw her.

They honest to God saw her.

I almost faltered, my knees buckling, and then she vanished. I only felt her beside me. Her hand touched mine. More strength transferred to me, but there was also peace. Contentment. She was letting me feel everything right along with her.

The door swung open. Someone saw me coming and was ready. The music cut off, and everyone who had been standing around on the walkway turned to watch. Some were smirking. Some were laughing. Some were sad. And the pity—that seared me the most.

I didn't want anyone's pity, but I was getting it. I gritted my teeth. Whatever was ahead of me, I would show them I didn't need it.

They were in the living room.

The crowd didn't part for me when the hallway forked off to the dining room and kitchen. But it opened to the living room, where people were sitting on the couches. Others were spread out, sitting all over the floor.

They were watching a movie on a large screen. It wasn't even the television. It had been projected onto the wall for maximum effect, and standing right to the side of it was Stephanie Witts, but she wasn't alone.

Zoe.

Gianna.

And next to them? Duke and Willow's ex-best friend, Serena. He had his arm around her. I turned away from them. They didn't even deserve my attention, but Duke dropped his arm as soon as he saw me. His eyes widened, and he jerked forward a step.

"Mackenzie—"

He was already groveling. I heard it in his voice, and I leveled him with a hard look. "Don't. Even."

I didn't need to ask how they got there. I looked right at Stephanie. "What'd you do? Go on my social media? Google my sister's name?"

Her eyebrows went up, and her lips pulled back in a haughty smirk. "You told me to come at you with the worst I could do." She waved at my ex-friends, at Willow's ex-friends. "Here you go. They've been telling me all about your sister—"

I finally looked at the screen, and I tuned her out. She was saying things, no doubt hurtful things, but it didn't matter in that moment.

Willow had been right. It was her. They were watching a compilation video of her winning the championship with that six-foot, papier-mâché dragon. She smiled, holding the dragon in one hand and the purple ribbon in the other. Her trophy was next to her, and she was so proud. She was beaming. Then the video skipped ahead to her nuzzling noses with Duke. Then I saw her and her friends, all in their cheerleading uniforms. Then older pictures of Willow—her school pictures when she was in third grade, fifth, sixth, seventh, eighth, all the way up to what should have been this year's picture.

They showed her senior picture.

I felt tears sliding down my face, but I didn't care.

So many pieces, one after another, connected, and they were strong. Twenty-five. Goddamn twenty-five, and I felt them in me. They were pulsating. They were buzzing. They were firm, cement, and more were coming.

"You guys had your pictures taken right before you moved," Duke murmured, coming closer. "She mailed that back to me. I got it a week after . . ."

She'd sent it before she killed herself.

I didn't respond to him. I wasn't sure if I wanted to yet. The video kept going.

Pictures of Willow and me: she was smiling, I was rolling my eyes.

Pictures of her in her track uniform and me in my soccer uniform.

Pictures of us hugging each other.

Pictures taken of us at school lunch one day. I had a bag of Cheetos, and she was eating a carrot. A goddamn carrot.

Pictures of us before school: Willow was in a dress. I was in jeans.

Willow wore a skirt, and I had holes in my shirt. Willow's hair was always perfectly styled, and mine was pulled into a messy ponytail.

I got the message Stephanie wanted to send, and I looked at her, wiping some of my tears away. "What? Are you going to follow this presentation with your decision that she shouldn't have killed herself, and I should've? That she was the twin who shined, and I wasn't? That I'm drab, and dull, and boring? And she excelled at almost everything?"

I had crossed the living room so my shadow hit the projector. Images of my sister continued to play over my face, but I kept staring right at Stephanie.

"Do you think I don't think of that every day since I found her?" I whispered. "Do you think I'm not haunted by her? By the thought that if I *had*—maybe she wouldn't have?"

My voice broke at the end.

Someone sniffled behind me.

I heard another whisper.

And I felt a presence at my back. I thought it was Willow at first until a hand—a real live hand—touched mine. It was Ryan. He didn't pull me back, though. He was just there for me.

I latched on to him, lacing our fingers together, and he moved a step closer so I could feel his heat against my back. His other hand rested on my hip.

Stephanie's malice had started to wane, and her forehead wrinkled as she began to frown. "I mean, come on." She glanced around for support.

There was none.

I didn't look, but I could feel the somberness creeping over the room. Anyone who had thought this was going to be funny didn't seem to anymore, and if it wasn't because of me, it probably had to do with Ryan, and the whole group that stood behind us.

"It's obvious your sister was popular, and you're . . ." She tried to sneer at me. And like everything else, that too failed.

"I'm what?" I raised my chin higher. "Mourning such a deep loss that I hope even you will never feel anything like it? Healing? Trying to keep going? Forcing myself to go forward because my family needs me? Because I've found people here who love me and support me, and I need to keep going for them? Is that what I am?" I raised my voice, grating out, "Does that somehow make me less than you? Less than anyone else in this room? Or maybe, just maybe, that makes me stronger than you? That makes me a goddamn survivor, when trust me, the thought of joining my sister is sometimes easier than breathing."

I was letting everyone see my insides.

All these months of not talking, and it was spilling out.

I could feel their surprise. It was in the way Ryan tightened his hold on my hand before letting it relax. The way the whole crowd seemed to waver, and the way Stephanie's eyes widened, and the blood drained, finally, from her face.

I turned to my two ex-friends and burned them with the same look of hatred I had for Stephanie. "How dare you come here. How dare you bring that video to a party. How dare you befriend someone you knew wasn't reaching out with my best interest at heart."

Zoe and Gianna blanched, but their mouths opened. I didn't let them speak. I kept going.

"How dare you turn your back on me? How dare you—just, how *dare* you?"

I didn't care why Duke or Serena were there, but I turned to them anyway. "Willow would hate you for this, and you know it."

Serena hung her head, but Duke surged forward again. "It isn't like that. I mean . . ." He gestured to Stephanie. "She said she was your friend."

Zoe and Gianna stepped forward, right behind him.

Zoe tried to smile at me. "We felt bad after you left, Kenz."

"And what Duke said is right. She reached out to us, saying she was your friend." Gianna glanced at Stephanie. "You haven't been on social media. I've been sending you messages almost since you left, but you haven't been getting them."

Because I was using Willow's account.

"We didn't know who you were friends with. Honestly, we had no idea. We aren't here to hurt you." Zoe started crying. "We really aren't."

I shook my head.

Ryan spoke over my head, "You thought showing a video of her sister at a high school party was a good thing?" His tone was hard, biting. "How the fuck do you make that right in your head?"

"We didn't—" Duke started.

"The laughter should've been the first clue!" Ryan cut him off, moving ahead of me. "Her face should've been the second." He jabbed a finger in the air toward Stephanie. "She looked goddamn evil when we first came in. If the other stuff hadn't sunk in, that look should've had you scrambling to turn the goddamn machine off!"

"We—"

Zoe interrupted Gianna, her shoulders sinking down. "We weren't thinking. You're right. We weren't thinking."

"I was hoping it'd all be okay," Duke said. "That's what I was hoping. But I swear, Mackenzie, we didn't come to hurt you. We came to apologize." He glanced to the others before placing his hand to his chest. "Or I came to apologize. You tried to talk to me after the memorial service, and I blew you off." He gestured to Willow's ex-friend. "Serena and I both did."

"It's just hard—"

I nodded, speaking before Serena could say more. "To see her when you look at me? To hear her when you talk to me? Trust me. I get it."

"You didn't expect her to stay, did you?" Erin stepped out of the crowd and folded her arms. She looked right at Stephanie, who had tried to blend in with her friends. "You thought she'd come in, see them, see the video, hear the laughter, and then run away crying? That was what you thought would happen, wasn't it?"

Stephanie's friends melted away, leaving her standing alone. She glared at them before facing Erin and then me. "To be honest, I was going to say everything Mackenzie guessed. That the wrong sister died, that Willow seemed like the better of the two. It's obvious from the pictures. So yeah." She jerked her head higher. "I was going to use the weapon she gave me, and destroy her with it."

She turned to me. "Imagine my surprise when I found out you hadn't been talking to your friends from home, and that Willow's boyfriend and best friend were dating. I mean, you were asking for it." Her eyes trailed to Ryan, pausing a beat before looking away.

"Because of him?" I dropped his hand, moving around him.

"Yeah!" Her head flared up again. "He's ours! He should be dating one of us, not you! Not someone who . . . you're mental! I've heard you talking to yourself in the bathroom. You freak out in the classrooms like you're nuts or something." Her hands went to the sides of her head. "You don't deserve him. You . . ."

My head tilted to the side. "I what?"

"You . . ." She gulped and then shrugged. "You aren't good enough for him."

Her words should've struck me at the core.

They didn't. Not this time.

"You're too late to make that stick. A week ago, I would've agreed with you." A hollow laugh left me. "I wouldn't have left him since I'm selfish enough to need him, but now I think you're wrong." I glanced up, seeing my shadow over my projected self. Willow was laughing, and when I leaned back, moving my shadow and letting the full picture hit the wall, there I was, laughing every bit as hard as she was.

"*You're the strong one, Kenz,*" said Robbie's voice.

"*You were the superstar in everything,*" Willow said. "*You just didn't know.*"

"*You were what we needed. You were our anchor.*"

"You're wrong." I looked right at her. "I *am* good enough; I'm better than you'll ever be."

And taking Ryan's hand again, I left the room. He followed. As did Erin. Cora. Tom. Kirk. Pete. Nick.

I was told later that almost everyone followed us out.

Stephanie Witt never had the same clout after that party.

She still had friends, but she wasn't popular anymore.

Erin became more of a friend to me, and somehow she almost took Stephanie's place at school—except for the bullying. I was very adamant that she couldn't do that, and she agreed.

She still somehow managed to rule with intimidation, though.

Cora and Kirk became exclusive after that party.

Nick and Pete hit on Zoe and Gianna before moving on to hit on other girls. There were no more wrestling matches, that night.

And Tom and Peach kissed, blushed, and held hands whenever they could.

The next day, I met Zoe and Gianna for breakfast before they went home. It still hurt that they hadn't been there for me in the beginning, but they'd been a part of my life for so long, and they loved Willow too. Plus, I was trying to be someone Willow would have been proud of. Yes, she'd told me so many times that she was proud of me, but I didn't fully believe her. I was still trying. And that meant meeting Duke and Serena too.

It was harder to talk to them than it was to talk to Zoe and Gianna. They knew Willow in ways I hadn't: as her friend, as her cheerleading accomplice and confidante, as her lover. And seeing them unable to hold back tears unleashed mine as well.

It was an awkward feeling to sit in that booth, first with Zoe and Gianna, and then with Duke and Serena as we all cried. But we were all mourning Willow, and for that I was grateful.

I was surrounded by people who loved her too. This was how it should've been from the beginning.

After that they all went back to Arizona, but I did talk to Zoe and Gianna more regularly.

And as for me and Ryan, well . . .

chapter forty

Five months later
Two hundred fifty-three pieces later

WITH HIS MOUTH FUSED TO MINE, RYAN PUSHED ME BACK AGAINST THE SHOWER WALL. Our hands clasped together, and he pinned them above my head before bending to my shoulder and scraping his teeth against my skin.

I gasped as he plunged into me.

He took my weight, and his left hand let go of mine to drop to my thigh. He gripped me there as he sank even deeper inside me.

God.

This guy.

Pleasure built and built low in my belly, and I used my free hand to hold on to him, sinking my fingers into his hair.

The shower beat down on us, but Ryan shielded me, taking most of the water. A slight mist coated my face, and as I drew in oxygen, I drank in some water too.

We had been together for almost a year. In forty-three days, it'd be the anniversary of Willow's death—the same day I'd first crawled into Ryan's bed. I'd gone through hell this last year, but he'd been with me the whole time.

I trailed my fingers down his back, feeling his muscles shifting as he thrust in and out, keeping a steady rhythm.

He bent forward, dropping his lips to my nipple and sucking.

I closed my eyes, feeling desire and the momentum building in me. I wanted him. I wanted him harder, deeper, and in the whole year, that hadn't lessened. If anything, I craved him more and more. Like tonight—we were going to prom later, but I'd stepped into the shower, knowing I had to feel him before we endured a night of mere touches and the whisper of being together.

All eyes would be on us.

All eyes would be on *him*. He'd be voted prom king, which was no shock to anyone. There was a prom queen, and there were rumors it would be me, but I doubted that. I'd only moved there a year ago. It didn't seem right, even though I was Ryan's girlfriend. I wasn't the most liked girl in the grade. But knowing everyone would be watching Ryan made me almost desperate to feel him first. I wanted to remind myself that he was mine, only mine. I wanted to feel him moving inside me, and I wanted to see him watching me the way he did when he took me at night.

I looked up to find him watching me once again.

His eyes were dark, heavy, primal.

Adjusting our bodies, he lifted me higher against the shower wall and began going harder. He was claiming me.

Pulling my hand free from his, I wrapped my arms around his neck, bending forward to kiss his throat.

He groaned, the sound rumbling deep, as his other hand found my hip. He slammed me against the tile, going harder and rougher.

I laid my head back, gasping in more breath as I tried to ride with him, but this was for him. He held me captive as he ground into me. An onslaught of pleasure assaulted me, and I sank into it. Hell, I felt half-drunk from this. All I could do was hold on to him until I felt my climax coming.

"Ryan," I gasped. My fingers bit into his back, my nails scraping his skin. "I'm going to come."

He slowed, grunting. "Not yet. Not." Thrust. "Goddamn." Thrust. "Yet." Thrust, and then he tensed, his hands tightening on me to almost bruising pressure. "Now." And he exploded.

I let go, the climax crashing into me, making my body jerk and shake.

He held me the whole time, waiting until both our bodies had calmed before carrying me out of the shower. My legs remained wrapped around his hips, and I clung tightly to him and rested my head on his shoulder.

He ran a soothing hand down my very wet back and took me into my bedroom.

"Fuck." I sighed as he laid me down and then eased out of me.

He laughed, skimming a hand down my side before following the motion with his lips.

I ran my hand through his hair and then down his shoulders and arms as he moved back up, bracing himself above me. His eyes found mine, still so dark.

"You okay?"

I nodded. "Yes." My hand cupped the side of his face. "I'm good. You?"

He nodded, falling down to kiss me again before settling onto the bed next to me. "Shit."

"Yep."

"I don't want to go tonight."

I laughed, curling on my side and kissing his shoulder. "Ship's sailed on that one, Prom King."

He groaned again, catching my hand and tugging me until I straddled him. "Yeah?"

"Yeah."

I matched his grin, both of us still riding the wave we'd just created in the shower. I was naked, and as his eyes trailed down my body, I tipped my head back. My hair had grown longer over the last year. I didn't have the heart to cut it. Willow always kept hers long, and I wanted it like hers tonight, though mine was darker. I felt the tips of it grazing my back, and it felt nice, but more than that, I enjoyed the feel of his eyes on me.

I knew, even before looking, that they'd be lust-filled, dark, carnal. As if on command, I felt him twitch under me again. He was growing hard, and unable to stop myself, I reached down for him.

"Holy shit, Mac." A guttural moan ripped from him, and he tensed under my hand. His hands went to my hips, but he didn't move me. I had him in the palm of my hand.

I began to rub him, making him even harder. "So if you're named prom king, we both know another girl will probably be prom queen."

He began to pant heavily as I stroked his length. "Can we talk about this some other time?"

"No." I grinned, enjoying the power I had over him. I touched the tip of him, pausing there. "You'll have to dance with this other girl."

"Goddamn, Mac." His chest rose up and down. His eyes were starting to go wild. "I'm going to get you back. You know that."

I was hoping for it.

I kept sliding my hand over him. "And when you dance with this other girl, you aren't going to like it." I held him, squeezing just slightly. "Right?"

He was almost trembling, and he shook his head. "No. Hell no." His fingers sank into me, flexing. "Keep fucking going."

So I did, but this time, I scooted back and bent to take him in my mouth. His entire body paused, his hands in my hair. I could've kept going, but I didn't want to torture him. At least not yet. I'd wait until after the dance, after Kirk's after-prom party when we were alone again. Then I'd torture him all night long.

He didn't wait long. Once my mouth settled over him and I began moving up and down, his hands fisted until he was ripping me away. He flipped me over, and grabbing my leg, he raised it over his upper arm and then slid inside, sheathing himself deep.

I sucked in a breath, letting the air out through my teeth at the sensations. Goddamn. That felt so good.

"Now you were saying?" He smirked at me, pushing deeper in before sliding out, only to go back in.

I sighed, letting the waves of torment roll in, and a half hour later, after he put on a condom, he had me whimpering and biting my lip to keep from screaming. Then my entire body went slack.

Afterward, he curled against my body and kissed my neck. "There's no one else I want to dance with," he whispered, his hand palming my breast. "It's only you." He kissed me again, his thumb grazing my nipple. "Only you, Mac."

I already knew this. I'd known this all year, but it felt good to hear because I felt the same. There'd be no one else.

Closing my eyes, I murmured, "Good, because I love you."

His arms tightened around me. "I love you too."

Thirteen pieces just fit back together, all at the same time.

chapter forty-one

"Your hair is so much darker now," Cora said, putting her eyeliner down on the counter.

We were getting ready at my house. Ryan had left, going to dress at his place, and he'd texted not long afterward to say the guys were already drinking there.

"Yeah." I pushed up some of the loose tendrils, patting them back into place. It wasn't that much darker, but I had put more brunette coloring in it. There were still some blonde, but I didn't want to look exactly like Willow tonight. I wanted to be me, and as I gazed in the mirror—I was me. I was Willow, but I was me too.

"And Ryan cut his hair short. I can't believe he did that. He's always had it where he could make it all messy."

I didn't smile; I heard the envy in her voice.

Cora was happy with Kirk, but she'd been harping on him to cut his hair too. Once she saw Ryan's new crew cut and how ridiculously hot it made him look, she started in. She hadn't been the only one. Peach had jumped on the bandwagon, asking Tom to cut his hair. Both guys refused, letting their hair grow even longer. Kirk's had grown to just past his ears, and Tom was closely resembling a shaggy dog these days.

Ryan had cut his for the summer. He was starting a new basketball training camp, and he didn't want to deal with too much hair and heat. I'd liked his messiness too. It always looked adorable on him, but I couldn't deny the spark I felt when he got back from the haircut place. It made him seem so much more grown-up, more of a man.

"Erin said Stephanie Witts is hoping for prom queen." Cora lifted her hand, inspecting her nails.

She missed the slight wince I couldn't contain.

It wasn't the prom queen thing. I didn't want it, but it'd become a sore spot over the last month. Erin, Cora, Peach, and all of their friends had been campaigning for me to win. I told them not to, but I knew they kept doing it. So, I started telling people to vote for Cora. She was the one who really wanted it, and after her transformation this year—from being one of the shiest girls in our grade to one of the most well-liked girls—she deserved it.

Not me. That was for sure.

I eyed her lilac-colored dress, the matching dusting of purple eye shadow, and the tiniest bit of glitter on her neck. "Have a speech ready," I told her.

Her eyes opened wide, meeting mine in the mirror. She quickly looked away, focusing on the bathroom counter. "You know that won't happen." But I could see her cheeks flushing.

"Right," I replied.

The doorbell rang, and pounding footsteps told me Robbie was running for the front door.

We looked to the door of my room, as if the guys would appear instantly, and a second later, we heard their voices. We grinned, glancing at each other.

Our men had arrived.

"Mac!" Robbie yelled from downstairs. "Ryan and Doofus are here!"

We heard Kirk grumbling, "It's Kirk, Little Dickwad."

That was another change over the year. Kirk and Robbie had developed this odd friendship. Kirk teased my little brother, and Robbie called him names. Ryan explained one night that Robbie reminded Kirk of Derek, and that silenced any concern I might've had about the situation.

"Ryan and Major Doofus are here!" Robbie added.

"Coming down!" I called back. "You ready?" I asked Cora.

She took a breath, staring at the mirror.

Her hair had been curled and was loose over her shoulders. Her makeup was on point. Everything was done up, complete with the mani and pedi we'd gotten yesterday. I'd had to touch-up my nails after this afternoon, but they were fine.

"Yeah. Ready."

"You look beautiful," I assured her.

"Thank you." She turned, taking me in, and a soft, awestruck expression came over her. I knew she'd been paying attention mostly to herself, which was understandable. She had the nerves, whereas I didn't.

That wasn't true.

I was nervous, just not for the same reasons as Cora.

I wasn't secretly hoping to win prom queen. And I knew she was nervous for Kirk's after-party, but she hadn't confided that in me.

"You look—"

I had to ask, and I reached for her hand. "Are you thinking of having sex with Kirk tonight?"

I noticed a shadow in the hallway at the same time I blurted that out, and I grimaced. But Cora was looking only at me, so she didn't see Ryan pause and then silently retreat.

"I . . ." She was back to picking at the counter. "I don't know. We talked about it."

I couldn't stop my frown. "At his party, though?"

"I know." She shrugged, looking to the side and biting her lip. "He'll be drinking. He's already drinking, but I don't know. I want to. I mean, he does too, but I think I'm just ready to stop worrying about it. If it feels right, I want to."

"Do you love him?"

All the self-consciousness in her vanished at my question. Her head came up. Her shoulders straightened.

"Yes. I love him."

It was the most confident response I'd ever gotten from her.

"Some people wait for marriage," I blurted that out—I have no idea why. "You could wait, if you're one of those people."

"Are you?" Her mouth turned down.

"No. Ryan and I—we already . . ."

"That's what I thought." She lifted her shoulder. "I know why you're saying this, because I do think like that, but I love him. And I don't know. I don't want to get married till I'm in my thirties, and I don't want to wait that long."

"Just—"

Shit. What was my problem? I understood what she was saying. But I felt like I had to say this to her—like I had to say to her what Willow would've said to me. Cora hadn't said a word about sex, but Ryan had said Kirk had stocked up on condoms. It wasn't a big leap for me to go from there.

"Do you regret it? Having sex with Ryan?"

I looked up, but I didn't see his shadow in the hallway. He might've been standing to the side, or he could've gone all the way downstairs, but I didn't lie when I said, "No. I regret not having my sister here, but that's it."

She jerked back. "I forgot about your sister."

My throat burned. "You didn't know her."

"But still." Her gaze lingered on my dress and then moved up to take me in. A wistful look softened her face. "You look really gorgeous, Mackenzie. I can't imagine your sister being more beautiful than you."

I—was shocked, and I couldn't talk for a second.

"And if I do win prom queen, I won't dance with Ryan. I'll dance with Kirk, so you don't have to worry about that." She darted toward me, hugging me and kissing my cheek. "I'll be downstairs." And then she was gone.

I felt Ryan's presence and without looking, I knew he was in the doorway. "You heard all that?"

"Yeah. Now you don't have to worry about the king and queen dance."

I grinned.

He took me in. He looked at my hair, my dress, and lingered on my lips. "She didn't lie. You look really beautiful, Mac."

That nickname.

I'd been in his arms just two hours ago, but a whole new wave of want came over me. I yearned to be in his arms again, to be held by him, to be kissed by him. And there was a whole host of other emotions intertwined there. I thought back to Cora's question, and no. There was no way I could've even considered regretting being with Ryan.

We went fast, but I had a feeling we went exactly the way we were supposed to. Either way, he was staring at me as if I were the most stunning creature he'd ever seen, and my entire body filled up with tingles. My knees were melting too, and my stomach flipped over, but in the good way. I had butterflies in there.

"Thank you."

I wore a shimmering pink dress, one that almost perfectly matched the one I'd seen Willow in. When I saw it at the store, the hairs on my neck had stood on end. Maybe she led me there. I'd been shopping with our mom, and I teared up when I saw it. We bought it immediately, and, like the last night I'd seen her, I put my hair up in a braided crown.

Cora's color was lilac tonight. I knew Peach was wearing yellow, and Erin was supposed to go silver. Not me.

I was pink. It was the most quintessential girl color there was, and it wasn't even my most favorite color, but it was Willow's.

I loved this feeling, seeing how I affected Ryan, but I hadn't dressed for him. I hadn't dressed for myself either.

I'd dressed for Willow.

And with everything feeling all sorts of right, Ryan came forward, his hand curving around the back of my neck as he bent to kiss me. His lips were soft against mine, and I closed my eyes, letting myself get lost in his embrace.

And then we went to prom.

More pieces fit together inside me, but I stopped counting. I didn't need to anymore.

epilogue

"Mackenzie."

I walked into Naomi's office and sat in the same chair I'd been using for the last ten months. I didn't want to do these sessions. I never even wanted to admit that I was doing them, but there I was. I'd promised six sessions to my parents, and this was my tenth. Go me. Pin a star on my file.

I nodded in greeting, folding my hands over each other in my lap.

Naomi took a second, probably evaluating my posture, and she leaned back in her seat. "What's going on?"

I knew what she was referring to, but I still played dumb. I didn't know why. I could've gotten a gold star in stall tactics too. "What do you mean?"

She smiled briefly, nodding at me. "You know."

There was our relationship, right there. She knew I knew. I knew she knew that I knew, and yet I still played the game. And she just called me on it.

I never wanted these sessions, but I'd dropped my wall slowly over the last ten months, even going after I didn't have to. But today was the day. It would be the day I clued everyone in on what was going on with me, because until then, it'd been another stall tactic of mine.

"Okay." She let out a sigh, leaning back in her seat. "For real, what is going on with you?"

I never wanted to talk about Willow.

She'd been the reason my parents wanted me to come to these things—because I'd walked in and found her body first. I hadn't known she was feeling like that. There'd been warning signs, but I didn't know how to read them. I knew that, but it wasn't the same for everyone. I knew that too.

I coughed, clearing my throat. "She had mood swings."

Naomi leaned forward.

"That's one of the warnings signs, right?" I looked away.

"Yes." I saw her nodding from the corner of my eye. "You looked up the signs, or are you guessing?"

I didn't have to guess. "She would go on these tangents, just raging about everything. I thought it was because we were moving."

"Yeah. I can see why you'd be confused."

But I wasn't done. "She withdrew from everyone too."

"Yeah. You mentioned that one time."

"She and Duke broke up, but I thought that was because of the move too. Later, Serena told me she'd stopped talking to her too."

"Serena was Willow's . . ."

"Best friend," I supplied. "I didn't know about that, but Serena told me when they came here a few months ago."

"Right. You mentioned their visit."

I wanted to laugh at that, but no sound came to me. I'd never told Naomi about the night with Stephanie Witts—not to keep it away from her, but because it wasn't something

I needed to process. Stephanie Witts never hurt me. She actually helped, and I didn't want to give her any more time in my mind.

"She was sleeping a lot too, and then some nights . . ." Some nights she would be working out. Some days she slept two hours, and some days she slept twelve hours.

"Some nights?"

I shook my head. "I thought she had an eating disorder. I didn't know she was suicidal. She never . . ." My throat was burning again. "Feeling hopeless, thinking about wanting to die, feeling trapped, feeling like being a burden, unbearable pain . . ."

I kept listing the symptoms. The checklist had been engraved in my memory since June thirtieth, last summer.

"I just thought she had an eating disorder, and I didn't take it seriously. I thought they would help her. I just thought . . ."

How do you do this? How do you talk about how it was missed in one person, but it shouldn't have been for another?

Naomi sat forward, leaning down so her arms were resting on her legs. "Mackenzie, I'm confused." Her voice was quiet. It was always quiet. She paused as if she was unsure of what to say, but I knew that couldn't be true. Counselors knew what to say. They understood things the rest of us didn't. They understood us even when we didn't understand ourselves.

Right?

Then Naomi spoke again, her voice still soft and delicate, as if she were trying to trick me into opening up to her. "I haven't pushed about your sister's suicide note, but I know you read it. Your parents told me. It was right next to her when she, when you . . ." Another awkward cough. "When you found her. Your mother told me it was in your hands, but you won't talk about it and acknowledge it. I think . . ."

Yes, Naomi. Tell me what you think. Tell me how I'm supposed to process and grieve, and more importantly, tell me how I'm supposed to tell the truth about the worst day of my life. Tell me, please.

I raged at her in my head, but not one of those words passed my lips. I was a statue, my head turned away, my usual stony expression firmly in place.

Yes, there were cracks. Yes, some of the cuts had healed. Yes, I had a new layer on the outside. My life had changed. It wasn't exactly better. There was no world where I would say it was better without my sister, but it was different.

There were days I felt good. There were days I was convinced I'd already gotten my happily ever after. There were days I felt stronger than before. But then there were days I missed Willow so much I wanted to curl up into a ball and cry. There were days the hole inside me ached so much that I was convinced I'd actually lost a lung or my liver or half my heart. Those were the days when I understood the unbearable pain she must've been in.

But there was still something no one knew. Only Willow.

It was something that tricked me at times—into thinking I was in an alternate universe. If I thought about it, a crack in my foundation would open completely, and everything would fall in. And I didn't know how I would survive if that happened, but I had to talk about it today.

Ten months of counseling. Almost a year since Willow died.

I had healed. I had gotten stronger. I had persevered, but this one thing still haunted me. Maybe this was the real reason Willow haunted me? She wasn't around as much, but I still felt her, and I always knew she wanted me to tell the truth, but it scared me.

My voice would leave me, literally, in those times. It was as if I were too scared to talk about it because I was too ashamed.

"Mackenzie?" Naomi had scooted her chair even closer. "What's going on with you?" Her hand came down on mine. "You're trembling."

"I'm getting better."

"I know you are." I heard the pride in her voice. Her hand squeezed mine. "You and Ryan are good?"

I nodded.

"You went to prom together? I saw pictures in the local paper. I didn't realize they did that, but I guess when it's Ryan Jensen, anything goes, huh?"

"He was prom king."

She lifted her hand and sat back. She was getting comfortable again. "Were you prom queen?"

I shook my head. "Cora was."

"And you were happy for her?"

I moved my head in the other direction, up and down this time. "Yes. She deserved it. She's one of the most popular girls now."

"If I'm remembering correctly, you had a part in that, didn't you? You took her under your wing, like Willow did with you. Am I right?"

God. My throat was searing.

It was never going to go away. I realized it then.

I looked at her, meeting her gaze, and the words choked out of me. "I'm never going to fully heal, am I?"

The sadness in her eyes answered me, but she said, "Losing a twin is like losing a mother, or a father, or a soul mate. I can only imagine that it would be worse in some ways. So no, Mackenzie. I think it's a hole you'll feel for the rest of your life." Her lips pressed together, and she scooted close again, leaning down so she was almost touching my knees. "I don't think this last year was about you healing or getting over Willow's death. I think it was about learning to cope, and I think you've done a remarkable job."

But she didn't know.

No one knew.

Except Willow.

"You wanted to talk about Willow's suicide note?"

Her eyes widened in surprise. I had brought it up, not her. That wasn't how this went.

"Yeah. I wanted to talk to you about it at our last few sessions, but you seemed so much better when you came in, so I didn't push." Her head inclined toward me. "Do you want to talk about it today?"

No. But I had to. "Willow never talked about feeling trapped or hopeless. She never talked about suicide, but those are some of the signs."

"There are others, but yes. The list you mentioned are some of the warning signs, if people are looking for them, but sometimes, it's really hard to see everything the way it is, or for what it is. Your parents were worried about your sister, but they were worried about you too. Moving right before your senior year can be upsetting for any teenage girl. But Mackenzie, you can't beat yourself up for not seeing the signs."

I shook my head. "Willow never talked about that."

"Maybe not, but it was what she was feeling. She talked about being invisible, feeling worthless, of not being able to compare to her siblings. I can tell you that even if she didn't say the words, she was feeling all of those things."

Naomi's tone shifted, and she frowned, looking at the ground for a moment. "I'm confused about the direction of this conversation. It seems as if you don't believe your sister's feelings. It was all in the suicide note." She took my hand again. There was usually a no-contact policy with Naomi. She didn't even like hugs, which I was fine with. I liked touching Ryan, and I liked hugging Robbie, but that was it. No matter my progress over the year, I still held back with my parents and everyone else. It wasn't that I didn't love them or like them; it was just me. It'd been me since Willow died.

I changed that day.

Everything I had been before June twenty-ninth was wiped clean. When I lay down beside Willow, it was as if she took my pain; she took my burdens.

I felt it pressing on me. I knew I would share, but before I did, I needed to make sure Naomi understood.

I murmured again, "She never said anything. Not about that."

She scooted even closer. "But you *are* talking. You *are* saying something."

Yeah . . .

"I'm fine," I told her.

"No, I know—"

She didn't. I had to make sure she did. "Willow died, and I lived. I laugh. I love. I feel happiness, but this year was so hard. I wanted to be with her at times, but I didn't. I couldn't. I had Robbie depending on me. My parents needed me. And I have Ryan. I love him, and I know we'll be fine. We'll be happy. I mean, yeah, we'll have problems, and we'll struggle. Everyone does. Every relationship has ups and down, but we'll be fine. I'll be fine."

"I know." But she still frowned, struggling to figure out what I was telling her.

"I'm not arguing with you about what Willow felt. I know she was hurting. I just didn't know how much she was hurting, and I wish—"

My voice broke. It went back to not working, and I had to wait a moment. One breath, two, three, and then I could speak again. "I wish I had seen more than I had. I wish I had talked to her, but I was wrapped up in myself. I could only see what I was dealing with, and I never thought—"

My voice stopped again. I had to wait longer this time. Thirty seconds, and then, I tried again. "It wasn't supposed to be her. I wasn't supposed to be the one to go on and shine. That was always her role." I repeated again, "She never talked. I am talking now."

Naomi sat up, a look of horror on her face, but I grabbed her hands before she could sit back in her seat, and I finally told her what I'd been hiding from everyone else.

"I don't know how she found it. I don't know why she had it with her, but she didn't write that note. I didn't read Willow's suicide note because it wasn't hers." I let go of Naomi's hands and sat back, finally, finally feeling some peace as I shared my last secret.

"It was mine."

www.tijansbooks.com

Dear Reader:

I have never written a book that changed me.

There were books in my past that changed a part of my life, where they moved my career forward, etc. That's happened. I've had books be so loved by readers, and I've also written books that seemed like a grimace, but I'm always proud of every single novel I write. I grew or learned some lesson with each one.

But *Ryan's Bed* is different.

I began writing Mackenzie's story when I would travel for book signings, and I think there's something so lonely about hotel rooms that it crept into me and then through Mackenzie. I remember writing some chapters and thinking in the back of my head, "Where am I going with this? What am I doing?" And that's how I felt for the first eight chapters, but I didn't want to take the book into a path that I didn't feel was right. I didn't want to be careless with this book because there was something more with Mackenzie and Willow.

I'm glad I waited.

When I started writing it again, I felt Willow wanting a voice and I don't know if she would've had one in the beginning if I just pushed through. And then as the book started to unfold, I heard Ryan's voice more and more and then his storyline unfolded too.

This book was so hard to write, not in the way where I felt like I was taking a chainsaw to a glacier, but in the way where I cried almost every time I wrote it or worked on it.

A friend talked to me about how taboo suicide is, and how teen suicide is even more so, and that conversation really affected me. I agonized over if I should dare write this book. I thought about parents I know who lost a child, friends I know who lost their siblings to suicide, and even the ones I know who have gone. And when I really considered putting it aside, telling people it was abandoned, I couldn't do that. I honestly couldn't. I felt a huge cry inside of me that it was wrong to shove this book back down and ignore it.

I even talked to friends about writing *Ryan's Bed*. I remember having conversations saying that I didn't know what I was going to do with the book, if I would just finish it for myself and not publish it. I was that scared to write this one and publish it, but I kept writing it because there was something in Mackenzie that wanted out.

I know, I know. If you're not a writer or an artist, you may not understand this and it makes me look crazy, but I kept writing this book because I had to. That's the ultimate truth. I felt it was more wrong not to finish it so I started writing it again.

I wanted to respect Willow. I wanted to respect the loss Mackenzie had about losing her twin. I wanted to respect grief itself, acknowledge it, and not have it shoved under a rug. I wanted to write about Mackenzie's relationship with Ryan, but I also wanted to focus on Mackenzie herself.

I always felt something dark with her, something that she was hiding from, even herself. It drove me nuts, trying to figure out what I was feeling from her, until I realized what it was. And even when I did, I was still so scared to address it in this book. If you've read any of my books before, you know that I'm not someone who will shy away from the real issue. I usually go head first into it, exposing it and making you, the reader, sit with it. I wanted to do that with Mackenzie, but I wanted to do it in a different way so if you've stayed with me this whole time, I hope this book will make you think, and I hope this book will sit with you because that's what it's done for me.

No sequel is planned and I left the ending how it is because I hope it will make you think. I hope it will make you reread the book, but see it in an almost totally different way.

Out of all the books I've written, this is the only one that has changed me as a person.

Sincerely,
Tijan

links
& resources

www.crisistextline.org
Text 741741 from anywhere in the USA to text with a trained Crisis Counselor.

suicidepreventionlifeline.org
Call 1-800-273-8255 or if you go on their website, you can chat online.

For more facts about suicide prevention and warning signals,
go to www.211bigbend.org/nationalsuicidepreventionlifeline
or call 1-800-273-TALK

books by TIJAN

www.tijansbooks.com
* Recently published

Standalones
* *Enemies*
* *Teardrop Shot*
Antistepbrother
A Whole New Crowd
Bad Boy Brody
Bennett Mafia
Brady Remington Landed Me in Jail
Crossover Mtg.
Evil
Fighter
Hate To Love You
Home Tears
Kian

Fallen Crest Series
Fallen Crest High
Fallen Crest Family
Fallen Crest Public
Fallen Fourth Down
Fallen Crest University
Logan Kade
Fallen Crest Home
Fallen Crest Forever
The Boy I Grew Up With

Crew Series
Crew
Crew Princess

Carter Reed Series
Carter Reed
Carter Reed 2
Cole

Broken and Screwed Series
Broken and Screwed
Broken and Screwed 2
Sustain

And more!

we own tonight

CORINNE MICHAELS

To all the girls who dreamed of what could've been while singing along to your favorite band on your Walkman. This one is for you.

chapter one

Heather

"Damn it, Heather. We're always late because of you!" Nicole yells from outside the bathroom. She's been my best friend since the sixth grade. You'd think by now she'd know to pad things by twenty minutes if she wants a snowball's chance in hell of getting anywhere on time.

"The peril," I taunt her as I finish putting my hair up.

"You drive me nuts."

"Such is life."

I hear her mutter something under her breath as she walks away. I don't know why she gets so upset. We have plenty of time. With the way Nicole drives, her lead foot will have us at the concert fifteen minutes before the opening act.

Of course, I'm taking my sweet ass time getting ready. I have zero desire to be forced to put on makeup or any version of pants.

Nicole's idea of girls' night out and mine are totally different. I could stay home, drink a martini, and be happy. My best friend wants to paint the town red. I'm too old for that shit. I end up smelling like a garbage can and feeling like I ate a jar of cotton balls. I'd rather be comfy in pajamas than wear these jeans that I had to lie on the bed to shimmy into. I can only imagine what I looked like while I was sucking it in and bending backward to get the damn button closed. Then I did about fifteen lunges to "stretch" the pants, all the while praying I didn't bust a seam. Nothing like a workout just to get dressed.

I make a mental note to call my trainer friend at the boxing ring.

She knocks again. "I'm leaving you."

No, you're not.

I open the door a smidge. "I have the tickets in here. So, you know what? Go ahead." I stick my tongue out and then quickly close the door and lock it. If they hadn't already left me twice before, I wouldn't have to go to such lengths. I learned quickly that I always had to have the upper hand with my three best friends. Then again, if I had let her leave me, I could be watching Netflix and shoveling popcorn into my mouth.

Nicole may not have figured out to pad time, but she has learned I have a spiteful side, so she lets me finish without another interruption. I could stay in here longer just to piss her off, but that would mean more time staring at the pink tiles on the wall that I loathe.

My house isn't bad, but it isn't great, either. When my parents passed away, it was passed down to me. It's old and probably falling apart more than I'd like to admit. Yet, I can't get rid of it. It's the only thing of them I have, and the only place I can afford.

The mortgage is paid off, which allows me to put what little money I have left over after my monthly bills to go toward my sister's medical care.

Once I'm happy with my appearance, I head out with a shit-eating grin.

She looks at her watch as I emerge and shakes her head. "I swear."

The best way to keep Nicole from blowing up is with diversion. "You shouldn't swear, it's unbecoming of you. Are we picking up Danni and Kristin?"

"No, and I'm grateful we aren't, because we would miss the opening band."

She and I are the two most sarcastic and the biggest assholes out of the group. When we start to bicker, it gets bad—quick. Without our two mediators, it's best not to engage.

"Are you sure?" I ask ignoring the jab.

"Yes, I'm sure. They're meeting us there."

Nicole and I walk out and get in her car. I wish she'd buy a normal size vehicle. I'm five-foot-five, and my knees mash my boobs because of how squished I am. Between my already tight jeans and this sardine can, I'm going to bust a gut.

"Please," I say dramatically, "tell me they're not bringing their husbands."

She laughs. "Dickhead One and Jackhole Two aren't coming. They're going for a boys' night." She sticks her finger in her mouth and makes a gagging sound.

Thank God for small miracles. Their husbands are the worst, especially Danielle's.

"Maybe the two loser husbands will fall madly in love with each other," I muse while I shift to get comfortable.

Nicole smirks as she watches me. "And figure out they were never meant to be married to such amazing women like them."

"And then we'll finally build that compound where the four of us can live."

"No. We're going to need penises. There's no way I'm living with you people without having someone to bang. You three will drive me so far up the wall that I'll need the release. Daily."

"You're ridiculous."

"You're damn near celibate."

Here we go again. "Shut your face." She whips out of my driveway so fast that I almost smack my head on the window. "Nic!" I yell as she takes another turn way too fast in this damn death trap. "Jesus! Slow down!"

"Stop being dramatic. I'm with you, and you have a badge. No one is going to ticket me."

"I don't care if you get pulled over." I right myself and grab the edge of the seat. "I care about dying."

"You're going to die from lack of sex if anything." She rolls her eyes and cues the '90s station. "Listen to Four Blocks Down, and get ready to watch the boys shake their delectable asses on stage. After that, you can remove the stick up your ass, maybe then you won't be so miserable."

"I'm not miserable." I slap her arm.

"Okay." She shrugs and ignores me, which is her typical way of blowing me off.

Am I miserable? No. I'm happy . . . for the most part.

I have a great job that keeps me fulfilled. Being a female police officer isn't easy, but I love it.

The only real downside to my job is that I come face to face with my ex-husband every day. Luckily, things didn't end *that* badly. But I'd be full of crap if I didn't admit how much it bothers me. Things with Matt are—weird. Sometimes people just don't work or you realize the person you married isn't what you thought. I wish I could transfer to another town, but my sister Stephanie and the twelve years invested in my pension keep me here.

Nicole belts out another round of lyrics. "Sing it with me, Heather!"

I don't want to, but I'm taken back in time when the four of us had bangs that were so high they could cause whiplash, wore colors that no one should ever wear, and drooled over Four Blocks Down without a smidgen of shame.

Smashed in the tiny death trap posing as a vehicle, I let go a little.

We both sing along, belting out the lyrics of our first crushes. "I wish I still had my Eli pillow case," I grin.

"I had a Randy towel. I would like to wrap myself up with him again." Nicole sighs.

I swear this girl needs sex more than anyone I know. "Does your vibrator ever get a break?"

She looks over at me with her usual you're-an-idiot face. "You're going to realize very soon, my love, if you don't use it . . . you lose it."

"And you're going to overuse it," I say. She's the only one of us who never married. Nicole lives in downtown Tampa. She has to schlep it all the way out to Carrollwood to pick me up, but she knows if she didn't, I wouldn't go.

Sometimes, I envy her life. She has everything she dreamed of. Opening Dupree Designs and then landing her contract with one of the wealthiest developers in the city was pure luck. She slept with him, got a few more jobs, and before she knew it—she was on top.

Then she dumped him.

We park the car at the arena, and Nicole shifts in her seat. "Listen, I know you're hell bent on being the responsible one of us, but tonight," she grabs my hands, "I beg you to let loose. You *need* a break."

I glare at her. "I do let loose."

"Your hair is in a bun," she raises her brow. "You're the definition of tight."

I touch my hair, hating that she has a point. But this is me. I like to make good choices. Other than marrying Matt, which wasn't *bad* per se . . . just hasty. Never mind that he was an asshole. And he sucked in bed.

Okay, so maybe it was a bad choice.

Moving on. "I'm not uptight, Nic."

"I didn't say uptight. But let your hair down. It'll make Danni jealous since she can't get her hair your color blonde no matter how much money she spends. Maybe one day she'll get over herself and stop trying." Nicole and Danielle have a love/hate relationship. This week it seems to be more on the hate side. I wish they'd get over this already and talk it out, but they both claim there's no issues.

From what I can gather, Nicole slept with Danielle's ex three days before she got married. I don't know if it's true or not, but I wouldn't be surprised since it is Nic we're talking about. When I heard the back story, I distanced myself from the entire thing. No way was I getting in the middle of it, but Nicole typically has something snippy to say about her and vice versa.

Feuds aside, Nicole is right. I don't ever go out. If I'm not being a couch potato, I'm with my sister.

I pull my hair out of the bun, allowing my blonde locks to fall around me. Thanks to the twist, it almost has curls. Nicole grabs her bag from the backseat and tosses her makeup pouch onto my lap. "Put some of that on. You know, look hot. Not like a frumpy divorcée."

"I often question why I didn't drop you after high school." I grab some eyeliner and darken my brown eyes. I add a little blush and lip gloss. "Better?"

"Much."

We head into the concert, and I can't stop giggling to myself. Everyone is around our age—all here to see a freaking boy band. The group we all lusted over as teens is now fully grown, but here we are, ready to swoon and scream their songs.

I can't remember how many dreams I had about Eli Walsh or how many notebooks

I filled with Mrs. Heather Walsh signatures. I'm sure I'm not alone, either. There are probably a few hundred middle-aged women here tonight who had done the same thing.

Some more scantily clad than others.

"What the hell is she wearing?"

Nicole glances over and makes a disgusted face. "Dear, Lord. Someone needs to tell her that a muffin top and a mini skirt don't mix."

I snort.

"I feel like this is our version of a high school reunion," I cogitate while scanning the crowd for Danni and Kristin. I know we're not spring chickens, but when did we get as old as some of the people standing in line? Sheesh.

"Heather!" Kristin waves as they rush toward us.

Even though we see each other at least every three months, I miss them. We made a promise when we graduated high school we'd have a quarterly date, and so far, we've all made a point of sticking to it. It helps that we all stayed in the greater Tampa area, but I think no matter the distance, we'd always be there for each other.

Some friendships are unbreakable—even if someone sleeps with someone else's ex.

"I've missed you," I say as she wraps her arms around me.

She plants a kiss on my cheek. "I missed you more."

We all stand here, hugging it out. We're dorks, but I couldn't care less. Other than my sister, they're the only family I have.

"How's Steph feeling?" Danielle asks.

"She's doing good, I think. I'm waiting for her to call me." It's so sweet how Danielle always asks about Stephanie.

"I'm glad she's doing okay." She smiles.

"Yeah, she should've called though. I should probably give her a call . . ."

Danni grabs my hand, stopping me from going for my phone. "I'm sure her nurse would let you know if there were something wrong."

She's right, but the worrier in me can't help myself. I've spent what feels like my entire life making decisions around Stephanie. I don't take any chances when it comes to her.

"I'm just going to check," I explain as I grab my phone from my bra.

Danielle laughs. "I should've known better than to try to stop you."

There are no missed calls or texts.

Breathe. I'm sure she's fine, don't overreact.

I send a quick text because I'll never let it go.

Me: Hey, you okay? I haven't heard from you today.

She answers right back.

Stephanie: Yes, Mother.

Brat.

Me: Have you had any more tremors?

My sister suffers from Huntington's disease. She was diagnosed at nineteen, and it took her independence before she even had time to enjoy it. I tried to care for her. I did everything I could to keep her with me, but when she started suffering from relapsing paralysis and struggling to speak, we knew it was beyond my capability.

Watching your twenty-six-year-old sister battle with early onset dementia is devastating. The last few weeks have been good, though. She's been cognitive, alert, and even happy. Her symptoms are sometimes so mild that I forget how sick she is, but then the disease rears its ugly face again and there's no forgetting.

Stephanie: *Nope. And aren't you out with the girls? Go have some fun, Heather. Tell them I said hi!*

"Is Steph okay?" Nicole asks when she sees me typing away.

"She's fine. I mean, you know . . ." My mood drops immediately as I think about how she'll never experience this. Danielle touches my arm, and I force myself to smile. "She says hi."

"Give her our love," Kristin replies. I type out their message and tell her I love her before tucking my phone away again.

"Okay!" Nicole exclaims. "Let's go see these amazing seats that our super-fan Kristin scored us."

Kristin gives Nic the stink eye, which would be way more effective if she weren't in their fan club. Yup, my thirty-eight-year-old best friend is in a fan club for Four Blocks Down. I'm positive she regretted telling us this piece of information, but it landed us front row seats, so we haven't been too hard on her . . . yet.

"You can sit in the nose bleeds if you want."

Nicole wraps her arm around her shoulder. "You love me too much to deprive me of Randy." She lets out a dreamy sigh.

I laugh. "As if you'll ever going to get that close to him. And he's married!"

I try to put Stephanie in the back of my mind. My sister's illness is ripping me apart. I wish I could help her, but I can't control any of it. It makes me feel helpless all the time.

Stephanie grew up listening to me blare the music and dance around like a loon, and instead, she's stuck in a damn assisted living facility while I'm out. It isn't fair. None of this is fair. She should be here with me.

"Hey," Danni nudges me. "You look beautiful."

I give her a small smile. "Thanks." I'm no longer feeling carefree. I can't stop thinking about how much I wish I could be doing this with her.

"I'm sorry." Her smile falls slightly.

"For what?"

She shrugs. "I made reality come crashing into our big fun night of no worries."

"Stop! Don't feel that way." I wrap my arm around her shoulder. "My reality never leaves me. My sister is dying. It's just the way it is."

Danielle's smile falls completely now. "I'm so, so sorry, Heather."

I know she didn't mean to bring me down. I wish I could be more like Nicole. No responsibilities, sex with random strangers, nothing to worry about . . . but that isn't how my life goes.

Nope. Mine is a series of tragedies. While my friends were partying in college, I was working full time. My nights and weekends weren't filled with formals or trips to the beach, they were consumed by doing homework with Steph. I'm not bitter. I'm actually grateful in some ways. It forced me to cherish life and the people in it. Every day I have with Stephanie is a gift.

I shake my head. "You have nothing to apologize for. Let's act like idiots and pretend there are no problems in the world."

"You want to party like it's 1999?"

"Yeah, just like that. If only we had our Four Blocks Down dolls."

"They are collectable memorabilia," Kristin corrects before blushing scarlet and mumbling about needing to go find our seats. Nicole, Danielle, and I laugh hysterically as we follow her inside.

I wave to two of the guys in my squad, who are apparently working overtime detail as security as we pass them. Shit. I didn't even think anyone from my squad would be here. Usually, it's the other district that handles the MidFlorida Amphitheater. They look thrilled to be here—not. I make a note to behave so my entire department doesn't find out that I came to see my favorite boy band. However, knowing them, they've already texted everyone. I swear, cops are worse than teenage girls with their gossip.

I'll never live this down.

Music plays from the two opening acts. I sing along because . . . their songs were my jams when I was a teen. I would blare their screw men anthems through my speakers, windows down, singing off key, and belting every note because they were my idols. I owe many of my breakups to them telling me that I didn't need to take it.

"Ah!" Danielle squeals after the second band finishes. "FBD is next! I had the biggest crush on—"

"Shaun," Nicole cuts her off. "We remember you licking his poster."

"Oh my God!" I giggle. "I remember that. She straight made out with it." I guzzle the rest of my beer and shake my hair around.

"I wanted him to be my first kiss," Danielle explains.

We all did. Hell, I may have had multiple fantasies with Eli, but I wouldn't have kicked any of them out of my bed. They were everything when we were younger. I think somewhere in my mind we're all frozen in time.

"Want another beer?" Kristin yells.

I've had three already. I'm halfway to drunk. I shake my head no.

"Yes, she does," Nicole answers for me. I look at her with my mouth open. "I'm driving. You're having fun." She turns back to Kristin. "She'll be drinking all night."

"Oh," Danni laughs, "this is going to be epic."

"Shut up, I'm a good drunk."

In my mind.

"You're good for a laugh," Danni tacks on.

The lights go out, and the mood shifts. All of us start to scream and hold hands. This is Eli and Randy's hometown, so it's extra special. Their homecoming concerts are always louder and longer.

"Are you ready, Tampa?" PJ's voice booms.

We all yell louder.

"We said," Shaun's voice comes through this time, "are you ready?"

I bounce with Nicole, unable to control myself. I allow the energy of the room to fill me. I'm probably the loudest of the four of us. I don't give a shit, either. "Hell yeah!"

Kristin looks at me with a huge grin. So unlike me.

"That's it, Tampa!" Randy's face flashes on the screen on the side of the stage. "The Walsh brothers are home. And we want to hear you!"

Eli's face. I sigh. "Did you miss us?"

"Fuck yeah I did," I scream.

"Good." The screen displays both Eli and Randy. "We missed you, too. And you're about to see a whole lot of us. FBD is back, and we're ready to blow your minds."

The arena goes black.

And slowly, I see something rise out of the stage.

I stand mesmerized.

The light shines in my eyes, blinding me, but when I can see again, I would swear that Eli Walsh is staring right at me.

Emerald-green eyes pierce through me. His dark brown hair is cut short on the sides and the top falls errantly around his forehead. I take in every ounce of his perfect body. The way his arms pull against the fabric of his shirt, the pants that hug his perfect ass, and the span of his broad shoulders, makes me want to climb him like a tree. Then, with our gaze connected, he winks and throws a wicked grin my way.

Holy shit.

I stand there and gaze back at him like a fish with my eyes wide and mouth open. He looks away, but it happened. Eli Walsh smiled and winked at me. I just died.

chapter two

Heather

"I'M HALLUCINATING," I SAY TO NICOLE AS I EXPLAIN WHAT OCCURRED, OR AT LEAST what I think did. "He wasn't actually looking at me, right? I'm being insane. I must be stupid drunk to be imagining this."

She lets out one of her evil laughs while shaking her head. "You have no idea how pretty you are. I swear. Blonde hair, petite, brown eyes, big tits . . . of course he winked at you. Hell, I'd do you."

I can't tell if this is her typical sarcasm or if she's being honest. Part of me doesn't want to know. I can continue to delude myself that he was zoomed in on me. What mega superstar/sex God who can have any woman he wants would hone in on me?

Sigh, I can't even lie to myself well.

The next song comes on, and he doesn't glance my way once.

Okay, I'm literally certifiable.

I knew I had to be off my rocker. Now I can continue on with my life.

We drink more, sing, and I do everything I can not to stare at him. But . . . I can't help it. He's too beautiful to look away from. I watch the way his chest heaves as he dances around the stage in perfect sync with the other guys. How his eyes scan the crowd but still make every woman think he's looking right at her. It's magnetic. Eli Walsh is ridiculously sexy. Even in his forties. He's aged so well it makes me wish I were a guy. They have it so much easier than women. My boobs were much perkier fifteen years ago.

His smile, though. That hasn't changed one bit. It still brightens every part of him.

"Heather!" Danielle calls to me over the music. "Matt," she jerks her head to the left.

Ugh. Why the hell is he here? I can't escape him.

One night. I wanted one single night with no Matt, Stephanie, bills, crumbling house, or any other issue. Once again, I get screwed, and not in the way that leaves me sated at the end of the night.

I grab Nicole's beer and chug.

"Whoa!" she says, taking the half empty can from me. "Easy there. You're a lightweight on a good day, but I can't remember the last time you drank like this. Pace yourself."

"You said to enjoy myself."

She smirks. "Touché."

I ignore Matt standing off to the side and looking authoritative in his uniform. It used to turn me on when he got ready for his shift. Watching him put on his vest and then take his time to make sure every crease was in line. Once he was sure his uniform was perfect, he would put his gun belt on and stand with his chest puffed out. Now he looks like an old guy who thinks his middle bulge is muscle. Sorry, dude, it's the bulletproof vest making your chest big, not what's under it.

Kristin wraps her arm around my waist, dragging my attention from him. "Ignore all men except those on that stage."

"I just can't seem to get him to disappear."

She touches my cheek. "Try to escape in the music."

I bob my head as we sing to our favorite ballad. "I love this song." I sigh.

"Love me till the end of . . . time," we both sing in harmony.

"I'll love you, Eli!" I scream.

His eyes lock on mine, and my face becomes an inferno. Heat floods my entire body as his lips turn up slightly, and he gazes at me a beat longer than last time. Everything inside me clenches. My breathing halts, and I don't look away. Eli finally turns to do some spin with the rest of the group, breaking our moment.

I just died of humiliation. I cannot believe I yelled that and he heard me.

Kill me now.

Kristin bursts out laughing, almost falling over from her hysterics. "I think I just peed a little."

"Shut up."

"You yelled . . . that you love him . . . and he . . . heard you!" she manages through her fit of laughter. "Only you."

I pretend it didn't affect me. We had a connection. I felt it, and I swear he did, too. My heart raced and not just because it was him. Part of me was mortified, but the other part of me was emboldened. He freaking looked at me. I know I didn't imagine it.

"Maybe he didn't hear."

"Oh, he heard," Kristin shakes her head.

The girls go back to dancing around and singing along while I feel like an asshole. I hate to be the center of attention, and I hate being embarrassed. That moment was as horrifying as it was exhilarating.

I need some air. There's no way I can look at the stage right now. If he isn't looking at me—which I know he's not—I'll feel stupid. If he is—again I know he's not—I may have a stroke.

"Be right back," I call out to the girls.

"You okay?" Danielle yells.

"I need another beer."

She raises her can and then I head up the stairs. The music plays in the background as I keep moving.

I arrive at the concession stand and grab two more drinks. I'm going to need them. But I decide there's no way I'm going to feel bad. I'm allowed to let loose. Besides, I'm sure he gets this all the time. Everyone here loves him, so why the hell do I care if he happened to hear me? I don't.

Lie.

But, no, this is the first time I've been out in how long? I'm going to enjoy every damn minute. I brush it off, sip my beer, and decide to own my pubescent love of Eli Walsh.

As I turn, I come face to face with Matt.

"Hey," he says.

"Hi." I muster all the enthusiasm I have . . . which is none.

He scans the crowd and looks at the beer in my hand. I can see the judgment in his eyes. God forbid I actually have a life. "I didn't expect to see you here."

"I didn't think I'd see you, either."

Matt puffs out his chest and puts his hand on his gun belt. "Well, I figured I'd get some overtime."

"That's good."

I'm not sure what to say at this point.

"So, how's life? Steph?"

Like you care.

"She's been good. Asked about you the other day."

Matt rakes his fingers through his short brown hair. Seeing him like this makes it hard to forget how good things were for a period of time. Right now, he's just a normal guy, not the asshole who broke my heart. "I'm glad she's doing good. So, Four Blocks Down? Didn't peg you for a groupie."

I'm honestly shocked he's surprised. Four Blocks Down was played at our wedding. He knows how much I love them. My bridesmaids serenaded me to my favorite Eli song.

"Attending a concert doesn't make me a groupie, Matt. I'm enjoying a night out."

His hand touches my shoulder. I wait for a feeling, any feeling, but nothing comes. I used to turn into a puddle when he was near me. He used to make my heart race, now he makes my head hurt.

I don't know if I can pinpoint exactly when it happened, but we fell out of love as quickly as we fell in love. I think I cried more over losing the idea of my marriage than losing him. I wanted a love like my parents had. Instead, I got apathy and a man who was extremely jealous of my sick sister.

Matt's thumb grazes my bare skin. "You deserve it."

The door opens, and Nicole catches my eye. The scowl on her face makes me grin. There's no love lost between these two.

She bumps my hip with hers, causing my beer to slosh over the rim of the cup. "If it isn't Deputy Dickless, or should we say, Captain Kangaroo?" Nicole says before grabbing the cup and taking a drink.

Here we go.

"Hello, Nicole," he says through gritted teeth. "And I'm a lieutenant not a deputy or captain."

"*Sooo* sorry to get that wrong." She touches her chest. "Well, as much as I don't give a shit . . ."

"Nic," I say, hoping to diffuse the situation. Nicole holds grudges, and the fact that Matt hurt me still enrages her.

Thankfully, she takes another swig instead of responding. When she finishes, she links her arm in mine. "On that note. I'm going to steal my best friend so we can enjoy our night without spineless men who leave their wives because they're selfish. Bye now."

She pulls me away.

"Bye," I say.

Nicole squeezes my arm. "I love you and want you to please not spend another second thinking of him."

"I'm fine. He was being really nice."

That was part of the problem. In the beginning, I was happy. Then Steph got sicker, and my attention wasn't directed toward him anymore. I needed to care for her, which meant Matt had to care for me. He either didn't want to or he didn't know how to, and it was the beginning of the end. We fought all the time and barely saw each other. Then, right before he left me, he was ridiculously nice. There wasn't passionate lovemaking or any big grand fights. Everything was even keel.

"Good. Let's go sing and see if you make an ass out of yourself again."

Ugh. I regret this already.

We get back to the front row as the boys are playing one of their older songs. I don't know why they play the new stuff. Really, no one cares. We want to pretend we're still thirteen singing into our hairbrush microphones.

"All right, ladies," Randy croons. "It's that time. We're going to take it down a notch. Maybe find that girl who only comes around once?"

My favorite song ever.

Eli walks around the stage, smiling and pointing to random women. "I feel like I need to sing to someone this time, Ran."

Randy smirks. "You need some inspiration, brother?"

Eli continues to walk around while tapping his chin. "I need a girl who's going to be mine. Are you her?" he asks the crowd.

People scream, jump around, and wave their hands frantically. I move behind Nicole, just in case . . . because I would rather take a bullet than go up there.

He comes around the stage and stands in front of me. His green eyes sparkle with mischief as they land on me.

He points. "You," his voice sizzles as he stares at me.

Fuck my life.

All the blood rushes from my head. No. No way. I vaguely hear the screams around me, but I can't move. I shake my head in protest.

Eli's finger hooks as the bouncer comes around. "Come up here, sweetheart."

"No," I whisper as Nicole pushes my back forward. "I can't."

"You're so going." She thrusts me forward, and the bouncer pulls me over the rail.

I look up as Eli stands with his hand out. "Will you be my once in a lifetime?" he starts to sing the lyrics.

My heart races as I place my fingers against his palm. I pray to God I can keep myself from passing out. I'm on stage with Four Blocks Down.

Breathe, Heather, I tell myself as he walks me around while singing.

"You're the only girl I see." Eli hits each note. His hand doesn't release mine as he begins to sway. This was the song that I always imagined him singing to me. "I want to wake up next to you."

Oh, Eli . . . if only. I feel the heat burn my cheeks. What the hell is wrong with me?

Eli sits me in the chair on stage. Thank God, because I may hit the deck. I say a silent prayer for the bright lights that obstruct my view into the audience. At least I can't see my friends doing who knows what. Or my co-workers. He kneels in front of me, holding my hand as if he were proposing. I can't feel my extremities. I'm shaking, and it isn't from being cold. "Will you be my once in a lifetime?" he asks again.

I know this is the damn routine.

I've seen them in concert at least four times, twice in high school and twice in college, but I'm completely lost to him. There are over twenty thousand fans here, but in this instant . . . it's him and me. A girl can dream.

His hand brushes against my cheek as he hits the final note. He helps me stand and then pulls me close. "Don't go anywhere after the show," he whispers in my ear.

I pull back and look in his deep green eyes waiting to hear: Just kidding. But it doesn't come.

Holy shit. He just asked me to stay? I'm being Punk'd. Seriously, where is the camera crew waiting to jump out at me?

The next song begins as the bouncer helps me back over the rail.

The girls attack me with their screams and flailing arms. I can't speak. I don't even know if I can breathe.

Nicole steps in front of them and holds my shoulders. "In and out, Heather."

I focus on inhaling and shake my head. "What the hell just happened?" My mouth hangs open.

"Well . . ." She grins before continuing, "You were serenaded by the hottest guy ever."

They ask me a million questions about what it felt like. The only thing I can say is: "Surreal." It was freaking surreal. I would never believe that actually happened if they hadn't shown me the video on their phones. Every glorious second is documented. I can see my face is flushed, my eyes wide, and I'm pale. Great. I look up, hoping he hasn't seen me and my friends freaking out, but his back is to us as he sings to the other side of the arena.

I think about what he whispered to me. Did he want me to wait—for real? And why? Maybe he wants to give me a signed souvenir? It would make sense. Embarrass the fuck out of some girl and then give her an autographed T-shirt.

"Nic," I call her over because there is no way I'm not telling someone.

"Yeah?"

"He wants me to wait after the show," I yell in her ear.

Her face brightens. "No way!"

"It's got to be a misunderstanding, right?" I ask.

"Or he wants you."

"No!" She's on crack. There's no way in hell he "wants" me. That's dumb.

"He already knows you love him." She smirks.

"Whatever. There's no way I am going to wait."

"The hell you aren't!" Nicole crosses her arms. "We're staying. We're going to find out what Eli Walsh wants because you'd be an idiot not to."

Yeah, I'm an idiot all right—not because I don't want to meet him but because I do. Very much.

chapter three

Eli

"Good show," Adam says as he cracks his neck. "I'm getting too old for this shit."

"You are old."

"You're older than I am," Adam reminds me.

Even though I'm forty-two, I enjoy the rush of performing. I'd just like it not to be so rough on my aging body. I don't remember having to take this many painkillers a few years ago, but between the traveling, shit food, and performing—I feel old as fuck.

Even though I love acting much more than I thought I would, I love the fans more. I don't have this kind of fun when I'm stuck on a set all day.

I look over at my brother, "Randy is older than all of us, so there's that."

"Fuck off," Randy tosses back. "We've got a few weeks before we need to meet up again since the tour is over. I'm going to head home to Savannah. She said the kids are acting up. It's time for Daddy to come lay the smack down."

"Right." I laugh. Those kids have him wrapped around his finger. "We all know Vannah is who they listen to."

"Don't piss in my Cheerios."

"We're heading out to the meet and greet." Shaun slaps my leg. "You coming?"

I gave my manager strict instructions to get that girl back here. I practically drew him a map on how to find her. She better be there or I'm canning his ass. I loved watching her face while I sang to her. She was like a deer in the headlights as I laid it on thick. I almost lost my shit when she yelled out that she loved me. She couldn't cover her face fast enough.

It was cute.

I like cute.

I also haven't gotten laid in about a month, so this seems perfect. Especially if she's good in bed. Plus, since we're done touring and my mother has been up my ass about spending time with her, I'm sticking around Tampa for a few weeks anyway. It may be nice to have a distraction until I start filming the next season of *A Thin Blue Line* in two months.

"Let's go meet the people." I stand, stretching my arms over my head. What I want to say is, "Let's go find the blonde."

We're contractually obligated to attend a meet and greet at every show. I fucking hate it. It's always the same shit. We sit back in the lounge and drink while girls tell us the same things over and over. I'm glad they love us. I'm glad they've been listening to us since they were thirteen, but I don't give a shit. It only reminds me how old I am.

If she's there, though, I'm going to thoroughly enjoy myself. I'm going to watch those brown eyes fill with pleasure while I make her lose her mind.

"You had Mitch bring the blonde back, huh?" Randy asks as he throws shit in his bag.

"Yup."

The guys leave the room while I hang back to talk to Randy.

He chuckles. "You're going to knock up one of these girls someday."

I roll my eyes. "The fuck I am. I learned that lesson on our first world tour. I've been at this for twenty years and haven't had that happen yet. No mini Elis or Eliettes running around here."

"That you know of," Randy retorts.

We could go back and forth, but the one thing is . . . I'm careful. There's no freaking way I'm getting saddled with some kid from a groupie. I know better. Plus, Mitch is a scary prick. We're his bread and butter. No way does he want some stupid shit taking away from his chance to make money. I know firsthand how easy he can make things disappear.

"Don't worry about me."

He stops putting things in the bag and gives me his serious look. "Like that'll ever happen."

Randy is two years older, and since our dad skipped out when we were kids and then died two years later, he thinks it's his job to protect me.

"Seriously, Ran. Stop. Be my fucking brother for once."

He huffs. "Fine. I think you need to grow up, Eli. You're over forty, never married, no kids, not even a serious girlfriend since—"

"Don't say her name." I put my hand up. "I don't want to even think about her tonight."

Randy knows better. I don't talk about her. At all.

"Fine, but Vannah is worried, too."

"Savannah couldn't care less about my love life. What you meant to say is Mom is worried. She's probably chewing Vannah's ear off about it, so she's coming to you."

My mother is the queen of meddling. She's like a damn parakeet, "Eli needs a wife. Eli needs a wife." I hear it all the damn time.

"No, it's not Mom. It's everyone. Stop the partying and random girls. Find someone who actually has a brain. You can't tell me you're satisfied with your life."

"I can tell you I'm done listening to you." I lean back and cross my arms.

Why do people think I need to be married to be happy? When did that become the definition of success and contentment?

Randy hoists his bag over his shoulder and smirks. I can practically read the thoughts in his mind. He thinks he has me. He has all the answers for why I need to live the life he thinks I should be living.

"And what about when things get tougher for you?"

And he just hit the only sore spot I have.

"Now I'm done."

I flip him off and walk out. As soon as I enter the hallway, I hear the screams. I'm really not in the mood anymore, but I have to at least appear. I wave to the girls who couldn't get in and head to the meet and greet where I hope she's waiting.

There are days when this life is exhausting. I work my ass off and don't get to enjoy it nearly as much as I thought I would. It's all work all the time in my life. This business has a life expectancy, and I'm past it, which is why my focus has shifted to my show and movie projects. That is where I feel normal. I'm surrounded by people who don't care who I was all those years ago. I'm an actor, a friend, a fucking human. When I'm on tour, it's different.

Acting gives me way more freedom than the band ever did, too. I have more days off, no days on the bus, and a nice long break between filming. I don't know how these other musicians constantly tour.

I turn the corner, and the music from the after party fills the air. The bass is loud, and the lights are dimmed, which means the girls are most definitely primed. My mind is set on one thing: convincing the blonde to spend the night with me. My mind has been consumed by her, and I move quickly, hoping she's there.

I haven't been this excited about a girl in a long time. There is no such thing as normal dating for performers. No woman wants to put up with the tabloids, groupies, and the fact that her man is never around. I sure as fuck wouldn't.

"Eli," a girl I don't know croons. "There you are."

She's hot, but not the girl I'm searching for.

"I'll find you later," I brush her off.

I glance around the dark room, but I don't see her. A few other girls approach me. I give them my customary smile while still scanning the faces for the one I'm looking for. She should be here. That's the one good thing about our manager—he does his damn job.

Finally, a few people move, and I see her. She's standing in the corner with her friend. Her long blonde hair is pulled to the side, showing off the skin on her shoulder, while she's sipping a beer. I love a woman who drinks from a bottle. It's sexy and down to earth. Shows me she isn't all high maintenance and can hang with the boys.

I push my way through the crowd and beeline right toward her. "You made it," I say, scaring her a little.

"Oh—" She clears her throat. "I-I . . . you said? I mean, you did tell me to, right?"

"Since you told me you love me, and I serenaded you, I figured we should meet officially."

Her brown eyes widen as her bashful smile flashes. She's even prettier than I remember. Her body curves in all the right places. Everywhere a man wants to lay his hands is carved to perfection. It's clear she's physically fit, and I'm ready to see what's beneath those clothes.

"I'm Nicole." Her friend extends her hand. She then gives me one of those looks that tells me she's watching me. I see why the blonde brought her. Smart move.

"Eli." I return the gesture with my most sincere smile.

"I'm Heather, by the way."

"Heather," I repeat, allowing her name to roll off my tongue. "Want another beer?" Her face turns red. "Did I say something?"

"No," she says as her hand touches my arm. "I'm sorry. I'm just nervous."

I like that I keep her slightly off kilter. Most of the girls that come back here are almost too sure of themselves. Like we should be so lucky to have chosen them. Then, it's sexual promises and over the top offers. Ninety percent of the time, I never even go there. I guess after this long, I've become picky.

I blame my niece and nephew. I'm not saying I want to settle down, because that's the last thing I need, but it would be nice to have someone to talk to once in a while. I'm surrounded by actresses most of the time, so I've had enough fake relationships.

"Don't be nervous," I try to reassure her.

Heather smiles and tucks her hair behind her ear. Is there anything this girl won't do that I find attractive? I must be losing my mind. "It was a great show."

"I'm glad you thought so." And I am. I sang and danced my ass off. Whenever we come home, we give a little more. "I enjoyed a few parts more than others."

"Me, too." Her eyes brighten.

"Why don't we go somewhere a little more private and talk? The after-show area is always crammed, and I won't be able to avoid everyone."

She looks at Nicole and then back at me. Nicole nudges her a little, and I decide that girl is my new best friend. Of course, I want to do a lot more than talk, but first, I want to get her away from all the noise.

I catch my manager's attention and jerk my head in Nicole's direction. He'll make sure she stays occupied.

"I don't know."

"I promise, this place will become something neither of us want to be a part of." I go for the truth, hoping she'll catch my drift. "I just want to talk, if that's what you want." So, I lie a little.

Nicole smiles, whispers in her ear, and shoves her forward. I extend my hand, hoping that her friend helped me out a little. Heather looks down and then entwines our fingers.

Fuck this is going to be a good night.

chapter four

Heather

OH MY GOD. OH MY GOD. I'M GOING TO A PRIVATE PLACE WITH ELI. WHAT THE HELL AM I thinking? I'm not. Clearly, I'm having some kind of out-of-body experience. I would never do this. Yet, here I am, holding his hand and walking away from the meet and greet.

"You okay?" His deep voice is laced with concern.

"I'm great." I'm such a liar.

"Yeah? Because you're shaking."

My entire body is trembling. I haven't pinpointed whether it's because I'm excited or scared out of my fucking mind. I'm pretty sure it's the latter. I focus on my breathing. I'm in high stress situations all the time, this should be a cake walk.

This is, as Nicole says, hooking up. Apparently, people do this all the time and it's normal. I can be normal. I can put all this crazy shit aside and be in the moment.

Just let tonight be what it is and enjoy it.

I clear my throat and smile. "This kind of stuff never happens to me."

He chuckles as he comes to a stop in front of the tour bus. "What kind of stuff?"

"This," I say a little high-pitched. "I don't typically drink, scream at random people, get serenaded, get asked backstage, and now . . ." I trail off. There's no way I'm finishing that statement, because I don't know what exactly is happening. Maybe he wants to ask me about something dumb. He may not want sex. I don't know that I want sex.

That's a lie.

I totally want sex. I want to let loose like Nicole told me to. To be completely without fear of consequence for just one night. I'm always responsible. My life is practically a billboard for sensibility. I uphold the law, care for my sister, work to support myself and Steph, volunteer at the youth center, but I never let loose.

I'm going to have fun. Well, if he wants to.

Thank you Jesus for beer. Or whichever person made it.

"What do you want to happen, Heather?" Eli's eyes smolder as he tugs me close.

Oh. Fuck. Me.

"I-I . . ." my mouth goes dry.

His hands move around my hips as he shifts us so my back is against the door of the bus. He's so close. Eli's touch travels up my sides until he stops at my neck. "Well? We can talk or we can do something else."

I think back to what Nicole said. *"Let go for one night."* And for tonight, I'm going to fulfill my teenage fantasy. I'm going to sleep with Eli Walsh . . . on a tour bus . . . after an FBD concert.

My back straightens as I muster my inner Nicole. I press my body against his, hooking my hand around his back. "I think we can find something else to do."

His green eyes flash with surprise before his mouth collides against my lips. Every inch of his body is flush with mine. Our lips move in harmony as he fumbles for the door handle. As soon as the door opens, we fall back. He walks me backward up the steps and through the vehicle without missing a beat or stumbling.

I lose myself in his kiss. He isn't soft or gentle. No, he devours me. It's passion unbridled. Neither of us worry about finesse. This is unlike any kiss I ever shared with Matt. He was slow, cold, and perfunctory. There was no *need*.

I need this. I need to escape my mind.

Eli pushes me where he wants me while holding my head in his grip. My fingers roam his body as we continue to move. He opens the door to the bedroom. "Bed," he mutters before his lips find mine again.

I pull at his shirt, breaking the kiss as I tear it off. "Wow," I say as my eyes take in his chest. My fingers move slowly over his pecs and then down toward his abs, rising and falling over each valley and divot. He doesn't have an ounce of fat on him, and I can feel every flex and pulse beneath my fingertips.

"You're beautiful." His soulful eyes lock on mine as he pushes my hair back.

"I'm average."

His gaze rakes over my body before coming back to mine. "There's nothing average about you, Heather."

That's all I need. My hand grasps his neck, and I bring his mouth back to me. No one has ever made me feel like this. And I'm still dressed.

He uses his weight to push me onto the bed. I revel in the feel of him braced above me. It's Eli fucking Walsh. Before I know it, my shirt is coming off, and I'm grabbing for his buckle. I undo it before he rolls me on top of him.

Our lips move in perfect unison, and my heart beats out of my chest. In the back of my mind, I know how out of character this is for me, but I can't stop. I want to be wild and crazy. The fact that I'm going to sleep with Eli is a little overwhelming, but it feels right. Maybe because I've dreamed of him since I was a kid. Maybe it's because I'm drunk as hell. Either way, it's happening.

I sit up, fully on display as I unhook my bra. My blonde hair spills in front of me, giving me a little coverage. Our eyes lock, and I glide the straps down.

Eli grins beneath me as the material falls away. I'm not fully exposed, but it's enough for him to see what he wants. "You have perfect tits," his deep voice is smooth as silk. "Move your hair, baby. I want to see all of you." Eli puts his hands behind his head, watching with rapt attention.

I do as he says. Again, totally out of character. I'm always in charge, but I surrender to him without question and pull my hair back before lowering closer to him. My breasts hang, just barely brushing against his chest. "I never do this."

"Do what?" He lifts his hand and rubs his finger across my cheek.

"Casual sex."

"Seems I'm breaking a lot of your rules."

I struggle to keep my voice steady. "I would say so."

"Do you want to stop?" His fingers slide down my neck and over my breast before he rubs tiny circles around my nipple.

"No."

He smiles. "Do you like the way I touch you? The way my fingers feel against your skin?"

"Yes," I admit.

"How bad do you want this?" Eli asks as he takes my nipple between his thumb and forefinger.

There are no words. I've been tasered, and this is more electric. Every inch of me is humming. I want this to never end. One-night stands aren't all that bad, I've been missing out.

I drop down and kiss his lips.

"Heather?" He pulls my attention back. "Answer me."

"What was the question?"

He chuckles. "Do you want me to fuck you?"

"Yes," I moan.

As soon as I say the word, he rolls me onto my back. His hands grip my breasts as he massages and kneads. I close my eyes and lose myself in his touch. Then I feel his tongue against my skin. The heat from his mouth and the cool air in the room sends shivers down my spine.

I need more. I rock my chest up, silently begging. He sucks and licks the right side and then pays attention to the left. Eli starts to move lower, and I lift my head. No way is he going down on me. I can't. I've only ever let Matt do that, and it was not a good experience.

He unbuttons my jeans that took me five minutes to get into, and I grab his hand. "You don't have to," I say quickly.

"I want to."

Want to? Matt said no man wants to do this, they do it because they have to.

"I'm serious." I give him another out.

Eli rises onto his knees then hooks his fingers in my jeans. "I'm serious, too. I want to taste you. I want to make you scream my fucking name so loud that everyone here knows what I'm doing to you." The heat in his eyes melts me.

"I know that most guys don't like it . . ." He stops, giving me a confused look, which makes me feel naïve and a bit stupid. "I mean, I've been told by . . . that . . ."

Eli pulls my pants lower. "Did you ever come on a man's tongue?"

"No."

"You're going to come on mine." He leaves no room for question. "A real man eats pussy. Only selfish pricks refuse to give their girl what they need."

I lie completely speechless. But I don't have time to think about what he said, because he's ripping my pants and underwear off. Eli lifts my legs, throwing them over his shoulder, and his gaze melts me. He watches me as he moves closer, taking his time, causing my heart to race.

At the first swipe of his tongue, I'm done.

But it only gets better. Eli knows what he's doing. His tongue presses against my clit, moving in circles, then up and down. It's like nothing I've ever felt. Sweat starts to bead on my forehead as my climax builds. He wasn't kidding about making me come.

My fingers grip the blanket as I try to hold back, try to stay on the ground. He forces me to climb higher and higher as he continues to drive me toward ecstasy. "Holy shit. Oh, my God," I mumble.

He stops for a second, slips his finger inside, and sucks even harder. I twist and start to tremble as he continues to drive me forward. Another finger joins the first, and he pushes deeper, crooking them just right and hitting the blessed spot that no man has ever found before. I burst apart.

Everything inside of me clenches as I fall over the cliff. I scream his name, exactly like he promised I would, and then become mush.

Holy shit. I'm dead. Died. Gone to heaven. I've met my maker because this man is a God.

My breathing is erratic, and my heart is thumping so loud that I swear he can hear it. "Wow."

"I told you." Eli crawls his way toward my face.

"You made good on your promise." My voice is low and full of appreciation. "I think you're a little overdressed, Eli."

"What are you going to do about it?" he taunts.

Making the most of the space between us, I slip my hand down and slide the zipper the rest of the way open. Then I remove his pants and boxers, allowing his impressive length to spring free. "This," I say as I wrap my fingers around him.

He lets out a low hiss as I slide my hand from base to tip. I watch his face, learning what makes his jaw tick or his eyes close. My thumb grazes the tip, and he pushes me back. "I want to fuck you."

Our mouths connect, tongues swirl, and our hands roam over each other. "I need you," I beg almost desperately. "I need you right now." I've never begged or been vocal during sex before. Ever.

Eli grabs a condom from the nightstand and rolls it on before getting back to where we were.

"You're making me break my rules, too," he confesses. I don't have a chance to ask what the hell he's talking about before he enters me.

My eyes slam shut as I stretch to accommodate him. He's big. Bigger than I've ever had before. He doesn't move like I expect him to, and I open my eyes.

"You okay?" Eli asks.

I nod quickly.

Eli drops on his forearm and kisses me with care. This kiss isn't the same as the ones before. It's slow, sensual, almost sweet. My fingers tangle in his hair as he begins to rock back slowly. He moans in my mouth as he continues to be gentle.

"Eli," I groan. It's too much. Everything about him is incredible. His thumb rubs back and forth on my cheek as he slides in and out. "You feel so good."

"So do you. What are you doing to me?" I glance up at him to find him watching me. "I want to make you come again."

Well, that would be nice.

He rolls over, forcing me to be on top. I never got to be on top much in the past. When I did, it was the only time I got off. Considering how good this feels, I doubt I won't climax again.

"Ride me, baby."

And I do. I glide up and down, allowing him to fill me to the brink. I rake my fingers across his chest, enjoying the way he groans. Eli is just as lost as I am. I move faster as my orgasm builds again. "I'm gonna come."

"Good. Hurry, baby. You're going to make me come the way you're gripping my cock." Eli grits his teeth as his fingers dig into the flesh of my hips, pulling me down harder as he thrusts up to meet me. I'm undone.

"Eli!" I cry out as my climax hits me hard. He continues to move me as he follows me to the end.

I fall next to him and try to catch my breath. Neither of us speak as we come down from the high.

As I lie there naked, it hits me that this really happened. It isn't just some dream. This is real. I had sex with a member of Four Blocks Down on his tour bus. Where he's done this with I don't know how many girls. I've never had sex with a random stranger before and now I'm lying here with a man that probably only does that. I'm not special, he probably doesn't even remember my name since all he did was call me "baby".

The bed shifts as Eli rises. "You need anything?"

A shower and a lobotomy. "No," I reply quickly.

"I'll be right back."

He heads into what I assume is the bathroom, and I jump up. I can't believe this. What the hell is wrong with me? What was I thinking? Clearly, I wasn't. I blame Nicole.

"What's your last name?" he asks from the other side of the door.

I quickly throw my clothes on. I need to get out of here. "Covey," I reply while pulling on my jeans. Where the hell did my underwear go? I look around and under the bed but don't see them. Damn it.

He flushes the toilet, and I'm out of time. I can't look at him. I need to go before he returns.

I grab my heels and phone and rush off the bus. I need Nicole, and then we need to leave. Now.

I spot her as soon as I walk through the door. Thank God. Nicole is making out with some guy in the hallway. Typical. I grab her arm and pull.

"We have to go," I explain.

She looks back at the guy, "I'm—"

"No. We have to go right *now*."

"Heather," she protests.

"Now!" I yell at her, and her eyes widen.

I'm not known for yelling, but when I do . . . I mean business.

"Bye." She says to the guy, and I drag her along. "Slow down."

I don't even acknowledge her. My mind runs in circles as I think about what just happened.

"We have to go." There's no way I can look at his face.

"You said that," she grumbles as we move. "What happened?"

I shake my head, pulling her into almost a sprint. I'm going to be sick. It was amazing, and so ridiculously good, but so wrong. I'm not a one-night stand girl. I'm a commitment and get-to-know-you girl. The guys at least know my last name. I'm a slut. I'm worse than a slut . . . I'm a *groupie* slut.

"Don't make me stop walking," Nicole threatens. "You know I will."

"Fine," I stop as we get to the exit door. "We had sex. Really good sex. You happy?"

The size of the smile on her face is all the answer I need. She looks like a proud mother at a talent show.

"Fuck yeah, I'm happy. Why are we running away?"

"Because . . ." I huff. "We had sex! I had sex with him! We have to go."

I push through the door, still dragging Nicole behind me. "That doesn't explain why you're running barefoot through the arena."

I'm not explaining this to her. "Just keep moving."

We finally exit, and I could literally cry. They closed the gates to the parking lot.

"Now what?" she asks, looking at the tall metal gate with big ass locks on it.

We could go to the south entrance, but that would take too long. There's only one option. "We climb."

"The hell we do!"

I let out a heavy breath and glare at her. "Nicole, I just did something so unlike me that I'm not even sure it was me. So, we're climbing the fence because you're my best friend and I need to get the fuck out of here."

"Babe." Nicole's eyes fill with sadness. "You didn't do anything wrong."

"I'm a groupie slut."

"You're so not a groupie. You're the furthest thing from a slut."

I don't respond. Instead, I chuck my shoes over the fence and start to climb.

When I was twelve, I could climb fences pretty quick. Especially growing up in Tampa where we would hop fences to get to each other's yards. But I'm not even halfway up and I'm winded, my foot has slipped more than once, and I can only imagine what I look like from below.

"Shit!" I yell as my toe misses the next opening. Nicole's laughter fills the air. "Stop laughing and start climbing!"

"This is priceless." she laughs harder. "Wait. Let me get my camera!"

"Nicole! We need to get out of here in case he comes looking for me."

"Fine. Fine. Chicken shit." Her shoes fly over my head, and the entire fence shakes. "You owe me."

"Stop moving!" I try not to laugh, but it's futile. This is hysterical. "I'm going to pee," tears fall from my eyes as I hold on.

"I need a Go-Pro for the next time we go out."

"I hate you," I say between giggles.

She purposely rocks back, causing me to almost fall. "You only wish you did."

"If I fall . . ." I warn as I sway and try to climb higher.

"It'll be what you deserve for making me climb a freaking fence at one in the morning!"

The amount of ways that I'm going to pay for this is unimaginable. My co-workers saw me being sung to on stage, I'm sure one of the guys from my squad caught me going backstage, I'm going to have scrapes from climbing a fence, and Nicole will never let me live this down.

I reach the top, one leg swung over on one side and one still in Eli-land. And that's when I hear him. "You're going to just run out?" Eli's voice is filled with disbelief. "Just like that?"

I get myself over the other side and climb to the ground so I have the fence between us. Nicole is near the top, watching this unfold. "This was a mistake. It should've never happened."

"So, you run?" He takes a step closer, and I thank God for the metal between us.

"Nic," I whisper-shout, urging her to come down, and she starts to descend. I glance back at Eli, who stands before me with no shirt or shoes. His chest heaves as if he ran here to find me. I stare at him. "It's better this way," I say, wishing Nicole would hurry the hell up.

"Why? Says who? You didn't even give me a chance!" Eli grips the back of his neck.

"This would never work. Seriously. You don't have to try."

Even if my life were completely peachy, which it isn't, Eli and I would never work. We had sex, it doesn't mean I want more, but there isn't even a chance I could. I've already seen that men are selfish, and I can't even provide enough attention for a local police lieutenant, there's no way I can do it for a world renowned actor and singer.

Eli takes another step, his hand gripping the steel separating us. "You said you don't do this before, well, I don't chase after girls who run out, so we're both doing something different. I wanted to talk . . . I wasn't asking for anything, Heather."

So, he does know my name, that makes me feel marginally better.

Nicole finally drops down beside me, and tears fill my eyes. I know she sees it. I'm not upset because of him. I'm upset because of me.

"Let's go."

She knows me well enough to know I'm in over my head. The reason I've never done casual is because I feel too much. I've had life-long friendships, one boyfriend who I married, and a sister who needs me—casual doesn't fit into my life. Now that I've come down from the buzz and adrenaline, I feel empty.

I release a heavy breath and shove down my emotions.

"Look. I'm sorry I ran out, but I have to go. I don't belong here anyway." I'm not sure what the proper etiquette is for running away from a man you've spent your entire adolescent and part of your adult life dreaming of and then slept with, but this seems appropriate. I grab my shoes and start to walk away.

"Heather, wait." I glance back at him over my shoulder. "I just—"

"Goodbye, Eli."

There's no way I'm looking back, because if I do, I might not keep walking.

As we start to sprint, my phone dings with a voice mail. It's Stephanie's facility.

With my fingers trembling, I press play. "Hi, Ms. Covey, this is Becca from Breezy Beaches Assisted Living. Stephanie had a . . ." She pauses as if she can't find the right words. "She's been transferred via ambulance to Tampa General Hospital. Please call me as soon as you can."

The tears I fought back fall without a thought. "It's Steph. We have to run."

chapter five

Heather

"I'M FINE," STEPHANIE SAYS WHILE SWATTING MY HAND AWAY AS SHE LIES IN THE HOSPITAL BED. "If you'd stop fidgeting."

Her seizure was the worst one yet. Thankfully, there hasn't been any damage that has manifested, but I've refused to leave her side, not even for a second. I hate myself for being at that stupid concert instead of here with her. She's my entire world.

"Go to work, Heather. I can't handle you being around me. You're like a fucking helicopter, always hovering over me. You annoy me."

One of the worst parts of Huntington's is the mood swings. Stephanie was a sweet, kind, and happy-go-lucky kid. When she was nineteen, she had her first onset of tremors. Her body would go stiff and she couldn't move. Immediately, Matt and I took her to the doctor, but they couldn't find anything.

Then her mood did a complete one-eighty. It was as if someone stole my sister's identity and replaced it with the angriest person I'd ever met.

"I am going to work today, thank you."

"Good. Do I go back to Breezy tonight then?"

"Depends what the doctor says."

According to the neurologist, we can expect her to continue to deteriorate, and she's at high risk of another seizure that could leave lasting effects. The younger you are when you become symptomatic with Huntington's the faster things get worse.

"Yet again, I have no say in anything. It's always you and the doctors. I'm a fucking adult!" She rolls her eyes and turns onto her side.

"I know you are, but yelling at me isn't going to help."

My patience with Stephanie is unending, but at times, I lose my cool. Being told how awful, worthless, and depressing I am eventually wears me down. I know it isn't her. She acts this way because she's frustrated and in pain, but I still hate it.

However, it was Stephanie who made the decision to move into Breezy Beaches. She knew I couldn't quit my job to take care of her. I needed to make whatever I could, and a live-in nurse was way over our budget since insurance wouldn't cover it. She needed aroundtheclock care that I could no longer provide.

It was the single most devastating day of my life. I cried harder after dropping her off than I did the night our parents died.

"I hate you. I hate this disease." She flips back over and throws the cover back, staring up at the ceiling. "I hate it all."

I touch her shoulder, and her hands start to move. They took her off the medication for the tremors when she was admitted, and it took less than forty-eight hours for them to come back.

"Steph," I say carefully. "Please don't shut me out."

"I c-ca-can't." Her eyes well with frustration and tears. "I h-hat-t-e th-this."

I move to the side of the bed and lace her fingers with mine, trying not to cry as well. Our hands move together as her body takes control. I do my best to comfort her. "I know, love. I hate it, too. Right now, we're just dancing. That's all."

In the beginning of the disease, this was what I used to say when her hands and feet would go. It was our dance break. I muster a smile and start singing as we move with no rhythm or purpose.

My heart breaks as I watch this disease rob my sister of a life she deserves. It isn't fair that she got the gene and I didn't. I would gladly take it for her if I could. So many times I've watched her and tried to stay strong, but sometimes there is no strength. Sometimes I can't help myself from losing it. My lack of strength sometimes won't be my demise—love will be. Love is what breaks me down. Love is what makes it so hard to forgive God for doing this to us. Stephanie should be hanging out with her friends, working, *living* life. Instead, she's stuck in a facility because we have no idea when the next symptom will arise.

The tear I was fighting so hard to push back, falls.

Stephanie's eyes lock on mine, and we both cry together.

"Is your sister better?" Matt asks as we finish roll call.

"Yeah." I nod. "She should be going back . . ." I stop myself from saying the word "home" because it isn't home. It's a fucking group home, and I hate that she's there. "to the place soon. Thanks for covering for me."

"I know this is hard for you," he says, trying to comfort me. "I hate seeing you like this."

Right. I'm so sure that's the case.

"Wouldn't have been if I had my husband's support." I toss back at him.

I watch his face shift to hurt. "Heather," Matt whispers. "It wasn't like that."

I roll my eyes and huff. While Stephanie takes her hurt out on me, I channel my anger toward Matt. "It was exactly like that. You left me. You moved out because I wasn't willing to put my sister in that home. You made it so that I had no other choice in the end. We were supposed to be a team, but you . . ." I pause and try to get myself back under control. "You left."

"You didn't give me any choice!" Matt's voice rises. "I was watching my wife drift away. I couldn't do anything. I couldn't make you happy. You act like I'm the villain here, but I had to sit around watching you lose yourself."

I can't believe him. "It was not about me or you, it was about her."

"Take a minute to think about who left who, Heather. You were gone a long time before I walked out that door."

Matt turns around and walks out. How fitting. It's a different time, but the same result—he walks away first. We've had this fight before, several times, and each time, it reminds me of what a selfish dick he is.

"You ready to hit the road?" My partner Brody asks as he slaps me on the shoulder, breaking me from staring daggers at the door Matt walked through.

I sigh and relax. Thank God for Brody. He's funny, gets my sarcasm, and is completely dependable. I know he has my back in the same way I have his. It's a relationship that is essential between partners. Aside from Nicole, Kristin, and Danielle, Brody is my best friend. We've been riding together for the last seven years, and there's no one in this world I trust more.

"Yup. I need lots of coffee today."

"Do you need me to sing to you?" he asks with a smirk. "Heard that does it for you. Or do I have to be rich and famous?"

My heart freezes, and I squeeze my eyes closed, mortified. I completely forgot about the concert. It all comes back like a freight train. The singing, the dancing, the sex with Eli Walsh. How the hell could I forget that there are probably videos and . . . oh God.

I look around the break room and there, on the bulletin board, is a photo of me sitting on the stage with Eli singing to me.

Damn it.

Shit. Shit. Shit.

I walk over and rip it down, trying to pretend as if I don't care. "Real funny guys."

"But," Whitman, one of the idiots on my squad jumps in, "you're my once in a lifetime girl."

"Shut up," I crumple the paper and toss it in the garbage. "You're all tools."

"We all know what you like, Covey. Maybe we should just pretend to be cops on television, then you'll think we're sexy."

"You need to lay off the greasy food and lose some weight. Then maybe the half blind lady down the street will think you're sexy."

A few guys laugh, and jab his side.

"Yeah? Tell your boyfriend that we don't all eat donuts! I work hard for this physique. Besides, we need to be in a boy band to get you tossing your panties at us."

This is never going to end. The more I feed into them, the worse this will be. I grab the keys from Brody's hand and walk off. They start to sing and yell at me, but I keep moving. Idiots. I work with idiots.

Brody climbs in the passenger seat and chuckles. "Oh, come on, Heather. We're just having fun."

"Clearly. It's not that, though." I toss my hat on the dash. "Stephanie had an episode, which is why I didn't come in yesterday."

Brody's eyes soften, and he sighs. "I'm sorry. I figured you were recovering from your night of singing and drinking. Is she better?"

"She's okay now, well, as okay as it gets for her."

Brody was the one who helped me move Stephanie in to Breezy Beaches. He's been more of a husband than Matt ever was. His wife Rachel has been great. I'm glad she and I have become as close as we are. There's a very strange bond between partners, which can lead to a lot of questions, and I've seen more than one wife accuse her husband of cheating. I've also seen more than one occasion where she wasn't wrong.

As much as I love Brody, it's a brother-sister kind of love. I would take a bullet for him, but his "gun" isn't going anywhere but in his holster.

"You should've called me, Rachel and I would've come to the hospital."

"No." I shake my head. "That would've been totally unnecessary."

"Let me guess, you had it?" His tone is laced with sarcasm.

I turn the key in the ignition and start to drive. I'm not going to let him goad me. He's way too good at it.

We drive toward the section we're patrolling. Even with Matt being the asshole he is, he always puts me in the section near Tampa General Hospital, which is something that I should probably thank him for. At least I'm close if something changes with her condition.

Brody tells me about Rachel's new kick with some crazy diet. She's so pretty and already skinny, I don't know what she's thinking.

"Well, when you finally have kids, she won't care."

He gives me side eyes and grunts. "I'm not sure we'll have kids."

"Brody," I touch his arm. "You need to let go of the past."

Two years ago, Brody was in a horrific wreck. He was doing code and a driver plowed through the red light, T-boning his cruiser. It was a miracle he survived. It was one of the nights we were shorthanded and weren't riding doubles. I've never been so scared in my life, and neither had Rachel. She was so terrified that the stress caused her to miscarry. Brody never recovered from that.

"Says the girl who refuses to date because she married an idiot. Hell, when's the last time you even had sex?"

My cheeks burn, and I hope he isn't looking at me.

"I know that look, Heather." Brody shifts in his seat and laughs. "Who did you have sex with?"

"None of your business."

Shit. He's going to keep prying until I have to tell him just so he'll shut up.

I focus on the road and want to throw my hands up hallelujah style when the radio cuts in.

"We have a report of a domestic in Hyde Park."

Brody's grin is gone, and he grabs the radio. "Car 186 is on it."

"Central copies, dispatching the address now." The dispatcher cuts out, and I flick the lights on.

I focus on the road as Brody gives directions. We head into the small upper-class suburb and pull in front of the house.

Both of us cautiously approach the door, we knock twice, and a woman opens the door with a smile.

"Hello, officers."

"Good morning, ma'am. We got a call about a disturbance. Is everything all right here?" I ask.

She smiles warmly and opens the door. "Yes, my son is autistic, and well, sometimes he gets really loud. My neighbor behind us keeps calling. No matter how many times we explain that there's nothing we can do but let him work it out, she continues to call the cops."

"Do you mind if we come in?" Brody asks.

We've seen too many instances of a wife covering for her husband because she's terrified of him.

"Of course," she steps back, giving us room to pass. "Please, come in."

"Thank you, Mrs. . . . ." I leave it open.

"Harmon. I'm Delia Harmon"

We step forward, and a boy around fourteen comes to the door, and I smile. "Hi."

He stares off to the side and grunts.

"Sloane doesn't speak, but he loves lights," Mrs. Harmon explains. "It's been a rough few months. His father took off a while ago, so it's just us, but we're doing fine. Aren't we Sloane?" She looks adoringly at her son.

I smile, thinking of how lucky this boy is to have a mother like her. The way she stares at him reminds me of how my mother looked at me, and my mother was always brimming with love. Stephanie and I were her life.

"Hi, Sloane," I kneel in front of him and his eyes dart outside.

"Can you say hello to the police officers?" Delia encourages.

Sloane doesn't say anything. Instead, he points to the cruiser outside. The look of wonder in his eyes is shining bright. He starts to pull on her arm while she tries to pull him back.

"Would he like to see the police lights?" Brody asks, breaking his silence.

"Oh, he'd love that."

Brody and I spend the next few minutes with Mrs. Harmon and Sloane. We show him the lights and watch as the joy spreads across his face. He seems much calmer, and I wish there were more we could do for him. Inevitably, another call comes in and we have to leave. Sloane starts fussing, and I know it's only going to get worse. He wants us to stay, and I hate that we are leaving Mrs. Harmon to calm him down.

We head back on the road, and our day is filled with bullshit calls. Two traffic accidents, a possible shoplifter who ended up being the owner's daughter, and a police report for a stolen car. Paperwork sucks.

"Do you mind stopping if we stop in and check on Steph?"

"You know I don't."

Brody calls in that we're on break, and we head over.

When we get to the turn in by Tampa General, a sleek, black Bentley comes peeling out of the side street, almost hitting two cars in the process.

"Oh, hell no," I say and flip the lights and sirens on. "I hate these assholes on this side of the island. They all think they can do whatever they want."

Having money doesn't mean you're above the law.

Brody and I approach the car and the tinted windows lower.

"License, registration, and insurance," I say without looking at the driver.

"Sorry, officer," a familiar voice causes my eyes to lift. I stare into the green irises I doubt I'll ever forget. A five o'clock shadow paints his face, and the sun only makes everything seem brighter. His mouth turns into a radiant smile, and my heart begins to race. "I was on my way to see someone. But it turns out she came to me."

chapter six

Heather

M Y LIFE . . . IS . . . A FREAKING COMEDY SHOW.
There's nothing I've done to deserve this amount of bad karma. I've been a good friend, sister, daughter, I uphold the law, and I'm a good person by most people's standards.

What the hell have I done to have this happen to me?

I release a deep breath and go back into work mode. "Do you know why I pulled you over, sir?"

"Are you going to pretend you don't know me?" Eli asks with his brow raised.

"Mr. Walsh, we all know who you are. However, that doesn't mean that nearly colliding with two vehicles is acceptable."

Eli looks over at Brody. "What's up, man? Is she always this way?"

"You two old friends?" Brody asks.

I clear my throat. "License, registration, and insurance . . . please."

I somehow get the words out without squeaking or sounding unstable. Brody laughs, and it takes everything I have not to look at him. I hate him right now.

"Sure thing, Officer Covey."

"Don't go anywhere," I warn as I take the paperwork from him.

"Don't worry, I'll be right here, Heather. I don't run away."

Bristling at his words, I walk away, feeling Brody's gaze on me. There's no doubt that as soon as we get back in the car, I'm going to get it—good.

Instead, Brody stays quiet while I assemble the paperwork. He may not be speaking, but he's saying a whole lot in the silence.

"Just say it," I mumble and finally look over.

"I'm not saying a word." He raises his hands. "Clearly, you two know each other, and it ain't from growing up here. You tell me everything, so there is no way you wouldn't have told me you know him," Brody pauses and leans back. "I'm not saying a word about who you may or may not have slept with recently. Even though, it's pretty obvious."

"You know, you not saying a word took you a long time."

"It's not like you've had a five-year drought since your divorce. Or that you slept with a singer/actor. Nope. I have nothing to say about that. Not a thing."

I groan. "Could you not say anything for real this time?"

"Sure thing, boss. I'll just be over here, watching Hell start to thaw."

This is not going to get any better. I'd almost rather hear the questions. This is Brody Webber. My partner, my friend, and the one person who I have enough dirt on to make his life hell if he repeats this.

"Okay, fine. Yes, I slept with Eli Walsh. I was crazy and dumb. I also had about six beers, which is two over my threshold, and I was trying to be in the moment for once. Fucking Nicole and her pep talks."

Brody coughs a laugh and then recovers. "Sorry, go on."

"I swear, you better keep this to yourself. If you tell anyone . . ." I give him my best threatening face. "I mean *anyone*, I'll make your life a living nightmare."

He shakes his head and laughs again. "I won't say a word, but you had a one-night stand with one of the most famous men in the boy band atmosphere. You're too cool for me, Heather. I don't think we can be friends. I'm sure you and the band will be happy without me."

I huff and grab the papers. "I'm getting a new partner."

I walk back over to the car, praying this will be painless. "I'm not going to ticket you this time," I explain.

"Because that would be awkward since I've seen you naked?"

Oh Jesus.

I ignore the comment and proceed as if he didn't say that. "Just slow down, Mr. Walsh."

"It's Ellington." He takes my hand in his as I hand the papers back. "I figure since we've you know . . . had sex and all . . ." He pauses and gives me a blinding smile before continuing, "You should at least call me Ellington."

Thanks to my obsession, I know most things about him, but I truly didn't know his full name. I guess back when I was searching for info, Google wasn't what it currently is. Now, though, I feel like he let me in on some secret.

"Fine, Ellington, please drive safe."

"We should talk about what happened the other night."

"That's not necessary."

Eli grips my hand as I start to pull back. "Dinner."

"What?" I ask with shock.

"Have dinner with me."

Is he for real? He wants to have dinner with me after I ran out? Either he's crazy or I'm still dreaming. "I appreciate the offer, but I'm really busy." I tug my hand back and smooth my uniform shirt. "Make sure you don't run anyone off the road."

"For you, Heather, I'll drive with both hands on the wheel and follow the speed limit."

"Oh, so you'll actually obey the law?" I smile without permission. Damn him.

He leans so his head is out the window. "I have a feeling you and I will be seeing each other again."

"I don't think so."

In fact, I know we won't. I know that I'll never pull over his car again, and he doesn't know anything about me other than my name and that I'm a cop. Okay, so maybe he knows a lot more than I'd like. Still, there's no reason for him to talk to me again. Ever.

"You and your partner be safe on the job. I hate seeing fellow officers in the line of fire."

My body twists, and I scoff. "You're not a cop. You play a cop on television."

"I have a badge."

"It's fake."

Eli reaches across the seat and puts his "badge" on his lap. "Doesn't look fake to me."

I roll my eyes. "We both know that's not real. Also, impersonating a police officer is a crime."

"Are you going to arrest me?" Eli asks with a coy smile.

"You're not worth the paperwork."

With that, I turn and start to walk away. I don't get too far when I hear him yell, "I'll see you soon, Heather."

Brody leans against the car with a huge grin on his face. I point at his chest and warn him again. "Not a word."

He chuckles and climbs in the car. "You better pray no one at the station hears about this."

I groan and rest my head on the seat. "I sure know how to complicate things."

"Yeah, you sure do."

With that, we both fall silent as I drive to the hospital. Brody and I walk to Stephanie's room without commenting further on my life choices. It's the one saving grace in my job, guys don't want to talk about it at all. Brody lets me say what I need to say, and then once he's had his input, he's done. I don't have three-hour-long discussions to analyze the "why" of things with him. Nicole, who I'm sure is dying to grill me for details, is the exact opposite.

I make a mental note to avoid her as well.

As soon as I see Steph, I can tell she's doing better. The shades are open, and she's sitting on the guest chair and looking out at the water. Her hands are steady, and the overall mood in the room is lighter. But I know my instincts are correct when I see Stephanie's big smile as we enter. "Brody!" she practically squeals.

Stephanie has had a crush on him for as long as I can remember. If I didn't see him as an annoying guy who has gas issues, I probably would think he's hot, too. He's tall, has dark blue eyes, a chiseled jaw, and he oozes confidence.

"Steph!" He grins and pulls her into his arms. "You're looking hot."

I fight back slapping him, but I know he's trying to make her happy. He is all too aware of her affections, and I'm grateful he doesn't ever make her feel silly.

Rachel thinks it's cute as well.

I think it's ridiculous.

"Stop," she says as the blush paints her cheeks. "How's work?"

Brody fills her in on the call we just came from, and she clutches her chest. I could leave the room, do handstands, or juggle and she wouldn't notice. When he's around, he's all she sees. He's the only man in her life that doesn't treat her like she's dying.

"But the best part," Brody leans in and my eyes widen, "was when your sister pulled over a famous actor!"

"Brody—" I try to stop him, but Stephanie waves her hand at me.

"Yup. Eli Walsh."

"Oh my god!" Stephanie yells. "Eli! Like, the same guy you went to the concert to see?" she asks, looking at me and then Brody.

"The same one." Brody grins. "Did Heather tell you they know each other?"

"Dead. You're dead," I state.

My hands start to sweat and regret washes through me. I didn't want to tell anyone this. And my big mouth told Brody. Yes, he sort of figured it out on his own, but still. Now, the last person I want to tell is my sister.

I don't know why, but I feel like an irresponsible adult who did something completely out of character. Letting her see that makes me want to crawl in a hole.

"Heather!" Stephanie shifts quickly. "Why the hell didn't you tell me?"

"There's nothing to tell. You need to focus on you and not me."

"What?" She looks affronted. "What does that mean?"

I walk toward her. "It's nothing that I want to talk about."

"But you'll tell Brody?"

I *was* enjoying her good mood.

"Because Brody is nosey and figured it out. You don't need to know about these things."

Her face morphs from annoyed to pissed off. "You're not my mom, Heather. You're my sister. You act like I'm some kid. I'm twenty-six, and I'm so tired of you treating me like this."

This the part of our relationship I absolutely hate. Stephanie doesn't get that, while she's technically an adult, she's still a kid to me. I'm twelve years older than she is and practically raised her because she was a minor when our parents died. I wasn't.

After that, we no longer had the relationship where she would try on my clothes and we'd spend hours watching movies. It became about homework, bills, laundry, and making sure she wasn't cutting class. I don't resent it. I would do it all over again. But it didn't mean I liked the way it changed the dichotomy of our relationship.

"I know I'm not Mom. Believe me, I know."

She's used every opportunity to wield that sword at me, and it cuts deep each time, leaving wounds that aren't superficial.

"Then stop treating me like your kid and treat me like your sister. I don't know how much time I have left, and I would like to have our relationship be different."

Tears fill my vision as she brings forth the truth of what time we have. Brody clears his throat and touches Steph's arm. "I'm going to grab some coffee. See you later, Squirt."

She fumes at his nickname and turns her head away.

I take Stephanie's hand in mine. "I'm sorry you feel that way."

"I ruin everything!" She bursts out and pulls her hand free from my grasp so she can cover her face.

"Why would you say that?"

"Because! I do!" Steph turns a little and a tear falls. "I know I'm the reason Matt left."

"Steph—"

"No, I know." She wipes the tear away and draws a long breath. "I hate that my illness brought you pain. You didn't need that."

My heart pounds in my chest, and I'm doing my best to stay strong. The fact that she thinks she's responsible for Matt's crappy decision is unreal. It isn't her fault he wasn't man enough—it's his.

I open my mouth to dispute her, but she puts her hand to my lips.

"I'm not done. It's been hard watching you scrimp and save because I can't work. There's nothing you wouldn't and don't do for me, and I love you so much. However, it doesn't mean you can't live, Heather. Jesus, live because I can't." Stephanie's voice is strangled on her last word. The tears I was trying to keep at bay fall. I pull my baby sister into my arms and hold her to my chest. "I can't live, but you can . . . and you should," she says as both of us fall apart a little.

I grasp her face and pull her so we're eye to eye. "You're living now, Steph."

"This isn't living. This is waiting to die."

The words I want to say all feel wrong. She has every right to be angry, sad, and anything else she grapples with. Her life was stripped from her in a way that took our world and knocked it over. There was no warning or planning for this disease.

Instead of demeaning her feelings, I hug her tighter and let her cry.

After a few minutes, she calms and leans back. "You okay?" I ask.

"No, but I feel a little better."

"You don't have to hide your hurt from me," I remind her. "I'm always here for you."

Stephanie nods. "I know, but I miss my *sister*. I want to know when you do dumb things, and I sure as hell want to know when you meet some famous person."

I groan, and my head falls back. "Fine. I'll tell you all about it, but it's so much more than meeting him."

"Oh. My. God. Tell me you actually hooked up with him!"

There's no way I'm getting out of this, and the joy that she has right now will be worth all my embarrassment.

I shift a little, trying to relax for this awkward confession. "I did. Get comfortable because I spent the other night being completely irresponsible."

"Finally!"

chapter seven

Eli

"LET ME GET THIS STRAIGHT, YOU SLEPT WITH HER, SHE RAN OFF, YOU SEE HER AGAIN, and she walks away—again?" Randy asks with a shit-eating grin. "Man, you really have the touch."

I regret coming here. After my run-in with Heather, I took a drive to Sanibel Island where Randy lives. I don't know why I thought it was going to help me in some way. I should've known my brother and sister-in-law would be all too happy about this story.

I'll get her, though.

It's just going to take some finesse and a lot of patience. Plus, I still have the ace up my sleeve.

"Yup. It was fucking unbelievable."

"You got out of the bathroom, and she was . . . gone?" Randy keeps pushing as he laughs.

"It was ridiculous. I couldn't find her, and then realized she took off. Who the fuck does that?"

Savannah giggles. "Umm, you!"

Exactly. That's my deal. I'm the one who runs out or finds someone to escort the stagefive clinger off the bus. I don't go searching for the girl, and I definitely don't go back for more when a girl brushes me off—twice.

"I never thought I'd see it happen." Vannah leans back in her chair.

"See what happen?"

"A girl has you all twisted in knots. For once, you're the one seeing what it feels like."

I shake my head. She has no idea what she's talking about. My sister-in-law is oblivious to the issue. It isn't about her, it's about how she seems not to care about me. I have feelings, too. I was in love before, but they forget that. "I'm not in knots. I'm goddamn confused. Why the hell would she push *me* away?"

"Oh, don't even, Eli. You're not some God. You're a spoiled shit who has had everything handed to you on a silver platter."

"The fuck I have."

It's her turn to give me a stare that would make any grown man cry. She looks around to make sure the kids aren't near and then her face softens. "Watch your mouth. It's bad enough Adriel told the teacher to kiss his ass the other day, we don't need the F-word thrown around."

Savannah is a great woman. She deals with a lot, but my seven-year-old nephew is a little shit. Adriel is the oldest, and he's beyond overindulged. Randy was gone a lot when he was a baby and then overcompensated when he was home. I feel bad for her since she's the one dealing with the fallout.

I put my hands up and flash her a smile. "Sorry. I'll be more careful."

"Good."

"I'm just saying that we didn't have it all that easy. There were no silver platters."

Randy laughs. "You were eighteen when we were signed. Since then, have you had any issues?"

"Have you?" I gesture toward the walls around us. They act like they're struggling. This nine million dollar mansion they're living in doesn't seem to be roughing it if you ask me.

"I remember Mom having to work an extra job for us to eat and take music lessons, do you?"

It always comes back to this. Of course, I remember. When our father passed away, everything changed. Yes, I was young, but that doesn't mean I have no memory of it. My mother was great at hiding things, but no matter how hard you try, some things show through. When his child support stopped coming, we stopped doing a lot.

"Why do you think I took care of her when we got money?"

"Because you wanted to be her favorite," he tosses back and chugs his beer.

"I already was, I didn't need to buy her that house to solidify it."

"Keep telling yourself that." Randy laughs and shakes his head at me.

"Okay, boys. Back to my point. You've had a pretty easy *adulthood*, Eli. Girls flock to you, the band succeeded beyond anyone's expectations, and then you landed the role on *A Thin Blue Line* without having any acting experience. Things fall in your lap, but this time . . . not so much."

She has a point, but it doesn't mean I don't bust my ass. Sure, I was scouted and asked to join *A Thin Blue Line*, but I immediately started taking acting lessons. I hired the best coaches to make sure I earned my money. I can't say anything about Four Blocks Down, that was a guy who promised us we'd be huge if we signed with him and a shit ton of luck.

Heather, though. She's something completely different. For the first time, I don't have someone chasing me because of who I am. Hell, she fucking ran.

I want to know why. I want to know what she's hiding behind her tough-girl exterior. I've never spotted a girl in a concert like that. It took every ounce of self-control not to stare at her all night. There's a pull between us, and I know she felt it.

I mentally scoff. It's absolutely ridiculous that some girl is having this effect on me. But yet I keep wanting to go back which only proves that there's something different. Why is this girl the only thing I can think about? The truth is, I wasn't going to kick Heather out of my bed that night. I wanted to hold her in my arms, breathe her perfume through the night, and feel her skin against mine. Instead of getting any of that, she bolted. The worst part is then, I fucking chased after her, and I'm debating doing it again.

Savannah waves her hand in my face. "Well?"

"I think you're wrong, Vannah. It has nothing to do with the thrill of the chase." And it's not, it's *her*.

"Oh?" she asks with surprise. Shit, I said that aloud. "What is it then?" Vannah pushes.

"I don't know," I admit and take a drink. "It was something in her eyes. I'm sounding like a pussy, but I'm serious. It was like there was this . . . thing . . . and I just want to figure out what it was."

Savannah does her best to hide her smile, but I see it. The eternal believer. She laid eyes on Randy and knew they'd be married. I've heard the story a million times, and each time, I fight back the need to puke. She swears that when it happens, you can't go back.

"I'm not in love with her," I quickly defend.

Randy elbows me. "Sounds like the first time I laid eyes on Savannah."

"You were an idiot. Hell, you still are."

"As is every man when he falls in love."

"For fuck's sake!" I throw my hands up and stand.

"Mouth!" Savannah yells.

"Sorry! But I'm not in love with anyone."

I can't believe these two. How does thinking about some girl equate to falling in love? It doesn't.

It means I need one more time with her to prove that it's all in my head.

That's it.

I grab my wallet and keys, grumbling as I walk off. They're wrong, and I'm not going to sit around with them as they try to convince me otherwise. All I know is her name, that she's a cop, and her address, that's it. How do you fall in love with a name? It isn't realistic, and I have no intentions of ever loving another woman.

Been there, and I'd rather be broke than give anyone that kind of power over me again.

The last bitch wrecked me and almost destroyed everything I worked for.

"Hey," Randy gets to his feet, "don't be like this."

"I'm going to prove you all wrong."

His brow raises, and he grins. "Eli, stop being an idiot."

"Untle Eli!" My niece runs over and leaps into my arms. "I missed you!"

"Hey, beautiful!" Daria is the only girl I'll ever love. She's three and owns my heart. I pity any asshole who ever tries to come near her. I don't give a fuck if I'm in a wheelchair, I'll kick his ass. "I missed you more."

"You and Daddy sing me a song!"

I look over at my brother and see the same adoration in his eyes. Adriel may be spoiled, but Daria... she had him wrapped around her little finger. There's nothing Randy won't do for Daria.

"I need to get home, pretty girl." I try to explain, but she crosses her arms and pushes her lips into a pout.

"Untle Eli, you don't love me."

"You know that's not true."

"Puuuuuleeeeeease," she begs and grabs my cheeks. "I lub you."

I'm just as screwed as Randy. "I love you, too. One song."

"Yay!" She claps her hands and wiggles for me to put her down. Three years old and has this whole world domination slash manipulation thing perfected already.

Eleven songs later, I'm finally standing at my car with my brother. "Listen, I know we gave you a load of shit in there, but you're not the guy who has ever been hung up on a piece of ass."

My blood pressure spikes a bit higher with each word, and I clench my fists. Heather isn't a piece of ass.

Fuck.

What the hell am I even thinking?

That's exactly what she is.

Randy smirks as if he expected this exact response and knows what I'm thinking.

He claps his hand on my shoulder and chuckles. "Go talk to her. If it's nothing, then come here and we'll tell Savannah how wrong she is. If nothing else, you'll know for yourself."

"You know that I refuse to do this again."

"Because of Penelope?"

Just her name makes me want to punch something. "Yes."

"That's sad, man. You and her were a lifetime ago, and you're older and wiser. No way you fall for another gold-digging whore like her."

"This is a moot point anyway. I'm not in love with anyone."

"Good." Randy nods in agreement. "It should be no problem seeing her then."

With that, my brother walks back up his drive, and I flip him off. I should've been an only child. It would've made life so much easier.

I start the car and turn all my focus to this Heather situation.

My eyes catch on the plastic card sitting in my cup holder, and I know exactly what I'm going to do.

chapter eight

Heather

After Brody and I left Stephanie, we had back-to-back calls. We were nonstop all day, and I'm exhausted. Thanks to shift work, I have the next three days off, and I couldn't be happier. Which is good since I need all those good vibes for the phone call I'm about to make.

I have to call Nicole back.

"Hey," I say as I flop on my couch.

"Hey yourself. Where the hell have you been? I called you four times."

I give her a rundown of the calls we had, purposely leave out the encounter with Eli, and lay my head back. "I'm beyond beat."

"Is Stephanie okay?"

"She seems to be. We had a really good talk." I fill her in on my hospital trip. It feels good that we got everything out in the open. I know both of us dance around each other sometimes. Stephanie a lot less than me. When her mind isn't in the right place, she lets it all fly.

"I'm glad. So, since that's out of the way, let's talk about the other night."

"Nic," I grumble.

"No. You made me scale a freaking fence. You're not getting out of this. I've given you space, but that's not happening tonight."

I can only imagine how much this has been eating at her, but I don't want to get into this right now. Maybe not ever.

Thankfully the doorbell rings.

"Shit, my pizza's here. Hold on, Nic."

I put the phone on the coffee table and grab my wallet before opening the door.

"Good to see you again, Heather." Ian the pizza delivery guy smiles. I try not to let the fact that the pizza guy knows me by name depress me too much. It's my go-to food after a twelve-hour shift.

"You, too." I return his smile, and he looks me up and down. He's a nice kid, but his roaming eyes are a bit much.

Ian hands me the pizza, and I head inside for a night of Nicole's interrogation.

"Okay," I put the phone to my ear. "I'm back."

"And you were about to tell me about your sex with Eli."

I take a massive bite of pizza and moan. All the gooey cheesy goodness is like a party in my mouth.

"Heather!" Nicole yells as I take another bite.

"I'm eating," I say as I chew.

"Pizza is not more important than my need for information."

The doorbell rings again, and I thank God for small miracles. "Hold again," I say as I hold the phone against my shoulder.

I walk over, smiling because I know that Nicole must be going out of her mind. "Did you for—"

"Hello, Officer Covey." Eli grins as he leans against the doorframe. "I was hoping you were home. We didn't get a chance to finish our conversation."

Not even thinking, I close the door and stand there. Holy shit. What the hell?

"Heather?" Nicole's voice is a buzzing in my ear. Or is that my suddenly frantic pulse?

"Hmm?" I can't speak. Eli Walsh is at my freaking house.

"Is that who I think it is?"

I rise onto my tiptoes and peek out the peephole. Sure enough, he's right there, smiling as if he has not a care in the world. "Yup."

"Are you fucking kidding?" Nicole screams.

"Holy shit, Nic. What the hell do I do?" My heart continues to race, and I'm completely freaking out.

Nicole chuckles and then proceeds to yell again. "Open the goddamn door!"

I look in the mirror and groan. I have on shorts and an oversized sweatshirt, which now has a beautiful pizza stain on the front. My hair is in a messy bun, I'm not wearing any makeup, and I have my glasses on instead of my contacts. I can't believe this.

Eli knocks again. "Heather, I can hear you on the other side."

My hand presses against the wood, and I close my eyes. "What do you want, Eli?"

"Heather! Open the fucking door right now!" Nicole's voice raises in my ear.

"Shut up!" I yell at my jackass best friend.

"I didn't say anything," Eli answers.

I sigh and drop my head against the door again, making a *thump* noise. "I know. I . . . I . . . just."

Nicole growls at me, "I swear that if you don't open it right now, I'm coming over and giving him your spare key."

There isn't a single doubt that she'll do exactly that. "Fine. Goodbye," I say and disconnect the phone.

With no other options, I fix my hair the best I can and pull the door open. Eli is still standing with his arm resting on the frame and a huge smile on his face. "Hi." His deep voice washes over me, making my toes curl a bit.

"Why are you here, and how did you know where I live?" I ask, trying to keep my heart from flying out of my throat.

He's ridiculously sexy. Even more so than earlier today. Everything about him screams heartbreak, but every muscle in my body wants to be close to him.

Eli doesn't say anything, he just stares into my eyes. "You going to let me in?"

"Are you going to answer my questions?" I counter.

"If you let me come in."

There's no way this is going to lead to anything good. Letting Eli any deeper into my life is not part of my plan. I can't get mixed up with some playboy singer slash actor and his overly problematic existence. I have enough complications, I don't need another.

I also don't think he's the kind of man to give up. If I send him away, he'll be back tomorrow. Saying no to a man who probably has never heard the word will only be a challenge. It's better to get this all out and over with now so I can move on.

"Fine, but you have five minutes." I push the door open more, and he stands in my doorway so we're chest to chest.

Eli's eyes don't stray from mine as his hand gently touches the side of my face. "We'll see about that."

I fight the impulse to crush my lips to his. To taste his kiss and feel his rough hands on my skin again. There's nothing I've wanted more than to stop replaying it in my head, but I can't.

It's been so long since a man has made me crazy, driven me to the point of complete madness, but Eli pulled it off with ease.

I shake my head and pull his hand down. "Start talking before I get my Taser."

"I'd rather you get the cuffs." He winks and walks deeper into my living room.

For the first time since I can remember, I look around and feel a wave of embarrassment. I live a modest life, I can't afford the repairs needed on my house, and I haven't bought new furniture since my engagement to Matt nine years ago. Here's a man who could buy the entire Pottery Barn catalogue, and I can't even afford a blanket.

"Eli?" I ask, trying to get him to stop looking around. "You found out where I live, how?"

"Relax." His smile is easy and warm. "I found something of yours. I figured you probably needed it."

"What? Something of mine?"

He pulls out a card, and my jaw falls. "Need this?"

"Holy shit! I didn't even know it was missing!" I walk over and take my license from his hand. "Thank you. I would be in deep shit if they did a paperwork check and I didn't have it before shift."

"I thought being the law-abiding citizen you are, it was important."

Relief floods me which is quickly followed by confusion. "But wait . . . you saw me earlier today."

"Yes, but I was in a rather precarious situation with a police officer who wanted to bust my balls, so I didn't have a chance to give it back."

My arms fold across my chest as I stare at him. "You had more than enough time."

He shrugs and plops himself on my couch. "I thought it would be better now. Plus, I wouldn't want to play all my cards on the first hand."

"So, this is what?"

"This is us becoming friends."

"Friends?" I ask.

His lazy smile grows, and he leans back. "Yup. I decided today we're going to be friends."

"Why is that?"

I'm not sure why I'm asking, but I can't help but want to know why he feels this is going to happen. Since it's totally not. I don't need any more friends, especially not rich sex Gods who out of nowhere want to make my life even more of a mess.

"Because that's what people do after they've slept together. Plus, I'm a good friend."

I huff and move closer, "I don't need any more—" Eli opens the pizza box and pulls a slice out. "Hey! That's my pizza."

"I'm starving." He grins and then takes a bite. "Mmm." Eli moans as he chews, and I would give anything to be what he's eating.

My eyes widen, and my cheeks burn as I chastise myself for even thinking that. What is wrong with me? Why do I become some addled teenager when I'm around him? I'm definitely not some sex-crazed woman. Since Matt, I've had one guy in my bed.

One.

And he sucked.

Now, I'm standing here thinking about Eli and all he did to me.

"Listen, new friend that I didn't particularly ask for, I appreciate you bringing my license back." I motion toward the door, but he leans back and throws his leg over his knee. "Really, I do, but—"

Eli cuts me off. "You're not going to eat?"

"No, I'm definitely going to eat, but you're definitely not staying."

"You can't share some pizza with me? I mean, isn't that what friends do and all? They break bread, have some fun, talk, hook up a little?" He wags his eyebrows with a grin.

I shake my head and sigh. "No hooking up, and while I love the idea of our newfound friendship, it's been a really long day. I was planning to head to bed."

"We can do that, too." He takes another bite as if he didn't offer to sleep with me again.

"What? No! I wasn't offering that!"

He laughs and tosses the pizza down before brushing some crumbs off his hands. "Jesus, relax, Heather. I was joking. I'm here because I wanted to talk about what happened. You ran off without a word, and when I found your license on the ground, I figured it was a sign."

"A sign?"

"Yes." He stands and then walks closer to me. "A sign that we have unfinished business. You know, most girls like to leave something behind so I have to come return it. Is that what this was? A game so you could see me again?"

Each step that Eli takes makes my pulse quicken a bit more. I'm not sure what unfinished business he thinks we have and what girls he's used to dealing with. I was pretty clear when I ran out that there was nothing more. I was half drunk, stupid, and pressured by my idiot best friend to do something outside my comfort zone.

"I don't have time for games. I never planned on seeing you again. The only sign was that I dropped something and you happened to find it."

Eli stands in front of me, and I have to tilt my head back to see his face. His gorgeous eyes hold me hostage, and his arm wraps around my waist. "I think we both know that's not the truth. You can feel it right now. I can see your breathing accelerating, your eyes keep moving to my lips, and while you can keep fighting it, I know you want me."

I shake my head, trying to make him wrong, but when his tongue slides against his lips, I know he hears the intake of breath. I know because it's loud, and in the silence, it might as well have been a sonic boom.

"Eli . . ." I try to move back, but his arm holds me in place.

"I'm not going to do anything, I just want to talk."

"This is crazy," I say, wishing I didn't want crazy with every cell in my body.

Eli's other hand slides up my back and holds me tighter. "What would be crazy is walking out the door without seeing if this is in our heads."

"If what's in our heads?"

"Whatever has us both so twisted that I'm here in your house, and you're running out in the middle of the night without a goodbye. There's something going on, and I want to see what the hell it is. Don't you?"

My gaze doesn't leave his, and the sincerity and conviction in his words stun me. If I tell him to walk out this door, I'll regret it. I'll think about this one moment for the rest of my life. Plus, Nicole knows he's here, so if I ask him to leave, she'll never let me live it down.

Before I can stop the words from falling from my lips, I agree. "Okay, pizza and talking only, though."

Eli's smile widens, and he squeezes me a little. "Pizza, talking, and who knows what else," he counters.

There will be nothing else, but I keep that to myself. Arguing with him seems to only lead to him staying, eating pizza, and thinking we're going to be besties.

We make our way back over to the couch and sit. He grabs a slice and hands it to me before going back for the piece he had. I curl my legs under me and try not to gawk. But Eli Walsh is sitting in the living room of my crumbling house. It isn't that I live in a shithole, but I'm sure it's nothing like his home.

My dad was a man of many projects. He started them and then quit before ever finishing. Matt helped a little, but he was in no way Bob Villa, if anything, he was Tim Allen from *Home Improvement* and broke more than he fixed.

After he left, I did my best to patch the holes of my home and my heart.

"So, a cop?" Eli asks after a few minutes of silent eating.

I wipe the sauce from my lips and then smile. "It was what I always wanted to be. My parents were killed by a drunk driver when I was twenty-one. After that, I knew I wanted to help even just one person be saved from that tragedy."

"I'm really sorry," Eli says and touches my arm.

"It was a long time ago."

"Still, that must've been tough."

I sigh and shrug a little. "It sucked, but I think it made me who I am today."

"I get it. My dad died when I was young, too."

"I'm sorry."

Losing your parents is never easy, but when you're young, it's impossible to navigate the emotions of it. So many times I wished I had my parents there to guide me. It would've been so much easier.

"Don't be, he wasn't a role model anyway." He waves away my condolences and says, "So, tell me, Heather . . . who are you?"

"I'm just me."

There's no way I'm going to divulge my deepest secrets. Eli will walk out this door tonight and never be back, which is exactly what I should want. Right? So, why don't I spill all the dirt? For all I know, I'm just some conquest to him. The girl who walked away from a man that girls flock to. It's what Nicole refers to as the rejection reaction. If I had stayed and pined for him, he would've brushed me off into the pile of other nameless, faceless girls he's slept with.

Eli removes his keys and wallet from his back pocket, tossing them on the table.

Sure, make yourself comfortable. I guess he plans on staying.

"I'm serious. I want to know more about you," he pushes for more.

"Why?" I ask with frustration. "You and I both know how this goes."

He grips the back of his neck and lets out a heavy sigh. "How is that?"

"You're going to go back to your lavish life, and I'll be here . . ." I gesture around the room.

"Maybe that's exactly what will happen, but only because you're so hell bent on pushing me out that door."

He isn't wrong, but that still stings a little. "I'm protecting myself."

Eli seems to recover and grabs another slice of pizza. "It's fine, you're going to have to try a lot harder. I'm basically a cop, too."

I laugh and roll my eyes. "We've already established that you're just a cop on television. Real police work isn't anything like that."

"So, you watch my show?" He says it so casually, so coolly, that if I weren't an actual cop, I would have missed his real reaction. He's practically preening inside over that little tidbit.

"I've seen it once because nothing else was on." I'm so full of shit. I watch his stupid show every week. At first, it was because I wanted to see how much they butchered the real way police are, but then I was hooked. Watching him is my guilty pleasure. After five seasons, I can admit that I'm officially addicted.

He'll never know that, though.

No way will I give him one more thing to try to use against me.

"Well, my partner, Tina, is a lot like you."

"Is she?"

She is so not like me. Tina is a hard ass who wants nothing to do with men, and her husband left her for another woman.

I want a man, I don't want another guy who will cut tail and run because life isn't perfect. And Matt left because he's a dick.

"Yeah, she lives alone and pushes any guy away."

Screw him. He doesn't *know* me. So what if I'm alone and I don't want to get involved with a guy whose life is the polar opposite of mine? I'm thirty-eight years old; I don't have to play by his rules or beliefs.

"I'm not pushing you away; I'm just living in reality."

Eli leans forward, and I force myself not to retreat. "The only reality is the one we make."

My reality isn't movie stars and playing a cop on television. I'm an actual cop. I deal with all kinds of shit, and there's no one to yell cut when it gets too intense. There are real bullets flying, people dying in car wrecks, immense amounts of paperwork, and shit pay. Keeping myself guarded isn't a choice, it's a necessity.

"Maybe in your world, but in the real world, we have crap to deal with."

Eli drops the slice and huffs. "I live in the real world too you know."

"Well, since we're friends and all, tell me about it." I toss the ball back in his proverbial corner.

I'm fully aware I'm coming off like a bitch. However, there's a reason I ran away after we had sex. I'm terrified of anything new. Things in my life disappear or fall apart, trying to start anything with someone else, isn't in my plans. I can't lose anything else.

Looking at Eli, though, makes me wish for another life.

One where we could be friends. One where we could maybe be more than friends, but that isn't the life I'm living.

Still, a girl can hope.

Eli shifts a little and clears his throat. "My full name is Ellington Walsh, I'm forty-two years old, never married, and grew up here in Tampa. I have one brother, Randy, who's two years older than I am. We've been in Four Blocks Down since I was eighteen, and now I'm an actor. I plan to go into movies soon, but I'm waiting for the right part. Oh, most importantly, I like blonde girls who tell me they love me."

I laugh. "Tell me something I wouldn't find on Wikipedia."

That look of silent preening is back in his eyes, and I want to smack myself. "You looked me up, huh?"

"Sure." I snort, trying to play it cool. "No, I've grown up watching you in a non-creepy way. It isn't like I don't know all your bullet points. How about you tell me something about your life that your *friends* would know."

Let's see how much Eli wants to tell me. I'm not sure he actually wants this friendship like he thinks. I'm not even sure what a friendship with a famous person even looks like. Will there be people following him around? Is there some crazy security team he has?

Does he have people? Do I even know what that means? Nope. The only people I have are my best friends and sister.

"Okay, I would've been here an hour earlier tonight, but a girl kept me held hostage."

My eyes widen. Is he seriously telling me about another girl? "Wow."

"Not like that!" he quickly says with his hands raised. "Shit. I'm not good at this. I'm talking about Daria, my niece."

"You have a niece?"

I haven't followed Randy's personal life since he's married. That crosses the line into creepy. I do know that he and his wife were together when the band formed, so he's always kind of been off limits. It was always Eli that was the heartthrob.

"Yeah, she's a man-manipulator already. My sister-in-law has trained her to terrorize my brother and me. She has this whole big eyes and squishy face thing down pat."

I smile, understanding how kids can get you to do what they want pretty easily. "Basically, she rules your world?"

Eli nods. "I promised her one song. One. And eleven songs and fifty minutes later, I was in the car. If that doesn't show you what one little 'I love you' from her does, I don't know what will. Basically, if she wills it, she gets it. She even got me to play with dolls." He shudders.

I can't imagine him playing with a little girl, but a part of me swoons at the thought. It's hard to picture him as anything but the elusive manwhore that the tabloids make him out to be.

"That's actually kind of sweet."

"You think I'm sweet?" he asks with hope filling his voice.

"I think *that* is sweet."

My clarification goes unnoticed.

"I'm taking that as you like me. I don't blame you, I'm quite charming."

I groan while grinning. "Wikipedia didn't mention that."

His finger grazes my bare leg before falling flat. The skin under where his hand rests tingles. "I'm saving the good stuff for you."

"Lucky me."

He laughs. "Well, most girls would think so."

"I guess it's a good thing I'm not most girls then," I throw back.

"Why is that?" Eli asks.

"Because you aren't trying to be friends with them."

Eli's deep, rich laughter fills the room. "Touché."

Eli and I finish the rest of the pizza as he tells me more about his niece and nephew. I love that he speaks about them with such affection. It's great seeing him as—normal. He isn't special sitting here in my rundown house. He's just a regular guy. A guy who eats pizza and talks about how much he loves annoying his sister-in-law.

We cover more about my job, his show, and about how happy he is to get to spend some time in Tampa.

I yawn and then look at the clock. Holy shit! He's been here for almost three hours. Wow.

It's been easy, fun, and filled with smiles.

"It's really late." He gets to his feet and shrugs on his coat.

"Thanks for bringing my license."

I walk him to the door, and when we get there, he turns to me. "Can I see you again?"

"Eli . . ." I hold the door in my hand, trying to find the right words. This was fun, but this is complicated. "I don't know if that's such a good idea."

He moves closer, keeping his eyes on mine. "I was hoping you'd see that I'm not just some dick who doesn't care. I thought we were getting somewhere, maybe even becoming friends. Seems I was mistaken."

"You're not!" I say quickly and grip his arm. "I'm being crazy, and I'm sorry. The truth is—" I sigh and decide to give him the truth. "You scare me. I'm not a one-night stand kind of girl. I have a lot, and I mean a lot, of shit going on in my life. Things that take up all my headspace, and I just don't have room for more." I take a deep breath, willing myself to continue. "I've had a lot of fun tonight with you, though. Honestly, it's been great talking, and yes, there's something . . ."

His smile is effortless as he leans in. "Listen, I head back to New York in a few weeks, but I'm staying around Tampa until then. I want to see you again."

"Why?" I ask with complete bewilderment.

"Because regardless of how hard you're pushing me away, I can't help but want to see you more. I liked hanging out, I don't get this with anyone but my brother. You don't treat me like I'm different." Eli winks. "Think about it."

He leans in and kisses my cheek before turning and walking down the porch steps. I stand like a statue, unsure of whether I could find my voice if I wanted to. I watch Eli walk to his car, not expecting him to turn around. When he does, he grins again and adds, "Besides, I know where you live and work, I'm sure we'll run into each other again anyway. Wikipedia should mention I'm relentless in pursuing what I want."

My lips part, but he's in his car before I can speak.

Damn it. This was not how that was supposed to go.

chapter nine

Heather

"You're shitting me!" Nicole yells as she almost drops her glass of wine. "I'm going to rub myself all over your couch."

"You would."

We're at her lush apartment in downtown Tampa working on killing off our second bottle of wine. I spent all day at the hospital with Stephanie and then refused to go home. So, instead of answering any of her twenty texts, I came here.

"What is wrong with you?" Nicole has probably asked me that ten times since I got here.

"Nothing is wrong with me! I'm being realistic. If Matt, who was a local cop that I've known for almost my whole life left because of Steph, what do you think an international superstar is going to do? Huh? Have you thought about that?"

"You're so dumb."

"You've been telling me that for a long time." I huff and take another gulp of wine. I get that she thinks I'm foolish, but I can't open myself up like that again. I'd be asking for my heart to be broken. I'd rather not. "There's no way that Eli is going to stick around Tampa, and I'm never going to move away from Steph."

Nicole takes the glass from my hand and places it on the table. Her eyes are soft, but I know what's coming. She's going to lay into me something fierce. "I've watched you make mistakes before, and I haven't said shit. Not this time. I'm telling you right now that if you don't do this, you'll regret it for the rest of your life. You can't tell me that you don't feel something for him."

"I don't know what I feel."

"Yes, you do. You had a crazy night with him, and it threw you for a loop. I get it. You're the straight-laced one of us. You don't do wild, and you don't take risks. Life has been a series of heartbreaks for you. I know this. We all do, but fuck, Heather, you have to live! There's no reason that you can't actually *live* the life you've been given."

Tears form, and my heart aches. I know she loves me and what she said is all true, but damn it, I hate her for it. I do the best I can, and I don't know how many times I can be hurt before I finally have enough.

When my sister dies, it's going to kill me. I'll have no family left, and I can't waste any of the little time I have with her. It's the truth I can't bring myself to say.

I sure as hell can't chase the idea of a guy who can essentially wreck my world. It's stupid, and I won't make mistakes like that. Not when my sister needs me. Eli is always photographed traveling, partying, and eating at all these expensive restaurants where I couldn't even afford a salad.

"Jesus, have you and Steph been swapping notes?"

"No, but if she's saying anything like I am, she's freaking right."

"You know why I'm this way." I wipe the bead that trickles down my cheek.

"I do." Nicole takes my hand in hers. "I'm not trying to hurt you, but I can't watch you like this anymore. Your sister doesn't want you to keep going this way and neither would your parents. It's okay to take chances and get hurt. It's okay to have regrets and triumphs, but it isn't okay to just . . . be."

"And what if he's like Matt?"

She smiles. "Then you dump his stupid ass and I'll feed you ice cream and wine."

I groan and drop my head against the back of the couch. "I hate when you make sense."

Nicole laughs. "I bet. It doesn't happen too often, so don't worry."

"I miss when all we worried about was if we'd go to prom with our boyfriends."

"I always knew that I wouldn't. Boys are dumb. I was much happier going stag and hanging out with you, Kristin, and Danni."

Crap. We're going to have to tell them about this. I've avoided their calls because I'm the world's worst liar. They will see right through whatever crap I try to sell them. "I have to tell them, don't I?"

"Nah, I'll tell them we couldn't meet him." I let my head fall to the side so I can look at her, and then I pull her against me for a hug. "Keep this to yourself for a while. You need to decide without anyone's influence."

"So, what you're saying is that I should just listen to you?"

"Precisely."

I laugh silently and let that go. My mind wanders to last night. I can't help thinking about how normal Eli seemed. He wasn't pretentious, he ate pizza from the box while we lounged on my ratty, old couch. There were no demands. It was only the two of us. It was comfortable even.

Just like the first time we were around each other.

Maybe I am being crazy and overthinking this. There's something about him that I can't stop thinking about. His smile causes butterflies in my stomach. His laugh is music that speaks to my heart. And even though I've spent all day trying to convince myself that he's the last thing I even want to think about, he's what I've spent all day talking about.

I'm screwed.

"What if he never comes back?" I ask Nicole.

"Then he's a complete idiot. You're worth chasing."

People can say what they want about Nicole, but she's the best person I know. Sure, she drives me nuts, but I love her. She's been there for me every step of the way, and I couldn't imagine my life without her.

I pass through the metal gates of the only place I feel close to my parents. Once I park, I grab the bouquet of flowers and head to their graves. It's been a long time since I've been here, but I haven't really had a reason to come talk to them.

If I'm completely honest, I've been angry for a long time.

Navigating the paths isn't difficult, and soon, I crouch in front of my parents' final resting places. "Hi, Mom and Dad." I start to pull overgrown weeds and wipe away some of the dirt. My fingers trace the cool stone, and I close my eyes, allowing sadness and the smell of fresh cut grass to fill my body.

"I know I haven't been here in a while, I'm sorry." I tuck my hair behind my ear. "It's sometimes hard to get here, especially lately."

After passing out on Nicole's couch, I woke this morning and drove here. There's a lot I need to say, and sometimes a girl just needs her mother.

This is one of those times.

"There's so much that's happened since I last visited. Matt and I are divorced now, but that's kind of old news. Let's see, I'm still partnered with Brody, he's annoying as all hell, but I can't imagine working beside anyone else. Stephanie is living in Breezy Beaches full time. It's hard not having her with me, but it got to be too much. Everything is a mess, Mom. I did something stupid, and now I don't know what to do."

I place the flowers on the ground and start to arrange them. "I met this guy, you probably remember my obsession with Four Blocks Down—Eli specifically. Well, we met at his concert the other night, and I . . ." I feel weird telling my mom about our one-night stand. Not that she can respond and tell me about her disappointment, but still. "Anyway, he showed up at the house last night, and we talked for hours. I like him, but it's so complicated. I'm not special or anything. I'm worried that he'll break my heart, and I really don't have much left of it as it is."

As much I want to talk to her about this, there's something else that forced me to finally drive here. The confliction I feel isn't just about Eli, it's about my whole life. All the things that I can't control, and I'm tired of spinning.

My fingers trace her name on the cool headstone, reminding me that everything here is dead. "I hope you understand why I've stayed away. Seeing your names like this hurts so much sometimes. Hell, pretty much all the time. And soon, Steph will be here with you." I drop my hand and fight the surge of tears that threaten to fall. "I don't know how I'll go on when that happens. I've tried so hard to accept this, but I can't. I've done everything I can for her, but she keeps getting sicker, and it's killing me. I love her so much." There's no stopping the tears now. They flow, and I know that I need this. I need my mother to hear me. "I know she isn't my daughter, but she's been mine to raise, and she's going to die. Just like you and Daddy. Just like everyone I love. You all get taken from me."

My hand finds its way back to the top of the stone, and I let my forehead rest against my knuckles as I fall apart. Fears that I've shoved deep for years all bubble to the surface. Losing my sister will be the nail in my own coffin. I will have lost each member of my family without any way of stopping it.

"I'm supposed to help people. I save people every day, but I can't save her, Mommy. I can't help her. I can't give her a life that she deserves. I'm so sorry. I know you trusted me to keep her safe." All the emotions I've been holding in pour out. The crying is loud and painful, but necessary. I've been strong for so long, I don't have it in me anymore. "How can you let God take her from me, too? I'll be alone and have failed you all. Please forgive me—" My words choke off and I fold in on myself, sobbing and trying desperately to draw air into my too-tight lungs.

Eventually, when my eyes are red and puffy and my emotions have run dry, I stand and touch my hand to my lips before pressing the kiss on the headstone. "I love you both. I miss you more than you'll ever know, and I hope it's a while before I'm back here again."

Because the next time will be Stephanie's funeral.

I walk back to my car, draw a few calming breaths, and then flip the visor down. I'm a mess. I wipe away the makeup that was ruined by crying.

There's a reason I don't come here often: it's too damn hard.

My phone pings with a text.

Stephanie: Are you coming to visit today?

Me: Of course.

Stephanie: See you soon?

Me: I'm on my way now. Just leaving the cemetery.

Stephanie: Tell Mom and Dad I miss them.

I close my eyes and try not to think about the fact that I lost it over her impending death.

Me: I did. They love you and miss you.

Stephanie: Glad they told you that . . . LOL.

My lips turn into a smile and a giggle slips from me. I can picture her rolling her eyes at me.

The drive to the hospital takes about ten minutes, all of which I use to collect myself and put my mask firmly back in place. If she sees that I've been crying, she'll do what she can to tell me about her acceptance of her fate. That isn't what I need to hear . . . ever.

Sometimes, I wonder if she would rather it happen already so she can stop suffering. I'm too selfish for that. I want every minute I can get with her. I'll take a hundred bad days as long as I can touch her, talk to her, and keep her close.

I enter the room and completely freeze. Stephanie is flirting with a male nurse. He's sitting on her bed, and her eyes move down as she smiles. I watch as she bats her eyelashes and tucks her brown hair behind her ears like I do when I'm nervous.

Then Stephanie's gaze shifts, and she spots me. "Heather!" She jumps, and the man leaps to his feet. "Hey! I didn't see you there."

I grin. "I see that."

"This is Anthony," Steph says with a sigh. "He's my daytime nurse and friend."

Oh, boy. I've seen this look before. This must be why she isn't fighting her doctor to be discharged anymore.

"Hi, Anthony," I say as I walk forward. "It's nice to meet you."

"I just finished my shift and was checking on her," he explains, as if I haven't already gotten his number.

"That's awfully nice of you." I look over at Steph, still grinning.

She gives me a look that clearly tells me to stop it. I haven't seen her even look at a man since she was diagnosed with Huntington's all those years ago.

"Well, she's a huge comic book fan, and I promised to show her my latest collector edition *Superman* I bought yesterday."

"Yes," Steph interjects and touches his arm. "He got the one I was looking for online."

"Really?" I bury my skepticism deep. Stephanie has never touched a comic book.

"Yes, *Heather*." Her eyes narrow, and she purses her lips. "Anthony is going to let me see it tomorrow."

Oh, I get it.

"I'll let you visit with your sister, Stephy, I'll see you tomorrow." Anthony squeezes her hand and moves toward me. "It was great to meet you. She talks about you a lot."

"It was nice to meet you also," I reply as he walks away.

As soon as he's down the hall, I rush over to her side, and we both laugh. "Comic books? Stephy? You hate that nickname! You are in *so* deep if you're already being all dorky."

"Shut up!" She slaps my arm. "I'm not dorky. I'm doing what *normal* girls do when they like a guy. He's cute. He kept coming to check my vitals way more than necessary, and I don't know . . . I wanted someone to talk to."

"I think it's great," I say to assure her. "And I am too normal."

"Yeah, you're normal my ass," Steph retorts.

She's right, I'm totally not normal.

"Anyway, I'm glad you're putting yourself out there a little."

I love that she's getting some human interaction other than with Brody and me. Nicole checks in on her once in a while, but usually it's just the people in the home and me. She has no friends that are around anymore, which is sad but unsurprising. Most people don't stick around long when something this serious happens. Not because they are cruel or uncaring. They just didn't know what to say or how to handle themselves. I understand to some extent, but I hate it for her.

Unfortunately, it's made it so there's a great amount of loneliness that my sister struggles with. I can take her anger, knowing it isn't really her, it's her illness. What I can't stomach is the thought of her feeling lonely. It breaks me in ways that I would sell my soul to prevent.

"I know there's no future," Her face falls, and her tone becomes sullen.

"Stop." I shake her hand. "You're allowed to have friends, and if you both like comic books, then let it happen."

She laughs. "Can you go buy me a comic book so I know what they look like?"

I burst into laughter. "Sure thing."

Stephanie looks away as her exhilaration fades. "I don't want to get attached."

"Babe, he's a nurse, he knows what he's getting into."

Of all the possible people she could have met, I'm happy it's him. He probably understands better than anyone what her future looks like.

"May—" she starts to say and begins to cough, which is deep and wet and sends me straight into panic mode.

I rub her back as she gets control. "I'll get the doctor," I say, but she grips my arm.

"No, it's fine. It's just from the air conditioner. I had them fix it."

"Are you sure?" I ask.

"Yes, it's fine. See? I'm fine."

She crosses her arms across her chest and waits for me to relax. I hate that I fuss over her so much, but I can't help it. I feel like my vigilance is the only thing keeping her alive. I'm not going to quit now.

"Fine, but if you cough like that again . . ." She doesn't need to hear the rest to know what I mean.

"You're so not normal." She rolls her eyes while shaking her head. "So, you went to the cemetery?"

"I did." I pause, thinking about what led me there. "I had an interesting night and needed Mom."

"Interesting how?" The curiosity seeps through her words.

I sigh, lie back on the bed with her, and tell my sister about my night with Eli Walsh.

chapter ten

Eli

"There's no need to fight us on this, Eli. We feel this is a generous offer," Paula says.

If it were so generous, I wouldn't have had to fly here to make sure my agent wasn't letting the studio try to give it to me up the ass. I could be in Tampa, working on getting Heather to stop fighting me.

I don't know what the hell it is about her. She's frustrating as all hell, but I like the challenge.

I'm not some young musician anymore. I'm older, wiser, and I know there's something with Heather that I shouldn't walk away from. I want to know her. I need to see her and touch her, which has to mean something.

"I'm not signing that, and you know why."

It isn't an ego thing. It's a value thing. If they don't pay me what I'm worth, then there's no reason they'll fight for the show. I'm not stupid. If they get this new contract to pay me less, there's no incentive for them to keep pushing it.

I don't work on dead ends. That's my only motto in this industry. Since landing the job on *A Thin Blue Line*, I've done a few movies. They were small parts, but I felt passionate about them. While I love my character and the storyline, I'm not working for less than what they've paid me the last five years.

"The show is lucrative, but they want to bring on some new blood," Paula tries to explain. I can see how frustrated she is, but that isn't my damn problem. "They need to free up money somewhere, and you're by far the highest paid actor on the show."

"Don't care." I lean back in the chair and scratch the back of my head. "It's not my problem."

Paula crosses her arms and goes silent. This is the thing about my agent I love. She's a shark. She smells blood in the water and circles until it's the right time to make her move. I see her predatory gaze as she studies me. She's on my team, but I'm also the only way she makes money.

Agents are awesome when you're making them money. When you're not . . . you're chum. I'm not about to be her afternoon snack.

"You know I heard they want a new love interest for your character. I heard that Penelope Ashcroft is back in town and looking for work. Isn't she a friend of yours?"

There's nothing friendly between us. Paula is definitely throwing out the bait.

I don't take it, though. The last fucking person I want to think about is *her*. I go years without a mention of her name and now twice in a week? "Another thing I don't care about." Which is total bullshit, but if I let Paula think this is a scab to pick at, she won't hesitate.

"She's auditioning for a few shows." Paula picks at her nails, letting the silence stretch. I know this game, so I stay quiet right along with her. "I didn't think much of it until Michael mentioned the casting director has her file."

"Michael? As in my director, Michael?"

So much for keeping my cool.

She shrugs. "It was just in passing."

Nothing this woman says is in passing. I have no doubt that Michael, if he did mention it, said it to push me. He knew I'd be reluctant to sign. I was lucky twenty years ago, I had a mentor. He told me that our careers start dying the day we sign our deals, and that if we want to make it in this world, we need to make as much money as we can, as fast as we can. I'm not about to take shit pay with them because they threw out that bitch's name.

I stand, place my hands on the desk, and stare in her eyes. "I'm not signing that contract until you get me the money I want. The way I see it, they—and you—need me. I'm not some small part on that show, and if you don't get ink on that paper, you don't get a check from me. So, push them harder. If they want to even entertain Penelope on the show, I'm done."

"What did that girl do to you?" Paula asks as if I didn't just say more than the part about her.

"She's a gold-digging, lying, slut. When I needed her most, she broke my fucking heart. I won't allow that bitch anywhere near me, got it?"

There are non-negotiables in life—this is one.

Paula gets to her feet and I straighten. "I'll do what I can, Eli. But I hope you're prepared to walk away from the show that you love so much. I don't know that I can get them to go much higher."

"And Penelope?"

She grins. "I wouldn't worry about that part. I'll handle her. She's a non-issue."

"Good, and don't bring her up to me again."

⁂

"You got balls, man," Noah laughs before throwing back a beer. "I just signed the damn contract."

I've been here three days working with Paula on renegotiations, and this is the first time I've allowed myself to relax. Normally, New York is where I feel settled. I know this isn't my native home, but I love it. The lights, people, smells, and food make me want to stay forever. I think it's also New Yorkers' ability not to see famous people. I'm at a bar without a single worry that some vapid fan will come bug Noah and me. However, tonight I would much rather be on the beach or sitting in a beautiful woman's living room eating pizza.

"It's not balls, it's negotiating."

"How was Tampa?"

My mind shifts to Heather. It's funny how after a few days, she's what I'm associating with my hometown. Not Ma, Randy, or the hundreds of things that I love about Florida. No, it's the beautiful blonde who has taken up residence in my goddamn mind.

"It's definitely more interesting."

Noah may play my brother on the show, but I still don't want to share her with him. As soon as people find out about her, she'll be swamped by publicity, which will send my shot with her up in smoke. My world comes with a whole new set of rules, right now, I want to play by hers.

I think back to the night we were together. We were laughing, talking, and hanging out. I can't remember the last time I did that with a girl. Usually, it's expensive restaurants, clubbing, and the talk about how great we'd be together if I give the random girl a shot.

With Heather, it's nothing like that.

I'm not even sure she actually likes me.

"Yeah?" he asks with a knowing grin. "What's her name?"

I lift my hand, motioning to the bartender to head our way. I need to get off the topic so that I don't outright lie to my closest friend.

It's clear she knows who we are but does her best to mask it. Another point for New Yorkers.

"What can I get you guys?" The bartender gives a seductive smile. I take a second to look her over. She's hot, but all I can think is that her eyes aren't brown and her smile is wrong. When Heather smiles, my heart pauses.

"Two beers, please."

"Not a problem." Her blue eyes travel to my mouth before coming back to my gaze. I know the look. It's her come fuck me eyes. I've seen them a lot, but once again, my mind isn't there, so I turn away.

Noah chuckles, and I glance back at him. "Smooth."

"I'm here for business this trip. I don't have time for a woman," I try to explain. It sounds plausible. I'm here to kick my agent and the network's asses. I'm not here to fuck some bartender. I have a goal, a mission, and that doesn't include detours.

I'll stick with that line of bullshit.

Noah shakes his head in disbelief. "Because you've never been known to mix pleasure when dealing with business?"

I'm not quite the playboy everyone has made me out to be. Sure, I'm not known for being a long-term relationship guy, which I blame on the bitch, but my public persona and the guy Noah, Randy, Shaun, and Adam are friends with are not the same. I'm different on stage or behind the camera. I look the part they've created—a bad boy with women in every town. It could be true, but it's not. I don't know what it's like not to always be putting on a show, but the other night with her, I felt . . . normal.

"Not since, Jo—" I almost said her vile name. "Her. I learned my lesson on the importance of keeping a clear head."

Noah's head snaps back. "Who? Penelope?"

Penelope is the reason I started acting. She pushed me to take something that would keep me around more, plus, the band was getting old and had lost a lot of its popularity. I loved her and wanted to make her happy. My heart was hers, and I thought she loved me, turns out she doesn't love anything except herself.

"Yup."

Noah eyes me carefully and pulls a long draw from the bottle. Then he proceeds to pick at the label as we both sit quietly. "I've known you a long time, and I like to think we're friends."

"We are."

"I know you've got secrets, I don't push because I've got them, too, but whatever happened between you and Penelope Ashcroft was years ago. She's married now, she's moved on, and you're still reliving the shit she did."

That has to be the deepest few sentences we've ever shared. I'm a private guy, you have to be in this world, but Noah is perceptive. Penelope married another actor—one more successful than I am—and lives her perfect life with her perfect bullshit. I refuse to let myself get close to anyone because I can't afford to.

"I'm working on it," I tell him.

"Yeah?"

I need a girl who will be there for me.

Stick out the hard times because life is chock-full of them.

Actresses are as fake as the characters they play, I want a real woman.

I smile knowing exactly what woman I want. The blonde who has invaded my mind. The girl who has no problem slamming the door in my face, telling me to leave, pushing me away, and making me want to stay.

I drain the remainder of my beer and slap Noah on the back. "There's someone who I have in mind."

He shakes his head. "She must be special to make you even pause."

She's more than special. Heather is the complete contrast to every woman I've ever known. She's strong, sexy, determined, and I don't care that she has some preconceived idea of how this is going to go. Too bad her idea is completely different from mine. She's about to see how persistence will always win out.

chapter eleven

Heather

A WEEK PASSES, AND I'VE FINALLY STOPPED LOOKING OVER MY SHOULDER, WAITING FOR ELI to magically appear on my doorstep. It's clear that whatever infatuation he thought he felt for me has passed. I'm not surprised. Eli doesn't seem like the patient kind of guy anyway. Friends my ass.

It's fine. I don't need friends. I've done fine on my own for this long, sans the complication named Ellington Walsh.

After telling Stephanie how I felt about the deteriorating state of the house, she pushed me to do a few projects. There are so many, but I decided to focus on the main living area. I'm spackling nail holes, painting the kitchen cabinets and the living room, and updating the light fixtures. Nicole said she had a few pieces of furniture from a staging she wanted to get rid of and was happy to donate them. Luckily, my best friends agreed to come help and bring their jackass husbands.

I may hate Scott and Peter, but they're good with tools, so I'll play nice for an afternoon.

I hear the doorbell, and I rush over, excited to see my girls.

"Hey!" I smile and we do a big group hug.

"Morning, Heather," Peter says and gives the customary kiss on the cheek.

"Thank you for doing this," I say to all of them. "I appreciate it."

Scott grunts and pushes through. "Let's get this going, I have a game to watch."

This is why I hate him. Peter is at least nice to us on the surface, but Kristin's husband is a prick all the time.

"Don't mind him, he's crabby because the Gators lost," Kristin says, gesturing in the direction where her husband just sulked off.

I touch her arm and shake my head. "It's fine. I appreciate any extra hands, and I'm good at ignoring him."

Nicole makes her way to us with her two guys on her arm. "I brought extra help!" I hope they're contractors she works with, but with her, we never know. "This is Jake and Declan, they worked with me on my last redesign and graciously offered to donate their time."

There's no way they willingly offered, they were incentivized, I'm sure. However, I'm not going to look a gift horse in the mouth. The number of things I'd like to do to this house is neverending, it's my cash flow that has a limit.

"Great!" I smile.

"We have a few of the pieces I was telling you about in the truck. I think the new tables will help, and I found a rug."

"You're the best," I say as I kiss her cheek. "Thank you."

"You're welcome. You should've told me earlier, I would've given you anything you wanted." She walks into the living room and pushes the guys aside. "Hold please. I need a minute to absorb the aura of a God," Nicole says as she flops on the couch and starts to squirm.

"Nicole!" I yell and grab her arm.

"Whatever! I told you this was happening."

She's unhinged.

"What the hell is wrong with you? Why are you rubbing yourself all over Heather's couch?" Danielle asks.

Nicole rolls her eyes and laughs. "Umm, Eli Walsh's ass was here, and I can now say I touched it."

Danielle and Kristin's heads twist to me, and their eyes widen. "What?" Danni practically screams.

Fuck. I haven't told them anything. I'm going to kill Nicole. My friends are great, but I wanted to keep this quiet as long as possible. Now there's no way I can explain away him being in my damn house. Not without making up some crazy bullshit, which they wouldn't believe anyway because I suck at lying.

"It's a really long story," I start to explain and glare at Nicole. "One that I promise I'll tell you about, but not now."

Kristin steps closer, and her voice drops. "Are you okay? Why the hell would he be in your house? What's wrong? What happened? Did you sleep with him?"

Her questions go so fast I couldn't answer them if I wanted to. "I'm great. I promise. It was a crazy night after the concert and then Eli returned something I dropped."

I guess it wasn't that long of a story after all.

"There's something you're not telling us," Danni says as she tilts her head. "Because how would he know where you live?"

My eyes move to Nicole for saving. She owes me that much.

"So, how about that work we're all here for?" Nicole says loudly. "I have two men who promised me a very fun night as payment for working here. Let's get to it. I'm all for my threesome that's happening."

That's one way to change the topic.

Danielle groans and shivers. "Yuck."

"You only say that because you're jealous."

"Danielle!" Peter calls from the kitchen. "I need your help."

Thank God for the interruption, because I don't know that I could've kept this conversation going without having to spill everything.

We spend the next few hours working on various projects. The cabinets are painted thanks to Danielle and Kristin. Apparently, there was some water damage on one of the walls, so Nicole's two helpers ripped it out, replaced it with new drywall, and helped repaint the living room. It's amazing how much all of us accomplished, and the house feels completely different.

I didn't have any motivation to spend time fixing anything until I saw Eli sitting in my space.

Everyone heads out with promises to call, and the looks that I got from Danni and Kristin say we'll be doing a lot more than talking about the weather.

I walk out onto the porch with my iced tea and sit in the swing that my dad hung the week before he was killed. I always feel a sense of calm when I rock here, as if the wind that blows is his spirit here with me. My dad was a quiet man, but he was full of so much wisdom. He loved my mother more than anything in this world. As hard as it is to admit, if my mother had been alone in that car, my father would've found a way to follow her in death. He would never have been able to survive in a world without her. It's the kind of love I want in my life.

It's the kind I thought I found with Matt. Boy was I wrong.

I lean my head back and close my eyes, hoping to feel that calm again.

Instead, I hear someone clear their throat.

My eyes open, and I come face to face with the man I didn't think I'd see again.

"Eli," I say, almost dropping the glass.

"Hey," he says as he climbs the stairs. "I'm glad you're home."

"What are you doing here?"

"I told you I'd see you again," Eli explains as if it makes total sense.

This is crazy. I thought we were done with him showing up. He's been in the wind, and I had no way to get in touch with him, not that I would have called anyway. I've already decided this will never happen, so I don't know why my heart is racing at the sight of him.

It makes no sense that the tight blue jeans and gray T-shirt that cling to his muscles have my mouth watering.

I'm completely unaffected by him in general. Yup. Totally. It's because I'm tired that I'm reacting at all.

I shake off the thoughts of how much more I'd like to see of him and take a drink. "You did, but that was . . ." I pretend to have to think about it. "Like, ten days ago?" It was eight, but I'm not going to tell him I'm counting.

He grins and takes a seat next to me. "About that."

I shift over a little, hoping some distance between us will help my racing pulse. "Were you out and about and then figured you'd stop by?"

I did not just say that, did I? Oh, God, I did.

"Nope." He chuckles. "I just got back from New York. My agent needed me to finalize some things for our next season."

"Oh." I take another drink as he moves a little closer. My heart races as his side touches mine. "I've never been to New York," I admit. I haven't traveled anywhere since my parents died.

Eli starts to move the swing. "You'll have to come with me one time."

"Come with you?" I squeak.

"Yeah," Eli laughs.

"That's a little presumptuous."

"Why? We can go away together if you want."

"What makes you think I'm going to go on a trip with you? We barely know each other. Hell, we're not even friends."

"I thought we established we were definitely friends last time."

It's going to circle back to my groupie slut status with us. There's no true friendship, there's a one-night stand and pizza. It hardly constitutes as anything. Besides, I don't need any more friends. I have my girls, Brody, and Stephanie. I'm set.

"Look, you don't know me, and I definitely don't know you."

Eli throws his arm around the back of the swing, and his fingers find their way to my neck. "I think I know you pretty well."

"Really?" I challenge.

"I know you're beautiful, like pizza, have the world sitting on your shoulders, and try damn hard not to like me, which you are failing at."

I smile and play with the ring on my thumb. "Whatever. I don't think about you."

I'm a big, fat liar. I think about him all the time, and last night, he managed to star in my dreams—again. As much as I tell myself I'm glad he stopped showing up, I was sad. There's something about being around him that makes me crave more, which is the dumbest thing I could allow myself to want.

Eli's thumb grips my chin, and he forces me to look at him. "I'm serious. Since the minute I laid eyes on you, I think about you all the time."

"Eli," I say, hoping he'll stop. I don't want to think about this.

"Why do you think I called you on stage? Why do you think I wanted you to come to the meet and greet?"

"Because you wanted me to sleep with you!" I say and try to shift away from him.

He cups my face and holds my gaze hostage. "No, because for the first time in all the years I've been doing this, I've finally met someone who managed to knock me off kilter. I didn't understand it until I was in New York. I kept wanting to look at you. Then I couldn't get to you fast enough after the show. That has never happened."

I want to believe him, but it's hard for me to even fathom. "Please don't feed me lines."

"It's not a line. It's you. I can't explain it, but you're all I think about. The way you hide your face from me when you're unsure of yourself. How your smile makes my heart stop, and how even now, with speckles of paint on your face, you take my breath away. Don't you see? I tried to stay away, but I keep finding myself back here."

My chest tightens as I wonder what alternate universe I'm living in. How does one of the sexiest men alive think that I'm in any way special? I'm average on a good day. He's extraordinary on a bad day. This is crazy.

"You can't mean that."

"I mean every single word. I've never chased a girl like this. I've never showed up at her house—repeatedly. I haven't felt like this in a long time."

No one has ever said anything like that to me, and suddenly, every reason to make him leave vanishes. I can't think of anything to say in protest. Plus, I've always believed that actions speak louder than words, and he's here. Even though I've done nothing to further his advances, he keeps coming back.

I shift a little, trying to break the physical touch because I'd be lying if I said I didn't feel something. When he touches me, I tend not to think straight. Eli makes me forget just how broken I am. I don't need to forget.

"Now," he prompts as he drops his hand. "What do you want to know about me? I don't want you to have that excuse anymore."

"Okay," I say with apprehension. "When did you get back?"

"I landed an hour ago, and I needed to see you."

"You landed and came straight here?" I shake my head in complete disbelief. "You can't possibly feel these things for me. You have no idea the mess my life is in, and I don't have time for games."

He retracts his arm from behind me and squeezes the back of his neck, "I'm not playing a game. We're not kids, Heather. We're both too old for that shit. If you don't want me here, I'll go." He moves to stand, and I panic.

"No!" I yell and then clasp my hand over my mouth. Why did I say that? Ugh. I'm giving off mixed signals everywhere.

Eli settles back down next to me, and the green in his eyes darkens. "No?"

"I don't know why I said that. I know I'm being complicated and stupid, but you have to understand my anxiety."

A shiver runs up my spine and I gasp. He gets to his feet and steps in front of me. "I think you're scared because you know what I'm saying is true and you feel it, too."

"I don't." I put as much steel in my voice as I can. He's right, though. Because when he said that he'd leave, I knew he would, and I want him to stay. Eli is the first man to make me feel anything since Matt. He looks at me without any pity or sadness. He doesn't know what I struggle with, and I'm not broken to him.

He looks at me the way I used to look at myself, and I can't help but want that.

"Tell me you don't think of me at all," he commands. "Tell me that in the week I've been away that you haven't wanted me to come here. Make me believe I'm the only one who feels this, Heather. Tell me, and I'll walk away right now. You'll never see me again."

Eli's hand cups my cheek as I get lost in his eyes. The desire swims on the surface, allowing me to forget all the reasons why I should push him away.

"I can't." The truth on my lips stuns me. "I can't say it because it would be a lie."

His lips move closer to mine, and my heart thumps erratically behind my ribs. He's going to kiss me. I *want* him to kiss me. There's no excuse of alcohol tonight. I won't be able to play this off as some drunken mistake. I'm sober, and I want him to make me feel again.

"I didn't think you could," he says before his lips press against mine.

Gone is the worry about my life, all that exists is us. Eli's mouth moves against mine, and his hands hold my cheeks. He keeps me firmly against him as our lips stay fused. It's everything that I remember and more. My fingers grip his shirt, holding him as much as he's holding me. It's reckless to be with a man that will never stay, but I don't have the energy to care.

Right now, he's here.

Right now, he's real.

Right now, he's kissing me.

And for right now, that's enough.

He slides his tongue against mine, pushing his way into my mouth. I've never been kissed like this. There's no way I'll ever kiss another man without comparing them to this one. Eli kisses me like he's been starved for it, which is completely absurd, but that's what he makes me feel.

Too soon, he pulls back and looks at me, his eyes blazing with heat as they dance along my features, his lips red from kissing me. If I pinch myself, would I wake from this dream?

"Tomorrow," he says in a strained voice. "I'm going to be here in the morning to pick you up."

"No," I say, shaking my head quickly.

There are so many things that I can't do with him. I can't get caught up in some tabloid scandal. I can't have my life get flipped upside down because of him. I can't date some celebrity who is only going to break my heart. More than anything, I can't seem to push him away.

"Do you have to work?" he asks.

"No, I mean I can't date you. I can't even think about whatever this is. I can't be hurt again, Eli. I wasn't kidding when I said I'm a mess."

Hurt flashes across his face before he masks it with a grin. "Who said anything about dating? I promise that no one will see us together. We'll talk about the mess you are and figure out how you're going to deal with me in your life."

"I'm not having sex with you again."

He laughs and kisses me. "Whatever you say. Wear sneakers and a bathing suit."

Before I can respond, Eli is halfway down the stairs. "Why are you fighting so hard to see me? I'm clearly pushing you away. What is making you keep coming back?" I ask.

He stops, rushes back up the stairs, and pulls me close. "Because you're not like every other girl. You're the first person I've met in what feels like forever who doesn't seem to want something from me." His hand pushes the hair back off my face. "You look at me like I'm just a guy, not a meal ticket. You're gorgeous, stubborn, and there's something more that I can't explain. I'm not saying this will work, but I'm willing to take a chance and see what this is, are you?"

Every word he said was exactly the right one. I'm not looking for anything from him. Maybe this won't work, but I don't know that I'm strong enough to say no.

"No strings?" I ask.

"No strings. Just a chance."

I'm not a fly by the seat of my pants kind of girl—I'm a planner. I like my life to have order because there's too much chaos everywhere else. I can't make my sister's disease fit into a box, but I can make my schedule solid. It's my only way of being able to control my life when everything else is spiraling. There was no way to plan for my parents to die when I was twenty-one, but I can make sure that each Thursday I'm at the youth center to teach self-defense. Eli is a variable, though. He won't fit into a box, so I won't let him become a fixture in my life.

I know without a doubt, he'll be the extra card that sends my house tumbling down.

chapter twelve

Heather

The clock reads four in the morning, and I groan. There's no way I'm going to get back to sleep if my mind won't stop running through all the possibilities of what Eli has planned. I didn't think to even ask him what time he's coming to get me today. For all I know, it isn't until late morning, which is going to leave me keyed up all day.

I decide to be ready for whatever will happen. I won't be caught off guard again and look like ass.

No, today I'm going to look as hot as possible. So, I climb out of bed and start a pot of coffee.

Two hours later, I'm showered and wearing my deep purple bikini, white off-the-shoulder top, and black lace shorts. I wanted to look like I didn't spend an hour trying to select my clothes. I've curled my blonde hair in loose curls, and I actually put makeup on. Nicole would be proud.

I grab my phone and dial her number. It's only six, but I don't care. She's the one who convinced me that I needed to let loose, so she can deal with my neurotic ass.

"Hello?" her voice is hoarse and sleepy.

"Wake up!" I scream.

"What's wrong?" she asks sounding more alert. "Are you okay?"

"I have a date with Eli! That's what's wrong!"

She groans, and I hear some rustling in the background. "For real? You call me at the freaking ass crack of dawn for this?"

"Well." I huff. "It was your genius idea I sleep with him, and now he keeps showing up, kissing me, and forcing me on random dates."

Nicole snorts. "Yeah, forcing you. I can imagine how hard it is to say yes to one of *People*'s Sexiest Men Alive. The torture."

Maybe "force" is the wrong word, but this outing wasn't my idea. I have no idea what we're even doing, except I need a bathing suit, which probably means my eyeliner was a stupid idea. I'm so not equipped for this. I'm much better when I'm in control.

Like at work.

"Not the point. And that was three years ago. Look, you need to come calm me down. I'm going to end up on the floor from a panic attack."

"I thought you didn't like him," she tosses back at me.

"I don't!"

I totally do.

I like everything about him so far. The only thing that keeps me hung up is the whole famous and wealthy thing. He lives on Harbour Island, and I don't even have enough money to dream of stepping foot there. Hell, the only time I've ever been there was on a call.

Panic starts to take hold, and my breathing becomes labored.

"Heather?"

"I . . ." I gasp. "Can't."

"Okay." Nicole's voice turns soft and controlled. "Breathe. Just relax. Think about the fact that he's chasing you. You're gorgeous, funny, and own a gun. You can shoot him in the dick if he upsets you."

Slowly, I gain control as I laugh at the last part. "What am I thinking?"

"You're thinking about yourself, babe. It's a good thing. You deserve to be happy and have some damn fun. Why are you overthinking this?"

My biggest worry is that I'll get swept up in this pretend life, and when reality comes crashing around me, I'll be broken.

Life isn't full of rainbows and sunshine. It's cloudy days and tornados that twist everything I love away.

"What happens when he finds out about my insane life and leaves?"

"What if he stands by you?"

It's my turn to laugh. "Yeah, what man doesn't love a woman who has no time for him?"

"Then you *make* time! You worry about shit that probably won't even be an issue. If he doesn't understand your life, then he doesn't belong in it."

"You're right."

Nicole sighs. "I know I am. Look, you're my best friend, and I love you when you don't call me before the fucking sun is up."

"Sorry." I lie back on the couch, hating my weakness. Self-doubt is a bitch.

"Don't be sorry, be Heather. Be the girl who is fearless, full of confidence, and knows what an amazing woman she is. Because that's who you are. You're not what Matt turned you into."

Another reason to hate him. When he left me, I started to wonder if I was worth anything. I know in some part of my rational brain that he's the idiot, but I couldn't help but doubt myself. I gave him my heart, and he tossed it away as if it meant nothing.

All because my sister needed me more than he did.

I've spent a long time trying to convince myself that he left because of his own issues, but the truth is, I wonder what's wrong with me.

"I wish I knew where that girl went," I admit.

"You'll find her. What time does he get there?"

"I have no idea. I forgot to ask."

Nicole bursts out laughing. "Well, this should be a fun day."

After Nicole gives me more of a pep talk, I get my emotions under control, and they are sent right back into meltdown mode when Eli knocks.

I take three deep breaths before opening the door.

Eli stands there in his mirrored aviators, white T-shirt, and dark blue board shorts. His dark hair is pushed to the side, and if I thought he was hot before, today he's on fire. In front of me is the man who every woman drools over. He drips with sex appeal.

And today, he's my date.

"Morning." I let his husky voice wash over me and try not to let it fry my nerves.

"Good morning."

"I'm glad to see you're awake."

I smile. "You never told me a time, but I get up early even on my days off."

It isn't a total lie, but I never would be awake at four in the morning.

Eli pulls his shades down and grins. "You ready?"

That's a loaded question. I'm ready in terms of being dressed, but ready to go on a date with him? No, not even a little bit. I'm not ready for any of this. I'm terrified of what today could lead to.

However, I'm more afraid of walking away and regretting this moment.

Instead of telling him any of that, I nod. "I am."

"Good."

"Can you tell me where we're going?" This is the only part of this whole thing that has me mystified.

"Nope," Eli says, his eyes dancing with mischief.

"Okay," I draw out the last syllable. "What do I need to bring?"

"Nothing."

This is so not how I function, but I've decided to go with him today, so I need to let it go. I grab my purse, leaving my gun in the safe, and try not to get lost in his smile.

He holds his hand out, and I take it, knowing that today, I'm going to let him lead.

The black Bentley is nowhere to be seen. Today, he walks me to a gray Audi Q5 sitting in front of the house. He opens the door, and I climb in. When he sits beside me, I can't help but look at him again.

His scruff is growing in, giving him a darker look than the first time we met. I like this so much more.

Eli's head turns, and I quickly look away. When my eyes shift back again, it's clear he caught me.

"So, how many cars do you have?" I ask after the silence between us has stretched to almost uncomfortable.

"A few."

"A few like three or a few like thirty?"

Eli smiles, focusing on the road. "Somewhere in the middle of that."

I shouldn't be surprised, his net worth is on Wikipedia, but still. It's hard to comprehend that he makes my yearly salary in a week.

Needing to shift topics again, I go with a safer question. "What was in New York?"

"I had to sign a new contract. *A Thin Blue Line* was renewed for another season."

"Oh, that's awesome!" I heard rumblings on a few of the news outlets that the show might get dropped. "I really hope you're finally able to get a new partner. I don't know why they keep pushing that story line. Tina is not a good match for Jimmy. Brody and I have been riding together for almost seven years, and I would punch myself in the face before I ever kissed him. The show needs to give Jimmy a woman who he saved or something. That would be an interesting plot. Also, your brother on the show *has* to stop sleeping with that model. Twitter went nuts when he went back to her. She's a bitch."

Eli's gaze shifts to mine, and he chuckles. "I thought you didn't watch the show."

Crap. I did say that. I chew on my thumb and shrug. "I guess I've seen a few seasons." I say the last word under my breath, hoping he didn't catch it.

"Seasons?"

No such luck.

"Whatever. It's just to see how bad you butcher my job."

Eli shakes his head and grabs my hand. His fingers thread with mine and then he gently squeezes. "Sounds like you're a little more invested than that."

"Fine," I admit. "I watch it religiously."

He brings my hand to his lips and kisses my knuckles. "I knew you liked me."

I laugh and hit his chest with our entwined hands. "You're crazy. I like your show, but seriously, tell the writers they need to clear that up."

"So, you and your partner have never . . ."

"Eww!" I twist in my seat. "Never. He's married first of all, and I was married to our lieutenant so that was never going to happen on Matt's watch, but . . ."

"You were married to your boss?" he questions.

I guess I haven't really been very forthcoming with information. Not that we've had a ton of time to get into much. I mentioned my ex-husband but didn't go into any great detail. "Yes, I was married, but we've been divorced for almost five years. It was amicable to a point, I guess. Not sure whenever a marriage dissolves that it's ever on good terms, but Matt and I see each other every day, so we're civil."

"You still see him every day?"

"He's still my boss. Unfortunately, it means that I have the pleasure of dealing with him almost daily. I hoped they would transfer me or him, but Matt has a lot of pull in the department."

Eli tenses, but he does a good job at hiding any further reaction. He has to know that I come with a past, just as he does. Might as well get some of this out in the open.

Besides, I'd much rather know what kind of man he is before we get too deep in a relationship or whatever this is. Matt couldn't accept my relationship with Stephanie, and she's a non-negotiable. If Eli can handle the Matt thing, I'll brave telling him about my sister.

"I can't imagine being around my ex. Especially with access to a lethal weapon."

I laugh. "In the beginning, it was tempting, but Matt is a selfish prick. He isn't worth the jail time."

His thumb rubs back and forth, leaving my skin tingling in its wake. Sure enough, we pull up to the gate on Harbour Island. Here's the contrast of my life to his. Eli scans the card that allows us access.

My anxiety starts to climb as the reasons why I should've said no start to swim back into my mind. I'm in his second of whatever number of vehicles, going through the metal gates to houses I couldn't afford to rent a bathroom in, and I'm completely out of my element.

I was crazy to think he and I were ever a possibility. I don't fit in this world.

As we drive down another road, the houses get grander, and my despair deepens.

The car stops, and he turns toward me. "You okay?"

"Yes. No. I'm not really sure," I finally settle on.

He releases my hand and turns to face me fully. "Care to explain?" His voice is light, but the concern is clear in his eyes.

My heart lurches when I see the house we're parked in front of. I point to the incredibly large mansion in front of us. "This. I live in a rundown house that could fit in your driveway. This is just one of the reasons I pushed you away. We're from different worlds, and this scares the shit out of me."

Eli sighs, exits the car, and walks around to my side.

Well, that wasn't what I expected. Is he going to tell me to get out of his car? Am I supposed to call a cab? Is he leaving me here?

My car door opens, and he grabs my hands, helping me out of the car. After releasing a heavy sigh, he speaks. "I didn't bring you here because I wanted to show you we come from different worlds. The truth is, I lived in the ghetto of Tampa, but I think you knew that already. Money doesn't define who we are, it's what's inside us that matters."

"I didn't mean it like that." I'm not sure if I could hate myself any more than I do in this moment. Eli has done everything right, and my insecurities are getting the better of me.

"I want us to spend the day together, talk, and it's private here. I'm just a guy, Heather. At the end of the day, no matter what you think I am, I'm a man."

"I'm truly sorry," I say immediately. "I didn't mean to freak." Our bodies are close, almost touching, and I pull one of my hands from his so I can cup his cheek. "You're more than just a guy to me. You're a man who reminds me that I'm a woman. You look at me as if I'm special, and that's difficult to accept. More than that, you're a guy that I spent my entire life dreaming of, but right now, you're real."

Eli's arm tightens around my back. "I want to be Ellington today. Not Eli Walsh the actor or FBD member. Can we do that? Can we just be . . . ourselves?"

It's a grand idea. To let go of the bullshit around us and just be two people getting to know one another. I want nothing more than to see who he really is. "Just the two of us?" I ask.

"No one else will be here today," Eli says and brushes his lips against mine.

"Then it's nice to meet you, Ellington."

His name falls from my lips, and I sigh.

"You, too, Heather."

I push forward, pressing a sweet kiss on his mouth. His smile is warm against my lips, and he releases his hold on me. Eli takes my hand as we walk toward the house.

He opens the door, and my jaw drops. This is beyond words. As we step inside, I look around, trying to take it all in. The foyer hosts two huge staircases that lead to opposite ends of a balcony. There are two rooms off to each side at the bottom, one of which is a library. I'm not talking about a few books on a shelf, either. The entire wall looks lined. We walk deeper, and the other room opens to what looks like a more formal living room.

"Wow," I say with awe.

"I bought this house a few years ago. I like to visit my mother here in Tampa, and Randy lives in Sanibel Island, so this is a good medium."

"There's nothing medium here, Eli. This is super-sized." My voice cracks a little as he continues to lead me down the hall.

I try to stop counting rooms because it's beyond what I thought it was from the outside. It's at least three times the size I assumed. The house seems to get deeper and deeper, and when we reach the back area, there are huge windows that overlook the water.

"Do you need anything before we go?" he asks.

"Go?"

"Yeah." He laughs and points outside. "That's my boat. We're going to spend the day on the water."

My eyes turn to his, and I plaster a smile on my face. I love the water. Some of my favorite memories of my dad are from when he would take me boating when I was a kid. His boat wasn't anything like the huge one currently docked to the pier, though.

Eli moves closer, and he pushes my hair back. "Is that okay?"

I nod. "It's perfect."

He shows me to the bathroom, where I put more sunscreen on, check my makeup, and say a few silent prayers that I don't get sea sick. It's been a long time since I've been on open water, and that would be my luck.

We get on the boat, which is equipped with two damn bedrooms, a kitchen area, bathroom, and a sitting area, therefore it's a house with a hull. He shows me around, and then eases the vessel out onto the water.

I watch him command the boat and fight back a sigh. Everything he does is sexy. The way his muscles flex when he turns the wheel. How his brow furrows when he's concentrating on steering. I don't want to do anything but watch him, so that's what I do. My focus is so singular, that I don't notice when we're out of the channel.

"Want to drive?" Eli offers, dragging me out of my staring.

"I've never driven a boat before."

"I'll help you." He gives an encouraging smile and steps back so I have room to stand in front of him.

Too excited to say no, I move toward him and slip into the space. My hands grip the wheel, and I glance at him over my shoulder.

"Good, hold it steady and move the wheel a little if you want to go in a different direction." Eli stands with his chest against my back, and I lean into him. "You're doing great," he says in my ear.

"I don't really know what I'm doing," I admit.

"Let's go right. There's a sweet spot for fishing over that way."

Eli's hands come around and settle atop of mine. He isn't steering, just holding on. I could close my eyes and get lost right now. Our bodies are so close, and his strong arms make me feel safe.

We stay like this for a while, not actually driving so much as drifting along together. Eli slows the boat and pulls me onto his lap as he holds the wheel. "It's like we're completely alone out here," I muse as I stare out into the ocean.

He kisses my shoulder. "We are."

I look back at him with a smile. "Let me get this straight, you're a sailor, singer, actor, and fisherman?"

"I'm a man of many talents."

My laughter is free and unabashed. "You're something all right."

"Come on, let's see if you can catch our lunch."

Eli and I move to the bow of the boat, where he has two fishing poles waiting for us. After we thread our lines and bait our hooks, we cast out into the water and stick the poles in the holders to wait. I settle back onto one of the benches and look out over the water. Deep blues and greens reflect the sunlight sending little bursts of light around. The cloud cover is light today, but they're big and fluffy. I turn to point out a cloud that looks like a dinosaur, but I can't speak. Eli stands there shirtless and my mouth waters.

Dear. God.

His body is exactly like I remember from our night together. Only now, I'm not in the dark. The sun shines on his perfect skin, giving me the most breathtaking view possible. I watch him move around the boat, securing a few things on the deck as I admire his chest. The tattoos etched on his arms, shoulder, and hip only make him look hotter. I swear that tattoos have never been sexier. My hands itch to trace the ink on his skin, the firmness of his muscles, feel his heat, and get lost in his touch.

"Come sit with me." Eli holds his hand out, and I force myself to drag my eyes away from his body to take it. He leads me to a couch under a retractable awning and takes a seat in the corner, pulling me down next to him. It's natural for me to rest my head on his chest, allowing the salty air and clean breeze to fill my nose.

"I'm glad you came." His deep voice seems to vibrate through me.

"Me, too."

"Tell me something," he requests.

"What do you want to know?"

"Something true. I don't get a lot of truth from people."

A wash of sadness comes over me from his words. I can't imagine what it's like to be him. Constantly battling the feeling of people trying to get a piece of him in some way. He probably doesn't get a lot of people being honest or just wanting to know him. I hate that for him. It must be lonely.

I sit up so I can look him in the eyes. "I won't lie to you. You can ask me anything."

He smiles and pushes himself closer to me. "Why do you keep saying you're a mess?"

I sigh and look away. "There are a lot of things going on in my life."

"Your ex?"

I laugh humorlessly. "I wish it were just that."

"Heather," Eli says my name with softness. "I want to know you. Really know you. I'm sure you know what the tabloids say about me, but that isn't who I am."

"Then who are you?" I would much rather hear more about him than air out my own life.

"I'm a brother, uncle, and son. My father died a few years after walking out on my mom. We were poor as hell, and I've done everything possible to make sure I never live like that again. Most days, I love acting more than singing, but I can't imagine not having Four Blocks Down in my life. I'm old as hell, tired of being so damn angry at things I can't control, and this is the first time I've ever had to chase a girl this fucking hard. Especially after giving her the goods."

I let out a soft laugh and lightly slap his leg. "I wasn't kidding when I said I don't do stuff like that. I don't date. I don't have time for men. I kind of gave up the idea of being with anyone after my ex left."

"Me, too," he says earnestly. "We all have our things, Heather."

I remember a few years back there was talk of Eli getting married, but you can't believe a thing you read. My curiosity spikes a little, and I have to swat away my inner cop who wants to interrogate him about it. "You had someone once, right?"

Eli shifts, bringing my attention fully back to him. "I don't talk about it much. She was playing me, though. Penelope was really good at it. I found out she was screwing my former agent when I came home early from a trip to surprise her. We were dealing with some personal stuff, and instead of coming to me, she went to another man. She fucked me up pretty good."

"I'm so sorry. That's awful." I squeeze his hand in solidarity.

He releases a deep breath through his nose. "I won't lie. I had no intention of ever having more with a woman, which is probably where all the rumors about my being a player come from. I don't fuck around and play games, but I'm not known for having relationships. It's been easier to keep my distance, and I'm always honest with the girls I've been involved with."

I've heard all of that, which is what leads me to wonder what we're doing here. Not that I need the promise of something magical, but I don't need a guy who has a girl in another city, either.

My heart races as I prepare to ask my next question. "Then what do you want with me?"

His eyes are open, allowing me to see all his emotions. "More. I want more."

"And what if you realize I'm not worth more?"

He shakes his head. "What if you're worth it all?"

"You've spent a few hours with me, Eli. You can't—"

"I'm giving you my truth," he interjects softly. "All I'm asking for is a little of yours."

The fear of falling for him is real. My mother and father left me, my husband left me, my sister will leave, and the last thing I want is to love someone else who will do the same. Eli doesn't know anything about me at this point. Nothing past the superficial things. If I give him my truth, I'll be giving him a part of me.

Fuck it. Not like he can go anywhere while we are still in the middle of the ocean. Plus, if I'm going to do this, if he wants to try, he should know.

"My sister is dying. She's twenty-six and has Huntington's disease, it's a rare degenerative disease."

His eyes widen as he sucks in a breath. "I don't even know what to say. Is there anything that can be done?"

I shake my head. "No, it's terminal. Stephanie's disease has become my whole life. *She's* my whole life."

Eli takes my hand in his. "I'm so sorry. I can't imagine how hard it is for you."

"Ha!" I laugh sardonically. "It's excruciating. She was diagnosed at nineteen and since then, we've been on a downhill slope. My husband left me because Stephanie needed full-time care. I guess I wasn't enough of a wife to him because I was too busy taking care of my dying sister."

"That's why he left?" Eli asks with disgust dripping from his words.

I look in his emerald eyes and sigh. "He couldn't handle it."

"He sounds like a fucking prick."

That's a nice way to put it.

"I'm telling you this now because whatever this is that we're doing here can't interfere with what I have to do for my sister."

Eli's hand tightens, and his head jerks back. "Interfere?"

"Yes, I won't be able to follow you around to New York, and I can't afford to spend time away from her. I can't get caught up in this . . . thing with you and miss spending what little time I have with Stephanie. It's what scares me. Well, that and the fact that you're . . . you, and I'm not in your universe. I can't allow myself to have regrets when it comes to my sister."

"I would never want you to. I'm not asking you to give anything up. And as for your ex, he's a piece of shit for making you think you should choose between your sister and a man. That's ridiculous. I have a brother, and if it were him, I'd be at his side."

A part of my bruised heart heals a little. I look in his eyes and wait for some kind of change in his thoughts. Anything to tell me that he's lying, but it never comes. "You can't be this perfect, Eli."

He laughs. "I'm far from perfect, baby."

"You're kind, funny, and unbelievably hot."

"Don't forget a God in the bedroom."

I shake my head. "Egotistical."

"Keep going with all my stellar qualities," he nudges.

Instead, I lean forward and touch my lips to his. "Don't make me think you're great and then break my heart."

Eli's fingers thread in my hair. "Don't make me keep fighting so hard to win you."

My defenses fall to the floor as he pulls my head closer. "What are you doing to me?"

He smiles. "I'm making you feel how you make me feel—helpless."

chapter thirteen

Eli

Kissing Heather is like nothing I've ever felt before. I've kissed a lot of girls, but she makes me lose track of the world around us. It's as if time is suspended when she's with me. The first night we slept together, I thought it was the endorphins from entertaining.

I figured that once I'd gotten her out of my system I would be able to move on.

Now, it's worse.

She's opening herself to me, showing me who she is and it's fucking beautiful. Everything about her brings me to my goddamn knees. How anyone can walk past her and not stop, blows my mind. The idea of her dickless husband leaving her is asinine. Who would walk away from someone as gorgeous as she is? It's more than just her beauty, though. She's smart, funny, strong—sometimes a little too strong, and she gives me a sense of hope that I haven't felt in a long time.

"God, you kiss good," Heather breathes, and then her lips are back on mine.

I hold her golden locks in my hands and plunge my tongue deeper. I taste the mint from the gum she was chewing. Heather's soft hands slide up my chest to cup my jaw, and I lean back, taking her with me. I'm practically lying flat so I can enjoy her weight as it settles on top of me.

Our tongues push against each other, giving and taking in a constant battle for control. I don't let up. I fight her for dominance. I struggle for her to let loose and give it over to me. The truth is, the harder she resists, the more turned on I get.

I tighten my grip in her hair, loving the moan she makes in my mouth. Her noises spur me further, wanting her so bad I think my dick is going to explode from fucking kissing. Because that wouldn't be embarrassing . . . I can see it now: "Pop Star Blows His Load While Making Out" on page seven. Thankfully, I'm able to keep myself in control because the only place I'm blowing my load is inside her. I might actually die if that doesn't happen soon.

My lips glide across the skin of her neck and down to her shoulders. "You're so beautiful," I rumble against her skin. "Every inch of you is perfect. I can close my eyes and see your body as if it's that night all over again."

She lets out a low moan as my hand cups her perfect breast. I let the weight of her fill my hand, and I roll it around, just brushing the nipple.

I'm a boob guy, always have been. Tits are like gifts from God. There's a reason men don't have them—if we did, we'd play with them all day. I would take a shit and cop a feel. I'd be showering and just rub them. I don't care if that sounds crazy, it's true.

"Tell me this is real," she demands.

"It's real," I say as I untie the knot of her bikini. I hold it there because I want her to lead this. If she wants to have sex and run away again, she's going to be swimming because there's nowhere to go.

She moves her hand to mine and pulls the strings down, giving me the view I am desperate for.

My mouth waters as I stare at her tits. I'm dying to taste her again. I shift our bodies so she's straddling my lap, and push my dick against the warmth of her pussy, wanting nothing more than to bury myself in her heat. My mouth latches onto her nipple, lavishing it as she holds my head where she wants it. The feel of her hands, controlling me has me sucking her harder.

Her head falls back, her long hair brushing the tops of my thighs as she grinds down hard. "I want you," she confesses.

I want her more than my next breath. I just don't want to scare her away. Yesterday was a turning point for us in some way. She didn't tell me to leave or push me away hard. It was almost as if she was finally agreeing to whatever this is.

The last thing I need is to go two steps back. However, I'm not going to tell her no, either. Not when my dick is so hard it could cut glass.

"Look at me, baby."

Her eyes meet mine, and I see the desire burning in her gaze. More than that, I see worry.

The way she looks at me stops my heart, and I feel like a prick. I may kick myself in the ass for this, but there's no way I can do this to her. If my whole goal is to get her to stop trying to get rid of me, I have to earn it. She has to trust me enough that, when I look in her eyes, the only thing I see is want and need. Not doubt.

The words feel foreign, but they're exactly what I know I need to say. This isn't a line of bullshit I'm spoon feeding her, it's the truth. "I want you. I want you so much that it's going to fucking kill me to say this, but I don't want to just fuck you."

"What?" Her eyes widen, and she quickly covers her chest.

I'm definitely kicking my own ass later.

"I feel like we're making progress, and I promised you we wouldn't have sex. I said we were going on a date."

Heather eyes me curiously, probably wanting to pull my man card and toss it overboard. Hell, I want to pull it myself, but I see something else.

Maybe hesitation.

Maybe a little doubt.

I also see a hint of respect.

For the first time in a long time, I revel in that last one.

She unhooks her leg and scoots off me so she's sitting next to me again. I watch as she re-ties her bikini, which makes me want to cry a little, and wait for her to say something. When she finally looks over, she smiles. "Thank you."

"Don't thank me yet, I'm seriously regretting it." I smile. I am, but I go for a more joking tone.

Heather giggles nervously, shifting again so her legs are under her. "I don't think you know what you just did truly means to me, Ellington." My cock strains against my board shorts when she says my full name in her soft voice. "I would've . . ." She stares off at the horizon before looking back. "I wouldn't have stopped you, and I probably would've hated myself for being so weak when it comes to you."

"I'm not sure it's you who's weak."

That's the truth, right there. I'm the fool who is chasing around a girl. Heather wasn't the one who showed up at my house, repeatedly, forced me to go on a date with her, or spent a week trying to negotiate a deal, only to take less money so she could get the fuck home to Tampa. I can lie and say it wasn't because I wanted to see her, but I won't. It felt like there was a magnet pulling me back to where she was. Heather may not see it, but I'm clearly fucked here.

"I keep waiting to wake up from this dream. That a guy like you could even look twice at a girl like me. More than that, I want to be close to you, even when I shouldn't." Heather sighs and then gets to her feet. "Don't mistake my pushing you away to mean that I'm not weak to you."

I get to my feet and pull her into my arms. "I don't. I know you want this as much as I do. I know that even though you keep fighting me off, you're fighting yourself more. I heard what you said about your life, but I'm not running away."

Her hands rest on my chest, and she tilts her head back to look at me. "I hope you mean it, because I'm kind of liking the idea of you sticking around."

"Ahhh," I squeeze her tighter. "I knew I'd wear you down."

"I guess I have a thing for actors who were once upon a time in a kickass boy band."

"Once upon a time?"

She shrugs. I'll give her once upon a time. "I'll have you know I'm multi-platinum. I'm more than kick ass."

"If you say so." She smirks.

She's going to pay for this.

"That's it." I move quickly, bending to hoist her into my arms. Then I walk with her toward the edge of the boat. "Say you're sorry!"

"You wouldn't dare!" Heather yells.

"Wouldn't I?"

I wouldn't throw her in, but I would jump so we both went together.

"Eli!"

"Say it, Heather. Say, 'Eli is the best singer in the world and every artist should bow to his talent.'"

I'm laying it on thick, but I want to hear those words from her lips.

"You're insane!" She laughs, and I move her closer to the edge. "Eli! Stop! Please!"

"This could all be over if you just say the words," I admonish her playfully.

She clutches the waistband of my shorts and yells again. "Please, I can't swim!"

I quickly put her down and grip her shoulders. "I didn't know. I wouldn't have really done it."

She bursts out laughing, clutching her stomach. "Who the hell lives in Florida and can't swim? You're so gullible!"

I move forward, but she moves quickly to the side. We play cat and mouse for a few more minutes before I finally catch her. Then, when her lips touch mine, I realize the girl I can't seem to get out of my head, is cementing herself in my heart.

◦∽◦

"Hello," I smile to the woman at the front desk. "I'm visiting a few patients today, one is Stephanie Covey," I say hoping it's the same last name as Heather.

Her eyes bulge as her jaw falls slack. I stand there, waiting for her to recover before she sputters out her words. "Oh. Oh, wow. Umm, Eli, I mean, Mr. Walsh, of course." The front desk nurse types on the computer, trying to hide the blush on her cheeks with her hair.

"Take your time." She glances at me, and I give her the panty-dropping smile that I use for concerts and photo shoots.

She bites her lip and then lets out a nervous giggle. "Stephanie Covey, yes. She's in room 334."

There are some serious perks to being famous, one of which is people tend to forget certain things like patient confidentiality. It's probably why I'll always have private care if I ever need it.

"Thanks, doll." I place one of the flowers from Stephanie's bouquet on the counter in front of her and wink. I don't know anyone that actually winks in real life, but apparently, if you're famous, it's a sure-fire way to get women excited.

The nurse clutches the flower to her chest with wide eyes. It really does work every time.

After I dropped Heather off, I started forming a plan. I have a big event coming up, and I want to do something special for her. She's a giver. She sacrifices everything for the people she loves.

Her ex-husband is a fucking moron, but, I'm kind of glad for it because it allowed me a chance to meet her. One man's mistake is another man's fortune and Heather is the fucking pot of gold at the end of the rainbow.

I grab my phone and text her.

Me: *Thinking of me?*

Heather: *Oh my God! You did not save your number under the name God's Gift to Women!*

I had to program my fucking number in her phone after our boat date. She refused to enter it, claiming she liked the arrangement where I randomly show up.

Me: *Well, I am. However, you still haven't answered if you were thinking of me.*

Heather: *Nope not once actually. Who are you again?*

I laugh.

Me: *Liar. And you know exactly who this is, baby. My ears were itching or ringing . . . whatever it is when someone is thinking of you . . . I figured I should do something about it.*

Heather: *You should see an ENT about that. Sounds like a medical condition.*

Me: *You wound me.*

I love that she has no problem giving me shit. So many girls would be falling over themselves, but not her.

Heather: *Actually, I was thinking of you before. I had a call, and this girl was going crazy over how much she loved Four Blocks Down. She was good people.*

Me: *See, if you would've taken my number and I didn't have to trick you, you could've called me. I would've made her a very happy fan.*

Heather: *Good to know. I'll be sure to call you each time someone talks about the God that you are. *eye roll**

I can picture her saying it and almost hear the sarcasm in her voice. Could I like this girl anymore at this moment? Doubtful.

Me: I'll be picking you up on Thursday at seven in the morning.

Heather: You will, huh?

Me: I will. I have something I want to show you.

Heather: Well, I guess I can squeeze you in.

Me: I'm honored.

Heather: Seriously, though. It depends on if Stephanie is released, can we play it by ear?

I will never stand in her way with her sister, which is why I'm here. It's one thing to say the words and another to actually follow through with action. She should never doubt me, I'm hoping to prove this to her now.

Me: Of course, I'll be in touch.

Heather: Thanks, Eli. I really was thinking of you. (Don't let that go to your head.) *wink*

I have a shit-eating grin on my face as I push off from the wall I was leaning against and start walking. Nerves that I don't normally feel start to build as I approach Stephanie's door. What if she doesn't know that her sister and I are . . . whatever we are? Am I going to seriously piss off Heather?

Instead of getting ahead of myself, I say fuck it and do what I came here to do. I knock on the door and hope for the best.

"What?" a hostile voice calls from the bed. "I'm sleeping."

"Sorry," I say, and then she looks over and lets out a high-pitched scream.

"Holy shit!"

"Hi, Stephanie. Can I come in?" I ask.

"Oh. My. God!" A younger, brunette version of Heather yells. "You're Eli Walsh! The one who my sister slept with!" I guess that clears up whether she knows about me. "Shit!" Stephanie clasps her hand over her mouth in a very Heather-like gesture.

"I'm one and the same, unless she goes around sleeping with other guys named Eli Walsh?"

She shakes her head with her hand still covering her lips.

"I wanted to come by and meet you, I hope that's okay."

It's clear that Heather's sister is her number one, and I want her to know I get it. Unlike her piece of shit ex-husband.

She tucks her hair behind her ears and sits up a little. "Of course! I mean, yeah. I can't believe you're here . . . in my hospital room. And you know my name."

"Your sister talks about you a lot," I explain.

"She needs a life."

I ignore the comment because it isn't my place to say shit. I know how easy it is to immerse yourself in whatever is going on in life. "So, tell me, how are *you* feeling?"

"Umm." She hesitates and scrunches her face a little. "Me? I'm having a good day. I'm going home tomorrow."

"That's good. I know Heather thought you'd be done today."

Stephanie chews on her lip while looking out the window. "They're keeping me one more day because I had a rough night last night."

Shit. Maybe this won't work. "I'm sorry to hear that."

"It's fine. My medication was causing my heart rate to spike, but the last twelve hours have been steady. Please don't tell my sister that last part. If I say anything about having a bad day, it's a yearlong lecture on all the reasons I should call her when things like that happen. As if my life isn't a series of freaking medical issues, I guess she just wants to be on the phone all damn day." Stephanie says the words so fast it almost comes out like one giant sentence.

My lips turn up, and I stifle a laugh. There isn't a doubt in my mind that Heather would be okay with that. She has a big heart, and her protectiveness of Stephanie is clear. My brother is the same with me. Randy may come off as an asshole, but if I needed him, I know he will be there.

"Your secret's safe with me." I move toward the side of her bed and extend the flowers. "These are for you."

"I can't believe you brought me flowers. You must really like my sister."

"I do. I like her a lot."

I never understood the saying, "You know when you know." I always thought that was some line of bullshit an idiot came up with. Yet, the older I get, the more reality I see in it. I've always known in some part of my head that the girls I was spending time with weren't worth it. They weren't going to be the girl brought to meet my mother.

Maybe it's because I'm old.

Maybe it's because it's her.

No matter what the reason is, I just know.

Stephanie's smile is wide, and I can feel the happiness rolling off her. "She needs someone to take care of her. I know she doesn't act like it, but she does."

It's clear that these two have each other's best interests at heart. Here Stephanie is worried about her while Heather is always trying to help her.

"We all do, right?"

She nods. "As much as I'd love to pretend you're here because I'm so amazing and you needed to know more about me, tell me what really brought you here."

I lean in closer and grin. Heather has no idea what's in store for our date, but I'm hoping it shows her there are other sides to me. I do a lot that has nothing to do with music or Hollywood. I'd like to have her sister be there as well as a surprise.

I can't wait to see Heather's face when I pull this off. "How good are you at lying to your sister for a good cause?"

chapter fourteen

Heather

"What do you mean you didn't want me to stop by?" I ask Stephanie as I try to organize her room the way it was a week ago. She came back to Breezy Beaches yesterday and refused to let me do anything last night. She said she needed to be alone and practically threw me out the door. Today, I didn't care what she said, I came anyway even with her bitch-o-meter being at an eleven out of ten.

She sits on the bed, glaring at me. "You never fucking listen to me! I don't want you to come! I'm tired, I'm finally back home and I want to just . . ." She pauses and then groans.

Today is a bad day. She's struggling to string words together and is getting frustrated.

I wait and then the words burst out. "Settle in! I want to be in this hellhole alone."

"I am listening. I haven't really been with you a lot lately." I try to explain. "I love you, Steph."

She starts to cough and swats my hand away. "You were at the hospital every single day. I'm asking for a d-d-day to myself! Why is that so hard for y-you? Why can't you let me be alone?"

I sit on the edge of the bed and sigh. "I'm sorry. I'm trying here. I'm doing the best I can."

It breaks my heart when she's like this. I never know what will happen, and fighting with her literally kills me. If tomorrow never comes, I don't want this to be our last conversation. Whenever it goes down this path, I have to swallow my hurt and anger. I hide the pain and do what I can to try to turn this around. I know what regret feels like, and I never want that for us.

Stephanie goes quiet for a few minutes, touches my shoulder, and then releases a heavy breath. "I hate this f-f-fucking disease!" Tears fill her eyes, and I pull her in my arms. "You sh-shouldn't have to be around me. I'm mean!"

Rocking back and forth with her in my arms allows me to keep my own tears at bay. It isn't her fault that she's having a bad day. It's the way it goes. Her symptoms are worsening, and we both know it. The outbursts have become more frequent over the last few months, her speech is declining, and the medicine isn't doing as much for her tremors. Yesterday, the doctor told me frankly that this is the beginning of the decline.

"You're not mean, you're doing the best you can." I know this isn't her fault.

"I didn't want to come back here. I wanted to stay at the hospital for longer."

"Why?" I ask and take her hand in mine. "You hate the damn hospital."

"I miss Anthony. I liked seeing him every day. I liked knowing he'd stop by the room and talk to me like I wasn't this poor d-dying girl. He saw me as a girl, woman, whatever . . . the point is that he saw *me*, Heather. Not the tremors, locking joints, problems remembering . . ."

I hate that anyone sees her that way at all.

"Did you call him?" I ask.

Anthony has been good for her. He was in her room after his shift each day, bringing her comic books and flowers. The bouquet of varying shades of vibrant purple and pink roses with plush hydrangeas mixed in that he brought her was breathtaking. I tried not to make a big deal of it, but the fact that Anthony cared so much made my heart swell.

"No, I'm not going to make him watch me die." Stephanie is stubborn. She always has been, and I worry she'll push him away without a chance of any happiness. On the other hand, I can't imagine what knowing she is dying and having people she loves watch feels like to her.

What can I even say to that? She's allowed to make her choices, and I have to understand that. Even though I think she's wrong.

"I wish you'd tell him how you feel. He brought you flowers, and by the looks of it, he cares for you."

I understand that Stephanie has her own set of issues, far more than I can comprehend, but it doesn't mean she should just give up.

She snorts. "Okay, whatever. First, the flowers aren't from him, which I've said three times. I told you they just appeared in my room. Second, is that what you're doing with Eli? Are you telling him how much you want to spend time with him? Are you giving him even the slightest inclination of how much you actually like the guy? No? I didn't think so." Gone is the anger in her voice, all I hear now is challenge.

I guess it's like the saying about glass houses and throwing stones. But it's different for me. He's complicated, rich, famous, and doesn't live here. Why am I going to let myself get tangled in some crazy mess? I'm not.

Do I like him? Yup.

Do I wish I didn't? Yup.

Does he listen to anything I've said regarding what he can expect? Absolutely not. He wormed his way in, and I'm pretty sure he has no intention to leave.

"It's not the same. He's got too many question marks around him."

"You're allowed to love again. You love me and I'm a giant unknown."

Loving Stephanie was never a choice, it was absolute. Even with knowing the ending of our story, I wouldn't make different choices. With Eli, I'm not there yet. I don't have to let it get that far. Loving another gives them power, it can be beautiful, fulfilling, and as easy as breathing, but if I lose it again, it will destroy me.

I twist the fabric of my shirt in my hands, feeling the threads loosen and notice the similarities in my own life. Each time I think I'm together and secured, something starts to break the bond, and I tear.

"I won't let myself fall for him, Steph. I like him, I won't lie, but he's leaving soon. His life isn't in Tampa. I'm not moving. I'm not leaving you."

"It's going to be me who leaves you, Heather. I don't know when, and I don't know how, but we both know it's coming." A tear falls down her cheek and another follows suit.

"Don't say that." I beg.

"It's the truth, and you have to come to terms with it."

Tears spring in my eyes. I don't want to lose my sister. The thought of living in a world without her is intolerable. I've lost more than any person should, and life isn't done taking from me yet. Stephanie, she's mine. I've cared for her, watched her grow, packed her lunch, dressed her for prom, and the idea that I won't have her in my life is too much.

Sometimes it's all just too much.

"We have time." I will the words to be true.

"I'm saying that when I go, I want to know you're okay. Don't you get it? As much as you love me, I love you more. You are my whole heart, and you have no idea how much anger I have inside me about this d-d-disease. It's taken everything from you, Heather. It took your money, your husband, your whole life! I need to know you have someone!"

"Stop it! Stop it right now!" I yell back at her, swiping the tears from my cheek. "We're not going to do this."

"We have to do this. We have to talk about it."

I don't want to. I want to forget and enjoy what time we have. I get to my feet and move around the room, trying to stop the tears that keep falling. I turn my back to her, looking out the window. Maybe I'm weak, but it's easier than facing her. "I can't lose you." My voice cracks with so much pain that I could splinter.

"Heather, look at me." I turn and meet her blue eyes that shimmer with unshed tears. "You will never lose me. We didn't lose Mom and Dad, we just can't see them anymore."

This time, it's my hands that are trembling. I move closer and reach out to touch her face. "I love you so much."

"I know," she murmurs.

"I hate this."

"Me, too."

"Do you forgive me for yelling? Are we good?"

Steph smiles and takes my hand. "If you want me to be good, you have to promise me you'll stop pushing everyone away. You have to tell me that you'll let your heart be open. Can you do that?"

I've never lied to Stephanie. It's one thing that I've always prided myself on. I tell her the truth, consequences be damned. Words matter and promises are meant to be kept.

"I promise to try."

Stephanie's eyes narrow. "Try?"

"Yes, I'll try to be open. I'll try to let Eli in a little, or if not him, some other jackass who will only fuck with my head."

That's really what it comes down to . . . men are liars. They say they're one thing and they never are. Matt said he loved me, that he'd honor and cherish me, and the first time shit got rough, he bailed. Cherish my ass.

"I swear, the older you get, the more dramatic you are. I think he's different."

"Based on all your time with him?" I challenge. She's never met him, so I don't know why she's so quick to defend him. Maybe because he's the first guy to actually try since Matt.

"No, based on the way your face lights up when you say his name."

I don't do that, do I? No. I don't think I do.

She laughs and points at my face. "You even do it when you think of him."

"Whatever." I'm going to have to work on that. I really hope he doesn't notice. He's good at getting me to do things as it is, if he has a read on me, I'm screwed. I think back to our last date and how sweet he was. Not many guys turn down a chance to get laid, but he did. I fell a little bit for him in that moment.

It was the first time in a long time that anyone put my needs above their own. I'm usually the one who has to sacrifice, and it was nice to have the shoe go on the other foot.

"Earth to Heather!" She waves her hand in my face.

"Sorry, I was just thinking."

"Uh-huh. Can you help me?" Stephanie asks.

My arm hooks under hers, and she slowly climbs out of bed. For the last month, her physical therapist has been pushing her to use her muscles as much as possible. She was in a wheelchair for four months, and with a lot of work, she was able to walk a little with the walker. That progress seems to be deteriorating as well. She sits up and stretches her limbs.

I watch my baby sister bite down whatever discomfort she's feeling and get to her feet with shaky legs. I quickly move to support her. Her eyes say everything her voice doesn't. The appreciation that I'm here and sorrow that she needs me shines as bright as the full moon outside the window. She and I take a few steps and grab the walker. We move without hurry through the halls as she tells me more about Anthony.

After another hour, I can see the exhaustion settling into her features.

"I'm going to head home. Can I see you tomorrow?" I know that I'm spending the day with Eli, but I need to see her. After the conversation earlier, I think we are both coming to grips with the future. My mother used to tell us to hold on to the things we can control and let everything else go. She insisted that wasting time was never a good thing. She was right. I can't control Steph's disease, but I can control how I handle the time we have left together. I'm going to make the most of it, cherish it, and hope I don't break when it ends.

Steph smiles and touches my arm. "I think that can be arranged."

"Do you think on our next date we can do something in the afternoon?" I ask Eli, who's standing in my living room while I pour another mug of coffee. Last night was tough. I couldn't fall asleep until after two, and not wanting to look like crap, I was up early fixing my face.

"Oh, we're going on another date?" Mischief is laced in his deep voice. "I thought you weren't into me? I thought you friend-zoned me? I knew you couldn't resist."

I walk out of the kitchen and roll my eyes. Damn him and all his arrogance. "You're the one who keeps calling these dates and showing up at my house. If anyone is into anyone . . . it's you who is into me."

There. Take that. I'm not chasing him, and I'm going to remind him of that.

He shrugs and pulls me against him. "I've never hidden the fact that I'm into you."

My arms rest on his shoulders, and I smile. "Sometimes I still think this is a dream."

"Would you believe me if I said I feel the same, too?"

I shake my head, because I can't see why he'd think that. Eli *is* the dream come true. He's the wish upon a star that girls spend their nights hoping for. Yet, he's in my living room. I can't tell you the nights I would dream about this very thing happening.

"Well, I keep waiting to find something about you that I don't like, but even the things that would normally annoy me, like trying to push me away so damn hard, only make me want you more. I'm just glad you're starting to cave."

"Who said I'm caving?" I goad him a bit. I enjoy our banter.

"I'd say the boat was a good indication I'm no longer friend-zoned."

"I can put you back there if you'd like?"

Not that whatever we're doing is serious. It's only been two dates and one hell of a night. But it's definitely more than friends. I mean, Brody is my friend, and we sure as hell don't rip each other's clothes off. We've gone fishing, and not once did I end up grinding against him.

Eli's arms tighten, forcing my body to be even closer to his. "I don't think I was ever there, and I don't think friends do this."

In an instant, his lips press against mine, and the flutter in my belly grows stronger. Eli's musky cologne envelops me, and I commit it to memory. I want to remember each detail regarding this moment. How his lips feel against mine, the way the callus on his thumb roughly grazes the skin on my cheek, and how he tastes. It's cinnamon and the hint of toothpaste. If this doesn't work out, I'll have this memory to hold on to.

His tongue seeks entrance, and I give it willingly. I don't even pretend to fight him. I want it. When he touches me, I can't help but find myself craving everything he'll give. I tell myself, and everyone else, that there's nothing here, but when he's close, I can't pretend. Eli breathes life into a heart that was deflated. A heart that never thought it would beat again is once again thumping at a steady pace.

He kisses me hard, forcing my feet to move with him. My back presses against the wall, and he pours himself into each movement. I'm trapped between the cool wood panel and the heat of Eli's body.

Everything is a contrast between wanting more from him and wanting things to end before it's too late to walk away.

I need him to leave, but I'm desperate for him to stay.

I say there's nothing between us, and yet the idea of him leaving is enough to make me scream.

I drop the mug to the floor, not caring that it shatters. My fingers grip his neck as I hold his lips to mine.

I drown in this kiss.

I die in this kiss.

I come to life in this kiss.

Eli pulls back and gives me a cocky smirk. "Do your friends kiss you like that?"

Instead of telling him the truth—that no one kisses me like that—I inhale and then sigh. "You know, I'm not even sure that was a kiss. It felt . . . a little . . . weak."

"Weak?"

"Yeah, it was okay, but you know . . . nothing to write home about."

"Really?" He pushes his hips forward, allowing me to feel that he's very affected by our kiss. My head falls back, and I use every ounce of strength inside to keep up my bravado. "You think so?"

"I'm just telling you how it is."

I'm playing with fire and I welcome the burn. I see the heat in his eyes, and I'm more than willing to dance closer to the flames.

Eli studies me like a lion about to strike his prey. Each movement is calculating, and I know I'm going to be one happy gazelle. His lips hover above mine, washing his warm breath over my own. I keep my eyes open, playing the part I've created. My pulse races as he stares at me.

His hand grazes my neck, sliding down my shoulder before he runs his fingers across my arm. "I know you're lying, baby. I know because of the way you kiss me." His lips barely touch mine before he retreats, and I smother a whimper. "I know because I can feel how hot you are. I can see the way your body is asking for me, even if you're not. If I touched you, Heather, would you come? Would you fall apart at my touch?"

I could come just from this. "Maybe you should find out." I dare him again.

Eli smiles and leans back so we're no longer touching. His hands frame my head, using the wall to keep him upright. "I have plans today for us, but tonight, baby . . . tonight we're going to find out a lot."

I move forward, kissing him softly. "We'll just see about that."

chapter fifteen

Heather

"Busch Gardens?" I ask with a groan. I love this place, don't get me wrong, but Eli isn't just a guy. He's Eli fucking Walsh. Everyone knows him, and I assumed today was another private or semiprivate day. For some reason, I figured he wouldn't take me where a million people with cell phones would see us.

"Relax." He takes my hand, twisting his fingers with mine.

"Eli, I'm not ready for this."

He tilts his head. "Ready for what?"

I sigh, not wanting to spell it out. "For us to be public when we're not even sure what this is."

"I promise, this isn't what you think."

I eye him carefully, not sure what the hell that means. "It's an amusement park that's always filled, what could I be misinterpreting? I'm not ready to be public. You have no idea what that'll do to me. To be exposed to the world when I'm not even sure what we are. If people see us, they'll know. I don't have the life you do. I'm a poor cop, living in a broken-down house, and I have a dying sister. My life isn't glamour, photos, and money. I just wish you would've warned me."

His thumb grazes the top of my hand before he lets go and exits the car.

I freaking hate that he does that. I like knowing what's coming, and Eli likes to keep me in suspense. I'm going to have a talk with him about this.

After a few minutes of trying to get myself prepared, I exit the car. He's leaning against the bumper and looking off toward the gates.

"Eli?"

"I know my world comes with a crazy amount of shit. I get that your life is pretty simple in that you have privacy, family, friends, and a job that doesn't come with paparazzi." There's a little bit of sadness in his voice. "I thought long and hard about today. I didn't come to this decision easily, and I assure you, your privacy won't be compromised." When I take another step closer, he moves back. "I have other sides that makes me who I am, Heather. Things that I want you to see and be a part of. Things that I value and have nothing to do with boats, houses, and cars."

He lets me move toward him this time and guilt twists in my stomach. I never realized that he may feel judged by me. That's never been my intention. I'm not one to judge anyone, and Eli has never made me feel small or less.

"I'm so sorry," I say as I touch his arm. "I shouldn't have said those things. I don't think your life is just glamour, and if I insinuated that, I'm truly sorry."

His eyes meet mine, and he rocks back on his heels. "I want you to see *me*, Heather. I want you to see the things that make me who I am, and they're not fame."

"I never thought that's who *you* are, Eli."

He extends his hand, and I don't hesitate to take it. He's right—this isn't about whatever people are going to think, it's about Ellington and me. It's about the man who keeps coming around, making me smile, and making me feel special.

Eli kisses my cheek and lets out a heavy sigh. "Let's go."

For the first time since we entered the parking garage, I look around. Where are all the cars? I count a total of twelve. Twelve cars on a Wednesday at Busch Gardens? I know it's a weekday, but this place is always packed.

"Where is everyone?"

"I told you it wasn't what you thought."

Did he rent out the damn park? My heart starts to race as my mind goes crazy. What did he do? "Eli," I say his name tentatively. "Why is no one here?"

He smiles and squeezes my hand. "I know your cop senses are flashing, but for once, just trust me and relax."

Cop senses? Huh. Now that he says that, I guess I do have them. I'm naturally untrusting and always want information. It's power in my job and allows me to stay safe. If I'm not informed when I run into a call, I might get shot, which would suck.

"I can do that," I say with as much conviction as I can muster.

Eli chuckles, which I ignore. He doesn't realize that I may have cop senses, but I'm also extremely competitive. If he doubts my ability to do something, I will find a way to do it. So, he wants me to relax, game on, buddy.

We get to the front gate, and they let us right in. I open my mouth to ask him another question and quickly close it.

We wait in the front and a man comes over. "Mr. Walsh, good morning. I'm Mr. Shea, I'll be making sure today goes smoothly. Your publicist called and gave all the names over, they've all been added to the list. Timothy should be here in the next ten minutes."

"Great." Eli's voice is full of authority. "This is Ms. Covey, she'll be with me through the day, and I'd like to ensure whatever she needs or wants during the day will be tended to."

Mr. Shea agrees. "Of course."

"Timothy is obviously my main concern. I want him to have the time of his life. Have the harnesses been acquired?" Eli questions. I probably look a bit crazy as my attention bounces back and forth between the two.

"Yes, we have everything that his team listed."

"Timothy?" I ask aloud. Does he have a kid? Am I meeting his son? Panic starts to flood, and Eli grips my hand tighter.

"He's an eleven-year-old kid from the Make-A-Wish Foundation. Timothy has terminal cancer, and one of his wishes was to meet me and ride some roller coasters. So, I rented out the park for the day so Timothy and I can ride until he's content. We have a big day in store for him."

That isn't at all what I expected, and it makes my heart sputter. Each emotion possible hits me all at once. Sadness for Timothy mixed with awe for Eli. He took time, and God knows how much money, to ensure this little boy has a day to remember.

I've been so wrong about him.

He's nothing like I could've ever known. He's everything.

Without thinking, I face him, grip his face in my hands, and kiss him. It isn't long or passionate, it's just all my emotions. I needed to kiss him because words wouldn't explain what I think.

His eyes shine with adoration, and his smile almost knocks me on my ass.

"Told you it wasn't what you thought." He taps my nose.

Mr. Shea shows us to the area where Timothy will be coming in. He has no idea that Eli is here or what the day is. Just that he's coming to the park. Eli made arrangements for his family and ten of his friends from the baseball team he played on before he was sick to come to the park, too.

We stand in an obscure part of the entrance so he doesn't see Eli until it's time. "Thank you for letting me be a part of this," I say when we're alone.

"You may not thank me if you're not big on rides." He laughs.

"I haven't been to an amusement park since Stephanie was a kid."

"Really?"

I nod. "She got sick when she was in her first year of college. It's kind of hard to fit in roller coaster rides when you're shuffling between doctor appointments and testing. Plus, sometimes, she loses control of her hands and legs."

Eli looks away and sighs.

"You okay?" I ask.

He looks back with a sad smile. "Yeah, just thinking . . ."

"He's here." Mr. Shea appears before I can ask what he's thinking about. "We'll lead you out this way if you're ready."

Eli pauses to glance back at me. My own excitement spikes at the thought of how happy he's about to make this kid.

"Go." I smile. "I'll be right behind you."

He follows Mr. Shea out, and I follow. I can't wait to see this. I've seen these things on television but never in person.

Timothy's family all have big smiles as they see Eli come into view. I stay back, not wanting to miss a thing. Timothy's back is to us and Eli moves quietly. A few kids see Eli, and their eyes get big, jaws go slack, and they point. Timothy spins his wheelchair around and covers his open mouth with his hands. The joy, surprise, and awe are bursting from this child.

Eli moves quickly and crouches in front of him. Timothy's arms wrap around Eli's shoulders and tears fill his eyes. He keeps shaking his head and looking back at Eli. I stand here with tears falling from my face. I think about my sister and how this family feels. The small amount of joy Eli brought them in a life filled with so much heartbreak. Knowing that Eli made this little boy's dream come true crumbles the last defensive wall I have against this man.

Eli takes the time to hug the kids and shake everyone else's hands. The boys jump around and snap pictures of him with Timothy.

His eyes meet mine, and I swipe my face, praying I don't have mascara running. He motions me over, and I plaster a smile on my lips.

"Timothy, this is my friend Heather. She loves roller coasters, too."

I squat and shake his hand. "It's nice to meet you. Though, I have to be honest, I'm a little scared of heights," I admit. "Do you think they'll be too scary for me?"

He grins. "No way, that's the best part, when you want to puke because it's so high."

"Good to know," I joke.

He looks back at Eli as if he's the coolest thing he's ever seen. "Eli, you're not scared, right?"

"Not a chance. I think we should try to make Heather as scared as we can. Maybe we can make her ride so many times in a row she gets sick," he says conspiratorially.

Timothy's eyes light up. "That would be so fun!"

Great. Now I'm going to have not only Eli but also Timothy and his friends trying to get me to puke.

"How about we go have some fun, bud? The whole park is ours so there are no lines!"

"Awesome!"

It is pretty awesome. If I were a kid, I would think this is like Christmas morning.

To get an entire amusement park to myself and my closest friends would've been the best thing ever. He and his friends make a plan on the most efficient way to get all the rides in as the adults try to get them to focus.

Timothy's mom, Cindi, walks over, wraps her arms around Eli, and cries while letting out a laugh. "I can't thank you enough for this. He never could have handled a day with crowds, and you're his idol."

"I'm happy to do it. He seems like such a great kid."

"He watches your show each week. He can tell you everything you've done to save the day."

Eli laughs. "I used to watch cop shows with my dad as a kid."

"He always wanted to be a police officer." She looks wistfully at her son. "I hate that he'll never be able to do that."

Eli places his hand on her shoulder and squeezes. "If there's anything I can do."

Cindi shakes her head. "You have no idea what this will mean to him. To hang out with you and have a day where it isn't about cancer. He can just be a kid today."

The parallels I feel for his mother are everywhere. I know the fear, the hate, and helplessness she feels. Watching her son smile because of the man in front of me will carry her through the dark days. He has no idea that this gesture will not only mean the world to Timothy but also to all those around him.

He turns back to me, taking my hand in his. "My girlfr—" His lips press together, stopping the word. "Heather is a police officer, I'm sure Timothy will love hearing real stories from her."

She smiles at me. "Oh, if he finds that out, you're in big trouble."

I laugh. "I'm happy to take him on a ride along if I can get clearance from my boss."

Her smile is huge, and she pulls me into her arms. "Bless you both."

"Mom!" Timothy yells, breaking the moment the three of us were sharing. "You gotta see this, Mom! Eli, are you coming?"

"I'll be right there, dude. I just need to take care of something."

Timothy waves, and his friends run with him in the wheelchair all screaming and laughing.

Eli turns back to me and grins. "Are you okay with this being our date today?"

"Oh my God, I'm more than okay with it. Thank you for letting me be here."

His hand cups my cheek, and I lean into his touch. He looks over my shoulder and then back to me. "I have another surprise for today."

"You do?"

His gaze shifts, and I follow it.

Never in a million years would I have guessed this would be the surprise.

But sure enough, my sister is coming toward me with a huge smile. Anthony pushes her in the wheelchair, and I gasp.

Stephanie holds her arms out, and I run to her. "I told you I'd see you!" She laughs.

I hug her tightly, overcome with another wash of emotion. "How?" I pull back. "How are you here?"

She smiles and lifts her chin, motioning to Eli. "He came by the hospital and told me about today."

I turn to him, eyes wide and full of tears. "You met Stephanie?"

"After our boat date," he admits.

"You went and spent time with my sister?"

"She's important to you, and she's pretty cool."

I move quickly, jumping into his arms and wrapping my legs around his torso. He catches me and laughs. I lean back and plant my mouth to his. He'll never truly get that this means more to me than anything else he could've done. I don't need fancy things. I need someone to care. I need to rely on someone, which isn't something I've had since I was eighteen.

Here Eli stands, caring about me enough to take time to go on his own and meet Stephanie.

"Get a room," Stephanie jokes.

I slide down his body and kiss him again. "Thank you."

"You're welcome, sweetheart."

We all enter the park, and Mr. Shea radios to find out where Timothy is. As we make our way there, I'm smiling so hard my cheeks hurt. My sister is with us, and we have the entire park to explore. Eli offers me a little bit more of his heart, and I give him a piece of mine.

As we all make our way to the first ride, I grip Eli's arm and stop him. I feel like I wasn't clear enough about how much I appreciate what he did. "I don't think I thanked you properly."

He smiles. "I think you leaping into my arms was clear."

"No." I shake my head. "I don't think you understand how much it means to me. For you not only to meet my sister but also to bring her here to something without me saying anything . . ."

Eli turns, cups my face, and presses his forehead to mine. When he pulls back, his eyes are filled with something that simmers on the edge of love. "She's important to you, which means that if you and I have any chance at a future, she's important to me, too. I wanted to meet her and let her see what I'm doing isn't a game. I'm not a guy who fucks around with people. I've always been honest of my intentions when it comes to you. I want your heart and your trust."

"I think you're going to win it all." The admission falls from my lips with ease.

He grins. "I sure plan on it."

I don't doubt he will, either. My heart races as I look in to his eyes, the determination stuns me. I'm not sure why this gorgeous man has decided he wants me. It baffles me, but I'm not questioning it anymore.

He's sweet, thoughtful, considerate, and I know that my heart has no chance of resisting him.

"Eli! Come on! We need to get Heather on this ride!" Timothy yells, and Eli laughs, breaking away from me.

"We're coming," he informs Timothy and takes my hand.

We walk toward him, and then Eli stops, grabbing his leg and massaging his calf.

"You okay?" I ask.

"I'm fine, I'm just getting old."

I laugh and pat his back. "Aww is the big sexy rock star not able to keep up?"

He pulls himself upright and smirks. "I'll show you later."

Heat pools in my core at the promises he's made about tonight. But Timothy cuts off my response.

"Come on, guys! I bet Heather is going to cry when she sees this one!"

Eli chuckles and looks at the roller coaster in front of us. "I bet she will, buddy. Wonder if the big bad police officer is too much of a chicken," Eli taunts me by using the words I just did.

I rise to the challenge. "Twenty bucks say you both scream like little girls!"

"Game on."

The rest of the day, I ride more rollercoasters than I care to admit, most of them for Timothy's amusement. He laughs each time my face pales at the peak of the incline and laughs hysterically each time I have to take a minute to settle my stomach. However, Timothy thinks that because I'm a cop, I have no fear. He eggs me on, and I agree because it's pretty impossible to say no to this kid.

Our day is perfect. I sneak kisses in with Eli and laugh with Stephanie after she actually does puke after the Scrambler ride.

She and Timothy take long breaks together, talking about their stays at the hospital and how much they hate needles. It's the first time in a long time that I've gotten to see her through the eyes of a big sister. Just as any good little sister would, she coerces Timothy to ask Eli to sing for the group.

"Please, Eli," Timothy whines. "I didn't get to go to your concert last time because I was in the hospital."

"Come on," Stephanie pipes in. "Timothy really wants to see this. You wouldn't want to disappoint him, would you?"

Eli lets out a nervous laugh and stands. "I don't have my group or music, though."

"Who cares!" Timothy says. "I have my phone!" He grabs the phone from his pocket and puts on the song Eli sang to me at the concert.

I smile at the memory of the night we met. It seems like so long ago, but it's only been three weeks. It's crazy how fast my feelings for him have changed. I giggle as he spins and does his best to entertain the crowd in a private concert.

Apparently, Eli isn't content being the center of attention, and decides to embarrass the shit out of me by pulling me out of the group. Once again, Eli serenades me. Only this time, it's much more intimate, and I'm not drinking. He gets on his knees in front of me, belting out the lyrics, and in true fashion, I turn bright red. My limbs are numb and each time I try to move away, he pulls me closer.

The song ends, and he bows as the group erupts with applause. Timothy claps the loudest and I bury my head in his chest, shielding myself from seeing anyone's face.

Once it's over, we go back to the rides for a while more. The sun begins to set, and I wish I could freeze time. If today could last forever, I'd be happy. It's been a day of celebration. It isn't focused on what the people who are suffering can't do, but all the ways they still live.

Stephanie wheels herself over to Timothy, who looks so tired I think he may fall asleep right here. "So, did you have fun?" she asks him.

He opens his eyes with a smile. "Today was awesome."

"I agree, kid."

"The cancer makes me so tired, and it's in my bones now." He rubs his arm and winces.

Stephanie reaches her hand over, touching his. "I understand. I'll need a lot of sleep tomorrow."

"It was worth it." He yawns. "It was the best day of my life."

Stephanie smiles at me and Eli. "Anthony and I have to go. I'm exhausted and need to rest. My head hurts, and my muscles are tight."

"Do you want me to come with you?" I ask.

"No!" She pretty much yells before dissolving into a giggle. "No, I'll be fine, Heather. Stay with Eli and come see me tomorrow or the day after, okay?"

Eli kisses her cheek, and her hand covers it. "Thank you. I really hope you stick around."

He grins. "I plan to."

"I love you," she says to me.

I kiss her forehead and smile. "I love you more."

I watch as Anthony fusses over her as they exit, and then we move over to Timothy hand in hand.

"I'm glad I got to spend the day with you," I say to him.

"Me, too," Timothy says and then looks at Eli. "I had so much fun."

Eli pulls his small body into his arms and holds him tight. "Thank you for giving me today, Timothy. I'll never forget spending the day with you."

Timothy looks up with tears in his eyes. "When I go to Heaven, I'm going to tell God about today. I'm going to tell him how meeting you was the best day of my life."

My hand flies to my throat, and I work hard not to fall apart. Eli doesn't do as well. He pulls Timothy to his chest again and shakes his head. "I hope that day is a long time from now."

Cindi, who has been watching the exchange, is crying as her family holds her tight. We all know the truth is that day is coming sooner than it should.

Eli tenderly places him back in the wheelchair before whispering something to him and kissing the top of his head. Then he makes his way to Cindi and does his best to comfort her. She thanks him repeatedly, and then he's at my side.

We watch as they leave, neither of us moving as he grips my hand.

After a few minutes, I turn into him. His arm is around my shoulder, and I hold his waist. "Today was . . ." I'm not sure how to express it, but I want to try. "It was everything. Not because you did something extraordinary for me, but because of the whole day. Seeing you with Timothy and his family, I can't tell you how much I'll cherish this."

Eli's gaze moves to mine, and I'm almost startled by what I see. There's an openness that is a gift. He's giving me access to his soul, and it's the most beautiful thing in the world. "I meant it, I want you to know me. I want to spend every possible day we have together in Tampa with you. I want to win your heart, Heather." He wraps his arms around my waist. "I'm forty-two and this is the first time in my life I've wanted to share myself. Randy used to say I was wasting time by not settling down, I think I was biding time until I found someone worthy."

I touch his cheek, waiting for him to disappear like an apparition. Guys like him don't exist, do they?

"And you think you were waiting for me?" I question.

"I think you make me feel like no one else has. I know that I want to give you things I've never given anyone else and make you proud to know me. It's a foreign feeling."

"You're not the only one who is feeling things that are foreign," I explain. "I promised myself after my ex that I wouldn't let another man in my heart. I lose everyone I care about. Until I met you, I was doing a great job keeping that promise. I've been able to shut it down before, but with you, I can't."

Eli has a way of making me forget that I'm not supposed to like him. He's leaving. He's famous. He's a heartbreaker . . . and yet, here I stand, wanting him anyway. The fact that he's so much more of a complication than I could ever want is scary, but maybe I need the fear. Maybe the fear is my way of knowing he's worth the chance.

His thumb brushes my lips. "I'm glad you can't."

"I'm starting to be as well."

chapter sixteen

Heather

ELI STANDS ON MY DOORSTEP AND I KNOW WITHOUT A SHADOW OF A DOUBT WHAT I WANT. I want to be with him. I want to be with him in every way.

"I'm going to see my brother next week, I'd love for you to come meet him," he says as I fumble with the lock.

Our ride home was quiet but comfortable. I was thinking about the events of today. How he orchestrated everything and cared to make it special for me. It's something that I still can't get a handle on.

"I'd like that. So, since I'm willing to meet your brother then you have to meet my friends."

"Do I?" he tilts his head to the side.

"It's only fair."

"I wouldn't want to have the scales tipped in my favor now."

He's too much. "One of my best friends, Danielle, has her big annual barbeque this weekend. I'd really love it if you'd come."

I don't have a big family for him to meet, but my girls are just as important to me. We're kind of a package deal and I want him to know them. It's also about time they learn about the relationship that's happening between us.

"You're inviting me to something?"

"It would appear so."

"For an event in a few days?"

It's amazing how much fun he seems to have giving me shit.

"Yes, Eli, an event, with my friends, in three days."

"I knew you liked me."

I smile and shake my head. "I guess you're kind of a keeper."

Eli's hands slide up my back and grip my shoulders. My hands tremble, and I finally get the door open. "Heather," Eli's voice is low with a hint of desire, "why are you so nervous?"

My eyes meet his. "Because I want you to spend the night." I blurt out before I lose my nerve. "I want you to stay."

"Are you sure?"

"Yes."

And I am. I've never been more sure of anything. It isn't only the emotions of today—it's him. It's everything about this man that has me so torn up. Eli wanted me to see him, I did, and now I want all of him.

He moves quickly, lifting me and then carrying me over the threshold. I press my lips to his as he kicks the door closed. My hands are buried in his thick brown hair as I kiss him.

"Bedroom?" Eli grunts as he bumps into the table.

I giggle and point. Our smiles are bright as he moves us. His mouth finds mine again, and he crashes into the wall. "Ouch." I laugh.

"Sorry. I promise I'll make it up to you as soon as we find your damn bed."

"Promises, promises," I tease.

"You know I make good on them."

Oh, yes, I do.

We get to my bedroom without further injury, and he places me in front of him. The moonlight shines through the windows, illuminating the planes of his face. My fingers lift, rubbing the stubble on his cheek. Slowly, my hand drifts to the other side, memorizing his features. The tip of my finger touches the small beauty mark under his left eye and then to the faint dimple on the right before moving across his lips.

I meet his gaze, and it feels like a thousand words pass between us. So many questions, promises, and worries, but I put my arms around him. I hope that, while we're wrapped up in each other's arms, we'll find the answers.

"I know you've been hurt, but I won't hurt you, Heather. I want to be the guy you can count on. I'm not sure how to make this work. But I'm not going to let you go. Not without one hell of a fight."

"I worry about tomorrow," I confess.

Eli brushes the hair off my face and kisses my lips. "We can't worry about tomorrow, we can only own tonight. And tonight, I'm going to make sure you never forget how good we are. When you want to run away, I want this to be what you remember."

I don't doubt I'll ever forget those words. There's moments in my life that I've cherished, and this will be one of them. The way he looks at me eradicates all the doubts I've held onto. The tenderness in his touch extinguishes the fears of our future together.

Even if this is the last night we ever share, I'll never regret it.

"I don't want to run anymore." My words are filled with honesty.

"I won't let you."

I hold his face in my hands, bring our lips together, and kiss him. Eli takes control, brushing his tongue against mine. Both our breaths are heavy as we drink each other in. This man can kiss like no other.

Eli pushes me to my back, and my heart takes off in a gallop. I watch his hands move from my hips, up my chest, and then he removes my shirt. "You're the most beautiful thing in the world," he comments while looking down at me.

My nerves bubble up, but the look in his eyes stop them. There's no mistaking the passion there, but under that layer is so much honesty, it knocks the wind out of me. "The way you look at me . . ." I mutter.

"Is the way you make me feel," Eli finishes my half statement.

Every thought in my mind is gone. I can't hold on to anything long enough for it to make sense. The only thing I know is that I need him. I need to touch him and make him feel everything I'm feeling.

"Kiss me," I request.

He doesn't make me wait, his mouth is on mine in an instant. His hand cups my cheek, providing the tenderness to offset the force of his lips. I try to pull his shirt off, needing the skintoskin connection, but I can't remove it.

Eli does that guy move where he reaches behind his back and pulls his shirt off in one move. God he's sexy. I love watching the muscles tense as my fingers explore him.

I stare at the ink I've come to love so much. The arrows on the inside of his bicep, the words on his hip and his arm, the cross on his shoulder, and wanting to see the birds on his back. My hands glide across the one that goes from his side down over his hip. "Tell me about this one," my voice is soft.

"It's to remind me that I don't have a right to judge anyone. To each his own."

"And the birds?"

Eli moves my hair from my forehead and hesitates. "To remind me that even though I feel caged, I'm free."

A part of my heart breaks at the sullen tone in his voice. "Do you feel caged?"

"Not when I'm with you."

"I'm glad." I move my fingers higher, loving that he allows me to touch him freely. "This one?" I graze along his shoulder following the shape of the cross.

"Perspective."

I regard him with bewilderment. I definitely didn't expect that answer, and I'm not sure what it means.

Eli seems to sense my confusion, and he gently brushes his nose against mine. "When things in life get hard to deal with, it's easy to be angry, blame others, and forget all the good. Each day I see that tattoo, it gives me strength, humility, and drive to live the way I want."

"Why do you have to be so perfect?" I ask.

His fingers slide against my neck and his lips brush against mine. "It's only because you're meant for me. I'm not perfect, baby. We're just perfect together."

His mouth crushes down on mine with so much passion I feel it through my toes. The power in his touch rocks me to my core. Our connection is so much stronger than the night of the concert. Tonight isn't about hooking up with Eli Walsh. It's about Ellington, the man that is stealing my heart so effortlessly. The man I'm quite possibly falling in love with.

He pulls the straps of my bra off slowly, placing soft kisses on my neck before fully removing it. Our mouths find each other again as his hand moves to my breast. Pulling the nipple between his fingers, rolling it, causing me to moan.

"I love the sounds you make," he declares as his mouth moves lower.

"You make me feel so good."

He groans, peeking at me as his tongue glides around my skin. "I love the way you taste, too. I'm going to savor you all night long."

Gone is the sweetness in his eyes, desire has burned it all away.

"Eli," I breathe his name as he licks around my nipple before taking it in his mouth. My hand is in his hair, fisting it and holding him there as his other hand moves to my shorts. Without much effort, he has me fully naked beneath him.

He moves back to my mouth, kissing me hard while he drives me crazy with his hands. I gasp when his finger finds my clit and he makes a circular motion. My body responds, causing warmth to flow through my veins. Everything he does feels so good. I move against him, wanting more and yet wanting to go slower.

"You're so fucking sexy when you're like this," he murmurs against my ear. "When my hands are on your body, making you feel good, it's so hot, baby."

Eli increases the pressure and then inserts a finger. My head lolls to the side as he continues to drive me crazy. "Please," I beg.

"Please, what?" he asks as his teeth nibble my lobe.

I don't answer him because I really don't know what I'm asking for. Just him. I need more of Eli. My fingers tangle in his hair while he continues to finger me and rub my clit.

My mouth falls open as I'm right at the pinnacle of my orgasm, and then I plummet over the edge. He moans against my neck while I scream his name.

Eli looks at me with a self-satisfied smirk.

The need to make him feel as good as he makes me feel takes over. I want to make him go crazy. My hand slides down his chest, and I remove his shorts quickly, freeing his cock. He allows me to push him onto his back with ease.

"Fuck," he grunts as I grip him.

"I want to hear you make noises this time, baby."

I pull my blonde hair to the side and kiss my way to his abdomen. My tongue leaves a trail leading to where I plan to go.

He leans on his elbows, keeping his eyes on me as I move lower. "I want to watch you suck my cock." His voice is thick with longing.

"Well . . ." I kiss all the way down his six-pack. "It looks like you're going to get your wish."

Eli does exactly what he wanted, he watches my lips kiss the tip of his cock. I want him to fall apart because of me. As much as he wants me to remember this night, I want the same. Our relationship is filled with obstacles that we'll either hurdle or trip over. I'm fully aware there are no guarantees, but I can give him this. I can give myself this.

I wrap my lips around his cock, pulling him deep into my mouth as I bob up and down, paying attention to the underside with my tongue. The noises that fall from his lips are exactly what I want to hear. He mumbles and moans as I take him deeper.

Hollowing out my cheeks, I force him to the back of my throat. Eli's fingers grip my hair, pulling just enough to spur me harder. I love that he's losing control. I bask in the fact that it's my body, my mouth, and our connection that's stealing his restraint.

"Heather! Fuck. Baby! Fuck! You have to stop." He groans. "I want to be inside you."

No arguments here.

He pulls me off him and flips me so fast I'm not even sure how it happened. But he throws my legs over his shoulder, and now it's my turn to watch. "First, I'm going to taste you. I'm going to make you scream my name while I bury myself in your pussy."

Dear God.

Eli does exactly as he promised. His tongue flicks my clit over and over, while I fist the sheets. He varies from fast to slow, drawing another orgasm to build. "Oh my God," I breathe as he continues.

I never want this to end. I fight it off, wanting tonight to last as long as possible. If we can make love all night, I'd be happy, but Eli has no intention of delaying my orgasm. He licks and sucks the bundle of nerves until I'm panting incoherently. Then his finger enters me, curling up, and I fall to pieces. "Eli!"

A sheen of sweat covers my skin, and I fight to catch my breath. The aftershocks of my second orgasm seem to be unending. I hear him tear open the condom wrapper, and when I open my eyes, he's braced above me.

I touch his cheek, and he kisses my nose.

Eli lines himself up, ready to enter me. "I need to be inside you. I can't wait another second, tell me you want this."

It's more than want, it's beyond that. I know that when we connect this time, it'll be different. This is me giving him so much more than just one night. This is special, meaningful, and a part of my soul will forever be his. I won't be able to brush this off, and I don't want to. No matter what tomorrow brings, I know that tonight, he owns my heart.

"I want you. I want this. I want us."

Eli fills me completely. My body, my heart, and my mind are consumed by him. The intangible connection that has been between us since the first moment, grows stronger, brighter with each stroke.

Our eyes stay trained on each other's as we make love. It's the most open I've ever allowed myself to be. There are no walls around us right now as we share ourselves. My every emotion is his to have and he shares the same gift.

I tip my hips back, drawing him deeper inside me than seems possible. Eli's jaw clenches as he picks up the pace. "Baby," he grunts. "Fuck. I can't hold back."

There's no way this can be happening, but it is, I build again. "Don't stop," I request as my body pulsates with pleasure.

Eli's hips slam into mine, driving himself harder. The sweat drips down his face, and his finger finds my clit. I close my eyes as I shatter apart, calling out his name as his release rocks though him at the same time. "Heather!" Eli yells and then collapses on top of me.

Moments pass, and I can't bring myself to open my eyes as I feel him slip from the bed. He isn't gone long, and when he comes back, he gathers me into his arms. Our legs are tangled together, my head rests on his chest as his fingers make patterns on my back. Neither of us say anything, we lie here, lost in all that just was.

In all my thirty-eight years, I have never experienced sex like that. It was truly two people coming together as one. We were one heartbeat, one breath, one moment in time where there was nothing other than us.

"You okay?" Eli asks.

"I'm more than okay. What about you?"

Eli makes a humming noise of contentment. I twist my head to look at his face. "That good, huh?"

His eyes open and he winks. "I'm pretty sure you've ruined me."

I laugh. "You ruined me right back."

It's completely true. I'll never recover from this night.

"Are you hungry?" I ask as his stomach growls.

"I'm not moving right now," he informs me.

Works for me.

I rub my hand on his shoulder and sigh. "I like this."

"Cuddling?"

"Cuddling with you."

He chuckles. "You could've had this the first night, but you ran out."

My cheeks burn, remembering the frantic way I threw my clothes on and rushed off the bus. "Because I had sex with you!"

"We had sex just now," Eli reminds me as if I could possibly forget.

"So not the same."

"We can't go backward this time."

I brush my thumb across his lower lip. "Please don't make me care about you if you're going to leave me."

That is the bottom line to all my issues. When I care about someone, they're gone. If I fall in love with him and lose him, I don't know if I'll endure.

"I'm not going anywhere."

"Good."

"So, was tonight better than the first time? Or do I need to go again to be sure?" His brow raises, and I smack his chest.

"Yes, Eli, your performance was stellar."

"Medal worthy?"

I push onto my elbow, but he pulls me back down. "You're such a guy."

"I damn well better be. I'm pretty confident I just proved it as well. How many orgasms was that? Two?"

Three, but I'm not telling him that. His ego is already inflated. "You should know if you were gifting them out."

"I'm like fucking Santa Claus, only I come every night with your presents."

I burst out laughing and roll off his chest. He shifts so he's braced over me and gives me a brilliant smile.

"You're really lucky you're so hot. If you keep saying shit like that, no woman is going to stick around."

Eli's emerald eyes pierce mine. "There's only one woman I'm worried about right now."

I smile, wrap my arms around his neck, and pull him in for a kiss. "Good answer."

His stomach growls even louder than the first time. He pulls back with a different need in his eyes. "On second thought . . . what kind of food do you have?"

"How do you feel about junk food?" I ask.

I throw on Eli's T-shirt and hop out of bed. I'm a closet junk food freak. There's something about cookies that I can't quit no matter how many hours I have to spend at the gym to burn off the calories. We make our way into the kitchen, grab a few things, and plop on the couch.

"No judging." I point at him. "I like food."

His hands rise. "None here."

I take the first Double Stuffed Oreo out and twist the cookie apart. The obvious thing would be to lick the icing before eating the cookie part, however, that isn't how I roll. Instead, I grab one of the Chips Ahoy cookies and place it between the two halves, making an Oreo and Chips Ahoy cookie sandwich. I like chocolate chip cookies, and I love the icing from Oreos—so, this is my perfect cookie.

Eli watches as I take a bite, a moan filling the silence. Heaven in my mouth.

"Did you just orgasm?" he asks with a throaty chuckle.

"Wouldn't you like to know?"

I scarf down two more cookies that way without feeling self-conscious at all. Eli doesn't make me feel guilty or as if I shouldn't be eating these things. Matt would always remind me that I wasn't in college anymore and my figure wouldn't remain. Just another vast difference in them.

"Your sister looked good," Eli says before he pops a chip in his mouth.

I nod. "Today was a good day, yesterday wasn't."

"Does she have more good than bad?"

I sigh and drop the Frankensteined Oreo I'm making. I wish I could tell him that she did, but the last few months have definitely been weighted toward bad. "Huntington's doesn't usually get better. It gets progressively worse. Because Steph was so young when she presented, we were told the decline would most likely be like falling off a cliff."

Eli takes my hand in his, probably hearing the pain in my voice. "What does that mean?"

"That once she starts to go downhill, it'll be very hard and fast. There won't be weeks and months of her suffering, though. That's the one thing she says is her silver lining. I don't know if it's better or worse that way. I've had a few years with her symptoms being pretty mild, but I can't say watching her struggle isn't the worst part. I don't know how I've survived so far. When my parents died, we didn't have a warning. There was no time to worry. With Stephanie it's the opposite, I'm literally watching her life slip away. I've been doing it with no one to help me keep it together."

His fingers go limp and he pulls his hand up, rubbing it with the other. "I wish I could say something to make this easier for you."

I shrug even though nothing we're talking about feels casual. "Tell me you're not going to leave me, Eli. Because I can't let myself keep falling for you if this is only going to end with you walking out the door."

"Come here," he says as he opens his arms. I don't waver, I move into his embrace, allowing him to hold me firm. "I'm not going to leave you."

Being vulnerable is a scary thing. It's hard to give anyone, let alone Eli, unfettered access to my biggest fear. I've been alone for a long time, and I've learned to handle it. This, though? I have no idea how to handle. Having a taste of Eli's affection is enough to make me an addict. The more time we spend together, the more I crave him.

"You're leaving soon."

It's the elephant in the room. We can pretend all we want that Eli isn't who he is, but there is a reality we need to face. He has to go back to New York in less than two weeks. Our time is fading before my eyes as well. I know it's his job, I would never ask him to stay, but I'll be without him. Three weeks ago, I could've said goodbye and walked away, but when my heart entangled with his, it complicated things. Why can't I fall for a normal guy? Why do I pick the one man who literally lives every single one of my insecurities? Because I'm dumb, that's why.

Eli's arm tightens. "That part sucks, but it won't be that long. We take breaks during filming, I can come here or you can come spend time in New York. I meant what I said, Heather, we'll make this work."

"I have work, too. And Steph."

"I know, I'm not asking you to give up anything, just make room for me."

When he says it like that, it seems so simple.

chapter seventeen

Eli

"Nicole, Kristin, and Denise?" I ask, trying to get the names right. Heather's best friends are her family, and I'd like not to look like a total douche in front of them.

"Danielle, or Danni for short. That's whose house this is." She corrects as she parks in front of a house in West Chase. It's a modest two-story house on a cul-de-sac, complete with a picket fence and all.

I'm adaptable, but my life hasn't ever been normal. I'm not sure what the hell I was thinking agreeing to this.

Heather watches me, and then I remember why—her. She wanted me here to meet her friends, and that's exactly what I'm going to do. "Are you okay?" she asks.

"It's going to be great, baby. Do they know I'm coming?"

I should've asked this earlier.

"Umm, well, I kind of didn't say anything."

I'm not sure if this is because she didn't think we'd make it to the weekend or because she didn't want her friends to freak. Well, here goes nothing.

I take her small hand in mine and smile. "Let's go surprise them."

Her one friend, I remember. Nothing specific, but she was who came back stage and urged Heather to come with me, I make a mental note to thank her.

There are a few guys standing over by the front of the yard, pointing at something on the ground, and the smell of food cooking on a grill fills the air. I'm in suburbia and completely out of my element.

We exit the car and the two guys who were shooting the shit stop and look. "Heather," guy number one calls her name.

"Hi, Peter." She smiles and waves.

They both head over and Peter extends his hand. "Hi, I'm Peter Bergen."

"Eli Walsh," I say, shaking his hand.

I watch as recognition sinks in. "Right, of course." He looks at the other guy. "Eli, this is Scott McGee."

We shake, and Scott stares me down. What the fuck is wrong with him? "Nice to meet you both." I try to keep my instant dislike to myself.

I wrap my arm around Heather, pulling her into my side. I don't like these guys, well, the one at least.

"Same here. The girls are around back," Peter says to her.

"Thanks." She smiles, but it isn't a real one. It seems I'm not the only one who doesn't care for these dickheads.

"What's their issue?" I ask once we're out of earshot.

She laughs. "Nicole and I hate them. Scott is the worst, but Kristin just makes excuses for him. Peter isn't that bad, he's just a sheep and follows what the first idiot says."

We make our way around the back of the house, and I take it all in. Kids run around in all directions, spraying each other with water guns. The women all have their backs to us, laughing and arranging the food table. It's exactly like the parties my mom threw when Randy and I were kids.

"Heather!" one of her friends yells and then drops the bowl she was holding. "Holy fuck!"

Heather steps forward, pulling me with her. "Danni, this is Eli, I hope it's okay that I brought a date?"

I flash one of my million dollar smiles and move toward her. Her eyes haven't moved from my face, and I'm pretty sure she's shaking. "Thanks for having me. Heather said you have the best party of the summer."

"I-I-I," she stammers. "You're . . . you . . . in my . . . Eli."

Heather laughs and nudges Danielle. "I wanted you guys to meet him officially."

The girl I remember comes walking straight up to me. "I'm Nicole, we met briefly, you may not remember because you were kind of busy trying to get in my best friend's pants, which you did. Good job on that."

"Thanks." I laugh. "And I remember you from climbing the fence."

She huffs and gives Heather a dirty look. "Yeah, she's an asshole for that, but it seems you found your way over it as well. Don't fuck it up, and I won't have to blow your nuts off."

"Nicole!" Heather screams and turns to me. "I'm so sorry. I should've warned you about her. We think she has a mental disorder that affects her ability to think before she speaks."

I burst out laughing. "I like her."

"Oh, God." Heather covers her face. "Don't feed the animals, Eli, they bite."

I say hello to her other friend, who I assume is Kristin since she stands there like a statue without saying a word. Her gaze moves from Heather to me and then back again. I've never understood the awe of famous people. We're normal and have the same issues that everyone else does. The only difference is that I travel, have no friends, and I deal with other famous assholes. It's not all it's cracked up to be.

Heather and two of the girls head inside to get some food together and probably talk about me. Nicole laughs when they ask if she's going to help, and instead, sits beside me with a beer in each hand. "You're going to need this." She hands me one of the bottles.

"Thanks."

"I want you to know that Heather is special."

I guess since there's no father or brother in the picture, I'm going to get the speech from her best friend.

"I agree."

She takes a swig and nods. "I think you're good for her. I've known her my whole life, and there's something different about her since you came around."

"Aren't you breaking some kind of girl code?" I ask.

I'm not sure how these things work with chicks, but if I'm basing it off my experience with Savannah, they're all deranged. She and her friends talk in some alternate language that Randy and I tried to decode once. In the end, we gave up and decided being on the inside wasn't worth it. However, I know she's talked about never breaking the code. Whatever the fuck that means.

"She knows me too well. I don't have a code."

"Good to know." I laugh as I take a pull from my beer.

"I heard about what you did for her sister."

I know this is a test. What I say now will determine if Nicole helps or hurts me. So far, I think she's been pro-Eli, but that can change. I'm not a fool.

"What's important to Heather should be important to who she dates, don't you think?"

She smiles and then catches herself. "Not all men feel that way. Some think they should be most important. I'm sure in your world it's that way a lot?"

There are days when I wish people could see the shit I go through. It may look all wonderful on the outside, but it isn't when you live it. I get hounded by the press, followed by the paparazzi, and forget having any kind of privacy. The only reason I have an ounce of it with Heather is because I'm here. Tampa is where I can be low key. But if Heather and I went to dinner in public, you can bet your ass I'll have photos taken, which will bring the headlines, questions, assumptions, and everything else. I don't think that was her point, though. I have a feeling it's about the loser she married before me.

I weigh my words carefully. "It can be, but not where the people I care about are concerned. Sure, the people who want something from me treat me differently, but if you met my brother or his wife, you'd know that's not the case. I'm fully aware of Heather's situation and only a selfish piece of shit would put her in a position to choose."

Nicole looks off at the kids running around and then back to me. "I'm protective of her."

"I'm glad."

"I won't let you hurt her," she warns.

"I don't ever want to hurt her."

Quite the contrary, actually. I want to be her protector, her sense of comfort, and the one who she can rely on. It's a primal desire to take care of her. I just don't know if she'll let me.

"Wanting and doing are two different things and people tend to protect themselves over another."

Her words strike me deep in my heart. Is that what I'm doing? Knowingly keeping things from her to protect myself? To be able to have whatever I can have with her at her expense? I hate myself in this very moment.

chapter eighteen

Heather

"There you are," I smile when I find Eli still sitting with Nicole in the backyard. His eyes are filled with sorrow when they meet mine. "Eli?"

With a blink, the sadness is gone. "Hey."

"What's wrong?" I ask quickly and glare at Nicole. I'll kill her if she said something stupid.

"Don't look at me." She waves her hand. "I was warning Eli of all the ways I'll make his life miserable if he hurts you."

Seriously, I wonder if I can have her committed. I know she's being a friend, but Jesus, she's a pain in the ass. "Could you not scare him off so soon?" I ask.

Eli pulls me to his side. "I'm good. It takes a lot to scare me off. Besides, I'm pretty sure Nicole would like to meet a certain member of the band, right?" He kisses my shoulder, and I chuckle.

In one of our recent conversations, I told him the stories of Kristin's tickets, Danielle licking the poster, and Nicole's obsession with his brother. He called his publicist right away and got something special for each of the girls. I laughed hysterically when he told me they took a photo of Shaun licking his own poster for Danielle. I'm sure her dumbass husband is going to be thrilled.

"Shut up!" Nicole yells. "I can't believe you told him!"

I shrug.

She turns her gaze back to Eli and huffs. "I know he's married and all, but seriously, your brother has always been my favorite."

Eli and Nicole are sitting on the table portion of the picnic table, and he pulls me so I'm sitting between his legs. I rest my hand on his thigh as they talk about how his sister-in-law would laugh so hard she'd pee herself hearing people talk about Randy. He tried to tell Nicole that he isn't all that special, but she's a dog with a bone, and there's no changing her mind.

Nicole heads inside for another drink and then the guys come over, striking up a conversation with Eli. I sit, bored and then I encourage him to go look at whatever the hell they're talking about. The three guys walk away, and I can't wipe the smile off my face. He looks so domestic right now, and it's adorable.

"Look what I got," Nicole calls me over by holding the sangria she's famous for.

"You're the best."

I take the glass, and we both take a seat away from everyone. "I think he really likes you, babe," Nicole says as she watched me watch Eli.

"Yeah?"

She smiles. "He's a good guy. Keep your heart open to him. I know you guys have a ton of obstacles, but he passes the best friend test."

I think Nicole forgets we're almost forty, and I don't need her approval. Still, I'm glad I have it. She tends to see through people's bullshit easier than anyone else. She also would never say it if she didn't mean it.

"I love you." I pull her close.

"I love you even though I'm jealous you're sleeping with a God each night."

"What about your threesome?"

She scoffs. "I'm over those two, I think they wanted to fuck each other more than they wanted to fuck me, and if I'm taking two men to bed, I better be the center of the world. I have my eye on someone else."

My jaw falls slack, even though I'm not sure why. This is Nicole. She's always been this way, and I'd be worried if she weren't. "I can only imagine what the hell you're up to now."

Danielle comes over and touches my shoulder. "I can't believe you kept this from us."

I wanted to keep Eli to myself for as long as possible. Plus, I don't talk to them as much as I talk to Nicole. They're in marriages that are hanging on by a thread, and their advice is always so off base.

"Oh, please," Nic pipes up. "Wouldn't you want to keep that a secret? Look at him, he's Eli Walsh. If I had him in my bed, he'd never leave, maybe bathroom breaks, but then back to the good stuff." She winks at me and grins.

"Well, cat's out of the bag now, tell us every glorious detail," Kristin says through a giggle.

We sit like we're kids again, gossiping about our first kiss, and I divulge my last few weeks with Eli.

"How about we go to my place tonight?" Eli offers.

So far, he's stayed at my house each night. I don't know if it was him trying to fit into my world or show he's fairly normal, but I've appreciated it. Tonight, though, I want to show him the same. His world and my world will need to mesh, and that won't happen by forcing him to fit only in my space.

"I'd like that."

Eli takes my hand and kisses the top of it. "I'm going to like seeing you in my home."

I like that he wants me there at all. I want to make him happy, too. Today was amazing. I knew he was uncomfortable at first, but he joked with my friends, did his best to put up with their husbands, and was all around perfect. I'd catch him watching me, smiling, or finding little ways to touch me. He was taking care of me without me even realizing it.

"Thank you for today."

"I had fun, your friends are great."

"They're something all right."

Eli laughs. "Nicole genuinely loves you."

"I'm lucky to have her." As much as she drives me batshit crazy, I could never imagine life without her. "All of them really, but Nicole and I have always been the closest."

I tell Eli a little about our childhoods, which makes me laugh. We were not all that bright back then. I don't know how we didn't land ourselves in jail. My mother would've beaten my ass if she knew half the dumb stuff we tried. Kristin was always the goody two-shoes out of our click, and our parents allowed us to do anything as long as she was there, too. I guess they hoped she'd somehow talk us out of it, the problem was, we usually talked her into things.

"Wait, you actually tried to hop the fence to get into Busch Gardens?"

"It was a dare." If you told Nicole and me that we couldn't do it, we found a way. "Nicole's boyfriend worked there and said it was impossible."

"Did it work?"

We pull into Eli's driveway and he parks the car. He looks over, waiting for me to answer.

"You saw firsthand how well we climb fences. We're no better now than we were then."

Eli's deep laughter fills the car, and he slaps the steering wheel as he lets it out. "That was the best thing I've ever seen."

I roll my eyes and cross my arms. "It was self-preservation." It was dumb. I know it, and I can't imagine how ridiculous we must have looked to someone else. At least I wore pants that day, otherwise, I'd have been even more mortified.

"From what?"

"From realizing I just slept with you."

Eli shakes his head at my rationality. "I'm not sure if I should be offended. It was definitely a first for me, though. Having someone sneak out after I gave them multiple orgasms."

I wish I could go back in time to change many things, but that isn't one of them. Sure, I could've done things differently, but my last few months would be very different.

"Let me ask you this, if I'd stuck around that night, would we be sitting here today?"

He goes quiet and runs his hand through his hair. "I wish I could say yes, but you walking out that night is what made me determined to know you. I've never had that happen."

"No one would dream of running from the Sexiest Man Alive."

He chuckles. "You did."

I lean over the center console so we're face to face. "I would do it the same all over again."

"Yeah?"

"Yup, because I'm here with you now, and I know if I'd stayed in that bed, you wouldn't have chased me."

Eli's eyes soften, and he gives one of his cocky smirks. "I guess we'll never know." He moves closer until our breaths become one as we both take in this moment.

I lift my hand, tangling my fingers in his brown locks without moving my gaze from his. I see the shift from contentment to fear and then to adoration. Is he afraid of us? It's twice today that I've seen something troubling him. There's a part of me that wants to ask him, but I pretend I don't see it.

My gut fills with dread because I know it's the wrong choice. I've felt this before, and I acted on it. I used to beg Matt to talk to me, to tell me what he was feeling. Each time I tried, he pushed me away more. Doing the same thing and expecting a different result is the definition of insanity. For all I know, it's nothing, yet somewhere inside me, I don't think that's the case.

Eli leans in, touching his lips to mine. I work hard to let whatever I saw go and focus on right now. Our futures are undefined, and if I set us on the wrong path, we'll crumble. I have to walk it with him and hope that we can endure the potholes and detours.

He pulls back, resting his forehead on mine. "Let's go inside. I want to get you in my arms."

"Sounds good to me."

We exit the car, and he seems to be back to normal. The sun has set, and strategically placed lights illuminate his house. It looks like a freaking palace. The grandness of it all hits me the same way it did the first time. I don't think it'll ever fade. With my hand in his, we tour the house again, only this time he shows me all the rooms.

On the second floor, he shows me his six guestrooms, all are double the size of my master bedroom at home, with a bathroom, and decorated with extreme detail. There's no way he chose this stuff, I can only imagine how much fun Nicole would've had in here.

When we enter his room, I almost pass out. It isn't a bedroom; it's a small house. There's a sitting room at the far end with a full living room set up, off to the left is a fireplace that's see through on both sides. Eli leans against the wall watching me as I walk around the room, trying to take it all in.

"This is incredible," I say with awe.

I continue looking around the other side of the fireplace. There's a master bathroom, if you can call it that, that leaves me speechless. The Jacuzzi tub sits off to the right, and there's a shower taking up the entire back wall. I swear at least ten people could fit in there.

Eli clears his throat, causing me to turn quickly. "You look good here."

I shake my head in disbelief. "I doubt that."

He moves forward. "One day, you're going to see how beautiful you are."

"One day, you'll realize that you need glasses." I try to joke, but it falls flat. I've never thought I was ugly, but I'm nothing special. It's still crazy to me that Eli thinks differently.

He wraps his strong arms around me, and I sink into his embrace. Just like that, Eli can make me feel whole. When I'm with him, my world doesn't seem so bleak. Sure, the issues are all there, but with him, shouldering them doesn't feel so hard.

"Let's go to bed." Eli's words are mixed with double meaning.

I smile at him. "I'd like that."

We both get ready for bed in the massive bathroom. I internally laugh at how vastly different this is from my house. I have one sink in my bathroom, and the double vanity occupies three quarters of one wall.

Once we're done, we settle into the king-size bed. As much as I love the space, I kind of like that we snuggle in my smaller bed. Eli puts his arm out, and I nestle into his side. "I like when we're close like this."

He makes a low rumbling sound in his chest as I drape my arm over him. "I never realized how much I like it until it felt like you were miles apart on your side."

"Aww, you like being close to me," I say, teasingly.

"I like being *very* close to you."

I grin and kiss his torso. "I like that you like that."

"Are you trying to seduce me, Officer?"

I look at him through my lashes and bat them. "Me?"

He twists, hoisting me so we're even. "I don't mind if you are."

"Are you seducible, Mr. Walsh?"

Eli's lips move to my ear so he can trace the shell with his tongue before gripping it in his teeth. "Maybe you should find out."

I move my hand under the covers, skimming over this hard body, until I find his erection. I love that he's always ready and I never have to wonder if he wants me. There are many benefits to sleeping naked, this is one.

Eli groans as I wrap my fingers around him and my lips find his. He roughly grips my hips, digging into my flesh as I start to jerk him off.

My phone rings in my bag across the room, but I'm too lost in his touch to care.

His moan is low, and I swallow it as we kiss. I feel his hands on my breasts, kneading the skin and pulling at my nipple. The sexual chemistry we share is unlike anything I've had before. I'm not the most experienced lover, but Eli pushes me. I want to please him. I love knowing it's my body he's seeking, claiming, and worshiping.

"You make me crazy," Eli admits before his mouth is on mine again. His hands exploring my body until his fingers brush my clit.

The phone goes off again. "Maybe you should get that," he practically growls against my lips, and I groan.

I drop my head on the pillow and curse the phone. "Don't go anywhere," I warn and hop out of bed. I glance back at him as he rests his head on his hand, watching me as I prance across the room.

My phone has six missed calls from a number I don't know. I didn't realize it rang that much. Something is wrong, I can feel it in my bones. No one calls me that much unless it's an emergency, and my dumbass ignored the call. "Hello?" I ask with a shake in my voice.

"Heather, it's Anthony."

"Anthony." My eyes shoot to Eli's, and he's already tossing the covers off him. "What's wrong?"

He pauses and dread fills my body. "You need to come to Tampa General. Please don't wait."

"Is she—" I choke the words as Eli's hands grip my shoulders. I can't say the words. I can't ask if she's gone, because if he says yes, I'll lose it.

"Just get here."

The phone drops to the floor, and Eli's arms encircle me. Everything I thought I knew about how I'd handle this moment is false. I feel my body start to protect itself. My mind goes to a place where I can't feel or do anything. I'm not sure how I got to the bed. I don't know how my shirt is on my body. Nothing is real right now. It's as if time has ceased to exist for me.

I feel hollow and lifeless.

Eli lifts me in his arms, carrying me like a child down the stairs. He barks orders to someone as we move to the car. He must be on the phone, but I truly can't process anything around me.

The car is moving, but I can't see anything passing by. I didn't need Anthony to tell me she died and I wasn't there with her. I can feel it.

My world is without my sister.

I'm alone.

chapter nineteen

Heather

"WE DID EVERYTHING WE COULD, MS. COVEY. I'M TRULY SORRY FOR YOUR LOSS." The doctor explains as I stand with a steady stream of tears trekking down my cheeks and dripping off the tip of my chin.

My sister has drawn her last breath.

Three days ago, we were at an amusement park. We were laughing, enjoying our time together, and now she's dead. No warning, no time to say goodbye, nothing but agony.

Now I stand in a cold, stark room while they try to give me some kind of answers.

"How did this happen so fast?" I ask. "I thought there would be a warning, something to tell me it was coming."

Anthony comes forward. "She begged us not to tell you."

"Tell me what?"

Dr. Pruitt touches my arm. "Stephanie was being treated for pneumonia after her seizure. It's why we kept her a few extra nights. The antibiotics weren't working, but she demanded we stop all treatment and discharge her. We did the best we could with the parameters she set."

Anger floods my veins, searing the pain in every limb. She chose this? She knew? They were lying to me? Don't they know what this cost me? My chest heaves as I struggle to understand how this could happen.

I look to Eli and then back to the doctor, and I erupt, "I don't understand! How could no one tell me? How didn't you think I should know?" I scream at them. "I was her caretaker! She wasn't thinking straight! I'm her sister! I should've known."

Eli pulls me into his embrace, and I wail. I smack his arm and then his chest, angry at everyone. Angry at him because I was with him when this happened. Angry at Stephanie because she didn't tell me. I could've had another three days with her. If they'd kept me informed, I never would've allowed her to come to a fucking amusement park. I would've pushed her to have treatment, not let it kill her. There were so many things I could've done, and now, it's too late.

My rage turns to Anthony. "You knew!" I rage at him. "You knew she was sick, and you brought her out!"

His head drops, and when he looks back at me, his eyes are brimming with tears. "I know you don't believe this, but I cared about her. She asked me if I would help to keep her stable so she could have that day with you. She wanted one day of normal with you. Your sister knew she was dying and didn't want to drag it out. I was there with her, holding her hand, and giving her what she asked for."

"You knew her for what, a week? I was there every single day throughout the last seven years! I should've been the one beside her. You took that from me."

A lone tear falls down his face, but there is no room in my broken heart to feel anything but hatred for him. "Believe me, your sister loved you so much that she wanted to spare you. It was all from love."

I hate myself. I hate him. I hate everyone, and I can't breathe.

I gasp for air as Eli rubs my back. "Easy, baby."

I look to him, his image blurry. "She's gone and I didn't say goodbye. I wasn't there, Eli. I wasn't with her."

"I know."

The doctor clears his throat. "We had specific instructions from Stephanie in her medical directive. They were followed to the letter. I'm truly sorry for your loss, Ms. Covey. Take as much time as you need."

He and Anthony both walk away, leaving me to do the last thing I ever wanted to do . . . say goodbye to my baby sister.

Eli and I walk down the hallway with his arm around my shoulder. I want to push him away, be alone and wallow in my grief, but I can't seem to do it. He's the only person here who didn't spend the last however long lying to me. I hold onto him as we move, following the line on the floor. We don't speak because there's nothing to say. I can't go back in time. I can't change the way everyone handled this. Once again, I've had the choice stripped from me.

The door is open, and I glance at her lifeless body lying there. I'm not strong enough for this. I've been fooling myself by believing I was prepared. There's no preparing for grief. Instead, I'm thinking of how I wasn't with her in the end. No, I was lying in Eli's bed, wishing my phone weren't ringing. I should've been holding her hand, telling her how loved she was. My beautiful little sister is gone, and I hate that she didn't hear my voice telling her all the things she needed to know.

Eli's hand is on my back, and I spin, crumple against his chest, and twist my fists in the fabric of his shirt. "No, no, no, no!" I thought maybe this was a lie. Somewhere deep inside I hoped she'd be alive, but she's not. "I'm not ready for this!" I cry. "She can't be gone. Please, God, give her back to me!"

He murmurs words of comfort and support, but they don't matter. There's no way to soothe the torture I'm feeling. Grief, guilt, anger, and desolation consume me. "Do you want to go in? You don't have to."

I know I need to. Even though she isn't really there, it's all that's left of her. "Yes, I do." I say to him and straighten my shoulders, finding a tiny bit of strength in his warm hand on the small of my back.

"I'll be right here."

My feet shuffle forward, and I pull the chair closer to the side of her bed as my heart splinters. Eli stays back, allowing me some privacy. I lift my hand, brushing the dark brown strands off her face. She used to love when I did this. In the beginning of her disease, it was the only thing that calmed her. I would spend countless nights running my fingers through her hair.

I close my eyes, not wanting to see her face, and repeat the motion. "I'm sorry, Stephy. I wasn't here, and I'll never forgive myself for that. I'm your sister, and I was supposed to be beside you. I don't know if you were scared or if it hurt. I don't know if you were looking for me—" A strangled sob breaks free.

Eli moves, but I put my hand up to stop him. I need to do this alone. Even if she isn't alive, I pray she can hear me.

"I would've been here, baby girl. I should've been by your side. You were my whole world, Stephanie Covey. I don't know how to go on. I love you more than my own life. You were the best sister in the world. Each day that I had you was a gift, and I wish it never ended. I wish I could tell you a stupid joke right now." The tears come so hard I can't see. "I wish I could hold you and tell you how special you were. Because you were everything good in this world." I wipe my face and suck down a breath. "The world was a better place with you in it. I was a better person because of you."

My head falls on the side of the bed, and I grip her lifeless hand in mine. I cry without restraint. It's ugly, full of pain, and I don't have the wherewithal to care. "It should've been me who was sick! You didn't deserve this."

I have no idea how long I stay hunched over the bed clinging to her. I never understood loss until this moment. I thought when my parents died that was the most grief I could've felt, but that was a splash in a puddle. Now, I'm drowning in the ocean, the current pulling me farther out into the murky waters.

I need air.

I can't breathe.

My lungs struggle to function. I gasp, trying to find any oxygen in the room, but there is none.

"Easy, baby. Easy. Look at me, Heather." Eli's kneeling by my side and cradling my face as he wipes the tears with this thumb. My eyes find his, and he stares until I calm down. "That's it. Breathe. Just breathe. I'm right here."

"She's gone."

"I know, baby."

"She won't come back."

His own eyes fill with sadness. "I'm so sorry."

The sound that escapes my throat is filled with despair. "Take me home, Eli. Please. I can't see her like this. I couldn't save her, and now she's gone!"

His arms become a vice around me as I fall apart. I want the numbness back. It didn't hurt when I didn't feel. The knowledge that tomorrow, I can't call her, text her, or touch her leaves me so bereft that I'm not even sure there's a way to live past this moment.

Eli tucks me against his chest, holding me as we move. I hear him talking to someone, but I've found my way back to the darkness. This is where I want to stay.

I focus on nothing.

The only thing that registers is Eli's arms wrapped around me as I close my eyes and drift to where not even death can touch me.

◦○◦

"Heather," a soft voice calls to me. "Wake up, honey."

Stephanie? Is she here? My eyes fly open, hoping to see my sister, but it isn't her. Instead, Nicole is leaning over me. Disoriented, I look around and realize I'm not in my house. A big bed sits in an enormous room. I'm at Eli's. When did we get back here?

"Hey." She stares at me with red-rimmed eyes.

She knows about Stephanie.

He must've called her.

"Nic—" I choke her name out, and she reaches for me. The minute she touches me, I break. The tears I cried before seem small in comparison.

The pain is back with a vengeance. Nicole rocks me back and forth, and I hold on to her for dear life. "Oh, honey. It's okay, let it out," she encourages. "Just let it out."

There's a connection between two people who understand each other. That's Nicole and me. We don't have to speak to know what the other needs. Sometimes, it's just falling apart in the comfort of your best friend's arms.

Nicole leans back when I quiet down. "Better?"

"No. I don't know that there is a better."

She wipes her own tears and nods. "It's going to hurt, but you're strong, Heather. Stephanie loved you so much, know that."

"She kept it from me." All the emotions of the night continue to assault me. My sister knowing that she was going to die and that she was sick. The fact that she hid her condition so we could have the day at Busch Gardens. "All at her own expense. If she were alive, I'd beat her for it. She should've stayed in bed, got better so that . . ."

"So she could just get worse again?" Nicole challenges. She loved my sister as if she were her own. Stephanie was always around when we were young, wanting to be exactly like us. I can remember finding Stephanie trying on my clothes and talking to her "best friend Nicole." It was annoying back then, if only I had the gift of foresight. "Is that what you'd really want for her?"

My gut reaction is to yell: Yes!

I open my mouth, but Nicole glares at me, daring me to say it. "I . . . I don't know."

I pull my knees to my chest and wrap my arms around them. I wish I could crawl inside myself and disappear. Living hurts too damn much.

"I know you, and you didn't want that. I can't imagine how you'd feel if this was months of her in agony."

Sure, I guess there's some comfort in that, but not much. The last seven years of Stephanie's life were a series of ups and downs. We struggled with everything, and she suffered through it all. I watched her life start to fade the day we got her diagnosis.

My eyes move to the doorway where Eli leans against the frame. In his hand is a glass of water and a plate of food. He hesitates before moving forward. I gaze at him, tears welling in my eyes.

"You've been sleeping for a while." His deep voice is filled with emotion. "I thought you should eat."

My lip trembles, thinking of how happy I was before I got the call. We were together, loving each other while my sister took her last breath. I wish I could go back in time. I would've gone to see her after the barbeque, but I was so wrapped up in him.

My heart aches thinking about the minutes wasted because I didn't answer the phone. The what-ifs are tearing me apart.

Nicole touches my arm. "Eli called as soon as you got back. I came right over, but you've been sleeping for about fifteen hours."

"I'm tired."

Eli and Nicole share a look, and she gives me a squeeze. "I'm sure. You need to eat, though. Do you want me to call Matt and tell him you'll be out for a few days?"

"Tell him I don't know when I'll be back."

Right now, I can't deal with anything. The idea of riding in a squad car and talking to people is too much.

"I'll tell him a week, and then you'll handle what comes after that." Her tone is firm, and I know what she's trying to do. The same thing I would do if she were giving up.

I'd push.

But you can't push someone out of a hole. You have to hope they'll claw their way up enough for you to help them. There is no strength left in my hands to help me move right now.

"Do you need me to stay?" she asks Eli.

"No, I'll take care of her."

I glare at both of them as they talk about me as if I'm not here. All I need is to go back to sleep and wake up when this isn't my reality.

Nicole kisses my forehead, and then they both leave the room. I grab my phone, scrolling through the texts and missed calls.

Danielle: I love you. I'm here if you need me.

Brody: Rachel and I send our love. Let me know what I can do.

Nothing. You can't do a damn thing.

Kristin: I talked to Nicole, I'm so sorry, Heather. Do you want me to come over?

I reply to Kristin right away. I don't want to see anyone.

Me: Thanks, but I'm not up for company.

It doesn't matter that I'm at Eli's house. She'll show up. That's Kristin's nature, she's the caretaker in our group, and I don't want to be mothered. I don't want anyone to make me feel better right now.

I try to remember what it was like when I lost my parents. Was I this devastated? I think I was, but I had Stephanie to worry about. I didn't focus on the sorrow. I had to be strong, give her hope, and make sure we would be okay. My friends were around, but we were also college aged. It wasn't like now.

Eli enters the room, and I use all my energy to stay upright. I tighten my arm, hugging myself together.

"Did you eat anything?" he asks.

"Not hungry."

The bed shifts slightly as he climbs in next to me. "Okay."

I look up, not expecting that. I figured he'd fight me to do something other than drown in my pain.

"Don't look surprised. You have to grieve the way you want. I'm just trying to be here in whatever way you need."

Tears fill my eyes, blurring him out a little. I lunge forward into his arms. I don't know why or what comes over me, but I need him to comfort me. He falls back, taking me with him and wrapping me tightly in his arms. The tears fall silently as I listen to the beat of his heart.

He's been here every second since it happened. Even when I couldn't care for myself, he made sure I was okay. I turn my head so that I can see his face. Eli gives me a sad smile, and appreciation overwhelms me. These have been the worst hours of my life, and he's stood by me.

"Thank you, Eli."

He threads his fingers in my hair. "You don't have to thank me."

"We haven't been together all that long."

"It doesn't mean that what we feel for each other isn't real. I told you I wasn't going anywhere, and I meant it."

I close my eyes and another tear escapes from the corner. "I'm going to be sad for a bit."

I might as well warn him now, let him run before I fall even harder. It would have to be him leaving, too. I don't think I'm strong enough to walk away even if I wanted to.

"Baby, look at me," he urges. I open my eyes, and he sits up, causing me to have to do the same. "You should be sad. I didn't know Stephanie like you did, and I'm sad. I don't think you understand how I feel about us . . . about you. I'm not going to leave you because you're sad. I'm not walking away, I'm staying here with you."

"You leave in a week," I remind him.

His hands grip my shoulders and then move to my neck. "I told my producers I'm not coming next week. I'll go to New York after we figure this out."

My fingers wrap around his wrist, and I press my forehead to his. "I don't know what to say."

"You don't need to say anything," he murmurs. "Just let me take care of you."

His lips brush mine with hesitation, and I make the movement to connect us. It isn't about passion. It's about something deeper. Our kiss is soft, sweet, and comforting. In all the sadness, he gives me hope that the sun will shine again. It's a brush of lips that temps me to believe he'll combat the clouds and ward off the storms so I can feel the warmth of the rays again. I hope he's ready for Mother Nature's fury.

chapter twenty

Heather

It's been seventy-six hours since my sister died. I've been cocooned in the comfort of Eli's home. He's been patient, kind, loving, and attentive. When we first met, I would've laughed if someone told me this is what he'd be like. I assumed he was a rich, selfish, arrogant prick who only cared about his wants. Because . . . that's the illusion of a celebrity.

I was wrong.

Eli is none of those things, except rich. He's definitely that, but he's never selfish with me. We've watched television, had takeout, and he's held me as I've cried.

I wrap my arms around him and snuggle closer, inhaling his scent. I love the mix of soap, sandalwood, and musk that is him. He's asleep, but he instinctively squeezes me tighter. I watch his face as whatever he dreams of makes him smile. I trace the lines on his cheek with the tip of my finger, grazing each little spike of his scruff.

"Hi." He smiles as his eyes flutter open.

"Hi."

He shifts a little lower to his side. "Did you sleep?"

I'm not sure that I've really slept since that first night. It isn't for lack of trying, but my body won't relax. The second night, I woke Eli with my sobs. I relived the entire event at the hospital, only this time I made it in time to watch her fade away.

My mind played every scenario out in the worst way. I don't know now if it's a good thing that I wasn't there. If it was anything like I imagine, I know I wouldn't be just mourning. I wouldn't have survived. I was never more grateful for Eli's presence than I was when I woke, covered in sweat and tears pouring down my face.

"I think I did."

"Good. How about we grab some food?"

I haven't eaten much, and thinking about food makes my stomach growl. "I guess I am hungry."

He laughs. "Come on, I'm starved."

I follow him into the bathroom and almost scream when I see my face in the mirror. My eyes have dark circles under them. Makeup is now dried on my skin, and I'm not sure if it's somehow become permanent. I won't even talk about the mess that is my hair. Jesus. I glance over at Eli, who looks as perfect as always. His hair only looks sexy in its disheveled state, there aren't any dark circles under his eyes. The deep lines of his hips are more prominent as the basketball shorts hang loosely.

Eli's eyes move to mine, and he appraises me. "What?" he asks with a grin.

I think he knows I'm checking him out, but I shrug, not caring that I got caught. "Nothing."

He comes closer, pressing his lips to mine. "You look at me like that, and I can't help but kiss you."

"Like what?" I ask.

"You'll figure it out soon enough." His kiss is quick and silences me from asking what the hell he sees in my eyes.

When he pulls back, I open my mouth to get my question out, but he moves toward the shower, slowly removing his pants. I stare at his broad shoulders, the way his muscles tense on his back, his now bare ass, and I can't speak.

For the first time in three days, I want something more to ease my pain. Not food, or him holding me. I need him to make me forget who I am. I feel alone, broken, and Eli has pushed me to stay out of the numbness.

I want to get lost in his green eyes and have him make me feel pleasure. He's spent every minute ensuring I felt safe. I think back to what Stephanie said: *You have to promise me that you'll let your heart be open. Can you do that?*

She was asking so much more than that. She was practically begging me to let myself be vulnerable enough to love again.

"Are you coming in?" Eli asks as he stands in the shower, water dripping down each delicious inch of him.

A thought strikes me, halting my feet. I was never more vulnerable than I have been the last three days. I let him see me at my lowest, and he's still here with his hand outstretched, calling me to him.

I step toward the man who I never thought I'd feel anything more than lust for. Each stride forward cements what I already knew was happening—I'm falling in love with Eli Walsh.

The steam circles around us as we stand in front of each other. My heart races with the knowledge of my deepening feelings. How did I get here so fast? Is it true that when two people are right for each other, time is irrelevant? Out of all the people in the world, is he really who I'm meant to be with?

His green eyes fill with wonder, as if we're sharing the same thoughts, and I know . . . I love him.

I lift my hand and place it on his chest. His heartbeat quickens as we both gaze at each other.

"Tell me what you're thinking." Eli's voice is heavy with confliction.

I'm terrified that if I say the truth, he'll laugh. I'm frightened that I'll lose him, like I lose everyone else. The crippling fear keeps me from saying it, but I give him what I can. "That I'm not alone because of you. That I'm afraid of losing you."

His arms wrap around my shoulder, clutching me as the water falls on us. "I told you, baby. I'm not going anywhere."

I tilt my head back, believing what he says. "I want you to make love to me."

He tenses, probably scared that I'm not ready. Each touch we've shared since that night has been in comfort, and he'll never grasp the intimacy he showed in that.

"Heather . . ." He hesitates. "I'm not . . ."

"I know." I put my hand to his lips. "I'm telling you that I need you. I need you to make me feel alive. I want you to make love to me because I *want* to make love to you."

His eyes don't leave mine, and I see the mix of desire and surrender. His fingers slide down my spine as I grip his neck. Both of us move in perfect harmony, and our mouths collide. Eli takes control of the kiss, entering my mouth, and pouring himself into the moment. Each swipe of his tongue solidifies my heart to him.

My hands move down his shoulders, over his thick arms and firm muscles, and then back up again. I love the feel of him beneath me. The way he emboldens me to give myself over.

The kiss continues as we touch each other. It's as if I'm experiencing him for the first time. His mouth moves against my throat, kissing me as his lips find purchase where it drives me wild.

He moves back to my lips and takes my head in his hands. My gaze meets his, and I see it all. He's as in love with me as I am with him.

Just as I was too afraid to say it, he doesn't utter the words, either. However, I know, and I show him the same love back.

The intensity of his stare is too much. My breathing becomes shallow, and he drops his grip and takes my hand. "I want to do something," he admits. "Will you let me take care of you?"

"You already have."

I'll give him anything he wants. I trust him more than I've ever trusted any other man.

Eli fills his hand with soap, turns my back to his front, and starts to wash me. He starts at my neck, lathering the soap and moving ever so slightly down to my shoulders. "You have no idea how you make me feel," he says against my ear. "How much I want to take away your pain. I want to make you smile, baby. I want to give you everything."

I lean back against him, as he moves to my chest. "I need you so much," I admit. "It scares me how much you mean to me."

He spreads the soap across my body with care. We're both naked, but it's more than foreplay right now, it's filled with meaning. Once he's done washing me, I'm desperate for him.

I need him inside me. I need to feel whole. I need him to fill me with life.

His gaze is brimming with hunger. Neither of us can wait any longer.

He presses my back against the wall and his mouth finds mine. I pour out every ounce of love I feel from my body. I want him to feel how deeply I'm in love with him. My hand reaches for his dick, trying to line it up. I can't wait. I have to have him right now.

"Heather," he says against my skin. "We don't have a condom . . ."

"I have an IUD, and I'm clean."

His head drops to my shoulder, and he moans. "I'm clean, but are you sure?"

I look up, watching his green eyes beg for me to say yes. But there's only one thing that falls from my lips. "I love you, Eli. I want you to make love to me."

I stun myself with my admission and wait for him to freak out.

He pushes the wet hair from my cheek and smiles. "I love you. I loved you the day we were on the boat. I loved you the day your face was covered with paint. I might have even fallen in love with you when you screamed my name at the concert."

The tears that fall this time aren't from grief, but from hope. I'm not alone or lost, I found my home.

<hr>

"You know, I've spent my entire life in Tampa, and I've never been here," I state.

Eli chuckles as we continue walking on the trail. "I love this park, Randy used to take me here to fish when my dad was too drunk to be around."

After our intense shower, Eli told me he wanted to show me something. I wasn't in the mood to leave our safe haven, but he wasn't budging, insisting that we were leaving the house before we had to meet with the assisted living director.

"Tell me about your parents." He doesn't talk much about his family. I know his mother lives in Tampa, but he hasn't mentioned her.

He sighs. "Not much to say. My father was a drunk, smacked my mom and Randy around. I don't remember if he hit me, but Randy says he took the hits so I didn't have to. From what I'm told, he lost his job and then left."

"Wow, is that why you and Randy are so close?"

"Yeah, my brother was more of a father than anything. Even though he's only a few years older, he took me under his wing. When we found out our dad was dead, that was when Randy really made it his job to take care of me."

It mirrors the relationship between me and Steph. When my parents died, I became the parent figure. It was different because we lost both Mom and Dad, but still, I can imagine what Randy experienced.

I rest my head on his arm as we continue through Lettuce Lake Park. The trees provide shade, allowing us to walk comfortably. It's Florida, so it's always hot and humid, but today is bearable. "What about your mom?"

"She's here in Tampa, but she spends half the year in New York visiting her sister. They do the whole snowbird thing. I don't get it, but they've been doing it for years." Eli stops in front of the opening by a small pond and grabs my hips. "I want you to meet them."

I give a small smile. "I'd like that."

"My brother is up my ass about bringing you to his house. I'd love for you to meet my niece and nephew."

A sharp pain slices through my chest. Eli having a family shouldn't hurt me. I know it's a little irrational for me to be jealous, and a part of me is angry with myself for thinking that way. In my heart, I know all of this, but it's there.

He rocks my hips back and forth when I don't say anything. "Yes, of course. I'm sorry I spaced out there." I try to laugh it off. "Maybe next week?"

"There's no rush, babe."

"Okay, I do want to meet them, though. Your niece sounds great."

I love that while the media portrays Eli as big and bad, he's a man with a beautiful heart. The fact that he's so smitten with his niece is proof. I can only imagine how much she rules his world.

Eli tosses his arm over my shoulder, tucking me into the crook of his arm, and we continue walking. I've been around tall and strong men my entire career and never felt secure. I've always been able to hold my own and am proud of that. With Eli, I can almost relax. I'm not looking for the next bad guy, I'm just happy to be in the moment with him.

"It's so peaceful here," he muses.

"I'm glad you brought me here. Stephanie would've loved it."

He smiles down at me, kisses my forehead, and rubs my arm. "That's the first time you've talked about her since the hospital."

"It hurts to think of her," I admit.

"Maybe talking will help."

I don't know that anything will help, but I know I don't ever want to forget her. If that's how I can keep her memory alive, I'll endure the pain. My sister loved when we'd talk about the funny things my parents did. She would tell me that by whispering their names in the wind, it brought their spirit to life.

I lean into Eli, needing his support. "Stephanie wanted to be a professional gymnast when we were kids. One time, she was practicing doing flips on the bed in my room." I smile as I remember how disastrous it was. "She missed the bed and her tailbone hit the wall, leaving a big ass imprint."

He laughs, and I giggle.

"My mom was so mad because we tried to cover it with pillows."

"Pillows?"

"Yeah, like we could hide the giant butt in the wall and she'd never know."

Eli shakes his head and grins. It was one of the stories Stephanie loved to tell. I ended up getting grounded because she lied and said it was me. Since it was my room and my bed, my mother never believed me when I told her Steph did it.

She was always doing those kinds of things, taking my clothes, mixed tapes, and any toy I loved. What I wouldn't give to be able to have that all back, I'd give her anything she wanted.

"You ready to head back?" he asks. "We need to meet the director."

This is going to be impossible. Collecting her things and getting rid of anything we don't want . . . I don't know how I'm going to do it.

"I guess—" I start to say but a woman shrieking stops me.

"Oh my God, oh my God, oh my God!" A jogger who is no longer running starts to yell. She stares at Eli with her jaw hanging open. "You're! You're Eli Walsh! Like, I love you. I'm your biggest fan!"

"Well, thank you." He flashes a smile and drops his arm.

This is the first time we've had this happen. I watch as the woman starts to prattle on about how amazing he is and how hot he is in person. A knot in my stomach starts to coil. I know he's hot, and I get that he's famous, but when we're together, it's so easy to forget.

"You have no idea, I've loved you forever. I know you're from here, and I kept waiting to meet you! And now you're here!" She screeches, and I barely contain my flinch.

Eli reaches his hand back, twisting his fingers in mine. "It was great to meet you, but I need to be going," he smoothly explains.

"Can you take our picture?" she asks me.

The last thing I want to do is be a photographer, but I have to remember *this* is part of who he is. To me, he's Ellington, the guy who watched awful comedy movies with me the last two days. He carefully picked each one to ensure nothing would trigger me breaking down again. He made sure I ate, slept, and functioned. He's the man who held me together when I was breaking apart. I don't share that man with these women, but Eli is a superstar. He doesn't belong to just me.

"Oh, sure." I grab her phone, and he shoots me an apologetic look.

The woman gushes some more, touches his arm, and doesn't even glance at me again. I take the photo and watch her hug him once more. She runs off, glancing back at him a few more times. What is wrong with these people? I know that I did that with Eli, but I was drunk and at a concert where I never thought he'd actually hear me. If I had been sober and in a normal setting, I would have waved or smiled, but telling him I loved him? No. That's ridiculous.

I love him. She doesn't even know him.

He walks toward me, and I can't get a grip on the emotions I'm feeling. "Hey," he says tucking his thumb under my chin. "I'm sorry."

"You have nothing to be sorry for." This is what his life is filled with, he shouldn't have to apologize for that.

"I brought you here because I wanted us to get some air, I forget that this can happen."

"How do you forget that?"

Regret flickers across his face. He reaches behind his neck, gripping it as he looks back at me. "When we're together, it's like I'm not that guy. You make me forget all of the shit that comes with singing and acting. I feel . . . normal."

"I was caught off guard, that's all. I'm pretty sure if this happened a week ago I wouldn't be acting crazy."

"You are not acting crazy, baby. Not even a little."

I don't trust whatever I'm thinking right now. It's a hint of jealousy mixed with a lot of grief. Not exactly the cocktail for sound decision making. I'm definitely filing this instance in my memory bank to recall later. I need to reconcile loving someone who I have to share. I'm not sure I know how to do that.

chapter twenty-one

Heather

TODAY WAS THE MEMORIAL.

It was the final formal event of my sister's life. Kristin and Nicole took care of the flowers and handled all the arrangements. Stephanie knew exactly what she wanted and laid it all out years ago. She had prepaid for the funeral home, memorial location, and casket, claiming that she knew I'd pick some ugly wood design and be too distraught to care. I thought she was being silly, but it turns out she was right.

I'm a mess and far worse than I thought I would be.

I figured because we knew it was coming, I would've been at peace. There's nothing peaceful about this.

When we got to Breezy Beaches the other day, I couldn't do it. As soon as Eli parked the car, I lost it. He went in, handled everything, and took me back to his house. He forced me to try to relax, so we had lain by the pool, and I read a book.

Well, I pretended to read because I don't think I absorbed a word.

Now, I'm back at my house, sitting on my bed, wondering what to do next.

"Knock, knock." Kristin pokes her head in. "You okay?"

After Stephanie's burial was over, I made a resolution to find a way to move on. My life has been my sister for almost twenty years. I went from being her guardian to being her caretaker. I don't remember a time when she wasn't my focus, and that hole is what I fear most.

What do I do when I don't have to worry twenty-four hours a day? How do I make choices that aren't regarding her needs? Where do I go after work or on Saturdays? My life has been her. Every choice has been made around her needs. I understand why Stephanie begged me to open my heart. She knew that I was going to be lost once she was gone.

"I'm doing a little better each day."

Kristin smiles. "I don't think we ever are any better, but we learn to accept it and find a new normal."

"That's what I'm hoping to do. I probably should decide what to do about going back to work."

"You have a lot of vacation days saved, maybe you should take some time for yourself. Go on a trip, do something fun for a change."

I can't remember the last time I went away. Maybe my honeymoon, but even then, we went to the keys because Stephanie wasn't mature enough to be trusted. Nicole was going to watch her, which meant they threw a party in my house.

"Maybe. I don't know when Eli needs to be in New York. He was actually supposed to be there a week ago, but he didn't want to leave me."

Kristin grins and takes my hand. "I really love you two together."

"I told him I loved him," I admit aloud for the first time.

"That's big for you."

"I know." I sigh. "It took me a year before I said it to Matt. And I wasn't even really sure I loved him, but he said it, so I said it back. With Eli, I couldn't hold it in any longer.

I had to say the words or I'd explode. But I haven't said it again and neither has he, maybe he didn't actually mean it . . ."

Kristin giggles. "You're such a freaking nutjob. You honestly think he doesn't love you? Think about it, the guy blew off his job, has practically moved you into his house, has taken care of you, and took care of all the expenses for today—"

"What?" I jump up. "They were prepaid, he couldn't have."

"I'm pretty sure that man can do anything he wants. He said he had all the money refunded a few days ago."

How could he do that? We took the money from the life insurance account that my parents left us. Stephanie didn't want us to use all the money on her care and leave me trying to scrape together funds.

I grab my phone and pull up my banking app. "Oh my God." My hands fly to my mouth. "It's all there."

My account is now ten thousand dollars heavier. He really did do it.

"A man doesn't do that for a woman he doesn't love. I see the way he looks at you." Kristin takes my hand. "Scott used to look at me that way. It isn't about what he says, Heather, it's about how he acts."

She's right. Since the very beginning, he's shown me how he feels. He doesn't have to say the words, because they've been in every one of his actions.

I'm such a fool to have been worried.

"I'm sorry that he doesn't see how wonderful you are." One day, I pray Scott will either do a complete one-eighty or she'll finally see her worth and leave.

"Don't worry about me." She taps my leg. "Tell me why you doubt your love at all?"

I tell Kristin about the park and the jogger. How I felt invisible and was worried that once we left our bubble, our love would pop. It was nothing he did. Even when he was performing, he touched my hand as if saying he saw me. I'm naturally a worrier, and Eli has an entire new can of worms that I can't contain.

"Well, my best advice is to talk to him. If anyone can navigate a public life, it's him."

Once again, Kristin proves I'm a fool. "Why am I so dense?"

"Because you're emotional right now, babe. Stephanie might have been a sister to us, but she was almost a daughter to you. We expect to lose our parents and people older, but never anyone younger."

She pulls me into her arms, and I'm reminded why I'm blessed beyond words. My sophomore year of high school, I met Kristin in study hall. She had broken her foot and she sat at my table because it was closest to the door. To anyone outside, we were the most unlikely friends. She was on the honor society, I was barely passing. I played sports, she was not athletically inclined. Yet, we clicked. Our friendship was instant and completely unbreakable. She introduced me to Danielle, and I brought in Nicole, from there, our group was indestructible. I couldn't ask for better people than them.

"I love you, Kriss."

"I love you. So, I came in here because I have to give you something." Kristin fidgets. "About six months ago, Stephanie reached out to a few of us. She explained that she could feel changes happening in her, and that she was sure she wasn't going to last another year."

My heart begins to race, and my chest aches. "Why didn't you tell me?"

"She begged us not to. Nicole, Danni, and I listened to her, and she explained that she wanted us to help her. So, the three of us have letters—" Kristin's voice cracks as a tear falls. I want to jump her and find the letter from my sister, but I restrain myself. She clears her throat and continues, "We have letters for you. Brody has one, too, I believe. I'm supposed to be the strong one, so I got today. Clearly, they all misjudged me." She wipes her face before letting out a nervous laugh and pulling an envelope from her purse. "She asked that you read it after her service."

"Have you read it?" My voice trembles as I take it from her.

"No, it's for you, honey. Do you want me to stay?"

Kristin is one of my best friends, she knows me inside and out, but it's not my girls that I want right now. It's really astounding how when I gave my heart completely over to Eli, he became so essential to me, and I want to sit next to him as I read this.

"Would you be angry if I said I wanted Eli . . ."

"Don't even finish that thought." Kristin gets to her feet. "I would never be upset. I'll go get him." She kisses my cheek and walks out.

I stare at the envelope with my name on the front, and my stomach is filled with knots. I feel Eli's presence as he enters the room.

"Kristin told me before she came in." The sound of his voice eases a little of the fear. "You want me in here?"

"I do."

He sits beside me, and I place my hand on his leg. I feel tethered to Earth around him. I need him to anchor me so I don't drift into the pain of whatever I'm about to read.

My finger slides under the glue, separating the flap to reveal a single piece of paper folded inside. I let out a deep sigh and pull it open.

My Sister who became my Mother . . . my Mister,

If you have this letter, I'm dead. Don't cry. Although, I have a feeling my asking that is like telling the sky to be yellow. You were always so dramatic, even when we were kids. You should stop that. We all knew this was going to happen, and I know you won't understand this, but I'm glad it's over. I have no idea how long it'll be after I've written this until it's in your hands, but know that I was ready. I was ready not to be a burden on you anymore. I was ready not to be in pain. Mostly, I was ready to be free.

You never let me be broken after Mom and Dad were taken from us. You were the rock. It couldn't have been easy to become my parent. Especially when I was going through that goth phase, which I still think I rocked. However, I never worried if you'd be there. The day I got my diagnosis, I lost my life, and so did you. We went from being in this relationship where I hated you for telling me I couldn't go on a date with Tyler Bradley—who, by the way, was not a bad guy for smoking—to having to worry about painkillers. Our Saturday nights weren't movies and popcorn; they were tremors and numbness. I hated watching you go from being happy and married to divorced and depressed.

You can try to convince yourself that you didn't care, but no one is that selfless. And if you truly believe my disease didn't rob you of anything, then I'll tell God you should be the next Saint. Although, I'm sure he knows about the time you had sex with Vincent in Mom and Dad's bed. Yeah, I totally heard you . . . gross.

My point to this letter is that you're free as well. You don't have to worry anymore. I know that you'll think I'm being stupid and I can hear you saying how you don't want to be free, but I do. I want you to be free. I want you to go out with your friends and have one-night stands, because I can't. I want you to find someone who isn't a loser and wants you to be a Stepford wife.

I want you to know this above anything else. You were the best Mister anyone could ever have. You are the only thing I will miss when I'm gone. On a side note, don't think I don't plan to haunt you. I'm going to be an awesome ghost. I figure it'll be like that movie you made me watch where Whoopi teaches the ghost guy how to move objects. So, when the remote goes flying because you're watching that awful cop show, you know it's me telling you to find something better to watch.

I'm going to stop rambling, but seriously, I love you so much. Thank you for being my Mister and not Momster.

So, in order to ensure you live your life after I'm gone, there are three more letters. I figured Kristin was the weakest link in your group, so she got the first one . . . the next you'll get on your wedding day. Because you need to find love again. You need to have someone who will take care of you for a change. Go find him so you can hear from me again! I promise, it's a good one!

I love you always and forever.
Stephanie

I fold the letter back with a mix of tears and a smile. It would be just like my sister to leave me on a cliffhanger so I'd do what she wanted.

I look at Eli, who's studying me closely. "She was always such a ballbuster, it's good to know even in death she kept that about her."

"What did she say?"

I laugh, thinking about the one thing she wrote about him. "She thinks your show is crap and doesn't want me to watch it."

He laughs and tugs me against his side. "Yeah, she mentioned that I needed to find better acting jobs."

chapter twenty-two

Heather

"Are you nervous?" he asks as we sit outside another ridiculous mansion on Sanibel Island.

"Of course I am," I chuckle. "I'm going to meet your family!"

It's been four days since the memorial, and while I've loved it being just Eli and me, I'm excited to spend some time with other people. I wish it wasn't the first time meeting them and it wasn't his famous brother's family. It's Eli's nephew, Adriel's birthday, so his family is having the adults over to celebrate.

"They'll love you," he assures me for the fifth time, and I know I can't put this off any longer.

When we climb out of the car, a little girl comes barreling forward. "Untle Eli!" she screams as her brown curls bounce in the wind.

"Daria!" He scoops her in his arms and twirls her around. "I want you to meet someone." He moves over to me. "This is Heather, can you say hi?"

"Hello." She smiles sweetly.

"Hi, you are even prettier than your uncle said."

She giggles and tucks her hands under her chin. "Untle Eli always tells me I'm going to be big trouble."

Daria wraps her tiny arms around his neck and squeezes. "You already are trouble," Eli says before blowing raspberries in her neck.

"You're silly!" Her sweet laughter fills the air.

"Look who's late again!" A woman with long brown hair, dark brown eyes, and a loving smile comes walking down the drive. From what he's told me, I assume this is Savannah. She's much shorter than I imagined, though.

"Look who's busting my balls, as always," Eli retorts.

She rolls her eyes at him and then turns to me. "Hi, I'm Savannah, I'm so glad you came."

"Thank you for having me. It's really nice to meet you," I say as she pulls me in her arms.

"We're all huggers, honey. Be ready, this family is small but crazy as hell." I laugh, and Eli grumbles about her being the leader. "Anyway . . ." She dismisses him. "I'm so sorry to hear about your sister."

"Thank you." I do my best to give her a small smile, but bringing up Stephanie is like a knife to my heart.

"We wanted to come for the memorial, but Eli said it would be better if Randy wasn't in Tampa when he was. The press goes a little crazy when both Walsh brothers are around. One is much easier to hide. I hope you understand."

I never knew they had planned to come. He never mentioned a word about it, and it touches me more than she'll know. It also reiterates what Kristin said about him showing me how he feels. He told his family, and they thought I was important enough to him to come to my sister's memorial.

"Of course. I'm so grateful you even thought to come." I glance at Eli with surprise and then back to Savannah.

Eli puts Daria to his side and grips my shoulder. "Savannah has a strong sense of family. She was adamant until I put her in her place."

She snorts, and her eyes narrow playfully. "You wish."

Their banter is hilarious to watch.

"You don't scare me, Vannah."

"Don't let him fool you," she whispers conspiratorially. "He knows who reigns supreme and it isn't either of the Walsh boys."

"Good to know." I laugh and jab his side.

"Everyone's out back," Savannah tells us and leads us through the house.

Eli holds my hand as I, once again, get lost in the wealth that he and his family have. This house is a little smaller than his, but it *feels* like a home. There are toys, warm colors on the walls, and it's clear a family lives here. Even with the size, it feels cozy.

We exit out back, and Randy puts his beer down and comes forward. "Heather, I'm so glad you could make it!"

"Thank you for having me."

Randy pushes Eli to the side and gives me a big hug. "Thank you." I look up, not sure what he's thanking me for until his gaze moves to his brother.

My cheeks burn, and I give a short nod.

"All right, asshole, stop embarrassing my girlfriend."

I won't lie, the fact that he called me his girlfriend gives me a thrill. Eli pulls me away from Randy, who chuckles over the possessive gesture. I meet his nephew, who reminds me of Danni's son, all proud and a total boy. He fist bumps Eli and gives me the chin lift.

Then Eli places his hand on my back and leads me over to who I assume is his mother. She has light brown hair, green eyes that match Eli's, and the sweetest smile. She's exactly like I pictured. Her hands are delicate, and she keeps them folded on the table. When she sees Eli approach, her entire face lights up.

"Mom." His smile is wide as he greets her.

She gets to her feet and takes his face in her hands. "Eli! My sweet boy!" His mother kisses both his cheeks before releasing him. "Are you eating? You look too skinny. I don't like you too skinny."

"I'm fine, Ma."

For the first time, he looks a little embarrassed. I didn't think that was something I'd ever see.

"He's all skin and bones," she says to the lady sitting next to her. When her eyes go back to him, she seems to notice me. She claps her hands together and then touches Eli's chest. "Is this her?"

"Ma, this is Heather, my girlfriend. Heather, this is my mother, Claudia."

Twice, but who's counting?

"She's so pretty." She's talking to Eli but looking at me.

"I'm so happy to meet you."

His mother walks over and takes my hands in hers. "I have waited a long time for Ellington to bring a girl to me, and here you are."

I'm not sure what that means, other than he told me that he hasn't really dated since his ex. Did she never meet her? I would've assumed they knew her considering how close to marriage they were.

I glance at Eli, and he rolls his eyes. "Don't start," he warns her.

"Oh, you hush. You don't date, and you don't call your mother. I have to read about your antics in those magazines. My Eli is too important to find a good girl. Makes his mother have to worry about being all alone without someone to take care of him."

I laugh as she gives him shit. He doesn't fight her back, he just tucks her in his side. "You love me."

She smacks his stomach and laughs. "Come sit, Heather. This is my sister, Martha."

I take the seat next to her, and Eli leans in, kisses my cheek, and wishes me luck. I watch him grin as he walks off. Asshole. Way to feed me to the lions.

His mother is absolutely perfect. She asks me a million questions about my job, my family, and her eyes fill with sympathy when I tell her about Stephanie. Her entire being is filled with warmth, and it's comforting being around her. Claudia tells me a little about Eli before he was famous, and I can't picture him that way. She talks about how scrawny he was, and that Randy was his only and best friend, which is something I assume followed him into adulthood.

He doesn't talk about any friends, and now, I can't imagine it's easy for him to trust anyone. When you're as successful as he is, it's probably impossible to figure out who wants to be your friend because they gain something from you and who genuinely cares about you. It's easier to shut them all out and not worry about it.

"You surviving?" Savannah says, handing me a beer before sitting.

"It's been such a great day so far."

"I'm glad. I have to tell you, we were shocked when Eli said he was bringing you to the party."

I'm not sure if I should be upset or relieved that he doesn't bring random girls here. I take a drink, hoping to mask my emotions. "I guess I was, too."

"Don't take that the wrong way." She gives me a reassuring smile. "We're all a little protective of Eli and haven't been a fan of his past choices. That said, judging by everything he told us, you're nothing like that. We were really happy he was finally going to get his head out of his ass and bring you around."

"Vannah," Claudia chastises her.

"You know you were happy, too, Mom. He's been so weird since the she-bitch."

I nearly choke on my drink. I think I love this girl. "I take it you don't like his ex?"

She lets out a loud laugh. "No. I hated her from the first second I saw her. You know how it is, I'm sure, women can read other women pretty easily."

"Oh, for sure," I agree. I feel like that's one of the advantages that make me a good cop. I have a pretty good gauge for whether someone is pulling crap or if they made a mistake.

"Guys are stupid and only care about one thing . . ."

Claudia scoffs. "Not my boys. They were raised right."

Savannah side eyes me and grins. "Yes, Randall and Ellington would never care about that."

If she only knew that's what Eli and I did after knowing each other twenty minutes.

Speak of the Devils, and they shall appear. Eli and Randy walk over with a plate of burgers and hotdogs.

"Don't scare her off with your evil ways." Eli points at his sister-in-law. "I'm watching you."

I inch closer to Savannah. "Don't be mean to my new friend."

"Great," Eli groans. "Now I'm really screwed."

Laughter fills the air and then we dig in. The family dynamic is fun and loving. They all make fun of themselves along with each other, and the conversation flows effortlessly.

Randy dotes on his wife, showering her with little tokens of love. It's clear where his brother learned how to treat a woman.

It's like watching Eli with me. He hands her a drink before she asks, or takes her hand for no reason. Once again, the Walsh brother's surprise me. People paint Randy as anything but a family man, but that's exactly what he is.

After the sun goes down, Savannah and I head inside to start cleaning up.

"You know that when your relationship goes public, things won't be easy," Savannah says as we wash dishes.

"I'm not sure what you mean."

She rests her hip on the counter, giving me her full attention. "It means that women are crazy, and Eli has been this attainable guy in some of their minds. You're not an actress or movie star, you're relatable to them, and you need to have some thick skin if you're going to get serious with him." She sighs. "I don't want to scare you, but I do want you to be prepared. Eli truly cares for you, believe me, I've never seen him like this. He may not understand this side of dating a famous person, but I do. I've been called horrible names, had photos photoshopped to make me look fat, and seen stories upon stories of Randy cheating."

"You don't think I can handle it?" I've wondered the same. I think back to the jogger and how uncomfortable I felt with her touching him. That isn't even what Savannah is talking about.

"I don't doubt you can if you want to. I'm sure there are awful things said about you being a female cop, right?"

I laugh. "You have no idea."

"Well, amplify that by a thousand. In the beginning, it'll be bad, but then it'll calm down. Just be ready, be on guard, and seriously don't listen to anything they say. It's truly disgusting the way the media portrays us, how people get a sick joy in watching famous people flounder. They will actually root for you and Eli to fail. Drama sells, and everything is about money in this world."

I hear the pain and disgust in her voice. She's been living this for a long time and must've experienced a lot of hurt at people's hands. "How do you deal with it?"

She looks out the window at her husband and smiles. "I love him. For better or worse, that man is my entire world. I deal with it because music is who he is." Her eyes turn back to me. "It's who Eli is, too. So, keep your head down and be open with each other. If you love him, he's worth it."

Without a shadow of a doubt, I know I love him. The mere thought of walking away from Eli is enough to make me want to cry. It could've been easier to fall in love with anyone else, but nothing in my life has been easy. I've had to bury my parents, my sister, endure a divorce, and been so broke I wasn't sure I could afford to eat, so dealing with people hating me is a cake walk. Nothing will ever compare to the pain of losing my sister. If they want to hate me because I love him, then so be it.

He's worth the risk, he's worth it all.

Hours pass, and his mother takes the kids upstairs for baths. Eli, Savannah, Randy, and I have been playing rummy for the last hour. I'm kicking ass.

"Well," Randy tosses his cards down as I win another round, "on that note. Heather is clearly a hustler."

"Never!" I pretend to be offended.

"Liar." He laughs and then turns to his brother. "Eli, you should search her for hidden cards."

"Are you cheating, baby?"

My jaw drops. "I would never. I'm an officer of the law." Savannah and I have been passing each other cards under the table.

His eyes narrow, but he doesn't refute me. I watch him look over at Savannah, and he yells. "I knew it! You little cheats!"

Savannah bursts out laughing, and I follow. "You guys are so blind."

"Unreal, Ran, we've been played by our women."

Randy smirks at his wife and kisses her. "She's been playing me since we were kids."

"Mommy!" Daria comes running in wearing her pajamas, her hair still dripping from her bath. "Will you read me a story?"

Savannah hoists her daughter up and gives an apologetic smile. "It's that time, Randall."

"We're going to hit the road."

"Don't be a stranger, you're welcome here anytime," Savannah says and pulls me in for a hug. "He doesn't need to be present, we don't like him much anyway."

Eli snorts and then we all say our goodbyes.

Today was a day I'll never forget. It was a family welcoming me without knowing me at all. I had worried before that meeting Eli's family would remind me that I was alone in the world, but instead, it showed me the opposite. Once again, Eli provided me with something I didn't even have to ask for.

chapter twenty-three

Heather

"I DON'T FUCKING CARE, THEN FIRE ME!" ELI YELLS INTO THE RECEIVER. "FILM WHAT YOU can without me. I'm not leaving Tampa until I'm damn good and ready." The phone falls to the floor, and he grips his hand. "Fuck!"

I move over quickly as he presses his thumb to his palm. "You okay?" I ask as I pick up the phone. He winces in pain, shaking out his hand. "Eli?"

"Yeah, give me a minute to finish the call." He grabs the phone and moves into the other room. I've never seen him this angry, but he's livid. I hear him continuing to fight with whomever is on the line.

I sit at the kitchen counter, picking at the fruit that his chef cut up. I took off the rest of this week and the next when Eli said he wasn't in a hurry to go back. I want to spend as much time as I can with him before our entire relationship shifts. We discussed the fact that he was in breach of contract, but he was relentless in telling me not to worry about it.

It appears that I should've trusted my gut in worrying.

Eli returns to the kitchen about fifteen minutes later and tosses his phone on the marble countertop. He pulls the fridge open, mumbling about asshole directors and egos. I try not to laugh, but he's so cute when he's pissed that a short giggle escapes.

His eyes shift to me, he slams the door shut, and then he moves to me so quick I gasp. Then, his lips are against mine and I have to grip his arms to keep from falling back. The brute force of the kiss shocks me. This last week has been all tenderness. This is anything but that.

He hoists me out of my seat with one arm, lifting me so my ass is now on the counter. My hands move to his neck, holding him now that we're even in height. He pushes himself between my legs, and I wrap them around his waist.

As much as I love the gentle Eli, I really missed the sex-God.

"Ellington," I say as I break away for air.

"Say it again," he commands. His lips suck at the skin on my neck, and I hold his hair. "Say my name, Heather."

"Eli," I moan as he starts to move lower.

"No, baby, try again."

I know now what he wants. Eli Walsh is the man I share. Ellington is all mine. I pull his hair back so he looks at me. "Ellington."

I watch the fire burn in his gaze, and I melt for him. "That's who I am to you, baby. Only you."

"Kiss me," I request.

He seems to struggle with moving, but I don't let him pull away from me. I'm not breakable. Eli made sure that, no matter what, I had what I needed, and now he needs me.

Instead of letting him decide, I push my lips back to his. He moans against my tongue, and it's the sexiest sound ever. There's nothing I love more than driving him to the edge. To have influence over this man is exhilarating.

He stops quickly, taking two big steps back, both of us breathing heavily. "Why did you stop?" I ask.

"Fuck!" He bellows as he looks to the ceiling.

I hop down. "What happened? Are you okay?"

His eyes close, and he takes a few deep breaths. "I'm fine, just pissed, and I shouldn't've taken it out on you."

I touch his cheek and smile. "Did it look like I minded? If that's how you handle being pissed, then I may piss you off constantly."

He bursts out laughing and shakes his head. "I love you," he says without hesitancy.

We still haven't said it since that night. I didn't need him to, either, but my smile is wide. "I love you, too."

My hands rest on his chest. "I was worried I imagined that night."

"It's been a long time since I've said that to anyone. I'll be sure to tell you more often."

"You show me every day."

He kisses my nose and sighs. "That was my agent. The producer is livid, demanding I return to New York in twenty-four hours or I'll be hearing from their legal team."

I've been selfish to think he could keep this up. We've both been living in our own dream world. He's under contract. I can't keep him here. "I'm doing fine now. You don't have to stay for me."

"I'm not here because I don't think you're okay, Heather. I'm here because I can't leave you. I don't want to go to New York and not see your brown eyes when I wake up. There's nothing up there for me, and you're everything I need here."

I know he's an actor, but there's no doubting the sincerity in his words. Knowing that he wants to stay because he wants to be with me makes me fall even deeper. However, if he loses his job and has this big legal battle because of me, it could possibly cause a rift in our relationship.

"You used to tell me you weren't going anywhere, the same goes for me, babe. I'll be right here when you get back. We have to trust that what we've found here is strong enough to endure a few months apart."

He starts to pace the room, and the air fills with his confliction. "I know that, but they're being fucking ridiculous."

There's nothing I'd love more than for him to stay, but it's wrong. I walk over to him, lacing my fingers with his. He needs to go, and I need to be on board with it. As much as he says he's not still here because he's worried about me, I know a small part of him is. Maybe he's not worried that I'm going to go catatonic again, but he's still concerned. I need to ease his mind and get him back to work.

"Eli, you have to go back to work. You've given them no timeframe so they're going to make threats. It would be the same in my department. I don't want you to leave, but we both know it's what needs to be done. I'm going back to work in a week anyway. With as amazing as our little world we've made is, the reality is we can't stay here." I hate the words because they're true. Our time together has been perfect. It's been what we've needed, but now we have other things that we both have to face. "I love you, and part of loving each other is trusting that we can handle this. You love acting, I love my job, and we need to build *our* life where we have balance."

Eli doesn't respond, he grabs the phone, dials, and waits. "I'll be in New York in one week. If they want to sue me, I don't fucking care. I'll be there next Monday ready for work. Let them know that I have other priorities now, and I'm going to be coming to Tampa on weekends."

The phone goes sliding across the counter, and I smile. He's going to come here on the weekends. Without a word, he takes my hands, guiding me upstairs. When we enter the bedroom, he pushes me onto the bed and climbs over me.

"I have seven days with you." His green eyes glimmer with lust. "Let's see how many times I can make you scream my name."

Eli continues to surprise me each time we're together. I've never known the kind of pleasure like he gives me. He's rather proud of the fact that I scream his name multiple times. I'm not complaining, either.

Sated, he passed out quickly and I lie awake next to him, watching him sleep. I want to do something special for him. When he talks about his life, it's almost surreal. People are always doing things for him, but it isn't like they care about him. They do it because it's their job. No one ever really thinks about him.

Thanks to my Wikipedia stalking, I know his birthday is going to be in two weeks. Since I'll be back to work, and so will he, I want to celebrate with him early.

So, I leave a note on my pillow that says I'd be back after I run a few errands and head out.

My first phone call is to Savannah. I ask if they'd be willing to come to the house for a party in two days. Of course, she agrees and then goes on to give me a list of his favorite things and then offers to help make sure everyone can make it.

After I have a list, I head to the grocery store. Eli's favorite cake is German Chocolate, which is not exactly the easiest thing to bake for someone who knows what they are doing. I'm not that person. I love to eat cake, but I can't make it. However, I want everything to be made by my hands. I can't give him fancy things. I'm not rich or have people to call to get things done, all I can give him is my heart and my time.

My phone pings with a text.

Best Sex of My Life: Hey, babe. Where are you?

He's ridiculous. I can't believe he changed his name in my phone again.

Me: A little full of yourself, huh?

Best Sex of My Life: I have no idea what you mean.

Me: Really? The name in my phone keeps upping your game.

Best Sex of My Life: Well, it's all true so far.

I laugh. It's these things. These little things that make him so endearing to me.

Me: I'm not sure about this one. I've had better.

Best Sex of My Life: The hell you have.

Me: Wouldn't you like to know . . .

Best Sex of My Life: I'll show you when you get back. Start stretching because it'll be one hell of a workout. Which leads me back to the first question, where are you?

I smile as I think about what his face must look like, the prowl in his eyes, and how his jaw is set. I know damn well he'll make good on his threat.

Me: I'm out. I'll be back soon. I love you.

Best Sex of My Life: I love you. See you soon . . . naked.

I snort.

I finish gathering ingredients and then stop at my house to unload them. I don't want to tip him off about anything. Not that I initially intended it to be a surprise, but if I can pull it off, I'd like to try. Eli and I have pretty much planned to do nothing but be together this week, but I can be creative.

I make my way back to his house—mansion—excited about my plans. I called my girls, inviting them as well. They love Eli, especially after seeing him with me these last few weeks, so they should be a part of his celebration.

"Honey, I'm here," I call out as I enter the house.

"I'm in the kitchen," Eli replies.

I move toward the back of the house where I find him walking to the fridge.

"You were gone a while, is everything all right?" Eli asks.

"Yeah, I had some stuff I needed to do, and then I stopped at my place for some clothes."

We've been staying here more than at my house, and I was running out of things to wear, even though we spend most of the time by the pool or in bed.

Eli moves back to the island and he winces. "You okay?"

"Yeah," he grumbles. "I did something to my foot getting out of bed."

"You really are getting old," I say in a joking voice. "You're falling apart, Gramps."

He cocks his head to the side and chuckles. "Keep it up, baby. You're not that far behind me."

"I am not old! I can kick your ass any day of the week and twice on Sundays."

Eli grabs the sandwich and takes a huge bite. "Try me," he says around a mouthful of food.

I think he forgets that I'm a cop. I've wrestled big guys in bar fights, taken down punks who try to run, and battled with prisoners who think they can take on the world. My training is vast, and I've worked hard to know my strengths.

Plus, most men don't want to hurt a girl. It's in their DNA. I take full advantage of that. It is also in their genetic make up not to get their ass kicked by a woman. I need to remember that.

"So," I say as I plop on the bar chair. "What do you want to do today?"

"I was thinking we go on a date . . . a real date. Where you get dressed up, and I wine you, dine you, and then sixty-nine—"

"Okay!" I cut him off. "Romantic."

He shrugs. "I thought so."

"People will see us."

"Good."

"They'll know you're dating."

Eli puts the sandwich on his plate and leans on the counter. "Good."

"We won't be able to hide."

He moves around toward me, still watching my reactions. "It's not my life that will no longer be hidden, Heather. I'm ready for every woman to know that I'm not interested, the question is . . . are you?"

My mind recalls the conversation with Savannah. I know that as soon as we step out behind our curtain, all of that will follow, but I meant what I said to him. I'm not going anywhere. His life and mine are becoming entangled, and I don't want to see what would become of me if the threads were cut.

✑

"People are looking at me," I whisper as Eli looks over the menu.

"Yup." He grins. "You're kind of hard to ignore."

I tilt my head and sigh. "Don't be charming."

"Can't help it. You bring out the romantic in me." Eli shrugs and goes back to reading.

I try to stop fidgeting, but it's hard when I can feel people's eyes on me. At least when we were in the park, I was invisible to the woman. Here, it's the complete opposite.

I straighten my back and follow his lead. I can do this. People look at me when I'm in uniform, so this is no different.

The waitress takes our drink order, spending extra time attending to Eli's request for water. I swear.

"You look beautiful," he says, taking my hand.

I glance at my navy one-shoulder cocktail dress and then back to him. I spent extra time getting ready, making sure I looked like someone who belonged with him. My hair is curled and pulled over to the side, exposing my neck. The nude pumps I stole from Nicole six months ago are killing me, but I wore them. And even with the extra makeup, making me feel less like myself, I'm totally freaking out.

"I feel like I'm naked in front of a crowd." Once again, I look around at all the people, some of whom are whispering and staring.

Eli's mouth turns into a sly grin. "I would be perfectly fine with that as well."

I glare at him. "Funny."

"Relax, Heather." Eli gives my hand a squeeze. "People look, and people talk, but we're the only thing that matters right now."

He's right. I'm on a date with Eli, and we both love each other. This is a part of who he is, and that means, it'll be a part of my life. I might as well get used to it.

"Okay, I'm sorry."

"Don't be sorry, it's an adjustment, I'm sure. You get used to it."

Something to look forward to.

The waitress returns, giving me a sour look. "Wine," she places it in front of me while looking at Eli. I go to open my mouth to let her know she's brought the wrong wine, but she turns her back to me. "And for you, Mr. Walsh, we've selected our top-of-the-line bottle of cabernet, on the house."

"Thank you," he says politely and then his eyes meet mine. "However, my girlfriend ordered the Pinot Grigio, but you brought her red wine. Why don't you fix her drink first since I only asked for water?"

"Oh, I'm so sorry." She grabs the glass and walks away quickly.

"I think she might cry." I fight back laughing. Her face was priceless. It's clear she's a fan, or at least thinks he's hot, and he just dismissed her.

Eli raises and drops his shoulder. "Maybe if she didn't ignore you, then I wouldn't have to be a dick."

I've never had someone love me like this. Thinking back, I'm not sure Matt ever defended me. I always felt like I was on my own. With Eli, he looks at me as if I'm special and treasured. He wants to protect and care for me.

"Is it like this in New York . . . when you go out?" I question.

He chuckles. "No, it's like I'm a normal guy."

"Yeah right." I don't think Eli could ever be normal. He's sexier than any man I've ever seen, and he's impossible to ignore.

"I swear. Celebrities there aren't treated as if they're special. It's why so many of them live there full time. Plus, there's always a movie or show being filmed. It's a part of life there."

The waitress returns with the right wine and a plate of appetizers. We place our orders, and I smile when he rubs his foot against my calf as she stands there. I can't remember the last time I played footsie.

Our food comes, and we enjoy the meal. I understand now what he means by no longer noticing the people around us. I'm sure they're watching, but I don't pay attention. I'm here with him, and that's all I care about.

Eli and I chat about his time in New York as I sit enthralled. It all sounds so exciting. We finish the meal and are enjoying our bottle of wine. He tells me about his co-workers, and I can't help but fangirl a little over Noah Frazier. After Eli, he's my favorite character, and hearing about how they hang out makes me a little giddy.

"Is Noah as cute in person as he is on television?" I blurt out.

Eli nearly chokes on his drink. "What?"

"I'm a fan," I reply with innocence. "Of the show, of course."

"Oh, of course." The sarcasm in his voice tells me he clearly doesn't believe me.

"Jealous?" I taunt.

Eli leans back, crossing his arms across his broad chest. I use all my restraint to hold back my laugh because he looks adorable when he's being stupid. "Not at all."

"Good."

"It's not like you're asking me about another guy on *our* date."

I giggle a little and recover quickly. "Eli Walsh, do you not know that I think you're the sexiest man I've ever laid eyes on?"

He leans forward, resting his hands on the table. "Do you now?"

I move closer and reach toward him. "Yes."

"Tell me just how sexy you think I am."

I extend my hand, and he mirrors my movement. When we connect, Eli laces his fingers with mine. My mouth opens to tell him all the ways I find him sexy when his phone rings. He grumbles as he looks at the screen.

"Hello, Sharon. Yes. No." His eyes meet mine, and I see the worry there. "We're on a date . . ." Eli huffs. "I don't have to tell you beforehand." A pause. "Well, then do your job and handle it and make it clear what it means." He disconnects the call and then runs his hand down his face.

It doesn't take a detective to figure out what's happened. She knew we were out, which means someone has leaked that Eli Walsh is no longer on the market.

Living in our bubble was great, but we knew it wouldn't last. I'm grateful for the time we had. It allowed us the time to get to know each other and fall in love. If we had people following us around, we may have never gotten past the first date.

"Well, I guess we're official now, huh?" I smile, hoping to reassure him.

He studies me, and when he finds whatever he was looking for, he smiles. "Yeah, baby. We're official."

I nod. "Maybe this means women will stop touching you?"

Eli laughs without reservation. "I doubt it, but I promise not to like it."

"And I promise not to shoot them when they do."

I think that's fair. He doesn't like it, and I don't lose my badge or go to jail . . . win, win.

"There will be photos tomorrow." Eli grows serious.

"I figured as much, people have been staring all night while holding their phones."

Eli's eyes turn playful. "How about we give them a good one to post?"

I'm not sure what exactly that means, but the look in his eyes is enough to make me go along with him. He gets to his feet, makes his way around the table, and places one hand on the arm of my chair, the other on the table.

"I'm going to kiss you," he warns. "I'm going to tell the world that you're mine, right here and now."

Warmth spreads through me as his hand moves to my cheek. He leans down, presses his lips to mine, and publicly declares our relationship.

chapter twenty-four

Heather

"Heather, where are the streamers?" Nicole yells from the living room.

"Check the bags where all the decorations were!"

Today is the surprise party for Eli. I'm shocked I've been able to keep him completely in the dark. His mother left for New York the other day and can't make it, but Randy and Savannah will be here. Nicole came over about an hour ago and started getting things ready.

I told Eli that Nicole needed some best friend time since he's been monopolizing me and asked him to come pick me up at eight.

"Found them!" She bounces into the room with a grin. "We only have about five more minutes till everyone gets here. What else do you need?"

"I think we're all set. The cake is done, the food is out, and we're decorated."

"Good. Now you can tell me about your big public date with Mr. Sexy Pants last night," she says as she flops on my bed.

Eli wasn't kidding when he said it was going to get crazy. Within thirty minutes of the call from his publicist, we had about fifteen paparazzi outside the restaurant. Before we left, he told me exactly what to do and promised he'd shield me as much as he could.

It wasn't all that fun, but we survived. Once we got back to Eli's house, he encouraged me to call my friends and the police department to let them know. I couldn't believe he thought they'd care that much, but he's the expert on dealing with it. No one seemed to care, except for Matt. That was a fun conversation.

"I'm sure you read all about it," I say with my brow raised.

Nicole is a gossip column freak, so I'm sure she knew before I did that the story was going to break. "Not the same. But you're right. Tell me about what happened with Barney Fife instead."

Her and her names for Matt. "He was very short with me. Just one word answers."

"I'm glad he knows. I hope he hates himself for walking out on you."

Eli was not happy about that conversation. He knew he couldn't say much, but I could see how angry he was that I had to tell Matt. It's the part about my job that sucks. I wish I didn't have to deal with my ex-husband, yet I can't say I didn't enjoy having to tell him.

"Matt made his choice, and he has to live with it," I say as I put the last of my clothes away. Not being here much in the last few weeks has made me a little lazy regarding my home. "All right, let's finish up. They'll be here soon."

"Is that what you're wearing?" Nicole asks.

"Yes."

"Oh no," she admonishes me as she looks at my outfit. "You need to change."

I glance at the shorts and top I'm wearing, confused as to what the hell her issue is. "There's nothing wrong with my clothes."

"Put a freaking skirt on."

"What I'm wearing is fine."

"No." She laughs. "What you're wearing is lame."

I'm not sure what the hell she wants. "What is the issue? Should I be wearing a ball gown for a party with friends and Eli's brother?"

She snorts and heads to my closet. "You need to dress a little sexy for the man. It's his birthday! I have two words—easy . . . access."

The one thing that will always be constant is that Nicole is always thinking about sex. I'm here, worrying about making sure the house is ready, and she's worrying about me getting laid. Nicole riffles through my clothes, and a few things fly from my closet.

"Here," she shoves a skirt and off-the-shoulder top at me. "Put that on, fix your face, you have like . . . two minutes."

Sometimes, I love this girl, other times I'd love to kill her, this is the latter.

Instead of arguing with her, I get changed. I don't think Eli gives a shit about what I'm wearing, but I want this to be special. After I get dressed, I check my makeup and decide Nicole is an idiot because I was perfectly fine.

A few minutes later, Kristin and Danielle arrive. Both of them left their husband's and kids at home. I explain again while it's the four of us that Randy will be here and they have to control their inner fangirls.

"I swear I'll behave," Kristin says. "I figure after Eli, this should be easy."

"I make no promises," Nicole says as she plops on the couch.

I glare at her. "I swear to God, if you do anything stupid, I'll pepper spray you."

Her eyes widen, and I know she's flashing back to the one time she accidently sprayed herself. Dumbass thought it wouldn't hurt and was acting like anyone could be a cop, she pushed the button, but it was pointed at her. After that, she's never even gone near my canisters.

"Not funny." She crosses her arms.

All of us laugh at her face. She's such a turd.

Brody and Rachel arrive a few minutes later, and I'm glad they made it. He got along well with Eli at my sister's memorial. They bonded over the Rays and their predictions for this season. I can't tell you how happy I was that Brody finally had someone other than me to talk to about baseball.

Five minutes later, the doorbell rings. Once again, a dose of fear hits me. I've only met Savannah and Randy once, and it was at their mansion on the beach, now they'll see my home. Will they think I'm a gold digger? What was I thinking having them come here?

I feel a hand on my shoulder, and I know it's Nicole. Sometimes our damn near telepathy is a blessing. "You'll be fine. No one is going to judge you, and if they do, famous or not, I'll kick their ass."

I nod and open the door.

"Hey!" Savannah says with her arms wide. "I'm so glad you gave us a reason to come out. I swear, Adriel is giving me gray hair."

"I'm happy you're here." I hug her back.

"Hey, Heather," Randy's deep voice booms as he pulls me into a hug.

"Savannah, Randy, these are my friends Nicole, Kristin, and Danielle. That's my partner Brody and his wife Rachel."

They all take turns saying hello and shaking each other's hands. It's clear that everyone but Nicole is nervous meeting Randy. However, Savannah's constant poking at him makes it easier to see he's just a guy. Brody and Randy grab a beer and head into the kitchen, leaving all the women to themselves in the living room. I love that my new friends and old are meshing so easily.

"So, what time will Eli get here?" Savannah questions as she scrunches her shoulders.

"Should be here in about ten minutes. I should text him to make sure."

I pull my phone out and search for the last name that he put himself as, but there is no Best Sex of My Life contact. I should've known he'd change it again. I scroll through the contacts from the start. Of course, he doesn't use his actual name, that would be too easy, so I continue checking each letter.

When I get to what is clearly the new name change, I burst out laughing. He's a mess, my mess, but a freaking mess.

Savannah looks at me with a mixture of humor and worry. "What's so funny?"

"He changes his name in my phone each time I forget to hide it."

"Oh, what has my idiot brother-in-law called himself this time?"

"Mr. Multiple Orgasms."

She doubles over with laughter, and I shake my head.

Me: *Hello, Mr. Multiple Orgasms . . . seriously? I wanted to make sure you're picking me up at 8? I can't wait to see you.*

Mr. Multiple Orgasms: *Yup, I'll be there by eight. I'm leaving in five minutes.*

My smile is automatic. I can't wait to see his face.

"He'll be here in about twenty minutes!" I tell everyone and go back to my conversation with Savannah. She laughs about the other names Eli's given himself, and then we all mingle.

Twenty-five minutes pass and still no Eli, so I shoot him another text.

Me: *Hey, you almost here?*

Another fifteen minutes pass, and he doesn't respond. Maybe he's stuck in traffic?

I mingle with my friends, watching the clock and trying not to jump to conclusions. I have to remember that not everything is a tragedy waiting to happen. Years of being preprogramed to expect the worst is sometimes a curse.

It's now half past eight, and he's definitely late, and I'm undeniably concerned.

"I'm not sure where the hell he is," I say to myself as I make my way around the room. I shoot off another text.

Me: *I hope you're okay . . . please text me back or call me.*

Brody comes over, places his hand on my back, and drops his voice to a whisper. "What's the matter, Covey?"

I look over with surprise.

"Don't look at me like that," he admonishes. "I can read you. You're worried about him being late?"

I subtly shake my head. "I'm fine. He said he'd be here over a half hour ago, and we both know it doesn't take that long to get here. He isn't responding to my texts, either."

I wait for my phone to buzz with a response.

"Everything okay?" Nicole asks when she sees me whispering with Brody.

"She's just being Heather," Brody explains.

I shoot him a dirty look, and he shrugs. "He usually texts me right back, and he's now forty minutes late. I'm wondering why he isn't responding."

"Maybe he fell asleep?" she suggests, which is ludicrous.

"After he said he was leaving?" I counter.

"Want me to check in at the station for reports of any accidents?" Brody offers.

I shake my head. "No, I'm probably being stupid. I'm going to call him now."

I can't explain it, but there's a niggling feeling in my gut telling me something else is keeping him. There are times that gut check has been the difference of life and death for me, I don't tend to ignore it, but I don't want to be a crazy girlfriend, either.

I make my way outside to see if maybe his car is here, but since there's no sign of him, I call. The phone rings and rings before his voice mail picks up.

"Hey, babe, I'm calling because it's been almost an hour since you said you'd be here, and I haven't heard from you. Give me a call when you can. Love you."

I disconnect the phone and start to pace the porch. My mind races from one extreme to the other as I go from fear to resolve. A big part of me wants to get in the car and head over there, the other says I have to trust him. He could be held up for a hundred reasons, and my being paranoid isn't going to be good for a long-distance relationship we're about to embark on. Not wanting to be dramatic, I convince myself to head inside and give him a little more time.

After another seven minutes, that niggling feeling is now a full-blown boulder threatening to crush me if I don't get in my car to go find him.

Randy comes outside, and I give him a fake smile. "You okay?"

"Eli isn't answering the phone or my texts, and he said he'd be here at eight."

He looks at his watch and back to me. "I'll go to the house and check on him."

I shake my head. "No, I mean, he has no idea you're here."

Randy's eyes flash with something, but I don't catch it. "You should do that . . . so it doesn't ruin the party . . ."

"Okay," I draw the word out.

"My brother has no idea how lucky he is."

I smile and shrug. "I think we're both lucky."

I'm fully aware of how blessed I am that Eli thought enough to chase after me. All those times I tried to get rid of him make me grateful that he doesn't like to be told no. Otherwise, I wouldn't know what real love is like.

I enter the house and explain to everyone that I'll be back. "I'm going to check on him. It's been an hour, and he still isn't answering."

I hop in my car, telling myself the entire way to remain calm no matter what. He's given me no reason to distrust him, and he's probably sleeping. Who am I kidding? He's not sleeping. The only reason I feel as though I'm a good cop is because of my intuition. It's something so many of us brush aside, but I believe it's a gift not to be squandered. How many times did I think Matt was unhappy and pretended I was being stupid? So many I lost count. I think back to when Stephanie's symptoms started, how the doctors told us she didn't need the extra tests, but I demanded they do them. I knew there was something we were missing, and I refused to budge.

Right now, my nerves are screaming that something isn't right, and he isn't where he should be.

I pull up to his house, and the lights are still on. I use the key he gave me and head inside.

"Eli?" I call out, but no one answers.

I hear noise coming from the family room off the kitchen. I turn the corner, but it's just the television. I check the pool deck before moving on to the rest of the second floor. This freaking house needs to be smaller.

My heart starts to quicken as I get closer to the bedroom. I don't know where he is, but each step I take makes my stomach grow tighter. I close my eyes, steeling myself for whatever I might find, and open the door.

He lies crumpled in the middle of the bedroom floor.

"Eli!" I scream and rush toward him. Sweat covers his body, he has a gash on his head where blood leaks from. His breathing is labored, and his eyes flutter open to closed. "Oh my God." My hands shake as I try to turn him over. "Eli, can you hear me?"

He struggles for breath, and I'm not sure if he's conscious when he mutters something incoherent. I lean closer, listening, and swear I hear the word "Help."

"Stay awake," I say as I tap the side of his face.

I dial 9-1-1, and my mind switches immediately into police mode. My voice shakes, but I'm able to give the dispatcher his address, my badge number, and a rundown of the situation. They instruct me to keep him awake if possible and to wait for help.

It shouldn't take long for the paramedics to arrive, but each second feels like hours.

I sit on the floor with his head in my lap. "Can you open your eyes?" I ask, but he doesn't respond. "Can you hear me, baby? Can you tell me what happened?"

"Heather," Eli's eyes open, and he starts to struggle. "Have to get . . . to . . . phone."

"I'm right here, Eli. Don't move, just stay with me," I command as I wipe a bead of sweat from his forehead. "Help is on the way."

He pants again, and I take his pulse several times, watching the clock move. His heart rate is all over the place. I hear the banging on the door below, and I now understand what it feels like on this side of the door. My fear of leaving him to let them in but knowing I have to makes my heart plummet.

"I'll be right back," I say, even though I know he probably doesn't understand.

I rush down the stairs faster than I knew I could move and throw the door open. Two of my fellow squad members, Whitman and Vincenzo, stand there.

"Covey?" Whitman asks with surprise.

"He's upstairs. Where are the medics?" I ask without answering the questions in their eyes.

"They're pulling through the gate now," Vincenzo replies. "Are you on duty?"

"Why aren't they here? He needs medical help!"

"Relax." Whitman touches my arm. "Wait, is this . . . this is . . ."

I don't answer him. I don't care if he's figuring out whose house this is and why I'm here. The man I'm so deeply in love with is going in and out of consciousness, and he needs help. My legs start to shake, and Whitman catches me as I start to crumble.

He steadies me, and I turn toward the staircase. I can't wait for help, I *am* the help. We need to get him to the hospital now. "You guys can transport him, fuck the ambulance. I can't carry him. I don't know what happened, but he needs help now!" I say with so much emotion that their faces fall. I'm not sentimental at work. I don't cry. I don't whine. I do my job and kick ass. I'm a warrior when I'm in uniform. Even through my sister's illness, I never once appeared weak. Right now, I can't hold it together. "He can't wait! I can't lose him!"

Tears spring in my gaze, and I can't stop them. I feel helpless.

"Heather," Vincenzo says in his calming voice. I know that tone. I'm the master at that tone. "They're almost here, relax."

"Go with her," Whitman instructs. "I'll get the medics upstairs. I'll radio when they arrive, okay?"

I know he's right. We can't take a patient with a head injury to the hospital in the cop car.

We rush back up the stairs and into the room where Eli still lies helpless on the floor. I move back to him, checking his pulse again. Tears continue to fall as I brush back his dark brown hair.

"They're here," I hear Whitman over the radio.

The paramedics enter the room, and I see the recognition as they realize they're in Eli Walsh's house. They look at both of us and back to him.

Questions are fired off as they try to gather information about his injuries and medical history. So many things I don't know . . .

"Is he taking any medication?"

"I don't know."

"Any medical conditions?"

"I don't know," I admit.

"Allergies?"

"I . . ." I shake my head. "I don't know."

"Has he taken any drugs? Been drinking?"

"No, I've never seen him take anything. And I wasn't here, so I have no idea if he drank anything."

They both look to each other and then ask more questions that I can't answer. It takes me three minutes to realize how much Eli and I don't know about each other. He has no idea I'm allergic to penicillin or that I had surgery eight years ago for an ovarian cyst. We're so in love and so oblivious.

He groans as they roll him onto the backboard and then carry him down the stairs. I grab my phone and keys off the front entry table and they're already closing the doors.

I quickly try to lock up, but my blood-covered hands are shaking so bad I can't get the key to go in.

Whitman comes over, places his hand over mine, steadying it so I can turn the key. "I'll drive you over," he says, guiding me to the cruiser.

I don't say anything, I'm in shock, and my mind can't fully absorb anything. I climb in the back and twist my hands together.

The only thing that goes through my mind is that I can't lose him. Not like this. Not so soon after Stephanie. Not when we haven't had enough time. We deserve more time.

Please, God, give me more time.

༄

"Randy!" I rush forward as he sprints into the hospital. It's been twenty minutes since we arrived. I was told to take a seat and they'd let me know something, but no one will answer me. They keep saying I'm not family. "They're not telling me anything, but they're working on him."

"Okay, I'll find out." Randy heads to the desk where the nurse grabs a file and then escorts him back.

Savannah's hand touches my shoulder, and I turn to her with tears streaming. "It's okay, Heather. Eli is strong."

"I don't know what happened. There was blood on the carpet from the bathroom to where I found him. I guess he hit his head and stopped there?" Now that I've had time to think, I'm trying to piece together the scene. My best guess is that he fell. I know his foot was giving him problems, so maybe he tripped? Either way, he hit his head, and then either fell again . . . or something. Why was he dripping with sweat? Did he have to drag himself from the bathroom? I don't know. "I couldn't tell the paramedics anything. I don't know what caused this or if he takes any medication . . . I called as soon as I snapped out of it."

Savannah guides me to the chair, and she's silent. "So, you and Eli haven't really gotten to that share everything point?" she asks after a few minutes.

"No, I guess not. We happened so fast and so strong. It was like this tornado that swooped us both up. Plus, I was dealing with my sister's disease, and he was trying to be there for me. I don't know."

She takes my hand in hers. "Randy should be out soon, he'll let you know what's going on."

"I should've gone and checked on him earlier."

Hindsight is a bitch. I had a feeling when he wasn't responding. I ignored it, and he needed me.

Randy comes into view, and we both stand. "He's going to be okay. He's confused, but he'll be fine."

"Oh, thank God." I sigh. The weight lifts from my chest, and I can breathe again.

"He wants to see you, but he needs a few more tests."

"Okay." I'll sit out here and wait forever if it means he'll be okay. He's going to be okay. I knew I was afraid, but I hadn't realized how tightly the fear had gripped me until it was gone. "Do you know what happened?"

Randy looks to Savannah and then back to me. "The details are fuzzy, but I'm sure he'll explain what he remembers."

"I'm going to call your mom," Savannah says and kisses his cheek.

"I'm glad you checked on him," Randy says as we take a seat. "I don't know what would've happened if you hadn't gone there. He's really lucky to have you, Heather. I hope you know how much he loves you."

It's weird hearing this from his brother. We've only met twice now, but Randy seems to understand Eli at his core. He clearly loves his brother, and it's a bond I can understand completely. What he said is something I would've felt toward someone loving Stephanie.

"I love him, too."

He nods. "I believe you do."

Savannah returns from her phone call right as the doctor comes out.

He explains that Eli finished his CT scan, and they're going to do some additional testing, but he's alert and receiving fluids. "He's back in his room if you'd like to see him, he's asking for Randy and then Heather."

"I'll be brief." He smiles and then follows the doctor through the double doors.

Relief floods my veins now that we've confirmed he's going to be fine. I close my eyes and say a silent prayer to Stephanie. I feel her here. This hospital was where we spent so much time together. Days of testing that turned into overnights because of her exhaustion. So many nights I slept in that God-awful chair that they said was a bed, hoping her pain would subside.

I hoped it would be a long time before I walked these halls again.

Randy returns to the waiting room not even ten minutes later.

"He's waiting for you." He smiles. "We have to get back to the kids, but if you need anything, just call, okay? I'll come back tomorrow to check on things."

Savannah pulls me in and kisses my cheek. "I'll call you tomorrow as well, okay?"

"Of course."

I make my way to Eli's room and knock softly. The door creaks and his eyes meet mine. All at once, my emotions burst forward. Relief that he's okay, fear that it could've gone another way, happiness that he looks a little like himself, guilt that I wasn't there, and most of all . . . love for this man.

"Eli," I say as a prayer. I move forward, and he pulls me to his chest. "God, I was so scared."

His arms are tight, and I breathe him in. "I'm going to be fine, baby."

I lift my head and touch his face. "You scared me."

He closes his eyes. "I was stupid."

"Stupid?"

Eli takes my hands in his. "I should've never pushed myself."

"What happened?" I ask, but the nurse enters.

"Hi, Mr. Walsh, I'm your nurse, Shera," she smiles. "I'm going to start the Solu-Medrol in the IV, and then I'll take your vitals again."

"Thank you," he says.

I know that drug.

I don't know why, but I swear I've heard it before.

I rack my brain to remember why the hell it sounds so familiar.

Then it hits me.

Solu-Medrol is what they gave Stephanie when her nerve pain flared. It's a drug she had several times to reduce the inflammation, and it's only used for severe conditions.

My eyes meet Eli's, and the floor drops out from beneath me.

chapter twenty-five

Eli

I SEE THE STORMS ROLL THROUGH HER BROWN EYES. I WATCH THE CONFLICTION WITHOUT saying a word. There's nothing I'm going to be able to say to explain this.

I've been lying to her.

The nurse takes her time as the tension fills the room. I almost want her to stay, any second to prolong the inevitable, I'll take.

There were so many times I could've said something. Randy laid into me pretty hard, and I deserved every word.

He has no idea the guilt I've felt for keeping my illness from her. The nights I lie awake with her in my arms, hating myself because I'm a pussy and couldn't let her go. I'm a selfish prick. I know this, but for the first time, I didn't care.

"All right, I'll be back to check on you in an hour," Shera explains and pats my arm. "I'm a big fan, Mr. Walsh. We'll take good care of you."

The knot in my throat doesn't allow me to speak. My gaze turns back to Heather, and I wait.

A single tear rolls down her perfect cheek. I watch as it lands on her lips, ones I know I'll never feel again, and my heart breaks. I wonder if this could've been different. If I'd told her I was sick, would she have stayed? I'll never know.

"You're sick." Her soft voice is filled with pain.

"Yes."

Heather's hands shake as she tries to wipe her face. "Do you have Huntington's disease?"

"No, I have relapsing-remitting multiple sclerosis."

Her lips part, and I watch her face fall. Fear beams from her eyes before another tear descends. "Are—" She clears her throat. "Are you okay?"

Agony like I've never felt before spreads through my body. Not because I'm actually in pain, but because even though she knows I've been hiding my condition, she's still worried about me.

I'm a fucking piece of shit.

I don't deserve her.

"I haven't been symptomatic in a while. I usually take medication that helps keep things under control."

She nods slowly while twisting her hands. "I see. And you're not taking them now?"

I've been reckless with my body the last few months. On tour, I didn't take the infusions regularly. Then I met Heather, and I thought I could be free for a little while. I didn't know we'd have something like this. Yes, I had feelings for her, but I truly thought they would fade, not intensify. My time with Heather has been the first time I felt warmth in my life, and I know the darkness will be that much deeper when she leaves.

"Not like I should."

Her gaze moves to where her hands are laced tightly together in her lap. "Okay. How long have you known you have MS?"

Her calm tone scares me more than if she were yelling.

"I had my first symptom ten years ago."

"Right. Ten years."

There's no anger in her voice, only resignation. She keeps her eyes down, leaving me no indication of what she's thinking. She has no idea how much guilt I've grappled with. But my need for her won out. Self-preservation came before anything else. I had to have her. I needed to keep her.

"I wanted to tell you," I admit.

"But you didn't."

Because I'm a fucking pussy. "I couldn't."

Her eyes lift, a mix of hurt and anger fill her gaze. "And you thought lying to me about it was the better option?"

"I couldn't tell you. I tried, but I couldn't do it."

She clutches her stomach and drops her head.

My chest aches and dread spreads through me. She's going to leave, just like Penelope. As soon as she found out I wasn't the perfect man, that I was damaged, she took off. When Heather returns her gaze to me, I see the same goodbye in her eyes, exactly like all those years ago.

"You kept the fact that you were sick from me. You . . . hid this." She chokes on the words. "Even knowing everything I went through? How could you do this to me? How could you make me believe that we were building a future together, when all the while you were keeping something so serious from me? How, Eli, how?" Her voice cracks at the end, and I curse myself for being weak.

Weakness in my heart. Weakness in my body.

I can't go to her. I can't grab her and force her to hear me out. Even though, I have nothing but excuses. Dread fills the room, weaving its way around my broken heart, squeezing tighter as I prepare for her to leave me.

"I've hated myself for it. I wanted you to see me, know me, love me, and then I was going to tell you. I know it's fucked up. But when you told me about your sister, I couldn't tell you. Then the day I was finally going to tell you, Stephanie died. After that, there was no way I could say it."

"And what about all the time since then?"

"Each day I kept it in, it became harder to tell you. I was afraid if I did, you were going to leave."

"What?" She turns with a mix of anger and shock. "You thought if I knew you were sick, that I'd walk away from you? You think that's who I am?"

"I think it's easy to love a man who isn't falling apart."

"And you think I'm that shallow? Do you know me at all? I would never have left you because you were sick!"

"I couldn't know that!"

Heather stands and moves toward my bed and tears fill her eyes as she touches my cheek. I want to relish in her touch, but I won't allow myself any of it. "You didn't give me a chance to show you."

"If you're going to go, then go," I spit the words.

She shakes her head, opening and closing her mouth before she collapses in the chair. Heather's body sings of defeat. I've broken her.

Anger toward myself builds like blocks. Each stacking higher and higher until I can't see over the wall. I punch my way through, each blow causing my panic to rise. She's going to leave me, and I won't be able to stop her.

"I want to fucking stand and come over to you," I say, hoping she is still listening. "I want to take you in my arms and be the man that you thought you had. But my fucking legs won't work. I can't walk, Heather. I can't fucking walk. I screwed up every goddamn chance I had with you. I know this. I hate myself for it, and I won't hurt you."

Her head lifts, and she wipes the tears with the back of her hand. "What do you mean your legs won't work?"

"I had shooting pain up and down my legs earlier. They're now numb."

Her lips part and she sucks in a breath. "Is that how you fell?"

"Yes, I knew it was happening, but I tried to pretend it wasn't."

Heather doesn't say a word. She watches me with her gorgeous eyes. Eyes that I know each speck of gold, each tiny piece of light brown, and every darker spot by memory. Eyes in which I've found everything I've ever wanted. She's loved me because I've been the man she needed. Because of my MS, I'm now broken, weak, and a liar.

I decide she needs to hear the entire ugly story. Let her get a glimpse into the hell my body is stirring. "My hand has occasionally been going numb over the last week."

Awareness flashes and she gasps. "Like when you dropped your phone?"

"Today, I was in the bathroom and realized I'd left my phone on the table in the bedroom. My foot started to tingle and there was shooting pain up my legs. I sat at the tub, thinking I could rub my legs enough to make it stop, which it did enough that I thought I could get to my phone." I look over, wanting to see her face when she hears it all. Heather is a statue, she doesn't move or even breathe, so I lay it out. "I took one step before I went down. My head slammed on the side of the counter."

"Eli," she gasps.

I lift my palm to stop her. "I don't think I passed out then, and I knew I was bleeding. But I couldn't feel my legs." Her hand covers her mouth as another tear falls. "I couldn't move, and all I could think about was disappointing you. I knew you needed me, but I couldn't get to you. I was lying on that floor, refusing to fail you. So, I used every fucking scrap of strength I had and clawed my way out of there. Using only my arms, I pulled, pushed, and struggled to gain each goddamn inch. Knowing that this was going to be how it went." She moves to my side, and I brush away her tears. I touch her blonde hair, memorizing the way it feels in my grasp. I touch her face, wishing I could go back in time. "I couldn't get far before my arms started to ache. My hands weren't closing like I wanted them to. I was weak, because that's what this disease has made me."

"You're not weak," her feathery voice rebuts. "All of this could've been avoided, Eli. Tonight could've been so much easier if you told me you were having symptoms instead of lying to me."

"You only knew me as Eli Walsh, the singer, actor, and man who could give you the world. I've lived this scene before, Heather. I watched it with Penelope, so go ahead and make your exit so we can go back to our lives!"

"No." The single word is steel, and it stops my pity party in its tracks. "Don't you dare make me out to be like your ex. I'm not her. I'm not running away. I'm still sitting right here, trying to understand!"

"Why?" I yell. "Why bother?"

"Because I love you!" She's on her feet at my side. "That's what you do when you love someone!"

I shake my head and smother the hope that tries to claw its way through. "What if I don't love you?"

I push the lie out of my mouth, needing her to have a seed of doubt.

Heather's eyes narrow, and she grips my face in her hands. "Say it to me again, Ellington. Tell me you don't love me. Look me in the eyes and tell me that."

One tear falls from her beautiful eyes, and it kills me. No matter what happens from this moment forward, I won't lie to her. I can't hurt her like that, because it would be like cutting out my own heart.

"I can't."

Her hands move from my face to cover her own. "You can't lie to me anymore, Eli. If we're going to do this together, we have to be honest."

"Do what?" I ask.

"If we're going to fight this. I need to know what all of your disease means."

I had so many brilliant reasons why I should keep this from her, but all of them seem ridiculous now, except this last one. The one I feared more than anything, that she'd look at me like this. Heather's eyes are no longer filled with fear or anger, now it's resolve. It's the same way she looked at her sister.

I love her more than anything in this world, and I won't be another thing she has to care for.

She's done it her whole life, and it won't be how we live.

"I won't do this," I say. "I won't become a patient to you. I can't."

"What?" she gasps.

MS doesn't have a guidebook. I don't get to predict my outcome, and I won't burden her. I knew the day I found out about her sister that I should've stopped pursuing her, but I've never been able to stay away. She needs to know the truth of what this means for us, but I cannot be the man she pities.

"I'm not your sister, Heather. Don't you get it? Don't you see that I want to be the one who takes care of you!" I yell, frustration rolling off me. Her body goes ramrod straight. I watch the anguish spread across her face, her shoulders slump, and her jaw drop. I say the dumbest thing I could. "Just leave."

Her eyes meet mine, and then Heather does the one thing I both wanted to happen and prayed wouldn't . . . she turns and walks out the door without a word.

I've just lost her.

Agony like I've never felt before engulfs me, and I fucking deserve every last bit of it.

chapter twenty-six

Heather

I LEAN AGAINST THE WALL OUTSIDE HIS DOOR, STRUGGLING TO CATCH MY BREATH. I CAN'T believe he said that. Of all the things that have come out of his mouth, nothing has ever hurt me like him bringing up my sister.

I've never looked at him like that. I loved my sister, I cared for my sister, and it's only been a few weeks since I lost her. I didn't need him to draw the comparison—I already had, and I was coming to terms with how different this is. He has no idea how much he hurt me. Not just because of the comment, either. I've shared everything with him. There's nothing I keep from him, and yet, he keeps vital things from me.

Anger sears my veins, and I fight the urge to go back in there and rip into him. Explain how things in an adult relationship are supposed to work, but I don't move.

"You okay?" Shera, the nurse assigned to Eli's room, asks.

I rub my eyes, hoping I don't look like a crazy person before righting myself. "Yeah, sorry. I just . . . I need a few minutes."

She rubs my arm. "Okay, honey. We'll keep an eye on him. Don't you worry. He's going to be okay, you'll see, the IV will help, and he'll be good as new."

Yeah, but what will we be? How do we move on from here when he's pushing me away? I don't voice that to her, I attempt a smile and nod. "Thanks."

My head falls back against the wall, and I close my eyes, trying to think through everything that happened. He had to know what he said would break my heart. Mentioning Stephanie like that was a low blow that I felt in the depths of my soul. She was my entire world, and I never pitied her, I did whatever I could to lift her up. How dare he wound me so deeply?

But Eli's never been callous, he's always been . . . perfect.

Perfection is an illusion we create to convince the soul to trust. Now that the curtain has fallen, I see how stupid I was. The thing is, I don't need perfect. I need real because Matt was perfect until shit hit the fan. Then he was gone. But this hurts so much more than that did.

I need air. I need to think and get control, because if I go back in there, I'm going to lose my shit.

I make my way toward the front of the hospital while my mind runs in circles. Tears roll down my cheeks as the warm air hits my face. I inhale, hoping to get some clarity, but I find something much worse.

"Ms. Covey!" My name is being called by a crowd of people all rushing toward me. Flashes of lights go off so fast I can't see anything around me. Over and over they blind me and create a circle so I can't move. They scream my name and bark out questions while I try to find a way out of their enclosure. "Is Eli okay? What happened? Is it true he collapsed? Ms. Covey, over here!" There is no time to answer even if I wanted to. "Are you still together? Are you crying? Can you tell us if there were drugs involved?"

My heart pounds too hard in my chest as I push through them without saying a word. I get back in the safety of the waiting room and release a heavy breath. One more thing to deal with today. God only knows what those photos will look like.

My phone pings, and I pull it from my pocket.

Nicole: Hey, don't want to bother you, just checking in. Are things okay there?

Me: No, things are definitely not okay. He's fine, but relationship wise . . . not so much.

Nicole: I'm sorry. Need me to kick his ass?

Me: I think I got this. We'll figure it out or we can both kick his ass.

Nicole: Regulators . . . Mount up!

I burst out laughing as I hear her doing her best Warren G impersonation. Nothing like Nicole to bring some humor in when I feel like I'm drowning.

I dial her number, and she answers on the first ring. "You're so not okay if you're calling me."

"I need you to remind me that I can handle this."

Nicole goes quiet and then clears her throat. "I don't know what happened to make you question yourself."

I tell her about what happened tonight. Nicole listens and allows me to spill my heart. I'm so hurt and angry. I'm also disappointed because I thought we were great. I didn't know he'd been lying to me and hoping I wouldn't find out. I'm angry because he hid his symptoms from me, which led to me finding him collapsed in his bedroom.

"I can't even get some air because I was assaulted by fucking photographers," I complain and sink into the chair.

"Do you want me to come kick some asses? I'll handle the paparazzi, and then I'll fuck Eli up for being a douche. I figure you're done with him so you won't be upset."

"I know what you're doing," I grumble.

"Either you're going to do it or I need to come and end it for you."

She's insane to think I'd let her handle this. "Stop being an asshole."

She lets out a cough that sounds more like a laugh. "You should talk. You're on the phone with me instead of in there fighting for him. Guys like Eli don't come around often, and if you're dumb enough to let him go, then you're not the fierce woman I've admired."

"I feel betrayed," I admit. "Him keeping this from me is a big deal, and then to be so cruel by bringing up Steph."

"You should feel that way and be sure to let him know that. But remember what happened to you not even two minutes ago, babe. Eli deals with that day in and day out, he has to protect himself, too. More than anything, you have to decide right now if you're willing to end things. If the answer is no, then get your tiny ass back in there and fix it."

She's right. I need to let him know exactly how I feel. I knew when I walked out of that room, I'd walk back in. He isn't the man I'm willing to watch leave my life. When Matt left, there was sadness but also relief. The idea of not having Eli causes my heart to drop.

I sigh and get to my feet. "I need to go."

I'm a strong woman who knows exactly what I want, and it's him. I'm going to tell him exactly how this is going to work. He doesn't get to decide this alone, it's as much my choice as it's his.

"I knew you'd do this," Nicole says with pride. "God help him, because my friend is a badass who doesn't take shit from anyone. Love you, call me if you need me."

"I will. Love you, too."

He isn't going to know what hit him. My life has always been a series of misfortunes, but I've never allowed it to define me. I may feel like I don't have a say in how things go, but I can decide how to deal with them. I'm a fighter, and I won't let anything stand in my way of the prize.

After a few deep breaths and an idea of what to say, I stand straight, crack my neck, and march to his room.

The door opens, and our eyes connect. Eli shifts slightly, and I clench my fists.

"You talked before, now you're going to listen," I demand. I'm determined for him to hear me. I move to the side of his bed and touch my finger to his chest. Our eyes stay on each other's, and I refuse to break away. "First, you will never use my sister against me. It was a dick move to do after everything I've been through the last few weeks. I will never allow you to hurt me like that again."

"I didn't—"

"No." I push my finger harder, silencing him. "You don't get to talk this time, got it?" I ask.

Eli nods and puts his hands up.

"Good." I ease back a little, still standing, needing the height to make me feel stronger. As much as I try to convince myself I'm going to just say what I need to, the truth is that I'm terrified this could end very different from how I hope it will.

Eli may decide that he doesn't want to be with me, and there's nothing I can do if that's his choice. However, I'm not going to allow myself to focus on that. I'm steeling myself for the outcome I desire, which is us moving forward—together.

My eyes close, and once I have my composure back, I continue on, "This situation is nothing like it was with Stephanie. I know you're not her, but it seems you don't get that. She was my sister, but she became my entire life when my parents died."

"I can't have you look at me like that again, Heather." He interrupts, and my eyes open.

The pain on his face causes me to let him have his say. I'm lost. I have no idea what he's talking about. During that entire thing, I wanted to make sense of it. All of it. I was focusing on not losing my shit on him, which I clearly didn't do a great job of. However, I can't recall whatever he says he saw.

"I didn't look at you like anything."

He sighs and glances at the ceiling. "You looked at me like you had to take care of me. I know right now my body is a mess, but I'll work through it. Usually, when you look at me, it's like you become bright and hopeful." He pauses. "When you were in here before, it was gone. Instead, I was a problem for you to solve. I watched your eyes go from days in the sun to doctor visits and hospitals. I know your sister was your life, but it was the same way you looked at her."

He couldn't be more wrong. That was not it at all. The fact that he feels that way sends a wave of fresh hurt through me. Why are men so stupid?

"First of all," I sit on the bed and rest my hand on his chest. "She was my responsibility. I was her parent for all intents and purposes, not to mention she was practically still a kid when she was diagnosed. I *had* to be the adult. It's not anything like that here. You're a grown ass man with a family that loves and supports you. I was her everything, Eli. There was no family or support system, I was it for her. So, yes, my entire life revolved around fixing or making things better for her. But us . . ." I sigh "It isn't that way. I want to be your partner. I want you to lean on me and then hold me up when I'm falling. That's not pity, that's love. Don't ever make this a parallel to Steph, because it's not."

He lifts his hand, touches my lips and releases a deep breath. "I'm so sorry, Heather. I never wanted to hurt you like that."

I believe him. Eli and I both have a lot of shit in our pasts that will be our demise if we don't work through it.

"I don't think you meant to hurt me, but it did, which is why I needed to walk away before I said something I'd regret."

"I thought you left," he admits with dejection laced in his voice. "I didn't think you were coming back and that I lost you because of this . . ."

I shake my head, partially in disbelief and partially in frustration. After all that we've endured, I don't know how he thinks I would be the girl to leave him because he's sick. There is no choice for me when it comes to him. The day Eli Walsh showed up at my door, he became a part of my world. I fought it, and failed. He's the other half of me, and there's no way that I could ever walk away from him.

Which brings me to my next part of this discussion. He has to see the distinctions in how we are from our pasts.

"I'm glad you bring that up." I lean back so we're not touching. I tend to think more clearly when we have a little distance. "I am not my ex-husband or your ex-girlfriend. I get that you have issues, and I do, too, but it's completely unfair to expect me to behave like them. Not only did you compare me to Penelope but also you made me Matt in the same breath. I hate her for what she did to you, and if you don't see the differences, then we should end things now."

People like her and Matt don't deserve a love like ours. Eli has given me more joy in our time together than anyone was able to give me in years.

Our relationship will be tested, but he has to know I'm not going anywhere. He's assured me of that more times than I can count. Not only in his words but also in what he's shown me. Now, I need to give him the same assurances.

Eli stays silent for a few seconds, and regret rolls off him. "Jesus, I'm just fucking up left and right. I know you're not her or him. I was pissed off at myself, and I needed to give you the reason to walk away."

"Is that what you want?" I ask.

His fingers wrap around my wrist and he tightens his grip. "No."

"I'm glad, because I have no intention of going anywhere. Even if you act like an ass sometimes. I'm not some fan who loves you because I have this idealistic dream of who you are. Love isn't some word to me, it's everything. I shared my heart with you, not because I want perfect, but because I want you. When I look at you, I see a life together. And no matter what life throws at us, I'm going to fight for you and with you, Ellington."

"Am I allowed to talk?" he asks.

"No, I have one last thing." He fights a smile, but it's probably the most important point we've yet to cover. "Don't ever lie to me again. This entire thing could've been avoided if you had talked to me. No lies between us. Ever."

"Okay," he replies, releasing my wrist only to take my hand in his. "I'll never lie to you again."

"You're going to share with me, Eli. You're going to have to let me carry your burdens just like I let you shoulder mine. But I'm not going to run from us. I've done that before, and you caught me."

Eli grips the back of my head and pulls me close so we're nose to nose. "I'm glad you say that, because as soon as I got control of my legs, I was going to hunt you down, and you weren't getting away again."

No matter what the future throws at us, I want to walk through it with him. I need him so much it's not even normal.

"I don't think you would've had to go far," I admit. "I never left the hospital grounds. I couldn't do it even though I was pissed."

Eli releases me. "Lay with me."

"Are you sure?"

He winces as he moves his legs over, making room. "Come on, I need to hold you."

I get on my side, nestling myself against his chest. I rest my chin on my hand and look at him. He smirks. "What are you smiling at?" For the first time, I can't help but laugh a little. He's too damn adorable.

"That you love me and couldn't leave. I'm glad I made you fall deep."

I roll my eyes. "Whatever, you're just as bad."

His smile fades, and Eli takes my face in his hands. "I'm far deeper than you even know. My life didn't make sense until that night at the concert. I thought I knew what love was, I didn't have a clue until you. I've never been more broken than when I watched you close that door. The pain I felt in that moment isn't something I ever want to feel again." Eli brushes his thumb against my cheek. "You're the strongest, most beautiful thing I've ever seen. I promise that there is nothing I won't do to prove how much I love you. Forgive me, Heather."

I kiss his lips and then rest my forehead against his, knowing we can face the storms ahead of us together. "I forgive you."

"I told you before that we could only own tonight, but that was bullshit."

My eyes meet his with confusion.

"I'm going to own all of our days, nights, and every tomorrow."

He presses his mouth to mine, and I melt into his touch. The weight that was sitting on my heart is lifted, and I know we're going to be okay.

chapter twenty-seven

Heather

"Are you sure you want to do this?" I ask him as we park in my driveway.

"You baked me a cake, and I'm going to eat it."

Eli was released from the hospital today, and he basically demanded we go straight to my house. He regained feeling in his legs after the first day, and he's able to walk now with his walker. His doctors reiterated how important it is to stay on track with his medications and infusions, and he claims he understands.

We've spent the last few days making plans and trying hard not to focus on his condition. Matt granted me another week off work, and I'm going to New York with Eli.

I help him from the car, and he grumbles when I bring the walker out.

"Don't gripe, you know you have to use it, Gramps."

"You do realize in a week, I could be perfectly normal and be able to kick your ass for that comment."

I smile, "I like my chances on outrunning you."

He huffs and pushes the walker toward the house. "Thinks she's all badass because she's a cop, I'll show her."

I've missed this playful, smartass, and horny-as-hell side of him. However, I swear, he tried to get me to blow him in the hospital. That was a fun fight, where I did actually help him a little, however I was not on board with hospital blow jobs. He threatened that if I didn't, he'd find a nurse to give him a sponge bath.

No one in that hospital was touching his junk but me.

We enter the house, and he sits on the couch. "You okay?" he asks for the millionth time. I don't need to even bother asking what he's referring to.

Tomorrow, Eli will hold a press conference to announce his condition along with our relationship. His publicist pretty much demanded we take control of the situation. They took thousands of photos of me coming in and out of the hospital. The constant barrage of questions was out of control. Eli was livid and demanded Sharon get here and handle things.

"Stop asking me that. I'm fine." For the most part. "Am I excited about this? No, but it's what has to be done. Honestly, I'm glad we had time before people figured it out."

Eli pulls me to his side and kisses the top of my head. "You're going to be great. You don't have to talk, just stand there and look pretty."

He's ridiculous. His publicist, Sharon, is a lunatic. I swear, she's her own brand of energy. She talks a mile a minute, has a Bluetooth constantly attached to her ear, and can carry on at least four conversations at once. She scares me—a lot.

"Sharon said they're going to hound me more if I refuse to speak. She practically demanded I answer questions."

"Baby, they're going to hound you no matter what. It's part of their game, but the beginning will be the worst. After that, some asshole will do something stupid, and they'll move on."

I look at him and grin. "Basically, we should hope for a celebrity shit show?"

"Pretty much. Give them a real juicy story, and they'll all flock to that."

This world is a little odd. I've never understood the appeal of stalking celebrities. Nicole tried to explain it to me once, but it was as if she were trying to explain quantum physics to a rock. I just didn't get it.

"Your life is bizarre," I muse while enjoying his warmth.

"And yours isn't?"

I sit up with my jaw open. "Umm, how is my life weird?"

He chuckles. "Let's see, you chase after criminals. People with guns."

"Yeah, bad people who need to be in jail."

"Even worse!" Eli laughs as his voice raises. "You're nuts."

"Oh, I see, now you're just an actor again?" I nudge him. Not so long ago, Eli was claiming he was practically a cop, I guess he forgets that.

Recognition dawns on his face, and he rolls his eyes. "I'm a man who is dying for some cake." He winks.

Smooth.

I kiss his cheek and get to my feet. I don't even know if the cake survived, but if I know Kristin, she wrapped it up and put it in the fridge for me.

I, on the other hand, would've just tossed it. I will never be the class mom or the wife who organizes some big event. It's not my style.

"You know," Eli yells from the living room. "I could skip the cake and go for a sponge bath."

"I bet you could, but I'm good, thanks." I laugh as I open the fridge.

Sure enough, the cake is wrapped in plastic wrap and aluminum foil, which is something I'm going to need to ask her about. Especially if it preserves cake for longer, that's a good tip.

Cake is always a good thing.

"Killjoy! Did you find the cake?" he asks.

I walk out with the whole thing and two forks.

"It looks great. Is it edible?" he jokes.

I move around to the couch and sit next to him. "Ass. I'm not sure, but since it's your birthday cake, you should totally have the first bite."

He eyes the cake and then looks back at me. Then, he dips his finger in the icing and moves it to his mouth. His green eyes move back to mine before he smears it on my chest. I go to jump up, but he grabs my wrist, holding me down. "Stay there," he instructs. "I want some extra sugar with my cake."

His lips kiss a trail down to my neck, and then his tongue slides across my skin. Heat pools in my center at the feel of him on my skin. Eli takes his time, licking the frosting from my chest. I've missed his touch. My fingers glide through his thick hair, and his longer-than-normal scruff scratches in the best possible way.

I make a mental note to tell him to keep it for a while.

"I think the cake is perfect," he muses.

"Yeah?"

"Oh, most definitely."

I dip my finger in and then pop the sugary goodness in my mouth. "Mmm," I moan. "It's good, but I think maybe it's missing something."

He takes a bigger swipe and places the frosting on my thigh. Eli grips my calves, pulling so I fall backward. "I need another taste," he explains.

"Well, by all means." I'm not going to stop him. Eli is the fire that I never want to extinguish. When he's around, I'm alive, and I never want to go back. I'm beautiful, special, and precious to him.

His tongue moves higher and higher up my leg before he stops. "Eli," I groan, wanting him to keep going.

He leans back, fire blazing in his eyes, and I know this cake is going to be eaten very creatively.

<hr />

"Mr. Walsh will read a brief statement, and then we'll allow a few questions at the end," Sharon says as we stand in front of a crowd of reporters.

Eli squeezes my hand before releasing it. I hate this for him. I hate this for me, too, but he's the one talking. Hours before, Sharon explained the importance of the wording and our body language before making us review each possible way to handle any questions. When she was satisfied we wouldn't screw it up, she berated me for another fifteen minutes about my outfit. After she finally found a black pants suit, red heels, and jewelry that she found adequate, we were on our way.

Now, it's really happening.

My heart races in my chest when Eli clears his throat. I wish this weren't necessary. He's kept his condition a secret for years, and today, he's going to tell the world.

"Good afternoon. I'd first like to take a moment and thank you all for the get-well messages. The staff at Tampa General Hospital is truly phenomenal, and I received the best care while I was there." Eli clenches his hand and then flattens it. "Six days ago, I was in my home where I fell and hit my head. Thankfully, I didn't sustain any lasting damage from the concussion, and my face is fine, so no worries about filming." He winks at the camera before tossing a smile to the reporters. "However, my fall was due to a condition I was diagnosed with ten years ago. I have relapsing-remitting multiple sclerosis and have been able to manage my disease with a fantastic team of doctors and regular medication."

The faces of the reporters vary from shock to worry. I listen as he explains more about his MS and how it affects him. He speaks about his medication, the fact that he wasn't symptomatic, and what it means going forward.

I wish I could take this for him and handle it, but a swell of relief washes over me at how well he's doing. Eli didn't need me to do anything but be by his side. We talked about how to deal with the press in regards to me, and we agreed as a couple that I wouldn't speak today.

Eventually, we got Sharon to agree to it, but we had to give her something in return. So, as soon as he's finished with this, he'll head outside where there are barricades to keep the fans at bay. Sharon thought it would be good for him to sign autographs and appear normal after he tells them about his illness. I thought he should get rest, but I was pretty much overruled.

"My girlfriend, Heather Covey, has been by my side through the entire week." Immediately, the press get to their feet, hands are raised, and people are calling his name, but Eli doesn't flinch. He gives them a second and just smiles. "I'm going to give you all the run down so hopefully you won't have any questions by the time I'm done. Although, I'm sure that won't happen." Eli laughs as a few of them do as well.

After he tells them a very abridged version of our relationship and who I am, I can breathe a little. My heart is still going a mile a minute, but he commands the entirety of their attention. He's truly in his element right now, and it's downright sexy.

He finishes, draws a deep breath, and asks, "Any questions?"

"Are you saying you're officially off the market?" A young reporter asks.

Eli rocks back on his heels with a grin. "Yes. I'm very much off the market."

He points to the next person with their hand up. "Do you plan to move back to Tampa?"

"I plan to fulfill my obligations to *A Thin Blue Line* and make time for my relationship as well. Does that mean I'll be in Tampa a lot more? Yes." I watch in awe as he takes each question with ease.

"Any plans to get married?"

My eyes widen at the leap from being off the market to marriage. We both love each other immensely, but Jesus.

Eli chuckles. "We're taking things day by day right now."

"So, it isn't serious?" The same reporter asks.

I can almost feel Eli's mood shift from amusement to anger. "If it weren't serious, I wouldn't be here, Joe. In the last ten plus years, when have you heard me talk about a girlfriend?" Eli challenges him. "It's serious."

Joe doesn't respond, and Eli moves to the next hand. It goes on with the same variations of questions, all centered around our relationship, none about his multiple sclerosis. Which is baffling since that's what the point of this was.

I stand one step behind Eli as he moves to the next question.

"Ms. Covey." She looks at me and a flash of fear hits me. "Do you plan to quit your job as a Tampa Police Officer?"

Eli starts to speak, but I touch his arm as I get closer to the microphone. I don't know how I got here, but my feet somehow moved toward him. "I don't. I love serving this city, and I'll continue to do so." I slide my hand down his arm and rest it on top of his hand. The smile on Eli's face is full of pride. He laces his fingers with mine, and I'm not afraid. He's up here taking the hits and standing strong.

I can do this because together, we're unrelenting.

"Is it true you were married before?"

I watch Eli's knuckles turn white from gripping the side of the table he's holding with his other hand. I squeeze my fingers and take a page from his book. "Yes, I've been divorced for five years. Eli is aware of my previous marriage."

Sharon moves to the other side of Eli and pulls the microphone out. "That's all we have time for today."

Sharon ushers us to a private room, where Eli takes a seat. He refused to use the walker today. I didn't even attempt to convince him otherwise. However, it's clear that it took a great amount of energy for him to stay on his feet and perform.

"You did great," I say, wiping his forehead.

"You weren't so bad yourself." He smiles and takes my hand in his.

"Yes, yes, you both were great," Sharon says as she types on her phone. "We need to get you out there as quickly as possible. They all need to believe you're the epitome of health."

I'm suddenly thinking this meet and autograph thing was genuinely a bad idea.

I roll my eyes and fight back the urge to slap her. "Are you good?" I ask him.

"I've got this, baby."

The instinct to protect him rises, but I repress the urge. I have to trust him, which means not trying to control the situation. It's so much easier said than done. I'm a cop. I thrive on being in control. It's who I am, but I also know that it's his greatest fear within our relationship.

Instead of doing what I really want to do, I smile. "Okay."

Eli bursts out laughing and pulls me on his lap. "You're such a shitty liar."

"Don't laugh at me." I smack his chest.

"You should see your face. Don't ever go into acting."

Whatever.

"Let's go, Eli." Sharon claps her hand. "I want you to go for as long as you can."

I glare at her. "Don't you think you should be a little concerned for him?"

"I'm concerned for his career, which is my job." Sharon doesn't even look at me. She goes back to her phone and huffs. "I'll meet you out there. Don't take long."

I get to my feet once she leaves the room. "I'm pretty sure she's Satan's daughter."

He chuckles. "Makes me glad she's on our team then."

Eli pulls me into his arms, and I wrap mine around his waist. "I love you," I tell him.

"I love you."

He drops his lips to mine, and I couldn't give a shit less about his fans waiting or Sharon, who is probably ready to butcher me. Right now, I have him all to myself. I love how centered he makes me feel. I never worry where his mind is. When we're together, it's on us.

"You should go," I mumble against his mouth. "And be careful, those women are crazy and will try to kidnap you."

He pulls back. "Don't worry, we have police protection."

"What?" I ask.

Eli shrugs. "I know you're able to take care of yourself, but this is a new set of rules. You're in my world now, and I'm going to do what I can to protect you."

I'm still not understanding. What the hell does any of this have to do with police protection?

He waits a second, and it hits me.

"Oh my God! You have people here to protect me? Other cops? I am a cop, Eli. I don't need protection." There's no freaking way this is going to work for me. I'm not getting other cops to shadow me. A lot of us do it part time. It's great money when the celebrities are in town. I've done it, and over my dead body will I become one of *those*.

"You have no idea what the hell crazy fans are like, I do. We do this my way, baby. No room for discussion, at least in the beginning. I have a bunch of off duty guys who will stay with me and some will stay with you."

My eyes narrow. There are so many damn things to say to him, but the worry in his eyes makes me swallow every single one of them. He's truly afraid and doing what he can to ease his own fears.

"We'll talk later. Right now, you need to go." I table the discussion.

His brow raises, but he doesn't say anything. We both know what this means . . . one hell of an argument followed by some fantastic sex.

We exit the room, and I see a bunch of my squad leaning against the wall.

"Hey! Look who it is, our very own celebrity officer!" Whitman laughs and looks around.

"Look, it's my over-aged security detail." I smile. "I've missed you jackasses!"

And I have. I've been off work since Stephanie passed away, and I've been itching to get back on the road. This squad is part of my family. We may give each other a hard time, but I would literally take a bullet for them. They're my brothers, and I don't forget how lucky I am to have these kinds of people in my life.

Whitman and Vincenzo pull me in for a hug. "It's good to see you with a smile."

"Yeah, it's all thanks to this guy. Boys, this is Eli Walsh."

"Eli, this is Whitman and Vincenzo." I point to each in turn. "They were who responded to your fall."

"Oh, wow." Eli shakes their hands. "Thank you, guys. I'm really grateful."

"We're glad we could help." They both brush it off. And in all honesty, it's our job. Being praised for doing what we took an oath to do is sometimes weird. I always feel awkward because I love it. I want to help others. I like the calls where I get to make a difference, and those two did so much—for Eli and for me.

"I'm glad Heather had someone she knew there to help," Eli says and then kisses the side of my head.

Federico coughs, and I glare at him before finishing the introductions. "You know Brody. This dumbass is Federico, that's Jones, and—" I stare in to the eyes of one man I didn't think I'd see here. I don't know why I never thought it was a possibility, but it's happening. "My lieutenant, Matt Jamerson."

"Nice to meet you guys." Eli shakes all their hands and then wraps his arm around my waist when he reaches out to grab Matt's hand. "I appreciate the help with the crowd."

I look to Brody and purse my lips, using my mind to yell at him about not warning me. In a weird way, he seems to understand my internal screaming and has enough sense to look contrite.

This is going to be so damn awkward.

"Well, we all love Heather and don't want anyone to hurt her," Federico says, as if I don't know they bitched about it.

"Yes, we do," Matt says in agreement.

Is he unhinged? Eli's hand constricts against my side. "Good to know."

Matt steps closer. "She's one of us. We protect our own."

I feel as if I'm having an out-of-body experience. I must be dreaming, because there's no way my boyfriend and my ex-asshole are having this discussion, right? I've had some weird shit go down in the last few days, but this isn't real.

"I completely understand," Eli says smoothly. I look up, slightly confused by how he managed to miss the hidden meaning in Matt's words. I'm not a guy and I get it. "It's why I hired you all. Heather's safety is paramount. I always take care of what's *mine*."

And there it is.

"She wouldn't need protection normally."

"When she fell in love with me, things changed. However, I clearly have all intentions of taking care of her . . . in every way. I don't walk away from my responsibilities, especially when it comes to people I love."

This conversation is going to get out of hand real quick. I look to Brody, who is about two seconds away from popping popcorn, and the rest of the guys are grinning. Matt is a good cop, but no one likes him as a person.

Time to end this.

"You guys about done?" I ask. "Want to measure who is bigger? Although, I already know the answer to that."

Matt huffs and shakes his head. "I've got paperwork to fill out, I'm sure you'll be fine with Brody."

I watch the man I thought I loved for so long walk away. Someone I made vows to, and would still probably be with if he hadn't left, and I wonder how I was so blind.

Matt would never have hired a bunch of police officers if my safety was at risk. He'd tell me I was being stupid. He wouldn't go out of his way to make me feel comfortable or just take my hand for no reason.

Eli does all of those things and more.

I turn back to Eli, who has his chest puffed out, his smile is ridiculously bright, and is probably two seconds away from him pounding his chest like a caveman.

"You're that happy with yourself, huh?"

He grins at me. "You're welcome."

I roll my eyes and drop my forehead to his chest. "You're a mess."

Eli's arms encompass me. "Your ex-husband is an idiot."

"I'm well aware."

"I'll handle him if he becomes a problem."

I'm not sure what he'll do, considering Matt's my boss, but I'll never tire of his desire to care for me. It's nice having someone there for me. We're truly partners in every sense of the word.

I lift my gaze back to his with my hand on his chest.

We don't say anything, we don't have to.

The depth of Eli's love is soul shattering, and I feel it in my bones. He gives me things I didn't even know I needed. He looks at me as if I'm the only thing that matters. It's the kind of love I saw in my father's eyes when he looked at my mother.

We could've fallen apart last week, but we didn't. We stand here, stronger and even more secure than before.

"Thank you," I say.

He takes my hands in his and smiles. "I should be thanking your ex."

"Huh?"

"I've never been more grateful than I am right now. If he weren't such a dick, I wouldn't be able to do this." He drops lower and kisses my lips. "And this." He places a kiss on my forehead. "Or this," he says before he cups my face and kisses me deeply. His tongue slides against mine, and I forget where we are. My hands grip his shoulders as I kiss him back.

I hear someone clear their throat, and we both pull back. Shit.

Brody stands there with a shit-eating grin. "Now that was some funny shit. Glad someone finally told him what a piece of shit he is."

"He's lucky I'm recovering or I would've kicked his ass," Eli concurs.

Oh, dear God.

I scowl at Brody and then look back to Eli. "Go be the famous hot guy who everyone loves."

He dips his head, giving me a sweet, short kiss. "Good thing I only love one person."

"Good thing she loves you back."

Eli smiles and taps my nose. "Once in a lifetime," he says before he heads out of the room.

I lean against the door, grateful that Kristin was in the Four Blocks Down fanclub. Otherwise, this chance would've passed us by, and *that* would've been a tragedy.

chapter twenty-eight

Heather
~ Two Years Later ~

"This is so exciting!" Danni jumps up and down as we get escorted to our seats.

"Dude," Nicole grumbles. "FBD is totally not as fun as the last time we were here."

I laugh. "Why because you know them all now?"

She rolls her eyes and huffs. "Duh! I swear, your boyfriend isn't even cute anymore."

"You're so full of shit." I smack her arm.

Eli Walsh is still a very sexy man, and she knows it. He's like a fine wine that only gets better with age. He's been on tour the last few months, and once again, he's doing his final show in Tampa. I spent two weeks with him jumping to St. Louis, Nashville, Chicago, Indianapolis, St. Paul, and Little Rock before I booked a flight home. Hell no was I doing that again.

They're all slobs.

I much prefer his apartment in New York than being cramped on the bus with the guys.

It's been a whirlwind the last few years. One that I'm sometimes amazed we've endured so well. The media responded well when I said I wasn't leaving my job, and I think being a cop shielded me a lot.

I'm clearly not after his money, even though he practically throws it at me.

The lights dim and déjà vu hits me like a Mac truck to the face.

Kristin grabs my hands, squeezing tight. "I'm so glad Eli hooked us up with these seats."

"Well, I didn't give him much choice." My smile is wide as she giggles.

"This is true. Still, I'm so grateful."

As much as this is like the first time we attended the concert, so much has changed. Kristin left her husband and now lives in my old home with her two kids. Danielle and Peter are actually doing extremely well after having a second honeymoon. And Nicole is still the same, having random sexcapades and God only knows how many threesomes. I stopped asking after it started giving Eli ideas.

I'm now permanently living in Eli's Tampa house. Though, at first it wasn't entirely by choice. Eli practically moved my stuff out of my place and into his the day after our press conference. My home was swarmed with photographers, and he wasn't having it.

I was exceedingly against it, we fought, and then did a lot of making up—in our new home.

The silhouettes of the band members are visible now, and the crowd roars. Lights come on and the concert begins.

I watch Eli the entire time. The way his dark brown hair catches the light, his green eyes meet mine every time he's close, and the way he only gives me his cocky smirk that makes my heart melt. I love him more each day, even on the days I'd like to wring his neck.

He dances around, and I study his movements, watching for any sign of his hands bothering him. He told me they were tingling after his last show. Today, he looks great.

The music shifts, and my adrenalin starts to thump. Anytime I hear this song, I can't help but smile. "I've got someone very special in the audience tonight," Eli says.

Oh, no. No, no, no. He promised. I try to move, but Nicole grabs me. "You're so going up there."

"My girlfriend is here tonight, and if you don't know, this exact concert a little over two years ago, was where I met her." He gazes at me and winks. "I'd like to bring her back up tonight and remind her just how much she loves me. So, come on Heather, get up here."

My lips purse, and he gets the meanest stink eye I can muster. But what does he do? Laughs. The asshole laughs.

The bouncer extends his hand. Eli watches me, and I mouth *I hate you* to him.

As soon as I'm on stage, he pulls me close and plants his lips on mine as the crowd goes crazy. "You love me," he says against my ear.

"Not for long."

"Randy," Eli calls his brother over. "Heather might need a little support for this number."

Randy laughs. "I see you're going to lay it on thick?"

"She is my once in a lifetime girl . . . she needs to feel it in her bones!" Eli yells.

Dear God this can't be my life. Here I sit, on stage while my boyfriend, Shaun, PJ, and Randy have fun at my expense. I'm going to kill Eli, and then I'm going to have Savannah kill Randy.

Damn Walsh brothers.

The music keys in, and Eli begins to sing.

After the first chorus of him being totally over the top, he stops.

He pulls me to my feet and sings to me. The audience disappears while he holds me close. We sway to the music, and suddenly, I don't care about the people or the lights. My embarrassment fades into the distance, and I pretend we're alone at home. Eli and I are in our kitchen as he tells me the words of the song.

I look out at the crowd and see the lights from the cellphones filling the room. It's like a million twinkling stars shine just for us.

My fingers rub the back of his neck, and I kiss his cheek when the song ends.

"My once in a lifetime . . ." He extends his hand.

Eli pulls me back to his chest and kisses me again. "Come backstage after the show. I've got another memory I want to recreate."

I shake my head and laugh. "I love you, Eli."

"I love you more."

Just like the first time, my friends all smile and are lost in the fanfare.

"What did he whisper?" Kristin asks.

"To go backstage," I say through a laugh.

"I totally thought he was going to propose," Danni says offhandedly. "I'm a little disappointed he hasn't."

My eyes widen, and my heart skips. I hadn't thought of that. I mean, I did, but he made a comment the other night that he was really happy that we're where we are. I've been married already, so it isn't like I need a ring, but there's a part of me that wants to be his completely.

Until now, I didn't even give it more thought, but having her say it, makes me a little sad.

Nicole smacks her arm and then comes in front of me. "You guys are happy, honey. Really happy, you don't need a ring to prove it."

I expel the rush of disappointment that hit me hard. I don't need it, and whenever Eli wants to propose, that's when it'll happen. I'd rather have him than anything else. "I was being dumb."

Nicole nods. "Trust me, there isn't a woman in this arena who doesn't hate you right now. Eli kissed you, sang to you, and then invited you backstage. If he proposed, we'd have to put you in protective custody."

I burst out laughing and agree. My press life with Eli is always . . . bizarre. When he was nominated for an Emmy, it was like nothing I'd ever seen before. People calling our names, taking so many photos I thought my face was going to be stuck with a smile. Not all the fans were awesome, though. Some were completely awful toward me. Not to mention the media picking apart our outfits, hair, makeup, everything . . . all for entertainment. If Eli draws attention to us, it only gets worse. It's why I prefer our happy little bubble in Tampa.

Not that he's here that much, but we've found a way to make it work, exactly like he promised.

We enjoy the rest of the show and then head backstage. The boys come out, and I hug them all. Shaun and PJ are always the first ones to enter the party. I swear, they have alcohol running through their veins instead of blood.

Then I see him, his perfect face and gorgeous smile heads right toward me. Eli's arms are around my waist and he lifts me, spinning around. "Hi, gorgeous."

"Hi there, sexy. I'm mad at you."

"You know I had to do it," Eli explains.

"Uh-huh."

Eli sets me down and kisses my nose. "Let's go somewhere private."

I hit his arm. "We are *not* having sex on the bus."

He tugs me against his chest and grins. "Oh, yes we are."

I start to protest, but he squats before tossing me over his shoulder. "Eli!"

"I told you, we're heading to the bus!" he yells as he spins around to face the party. "We'll be done in a few hours. I'm going to make my girlfriend scream for a bit."

"Oh my God!" I slap his ass. "You're a dead man."

I hear the door to the bus open, and he slides me down the front of his body. "I think you'll let me live," he says against my lips.

"Don't be so sure."

Eli climbs the stairs backward, and my eyes take everything in. The bus is filled with candles and red roses. Dozens and dozens of flowers fill the space. There's no surface untouched by soft delicate petals and warm candlelight. I spin around, my eyes filling with tears as I see how absolutely gorgeous it looks. The floor has a line of petals leading to the bedroom. I turn back around to Eli and my breath hitches.

This isn't happening.

"What are you doing?" He's on one knee before me.

"I'm doing what I've wanted to do for a long time."

My hand covers my mouth as he pulls the lid back on the black box. "Heather Covey, I've spent a lifetime waiting for the woman I'd want to share my heart with. We met at this concert, we made love on this bus, and you're the only person I want by my side. I know we've said we were happy with how things are, but—"

"Yes!" I scream out, unable to hold it in any longer.

"I wasn't done yet," he complains with a laugh.

I get on my knees with him and giggle with tears in my eyes.

"I want it all, baby. I want you to be my wife. I want us to share everything. I need to give you my name just as I've given you my heart. So . . . will you marry me?"

I launch myself into his arms and kiss him hard. "Yes, yes, yes!" I say and then kiss him again. "I love you so much."

"Good." He kisses my tears of happiness.

Then I watch as he puts the stunning princess cut diamond on my finger. I stare at it shimmering in the candlelight. I'm going to be his wife. Our lives have fit together seamlessly. We find true happiness in each other like I've never known. My eyes meet his again, and I touch his cheek.

"I don't know how I ever lived before you." I rub my thumb against his stubble. "I love you so very much."

Eli stands and then pulls me to my feet. His arms cinch around me, and we hold on to each other. "I wasn't living before you. I was waiting."

"No more waiting." I smile, remembering the same words I spoke to him years ago.

His eyes meet mine, and there's so much love in his gaze, it takes my breath away. "I'd wait forever if it meant I found you."

I can't wait another second to kiss him, so I do. Eli leads us to the bedroom where we make another memory. This time, there will be no running away after.

I lie in his arms, loving the way we fit together. After some time, my mind fills with a pinch of sadness. My first wedding was a justice of the peace deal, but with Eli, I know he'll want it all. My sister isn't here to see us get married, and I have no one to give me away.

"Hey, what's wrong?" he asks.

He can always tell when my feelings go dark. I seriously need to work on hiding that.

"I wish Stephanie could be here, and my parents. I know my dad would hate you, but my mom would be completely over the moon."

His arms tighten. "I wish I could give you that, but it's the one thing I can't."

"I know, and I know if you could, you would."

"There's nothing I won't do for you," Eli promises. "And wait, what do you mean, your dad would hate me?"

I sit up, smiling as I think about my daddy. "No one was good enough for his little girls. Also, he didn't like you. He had to hear all about how I loved you and how amazing you were. On top of that, he had to listen to all your songs—he wasn't impressed. He told me to avoid dating any musicians. Clearly, I didn't listen."

When Four Blocks Down came out, I was obsessed and told my father one day I would marry Eli. My father told me boys were all stupid and I should stay away, but boys in a boy band were the ones I should run from. I want to believe he'd have changed his tune after meeting Eli. Regardless, it would've been funny to watch.

Eli moves so we're eye to eye and smiles. "I would've won him over."

I touch his cheek; the diamond on my finger catching the light and sparkling. "Daddy would've seen that you weren't a spoiled, self-centered, egotistical jerk who uses girls and leaves them."

"That's what he thought?"

I laugh. "Probably."

He moves quickly, pulling me beneath him. "Well, in a few weeks you'll be my wife."

"Weeks?"

He nods. "Weeks. Three to be exact."

"Wait!" I push him off me. "You want to get married in three weeks? I don't have a dress or anything! We can't get married in three weeks!"

Eli is always doing this to me, like the trip he surprised me with to Antigua. He came home, told me to pack, and took me away four hours later. He even had Brody get my time off cleared, he's crazy. And yet, he's everything.

"The date is set, everyone knows."

"Everyone knows?" I push his chest. "You just asked me! We haven't left the bus, how the hell did you plan a wedding?"

He shrugs and then gives me a smug grin. "I knew you'd say yes."

I groan and flop back on the bed. I'm not angry, but he kills me. "Okay, I'll bite, when is our wedding?"

My life is filled with love and a crazy man who plans a wedding before he gets the bride.

He tells me all the details while I stare at him with a stunned expression. He actually planned the entire damn thing. I'm not sure if I should jump his bones or beat the crap out of him. Eli said it was more because of his schedule. He's starting a movie in Vancouver in a month, so he wants to tie the knot before he leaves.

"You really want us to get married on a boat?" I ask.

This is the one detail I don't understand.

Eli climbs over me and pushes my hair back. "This is for many reasons," he explains. "Number one being that I can control the security and guest list. Number two is because I like boats and our first date was on one." I smile at that one. "Number three is that there's nowhere for you to run."

"Run?"

"Yeah, there are no fences for you to climb if you get cold feet. I'll have you right where I want you, right next to me—forever."

epilogue

Heather

HOLY CRAP. I'M GETTING MARRIED TODAY.
I stand in front of the full-length mirror in the master bedroom, stunned. The day after our engagement, I met my wedding planner, Kennedy. She arrived with a van packed with options. I thought his publicist was scary, but she could learn a thing or two from Kennedy.

In two days, I had a dress, flowers, colors, bridesmaid dresses, and the menu selected. It's amazing what you can get done with a woman who doesn't understand the word "no" and an unlimited budget. When a vender said they couldn't do it, she told them they didn't have a choice.

"Oh, Heather." Nicole enters and her eyes fill with tears. "You look gorgeous."

My eyes go back to the mirror, and I take it all in. The hairdresser arranged my hair to be mostly up with tendrils of blonde hanging around my face. My makeup is flawless. It's soft but still slightly dramatic. However, the dress . . . I still can't believe it's me in it.

"You think?"

She stands behind me in the aqua-colored dress I chose and places her hands on my shoulders. "Yes, honey. You're breathtaking."

I glide my hands against the satin fabric, loving how perfectly it fits me. Nicole and Kennedy argued over their top choices for what I should wear, and Nic demanded I try on her choice. The scoop neck shows off the right amount of cleavage and is skin tight through the bodice before it trumpets out at the bottom. It's classic, elegant, and I love every inch of it.

"I can't believe he planned all this," I muse, still looking myself over.

"Lucky bitch." She snorts, and we both laugh.

I know I'm lucky. Each time I look at my ridiculously sexy fiancé, I remember how special what we have is. Sure, we have our ups and downs and things are never always easy, but he's worth it all.

Kristin peeks her head in. "You guys ready? We need to get to the dock and send the limo to the park."

I roll my eyes at the lengths he's gone to, but he said he refuses to let one photo be leaked. Therefore, there are fake limos, and he rented out the park we went to after Steph passed away.

Kristin, Danielle, Nicole, Savannah, and I climb into the other limousine and head to the boat. The wedding is only immediate family and friends, we want to be surrounded by those we love without any fanfare.

"Are you ready?" Savannah asks as we pull up.

Our relationship has become incredibly close. She's been there each step of the way, helping me find my footing in this crazy public life. I'm so grateful to her, and I'm excited to become sisters-in-law.

"I really am."

"I'm so happy for you guys," she takes my hand.

Kennedy opens the door and ushers everyone out. "Let's go. So far, we've evaded any possible press, so let's get you out to sea before that changes." When we don't move fast enough she claps her hands. "I'm not kidding ladies, let's move your butts."

We all glance at each other, and I stifle a laugh.

Once safely aboard, we head to the first level, where there's a plush living room type area. The boat is magnificent. It has a dining area with a dance floor, a bathroom that doesn't make me cringe, and even a few bedrooms. It's basically a miniature cruise ship.

"Do you think he's nervous?" I ask the girls.

"I'm sure he's being restrained by Randy so he can't come find you." Savannah laughs. "Eli isn't known for his patience."

"No shit," Nicole agrees. "Who the hell plans a wedding before asking the bride?"

"I think it's romantic." Kristin grins.

I agree with Kristin. On one hand, he's crazy, but on the other, he's sweet. "Well, he does leave for filming soon, so we either did it now or waited a few months."

After a bit, Kennedy comes in and instructs us where to go. She fusses over each of my girls, getting their dresses perfect.

Nicole turns to me and pulls me close. "He's the one, Heather. The one who deserves you." She pulls a note from her freaking cleavage, and I know what that is. "I wanted to do this before we left, but I forgot until now. Stephanie said this was only to be given to you on your wedding day to a man who truly deserved you."

My hand reaches out, shaking as I take the paper. "I can't read this," I admit.

"Do you want me to read it to you?"

"No," I sigh. "I just mean I'm going to lose it."

She touches my hand. "I'll hold Kennedy back. Take your time."

Nicole makes good on her promise, informing Kennedy that she'll make her walk the plank if she comes in here. I sit on the chair and open the note. My sister is always with me, and today has been tough, but I pray this won't wreck me.

Heather,

I really hope you get to read this, and for real, don't cry!

You were meant to be loved by someone special. You have given yourself to everyone around you, and I hope you've found a man who will finally fill you up. I don't remember Mom and Dad's marriage like you do, but from what you've told me, I pray you've found that kind of love. I hope the other half of your soul is a fraction as wonderful as you are.

While I can't be there, know that when you finally open this note, I'm smiling down on you. If it's sunny, it's because I'm shining. If it's raining, it's because I wanted to make your makeup run, because that's what sisters do. However, if it's a hurricane, then Daddy is probably trying to send you a message or you just have really shitty luck.

I hope you're happy today. I want you to smile all day, even when you miss me. I'm never far from you because you're a part of me. I love you so much. I wish I could tell you how special and beautiful you are right now, but this letter will have to do.

Last, let him know if he messes up, I probably have other ghost friends by now, and I'll make sure he never sleeps again.

I love you.
Stephanie
P.S. You get the next letter when you either have a kid or turn fifty. Either way, I'll be back . . .

I tuck the letter into my bouquet of flowers so she's with me down the aisle and look out at the now coral-and-purple sky with a smile. She's such a turd, even from the grave she still messes with me.

My sister would've loved this. I can imagine her giving me crap about the color dresses, the flavor of cake, and pretty much anything else she could make a fuss about. The way she would've gone to war with Kennedy and then with Nicole. She would've loved Eli. They only met a few times, and I know she'd be completely on his side. He has this way about him that she wouldn't have been able to resist. It's annoying how charming he is.

There's a soft knock on the door, and I open it.

"Ready?" Brody asks with a smile.

"I'm ready." I loop my arm in his.

Brody kisses my cheek, and we start to walk. "I'm happy for you. Eli's a good dude."

I chuckle. "He is."

"You doing okay after the letter?"

"I actually am. I miss her. I miss her so much, but she's with me all the time."

Brody stops me at the bottom of the stairs. "She would be so proud of you."

Now the tears start to come. I look up, fanning my eyes and hoping to keep them until at least the vows. "Damn it." I laugh. "No more talking. I'm not crying before the wedding."

"All right, let's focus on you not tripping."

"Agreed."

We make it to the upper deck, and nerves have me gripping Brody's elbow a bit tighter. I think about how different my life is. I'm not afraid anymore, and that's all thanks to Eli. I don't sit and wait for the floor to drop out, I dance on it, enjoying what we do have. He's been there each step of the way, always holding out a hand for me to hold. When he wanted to leave his show, we talked about it. He wanted me to quit my job, and we talked through my staying. I'm there by his side at his doctor appointments, but I'm not the one running it all. There may come a time when things will change for us, but that's okay. If it does, we'll do it together.

Kennedy makes her way over and fixes my veil. "Here we go."

The double doors open, and I continue to cling to Brody's arm so I don't falter in my steps. The space is more stunning than I could have imagined. There are blue and green flowers, beautiful white chairs, and twinkling lights fill the space. It's absolutely perfect.

The music cues, and the room no longer is what I see. The man I love more than life comes into view, and I melt. His black tuxedo frames his body, showing off his broad shoulders and trim waist. Our eyes connect, and he smiles. My chest clenches, and I fight the urge to run toward him. Suddenly, I can't wait.

I start to move, but Brody holds me steady.

Each step I take eases the tightness around my ribs. The closer we get, the easier I can breathe.

We reach the end, and Brody places my hand in Eli's as a tear falls. I look at my best friend who has been a brother to me. He winks and kisses my cheek. "You have a new partner now."

Another tear drops, and I nod. "Thank you."

"Be good to her," Brody says as Eli shakes his hand.

"Always."

The minister calls attention to us all, and I feel the greatest sense of calm. Here, surrounded by our family and friends, we confess our love. Eli slips a diamond eternity band on my finger, and I place a titanium ring on his. When we picked out our rings, Eli said my ring was to be wrapped with no break in stones. I chose one that was the strongest metal.

"Ellington and Heather have decided to write their own vows," the minister explains. "Heather, you're first."

I take a deep breath and confess what's in my heart. "I never believed in fate. My world was exactly what I made it to be. I felt that by believing there was something else controlling the things around me, it meant I wasn't worthy of much because my life was a mess. Therefore, I controlled anything possible. And then I met you. A day that was a way for my friends to force me out of the house for a good time, became my future. I didn't know that one instant could alter everything I ever believed in, but you did that. You showed me that it was okay to take chances. You gave me a safe haven through the storm. You give me the ability and the strength to believe in tomorrow." A tear rolls down his face, and I swipe it away like he's done for me so many times. I take his hand in mine and squeeze hard. I want him to know how much I believe in us. "I promise that I'll never run from you, not even if you push me outside my comfort zone. I promise that even when our lives feel like they're crumbling, I'll stand beside you. I will be your strength when you need it. I promise you will never have to wonder if I love you because I'll show you in every way. You are the other half of me. You are my belief in fate. You're my reason for going on. You're my salvation, and I love you so much. I give you my heart, my soul, and my life from this day forward."

I release a shaky breath and try not to cry, but I fail. Nicole hands me a tissue, but Eli wipes it away before it falls. We smile at each other and the minister nods at him.

"Love wasn't something I was ever looking for. I didn't seek it out or hope it would come along, but then I found you. Through a sea of people, my eyes met yours. I suddenly didn't know how to breathe. All I wanted to do was talk to you, touch you, know you, and I had to find a way. I had no idea that moment would flip my entire world upside down. That the words to that song would be exactly what you are, my once in a lifetime. I had no way of knowing that one night could alter every tomorrow. Knowing that you're with me gives me all I need. Heather, I would chase you over a thousand more fences if it meant I had the next day beside you." I giggle through the tears, and he grins. "I won't ever give up on us. I'll fight every darkness that threatens to blind our love. I'll never let you feel alone because you'll always have me. On my bad days, I promise to come to you and lean on you for support. On your bad days, I promise to be your rock. I will love you through every doubt, fear, laugh, cry, and emotion that you may have. When we're apart, I will love you through the distance. From this day forward, I promise that you'll be my day, night, and my tomorrow."

Tears of happiness fall down my cheek, and all I want to do is kiss him. Eli slips the eternity band on my finger, and then he steps closer and brings his hands up to cup my face. Before the minister is finished declaring us man and wife, Eli's lips are on mine, sealing all our promises until the end of time.

Bonus Scene

Dear Reader,

Thank you so much for all your love and support and I hope you enjoyed *We Own Tonight!* Do you want more Eli Walsh? If so, just sign up for my newsletter and you'll get an exclusive bonus scene that you can't get anywhere else!

www.subscribepage.com/BonusWOT

keep up with Corinne

If you'd like to just keep up on my sales and new releases, you can follow me on BookBub or sign up for text alerts!
BookBub: www.bookbub.com/authors/corinne-michaels

Text Alerts: Text cmbooks to 77948

If you're on Facebook, join my private reader group for special updates and lot of fun.
Corinne Michaels Books Facebook Group:
www.facebook.com/groups/corinnemichaelsbooks

New York Times, *USA Today*, and *Wall Street Journal* Bestselling author of *Beloved, Beholden, Consolation, Conviction, Defenseless, Say You'll Stay, Say You Want Me, Say I'm Yours, Say You Won't Let Go, We Own Tonight, One Last Time, Not Until You,* and *If I Only Knew*. Co written novels with Melanie Harlow: *Hold You Close* & *Imperfect Match*

Check me out on Amazon: amzn.to/1NVZmhv

books by
CORINNE MICHAELS

The Salvation Series
Beloved
Beholden
Consolation
Conviction
Defenseless
Evermore: A 1001 Dark Night Novella
Indefinite
Infinite

Return to Me Series
Say You'll Stay
Say You Want Me
Say I'm Yours
Say You Won't Let Go

Second Time Around Series
We Own Tonight
One Last Time
Not Until You
If I Only Knew

The Arrowood Brothers
Come Back for Me
Fight for Me (Coming 5/19/20)
The One for Me (Coming 8/18/20)
Lie for Me (Coming 12/8/20)

Co-Write with Melanie Harlow
Hold You Close
Imperfect Match

Standalone Novels
All I Ask

acknowledgements

I keep joking that I'll just write a blanket thank you, but then I remember how nuts I am when I'm working on a book. If you deal with me during this process, you deserve so much more than what's back here.

To my husband and children. I don't know how you deal with me, but I can't tell you how much I appreciate you. I love you all with my whole heart.

My beta readers, Katie, Melissa, Michelle, Clarissa, and Shera: Thank you so much for your support and love during this book. I had so much fun going through this journey. You keep me laughing when I feel like punching myself in the face.

My assistants Melissa and Christy: You guys are my heart. No matter how insane I am, you keep me around.

My publicist, Danielle, thank you for dealing with my rambling messages and still somehow making sense of what I mean. I'm grateful for you more than you will ever know.

My readers. There's no way I can thank you enough. It still blows me away that you read my words. You guys are everything to me.

Bloggers: You're the heart and soul of this industry. Thank you for choosing to read my books and fit me in your insane schedules. I appreciate it more than you know.

Ashley, my editor, for always pushing me to write outside of my comfort zone. It's truly a blessing to work with you and I love our crazy process. Sommer Stein, from Perfect Pear Creative, for being my friend and creating the most amazing cover ever. Janice and Kara for proofreading and making sure each detail is perfect! Christine, from Type A Formatting, your support is invaluable. I truly love your beautiful hearts.

Bait, Stabby, and Corinne Michaels Books—I love you more than you'll ever know.

My agent, Kimberly Brower, I am so happy to have you on my team. Thank you for your guidance and support.

Melissa Erickson, you're amazing. I love your face.

Vi, Claire, Mandi, Amy, Kristy, Penelope, Kyla, Rachel, Mia, Tijan, Alessandra, Syreeta, Meghan, Laurelin, Kristen, Kendall, Kennedy, Ava, Leylah, and Lauren—Thank you for keeping me striving to be better and loving me unconditionally.

about the author

New York Times, *USA Today*, and *Wall Street Journal* Bestseller Corinne Michaels is the author of nine romance novels. She's an emotional, witty, sarcastic, and fun loving mom of two beautiful children. Corinne is happily married to the man of her dreams and is a former Navy wife.

After spending months away from her husband while he was deployed, reading and writing was her escape from the loneliness. She enjoys putting her characters through intense heartbreak and finding a way to heal them through their struggles. Her stories are chock full of emotion, humor, and unrelenting love.

irresistible attraction

WILLOW WINTERS

a single
glance

I saw her from across the bar.
My bar. My city. Everything in that world belonged to me.
She stood out from the crowd, looking like she was searching for someone to blame for her pain.

That night, I felt the depths of my mistakes and the scars they left behind. With a single glance, I knew her touch would take it all away and I craved that more than anything.

I knew she would be a tempting, beautiful mistake.
One I would make again and again... even if it cost me everything.

Dedicated to both TJ and Gem. In no particular order.
Your love for my books and these characters knows no bounds. You have no idea how happy it makes me to hear you guys fighting over who licked Jase first. I love you both… and I'm staying out of this one!

MUAH!

prologue

Bethany

I've learned to love the cold. To love the heat that comes after. To love his touch. Whatever bit of it he'll give me.

Only when we're in this room though. Outside of it, he's still my enemy. And I'll never forget that. But when I'm tied down and waiting for him to use me as he wishes… I live for these moments.

The edge of the knife drags down my body, the blade running along my bare skin and taking the peach fuzz from every inch of me. It doesn't cause pain, but it leaves a sensitive trail that awakens every nerve ending it passes. Making me feel alive, so desperate and so conscious of how good it feels to long for something.

The knife travels down my collarbone carefully, meticulously, leaving a chill in the air that dares me to shiver as the sharp knife glides lower, down to the small mounds of my breasts. It's so cold when he's not hovering over me. The icy bite of the air alone has never brought pleasure, but knowing what's to come, the draft is nearly an aphrodisiac.

All the heat I need is buried between my legs, waiting for him to move the knife lower, bringing with it his hands, his breath… his lips.

The desire stirs deep in my belly, then lower still. With my legs spread just slightly, my thighs remain touching at the very top, closest to my most bared asset. The temperature in the room is low, low enough to turn my nipples to hardened peaks. Sometimes he drags the tip of his knife up to the top of my nipples, teasing me, and when he does this time, I let my head fall back, feeling the pleasure build inside of me. The smallest touches bring the largest thrills.

He tortures me just like this; he has for weeks. At one point, it did feel like suffering, but I crave it now. Every piece of it. I only feel lust when I think about being at his mercy.

"I love you naked on this bench." Jase's deep voice is so low, I barely hear him. But I feel his warm breath along my belly as he moves his tongue to run right where the blade has just been.

He does this first every time, teasing me with the knife, shaving any trace of hair before moving on. He always takes his time, and part of me thinks it's because he doesn't want this to end either. Once the flames have all flickered out and darkness sets in, and the loud click of the locks in the barren room signal it's over, that's when reality comes rushing back.

The war. The drugs. All of the lies that leave a tangled web for me to get lost in.

I don't want any of it.

I want to swallow, the need is there, but I know to wait until the blade is lifted, leaving me cold and begging for it back on my skin. Teasing me. It's only once he pulls it back that I dare to swallow the lump in my throat and turn my head on the thick wooden bench to look at him.

Jase Cross.

My enemy. And yet, the only person I trust.

Fear used to consume me in these moments, but as the rough rope digs into my wrists, not an ounce of it exists. His dark eyes flicker, mirroring the flames of the fireplace lining the back wall of the room.

My gaze lingers as he swallows too, highlighting the stubble that travels from his throat up to his sharp jawline. That dip in his neck begs me to kiss him. Right there, right in that dip, as if he's vulnerable there.

With broad shoulders and a smoldering look in his dark eyes, Jase is a man born to be powerful. His muscles rippling in the fire's light as he looks down at me force my heart to flicker as well.

The gold flecks in his irises spark, and I'm lost in a trance. So much so that I freely admit what I never have before as I say, "I love it too."

I swear I see the hint of a smile tugging the corners of his lips up, but it's gone before I'm certain.

I shouldn't have said that. I shouldn't have given him more power than he already has.

Jase Cross will be my downfall.

chapter
one

Jase
One month earlier

It's a sloppy mistake. I never make a mistake like this. ***Never.*** Yet, staring at the bit of blood still drying on my oxfords, I know I've made a mistake that could have cost me everything.

And it's all because of her. She's a distraction. A distraction I can't afford.

The thick laces run along my fingertips as I untie them, and as I do, a bit of blood stains my fingers. Pausing, I contemplate everything that could have happened if I hadn't seen it just now. I rub the blood between my fingers, then wipe it off with a napkin from my desk. Carefully, I slip off my shoes, shoving the napkin inside of one before grabbing a new pair from behind my desk and putting them on.

The pair with evidence of my latest venture will meet the incinerator before I leave my bar, The Red Room, tonight. Where all evidence is meant to be left.

"What do you think?" Seth asks me, and I turn my attention back to him. Back to the monitors.

She's gorgeous. That's what I think. With deep hazel eyes filled with a wild fire and full lips I'd silence easily with my own, even if she's screaming on the security footage, she's nothing but stunning.

Her anger is beautiful.

The bar and crowd would normally take my attention away from her, but I was there that night and I only saw her. The patrons from last week get in the way of seeing her clearly on the security footage though. I can barely make out her curves... but I do. Even if I can't fully see them here, I remember them. I remember everything about her.

If I hadn't been with my brother at the time and in a situation I couldn't leave, I would have been the one to go to her. Instead, I had Seth throw her out. No one was to harm her, which isn't the best example to set, but I wanted to tempt her to come back. I needed to see her again. If for nothing more than to serve as a beautiful distraction.

Running my thumb over the fleshy pads of my fingertips, I lean back in the chair, crossing my ankles under my desk and letting my gaze roam over every bit of her as he leads her out.

My voice is low, but calm as I comment, "She's different here than she is in the file."

"Anger will do that. She lost her fucking mind coming into your bar talking about calling the cops."

Although my lips kick up into an asymmetric smile, a heaviness weighs down on me. There's too much shit going on right now for us to handle any more trouble.

She's a mistake waiting to happen. A delicate disaster in the making.

"How many days ago was this?" I ask, not remembering since the days have melded together in the hell that this past week was.

"Eight days; she hasn't come back."

"What do you want me to do?" Seth asks when I don't respond.

"Show me the footage again."

He's my head of security at The Red Room, and over the years I've come to trust him. Although, not enough to tell him what I really want from her. How seeing her defy the unspoken rules of this world, seeing her slander my name, curse it and dare me to do anything to stop her... I'm harder than I've been in a long fucking time.

"She's irate about her sister," Seth murmurs as the screen rewinds, then plays the footage of her parking her car, storming into the place, and demanding answers from a barkeep who doesn't know shit.

None of them could have given her the answer she wants.

I recognize every movement. The sharpness of her stride, the way her throat tenses before she even says a damn thing. I bet she can feel each of her words sitting on the tip of her tongue, threatening to silence her before she's even begun.

Even still, I find her beautiful. There is beauty in everything about what she did and how she feels.

"She lost her fucking mind," he mutters, watching along with me.

Seth is missing something though, because he doesn't know what I know. He doesn't see it like I do.

She's not just angry; she's lonely. And more than that, she's scared.

I know all about that.

The days go by so slowly when you're lonely. They drag on and bring you with them, exaggerating each second, each tick of the clock and making you wonder what it's all worth.

I can't deny the ambition, the desire for more. There's always more. More money, more power, more to conquer. And with it more enemies and more distrust.

It's a predictable life, even amidst the chaos.

"I can understand why she's looking for someone to blame." I pause to move my gaze from the screen to Seth, and wait for him to look back at me. "But why us?" I ask him, emphasizing each word.

He shakes his head as he skims through the file he's holding, an autopsy report and photographs of a body catching my eye in particular, although you can barely tell that's what she was after washing up on shore. Dental records were needed to identify her, the poor woman.

"She thinks you and your brothers are responsible."

"No shit," I answer him, waiting for his attention before adding, "but why would she think that?"

Again he shakes his head. "There's nothing here that would lead her to that conclusion. We didn't touch the girl. Her sister wasn't a threat to anything that we know of."

My fingers rap on the desk as I think about Jennifer, the girl who died so tragically. I met her once, and I can imagine she got into far more trouble than she could handle.

"I'll figure it out, Boss," Seth tells me and I immediately answer, "Don't go to her."

His brow raises, but he's quick to fix the display of shock. "Of course," he replies.

"I'm arranging to see her shortly. Dig up everything you can on her and on her sister's death."

"Will do," Seth says as he slips the papers back into the folder and then glances at the monitors once again. The paused image of Beth shows her leaning across the bar midscream, demanding answers. Answers I don't have for her. Answers she may never get.

"The other reason I wanted to see you... I have those papers you wanted," Seth says, interrupting my thoughts.

"What papers?"

"The ones about your brother."

My brother.

There's always someone to fight. Someone to blame.

It never stops.

chapter two

Bethany

PEOPLE MOURN DIFFERENTLY. MY MOTHER WOULD TURN IN HER GRAVE IF SHE KNEW I WENT to work last night instead of going to my sister's funeral. My sister, Jennifer, was the only family I had left.

And instead of watching Jenny be put in the ground, beside my mother who's been there for a decade, I worked.

Yes, my mother would turn in her grave if she knew.

But that's because my mother had never been able to stand on her own two feet whenever there was a loss, or any day of the week, really. Let alone take on a sixteen-hour shift to avoid the burial of a loved one. The last loved one I had.

As I let out a flat sigh, remembering how she used to handle things, I watch my warm breath turn to fog. It's not even late, but the sun has set and the dark winter night feels appropriate if nothing else.

The laughter coming from inside my house doesn't though.

My heart twists with a pain I loathe. *Laughter*. On a night like tonight.

Gripping the door handle a little harder than I need to, I prepare myself for what's on the other side.

Distant relatives chattering in the corner, and the smell of every casserole known to man invade my senses.

The warmth is welcoming as I close the door behind me without looking, only staring straight ahead.

Even as I lean my back against the cold door, no one sees me. No one stops their unremarkable conversations to spare me a glance. Bottles clink to my right and I turn just in time to see a group of my sister's friends toasting as they throw back whatever clear liquor is in their glasses. *My glasses.*

With a deep breath, I push off the door. Focusing on the sound of my coat rustling as I pull it off, I barely make eye contact with an aunt I haven't seen in years.

"My poor dear," she says, and I notice how her lips purse even while she's speaking. With a wine glass held away from her, she gives me a one-armed hug. "I'm so sorry," she whispers.

Everyone is so, so sorry.

Offering her a weak smile, and somehow not voicing every angry thought that threatens to strangle me, I answer back, "Thank you."

Her gaze drifts down to my boots, still covered with a light dusting of snow and then travels back up to my eyes. "Did you just get done with work?"

I lie. "Yes. Did the scrubs give it away?" The small joke eases the tension as she grips my shoulder. This isn't the first time I've ventured to the bar before coming home. Although, this is the first time the house isn't empty. And it's the first time I've felt I truly needed a drink. I need something to numb... *all of this.*

"Would you like a drink?" she offers me and then tells a group of people I've never met goodbye as they make their way out of my house.

"How about some red wine. A nightcap, since it's almost over?"

It's. Is she referring to the evening? Or the wake?

The tight smile on my face widens and I tell her, "I'd like that." My gaze wanders to the living room and I spitefully think that I'd like the four-year-old rummaging through the drawer of my coffee table to get out. They can all get out.

That thin smile still lingers on my lips when she brings me a glass and I nod a thanks, although I don't drink it. Not because I don't need one, but purely out of spite.

"Did the caterers bring everything?" I ask her politely, nodding a hello at a few family members who offer a pathetic wave in return. My mother was the black sheep of the family. Because of that, I couldn't name half of the people in here even though I recognize their faces. She got a divorce when my dad skipped out on us, and the family essentially divorced her for not "trying harder" in her marriage.

So the majority of the people here, I've met only once or twice... usually at funerals.

"They did," Aunt Margaret answers and I'm quick to add, "I'm glad everyone could come."

I hate lies, but tonight they slip through my lips so easily. Even as the emotions make my throat swell up when I see the same group of girls doing another round of shots.

Maybe it makes me a hypocrite, seeing as how I just came from drowning myself in vodka and Red Bull at the bar down the street, Barcode. I tend to swing by after a lot of hard shifts, but that particular group doesn't need any more drugs added in the mix.

"The funeral was beautiful." My aunt's words bring a numbness that travels down my throat and the false expression I'm wearing slips, but I force the smile back on my face when she looks up at me.

I take a sip of cheap Cabernet and let the anger simmer.

Beautiful.

What a dreadful word for a funeral.

For the funeral of a woman not yet thirty. A woman who none of these people spoke to. A woman I tried so desperately to save, because at one point in my life, she was my hero.

The glass hits the buffet a little harder than I wanted.

"Sorry I didn't make it. I'm glad it went well." My voice is tight.

"It was really kind of you to pay for everything... I know there's nothing in the estate or..." she says, but her voice drifts off, and I nearly scream at her. I nearly scream at all of them.

Why are they doing this? Why put on a front as if they cared? They didn't come to visit any of the times she was in the hospital. They didn't pay a cent for anything but their gas to attend the funeral and come here. And whatever those fucking casseroles cost. All the while I know they were gossiping, wondering about everything Jenny had done to land herself in an early grave.

They're from uptown New York and all they do is brag on social media about all their charity events. All their expensive dresses and glasses of champagne, put on full display every weekend for the charity that they so generously donated to.

I'm sure that would have been so much better.

Or maybe this alternative is their charity for the weekend. Coming to this fucking wake for a woman they didn't care about.

I could scream at myself as well; why open my door to these people? Why tell my aunt the reception could be held here? Was I still in shock when I agreed? Or was I just that fucking stupid?

They didn't see what happened to her. How she morphed into a person I didn't recognize. How my sister got sucked down a black hole that led to her destruction, and not a single one of them cared to take notice.

Yet they can comment on how beautiful her funeral was.

How lovely of them.

"Oh dear," my aunt says as she hugs me with both arms this time and I let her. The anger isn't waning, but it's not for them. I know it's not.

I'm sorry they didn't get to see those moments of her that shined through. The bits of Jenny that I'll have forever and they'll never know. I feel sorry for them. But her? My sister? I'm so fucking angry she left me here alone.

Everyone mourns differently.

The thought sends a peaceful note to ring through my blood as I hear footsteps approach. My aunt doesn't pull away, and I find myself slightly pushing her to one side and picking up a cocktail napkin to dry under my eyes.

"Hey, Beth." Miranda, a twentysomething string bean of a girl with big blue eyes and thick, dark brown hair, approaches. Even as she stands in front of me, she sways. The liquor is getting to her.

"Do you guys have a ride home?" I ask her, wanting to get that answer before she says anything else.

She blinks slowly, and the apprehension turns into hurt. She shifts her tiny weight from one foot to the other. Her nervousness shows as she tucks a lock of hair behind her ear, swallowing thickly and nodding. "Yeah," she croaks and her gaze drops to the floor as she bites the inside of her cheek. "Sorry about last time," she barely whispers before looking me in the eyes. "We've got a ride this time."

It's when she sniffles that I notice how pink her cheeks are – tearstained pink – not from drinking. Fuck, regret is a spiked ball that threatens to choke me as I swallow.

"I just don't want you guys getting into another accident, you know?" I get out the words quickly in a single breath, and pick up that glass of wine, downing it as Aunt Margaret turns her back on this conversation, leaving us for more... proper things maybe.

Miranda's quiet, looking particularly remorseful.

I don't mention how the accident was in front of my house, five fucking feet from where they were parked. Miranda passed out after getting drunk with Jenny and some other people nearby. Her foot stayed on the gas and revved her car into mine, pushing both cars into my neighbor's car until mine hit a tree. She could have killed them all. All four of them in the car, high and drunk and not caring about the consequences. Consequences for more than just them.

Her voice is small. "Yeah, I know. I'm sorry. It was a bad night."

A bad night? It was a bad month, and the start of me losing my sister. That night, I couldn't turn a blind eye to it any longer.

"I just wanted to say," she begins, but raises her voice a little too loud and then has to clear her throat, tears rimming her eyes. "I wanted to tell you I'm really sorry." Her sincerity brings my own emotions flooding back, and I hate it. "I loved your sister, and I'm..." This time I'm the one doing the hugging, the holding.

"Sorry," she rasps in a whisper as she pulls away. I look beyond her, at the groups of people in the dining room and past that to the kitchen. There are maybe twenty or thirty people in my house. And not a single one looks our way. They're too busy eating the food I paid for and drinking my alcohol. I wonder if they even feel this pain.

"She had this for you." Miranda pushes a book into my chest before running the sleeve of the thin sweater she's wearing under her eyes. Black mascara seeps into the light gray fabric instantly. "Right before she went missing, while she crashed at my place, she couldn't stop reading it."

It takes me a moment to actually take the book from her. It's thick, maybe a few hundred pages... with no cover. The spine's been torn off and my name replaces it. *Bethy*. That's what Jenny used to call me. The black Sharpie marker bled into the torn ridges of what the spine would have protected.

"What is it?" I ask Miranda, not taking my eyes from the book as I turn it over and look for any indication as to what story it is. I can feel creases in my forehead as my brow furrows.

Miranda only shrugs, the sweater falling off her shoulder and showing more of her pale skin and protruding collarbone. "She just kept saying she was going to give it to you. That you needed it more than her."

My gaze focuses on the first lines of the book, skimming them but finding no recollection of this tale in my memory. I have no idea what the book is, but as I flip through the pages, I notice some of the sentences are underlined in pen.

He loves like there's no reason not to. That's the first line I see, and it makes me pause until the conversation pulls me away.

"Before she died, she told me things." Miranda's large eyes stare deep into mine.

Jenny told me things too. Things I'll never forget. Warnings I thought were only paranoia.

As Miranda's thin lips part, my boss, Aiden, walks up to us in a tailored suit and Miranda shies back. My lips pull into a tight smile as he hugs me.

"You're dressed to the nines," I compliment him with a sad smile, not bothering to hide the pain in my voice. Miranda leaves me before I can say another word to her. She ducks her head, getting distance from me as quickly as she can. My eyes follow her as Aiden speaks.

"You okay?"

My head tilts and my eyes water as I reply, "Okay is such a vague word, don't you think?"

He's older than me, and not quite a friend, but not just a boss either. The second my arms reach around his jacket, accepting his embrace, he holds me a little tighter and I hate how much comfort I get from it.

From something so simple. So genuine. My circle is small, but I like to keep it that way. And Aiden is one of the few people in it. He's one of the few people I can be myself with.

"I heard you didn't go... that it was today?" he asks me, although it's more of a statement, my face still pressed against his chest.

I won't cry. I won't do it.

Not until I'm alone anyway. I can't hide behind anger then. There's nowhere to hide when you're lying in bed by yourself.

"I couldn't bring myself," I tell him, intending on saying more, but my bottom lip wobbles and I have to pull away.

He's reluctant, but he lets me and I find my own arms wrapping around myself. Looking back to where Jenny's friends were, I notice they're gone, along with a lot of the crowd.

Maybe they heard my unspoken wishes.

"You need to take time off." Aiden's words shock me. Full-blown shock me.

My head shakes on its own and I struggle to come up with something to refute him. Money seems like the most logical reason, but Aiden beats me to it.

"There was a pool at work, and the other nurses are giving you some of their days for PTO. You have your own banked, plus the bereavement leave. And I know you have vacation time too."

"They don't have to do that..." My voice is low, full of disbelief. At Rockford, the local youth mental hospital, I know everyone more than I should, especially the night shift. But I wouldn't ever expect any of them to give me their time off. I don't expect anything from anyone.

"They can't do that. They'll need those days for themselves." They don't even know me really. I'm taken aback that they would do such a thing.

"It's a day here and a day there, it adds up and you need it."

"I'm fine-"

"My ass you are." Aiden's profanity draws my gaze to his, and the wrinkles around his eyes seem more pronounced. His age shows in this moment. "You need time off."

Time off.

More time alone.

"I don't want it."

"You're going to take it. You need to get your head on right, Fawn." His voice is stern as my body chills from a gust of air blowing into the dining room when my front door opens once again. More *guests* leaving.

"How many days?" I ask him, feeling defeat, so much of it, already laying its weight against me.

"You have six weeks," he informs me and it feels like a death sentence. My heart sinks to the pit of my stomach as my front door closes with a resounding click.

With his hands on my shoulders he tells me, "You need to get better."

Holding back the pain is a challenge, but I manage to breathe out with only a single tear shed. Six weeks.

The next breath comes easier.

I tell myself I'll take some time off, but not to get better.

My breathing is almost back to normal at my next thought.

But to find the men responsible for what happened to my sister.

―❦―

My eyes are burning and heavy, but I can't sleep.

I'm exhausted and want to lie down, but my legs are restless and my heart is wide awake, banging inside of me. I need to do something to take this agony away. Staring back at The Coverless Book beside me on the side table, I lean to the left, flicking on the lamp while still seated on my sofa.

The Coverless Book

Prologue

I'm invincible. I tell myself as I pull the blanket up tighter.
    My heart races, so fast in my chest. It's scared like I am.
    Jake is coming.

He's going to see me here in my house, and then where could I possibly hide from him? Where could I hide my blush?

Maybe behind this blanket?

"Miss?" Miss Caroline calls into the room, and I perk up.

"Yes?"

"Your guest is here," she announces and I give her a nod, feeling that heat rise to my cheeks and my heart fluttering as she gives me a knowing smile and I hide my brief laugh. Caroline knows all my secrets.

Before I can stand up on shaky legs, he's standing in the doorway, tall and lanky as most eleventh-graders are. But Jake is taller. His eyes softer. His hands hold a shock in them that gets me every time he reaches for my calculator in class.

"Jake." His name comes from me in surprise as I struggle to lift myself.

"Emmy." The way he says my name sounds so sad. "I heard you were sick."

∽∘∽

I read the prologue and the first chapter too before falling asleep on the old sofa that used to belong to my mother. I'm cocooned in the blanket I once wrapped my sister in when the drugs she'd taken made her shake uncontrollably.

The only sentence Jenny underlined was the one that read, "I'm invincible."

Jenny, I wish you had been. I wish I were too.

chapter three

Bethany

My eyes feel so heavy. So dry and itchy.

Rubbing them only makes it hurt worse.

I would have slept better had I worked. I know I would have.

My gaze drifts back to the book. I'm only a few chapters in, but I keep walking away from the pages, not remembering where I left off and starting over each time.

Knowing I can't focus on work, knowing it's been taken away, has brought out a different side of me.

The side that remembers my sister.

Not the way she was in the last few years, but the way she was when we were younger.

When we were thick as thieves, and my older sister was my hero. Those memories keep coming back every time I read the chapters written from Emmy's perspective. She's young, and sweet, but so damn strong. My sister was strong once. Held down by no one.

Once upon a time.

Letting out a deep breath, I stretch my back, pushing the torn-up book onto my coffee table. I sit there, looking out the front bay window of my house. The curtains are closed, but not tightly and I catch a glimpse of a car pull up.

A nice car. An expensive one.

All black with tinted windows. Jenny came home in a car like that once, shaken and crying. Back when all of her troubles started. My blood runs cold as the car stops in front of my house.

If it's someone she was associated with, I don't want them here.

Anger simmers, but it's futile. You can only be angry for so long.

Once it's gone, fear has a way of creeping into its place.

My pace is slow, quiet and deliberate as I head to my coat closet and reach up to a backpack I haven't used in years. I figured it would be the perfect place to hide the gun. The one Jenny brought home for me, the one she said I needed when she wouldn't listen to me and refused to stay. I was screaming at her as she shoved it into my chest and told me I needed to take it.

It was only weeks ago that my sister stood right here and gave me a gun to protect myself, when she was the one who needed help. She needed protecting.

Jase

I can't handle one more thing going wrong.

My keys jingle as the ignition turns off and the soft rumble of the engine is silenced.

Wiping a hand over my face, I get out of the car, not caring that the door slams as my shoes hit the pavement. The neighborhood is quiet and each row of streets is littered with picture-perfect homes, nothing like the home I grew up in. Little townhouses of raised ranches, complete with paved driveways and perfectly trimmed bushes. A few houses have fences, white picket of course, but not 34 Holley, the home of Bethany Fawn.

Other than the missing fence, the two-story home could be plucked straight from an issue of *Better Homes & Gardens*.

Knock, knock, knock. She's in there; I can hear her. Time passes without anything save the sound of scuttling behind the door, but just as I'm about to knock again, the door opens a few inches. Only enough to reveal a glimpse of her.

Her chestnut hair falls in wavy locks around her face. She brushes the fallen strands back to peek up at me.

"Yes?" she questions, and my lips threaten to twitch into a smirk.

"Bethany?"

Her weight shifts behind the door as her gaze travels down the length of my body and then back up before she answers me.

The amber in her hazel eyes swirls with distrust as she tells me, "My friends call me Beth."

"Sorry, I'm Jase. Jase Cross. We haven't met before... but I'll happily call you Beth." The flirtatious words slip from me easily, and slowly her guard falls although what's left behind is a mix of worry and agony. She doesn't answer or respond in any way other than to tighten her grip on the door.

"Mind if I have a minute?"

She purses her full lips slightly as the cracked door opens just an inch more, enough for her to cautiously reply, "Depends on what you're here for."

My pulse quickens. I'm here to give her a single warning. Just one chance to stay the hell away from The Red Room and to get over whatever ill wishes she has for my brothers and me.

It's a shame, really; she's fucking gorgeous. There's an innocence, yet a fight in her that's just as evident and even more alluring. Had I met her on other terms, I would do just about anything to get her under me and screaming my name.

But after this past week with Carter and all that bullshit, I made my decision. *No distractions.*

The swirling colors in her eyes darken as her gaze dances over mine. As if she can read my thoughts, and knows the wicked things I'd do to her that no one else ever could. But that's not why I'm here, and my perversions will have to wait for someone else.

I lean my shoulder against her front door and slip my shoe through the gap in the doorway, making sure she can't slam it shut. Instead of the slight fear I thought would flash in her eyes as my expression hardens, her eyes narrow with hate and I see the gorgeous hue of pink in her pale skin brighten to red, but not with a blush, with animosity.

"You need to stay out of the Cross business, Beth." I lean in closer, my voice low and even. My hard gaze meets her narrowed one, but she doesn't flinch. Instead she clenches her teeth so hard I think they'll crack.

With the palm of my hand carefully placed on the doorjamb and the other splayed against her door, I lean in to tell her that there are no answers for her in The Red Room. I want to tell her that my brother isn't the man she's after, but before I can say a word she hisses at me, "I know all about Marcus and the drugs and why you assholes had her killed."

The change in her tone, her expression is instant.

My pulse hammers in my ears but even over it, I hear the strained pain etched in her voice. Her breathing shudders as she adds, "You'll all pay for what you did to my sister." Her voice cracks as her eyes gloss over and tears gather in the corners of her eyes.

"You don't know what you're talking about," I tell her as the rage gathers inside of me. *Marcus.* Just the name makes every muscle inside of my body tighten and coil.

The drugs.

Marcus.

Before I can even tie what she's said together, I hear the click of a gun and she lets the door swing open, throwing me off-balance.

Shock makes my stomach churn as the barrel of a gun flashes in front of my eyes. She leans back, moving to hold the heavy metal piece with both hands.

Fuck! Lunging forward, still unsteady as dread threatens to take over, I grip the barrel and raise it above her head, shoving her small body back until it hits the wall in her foyer and she continues to struggle, pushing away from me and getting out of my grasp.

Bang!

The gun goes off and the flash of heat makes the skin of my hand holding the barrel burn and singe with a raw pain. Her lower back crashes into a narrow table, a row of books toppling over and a pile of mail falling onto the floor as I stumble into her and finally pin her to the wall.

My chest rises and falls chaotically. My body temperature heats with the adrenaline racing through me.

Her small shriek of terror is muted when I bring my right hand to her delicate throat. My left still grips the gun. I can't swallow yet, I can't do anything but press her harder against the wall, smothering the fight in her as best as I can.

She struggles beneath me, but with a foot on her height and muscle she couldn't match no matter how hard she tried, it's pointless. Her heart pounds hard, and I feel it matching mine.

"Knock it the fuck off," I grit between my teeth.

She yelps as I lift the gun higher, ripping it from her grasp. Both of her hands fly to the one I have tightening on her throat. On instinct, like I knew she would. Did she really think she could get one over on me?

"You tried to shoot me." I practically snarl the words, although they're nearly inaudible.

Struggling to catch my breath, I don't let anything show except the absolute control I have over her. The door is wide open and I'm certain someone could have heard, although it's a Monday and during work hours. It's why I chose this time to pay her a visit.

A faint breeze carries in from behind and I take a step back, pulling her with me just enough so I can kick the door shut and then press her back to the wall. Her pulse slows beneath my grip and her eyes beg me for mercy as her sharp nails dig into my fingers.

The way she looks at me, her hazel eyes swirling with a mix of pain, fear and anger still, makes my chest ache for her, because I see something else. Something that fucking hurts.

She doesn't want mercy. She wants it to end. I can see it so clearly. I've seen it before, and the unwanted memory is jarring in this moment.

A second passes before I loosen my grip just enough so she can breathe freely.

Through her frantic intake, I lean forward, crushing my body against hers until she's still. Until her eyes are wide and staring straight into mine. The sight of her, the fear, the desperation... I know I'm not letting her go. Not yet.

"You're going to tell me everything you know about Marcus." I lower my lips to the shell of her ear, letting my rough stubble rub along her cheek. "And everything you know about the drugs."

My mind is whirling with every reason I should walk away. Every reason I should simply kill her and leave this mess behind. She tried to kill me; that's reason enough.

But I don't want to. I need more.

With a steadying breath, my lungs fill with the sweet smell of her soft hair that brushes against my nose.

I comb my fingers through her hair and let my thumb run along her slender neck before I lean into her, letting her feel how hard I am just to be alive. Just to have her at my mercy.

"And because of that little stunt you just pulled, I'm not letting you go."

chapter four

Jase

Fuck! The palm of my hand bangs on the steering wheel, sending a sharp pain radiating up my arm. Fuck! Over and over I slam my hand against the wheel while gritting my teeth to keep from screaming out profanities.

Even with the adrenaline still racing and the anger still present, I force myself to sit back in the car, listening to the dull thuds coming from the trunk.

I shouldn't have done that. *What the fuck was I thinking?*

I put cuffs around her wrists, her ankles too, and then gagged her to keep any more screams for help from crying out between those beautiful lips of hers.

I backed my car into her garage and dealt with the kicks and her feeble attempt to fight back as I forced her into the tight space.

I can only imagine what she's thinking with the handcuffs digging into her wrists as she's trapped, dark and alone and having no idea what's going to happen.

Thump. The sound reminds me—I shouldn't have done that shit.

Her garage door opens with an abrupt, jerky motion and then slowly rises, bringing with it a vision of the suburban street, lit by the warm glow of the inevitable evening. A sarcastic huff leaves my lips as I pull away, gently stepping down on the gas and blending in.

Knowing she's bound and gagged in the trunk, unable to do a damn thing until I decide what to do with her, time slips by as I drive down her street, thinking about how the hell I'm going to fix this shit.

The second I give her freedom again, she'll go to the cops, which is fine, since they're in our back pocket.

Every way I look at this, I know she's going to have to go. A threat is a threat is a threat. I underestimated her, but now that I know what she's willing to do, there's no excuse for keeping her alive.

No reason except for that look in her eyes.

The blinker ticks as I round the corner, turning right out of her neighborhood and down the main drag. I'm not taking her to the back of The Red Room. I don't want a damn soul to know about her pulling out a weapon. She's merely a nuisance, nothing more.

No one can know. If they find out and I don't silence her, they will.

"Call Seth." I give the command and instantly the cabin of the sedan fills with the sound of a phone ringing. Before it finishes the second ring, Seth answers.

"Boss," he greets me.

"I need you to do something."

"I'm listening." I can hear the shuffle of papers in the background and then it goes quiet on the other line.

"Drive out to the address you gave me yesterday. You know which one?" I ask him and keep my words vague. I'm careful not to risk a damn thing, not when calls can be recorded and used against me.

"Of course," he answers and I can practically see him nodding his head in the way that he does. Short and quick, with his eyes never leaving mine.

"I went over there and I may have made a mess."

"Just clean it up?" he asks. "Anything in particular to look out for?"

"The hinge on her door broke, and there's a bullet hole in her ceiling, but everything's fine otherwise. No one will be there, so lock it on your way out." A thought hits me as I get closer to my own home and my fingers slide down to my house key, dangling from the ignition. "I'm going to need you to make me a copy of a key too."

"For the address I gave you yesterday?" he clarifies and I nod while answering, "Yes."

"Anything else?" he asks and I'm silent for a moment, thinking about the next step and the one after it.

Seth is a fixer. Every fuckup I make, or better yet, any fuckups from my brothers, he cleans up. He's also my right-hand man when I want to keep things from Carter.

"If anyone asks or comes looking, let them know you were hired to fix it."

"No problem."

Thump, thump, THUMP! My gaze lifts to the rearview mirror as I listen to Beth trying to escape. The trunk can't be opened from the inside; she'll learn I'm smarter than that. She caught me off guard once, but it won't happen again.

chapter five

Bethany

My heart won't stop racing. It's pounding hard and fighting back from inside my chest; I can't imagine I'll survive this.

It's throbbing so loud, it takes me a moment to realize the car's stopped. The hum of the engine has vanished and there isn't a damn sound other than my own chaotic heartbeat.

I hear a crunch, I think, and my head whips around to the side, so sharply it sends a bolt of pain down my already aching shoulder. Traveling up and down my shoulders is a dull fire that blazes. Between the way I was forced in here, practically thrown in, and lying on my arms with them cuffed behind my back, my shoulders are in absolute agony. The metal bites into my wrists and ankles, and I know I'll have bruises on my knees from slamming them as hard as I could into the top of the trunk. My entire body is cramping.

Every trunk has a latch somewhere on the inside. It's to save children from being locked within and trapped. I know because I once played hide-and-seek with my sister and tried to get in the trunk, only to have my mother scream at me. She said it was dangerous, and the neighbor girl we were playing with told my mother what her mother had told her. That there was a latch on the inside. Sure enough, there was. My mother still didn't let me hide in the trunk though and after she grabbed me by the hand and brought me inside, I didn't want to play anymore.

Since being dumped in here, I've spent all my energy maneuvering through the pain to search for the latch. I can't fucking find it. So I resorted to bucking my body in a desperate attempt to force the trunk open or to kick out a taillight. Anything. Anything at all to get the hell out of here.

No luck. And now it's too late.

It's funny what you think of while you're waiting for the inevitable. Maybe it's a coping mechanism, a way to take your mind elsewhere when darkness is looming. Or maybe my memory was simply triggered by the lack of a handle and how I learned such a thing should be here because of hide-and-seek. Maybe that's why as I close my eyes and listen for something, for anything at all, my mind takes me elsewhere. I hear my sister call my name down the hall of our childhood home.

I'm in the closet upstairs, and it's so hot. I buried myself under all the blankets my mother stored on the floor in there and carefully laid them on top of me, hoping that when Jenny opened the door, searching for me, she wouldn't see me.

She was always better than me at everything—every game, every sport, every class. But today, when she opened that door, and I waited with bated breath, she closed it and continued silently searching the house.

With the smugness to keep me company, I stayed there under those blankets and I must have fallen asleep. It was Jenny's voice that woke me and when I came to, I felt so hot. I was absolutely drenched in sweat and the blankets felt so much heavier than they did before.

"Jenny," I cried out for her, feeling an overwhelming fear that didn't seem to make sense, but I knew I needed to get out from under the blankets. I couldn't shove them forward though, the door was closed and I couldn't lift them up because a shelf was above me. "Jenny!" I cried out again. Louder this time, as I tried to wiggle my way free under the weight of the pile. I didn't have to free myself alone though; Jenny opened the door and helped me out, telling me I was okay all the while and when I did crawl out into the hallway, I knew I was okay, but it didn't feel like I was.

I never hid there again. I don't think I ever played hide-and-seek again at all.

There's another loud crunch, and another. My eyes pop open and suddenly I am very much in the present, leaving the memory behind. I'm listening to the sound of shoes walking along small pieces of gravel maybe. The beating in my chest intensifies and I can't breathe as I hear the steps get closer. I even squeeze my eyes shut, wishing I could make myself disappear, or go somewhere else. Like I used to do when I was a child. As if this could all just be a dream or I had somehow gained impossible abilities.

I would try to scream, but the balled-up shirt in my mouth is already threatening to choke me as every small movement sends it farther into my mouth. Any farther, and I think I'll throw up.

When the trunk swings open so loud that my instincts force me to look up, the light's bright, almost blinding.

I wish I could beg; I wish I could yell. I wish I could fight back when I see him towering over me and taking his time to consider me.

"That looks like it hurt," he says as if he finds it funny. The words come out with condescension as he reaches down to let his fingertips glide over my already bruised knees. Even the small movement makes me buckle, forcing my weight back onto my shoulders and it starts a series of aches cascading throughout my body all over again.

The agony begs me to cry, but in place of tears, I find myself screaming the words, "Fuck you," over the gag in my mouth. The soft cotton nearly touches the back of my throat, and for a moment I think, if I were to vomit right now, I'd choke on it.

I won't die like this. Not like this.

My gaze doesn't leave his as he angles his head, reaching up to grip the hood of the trunk with both of his hands. The sun's gone down and wherever we are, there are trees. Lots of trees.

Staring up at him, searching for a clue as to where we are, it's hopeless. Yellow light slips through the crisp dead leaves above us, giving way to a deep blue sky that'll soon turn to black night, and there isn't a damn thing else to see.

Nothing but his handsome face, and the way his broad shoulders pull that jacket a little too tight.

Let him think you've given up. Don't die like this. Use him. Use him to find out what happened to your sister.

The voice in my head comes out as a hiss. And with the reminder of Jenny, tears prick at my eyes. Through the glossy haze, I see the man's expression change. Jase's hardness, his cockiness, it all dims to something else.

My breathing slows, and the adrenaline wanes.

My fight isn't over, but I'll give in for now.

"We're going to have a conversation, Bethany." Jase's words sound ominous and they come with a cold gust of wind from the late fall air. Both send a chill down my spine and leave goosebumps in their wake.

"Nod if you understand." His hardened voice rises as he gives me the command. Loathing him and everything he stands for, I keep perfectly still, feeling the rage take over anything else. His eyes blaze with anger as he grips the hair at the nape of my neck, pulling my head back with a slight sting of pain and forcing me to look at him. "You need to play nice, Bethany." If I could punch him in the throat right now, I would. That's how *nice* I'm willing to play.

He lowers his head into the darkness of the trunk, sending shadows across his face that darken his stubbled jaw and force his piercing gaze to appear that much more dominating.

A heat flows in my blood as my breathing stutters and he brings his lips down to my neck. They gently caress my skin and with the simple touch, a spark ignites down my body. A spark I hate even more than I hate Jase himself.

His next words come with a warm breath and another tug at the base of my skull as he whispers, "You're going to listen to me, Bethany. You're going to do what I tell you... *everything* I tell you." The way he says the word everything dulls the heat, replacing it with fear, and for the first time, I truly feel it down to my bones. Standing up a little straighter, but still keeping his grip on me, he asks with a low tone devoid of any emotion, "We're going to have a conversation, isn't that right?" He loosens his grip on the back of my neck as he waits for my response.

I wish his gorgeous face was still close to mine, so I could slam my head into his nose.

With a tremor of fear running through me and that image of him rattling in my head, I nod.

As a small smile drifts along his lips and he nods his head in return, I welcome the cold gust that travels into the trunk.

He may think he can use me, but I swear to everyone, living and dead, I'll be the one using him.

chapter six

Bethany

HOPE IS A LONG WAY OF SAYING GOODBYE.
I told that to Jenny a few weeks ago. No, it was longer than that. It doesn't matter when, because by then, I'd lost my faith in her. Disappearing for days on end and talking about a man who had what she needed ... my sister was never going to get help. I begged her to come back home, and she just shook her head no, and told me to hold on to hope.

I wanted her to stay with me. To get better.

I could have helped her, but you can't help those who don't want to be helped.

I can still feel her fingers, her nails just barely scratching the skin down my wrist as I ripped my hand away.

The memory haunts me as I think in this moment – this terrifying moment of waiting for his next move - I think, *I need to have hope that it's not over*. I need to have hope that I can get the fuck away from this man. That I can make him pay if he had any part in her death. *Jase Cross will fucking pay.*

The last thought strengthens my resolve.

"You'll be quiet," he tells me as if he's certain of it, a hint of a threat underlying each syllable, and I nod.

I nod like a fucking rag doll and try not to show how much it hurts when he rips the duct tape off my face in one quick tug. The stinging pain makes me reflexively reach for my mouth, but I can't; that act only exacerbates the cuts in my wrists, still cuffed behind my back. I try not to heave when he pulls the wet cloth from my mouth, finally giving me the chance to speak, to scream, to fucking breathe.

My body trembles; it's not from a cold breeze or the temperature though, and not from the fear I know is somewhere inside of me. Instead it's from the anger.

His eyes stay fixed on mine as he reaches down and lifts me into his chest before heaving me over his shoulder.

My teeth grit as he slams the trunk shut, turning to the side and giving me a view of a forest. All I see is a gravel drive and trees. So many trees. My heart gallops, both with that tinge of fear and with hope. *I could run.*

Fuck that.

I'm not running. I'm not giving up this chance to find out more about the family name I've heard so much about lately.

Somewhere in the back of my mind, I see my sister, and I hear her too. *The Cross brothers*, she whispers. She mentioned them so many times on the phone. He knew her. Or one of his brothers did.

As time stands still while I wait for the verdict I'm about to receive and what this man has in store for me, I remember the week my sister first went missing. I started with Miranda to try to figure out where my sister had gone. It made the most sense because Jenny told me she'd crash at a friend's place whenever we got into a fight. Miranda and she were close. But Miranda didn't have any idea what happened to her, only that she went out for drinks at The Red Room before she disappeared, a place I'd heard Jenny mention before. A place I knew I was headed to next.

All I had were two names and a single location. One name, Marcus, proved elusive—no one had any information on him at all. Not a single person inside The Red Room had any idea who he was. They wanted a last name, and I didn't have one. He was a dead end.

I'd spent hours at that bar, waiting for something. Waiting for anything. Any sign of her, or for anyone who knew them. Everyone knew of Jase, but no one *knew* him. They couldn't tell me anything about him. Nothing more than the dirt I dug up online.

They said he was one of the Cross brothers. The owner of The Red Room.

They said you don't cross a Cross; they laughed when they said it, like it was funny. Nothing was funny to me then.

And when two men appeared from the back of the club, heading toward a side entrance, the woman next to me pinched my arm and pointed as the side door was opened for them.

"Those are the Cross brothers," she said and then bit down on her bottom lip as she sucked it into her mouth. She was skinny like a model, with the straightest black hair I'd ever seen. Her icy blue eyes never left the two of them and I stared at her for far too long, missing my chance to catch the Cross brothers. The thick throng of people kept me from making it to them, and by the time I got outside, they were nowhere in sight.

I stalked that place for four days straight, waiting for Jenny to show up. An aching hollowness in my heart reminds me how it felt, sitting there alone at the bar, praying she'd walk up to me or someone would message me that they found her.

It was late on that last night, and hopelessness was counting on me to give up so it could take over, but I never would.

It was 1:00 a.m.; I remember it distinctly because I had an early shift the next morning, and I kept thinking I wouldn't make it through my twelve-hour shift if I stayed out any later.

All the time I'd spent in the bar hadn't given me any new information. Countless hours had been wasted, but I didn't know what else to do or where else to go.

It was that night I got a better view of Jase. Only his silhouette, but it grabbed my attention and held me in place. The strength in his gaze, accompanied with a charming smile. He was handsome and beautiful even. I remember thinking he was the kind of man who could lure you in so easily and you wouldn't know what hit you ... until he was gone. He had that pull to him, a draw that made you want to go to him just to see if he'd look your way.

He came and he went and I sat on that stool, knowing my sister wasn't coming.

That was then. This is now.

A grunt of pain slips from me as he hoists me up higher on his shoulder, one hand wrapped around my waist to keep my body from falling backward, and the other hand swinging easily at his side.

Every step hurts, and the agony tears through me with my hands still restrained behind my back. Biting down on my bottom lip, I don't scream, and I don't try to fight him. Not like this.

I'll be good until I'm uncuffed. Then this fucker will get what he has coming to him.

His hand splays on my ass, immediately heating my core as I hear the jingle of keys. Craning my neck, I get the first view of where he's taken me.

A house in the forest. A big fucking house, to boot. It's three stories with white stone leading all the way up. My body reacts on its own; the need to run takes over, as if I could still run, cuffed like I am.

"Don't struggle." Jase's words come out hard, and I bite down harder on the inside of my cheek to keep from telling him to go fuck himself. If I could struggle, really struggle, I would.

He holds me tighter with both of his hands this time, and the sharp metal of the keys digs into my thigh. Even when I keep myself perfectly still, he doesn't let go.

With a tight throat and resentment flowing through my veins I attempt to answer him, but I can't think of anything to say. Maybe it's the blood pooling in my head, or maybe it's the pain finally taking over, but I have to close my eyes just to keep from passing out. The moment I do, he takes his hand away and I hear the keys scrape into the lock along with a beep from something that startles my eyes open, followed by the telltale sound of a door opening.

The beep... There's some sort of alarm beyond the key. It's then that I see my purse swinging. He brought it with him, and I force myself to think about everything in that bag that can be used as a weapon.

Knowing that and gathering information keeps me calm. Anything that can help me fight.

The warmth is welcoming, even as I bid farewell to the forest that leads somewhere to freedom. I intend for the goodbye to be temporary anyway.

I don't expect him to be careful as he sets me down in what looks like a foyer. But he is.

Thud. My heart flinches as the jangle of keys being tossed somewhere to my right hits me. And then I see him again.

His back is to me as he removes his jacket, revealing more of him. Everything is in place. The cuff links, the neatly trimmed hair on the back of his neck. He screams wealth, power... sex appeal.

My eyes close slowly at the thought, hating myself for recognizing that primal urge. They open just as slowly when his footsteps grab my attention. Even the sound of his steps hints of elite status. He walks toward me and my eyes stay on his, even though the depth of his stare dares me to defy him.

My stupid heart races, dying to get away.

He makes me feel weak and I hate him for it.

"I hate you." The hoarse words come from my throat unbidden. The fact that they only make him smirk as he crouches in front of me, pisses me off that much more. It hurts, though. I can't deny it does more than aggravate me to be at the mercy of this man.

Craning my neck and straightening my back so I can bring my eyes to his level only forces more weight onto my hands.

I seethe through clenched teeth, giving away the pain and that's when he breaks his stare.

I turn away from him to my right as he reaches behind me and uncuffs my hands first. He reaches for the pair on my ankles, but pauses.

"How much?" he asks me, his voice deep and husky.

My gaze flickers to his as I pull my hands into my chest, my fingers gripping around the small cuts, trying to rub some feeling back into my wrists. I hesitate only for a moment, confused by his question. "How much what?"

"How much do you hate me?" he asks, and my heart does it again. It scrambles in my rib cage, wanting so desperately to escape. The heart is a wild thing, meant to be caged after all.

I try to swallow, swallow down the spiked lump, but I can hardly do it. Staring into his eyes, I answer him, "It depends."

"On what?" he asks, letting his fingers drift over the metal cuffs, his eyes roaming from mine down my body. He tilts his head, looking back at me once again when I answer, "Whether you tell me the truth or not."

Thump, thump. My heart hates me.

"You're in no position to question me."

"What makes you think I'm not?" Somehow my words come out evenly; controlled and daring. I revel in it as his dark eyes flash with the heat of a challenge, but then he moves his hand away from the cuffs, the small key still resting in his palm.

I could try to reach for it, but I wait.

When he peers down at me, I stare back without flinching, but the second his eyes are off of me, my gaze scatters across every inch of this place. Every window, every door. Every way out.

"You're not getting out of here until I let you out," Jase says absently when he catches me. So casually, as if he doesn't care.

My lips purse as I wait for more from him. If he thinks I won't try to get out, he's dead fucking wrong.

"You don't believe me?" he asks with a trace of humor lingering in his tone. I can feel my heartbeat slow, my blood getting colder with each passing second.

"There's always a way out." My words come out low, barely spoken, but he hears them and shakes his head before crouching in front of me again.

"Every window and door requires a fingerprint and a code, Bethany." The way he says my name sounds sinful on his tongue. I wish he'd take it back. I don't want him to speak my name at all.

My jaw clenches as I take in this new information and then ask him, "What do you want from me? Are you going to kill me?" The second question catches in my throat.

He runs the pad of his thumb along his stubbled jaw and then up to his lips, bringing my eyes to the movement as he says, "I went to your house with decent enough intentions. I wanted to tell you that you weren't going to get anywhere and whatever rabbit you were chasing was only going to lead you down a dead-end road and get you hurt, or worse."

I have to grab on to my fingers, squeezing them as tight as I can to keep from slamming my fists into his chest, to keep from slapping him or from punching him in his fucking throat as he gets closer to me.

"I don't have the answers you're looking for. I'm sorry about your sister," he says and my stomach drops, it drops so quickly and so low I feel sick. "I don't know how she died and I sure as shit didn't play a part in her death..." He pauses and inches closer to me, a hint of sympathy playing at his lips before he adds, "She owed us far too much money for me to kill her."

Dread is all-consuming as he stands, leaving me with a chill and turning his back to me. "I was being nice, giving you a warning and then you tried to shoot me."

He takes three steps away, three short steps while staring down at his own shoes as if contemplating. The hard marble floors feel colder and more unforgiving as I struggle with whether or not I believe him.

He's a bad man. Jase Cross, all of the Crosses are bad men. I don't believe him. I believe what Jenny told me.

She'd said the name Cross over and over again. Cross and The Red Room were my only real clues to go by. At that thought, there's a prickle at the back of my neck and I struggle to stay calm as the exhaustion, the sorrow, and the hate war with each other.

"I don't believe you," I whisper weakly but with his back to me, he doesn't hear me.

"I'll be nice again. Only because you remind me of someone I once knew." Looking up through my lashes, I wait for him to continue.

His dark eyes pierce me, seeing through me and causing both the need to beg for mercy and the need to spit on him, simply for not having the answers I crave.

"If you're lying to me... you'll pay," I utter and keep going. "I'll... I'll," I attempt a threat, but my last word cracks before I can finish.

Without warning, Jase closes the distance between us in foreboding steps I both loathe and refuse to be intimidated by. So I react. All I've been doing is reacting. I spit in his face the second he lowers himself to tell me off.

The shock from what I did is enough to outweigh the fear as Jase wipes his face, his expression morphing into fury as he stares at my spit in his hand.

Before I can say anything, he grips my throat. His large, hot hand wraps tightly around my neck, and my own hands reach up to his in a feeble attempt to rip his fingers off of me.

The heat from his body engulfs my own as I struggle to breathe. My nails dig into his fingers. His body is heavy against me, practically burning me. His entire being overshadows mine with power.

"I'll allow you to ask questions," he says and pauses, letting the air leave my lungs and the panic starts to take over, thinking there's no air to fill them, "but you will never," he pauses again for emphasis, staring into my eyes as they burn while he concludes, "threaten me again." Small lines form at the corners of his eyes as he narrows them, gazing at me and squeezing just a little tighter. So tight it hurts, and I struggle, scratching at my own throat in an effort to pry his grip loose.

My head feels light as my body sways in his grasp.

Just as I think he's going to kill me, that I'll die like this, he releases me.

Heaving in deep gulps of air, my shoulders hunch over.

I practically suffocate on the sudden rush of oxygen. My clammy palms hit the cold floor and my body rocks on its own.

"Don't make me regret this, Bethany." He does it again, saying my name like he had to spit it out of his mouth.

I grind my teeth against one another so hard that my jaw aches from the pressure. I have to stare intently at the spiral staircase behind him to keep from saying anything.

Time passes, the ticking of my heart somehow finding its normal rhythm once again in the silence.

"Your sister owed a debt, and you're going to pay it."

chapter seven

Jase

LIES. I HEAR THE WORD IN MY HEAD OVER THE SOUND OF THE ARMOIRE CRASHING TO THE bedroom floor. I turn the speakers down, but continue to watch her trash the guest bedroom.

I'm not surprised she's destroying everything she can.

As I dragged her to the guest bedroom, she never stopped fighting, and I never stopped hearing the hiss in my head. *Lies.*

Never tell a lie, my younger brother, Tyler, once told me. I was fucking around with him about something when we were kids. I don't remember what, but he looked up at me and the words he spoke stuck with me forever.

A lie you have to remember. So never lie, it will only fuck you over.

I can still see the smug look grow on his face as I felt the weight of his words. He was an old soul and had a good heart. *Never tell a lie.* He'd be ashamed of the man I became.

The screaming that comes from the faint sound of the speakers brings me back to now, back to the present where I keep fucking up.

One mistake after the other, falling like dominos.

I stare at her form on the screen as she pounds her fists against the door, screaming to be let go. Bethany Fawn's throat is going to hurt tonight. It already sounds sore and raw from her fighting.

It's useless. Part of me itches to hit the release on her door to let her roam throughout my wing, struggling with every locked window, with the doors that will never open for her. Just to prove a point.

I can't blame her though and as she falls to her knees, violently wiping away the tears under her eyes as if they're a badge of dishonor, I hurt for her. For the woman she is, and for the woman I once knew who did the same thing.

She fought too. She fought and she lost.

It's so easy to hide behind anger, but it gets you nowhere. I can help her though. I need this too. The very thought of what I could do for her makes my blood ring with desire.

"I hate you!" Bethany's words are barely heard through the speaker, seeing as how I've turned them down so low.

In an attempt to ignore the thoughts and where they're headed, I check my phone and notice a flurry of texts, coming one after the other.

I text my brother, Carter, back without reading much of what he wrote. *I'm busy. Can we talk tonight?*

His response is immediate. *We need to talk about how we're going to deal with this situation.*

This situation ... meaning Romano. The next name on a list of men I'll put ten feet in the ground.

A grunt barely makes its way through my clenched teeth as I write him back. *Push him out of his window, his own property.*

Let his body fall onto the spiked fence surrounding his estate.

Make an example of him.

I keep messaging him as the thoughts come, one line after the other.

Carter's answer doesn't come for longer than I'd like. My gaze is drawn again to Bethany, lying exhausted on the floor, and covering her face to hide the pain.

Fuck. I don't know how the hell it came to this.

Finally, he answers. *It's not that easy. There are complications.*

I stare at my phone, but my attention is brought back to the security monitors when Bethany finally stands, making her way to the bed. She stares at the door for a long time, sitting cross-legged and tense.

Jase, we need to wait for this one.

I don't have time for complications. I don't have patience for this. I don't have a desire for any of this. He should be dead already.

I turn off the phone, unwilling to spend another second dealing with this shit.

I want to get lost and find myself somewhere else.

Glancing at the screen, I watch Bethany pull a book into her lap. She must've gotten it from her purse. I went through the contents of her bag before I retrieved her from the trunk. Everything's there, except for her keys and a pen. I've seen both used in more violent ways than one could imagine.

She brushes the hair away from her face, showing me her vulnerability as she closes her eyes, and calms herself down.

I can get lost in her.

I lock the door to my office as I make my way to her, letting the keys clink against one another. My thumb runs along the jagged teeth of the key to the guest room as I think about stealing the fight from her, dragging it out of her and giving her so much more.

I'm careful with the lock, even more careful as I silently push open the door to her room. I don't stop at a crack, I keep pushing until the door is wide open and I can easily step through the threshold. It's quiet, so quiet in fact, that at first I don't see her.

Her small form is still on the bed, and only the sound of a page turning alerts me to where she is. With the overturned dresser, splintered wood and ripped curtains, she could have been hiding anywhere in here.

She ripped out every drawer. She threw two across the room, denting the drywall and cracking the walnut furniture.

Fragments of wood litter a corner of the room where she demolished a drawer, slamming it on top of another.

What a waste of energy. She should've saved it for this moment.

Instead the poor girl is still, curled up in a ball, and has her nose buried in the book.

She still doesn't see me, not even as I take a step forward, carefully stepping over a broken drawer.

The empty dresser, thick damask curtains and neatly made bed with bright white linens were all that were in the room. And now the fabric is heaped on the floor, the curtains ripped from the oil-rubbed bronze finishings and the armoire is … wrecked.

And little Miss Bethany sits in the middle of the bed, worn out and oblivious.

Her hair's a chaotic halo around her shoulders. The faint light from the setting sun casts a shadow around her, but it highlights her hair and when she tucks a strand behind her ear, it hits her face. Her fair skin's so smooth, it tempts me to brush my fingertips against it. The light falls to the dip in her neck, to the hollow there and it dares me to kiss her in that spot.

My cock hardens as I wonder what sounds would spill from her lips if I were to do just that.

"Looks like you had some fun." My voice comes out harder than I anticipated, startling her. She practically screams and slams her book shut as her body jostles.

She stands abruptly, backing off of the bed and clutching the book to her side as she squares her shoulders. "Let me go."

The huff comes back to me, but this time it's with a hint of humor.

"You're good at making demands when you have no authority, aren't you?" I question her, feeling a smirk play at my lips.

Silence. It's so fucking silent in this room, I think I can hear her heart pounding.

"Did you think destroying your room would … upset me?" I ask her with a deliberate casual tone to my question. Rounding the bed, moving closer to her, I kick a scrap of broken wood away from me. I follow her gaze as she glances at it, and then to the chunk of wood she left on the bed where she was sitting.

"Leave it there." I give her the command and watch her resist the urge to lunge toward it.

Her plump lips tug into a feigned smile. It's faint, but it's there. She is a fighter. There's no denying that.

"Did you want to anger me, Bethany?"

She flinches every time I say her name. That hint of a smile vanishes and the smoldering hate returns.

"I don't care what you do with this room. I won't be cleaning it up." I shrug as I add, "I hope it calmed you down to make such a mess."

With a gentle shake of her head, she huffs a humorless laugh at me then says, "Whatever you do to me, know that it won't hurt me. Whatever it is, I'll give you nothing."

She practically sneers her words, even as her eyes gloss over.

"We need to come to an agreement, and seeing as how you've gotten some of your… displaced anger out of the way--"

"Fuck you. I'm not agreeing on a damn thing with--"

"Not even to get the hell out of here?" I ask and cut her off.

The anger wanes from a boil to a simmer as her glare softens. "Just like that?" she asks skeptically.

"I don't want to keep you locked up… breaking all my shit." I make a point of kicking a piece of broken wood to the side. "I didn't plan this. And I want something else."

"So you're going to just let me go?"

"Once we come to an agreement, that's exactly what I plan on doing."

Shock lights her eyes, but so does skepticism.

"Do you think you can be reasonable this time?" I ask her, feeling I have the upper hand via the element of surprise.

"You fucking kidnapped me," she scoffs, the control leaving her in an instant. I watch as her knuckles turn white from how she grips the book so damn hard.

I take another stride forward to the end of the bed, and now only a few feet and a puddle of cotton linens stands between us.

Bethany takes a half step back, but when she tries to take another, her heel hits the balled-up curtain on the floor behind her. The wall is next.

"You tried to shoot me." My words cut through the air, leaving no room for negotiation as I add, "You should be dead for trying something so stupid."

At my last word, she steps behind the bundle of fabric at her feet, pressing her back to the wall. Her body trembles even as she utters the words, "Fuck you."

"I'm sure a well-read woman such as yourself has a wider vocabulary to choose from," I taunt and then nod to the book in her hand. "What is it?"

She breathes in and out, staring at me and refusing to speak.

"What book are you reading?" I ask her with less patience.

"I don't know," she answers, not taking her eyes from me.

"Now you're deliberately pissing me off," I tell her without any attempt at hiding the irritation.

"I don't know," she repeats, raising her voice, and her words come out hoarse. All that screaming she did caused more harm than good.

"Bullshit," I grit out and reach for the book, pissed off that she's being so stubborn, so resistant. With a single lunge forward, I grip the book in my hand, the other finding her hip to pin her against the wall.

"No!" she screams out at me, ripping the book away, and the thin pages on top nearly rip off without the cover to shield them. She turns her small body away from me as I press my chest against her. Barely managing to turn herself to face the wall, she cradles the book against her chest with both hands, concealing it from me. "It's my sister's." Her words are more of a cry than anything else, but the tone of them holds her explanation. "It's the last thing she gave to me," she bellows against the wall.

"I just got it yesterday; I don't know what book it is." Her voice lowers as her shoulders shudder. "There's no cover and I don't know what it is."

So this is what it takes to make her cower? An attempt to steal a book from her?

She's a trapped, scared, wild creature with nowhere to run and not sure how to fight, holding on to defiance because she has nothing else. I see her so clearly.

One breath, and then another. I stand there and just let her breathe.

"I believe you. Calm down."

"Calm down?" she shrieks at me, her voice wavering.

"Lower your voice or you'll stay in this fucking room until I feel like letting you out." I practically hiss the low threat, backing away slightly, but still remain close enough that she doesn't turn around. "Let me see it," I demand, holding out my hand. "I'll give it back."

She's still and quiet for a long moment as my hand hovers in the air.

"There are times to fight and times to give in," I say calmly and then add, "I might know what book it is."

Thump. My heart pounds in my chest as she still doesn't react. Hope starts to wane, but before I have to decide what to do with her, she turns to face me, and hesitates only a second more before giving me the book.

"Do you read a lot?" she asks me as I skim the first page and then turn it over to examine the back.

Before I can reply, a small sigh of amusement erupts from her lips and then she covers her mouth. I can't help but to watch as her fingers trail down her lips before she lets her hand fall to her side. "Sorry," she says. "That's a ridiculous question."

"It's a ridiculous situation, so it's a fair question," I answer her evenly, letting her see how easy it could be if she just gives in.

Holding the book out to her, I shake my head and say, "I don't anymore, and I don't recognize it either."

Her fingers barely brush against mine as she takes the book back, and the heat in her touch is electrifying. So magnetic, I nearly slip my hand forward, desperate for more. Her lashes flutter as she moves away from me, pulling back as much she can and wrapping her arms around herself. "What do you want from me?"

The immediate response is disappointment, and something else. There's a twisting feeling inside that feels like a loss, but I would have had to have possession of her in the first place to justify this feeling deep in the pit of my stomach.

"I have an offer for you and then I'll let you go," I tell her simply, acutely aware of the way each word sounds controlled.

"Is that a promise?" she asks as her gaze lifts to mine and she shakes her head in disbelief.

"Only because you'll be coming back."

In return she bites her bottom lip, effectively silencing herself, but the rage is clearly written on her face.

"You want to hate me." I address her anger before anything else.

"Yes," she answers quickly and honestly.

"That's only going to hurt you." The rawness in my words comes from a place I don't recognize.

She answers me, but she chokes up as she says, "I'm fine with that."

The twisting in my gut gets sharper. The seconds pass, and the air changes subtly between us, each of us staring at the other and waiting for the next move.

"What do you know about Marcus?" I ask her pointedly.

She shrugs like none of this matters, as if she isn't breaking apart. "I heard my sister say his name. He had something for her."

"What else?" I push her for more.

"Nothing." She looks me in the eyes and says, "All I had was his name and yours when she left."

"Nothing else?" I finally ask her when I judge her response to be sincere. "Nothing about the drugs?"

"You're all drug dealers," she bites back.

"Now Marcus is a drug dealer?"

"He must be. Just like you must be."

"Why do you say that?"

"Because my sister bothered to learn your name."

"What name is that?"

"Cross."

"So when you said you know all about Marcus and the drugs…"

"I wanted to …" She can't finish. Her lips press into a thin line before she finally says, "I wanted it to sound like I had you."

Time moves quickly as I stare at her and she stares back.

"I wanted you to feel like you weren't going to get away with it," she whispers, breaking the silence and rubbing her arms.

"That's all you know?"

"One of you had her killed." She croaks the quick response and I can see the frustration on her face from not being able to keep it together.

"It wasn't me or anyone who works for me," I tell her calmly, keeping my voice low and steady and looking her in the eyes just like she did me.

When she doesn't react, I add, "You have questions; I can give you answers."

"What happened to my sister?" she asks me without allowing a second to pass.

"I don't know exactly, but I can find out. And more importantly, it's not going to happen like this. I have a way of doing things and a desire to handle things in a certain manner."

She stares at me like I'm the devil and she's searching for a way to escape. There's no escaping from this though.

"You'll get the answers you want and pay off the debt your sister owed."

"What do you get?"

"It will be tit for tat. I seem to remember you mentioning Marcus and something else about drugs?" I press and she blanches. "But I like things done a certain way. When I have questions to ask and I need to make sure the person giving me an answer is telling the truth."

"What way is that?" she asks in a single breath. The nerves are making her shoulders shake slightly.

There's no way I can tell her; I have to show her instead.

"Every ten minutes is a hundred dollars." I make up the amount on the spot and before I can calculate anything else, she questions, "Ten minutes of what?" She doesn't bother to hide the trepidation in her voice.

I can see her nervousness, the anger barely hidden.

"I'm not going to lie, Bethany. One of the reasons I didn't kill you where you stood in your foyer is because I find you…" I trail off as I debate on the next words I want to say, but take a risk.

"I think you're beautiful and I love the way you fight me."

Her lips part, her breathing coming in short gasps, and her chest flushes with a subtle blush that trails up her neck. The compliment leaves her more amenable. Her eyes widen, the depths of the darkness taking over as what I want sinks in.

"And what do you expect me to do?" she asks and her words are rushed as if she doesn't already know.

"You'll see."

"I'm not a whore." Her barb is immediate and raw. "I don't care what my sister owed you." She lowers her voice to add, "I don't owe you anything."

A smirk tugs at my lips and I lean forward, letting my palm rest against the drywall just above her right shoulder. Bringing my lips to her ear, I tell her, "I don't have to buy sex and if and when we do fuck, it will be because you're begging me to be inside of you."

"Fuck you."

"Those words again." I tsk and then add, "You do owe me."

"I don't owe you shit. The person who killed my sister owes you, not me."

With her raised voice, the tension rises as well until I tell her, "Three hundred thousand dollars."

"I don't… my sister…" She struggles to finish her sentence, choking on her words, letting the number hit her. *Three hundred thousand dollars.*

That's more than she'll make in five years of working her ass off at the mental health hospital. I know what she makes, and every cent she has to her name was in the file Seth gave me.

I can see the way number piles on top of her; the very idea that she would have to pay that amount suffocates her. Stealing the life from her for only a moment before she tries to back away from me, but there's only the wall behind her. Nothing more, and nowhere to go.

"You have no choice."

"Jenny couldn't have…" It's not the debt that causes grief to settle in the depths of her eyes, it's the very idea that her sister owed that much money to men like my brothers and me.

"You have questions and want answers. I want my bar to be free of your bullshit." Although my words are harsh, my voice is calm, as soothing as it can be given the situation.

Her gaze whips up to mine, and she battles the need to hold on to the anger as my eyes roam down her body. The sleeve of her shirt is ripped, probably from her own doing. Her nails are chipped—again, probably from the way she's struggled in all of this and then destroyed everything she could get her hands on.

"You have aggression and you need a release; I can give you that."

She breathes a little heavier then says, "I want to leave."

"I want an answer."

Silence.

"You have a debt, an inherited debt and I'm giving you a way to pay it, free and clear."

"I don't owe you shit," she whispers, her pain laced in between each word, woven in the air between us. But more than that... I can hear the consideration evident by the lack of her animosity.

"It's your house, Thirty-four Holley Drive? Your sister was on your deed, wasn't she? I'm guessing she helped you get the loan before she fell down the path that took her away from you?"

I'm an asshole, a prick. I'm going to fucking hell for this. With every second that passes, Bethany struggles more and more to fight, because she can barely hold herself together. "She used your home as a marker for this loan. It's going to be paid."

It's cruel how I stand here, watching these words strike Bethany over and over. Each time taking a larger piece of her sister's memory and changing it. Changing how she remembered her. And how she feels about her now.

I am the devil she thought I was.

"It's not about the money for you though."

My statement brings her gaze to me as I add, "And I'm not interested in taking from you what you don't want to give."

Her lips part, bringing me closer to getting what I want.

"You want to do it, Bethany. You will do this. The curiosity will win out. And if you don't go through me, if you go back to pounding down doors and calling the police..." I let the unspoken threat dangle in front of her, allowing her to come to her own conclusion. "I'm a powerful man, but even I can't save someone from themselves."

My words seem to strike a chord with her, stealing what's left of her composure.

"I just want- "

I cut her off and say, "I can give you what you want. And you can give me what I want too. Or you can pay me three hundred thousand by the due date, which is in...eleven days." I make up a date, and then regret the fact that I didn't say tomorrow.

chapter eight

Bethany

I don't know how long I've sat here, wondering why he let me go. I know I should be dead after what I did. He's a criminal, and he could have done whatever he wanted with me. Before or after I shot that gun. He's strong enough to, and he has the means to do it. I've learned that much.

The sun's gone down, leaving my small living room bathed in shadows. My eyes burn, and my left ankle is numb from sitting on it for so long.

There's a bus that runs from the next block over all the way to Jersey City. I've been thinking about that too. And whether or not I would be able to use my credit cards, or if he'd be able to track me. I don't have enough cash to live without cards. I barely have any cash, in fact. There's a lot of debt in my name if I were to run and somehow try to come up with a fake ID.

I guess I can add three hundred thousand more to that debt. My stomach sinks at the thought, somehow finding its way to my throat even though it's in the opposite direction.

I've been waiting for some miraculous plan to smack me in the face. An easy way out, or even a difficult one. Something tells me Jase Cross will find me though. He'll find me wherever I run.

I can hear my back crack as I slowly rise from the sofa. My body is so stiff and sore, an obvious reminder of what happened. I need to give in to sleep and rest, but I can't bring myself to do it. To go lie in my bed when I'm so fucked.

Three hundred thousand dollars. What did you get yourself into, Jenny?

I have nothing. No money saved, only debt from school and from bailing Jenny out countless times. No answers to what happened.

He has answers. The nagging voice reminds me of that fact as I walk around my coffee table, leaving the book where it sits, and heading to the kitchen.

He wants to use me and pressure me into this when I don't deserve this shit. And he's the one with all the power. The one with all the answers.

Answers that belong to me. If he wants that debt to be paid, he'd better hold up his end of the deal. He'd better give me answers.

Grabbing a glass from the dishwasher and one of the many open bottles of red wine from my fridge left by all my unwelcomed guests, I decide on a drink. A drink to numb it all.

It's what I relied on last night too, after hours of searching my sister's old room for anything at all. Drugs she could have bought, cash she stored somewhere. I have no fucking idea how she owes so much, but her room was barren.

When Jase Cross dropped me off and told me he'd be seeing me soon, that was the first thing I did. Then I searched everywhere else. I searched and dug until my body gave out. And then I drank, somehow finding a moment of sleep, only to wake up with a pounding headache and that sick feeling still in my gut.

The way he said he'd be seeing me soon, before unlocking the car doors and walking me to my front door, the way he said it was like a promise. Like a promise a long-lost lover makes.

Not at all like the threat it really is.

The cork pops when it comes out, that lovely sound filling the air, followed by the sweet smell of Cabernet.

One glass quiets the constant flood of questions and regrets.

Two glasses numb the fears and makes me feel... alive. Free? I don't know.

Three glasses and I usually give in and pass out and everything's better then. Until I wake up and have to face another day with nothing to take this emptiness inside of me away.

He has answers.

Jase fucking Cross.

Ever since he let me go, my wrists and throat have felt scarred with his touch, and his voice has lingered in the back of my   thoughts.

I hate that he makes me feel so much. There's a spark between us I can't deny. He doesn't hide it, and that only makes this all hotter. It's in the way he talks to me, his candor and tone. The way his gaze seems to see through me while also seeing all of me, every bare piece of me. There is nothing that isn't raw in the tension that ties us together. Raw and thrilling... and terrifying.

I shouldn't find the arrogant prick so hot. He's a criminal and an asshole.

It doesn't matter if I want to fuck him. I still hate him. I hate what he does to earn a living and what he stands for. I hate that in her last months, he may have seen my sister more than I did.

Hate doesn't do what I feel toward him justice.

He has to know there's no way I can pay him three hundred thousand dollars.

He has to know and that's why he's given me this "out" – it's coercion at best. I could take him to court, but I already went to the cops. And going to them got me nothing. Not a damn thing but Jase fucking Cross knocking at my door.

"I don't trust him," I whisper to no one, letting my fingertip drag along the edge of the wine glass before tipping it back, gulping down the chilled liquid. "I don't trust anyone anymore."

I almost called the cops. The very second I shut the front door after saying goodbye as if he was an old friend, not a bad man wrapped in a good suit, and pushed my back against it. I almost did it and then I remembered doing the same damn thing yesterday, and the day before and the day before that. No one can help me.

Jase has answers. The voice doesn't shut up. I slam the glass down hard on the counter. Too hard for being this sober. Barely caring that the glass isn't broken, I grab the bottle and pour the rest of it into the glass. It's more than enough to help me pass out and to leave me with a hangover in the morning.

With both of my hands on the counter, I lean forward, stretching and going over every possibility.

If I stay, he's either going to try to fuck me or kill me. And I must be insane, because I think it's all worth it if I get answers.

I'm willing to risk it just to feel something else – something other than this debilitating pain. "I've lost my fucking mind."

Just as the words leave me, I hear a ping from the living room and turn my head to stare down the narrow walkway of my kitchen.

My gaze moves from the threshold, to the fridge and I purse my lips before making my way to where the other bottles are hiding from me.

My bare feet pad on the floor and it's the only sound I hear as I grab the next partially drunk bottle from the fridge, the glass from the counter, and move back to where my ass has made an indent in the sofa.

Pulling the blanket over my lap, I sit cross-legged and read the text. I'm trying to prepare myself for any number of things. The trepidation, the anxiety, both are ever constant, but dampened with yet another sip of the sweet wine.

It's only Laura, though. Seeing her name brings a small bit of relief until I read what she wrote.

Where the hell are you?

Home. What's wrong?

I went there yesterday. What happened to your door?

That sick feeling creeps up from the pit of my stomach and rises higher and higher until I'm forced to swallow it down with another gulp. This wine is colder, and it gives me a chill when I drink it.

Lie.

Just lie.

I know I should. I need to. I won't bring her into this bullshit. It's my problem, not hers.

You know I'm Italian, I answer her. Hoping the bit of humor mocking my hot-tempered heritage will lighten her mood.

You broke your door?

Italian and Irish, can't help it. Even I smirk at my answer. My mom used to tell us we're mutts, a mix of Italian and Irish, so people should know we'll hit them first if they're coming for us, and we won't stop hitting until we hit the floor. She was a firecracker, my mom.

The memory of her, of us, stirs up a sadness I keep at bay by filling my glass again. Three glasses, in what, twenty minutes? Even I can admit that's too much.

What happened? Laura asks.

Staring at the full glass, but not taking a sip, I settle with a half-truth. *My boss told me I have to take time off.*

Is it paid?

I get a little choked up thinking about how everyone chipped in to donate their PTO and debate on telling her the details, but hell, I can't deal with all this shit right now. I've never felt so overwhelmed in every way in my entire life. So I keep it simple.

Yeah. It's paid.

I miss you, she writes back. Thankfully, not continuing a subject that's going to push me over the edge.

I'm teetering on the wrong side of tipsy, exhausted, mourning, angry and in denial of fear and loneliness. And being coerced into ... probably sex, by a man I thought was going to kill me.

Fuck any kind of therapeutic conversation right now. Whether it's with Laura or anyone else. I don't have the emotional energy for it.

I miss you too.

We should go drunk shopping next weekend. Laura's suggestion sounds like a good way to have a minor public breakdown and max out my credit card. Which is fine if I do decide to leave town on the bus to Jersey City.

We can start at the mall, hit the restaurant bars in between the department stores? she suggests. The best times I've had with Laura were on the edge of a barstool holding a bag in one hand and a drink in the other, all while laughing about old times.

Hell yes, I answer her, because that's how I always answer her. Whether I'm going or not, I'll let her think I am so she feels better.

I promised I'd make you go out, so boom. Look at me keeping my commitment. I can practically hear the laughter in her voice from that text.

Who would have thought drunk shopping was a commitment you could keep, I joke back.

Seriously though, we haven't talked. How are you? Do you need me to come over? Laura's message makes me pause. But I can't hesitate for too long. She's sent me that message before, *do you need me to come over*, when in reality she was five minutes away and already headed here. She's notorious for just dropping in on people like that and thinks it's cute. In all honesty, I'm glad she's done it in the past, but I can't tonight. I will break down and tell her everything.

Don't come, I'm fine. I think I needed the time off, I admit to Laura after writing several messages and deleting them all.

If she came over... it would be disastrous.

Life moves too fast. It's whirling around me, demanding, taking, and I don't even have time to do an inventory of what's left of me. I don't know how to be okay, and I want someone to hurt for what happened to Jenny. I want someone who deserves it to be in this pain.

Someone other than me. It's so easy to blame myself. I deserve some of it. I can admit it.

I don't tell Laura any of that though. A small part of me knows she already knows I blame myself. No matter how many times she's told me you can't help someone who won't help themselves. It doesn't change the fact that Jenny was my sister. It doesn't change the fact that I keep thinking if only I'd been with her, or if I'd followed her, if I'd pushed her more, maybe she'd still be with me.

I don't even realize I'm crying until I feel the tears on my cheeks.

Angrily, I wipe them away and toss my phone across the coffee table. It makes the glass clatter against the table as I cover my face with my hand and force myself to calm down.

I just need to know what happened. I need to know.

Jase Cross will get me answers.

The very thought has my eyes opening, and the need to mourn subsiding.

My gaze wanders to the foyer. To the small table that sits right where it should, but was pushed to the side only hours ago. To the wall he pushed me against. The scene plays out in my head, complete with the bang of a gun and his husky voice whispering against the shell of my ear.

As I remember his words, shivers run down my shoulders. I'll blame some of them on the wine.

He may not have hurt her, but he knows who did, or he knows someone who can find out. He knows *something* about the side of my sister I never fully knew.

I want it. I need it. I need to know.

As my phone pings with another text, there's a knock at my door.

Fucking Laura. I love her, but I cannot deal with life right now. I don't bother picking up the phone to see what she wrote this time.

Instead I'm focused on one glaring thought that won't leave me alone as I stand up. I know nothing about the world my sister inhabited. I know nothing about the life she led.

All I know is this, my work, my small circle, and the daily patterns that haven't changed in years.

But Jase Cross knows it all.

Making my way to the door, I come up with every excuse I can to make her go away;

looking down past my baggy pajama shirt all the way to the stains on my old sweatpants, my very appearance is excuse enough. I need to pass the hell out and be alone.

I'm already telling her to go home when I open the door, wide and easily, not even considering for a second that it isn't her.

"You aren't touching my wine-" I start to joke with her, but then my jaw drops open and my heart stutters. My body heats with both fear and desire, making my grip on the doorknob slip as Jase stares down at me.

He's taller than I remember; how is that even possible? His shoulders are wide and dominating as he stands in my doorway. A ribbed black Henley under a thick wool coat and dark jeans are all he wears this time. For some reason, comparing the two sides of him, this casual man with an edge of seduction and the buttoned-up powerful man of control... it stirs a heat in my core.

"What do you want?" My words are rushed and I try desperately to hold on to what little sense I have.

"You look surprised." His voice is smooth like velvet, caressing every one of my senses.

"What are you doing here?" I question him, feeling panic rise inside of me.

With a sexy smirk kicking up his lips, he runs the pad of his thumb down the sharp line of his jaw before telling me, "I'm here with your contract."

chapter nine

Jase

She's less than sober. The winestained lips tell me that.

She hasn't slept, judging by her messy hair and the darkness under her eyes.

And I can tell by the response of her body when she looks into my eyes that she needs to be fucked. Hard and ruthlessly. Fucked into her mattress until she can't do anything but sleep away everything that plagues her.

Good fucking timing for me. I've never given in to these desires. It's only been a fantasy. I know she's hurting and so am I. There is a certain kind of pleasure that can soothe such a deep pain. I fucking need it. Right now.

The thoughts run wild in my head as I wait for her to let me in.

The foyer is just how I remembered it. A classic '50s house with a mix of modern and antique furniture that give it a comfortable feel. She's eclectic. Or at least her belongings are.

The chill of the winter air moves with me as I take a long stride inside, forcing Bethany to take a step back. Her stride is shorter though and she bumps her ass into the hall table, turning around as she startles, and I take the moment to close the door.

"I didn't say you could come in." She breathes out her words and stumbles at finding her anger and her strength to keep me away. I almost feel bad catching her off guard. But then again, that's how she caught me yesterday.

"We got off on the wrong foot." I ignore her statement, taking a step toward her but making sure to be as nonthreatening as I can. With my hands slipping into my front pockets I meet her questioning gaze, and each passing moment it heats with an anger she's barely concealing.

"I apologize," I offer, seeing that fight come and go inside of her. She has no idea what to do, and my apology gives her whiplash.

Her lips part, but no words come out. Her hands move behind her, gripping the small table and I swear I can hear her heartbeat loud and clear. As if it's pounding inside of her just for me.

Still no words have come but her lips stay parted, and her gaze remains questioning.

"I shouldn't have come in here like I did, making demands. I think we can come to terms in a civilized manner."

A crease mars her forehead as Bethany brushes the hair from her cheek and tucks it behind her ear.

"You're a criminal," she speaks lowly to the floor, but her eyes rise to mine as she adds, "You think you can force your way into getting what you want and if that doesn't work, charm will?" Although she poses the statement as a question, I know she believes what she said wholeheartedly.

She's not wrong, but I won't give her that satisfaction.

"I've never been called charming, Bethany," I tell her, playing with the way I say her name. Softening it, letting it fall from my lips gently, as if simply whispering it allows it to hang in the air, hinting at all the things we're leaving unspoken.

It takes her a moment to say anything at all. The force in her words is absent, and she doesn't look me in the eyes.

"Apology accepted, please leave."

"We have unfinished business." My response is immediate.

I watch as she swallows, hating me but knowing I push more boundaries than just anger.

"I stand by what I said, you owe a debt." Her gaze snaps to mine and her exhale is forceful. I continue before she can object. "I wrote up a contract I think you'll find agreeable."

She's silent as I pull out the folded paper from my back pocket, along with the pen I lifted from her purse.

Her gaze narrows as she recognizes it. "You'll need to sit down for this. Standing in the hallway isn't how I conduct business."

Silence.

Ever defiant.

I fucking love it. I relish standing here while she makes me wait, as if she could actually control what happens next. Our story is already written, and she knows it. She'll give in. She knows that too.

Without saying a word, she stalks to her living room, her arms crossed over her chest until she sits.

Although I haven't been in the living room, I've already seen it. And the kitchen and dining room. I'm prepared for what's in every drawer. Seth took care of that for me.

There's a heavily poured glass of wine on the table, and she pours it back into the bottle rather than downing it like I thought she was going to do when she grabbed it.

"You can sit wherever you want, intruder."

"Intruder?" I question her and the only acknowledgement I get is a firm, singular nod in time with the glass being placed gently on the coffee table.

"All right then, *attempted murderer*," I quip back and take a seat on the armchair beside the sofa.

Her mouth drops open and then slams shut, her jaw tense as she stares back at me as if I've said something offensive. "Just calling a spade a spade," I say and hold her gaze as I raise my hands, palms toward her in defense.

She hesitates to respond and I know I see remorse in her eyes. I know what it looks like; I see it every fucking day.

"I would have done the same, just so you know," I confide in her and her tense shoulders ease a bit. Only a fraction though. "I don't blame you."

She's still silent for a moment, assessing me and everything she's dealing with.

I'll be gentle with her, I'll give her what she needs. I can be that man for her. And she can be what I need.

"What do you want?" she asks after a moment. "What contract?"

Leaning forward, I rest my elbows on my knees and lace my fingers together. "You have questions, needs, and so do I. You owe me a debt, whether you like it or not, and I can give you something you never knew you wanted."

Her thighs tighten as she swallows thickly, tensing her neck. She pulls the blanket closer to her and asks, "Did you know my sister?"

"Not personally, but I know things she was doing. She got into some trouble."

The reaction is immediate, her expression falling and for the first time I came in here, the pain shows, but she's quick to hide it.

"I'll answer your questions," she says softly, gaining control of her composure before looking at me and finishing her negotiation. "And you'll answer mine?"

A sorrowful smile plays at my lips. "That's not how this works." Her bottom lip wavers and her fingers dig into the comforter on her lap. "I want more."

The tension thickens between us with every passing second of silence.

The paper crinkles in my hand as I unfold it and read it to her.

"For the payment of three hundred thousand dollars, not a penny will be paid in currency. The party agrees that sessions will take place, in which Bethany Fawn allows Jase Cross to question her as he sees fit, questions she will answer honestly to the full extent of her knowledge, and in a manner that will entail no physical harm whatsoever to Miss Fawn. The ability for Bethany to stop all proceedings whenever she wishes, verbally, will halt the session, allowing Miss Fawn to leave as she wishes."

I watch her expression, noting how she squirms uncomfortably and pushes her hands into her lap and she then reads the last line.

"Every ten minutes is equivalent to one hundred dollars."

"That's thirty thousand minutes total, that's five hundred hours," Bethany says aloud with no indication in her tone as to what she makes of that sum.

"Correct."

"I couldn't possibly... that's a full-time job for a quarter of the year. I won't let this interfere with my job."

"It won't. We can add in a line if you'd like, stating that it will come second to your occupational needs."

"I would be in debt to you for a year at least."

"Yes," I say, and there's no negotiation in my tone.

"What about my questions?"

"They're yours to ask, but not a part of this contract."

"That's-"

I cut her off. "Not necessary to be included in a contract regarding how you'll be paying me back." I lean forward, holding her gaze. "I choose to answer your questions as a gesture of goodwill."

"And you'll continue to?" she pushes.

"I don't have a single problem answering every question you have. Tit for tat." She gives a small nod of acknowledgement, but nothing else.

Time passes and Bethany chooses not to push for that to be in writing.

"How will you be questioning me?" she asks and a warmth flows through me, the tension lighting slowly, crackling between us like a smoldering fire.

"Sign first," I answer, swallowing thickly as I pass the paper to her, followed by the pen. Her fingers brush against mine, gentle but hot. The sensation travels from my knuckle all the way up my arm, the nerve endings coming alive with heat.

My throat's dry and my blood hot just thinking about her allowing me to show her.

"You realize I'll never believe I owe you anything?" she questions me, a simple statement, so matter of fact.

"You owe me your life for that stupid shit you pulled. Whether you want to believe that or not."

She picks at some indiscernible fuzz on the blanket before whispering, "I'm sorry."

Remorse and conflict swirl in her gaze, but she's quick to hide it from me.

"I like that you're less angry."

"That happens when I greet the bottom of a green glass bottle with a label that reads Cabernet." Her tone is muted, but she gives a small huff of a laugh, and lets a smile kiss her lips for only a moment.

"I need to know what you're going to do to me," she says before clearing her throat. "I'm not naïve. I know ... I know you can do what you want. I know you may lie to me, hurt me, fuck me, whatever it is you intend to do, I'm not stupid." I can hear her swallow and then she adds, "But what if I did go along with it? Would you really tell me what happened to her?" Her eyes gloss over and her voice softens.

"A question for a question," I tell her. "An answer for an answer."

"You're going to be disappointed with my answers," she says with a weary note to her voice. "She barely told me anything. I was speaking out of anger when I saw you."

"You came to my bar, you looked for my family. You tried to shoot me." With every sentence, she cowers more and more. "There's a reason for those actions." She nods solemnly.

"What are you going-"

"Just sign," I cut her off and she moves her focus to the empty glass. My pulse is racing, my nerves on edge. And yet, she looks so ... unaffected by the weight of what's to come. Like some part of her has given in.

"I need this as much as you do."

Her huff is nothing but sarcastic. Easy, I remind myself. Go easy on her now. It will be different later.

"It will be an escape from the pain if nothing else. You need it," I tell her and this time her expression changes slightly, as if she's so very aware of the agony that mourning is. It's also an aphrodisiac. There is never a more relevant time to be touched, or to be loved than when someone you love is gone.

"You want another glass?" I offer with a slight teasing tone to lighten the mood, an asymmetric grin pulling at my lips when she peeks up at me through her thick lashes.

"I may have had more than enough already."

The sofa groans as she leans back on it, reading the single sheet of paper once again.

The faint light from the disappearing sun kisses her skin as the loose shirt slips down her shoulder and she has to readjust it. She doesn't look back at me as she does. With her legs bent, her bare feet resting on the edge of the sofa and a thin blanket thrown over her lap, she looks far too casual for this moment.

As if that exposed skin of hers wasn't everything I've been thinking about since I first saw her across the bar. As if I don't want to rip that shirt off of her and devour every inch of her body with open-mouth kisses, dragging my teeth along her skin and making her that much more sensitive for what I'm going to do to her.

There are moments in time, pauses in your reality, where you realize this instant will be a memory forever. Something that will never leave you. I'll remember this one forever.

I hope I never forget how the adrenaline is rushing through me, how eager I am. I want to remember it all. Every single detail.

I'll remember it, and I'll have to, because I'm going to lose her. She's not meant to be mine.

That doesn't mean I won't take her, though.

"If I say no?" she asks, her wide hazel eyes searching mine for something.

"It doesn't happen." There's no hesitation in my answer.

"If I say stop?"

"It stops."

"Why do it then? Why would you do this?" she asks with her brow furrowed.

"Because I know you want it. I know you need it." She's silent in return.

"This would never hold up in court," she says, finally breaking the quiet.

"I have no desire to ever see you in a courtroom, Miss Fawn. I didn't even intend to write this down; I only did it because I thought you would respond better, maybe even listen to what I'm offering, if it was written in black and white."

"And what is it you're offering exactly, Mr. Cross?"

"Answers, and an escape, a way to pay a debt I know you can't afford." My gaze stays on hers, holding her in place until she gives me an answer. "This is a world you know nothing about, Bethany, and I'm willing to bring you into it. I'm willing… and you'd be wise to take this deal."

"Call me Beth." She corrects me without looking at me as the pen scribbles her signature, right on the line next to mine.

Desire sinks into my blood in an instant, surging through every fiber of my being as the paper and pen find themselves on the coffee table. Signed on the dotted line.

"I'll go easy on you," I tell her as I stand up, preparing myself to show restraint. She stays where she is, pretending not to be affected in the least.

"Is that right?" she asks as I pour a glass of wine. She stares at the dark liquid swirling before speaking out loud. "I'm already a little further than the right side of tipsy, Mr. Cross."

I fucking love the way she said my name. My cock stiffens, immediately hard just from having her obey me, having her speak to me like this. There's something about a fiery woman submitting that makes me lose all control and focus, giving it all to her.

"It's for me," I point out and take a sip. It's cheap wine, but decent enough.

"Don't confuse me going along with this for something it isn't," she says a little harder, with more resolve than I expect.

"Oh, and what isn't it?"

"I'm not just going to let you do what you want and get away with it. I'm not that easy, and I'm not submitting to your every wish if that's what you think this is."

A beat passes before I ask her, "Then what are you doing?"

"I'm simply learning the ropes of your world, Mr. Cross."

"This is how you'll learn. You'll do what I say. I ask the first question, then once I'm satisfied with your answer, you can ask me whatever you want. Those are the ropes, Miss Fawn."

Her long brown hair brushes against her shoulders as she nods, making her shirt fall once again and a shiver run across her skin. She's quick to lift the thin fabric back into place, as if it will be staying there.

"Lie down." I give her the first command and just like yesterday, in the guest bedroom when I waited for the book she held so tightly, she hesitates, testing me before obeying.

"I'd like to address an important matter first," she states innocently enough, arching a perfectly plucked brow at me.

"What's that?"

"It's seven seventeen," she tells me and I grin, letting the rush of desire take over.

"I already started the clock at six fifty-two when I pulled into your driveway."

Surprise widens her eyes.

"Lie down."

"I'll say no if you tell me to spread my legs for you."

The determination in her voice is surprising, considering how badly she wants me.

Although I don't speak the sentiment out loud, I make her words a personal challenge.

"You'd spite me to deny yourself a basic need?" I ask her and before she can respond I add, "I have no intention of fucking you today, but I know you need to be fucked long and hard … both that mouth of yours and your cunt."

Indignation flashes in her eyes, darkening them, which only makes the golden hues that much more vibrant.

"If I put my hands between your thighs, would I find you hot and wet for me?" My voice is calm, although my dick leaks precum, throbbing from the very idea that her cunt is ready for me.

"You'll never know," she says offhandedly before lying down, covering herself with the blanket and resting her head on the one pillow that was tucked in the corner of the sofa.

"I asked you a question." My words are hard, and her hazel glare whips to mine. "Is your cunt soaking wet for me?"

"No." She answers savagely and begins to ask her own question, but I tell her, "I'm not satisfied with that answer."

I drop to my knees one by one to get closer to her, feeling her heat, but not touching her. Not yet.

Somehow I keep my voice low and controlled when I repeat my question, "Is your cunt soaking wet for me?" My breathing is short, my palms hot with desire raging inside of me.

Give in to what's to come, my cailín tine.

The Gaelic phrase fits her, everything about her, perfectly. My cailín tine. My fiery girl.

Lifting her head and staring boldly into my heated gaze, she answers, "You're an attractive man, Mr. Cross. I've been wet for you since you pinned me against my foyer wall." Her blink is slow and deliberate. When she opens her eyes, she stares at the ceiling as if her heart isn't racing out of her chest, as if the blush on her cheeks is only from the wine. With her hands on her chest, she gently places her head on the pillow and asks politely, "Is it my turn to ask a question?"

Sitting back, I rest my hands on the rustic wood floors on either side of my thighs, forcing myself not to touch her. It's so cold, and a much-needed reminder of how hot I burn for her.

"You aren't in the position I want yet, but yes, I did say I would go easy on you this first time."

"Who killed my sister?" Her words are blurted out and her body tenses. "I want a name," she adds quickly.

"I don't have a name, but I'm looking into it and when I do – which I will, I promise you – when I do have a name, I will tell you."

"So you're saying you had nothing to do with it?"

"That's another question, Miss Fawn. I'll gladly answer it now, but then I get two in a row."

Her wild eyes search mine for a moment as she clenches her jaw before nodding in agreement.

"Not only did I have nothing to do with her death, neither did my brothers or anyone who works for me. I have no idea why she was killed... yet."

She swallows thickly and her forehead scrunches as she wars with whether or not to believe me.

All I can think about is the one night at The Red Room. I bet her sister told her about that night and that's why she came searching for me and knew to go to my club.

"Move your hands above you, to here," I say then reach up and pat the arm of the sofa. She's slow to obey, but she does. Her nails sink into the fabric and that loose shirt slips down her shoulder again, showing me more of her soft skin. I run a finger along the curve of her arm, leaving goosebumps along my path.

"I don't know—"

I cut off her objection. "I want to know when you're lying to me, and I'll do as I see fit." My words are barely spoken, because my focus is on how flushed her skin is already from such little contact.

I take my time, moving her hair to the side so I can see her slender neck and the dip in her collar.

Reaching into my left back pocket, I pull out a simple, black silk tie and tell her, "Your wrists will be bound." Her eyes flash to mine, and I take another sip of her wine. It's so much sweeter the second time, not unlike herself.

Although she watches as if she'd like to object, she doesn't. Instead all she says is, "Seven thirty-four."

"One thing you'll find benefits you greatly in this arrangement is that I enjoy taking my time," I tell her, picking up her left wrist, wrapping it and then the other before tying the two together. "Your body will tell me if you're lying to me. Your body will tell me *everything*."

All the while I watch her body. How her back arches slightly, how slowly she's blinking, how quickly she's breathing. I'm captivated by her and I couldn't give two shits if every word out of her mouth is a lie.

"You said you'd stop if I want you to?" she asks me and I answer with a question of my own. "Are you already having doubts?"

"Just checking," she whispers as I tighten the knot and place her wrists back on the arm of the sofa, above her head. The nervousness colors her every move. She can't hide anything from me like this.

I don't ask her or warn her before I pull the blanket down, exposing her to the cool air, so at odds with her heat.

I'll go slow. I'll be gentle this first time and ease her into what I want.

Her hips dig into the sofa as if she's trying to get away or hide, before ultimately relaxing. Her thighs are pressed firmly together, all the way down her legs to her ankles, barely covered by the thin sweatpants. With her shirt pulled up from the way she's laying, there's a sliver of her midriff exposed.

"Let me tell you a secret." My fingers fall to just above the exposed skin, playing along the hem of her shirt and gently lifting it higher. "I often have to get answers from people. It's what I do; it's what I'm good at."

It's because of me that Carter was able to create this empire so quickly. Everyone had secrets and I was able to get them all. With a knife and ruthlessness he didn't have quite yet. Power is limited if you don't have the knowledge to enforce it.

Her body stiffens and the breath she releases is strained.

"When someone is put in a state where they can't control their body, their emotions," I say, watching her as she stares at the ceiling, waiting for her eyes to find mine before continuing, "their pain or their pleasure, they give so much away." I let my words linger in the air before my fingers finally fall to her exposed belly. I run the tips of my fingers just inside the waistband of her sweatpants. Just barely venturing lower. "I intend to tie you down, to push your limits, and to enjoy every detail you give me about whatever it is I want to know."

"I can say no," she gasps as I slip my hand lower, finding the elastic band of her underwear. The way her shoulders rise and hunch with every quick breath reveals her desire just as much as it displays her need to run.

"Of course you can, but why would you deny yourself if you have nothing to hide?"

"I don't have anything to hide."

"Prove it," I tell her.

"You just want to touch me." Her words fall carelessly from her lips.

"I want to do more than touch you," I admit to her and feel a pang in my chest. A longing that's desperate to be spoken. "You aren't the only one in this room who's in need."

At my words, her gaze drifts lower, down to my zipper and I'm sure she can tell how hard I am for her. Her mouth parts slightly and she looks away, not commenting but showing her cards all too easily.

My gaze wanders to the crook of her neck, and as she breathes, a lock of hair falls right where I'm looking.

Leaning forward, I brush it to the side and bring my lips closer to her ear. Intent on whispering, intent on sharing a part of me I haven't shared with anyone.

I want to run my lips along her neck, kissing and sucking and confessing all my sins, begging for forgiveness.

Her chest heaves as if she knows I want to kiss her.

None of that happens though, because she turns her head just as I start to make my move, and she steals the kiss from me.

Her lips brush against mine at first, soft and hesitant. Yet she nips my bottom lip before I can deepen it. The gentleness of her touch is at odds with how my hands reach up to her hair, gripping it at the base of her neck and pulling her head back to expose more of her throat.

With my breath stolen, once again caught off guard, and with the desire running rampant in my blood, I stare down at her. Her eyes half lidded, her breaths coming in short pants as if I'd just devoured her and it wasn't at all a tempting taste of a kiss.

I'm drunk off her.

Breathing in her lust and not breaking her gaze, I lower my fingers to her swollen nub, spreading her arousal up to it, and then circling it. "What was that for?" I ask her and she tells me, "I wanted to take it first. I deserve that much at least." Her last word skips in the air, like a flat rock thrown across a summer lake. Her speech moves from a higher pitch to a whisper as I move my fingers lower, playing with her and watching every reaction she gives me.

"How many lovers have you had?" I ask and my question catches her off guard as she struggles to hold back her gasps.

"Few," she answers in a strained voice as I circle her clit again.

"Recently?"

"Not since college."

"Did they touch you like this?" I ask her, imagining a younger version of her under the sheets in a dorm room, letting some dumb fuck put his hands on her.

"Yes," she breathes with her eyes closed and I gently press down on her clit and then smack it.

She sits up and when she does I aim for another kiss, but she bites down hard on my mouth. Her teeth plunge into my bottom lip, the bite sending a pain shooting through my body. It's hard enough to draw blood and I swear to God it does nothing but make me that much harder for her.

She releases me all too soon, sucking in a deep breath with her mouth still open, her chest heaving and her eyes pinned on me.

Lifting my fingers from her heat, I bring them to my throbbing lip.

"No blood," she murmurs and a soft smirk plays on that pouty mouth of hers. "Don't get the wrong idea, Mr. Cross. Even if the thought of you getting me off makes me all hot and bothered, I still hate your fucking guts."

My dick responds, getting harder by the second as she utters the threatening words so sensually, words that would get others killed.

Her anger's at war with her desire, but it's losing the battle. Maybe it's the wine, maybe it's the exhaustion, but I can give her desire the upper hand.

I watch her every move. The way she clenches her hands and struggles to keep them motionless above her head. The way her skin flushes and goosebumps run up her chest, then down her arms. She's fucking gorgeous like this. Bared to me without reluctance. Without a single hint suggesting she's hiding a damn thing.

She's lost in the lust.

I spread her arousal around her swollen nub before bringing my middle finger back to her opening. With a gentle press, her lips part, and the word *stop* is there, just behind her clenched teeth. The hiss of an S was coming.

I push her, barely sliding the tip of my finger into her hot entrance, and her jaw drops open, the word lost somewhere and remaining unspoken.

Bringing my fingers back to her clit, I let her come down from the high, simply toying with her as she regains her composure.

"That's your limit?" I ask her, bringing my fingers back up to her clit, watching as her eyes go half lidded and she exhales with pleasure. My fingers drift back down and press against her slick entrance slightly before she nods a yes to my question.

Her control is as surprising as my restraint. If I hadn't decided I wasn't going to fuck her tonight, not until she truly begs for it, she'd be screaming my name as I ravaged her on the carpet beneath me. Maybe bent over the coffee table to leave bruises on her hips as a reminder. Making sure she'd feel it tomorrow, so it would be all she could think about.

I need to be gentle today. I'll ease her in until she's drowning in the pleasure I'm so desperate to give her.

She can barely breathe. Her gasps and held breaths are making her body tremble just as much as my touches are.

"Cum." My singular word bites through the air as I land a hard smack on her clit and then capture her scream of pleasure with my own kiss. My kiss is more ruthless than hers as I let my tongue delve into her hot mouth. It's quick like hers though; I pull back both the kiss and my touch, just as soon as it began.

She can barely keep herself still, her body begging her to move away from the sensation, but she needs more. Pulling her shirt down, I move her bra so it pushes her breast up, and before she can object I lean forward and swirl my tongue around her nipple. Her thighs move together and stagger to the side.

Still sucking on her, I smack her thigh with the back of my hand, pushing her legs open and moving my hand to cup her pussy.

Letting her nipple out of my mouth with a pop, I pull back to tell her, "Your cunt is soaking wet for me," and rub ruthless circles around her clit, making her brow pinch, her mouth open and her body shudder with another climax.

Her entire body spasms with the second orgasm. And I can barely fucking stand to watch with how hard I am. Everything in me begs me to shove my cock down her throat.

Still panting and struggling, Bethany lets her hands fall forward and then quickly moves them back into place on the arm of the sofa. Her eyes search mine for direction with a desperate apology to forgive her swimming in their darkness.

In answer, I pull the tie loose. She came, she let me touch her. I need to get the hell out of here before I fuck her and ruin it all before it's even begun.

"Next time will be more intense. You should prepare yourself."

Her first words as I reach for the contract, still on the table, bring a genuine smirk to my lips. "You didn't ask your question."

"I know."

It's quiet for a moment as I tuck the contract into my back pocket.

"Why are you doing this?" Her bright eyes are wide and full of fire. Full of an intense desire and a curiosity that are addictive. Every look she gives me brings out more life, more heat, more passion in me to coax more of this from her. She burns like wildfire and I want to add fuel to her flame.

"I wanted you to see why I let you live. What I wanted from you against that foyer wall after you pulled that trigger." Although her chest rises and falls rapidly, the memory of yesterday adding fear into the cocktail of emotions she's drunk on, the golden flecks in her hazel eyes stay lit. Her lips part slightly, and I know the memory only gets her off just like it does to me.

"It was an accident," she admits to me.

My smirk widens into an asymmetric grin. "Is that supposed to make me feel better about it?" I ask her and she simply shakes her head, pulling her shirt down and reaching for the thin blanket to cover herself. Her skin is still flushed, the pleasure still rocking through her, but her eyes are focused on the digital clock below her television.

Ever a reminder.

My smile falls as I tell her, "You're reckless."

"You're the one who was almost murdered by someone like me. So who's really reckless?"

"Maybe I'm just reckless for you," I answer without thinking, barely hearing my words before recognizing them.

I warn her, "Next time I won't ask for your boundaries."

"I would have--"

"Next time I'm going to fuck you like both of us want me to."

chapter ten

Bethany

I FEEL LIKE I'M DROWNING. LIKE I'M IN OVER MY HEAD, AND I DON'T KNOW HOW I VENTURED into the dark abyss of the ocean, sure to swallow me whole.

I dreamed of him. I dreamed of Jase fucking me, taking me ruthlessly on the sofa. I dreamed of telling him no, only to have him pin me down and take me regardless.

The thought sends a blush of desire to grace my skin, kissing it and leaving a shiver in its wake. The way Jase did last night. Every small touch brought more and more heat, more sensitivity, more life. I felt alive under him.

And I want more. I'm not ashamed to admit I want more of Jase Cross.

Bringing my fingertips to my lips, I remember the kiss I drunkenly stole—thank God I can blame it on the alcohol. He tasted like bad decisions and lust. A sin waiting to happen.

When did my life become like this?

Working every day has kept my thoughts at bay. And now I have nothing to occupy my time. Nothing but a debt to Jase Cross and unanswered questions I have no way of answering on my own.

The only thing I've been working on is looking up every detail I can on Jase Cross. Hardly anything comes up at all about any of his brothers. All I can tell is that they were a poor Irish family, raised in the hellhole that is Crescent Falls. Back then they were nothing. And now they're everything.

There are only four pictures of Jase that I could find. Two had the same woman in them. In one, she's in the background, laughing at something. It's a candid photo and it seems harmless enough. But in the second, her arm is around him. It was taken nearly five years ago, and Jase looks much younger.

I have no fucking clue who she is.

Although, she looks a little like me in this picture, the second one. Only slightly. But the resemblance spreads an eerie chill over my body when I think about it.

Is this who I remind him of?

Was he with her? The fact that I feel any hint of jealousy is ridiculous.

I haven't been touched since college, and I haven't wanted a damn thing from a man since that catastrophe.

Maybe I've always been jealous like this, and I just didn't know it because I had nothing to be jealous of. It only took the strike of a single match to ignite a blazing desire to overtake every piece of me.

Maybe this is what it was like for Jenny. One small change, and everything fell from there. Addiction is like that, isn't it? No matter what your addiction is.

The sound of my phone vibrating on the kitchen counter saves me from the downward spiral of my thoughts.

It's only Laura, checking in again since I didn't respond to her last night.

A few quick texts and I'm free of her prying questions, plus I've booked a date with a bottle of tequila, her, and the outlet mall next weekend.

The phone clatters on the kitchen counter when I toss it down, staring at it and wondering what that night will end up being. A few drinks, and I'll tell her the sordid details.

I know I will.

I can see it unfolding in front of me.

She won't judge me, seeing as how she's had a few one-night stands. She's gone backstage with an out-of-town band before, only to be seen again at 2 p.m. the next day, walking a little funny but smiling so hard that it didn't matter.

It's not the judgment that concerns me. I couldn't care less about what people think of me.

If Laura thinks I'm in danger though, she'll get involved. The very thought makes me let out a slow quivering breath, calming the rush of anxiousness.

I can't keep Jase my dirty little secret, but some things will have to be just that. A secret. I'll let him use me, and I'll use him. Every encounter with him is a step closer to the world my sister lived in before I lost her. It's closer to where she was and closer to finding out what happened. At least the thought is somewhat calming.

Knock, knock, knock.

Three raps in quick succession sound through the first floor of my house. I've never been so grateful for a distraction before.

Looking out through the peephole, I see a man in a gray wool coat, a man I don't recognize.

Maybe he has a package, or maybe he's a neighbor. I hesitate to open the door, my hand gripping the knob tight as I consider getting the gun. That didn't turn out well last time though, and I refuse to live in fear.

It's just a man. Not everyone is a villain.

The last thought firms my resolve and I pull open the door halfway, wincing when I feel the sharp coldness in the air.

"Hello," I greet him easily, immediately struck by how handsome he is.

Classically handsome with striking blue eyes and a charming smile. This man has definitely left broken hearts behind in his wake.

The small smile from the thought fades.

Nervousness pricks along the back of my neck. Every hair is standing on edge when I glance behind him, only to see a cop car.

He's a fucking cop.

"Ma'am, I'm Officer Cody Walsh," he tells me, taking off his gloves and reaching out his hand to shake mine.

Every ounce of me is consumed with fear, nausea, and the suspicion that this is a setup. I shake his hand without thinking, without considering a damn thing.

Even though he was wearing gloves, his strong hand is ice cold and I feel the chill flow from his touch straight to the marrow of my bones.

It's not until I swallow my nerves, nearly ten seconds after shaking his hand while he only stares at me curiously, that I'm able to speak.

"Could I see your badge?"

He's quick to take it out, passing it to me and when he does, his fingers brush against mine. The physical contact is a little too close I think at first, but then I peek up at him and he's all business. It's all in my head.

"Sorry, I just didn't expect to see any more cops now that the funeral's passed," I tell him, whipping up the excuse on a dime and praying it explains my hesitation as I pass back his badge. Again his fingers brush mine and although I'm well aware of that fact, he doesn't show any sign that he noticed.

"The funeral?" he questions and I feel the blood drain from my face.

"My sister's; isn't that why you're here?" My voice is calm but drenched in sorrow. Real sorrow. I stand there pretending I know nothing of the past few days but my grief. I think back to what I felt the night my estranged family left me alone and I had to sleep knowing Jenny was really gone. That the world has accepted that, and I needed to as well.

I'm only a sister in mourning. That's all I choose to be right now.

"I'm sorry to hear about your loss." He clears his throat, bringing his closed fist to his mouth as he looks to his right, away from me and then adds, "I'm here on different matters."

Finally, he looks back at me, and at the same time I feel my heart pounding, filling with so much anxiety, it feels as if it will burst.

As I grip the edge of my door, letting him see the nerves and apprehension, he asks, "Do you mind if I come in?"

A second passes as I look past him to his cruiser. The pounding inside my chest intensifies.

I don't know what to do, and I'm terrified to make the wrong decision.

"Is this a bad time?" he asks when I don't answer, his voice carrying my attention back to him.

The light blue eyes that pierce into me tell me it's all right, there's a kindness there, a caring soul somewhere deep inside. A small voice inside my head is screaming at me to tell him about Jase. The voice says I'll be safe. There will be no debt, and all of this will be over.

But a bigger side, the side of me that's taken over, the side I don't recognize, isn't ready for this to end. Already I love being touched by Jase Cross. I crave for that powerful man to use me, and I'm determined to use him in return to get answers.

I can practically hear his sinful voice, luring me into a darkness I may never come out of.

And that's why I tell him, "I'm sorry, it's just a bad time. I wasn't expecting anyone."

The officer nods his head in understanding, but his eyes are assessing and my body tenses. *Just go. Please, go.*

"I'm new here," he tells me. "I came down from upstate New York."

I nod, blinking away the confusion. I anticipated him saying goodbye and apologizing, but instead he shuffles his feet on my porch, shoving his hands into his pockets as he speaks.

"I wanted to come to a smaller city, somewhere with fewer problems and a slower pace."

A genuine, soft sound of amusement comes from me, forcing the semblance of a smile to my lips. "You aren't going to find that here," I tell him.

"So I noticed. Born and raised?" he asks, and I nod.

"My mom moved here when she was pregnant with my sister, before I was born. It was just us three for the longest time."

"Your sister who just passed?" he asks, inflecting his tone with an appropriate amount of sympathy as his voice lowers, and again I only nod. With the small movement comes a pang in my chest. Every reminder of her is like hearing the news that she's missing all over again. Or worse, the news that they found her and my worst fear was realized.

"I'm sorry. I lost my brother a while ago. We were close, so I can understand the loss."

I have to look up to the sky, letting out a slow exhale to keep from tearing up. He doesn't know. No one could know what we went through this past year.

"I'm getting the lay of the land here, and it seems like there may be a bit of trouble from a man who owns a vehicle spotted at your address recently."

My teeth sink into my bottom lip and I try to keep my expression neutral until I can ask, "Who would that be?"

"Jase Cross. His entire family and a few others are associated with murder and drug rings, along with other criminal activity."

Silence.

It's a long moment that passes, a frigid gust of wind traveling between us before I tell him, "Like I said, this isn't a good time for me."

Officer Walsh takes a large step forward, coming close enough to startle me. Staring into my eyes as my lungs are paralyzed, he lowers his voice and says, "I can help you, Bethany. All you have to do is tell me that's what you want."

Thump. Thump.

Staring into his light blue eyes, feeling the authority that comes off him in waves, I can't speak. I only know when I do say something, no matter what I say, there's a very large probability that I'm going to regret the words that come out of my mouth.

chapter eleven

Jase

The door opens before the knuckles of my loosely curled fist can even hit the hard wood. The bite of the cold night nips at my neck at the same time the warmth of Beth's home welcomes me into 34 Holley Drive.

I'm only slightly aware of either, and neither could beckon me inside the way Bethany's eyes do. Wide and cautious, but curious more than anything. In this split second, the way she's breathing, heavy with anticipation—nothing's ever made me so fucking excited.

"Jase." She murmurs my name, but not in a greeting. It's more like an omen.

As I take a step inside, dropping the duffle bag just inside the foyer, she takes a step back, releasing the door and allowing me to close it. It's quiet; the only sound is the foreboding click of the door shutting.

Bethany nervously picks under her nails as she waits silently.

"You scared?" I ask her and she responds with a huff of a sarcastic laugh and the faintest hint of a smile that comes and goes.

"Is that your question?" she asks me and it's then that I catch something's off. Something happened. Squaring my shoulders, I peek behind her. The front hall leads to the kitchen in the back, with the living room to the left and the dining room to the right. It's all quiet, all dark with the exception being the living room.

"If it's my turn to ask a question … who do I remind you of?"

My gaze returns slowly to her. I let it travel down her body, noting that she's in sweats and a baggy t-shirt that reads, *Coffee Solves Everything*.

"No questions yet," I answer her and then brush her thick locks of gently curled hair behind her back. "You need to see what I want from you first."

She leans her weight onto her left heel, tilting her stance and the nervousness wanes some. That's better.

"I think I got a good idea of that last night," she says and tries to hide the breathiness that came with "last night" and the rosy blush that slowly rises to her cheeks.

My smirk kicks up, and a warmth flows through me. I knew she needed it. I knew she'd love to be played with.

Lowering my lips to hers, but just barely keeping our mouths from touching, I look her in the eyes and tell her, "That was hardly a nibble of what's to come."

Instead of stepping back slightly as I expect her to do so I'm not in her space, she stands her ground and shrugs as she replies, "No need to hold back tonight." Her words caress my face, causing a longing desire to travel down my body, all the way to my cock.

Keeping my gaze pinned on her, I stand up straighter and gesture to the living room. "After you then," I offer.

"Not in the bedroom?" she comments under her breath as she walks ahead of me, and I don't hesitate to grab her hip in my left hand and pull her back into my chest. Her yelp of surprise only makes me harder.

With my lips at her ear, I whisper, "The bedroom is reserved for the nights you beg me the second I walk in to fuck that pretty little cunt of yours."

The second the words are spoken, I let her go and she falls forward slightly. Barely catching herself although she plays it off, just like she tried to hide her lust for me as she walks ahead of me. I watch her wide hips sway and grab the black duffle bag I'd dropped by the door.

"What's that?" she asks when she sees it, taking a seat on the sofa easily. As if she's not nervous at all, and that moment a few seconds ago never happened. It's cute that she thinks she's playing hard to get when she's nothing but eager.

"Rope, for starters." Her eyes flash, but she says nothing more.

The bag drops with a thud and as the sound of the zipper opening fills the room, she leans closer, attempting to peek inside.

"Ethanol?" she questions with a hint of hesitancy as I pull out several feet of thin nylon rope.

"I'm not sure we'll need that tonight," I tell her absently as I let the rope fall to a puddle on the floor and move the coffee table out of the middle of the room. It drags along the floor, and in true Beth fashion she focuses on the bag, walking to it and taking into account everything inside.

A bottle of ethanol, a lighter, candles, a torch, balm, four sections of nylon rope, two large flame-retardant blankets, a weighted blanket, and last but not least, a knife.

Her lips purse as she stiffens by the bag. The worst thing that could happen is that I scare her off. I've never wanted anything more than I want this right now.

"Don't be scared," I tell her softly with a bit of humor I know will challenge her.

"I'm not," she bites back, even though she is. I can see it.

"If you could supply a bucket of ice, I think you'll be grateful for that."

At my words, she turns her head slowly toward me.

"What exactly is this?" she asks softly, backing away from the bag.

"I'm going to show you."

Her eyes move to the digital clock and she says, "Eight fourteen…"

"We'll start the clock at eight if you'd like," is all I offer her.

When I stand up, the coffee table now repositioned, her arms are crossed and she's staring down at the bag.

"Your reluctance is understandable, but I promise you, you want this." My last word hisses in the air, the tempting snake that led Eve to the apple.

"I want at least one question answered first," she tells me, lifting her gaze from the bag to meet my own.

"One."

"What kind of business is done at The Red Room?" she asks and a glimmer of a smile pulls at my lips.

"Once you're tied up with your hands behind your head, I'll allow you to ask the question again, and I'll answer it completely."

The skepticism is there, the hesitation, but slowly she stands tall and leaves the living room, heading to the kitchen. Presumably she's getting the ice.

I lay down the first flame-retardant blanket and leave the second within reach.

Beth makes her way back into the room holding a glass wine decanter filled with ice. "I don't have an ice bucket," she admits to me while I'm still on my knees, fixing the corner of the blanket.

"You nervous?" I ask her, reaching for the decanter.

"You fucking know I am." She rushes her words like she can't get them out fast enough, and a deep, rough chuckle leaves me.

"I'm going to need you naked for this," I tell her as I set the ice down next to the folded-up blanket.

"Of course you are," she says skeptically, turning away from me and breathing out deep as she shakes out her hands.

"If you want to stop, it stops. I'll learn your limits. You'll still get your answers and your debt paid." I start with addressing her logical concerns, but move to the other side of her thoughts. "The exotic becomes the erotic. Have you ever heard of that?" I ask her.

"I understand temperature play and that this is meant to be ..." she trails off and swallows as she turns to face me, her features riddled with a mix of nervousness and fear. "Why like this?"

"Because I crave this," I admit to her without thinking twice. "It soothes a part of me that isn't easily kept at bay. I will enjoy every second of this. It's worth more to me than secrets and a debt." I didn't realize how much I needed this, how much I coveted her body beneath mine as I brought out the most intense reactions from her until those words were spoken.

Her eyes close and her body trembles.

"Does this excite you?" I ask her and when I do, her hands move under the hem of her baggy shirt, to the top of her sweatpants and she slowly pushes them down, stepping out of them and then opening her eyes.

Her lips part slightly, ready to answer. But she closes herself off, shutting her mouth and balling her hands into fists at her side. Clearing her throat, she looks away and I remind her, "I'll answer your question tonight, the single question. But after tonight, it's tit for tat. Tonight is so you can see what I want."

She nods her head once and then again, standing only feet from me in nothing but her socks and a t-shirt. "Yes, it excites me," she finally answers and as she does, the radiator kicks on behind her, making her jump slightly.

"And it scares you?" I ask, although it's more of a statement. She doesn't waste a second to answer, nodding furiously.

"I don't like not being in control. Tied up and..." She doesn't finish her thought, and swallows thickly.

"You're thinking too much," I tell her and her gaze narrows. All the jitters leave her in that instant and I have to smile. "There you go, just remember how much you hate me and this should be easy."

With her lips pressed in a thin line, she removes her socks first and then reaches behind her back to unhook her bra, revealing a simple white cotton bra with no lace, no frills, no padding.

And with her arms crossed in front of her, she prepares to lift her shirt over her head, but I stand abruptly and stop her, gripping her wrists.

Her skin is hot to the touch.

"I want to do it," I tell her softly. Slowly, she releases her grip on the hem and I circle her, taking my time to observe how the shirt, hitting just below her ass, is more tempting than I'm sure she thought it would be.

"You didn't try to impress me, did you?" I ask, although the light in the room shines off her freshly shaved legs, smooth and glimmering.

"This is business, Cross," she tells me and I simply nod.

"It is."

Making sure not to touch her skin, I grip her hem and lift the shirt above her head, revealing one inch of skin at a time. The movement is achingly slow. Her body quivers as I let a single finger run along her side. The lone touch causes such a strong reaction in her, and it only makes me that much harder for her.

She doesn't look at me; instead she stares straight ahead, but she doesn't cover herself either.

She's fucking beautiful. Every inch of her. From the freckle on her lower stomach, to the pale rose pink of her nipples. Her hips are wide enough to grip during a punishing fuck, and her ass begs me to smack those perfect curves.

Time ticks as I circle her one more time. "You're beautiful," I whisper and the small compliment does wonders in relaxing her stiff posture. "How long has it been since someone's told you that?" I ask her, standing in front of her and allowing my gaze to roam to her hazel eyes.

She blinks and her lashes seem thicker, her lips fuller, her chestnut hair ready to be fisted as I kiss her. Everything about her is fuckable and desirable.

"I don't know," she whispers. Her eyes drift to the blanket and then look back to me. "It's been a long time."

I search her expression for an idea of just how long, but she doesn't give an answer.

"Lie down on the blanket."

Her shoulder brushes my arm as she obeys.

The blanket moves under her slightly, but her entire body is positioned in the center of it.

Using the longest section of the thin rope, I lift up her thighs, making her knees bend so I can lay the middle of the rope under her ass. I secure her hands with the remainder of the rope on either side of her with a simple bondage knot. I'm effectively making sure she won't be able to reach up. Half the rope is knotted around her left wrist where it slips under her thighs, right below her plush ass and the other half is knotted around her right wrist. Perfect.

"I'm going to put a weighted blanket across your ankles," I tell her as I pull it out of the bag, reaching past the sealed bottle of ethanol and one of the two candles.

"Why?" she asks, and I answer easily in an attempt to calm her nerves. "So you'll have a resistance to lifting them up. It'll make everything feel more intense."

With the weighted blanket laying across her ankles, she's bared to me, bound and somewhat calmer than I imagined.

"You fought very little tonight," I note.

"Learning the ropes," she answers softly, opening her eyes for the first time since she looked down and saw the rope twined around her wrists.

"You're going to enjoy this," I tell her, lightly brushing my fingers down her stomach. When I do, I hear the weighted blanket rustle, but her legs stay still, immobilized from the weight. Her shoulders shudder and her head lifts slightly before falling back down into a halo of brunette hair.

"I'm ready for you to answer my question," she says confidently. As if we're in an interview and she's not bound on her living room floor, available for me to do whatever I'd like to her.

Her breasts are perky and full; taking them in my hand, I play with their weight and bend down to suck her nipple into my mouth. I moan around her nipple and then let my teeth drag up them. One, and then the other.

Bethany lets her back arch and her body sways to the side, moving further from me as she puts her weight on her left hip. Pushing her back down on the blanket, I blow across her nipple, chilling the moisture I left there and she sucks in a shuddered breath, her head falling back and a sweet sound of rapture leaving her lips.

"I'm going to take my time touching you, playing with you," I say without acknowledging her earlier remark. "Does that scare you?"

"What are you going to use from the bag?" she asks me and a slight laugh slips from my lips.

"That doesn't answer my question."

"My answer relies on it." Her eyes darken, her pupils dilating as she answers me honestly. I can see the plea in her eyes to not push her boundaries, to not touch the bag of supplies.

She should know better than that.

"Everything, Bethany. I intend on taking full advantage of tonight."

Bethany

I'm scared, I can't deny that. My entire body is alive with both fear and something else. Something sinful.

Every tiny hair on my body, from head to toe, is standing on end. My nipples have hardened and every touch from Jase sends a trail of goosebumps down my body that makes me shiver with hunger for more.

More of his warm breath on my chilled skin, more of his fingers barely touching my sides as he brings them down to my hips.

But only if he answers me. He'd better fucking answer me. *We have a deal.*

"What kind of business do you do at The Red Room?" I ask him as he turns his attention away from me and reaches to the decanter of ice.

He makes me wait for my answer, but not too long.

"I first created The Red Room as a place to conduct other business. My brother's business, really."

His voice is far too low, too soothing and seductive for the information he's relaying. The ice clinks in the glass before he places a single piece at my lips.

I part my lips, intent on sucking the ice, but he moves it too soon, tracing my lips and then bringing it lower. A cold sensation flows over my skin in a wave.

"Eager thing, aren't you?" he teases me.

"Fuck you." The words come out quickly but his are just as quick as he says, "Only when you beg me, cailín tine." I don't know why he calls me that, *cailín tine*. Or what it means. And I hate that I swallow down my curiosity rather than ask him. But I want him to answer my damn question.

"My brother was dealing. Drugs, guns, all sorts of things," he tells me and my focus returns to the one reason I have to allow this. The one logical reason I'd ever willingly put myself in this situation. *Jenny.*

I ready myself for another question to clarify, but Jase places a finger over my lips. His touch is so hot compared to the ice. "I'm still answering. Let me tell you everything," he whispers.

He runs another cube from the dip just below my throat, down the center of my chest. His hand brushes my breast until he brings the ice farther, all the way to my belly button, circling it and then moving lower still, letting it sit just where my thighs meet.

The ice itself is numbingly cold, sending a spike of awareness through my body. But it's the path that I'm so highly aware of. Each trail leaves a bit of water behind and the air cools it, causing every nerve ending there to prepare to spark.

Even though he lets the ice linger at the top of my pussy, he's quick to repeat the pattern, and I don't know how it's possible, but it makes my body feel even hotter. My toes curl on the third round, and my core heats.

All I can do is turn my head, close my eyes and my fists, and try not to let the ice excite me.

It's an impossible feat, though.

In between every round, he gives me more information, and occasionally asks me insignificant things. Things I don't mind answering, all the while Jase promises to tell me more. It's not quite tit for tat, since he's giving me more and more information about The Red Room and what happened to make it become what it is, all while asking me simple questions that don't require more than one-word answers. But he's gauging how my body reacts when I tell the truth. Taking the time to learn my body. My only response to that is that I'm not a liar. I don't have the time to tell him that though as he continues to feed me information.

"I enjoyed the control. Knowing when and where everyone would meet up. Giving them a space where they could enjoy themselves, and observing them in the meantime. I wanted to know the ins and outs of every partner we had. I wanted their secrets…"

I can barely breathe as he gives me his past so easily, all while bringing the mostly melted ice down farther than he ever has to my pussy, and gently pushing it inside of me. My lips make a perfect O as every nerve ending in my body lights.

He continues his story as my lips part, feeling the rush of desire spark inside of my body. "So we could blackmail them. I used the bar to set everyone up to owe us in some way, or to have information we could use against both our partners and our enemies. In this industry, everyone is an enemy at some point, and we would be ready the second anyone thought they could turn their backs on us."

It's exhilarating.

Both his touch, and the tale of how they rose to power. Creating a place for divine pleasures and allowing everyone to taste, for everyone to fall into their grasp to be controlled and their actions predicted so easily.

He lowers his lips to the crook of my neck, letting his warm breath be at odds with the chill that's slowly melting at my core, being consumed with his criminal touch.

"I sell every addiction possible and I don't have rules within those walls." As he speaks, he pushes his fingers inside of me, dragging them against my front wall and bringing me closer and closer to the peak of an impending orgasm. I close my eyes tight, trying not to give in although I know it's useless. My toes have curled and the pleasure builds inside of me so quickly like a raging storm, unstoppable and demanding its damage be done.

"Every corner of that place is defiled; every square inch has been touched by sin. That's the kind of business I conduct in The Red Room."

My neck arches as I give in to the need, a wave of pleasure rising from my belly outward, followed by another, a harsher, more severe wave crashing through me. I can't move an inch as Jase grips my throat with his free hand and continues to torture me, fucking me with his fingers and drawing out every bit of my orgasm. I wish I could move. I want to get away from the third wave threatening to consume me, but I'm paralyzed as it rages through me.

Every nerve ending in my body ignites, my body shuddering and trembling as my release takes its time, wandering through my body and slowly dissipating. Jase removes his fingers carefully, and I gasp in pleasure as he circles my clit before bringing his fingers to his mouth.

My arousal shines on his fingers as he sucks it off, one by one. I can't bring myself to look away when he groans in sheer delight.

Even as my heart races and adrenaline and excitement race through me, fear freezes my body when Jase picks up a knife from his bag. It's only a pocket knife.

It's just to get the ropes off, I tell myself. It's amazing how the sight of it destroys the previous moment. I close my eyes, waiting to hear the sound of the blade sawing at the rope, but Jase doesn't allow me to.

"I need your eyes open for this. You need to stay still and I don't want the touch to startle you." He sounds so calm and in control as he splays a hand on my chest. His elbow rests on my shoulder and pins me in place as my heart lurches inside of me, ready to escape.

My gaze begs him to explain, to stop, to reconsider whatever he's doing as he brings the knife closer to me.

"It's only to shave the small hairs from your body," he says, answering my unspoken questions. "I won't hurt you," he tells me soothingly as the blade just barely touches my skin. He drags it slowly across my breast, all the way down my mound and then back up, avoiding my sensitive, swollen nub.

"Can I let you go?" he asks me, gently lifting his elbow. "Or are you going to move?"

I can only swallow, I can barely even comprehend what he's saying since the panic is so alive within me.

"If you move, it will cut you," he tells me.

"I'll be still," I whisper and as the blade lowers to my skin I consider the word, stop. So easy to say. I could say it; it's right there, waiting to be spoken. But Jase drags the knife along my chest before I can utter it and then he kisses the sensitized skin. An open-mouth kiss that feels like everything. Like this is the way a kiss is meant to be, and every other way is wrong.

My head's fuzzy and a haze clouds it as he scrapes the knife along my body, leaving a pink path occasionally, but his kisses and the ice make the evidence vanish.

It's all overwhelming and agonizingly slow. By the time he gets to my pussy, I'm on the edge of another release. My impending orgasm is waiting for the knife, for his touch, for a kiss. But it doesn't come.

After the longest time, my body feels his absence and I open my eyes. He pours ethanol onto a rag, then wipes down my body in one swift stroke and before I can say anything, a flame lights on a candle and he lowers it to the ethanol, lighting my skin ablaze.

The scream is trapped in the split second, but before its escape, his hand follows the path, quenching the heat and leaving me wide eyed and breathless.

So hot, and then so cold.

With a pounding heart, I take in the reality. "You lit me on fire."

"No, I lit the alcohol just above your skin on fire." He does it again and this time hot wax drips with it and I suck in a tight breath, my hands turning to fists from the slight pain, the immediate heat, and the cold absence that comes afterward. My head thrashes from side to side as he does it again and again. The pain morphing to unmatched pleasure makes my body feel alive in a way I never knew was possible.

Every climax feels higher and more unbearable than the last. My words fail me as Jase moves down my body, not sparing any inch of my skin.

The alcohol, the fire, his touch. Over and over. He massages the wax onto my breasts before using the knife to pick it off, and the third time he does it, I cum violently.

The pleasure rages through my body with no evidence of it even approaching until the blinding pleasure rocks through me, from my belly to the tip of my toes and fingers.

It's as if my body has rebelled, choosing his touch and this heat over any sense of calm. It prefers the chaos, the unknown, the absence of all control and stability.

With my bottom lip still quivering and my belly trembling as the tremors of the aftershock subside, Jase kisses me, madly and deeply. I feel all of him in this kiss and it kills me that I can't lift my hands up, keeping him where I want him.

I'm at his mercy. Fully and truly, and that very fact plays tricks on me. Telling me I love it. Telling me he knows what I need more than I do.

With every pleasure still ringing in me, he pulls away and stands up, removing his shirt and the light from the candle plays along the lines of his defined muscles. I can see his thick length pressing against his zipper and when he palms it, I have to look away. I'm so close to another orgasm. My clit is throbbing; I feel swollen and used, but he's hardly touched me there.

The sound of a zipper makes me look back at him and the instant I do, his pants, along with his belt, drop to the floor with a clink and a thud and his dick is all I can see.

His girth is so wide I'm not sure I could wrap my hand around him. I can practically feel the veins pressing against my walls and pulling every ounce of pleasure from me, practically imagine his rounded head sliding back and forth over my clit. Oh my God. He's massive. He grabs his cock and rubs the glistening precum over the head and that's when I lose it.

Cumming again, and he didn't even touch me. That's how much power he has over me. Just the thought of what he could do to me, how he could ruin me, how he is so much more than any boy I ever thought of letting touch me… all of it is fuel that ignites a raging fire inside.

Jase groans deep in the back of his throat, dropping to the floor so quickly and so hard, I know it will leave bruises on his knees. "Cum again," he commands me breathlessly, leaning over my body to kiss and bite the crook of my neck as he pushes three fingers inside of me and ruthlessly fucks me with them.

The waves of my last release have barely left me when the next orgasm crashes through me, harder and higher than any of those before. My scream is silent, my body stiff as it commands attention from all of me. My body, my soul.

And Jase doesn't stop, even as my arousal leaks down my ass, he continues. Even as I feel myself tighten around his fingers, he doesn't stop.

I can't. I can't take it. I can't breathe.

I can't move. I can't speak.

I'm helpless and consumed by fire and lust.

I try to focus on Jase when he whispers in my ear, but my body won't stop shaking and my neck is rigid. "When you look at me, know this is what I want from you. Only I can give you this." His words hiss in the air, crackling and demanding to be burned in my memory.

Jase Cross destroyed me and what I thought was pleasure.

And where I thought my boundaries lied with him.

chapter twelve

Bethany

MY EYES OPEN QUICKLY, THE DARKNESS CONSUMING ME EXCEPT FOR THE MOONLIGHT FROM the bedroom windows. My heart's racing and it's then that I realize the trembling isn't a dream. I can't stop shaking and I'm so fucking cold.

"Shhh." Jase's voice is anything but calming. After the initial shock of realizing he's in bed with me, I barely turn around before the bed groans and he pulls the weighted blanket up and around my entire body.

Frantically I try to recount it all, every moment that I can remember.

"What did you do to me?" I ask, and the question comes out viciously. I'm fucking freezing, and I can't stop trembling.

"I brought you to bed," he says lowly, a threat barely there, warning me to be careful but fuck that.

"What did you do?" The words are torn from my throat. It's not even the fear that's the most overwhelming. As my throat dries and a sinking sensation in my stomach takes over, I look him in the eyes and realize how much trust I had in him. It wasn't just business. I gave up more than I should have, and he did something to me. He hurt me.

How could you? I want to say the words, but I can't bear to bring them up and admit to the both of us that I thought he wouldn't hurt me. That I was that fucking naïve.

Jase's arm is heavy and pulls me closer to him, even though I attempt to push him away as he says, "It's just the endorphins crashing." Although his words are drenched with irritation, there's something else there, something buried deep down low in his words that I can't decipher. "You're okay," he nearly whispers and then pulls me in closer, dragging my ass to his groin, my back to his chest and nuzzling the nape of my neck with the tip of his nose. "It's okay, I've got you."

His voice is a calming balm. Even as I continue to shake. As my fingers feel numb and then like they're on fire. Cold again. "I'm so cold."

I almost expect my confession to turn to fog in front of me. Like warm breath in the winter air.

"You were on a high," Jase tells me and then presses his arm against mine, pushing it closer to me and acting as if I'm not trembling uncontrollably. "It's all coming down. I thought you may have a little aftershock. That's why I stayed," he explains.

Aftershock. Endorphins.

He didn't drug me. It's not drugs. I can barely swallow for a long moment, trying to make it stop, but my body's not listening.

"Does this happen all the time?" I ask him, attempting to let go of the anger, swallowing my regret that I immediately assumed the worst of him. It was my first instinct, and shame hits me hard as I realize he did quite the opposite.

I'm a bitch. I am an asshole. An embarrassed asshole.

With sleep lacing his words he tells me, "Not often, but I imagine that was your first?" and I instantly clench my legs. Remembering the ice, the cold, his touch, the fire.

My shoulders beg to buck forward, my eyes closing at the memory and the heat flourishing in my belly.

"Was it?" he teases me, nipping my neck and just that small touch threatens to push me over again.

"I can't," I say, and the words leave me in a single breath. A single plea. Instantly a chill creeps up my neck, the open air finding its place there as Jase moves his head to the other pillow.

A shaky breath leaves me as I turn my head to peek at him, craning my neck as my back is still positioned firmly against his chest. "Did we have sex?" I ask him, feeling a weight press down on my chest.

Jase merely gazes back at me. The depths of his dark eyes deepen as I stare into them. Licking my lower lip first, I explain, "I don't remember everything."

"We didn't. No," he answers me, and his expression remains guarded. "I told you, you'd have to beg me for it."

His warmth calms me and slowly I stop trembling as hard. Very slowly, but the tremors are still there.

"For all I know, I did tell you to fuck me," I tell him.

"You could barely look at me, let alone speak."

"Holy shit," I murmur beneath my breath.

"When I fuck you, trust me when I say you'll remember it."

His words force a shiver of pleasure through me when I remember I saw ... I saw *all* of him. "Why am I shaking so much?"

"From you getting off so many times. Your body can only handle so much."

"I can't believe it can feel like that," I say, thinking out loud.

"Sometimes the things that cause you pain can bring you so much pleasure."

"Not everything that brings you pain." The hollowness in my chest expands at my thought, drifting to darker places.

The shaking and trembling stop altogether, but Jase doesn't let me go and I'm happy for that. There's so much comfort in being held right now.

"Tell me something," I ask Jase, resting my cheek into the pillow, feeling the warmth come back to me and the lull of sleep ready to pull me under once again.

"Tell you something?" He ponders and then readjusts on the bed, making it shake slightly. "What do you want to know?"

"Anything," I answer as my eyelids fall heavily without second-guessing and my eyes pop open wider, remembering all the bits and pieces he told me about The Red Room. "Maybe about your brothers?"

Once again Jase's lips find my neck, and this time he leaves an open-mouthed kiss there. I'm starting to love those kinds of kisses. I think they're my favorite. "I had four brothers, now I have three and I recently learned that my younger brother, the one I was closest with..." He hesitates and again that small space on my neck feels the prickle of the air instead of his warmth. "I found out his death wasn't an accident; it was murder. And it was supposed to be me, not him."

"Oh my God," I whisper, completely shocked. My heart breaks in half for him. I know the pain of losing a sibling, the agony of blaming yourself. But knowing it was supposed to be you instead? "I'm so sorry." I put every ounce of sincerity into my words and pray it doesn't come out the way everyone else says, like the people who say it simply because they don't know what else to say. "I'm really sorry."

Jase doesn't say anything at all. Not for a while until he requests the same from me. "Tell me something."

"I can't figure you out, Jase," I answer him almost immediately.

"You already know who I am, cailín tine. Don't let me fool you."

I look over my shoulder to ask him, "What's that mean? Cailín tine?"

He gives me one of those smirks, but it's almost sad and short lived. "Fiery girl."

My entire body betrayed me earlier, and so does my heart in this moment, beating just for him with a warmth I've never felt before.

As I nuzzle back down into the pillow, I remember Officer Walsh and I spit out the words before I hide them forever. "A cop came asking about you today. He knocked at my door."

Nerves prick down my neck, but Jase's touch remains soothing and his voice calm when he asks, "What was his name?"

"Cody Walsh," I answer and then feel Jase's nod as his nose runs along my neck.

"He won't be a problem. He's just new."

"Don't you want to know what I told him?"

"If you want to tell me."

"I didn't tell him anything."

His response is to kiss my neck. Then my jaw. He tries to lie back down, leaving my lips wanting but I take them with my own. Reaching up to grip the back of his neck, and pulling myself off the comfort of the bed.

It's a quick kiss, but it was mine to have. And mine to give.

"What was that for?" he asks me, and I answer him honestly. "I wanted you to have it."

Turning my back to him, I lie back under the covers. There are no more questions or conversations. With my eyes wide open, I pretend to sleep. After a short while, the bed protests under the weight of him moving, the covers are shrugged off behind me and I listen to him leave. Across the wooden floorboards, down the stairs. I can only faintly hear him in the living room, but I recognize the sound of the front door opening and closing.

All the while, there's this vise wrapped around my heart. Keeping it still, not allowing it to move the way it used to.

chapter thirteen

Jase

"WHAT HAPPENED TO HER? TO JENNIFER PARKS?"

Seth hesitates. Seated across from me, he slides forward to readjust before leaning back into an auburn leather armchair. It's silent in the back of The Red Room. Not a single beat of the music or murmur of the guests makes its way through these doors.

Nothing makes it out of them either.

It's a decadent but vacant space. A simple, but too-fucking-expensive iron and driftwood desk with no drawers stands in the middle of the room. My chair is at one end, while two matching chairs are on the other side. Not a damn thing else in the room.

The stubble on my jaw is rough; I'm way past due for a shave as I run my hand along my jaw as I wait for Seth's answer.

"I'm still working on it, but let me tell you what I've got so far."

"Are you fucking kidding me?" The rage is inexplicable as I slam the edge of my fist down on the desk. It jolts and I clench my jaw, hating that something like this can get to me.

I focus on calming my shit down, ignoring the irritation and Seth's questioning gaze. All day I've been on edge. Ever since I left Bethany's place, the second the sun rose.

"It goes deeper than you think, Boss." His voice is low, testing my patience and apologetic even.

"Let me have it," I speak and gesture for him to get going.

"She went missing on December twenty-eighth, but before then she was in and out of her sister's home and several friends' places. It was January seventeenth that the burned remains, including several of her teeth, were found in a trunk at the bottom of the Rattle River on the west side of town."

I remember the flash of an image I found myself, searching through the archives at the downtown station hard drive. It was all the information Kent, one of the detectives we keep on our payroll, had to give.

"Fucking brutal," I murmur. The remains were charred, but some of the bones were broken before being burned.

"She was tortured, but time of death couldn't be determined."

"I already know this. Get to something I don't know."

He starts to speak, but before he can even suck in the air needed for the first word, I ask, "Did you find anything on the sister?"

My fingers rap on the desk, one at a time with brief pauses, one after the other. As if it's only a casual conversation.

"Bethany Fawn?"

At my nod, he begins. "Jennifer was born out of wedlock to a Catherine Parks. Shortly after her birth, her mother and father got hitched, then conceived Bethany. Not long after her birth, the father took off. Leaving their mom with no job, a toddler and an infant."

"Where did he go?"

"Nebraska, where he died of a heart attack in a casino three years ago."
"Did they keep in touch?"
"Not a word," Seth answers professionally, but his eyes are questioning.
"Go on."
"Bethany Fawn, the younger of the two, did well in school. And it seems like that was all she was interested in. She's a nurse on the psych ward at Rockford. She's worked there since she graduated. Apparently her mother had issues in the last years of her life and she chose this path because of it. Her sister--"
"What issues?" Again, I cut him off midbreath.
"Alzheimer's."
"How old was she?"
"Bethany? Twenty. Her mother was fifty-two when she died."

I watched my mother die slowly, but I was young. Cancer is a bitch. I can only imagine being more aware and having to go through that. Being old enough to understand. Back when I was a kid, I was sure Mom was going to get better. Knowing there is no getting better and having to watch someone you love slowly die? That's a cruel way to live. A cruel way to die as well. But that's life, isn't it?

"One thing you may find interesting is that she was spotted with you recently," Seth says and sits back further in his seat. It's the only note on her in the entire department. "A possible associate."

"And who put that in? Our new friend, Walsh?" I surmise.

"You got it," he says and snaps his fingers. "And you two aren't the only ones doing some digging. Miss Fawn's search history is interesting ... limited, but interesting."

"Is that right?" I ask, bringing my thumb up to run along my chin.

"Little Miss Fawn was looking you up and Officer Walsh after he paid her a visit."

I shrug impatiently, and Seth continues.

"She didn't find much, obviously, since there's nothing on the internet to find... although it seems she's interested in Angie. She's searching for pictures of her, doesn't look like she knows her name. *Jase Cross with brunette. Jase Cross lover. Jase Cross date.* Things like that."

"Angie?" The only piece of information that surprises me so far is this. "Why?"

"I guess she saw her with you in pictures online. But she doesn't have her name, or any information on her."

Who do I remind you of? I remember her question last night. That's why.

"Shit." I breathe out the word. "Anything else?" I ask him, ignoring the dread, the regret, the deep-seated hate for myself because of everything that happened four years ago. All of those ghosts belong in the past. They can stay there too.

Seth passes me a folder; opening it up reveals six profiles. All are of women in their late twenties, and two I recognize from the club. Jennifer is the first. The second is Miranda. She's gotten thrown out a handful of times. Too high to know she was messing with the wrong guys. Causing problems that aren't easy to fix.

"She ran with quite a crowd," I comment as I sift through the papers, reading one charge after the next and notes about the men they each were associated with. Men I don't trust or like.

"You could say that. It was all recent though. She only came into the scene this past year," Seth comments and leans back in his seat. The leather protests as he does. "College grad who struggled to keep a job after school. Taking one after the next. All had nothing to do with her degree."

"Quit or fired?"

"She quit them all. Everyone I talked to said they loved her, but they knew she wasn't going to stay long. It wasn't *interesting* enough for her," he says but forms air quotes around the word "interesting."

"You think that's why she quit them? Boredom?"

"I'm guessing she just needed to pay her bills." He shrugs. "From what I gather she was eccentric and wanted to solve the world's problems. The last job she had was working at The Bistro across the turnpike."

That particular information catches my attention and I look up from the papers to see Seth nodding. "Romano's place?"

"The one and only."

Just hearing that name makes me grit my teeth. "He's a dead man." My throat tightens as I speak. All I can see when I hear the word Romano is the picture of Tyler, dead on the wet asphalt; the water soaked into my hoodie he wore that day.

It was supposed to be me.

"Damn right," Seth says and I check my composure. Refusing to let that fuck get in the way of this conversation.

"So, The Bistro," I say to push Seth to continue the conversation, picking at the pages in the folder, and trying to rid my mind of the sight of Tyler. He was a good kid. That's the worst part. No one really deserves to die, but if anyone in this world could have been spared, it should have been him.

Tossing the folders down onto the desk, I lean back, letting the information sink in. "So she's got debt from college, can't get the right job yet so she's bouncing around to pay the bills. She lands a job at The Bistro and something there's leading these girls down a dark path."

"We have eyes down there; what'd they say?" My voice rises on its own, demanding information.

Seth winces slightly before telling me, "You aren't going to like this."

"Don't be a little bitch," I tell him, losing my patience.

"They said she was there and gone. She was friendly and nice, but then up and quit. Miranda was working there at the same time and quit with her. No reason. She didn't stand out and nothing did about the two of them leaving. Just two open waitress spots to fill when they left."

"So they've got nothing?" I ask as my heart rate rapidly increases and the blood rushes in my ears. "We have a group of women," I enunciate each word and Seth takes the opportunity to butt in.

"Two of them working there at the same time and quitting at the same time," he adds and I meet his gaze, daring him to interrupt me again.

"A group of women with no prior history of any of this bullshit, getting hooked on some shit, all of them racking up charges in the past year and some of them stepping foot into my club. And you're telling me the boys we're paying to watch that shithole have no fucking idea what happened, or who influenced this shit?" I slam the bottom of my oxfords again on the inside of my walnut desk, kicking it as hard as I can on impulse. Needing to get out the rage. My muscles are tense, my body's hot and I need to beat the shit out of something.

I have no fucking impulse control, no restraint today. Not a damn thing keeping me under control.

Moving my chair back into place, I set my elbows on my desk, lower my head and smooth my hand over the back of my neck.

"I'm losing my patience," I tell him. Staring at my desk, I admit the obvious. "I don't like not having answers when I want them. She's one girl. A girl we've seen; a girl we've watched before. We should know who the fuck killed her and why."

Seth grips the armrest, looking away from me, toward the blood-red leather walls that line the room.

"It's like someone's hiding it," Seth speaks quickly.

"Hiding?"

"I can't find a damn thing on her after she started working there other than what we had already with the sweets," he says, and his frustration grows with each word.

"We know she was buying our shit in bulk, high on what was obviously coke. She gave the name of a fake brother when we questioned her, that was early December. Then there's not a trace of her."

"She ever come back after that night?" I ask him. I remember that night. Carter came down here, looking for answers about his drug. It hardly sold shit, it's something that puts you to sleep. We only push it on addicts that can't handle any more. It knocks their asses out as they go through withdrawal. They always come back though, but never for the sweets.

Not until recently.

"No. She never came back and the demand for the sweets dropped simultaneously."

"She was buying for someone," I remark. "Someone who backed off when they found out we were onto them.... maybe that's who did this? He wanted her silenced so there were no loose threads?"

"It's not Romano, we have ears on him, we would know. I've been through every fucking recording from December twenty-seventh to the fucking week she was discovered. He didn't say a word about it. I don't think she's on his radar."

"So it's just a fucking coincidence that all her shit starts going downhill when she starts working for him?" I raise my finger, feeling the lines in my forehead deepen with anger.

"He got her hooked; I think he did. Or someone there did. I think that's when it started, but her dying... whoever it was, they got to her at his place, and Romano doesn't know about it or even realize someone's taking those girls from him."

The pieces of the puzzle fall slowly into place, giving me the rough edges of a watered-down image someone doesn't want me to see.

"It would be easy if it was Romano; he's already a dead man."

"As soon as this new cop is off our fucking backs, he's dead," I tell him, opening up the folder again to see Jennifer's profile on top and Beth's name listed as her only living relative staring back at me in black and white. "If Officer Cody Walsh doesn't watch his step," I say and lift my gaze from Beth's name, where the tips of my fingers still linger to tell Seth, "he's a dead man too."

chapter fourteen

Bethany

The Coverless Book
Third Chapter

I'm pretending not to be tired. Like the weight and pull of sleep isn't a constant battle tonight. Every day after seeing the doctor, it's like this. Well, every day for the past five years except today. Today will be the exception, because of Jake. He makes me smile, and just smiling reminds me I still have so much left in me.

"I'm really happy you do this for me," I tell Jake, pulling the blanket around my shoulders a little tighter. We're having a picnic in the backyard overlooking the hill. The spring air brings a strong scent of lilac and I breathe it in. As much as I can, and for as long as I can.

This is what living feels like.

"The soups were perfect," he comments and adds, "I didn't know it'd get this cold at night."

"The summer nights are warmer," I tell him easily and then feel embarrassed. Of course they are, I think inwardly and my stomach stirs with nerves.

"We'll have to do it again in summer then."

The nerves turn to something else and they spread higher up to my chest at Jake's words.

"I'd really like that." I almost whisper the words and then have to clear my throat. As he picks two blades of grass, no doubt to whistle with them again like he showed me earlier, I take a chance.

"Maybe even before summer?" I ask him and lean close to nudge his shoulder with mine. Just a nudge, then I sit back upright, but he's quick to nudge mine against his.

"Definitely before summer too."

Time passes and the sun sets too quickly. I know time is almost up, and that's so bittersweet.

"Are you really sick? Like... like, sick sick?" Jake's question pulls the smile from my face in a single swoop. And the nerves settle back in my stomach. I pick two blades of grass, thinking maybe I could whistle too. But instead I let them fall, and the wind takes them.

"The doctor said I was sick years ago..." Instead of letting any bit show of what I felt that day Mama cried and cried in the car, I actually let out a small laugh. It's only a huff of laughter. Even though I'd like to pretend I'm not affected by the pain of the memory, my eyes gloss over.

"Why are you laughing?" Jake sounds truly concerned, and I'm quick to put a reassuring hand over his. That small move changes everything. The electric spark, the sudden heat. I'm quick to take my hand back.

"Sorry, it's just a little joke I tell myself," I explain, shaking off both the memories and the touch with a quick sip of water.

"What do you tell yourself?" he asks skeptically as I set the cup down. I can't take my hand off of it as I nervously peek at him and answer, "That I'm invincible."

His smirk is slow to form, but it grows quickly, turning into a grin. "I like that."

His smile is contagious, and I find myself telling him, "I like that you like it."

I'm still biting down on my bottom lip and hoping I'm not blushing too hard when he looks me in the eyes and responds, "I like you, Emmy. I think I more than like you."

Three days came and went. I got lost in the pages of The Coverless Book, falling in love with both Emmy and Jake, rooting for them as he fell in love with her and she with him. I spent all of yesterday checking in with my patients at work before Aiden told me that wasn't what my leave was for. I spent every waking hour trying to occupy my thoughts and time. All so I wouldn't think about Jase Cross or my sister, and every moment in the months that I lost her.

Every moment I wish I could have changed.

Between the two, I thought about Jase the most. Because it felt better to think of him than her. Choosing pleasure over pain.

Three days went by, and I thought of him every morning and every night. I started to think I'd made it all up because I didn't hear from him, not one word. Not until this afternoon when I got a text from a number I didn't know, giving me an address signed with "J." Followed shortly by the number of hours we'd already spent together. Eleven. I imagine he must've included the time he was in bed with me. One hundred dollars every ten minutes, six hundred dollars an hour, so I've barely made a dent in the time I owe him.

And I haven't gotten anywhere. I have no new information that sheds light onto what happened to Jenny. He says he didn't do it; I already knew The Red Room was a place for drug deals and a criminal hangout.

Nothing new. Time is stagnant and I can't hold on much longer. I can't rely on someone who isn't coming through.

I made it down the long winding path around the massive estate and parked in the back where Jase told me to; I made it all that way without breathing.

Maybe that's why I feel faint as I shut my car door, the thud echoing in the depths of the thick forest I stared into only days ago. The dark greens are covered by a slight dusting of white as the snow falls gently, creeping into the crevices of everything.

Pulling my scarf a bit tighter, I take the steps one by one to the front door.

Answers. I will get answers. Even if it's only one question at a time. *He has to know something.*

The bite from the wind creeps up quickly as I raise my fist to knock on the door, only to hear a beep and a click before I even touch it. Someone else grants me entry. *He already knows I'm here.*

Warily, I push the large, carved wooden door open, and it glides easily with the softest of pushes.

Thump. My heart slams as I remember the last time I gazed at this wood, but the engravings were upside down as I dangled from Jase's shoulder.

It's only been days, but it feels like everything's changed.

The massive foyer greets me with warmth, but not much else. The lighting of the wrought iron chandelier reflects on the shiny marble floor, radiating wealth with the spiral staircase, but that's all this room contains. It's empty and even in the warmth, even coming in from the blustery weather, it's cold in here.

Click.

The door shuts behind me, and the small sound startles me. My quick gasp echoes in the room.

Clenching my fists, I inwardly scold myself. *Pull it together.*

He's only a man. A man with answers. A man who will bring me justice. Justice Jenny deserves.

A man who is not here. I have no idea where he is. But I'm alone in the foyer.

My lips purse as I breathe out, letting my heavy bag drop to the floor. It's topped with the weighted blanket Jase left.

My gaze moves from window to window, to the heavy front door.

I can't help but to test Jase's statement. That the doors are locked on the inside and there's no way out. Something about Jase makes me feel like he wouldn't lie. Like he doesn't make threats, only promises of what's to come.

I think it's the severity of his presence. The confidence in his banter. Everything is always just so with him. It's how he wants it to be, and everything is exactly that. How he wants.

It's the impression he gives me and that impression is why I pull off my gloves and shove them in my coat pocket. Gripping the knob with both hands, I turn and pull. I yank it harder when it doesn't give, feeling the stretch in my arms from tugging on an unmoving door.

Huffing the stray hair out of my face, I glance up at a small black square, smaller than the size of a sheet of notebook paper. It's digital. Whatever lock he uses, it's digital.

"Fingerprints and hand scans," Jase's voice bellows from the empty hall behind me, forcing me to whip around to face him, my hand on my chest. "That sort of thing," he adds, slipping his hands into his pockets.

"Jesus fuck," I gasp with contempt. "Are you trying to give me a heart attack?"

My heart thumps a *yes*, my core clenches with affirmation and my gaze drifts down his body, agreeing with the two of them.

He's not wearing a suit today. And he looks damn good in his perfectly fitted suits. In jeans and a t-shirt stretched tight across his shoulders, showing off those corded muscles in his arms... he's doing that shit on purpose.

Swallowing down my heart, I try to relax again. "Just testing what you said..." My explanation dies in the air as he stalks closer to me with powerful strides and in a dominating way that almost has me stepping back, bumping my ass into the door. Almost, but I hold my ground.

"Well then, I'm relieved you weren't leaving already," he comments, the words spoken lowly as he stops right in front of me.

The air between us crackles like a roaring fire.

How does he do this to me?

"I like it better when you're an asshole," I speak without thinking. I'm rewarded with a charming smile, and a deep rough chuckle.

"I'll remember that, cailín tine." Holding out his hand, he commands me, "Come."

As I reach for my purse, Jase leans down, grabbing the handle before I can. His blanket is in plain sight on top and before I can speak, he comments, "You could have kept it with you; it may help you sleep."

One step in front of the other I follow him, with only the sounds of our footsteps keeping us company while I try not to think too much about what he said and why.

He doesn't care about my sleep.

He doesn't care about how I'm feeling.

He wants to get his dick wet. He wants to tie me up and do with me what he wishes.

All of this is simply to keep me amenable.

Jase Cross may have the upper hand, but I'm doing this for me.

The echoes of my footsteps get louder in the narrow corridor as I think, *I'm doing this for Jenny.*

One step, one beat of my heart, one tick of the clock.

I have my questions lined up in a pretty row. Without warning, Jase halts and unlocks a door, but how? I don't know. It simply clicks the moment he stops in front of it and with a flick of the handle, it opens.

I've never seen wealth like this before. And I imagine it shows in my expression, judging by the smug look on Jase's face when he opens the door wider and says, "After you."

"Where would you like me?" I ask him the moment he opens the door and I step in before taking a look. "Oh," I murmur, and the word leaves my lips without my conscious consent.

The click of the door closing behind me is followed by a dull thud of a lock, some sort of lock, moving into place.

My belly flips in a way I don't understand. Almost like when you're driving down a hill too fast, or on a roller coaster. The anticipation of the fall, the sudden drop of reality making your stomach somersault.

As I spot the table in the middle of the room, that's exactly what I feel. Followed by the same exact cold prickling I remember so well from three nights ago traveling along my skin.

"What do you think?" Jase asks me, and at the same time he reaches up to my shoulders to take my coat. I anticipate the feel of his fingers trailing along my skin as he does, but he's careful not to touch me. I think he does it on purpose.

I think he does more things with intent than I first realized.

"It's not at all like your foyer," I comment and then drag my eyes back to the wooden bench in the middle of the room. It's at odds with the large plush carpet that takes up most of the space. I have to look out further to the edge to note that under it is a barn wood floor, or something like it. A darker wood, with wide planks. The cream rug is the brightest thing in here, and thank goodness it's large. Even with the three chandeliers at varying heights with a mix of iron and wood, the room has a soft, airy feeling. Dim and romantic even.

As my coat falls off my shoulders, I take a half step forward and touch the wall. It's a thick wallpaper in a damask cream, but it's darkened by the blood-red pattern within it.

Besides the bench and a matching dresser, there's a whiskey-colored leather chaise lounge and a white crystal fireplace that would certainly be the focus, if not for the wooden bench dead smack in the center of it all.

With the flick of a switch from behind me, I hear the gas turn on and the fireplace roars to life. Jase's hand is still on the switch when I peek behind my shoulder.

I dare to step forward and touch the edge of the wooden bench, noting it's lined with padding upholstered in a soft black leather.

"It's beautiful. It's primitive and raw. Elegant, yet seductive in a way that borders on decadence."

He doesn't respond to my comment, although his eyes never leave me as I walk around the table. "The wood won't catch on fire?" I ask him, remembering how the flames felt like they consumed everything. I've never felt so alive.

"It's for fucking, not fire play." Jase's words come with authority and a heat that could match that raging from the fireplace behind me.

My lungs still as I'm pinned by his gaze. "Is that what you think you'll be doing today?"

Thump, thump, thump. The pace picks up.

"I think you'd enjoy it and my temperament hasn't been... appropriate. I'd appreciate a good fuck."

"I can say no," I remind him, feeling the warring need to give in, to have it all, and to keep my head on straight.

"You could." His dismissive nature would piss me off if it weren't for the way he looks at me. Like he can see right through me, but he doesn't want to. He wants to see *me*.

"I don't fuck every man I find attractive. Even if I'm willing to admit," I pause a moment, wondering if I should say it out loud. It brings the truth to life when you speak it, but he already knows. This cocky bastard is well aware of what's between us. "Even if I'm willing to admit there's chemistry between us and I like what you do to me. If it weren't for the fact that I have questions and a debt you're holding over my head... I wouldn't give you the time of day."

The heat sizzles between us, although the nerves rack through my body. He intimidates me. Maybe it's something I hadn't admitted to myself before, but in this moment, as he stares down at me, making me wait for a response, I'm so sincerely aware of how much he intimidates me.

"Business then?" Jase asks with an arched brow; his expression doesn't hold a hint of emotion, or amusement. He's a man in control and nothing more.

Standing toe to toe with him, I swallow as I nod. "It's business."

"I have the first question, you have the next." He speaks as he turns his back to me and strides to the dresser, laying my coat over the top of it. He stands there a second too long. The silence is only broken by the pop of the fire to the left of him. The bright light sends shadows down the side of him, and when he turns around those shadows make his jawline seem sharper, his eyes darker and every inch of his exposed skin looks taut and powerful.

He exudes raw masculinity.

"Strip." He gives the command and whatever hint of defiance had come over me flees in an instant.

I have to lean down to unzip my leather boots, then slip them off. I'm ashamed to say I put more effort into this outfit than a woman with self-respect would. The dark denim skinny jeans take a little more effort to shimmy out of, and all the while Jase stands there with his muscular arms crossed in front of him as he leans against the dresser, watching in silence.

I can't even look at him as I second-guess everything in this moment.

I'm not a whore, but that's exactly what I feel like. I can't pretend it's anything else.

When I'm left in nothing but my silk undershirt and lace bra, both covered by an oversized, cream cashmere sweater, Jase's steps destroy the distance between us. It only takes three steps until he's in front of me, his hands at the hem of my sweater. I'm quicker than he is, my hands wrapping around his powerful wrists. My arms are locked and my nails nearly dig into his flesh as I glare into his prying gaze.

"I can do it myself," I say, pushing the words through clenched teeth.

"I'm paying very well for this time with you. I intend to enjoy every minute. If you'd like for it to stop, you know how to tell me just that."

There's no reason I should feel a sudden stab of emotions up my throat, drying it and tightening it. Or the hollowness that grows in my chest.

"It's just business, isn't it?" he questions and with another thump of my treacherous heart, I release his wrists, waiting for him to undress me like he wishes.

Whore. Whore is the first word that comes to mind, and how I made it this long without feeling like one is beyond me.

"May I ask a question then? I know you have yours first, but I'd like to ask one, if you'll ... allow it." I keep my tone professional as I can, holding back the desire to smack my hand across his arrogant, handsome face.

Jase doesn't touch my sweater. Instead he walks around me to stand behind me, leaving only the fire for me to look at. His voice hums a "mm-hmm" behind me. His chest is so close to my back, I can feel the vibrations of it, even if he's not touching me.

"Are you looking in to who did that to my sister? If she owed anyone anything?" My words waver in the air and I wish I could hold them steady. I wish I could sound as strong as I feel on my best of days. Not in this moment, not when I'm acutely aware that I'm whoring myself out to this arrogant bastard who could be using me, lying to me and toying with me just for his own sick pleasure. All so I can chase the ghost of whoever hurt my sister. Whoever took her from me.

"I already told you I was." His answer is clear and lacks the arrogance and dismissiveness he's given me so far today. I don't have to ask him to expand on his answer, since he does that himself. "Her death has caused ripple effects. When I have a name and a reason, you will too."

I can't help that I flinch when he lays a hand on my shoulder. I can't control the way I feel, and I struggle to hide that from him.

I'm so alone. In a room with this man I've been thinking about for days, I feel so fucking alone. Maybe I made the memory of that night more than what was actually there.

I stare at the flames lingering among the pure white crystals. I let them mesmerize me and tell myself I don't have to go through with this. I don't have to rely on Jase Cross.

But the alternative crushes me; I can't risk never knowing what happened and having to say goodbye without giving her justice.

His left hand finds my hip and he rubs soothing circles there over the sweater. Which only makes me hate him more until he lowers his lips to my ear and whispers, "Does it make a difference to you... if I admit I feel that chemistry too? That I have a desire to be near you?"

With a gentle kiss on my neck, that hard wall around me cracks and crumbles.

"It's no longer only business for me, cailín tine."

His words are a soothing balm. One I didn't realize I needed. My hand covers his, and I lean back into his chest, where he holds me. This man holds me because he wants to do just that. And I lean into him, because I want to do just that.

"I like it when you touch me," I whisper into the room, hoping it will keep my secret.

"And I like touching you," he says softly and runs the tip of his nose down the back of my neck, causing my eyes to close, my head to loll to the side and the pain to drift away slowly.

I don't want to be alone. I almost speak the realization aloud.

"I promise you, I will find out who hurt her." His words cause my eyes to open and when they do, I stare at the fire as Jase pulls my sweater over my head. It falls to the floor and then he whispers against the shell of my ear, "I will make them pay for what they did. And you will know every detail."

chapter fifteen

Jase

When she turns in my arms, I don't expect her to devour me with a kiss full of need and hunger. She can only hold up the hate routine for so long before her arms get weak and tired, and her body gives in to what it needs.

Pressing her lips to mine and spearing her fingers through my hair, she pulls me lower to her, standing on her tiptoes and holding her body against mine.

My tongue dives into her hot mouth, feeling the heat and need and lust she has to offer.

Her head falls back so she can breathe, deep and chaotically. I don't need air. I need to devour her.

With my arms wrapped around her and my lips traveling down her neck, down her bare shoulder, I take in every inch of her. Inhaling her sweet scent, memorizing the alluring sounds she lets slip from her lips. Dragging my teeth back up her neck, I hear her hiss my name, "Jase."

"Make me forget," she whimpers against my lips before I can ravage her.

Make me forget.

I don't speak the only response I can give her. *I will, if you do the same for me.*

Slamming my lips against hers, I grab her ass and lift her into my arms. Her legs straddle my waist as I carry her to the table.

Her hips need to be nestled against the padding, and the strap is meant to keep her in place. But I have no time for any of it. The urgency of our heated kiss fuels a primitive side of me with the need to have her under me as soon as possible.

With her heels digging into my ass, spurring me on, I groan in the hot air between us, "I need to be inside of you."

Her lips part, and I can almost hear her say the words. I know what she's going to say before she says it, *I need you too.*

But her gaze lingers, time pauses and the truth is lost in a haze of want and need.

Instead she kisses me, long and deep. Massaging my tongue and taking everything she wants with our kiss.

With her ass supported by the bench, I unbutton and unzip my jeans, letting them fall as I stroke my cock.

"I need you," she whispers into my mouth and then kisses me reverently again.

She's already wet, but so tight. Pushing two fingers inside of her, I stretch her until she can take three. "Your cunt was made for me to fuck," I tell her as I drag my knuckles against her front wall.

Her grip on the edge of the table nearly slips as her pussy spasms around my fingers.

I don't stop fucking her until her release is passed and her chest heaves for air and her face is flushed.

"Flip over," I command her but it's unneeded. I take the task on myself, gripping her hips and butting them against the bench.

Moving the head of my cock to her core, I press against her gently, not pushing in just yet.

A deep groan leaves me as I bend over her, my chest against her back. "You feel so fucking good," I whisper against her and just as she lifts her head to respond, I slam myself inside of her. Every inch of me in one swift stroke.

Her mouth drops open with a scream and her nails dig into the wood. Fuck, she's tight, so tight it almost hurts and I have to clench my jaw and force myself to slam into her over and over again.

Her small body jostles against the table and I know there will be bruises tomorrow. I'll be a happy man if she can't even walk.

A strangled noise leaves her as she gets impossibly tighter, cumming all over my cock.

"Jase," she moans my name, arching her back and scratching the wood as her body stiffens with her release.

With one hand on my shoulder, keeping her arched, and the other on her hip to pin her against the table, I ride through her release, taking her savagely and with no mercy.

It's more than just fucking her, this is about owning her and I don't know when that happened.

She adjusts to me soon enough and my thrusts pick up, my balls drawing up with the need to release, but I can't give in just yet.

A desperate moan, loud and uncontrolled, fills the air. In an attempt to silence it, Beth covers her mouth with both hands as I thrust again and again.

"Don't you fucking dare." The words leave me at the same time that I grab her arms, pulling her hands away as I continue to fuck her with a ruthless pace.

Her upper body sways with every hard push of my hips against her ass.

"I want to hear every fucking sound." The words come out rough, from deep in my chest. "Scream for me."

chapter sixteen

Jase

"I THINK I SHOULD LEAVE." BETHANY'S CADENCE IS SOFT AND INNOCENT, AND IT DOESN'T hold any of the regret I'm sure she's feeling.

She's been silent since I brought her into the bedroom. Limp, well fucked, and sated.

And questioning everything.

I know the war that rages inside of her. I feel the same.

It's not just business. And there's no justification for the two of us being together.

She knows it. I know it. It's easy to get lost in each other's touch, but when it's over, what's left?

Beth turns in my bed, careful not to disturb the sheets to face me. Her small hand rests against my chest and I lift mine up to hers, holding her hand and bringing it to my lips so I can kiss her knuckles.

I don't know what this is. Or where it's going. All I know is that we shouldn't be doing it. She knows it too.

"Do you mind if I use your bathroom?" she asks, not even looking me in the eyes.

I nod, forcing her to peek up at me, and the well of emotion I'm feeling sinks deep into the soft browns and hints of green in her gaze.

I move to lie on my back as she scoots to the edge of the bed and quietly picks up her sweater from the pile of clothes we carried in from the den. I watch the dim light kiss the curves of her body until it's covered by the soft fabric.

Listening to her bare feet pad on the floor, then the flick of the light switch and the running water, I stare at the ceiling, knowing I need to give her an answer to her unspoken question, but the moment I do, I may lose her forever.

"You take medication?" Beth's question brings my attention to her as she stands in the threshold of the bathroom. One hand on the door, the other on a bottle of unmarked pills.

"No," I answer her, feeling the tension thicken.

Her weight shifts from one foot to the other. "So... you just keep your product in your bathroom then?" she dares to speak.

"My product?" I'm quick to throw off the covers and stalk toward her. My shoulders feel tense, hearing the confrontation in her voice. Maybe she just wants to pick a fight. Something she knows will end whatever it is between us and she can go back to pretending, *it's just business*. Bull-fucking-shit. I won't allow it.

"For a moment, I forgot. For a moment," she says under her breath, shutting the medicine cabinet. She turns around before I get to her and looks me in the eyes as she takes a step forward to meet me. "I was looking for Advil. And I thought..." She trails off and swallows hard, pulling her hair into a ponytail before continuing to speak. "For a moment, I forgot and I don't know how that's fucking possible."

I expect anger, but all I see in her features are disappointment and sadness. "Of course you have drugs here. You're a drug dealer."

Even as she stares at me, her eyes gloss over. She's so close to the edge of breaking.

Looking for anything to push her over so she doesn't have to deal with the real cause of her pain.

Reaching around her, I open the medicine cabinet door and pull out the pills. "They're for sleeping," I tell her, and my voice comes out hard.

She tries to maneuver around me, but with my other hand, I grip her hip and keep her right there. "That's all they are. I don't do drugs and I don't like what I do, but I have to do it."

"You don't-"

My finger over her lips silences her. Her eyes spark and rage, but beneath the anger there's so much more.

"You don't have to understand." She pulls my hand away from her mouth just then.

"Yes, I do," she says and shakes her head. "You don't understand. I am not okay." Her last word cracks. "I don't know when I became this woman, or if I was always like this and never knew it because I was too busy solving someone else's problem. But right now, I have nothing." She swallows thickly, holding on to her strength. "I feel like my life is on the precipice of changing forever. And I don't want to go back to the girl I was, but I don't like where this is headed either. I don't have answers, and I need answers."

Her hand is still firmly gripping my wrist, and I stare at it until she loosens her hold.

"What answers do you need?"

My patience with her is higher than it should be. I'm softer and more willing to be gentle with her.

"I don't like what you do."

"That's not a question to be answered."

"Well I don't like it. I don't like that I like you."

I let her raised voice and condescension slide. For now. Only because it's true. She's only being honest, and I get it.

"Someone's going to do it, Bethany. There will always be someone in my position. You can't stop that. I can at least have control if I'm that someone."

"You sell drugs?" she asks, staring at the door to the bathroom before looking me in the eyes.

"You know I do. That answer isn't going to change."

"Why?"

"It's a long story," I say, keeping my voice firm.

"I have time."

"I don't want to tell it right now."

"Why are you making me pay Jenny's debt?" Her wide eyes beg me to give an answer that will calm her fears. I can see it clearly. "You didn't mention it when you came to the house. It wasn't until after you brought me here. And you don't need the money, that's for damn sure." Her gaze searches mine, looking for the only words she wants to hear.

"I wanted to let it go," I lie, hating myself for every word that comes out of me.

"How could she even owe so much? What did she use the money for?" she continues, not finding my answer satisfying enough.

Every question is another cut in the deepening gouge.

"You already got a question. Mine first." It's the only thing I can think of to hold her off for a moment. She quiets, watching me and waiting. Willing to give me whatever answer I need.

"How did you know about The Red Room? Why is that where you went to find answers?"

I already know the truth, so all while she speaks, I grasp for what answer I can give her in return.

"Jenny; she used to talk about it. The back room of The Red Room. All the time. I heard her on the phone."

"Who was she talking with?"

"I don't know." She's quick to add, "That's another question."

"Semantics."

"Answer my question!" Bethany pushes her hands into my chest. Not to hit me, not to push me, but to get my attention, to demand it. My blood simmers simply from her touch. "Why did she owe you so much money?"

"She owed it to Carter," I answer her, unable to deny her at this point. Blaming the debt on someone else like a coward. "He didn't want to let the debt go and be made to look like a fool."

"I don't understand what she did with all that money," she nearly whispers, looking past me as she searches through her memories for answers. Answers she'll never find.

"Debt adds up fast." I try to keep my tone gentle as I speak. "I can tell you I met her once," I add, and my confession brings her gaze to mine. "She was looking to buy that drug you just had."

"Sleeping pills?" She looks confused.

"Sweets is what they call it. Sweet Lullabies. We mostly use it for addicts to wean them off, put them out during their withdrawal." Bethany stares up at me, hanging on every word as I speak. I only wish this story had a better ending for her.

"She was strung out on coke; every telltale sign was there. And she was buying too much of the sweets. It didn't make sense. It wasn't for her. When we questioned her, she said it was for her brother. She left and never came around again."

"We don't have a brother."

"I know. We could tell she was lying to us, so we sent her away."

"That's what you know of my sister?" Shame and sadness lace her words.

"That's the only time I met her," I answer her and her gaze narrows, as if she can see through my truth to the lies I just told her moments ago. But this is the truth.

"I don't know who she was buying it for, or if it has anything to do with why she was killed."

I've lost a piece of her in this moment. I don't know how, but I did.

"Don't judge me, Beth. I'm the one who will pay for this."

She stares up at me, but she doesn't say a word. Still assessing everything I said, or maybe trying to see her sister as she was in her last days.

"You've got to calm down."

"I don't just calm down," she says, wrapping her arms around herself and I think she's done, but she tells me a story. "I was a preemie when I was born, and I almost died. My mother told me she thought it was God punishing her. She hadn't wanted my sister; she almost gave her up. Not that she was a bad person," she adds, quick to defend her mother. "She didn't think she'd be a good mom to her, and had broken up with my father just before she found out she was pregnant. She came very close to giving her up, but my father came back around and wanted to try to make things work. And then a few years later, they wanted to have me. And she told me she'd thought God was going to take me away. My lungs didn't work and the hospital couldn't do anything, so they put me in a helicopter and sent me away to a hospital that could save me. My mom couldn't come at first, because she lost a lot of blood.

"My grandfather used to say I came into this world fighting and I never stopped. He told me once, 'You'll leave this world fighting, Bethy. And I'll still be so proud of you.'" Tears cloud her eyes, but she doesn't shed them. Not my fiery girl; she holds on to every bit of her pain.

"It's okay," I tell her, rubbing her arm and then holding her when she falls into my chest.

"I'm sorry I'm a bitch," she tells me, sniffing away the last evidence that she may have been on the verge of crying. "I don't know why I'm always ready to fight. I just am."

"It's okay, I already told you that."

"Why is it that when you say that, it feels like it really is?" The way she looks up at me in this moment is like I'm her hero. It's nothing but another lie.

"Because I'll do everything I can to make sure it is okay, maybe that's why?"

She sniffs once more and takes a step back to the counter as she says, "I should leave."

"I want you here. I don't want you to leave tonight."

"Why?" she asks. "Why do you want me to stay?"

"Do you really want to go to bed alone?"

"No," she whispers.

A moment passes between us. The look she gave me a moment ago is coming back.

"Jase, promise me one thing."

"What?"

"Don't hurt me."

I lie to her again, knowing that I hurt everyone I touch. Knowing I've already hurt her, although the truth of that hasn't revealed itself yet. "I won't hurt you," I tell her. I would have told her anything. Just to get her to stay.

chapter seventeen

Bethany

One thing the kids at the hospital do all the time is lie. They lie about taking their medication. They lie about their symptoms. They lie for all sorts of reasons all the time.

It's my job to know when they're lying. I can't save them if I don't know the truth.

When Jase looked me in the eyes hours ago, he lied to me.

I don't know what piece of the conversation contained the lie. I don't know how much was a lie. I don't know why.

But I know he lied to me. And I can't let it go. The nagging thought won't let me sleep. He fucking lied to me. I put it all out there, allowed myself to be raw and vulnerable. My imperfect, broken, bitchy self. And he lied to my face. The worst part is that I'm sure it had to do with my sister.

That's what hurts the most.

Every minute that passed after seeing that look on his face when he lied, every minute I thought of how I could get it out of him. How I *needed* to get it out of him. How I was failing Jenny by letting it happen. How I was failing myself.

I'm careful as I slip off the sheet. I haven't slept at all, but he has. His breathing is even, and I listen to it as I gently climb out of the bed. My body is motionless when I stand up, listening to his inhales and exhales.

I already have my excuse ready in case he wakes. I never got that Advil, after all.

Every footstep is gentle as I move to the dresser, opening a drawer as silently as I can. The first drawer proves useless and as I shut it, Jase breathes in deeper, the pace of his breathing changing. I stand as still as I can, holding my own breath and praying he falls back asleep.

And he does. That steady, even breathing comes back.

With the rush of adrenaline fueling me, I move to his nightstand quietly, slowly, wondering if I've lost my fucking mind. I'm so close to him that he could reach out and grab me if he woke up. I watch his chest rise and fall as I open the drawer. The sound of it opening is soft, but noticeable. All the while, Jase sleeps.

I watch his chest for a steady rhythm; I watch his eyes for any movement. He's knocked the hell out.

The faint light from the room is enough to reflect off the metal of the set of cuffs. I only have two, but if I can get one wrapped around his wrist and linked to the bed, I'll have him where I need him.

Trapped, until he tells me the fucking truth.

I almost shut the drawer, almost, but then I realize he would be able to reach it, and nestled inside are both a gun and a knife.

The metal gleams in the night and I carefully pick up both weapons and move them to the top of the dresser on the other side of the room, away from his reach.

Thump. Thump. The heat of uneasiness creeps along my skin. My own breathing intensifies, my hands shake slightly and the metal of the handcuffs clinks in the quiet night.

Freezing where I am on the other side of the bed, I wait. And wait. Watching him carefully. If he woke up right now, I don't even know what he'd do to me.

But it's better to suffer that consequence than to accept him lying straight to my face, all the while, I fall for him ... him and his lies.

It's what my mother did. She accepted my father's lies. And it left her a lonely woman. I won't be with a liar. I don't care about any debt or any other bullshit reason. I can't trust a liar.

I don't realize how angry I've become, not until Jase rolls over slightly in bed and my heart leaps up my throat.

The thought runs through my mind not to do it. That I'm out of my element and this world is more dangerous than I can handle. This isn't the person I am.

But he lied to me. ...About Jenny.

Biting down on my bottom lip, I creep back up onto the bed and close one of the cuffs around an iron post of Jase's bed. There are four metal posts that surround his bed. The soft clink of the locks goes by slowly, *clink, clink, clink* and I swear he'll hear it, but his chest rises and falls evenly while he shows no signs of waking.

As I lean closer to him, closer to the other side, and ready to slip the other cuff through the post on that side of him, I gaze down at his face. In his sleep, he's still a man of power. But even with his strong stubbled jaw, there's a peacefulness I haven't seen.

He's only a man.

It fucking hurts to look at him. When someone can hurt you, it means you care. I have lived my life making sure not to care, so that I won't be hurt. And yet, Jase Cross pushed his way in, only to lie to me.

It solidifies my decision. I'll be damned either way.

Clink, clink, clink. With both handcuffs in place, I know securing the one on the left to his wrist will be easy. His wrist is close to the first cuff already. I'm sure he'll wake and then I'll be fucked, but I have to try. I'll have him where I want him.

With that thought, I go through with it, not second-guessing a thing.

I grab his wrist and it's by sheer dumb luck that he wakes up and grabs my throat with that hand. His dark eyes open wide and he stares daggers at me. Pinning me with a fierce look, the fear I knew I held for him deep down makes me still.

The look he shows is of startle and shock, and I don't let it distract me, even if I do scream out of instinct.

I drop my head down, shoving my face into the headboard, feeling the burn rising over my head from hitting my nose, and slip the metal around his wrist, scraping it against his skin as he screams at me, locking it into place.

"What the fuck are you doing?" his voice bellows in the room. His grip tightens for a moment, right before releasing me altogether.

I can still feel the imprint of his hand on my throat, the power he has to hurt me. I can feel it as I kick away from him, fighting with the sheets to get far enough away.

Scrambling backward, I fall hard off the bed onto my back, gasping for breath as my heart attempts to climb out of my throat.

Jase rips his arm back, yelling in vain as the metal digs into his wrist and the bed shakes, but he remains attached to it. Cuffed to the bed. He does it again and again and each time I lie on my back like a coward, my elbows propping me up on the floor as I wait with bated breath to see if I have trapped the beast.

"What the fuck did you do?" he jeers. "Where's the key?" he asks in a snarl.

Silence. *Did I really do it?* Thump.

"Where's the fucking key!" he screams until his face turns red. The anger seeps into the air around us as I slowly stand.

"I have the key," I manage to say somehow calmly, still in disbelief. He blinks the sleep from his eyes, breathing from his nostrils and slowly coming to the realization of what's happened. The way he looks down at me, like I betrayed him—I'd be a liar if I said it didn't kill something inside of me.

I ruin what I touch. I should have known this would end with him hating me.

"Give it to me," he requests with an eerily calm tone, one that chills me to my bones.

"No," I say, and the word falls from me easily. More easily than I could have imagined as I stand up straighter, walking slowly around the edge of the bed. Not unlike the way he does to me when I undress for him.

His dark eyes narrow on me. "Don't do this. I won't be mad. Just give me the key."

Thump. Thump. Fear burns inside of me. The fear of both repenting, and the fear of going through with it.

I keep walking, slowly making my way to the dresser and Jase's eyes move to it before looking back at me. "What are you doing?" he asks me, and then I hear him swallow. I hear the hint of fear creeping into his voice. "Give me the key."

I ignore his demand and pick up the gun. I don't aim it at him, I merely hold it and tell him, "Put the open cuff around your other wrist." Although I lack true confidence, the gun slipping slightly in my sweaty palms.

"And how would you like me to do that?" Jase questions, a lack of patience and irritation are the only things I can hear in his voice. Like I'm a child asking for something ridiculous.

"You're a big boy," I bite back, "I'm sure you can figure it out."

All the while I watch him and he watches me, my heart does this pitter-patter in my chest making me think it's giving up on me as it stalls every time Jase looks back. Using the pillow and occasionally leaning down to hold the cuff between his teeth, he struggles to lock it. I don't trust him enough to do it myself though. There's no way he wouldn't grab me.

My heart beats faster with each passing second as he attempts to close the cuff himself.

Every moment his gaze touches mine, questioning why I'd do this, I question it myself.

"I don't want to hurt you," I whisper when I hear the cuff finally pushed into place. He rests his wrists against the iron rod, pushing it tighter and securing it.

"Then put the gun down," he urges me and I listen. I set it down on the dresser where it sat only minutes ago and hesitantly turn to him, each wrist cuffed to his bed.

"You can still uncuff me," he suggests with more dominance than he should have. Especially because I lift the knife at the end of his sentence.

"More cuffs." I speak the words and fight back the bile rising in my stomach from knowing my own intentions.

Jase's eyes stay on the knife as he answers me, "In the top drawer of the dresser. To the right side... with the ropes." His voice is dull and flat. "You're going to cuff my ankles?" he guesses correctly and I nod without looking at him, simply because I can't.

Thump. Thump. My heart feels like it's lagging behind as I pick up the cuffs from the drawer, right where he said they were.

"Why are you doing this?" he asks me; any hint of arrogance or even anger is gone.

I can barely swallow as I move toward him. With the sheet barely covering him but laid haphazardly over his groin still, the rest of him is fully exposed. He is Adonis. Trapped and furious, but ultimately mortal.

"I want answers," I say, and I don't know how I'm able to speak. "You lied to me. I know you did."

His only response is to stretch out his legs, not fighting, not resisting. Putting his ankles close to the rods.

He's helping me. Or it's a trick. I decide on the latter, moving closer, but hesitantly.

"Go on," he tells me, staring down at me.

I stand back far enough away from the footboard, cautious as I click the first cuff into place.

"Go ahead, cailín tine," he tells me, staring into my eyes. His nickname for me breaks my heart. Even as I look away, feeling shame and guilt consume me even though I know I have a good reason to do this. But it doesn't make it hurt any less.

With the last cuff in place, and Jase half sitting up in bed, leaning against the headboard and staring at me, I observe him from where I stand.

"What are you going to do now?" I ask him.

"Wait."

"You lied to me." I whisper the ragged words and turn the handle of the knife over in my hand.

"When?" he questions, and the muscles in his neck tighten.

A sad laugh leaves me and I'm only vaguely conscious of it when I hear it.

"So you did lie?" I ask weakly, feeling the weight against my chest. "And here I was hoping I was just crazy."

"I'd be hard-pressed in this moment to call you sane," Jase comments, and my eyes move to his. "Yes, I lied to you."

"What was a lie?" I ask him and take a step closer to the bed. The floorboard creaks under my step and I halt where I am, taking it as a warning.

"I don't want to tell you. It doesn't matter." He speaks a contradiction.

Wiping my forehead with the back of my hand, still holding the knife, I walk closer to him, gauging his ability to move, even though he's still as can be.

"I don't think you could do anything," I start to tell him as I stand right in front of the nightstand, "if I stand right here." Holding out my arm, I gently place the blade of the knife on his chest, not pushing at all, but letting him see how far away I can be while still capable of hurting him. "What do you think?" I ask him, wondering if I truly am crazy at this point.

"What do you want to know?" he asks, not answering my question.

"What did you lie about?"

"It's irrelevant."

"Anything relating to my sister is relevant." I grit out the words, pushing the knife down a little harder. Enough so the skin on his pec surrounding the knife, tightens under the blade.

"Did you hurt her?" The words come out unbidden.

"No, I told you that."

"And you told me you lied," I counter.

"I lied to protect you, Bethany." He almost says something else, but instead he rips his gaze away from me, gnashing his back teeth to keep him from talking.

Before I can continue, he tells me, "I have a name, but it's useless." His dark eyes lift to mine. "We think he got her hooked, intentionally or not, but he can't be tied to anything else. Nothing ties him to her death."

"Give me his name." The strong woman inside of me applauds my efforts, rejoicing in the fact that it took this much to make him speak and that I was able to push myself to this point.

And that I have a name.

I have someone I can blame and punish, someone I can make pay for what they did to my sister. They tortured her. Broke her body. She was gone for so long, I don't know how long it went on. And then they burned her. They left nothing of her for me.

There will be nothing of them left when I find them.

"No." His answer dies in the tense air between us. It takes me a long moment to realize what he's even saying no to. My mind has gone to darker places, and tears streak down my cheek thinking about what she went through and that I wasn't there. I couldn't save her.

"Tell me who it was," I say as I move a bit closer, holding the knife with both hands, barely keeping it together. I let the tears fall with no restraint, and no conscious consent either. "I want his name!" I raise my voice and even to my own ears it sounds violent and uncontrolled.

Jase stares straight ahead, ignoring me, not answering.

"I don't want to hurt you." The confession sounds strangled.

"You don't have to," he answers.

"Give me the name, Jase!"

"You'll get yourself killed!" he yells back at me and the sound bellows from deep within him.

"You don't understand what they did to her!" I scream at him, feeling the well of emotion filling my lungs. I remember the fear when she went missing. "She would text me every day when she woke up, regardless of what time that ended up being. Sometimes she forgot. But every day, there was at least one text…" I trail off, remembering how angry I'd been when she messaged last. She wouldn't come back after I made her admit she had a problem. She refused to come back and get help. But she still messaged me every day. Until she didn't.

"And then there was nothing," I speak so softly, using what's left inside of me as the tears fall freely down my face.

"For days and then weeks, there was nothing but fear and hope. And fear is what won. Every day she didn't text me. The fear won." As I try to regain my composure, I wipe haphazardly at my face and focus on breathing.

"I waited in silence for nothing. The first forty-eight hours, no one did anything at all," I say and my words crack. "Why would they? She was reckless and headed down the wrong path."

The knife is still in my hands, still pressed to his skin when I tell him, "I knew something terrible had happened to her, and I could do nothing. She was still alive then. I know she was. I remember thinking that. That she was still out there. That I could feel her."

I'm brought back to my kitchen, crying on the floor, hating myself for pushing her away, regretting that I yelled at her, all alone and praying. Praying because God was the only one left to listen to me. Praying he could save her, because I couldn't.

"I had no name. No one had a name for me. But you do." I twist the knife just slightly, and suddenly feel it give, but I don't dare look. I don't look anywhere but into Jase's eyes, even as he seethes in pain.

"Give me the name."

"He'll kill you, Bethany." Sorrow etches his eyes and I know his answer already even before he says, "I won't do that."

I scream a wretched sound as I pull back the knife. It slices cleanly, so easily, leaving a bright red line in its path. Small and seemingly insignificant, but then blood pours from the wound and he bites back a sound of agony.

It's bright red. And it doesn't stop.

What have I done? Jase's intake is staggered but he doesn't show any other signs of pain.

"Fuck!" The word leaves me in a rush. "Jase," I say, and his name is a prayer on my lips. "No," I think out loud as my hand shakes and the knife drops to the floor. There's so much blood. There's so much soaking into the bed as it drips around his body.

It doesn't stop.

"Jase," I cry out his name as I ball up the bed sheets and press them to the laceration.

He breathes deep, staring at the ceiling. Silent, and ignoring me as I press more of the cotton linens to his chest, only for it to be soaked a half second later.

There's so much blood.

"I'm sorry," I utter as I rip the sheets out from under him, desperate to make it stop. "I'm so sorry."

The blood soaks through the fabric within seconds, staining my hands.

Staring down at the blood that lines the creases of my palms, I take a step back and then another.

What have I done?

chapter eighteen

Jase

It's like when you wake up from a nightmare. There's a moment where it all feels real and then, sometimes slowly, sometimes quickly, reality comes back to you. The horror stays, the damage done, the terrors in your sleep lingering as you walk down the steps of your quiet house to get a drink of water. And sometimes those monsters stand behind you. You can still sense them, even when you know they're not real.

That's what this feels like as the slice on my chest rips agony through my body. Like I can't get away from the ghosts in her eyes, even if she's woken from her dream. Even if disbelief and regret are all she feels, all she sees, all she recognizes.

The ghosts will still be there, waiting in the dark.

Every time she presses the sheets to the wound, a renewed sense of pain spreads through my body, but I refuse to make a sound. My hands turn to fists and I pull against the cuffs, feeling the metal dig into my wrists.

"I'm so sorry. I don't... I didn't mean..." she says, choking on her words.

"I told you I would tell you," I remind her, flexing my wrists and breathing through the pain. I've had worse shit done to me. "When I know who it was, I will tell you and I will make them pay."

Besides, I fucking deserve this.

"I'm not going to give you a name without knowing for sure," I confess to her, letting her believe that's the only thing I've withheld, the only lie I've spoken. "I promise you."

Her beautiful hazel eyes lock onto mine, begging and pleading for forgiveness but more than that, an out. A way out of the nightmare she's in.

There's no way out of this shit though. This is what life is. It's what mourning is. A waking nightmare.

"I'm sorry," she blurts out before turning her back to me and running to the bathroom.

I hear her open the medicine cabinet and when I do, I push the escape lock on the cuffs with my thumb. It would be all too fucked up for her to have found the cuffs in my car; the ones I put on her, the ones I keep in my car. And not these safety cuffs I intend to use when I light her ass on fire with my paddle. The ones for play sold at sex shops.

Maybe I shouldn't have let it go on for as long as I did, but I think she needed this. She needed to get it out of her system.

I'm quiet as I unlock the ones on my ankles, taking my time to put them away, gritting my teeth every time the sharp pain reminds me that she cut me.

With the drawer open, I drop the cuffs in, one by one when I hear her close the cabinet and I wait.

Her gasp is telling and I turn around slowly to see the halo of light surrounding her from the bathroom door. A bandage and gauze in one hand, and hydrogen peroxide in the other.

Horror plays in the depths of her eyes as she freezes where she is. She's a beautiful, broken mess.

I take a single step toward her; the floor groans and the only other sound is the hushed gasp she makes.

"Jase," she pleads, not hiding her fear. She doesn't hide anything; it's a big part of what I admire about her.

"Jase," she says again and this time my name is strangled as it leaves her. So much begging in only a single word as I take another step.

She trembles where she stands. I reach out for the bandages, and her arm drops dead to her side as she awaits her sentence. I place the bandage over the cut without sparing it a glance and wipe up the remaining blood with the gauze before tossing it behind her into the bathroom and onto the floor.

And she flinches from the movement. From my arm moving her way.

It fucking kills me. My chest doesn't feel a goddamn thing from the cut. But it feels everything knowing that she thought I was going to hit her. That I would strike her.

Everyone deserves punishment for their sins. And I accept mine. But I won't accept losing her.

Her eyes never leave mine, and mine never leave hers.

She doesn't beg for mercy; she doesn't try to run.

The world is full of broken birds and pain. I won't add to it.

Not her. Not my fiery girl, my *cailín tine*.

"Jase." She says my name thickly and swallows after a second passes of silence. Just the two of us knowing the other's pain, knowing what's happened wasn't a nightmare, it was real.

"I'm sor-"

I cut her off with my own apology. "I'm sorry I can't bring her back." The emotion wells in my throat as I add, "If I could, if I had that power, I wouldn't be feeling the same shit you are."

The tense air changes, and everything falls around us. For me it does. Nothing else exists for me but her.

"If I could, I would," I tell her as I brush her hair off her shoulder and lower my lips to hers. It's all done slowly. I'll be sweet with her tonight.

Her lips brush against mine gently and then she deepens our kiss.

Her fingers are hesitant at first, as if she's still expecting me to snap like she did.

I have all the time in the world for her tonight. To see what's really here. To know what's between us.

I can show her, and I do. Slowly, gently, and with every small touch, I chip away at any armor she has.

I don't want the hate; I don't want the fight.

Not tonight.

Tonight I make her feel loved.

A part of me knows it's selfish, because I don't deserve her or any of this. But tonight I need to feel loved too.

chapter nineteen

Bethany

The Coverless Book
Fourth Chapter

"Do you think Mama will be okay with it?" I ask Caroline, nervously peeking up at her. The silk is like water under my fingers. So smooth and easily flowing. "I've never worn anything like it."

"It's perfect for your first date," Caroline tells me with that sweet Southern charm.

I turn around fully to face her, repeating my question, "But do you think Mama will be okay with it?"

Caroline's expression falters.

"I think your mama would love it, Emmy," Caroline says, forcing that false smile to her lips. She's worked for our family since just before I got sick. I know all her tells and that smile she's plastered on her face is only there to hide the truth. She hates my mother, but I don't know why.

"She's sick too," I whisper defensively. "That's why she's not here." The excuse falls flat, just like it does every time.

"She's not sick like you. She's just in pain," Miss Caroline corrects me.

Those in the most pain, cause pain. My mother told me that once. It was a while ago and she said that's why she doesn't see me very much. She doesn't want to hurt me. I know it kills her inside to know what's happening to me. "Pain is a sickness, isn't it?" I ask Caroline.

The false smile wavers as she reaches down to pick up the pair of shoes. "Your first pair of heels," she states and pretends she didn't hear me. She does that sometimes. She doesn't answer me when I ask questions. I know they're insignificant, but I have no one else to talk to. Some days I wonder if I've spoken when she does that.

I only know I have when I hear her sniffle. They don't like to see me like this, frail and losing weight and muscle like I am. No one does. I'm not just sick; I'm dying. That's what the doctors say.

Smoothing the ruby red silk fabric with my hand, I turn to the mirror thinking, Jake will like me in this dress. He won't mind seeing me sick. He doesn't cry when I tell him I'm invincible, not like Mama and not like Miss Caroline.

Jake thinks I'm pretty. He thinks I'm sweet.

"Soup, Emmy," Caroline calls out and I can hear the spoon clinking against the porcelain.

"Is it- "

Before I can finish, Miss Caroline nods and says, "Of course it is. I had to make your favorite for today. Drink up, baby, you need to be strong."

"I already am strong," I tell her with a smile, feeling the excitement of tonight. "Haven't I told you? I'm invincible."

The story grips me as the pages turn. A young boy and a sick girl, falling in love even though they know it won't last. I can't help but to think it's not that simple. I hate her mother and I like Miss Caroline, but I feel sorry for Emmy. It's funny how they feel so real when I curl up under the blanket and let the night disappear in between the pages of The Coverless Book.

Lines of a dark blue ink run along the pages. And with every line, I add it to the list in my notepad.

I'm invincible.
Those in the most pain, cause pain.
I don't feel sick when he looks at me like that; I can only feel cherished with his gaze on me.
Agony is meaningless; only love can relate.

There is no pattern. No reason to think there's a hidden message lying inside. But I do. I can't help but to hope that I'm missing something. Anything. I just want my sister to tell me something.

Or at least I did. Days ago.

Before that night with Jase. The night everything changed. Somehow, he took my fight away, but with it, there's relief.

It's been two days and he hasn't messaged me, and I haven't messaged him either.

I don't know how it happened, but everything feels different now.

With every thrust against his bedroom wall, he forced the air from my lungs. He took it, he made it his. The air, my body... and more.

Forgiveness and understanding can do something to a person. Especially when you don't feel worthy of it.

When I stepped out of that bathroom, not knowing what the hell I was going to do or what the hell I was thinking when I cuffed him, I wouldn't have fathomed he'd be there facing me.

What did I think would happen even if I did get a name from him?

That somehow he would let me out of his gilded cage after he admitted what he lied about? That he wouldn't hold it against me that I'd cuffed him up and threatened him?

I don't know what the hell I was thinking. I've never been sorrier for hurting someone. I can't believe I did that.

There will be consequences, I remember Jase's words last night. Just before I fell asleep, he told me the night wasn't forgiven wholly, until there were consequences.

And I accept it. Whatever those consequences may be.

I don't know what happened to make me think I could, and that I should, lay a knife to his skin.

The only way I can justify it, is that I think it happened for a reason.

I think we were meant to have that moment. The moment when he kissed me, and he made it feel okay to let go. He made me feel like if I was with him, everything would be the way it should be.

He made me feel like I wasn't as broken as I thought I was.

And I gave him everything I had to give. Even if it's not much.

I would give him everything and anything from this day forward.

His forgiveness and touch are worth more than I'll ever have.

Ping. My phone goes off with a text message, followed by another.

Are you okay?
How are you feeling?

Two different texts, from two different people. And I'm grateful for the distraction.

One's from Laura and one's from Jase.

I'm feeling good, how are you? I text them both the same thing. I don't even realize it at first.

I just haven't heard from you. Anything new? Laura writes back first.

I write a few words and delete them. Write some more and delete those too. I finally settle on, *Maybe. I'll know more when we go out this weekend.*

My heart does this little pitter-patter thing and my head tells it that it's naïve.

The three dots at the bottom left of the screen tell me she's writing something, but before she can finish, Jase messages.

I was hoping to see you tonight. But things came up. Tomorrow.

He doesn't ask. He tells.

I debate on what to say, focusing on the first part and then the second. *He was hoping to see me.* The butterflies Emmy feels ... I feel them too. They kind of scare me. Everything that's happening scares me.

Before I can respond to him, Laura writes back.

What's new? I can't take the suspense. You know I thrive on instant gratification.

Shifting on the sofa, I pull the blanket up my lap, hating the draft coming from the old window and focusing on that rather than the butterflies.

I pick up my mug and take a swig of it; the decaf tea is lukewarm, but still satisfying.

I don't know exactly what it is yet, I tell Laura. *But when I do, I'll let you know.*

I press send and then realize I sent it to the wrong fucking person. The mug slams down onto the table when I realize, but thankfully my tea's almost gone so none of it splashes out.

"Fuck, fuck, fuck, fuck," I mutter under my breath, feeling my heart race.

Sorry, I meant that for someone else. See you tomorrow. I type out the response quickly, before Jase can respond. My heart's a damn war drum as I copy and paste what I sent him to send to Laura.

"Fuck a duck," I say out loud, letting my head fall back on the sofa. I am ... a mess. A living, breathing mess.

Omg that's so exciting! Tell me everything! Laura writes immediately.

You don't know what "what" is? What is "what?" And who are you talking to? Jase writes back. Fuck, he knows. It doesn't take a genius to know what I'm talking about.

"Shit, shit, shit," is all I can think and say as I stare at his message.

Rubbing the stress away from my forehead, I decide they can get the same message again.

I'm heading to bed. Sorry, we'll talk later. As soon as the text is sent, I toss the phone on the other side of the sofa and stare at it as it goes off. Again and again. Taunting me every time. And with each one, I wonder if it's Jase, or Laura.

Fuck both of those conversations. It's late, and I'm obviously not with it. I'm tired, but I haven't been able to sleep. They can wait. Everything can wait.

Rubbing my eyes, and ignoring the sick feeling I have inside, I finally get up off the sofa and wonder if I should grab another cup of tea, or just pass out like I said I was going to do.

My mind won't stop with all the questions though. So sleeping is nonexistent.

I don't know what we are. Jase and me. I don't know where this is going. And I don't know how I'll be all right if I don't have Jase in my life. I owe him a debt, and the hours are numbered. It will come to an end. I'm fully aware of that, and it's terrifying.

Sleep doesn't come easy for me and with that thought in mind, I pick up the small bottle of pills from my purse. The handwriting on the back merely says, *All you need is one.*

I can add assault and theft to my résumé after what happened two nights ago.

Before I left Jase's home, I swiped the bottle of sleeping pills from his medicine cabinet. I don't know if he knows yet, or what he'll do when he finds out, but he can add them to my tab.

This goes against everything I know; everything I've ever done. Both the stealing and taking the drugs. *They're only sleeping pills*, I remind myself. And I desperately need sleep. Holding the pill up, I see it's a gel capsule with liquid inside. Just like an Advil.

But everything about this week is more than morally ambiguous. And everything has changed.

The phone pings again and I check to see what they said after getting a glass of water and a single pill.

Laura wrote back a novel. Text after text demanding I give her every detail. To which I reply, *I still love you! I'll tell you all of it soon!*

And Jase wrote back, *Sleep well*. To which I reply, *You too*. And feel far too much just from being able to tell him goodnight.

It's so cold here. At first I don't know where I am. Sleep came too easily. I remember feeling my entire body lift as if I'd become weightless, right before falling so deeply into darkness. Even now I can remember it, as if I could touch it and relive it. Although I know it's already passed.

I fell and fell, but it didn't feel like falling. Everything else was moving around me until I landed in this room. A small room with dirty white walls. There's a radiator in the corner with a thick coat of paint, or maybe many coats of paint. It's white too, like the walls. The thin wooden boards on the floor are old and they don't like me walking across them. They tell me I don't belong here. They tell me to go back.

But I hear the ripping.

Something is being torn behind the old chair. It's a tufted chair, and maybe it was once expensive, but faded fabric is being torn down the back of it.

Rip, another tear and I hear something else. The sound of a muffled sob. A shuddered breath and the sound of gentle rocking. Just behind the chair.

I take another step, and a freezing prick dances along every inch of my skin. It's so cold it hurts, like an ice pick stabbing me everywhere.

It doesn't matter though. Nothing does. Because I see her.

She's there, Jenny's there. Sitting cross-legged on the floor, rocking back and forth with a book in her hand. The Coverless Book.

"Jenny," I cry out her name and try to go to her, but the chair doesn't let me; its torn fabric holds me where I am, making a vine around my ankles. My upper body tumbles forward, falling onto the back of the chair. "Jenny!" I scream as I reach out to her. But I can't reach her, and she can't hear me.

Her hair is so dirty, long and stringy now. The tears on my cheek turn to ice.

"Jenny," I whisper, but her name is lost in the cold air as I try to move from where I am. How is it holding me back? Let me go! She's my sister! She's here!

I fight against it all, but my hips are now tied down as well. I can't move to her; I can't even feel my legs. Please, let me go. I have to go to her!

The book falls, and the sound whips my eyes to her once again as Jenny covers her face to cry. Her arm has a marking, is it a quote? A tattoo?

What is it?

Her shoulders shake as tears stream down her cheeks and I tell her not to cry. I tell her it's okay, that I'm here. Her wide, dark eyes look up at me. Her pale skin is nearly as white as the fog from her breath.

It's so cold here.

"You shouldn't be here," she says, staring straight into my eyes. Both pain and chills consume me.

"Come with me," I beg her, licking my chapped lips and I swear ice coats them after. "Come

with me, Jenny!" I scream, feeling the bite of a chill deep in my lungs, and she only tilts her head as if she doesn't understand.

The torturous feeling of being trapped makes me scream a wretched cry. And Jenny only stares at me.

"I just wanted them to be okay," she tells me as if she's apologizing. "Someone needs to be okay."

"Who?" I beg her for an answer. "Who did this to you? Where are you?"

Her voice cracks and she tells me repeatedly, "You shouldn't be here." Over and over in the same way, all while she shakes her head and rocks. "You shouldn't be here."

Darkness descends, like a storm brewing inside of the small room. "Jenny, come with me!" I scream again, "Jenny, come with me!" as the room stretches, tearing her away from me. No!

"Don't believe them," she whispers and I hear it as if she's next to me. As if she's whispered it into my ear.

"Don't believe the lies. They'll all tell you lies."

Even when she's gone and there's only darkness left, she tells me, "Don't believe your heart; it lies to you too."

chapter twenty

Jase

"What happened?" I ask her the second I shut her front door. I've only just gotten here, intent on implementing consequences, and I'm already changing my mind.

Her eyes are bloodshot, and her skin is pale. Hugging her knees into her chest, she's seated on her sofa, staring at nothing.

"Nothing," she's quick to tell me. "I didn't think you'd be here in the morning. I thought you'd come at night," she adds and then wipes under her eyes as she tosses the blanket to the side of the sofa.

"I don't like it when I ask a question and you lie to me," I speak as I walk into the living room. Not a single light is on and the curtains are shut tight. It's too dark.

That gets her attention, and a hint of the girl I know shows herself when she answers smartly, "Oh, it's not the best feeling, is it?"

The sarcastic response leaves her easily, and she watches me as I narrow my gaze at her. From bad to worse, the air changes.

"Something happened from the time you left me to just now." I speak clearly, with no room for argument and Beth crosses her arms, staring just past me for a moment before looking me in the eyes.

She's in nothing but a sleepshirt that's rumpled, and dark circles are present under her eyes. Even still, she's beautiful, the kind of beautiful I want to hold on to.

"Are you going to tell me?" I ask her, not breaking our stare.

Time ticks by and I think she's going to keep it from me, but finally she looks to the kitchen and then back at me. "Over coffee," she tells me.

She turns toward the kitchen like she's going to walk there, but then pauses and looks over her shoulder. "You coming?" she asks, and I follow. Watching every detail, noticing the way her movements lag, the way she sniffs after a long exhale, like she's been crying. The way she leans against the counter after putting the coffee grinds in the pot, like she can barely stand on her own.

"What the fuck happened?" I ask her and lean against her refrigerator. Standing across from her, we're only feet apart but it feels like so much farther away. I should know everything that happens. I'll correct that mistake immediately.

"Where do we stand on the debt?" she asks and then clears her throat as the coffee machine rumbles to life.

"I wrote it down; don't have it with me." I give her a bullshit answer and ask again, but harder this time, "What happened?"

Lifting up her head to look me in the eyes, her lips pull down and she tells me in a tight voice, "I wasn't sleeping… not at all since Jenny…" She leaves the remainder unspoken. "So I took those pills you had." She crosses her arms, looking down at the coffee pot and licking her lower lip before telling me, "I'm sorry. It was shitty of me and I don't know why I'm doing so many shitty things, to be honest."

Her arms unfold and she rests her elbows on the counter, like she's talking to the coffee pot instead of me. Her fingers graze her hairline as she keeps going. "That drug doesn't work; I'll tell you that." As she speaks her voice is dampened, although she tries to keep it even. "I had the most awful dream, but it felt so real." I take a tentative step forward, getting closer to her, but am careful to keep far enough back so she won't feel threatened.

She reminds me of a caged animal backed into a corner. One who's given up and given in, but still frightened and not ashamed to admit it. One who would still try to hurt you, and you'd be the one to blame, because it warned you so.

"It was so real, Jase," she whispers and before I can ask what her dream was, she tells me. "Jenny was there, ripping the cover off the book." She turns around to face what little of the living room she can see from this angle. Her hand falls to her side as she peeks up at me.

A deep well of emotions burns in her gaze, enrapturing me and refusing to let me go. "She said I didn't belong there and she wouldn't come back with me." She has to whisper her words, her voice is so fragile. Like she really believed it happened.

"I'm sorry I stole from you, and I'm sorry I even took it. I don't know what's happening to me." Bringing the heels of her hands up to her cheeks she wipes at the stray tears and that's when I hold her, rocking her in my arms and shushing her.

"I hate crying... why am I crying?" Her frustration shows as she holds on to the pain, still not having learned to let it go.

The coffee pot stops, and I can't hear anything. She's stiff in my arms, not crying, but not getting better either.

She's stuck in that moment. The monster in her dreams, following in her shadows.

"You want to go upstairs?"

She doesn't answer right away and I add, "You need to sleep."

It takes a moment, it always does with her, ever defiant, but she nods eventually. She pushes off from the counter, leaving the black coffee to steam in the mug where it sits, knowing it'll go untouched and turn cold.

Her arms stay wrapped around her as she walks up the old stairs, and I follow behind her, listening to the wooden steps creak with every few steps.

I keep a hand splayed on her back and when we make it to the bedroom, she stops outside of the door. "You don't have to babysit me," she tells me, craning her neck to look up at me in the dimly lit hall.

"Maybe I want to lie in bed with you, ever think of that?" I ask her softly, letting the back of my fingers brush her cheek.

She takes my hand in both of hers and opens the door to her bedroom. It's smaller than mine, but nice. Her dresser looks older, maybe an antique like the vanity she has in the corner of her room.

Everything is neatly in place, not a single piece of clothing is out, nothing is askew. Nothing except for the bed. It looks like she just got out of it. The top sheet's a tangled mess and the down comforter is still wrapped up like a cocoon.

"When did you get up?" I ask her.

She shrugs and pulls back the blankets, fixing them as she answers, "I think around three... I don't remember."

"It was almost midnight when you said you were going to bed."

"Yes," is all she answers me.

"Come here." I rip her away from straightening the sheets to hold her, and she clings to me. "It wasn't real," I whisper in her hair.

"I wish..." she pauses, then swallows thickly before confessing, "I wish it was in some way, because at least I got to see her."

Her shoulders shudder in my arms. I don't have words to answer her, so I lay her in bed, helping her with the blankets and climbing in next to her.

The kisses start with the intent to soothe her pain. Letting my lips kiss her jaw, where the tearstains are. Up her neck, to make her feel more.

And she does, she breathes out heavily, keeping her eyes closed and letting her hands linger down my body.

Slowly it turns to more. She deepens the kisses. She holds me closer and demands more.

"You're still in trouble," I whisper against her lips, reminding her that she needs to be punished. Her response is merely a moan as she continues to devour me with her touch.

"Not tonight, but it's coming."

Her eyes open slowly, staring into mine and she whispers, "I know."

"Tell me what you want." I give her the one demand, wanting her to control this. Giving her something I haven't before.

"Don't make this harder on me. Please," she begs me and I nearly turn her onto her belly, to fuck her into the mattress like I've wanted to do since the day I first laid eyes on her, but then she says, "I don't want to beg you for something like... like..."

"Like what?" I ask, not following.

"I don't want to consciously ask... for... for this," she whispers and opens her eyes to look back at me.

It takes a long moment to feel how deep that cut me. Maybe it's the disbelief. "To ask for something ... like for me to fuck you?" My tone doesn't hide a damn thing I'm feeling as I sit up straighter in bed. "Is it offensive? Or do you just not want to admit that you want me?"

"Jase." Bethany wakes in this moment, her eyes more alive than they were downstairs. Brushing the hair out of her face, she sits up straighter, and blinks away the haze of lust.

"Tell me what you want." I give her the request again. Waiting. Every second the fucking agony grows deeper and deeper.

"Jase," she pleads with me. But I ask for so little now. I'm trying to give her everything to make it right, but I need this. "Tell me," I say. The demand comes out hard and her expression falls.

A moment passes and she takes my hand, but her grip is weak.

"Please," she begs me, "I don't want to be alone."

"I know that, but you don't want to be with me either. Do you? We shouldn't be doing this anyway." I say the words without thinking. I know we've both thought it. That what this is today isn't what it was that night I had her sign the contract. And two nights ago, we should have parted ways. It's volatile and wrong. Being with her is going to be my downfall, I already know it.

And yet here I am waiting for her answer, because she's the only one of the two of us who has the balls to admit out loud that we shouldn't be together.

She hesitates, although she doesn't deny it. She doesn't say anything. The silence grows between us, separating us and making it seem as if the last time we were together never happened.

Thump, there's the dull pain in my chest. It flourishes inside of me as I stand there in silence.

"After what I did for you, I deserve better than that," I snap back. It fucking hurts.

There's a splintering sensation in my chest as if the absence of her words truly injured me more than that cut she gave me the other night. Only one will scar.

Her lips turn down as she swallows, making her throat tight. Her inhale quivers but instead of saying anything, she shakes her head, her hair sweeping around her shoulders as she looks away.

Nothing. She gives me nothing and with that I turn my back to her, slamming the door shut behind me. As hard as I can. The force of it travels up my arm, lingering as I walk away from her.

I could tell her she still owes me; I could tell her that. But right now, I don't want to.

An awful sound travels down the hall, following me. A sob she tries to cover. The kind you hope comes out silent, but it's ragged and fierce. My footsteps thunder behind me as I take the stairs as quickly as I can.

The kind of sobs that you can't control. The kind that hurt.

Both the pounding of my shoes as I leave and the evidence of her misery, both are uncontrolled and painful.

I have seen so much brokenness in my short life. I hate it. I hate how easily everything can be destroyed and wasted. It's so useless to live day by day, not just seeing it all around you, but making it so.

Standing at the bottom of her stairs, with one hand on the wall and the other gripping the banister, I listen to her cry. Crying for me? And the pain she's caused me? Crying for herself and how alone and empty her life truly is? Crying for us?

And it takes me back to the time I heard similar cries. A time I left.

And I remember what was left of me when I came back to see the damage done.

My body tenses and my throat dries as I stand in between the man I was before and the man I'll be tomorrow.

Tonight is mine regardless and knowing that, I turn on my heels and make my way back up the stairs as quickly as I can, pushing her door open without knocking. Her wide eyes fly to mine as I kick the door shut behind me.

"Jase?" She whispers my name in the same way the snow falls around us. Gentle and hopeful the fall won't last for long.

She moves on the bed, making a spot for me easily enough although her eyes are still wide and searching for answers. She stays sitting up even though I climb in and lie down back where I was, pulling the covers over my clothes.

It's too hot, but it's better than taking the time to do something other than lie down with her.

Patting the bed, I tell her to lie down, noting how gruff my voice is. How raw.

"Are you angry?" she asks and I tell her I've always been.

Molding her small body to mine, she rests her hands on my chest, still wary, still exhausted. Still hoping for more. "I'm sorry," she whispers and I tell her so am I.

Hope is a long way of saying goodbye. Even I know that.

Her hair tickles my nose when I kiss the crown of her head. The covers rustle as I move my arm around her, rubbing soothing circles on her back.

Time marches on and with it the memories of long ago play in my mind. Making me regretful. Making me question everything.

"Why did you come back?" she asks me before brushing her cheek against my chest and planting a small kiss in the dip just beneath my throat.

I confess a truth she could use against me. Even knowing that, still I admit, "I don't want you to be alone either."

chapter twenty-one

Jase

THE SNOW'S FALLING. It's only a light dusting, but it decided to come right this moment, right as my brother leads his love across the cemetery.

One grave has been there for half her life. The one next to it has freshly upturned dirt. The snow covers each of the graves equally as Aria silently mourns, her body shaking slightly against Carter's chest.

I spoke to her father only days before he met his death. A death he knew was coming. A death that always comes for men like us.

The powerful man asked me to find a way. Swallowing his pride when he thought his daughter was going to die because of him.

Talvery wasn't ready to lose his daughter. She swears he was going to kill her.

That's the irony in it all.

He was a bad man. And that's the crux of the problem. She expected him to do bad things, even if she loved him in his last days, although I don't believe she did love him anymore.

She swears he was going to shoot her, but there was only one gun cocked and it wasn't her father's. She heard it, she speaks of it, but she doesn't realize what really happened and I don't have the heart to tell her.

The man who pulled the trigger confessed to me. He said in the old man's last breaths, he laid down his gun and said goodbye to his daughter. But she didn't see, clinging to a man she loved and not to the man who gave up fighting to ensure she would be loved one more day.

That's what this life brings. A twisted love of betrayal. A reality that is unjust and riddled with deceit.

Aria lays a single rose across her mother's grave, but not her father's, even though when he called me, he said he would give up everything right then and there, if I promised we'd keep her safe.

There was no negotiation we could offer.

Her father had to die. And Aria was never in harm's way. The man had nothing to barter with, not when he knew we'd take it all. I never told Carter. And I never will. The perception that her father was a ruthless crime lord past his date of redemption is what makes it okay. It makes it righteous that she only lays a rose down for her mother, a woman who betrayed everyone to benefit herself.

Watching Carter hold her hand, kiss her hair and comfort her, only reminds me of what could have been. If the gun cocked had been Talvery's and my brother was in that grave instead.

Bright lights reflect a section of falling snow. Headlights from a cop car pulling in across the parking lot I'm sitting in.

Gripping the steering wheel tighter, I take into account everyone here. It's only me, still in the driver's seat waiting for Carter to bring Aria back and the sole cop parking his vehicle across from mine.

Before Carter has a chance to look behind him, taking attention away from Aria, I message him. *I've got it. Stay with her.*

A second passes, and another before Carter looks down at the message, back at me, and then to the cop, who opens his door in that moment.

Officer Walsh.

The sound of his door closing echoes in the vacant air. It's hollow and reflects its own surroundings.

As I open my car door, welcoming the cold air, breathing it in and letting it bite across my skin, I nod at Carter, who nods in return, holding Aria closer, but not making a move to leave.

The snow crunches beneath my shoes, soft and gentle as it falls. It vanishes beneath my footprints as I make my way around to the front of my car, leaning against it and waiting for him.

As I take in the officer, a crooked smile forms on my face. We're wearing the same coat. A dark gray wool blend. "Nice coat, Officer Walsh," I greet him and offer a hand. He's hesitant to accept, but he does.

Meeting him toe to toe, eye to eye, his grip is strong.

"So you've heard of me?" he asks. I lick my lower lip, looking over my shoulder to check on Carter one more time before I answer him, "I heard someone was asking about me, someone who fit your description."

"Funny," he answers with a hint of humor in his voice, although his pale blue eyes are only assessing. "I heard the same about you."

"That I was asking about you?" I ask with feigned shock as I bring my thumb up to point back at me. "I only asked who was asking about me and my club."

"The Red Room." The officer's voice lowers and his gaze narrows as he speaks. He slips his hands into his coat pockets and I wait for more, simply nodding at his words.

Some cops are easy to pay off. They need money, they want power, or even just to feel like they're high on life and fitting into a world they could only dream of running themselves.

I can spot them easily. The way they walk, talk—shit, even the clothes they wear on their time off. It's all so fucking obvious. The only question that needs answering is: how much do I need to pay them until they're in my back pocket?

Not Cody Walsh.

"What is it that you want, Officer?" I ask him and then add, "Anything I can help you with?"

"Anything you had in mind?" he asks in return, tilting his chin back and waiting.

The smirk on my face grows. "I don't dislike having conversations with cops." I follow his previous gaze just as he looks back at me and see Carter and Aria making their way back to the car that's still running. "But I don't really like to start a conversation either."

He's playing me. Thinking I'll try to bribe him for nothing. What a fucking prick.

"Is that his wife?" he asks me, and I tell him the truth. "His fiancée."

"Aria Talvery," he comments.

"You know a lot of names for being new around here."

"It's my job," he answers defensively.

"Is it?" I rock back on my shoes as I slip my hands into my pockets. My warm breath turns to fog in the air. "You know everyone's name who you pull over then?" I ask him.

"Not unless their name is in the file of the case I'm working on."

"A case?" I ask him as the cold air runs over my skin, seeping through my muscles and deep down into the marrow of my bones. I feel the shards of ice everywhere, but I don't show it. "It's the first time I'm hearing about a case."

"A house burned down, killing over a dozen men, explosives."

"Aria's family home," I remark, acknowledging him with a nod. "What a tragedy."

"It was arson, and one of a string of violent crimes that leads back to you and your brothers."

With the sound of the car door opening behind me, indicating Carter is helping Aria into the backseat, my patience is gone.

"If you have questions, you can ask my lawyer."

"I don't have any for you," he tells me and I huff a humorless laugh before responding, "Then why come to pay this visit?"

"I wanted to see her reaction; if she was remorseful at all."

"Aria?" The shock is apparent in my tone and my expression, because I didn't hide it in the least. I shouldn't be speaking her name. I shouldn't even engage with this fucker. And that's the only reason I'm silent when he adds, "Knowing she's sleeping with her father's killer…"

He shakes his head, although his eyes never leave mine.

"Is that all then?" I ask him.

A moment passes, and with it comes a gust of cold wind. Each day's been more bitter than the last and with a snowstorm coming, the worst is yet to come.

"That's all," he says and then his eyes drift to my windshield before he adds, "And pay your parking tickets. Wouldn't want that to be what gets you."

All I give him is a short wave, right before snatching a small piece of paper off the windshield. It's not a parking ticket, it's a thick piece of yellow paper folded in half. It's been here for a while, partially covered by the snow. And knowing that, I look back to see if Walsh is watching. His eyes are on Carter, not me. Thank fuck.

I don't know who the fuck left it, but I'm not going to figure that out while under the watchful eyes of Officer Walsh.

Lacking any emotion at all, I bid the man farewell. "Have a good night, Officer."

With my back to Walsh I share a glance with Carter, who's waiting by the backseat door on the driver's side, one hand on the handle, his other hand in his pocket.

"You too," the officer calls out in the bitterly cold air, already making his way back to his car.

It's silent when I close the door. Aria tries to speak, but I hear Carter shush her, telling her to wait for the officer to leave. Peeking at her in the rearview mirror, worry clouds her tired eyes.

"Everything's fine," Carter reassures her and she lays her cheek, bright red from the frigid air, onto his shoulder.

My gaze moves from the cop car, reversing out of the spot, to the note. The sound of the thick paper opening is all I pay attention to as Officer Walsh drives away, leaving us alone in the parking lot.

A sharp ringing in my ear accompanies my slow breaths and the freezing sensation that takes over when I glance at the note, a script font I recognize as Marcus's.

How the fuck did he leave a note? And when? I read his message and then read it again. The psychopath speaks in riddles.

You took my pawn. I have another.
The game hasn't stopped. It's only changed slightly.
Just remember, the king can only hope to be a pawn when his queen is gone.

Every hair on my body stands on end after reading the note, knowing he was here. How the fuck did I not see him?

"What's wrong?" Carter asks me as I reach for my phone, needing to tell Seth and everyone else what happened and get security footage immediately.

But Seth's already texted me.

And I sit there motionless in my seat, reading what he wrote as Carter bites out my name, demanding an answer I don't have to give.

We found the sister.
She's alive.
Marcus has her.

chapter twenty-two

Bethany

I CAN'T STOP READING. WHEN I DO, I HAVE TO FACE REALITY AND I'M NOT READY TO FACE THE consequences of my decisions yet. I'd rather get lost in the pages.

Every time they kiss, I think of Jase Cross.

I think I love him.

I love my enemy.

Why couldn't I be like the characters in this book? Why couldn't I be like Emmy and fall for the boy who loves her just as much and the only thing they have keeping them apart, is whether or not they're both still breathing?

Why did I have to fall for a villain? Maybe that's what I deserve. Deep down inside though, I don't think I even deserve him.

Books are a portal to another world, but they lead to other places too. To places deep inside you still filled with hope and a desperate need for love. Places where your loneliness doesn't exist, because you know how it can be filled.

Jase isn't a good man, but he's not a bad one either. I refuse to believe it. He's a damaged man with secrets I know are lurking beneath his charming facade, a man with a dark past that threatens to dictate who he will become.

And I think I love him.

I can't bring myself to tell him that. I just had the chance a moment ago when he told me he wasn't able to come tonight because he was with his brother and Carter needed him.

But he still asked if I needed anything. I could have told him I miss him. I could have messaged him more. Instead, I simply told him I would be ready for him when he wanted me.

The constant thumping in my chest gets harder and rises higher. I have to swallow it down just so I can breathe. This was never supposed to happen. How could I have fallen for a man like him?

I'm drowning in the abyss, and he's the only one there to hold me. That's how. I need to remember that.

He made it that way, didn't he?

The sound of the radiator kicking on disrupts the quiet living room. I take the moment to have a sip of tea, careful not to disturb the open book in my lap. The warmth of the mug against my lips is nothing compared to Jase's kiss.

With my eyes closed, I vow to think clearly, to step back and be smart about all of this. Even though deep inside, I know there is no way that means I could ever stay with Jase Cross, and the very thought destroys something deep inside of me. Splintering it and causing a pain that forces me to put the cup down and sink back into the sofa, covering myself with the blanket and staring at the black and white words on the page.

It all hurts when I think about leaving him.

That's how I know I've fallen.

The Coverless Book
Eighth Chapter

Jake's perspective

"Kiss me again?" Emmy's voice is soft and delicate. It fits her, but she's so much more.

"You like it when I kiss you?" I tease her and that bright pink blush rises up her cheeks.

"Shhh, she'll hear us," she says as her small hands press against my chest, pushing me to the side so she can glance past me and toward the hallway to the kitchen.

"Miss Caroline knows I kiss you." I smile as I push some strands of hair behind her ear, but it falls slowly. It should be her mother who Emmy's afraid will catch us. But her mother is never here.

"Maybe go check on her?" Emmy asks, scooting me off the chair. "See what she's doing and if we have a little more time?"

It's her elation that draws me to her. There are some people in this world who you love to see smile. It makes you warm inside and it feels like everything will be all right, if only they smile.

That's all I can think as I round the corner to the kitchen. I've only been here to Emmy's house twice, but I know the help's kitchen is through one of these two doors. I'm right on the first guess and there's Caroline, hovering over the large pot with a skinny bottle above it. Clear liquid is being poured into the steaming pot of soup.

Although I'd planned to offer to help, just so I can gauge how much time we have, my words are stolen.

The glass bottle she's holding doesn't look like it belongs in a kitchen. I feel a deep crease form between my furrowed brows and I stare for far too long as she pours more and more into the pot. She's humming as she does. A sweet tune I'm sure would lull babies to their dreams.

Emmy has soup every night. Every night the caretaker makes her soup. And Emmy stays sick, every day.

"What did you put in there?" My question comes out hard and when Miss Caroline jumps, the liquid spills over the oven and the bottle crashes onto the floor with her startled cry.

I debate on grabbing the notebook from the kitchen counter where I left it. Just so I can add to the collection of underlined sentences. I'm reading without really paying attention, just letting the time go by.

My gaze skims the page, finding four sentences underlined this time and none of the four hold any new meaning. One is the same as it's been for a while now. *I'm invincible.*

If it weren't for the distraction of this story, the suspense and the emotion, I'd feel hopeless. I'm hopeless when it comes to Jase.

If hope is a long way of saying goodbye, hopeless can only mean one of two things. As the thought plays in my mind, my thumb brushes along my bottom lip and I stare at the page.

And that's when I see it. What I've been waiting for. What I was so sure was here.

A chill spreads across my skin as the mug slips from my hand, dropping to the floor, crashing into pieces. If the letters weren't staring right at me, I never would have seen them.

It's not the underlined sentences. *It's the lines below them.* The first letters of the sentences *beneath* the pen marks. C. R. O. S. S. She buried the message so deep, I didn't see it before.

At first it hits me she left me a message, and there's hope. And then I read the word again.

C. R. O. S. S.

"No." The word is whispered from me, but not with conscious consent. My head shakes and my fingers tremble as I stare at the evidence.

C. R. O. S. S.

She did leave a note. My blood turns to ice at the thought. Jenny left me a message in this book, and it has to do with the Cross brothers.

"No." I repeat the word as I lay the book down, although not gently, but forcefully, as if it will bite me if I hold it any longer. I nearly trip over the throw blanket in my rush to get off the sofa.

Thump, thump, thump. Ever present and ever painful, my bastard heart races inside of me.

My limbs are wobbly as I rush to the kitchen, searching for the notebook. I need to write it down. "Write it all down," I speak in hushed and rushed words as I pull open one drawer in the kitchen, jostling the pens, a pair of scissors, and papers and everything else in the junk drawer. It slams shut as I bring the notebook to my chest, ready to face the book. To face the message Jenny left me.

Knowing she wrote something about the Cross brothers.

Knowing Jase Cross lied to me.

They had something to do with her murder. Maybe even him.

Tears leak from my eyes as I stumble in the kitchen.

"No," I whisper, and force myself to stand. *It will say something else.* I tell myself it will, and the sinful whisper in my head reminds me, *Hope is a long way of saying goodbye.*

Swallowing down my heart and nerves, I push myself to stand, only to hear a creak.

Thump, goes my heart, and this time the beat comes with fear.

I couldn't have heard that right. No one is coming. No one is here, I tell myself, even though my blood still rushes inside of me, begging me to run, warning me that something's wrong, that someone's here who isn't supposed to be.

I keep silent and hear the sound of my front door.

Thump. Terror betrays my instincts. Stealing my breath and making me lightheaded.

The foyer floor creaks again and the front door closes, softly. A gentle push. A quiet one meant not to disturb.

The creaking moves closer and I listen to it with only the harsh sound of my subdued breath competing with it.

And I'm too afraid to even whisper, "Who's there?"

a single kiss

From *USA Today* best-selling author Willow Winters comes a gripping, heart-wrenching tale of romantic suspense that will keep you on the edge of your seat.

I should feel shame for not wanting this to end, but he doesn't want it to end either.

When the darkness sets in with the flames all flickered out, and the loud click of the locks signal it's over, that's when reality comes flooding back.

The war. The drugs. All of the lies that weave a tangled web for me to get lost in.

I don't want any of it.

I only want him. Jase Cross. My enemy. And yet, the only person I trust.

With broad shoulders and a smoldering look in his dark eyes, Jase is a man born to be powerful.

I shouldn't give him more power than he already has…

Jase Cross will be my downfall.

A Single Kiss is Book 2 of the Irresistible Attraction series. *A Single Glance* must be read first.

"Grief does not change you, Hazel. It reveals you."
—John Green, *The Fault in Our Stars*

prologue

Jase

It's odd the things you remember in the midst of fear. Fourteen years later, and I still recall the cracks in the cement; the sidewalks were littered with them. This particular one though... I remember it in vivid detail, probably because of what happened immediately after.

Against the old brick building of the corner store, a green vine had found its way through the broken cement and climbed up the wall. I remember thinking it had no business being there. The crack belonged, but the new life that had sprouted up and borne what looked like a closed flower wasn't supposed to be there. Nothing beautiful belonged on that street.

The dim streetlight revealed how lively it was, even that late at night. With shades of green on the perfect vine and its single leaf with the bud of a flower just waiting to bloom, it made me pause. And in that moment, I hated that it was there.

I was almost eleven and maybe that childishness is why I scraped my shoe against the leaf and stem, ripping and tearing them until the green seemed to bleed against the rough and faded red bricks. I know I wasn't quite eleven, because Mama died right before my birthday that year. It was her medicine that almost fell out of the overfilled paper bag I was gripping so tight as I continued to kick at the wall before feeling all the anger and hate well up and form tears in my eyes.

Life wasn't fair. Back then I was just learning that truth, or at least I'd felt it somewhere deep in my bones, although I hadn't yet said it out loud.

Mama was getting sicker. Dad's condition was getting worse too, although he couldn't use cancer as an excuse. Thinking about the two of them, I continued to kick the wall even though my sneakers were too thin and it hurt to do so. The bottles the clerk had given me to give my dad clinked against one another in the bag, egging me on to keep kicking until I felt a pain that I'd given myself. A pain I deserved.

All the while, the bottles clinked.

That's what I had gone out to get, even as my stomach rumbled. I had enough money left over to get something to eat, but Dad always demanded the receipt. If he saw that I spent his change, I knew it'd be bad. I knew better than to take his money. Times were hard and I would eat what I was given to eat and do what I was told to do.

I picked up the medicine and beer for my folks on the way home from dropping off something at a classmate's house on the other side of town. Maybe a book I'd borrowed. Those details are fuzzy over a decade later. I didn't have many friends but a couple of students pitied me. I was the smallest one in the class and we couldn't buy everything I needed for school. The other kids didn't mind letting me borrow their things every once in a while. I never asked the same person in the same week and I always gave stuff back promptly. Mama always smiled when I told her I'd just gotten home from giving things back to my friends. I told her they were my friends, but I knew better. She didn't though.

I'm not sure what I'd returned that night or to who. Only that I had to go by the corner store on the way home.

None of that mattered enough to remember, but the damn flower I'd killed, I remember that.

It was the shame of nearly crying that made me take that detour, right at the damaged sidewalk that was free of what wasn't supposed to be there anymore. I cried a lot and that's why everyone looked at me the way they did. The teachers, the other kids, the clerk at the corner store. They always got a certain look on their faces when they saw the dirty, skinny kid whose mother was dying.

They didn't look at my older brothers that way. They were trouble and I was just... not enough of anything other than a kid to feel sorry for.

I stalked down the alley to hide my face in the darkness, only to meet a man I thought was a figment of everyone's imagination.

He was like the boogeyman or Santa Claus; all myths I didn't believe in.

A lot of people called him the Grim Reaper, but I knew his name was Marcus. It's what my brothers called him. I thought they were messing with me when they'd told me stories about him, right up until I looked into Carter's eyes and he shook my shoulders because I wouldn't listen.

Don't ask for Marcus, don't talk about him. If you hear his name, run the other way. Stay the fuck away from Marcus.

Swallowing thickly, I remember the harsh look of fear that Carter never allowed to cloud his expression and his tone that chilled my spine.

The second I lifted up my head about halfway down that alley, staring at where I'd heard a soft cough in the darkness, in that moment, I knew it was him.

I thought I knew fear before that night. But no monster I'd conjured under the bed ever made my body react like it did when I saw his dark eyes focused on me. His breath fogged in front of him and that was all I could see as my grip involuntarily tightened on the paper bag. It was late, dark and cold. From the icy chill on my skin, down to my blood and even deeper to the core of what makes a person who they are, suddenly it was freezing.

So I stood motionless, paralyzed in place and unable to run even though every instinct inside of me was screaming for me to do so.

I remember how gracefully he jumped down from his perch atop a stack of crates, still hidden in the darkness. The dull thump of his shoes hitting the asphalt made my heart lurch inside of my chest.

"What do you want?" I braved the words without conscious consent. As bitterly cold as I'd been seconds ago, sweat began to bead on my skin. Sweat that burned hotter than I'd ever felt, knowing I dared to speak to a man who would surely kill me before answering my question.

A flash of bright white emerged in the blackness as he bared a sick grin. I could feel my eyes squint as I searched desperately for his face. I wanted to at least see him, see the man who'd kill me. I'd heard the worst thing you could see before you die was the face of the person who ends your life. But growing up here, I knew it wasn't true. The worst thing you could see were the people all around you who could help, but instead chose to do nothing and continue walking on by.

The streets were quiet behind me, and somewhere deep inside, I was grateful for that. At least if I begged for help, no one would be there to deny me a chance to be saved. It would end and there would be no hope. Having no hope somehow made it better.

"Your brother has an interesting choice of friends."

Again my heart spasmed, pumping hard and violently.

My brother.

I was going to lose my mother; I knew I would soon. She was holding on as hard as she could, but she'd told me to be strong when the time came and that was a damn hard pill to swallow. I'd already lost what semblance of a father I had.

My brothers…. they were all I had left. I suppose life is meant to be suffered through loss after loss. That would explain why the Grim Reaper showed up, whispering about my brother.

I don't know how I managed to answer him, the man who stayed in the shadows, but I questioned, "Which brother?"

He laughed. It echoed in the narrow alley, a dark and gruff chuckle.

For years that followed, every time I heard footsteps behind me or thought I saw a figure in the night, I heard that laugh in the depths of my mind. Taunting me.

I heard it again when my mother died, loud and clear as if he was there in that empty kitchen. It was present at her grave, when I saw my closest brother dead in the street, when my father was murdered and I went to identify his body—even when I first killed a man out of vengeance when I was nineteen years old.

That demeaning laugh would haunt me because I knew he was watching. He was watching me die slowly in this wretched world and yet, he did nothing.

"Carter," he finally answered me. "He's making friends he shouldn't."

"How would you know?" I asked without hesitating, even though inside I felt like a twisted rag, devoid of air and feeling.

"I know everything, Jase Cross," he told me, moving closer to me even as I stepped back. The step was quick, too quick and the one free hand I had crashed behind me against the rough brick wall from the liquor shop. It left a small and inconsequential gash just below my middle knuckle. Eventually the gash became a scar, forming a physical memory of Marcus's warning that night. His laugh stayed in my mind after that night, and like my scar, served as a permanent reminder of him over the years.

He neared the dim strip of light from the full moon overhead, the bit that leaked into the alley, but still he didn't show himself.

I nearly dropped the bag in my grasp when he came even closer and I had nowhere to go.

"I have a message for you to deliver to him," he told me. "If he ever goes against me, your entire family will suffer the consequences."

"Carter?" I breathed his name, shaking my head out of instinct from knowing Carter hadn't done anything. "He doesn't know anyone. You have the wrong person."

All he did was laugh again, the same sick sound coming up from the pit of his stomach. I repeated in the breath of a whisper, "Carter hasn't done anything."

"Not yet, but he will." The words were spoken with such confidence from the darkness. "And I'll be watching."

He left me standing there, on the verge of trembling as he walked away. The pounding in my chest was louder than his quiet footsteps although I didn't dare breathe.

That was the first night I met the man I would now call my enemy. Whatever fear I had for him as a child has turned to resentment and spite.

That's all he is. He's only a man. A man with no face, a hefty bag of threats and a penchant for eliciting fear in all who dare to walk the streets he claims as his own.

These aren't his streets. He has no right to them, but I do.

He treats this world like a game; the lives and deaths of those around us are only pieces on a board to be lost or taken, used however he'd like.

But the mistake he made is simple: He dared to meddle and bring Bethany into this game.

She's mine. Only mine.

Not a pawn for him to play with.

It's time for Marcus's game to end.

chapter one

Bethany

F*uck. Fuck. Fuck. Fuck. Fuck.* A numb prickle of fear races up and down my body like a thousand needles keeping me still. All the while, my heart's the only thing that's moving. It's frantic and unyielding as it thrashes inside of me.

The floorboards creak again as someone moves toward the stairs while I keep my feet firmly planted in the kitchen. *Someone.* Who? I don't know.

No one has ever walked into my home unannounced and I know it's not Laura; I know it's not Jase. Just thinking his name sends another chill down my spine. The fear, the regret, the unknown from what I just read in The Coverless Book are all things I can't dwell on right now. Blinking furiously, I shut the wayward trail of thoughts down.

No, it's not Jase.

It's someone else, someone with bad intentions. Deep down, I can feel it.

If I'd just been back in the living room when the door opened, back there where I was a moment ago, reading The Coverless Book and using this notebook to jot down the underlined words... if I'd been there, whoever just opened the door would have seen me instantly. If I'd left the notebook in the living room, and not in the drawer in the kitchen, whoever it was, would have seen me. I wouldn't have had a chance to run.

Fate spared me, but for how long?

My fingers tremble as I silently set the notebook down on the counter, devising a plan.

Get my phone. Run the hell out of here. Call the cops.

It's as simple as that. If I can't get the phone, *just run.*

Whoever it is, they're heading upstairs and once I hear the creaking from the floorboards move from the stairs to one of the bedrooms, I'll move as quickly and quietly as possible. I can barely keep it together while I'm waiting, listening, and feeling the numbing fear flowing over my skin.

Hot and cold sensations overwhelm my body at once and I don't know how I'm even capable of breathing with how tight and raw and dry my throat is. All I know is that I can't fail. I can't let him know where I am.

My movements are measured as I release the notebook. The second I do, I hear another person open my front door. *Thump, thump, thump.* My heartbeat is louder than anything else. Another person's here. I'm not in control as I instinctively back away from the threshold of the kitchen, closer toward the back of the house.

One person and then another.

Thump, thump, thump.

Abandoning all reason, I turn my back to where they are, ready to hide somewhere as quickly as possible. *Somewhere. Where? Where can I hide?* My head whirls with panic. I need to hide.

My body freezes when I hear my phone go off. It's still where I left it in the next room over, the living room. Footsteps come closer, closer to me, closer to the threshold of the kitchen where they can see me. *No, fuck, please no.* Inwardly I beg; I plead.

I'm trapped in the narrow kitchen with three people sneaking into my home. I can't die here. Not like this. Not after everything that's happened. It would be more than cruel to make me suffer in the last weeks of my life, like this.

I know if whoever it is stops at the coffee table where my phone is, he won't be able to see into the galley kitchen, but that won't stop him from moving on once he picks up my cell. Even more, he'll know for certain I'm here. I wouldn't leave without my phone, so they'll know. *Fuck!*

Thump, thump, thump. I wish I could quiet the pulse that's banging in my ears faster by the second.

Forcing myself to calm down and think as I hear a murmur from only ten... maybe twelve feet away in the other room, I focus on anywhere I could conceal myself. The pantry is the obvious solution, but it's so full, there's no way. Plus the shelves come out too far.

With numb fingers, I pry open the cabinet door for the recycling. The bin is still outside where I left it for pickup yesterday. It'll be cramped, but I think I can squeeze myself into the small space. I don't know the chances they'd open every cabinet of the kitchen, but I don't have anywhere else to hide.

My feet are heavy and my limbs rigid. I'm not as quiet as I wish I was. But I'm quick. I'm damn quick as I cram myself inside of the cabinet, the faint scent of spilled wine that's leaked from empty bottles hitting me at full force, along with other less than desirable odors.

I couldn't give two shits about what it smells like. All I care about is if they heard. *Please, please.* The telltale sound of shoes on the tile lets me know someone's here.

The weight of the steps is heavy; they have to be from a man. Both hands cover my mouth out of an instinct to be quiet, just as my eyes slam shut tight and refuse to look. I pray he didn't hear. If he heard the sound of a cabinet... *fuck. Please, no.*

I swear whoever it is can hear my ragged breaths and the ringing in my ears that's so fucking loud I can barely hear them walk into the kitchen. Them. Multiple footsteps.

Fuck, fuck, fuck, fuck.

I can't think about it. I can't be here right now. Not my mind. The stress and fear wrap around my body like barbed wire, tightening by the second and forcing me to fight it, to move, to react. I can't be here. This can't be happening.

Go somewhere else. My own words, words I've told patients many times slip into my consciousness. *Go somewhere else.*

"Have you ever thought about what it would be like to be pregnant?" my mother asks me with a devious grin. Her knee rocks back and forth as she sits in the chair, playing with her long hair that's draped over one shoulder. "Like, to be Talia right now? Could you imagine?"

I was hoping she'd remember today, but at least she's talking. That's good, I tell myself. It's good that she's happy today, in whatever time she's living in, it was a happy one for her.

"Who's Talia?" I ask her, feigning the curiosity I think she'd expect from whoever it is she thinks she's talking to. It's never me. She never knows it's me.

"You know, the blonde in Mr. Spears's class. She's almost six months along now," my mother says, enjoying the gossip.

"Mr. Spears?"

"Tenth grade English. The really tall one and kind of young? I think he's hot."

My mother's comment makes me smile. I wish I were back in high school. She didn't have Alzheimer's then.

"So have you thought about it?" she questions again and I shake my head honestly.

"I can't imagine having kids right now."

"I can. I want a boy. A boy with James Peters's eyes and smile."

"James Peters." I repeat the boy's name and set two cups of water down on the end table.

"One day I'm going to ask him out."

"What if you have a girl?" I ask her.

"Oh no," she says and shakes her head. "Girls are too much trouble." I have to remind myself that she's only a teenager today. I'm sure all teenagers think that. They have perceptions before having kids.

I remind myself of it but still, I have to get up and get away. Just for a minute.

"Where are you going? Is class starting soon? I thought we had another half hour of lunch?"

"We do," I answer her, forcing a smile. "I just have to do something."

"You forgot your books, didn't you, Maggie?" She taunts me. "You're so forgetful."

I can feel it when I hit my breaking point. It's not getting easier like I thought it would.

Resting against the wall in the kitchen, all I can do is breathe. All I can do is hide from my mother and hide from the truth.

"Does Mom remember?" Jenny's question comes from the threshold of the kitchen. She leans against it with a mug in her hand although I can smell the whiskey from here. I'm not sure if it's in her mug or just a leftover stench from wherever she was last night.

"No," I answer her.

She takes a sip in response and with it, I'm given an answer to my own unspoken question. It's nine in the morning and the whiskey is in the cup she's currently clinging to.

"She's talking about having kids right now. Back in high school."

"Kids," my sister repeats, rolling her eyes and taking another sip.

"Yeah, she said she wants daughters." I don't know why the lie slipped out. I think I just wanted to comfort my sister.

My sister throws the mug back, downing its contents before tossing it into the sink.

"Really? She told me the other day she'd hate to have daughters."

A bang close by brings me back to now. Back to the present. Away from my sister and away from my mother.

My eyes open unhurriedly, not wanting to see but forcing myself to take in anything I can in the dark space. Tremors run through my legs and up my spine to my shoulders, leaving goosebumps in their wake. With a single unsteady exhale, I stare through the bright slit in the cabinet door as faded, broken-in blue jeans show themselves. I can see the seams and the stitching even. He's that close to me. Just behind the door. I nearly whimper when the creak of the pantry closet proves he's searching for me.

He heard me moving around in the kitchen. I feel lightheaded for a moment, maybe from fear, maybe from holding my breath.

A buzzing from the other room makes him turn on his heels and I watch all the while with both hands over my mouth, my palms sweaty and clammy. He stands still as the other person walks out of the kitchen. They're louder now, reckless and bold as they open doors and search for something or someone.

It doesn't have to be me. Please, don't let what they're looking for be me. Be looking for something Jenny left here. Please, for the love of God, be that. Find it. Find it and get out.

The thoughts don't go unanswered. Fate lets me know the worst-case scenario is in fact my reality.

"Her car is still in the driveway. You think she heard us and ran?" A muted voice I don't recognize is coming from the living room. Another voice, one from farther away, maybe in the foyer answers, "Nah, she has to be here still. She wouldn't leave her phone."

The man just beyond the cabinet door walks away swiftly and moves toward the voice—that's when I catch a glimpse of the red stripes on his white sneakers. A single horizontal stripe runs along the length of each shoe midway up the side. White shoes with red stripes. I can hear him smack the man after a gruff response from his throat and then it's quiet again.

The man who was so close to me knows better than to talk and give away their thoughts.

Thump, thump, thump. They don't say another word as I inhale the musty smells from the cabinetry, willing my body to obey me and not betray my position.

Every time a loud bang or the crash of something being overturned startles me, my shoulders push harder against the rough wood behind my back and I bite down on the inside of my cheek to silence the instinctive scream.

My nails dig deeper into my skin on my thighs as the bangs get closer and louder. It's obvious they're trashing the place. All the while, I pray. *Please don't find me. Please leave.*

For a moment, I think they might.

The recognizable noise of the front door opening is suddenly clear. As are the sounds of them leaving, one by one, but I don't believe they're truly gone. It's too obvious. It's a trick and a trap; one I won't be caught in. Time passes, each second seeming longer and longer, gauged by the steady ticking of the clock above the kitchen sink.

All I can think about is every time a girl is in the middle of the woods running from someone in the movies. She hides behind a tree or bush—something that offers her a hidden spot—and she waits until she thinks they've run by and can't hear them anymore. She thinks they've moved on, as if they've kept running through the tall trees and didn't see her. She doesn't hear them, so she takes off.

That's when they catch her. They know she's hiding and they're just waiting until she comes out to snatch her up.

Not me. They won't catch me that way. For the first time since I heard someone come in, strength and conviction outweigh the fear. I'll stay here until I know for certain it's safe.

I don't know what these men wanted with me, but I know they were looking for me and that's all the reason I need to stay right where I fucking am.

My body stays tense for I don't even know how long. It feels like maybe ten minutes. Only ten minutes or so, maybe twenty? I can't track the sound of the clock; it's going too fast and then too slow and then it blurs together and I can't focus on it. It feels hotter and hotter in this small space, but I don't waver. Never daring to move. Not even after it's silent. With stiff legs and an aching back, I finally lower my hands and that's when I realize how my neck is bent. It hurts; everything hurts from being shoved in this small space and hunched over, crouched down. My ankle dares to stretch forward, causing my toes to brush against the cabinet door.

Did they really leave?

Not a sound is heard when the cabinet pushes open, ever so slightly. I didn't do it on purpose, I just needed to move.

Nothing happens. There's no sign they're still here and I could see myself sneaking out slowly, risking a look.

I still don't trust it though. What happens if they're right outside and they see through the windows that I'm here? A black vision passes before my eyes and my head falls back, feeling the anxiety rush through me.

Staying as still and as silent as I can be, I wait, praying for a sign that I'm safe.

All I'm given is silence. God didn't answer my prayers for my sister. Why would he answer me now?

For the longest time, there's nothing but silence. The tick of the clock goes on and on, and I endure it. Not daring to move.

And then everything happens all at once.

The slam of the front door, and then the back door to the garage. My hands whip up to my mouth to cover the silent scream as my entire body tenses and my skin scrapes against the wooden walls of my hiding spot.

The crash of glass breaking, I think a window in the back room, makes my shoulders hunch and I wish I could hide even further back. All of it is followed by the sound of tires squealing from outside my house. At least two cars. At least three men. And one with a pair of white shoes with red stripes.

I don't think I inhale the entire time. It doesn't seem like they came back in. They merely broke something from the outside. Did they throw something inside the house? A bomb? That's the first place my head goes. They threw a bomb in here and I'm going to die anyway. Still, I can't move and nothing happens.

There's no noise, no explosion. Just silence again.

Possibilities run furiously through my mind as I try to calm down. The back of my head rests against the wood as my thoughts turn dark. I think about how desperate I was to move, and how they were right there waiting. How close I was to playing into their trap.

I don't have long to drown in gratitude and the horror of what could have been. Maybe five or ten minutes go by before I hear another car. That's all the time that passes from the squeal of one set of tires leaving and then the shriek of another set slamming to a halt in front of my house.

I nearly upheave at the prospect of what they came back to do.

The front door opens, loud with intention, banging off the wall. Then I faintly hear a gun cock, followed by his voice.

Jase.

"Bethany!" Although he screams my name with a demand, his cadence is laced with panic. "Bethany, where are you?" he calls out as I hear the crunch of glass beneath his feet. "Fuck! Bethany!" He screams my name louder and still I don't move.

There's a moment where I feel relief. Where I want to run to him and get out of here, climbing into his arms and begging him to take me away from here and spilling everything.

But then I remember. The black words on cream paper with the blue underlined ink left from Jenny. All I can think about is how CROSS was in The Coverless Book. A hidden message from my sister.

The unknowing fear is crippling and the pain in my chest makes me grip my shirt, right where it's hurting.

I hear the faint sound of a phone dialing—muted and barely heard, followed by my cell vibrating on the coffee table. *They left it?*

"Fuck!" Jase screams and then hurls something across my living room that makes my entire body jostle.

My thoughts scramble, my emotions stay at war with one another, but one thing is for certain: He'll protect me. The selfish thought forces me to lurch from where I am.

I push the cabinet door open, the creaking a companion to the aching pain of my muscles screaming from being cramped up for so long. "Jase." I try to call out his name, but it comes out jagged and hoarse from my dry throat. I fall on my ass and right thigh as I make my way out of the cabinet, wincing from a cramp sending a sharp pain shooting up my side just as Jase sees me.

"Bethany," he says, and my name is wretched on his lips. Slipping out with relief and his own fears ringing through.

I'm stiff as he drops to his knees beside me, pulling me into his hard chest. Both of his arms wrap around me and he tucks my head under his chin, rocking me and kissing my hair. I can't focus on him though; my body is screaming in pain. I just want to breathe and stand up. Why do I hurt so much? I don't know what to think or what to say or what to do. It's all too much. I'm breaking down.

All I can focus on is keeping my eyes open and staying aware. He's still shushing me when I finally push a logical thought out.

"Let me go," I tell him, my words rushed. I have to clear my throat, but that just makes it more hoarse. My body's still stiff and it's then that Jase seems to notice I'm not quivering in his arms and begging for him to save me. Maybe that's what I should have done, but I've always been a bad liar. "I need to move; let me go."

The change in Jase's demeanor is immediate and palpable. His grip moves to my upper arms, his fingers digging into my flesh and nearly hurting me.

"What happened? Are you okay?" he questions and the hardness in his words echoes the look in his gaze. Piercing me, demanding information. He doesn't let go. There's no sympathy from him, and for the first time, I see the man he really is. The man who rules with fear and unrelenting force.

I try to answer him, but my throat is so dry I could choke on the words. With a heavy breath out, I feel faint, staring into his eyes. I watch as his stern expression changes slowly. Before, I felt like I'd been given a glimpse, but thought I'd imagined it. This time I know I saw it.

"Why didn't you answer me?" The words of his question waver. The guilt and betrayal flicker on each syllable and make my chest feel hollow and vacant. I'm pinned by his gaze and the nausea comes back full force.

A dry heave breaks the tension, forcing Jase to lift me to my feet and bring me to the sink. Pushing him away with one shaking hand, I turn the faucet on, my fingers slipping around the knob at first, unable to grip it tight enough. The cold water is more than a relief against my face, dripping down my neck and throat, even though it soaks into my sweater. And then drinking it from my cupped hands. I hear Jase go through a cabinet to my upper left and then he pushes a glass toward me for me to take.

One breath. And another. One breath. And another. The water swirls around the drain and I focus on two things.

1. I'm alive.
2. Jase doesn't know about the message in the book.

It's hard to remember where we were before I read those lines. It's always hard going back.

The knob protests with a squeaking sound as I turn it off, still not daring to look Jase in the eyes. Leaning my hip against the countertop to stay upright, I force myself to calm down. Still feeling dizzy and as if I don't have a grasp on anything at all, bringing my arms up to cross in front of me, I spit it out, one line at a time.

"At first one man… or woman," I breathe the words out. "I didn't know who it was but…" I trail off slowly, because that's when I remember Jase said he wasn't coming over tonight. I knew it wasn't him because he'd told me he wasn't coming.

"Why are you here?" I ask him and stare into his dark eyes as I feel how heavy my own are.

"Things changed and I wanted to make sure you were all right." Every word is spoken with a sense of calm but also forcefully. His hand on my upper arm steals my attention. Though gentle, it's demanding just the same. It strikes me that "gentle but demanding" is exactly how I'd describe this man. The knowledge makes something in the pit of my stomach flicker to life, a dull burn.

"One man came? One man did all of this?" he questions.

One breath, one beat of my heart and I move my gaze to his. "I was in the kitchen and heard someone come in. Whoever it was went upstairs and before I could do anything, two more people came in and I hid."

It sounds so simple when I say it like that. Only two sentences to describe the last half hour? Or maybe an hour? I peek at the oven and then swallow thickly at the red digital numbers staring back at me. Over an hour and a half. Sucking in a hesitant breath and closing my eyes, I tell him just that. "I hid for an hour and a half and they just left."

My eyes are still closed when he asks, "They just left? How long ago?"

The irritation that flows from my words is unjustified, but it's there nonetheless. "Yes, that's what I just said. They just left." My voice cracks as I raise it and pull the hair away from my hot face. "Minutes ago. They could come back." I lie and say, "That's why I couldn't answer you when you first came in. I wasn't sure if they were really gone yet."

He sees right through my lie; I can tell with the hint of a tilt of his head.

The realization leaves me just as it comes. Jase is here. Relief is hesitant to console me when he says, "No one's going to hurt you," instead of calling me out on the lie.

"You sound so sure of that," I speak just under my breath and finally look into his eyes. Into the eyes of a man I was falling for. A man I trusted and slept with. A man who makes me question everything now.

I have to break his gaze and let out an uneasy breath as I stare past him and see the destruction. "Oh my God." The words fall from my lips. "What the hell did they do?"

He follows me silently as I walk without thinking into the living room. The sofa is moved away from the wall, the cushions scattered on the floor. Maybe they did that when they were searching for me, but the lamp is busted, the light bulb shattered on the floor where it fell, the coffee table is overturned and that's when I realize the book is gone.

The Coverless Book. Disbelief runs through me in a wave as I fall to the floor searching for it, but knowing it's not here.

These were my mother's things and the first pieces of furniture I bought on my own. Pieces I picked out with my sister. Each and every thing in this house comes with a memory. They violated it. I've never felt like this before.

"A robbery," Jase says behind me and I shake my head. Denying the lie he speaks.

"They wanted it to look like that." I'm barely conscious of my response as I take in the place. "That's why they did it," I add as the thought hits me and I stand up, looking toward the door. "They broke the window after they left to make it look like a robbery. Like they broke the glass to unlock the door."

I feel sickened more than angered.

Pushing the hair out of my face, I try to think about what they could have been after, but it's obvious. "They came here for me, but they thought I ran, so they made it look like a break-in." I whip around to face Jase and tell him, "They knew I was here… or maybe they thought I took off. So they staged it…" My gaze falls as I swallow the lump in my throat. "They thought I took off when I heard them so they staged it as a robbery."

"It's a setup," Jase agrees, searching through things and telling me Seth is nearby watching the entrance to the neighborhood and that everything's okay now. He promises me he'll fix it, he says he'll find whoever it was and make them pay. He tells me he's happy I'm okay and tries to comfort me with his touch, but I pull away. I don't listen to his promises. I'm not in the habit of relying on promises. The seconds pass as I give myself a moment to actually process what happened.

It makes sense. All of it makes sense.

But why take the book? Every hair on the back of my neck stands up when the question echoes in my head.

My phone's on the floor, as is a stack of envelopes from the pile of opened mail, but the mail itself, is missing. They were only bills, nothing of importance. But my laptop is gone too. Fuck! I need that for work. As I halfheartedly lean forward searching through my things, I take everything into account, but the one thing that matters... It really isn't here.

"The book." I can't help but to say it out loud and when I do, my lips feel chapped and the sentence comes out raw. "They took it?" Denial is apparent. "Why take the book?" I shove everything out of the way, searching all over the living room until I get to the hallway only to see it's trashed too. My mother's vase sits perfectly where it is, thank God, but the light in the hall is broken. All the lights are broken.

They upturned the furniture, then busted the lights and stole meaningless items with no worth. Meaningless to them, but to me... "I want my book back." I'm surprised that after all this time, the back of my eyes prick and my hands ball into fists at the thought of someone coming in here and taking The Coverless Book.

I don't even realize I'm shaking until Jase holds me from behind, pulling me into his chest. And again, I'm stiff.

His embrace is calming and masculine, wrapped in warmth. It's designed to comfort, just like the small kiss he plants on my neck. But I can't relax. I can't.

"Why did they do this?" My question turns to broken pieces of whispered syllables in the air.

"Stay with me. I'll make sure we find them and get your book back." His soothing words do nothing to change what's happened and where my mind leads me.

None of this would have happened if Jenny hadn't died; if she hadn't gotten herself into this mess. It always leads back to Jenny and with her name on the tip of my tongue, tears threaten again to fall.

All the calm words and pretty promises couldn't keep the tremors at bay.

"I want to know who they were. They knew what they were doing. It's the men who murdered Jenny. That's why they took the book."

Every memory of my sister always brings out the worst in me.

Angry tears form but don't fall as I take in a heavy breath and shove Jase away. I'm good at doing that. At shoving people away.

Those bastards came here. They took her book from me, the last thing she left me and the only thing that had a message from her. The only key I had to finding out what happened to her.

"Call the cops," I demand, wiping at my eyes with the sleeve of my sweater. The words scratch my throat on their way out.

"No." He answers hard.

"Call them!" I screech, shoving my fists into Jase's chest to get him away from me. Anger is nothing compared to what I feel. He grabs my wrists quicker than I can register, forcing me to stare up at him. He can stare all he wants; he can try to hold me, try to bend me to his will, nothing will get through to me. Once he learns that, he'll leave.

It's only when I look into his eyes in this foyer, with this fear and the memories of Jenny that I realize it's just as it was a week and a half ago when he first knocked on my door. Nothing has changed.

"Just go," I seethe.

"Calm down." He grits the words through his teeth, the irritation barely contained in his voice.

"I'm calling the cops." I stare into his eyes as I speak.

"No, you're not. You're going to come with me. You're going to wait while I find the men who did this and make this right." Every word from his mouth is a demand. They strike me and dare me not to obey.

Ripping my hands away from him, I step back and then step back again. My teeth grind so hard against one another they could crack.

Jase knows better than to approach me as I reach for my shoes and then gather my phone without a word spoken. He thinks I'm obeying him. Going along with what he says and listening like a good girl.

Never in my life has someone bossed me around and told me what to do. Not until Jenny went away and Jase came storming into my life. The bitter acknowledgement stays with me as I prepare to get the hell away from here.

He walks around my place as I silently put on my shoes and grab my coat, my car keys still in the right pocket. Beneath the heavy fabric is my purse, the wallet still there.

And the knowledge is a smack in the face.

They had to know it would be obvious that it wasn't a robbery. Maybe they were counting on me not calling the police. Maybe they know about Jase. They thought I'd run to him?

A chill flows down my spine as I stare up at the man I've been sleeping with, the man I thought I was falling for. He nods toward the door, telling me he has to make a call before we leave.

I don't answer him, not trusting myself to speak.

Instead, while he's on the phone on the porch I walk right past his car and get into my own, speeding off quickly enough so that all he can do is run into the street as I stare into my rearview mirror watching him.

The deafening silence is my only companion as I run away from it all, toward God knows where. I have no idea where I'm going or how I'll find a way out of this mess. The second I get around the corner, panic takes over. Realizing this is my life; this is what my life has become.

The tires screech as I yank the wheel to the left and turn into the neighbor's long drive. Slamming on the brakes and parking, I turn off the car, feeling a sickness churn in my gut.

I did what she used to do to me.

This is what Jenny used to do when she'd leave in an angry fit. We'd get into fights about her new friends and new habits. She'd threaten to leave and I'd threaten to follow. She thought I didn't know that she would just pull in here until things calmed down and then she'd drive home. She'd drive away, just to hide down the street, all alone crying in her car. The house itself is empty. The owner lives in a retirement home and his kids aren't willing to sell it yet.

I knew. I knew exactly what Jenny was doing. Not the first time, but the time after, she was too slow and I saw. I'd drive past every time though and park a few streets down and then walk back up here, watching her cry in the driver's seat. At least she was safe.

That's all I ever wanted.

Safe is what matters.

That's what I told myself back then. As I see Jase speed down the road behind me, not glancing my way at all, that's what I tell myself now. I need to keep myself safe. Safe from everything.

I don't trust anyone.

All I know is that I need my book back.

I need to know what Jenny's last words to me were.

chapter two

Jase

The leather is hot against my palms as I twist my hands around the steering wheel. My knuckles are turning white with every second that passes.

I force myself to focus on every detail around me to keep from losing all sense of control.

The ringing of Seth's phone echoes in the silent car. It rings once, then halfway through a second ring before he picks up.

"Where is she?" My question comes out hard and I don't bother to hide the fury. "How the fuck did she get away?"

"Boss?" Seth questions and it only makes the irritation grow.

A seething anger is in command of every aspect of my being right now. Nothing is going right and nothing is under control. "Where the fuck is she?" I scream the question, feeling each word claw up my throat on the way out.

"Bethany Fawn's car is located at Forty-two Bayview."

"Forty-two Bayview." I breathe out the address, craning my neck beneath the windshield to look at the small green street sign and then to my left as if one of them will magically be Bayview. Neither of them are and that fact is why I slam my fist on the dashboard as I simmer with pure rage. She fucking left me. Knowing there are men after her, she fucking ran from me!

"Four streets behind you, Mr. Cross." I focus on what I can control and then finally breathe.

"Four streets?" I swallow after repeating what he said, knowing she's safe. She's within reach.

"Make a U-turn when you're able. It looks like she stayed there for…" The word stretches out as he pauses and then continues, "…two minutes. She's on the move now, backing out of the driveway." Seth uses the GPS in her car to track her and gives me directions. "I'm still at the back entrance to the neighborhood and it looks like she's coming this way. She'll be driving by me if she stays on course."

"Follow her." Resolution takes over, following a pang of regret. Running my hand down my face and pinching the bridge of my nose, I try to pinpoint the moment I lost her. Truly lost her. She shouldn't have done that. Something happened.

The break-in. I slam my head back, exhaling a tight breath and loathing the life I live. No shit, something happened. What the fuck is wrong with me?

"On her tail," Seth says over the speaker. His obliviousness to my state is a kind gift in this moment as I press my palms to my eyes and focus on what I can do to keep her safe.

"Call for backup and continue following her but keep your distance and keep me informed. I want to know where she's going and I never want her out of your sight."

"Understood, Boss."

"I'm not letting her go," I tell him. My voice is firm and resolute, although my words are more for me than for him.

"Of course not," he answers although his tone has changed. Softer, not consoling, but understanding. A sedan skirts around me, a newer Mazda with an older man at the wheel who looks at me with a crease marred into his wrinkled forehead as his car passes mine.

Forcing a semblance of a smile to my lips, I offer him a small wave and pretend to be someone just passing by. As if I could ever just pass by Bethany. I would never be able to not feel her presence in a crowded room. I could never ignore it. Let alone allow her to ignore me.

"Is everything all right?" Seth asks after a moment of quiet.

"No, I'll brief you once she's secure."

There's a pause before he asks, "Is there anything else I can do?"

"She is your only priority at the moment."

It's quiet again, but I can't hang up yet. Not without Seth acknowledging what I just said. My gaze lifts to the rearview as a man exits his front door. As he walks to the car in his driveway, the headlights flash and it's only then that I'm aware of how dark it's gotten.

It wasn't that late when I left the cemetery. I just wanted to make sure she was okay. It was foolish to think she would be.

It took me far too long to get to her. I never would have guessed when I got there that her brunette hair would tumble into a halo upon the tiled floor, followed by her small frame. My hand stings from the impact of bashing it against the dashboard a moment ago and I clench it into a tight fist, staring at the silver scar below my knuckle as I remember how she fell.

Fuck, she didn't even make a sound for the longest second.

I thought she was dead. I thought he'd killed her. I thought Marcus had ripped her away from me, getting to her first, when she fell out onto the kitchen floor. I hate that the scar stares back at me in this moment.

It's hard to ignore the splinter of pain that tears through me.

Why else would she not have responded? He'd killed her and shoved her in a cabinet for me to find. I thought it was merely her body falling and that she was already dead.

"Does she know about Jenny?" Seth's question brings me back to the present. To her running away from me.

"That he has her?" I clarify and breathe in deep, staring at the picket fence in front of me. "She doesn't know anything. I didn't tell her about the note."

She'll live her life with unanswered questions unless I can give them to her, and right now, I wouldn't be so cruel.

Even if she'd been fine. Even if she'd spilled out of that cabinet and ran to me like I wanted her to, I wouldn't tell her. She's barely holding on as it is. It's not pity I feel for her, it's worry.

"I'm not telling her that her sister's alive until I know we can bring her back." It's one mess after the other. "False hope can kill what's left of a person." That's the only explanation I give him. He knows about the note from Marcus. He knows Marcus has Jenny.

I'd rather she continue thinking Jenny's dead. Just in case that's how this all ends.

"We'll discuss everything moving forward tonight." Even as I give him the command, I hear the fatigue in my voice. The day has taken its toll. More than its fair share. "Has my brother gotten in touch with you?"

"About the men we sent out?" he asks to clarify.

"Yes."

"We have men trailing the man seen with Jenny. His name's Luke Stevens. He's driving out west. We don't know where to but he's definitely taken orders from Marcus. He's mentioned him twice on the calls taken from his car."

"Don't let him get far; I don't give a shit if we blow our cover. Have our men grab him and bring him back here."

"Consider it done."

"Good. I want him brought in and questioned. I want to know everything about Marcus. About Jenny. Everything that bastard knows... I'll get it from him." There are enemies everywhere and everything is moving quickly. "Bethany needs to stay put tonight. Let her run it off. But stay on her and don't lose her. I want an update every five minutes."

"Of course," he answers me.

Glancing at the clock, I change my mind. "Every three minutes. An update every three minutes." I give him the order as I make a U-turn and head back to Bethany's home, preparing myself for the evidence of what happened. "Briefing is tonight, war starts tomorrow."

chapter three

Bethany

I SHOULDN'T CALL LAURA. I KEEP THINKING IT OVER AND OVER AGAIN EVEN AS I STARE AT THE bright white screen of my phone with her contact info staring back at me.

I'm so fucking alone. After driving to nowhere in silence for an hour, that's what I've realized more than anything. I'm so fucking alone.

It's sad when you realize there's only one person left, and you can't reach out to them, because God forbid if what happened to me affects her. I'd never forgive myself.

The darkness outside drifts in as I sit listless in the driver's seat. There's not a star in the black sky and the moon is merely a sliver. Not even the lingering snow reflects the light. It's no longer white and bright, it's dulled and nearly vanished as well.

My teeth scrape against my bottom lip as I pull it into my mouth and look out of my window, still strapped in to the driver's seat. From the outside of my house, no one would ever know what happened.

Closed doors hide a variety of crimes.

Wiping under my tired, burning eyes, I then press the button to exit my contacts to prevent myself from giving in and being weak. I won't call her.

But that only leaves Jase.

CROSS. I can't think of him without being reminded of the book, the underlined hidden message inside it, followed by the break-in, and then Jenny. Every thought, question, and mournful memory assault me one after the other just from thinking his name. I'm so confused and lost... and alone.

I stare down at the white plastic bag on the passenger seat. The logo of Martin Hardware stares back at me in a bold red font and beneath it I know there are three packs of light bulbs, each containing four apiece. It took me a while to feel safe enough to go in. Shit, it took me a while to stop looking in my rearview mirror and keeping track of cars who could be following me. There was no one there for all the hours I've been away from my home.

There's no one here now either. It's just me and the aftermath.

All I have to do is get out of my car and replace the bulbs so I can at least turn on a light.

I have to know what happened. I have to search my place and see what they took. The puzzle keeps me from breaking down. It keeps me from remembering Jenny and the fact that she's gone. As well as Jase, and the fact that he may be to blame if the message in the book is about him.

Why did they take the book and my bills? I think back to the living room. Everything turned over, but systematically. Everything was done with the purpose of making it look like a robbery... but they didn't steal what a random burglar would take.

A long exhale and I'm able to pretend like it isn't devastating. Like I don't feel violated. Like there's no reason for me to be terrified.

My bills and mail, plus whatever other papers were in the coffee table, although I can't even imagine what else I had stored there. And my laptop.

But not my phone or my wallet.

They stole information.

Resting my elbow against the window frame of my car, I press my thumbnail between my teeth and bite down gently, mindlessly. All I can do is stare at my front door and see a man. He had to have been tall, wearing faded, broken-in blue jeans and white sneakers with a red stripe along the sides of each. My mind plays the scene for me. Him quietly picking the lock, pressing his shoulder against the door and opening it as silently as he could. Did he know I was in the living room before he stepped in? Did he peek into the curtains in the bay window beforehand?

Again the series of thoughts plays out. The break-in will always lead to Jenny.

Did he hurt Jenny? Did he know her? I can barely stand to look at the stark white door as the realization hits me.

The men I've been after, the ones I've demanded be served justice were only feet from me today. And I cowered.

My breathing comes in staggered pants as I look at my front door again and instead of seeing him, I see my sister sitting on the front step. Just as she was the last time I saw her. Bloodshot eyes full of fear staring back at me. It was the day she gave me the gun.

The image washes away as my eyes turn glossy, but the emotions are short lived.

Bright lights from a passing car distract me and the fear I can't deny takes over. It lasts only for a second as the car continues on its way, never even turning down this street.

The sliver of strength I had pulling into the driveway is long gone.

The adrenaline doesn't wane though. And I know there's no way I can go back inside.

I can't sleep here.

I'll never feel safe in this house again.

My thoughts aren't cohesive when I call him. I don't even realize what I've done until Jase's phone is ringing with my cell pressed to my ear. He doesn't make me wait long to answer. Which is a damn good thing, because I nearly hang up on the second ring.

"Bethany." He says my name with a quiet emotion I can't quite place. Longing is evident though and somehow that makes me feel like it's all going to be okay. But how could it ever be okay at this point?

Time goes by and words evade me. Jase doesn't speak either.

"Are you angry?" I eventually ask him and I can't fathom why. It shouldn't matter if he's angry at me or not. My life does not revolve around this dark knight. I won't allow it. I don't want this life.

"I'm disappointed."

"You sound like my mother," I answer with feigned sarcasm and not really meaning it. It just seems like something someone would say in response to, *I'm disappointed.*

All I can hear is a huff on the end of the line followed by a resigned sigh. "I keep having to remind myself that you're going through a lot, but that doesn't mean you can do this shit, Bethany."

Shame heats my cheeks and my throat dries, keeping me from being able to swallow as I look back to the house. With every passing second, I'm sinking deeper into the dark pit of emotions that's expanding around me.

"You don't know what I'm going through," I tell him simply. And all the voices I've heard before at the hospital echo in my mind. So many people think no one else feels the way they do when they're mourning, when they're sick. When life has got them by the throat and they have nowhere else to turn to but a mental hospital.

"I know people have it worse, people have more pain and more tragedy... but that doesn't mean I'm not handling things the best way that I can." Dignity is slow to greet me and I strengthen my voice to tell him, "I'm trying to just hold on right now." As I finish, my words crack and it's then that I feel as crazy as my patients. I'm losing it. I'm losing everything, watching it all slip through my fingers like the sand of an hourglass.

"Why did you run?" he asks me, not commenting on a word I've just spoken. Somehow, I'm grateful for that.

"I wasn't in the right mindset to be bossed around and whisked away." It's semi-honest. At the very least, it's not a lie.

"And now?"

"I don't know what to do," I admit, feeling the insecurity and the weight of what's happened push against my chest. "And I'm scared," I add. The confession barely leaves me; I don't know if he heard me or not. Another car passes down the street that crosses mine, forming a T-shaped intersection. This time I'm not as scared, but I'm conscious of it. I'm conscious of everything around me.

"Do you want to stay with me?" he asks.

"No," I say, and it hurts to answer him honestly. Physically hurts and drains me of what little strength I have left. I should add that I don't trust him after what I read in the book. But without the book, I can't be certain that I shouldn't trust him. Which makes everything all the more complicated.

"Why is that?" There's no hint of what he's feeling in his question; it's only a string of words asked for clarity. And that makes it easier, but not easy enough to tell the truth. How could I tell him I saw his last name in a coded message in The Coverless Book? I already feel like I've gone insane. I don't need someone else to confirm it.

"I'm just confused and I want to be alone." Nodding to myself although he can't see me, I repeat the sentiment, "I'm not sure exactly what I want right now, but I think I'd really like to be alone."

"I'd prefer you weren't alone right now... And you still owe me time." He adds the second statement when I don't respond to the first.

"I can always say no."

"I never should have put that in the contract."

His response forces a weak smile to my face. It's just as tired and sad as I am. "Your contract is bullshit." Our quips are a quick tit for tat. The rough chuckle from the other end of the line eases a small piece of me. As if slowly melting a large sheet of ice that encases and presses against me constantly.

"You're not going to be happy." He pauses after his statement and I simply wait for what's next, not responding until I know what he's getting at.

"Seth is behind you. He's parked a few houses down. I'll have him flash his lights for you." *Thump*, my heart squeezes tight, so tight it hurts and I actually reach up to place a hand over my chest as bright white lights shine behind me and then disappear.

"How long?"

"The entire time. Did you think I'd risk anything happening to you?"

Gratitude is a strange thing. Sometimes it feels warm and hugs every inch of you. Sometimes it strangles you and makes you feel rotten and unworthy. The latter is what I struggle with as Jase continues to tell me what to do.

Follow Seth to a hotel.
Stay there tonight.
Meet Jase tomorrow for dinner.

He ends the rattled-off list of things I'm required to do with, "We need to have a conversation."

The pit of my stomach sinks as I take in my current reality.

"I was a fool to think I'd outrun you, wasn't I?" My words are whispered and as they leave me, Seth's car comes to life. As he pulls up in front of my house, his eyes meet mine in the faint darkness. I rip my gaze away.

"You're far from a fool, but running from me ... it won't be tolerated, Miss Fawn."

chapter four

Bethany

There's a saying about life and how it can be anything you want it to be. I forget how it goes exactly. Not that it matters, because the saying is a fucking lie. You can't just decide one day you're going to change and everything will change with you. That's not how it works. That's not life. It's more complicated than that.

Life is a tangled mess of other people's bullshit and other people's decisions. Even decisions they make on a whim.

Sometimes, you get to decide whether or not you care about them and their issues. If you do, you're fucked. Their problems become yours and sometimes that means you fall down a black hole and there's no easy escape. "Today I choose to be happy," is a joke. You can't be happy when there's a rope around your neck and another around your feet. You can't step forward, and even if you could, you'd just hang yourself.

Sometimes you don't get to decide a damn thing at all. There's not a choice you could have made that would have prevented what's to come. My sorry ass has been thinking about that all day. Whether I had a choice or not. And if what I choose is what I deserve.

Because right now it feels like that rope is pulled snug under my chin with another wrapped tight around my ankles, scratching against my skin with every step I take.

As I stare at the slip of paper I've kept in my wallet that says, *in a life where you can be anything, be kind*, I don't think twice about balling it up to toss the crumpled scrap in the trash can outside the restaurant.

I miss on the first try. *Figures.* It mocks me as it falls to the ground, daring me to pick it up and really discard it. Which I do, albeit spitefully.

A strong gust of wind blows the hair from out of my face, and without the scarf I left in my car, the chill sweeps down my collarbone and seeps into my jacket. The weather is just as bitter as I am.

I don't know how long I've been standing outside of Crescent Inn, one of the nicer restaurants in this town. I've always wanted to come here, but I could never justify it because of the price. Pulling my coat collar tighter around myself I peek in through the large floor-to-ceiling windows, past the wooden blinds that only cover the top third of the windows and search for Jase.

He's not hard to find. In the center of the room, filled with bright white tablecloths amid a sea of small cobalt blue vases, each housing an array of fresh flowers next to tea lights for ambience, he stands out.

Just seeing him does something to me. Even as a couple passes around me, giving me a disconcerted look for blocking the door and staring inside the place, I can't bring myself to go to him. I couldn't sleep without dreaming about him.

I can't think without wanting to know what *he* thinks about it all.

It's only when he brings his gaze to meet mine, as if he could feel my stare, that I dare consider taking the necessary steps toward him.

How did I get in this deep? How did I let the ropes of his life and my sister's death wrap so tightly around my every waking moment?

More importantly, *how the hell do I get out of this?*

I tell myself the only reason I came is because he said he found my things they stole when he called this morning. They were all thrown in a trash can a few blocks down from my place. There's no way it was a break-in. Jase is on my side; it was staged to disguise something else.

It's easier to enter though, knowing I'll get my book back.

"Good evening, Miss Fawn." The host greets me the moment I walk in. Without another word, he graciously takes my coat from me, ignoring the shock and apprehension that must show on my expression. With my jaw dropped, and the air absent from my lungs, I don't have a chance to ask him how he knew my name, as if the answer isn't obvious.

"Mr. Cross is right this way. Follow me, please." The skin around the man's light blue eyes crinkles when he offers me a gentle smile. His suit is perfectly fitted to his proportions; his shoes are shined so well the chandeliers in the foyer of the restaurant sparkle against the black leather.

He's professional and kind. Still, I don't move. I stay where I am, knowing with every step I take that Jase Cross tells me to take, those ropes get tighter and tighter. Holding me right where he wants me.

The only saving grace is that if I don't think about it, if I just surrender to him... it will feel weightless, easy and deliciously thrilling while it lasts. If only I could think of anything but the demise of what my life once was.

The polite smile falters on the gentleman's face, emphasizing the lines around his eyes even more. The chatter of the crowded restaurant is what breaks me in this moment. There are plenty of people here, witnesses if anything were to happen. And I do need The Coverless Book. I need to know what Jenny said.

With her in mind, one imaginary rope around my ankle loosens. I'm all too aware that it belongs to her.

With every step I take, I think back to what's led me here:

Jenny's disappearance and how I couldn't let it go.

Jase's bar and how I couldn't keep my mouth shut.

Jenny's death and how I need to have justice.

The gun Jenny gave me and how I shot at Jase rather than playing dumb.

The contract I signed giving away my time and body in exchange for a debt.

And the break-in I don't know enough about. The book and the message inside I have to obtain.

They may have left the ropes for me to take, but I damn sure slipped them into place myself.

The host pulls the chair out for me as Jase stands, buttoning his jacket and pinning his gaze on me. A gaze I return.

"Thank you." My words are soft and I'm not certain if the host heard me or not, but I'm well aware that my hand is trembling as I reach for the water. Even more certain when the ice clinks against the edge of the pristine goblet.

I can tremble as much as I need. I'm in this mess of tangled lies and secrets, the violence and the need for vengeance. Even if it ends up killing me, I would have taken every step just the same if I had to do it all over again.

"You didn't sleep." Jase speaks first and I shake my head, staring at the cold drops of water that drip down the goblet as I set it on the table.

When I lift my tired eyes to his dark gaze, I answer him, "Maybe an hour. I was in and out." I swallow and place my hands in my lap before continuing. "Just couldn't stop thinking about everything."

He nods once and doesn't speak; instead he searches my expression for answers. Or maybe for where my boundaries lie with him today.

"What you did yesterday is unacceptable."

The tremors inside of me tense with irritation. "Which part exactly?" I question and the defiance is clear in my tone.

"The part where you ran from me."

"Who are you to me where that is unacceptable?"

His fixed stare narrows. "Your lover."

"Do all of your lovers owe you thousands of dollars?" I dare to question him, feeling the anger simmer from his taut skin. It's so much easier to be angry. It's easier to yell than listen. Easier to hate what's happened, than to suffer through the aftermath.

The muscles in Jase's shoulders tighten, making him look all the more dominant and I don't stop pushing him. Maybe I have a death wish. "You're a man who coerced me, a man I fell for when we both know we shouldn't be together. And whatever's between us will end when the debt is paid. I will not listen to your every command because you happen to give one to me. If I don't want to be with you... I won't." His chest rises and falls quicker as his jaw clenches at my final words. "You'd be wise to remember I am not interested in being told what to do. This agreement was for information. That is all I want from you."

Thump, my heart wrenches inside of me knowing it's a lie. All I can do is remember CROSS in the hidden message of The Coverless Book and it stops its furious beating, but the beat it gives me in return is dulled and muted, slowing more and more by the second.

"I've already told you, I don't like it when you lie to me." He hardens his voice further as he adds, "Knock off your bullshit." Jase speaks through clenched teeth and before I can answer, a waitress appears with a bottle of wine draped with a white cloth napkin in an ice bucket and two glasses. It's a dark red with a silver label although I can't read what the label says.

I could use a glass of dark red wine. Then a long nap. One that lasts forever and takes me somewhere far away from the hell my life's become.

"Drink," he commands me when the waitress leaves and I smirk at him.

"If you thought I wasn't going to drink, you're just as much of a fool as I am." Some spiteful side of me wants to deny the wine, just because he told me to drink it. But fuck that. It's the only good thing I have going for me.

I take a sip and time passes with neither of us saying anything. The first breath is tense, but the next comes easier. With every second that passes, the hate and anger wane, leaving only raw ugly feelings to fester inside of me. When that happens, I don't want to think. That's my harsh reality. I'd rather get lost in him when I don't have the anger to hide behind anymore.

"What changed?" he asks casually, breaking the silence.

"I don't trust you," I reply, and my answer slips out just as easily. An anxiousness wells up inside of me. I didn't mean to say it out loud. He doesn't know about the message in the book. That's really what changed although without it, I can't even say for sure what it says. The table jostles as I plant my elbow and rest my forehead in my hand while I refuse to look at him. I can't look him in the eyes; I can't take this shit. A moment passes and another.

"Is there anything you do trust about me?" he asks, not bothering to question why it is I don't trust him. Maybe he has his own reasons.

Peeking past my hand and then lowering it altogether, I answer honestly again, only this time it's a conscious decision. "I don't think you'd hurt me. Not physically... which is truly ironic considering how we met."

Only after I answer do I look into his eyes. And I see turmoil raging within them.

"I would never hurt you. Not in any way if I can help it."

"And what if you can't?" I ask him with the sorrow that's buried its way into my every thought finally showing. "What if there's no way for me to come out of this undamaged?"

"That's what you're afraid of? That's what you don't trust?" he questions.

I hadn't expected to be so transparent with him. I don't even think I was cognizant of what I'd said until the words were spoken. I could blame it on the lack of sleep or the wine. But a part of me wants him to take it all away. A part of me thinks he can make me believe he'll fix my problems. I don't even care that he can't. I just want to believe that he can for a moment. Just a single moment of peace. That part of me is so tired of fighting. I hate that part of me.

"I'm scared in general, Mr. Cross." Emotions tickle up my throat, but with a short clearing of my throat, they're gone. "I've found myself deeper and deeper in a hole that I don't know I'll be able to get out of." My eyes feel heavy, as does the weight against my chest.

I don't know how I'm still sitting upright at this point. That's the truth.

"The debt? Is that what you mean by the hole?" he asks although the look in his eyes tells me he knows that's not what I'm talking about. I shake my head, no, confirming his assumption.

"It's because of the break-in?" he asks and I don't answer, swallowing down the half truth and hating that it's all I'm willing to give him. "Bethany?" he presses and I finally speak, "Yes."

It's a lie though. Things changed before it. "Do you have my book?" I ask him the second I think of The Coverless Book. Seeing the underlined words in my mind and needing to read the hidden message. Clearing my throat again, I ask, "Did they find it?"

I don't know where to go from here until I know what my sister left for me.

I don't know what to think of Jase until I see what my sister said. That's what hurts the most.

Leaning back into his chair, he lets out a long exhale, staring into my eyes and not answering. His thumb rubs circles over the pad of his pointer finger and he leaves me waiting.

"Jase, please," I plead with him, seeking sympathy and mercy. "I just want the book back."

He leaves me without an answer still, but only for a moment.

Wordlessly, he raises his hand and I expect the waitress to come, but instead Seth walks forward. I hadn't seen him before this, not since last night when he brought me a duffle bag of the things I asked him to bring. With my head buried in the hotel pillow, he opened the door and left my bags for me. I barely even got to see him before he left, muttering a thank you into the pillow as the door was already closing.

He's quiet and businesslike, but he gives me a soft smile every time. He's like a warden with sympathy for his prisoner. The thought makes a sarcastic huff of a laugh leave me, although it's barely heard.

I don't know where he was hiding or if he was seated, perhaps standing. I have no idea. But Seth nods at me with the same polite smile the host had for me in the foyer. As if no one in this world would dare admit what a shit-show my life is and how I look the part for it right now.

I can't hear Jase's murmur but I don't need to. Seth disappears for a moment, swiftly walking away when the waitress arrives with oysters Rockefeller and seared scallops. Setting the large plates in the center of our table, she then places two small plates equipped with tiny seafood forks as well in front of each of us.

She's courteous and polite, smiling at me but more so at Jase before asking if we need anything else. Jase shakes his head once and I do the same, not trusting myself to speak.

"I chose the courses while waiting for you," he explains.

"I'm not hungry," I tell Jase, spotting Seth making his way back to us with The Coverless Book in his right hand by his side.

"You haven't slept; you should at least eat."

The tight smile graces Seth's lips once again and then holding out the book for me to take, he tells me, "The rest is now in your car, Miss Fawn."

"Thank you," I say, and somehow the words are spoken; how? I don't know. My head feels dizzy as I hold the book tighter than I've held anything in my life. It could give me the answers to everything.

"That's all," Jase says lowly and Seth is gone before I can say anything else. Before I can even swallow down the ball of dread that's cutting off the oxygen in my throat.

I should ask him where he found it; I should say something or attempt to carry on conversation so it's not obvious that this book may change the way I think about him. He has no idea and he's given it over to me freely. I should try to keep my cover, but I'm an awful liar.

"I have to go to the restroom," I tell Jase as I stand up from the table and reach for my purse, setting the book inside before slinging the bag over my shoulder.

Jase only nods. I have to grip the back of my chair, taking him in for what could be the last time. The air changes around me, it moves around him, pulling me toward him, begging me to stay there... *just in case*.

I think if I ran, which I know very well I may do depending on what's in the book, I'd miss the way he looks at me the most. He doesn't just glance at me, he doesn't observe me the way others do, inconsequentially and only with little curiosity. He stares at me with a hunger and a need for more, to see more of me and what's inside of me. He looks at me like he never wants to stop seeing me.

Even knowing he's angry with me and how we're surrounded by prying eyes in a crowded restaurant, he only sees me. Yes, that's the way he looks at me. Like I'm the only one worth seeing. With my back turned to him, I know it might be the last time, and it hurts. I wasn't expecting that. I should stop expecting anything at all.

As I'm walking away, I feel the vibrations of my phone ringing silently, but I ignore it, quickening my pace to get away from Jase and from these thoughts.

The women's restroom door pushes open easily and I don't hesitate to lock myself inside of the stall farthest from the entrance, dropping my purse to the floor and quickly opening the book to where I was.

I check my phone just before opening the book, and it says Rockford called. For a second I hesitate, wondering what work wanted and why they called.

I drop it back into the inside pocket when I hear the door open and someone walking in. I can just barely make out a pair of red heels by the sink and I hear the telltale zip of a bag as she stands there. Maybe she's reapplying lipstick or checking her appearance. I have no idea, but either way, alone in the stall, I open the pages of the book, searching for the last page I read.

My eyes are tired and the black and white is more blurred than it should be. But the underlined words are still there and just beneath the lines, the first letter of the sentences are just as I remembered.

C starts the first sentence. R is next. Followed by O, S, S.

My fingertips slide against the indented lines. When Jenny left this message, I can only imagine the fear she must have felt, hiding it so deeply in this book.

With a deep, but staggering breath, I dig in my purse for a small Post-it note and a pen.

The next letter is an I. I write it down, then search for the next. M. M. I stop at the P for "Promise me you'll never leave." MMP makes no sense.

CROSSIMMP. Rubbing under my eyes and double-checking them, that's right. But it makes no sense. With my brows knit and the adrenaline pumping harder, I keep going. Q in "Quite the way to lead life." S for "Secrets always come out."

It makes no sense at all. There are no other words that can be made from the jumbled mess of letters. I search another chapter and another. Not reading at all, just gathering letters. And there's nothing else. No other words hidden.

My blood cools and I struggle not to cry.

There is no message.

Deep breath. Deep breath. Don't cry. Crying is useless.

A snide voice in the back of my head reminds me, so is searching for messages from the dead. They're gone. They don't come back. And they have nothing new to tell you.

I swear I can hear the crack that splits down my chest, through my heart and onward.

Hope is a long way of saying goodbye.

My own voice echoes in my head. Mocking some of the last words I ever spoke to my sister. And that's the moment I break down entirely. I suppose I can take the death, the coercion, the break-in, the fear of losing my life. But losing hope?

Even I can't live without hope.

So I read the lines again and again, although this time, they're blurry.

There is nothing here but false hope and lines from an old book with no title. Lines that for the life of me, my addict of a sister thought worthy of underlining, though I can't imagine why.

However gentle the knock at the stall door is, it still startles me.

Hiding my sniffling with the sound of pulling on the roll of toilet paper, I respond, "Just a minute."

"Are you all right?" The question comes out hesitantly. "I just… is there anything I can do?"

How sweet a stranger can be. Kind and caring for someone they don't know. If she knew, she'd stay far away from me. Everyone in my life dies tragically.

"Just allergies. I'll be fine."

She stands there a second longer until I add, "Thank you though. That's very sweet of you."

"I haven't heard someone use allergies before," the stranger in dark red heels replies, letting me know she's well aware of my lies. "Is there anyone you'd like me to get for you?"

Although I owe this woman no explanation, I answer her. "No, I promise I'm fine. Just a really rough… month." I say that without thinking, because my mind is riddled with thoughts of Jenny. And how I wish this stranger could simply go get her for me.

If only it were possible. That's what I really want and need, far more than I should.

The woman leaves and another enters. I sit there for longer than I'd planned, drying my eyes and rearranging my bag before heading to the sink. There isn't a lipstick in the world that could make me look better. But I try to hide my crying with the stick of concealer and powder in my bag. And then a coat of pale pink lipstick.

Letting it all sink in, the only relief I have is that there was no message about Jase or his brothers. There is no warning to stay away from him.

That knowledge releases the only inhibition I had for not losing myself in him. What a way to mourn. Grief is an aphrodisiac, or so I've been told. Although I've done damage the last twenty-four hours and I don't know where we stand.

With my purse on my shoulder and the book safely tucked inside, I head back to the table feeling flushed, overwhelmed and with no appetite at all.

"So you weren't tunneling an escape after all," Jase jokes weakly as I sit down across from him. He sets his hand palm up on the table, but I don't reach for it.

"I was... just realized it would take a little longer than I'd like," I joke back, just as weakly. "No appetite?" I question, noting that he hasn't touched the appetizers.

He shakes his head in response, his eyes ever searching, ever wondering what I'm thinking. "I need an answer first."

"An answer to what?" I ask.

"I need you to agree to stay with me."

"No." My answer is immediate and I question my sanity. He could protect me. Jase Cross could do that. At the cost of losing my only sanctuary and the place that houses the memories I have. Living in fear is the worst thing I could agree to. I refuse to do it. I refuse to choose staying with him because I'm scared.

Angling the small fork to ease the oyster from its hold on the shell, I struggle for an excuse and the only one I can offer him. Thinking eating will appease him, I lift the oyster up so he knows I'll do just that but first I tell him, "I'd like to stay with my friend for the time being."

With a salty bite left in my mouth, I swallow the heavenly oyster and set the empty shell back down on the bed of ice. The tension doesn't wane, not even when I eat another, refusing to look Jase in the eyes.

"Don't do this," he warns me.

My gaze flicks to his. "Do what?"

"Don't make this harder. I don't understand what's gotten into you. But you should consider your options carefully."

"Is that a threat, Mr. Cross?"

Exasperation grows in his expression as he tells me his patience is wearing thin.

"What changed?" he finally asks. "You treat me like I'm an enemy and I'm starting to think I am to you now."

Thump. My heart is a treacherous bastard, begging me to tell him about the book. Begging me not to lie. Telling me he'll understand.

He pushes the issue, asking, "Is there something you're not telling me?"

Thump.

"You wanted me, and I wanted you. I thought that's where we were."

"Did you forget the other night?" I ask meekly, remembering crying in the bedroom, remembering him walking away because I couldn't admit it out loud like he has just now. Raising my eyes to him and staring back with nothing but sincerity I remind him, "It's not like the two of us should be together."

"Do you want me?" he asks, not letting anything change in his expression.

With a single hard swallow, I answer him with raw truth, "Yes. More than anything else."

"Nothing else matters then."

"Not the debt? Not the fact that someone's after me?" I feel my expression fall, the kind of crumpling that comes with an ugly cry, but I don't give a shit, I let it out, I let it all out. "Not the fact that a part of me hates you because I hate what you do and that the life you lead is why my sister's dead?" I'll never be able to say those words without tears flooding my eyes. I don't blink and a few tears fall, but I won't cry after that. Crying does nothing.

As I'm angrily wiping my tears away, I note his lack of a response and continue the onslaught. I ask him, "How much is it that I owe you again?"

"I'm fucking tired of you asking me that. It'll be months before you've paid the debt."

"*The* debt…" I whisper, sniffling and looking away thinking about how it's *her* debt, not mine. But the thoughts vanish as I note how the restaurant is slowly thinning in attendance. It's sobering, the sight around us.

It's not just thinning, everyone is leaving. There are only two couples left. And both are preparing to exit. The young woman glances at me as she pushes her chair in, her eyes wide with worry.

"Jase." I can only whisper his name as my pulse races with concern.

"I was wondering how long it would take you to notice."

Thump. Thump. Thump. It's like a war drum. I whisper the question, "What did you do?"

Leaning forward, he places his forearms on the table. His eyes darken as they sear into me. "I've let you get away with too much."

I can't breathe, and I can't move; even when I hear the door click loudly behind me and bringing with it utter silence, I don't dare to do anything but stare into his eyes.

They contain a mix of hunger and depravity. His hard jawline tightens as he clenches his teeth and lets his eyes roam down the front of me then back to my apprehensive gaze.

"They couldn't stay here any longer, because I need to punish you. You've known this was coming. I should have done it sooner." Frustration and regret ring clear in his voice and guilt overrides my other emotions. "I take responsibility. You wouldn't behave this way if I'd punished you like I should have."

The way he says punish evokes a mix of reactions from me. I heat with desire and longing, wanting him to take control so I can stop thinking, stop doing, and just obey and receive what he's willing to give. The other reaction though comes from the knowledge of who this man is and how it will never change. Fear is ever present when he takes control.

"There are consequences. And like I've said, you've gotten away with too much."

chapter five

Jase

With the door securely locked, I check to make sure the blinds have been lowered, and they have. Although the front door window is visible from this table, meaning someone could see if they dared to peek, but Seth is waiting outside and he'd take care of that problem before any prick would have the chance to see a damn thing.

"Jase, I'm sorry." Bethany's voice wavers as she speaks, showing her fear. I wondered which side of her would take over. I was hoping it wouldn't be this one. It makes everything more difficult, but she must be punished. This has to stop.

"You aren't. If you were sorry, you wouldn't continue to defy me." A deep inhale barely keeps me grounded as my temper flares. "You are the only one who has ever made me lose control like this. Do you know that?"

"Jase, I don't mean to," she nearly whimpers with more than a hint of fear and finally glances away from me, toward the door.

Her breathing is erratic and her fingers wrap around her silverware as if she'll use it against me. She may do just that, my fiery girl, if I give her a reason.

"Jase," she says and whispers my name.

"You're scared?" I ask her.

She hesitates to answer before closing her eyes and nodding. The fear is a constant. I'm not sure it'll ever leave her and I can't blame her.

"You just said you trusted that I would never hurt you." The pain inside of my chest is sharp like a knife, piercing and twisting, never stopping to offer a moment of relief. I'd bleed out here if I had to watch her paused in this moment, truly afraid that I'd hurt her. "I'm not going to hurt you, Bethany. This is a punishment that you can take. One that you obviously need."

"I'm scared," she whispers.

"Don't be. Parts of it you may even enjoy." That comment gets her attention. I keep her gaze to tell her, "I'm not going to let you get away with this shit any longer. You will be punished. Whether you're upset or scared or otherwise. I should have already punished you." At the word punish, she licks her lips. Her body will always betray her regardless of the brave front she puts on around me.

"You've run from me, lied to me, stolen from me, raised a knife to me... And you thought I'd do nothing?" I question her. "How much did you think I'd let you get away with, cailín tine?"

Using her nickname is what does it. I can feel the tension break, I can feel it warm and I notice how it melts around her. Her bottom lip drops, pouty and trembling, but her breathing has changed. No longer tense, but still quick with anticipation.

I give her a moment, letting everything settle for her.

"Still your cailín tine?" The Gaelic phrase sounds foreign on her tongue.

"Of course," I answer, reaching across the table to offer my hand and she still hesitates to reciprocate, but she does, setting her small hand in mine. Brushing my thumb across her wrist, I try to keep it soothing to calm her before the inevitable will happen. "I hate that it comes to this before you'll let me in. Do you know that?"

She exhales deeply before telling me, "I'm not exactly used to this. And I don't exactly like it either."

"You don't like what?"

"Having to be accountable to someone like…"

"To someone like me?" She only nods at my question until I narrow my gaze and pause the motion of my thumb against her pulse. "Yes," she answers verbally.

"Well I enjoy your company, Miss Fawn, and from what I gather, you enjoy mine." Again she nods and this time whispers her yes along with it, nearly defiantly.

"When you're with someone, you have to make allowances for them. I have done my best to make allowances for you given this… situation."

"And I have not," Beth speaks before the judgment can fall from my lips. "I realize I am difficult and…" she pauses, swallowing thickly before adding, "I do appreciate some things… I am just very aware of others that…"

"That you will have to make certain allowances for," I say, finishing her sentence for her with the only outcome I'll allow. "Is that understood?"

She nods and speaks simultaneously, "Yes."

Pulling my hand away from her, I let the warmth of her words—that she appreciates me, no matter how small a part of me— flow through me, feeling my cock harden as I think about what I'm going to do to her. "This situation being new for you is no excuse. It's new for me too."

"What are you going to do?" she asks breathlessly.

"You're going to need the rest of your wine."

I'm careful and calm as I stand up, pulling the chair back and unbuttoning my jacket.

Her fingers linger on the glass but she doesn't pick it up until I pick up my own glass, downing the full-bodied red I know she loves. It's sweet and decadent, like her when she lets go and gives me control.

I set the empty glass on the table behind us. The aftertaste is smooth and I focus on that as I calmly remove everything from our table one by one. The candle, the vase, the small plates and then the large one still littered with hors d'oeuvres I thought she'd enjoy.

She doesn't just calm down; that wouldn't fit the woman she is. She's intense and wrought with emotion. She feels everything in exaggerated stages.

Every second that passes, the air gets hotter around us.

Each breath she takes picks up its pace.

After loosening my tie, I remove the last few pieces of silverware from the table, placing it easily on the table to our right.

"Sit here." My hand splays on the barren table in front of me. My palm is flat against the surface. "Right here," I say and pat the table again, closer to the edge this time and although she's slow, she obeys. Climbing onto the table, she's fully clothed. The blush that creeps up her cheeks is an indication that she knows damn well she won't be staying that way.

"Come closer," I command once she's on all fours on top of the table and when she's close enough, I position her body how I want it, feeling the race of adrenaline and desire run through my pulse.

"Jase." My name is merely lust wrapped in words that don't matter. "I really am sorry."

"I have a question for you," I say, and I don't bother accepting or denying her apology. "Are you terrified of me? Or of what I could do to you?" I ask her, placing my forearms on the table on either side of her. She's close to me, her luscious curves within reach. Her pouty lips near mine, ready to capture. But I don't kiss her. Not yet.

"Both," she admits and I don't blame her.

"I've done terrible things in my life. It makes sense you'd be afraid," I admit, feeling a crease in my forehead as her expression stays etched with concern. "But leading with fear is a bad move to make."

"I know," she whispers just beneath her breath. "I don't know what I'm doing. I don't know what I've gotten myself into. I'm angry, I'm lost and I'm terrified."

"I'll be angry alongside you. I'll find you a way. I'll make sure there's not a damn thing that will touch you. Nothing should scare you when you're with me." Reaching out, I cup her chin in my hand, feeling her smooth skin and continuing to caress her when she presses her cheek into my embrace. "Even me. I shouldn't scare you."

"Knowing how much I want to be around you is terrifying in itself. Which is ridiculous, all things considered." Her eyes open on her last point, her thick lashes barely revealing her eyes beneath them.

With one leg on either side of me, I press my fingers against her pussy, through the fabric that separates our skin and she keeps her eyes on mine, but her head falls back just slightly.

"Already hot," I comment. "Are you already wet for me too?"

She only nods and as I open my lips, moving closer to her to reprimand her for not answering verbally, she halts any inclination I have to do so.

She kisses me first. Without warning. Surprised, I moan into her mouth, feeling my rigid cock twitch with need to be inside of her. This greedy woman who takes from me when no one else would dare to do so.

"Even when you're in trouble, you still defy me and take from me."

She only answers with the hint of smile.

"You like to be the first to kiss, don't you?" I ask her.

"It's my call." I don't bother to hide the smirk that lurks on my lips.

I don't bother to hide the lust either as I answer her, "It was going to happen anyway."

"I could have run, I could bite you, or deny you."

"Why would you?" I ask her with genuine curiosity, my lips just barely away from hers.

"That's what people do when they're scared, Jase. You should know that by now."

Words catch in my throat, tightening it and warring with each other inside of me. "Strip" is the only one that manages to escape.

"Jase." I watch her swallow, I can even hear it before she tells me, "They'll see. Anyone could see from the door."

"I don't give a shit about anyone but you right now."

Words are lost to her as we stare into each other's eyes until I tell her, "Any man who dared to look through that door would die."

Her breath hitches and her thighs tighten at my words.

"Does that make you hot?" I ask her, feeling my own desire rising.

She nods as she whispers yes. I allow my gaze to wander down her body, although it stops too soon as I focus on her breasts when she pulls her sweater over her head. Through the tank top underneath, I see her pebbled nipples.

"Maybe he'd get a glimpse of you cumming with my lips between your legs."

Leaning in closer, I whisper in her ear as she pulls the straps of her tank top down, "What a way to die... for that to be the last thing he sees."

The exhale she releases is tempting, but I maintain control. I don't touch her again as she peels off every bit of clothing and lies bared to me, pushing her bra off the table for it to fall carelessly on the floor below with its companions.

Both of my hands grip her hips and I pull her closer to me. Keeping her gaze with mine, I lower my lips to her swollen nub and suck. With a single lick of her sweet cunt, I go back to her clit, sucking it until she's letting those sweet sounds flow into the air.

Her body rocks, her hands spear my hair. I love the way her nails scratch me as she gets closer and closer.

I have to remind myself that this is a punishment. I can't get lost in her.

The moment her back arches and her bottom lip drops with a deep moan, I pull away from her, smacking the inside of her thigh to take her away from the edge of her forbidden fall.

"No," I tell her. With flushed cheeks, she stares back at me breathlessly and wordlessly. "You don't get to cum tonight."

As she blinks away the haze of lust and confusion, my middle finger plays at her folds, spreading her arousal as I talk. "I will play with you, fuck you, and get myself off with the things I plan to do with you. But you will not cum."

All I can hear is her single breath before she nods.

"Verbally."

"I understand."

Rewarding how easily she accepts the punishment, I plant a kiss on the bright red patch of skin on her inner thigh. And then another, traveling up her body, over the curve of her waist and then higher. Standing up and dragging my open-mouth kisses up her neck, I unbutton my pants, letting them and my boxers drop to the floor so I can stroke myself.

"On your back," I command her and pull my shirt over my head. She positions herself with her heels on the edge of the table and her back flat against the tabletop.

She struggles not to lift her head and watch me as I undress entirely.

I can't resist toying with her breasts, plucking her nipples and pulling them back to bring those sweet sounds to leave her.

Her pussy clenches around nothing. I watch her, hot and flushed, ready to be fucked. The taste of her and red wine still remain on my tongue.

"You're taking this punishment well," I commend her and then pull her ass closer to me, nearly falling off the edge of the table.

She starts to answer, but I grip her hips in my hand and slam myself inside her. Fuck, she feels too fucking good. I can't close my eyes even though my body begs me to enjoy the rapture of pleasure fully and do so.

Her neck arches and her eyes scrunch as her heat clenches around me. The table jostles with the thrust of my hips and her breasts sway as I fuck her. I'm careful not to allow her to enjoy herself fully.

Her hands move to her breasts, her nipples barely peeking through her fingers as she gets close, inching her way toward her release.

I pull out fully, instantly missing her warmth.

She whimpers and struggles to stay still as I step back. It's hard to keep my breathing controlled, even harder to do it again, fucking her relentlessly on the table and stopping just before she reaches her climax.

The third time, I lower my body close to hers, feeling my skin heat and needing to be closer to her. She doesn't kiss me when I bring my lips close to hers this time.

She pushes her head back against the table, so I drag my teeth along her throat and up to the shell of her ear, loving how she moans even though she knows she'll be left wanting yet again.

"This is what a punishing fuck is," I hiss as I pound into her again and stay buried deep inside of her as I almost lose myself in the moment. "I take all my pleasure," I push the words through clenched teeth as I move myself slowly out of her and then slam all the way back in.

A strangled cry leaves her and she drags her nails down my back. The mix of pleasure and pain nearly has me finding my release too soon. I'm not ready for it to be over though, not by a mile.

"I get my pleasure, and you get nothing," I whisper in her ear as the intensity of the pleasure stirring inside of me subsides. Only then am I able to pull away from her enough to look her in the eye.

Daggers stare back at me, but not in anger. I can see the challenge clearly written on her face. My poor cailín tine has no idea how painful orgasm denial is. To be taken to the highest high each time, finding the edge of release so close, only to have it ripped away from you and the waves of pleasure yanked from you.

"I dream about the noises you make when you get off. I want to hear those sounds over and over again," I tell her and then recklessly fuck her, feeling the stir of my climax approaching in time with hers. Only to pull away at the last second.

"No," this time she whimpers and her body rolls to the side, wanting to get away. "Please," she begs me, her face pained.

"How can I reward either of us with that, when you don't listen to me? When you fight me every step of the way?"

She visibly swallows and tells me she's sorry again. I'm not interested in an apology.

I fuck her again, listening to the sound of me fucking her, of the table banging against the floor as my movements get stronger with my own needs taking over.

I suck in a deep breath as I pull away again. She can't resist touching herself, knowing it's only a small touch she'll need at this point and I grip her wrists, pulling them away and pinning them to the table.

The frustration, even the contempt, show in her expression. "Keep your hands here." My voice is deep and the threat is there. I can tell she's biting her tongue and I love it. I love taming my wild girl.

"Let me be very clear. I would have loved to get lost inside of you and give you every pleasure imaginable. But I will not be made a fool, Bethany. Do you understand?"

"I'm not a fucking idiot."

"You put a knife against my chest," I rebut. "That doesn't make you a smart woman, does it?"

"I'm sorry," she tells me again and her gaze falls to my chest, but I grip her chin, stealing her attention back to what matters.

"Do you think words are enough? Words are meaningless."

She shakes her head. "I can't go back. What more do you want from me?" She screams her question, the hoarse words ricocheting in the restaurant.

Even now she pushes me. She'll never stop. I know she won't. The fire inside of her will never die.

And I love it. I will live for the moments she defies me.

Knowing that to be the truth, I pin her hands above her head when I thrust inside of her this time and push my chest to hers. My muscles scream and a cold sweat breaks out along my back as I rut between her legs, hard and deep, listening to her strangled cries of pleasure.

I nearly don't stop. I nearly ruin the punishment, but fate would have me go through with it. The leg of the table that's closest to me, buckles and breaks. Forcing us to fall as the table crashes to the floor.

Silencing her scream with a desperate kiss, I pull her body on top of mine as my back falls against the broken wood. With an arm wrapped around her back, I roll over to lay her on the floor.

I only take a moment to make sure she's all right, and her response is to writhe under me, begging me to keep fucking her.

I slam myself as hard and deep as I can inside of her and stay right there. She claws at the floor, screaming and moaning with nothing to silence her cries.

Watching her gasp for air and struggling to contain herself, I push the question out with what little control I have left. "Tell me what you really think of me."

I shouldn't have asked and it shouldn't matter, but in this moment, being inside of her and having her at my mercy, I need to know. More than anything else, I need to know the truth.

She struggles not to thrash under me as I rub her clit, still buried inside of her. "Tell me the truth, cailín tine."

"I love you," she practically screams the repressed truth and I still. My body tenses, even as she continues to thrash beneath me, heaving in air and still pushing me away, although weakly.

I have to move. Before I lose myself inside her, and before she says anything else.

She loves me.

I fuck her with long strokes, each of them penetrating her as deeply as I can and pulling out until I'm barely inside of her.

Each time she lets out a moan of sudden pleasure and then her eyes seek mine, wanting more, needing me again and again.

I draw out her release, teasing her like this and nipping her lips. All the while hearing her say those words over and over in my head. *She loves me.*

She whispers it again, right when her pussy tightens and she cries out her orgasm.

When I finally feel my own release, I sink my teeth into her neck, not biting her, but needing to do something so I don't groan out words I'll regret.

The haze of desire fades slowly and then all at once when I sit up, pulling myself away from her, and she finally looks me in the eyes.

For a long time, the only thing I can hear is both of us breathing, both of us getting a grip on what just happened. She said she loves me.

As I clean between her legs, pressing the cloth napkin against her clit and forcing her head to fall back from the pressure, I'm all too aware that I didn't say the words back.

And I don't plan on it.

"You're not going to your friend's house to put her in danger and you're not going to a fucking hotel and leaving my men out there to watch over you. You're coming home with me."

Shock colors her expression at first when I stand up and leave her where she is. She reaches for her tank top before anything else and then finally looks up at me.

"I don't love you." The words rush out of her, the hurt written on her face. She tries to swallow up the evidence of her lie, but it doesn't work.

"Of course you don't," is all I answer her, burying the sensation that grows inside of me. I turn my back to her while putting my pants back on as she cleans herself up. "You're coming home with me," I repeat, focusing on what matters. A truth she can't deny, unlike what she's doing now.

The chair behind me groans against the floor as it's moved and I peek over my shoulder to see her nearly dressed and avoiding eye contact. "Did you hear me?" I ask her, feeling something stir inside my chest with restlessness.

Bethany kicks aside a scrap of wood to stand and nods her head while answering me, "Yes, and that's fine. I don't want to go back to my place anyway." Her voice is low, too low and devoid of any of the fight I'm used to from her.

The silence of the restaurant is uncanny as we wait there, with my eyes on her and her eyes anywhere else.

"Seth's waiting for us outside. You'll follow me and he'll be behind you."

She nods and audibly swallows but doesn't say anything else as she wraps her arms around one another. Not crossing her arms in front of her chest, but laying them atop each other. Her gaze lingers on the front door, but she doesn't move until I splay my hand on the small of her back.

That gets a reaction from her. She walks faster, fast enough for the pressure of my touch to be meaningless.

No one's out front of the restaurant, no one except Seth leaning against the hood of his black Audi and keeping watch. The light dusting of white on the ground outside is evidence that the snow must have come and gone already. Leaving behind it a thick white fog, and the curtain of white across every surface.

Bethany lets me open the front door for her and I'm granted a muted thank you. Same with her car door. She doesn't look toward Seth at all; she merely focuses her attention on each of her steps.

Seth's gaze turns questioning. Anyone with any common sense can see she's not well.

"Upset" is hardly a word I would use to describe Bethany. It's too weak. She's too volatile to simply be upset. But right now, it's the only word I can find. She's upset and I fucking hate it.

I love you.

She said it and then took it back. She's confused and upset. Confusion runs deep in my mind as well. For the first time since I've set eyes on her, I'm uncertain what to do with her.

I want to hear her tell me those words again, and to mean it. But I would never wish for a girl like her to fall for me, either.

"You can close the door, Mr. Cross," she tells me, staring at my shoes from where she sits in the driver's seat. The clinking of her keys is all I can hear as I stare down at her, waiting for her to look up at me. My hand is still firmly on her car door.

A gust of wind passes and I can hear Seth clear his throat in the distance. Still I don't look away, and neither does she.

"Bethany," I murmur her name and she hums back, a sweet sound, seemingly just fine, but still doesn't look at me.

"What's wrong?" My grip tightens on the door when the question leaves me. I already know and I feel like an asshole. She's a mess. That's all she's been since I've come into her life. A mess, but a beautiful masterpiece. She'll do more good in a week at the hospital than I'll do in my entire life. There's no questioning that.

"Nothing," she answers in a whisper, then peeks up at me, toying with her keys in her hand and offering a sad smile.

"You look like you're going to cry."

Her voice in response is stubborn, but it also cracks. "I'm not."

"Get out of the car, Bethany." I give her the command and step back although I keep my grip on the door, pulling it open wider and waiting on the vacant street. I can't help but notice our footprints on the sidewalk. Hers are so much smaller than mine, but the spacing is the same. They're in complete rhythm and time with mine.

She clears her throat as she steps out, moving over the curb and onto the sidewalk. Toe to toe with me, she stands there, both of her hands cradling the keys. Maybe to keep them from making noise, maybe to give her something to focus on other than me.

Either way she looks me in the eyes, daring me to accuse her of being on the verge of tears again. I can see it.

Instead I tell her, "I don't love you too." I don't think about it; I just say it. Feeling the restlessness sway inside of me, panicking and not knowing how she'll react.

Her large hazel eyes widen even more, for only a moment as her lips part just slightly and other than that, there's no response at all. No telling as to what she thinks. Until she tries to speak and the first word can't even make it out unbroken.

Instead of carrying on with the intention of speaking, she snags her bottom lip between her teeth to keep it from trembling and stares at the window of the car door rather than at me.

I add, leaning closer to her, close enough to feel her warmth and for her hair to kiss against me with the upcoming gust, "I lied to you and you lied to me. Now we're lying to each other."

I hate myself in this moment, for daring to lead her into this path. But the other path is away from me. I want her close, I need her as close to me as I can have her.

Her hazel eyes swirl with a mix of emotions. Complicated and in broken disarray, the amber colors bleeding into one another, but each still visible and adding to the beauty of her gaze.

"I don't love you." She shakes her head as the statement leaves her. Her body consciously denying the very words she speaks.

"I don't love you too," I repeat.

She's searching. Trying to figure out whether or not I'm lying to her and I don't know what she'll find. I don't know if I'm even capable of loving anymore. Not the way she needs. Not the way she deserves.

Before she can find whatever truth there is, I crash my lips against hers, letting go of the door to pull her into my arms. Her soft lips melt as I deepen the kiss. Her small hands reach up to push against my chest, but instead she quickly fists my coat and pulls me in even closer.

With a swift glide of my tongue against the seam of her lips, she parts them for me and lets me in. In the middle of the empty sidewalk, I pour everything into that kiss, holding her body against mine. Letting her feel what it is that I have. Maybe she can feel what I have for her. Maybe she'll know it better than I can.

I can feel her heart pound against her chest, maybe hating my own, maybe needing another to commiserate with.

chapter six

Bethany

THE QUIET IS UNCOMFORTABLE. OR MAYBE IT'S JUST MY THOUGHTS FILLING UP THE SILENCE that are uncomfortable. Every second, I go through an entire day. Each day since Jenny's gone missing, even worse when she was found dead, and then each day that Jase tore through the shambles of my life.

That's what the mind does when placed in a quiet room.

His bedroom is a subdued masculinity. A calming presence that begs me to lie down and sink into the plush linens. But then... the thoughts come back. The memories. The what-ifs.

Sitting on the edge of his bed, I focus on the chaos that used to be. The Rockford Center kept me busy, kept me going. And I miss it.

I miss my patients. Marky Lindgren in particular. He always had a story to tell. Sometimes the patients are violent. Sometimes they're vile with what they say. Sometimes all they do is cry, and I keep reminding myself of what I'd tell them when they apologized.

"You're having a moment and you can have as many as you need."

People mourn differently. Funny how on this side of it all, I find my own advice something to ignore. I don't need moments; I need a way forward.

And that's why I miss Marky. Marky's a liar and he spins stories about the other patients to occupy his time. I remember one night he told me how the male patient at the end of the hall had slept with one of the patients that had just been admitted.

He said it so confidently, so seriously, I almost believed him.

And then he told me how she just had to break it off with her husband who was in room 3B. But the man in 3B wasn't going to let her go without a fight and that's what all the commotion was about. Why everyone was crying and yelling.

He said it was a love triangle and then he added... the man at the end of the hall would be fine with a threesome, but he'd never admit it to the woman. I shake my head remembering how he said it, baiting me and waiting for a response I didn't give him.

Each time someone would walk past his room, he'd create a dialogue on what they thought of the adulteress and the sordid affair that never took place. Some of his comments made me genuinely laugh.

The first time I let the smile show on my face, he laughed and then I with him.

He would break up the time with stories that didn't matter, stories you could get lost in. I let myself get lost in them too, because the man in 3B was always angry due to having Alzheimer's and not knowing why he was there. And the man at the end of the hall was violent because he wanted to end it all and we had to strap him down to keep him from doing just that. All over a job he'd lost. It was just a job and just an income. But the debt was too much for him to bear.

Real life didn't matter in Marky's stories though, and amid the chaos, the rounds of delivering pills and checking on patients, Marky's stories made some horrific days tolerable.

No matter how bad the days got though, going home I felt accomplished, needed, and like the chaos was worth it.

The man at the end of the hall found a way out of the hole he'd dug himself with bankruptcy. The man in 3B remembered some of the best times of his life when his family came and they'd just come two weeks ago before I was told to go on leave; it made all the difference for him.

I still don't know about the woman who just came in. She's not from around here and we were told to keep her "attendance"—as they called it—private.

I wasn't even given her full name, only initials.

I miss the chaos, I miss Marky's stories, I even miss my boss and the bullshit rotating schedule. I miss my mind being occupied.

Right now, in the quietness of Jase's bedroom, I'd prefer to be in the halls of the Rockford Center, wondering what everyone else's story is and helping them with their tales, rather than having to face my own.

A creak in the hall catches my attention. A sputtering in my chest echoes to the pit of my stomach. "Jase?" I call out when the door doesn't open.

It's his own bedroom, so if he wanted to come in, surely he would.

But the door doesn't open and I'm left staring at a doorknob I haven't dared touch and wondering what the fuck I'm doing.

Neither of us spoke last night really. Which is for the best. I don't trust the words coming out of my mouth when he's near me.

So we didn't speak, apart from the necessary details.

Half a bottle of zinfandel, a full dish of chicken parmesan, and a soft pillow in a quiet house, with the firm chest at my back of a man who says he'll keep me safe... and I fell asleep. A deep sleep, one where you don't move and you don't dream, because your body sleeps just as heavily as your mind.

That's the kind of sleep I had and then I woke up to a note from Jase, letting me know that he'd be back later tonight and to "make myself comfortable."

I've been torn and now I'm breaking down. If I were at work right now, visitors might think I should be in one of the rooms, rather than in my scrubs holding a tray of medication to dish out.

Do I love Jase? I don't know. It's easy to want love when you're hurting. It's easy to hold on to anything that could fill the void pain has caused. I don't know what's real, and what's the product of coping.

Does Jase Cross love me? No. He doesn't. Not at all.

I think he feels bad for me. It's all sympathy. The way he looked at me tonight said it all. He feels sorry for me.

It's such bullshit. But at least I'm safe. All I need to be, right now, is safe.

And that's the dichotomy I'm supposed to *make myself comfortable* in.

He left me two rules on the slip of paper as well:

If the door is locked, stay out.

Your handprint opens the front door and the hall door behind the stairwell. Don't open the hall door at the moment and don't leave. I'm trusting you.

In other words, stay right where I left you. If I didn't feel so tired, I'd have my ass out of that front door, and walk in knee-deep snow to some shady hotel I could afford. Just to spite him.

But I'm tired. All the sleep in the world can't help the type of tired I am.

You may be tired, Bethany Ann Fawn, you may be sad and in a shit position, but you are still a badass. You are not going to take any shit. And those rules Jase left you, those rules that sexy motherfucker thinks he can lay down while trapping you here, those rules can go fuck themselves.

My little pep talk kicks my lips up into a grin and the lyrics to a Pretty Reckless song play in my mind.

Tell them it's good. Tell them okay, but don't do a goddamn thing they say.

It's been my life's motto. Nothing's going to change that.

My first move is to push the curtains in the bedroom as far open as I can. They're heavy and the sky is full of white fog, not offering much light at all. I think it's the winter that's gotten me so down, at least it's part of the reason. The season can take some of this blame.

With a little more light in his too-dark-even-with-the-light-on bedroom, I go drawer by drawer. I don't find anything interesting. Socks, neatly folded in a row. Same with his ties. I let my fingers linger over them, feeling the silk and wondering how he could even choose a tie like this, given the patterns are hidden this way.

I finally find a drawer that's mostly empty; it only houses two pairs of jeans I'm able to put in his undershirt drawer, which is filled with white and black cotton undershirts... and now two pairs of jeans.

All of my things don't even fill the drawer: two pairs of PJs, a pair of sweats, a pair of jeans and a few tops. It's everything that was in my clean laundry basket. I have a closet full of clothes, but I wear these garments over and over again. What can I say? I like what I like and I damn well like to be comfortable.

The toiletries are next, but there's not a space in the medicine cabinet, nor under the sink. I'm able to clear room in the linen closet and shamelessly rearrange what was under the cabinet, putting most of it in the closet and finding a place for my own things there.

A tightness starts in my abdomen and works its way up every time I peek at the medicine cabinet. The pills are still at my house; the ones I stole from Jase. That's the only spot available to put anything in there, but I don't bother to touch anything else in that cabinet.

All in all, I waste about an hour. That's all the time I could fill. Then I'm back to staring at the doorknob, wondering when Jase will be back, wondering if I should leave, if I should go. All the wondering that drives me mad.

The clouds shift behind me, as does the faint light in the room. A band of white light shines across the room until it lands on my purse. It's only then that I realize my phone is probably dead since I haven't charged it.

As I'm rummaging for it, I take out The Coverless Book. I have no right to feel betrayed by it, but I do. Jase's charger on his nightstand works for my phone and once it comes to life, I stare at a blank screen. No missed calls and no missed texts.

I call the Center, keeping the phone plugged in and sitting on the edge of Jase's side of the bed. I'm given the voicemail before the second ring occurs. They shunted me there intentionally. If they were just going to ignore me, why bother calling yesterday?

I listen to the voicemail message far too long before hanging up. I have no one right now. No one.

The only people waiting for me, are the fictional characters in The Coverless Book.

chapter seven

Jase

I could hardly focus on the update from Carter this morning. Romano's planning something judging by how he's moving storage units and Carter thinks he might take off, so we have to strike now if we want a chance at getting him before he leaves. He said Officer Walsh has members of the FBI in town, something about them being involved with Romano's indictment. They're all over him and watching his every move, which makes it impossible for us to do a damn thing.

I couldn't focus on anything he was telling me in his office. All I could think about was how Bethany had wrapped her arms around me in the middle of her sleep. She clung to me without knowing, nestling her head against my chest. I could live a thousand lives in that single moment.

All I could picture was how serene she looked in her sleep. All throughout the conversation with Carter and all throughout the drive to the club.

If she knew her sister was still alive, she wouldn't sleep like that. If she finds out I knew and I didn't tell her, she wouldn't cling to me like she had last night.

I only have one lead that could change the course of where this is all going. One chance, one moment, to hold on to Bethany like I want to. One lead, who's waiting for me just beyond the glowing red lights of the sign ahead of me.

The Red Room isn't just a cover. It's not just for laundering and meetups. Just like the storage shed behind it isn't exactly what it looks like. It's inconspicuous, large and organized with wide open spaces. Everything clearly seen on first glance when you walk into the storage shed which measures forty feet on each side. I demand it be kept clean and tidy. So anyone looking for any hint of it being anything other than a place to keep the extra bottles of liquor and tables would know at first glance there's nothing else here.

Unless they opened the safe and found the secret door in the back of it. It leads to a winding iron staircase, down to a long hall in the basement with a vault door to a room.

The skinny hallway that leads to the room reminds me of the old warehouse I'd sneak off to when I was a boy. Back when I needed to be alone and get away. It was quiet, and offered the comfort of both safety and a place to simply be alone.

The room in that basement exists for one purpose. And one purpose only.

The men who find themselves here aren't feeling the security I did when I was younger and hiding in the warehouse.

No, the men who end up in this room are here to die, although they would say and do anything to believe that they'll get out of here still breathing.

The vault door opens with a slow, plaintive cry. It's heavy and made of thick steel. With Seth behind me, we enter the room comprised of four smooth concrete walls. It's soundproof and the floors are made of steel grids with a drain in the center of the room.

There's no furniture in the room, save an old iron chair bolted to the floor over the drain. I bring everything I need with me each time.

This time I've brought a pair of hedge clippers, the kind most people use for their gardens. They're in my back pocket, as is my pocket knife.

The muffled screams that come from behind the balled cloth in Luke Stevens's mouth fill the room as the two of us walk in.

His skin's paler and almost gray in this light than it was in the video we had of him and another man talking about where Marcus wanted Jenny Parks delivered. That's the word that came out of his mouth. Delivered. As if she were only an object to be shipped off.

The steel cuffs leave bright red marks around his wrists and ankles, along with a trail of dried blood as he wrestles with his restraints, still screaming. Like it would do him any good to fight.

My nostrils flare with the stench of piss in the damp underground as I get a few feet from him and then look to my right to ask Seth, "How long?"

"Twelve hours now."

He stands closer to the prisoner than I do. We have a system that works. When something works, you don't fuck it up. He knows that and he stands where he always does, just behind the subject of our interrogation, where he can't be seen.

Crouching in front of Luke, a man who may know where Jenny is, I look into his dark eyes, taking in how dilated they are. Wondering what the hell he's on.

"You think twelve hours is enough?" I ask Seth and he shrugs. Luke struggles to look behind him, and his ass comes off the chair just slightly, but the chain wrapped around his waist keeps him down.

Standing up straighter, I pull the clippers from my back pocket and unlock them to look at the blade. "They're dull," I comment as if I didn't notice before.

"They'll still work," Seth says and this time he places a hand on either side of the back of the chair, close enough to Luke so our victim notices, but still not touching him.

I can imagine how Luke's heart races, how the adrenaline takes over. The fight or flight response failing him and every instinct in his body screaming for him to beg. Just like he's screaming now, behind the old shirt shoved in his mouth. Seth's silent and that's how he'll stay until I ask him if there's any reason not to kill the man in the chair.

"Take it out." On my command, Seth removes the shirt from Luke's mouth, ripping the duct tape across his skin in a swift motion. The bright pink skin left behind marks where the tape once laid.

"I didn't do it," Luke screams immediately. Even as the pain tears through him and he's forced to wince, he continues to plead. "Whatever it is, I didn't do it. I didn't fuck with you guys."

"Jenny Parks," I say quietly, and it's all I say. Realization dawns on the man that he did, in fact, do it. He fucked with us. And it shuts him up, although his bottom lip still quivers.

There's a knowing look of fear in his eyes. The lack of an exhale, the stale gaze he gives me. "You know her name."

His mouth closes before he speaks and he visibly swallows.

"Every time you hesitate, I take something from you," I tell him easily, crouched in front of him and waiting for him to acknowledge what I've said.

The second his mouth opens to speak, I grip his hand, choosing his pointer first. The clank of the cuffs and his protests mix in the damp air that still smells like piss. Seth does his part, shoving the shirt in the man's mouth as I clamp down on the clippers. My left hand keeps the other fingers bent, stopping them from interfering. My right hand closes the blades around his pointer. The flesh cuts easily; blood flows just as easily as he lets out a high-pitched muffled scream, but the bone I have to break away from the ligament first before it's cleanly gone.

I take a half step back, watching the blood pour from where his finger was moments ago. It streams out steadily and more blood creeps from under the metal cuffs that keep him held down as he struggles. Seth keeps his hand over the shirt, and watches Luke's face turn bright red, struggling to breathe, screaming with everything he has in him.

His chest heaves. But it never lasts long. The screaming is only temporary. Just like the hesitation and the lies.

"I've done this a few times, Mr. Stevens," I comment as I wipe the blade on his dark blue denim jeans. Although he's stopped screaming, the shirt stays where it is. Seth knows to only remove it once I'm ready for the man to speak.

I let out a heavy exhale and then crouch down in front of him again as I say, "I don't like to waste my time." My tone is easy, consoling even as I stare into his bloodshot eyes, noting the desperation that flows from his sweaty skin. I tell him, "I just want answers, and then all of this is over."

He tries to shriek through the shirt, his neck craning as he more than likely pleads with Seth to remove the gag. The tendons in his neck tense and he keeps it up, which only pisses me off.

"We don't have time for your comments or questions. Now answer mine. Do you know Jenny Parks?"

With the question asked, Seth removes the rag and the man in the chair stumbles over his words.

"She's the girl I took to the bridge." He does well with the first statement, but then he backtracks and barters. My irritation would show, if I weren't expecting it. After all, I have done this more than a few times. He started off strong, thinking it was a negotiation, but the tilt of my head changed his tone to one of a beggar.

"If I tell you everything… will you just let me go? Please! I'll tell you everything!"

I stare at the clippers and take in a breath. A single breath waiting for more information and then my gaze moves to Luke, my eyebrows raising in warning.

He looks to his left quickly, as if anything is there. He tries to get up as if the cuffs had disappeared. What he doesn't do, is give me the information I need.

The shirt is shoved back into his mouth and his ring finger goes next, leaving the middle finger on his left hand easily available for the next time I need to prove a point.

Tears leak from the man's eyes and his cries turn morbid as he mourns his mistake. I feel… I feel nothing but anger for him. Anger I don't show.

"Mr. Stevens, I read your file. You killed your mistress and then your wife. Or no," I feign a correction as I keep eye contact with Seth, not the man I'm determined to kill tonight. "Was it his wife first and then his mistress?"

"You've got it a little wrong, Boss," Seth tells me casually, the shirt still balled up in Luke's mouth, even though he's only crying, no longer screaming. "It was his sister and then his wife."

"No mistress then?"

Seth shakes his head in time with a sputtering of heaving coughs from Luke. "They stole his dope, or something like that." I stoop in front of the man and ask him, "Is that right?"

He's nodding his head even before the shirt's taken from him. As the damp cloth leaves his mouth, he nearly chokes trying to speak too soon. With a quick intake of air he explains himself. "They were going to take it all."

"Oh," I say and nod in understanding. "I see." Again I wipe the blades of the clippers on Luke's jeans. He glances down and then his head falls back as he tries desperately not to cry again.

"And you took Jenny Parks."

"I didn't take her!" He shakes his head as he denies what I said. And I wait a fraction of a second for him to explain. Which he does this time, the information flowing from his lips. "She wanted to go to Marcus. I was dropping her off! I was just supposed to drop her off at the bridge!"

"What bridge?"

"On Fifth and Park. The overpass." He nearly says more, but stops himself. With a knowing look I lean forward, but he continues. Just barely in time. "It's where I do all the drops for Marcus." His pale skin turns nearly white and his voice lowers. "Every three weeks or so, I have a pickup from out of state and a drop-off at the bridge. He gives an address. I go, pick up the unmarked package and drop it off at the bridge. A few weeks ago, he gave a name instead of an address. He told me to go to her, and to tell her Marcus was ready."

I can feel my brow pinch and a crease deepen in my forehead as I ask, "Do you know what he wanted with her?"

"No!" His head shakes violently with the answer. "I just had to pick her up and drop her off. That's all!"

"And what about the other drops?" I question him. "You ever take a peek at what's inside?"

Instead of answering, he swallows. Poor fucker.

His cry this time isn't at all like the last two. Seth covers his mouth as Luke's head falls back, and his middle finger drops to the grated floor alongside the other two severed extremities.

"Please, please." I know that's what he's saying behind the gag. *Please, stop.* I've heard it so many times in my life.

But in this world, there is no stopping.

I take a moment, wondering how he killed his wife. How he looked her in the eyes and stabbed her to death. Fourteen stab wounds. His sister was a gunshot to the back of the head. That one, that type of kill sounds like someone who stole from him. But fourteen stab wounds... that's anger. The twin sister of passion.

When Seth removes the shirt, Luke's head hangs heavy in front of him. He sucks in air like he's been going without it for too long. I could change that, but that's not in my favor.

"I want answers, Luke."

"Drugs. Lots of them. That's what the packages were."

"What kind of drugs?" I ask and for the first time, I grit my teeth, letting him hear the frustration.

He doesn't answer immediately and I stand up straighter, quickly gripping the hair at the back of his head and pulling it back so I can bring the clippers to his throat.

Seth takes a step back and I can feel his eyes on me, knowing this isn't the way it goes down. I couldn't give two shits about that right now.

"Heroin, coke, pot, you name it." Luke's answers are strained with his throat stretched out.

"And sweets?" I ask him.

The dumb fuck tries to nod and the blade slips across his skin. It's only a scratch, one he probably can't even feel with all the other pain rushing through him.

"Marcus doesn't need to deal. What's he doing with it?" I ask as I release him, turning my back to him and taking a few steps away to calm down.

"I don't know," is Luke's first answer but before I can even fully turn around the words rush out of him. "I think it's experiments and setups. He needs the drugs for planting them and I think a month or so ago, that deputy who OD'd? I think that was Marcus."

He insists he doesn't know after that, giving examples that he thinks Marcus may be responsible for, but not saying for sure that his guesses are true.

"You were in it for the money?" I question and to my surprise, the man shakes his head.

"At first… but then I wanted to be in with him. I wanted a place on his team."

The last sentence brings a chill to flow over my skin. "His team?"

Luke nods once. "I wanted to work with him."

"Marcus works alone," I tell him and he actually laughs. It's a sad, sick kind of laugh that graces his lips for only a fraction of a second, but then he shakes his head, looking me in the eyes. "That's not what Jenny said. She said he needed her. That she was going to make things right with Marcus."

"And what did you think that meant?" I ask him, feeling a frigid bite taking over my limbs. It grows colder and colder.

"That he was giving her an in to control it all."

"Control it all? You think that's what Marcus does?"

With hope fleeing Luke's eyes, he nods. "He has an army."

"And you think that's what Jenny was there for? To be in his army?" I ask him, getting closer to him.

He nods.

"Do you know anyone else in his army?"

He slowly shakes his head. "But she told me that's what she was doing. She said she was joining his army."

An army of men working under Marcus. I share a look with Seth and he shrugs but doesn't look so sure.

"I'm not convinced," I say offhandedly and Luke's body jolts up as his voice raises. He's adamant it's the truth. All the while he continues to spill his thoughts that mean nothing to me, I consider what he's saying. There's simply no way Marcus would trust anyone to be involved with his plans.

"So what's he doing with Jenny then?" I raise my gaze to the now silent Luke Stevens. "What is he going to do with her?"

"I don't know. All I know is that I dropped her off securely. I held up my end of the bargain."

"And what did you get in return?" I ask him. He hesitates, but I don't bother removing anything else from him.

"Money," he finally answers. "Four grand."

"Is there anything else we should ask him?" I direct my question to Seth, who merely shakes his head before suffocating the man with his shirt.

Luke fights to breathe, but it's useless. It takes a few minutes and still Seth keeps the shirt over his face when Luke's body is motionless for another minute longer.

"You think he'll keep her alive?" I ask Seth once the rustling and muted screams have settled to silence.

"To start an army?"

I shake my head and agree with the expression on his face. That it's unrealistic for Marcus to have an army. It may have been what he led her to believe, but there is no army.

"Any reason at all that he'd keep her alive," I answer him.

"Marcus doesn't do loose ends." Seth's answer causes a chill to travel down the back of my neck. The feeling of loss and failure intertwine and wrap around my throat as I ask him, "What am I going to tell Bethany?"

His answer is simple and I already know it's what I should do, even if it's not what she'd want. "Nothing. Don't bring her into this any more than she already is."

chapter eight

Bethany

THE COVERLESS BOOK PLAYS TRICKS ON ME. I WAS CERTAIN EMMY'S MOTHER WOULD FIRE THE caretaker for poisoning her daughter. But she says it's only medicine that was poured into the soup. With the bottle in her hand, the mother does nothing but reprimand Emmy. She doesn't look any deeper into it. She only tells Jake that he's out of line and that Miss Caroline did nothing wrong. Emmy begs her mother to hire someone else and fire Miss Caroline, all to no avail.

Hate consumes me. For the women who are supposed to protect and love Emmy. And for the situation the young girl is in.

I read about how Jake is no longer welcome on the property, but Emmy sneaks out to see him, refusing to go on with life as she has been.

She doesn't eat what Caroline cooks so Caroline stops cooking for her altogether, crying outside of the kitchen all while Emmy cries in her bedroom and her mother does God knows what.

It's only at night that anything seems right. Only when Emmy climbs out of her bedroom window to meet Jake. It's the two of them against the world.

There's a passage that makes me feel alive, a passage that warms everything in my body.

"Take my hand and trust me," he tells her. "I promise to save you, because I love you."

That's what you do when you love someone, he said. You save them.

And that's where I had to stop.

Three more sentences are underlined. I don't have my journal with me though to add them to the list. It's useless to add them anyway. I've accepted that there's no message buried in the lines. Maybe Jenny just wanted me to read the story. Maybe she fell in love with Emmy and Jake like I have. So many maybes and questions that will never be answered.

I lay the book on its pages, so I don't lose where I'm at. I have to rub my eyes, and take a break after reading the last line I underlined, the line Emmy's mother told Jake. *Hope is a long way of saying goodbye.* It's in the book.

The words I gave to her, she saw it here. I wonder when she read it. Which came first. Not that it matters. None of it matters anymore.

I don't know why I bother to keep reading when it only makes me sad inside. When I know there's no message buried beneath the black and white letters.

It makes no sense at all, either, that I reach out to the phone to text Miranda, Jenny's friend who gave me the book.

I want to text Jenny and I'm conscious of that. I nearly do. I nearly text her, *Why this book? What did you want me to get from it?*

I'm not that crazy yet, so I text Miranda instead. Or maybe that makes me crazier. I'm not sure anymore.

Thank you for giving me the book.

It takes a minute before my phone vibrates in my hand with a response. *Bethany?*

Of course she wouldn't know it's me. Feeling foolish, I answer her, *Yes, I'm sorry to message, I just wanted to make sure I'd thanked you.*

You should know, when I saw her with that book and she was underlining it.... She said you would understand better then. She said you'd be happy.

I'd be happy?

Miranda is no one to me. I'd have been just fine never seeing her again... until my sister died. That changed so many things. She's a person I would never confide in, yet here I am, not hesitating to bleed out my every thought and emotion without recourse into a stream of texts. *I'm anything but happy. Maybe if she was truly invincible, I'd be better.*

Feeling the need to explain, I follow up my messages. *Sorry, it's a line in the book. She keeps saying she's invincible.*

I stare at her next message, reading it over and over. *So that's where she got it... she was saying that for a while before she packed.*

Packed? I think to myself. Why would she have packed? Jenny didn't tell me that before.

I text her back, *Where did she go?*

Her answer is immediate. *I thought she went home to you. She didn't tell me where. I just assumed she was going back to you because she said she needed help.*

Jenny always said she wanted help, but she didn't really mean it. She only said it to get me off her back. It was always lies she told me.

But maybe that day, she was coming home. Maybe she finally wanted to get better. It's the sliding doors of life. If only one thing had changed, everything would be different. Maybe she was coming back home. Maybe that's when they got her. Maybe I was only minutes away from being back with her and they tore her from me.

I drop the phone onto the nightstand, not bothering to reply anymore.

Hating all the maybes, all the possibilities that could have, should have happened.

Everything stills for a moment, going out of focus. As if forcing me to embrace only one thing: She's gone. My sister is gone. My sister is gone, and I have nothing left. No one left but a man who I know is bad for me and one who will never love me.

The first tear that comes, I thought I could control. I can feel the telltale prickle, and how the back of my throat suddenly goes dry in that way that I know it's coming. I think I can keep it from slipping with a single long, deep breath. I think I can stop it and be just fine. I don't need a moment.

I thought so wrong. The first sob comes and in its wake and my failure to control it, heaving ugly sobs come bearing down on me. They're reckless, and unwarranted. Turning to my side, I bury my head in the pillow, wishing I could suffocate the sniveling wails that come from me without any consent at all.

I hate crying. I've always hated it.

The tears are hotter and larger as they slip down my heated face. Falling to my chin just below where my bottom lip quivers.

Jenny is gone. Such a simple thing, something I deal with constantly in work and have dealt with all my life. She's gone and there's nothing I can do about it.

The nightmares aren't real. She isn't hiding somewhere waiting for me to save her.

The book is only words; there's no deeper message within. It's only words, meaningless like Jase said they were.

It all means nothing.

I have nothing and I feel like nothing just the same. But why does nothing hurt so much? Why does it hurt this bad when you give up hope?

Something must find its way into hope's place in your heart. And that something feels like burning knives that keep stabbing me. I just want it all to stop. I want this chapter to end. Fuck, I need it to end. I can't live like this. I can't live in constant, all-consuming pain with nowhere to run.

Jenny, I hate you for leaving me. I hate you, but even hating you doesn't make the pain stop. I still love you and I don't think love can exist without hope.

It's funny how I cling to something that's not there. That I have faith that I'll see her again in another life. Or that if I somehow bring her justice, she'll know. That it will mean something to her, even if she's not here.

Settling back into the pillow, I lie there tired and feeling like I'm drowning. I start to think that it's okay to drown, that I shouldn't fight it anymore. I'm scared of what will happen when I stop fighting though. What happens when I sink lower and lower into the cold darkness?

That's the imagery that meets me in my sleep.

Jenny

It's almost been a month. Every day drags, achingly slowly. Every second wanting me to suffer more and more. It's worse than what I thought it would be. The nausea and shaking. I can't get over how cold I am all the time here.

There's nothing but cinder block walls and a mattress on the floor. If I could think for a moment, I'd remember where I am, but I don't remember. I can barely stand up without vomiting.

My bare knees scrape on the floor as I brace myself. The floor feels damp at first, like it's wet, but the palms of my hands are dry. Rocking my body back and forth, I try to just breathe through the aching pain, the sweating, the constant moving thoughts that only stay still when I see her. That's the only time everything settles, but it falls into the darkness where I hate myself for what I've done and what I've become.

The rumbling happens again, the gentle shaking of the light above my head. I'm not crazy. It's real. The room shakes every so often.

He told me I could sleep through it. Weeks of sleeping while my body goes through withdrawal. He said he'd take care of me, that I had a purpose in this world.

He said he'd help me. Marcus can't help me through this though. No one can help me. No one can save me from where my mind goes when I lie down.

I can't sleep anymore. Bethany's there every time I close my eyes and I feel sicker and full of guilt. I can't sleep through this, knowing what I did to her. What I sacrificed to be here.

"It'll all be worth it."

My eyes whip up to his when I hear his voice. "It hurts," is all I can say and I feel pathetic. Hurts isn't adequate. "I feel like I'm dying." The sentence is pulled from me, slowly, as it drags too. Everything drags so slowly.

"A part of you is dying." His voice holds no emotion, no remorse, no sympathy. It's only matter of fact. "And that's a good thing."

My head nods although I don't know that I agree. Some moments I do. Some moments I just want it to end. I know what would make it all stop; I know a needle would make it go away. I nearly beg for it, but the last time I did, he left me alone in here. "I thought it would only be weeks," I tell him, gripping on to that thread of a thought.

"It has only been weeks."

Shaking my head violently and then hating the spinning that comes after, I grip the sides of my head and rock again, trying to settle.

His voice carries softly to me, as if it's rocking me as well, "It's been close to a month. It's almost over. Just sleep."

"I don't want to sleep!" I scream at him, the words clawing up my throat and scarring the tender flesh on their way out.

"Then don't." His answer is simple. In the dark corner of the room, he sits and watches. That's what he does. He observes. That's not what Beth would do. Licking the cracked skin on my bottom lip, I remember how she always had to be there, always involved, always telling me what I was doing wrong.

I wish I'd listened to her.

My rocking turns gentle just thinking about her.

"You said you'd tell her I was okay."

"I said I'll make sure she finds out." He corrects me sharply.

"Did she see it? The note Jeremy left for her?" His gaze meets mine when I say the name, we're not supposed to say each other's names. I know it's Jeremy though. He came in here to check on me the first few days. It had to be him because of the bandage on his chin.

Jeremy told me what Marcus did to his chin though. He said it was necessary and that's how I know it was him in the video Marcus showed me.

Jeremy's scar is not nearly as bad of a fate as what Luke would endure. Marcus said he deserved it. That it was meant to happen and to only tell him certain things. I listened; I was a good girl, but I regret it all right now. I want it all to stop. "Please," I whimper, "make it stop."

"It will stop in time and your sister will know in time." My sister. Bethany. I need her to know. "Things are going according to plan."

I comment, feeling hollow inside, "I just need her to know."

"Go to sleep, Jennifer." He knows the only person to call me Jennifer was my mother. I told him to stop, but all he says is that it's my name.

"I feel guilty," I confess to him as shivers run down my arms. I don't know why. Maybe because there is no judgment from him, only truth and facts no matter how cold and callous they are.

"You should," is his only answer.

"When will she know that I'm okay?" My eyes burn searching for him in the dark corner.

"That depends on something I can no longer predict."

"On what?" I ask him, feeling a new pain run down the seam of my chest.

"Jase Cross."

chapter nine

Jase

SOME DAYS, BAD SHIT HAPPENS.
Some days you take a loss.
Other days, like today, the puzzle pieces to the overall bigger picture form and you can feel the bad shit and losses preparing to come. It's like watching it all tumble around you.

It's all I can think on the drive back home. That's it falling, everything is going to fall and I'm not sure how to stop it.

As I turn right onto the long gravel road, I feel the vibrations in the car and remember the footage played for Seth and me in the back room after we took care of Luke Stevens.

Declan finally got hold of video from a coffee shop's security feed of their parking lot that showed a section of the graveyard.

A young prick with a bandage covering half of his face snuck up on us and we had no fucking clue. He was right there, hiding behind the car and then at the windshield when the cop car came into view and I was focusing on that, rather than on him tucking a note in the wipers. He hid, crouched down by the wheel, but I should've seen his hand, I should have seen him walking up in the rearview by the tree line. I should have seen, but I didn't.

Marcus may truly be building an army; an army of faceless men like this prick. An army I don't have names for.

Seth's taking care of the surveillance at the bridge Luke mentioned. We have eyes everywhere, watching and waiting. But in order to see what's going on, something has to happen. Something has to fall. And I need names and faces to recognize.

The only one I have right now is Jenny Parks.

"Shit." The curse falls from my mouth as I pull up to my driveway to the estate, seeing the cop car in plain view. Officer Walsh is standing off to the right of the yard, looking out into the woods.

Just what I fucking need.

It's one thing after another. With the rise of adrenaline, my gaze instinctively goes to the second story window on the right, the curtains wide open, but Bethany nowhere to be found.

As I park the car and the faint music I wasn't listening to shuts off, a thought passes through me: *She wouldn't have called him.* There's no way he's here because of her.

With the car door opening, the bitter air hits me and it only makes the sweat on my skin feel hotter.

"Officer Walsh," I call out, and my voice carries through the cold air. That's all I say to greet him, walking steadily past the cars to the yard where he stays put. He rocks on his heels as I slip my keys into my pocket. "Anything I can help you with?" I ask when I'm close enough to him.

"Beautiful view," he comments, taking his gaze back to the forest.

With the thin layer of snow and the white fog along the tree line, it's eerily beautiful.

I don't bother to comment, or to play with his niceties. If she called him, if she wanted to break me like that, get it over with. So I can deal with her and fix this shit.

She wouldn't do that, I think as I swallow, shoving both my hands in my pockets. The moment I glance at the trees, Officer Walsh finally looks back at me.

"I thought maybe if I told you something, you could tell me something," he says, and then clears his throat. A look crosses his face like he doesn't know if he's making the right move. Curiosity sneaks up on me and I give him a small nod as I say, "You first."

"My last case in New York… I failed to save a girl. She's all right now… but I didn't protect her like I should've. It's why I asked for reassignment. I failed her."

He doesn't look at me when he talks, so I take in every bit of his expression. Noting the sincerity in his voice. But wondering how good of a liar this prick is.

"She moved back here. Close to here, anyway."

"That why you're here?" I ask him. "Are you looking for her?"

"No, not looking," he answers me but still doesn't look at me. "I know where she is."

A breeze rushes by, causing his coat to slip open for a moment. His badge shows, just as the gun in his holster is on display for the moment. He shifts and buttons up his coat as he talks.

"I'm looking for someone else. A man named Marcus. He's the one who *saved* her." He rolls his shoulder back as he says "saved" and a grimace mars his face. "He's the one who got her out of that mess." His gaze finally meets mine when he adds, "He got her into it though. He used her, and then claims to have saved her."

His jaw clenches and an anger I haven't seen from him is left unchecked. It's evident in the way his shoulders tense, plus the way he breathes out heavily. And in his voice when he says, "Marcus put her through a hell that I can't even imagine surviving."

Emotion drenches his confession and I can feel the vendetta that wages war in his eyes.

"What is it you want from me?"

"I want Marcus." His answer is immediate. "Anything you have on him."

I swallow, hesitating and Officer Walsh shakes his head with disgust. "You know him. I know you do. I've read the files and all the paperwork. For a decade or more, you and your brothers' names have been right there along with his."

"Sure," I tell him, "Names on paperwork. But Marcus doesn't have a face, he doesn't have a number to call, he doesn't have a location. There's not a damn thing I can give you on Marcus." I'm surprised by the resentment that laces itself around every sentence that's spoken.

"If I could hand over Marcus to you, I would. Because I don't know what he's thinking or why he does the shit he does," I say with finality, and then question my own statement.

Officer Walsh considers me for a long moment, maybe waiting for more.

"I don't have anything for you, Officer."

"If you're not with me, you're against me," he responds lowly. "You know that?"

"Words to live by," I comment with a nod and this time I'm the one staring off into the woods.

"If you do find something, would you even consider telling me?" he asks and I can feel his eyes burning into me.

"I wish you all the luck in the world," I tell him and then breathe in deep, debating on answering his question truthfully, lying or simply not answering at all. I settle for the last option and ask him, "Is there anything else I can help you with?"

"What's that?" That's the first thing Bethany says to me as I set the large cardboard box down in the middle of the bedroom. She didn't respond when I walked in; she remained under the covers, in the same position she was in when I left.

Her brunette hair tumbles down her body as she raises herself off the bed. Off my bed. That knowledge does something to me, as does the white light from the open curtains kissing her skin.

"Did I wake you?" I ask her rather than answering her question. The look of sleep plays on her face, making me eager to get in bed with her. As she sits up, crossing her legs in bed and pulling the covers into her lap, her baggy sleepshirt falls off her shoulder and she has to readjust it.

"Only for a minute I think. It's been hard getting to sleep," she answers as I climb into bed, and it groans with her words.

"Just a single minute?" I tease her, wanting to put a smile on her face. She gives me a small one, accompanied with the roll of her eyes. It's my cue to lean forward, taking a single kiss from her. She's still guarded, still giving me questioning gazes and still stiff when I reach out and place my hand on her thigh.

Tucking her hands into her lap she doesn't answer me, she only shrugs and then those hazel eyes look up at me, peeking through her thick lashes.

"I went to your place," I say to change the subject, getting off the bed to go to the box and needing to get away from the look in her eyes.

I grab the pills out of the box. They're years old; we don't even make sweets in the pill form anymore. But I would never throw this bottle away. "I thought you may want some more of your things. Grabbed some mugs, your throw blanket, stuff like that."

She says thank you softly and then clears her throat to say it again louder.

"You brought my mugs?" she questions me with her brow furrowed and it only makes her look cuter. Her legs are bare as she makes her way to the box, the t-shirt stopping just past her ass.

"You have a lot of them on the counter with that box of tea." I shrug as I sit on the bed, watching her go through the box and staring at her ass as she does. "Thought you'd like them."

She takes a few things out of the box, setting them on my dresser behind her and lining up her computer, charger and a few other things in a row.

"Why are you like this?"

Her question catches me off guard. "Like what?"

"Why are you trying to make me happy... I don't understand what you want from me."

I would be frustrated if she wasn't genuinely curious. "Did you expect me to keep you here with nothing of your own?"

"I don't know what to expect," she says, and the honesty in her voice is raw and transparent.

"Right now, I want you to stop fighting me."

She smiles wide for the first time since I've walked in, staring down at an owl mug in her hand. It's a sad, soft smile. "Fighting is what I do best though. Came into the world fighting, I'll leave it that way."

I can't help but return the smile to her. "That's fine with me, cailín tine. Just don't fight with me."

"You okay?" she asks me, setting down the mug and stalking over to me. I lean forward and pull her petite body between my legs, resting my hands on the small of her back before I answer her.

"I had a long day."

I lower my head to rest in the crook of her neck and she does the same. Her lips leave a small kiss that rouses desire from me.

Just as I'm ready to take her, to lay her on the bed and fuck away my problems, she stops me, pulling away to tell me, "I did nothing today."

"Some days that's good to do, to just heal and let the world move around you."

"That's one way to put it."

Every ounce of lust dampens, seeing her lack of life. Fire dies when it's closed off and not allowed to breathe.

I want her to breathe, but she's suffocating herself.

"Did you go to the kitchenette?" I ask her and she shakes her head.

"I didn't leave the bedroom."

"I need to show you around," I comment, noting that she's been like this for a few days. Listless. Depressed. "You can't just lie around and expect to get better."

"Get better?" she bites back, her eyes flashing with indignation. "There is no 'getting better,' Mr. Cross. I'm simply trying to adapt to my new reality and I don't have a damn thing to distract me."

She stands up straighter, squaring her shoulders and leaning closer to me. "I may be taking up residence in your bed. I may do all sorts of shit with you I'd never tell a soul I craved so badly, but you," she points her finger to my chest and then licks her lower lip. The act distracts me and instantly I want to take her, punish her for tempting me. "You can tell me how you want me in bed. You can boss me around while I crawl on all fours for you, I don't give a fuck." She shrugs halfheartedly and her shirt slips off her shoulder. She knows what she's doing to me. The little smirk on her lips dims though when she looks me in the eyes and tells me, "You don't get to tell me how to live my life."

"I wasn't," I respond and I'm surprised by the sudden change. The hot and cold between us.

"I want you, I'm not afraid to admit that. Even now, when I'm not able to do what I love, I can't go into work. I'm afraid to go back to my own home," she admits and swallows, looking anywhere but at me and crosses her arms. "And I'm coming to terms with the fact that everyone in my family has died tragically and there wasn't a damn thing I could do about it." She shakes her head.

"Even now, I want you and I love the distraction of you." Her fingers linger on my chest and she steals a quick kiss before whispering down my neck as she pulls herself away from me. "But you don't get to tell me what to do or how to mourn. You'd be wise to remember that, Jase."

That's my cailín tine. Not hidden deep down, just failing to find a reason to come out. I'll give her a reason. I can give her that.

"Tell me something," she says and takes a seat on the black velvet chair next to the dresser. She lays her head back against the wall and pulls her legs into her chest.

"What do you want to know?"

"Who is Angie? What happened to her?"

Surprise lights inside of me, along with dread. "Why are you asking?"

"One time you said I reminded you of someone. Do I remind you of her?"

"She's not the one you remind me of." As I answer her, every muscle in my body tightens.

"Is that where you learned to do those things? The fire? With Angie?"

"No," I answer her again, feeling my throat go dry.

"Well then who the hell is she?" she questions flatly, shaking her head.

"She's someone who died a while back."

"I'm sorry," she whispers and I tell her it's okay although the tension grows between us.

"Do you want to talk about it?" she asks and I shake my head no.

"Everyone dies, Jase, that doesn't define her as to who she was." I don't think Bethany's aware of the magnitude that her words have. "Who was she?"

"A girl who died because of my mistakes."

"And I don't remind you of her?" she questions again, a dullness taking over her gaze.

"No."

As she goes through the things I brought her, I go to the bathroom, placing the pills where they belong. In the same spot Angie left them. The pills were hers and they've been there since the day she died. Not this same medicine cabinet, but the same location. Bottom shelf on the right. That's where she put them.

The irony isn't lost on me that Bethany took them. I stare back at myself in the mirror after I close the medicine cabinet and wonder if I should've left Beth alone. If I never should have tainted her by knocking on her door almost two weeks ago.

"Well," she says, sitting up straighter and making her way to the bed behind me. "Since it's already uncomfortable I might as well tell you, I did some math."

"Go on," I tell her when she breathes in deep, pulling the comforter all the way up. I suppose she got cold.

"One hundred dollars every ten minutes. That's fourteen thousand, four hundred every day. Which would mean the debt is paid in twenty-one days. Not months."

The semblance of a grunt leaves me and I run my thumb along my bottom lip. The only sweet distraction from this conversation is that her eyes lower, lingering on my lips and her own lips part.

"So if you're wanting me to stay here," she starts, staring at my lips as she speaks. Standing up, I walk as she talks, so I can stand across from her. "I want it in writing that the debt won't exist after twenty more days."

Leaning against the dresser, I cross my arms and gaze down at her. "You think you earned fourteen thousand dollars yesterday?"

Indignation flashes in her eyes. "The deal was time, nothing else. And I gave you all my time and listened to you." Her throat tightens as she swallows and my gaze falls to her collarbone and then lower.

"You stay with me for twenty days, which I'm doing to protect you-"

"Which I didn't ask for." She's quick to cut me off. "In fact, I think we can both agree I was resistant but did it because it's what you wanted."

"No good deed goes unpunished, huh?"

"It was never my debt," she rebuts.

Time passes with each of us staring at the other, waiting for the other one to give.

"You listen to everything I say for forty days—"

Again she cuts me off. "Twenty."

"No fucking way," I answer her, keeping my voice low. "Sleep doesn't count as listening to me."

"Thirty max, including yesterday, so twenty-nine days." Her voice is strong as she negotiates. I have to focus not to glance down at her breasts and the way they peek up from her crossed arms.

"Twenty-nine days of you doing whatever it is that I want?" I ask her, feeling my cock go rigid. I unzip my pants and let them drop to the floor so she can see.

Color rises from her chest to her cheeks. She swallows, watching me stroke myself as she answers. "Twenty-nine days," she agrees.

"Get over here and get on your knees." I barely get the words out before she's moving, kicking the sheets away so they don't trip her up.

She takes me into her mouth and I shove my cock in deeper, gripping her hair so I can control it.

Before she can choke, I pull her back and listen to her heave in a breath. She stares up at me with eagerness, her hands grabbing the back of my thighs.

"I'm going to use you and get my money's worth, cailín tine."

∽

Sleep's dragging her under. I can admit I'm exhausted as well. Not in the same way, but I can't go to sleep. I don't want tonight to end.

"I can still feel you," she whimpers. The sheets rustle between her legs as she moans softly, pushing her head into the pillow and letting the pleasure ring in her blood.

Her eyes are half lidded as she peeks up at me. "Does it feel the same for you?" she asks.

I let the tip of my nose play along her cheek and then nip her earlobe. "Does it feel drawn out to you? Like wave after wave and a single touch would make the next crash on the shore?"

Her eyes close as she breathes in deep and steady.

"Sex certainly changes things, doesn't it?" I ask her, remembering how only hours ago I worried about where her mind was headed. She hums in agreement.

I pull the sheet down from her chest slowly, exposing her all the way down to her waist. A shudder rolls through her and with a single tug on her nipples, they harden for me.

"Jase," she murmurs my name.

"I'm not done with you yet," I tell her and her hazel eyes widen.

"I stored the lighter and alcohol pads in the nightstand yesterday, hoping to play with you this morning, but you were asleep."

She huffs a small playful laugh as I open the drawer, still lying in bed. "Is that why you said sleeping doesn't count?"

Keeping one small pad folded, I run it along her closest breast and then pluck the other one, letting the moisture cool on her skin and sparking her nerve endings.

Sweet sounds of rapture slip through her lips as her hands make their way between her legs. She doesn't touch herself though, not until I tell her, "It's all right to play with yourself, but be still."

The fire blanket is in the drawer, I remind myself of that as I flick the lighter, staring at the flame and then gently bringing it to where the ethanol is still lingering on her skin. The flame grows along her skin, licking and turning a brighter yellow, but it's gone just as quickly as it came. By the time her mouth has parted, the evidence of it is all gone.

"Again," I tell her, sucking the other nipple into my mouth and running my teeth along her tender flesh before moving back to her right side, wiping the alcohol pad around her areola and then lighting it aflame again.

This time she moans louder, her knees pulling up the sheet that's puddled around her waist.

"Do you know why I enjoy fire?" I ask her, massaging and pinching her left breast once again.

"Because it's dangerous," she answers me softly and I shake my head no.

"Because it's wild," I correct her and then do it again, a larger portion this time.

Once the fire's gone, I grip both her breasts in my hands and run my thumbs over both nipples.

"Which one makes you feel more alive, cailín tine?"

chapter ten

Bethany

I SUPPOSE I WAS NEVER UNDER THE ILLUSION THAT IT WAS A TIT FOR TAT OF INFORMATION. So long as he answers my questions and keeps searching for answers I'll never be able to find, I'll willingly warm his bed.

In fact, I have little to no objection to it at all.

It's obvious I'm a fool, that I have no grip on reality, let alone my own mind. I feel like I'm losing it to be honest. What's the point in trying to stay afloat in the middle of the deep dark ocean when there's no land in sight? I could fight it, and I feel like I have, like I'm exhausted from fighting to stay above water. Or I can fall into Jase's arms, and let him hold me for a moment.

Fear plays a small part, but it's shocking how small a part it is.

Someone is after me, and this arrangement prevents them from getting whatever it is they want from me—which can't be good—and could lead me to information. Although that piece… that last piece about information. I'm starting to lose hope for that to happen.

I'm starting to accept it never happening.

If I think about it like I'm an undercover cop, suddenly it's all okay in my mind.

That's what I tell myself anyway. It's all pretend. My life is turning into a tall tale like Marky used to feed me. And that makes the jagged pill easier to swallow.

These are the thoughts that lead me to biting my thumbnail as I lie in Jase's bed. The clock on his nightstand, a beautiful contemporary clock with a minimalistic face of sleek marble and only hands to tell the time, must be lying to me because it reads that it's after noon already.

I sink back under the covers, pulling them up easily since I'm in bed alone and listen to the ticking. My hand splays under the sheets onto the side of the mattress where Jase lay last night. The thought of last night brings a faint kiss of a smile to my lips, but it falls just as quickly as it came, finding the bedsheet cold to the touch.

I called work again when I first woke up, ready to leave a message this time. Half of me wanted to be professional and ask what the phone call regarded, the other half wanted to call my boss an asshole, assuming it was him. Instead of leaving a message, I found myself talking to the lead nurse on Michelle's case.

"I'm so sorry," she started and then immediately dove into discussing the restraints they had to use on her arms. "She was eating the gauze, Beth. I have no idea what to do with her other than restrain her. I've never had a patient with pica and I don't know what to do."

"She loves pickles. So make pickle ice." I rattled off what I'd been doing with Michelle. She's a new patient, pregnant and newly diagnosed with pica. It's a psychological disorder where patients have an appetite for non-nutritive foods, or even harmful objects. "It'll most likely diminish after the pregnancy."

"I know, but what am I supposed to do?" The stress and frustration were all too relatable. "She can't stay restrained for six months."

"Listen to me," I said as I gripped the phone tighter. "Mix half pickle juice and half water, add in a soluble supplement, freeze into ice chips and then give them to her throughout the day, constantly."

"That can't be it."

"I'm telling you, you keep that by her bedside and she eats it slowly. Something about the cold makes her pace herself."

"Okay... okay," Marilyn sounded hopeful and I felt it too, until I heard someone ask who she was talking to and then the line went dead. When I get back to work, I'm going to kill my boss. I can hear his excuse now, that I'm a workaholic and I wouldn't be able to help myself, but that they should know better.

That was the only distraction I had.

I'm slow to sit up, forcing myself to rise although I have no plans, no control, nothing at all I want to do... but read I suppose. Thank all that's holy for books.

The small piece of me that anticipated—and looked forward to a note from Jase—is disappointed when I find his nightstand empty of any slip of paper.

I shouldn't feel so hollow in my chest. I shouldn't feel this kind of loss.

Bringing my knees up to my chest, I rest my cheek on my right knee and wonder what happened to me. What the fuck happened to the woman I was? Without work... I'm no one. My life is utterly empty and the one thing that's filling it shouldn't be in my life at all.

One breath, and the screaming thoughts quiet. Two breaths and I find it hard to care. This will all be over soon. It's temporary and nothing more. I'll be back to work, unraveled or not.

Until then... I'll read and let Jase fuck me. Maybe one day, I'll even get out of bed.

The Coverless Book
Three quarters through the book

Emmy

I remember all the times Miss Caroline took me to the appointments. Mother always met me there. It was Miss Caroline who took me on long drives and told me stories the whole way. No matter how many hours it was. That's all I can remember as we sit outside of the shed. It's a large shed, with running water and an outhouse with plumbing around the back.

Jake said it's his cousin's place, so it's okay that we stay here.

I can remember the trips to the hospitals. The long drives we took to get to them. The hotels we stayed in. Miss Caroline always stopped for ice cream on the way to and back. And she let me eat all sorts of things I never had at home.

I remember all those trips... but those are the only trips I've ever taken.

Until this one.

"What's wrong?" Jake's voice breaks my thoughts. His hand cradles my chin. "You look like you regret this." I hate how his voice sounds like he really believes that.

My hair tickles my shoulders when I shake my head and tell him, "You're crazy to think that. I love you, Jake." He needs to know that. "I was just hoping to go inside. It's been a few days since we've slept on a bed." I want to give myself to him. But not like this.

His lips part and instead of words coming out, he closes them again, kicking the rubble under his shoes. "We can't go inside, Em." He stares off at the large farmhouse. "Your mom filed a report and the sheriff called. We can't go inside."

Feeling a wave of nausea, I lower my head to my hands. "Your family doesn't know we're here?"

"My cousin does, and he's bringing us blankets. I've got money once we get out of this town. But, for tonight... Our parents are looking for us."

The crickets from the cornfield get louder as the sun sets deeper behind the crimson sky. It's nearly dusk already.

"I'm sorry I can't give you more right now, but soon I can."

I find his hand in mine, and tell him, "It's why running away is so scary. The unknown."

His eyes stare deep into mine as he says, "The only known in my life I need, is you beside me. As long as I have you, nothing else matters."

He tells me he loves me and I feel that drop in my stomach again, but I make sure I tell him I love him too and that I can't wait for all of the unknowns I'll face with him.

That's just before I go around the back of the shed to where the faucet is to wash my face. It's just before I get sick in the field. It's just before I look down at my hands as I'm cleaning myself up and see nothing but blood.

Three more times, I cough up blood and my eyes water. My face heats and then all at once, it stops. It's not a lot, it's not a lot of blood. It's because of whatever Miss Caroline put in the soup for all that time. I know it is. She made me sick. I'll get better now; Jake knows that too. I'm not sick, I'm recovering from what she did to me.

I hide what happened from Jake, though, all the blood I just coughed up. I don't want him to see.

I just want to be loved and to love him. Isn't love enough?

"Are you okay?"

Hearing Jase before I see him startles me. I hadn't noticed how erratic my breathing was until he came in. I set the book down on the nightstand.

"Yeah, why?" I ask him as I rub my eyes, and try to come back to reality. I catch a glimpse of the clock and realize nearly two hours slipped by. The uneasiness and shock that the book left me in won't shake off when I look back up to Jase.

"You look horrified."

I answer him, "It's just a book."

"What happened?" he asks me like he really cares as he takes off a black cotton shirt, damp with sweat. His body glistens, his muscles flex with every movement and with the increase of lust, the problems of my fictional world fall away.

"She might really be sick," I tell him, although my eyes stay glued to his chest.

"Who?" He stands still, a new shirt in his hand as he waits for my answer.

"Don't worry about it," I tell him. "She's invincible." Hearing those words come from me with confidence makes my stomach drop.

Jase has a different reaction. His lips pull up into an asymmetric smile at my remark and the way his eyes shine with humor is infectious. I feel lighter, but still, the sickness of the unknown churns in my stomach.

"I can't stay here," I tell him, knowing I need to do something and just as aware that there's nothing for me to do here. He removes the space between us, climbing up onto the bed to sit cross-legged in front of me. He doesn't love me like... like I feel for him. That's the truth that sinks me further into the bed.

Being around him, knowing what I feel for him and coming to terms with that, but not feeling the same from him... it's killing me. It makes me want to run. It's scary when you realize you love someone and that they may never feel the same for you. Not in the same way. Nothing like what I feel for him.

It doesn't stop me from breathing him in though.

The sweet smell of his sweat is surprising... and heady. The way he looks at me, it's all the more intoxicating.

"You agreed to twenty-nine days," he reminds me.

"Twenty-eight now," I correct him in return.

"Twenty-eight then."

"I can't stay here like this. Doing nothing day in, day out."

"I don't expect you to."

"What am I supposed to do?" I ask him, truly needing an answer.

He considers me for a moment. "I really don't know what to do," I tell him when he hesitates to answer me. It's harder for me to admit that than I thought it would be.

"I don't have any answers for you," he tells me beneath his breath, quietly, like he's sorry.

"I love work. I want to go back to work."

"I don't know that you're in the right mindset to do that."

My voice rises as I ask, "How am I supposed to get better when I have nothing to do to make me better?"

"Time." He answers me with a single word, joining me on the bed. "You could start with putting your mugs in the kitchen." Looking at the box still where he left it yesterday, he tells me, "You could do whatever you like."

"I can't leave," I answer him boldly, letting him know it pisses me off.

"Yesterday I didn't want you to, no. But that doesn't mean you can't leave. I'm not trapping you here, you're locking yourself in this room."

I hate him for his answer, although I don't know why.

"Where would you go after you're done with work to let loose?" he asks me.

"A bar."

"I like that," he says and scoots closer to me, pulling me into his lap. I settle against him, resting my back to his front.

"You order wine or mixed drinks at the bar?"

"Mixed. Vodka and whatever the bartender wants." The rough chuckle makes his chest shake gently and I love the feeling of it. His stubble brushes my neck as he asks, "And then?"

"Grocery store if I need to, although I really only keep K-cups and cardboard pizza in the fridge."

"Cardboard pizza?"

"You know, the kind that come in a box and you put in the toaster oven?"

That makes him laugh too. The sound of him laughing eases everything.

"You have a pretty smile," he tells me and his voice is calming.

"You have a pretty smile too," I tell him back and he makes a face.

He changes the subject quicker than I expect. "We don't know who broke in."

My own smile falters and I stare at my fingers, picking absently under my nails at nothing.

"I know that's not what you wanted to hear and it's not what I was hoping to tell you. But there are no fingerprints, no cameras anywhere."

With his hand on my chin, he forces me to look at him as he explains, "We looked into everyone's surveillance cameras, Beth. It's not quite legal, but they'll never know. Whoever it was left no trace at all."

"So I'll never know and they could come back." I'm surprised how much pain accompanies that knowledge. My chest feels like it's been hollowed out and bricks put in the place of whatever it is I need to survive.

"No. That's not true. We have a lead on your sister," he tells me with hope and authority.

"A man named Luke Stevens. He's no one around here, but he was seen with your sister before she went missing."

He hands me a picture of a man I've never laid eyes on. He's got to be in his forties, with a clean-cut look to him and I could only imagine what the hell Jenny would have been doing with someone like this.

"You think he did it?" I dare to ask Jase.

"I'm not sure, but I'm going to find him and get as much information as I can from him, cailín tine."

"Miranda told me she packed her bags," I say and swallow thickly, needing to calm the adrenaline racing in my blood. "She said Jenny packed before she went missing." The image of my sister doing just that and then leaving with this man plays in my mind. "Maybe she was in love with him," I surmise.

"I don't think—" Jase bites down to stop himself from saying something else.

"What?"

His inhale is uneven and he looks past me before saying, "I just wanted you to know that I'm working on it. But don't do this. Don't let your mind play tricks on you. All we know is that he was seen with her."

"Seen doing what?"

"Getting into a truck around the time she went missing but they aren't positive of the date."

I have no words as the theory in my mind unravels.

"It could be nothing, but we have a name and I'm working on it," he tells me and takes my hand in his, stopping me from my mindless habit.

"So now there are two names?" I ask, remembering the last time we talked about information.

He nods once, but doesn't give me the other name. The one he promised wouldn't help me.

"Which do you think broke into my house?" I ask him and instead of answering, he tells me, "I'm having Seth install a top-of-the-line security system. Everything will be repaired, and all the locks will be changed."

The information sparks a reaction I don't expect and I have to pull my hand away, but he doesn't let me so I blurt out the question, "You want me to go back... to my place?"

"No," he says and his quick answer alleviates some of the unwanted stress. "I'd prefer you here by my side and for the next twenty-eight days, I want you here at my place. But you need to be able to go home and feel safe. I get that and I wanted to make sure it was safe."

I can only nod, feeling overwhelmed and not knowing what to do. When he squeezes my hand, I squeeze back and tell him, "Thank you."

"I have to go. Late-night meeting."

Late meeting. My lips stay closed although I don't have to say anything at all. My gaze drops just as my lightheartedness does. I can never forget the life Jase leads. I need to remember.

"Don't look at me like that." His voice is low and a threat lays behind the words.

"Like what?" I ask him as if I don't know what he's referring to.

"Like I'm less than you for what I do."

"I don't," I protest, hating that it's obvious.

"You do."

Biting back my pride, I apologize, "I'm sorry."

"It's never going to change, Bethany. This isn't something I can run away from."

He stares at me like he's repentant. Like he'd change it if he could, although I don't believe him. All I can tell him back is, "I didn't ask you to."

chapter eleven

Jase

I'M THE LAST TO ENTER THE KITCHEN AND AS I MAKE MY WAY TO THE COUNTER, CARTER PUSHES a tumbler with ice and whiskey my way.

"You want to meet her, huh?" I ask Carter, looking him in his eyes as I bring the glass to my lips and let the liquor settle on my tongue to burn.

Carter only lets a smirk show, filling the empty tumbler in front of him and then asking Declan if he wants a glass too.

"I'll have beer," Declan announces and Daniel looks over his shoulder at Declan, a grin on his face too before reaching into the fridge. The bottles clink together and the telltale sound of the beer fizzing fills up the silence as I wait for my answer.

"You told her not to come in here, didn't you?" he asks, the smile only widening.

"You're a prick," I tell my oldest brother and when they all chuckle, I finally let myself smile and pull out the barstool. I'm a prick for lying to her too, but they don't need to know that.

"If she met us, if she knew what was going on, maybe she'd feel a little differently," Sebastian says as he enters the room, touching his elbow to Carter's in greeting and taking the last tumbler of whiskey.

"Maybe," I agree although I'm quick to take another swig of the whiskey.

"What's the update on Addison?" Sebastian asks Daniel. His response is to share a look with Carter first. They're going through the next stage of life together. All three of the men although Sebastian's wife is furthest along. Daniel and Carter just found out about the pregnancies.

Daniel picks at the label on his beer bottle as he answers, "They said it's just high blood pressure. She just needs to take it easy."

A moment passes where no one knows what to say. Addison never thought she could get pregnant and for good reason. She went through a rough life as a child.

"Aria's happy that she gets to pick out everything with a friend," Carter says to break up the tension.

Sebastian contributes to the easy feeling by remarking, "Chloe's happy she won't be the only fat one." He adds quickly, "Or so she said," which gets a good laugh and a clink of beers and glass tumblers.

"It feels good having all five of us in here, doesn't it? Like old times," Declan comments.

All four of my brothers and the one man, Sebastian, who sticks out because he's older.

"We do have a real reason to meet," Carter says and glances at the closed door behind me. She can place her hand to the panel and enter, or simply try to listen from the other side of the door.

"Romano." Daniel and I say our enemy's name at once.

Carter nods. "He's scattered. There's no doubt."

"What made him run?" Sebastian asks.

"He's outnumbered. It's not just Talvery men looking to settle a vendetta, but us too."

It's quiet with Officer Walsh and the FBI leaning hard on the local cops," Daniel answers and Carter nods along with him. "If he was ever going to leave, now is the time to do so."

"If he comes back, which he has to in order to get everything out of his warehouses, all of his supply and the stashed guns are on Fourth. If he comes back, there are only two roads he can use to come into town," I comment, knowing if he comes back, I don't want to give him another chance to leave.

"You think he'll come back for it?" Sebastian asks.

"He's got money hidden away in the warehouse on Fourth, we've staked out that street and he knows, but he doesn't know that we're aware his money's there. Maybe he thinks with him gone, we'll forget about him," Carter answers him.

"Forget about him?" There's a tension in Daniel's voice, akin to outrage. "We aren't going to let him run."

Daniel's comment goes unanswered.

"I say we blow up his estate and the warehouse too. Destroy everything."

"He left men behind." Carter's quick to rebut my suggestion.

"Not enough," I answer him, staring into his eyes.

"With the FBI and former agent on our asses, do we really want to risk it?" Declan asks, wanting to be safe.

"Yes. We do. We can't let what he did go unanswered. We can't let anyone think they can run from us," Daniel says, his body tense and the beer he has in his hand tapping against the granite.

"Calm down," Carter tells our brother, but I'm with Daniel.

"He's right," I say to voice my opinion.

"Destroy everything in his name and send Nikolai after him," Daniel suggests.

"Nikolai?" A tension coils in my stomach. "He tried to kill me; he tried to take Addison, your soon-to-be wife." I can't help that my voice rises, the same outrage Daniel had a moment ago slipping into my cadence.

"Do you plan to chase him, Jase? You going to risk your… what's her name? Bethany? Are you going to risk her to chase after him?" he questions me.

"Sending Nikolai is smart," Declan adds and Sebastian nods in agreement. I crack my neck, not looking at my brothers, knowing they're not on my side. All while questioning if they're right. If I could really risk leaving Bethany behind.

"With Marcus still here… you're right. We should send Nikolai."

"Aria will never forgive me if something happens," Carter admits and stares into the swirling whiskey in his glass.

"She doesn't have to know," Declan says which brings all of our eyes to him.

"It's easy to say that, but they always find out. The truth always rises to the surface." Sebastian's sentiment sends a chill down my spine. I warm it with the remainder of the whiskey in my glass.

The empty tumbler hits the granite in time with the door opening behind us. All five of us turn to see Bethany, standing in the now open doorway with her hand still in the air.

The sight of her is enough to ease the tension in the room.

"You look like a deer in headlights," Daniel comments and then waves her in.

"I'm sorry," she says immediately, not moving an inch. "I didn't mean to interrupt."

"Were you planning on just sneaking around then?" Carter asks and grins at her. "We can pretend we didn't see you if that's the case." The ice in his tumbler clinks as he brings it up to his smile and takes a sip.

The long sweater hangs loosely on her, but when she wraps her arms around herself,

I can just barely make out the dip in her waist. With keys jingling in her hand, and seeing as how she's slipped on leggings and boots, it's obvious she's heading out.

Doubt sinks its claws into me. Holding me in place as she stands there. Bethany's wide eyes meet mine and she nearly turns around when I don't say anything.

"Come meet my brothers," I say loud enough to stop her in her tracks before she can run off completely.

She hesitates a moment and then walks to my side, her insecurity showing. The moment she's beside me, I wrap my arm around her waist.

"I'm sorry," she whispers although it's not low enough that the rest of the guys wouldn't hear.

"Guys, meet Bethany. Sebastian, Carter, Daniel and Declan." I point at each of them one by one and she gives them a small, embarrassed wave. "Sebastian's not blood, but still family," Carter comments and then fills his glass and mine again. "Want a drink?" he offers her.

"That's actually why I came in here," she says and Daniel interrupts her by saying, "I like her already," which gets agreeable laughter from the rest of the guys.

Her nerves are still high, no matter how much I run soothing circles along her back. Her voice is strained when she looks up at me and says, "I forgot I told a friend I was seeing her tonight. It's the weekend. I was just going to head out."

It's more than obvious to not just me, but to all of the men standing here that she's searching for permission.

It's not like her, I wish they could see her. Really see her. I tell myself she just needs time.

"Have fun." With that I smile down on her, not giving her any restraints. Seth and his men will watch her and inform me.

Blinking, she holds back the obvious questions that beg to be spoken. Instead she only nods and nearly says thank you, but those words turn into an, "Okay, I'll see you tonight?"

My brothers and Sebastian say nothing, only observing and drinking. I know they're judging, and I hate them for it.

I can see her need to run and before she can turn and leave me, I capture her lips with mine. Her lips are hard at first, and she utters a small protest of shock, right before she melts into me. Her lips soften and her hands move to my back when I deepen the kiss just slightly.

It doesn't last long, but it lasts long enough to bring color to her cheeks. With her teeth sinking into her bottom lip, she smiles sweetly and barely glances at my brothers, giving them a wave before quickly walking away.

I leave the door open, watching her walk out of sight.

"She seemed nervous."

"No shit," Carter says and laughs off Declan's comment at the same time Sebastian asks for another beer.

"What are you doing with her?" Carter asks me and everyone goes quiet. "It seems different from what you mentioned." All eyes are on me as I stand alone.

I can feel all of their eyes on me, the questions piling on one after the other in their gazes. With my forearms on the cold, hard counter, my shoulders tense. I lower my gaze to my folded hands firmly placed on the granite.

"That's a damn good question."

chapter twelve

Bethany

It feels like there was a heavy bell that rang too close to me. That's the only way I can describe how I'm feeling. The sound left a ringing sensation on my skin, maybe even deeper.

Every minute on my drive home I thought it would go away, but it didn't.

It tingles, and refuses to go unnoticed. Even now as I sit with Laura in the parking lot outside of a strip mall with a bottle of cabernet half gone and tempting me to take another swig... the ringing doesn't stop. I'm trapped in the moment when it happened. When the world shifted and made it impossible for me to get away from the giant bell.

The moment Jase kissed me like a lover in front of his brothers.

I've heard of Sebastian Black; my sister went to school with him. I've heard of the Cross Brothers. I've seen Carter from afar at The Red Room once. To be in a room with such men, with intimidating, dangerous men, I couldn't think or breathe. It was a mix of fear and something else. Something sinful.

Even with them talking, joking, acting as if it was just an ordinary day and ordinary people in an ordinary kitchen, I couldn't shake all the stories I'd heard of these men.

But then Jase kissed me.

Every part of my body has woken up, and it refuses to let the memory become that, a memory. It's holding on to it instead, trying to stay there. Going out with Laura has definitely dampened the ringing, but not so much though that I can't feel it still, even hours later.

"What's wrong with you? You love this song." Laura cuts through my hazy thoughts and my gaze moves from the yellow streetlights and lit signs of the chain stores to focus on her instead.

I hadn't even noticed music was playing.

"Hey," Laura says and pats my arm as she leans forward with a hint of something devious in her voice. "You know how..." she shifts uneasily and restarts. "You remember how you helped me interview for the position at the center?"

"Of course," I answer her and wonder where she's going with this.

"Aiden didn't like me during the interview."

I cut her off and say, "He was a grade-A dick for no reason." I still remember how shocked I was at his unprofessionalism.

"I hit his car a week before," she blurts out.

"What?"

She can't stop grinning. "I was so embarrassed. It was a rough day. Like really bad and he backed up out of nowhere in the parking lot and I just tapped him." Her thumb and her pointer are parallel as she holds them up and whispers, "Just a teeny tap."

"You hit his car?"

"And then I might have... you know," she stops and laughs again. "I called him a dickhead when he was yelling at me. Like he was screaming in my face and it wasn't like it was helping anything and like I said, it was a rough day and I just snapped." Her shoulders shake with another giggle. "And then I showed up for the interview the next week."

"Oh my God! And you never told me?" I can't help laughing either. I can absolutely see Aiden and her screaming at each other in a parking lot over a scratch on a car. They both have a habit of taking out their aggression on the least suspecting.

"I was so embarrassed I couldn't tell you."

"Well no wonder he didn't want to hire you," I comment.

"I know. I had to go back in and apologize. I'd already sent him insurance information that he didn't even need, but still. I felt awful. It was so awkward and... unfortunate."

"But he still hired you," I say and hold up my finger to make that point clear.

"Because of you. He never would have if you weren't there backing me up."

"Knowing about the car... I'm going to have to agree with you now. I just thought he was an uncalled for asshole at your interview."

"I never told you and I want to thank you again, Beth. Thank you."

"Of course, I love you." I almost add how she was by my side through everything with Jenny before she died, and that getting her a job is insignificant in comparison, but I leave that out. I'm not wanting to drag the mood down.

"I love you too."

She spears her hand through her golden locks, moving all her hair to her left shoulder and glancing at her split ends. "You're off, like even more than you have been. And don't tell me *you're fine*," she says, mocking the words I've been giving her all night.

Reaching out for the bottle of wine, she gives me a pointed look. The swish of the liquid is followed by the sound of a car riding down the half-empty lot and I look at it instead of her.

Again not answering her. It's only about the dozenth time she's asked me what's going on.

"A cop came to your house today." Her voice is clearer and when I look back, this time she isn't looking at me. I wouldn't call her expression a frown, it's something else, something etched with worry.

"When I was waiting for you to get home, which—by the way, where the fuck were you?" She pauses and sucks in a breath before relaxing into the seat and then taking another swig. She offers it back to me and then repeats, "I was waiting and a cop came by. I told him you weren't home and he said he'd come back later."

"Officer Walsh?" I question her and she nods, then takes the wine back before I can take another sip.

"I was going to tell you at dinner, but you seem really not with it. So like... I don't know."

This time I grab the bottle and take a drink before it's all gone.

Laura looks at me with a slight pout, although I'm not sure it's quite that. It's genuine and sullen, but there's a sadness I can't place.

I watch her look out to the shoe store we just left before she exhales with frustration. "You always tell me everything," she starts. "I know this is hard and you're not a 'speak your feelings' type of girl, which is ironic since you tell everyone else to do just that."

The wine flows easily until the bottle is empty, but I don't let it go.

"It just seems like this isn't mourning, it's something else and I don't know what to do or how to help you."

Laura's voice cracks as she raises her hands into the air, trying to prove a point but needing to wipe under her eyes instead.

"No, no, don't cry." My reaction is instant, reaching out to clutch her shoulder. The leather of her seats groans as I sit up and reposition myself on my knees to face her in the small car. "Everything's fine," I tell her but she only shakes her head.

With her eyes wide open and staring at the ceiling of the car, she responds, "It's not though. You're not okay."

"Seriously," I start to tell her and then catch sight of a car I recognize, and a prick I know too. Seth raises his hands in surrender at the wheel of his car, although his wrists stay planted on it, and my throat tightens. I can't hold on to my train of thought and I have to sit back in my seat, taking a steadying breath.

Jase sent Seth to follow me.

Maybe I should have guessed it. Maybe I should have known I'd be followed.

It's a strange thing, to feel safe, to feel wanted and protected by someone I know I fear and hate on a level that's unattainable to my conscious.

I rest my head against the cold window and close my eyes.

"We were having a good time," I tell her softly. Feeling the tingle of the bell, and falling back into old habits with Laura, I felt like I escaped for a moment. I'm nothing but foolish.

"Shit, no, don't you cry too." Laura presses a hand to her forehead and then over her eyes.

"I swear, I'm fine," I tell her although I can't help but to look past her and at Seth instead. "I…" I trail off and have to swallow before I lie again, "It's just hard to stop thinking about Jenny."

Fuck, that hurts to say. To use her as an excuse. To bring her up in conversation at all.

"And now we're both crying," I tell her with a huff and pull my sweater to the corner of my eyes. "I don't want to cry. It's just my eyes glossing over. It's not crying… I'm not crying."

"You're an awful liar." Laura's voice is soft and I'm pulled to her, to tell her everything. To lean on her like a friend would do.

How selfish is that?

"Tell me about work. I miss it. What kind of person misses work?"

Laura works in Human Resources at the center, but they get all the gossip just the same as the nurses who do the rounds like me.

"Well there's a cute guy who came in last week," she starts to tell me with feigned interest. Then her head falls to the side to look at me as she says, "But his name is Adam and we both know Adams are dicks."

Her comment forces a small laugh from me and then she reaches for the bottle.

"I don't know what's funnier, your taste in men or your pout when the wine's gone."

Instead of commenting, she pushes her hair back and tells me about a few new patients, all of which piss her off for good reason. A man who was drunk at the wheel and killed two people. She thinks he's faking insanity because ever since he was admitted all he can talk about is how totaled his truck is and he hasn't shown a damn bit of remorse for the couple he killed even though he knows he's being charged with their murder. We get those kinds of people sometimes. Assholes who fake mental illnesses to get out of legal trouble. Or even to get out of work for a week.

"Oh, I do love this one old woman who came in though. She said it's actually the 1800s and she's talking to dead people. I like Sue a lot. She's so sweet."

"I wish I were at work."

"I wish you were too," she adds and pats my thigh. "You'd love Sue."

"I'm sure I would." It's never a boring day at the Rockford Center. That's a truth no one can deny.

"I can't drive us home." Laura's statement makes me look at her and then at Seth. "You want to Uber?" she asks me and I shake my head no, getting out without thinking.

"What are you doing?" she calls out as I step out onto the asphalt and make my way to Seth's car. I ignore her calls for me to *get my ass back there*. I'd smile at the way she whispers it and tries to keep me from knocking on Seth's window if it weren't for the anxiousness creeping up on me from what I'm about to do.

I don't have to knock though; he rolls down his window but doesn't say a word.

"Oh my God, I'm so sorry," Laura says and tries to pull me away again. "My friend is a little bit more drunk than I thought." She tugs at my wrist and again I ignore her efforts.

"Will you give us a ride home?" I push out the question. Seth lets out a smile, a handsome smile with perfect teeth, all the while staring at Laura and her wide eyes.

"We don't need a ride," Laura's quick to tell him. "I'm so sor-"

"I don't mind," Seth cuts her off and asks, "Where are you going?" I'm still staring at Laura and the way she's looking at Seth that I don't notice he asked me.

"Home," is all I answer him and he nods once, the playfulness gone from his expression and tells us to get in the back.

I don't know what came over me or why. Maybe it's the piece of me that wants Seth to pay for watching me like a hawk. I can't explain it, but it feels like a step forward. Not the literal step forward I take to get in the back of the car, but a step out of whatever place I was in just hours ago.

Laura snatches me when I open the door, and she immediately slams it shut instead. The thud is loud and nearly violent.

"What the fuck?" she hisses. "Do you even know him? Do you want to get us killed?"

"Yeah, I've met him a couple of times," I tell her and shrug, feeling like the worst liar in the world. A heavy weight presses against my chest as I escape the harsh wind, opening the door again and scooting over to the other side so Laura will get in too.

She takes a little too long to decide so I tell her, "Hurry up, it's cold out there and you're letting all that cold in here!" My admonishment works.

"Let me get my bag."

As she turns to walk away, Seth asks me all the while watching her, "Whose home?"

Whatever's settled into my stomach feels thicker. "Can you drop her off first?"

"You think she'd be okay with that?" He finally turns in his seat to look at me. "Because I don't."

I watch her texting on her phone a few spaces over with her driver's door open although she still stands on the street.

"I want to tell her," I admit to him. "You can stop me if I say something I shouldn't."

"You shouldn't say anything, Bethany."

"Well, I'm going to say something. I have to tell her." We both hear her car door shut and he says lowly, "You really shouldn't." The way his shoulders tense and he grips the wheel makes my chest feel hollow and I almost reconsider, but I have to tell her something.

She's my best friend and she deserves to know. I can't not tell her. I can't let her cry for me like she's doing.

Her car beeps from the alarm and then she's seated beside me, thanking Seth and referring to him as the "handsome savior" of our night although I can still hear the hesitation and worry in her tone.

She gives Seth a tight smile and then he asks again, "Where are you guys headed?"

"Can you take me to Jase's?" I dare to ask Seth, knowing Laura's going to ask me about Jase, paving the way for it to happen.

Seth's returning smile is tight, but he nods.

"Who's Jase?"

Ignoring Laura's question and her stare of confusion, I ask Seth, "Can you take Laura home first?"

"No fucking way are you staying in this car, drunk and with a guy you don't know." She glances at Seth who puts the car in reverse to leave as she adds, "No offense."

"He works for Jase," I answer her, finally looking her in the eyes.

"Who the hell is Jase?"

"Jase Cross," I tell her, gauging her expression when I mention "Cross." Everyone knows about the brothers and I can see the exact moment when it sinks in.

"You're with Jase?" she questions me softly and then swallows so loud, looking between me and Seth, that I'm sure even he can hear it. I only nod.

"With him? Like what does that even mean?"

My hands turn clammy and I have to wring my fingers around one another in my lap. "I can't even look you in the eyes," I tell her and then cover my face with my hands as my head sinks back into the seat.

"No, Bethy, no. Don't cry."

"I'm not going to cry," I protest, forcing my hands down and staring straight ahead at the back of the black leather seat in front of me. "I'm just…" I can't finish. "I don't even know what I feel. Ashamed, I think."

"Ashamed because you're with him? Or ashamed at what you've done?" she asks cautiously. She whispers, "Did he make you do anything? I will fuck him up. I don't care who he is."

"No, stop. No, he didn't make me do anything." Although I tell her that, the first time we met flashes in my memory. I think I'll leave that out of this conversation.

I have to shake out my hands, feeling them turn numb and having a wave of anxiousness hit me. "I'm ashamed because of both… neither. I don't know. I'm confused."

"Okay." Laura's patient with me although she keeps looking at Seth like he's not to be trusted.

The way she looks at Seth, questioning him and his intentions gives me an uncomfortable feeling. More than that, I feel like I should be defending them. Which is outrageous, yet it's exactly how I feel in this moment.

"He's a good guy," I tell her to ease her worries. "Jase treats me really, really good." Emotions tickle up my throat and I have to swallow them before I tell her, "Seth watches out for me for him."

She asks the obvious question. "Watches out for what?"

With Seth as my witness, I tell her everything.

I don't even leave out the part where I almost shot Jase. I tell her literally everything that I can remember. Including the part where I think I love him. Fuck my life.

chapter thirteen

Jase

It's not every day that I feel like a prick.

Taking advantage of someone's weakness is how I survived, how my brothers and I rose to the top.

There's not a single doubt that I'm taking advantage of Bethany. It's easy when you're hurting to fall for someone, to trust them, to want there to be a way out of the pain.

Listening in on her conversation in the car, listening to her recount the events with Laura Devin, makes me feel like the worst fucking prick alive.

I made her love me. I made sure she had no other option. And worse than that, I don't know that I will ever say the words back to her.

"Boss." Seth nods when I see him and I nod back although my gaze travels to Bethany. Watching her climb the steps as I open the door for her.

Her cheeks are tearstained but there's a sense of lightness around her. Even more than that, her small body brushes against my chest as she walks in. She did it on purpose. She wanted to touch me and I fucking love it. Prick or not.

"Have a good night," I tell him and he smirks at me as he replies, "You too."

Bethany rocks from one foot to the other, watching me as I close to the door to the cold and then turn to her fully.

"Let me help you," I tell her and then act like a gentleman, helping her out of her coat.

With my fingertips lingering on her bare skin, I lower my lips to the shell of her ear and whisper, "Seth put you on speaker from the moment you knocked on his window."

She shudders from my touch and lets her head fall back into my chest. "Are you angry?" she asks with her eyes still open, staring past me at the now closed door.

"No, I'm not."

"I had to tell her." Her words slur slightly and I can smell the hint of alcohol on her.

"Of course you did."

"And you heard everything?" she asks and that's when her expression falls. No doubt she's questioning where my opinions lie. When I nod in response, she doesn't voice her question.

She takes a different approach, changing the subject altogether.

"What were you talking to Seth about before I went to him?" she asks me, her own curiosity showing.

"Maybe about you?" I give her a flirtatious response that's only a half lie, rather than telling her about Marcus.

"Oh... and what about me?" she asks although the flirtation isn't quite there.

"I wouldn't tell you, you like to gossip too much," I tease her, giving her a kiss on the crook of her neck. She rewards me by wrapping her arms around my shoulders, and planting one of her own on my neck.

The knowledge of what I'm going to do tonight keeps me from pushing for more. It keeps me from wanting more, it keeps me from lifting her ass up and pinning her against the wall.

"Are you okay?" I ask her, holding her close and not letting her go just yet.

"Me?" she questions and I nod against her, feeling her hair tickling along my stubble as I reply, "Yes, you."

"I feel better in a way," she confides in me and stands upright so I let her go. "It feels good to say it all out loud and still be able to stand afterward."

Staring into her gaze I admit to her, "You don't strike me as a girl who would ever not land on her feet, cailín tine."

"You know, I forgot to tell Laura that," she murmurs and sways slightly. Enough that she feels the need to take a step back and steady herself.

"How much did you drink?"

She shrugs and then says, "The normal amount when we go drunk shopping."

"No bags though?"

"Oh, well there's this thing where I owe this guy some money so I'm on a tight budget at the moment," she jokes with me and her smile is infectious. "Really, I just wasn't interested tonight in shopping."

"Only gossiping?"

"Yeah," she answers and then says again, "I can't believe I forgot to tell her."

Walking her to the bedroom, I ask her what she forgot to tell Laura.

"The nickname." Her answer stops me just outside the door although she continues, "I think she'd understand better, if she knew."

chapter fourteen

Bethany

It's different here. Maybe because it's his room. His house. His place.

He's different here. He's more transparent. Less hidden with his emotions. Other than anger and dominance… and lust, he hasn't shown me more than that beyond these walls.

Or maybe it's just tonight. Maybe it's just the wine talking or the relief that I finally told Laura what's going on.

I don't know, but when I look at Jase, he's different.

And he's not okay. Pain riddles every move he makes. Not the physical kind, the kind that wears away at your mind.

His head hangs lower as he asks me what we did. As if he doesn't already know. His voice is duller, his grip less tight on my waist as he pulls me into the bedroom.

With every step my heart beats slower, wanting to take the agony away from his. The answers I give him are spoken without thinking. I'm more concerned with watching him than I am with making small talk.

With his back to me, he pulls the covers back and tells me to strip and get into bed, which I do.

My mind starts toying with me. Insecurity whispers in my ear, *"Maybe it's you."*

"Are you okay?" I ask him, letting a tinge of my insecurity show.

"Fine," he answers shortly, but he gets into bed with me.

"You're still dressed," I comment, listening to my heart which is quiet. I think it's waiting for him to say something too. For him to tell us what's wrong.

"I know," is all he gives me as an answer and the high I was on, all that relief I felt, vanishes.

I feel sick. Not hungover or drank too much sick, but the sickness that comes when you know something's wrong. The awful kind where you can guess what it is, but you don't want to just in case it'll go away if you never voice it.

I know what I need, but I don't ask him for it. Instead I pull the covers up close around my chin and lie there. My pride is a horrid thing.

I'm aware of that.

If I could simply let it go, I could communicate better. I know that. I've known it all my life. But still, I don't ask him to hold me.

I don't have to though. I don't have to tell him what I need to feel better.

The bed groans as he moves closer to me, wrapping a strong arm around my waist and pulling me closer to him. It's a natural reaction for me to close my eyes and let out an easy breath when I take in his masculine scent. It engulfs me just as his warmth does, just as his touch does.

"You promise we're okay?" I ask him and then my eyes open wide, realizing the mistake I made. The Freudian slip.

Kissing the crook of my neck, he murmurs a yes.

He gives so much and I feel so undeserving. The ringing on my skin comes back, the bell of what happened earlier reminding me that it's okay. That it's better than okay.

My hand lays over his and he twines his fingers with mine before planting a kiss on my cheek.

Before he can pull away, I kiss him again. Putting everything I have into it, trying to give him what I can in what's a very unbalanced relationship.

That's what this is. A relationship. Fuck me, when did it happen?

The second I pause, pressing my forehead to his and pulling my lips away, he does what I just did to him, kissing me and giving me more.

With a warmth flowing through my chest, I settle into his embrace.

"I want to ask you something." His whispered question tickles my neck and makes a trail of goosebumps travel down my shoulder.

"Yeah?"

"How are you feeling about your sister? Are you okay? You didn't mention her to Laura. Or how you were handling it. And the last few days you seem…"

"Seem what?"

"A little more than sad today before you went out and yesterday," he answers honestly, and I want to pull my hand from his, but he doesn't let me. He holds me tighter and closer as my composure cracks.

"Tell me, cailín tine," he whispers at the back of my neck, running the tip of his nose along my skin. I love it when he does that. I love the soft, slow touches. I love how he takes his time with me.

It takes me a long moment to answer him. "I feel like I've slowed down, which makes sense because I'm not working anymore. I am crying when I hate it and I can't stop myself, but that damn book is sad too, so it could be the book's fault right? I don't know."

"You can't hide behind a sad book," is all he says and then he looks at me like he wants more.

Staring at the still curtains and listening to the heater turn on with a click, I let it all out; I don't think, I just speak. "Everything is moving so fast. That's what it feels like. Like the world didn't just refuse to slow down with me while I mourn but it sped up too."

Kind eyes look down on me when I peek over my shoulder to see his response. He's propped up on his elbow, his hard, warm chest still pressed against my back. I roll over to face him and look him in the eyes as I say, "It became chaotic and unpredictable and I'm a person who likes consistency and schedules and predictability and it's all gone. In one second everything changed, and now I can't be anything but slow and everything is going so fast." He's silent, so I continue.

"Except when I'm with you. Everything slows down then. It stops and waits for me when you show up."

I don't expect to say the words I've been thinking out loud. I say them all to my folded hands in my lap rather than to Jase. I need to see what he thinks though. If he understands or if I'm just crazy.

He leans down to give me a small kiss. It's quick and gentle. I want more but I don't take it. Even when the tip of his nose nudges mine, I don't do anything but wait for him to say something.

"That's a good thing, right?"

"Yeah… but I think the world is going so fast because of you too. Because of lots of things. And here I am stuck with a rope around my feet."

"I could see that," he comments, brushing the stray hairs away from my face and his touch brings back that tingling full force.

"You make it easy to talk," I murmur.

He doesn't say anything at all, he merely touches his fingers to my lips and gives me a small smile.

"I do that with my patients. I put on a smile all day long and they trust me, they open up to me. Jase, don't treat me like a patient."

"Well, first off all, you're not a patient. Second, you better not touch your patients like I touch you."

"You're awful," I tell him halfheartedly, but still feeling a hollowness in my chest that I can't place.

"I smile at you because sometimes you smile back, and that's all I want. I want to see you smile."

Breathe in, I remind myself. *Breathe out*. I have to, or else I think I'd forget in this moment. It's not often you can feel yourself falling, but I'd be damned if I didn't feel like that right now. Even knowing who he is and what he does.

"Why are you so sweet and charming... yet the very opposite too?"

He shakes his head gently, not taking it like I thought he would. Then he answers with another question of his own. "Why are you so strong and confident, yet... feeling like this?"

I don't have an answer. The old me would though. The me from only two months ago before Jenny went missing, would know why. I work in a psych center, for fuck's sake. I would have known. I could have answered. Being in it though... I've lost my voice. I have nothing to say, because I don't want this reality to be justified.

"Because that's life, cailín tine. We aren't just one thing. Life isn't one story. It's a mix of many and they cross paths sometimes."

I swallow thickly, understanding what he's saying and hating it. Some parts of life are simply awful. When I close my eyes and focus on one more deep breath, Jase's strong hand cups my chin and my eyes lift to his.

I nearly apologize for being the way I am. But it's not some stranger I've lost it in front of. Or my boss. Or my fucking family from New York. It's Jase.

I expect him to say something, but he only pulls me closer to him, letting time pass and the wretched feelings that have welled up, slowly go away.

Mourning is like the tide of the ocean. It comes and it goes. It's gentle and it's harsh. Slowly, the tide always subsides. But it always comes back too. It never goes away for long.

"The world stops when you see me, huh?" he questions softly after a moment, teasing me and letting the sad bits wash away like they're meant to. I love the teasing tone he takes. I love this side of him. I love many sides of him.

"I didn't say that," I'm quick to protest.

"You practically did," he teases, although the smile on his handsome face tugs down slightly as his eyes search mine.

"I don't love you," I murmur the words, feeling the hot tension thicken between the two of us. He leans closer to me, nearly brushing his lips against mine. All the while, I keep my eyes open, waiting for what he has to say.

"I don't love you too," he says and I can practically feel the last bit of armor fall as I lean into his lips. His hand brushes my shoulder, my collarbone and then lower, barely touching me and feeling like fire as he caresses my skin.

The covers swish around us as I lean back, giving him more room and urging him closer. I've never wanted a man like I want him. I've never memorized the rough groan a man gives as he kisses me like Jase does, with reverence and hunger.

I let him take me as he wants. What he wants is exactly what I want.

Time doesn't pause for us though. It doesn't go by slowly either.

It's all over far too soon. Maybe because I never want this one moment to end.

"I have to go," he tells me after glancing at the clock on his nightstand. He makes no effort to move though, other than to run his thumb along my bottom lip.

"Okay," I whisper, not wanting to chance that he'll stop touching me. All I want is for him to keep touching me and for my world to stay still and in pace with me, not wanting to take the next step forward.

"Don't follow me, Bethany," he warns, his voice sterner, but the lust still there.

"Okay," I repeat and my eyes finally close as he leans down, pressing his lips against mine once again. He tries to move away before I'm ready for him to go, but I reach up, pulling him back to me with my hands on the back of his neck. I hold him there, deepening the kiss and listening to his groan of satisfaction as I do. Kissing this man changes everything. I can't think about anything other than wanting him with me. I'm highly aware of it and I know it's dangerous, but still… I want it.

It's wild and dangerous, and I love it just as much as I love the fire.

When he finally leaves me, I hold on to the warmth he left in the covers, and I bury my head in the pillow he slept on, rather than the one he gave me. I stare at the clock, watching the hands move slowly. Trying to keep it moving slowly with me.

I don't follow him. Not because of a debt or an agreement. But because he asked me not to. Because it means something to him.

I would have stayed like that longer than I'd care to admit, really I would have, but that's when my phone chimed with a message from Laura.

chapter fifteen

Jase

I KNOW HE'S HERE BUT HE HASN'T SHOWN HIMSELF YET. I SAY ALOUD TO NO ONE, "When I was a kid, I hated the dark."

The playground is quiet tonight. With its broken swing that creaks as a gust of wind blows, and the full moon's faint blue light that shines down and covers every inch of the fallen snow, it's the perfect setting for Marcus. The kind of setting that's eerily familiar. The place where you don't go and you walk as quick as you can to get far away.

The backyard playground of the abandoned school is where no one goes unless they're up to no good. Like I am tonight.

"Most kids do," a voice answers from somewhere to my right, under the old, ten-foot rusty slide. I can just barely make out the brown broken bits through the veil of snow.

"I figured you'd be there. In the dark, just watching." I make my way to where he is, but stop short. I stay by the swing set, close enough to hear, but not bothering to look at him.

I'll play by his rules. He has what I want, Jenny Parks. We both know that I know.

I can hear the faint laugh carry in the night, but he makes no other comment and instead there's nothing but the bitter cold between us.

"What about now?" he asks me and I resist the urge to turn my head to face where he is. Instead I stare at the graffiti on the back of the brick building.

"What about now?" I question.

"Are you still afraid of the dark?"

His question makes me smirk. "I never said afraid... I said I hated it."

"You didn't have to say you were afraid, Jase. Every child is afraid of the dark."

A moment passes and I stalk forward to lean against the metal bar of the jungle gym.

"You wanted something?" I ask him, knowing that my back is to him and knowing he could sneak up on me if he wanted. I'll risk it.

"You wanted something," he answers me as if it's a correction. His voice a bit louder this time, followed by the sound of footsteps. "Don't turn around just yet."

"Understood," I respond quickly, knowing in my gut I'm walking away from this. He wants me to know something. And I want to know what it is.

I can hear him stop just a few feet behind me and I stay where I am although the need to turn rings in my blood. I've never crossed Marcus and from what I know, he's never crossed me. But he isn't on our side either, and that makes me question where his intentions lie.

"You're looking for information and I came with... a gift."

My pulse quickens as I hear more movement behind me. Gripping the bar tighter until my knuckles have turned white, I ignore every need to turn, making my muscles tense.

"A gift?" I press him for more information.

"Yes," is all he gives me.

"Is it Jenny Parks?" I dare to ask, giving up information, but in the hopes of cooperation.

"Jenny is fine."

A beat passes and the muscles in my arms coil, my grip too tight, the adrenaline in my blood racing to get somewhere, or to do something. To simply react.

It's a puzzle with Marcus, attempting to ask the right questions, because he has all the answers.

"What are you doing with her?"

"I'm helping her." His voice is faint this time, as if he's farther away now. The crunch of the snow beneath his feet makes me realize he's pacing. Maybe considering telling me something.

"You know I want answers... I want her sister to have a life with her. She wants her back." There's only the soft call of a midnight wind that whistles in the lack of his answer. "What do you want me to know?" I ask him, acknowledging to both of us that's all he'll tell me anyway.

"Did you have a nice conversation with Mr. Stevens?"

An exhale of frustration slips through my lips at the change in subject. I answer him, "It went well."

"What did he tell you?" he asks.

"He said you were building an army," I say and raise my voice to make sure he can hear me. He does the same and takes steps to come closer, but still stops far enough behind me that I can't see his shadow yet against the pure white snow.

"Building one?" The tone of his voice lingers in the air, and his answer leaves a chill to run down my spine. "Did you think I did all of this on my own? There's always someone looking for salvation, for redemption, for something to believe in."

"You're their savior?"

"I'm no savior and the things they do... it's no redemption."

"So you're using them?" I ask him and rein in the simmering anger as Jenny's face from the pictures in Bethany's house flickers in front of me. Back when things were different.

"I'm giving them what they want," he answers.

"And then?" I ask him. "What are you going to do with Jenny when she's done doing your bidding and you have no use for her?"

Silence.

My head falls forward, heavy as I struggle with the need to force an answer from the man I used to fear. I focus on staying still. On not facing him so I can gather more information. I need an answer. I need to know where Jenny is. I have to know if she'll ever come home.

"Did you know wolves used to live here? Back in the day, so to speak."

My eyes open slowly and I stare straight ahead as my shoulders tighten. "You love your stories. Don't you?" My voice is menacing, not hiding my disappointment and outrage.

"Oh I could tell you a story, but the truth will hurt the most."

My teeth grind together, my patience wearing thinner and thinner as all the pictures I've seen of Jenny from when she was a girl hugging her sister, to only a few years ago when she was in school, play in my mind.

"They'd run in packs and terrorize the people." He paces again, I can hear him doing it and a part of me wants to turn around; I want to look him in the eyes and see the man who plays with fire like he has. The only reason I don't is because he has the upper hand. He has Jenny. He has the answers.

"They attacked people, but farms mostly, leaving the families little food for themselves..." He pauses and lets out a soft sound, nearly a chuckle although I'm not certain it's humorous; it sounds sickening.

"They ruled and there was not much to be done. Much like you and your brothers," he says and the S hisses in the air. "They don't run wild here anymore though, because hunters found a way. Well, there were two ways." I remain silent, biding my time, struggling to stay patient with him.

"The first, I'm not a fan of," he says and steps closer to me, but still I don't react. "They'd find the female mates and put them in cages for the males to see. When the males would inevitably come to find their mates, they'd try to release them, to no avail. And then they'd wait there for the men to come, with their tails tucked under them, begging in whimpers for their mates to be freed." Every hair stands on end as he tells his tale. All I can think about is Bethany. "I've been told you didn't even need a gun to kill them when they did this. When they came to get their mates, they were so willing to do anything and accept anything in order to free their mates, you could turn your gun around and beat them to death with the end of a rifle."

My skin pricks with the imagery that floods my mind. The fog of my breath in front of my face paints the picture of a wolf, bloodied and dead and next to it a caged mate, with bullet wounds ending her life.

"Are you implying something, Marcus?" I dare to ask him, feeling the anger rising. "If you're threatening-"

"Bethany is safe," he answers before I can finish and the simple confirmation is more relief than I thought imaginable, given my current position.

"The other way though... I... I find it more fitting," Marcus says, and continues his story. "The farmers would dip a knife into bloodied water. Wolves love the taste of blood. They knew that, so they'd tempt them. They'd dip it and freeze it over and over. Practically making a popsicle, made just for wolves."

The swing blows and creaks again as he tells me, "They'd leave the knife for the wolves, and the wild animals would lick and lick, enjoying their treat and numbing their own tongues with the ice. They'd continuing licking, even after they'd sliced their own tongues. After all, they love the taste of blood and they couldn't feel it."

"The wolves would bleed out?" I surmise.

"They would. They would lick the knives even after the ice was long melted, and bleed themselves to death."

"Now, if only I'd heard that at bedtime, maybe I would have had better dreams," I lay the flat joke out for him, downplaying the threatening tone he chooses, and keeping my voice casual.

"Humor is your preference, isn't it?"

I don't bother answering.

"What's the point to your story, Marcus?" I ask him bluntly.

"I brought you a gift," he answers. "I brought you a bloody knife."

My jaw clenches as I wait for more from him.

"Trust me, you're going to want this one, Jase. I think you've been waiting for it for a long, long time."

"What is my bloody knife?" I ask him, gritting my teeth and praying it's not the body of Jenny Parks. That's all I can think right now. *Please, don't let it be her.*

"Inside the trunk of the lone car across the street is your package. I sent you a video, you should watch. He's had a high dose of your sweets. I'd think it'll wear off by tomorrow... Good luck, Jase."

chapter sixteen

Bethany

"This is completely and totally shady," I mutter under my breath and then look over my shoulder to make sure no one saw me walk into the alley behind the drugstore. It's nearly 3:00 a.m. so the store is closed, as is everything else around here. "Could you freak me out any more?"

Meet me behind Calla Pharmacy. I have something for you.

That's the text Laura sent. And the messages afterward were a series of me asking why the fuck we were meeting there and her not answering my question, but insisting that I come.

"You have no idea the shit I was imagining on the way down here," I scold her although it's only concern that binds to the statement. The buzz from earlier has worn off completely, as if the current situation isn't sobering enough.

"Sorry." Laura's hushed voice is barely heard as she grips my arm and pulls me farther down the alley to where she parked her car.

"We can do shady shit at my house," I say, biting out the words.

"What if it's bugged or something?"

All I can hear is the wind as her words sink in.

Concern is etched in her expression as she looks back at me and then nearly opens her trunk, but she stops too soon and places both of her palms on the slick metal.

The streetlight from nearby barely illuminates us.

"It's dark and cold and you're freaking me out," I finally speak and ignore the way it hurts just to breathe in air this cold. I lift my scarf up to cover my nose before shoving my hands in my pockets and asking, "What the hell are we doing here?"

Every second it seems scarier back here. It's a vacant small lot, no longer asphalt as the grass has grown through patches of it. It's all cracked and ruined. Even though it's abandoned, there are still ambient noises. The small sounds are what spike my unease.

Like the cat that jumped onto the dumpster and the cars that speed by every so often out front. I should have told Jase. I should have messaged him, but I didn't.

"Why did we have to come down here? And why couldn't I tell Jase?"

"We just had to, okay." Laura's fear is barely concealed by irritation. "And he doesn't need to know about this. I did something," she quickly adds before I can get in another word. Her soft blue eyes are wide with worry and she looks like she can barely breathe. Her gaze turns back to the trunk and chills run down my arms.

"There better not be a body in there," I tell her more to lighten the mood, but also out of the sheer fear that she fucking killed someone. At this point, I don't know what to predict next.

"Jesus," she hisses. "I didn't kill anyone." She searches behind me and then over her shoulders like someone might be watching. "I'm not one of the crazies in your nut hut."

There's a small voice in the back of my mind telling me that Seth is somewhere. Seth is watching and Jase will know everything she says and does right now. But only if Jase knew I left, only if Seth is watching me nonstop. The thought is comforting for a split second, and then I regret not telling Jase.

"You promise you didn't say anything?" she asks and I nod.

I remind myself, this is Laura, Laura the friend I met in college, the girl who I ran to when I got dumped and needed to consume my weight in ice cream and fall asleep in front of romcoms. *My* Laura. My best, and really, my only friend.

There isn't a damn thing she could do that would be problematic. With that thought lingering, I get to the bottom of it. "Why are we here?"

"Look... first..." It's a heavy sigh that leaves her when she stares at me. The look she's giving me is begging for forgiveness and acceptance.

"You're freaking me out," I admit and grip her hands in mine. They're cold, just like the air, like my lungs, like everything back here on the cold winter night. "Just tell me; I won't be mad."

Laura's never done anything like this and I don't know what to expect. I always know what she's going to do and say. She's the voice of reason more times than not. But this... "I have no idea what you did, but it's okay. Whatever you have to tell me or show me, it's okay." I hope my words comfort her like they do me. Even if they are only words.

"You have to accept it," she tells me and her voice is sharp. The worry is gone in her cadence, replaced by strength.

"Accept what?" The question I ask goes unanswered. Instead a breeze blows, forcing Laura's blonde hair to blow in front of her face although she makes no move to stop it. Bits of soft snow fall between us and all she does is stare at me and then make me promise.

"Promise you'll take it. Promise you'll never mention it again." She inhales too quickly and finally moves, shifting on her feet to look behind me before adding, "Promise it leaves with you and you forget where you got it."

My stomach coils and I nearly back away from her, but she grips my hand instead. "What the fuck is it, Laura?"

"Promise," she demands.

"Whatever it is, I promise." The pit in my stomach grows heavier as the trunk creaks open, darkness flooding it and hiding what's inside at first glance.

It's only when she pulls it out and shoves it into my chest that I see it's a black duffle bag.

The trunk shuts and the thud of it closing is all I can hear as I hold the bag. It can't be more than fifteen pounds, but until the hood is shut I have to hold it with both hands and then rest it against the flat back of the car.

"Don't open it. Just take it."

I look Laura dead in the eyes as I answer her, "You've lost your fucking mind if you think I'm not looking at what's in here."

"Don't. In case someone's watching."

"What is it, Laura?" I ask her again, my voice even but somehow sounding eerie in the bitter air.

"Your way out of the debt," is all she tells me until I grip her wrist, forcing her to look at me instead of walking back to her driver's seat like she intended.

She glances at my hand on her wrist, and then back up to me before turning to face me toe to toe.

I don't expect the words she says next. The casualness of her statement, yet how matter of fact it is.

"If you want to be with him, this is the world you live in. There's a risk of people going after you. If you don't... I think you're still in that world, regardless. It has a way of not letting go."

A silent shrill scream rings in my ears from the need to run, the need to do something. It comes from anxiety, from the need to fight or flee. I choose fight. I was born to fight.

She finishes, "But at least this gets rid of the debt."

It takes a second and then another for me to comprehend what she's saying.

"The debt? I owe him-"

"Three hundred grand." She nods as she speaks. "And now you have it to pay off."

"No fucking way." I'm adamant as I shove the duffle bag into her chest but she doesn't take it, she doesn't reach out for it and the bag falls to the icy cracked ground. "Where did you get it?" I hiss the question, with a wild fear brewing inside of me. "Take it back," I beg her before she even answers.

Her baby blue eyes search mine for a moment and I'm left with disbelief and confusion.

I tell her with a furious terror taking over, "You don't have that kind of money."

"I didn't and then I did," she answers simply.

Emotions well in my throat. "Take it back, Laura. However you got it, give it back."

"No," she says first and then adds, "I can't anyway."

"No, Laura, fuck! No." I have to cover my face as it heats. "Please tell me-"

"I'm more than fine," she cuts me off. "I wanted to do something for a long time. An offer I had and wasn't sure if I wanted to take or not."

It's only the ease of her confession that settles me slightly.

"You can always go back."

"No," she answers me, "I can't and I don't want to. I'm not taking the bag back either and I have to go, I have the night shift and you promised me. You promised you'd take the bag."

"What did you do?"

"I can't tell you," she murmurs. There's no fear or desperation when she speaks to me and my head spins with the denial that this is even happening.

"You can, you can tell me anything." I feel crazed as I reach out to her, stepping forward as she steps back and kicking the bag at my feet.

"I can't tell you," she says, stressing every word and pulling herself away from my grasp. "That bag is yours. And I have to go."

She leaves me there with the duffle bag at my feet, the snow clinging to my hair and the cold of the night settling in to wrap its arms around me, the same way I wrap my hand around the strap to the duffle bag.

chapter seventeen

Jase
Years ago...

I knew something was off before I even opened the door. I spent the hour before coming here arguing with Carter about even bringing Angie here.

I didn't trust her at The Red Room though. Not with the shit I have going on and the people that come and go. I tried to help her before and she took off, coming back worse. And the last three nights she destroyed the place, searching for anything to numb the pain she was in. She was fucking skin and bones. Her cheeks were so hollow. Addiction will do a lot of things to a person. It turns their curious smirks into glowers of pain, their bright eyes into dull gazes to nowhere.

It wasn't just the addiction though. She couldn't be sober because then she remembered what she'd done.

Fuck, the memory of it makes me sick.

"She's not with me, but that doesn't mean I can't help her."

"You can't help everyone, Jase." Carter's hardened voice is clear in my mind. He looked me in the eyes and told me, "You can't help her. You can't and shouldn't. You shouldn't have brought her here."

"I don't want to help everyone." I bit back the answer, feeling the anger rise inside of me. It was the first disagreement we'd ever had. I had to do it, though. "I want to help her. Just one person."

"Why? She's not yours."

He didn't get it. For the first time, he showed his confusion. He didn't understand that I didn't want her, I just wanted her to be okay. Even if she was nearly a stranger, even if I'd never want her to walk through the doors of the bar again once she left.

I needed to feel like I could make it right. We all make mistakes, but it's okay if you can make it right. I just needed to make it right.

"You shouldn't have brought her here." That was the last thing he said to me as I made my way back to the guest bedroom, questioning everything I'd done. I'd like to think that was why I thought things were off when I got to the door. But it was something deeper than that.

With my hand on the doorknob, I remember how I told her to just sleep before I left. Get some fucking sleep to help her with the withdrawal. Her eyes were so sunken in and dark as she screamed at me. It could have been the cocaine or the heroin. She looked nothing like the woman I'd known before.

I had to empty the room out to keep her from throwing things. She liked comic books, so I went out to get her some. It would only be weeks. Only weeks of helping her get back on her feet, then she was someone else's problem. Then she'd be able to think clearly and choose whatever she wanted to do next. But as it stood, the addiction made every choice and it was leading her to an early grave.

I remember the way my scar shined on my hand, the light brighter there than on the metal knob as I pushed the door open.

It was quiet, too quiet for her not to be sleeping in the empty bed.

The bathroom door was closed and I glanced at the clock. 3:04 a.m. Someone once told me the Devil gets a minute every day. 3:07 to come and do his darkest deeds. I stared at the clock, knowing the Devil's deeds were done all day long, whether he was here or not.

Every second I sat on the chair in the room, I thought about what to tell her. I didn't know her well enough to know what to say. All I could think of telling her was that it would be better tomorrow. That she just had to take it day by day. It takes weeks to get through the worst of it, sometimes longer.

She didn't listen the first time, or the second, but maybe she'd listen now. Maybe tomorrow. Back then, I had hope.

The next time I looked at my watch, nearly forty minutes had passed. It was then that I realized it was still too quiet. Far too quiet.

I knocked at the door, but she didn't respond. "Angie?" I called her name, and still nothing.

I knocked harder, feeling that gut instinct that something was wrong. I remember the way her name felt as I screamed it and hammered my fist against the door, all the while, it was far too quiet.

Testing the knob, it wasn't locked, so I pushed it open. I knew then though, the Devil had come and gone. And that I was too late.

She'd shut the shower curtain, but even through it I could see the slash of red on the tiled wall. I'll never forget that first sound I heard that night when I went to check on her. It was the sound of the shower curtain opening.

The blood was all over her hands and arms. The first thought I had, was that she must've regretted it and tried to stop the blood from the cut at her throat.

She tried to take it back.

I didn't cry for her in that moment, but I leaned back against the wall, taking in her red hair and how it matted to her bloodied skin. Her eyes were still open, so once I could move, I closed them for her, even though my hand shook.

I failed her. I did this to her. It was all I could think.

Falling to my knees next to the tub, I prayed for the first time since my mama died. I asked God to take over for me. To help her and forgive her and forgive her sins.

I didn't ask him to forgive mine though. I'd be more careful about mine, but I knew I'd keep doing it.

I couldn't take back the years of what we'd already done. I couldn't take any of it back.

Carter was right, I never should have brought her there.

"I remember the first time I met Angie. I thought she was a sweet girl although a little too loud when she was drunk. She was older than me, and didn't want a damn thing to do with me other than to score drugs for a party. Which was fine, because the feeling was mutual." I talk easily, like I'm only telling a story.

"Coke or pot for the weekend. Whatever the flavor of the week was, she wanted it. It was easy to sell it to her. With her long red hair and wild green eyes, she wasn't my type, but I couldn't deny she was kind and polite. She used to stand on her tiptoes to turn around after getting her stash, doing a little curtsy of thanks that would at least get a chuckle from me.

"You remember Angie, Seth?" I speak clear enough that both Seth and Hal can hear me. The basement room today feels hotter than ever. More suffocating than it's ever been before.

"Of course." Seth answers calmly as I roll up the sleeves to my shirt. I'm careful and meticulous, but even so, I know I'm on edge. I'm on the verge of losing it and I haven't even touched the surface yet. He adds, "One of our first regulars," when I don't respond.

I made the mistake of watching the video Marcus sent me the second I got out of the park. I brought Hal here and waited. I didn't sleep, I didn't go home. I just waited until Seth said Hal was alert enough to go through with this.

Like always, he's standing behind Mr. Hal, who's in the interrogation chair. Although there's no interrogation today.

There are no questions for him. No need for a shirt to smother his screams. I want to hear them. I want the memories of tonight to somehow mask the memories I have of Angie's last day.

"You remember her?" I question Hal, feeling that crease deepen in the center of my forehead as I pick up the hammer. It's an ordinary hammer.

The tool of choice is fitting. Angie's dad worked as a carpenter. When he died, she went off the rails, that's what she told me once when she was struggling with her sobriety. It was easier than dealing with reality and the party drugs she bought for weekends became necessary every day. And then a few times every day. And then harder drugs. Just so she didn't have to think about her dead father.

So it made sense to me to choose a hammer.

"I don't know who you're talking about," the man answers. Confidently, stubbornly, like somehow he's got the upper hand here. Maybe he thinks I actually have questions, but I don't. All I have for him is a story.

I watch the light shine off the flat iron head of the hammer as I walk closer to him. There are no cuts on his wrists from trying to escape, nothing that shows any fear. And that's fine by me. I don't want him scared, I want him in pain. In fucking agony the way Angie was.

In the same agony Bethany's stuck in. The thought strikes me hard, and I hate it. I want it to go away. More than anything, I want her pain to stop.

My arm whips in front of me, the metal crashing against the man's jaw and morphing his scream into a cry of agony in a single blow.

The left side of his jaw hangs a little lower and the man fights against his restraints as he screams from the impact.

Glancing at the splatter of blood across my dress shirt, a huff of a breath leaves me, trying to calm the rage, trying to calm the need to not stop.

But Bethany's pain never stops. It never fucking ends.

"Marcus showed me a video. Only one. You knew her," I say and shrug, like it's not a big deal. Like he wasn't forcing himself down her throat while she was high and crying on a dirty floor.

"You knew her better than me," I comment. Thinking back to who she was before it all went downhill and trying to get the loathsome video out of my mind. If I could bleach it away, I would.

"She came in a lot, but only to get what she needed," Seth speaks from behind the fucker. He's reading me, his eyes never leaving me as I pace in front of the chair, waiting for Hal to stop his bitching and moaning.

"I want him to hear this," I tell Seth, raising my voice just enough for him to know not to console me like he's trying to do. I don't need that shit. I don't need to be told I couldn't have helped her or I couldn't have stopped it. I could have. I know I could have if I wasn't so fucking high on power and young and stupid. It's more controlled now. But back then, there was no protocol, and we sold to anyone and as much as they wanted.

"She was young, I had the drugs, I couldn't tell her no at first. She was the first person I told no. The first one where I realized I ruined her life." I'm staring at this asshole, and he's not looking at me. He's whimpering, looking down at his bare feet that are planted on the steel grid beneath him. He's not paying attention, so I swing the hammer again. Down onto his right foot. Crack! And then the left. The clang of the metal and the crack of small bones ricochets in the room. The black and blue on his skin is instant.

He screams and cries, but all it does is make me angry. He didn't care that Angie cried. He didn't care about what he did to her. He can mourn for his own pain all he wants, but it's not enough.

I have to walk away, seeing Bethany's face and knowing she wouldn't approve of this. What alternative is there though? To let this world turn with no consequence?

It's the fact that we feel pain when others feel nothing. This man feels nothing. The regret is hard enough and the guilt too, but walking around in a world where it isn't acknowledged, where those feelings travel alone... it's a hell that hides in every corner.

Hal cusses at me, spitting at my feet and sneering an expression of hate. He can't hold it long though. I slowly draw the sharp edge of the hammer across his throat as I speak.

"It was my fault, Hal. My fault that she got hooked and when she did, I sent her away. We'd only just begun in this game. We were bound to make mistakes. And Angie Davis was one of them."

Fuck, the guilt comes back full force just saying her name.

"I told her no, only a few months after I met her. I gave her the sweets, I told her to get better and then she could come back. Instead, she found you."

If she hadn't come to me, if Angie had gone to Bethany instead... My fiery woman, she would have known what to do. "Angie wanted help, she really did." I equate her to Jenny in this moment. Wondering if it really would have been different. If she really wanted help and if Bethany could have fixed her. I wish I could go back.

I can smash this hammer into his head, but I can't take her pain away. There's not a damn thing I can do to take Bethany's pain away

I think the words Hal's trying to say are, "Please, don't," as he spits up blood. It only reminds me of the way Angie said it in the video I saw hours ago. *Please, don't*.

"It's fine to party and have a good time, but she was slipping. She wasn't herself. Addiction grabbed hold of her and wasn't letting go. Anyone and everyone could see it."

"Yeah, I remember," Seth comments, nodding his head even as looks at me like he has nothing but sympathy for me. Fuck that. I don't need sympathy. I don't deserve sympathy.

"I remember. She was clinging to you crying, begging you for more." Seth still hasn't accepted what I have. Every word he says sounds like an excuse. "You sent her away with a way to help her."

Fuck, I should have known better. I wasn't in it like Carter was. I'd only just started and I didn't realize the ripple effect and the tidal wave it was capable of creating.

"I was young and I was stupid. I gave her whatever she wanted and however much she said she needed. Even when I knew it was getting bad. It took a long time before I sent her away..."

"Jase," Seth's tone is warning, cautioning me in where my mind is going, but I cut him off.

"No." My response echoes in the room even though it's pushed through gritted teeth while I tap the hammer in my hand, blood and all, as I add, "I take that blame. It's my fault. All of it."

Lifting the hammer up, I point it at Hal. "But you," I start to speak. I can't get the rest out though. I can't voice where this story inevitably turns.

Instead I crash the hammer onto his knees. Bashing them relentlessly. Then his thighs. His arms. Every bone I can break.

Screams and hot blood surround me. The man's cries get louder and louder. Does he cry in front of me at the memory? Or at the realization that there's no way he's getting out of this room alive?

It's what I've wanted for so long, some kind of justice for Angie, but I thought it would feel different. I thought it would feel better than this.

Instead the pain seeps into my blood, where it runs rampant in my body. The memories refuse to stop.

With a deep inhale I back away, letting the screams dull as I think about how sunken in her face was when she came to me after a month of being gone. I didn't know. I didn't take responsibility for what I'd done, and I let her walk out, thinking she'd be fine.

Because that was the story I wanted to hear.

"She told me things you had her do, but you didn't have a name then. How you took advantage of her. You had others come in while she was tied down on the table. She told me how she didn't even care when you tossed the heroin at her. That she remembers how badly she needed the hit. Even as you and the other men laughed at her and what you'd done."

Seth isn't expecting the next blow I give to the guy, straight across his jaw. He lets out a shout of surprise as the blood sprays from the gushing wound, down Seth's jeans and onto his shoes.

The once clean, bright white sneakers with a red streak are now doused in blood.

He takes a step back, getting out of my way and keeping his hands up in the air. He's acting like I'm the one who's gone crazy. But how could I be sane if the very thought of what happened didn't turn me mad?

"Seth, she ever tell you the things she did when we sent her away?" I ask him. Feeling a pain rip my insides open.

He shakes his head. His dark eyes are shining with unwanted remorse.

"She said she did shit she was so ashamed of, she couldn't tell me. She said she didn't deserve to live."

I smash the hammer down onto Hal's shoulder. But he doesn't scream this time and that only makes me hit him harder. Still, he's silent. His head's fallen to one side and I don't care. Maybe his ghost will hear me.

"All the money and all the power in the world, and I couldn't save her," I scream at the man. "You know why?" I keep talking to him. To the dead man. Feeling my sanity slip. "Why I couldn't save her?" I ask him, knowing Seth's eyes are on me, hearing his attempts to calm me down but ignoring him.

"Because she couldn't live with the things she'd done when she wasn't sober. She remembered it all. And she couldn't deal with it."

There is never true justice in tragedy.

You have to live with yourself after what's done is done.

"Angie couldn't do it," I tell him. "She couldn't live with the memories and she couldn't forgive herself."

I locked her in a room to help her get over the withdrawal. I gave her the pills and I gave her a safe place.

She killed herself.

"She had a sister. She had a mother who needed her. I couldn't even get out of the car at the funeral because of how they were crying."

It's the endings that don't have an honest goodbye that hurt the most. They linger forever because the words were never spoken.

I don't know who I'm talking to at this point. Seth or a man who didn't feel remorse for what he'd done, only for himself. I should have made him suffer longer. I should have controlled myself.

I hate that I ever sold her anything. I hate that the beautiful redhead at the bar would never smile again. All because of a dime bag of powder that took her far away from the world she wanted to leave. All because I sold it to her.

Every blow, I would take too. I deserve it.

Bethany should do to me what I've just done to this man. I led Jenny down that path. We sold her drugs, we bribed her with them for information. Even if it wasn't her first or her last, I know we sold her something and then let her walk away.

The thought only makes me slam the iron of the hammer down harder and more recklessly. Crashing into his face, his shoulders and arms. Every part of him. Over and over again, feeling all the anger, the pain, the sadness run through me, urging me to do it again and again.

When my body gives out and I fall to the floor on my knees, heaving in air, I finally stop. Letting my head fall back, and closing my eyes.

I could never tell Bethany. She deserves to hate me. I don't deserve her love, let alone her forgiveness. Not any of it.

chapter eighteen

Bethany

The very idea of leaving three hundred thousand dollars in the back of a car makes me want to throw up. People kill for this kind of money.

I can hardly even believe I actually have that amount. I didn't count it and I don't intend to. I don't want to touch it. All I did was unzip the bag once and then close my eyes again, pretending like I didn't see it.

Three hundred thousand dollars. I don't know what Laura did to get this money, but maybe I can give it right back to her. I don't think Jase gives a shit about the debt. A very large part of me believes it's more than that.

I won't know until I do this. Although sickness churns inside of me at the possibilities, I focus on the one thing I want to happen. I hand it to him, telling him honestly where it came from. He hands it back, telling me it's not my money and he doesn't want it.

"That's what will happen," I say for the dozenth time under my breath to no one. Maybe the dozenth is the trick, because I'm starting to believe it.

He wasn't home when I got back last night and he wasn't home when I woke up after only sleeping a handful of hours. He didn't answer my texts. He's nowhere to be found. The money was in the car while I paced inside waiting and waiting. I finally had to come out and make sure it was still there. I ended up getting in, just to kill time rather than pacing and pacing. I drove past the graveyard a few times, but I never got out of the car.

Pulling out the keys from the ignition, I stare up at the large estate, going over the dialogue in my head one more time.

The debt is paid. The time we had together was time I spent with you and nothing more and nothing less. That's what I'm going to say to him. I can do it.

I'm burning up in the car, the sweat along my skin won't quit. I know part of it is from the duffle bag in the back. I look over my shoulder once again, just like I have the entire drive down here last night and even an hour ago to make sure it didn't magically disappear.

Part of this anxiousness though is because I don't know what Jase will say or what he'll do with me once the money's handed over.

It's not just a debt. I know that. It can't be just a debt to him.

Opening the car door lets the cool air hit me and I relish in it. Calming down and shaking out my hands.

This world Jenny brought me into... I'm not fighting it anymore. I'm walking into it, ready for what it will bring me. It's another step forward. I can feel it. Just like telling Laura everything. Maybe it's a small step, but it's one I'm taking.

My heels click on the paved path to his door. The door that I open on my own.

He could take that away, but why would he? The doubts swirl and mix with the fear that what we have is only about the debt. Maybe he likes holding it over my head; maybe he thinks he won't have the upper hand if I pay it off.

That thought actually eases the tension in me. He's never going to have the upper hand when it comes to me. He should know that by now.

Calm, confident and collected I walk into the foyer and then past the hall, listening to my heels click in the empty space. The clicks, the thumps, they all only add to the urgency to tell him. To get it off my chest and to get that cash out of the back of my car.

"Jase," I call out his name, seeing the bedroom door open, but he doesn't answer.

A chill follows me, bombarding me even as I stand in the threshold of the dark bedroom and see only the light from the bathroom.

There are moments in time when you know instinctively everything is wrong. You know you're going to see something that you don't want to see. It's like there's a piece of our soul that's been here before. A piece that's preparing you for what's to come. Warning you even. And maybe if I was smarter, I'd take the warning and I wouldn't step foot into his bedroom.

I'm not smart enough though.

With the sound of running water getting louder as I approach, I creep quietly to his master bath.

The water's so loud I'm sure he couldn't hear me. That's what I tell myself.

Thump, my heart doesn't want to be here. *Thump*, it wants me to stop. I test the doorknob, and it's not locked. Something inside of me screams not to take this step. Not to go forward. *It's the wrong time, I'm not ready for it.* I can feel it trying to pull me away.

But I'm already turning the knob and with a creak, I push the door open.

I catch sight of his clothes on the floor first; he's still hidden from view from where I'm standing. The mix of bright and dark red splotches and smears wraps a vise around my lungs.

I can't breathe, but I still move forward.

Blood. There's blood on his shirt. That's blood, isn't it? Fear wriggles its way deeper inside of me, like a parasite taking over.

"Jase," I barely speak his name while taking a small step forward. My gaze moves from the blood on his clothes piled on the tile floor, to his naked body seated on the edge of the tub. He's covered with the way he's sitting, and his head's lowered, hanging heavy in front of him. I'm not sure he heard me the way he's sitting there. Like he's stunned, like his mind is elsewhere, lost in another place or another time.

Despair is crippling and I swallow hard. My trembling fingers reach out to pick up his shirt, wanting to believe it's not blood. There's not a mark on his skin, no cuts or bruises that are fresh. The cut I gave him is scabbed over.

The warmth of the air flows around me as I step closer and lift the shirt off the floor. It can't be blood, Jase isn't injured. Jase is fine.

But it looks like it. I don't understand. There's so much blood, in different patterns. Smeared and stained into the undershirt. I still don't want to believe it. I wish it would be anything else. My head spins as I grip the shirt tighter, staring at it as if it'll change, it'll go back to being clean if only I look at it the right way. But it's blood. There's so much blood, my hands are wet with it.

"Bethany." Jase's voice catches me off guard and I scream, pulling the shirt into my chest out of instinct before shoving it away when I realize I've pressed the bloody clothes to my own.

I could throw up with the revolting disgust and fear that sink into my bones. The blood is on me.

"Whose blood is that?" The question tumbles from me as I take a step backward and Jase stands up tall. My hands grip the doorway and my fingers leave a trail of blood.

There's a look in his eyes I will never forget when my gaze finally reaches his.

A darkness I haven't seen before and the fear that accompanies it is all-consuming.

In sharp spikes, the chills take over and I take another step back. Out of the bathroom and away from him.

That piece of my soul that was warning me before... it wasn't about the blood, it was about Jase. I know it to be true when he takes another step forward, so much larger than mine with his hands raised and he tells me to calm down.

If I could speak, I'd tell him he's crazy to think I should calm down. If I could speak, I'd scream at him, demanding he tell me what he's done.

But I can't. Every syllable catches in the back of my throat in a way that feels like I'm choking.

"Let me get a shower and we can talk," Jase states calmly, the savage look in his eyes just barely dimming.

My head shakes, all on its lonesome and I turn and run. As fast as I can, I run away from him.

"Fuck," I hear him mutter as I bolt to the door, sweeping myself around it and crashing into the hall wall. I don't stop running, even though I don't hear him behind me.

Thump, thump, thump, thump. My heart pounds faster than my heels, ushering me away.

As I reach the door, I hear him call out. With my hand on the scanner, I turn around to see him with a pair of sweats, walking toward me, not running.

Maybe he thought that would keep me from leaving. Maybe he thought I wouldn't be threatened or I wouldn't be scared.

But he was wrong.

So fucking wrong. The second I swing the door open, I hear him scream my name and start running. I slam the door closed knowing he'll have to use the scanner too. It's another second I have ahead of him. Only seconds.

Run!

I scramble to my car and to find my keys. With terror raging through me at Jase getting his hands on me and forcing me back inside, at not knowing what he'll do to me or what he's capable of, I shove the gear into drive and reverse out of the driveway. I'm senselessly speeding away with the sight of him swinging the door open the moment my car hits the gate. Crashing it open and denting the hood of my car.

Even as I scream, I keep my foot on the gas, not caring about the damage, just needing to leave as quickly as possible.

I need to run and never stop.

Run far away and not look back.

The car jostles as I go over a curb and then another, my tires screaming as I race out of the long drive and backroads to get to the busy streets.

My gaze spends too long in the rearview, waiting for his car to show. It doesn't, but that doesn't keep me from tearing down the road.

My grip is hot, my pulse fast. I need to get the fuck out of here.

It's only once I've gotten onto the main road and I'm minutes away from my home that I let myself think of anything other than the need to go faster.

How could I love him? How could I want to love him?

Thoughts run wild in my mind, fighting with each other to be heard. There's a pounding in my temple and I don't even realize when I've run the red light until a car beeps their horn at me.

Fuck! I have to veer to the right to miss hitting the SUV. A wave of heat flows over my skin, far too hot as my tires squeal and I barely keep my car on the road.

That doesn't stop me. I keep going. I don't stop. I can't stop. I need to go faster. I need to get away.

With my chest heaving, I catch sight of the blood. Oh my God, the blood.

I need to get it off. I need to get this off. Bile climbs up my throat and I have to swallow it as I pull into my driveway. It's a reckless turn but I don't care. I need to get inside and get this off.

Get this blood off of me. Get Jase Cross off of me.

It's all I can think about as I slam the door shut to my car and run to the porch. The gust of cold air brings with it the white mist of an incoming storm tonight.

My hands are still shaking as I search for my key and that's what I'm staring at when I hear Officer Walsh's voice. "Bethany?"

The surprise and shock make me scream and drop my keys. They bang as they hit the ground and I stay perfectly still.

"Fuck." The word is spoken faintly as I stare back at him on the other end of my porch as he gets up from the chair. Like he was waiting for me.

I know my expression is one of fear and guilt, a doe-eyed woman caught in the act of something awful and I can't change it as our gazes lock.

"Is that blood?" he asks, standing straighter, but with his hand behind him as my feet turn to stone and refuse to move.

"No," I lie and his head tilts as his hand pushes his coat back and his fingers rest on his gun.

"I didn't do anything," I spill the words out, pleading with him to understand. My pulse rages and I can barely stand up straight. Fuck, no. How did this happen?

"Tell me everything. I can help you," he urges, but it doesn't sound sincere.

"You have to believe me. It's not me. I didn't do anything."

"Tell me whose blood that is."

"I don't know," I practically shriek.

"It is blood then?" he questions. Immediately, I feel caught. I feel trapped. The bite of the air creeps in, cracking the heat that's consumed me.

My lips part, but instead of giving him words, all I can do is swallow as my vision becomes dizzy.

"Tell me everything, Bethany; what happened?" His question comes out harder this time and he takes a step forward. I instinctively take a step back and my back hits the wall of the house.

With a trembling voice I whisper, begging him to let me go. "I can't," I tell him. "I don't know."

My inhale is ragged as he takes another step closer and I have nowhere to go.

"I wish I didn't have to do this." Pulling out the cuffs from behind his back, he tells me, "Bethany Fawn, you're under arrest."

a single touch

From *USA Today* bestselling author W. Winters comes the conclusion to the breathtaking, heart-wrenching romantic suspense trilogy, Irresistible Attraction.

Sometimes you meet someone, although maybe *meet* isn't quite the right word. You don't even have to say hello for this to happen. You simply pass by them and everything in your world changes forever. Chills flow from where you imagine he'd kiss you in the crook of your neck, moving all the way down with only a single glance.

I know you know what I'm referring to. The moment when something inside of you ignites to life, recognizing the other half that's been gone for far too long.

It burns hot, destroying any hope that it's only a coincidence, and that life will go back to what it was. These moments are never forgotten.

That's only with a single glance.

I can tell you what a single touch will do. It will consume you and everything you thought you knew.

I felt all of this with Jase Cross, with every flicker of the flames that roared inside of me.

I knew he'd be my downfall, and I was determined to be his just the same.

A Single Touch is **the third and final** book of the Irresistible Attraction trilogy.

A Single Glance and *A Single Kiss* must be read first.

> "Past is a nice place to visit,
> but certainly not a good place to stay."
> —Anonymous

prologue

Bethany

My calculus grades are slipping. The large red D scribbled in Miss Talbot's handwriting stares back at me. One look at it shoves the knot in the back of my throat even deeper down my windpipe. My bookbag falls to the floor in the nursing home with a dull thud as I whisper the word, *"fuck."* With my hand rubbing under my tired eyes, I let out a heavy sigh and stare at the ceiling in the hallway.

There's no way I'm going to be able to stay in college if I don't pass. There's no coming back from this. My grades didn't slip like this last year when Jenny was here with me every day at four o'clock on the dot. I only have one more year to go, but this class is a core requirement. I'll never need to know how the hell derivatives work in order to be a nurse, but I can't fail this class. *I can't fucking fail.*

"Bethany?" The soft voice belongs to Nurse Judy. She told me exactly how she got her degree and that I could do it just like she did. She's the reason I changed my major sophomore year to pursue a nursing degree. Just as she creeps into the long hall, I shove the test into a notebook while stuffing it into my worn leather backpack, listening to the sound of the zipper rather than what she's saying.

I'll fail calculus, lose the scholarship that's paid for more than half of my college education, and be left with even more debt and no degree to show for it. *Perfect.* I don't know what I'm going to do. Other than work a nine-to-five at whatever minimum wage job I can get. If they'll even hire me.

"Did you hear me?" Nurse Judy coaxes me out of my downward spiral and it's then that I see the worried look in her dark brown eyes. "Your mother had a relapse."

"A relapse?" The confusion leaves a deep crease on my forehead.

"We don't know what caused it, but she's with us, Bethany. Mentally aware."

"Aware?" All the air leaves me with the single word.

"She woke up, not knowing what happened during the last three or so years. But she knows time has passed. She knows you and your sister have been on your own and that she has Alzheimer's."

"I don't understand how that's possible." Fear is something I never expected to feel in this moment. I've had so many dreams come to me in the middle of the night where my mother would be lucid. Where she'd tell me it was okay, that she was back now. Back for good and that she remembers everything. They were only dreams though. It's only ever a dream.

I can barely swallow as I stare past Nurse Judy and walk forward without conscious awareness. "Is she okay?" It's the only thing I can ask. I can't imagine what it's like to wake up one day to have lost years of time. To wake up and find your children look different and everything's changed.

The oddest thing in this moment is that I hope she still loves me. I just want her to love me still. Even if I'm failing. Even if I'm no longer her little girl. It's been years since she's been lucid and this is what I want most of all.

"She'll be better when she sees you," is the answer Nurse Judy gives me. With each step, I know I'll always remember this moment. It's like something flipped a switch in my head and a voice gives me reassurance. *This moment will never leave you. This moment will define you.*

"Are they here?" my mother's voice calls out. Echoed in her voice, I can hear the strain of past tears. "Did they get your messages?"

My answer drowns out Nurse Judy's as I round the corner to the living room in the home, my steps picking up pace just as my throat tightens. "Mom," I croak.

She's frail and thin, as she was yesterday and the day before. Somehow I thought when she came into view, she'd look like she did the last time I held her hand and she asked me again who my sister was.

She had her makeup done perfectly although she didn't need it. Mom used to say she'd never grow old. Even joked about it that day as she brushed her blush up to her temples. That was the day we took her to the hospital. She'd forgotten who my sister was and it took me a long time to realize she'd forgotten who I was too. She thought I was her best friend from high school, the girl she named me after. A girl who had long since died.

My mother squeezes me harder today than she did back then and the tickle in the back of my throat grows impatient as I hold my breath and squeeze her back just as tight.

I don't cry until her body wracks with sobs against mine. "Sorry," she tells me. "I'm so sorry," is all she can say over and over.

As if she chose this. As if she wanted to forget the life she had and let the memories fade and die. That's what forgetting is, it's the death of the life you had. It doesn't just kill you though. It kills everyone else as well.

I only pull away from her for a moment, just to tell her there's nothing to be sorry for, but the words are lost when she looks into my eyes. Her own are gray and clouded with a gaze of sorrow.

"Mom?"

Her expression changes in an instant. Confusion clouds her face, where just minutes ago there was clarity.

My mother is in there, or she was, but the moment is gone.

"Who are you?"

"Mom, come back," I beg her, feeling my chest hollow and then fill with agony. "Where'd you go?" I ask her, not giving into the fear this time, only the loss. "Mom!" Hope is undeniable. "I'm here, Mom; I'm here!"

Her hand tightens on my forearm, too tight.

"Mom," I gasp, trying to pry her hands off of me as she refuses to look away, refuses to react to anything at all. She's merely a statue and the realization frightens me. I turn to look over my shoulder just as I hear the front door shut from the hall. My heartbeat races. Where'd Nurse Judy go?

"Mom," I protest, writhing out of her grasp. "Help!" I finally call out, the fear winning.

"Everyone I loved has died," my mother says, and her voice is ragged. Despair and loss morph her features into one of pain and her grip on me loosens.

Staring into my eyes with sincerity, she tells me, "Everyone you love will die before you do." As if she's talking to a stranger she only intends to bring pain, they're the last words she speaks before her slender body relaxes into the chair. Her gaze wanders aimlessly as I stand there breathless from both fear and despair, knowing I was too late. That's when I hear the quickened footsteps of my sister running into the room.

Running to see her mother. Who's already gone.

Seconds pass, and I can't look at Jenny. I brush the tears away as Nurse Judy pushes past us both, aiding my mother, whose consciousness has drifted to another place and another time.

"Mom," my sister cries. And I don't blame her.

That was the last time my sister cried for our mother. She didn't even cry at her funeral nearly a year later. Jenny always held it against her that our mother didn't wait for her. She held it against me too, knowing I at least got to hear Mom tell me she was sorry.

I never told her what else our mother said. I tried to forget it. I did everything I could to kill that memory.

It's come back though. It refuses to die, unlike other things in my life.

chapter one

Bethany

THE CLOCK DOESN'T STOP TICKING.

It's one of those simple round clocks. There's nothing special about the white backing and thick black frame. *Tick, tick, tick.* It's loud and unforgiving. The torture of it is all I can focus on to bring me sanity as the last hours of my life fall like dominoes in my memory.

The money in the trunk.

"You still haven't explained where you got the three hundred thousand dollars." Officer Walsh's voice is hard.

The blood on Jase's clothes and the look in his eyes when I came into his bathroom.

"Or why you were covered in blood. Whose blood is it, Miss Fawn? You need to tell us."

Fear is what motivated me to run from him. Fear is the cause of all of this. It's left me now, though. In its place is something more resigned.

One long, deep breath falls from me as I stare at the painted white bricks of the interrogation room's walls and listen to the *tick, tick, tick.*

My piss-poor decisions have led to this point in my life.

The point of waiting. I've fucked it up enough; I may as well just let it all fall. When Alice fell, she landed in Wonderland. I'm thinking that's not where I'll land, but I'm ready to feel the weightlessness of what's to come. I'm simply tired of fighting it.

There's another officer in the room. He's younger. When I first listened to their demands for me to answer their questions, I sat here hours ago with my shoulders tense and feeling the need to curl up into a ball and hide. The young cop sat across from me, his arms crossed and his gaze never wandering from me.

I don't like him or the way he looks at me.

"We're doing a DNA test now. You think it's going to hit, Walsh?" The other officer, Linders, finally speaks to Walsh, even if his eyes are still pinned on me. There's a certain level of disdain that seeps into my skin every time I meet his gaze.

"I'll tell you what I think," Officer Walsh answers. He's staring at me too, even as he taps the stack of papers in his hand and continues, "I think she was in the wrong place at the wrong time and that she has names."

Tick, tick, the clock goes on. It's been like this for hours in this cold interrogation room. An ache in my back reminds me how uncomfortable this metal chair is.

"I don't think so. I think she was hired for a hit or was hiring someone else and it went wrong." Officer Linders speaks clearly, although his voice is low and rough. "A hit or drugs. There's no other explanation. Who'd you get the cash from?" he asks me. It has to be the hundredth time they've asked about the cash. "Where did it all go wrong?"

"I already told you," I start to say but don't recognize my tired voice anymore as I lift my gaze to Officer Walsh's and then to Linders's. "I don't have anything to say."

Officer Walsh leans forward, exasperated. The metal legs grind against the floor as he repositions in his chair. "I saw how scared you were," he says. Compassion wraps itself around every word and his gaze pleads with me to give him something. "I can help you."

A second passes and then another.

I could let it all out. I could tell them the truth. I know I could. Maybe they'd give me a new name and send me off to some place where bad men can't find me. Somewhere free of all these memories. A place where I didn't have to think of my sister or my fucked up life.

Where I wouldn't feel the presence of Jase Cross on every inch of surface I can see, smell, touch.

As I swallow, the click of the the heat switching on is all that can be heard in the room.

I don't want to live in that world. In a world where Jase Cross doesn't hover over me. Even if he scared the hell out of me. Recalling the sight of him sitting there on the edge of the tub, tilting his head to look me in the eyes, makes me close mine tight. I don't know what happened, but I can't leave him.

More than anything, the incessant ticking of the clock reminds me that every second that passes, I'm not with him. He's not okay and I'm not with him.

Let me fall to whatever may await me, and I'll crawl my way back up to Jase. I'll find him or he'll find me. And when that happens, he better fucking confess. I deserve to know what happened.

Strands of my hair wind around my finger as I ignore Officer Walsh. He hasn't charged me yet, but I know he will. I'll be charged with obstruction of justice for not giving them information about the blood on my shirt when it comes back confirmed from a human… or maybe with a name. God forbid it comes back as from a missing person. And who knows what I'll be charged with because of the cash in the back of my car. I don't even know what the offenses will be, since so many have been listed off in their speculation of what I've done.

But I'll never say a word. And that's how I know I care more for Jase than I should. And why he needs to tell me *everything*.

"There's no helping anything. Whatever she says will be a lie." The dark stare of Officer Linders makes my stomach curl.

Good cop, bad cop, I suppose. I manage to offer him a hint of a smile. My mouth moves on its own and I didn't mean for it to do that. It just happens. As if I need to tempt fate any further.

"Let me make you an offer," Officer Walsh starts and Linders huffs in disdain, rocking back in the chair and for the first time his gaze shifts from me. He's young, very Italian in appearance although he doesn't have an accent. He scratches at his coarse dark stubble as Officer Walsh draws my attention.

"I used to work for the FBI and I have some friends in town, looking into things." There's a sense of compassion and empathy in Cody Walsh's voice that's hypnotizing, like a lullaby that draws you in. "What I'm trying to tell you is that I have connections. I know what happened to your sister. I know Jase Cross has been seen at your residence."

His light blue eyes sharpen every time he says, 'Cross.' "What I know is that you can have a happy life. You can start over, Bethany. All you have to do is tell me what happened."

It's like he read my mind. A way out. This is the bottom of the barrel, isn't it? When you need witness protection to find a way out of the hole you've dug for yourself.

Officer Linders clears his throat and the spell from Walsh is broken for only a moment as my eyes flick between the two of them. A man with hate for me, and another who I've felt from the first day I saw him, that he wanted to help me.

"All you have to do is tell me what happened." His hand gestures an inch above the table as he adds, "No matter how guilty you may feel; no matter what you've done."

Everything seems to slow as a part of my conscience begs me to consider. The part that remembers how dark Jase's eyes were when I last saw him. The part that's fear's companion. The part that questions if I'm strong enough for all this. Even if Jase tells me what he did and why he was sitting there like that, like he was someone else. Even if I pretend as though what happened earlier today will never happen again.

And yet another part of me is like a signal amid all the noise. A part that's fading away. A small part that remembers this all started because I wanted a single thing from Jase Cross.

A name. The murderer who made the one person I had left in my life disappear. Justice for my sister.

A name Jase has yet to deliver.

I have to blink away the thoughts, and Officer Walsh seems to take it as me considering his offer.

Say nothing, do nothing. Say nothing, do nothing. Fall down the rabbit hole; they can even throw me in that pit if they want. When I finally land, I'll do what I've always done. I'll stand up on my own and keep moving. With Jase or without.

Three knocks at the door startle me, causing the chair I'm firmly seated in to jump back. Officer Walsh is the one to stand and rise, leaving Linders staring at me, relishing in the hint of fear I've shown. I can barely hear someone outside the slightly ajar door speaking to Officer Walsh over the sound of my heart racing.

All my life, I've lived by elementary rules. *Do what is right and not what is wrong.* It's the simplest way to break down the laws of life. And yet here I sit, not knowing my judgment and wondering when the black and white of right and wrong turned so gray for me. Especially since I can't even list all the wrong things I've done recently. There are too many to count, yet I'd defend them all.

"Be right back." Officer Walsh is tense as he grips the door, locks eyes with me, then leaves the room. With only Linders across from me, a new tension rises inside of me.

I don't like the way he looks at me. Fear and anger curl my fingers into a fist in my lap.

Say nothing, do nothing.

He stares at me and I him, neither of us saying a word until a small red light goes off to my left. It's oddly placed in between the painted bricks. If it had never come on, I would've never known of its existence. And the little red light changes everything.

"It's clear for the moment, but I don't know how long we'll have, so I'll be fast," Linders says quickly with a new tone I haven't heard from him. Leaning forward, the distaste vanishes, and the hate I felt he had for me is nowhere to be found.

"It's all being scrubbed; every shred of evidence on you is going to vanish. Or it already has. Officer Walsh won't have anything to hold you on and no charges will be pressed."

"What?" Disbelief takes the form of a whisper.

"He already knows someone here at the station is in their back pocket. It'll be all right," he assures me when my expression doesn't change. "If you want to go to a cell, tell me. If you'd rather stay here, we'll have to keep this up when Walsh comes back, but I'll make sure he doesn't cross the line. There are others too who are loyal to Walsh, but I'll stay with you the entire time. Unless you want to be alone."

"I don't understand." I don't know why that's my reply.

Because I do understand. The pieces line up with one another perfectly. The Cross brothers control the police department. I knew that. I know that now, even. But to be a part of it, to see it happening...

"Mr. Cross told me to protect you and get you out of here." His eyes search mine, although there isn't a bit of judgment to be found.

"Thank you," is all I can say although I wrap my arms around myself and contemplate what would have happened if I was in a different mindset. If I was ready to spill my guts. If I was wanting that new life Walsh sold me so well.

I should feel relief, which I do. The more nagging thoughts are of how powerful Jase is. How much damage a single man could do. And how little I know about him. Yet how willing I was to fall for him.

What if I had said something? What then?

"The shirt's been destroyed and that's really the only damaging piece he had on you," Linders tells me, clearing his throat.

The money.

"What about the money?" The question leaves me with haste just as the red light vanishes, blending in with the wall once again.

"Are you going to sit there and deny everything? Maybe I should put you behind bars and see how you like that," Linders sneers, forcing my body to turn ice cold. I can feel the blood drain from my face, even if I'm consciously aware this time that it's all an act.

"What's it going to be, Miss Fawn? Are you going to talk? Or do you want us to stick you in a cell like the criminal you are?" Those are the options he offers me as the door opens and Walsh returns. Walsh's demeanor is defeated as he motions for Linders to follow him out of the interrogation room.

Linders doesn't though. He doesn't obey the command from his superior. He waits for me, wanting to know an answer.

Words get stuck in my throat and I try to swallow them, I try to speak.

Nothing comes. Not a word is spoken as I stare into Linders' gaze, knowing he's one of so many men who do Jase's bidding.

Jase is still here, still in this room, protecting me even when I didn't know it.

chapter two

Jase

"It's risky with the FBI already involved," Seth speaks from the driver's seat as we're parked out front of the police station. His eyes seek mine out in the rearview mirror and I meet them, but I only nod, not bothering to speak. "Four men now, active agents, coming all the way down here from New York." He sucks his front teeth in the absence of a response from me.

It's all my fault. It's my fault she's in there. I know it is. What I don't know is what the fuck came over me.

A voice in the back of my head answers instantly. *She did*. Bethany Fawn came over me.

"We should prepare for someone to take the fall," Seth continues and a grunt of acknowledgment comes from my chest.

I've already been thinking about it. How best to handle this particular fuckup of mine. It involves a dead former FBI agent by the name of Cody Walsh and one of my men in a jail cell taking the fall. Judge Martin will give the minimum sentence. All because I fucked up at a time when fucking up isn't a possibility.

"Someone who needs the money for their family. Someone who'd go away for a year and be all right with that." Seth rattles on.

"Chris Mowers," I finally answer him and then clear my throat although my eyes stay glued to the double doors at the front entrance. "He's new to the crew, young and seemingly naïve. His dad isn't doing well. Medical costs and looking out for his mother while he's serving time should do it. Besides, we've primed him for this." Chris wanted to work for me. I told him to go through the police academy, to earn a position we could use to our advantage. "He's not going to like it. But we can make it worth it."

My answer receives a single nod from Seth followed by the impatient tapping of his foot in the front seat.

"You're too nervous," I comment. I'm well aware of the consequences and everything at stake in this moment. The nerves he feels are nothing compared to the turmoil rattling inside of me. "Knock it the fuck off."

With his hand running over his chin he takes in a deep breath, but doesn't speak. Instead he releases a long sigh.

"You have something on your mind?" I push him.

I start to think he's going to keep it from me, whatever it is he's thinking, and then he finally says, "She's different."

Bethany. Every muscle in my body tenses at the mere mention of her.

"Yes," I answer him, feeling a pressure inside of my chest that makes me grit my teeth.

"She's in your head." He swallows after speaking.

Narrowing my eyes, I answer him with an acknowledging yes.

"I don't know how to help that," Seth admits, breaking eye contact in the small rectangular mirror for the first time. I hear him readjust in the seat in front of me as he adds, "I don't know what I should have done differently." When I don't immediately respond to that, he doesn't say anything else.

The sound of a car driving past us intrudes on the silence and I watch the tires leave tracks on the asphalt after driving through a small puddle. The brutal cold hasn't stopped the early spring flowers from pushing through the dirt out front of the police station.

Staring at the double doors that hold my cailín tine behind them, I finally answer him, "This is all on me. I know where I fucked up and you did everything right."

"What if it happens again?" he questions and a coil of anger tightens inside of me. He adds, "What do you want me to do? When you took off, I knew I should have stopped you."

I don't have time to answer him. Instead my attention is drawn to the doors being held open by Curt Linders while Bethany walks through them. With her arms crossed, she stands at the top of the concrete stairs, looking smaller than she ever has to me. Her hair is wild as the wind blows from her left and it's then that her gaze lands on our car.

"You don't have to worry about it," I say without taking my eyes off of her. "The next time I'll be the one taking the fall," I answer him and push my door open, not hesitating to go to her. Curt's shock doesn't go unnoticed. Neither does Seth's protest to simply wait for her and for me to remain inside the vehicle.

Neither of them understand. At this point, all I want is to be seen with her.

Let them all see. They need to know she's mine.

I'm drawing the line here, hoping it keeps her beside me regardless of what happens.

Bethany manages to take two steps by the time I've closed the distance between us. She's hesitant even as I wrap my arm around the small of her back.

A sharp hammering in my chest beats faster than my shoes thud on the pavement to get her in my car and away from this situation.

The feeling of failing her, of her knowing and seeing who I truly am grips me and in turn, I hold her closer. I'll never forget the way she looked at me before running off.

"It was a mistake," I mutter beneath my breath, but the tension in her body doesn't lessen and she doesn't look up at me in the least.

Seth's quick to get out and open the door for us. I'm only grateful she doesn't pause before slipping inside.

The door shuts with a resounding click as another gust of wind blows.

"You all right?" Seth asks me and I look him dead in the eyes to answer him. "No more fucking questions."

I don't have the answers to give him. None that I'm willing to give, anyway.

The bitter cold from outside doesn't carry into the back of the car. The warmth is lacking nonetheless as we leave the police department behind in silence.

The dull hum of the car doesn't last long. "Nothing will happen to you. I promise you." My words are quiet, but I know she hears them.

Her hands stay in her lap and she answers while still looking out of her window, "Thank you."

I didn't expect this distance between us. I didn't expect the damage to be so obvious. Regret urges me closer to her, leaning across the leather seat to grip her chin between my thumb and forefinger and forcing her to look at me.

She doesn't resist, but uncertainty lingers in the depths of her hazel eyes and her breathing becomes unsteady.

"I'm sorry," I whisper. "I should never have let you see that."

She only swallows, the sound so loud in the quiet space between us.

"No, you shouldn't have. But I shouldn't have run."

"It would have been better if you hadn't." There's no fire, no fight, nothing except hurt. "I know it scared you."

It's the way she hesitates before answering. The strained way she breathes in when she looks into my eyes. *She doesn't trust me.*

"I don't know what to think right now. I'm going back and forth."

"Back and forth?"

"Whether or not I'm capable of standing beside you. Of demanding you tell me what the fuck happened." Her voice drops as she adds, "And whether or not I can stomach the truth."

It's been a long damn time since I've felt the sense of losing someone. Of feeling them slip through my fingers. I can feel it; I can fucking *see* it. I just don't know how to change it.

"Marry me." I let the idea slip out, but keep my composure. I can't lose her. I fucked up, but everyone fucks up at some point. She'll get over it. I just need time. "They can't make you testify if you're legally married to me." The excuse comes out easily enough.

Her eyes widen as I lean back in my seat. I thought about it every second we sat outside the department. She needs to be my wife.

"You're fucking crazy to think I'd take that proposal seriously."

"If something happens--"

"I'd go to jail," she cuts me off, her fire blazing as the irritation grows in her eyes. "I'd rather go to jail than marry someone because I accidentally saw something I shouldn't have." She eyes me as if I've lost it, and maybe I have. "I'll stick to my story that I don't know how any of it happened and I don't have anything else to say. Thank you very much," she says, and her final quip comes with the crossing of her legs away from me. She stares out the window again and it's then I realize where the term 'cold shoulder' comes from.

"I had a moment, Bethany. Don't hold this against me." My voice is calm and like a balm it visibly soothes her prickly demeanor.

She's slow to look over her shoulder, peeking at me before saying, "Everyone has moments, but it scared the fuck out of me, Jase."

"I'll apologize again, I'm sorry-"

"I don't want an apology." Her entire tone changes, and a different side of her I've never seen presents itself. She's calm, receptive, concerned even. "What the hell happened?"

I've never spoken about Angie to anyone so openly. Not even my brothers know all the details. Not Seth. No one.

I repeat forcefully, "I had a moment."

She pauses, considering me, but returns to the cold condition she had moments ago as she says, "I want to go home."

"No." I answer her with more force than I intended.

"Yes," she snaps back. "You can have your moment. But if you aren't going to tell me what the hell happened, I'm not going back to your place right now so I can have my own damn moment."

I shouldn't be so turned on by her anger.

"You still owe me twenty-seven days." I remind her of the only card I have to play, leaning closer and daring her to fight me. The tension in the car thickens and heats.

"Fuck you," she retorts far too casually, pulling the sleeves of the large white sweater she was given in the department down her arms. It's a simple plain sweatshirt material, and it does nothing to show off her figure. I had Linders offer it to her since her own shirt was confiscated... and now incinerated back at The Red Room like it should have been initially. Before she ran.

"Did you forget about our deal?"

She ignores my question and replies, "I had three hundred thousand in cash in the back of my car."

"They destroyed it."

The question's there, lingering in her gaze. "I'm well aware of that," she says, then swallows loud enough to hear. "Is it really about a debt for you?"

"Would I ask you to marry me if I only cared about a debt?" I question her unspoken thoughts.

Time pauses and it feels like I have her back, like she's close enough to hold on to forever so long as I don't slip up.

"The suggestion wasn't asked, it was told. In order to save me from having to testify... It's not the same."

When she speaks, she's careful with every word. "I don't want to be under your thumb, Jase," she admits. "That's all this is. I'm playing into your hands over and over. I think I have control in situations when I don't."

I'm just as careful with my reply. "I know I fucked up. I shouldn't have let you see me like that--"

"Why?" she cuts me off. "Why wait there for me to see? You had to know I would."

And just like that, she's slipping away again.

I can't fucking breathe. This damn shirt feels like a noose around my neck; I clutch at it, unbuttoning my collar.

"I need you right now." The words fall from me and I'm not even aware that they have until she threads her fingers between mine and squeezes.

"You can tell me," she whispers.

How do I tell her the truth: I killed a man who hurt a woman I barely knew and it doesn't feel like it was enough? How do I tell her I can't get what happened years ago out of my head and the sight from that night will never leave me? How do I share that burden with anyone?

Let alone with her, a woman I can't lose? I'm barely conscious of it myself.

"Jase, I deserve to know."

My gaze drifts from hers and finds Seth's in the rearview mirror.

"I don't have answers right now."

"That's becoming a theme for you, isn't it?" she bites back, pulling her warm hand away from mine. Leaning forward she places her hand on the leather seat in front of her. "Seth, please take me home."

There's no room for negotiation in my tone. "You're coming home with me."

"The hell I am--"

"You belong with me!" The scream tears from me before I can stop it. Chaos erupts from hating the blur of failure around me and the uncertainty.

I feel insane. The stress of everything that's happened is driving me mad and I'm losing the only person who can keep me grounded. I can't look her in the eyes, knowing how badly I've failed her but she makes me, her fingers brushing the underside of my jaw until my gaze lifts to hers.

"I didn't say that I wasn't still with you. I didn't say I don't belong to you." She pauses, halting her words and seemingly questioning her last statement.

I won't allow it. She can't question that. Above all else, she needs to believe with every fiber in her that she belongs to me.

My fingers splay through her hair as I kiss her. With authority and demanding she feel what I can't say. She meets every swift stroke of my tongue with her own demands.

Reveling in it, I remind her of what we have.

This won't come around again. I can feel it in my bones. What we have is something we can't let go of. I've never been surer of anything in my life as I am of this.

It takes her a moment to push me away, with both hands on my chest. It's a weak gesture, but I give it to her and love how breathless I've left her.

Barely breathing, she alternates her stare between my lips and my eyes before nipping my lower lip.

The small action makes me feel like everything will be okay. I'm all too aware that's exactly what it's intended to do.

"Come home with me." It's not a command; I'm practically begging her.

She doesn't say no, but she doesn't say yes either. "You scare me. *This*," she says and gestures between the two of us, "scares me."

"Do you think it doesn't scare me too? That fear doesn't have a grip on me sometimes?"

"I didn't ask for this," she answers and when she does, her voice cracks, the emotion seeping in.

"I didn't either, but I'm not afraid to make known what I want. I won't let fear do that to me."

"I'm not saying this isn't what I want. I'm saying I need to breathe for a minute. You need to take me home."

It's then that I realize the car has stopped at the fork that determines which way we'll go.

"Take me home." Bethany whispers the statement like it's a plea. Seth waits for my order and when I nod, the car goes right, heading toward her house.

"I'm giving you space, Bethany. But it's temporary."

She doesn't let me off so easily. "Are you willing to tell me whose blood was on my shirt?"

I shake my head, but offer her a question in its place. "Are you willing to seriously consider my offer?"

"Offer?" The fact that she's forgotten so easily hurts more than I'll ever admit.

"Marry me."

"Tell me what happened."

"Say yes." Neither of us budge, neither of us give anything more than the gentle touch of our fingers meeting on the leather seats.

"When I marry someone, it will be because I never want to be away from them. Not because I involved myself with someone who doesn't trust me, who keeps secrets from me. Someone I know I shouldn't be with and who's giving me every reason to run."

I can't come up with an answer. I have nothing. Words never fail me like this.

"Everyone's entitled to a moment. But if you're going to keep it to yourself, prepare to be by yourself."

All I can give her is a singular truth as the car slows to a stop in front of her house. "I won't be by myself for long, Bethany."

"You will if you don't figure out how to answer my questions, Jase. I'm not in the habit of helping those who don't want to help themselves."

chapter three

Bethany

The Coverless Book

Twentieth Chapter

Jake's perspective

"She's a healer. She'll help you get better."

"I'm fine, Jake," Emmy pleads with me. I know she's scared to be in the woods searching out a woman some call a witch, but I won't let her die.

Staring at the dried herbs that hang from a line outside the leather tent, Emmy hesitates. "It's nearly twice a week," I tell her and my fingers slip through hers. She's lost weight and she looks so much paler than she did nearly a month ago when we ran away.

"The farmer's sister is nice, they're all nice, but she's not helping you."

We've been staying in a small cabin on the back of a farm in exchange for labor. It would be perfect this way… if Emmy didn't get sick and spit up blood so often.

"Please. Do it for me."

Her eyes are what draw me to her. She can't hide a single thought or feeling. They all flicker and brighten within her gaze. Her lips part just slightly but before she can kiss me or I can kiss her, a feminine voice calls out to our right, "Are you ready?"

Emmy immediately grabs me and hides just behind my left side. She doesn't take her eyes from the woman though. Shrouded in a black cloak, it's harder to see her among the shrubbery, but as she unveils her hood and walks toward the fire, the light shows her to be nothing more than human.

"Jake…" Emmy protests.

"For me," I remind her, squeezing her hand after prying it from my hip and following the woman under the various tanned hides that protect her potions and remedies.

"I know what ails you, but tell me what you think, my dear?" The healer doesn't look at me; she doesn't speak to me at all. Emmy's quiet, assessing at first, but quickly she speaks up.

I only watch the two of them taking a place in the corner, quietly praying to whatever gods may be listening, to help Emmy. I can't lose her.

"When I'm with him, I'm invincible."

The healer's smile wanes as she places her hand just above Emmy's but quickly takes it away, snatching a bag of something dried… flowers maybe? "Take these," she says as she hands the bag to Emmy. "You like soup, don't you?" The chill of the night spreads under the tent, the wind rustling everything inside. "It'll take the pain away."

"When I'm with him, I'm invincible."

I keep dragging my eyes back to that underlined line. She's changed. Emmy's changed. When did she need Jake to be invincible? And more importantly, why did he let that happen?

I have to remind myself that it's fiction. With that thought, I put down the book and force myself to face my own reality. I'm sure as hell not invincible. Not with Jase Cross and not without him either.

Laura's never going to believe me.

It's funny how I keep thinking about telling her what happened as if it's the worst hurdle to overcome at this point.

Telling your friend you lost hundreds of thousands of dollars they loaned to you... or gave to you, whichever... the thought of telling her that makes me feel sick to my stomach.

I have to rub my eyes as I get up off the sofa, The Coverless Book sitting right in front of me, opened and waiting on the coffee table. I couldn't close my eyes last night without seeing Officer Walsh, the blood on the floor, or Jase's intense gaze and the demons beneath that darkness.

Rest didn't come for me last night, no matter how badly I prayed for it.

Beep, beep, beep. Gathering my mug of hot-for-the-third-time coffee, I promise myself I'll remember to drink it this time as I test the temperature and find it acceptable to drink.

The last time I burned the tip of my tongue.

My cell phone stares back at me. The book stares back at me. The door calls to me to go back to Jase.

And yet all I can do is sit back on my sofa, stretching in the worn groove and staring across the room at a photo of my sister in her high school graduation cap with her arm wrapped around a younger, happier version of me.

Life wasn't supposed to turn out this way.

She was never supposed to go down that path and leave me here all alone.

"I still hate you for leaving me," I speak into the empty room even though I don't believe my own words. "But damn do I miss you." Those words are different. Those I believe with everything in me.

I wish I could tell her about Jase and the shit I've gotten myself into.

If only I had my sister back.

There are multiple stages of grief. I had at least three courses that told me all the stages in detail. I had to take all three to work at the center. If you're going to work with patients who are struggling with loss, and a lot of our patients are, you have to know the stages inside and out.

Acceptance comes after depression. It's the final stage and I've heard people tell me that they can feel it when it happens.

I used to think it was like a weight off their shoulders, but a woman told me once it was more like the weight just shifted somewhere else. Somewhere deeper inside of you, in that place where the void will always be.

Denial.

Anger.

Bargaining.

Depression.

Acceptance.

The five stages in all their glory. I've read plenty about them and at the time I associated each one with how I felt when my mother died, but maybe every death is different. Because this feels nothing like what I felt with her.

There are so many reasons to explain the differences. But one thing I can't make sense of is how I feel, with complete certainty, that I've accepted Jenny's death too soon. A month since she's been missing, weeks since her death.

I'm not ready to accept I'll never see her again, but I have. How fair is that?

"Do you hate me for it?" I ask the smiling, teenage version of my sister, with her red cap in her hand. "Can you forgive me for accepting you're gone forever so soon?"

Wiping harshly under my eyes, I let the exasperated air leave me in a sharp exhale. "And now I'm going crazy, talking to no one." I swallow and sniff away the evidence of my slight breakdown before confessing. "Not the person you were in the end, but the real you. Could the real you forgive me?"

As if answering or interrupting me, or maybe hating my confession—I'm not sure which—the old floor creaks. It does that when the seasons change. When the weather moves from bitter cold to warm. The old wood stretches and creaks in the early mornings.

Still, I can't breathe for the longest time, feeling like someone's with me.

Any sense of safety has vanished.

I wish Jase were here. It's my first thought.

Even when he hides from me, I still wish he were here. I'm choosing to stay away and yet, I wish he were here. How ironic is that?

The back and forth is maddening. Be with him, simply because I want to. Or hold my ground because he can't give me what I've given him. Truth and honesty in their rawest form. He makes me feel lower than him, weaker and abandoned. It's hard to turn a blind eye to that simply because I want his protection and his touch.

It hurts more knowing I went through my darkest times naked in his bed. Bared to him, not hiding this weakness that took me over. He couldn't even tell me what happened that landed my pathetic ass in jail.

Without a second thought, I snatch my phone off the table and dial a number. Not the one I've been thinking about. It's not the conversation I've been having in my head and obsessing about for the last hour.

No. I'm calling someone to get my life back. My life. My rules. My decisions. My happiness.

The phone rings one more time in my ear before I hear a familiar voice.

"There's only one thing I've ever had control over in my entire life, and it's been taken away from me."

"Jesus Christ, Bethany. Could you be any more dramatic?" My boss sounds exasperated, annoyed even and that only pisses me off further.

Leaning forward on the couch, I settle my heels into the deep carpet and prepare to say and do anything necessary to get my job back.

"I need this, Aiden," I say and hate that my throat goes dry. "I can't sit around thinking about every little detail anymore."

"Did you take a vacation?" he asks me.

"No."

"You need to get out of town and relax." The way he says 'relax' feels like a slap in the face. Is that what people do when they're on leave for bereavement?

"I don't want to relax; I just want to get back to normalcy."

"You need to adapt and change. That takes a new perspective."

Adapt and change. It's what we tell our patients when they're struggling. When they no longer fit in with whatever life they had before. When they can't cope.

"Knock it off," I say, and my voice is hard. "I'm doing fine. Better than fine," I lie. It sounds like the truth though. "I need to feel like me, though. You know me, Aiden. You know work is my life."

"Go take a vacation and I'll think about it while you're soaking in the sun."

"I can't." I didn't realize how much I needed to go back to work until the feeling of loss settles into my chest like cement.

"Well, you can't come back."

"Why the hell not? Why can't I go back to what was?"

"Why can't things go back? Do you hear yourself, Bethany?"

"Stop it," I say and the request sounds like a plea. "I'm not your patient."

"Your leave is mandatory. You aren't welcome back until the leave is over."

"My patients are my life."

"That's the problem. They shouldn't be. You need something more."

"I don't want something more." The cement settles in deeper, drying and climbing up to the back of my mouth. It keeps more lies from trickling out.

"I'm looking out for you. Go find it." The click at the other end of the line makes me fall back onto the sofa, not as angry as I wish I was.

Fuck Aiden. I'll be back at work soon. I just have to survive until then. I hope I remember this moment for those long nights when I can't wait for my shift to end.

Swallowing thickly, I consider what he said.

I need something else.

Something more.

A memory forms an answer to the question: what is my "something more?"

Marry me.

My palm feels sweaty as I grip the phone tighter, then let it fall to the cushion next to me.

Marry me. His voice says it differently in my head. Different from the memory where he told me to do so because then I wouldn't have to testify against him.

I can't see straight or think straight. I'm caught in the whirlwind that is Jase Cross.

Knock, knock, knock.

Startled by the first knock, feeling as if I've been spared by the second, I stop my thoughts in their track. Someone at the front door saves me from my hurried thoughts, but the moment I stand to go to the door, I hesitate.

I shouldn't be scared to answer the door. I shouldn't feel the claws of fear wrapping around my ankles and making me second-guess taking another step.

I will not live in fear. The singular thought propels me further, but it doesn't stop me from grabbing the baseball bat I put in the corner of the foyer last night. The smooth wood slips in my palm until I grip it tighter and then quietly peek through the peephole.

Thump. Thump.

My heart stops racing the second I let out a breath, then put the baseball bat back to unlock the door and pull it open. "What the fuck is wrong with me," I mutter to myself.

"Mrs. Walker," I say and then shut the door only an inch more as the harsh wind blows in. "I wasn't expecting you."

The older woman purses her thin lips in a way that lets me know she's uncomfortable. She has the same look every time she stands to speak at the HOA meetings. Which she's done every time I've been there. I glance behind her to check my lawn, but the grass hasn't even started to grow yet.

"Is there something I can help you with?"

Her hazel eyes reach past me, glancing inside my house and I close the door that much more until it's open just enough for my frame, and nothing more.

"Is your grandson doing all right?" I ask her, reminding her about the last time we spoke. When she needed help and I came to her aid. Technically to her grandson's aid, who'd been struggling with his parents' divorce and needed someone to talk to.

"I was wondering if you were all right?" she clips back.

"Me?"

"There's been some activity… some men around your house lately." Her eyes narrow at me, assessing and I'm not sure what she'll find. I close the door behind me to step outside on the porch.

"Men?" I question.

"A number of them. In cars that seem… expensive. Same with the clothes."

"Are you suggesting I'm some sort of escort, Mrs. Walker?" I throw in a bit more contempt than I should, in an attempt to get her to back off.

"No. I think they're drug dealers." Her answer isn't judgmental. Just matter of fact.

The tiny hairs on the back of my neck stand on end and I have to cross my arms a bit tighter.

"This is what happened to your sister. Isn't it?"

Words escape me. The memory of my sister on the steps right in front of me causes the cold to seep into my skin, and then deeper within. I can see her there still. I can't tear my eyes away from her. God help me, I'm losing it. She looks just as I saw her last. Except for her hair, she's wearing it like our mom used to. Memories flood my thoughts. None of them good.

"Are you all right? You're as white as the snow," Mrs. Walker says as she grips my shoulder and I snap, pulling myself away from her.

"Please leave me alone," I tell her and refuse to look back at my sister. I can feel Jenny's gaze on me. It's like she's sitting right there on the porch steps. Watching us now, but not saying anything.

I don't move until Mrs. Walker does, leaving in silence. It's only when she's walking down the stairs that I dare look at them.

My sister's not there. Of course she's not. She's gone. My sister's gone.

Whipping my door open, I pace in the hall.

What the fuck is wrong with me? I need to get the fuck out of here.

My keys jingle as I lift them from the hook in my foyer. I nearly leave just as I am: unshowered and in pajamas. I haven't even brushed my hair yet today. With my hand on the doorknob, I settle my nerves.

Just take one breath at a time. One day at a time.

Shower. Dress. And then I'm heading to Laura's.

She'll help me. She has to know a way out.

If Jase loves me, he'll give me space. I just need to breathe. He'll understand if I go away for just a little while. I'll do what Aiden said. I'll go away. Somewhere no one knows. I have to get away from here. Somewhere in the back of my mind, my inner bitch is laughing at me for thinking Jase would ever let me leave. He doesn't know what my mother told me though. I can't fall for him. I can't risk it and knowing that makes me want to run faster than I've ever run in my life.

chapter four

Jase

It's always quiet out here. Although it was quiet last time as well, and that's when everything fell apart.

Rows and rows of stones. Centuries have passed and nothing's changed. I think that's why I come here. It doesn't matter what happened before or after, the stones stay in familiar rows like silent sentinels.

I've lived with many regrets and many failures. It's not often that I can see them the moment they happen. I shouldn't have told her to marry me. Now that it's done though, I can't stop from wanting to tell her again and again until she agrees.

I can make that right.

Unlike so many other things I can't fix. The gust of breeze blows dried flower petals across the gravestone before me. With the petals clear of it, it's easy to read my brother's name etched in stone.

I'll make it right with her. There's only so much I can make right, and she deserves it. Not many do.

If I had to pinpoint a time when everything changed, a single moment when everything went wrong, I'd be forced to choose between two.

The first is the moment Romano hired a hit on me that went awry and resulted in a funeral for my closest brother. An old soul at such a young age, he never did anything to anyone. Tragedy changes a man forever.

If fate had ended its interference there, I don't think my brothers and I would have a normal life, but it wouldn't be one so cruel. Maybe one more empty though.

"I figured I'd find you here," Seth calls out from a distance. Shoving his hands into his black windbreaker he makes his way to me. I'm not ready to leave though.

The second moment is when Carter was taken by Nicholas Talvery, beaten, and changed into a broken boy hell-bent on fighting the men who lived to destroy us. He blazed the path for us, viciously and mercilessly. Because of him we stayed. We didn't have to run; we were more than capable of fighting together.

Two old men, men who ruled ruthlessly, they're the ones so easy to blame.

Since then, everyone has left us and no one could be trusted. Pillars of life crumbled to insignificant dust in favor of simply surviving and adapting to be more like them. To dedicate our lives to destroying them before they could do the same to us.

I hate what we've become, but I can't let go of how it all started and what still needs to be done.

Talvery is dead; Romano is close to gone, but Marcus is still here. Still giving orders, still deciding everyone's fate as if it's his right. They may be the root cause of it all, but Marcus planted the seeds, Marcus knew.

"I'll make them all pay." The promise to my brother drifts away in the bitter wind.

"What's that?" Seth asks and then braces against the harsh chill, zipping his jacket before glancing at the stone on the ground. I can see the question written on his face, but he doesn't voice it. Instead he tells me, "I didn't hear what you said."

He's taller than me, just barely. But on the hill of the grave he looks taller still.

"You found me," I comment and huff a sarcastic laugh. "Should have gone somewhere else."

"I have good news and bad. I didn't think you'd want to wait for either," Seth tells me, and the way he lowers his voice suggests an apologetic tone.

"Let's have the good news first," I tell him, staring off into the distance past the rows of gravestones to the green grass, waiting to be filled.

"There are patterns in the movements of the men we've been watching." Seth takes a half step closer and adds, "Marcus's men."

I focus all my attention back to Seth. "Patterns?" He nods and says, "Between the ferry and the trains. They're transporting something."

The smell of fresh dirt and sod blow by us as he adds, "They're spending a lot of time at each location. Declan thinks there are holding points."

"And what about Marcus? Where is he?"

"We don't know yet."

"Find him." My answer is clipped, but easy enough. It's progress in this slow game of chess and we're carefully moving pieces on the board.

"Bethany still doesn't know about Jenny?"

"No. I'm not telling her until I know where she is and that she's alive still."

"Right," he says. The single word brings defeat to the air and I can't place my finger as to why. "I don't know that we'd be able to sneak up on him or set something up without him knowing. He has eyes everywhere. The more people we follow, the more are involved--"

I cut him off, knowing the risk involved, knowing Marcus will more than likely know when we come for him. "Just find him."

"Of course. I'm on it."

"And the bad news?"

chapter five

Bethany

"W**HY DON'T WE TAKE IT FROM THE TOP?**" Laura asks me in her living room as I pace in front of the floor-to-ceiling windows that look out over the park. Although, from up here on the twentieth floor, it's merely a square of green.

"Which top?" I ask her. "The one that involves Jase or the one that's easier to swallow?"

"I get the easy one, you're on leave and need to go on vacation before Aiden will quit being an ass. That one I've got. How about the one where you went to jail?"

"I don't think I was technically in jail since I never saw a cell." I don't stop my pacing.

"So the money is gone, but Jase doesn't care. All the evidence is gone and he wants you to marry him just in case this happens again?"

I only nod.

"See, it's the marriage thing that I may be hung up on…" she trails off as she lowers herself to a dusty rose velvet chair and takes a sip from her tall wine glass. She settled on prosecco when I said I didn't want any coffee and word-vomited up everything—including seeing my sister on my front porch steps. I'm surprised she didn't go straight for the vodka.

"The 'marry me' part? Not seeing my dead sister and feeling her there?"

She shrugs. "Sometimes we see what we want to see. You feel alone and need someone to talk to. You didn't want to tell me about the money. She was your rock for a long time…"

Was. Past tense. My steps slow to a stop as I pull my still-damp-from-the-shower hair away from my face and look back down at the park.

"I'm sorry about the money," I say and have to clear my throat after speaking. I'd say anything for her not to bring up Jenny again. She's gone. Truly gone.

Fuck. It shouldn't hurt like this still, should it?

"Don't worry about the money--"

Cutting her off, I ask, "Will you hide me?" Shock flashes in her eyes. Swallowing thickly, I continue, "I don't know how you got the money, but there's obviously a lot I don't know. If there's any way to hide me—please do it. I just need to get away for a while."

"Away from Jase, you mean?" She barely says the words and I nod.

"I need to cope and think on my own and he's just…"

"All consuming," she finishes my statement for me, but somehow the words seem to be meant for someone else as she looks past me, staring at the white and blush striped curtains instead.

"Yes."

She nods once, downing her glass and then standing up, all the while not looking at me. As she rounds the corner to her kitchen, no doubt to fill her glass, she tells me, "I have someone I can call. I can ask him for a favor."

Hope is nowhere in her cadence; her tone is resigned.

I can feel some hope though. A tiny bit at the idea of being away for just a little while. Enough to get out of the chaos. Enough to breathe. Taking out my phone, I contemplate telling Jase just that. To give me space and time. That I'll be back.

I slip my phone back into my jeans. Not yet. He's not going to like it. He needs to get over it, though. There are plenty of things I don't like about this arrangement either, and I've rolled with the punches as best as I can. I return to gazing at the park and brush my fingers against the cool glass. I've never felt like this before. I've never been so... so helpless.

I hear Laura before I see her and I'm quick to turn my back on my reflection as she lets out a long breath.

"Did you call?" I ask her and she doesn't answer immediately. Instead she stares through me, looking to the park outside.

She snaps out of it as I bite out her name.

"What?"

"Did you call?" I ask her again and an eerie feeling crawls over my skin at the way she swallows before answering me, although she only nods.

"What's wrong?" I question her and she shakes her head, then returns to her seat.

"It's just work. Not you."

Relief isn't so forthcoming, but I don't think Laura's lying to me. Especially not when she offers me a tight smile.

"Is it Michelle? Is she okay? I heard dealing with the pica condition has been difficult."

Her hair swishes as she shakes her head. "She's doing fine. All your patients are fine," she says as she leans back, moving her hair to one side and braiding it. "Don't worry about them, you workaholic, you."

"What is it then?" I ask her. "Anything I can do to help?"

"Did I tell you about the patient with no name?" she says and her features turn serious. A haunting memory reveals itself in her eyes.

"Just initials?"

"Right. The woman with only initials..." She pauses before telling me the rest. "Somehow... someway, she got hold of a bottle of antifreeze."

"What the hell?"

"She tried to kill herself. She drank the entire thing and needed an emergency transfusion. Every ounce of her blood had to be drained for her not to die."

"How could that have even happened? That's impossible." She shakes her head only ever so slightly, but her expression holds a different answer. My hands tremble as I walk toward her. I can't believe it. "When did this happen?"

"Three days ago."

"How the hell did it happen?" I walk closer to her, unable to contain the horror and shock that a patient in our facility was able to obtain a means to end it.

"That's the thing," she says and looks me dead in the eyes. "There is no investigation."

Chills flow down my arms. All my concerns seem so meaningless in comparison. I've never been so grateful for a tragedy.

"She had to have dialysis, the antifreeze did so much damage. We were waiting to hear what kind of inquiries would be made. What paperwork and interviews we needed to prepare for... but Aiden told us that it never happened. To act like there was no incident and not to speak a word of it. So you... you better not tell him I told you."

"How can there be no investigation?" The question leaves me slowly, barely able to form itself.

"Whoever is paying for her to be there paid for the antidote, the dialysis... all of it with cash and they don't want any attention brought to it."

I drop into the seat next to her, processing it all and unable to shake the cold sensation that's taken over.

"Whoever it is, they want her there and they don't want anyone to know about it."

"Did they give her the antifreeze?" I dare to question.

"No. Aiden's the only one on her charts. After he told us, I followed him to his office." She swallows thickly. "I think it was an accident. He's on her charts, bringing her items she asked for. I think he made a mistake. But I don't understand why he's not fired. He should have checked it."

"Aiden? No." I can't believe that. Aiden's better at his job than that.

"I think he fucked up. She's smart and wants to die. Really wants to die." She licks her lower lip and then tells me, "But whoever's paying for all of this? They want her alive."

A cheerful series of dings in different octaves fills the room, forcing her knuckles to turn white as she grips the chair and then cusses beneath her breath.

"Your doorbell is going to give you a heart attack," I comment and then look to the large cobalt door. "Who is that?"

She doesn't look back at me as she stands and tells me, "The person I called."

There are little moments when you know someone's screwed you over before they show their cards.

It's in the way they talk; the way they look at you. Even the way Laura walks right now. Unlocking the deadbolt and opening the door without speaking, without checking to see who it is.

All the while I sit there, denying this feeling of betrayal as if it's not really happening.

Even when Seth walks through the door, tall, handsome and demanding Seth, I still want to deny it.

"I'm tired of being the last to know," is all I can mutter, leaning back and hating that the last person I had in my corner denied me a chance to get out of this mess. "I suppose it's my problem to deal with, isn't it?"

I can hear her apologies, her pleas for me to understand all the while Seth is saying something, but it's all white noise. I'm not interested in hearing what her excuse is. She of all people should know I need to get away. She lives in solace. She preaches it to me constantly.

"So, Seth?" I finally speak up although my ass is still firm in the chair. "Seth's who you called? Or did you go straight to Jase?"

They both speak at the same time.

"You have to forgive me, Bethany—I didn't have a choice."

"Jase doesn't have to know you were thinking about leaving him."

The chair pushes back against the wall; it would have tipped over if the wall hadn't been there to block its path because I stood so quickly.

"First off, you always have a choice," I push the words through clenched teeth at Laura and then turn to Seth. "Secondly, I wasn't leaving him. I wasn't running, so fucking tell him for all I care!" I don't mean to scream.

I don't mean to lose control. *Who the fuck am I kidding? What control did I ever have?*

"Beth, please," Laura says as she reaches out for me and I snatch my arm away.

"How could you?" I can't look at her. Not because of anger. Because of the hurt that rests across my chest.

"One day I'll tell you why. Just forgive me," she pleads with me.

"I love you," I tell her. "But right now, I really hate you."

She covers her mouth with one hand and watches me walk to Seth, who hasn't moved from the threshold.

"Seth."

"Bethany." He says my name sweeter than I say his. He even affords me a smile. "Are you ready?"

"No. No, I'm not. I wasn't expecting you. When I asked my *good* friend," I pause to look at her from the corner of my eyes, only to see her leaning against the wall. Her arms are crossed over her chest and her focus is straight ahead at the window rather than at us. "When I asked her to call someone, I wanted to leave. Not go back to Jase." Before he can respond I add, "Not right now. I just need to breathe."

"No, you don't," he tells me as if he knows what I need. As if he knows what I'm going through.

"I hear things. I see things. I don't feel okay." I don't expect my voice to crack or the admission to stir up so much emotion, but it does.

"Hey," he says then reaches out to brush my shoulder, and I notice how that gets Laura's attention, how she watches him touch me.

He squeezes my shoulder gently when he tells me, "It's going to be all right." His voice is soothing, his dark eyes calming. "Come on, come with me." Seth holds out his hand for me to take once he's released his grip, as if he's some sort of savior. "Jase doesn't know, but you should tell him what you're feeling."

Guilt isn't something I expected to feel.

"If she wants to, she will." Laura speaks up for me, and when I look back at her over my shoulder, I can see her swallow and it's not until I nod that she nods too.

I already forgive the two-timing bitch. I don't understand, though. I'll never understand why she sold me out.

Seth's eyes stay on Laura's a moment longer as he speaks, right before he looks back down to me, letting his hand fall to his side. "He's going through something right now. He's making mistakes and focusing all his time and energy on you. It's causing problems."

"He shouldn't." I refuse to be used as an excuse for someone else.

"I know that. He knows that too."

He starts to say something else but I cut him off. "I'll drive home myself."

"I wanted to show you something."

"I don't want to see anything, talk about anything, or do anything at all but have a moment to just be away from all of this," I practically hiss. "What can't you understand about that?" Anger and desperation twine together. "I'm not okay, but I'm trying to be."

"I wanted to show you something. But it can wait. We have time. Plenty of time. If you want to go home, know that I have to keep an eye on you."

"How's it feel to be a babysitter?" I can't help the snide comment although I immediately apologize. "I'm not usually such a bitch," I comment after he accepts.

"You could tell me whatever it is. I could go there myself."

He only shakes his head.

"If you could be a non-problem... he has enough of them."

"Wouldn't me leaving be exactly that?" I already know the answer before it's fully spoken.

"The fuck it is." His quick response and even scorn at the thought throw me off. "He needs you by his side." His statement strikes me at my core. The emotional crack destroys what little resolve I have left.

"I just don't know if I'm the woman that can be by his side." I almost tell him I don't know if I can be by anyone's side. Especially not now, with every day passing and the warning my mother gave me sounding louder and louder in my mind.

"Well, he chose you. And between the two of us, I know you are."

chapter six

Jase

"How could you be so fucking reckless?"

I don't answer my brother. The silence is deafening as my shoulders tense and I lean against his desk with both my fists planted on the edge of it. He refused to wait for this meeting and demanded it happen right now; that's how I knew he was aware of my fuckup.

Neither of us say anything. I can feel his eyes on me as he turns from the windows in his office and slowly takes his seat. The smell of polished leather and old books invades my senses as I do the same, sitting across from him and feeling the disappointment flow through me.

The need to check on Bethany rides me hard as I sit there. All I can think about is Bethany and how I hurt her.

Seth's watching her though. *She's fine.* I've been telling myself that repeatedly since I left her. That, and that she'll forgive me. That she just needs space.

She loves me. I remember that she told me she did once. The reminder doesn't feel so truthful anymore.

"It's unacceptable." I say the words so he doesn't have to. "What I did could have cost us everything." All I can think about is Bethany, and all he can think about is the mistake I made. The first one in a long damn time.

"The fucking FBI is breathing down our necks and you do that?" Carter doesn't hide the rage as he slams his fist down.

I don't react. This is how he is and how I knew he'd be. He can scream all he wants. What's done is done and his display of anger won't change that.

I don't say anything for the longest time, until finally, "I know," is somehow spoken from my lips.

"What the fuck were you thinking, leaving like that? You drove in public while covered in blood. It would have taken a single phone call. We don't flaunt this shit. It's one fucking rule none of us has ever broken." His chaotic breathing has lessened. The cords in his neck are no longer as tense.

In this moment, he reminds me so much of our father. Maybe because he's focusing his rage at me for the first time that I can ever remember. "Everything we do is with reason and intention. Careful. Meticulous. We don't leave evidence." Every word is spoken calmer and more relaxed. He even sits back in his seat before running a hand down his face.

"What were you thinking?" he asks again.

"I don't know."

My answer is quick, as is his rebuttal. "Bullshit."

"Bull-fucking-shit," he repeats and with his words, the sky darkens behind him. The night is settling in, as is his disbelief. My knuckles rap in synchrony on the wooden armrests of my chair as he looks at me, and I look at him.

"You always know what you're doing. You're always in control, yet you did it anyway." His voice is calm, his composure returned. Tilting his chin up, he asks me, "Why?

You had to have known she'd see and that you were risking everyone else seeing just so she could see."

"I shouldn't have-"

"But you did. You wanted her to see you, Jase. There's no other explanation. You don't fuck up like this. None of us fuck up like this."

My brother's words hang heavy in the air. Waiting for me to accept them.

"She doesn't need to see what I do. What I'm capable of."

"You wanted her to, though."

"I won't do it again," is all I answer him, still not wanting to accept I'd do something so stupid and reckless. "I was emotional. I was caught up in the past."

"You wanted her to see," he repeats and I lift my gaze to his dark eyes.

"It doesn't matter. It'll never happen again."

He looks like he wants to say something else. Like the words are just there, right on the tip of his tongue, toying with the idea of falling off.

The room is silent though. For a moment and then another.

"She doesn't need to see that," I tell him, content with that truth and then I crack my knuckles one at a time. "I won't do it again."

"She already knew, Jase." I pin my gaze to my brother's. "Even if she doesn't admit it. She already knew."

"Knew what?"

"What you were capable of. She knows what you do. She already knows. You're right that you don't need to show her. But you're wrong to think she didn't already know."

With an open palm, my hand moves to the harsh stubble surrounding my mouth and then to my jaw.

"Some part of you wanted to know what she really thought of it all. Is that it?"

I ignore his question. "I scared her."

"She should fear what you're capable of. It's new to her." Carter leans forward on his desk, resting his elbows on the hard wood and it gets my attention as what he says registers.

"What do I do now?"

A flicker of a grin shows on Carter's face. "Because I should know what to do when the woman I love fears me?"

"I didn't say that."

"What are you saying then?"

"I'm saying I fucked up, she's scared, and I don't want her to run." My voice lowers of its own accord and a confession escapes as I say, "I can't let her run." With my head lowering, I think back to the way she looked at me before closing her front door. She looked back at me the way she did in the restaurant. Like it may be the last time.

"She's not the only one afraid then, is she?"

"I'm asking for advice, Carter. It's not something I care to do often," I comment, hating the way something in my chest twists with agony.

"She's not like us; she didn't grow up in this world."

"She fixes the ones we break though. Addiction and loss... she stares that in the face every day."

"You think because she works at the Rockford Center that she could handle seeing you covered in blood?"

"I wasn't covered in it," I say. My rebuttal is useless.

"Not to her. She doesn't see *this*. This is different. It's not something she can control with a bed, pills and a conversation."

"Neither is loss. Loss isn't controlled." The need to defend her overrides my sensibility.

Carter's gaze is assessing. Running my hands through my hair, I question my own sanity.

"She's under your skin." Carter's tone verges on discouragement.

"Which is right where I want her to be," I admit freely, correcting him. "I'm not letting her go."

"Then don't allow her to see what frightens her without first giving her a way to handle it. You blinded her to what's going on, then showed Bethany her own worst fears without warning. What did you think would happen?"

"I wasn't thinking," I mutter, staring at the dark red in the carpet beneath our feet.

"Start using your head again. How's that for advice?"

It's hard to hold back from rolling my eyes. "Any other advice you want to offer?"

"Promise her she doesn't have to be a part of this world if she doesn't want to. You should have never come back like that... She's seen already, she knows and she hasn't walked away."

"What if I can't hide it all from her? What if I don't want to hide it?" The truth is buried in the questions, something that loosens the tension. Something that makes me feel like I can breathe again.

"She knew before, Jase," he repeats himself again. "You're fooling yourself if you think she didn't know who you were and the world you inhabit before."

"Knowing isn't the same as seeing," I comment and regret what I did. I regret losing it and putting her in a place to be shocked and frightened. "I'll do better." I make the promise to her, although Carter's the one who hears it and the one who gives a single nod.

"Do you know how I knew I should fight for Aria, rather than let her go?" Carter asks me and I wait for his answer. "Without her, I just can't go back to being without her. There is no version of my life where I'd be okay knowing she wasn't with me and not knowing if she was okay. I needed to make sure she was loved. I couldn't move forward not knowing if she would be loved if I weren't there."

There's that word again... *love*.

"If you want her, make her see that. She knew what she was getting into. She'll be exposed to more of our world over time and she'll learn to deal with it in a way she can. She didn't run, though. She's not going to leave you, Jase."

"Is that why you called me in here?" I ask him, watching the wind blow the trees in the distance behind him. "To give me advice and watch me sit here with my tail between my legs?"

The leather groans as Carter sits deeper in the wingback chair. "Romano's been indicted."

"Indicted?"

"The FBI agents that have set up camp aren't going to be leaving anytime soon. They're fucking everywhere."

"Did they find the explosives on the east side?"

"No, we got there first. Any evidence of an association with him has been wiped. But they're digging. So we need to be careful." I don't miss the way Carter looks at me when he says the word *careful*.

"You think he'll pay them off?" I ask.

"I think he'll try. I would."

His phone vibrates on the desk, halting the conversation momentarily. With a glance he sits up, and messages back. It must be Aria. "I've got to go; do you have anything else?"

"I want her to marry me." I say the words out loud. Freeing them. He's the one who brought up love. I've never considered him helping me, but he has Aria and if he can have her, I should be allowed to have Bethany.

"Then tell her." Carter's response is easy enough.

"I did."

"Was that before or after she was arrested?" I look past him, letting out a frustrated sigh. "You've never waited for anything. Why would a marriage proposal be any different?"

"Timing may not have been the best."

"Best?" Carter actually laughs. He has the balls to let out a deep, rough chuckle that fills the room and forces me to crack a smile.

"I told her she wouldn't be able to testify if we were married."

"You're a fucking dumbass, Jase. I'm a goddamn bull in a china shop and even I'm more graceful than that."

"It felt right." I drag my hand down my face remembering how her eyes widened.

"Like I said, you're a dumbass. You like shocking her," my brother comments. "I'm not sure that's exactly what she wants or needs from you at the moment."

"What does she want?" I say out loud and Carter answers as if he's known Beth her entire life.

"Someone to help her with the things that matter most to her. Someone to love her."

His phone vibrates again and that's when I check mine and my stomach drops. "She needs someone to kick her ass. That's what she needs," I murmur under my breath.

chapter seven

Bethany

"Seth told me."

The heat in Jase's car is stifling. For the first time, he's driving and Seth is nowhere to be seen. It's just us.

"What did he tell you?" I ask.

"You said you wouldn't run," he says and his tone is accusatory.

A small and insignificant sigh falls from my lips as I stare at the passing trees, small buds forming on the branches and lean my head against the passenger side window. "I wasn't running."

The steady clicking of the blinker is the only sound until we turn at the end of the street. "What would you call it?" he asks me and I answer.

"Following my boss's orders to take a vacation while getting away from the chaos for a moment."

"You really think you would have come back?" I can tell from the huff that leaves him that he doesn't believe I would have.

"I would have missed you, worried about you and thought about you every second I was gone. You're a fool to think otherwise." I second-guess my harsh manner and turn to look at him. He only gives me his profile; he's still staring at the road. His stubble is longer than it's ever been, but I love the masculinity of it, along with his dominating features. "I'm sorry. I shouldn't have called you that."

Quiet. It's quiet and that's how I know he doesn't believe me. I suppose it works both ways. The mistrust between us runs deep with not just everything that's happened, but the way we've handled it all.

Laying a hand between us, palm up, I offer a truce. "I thought you'd come last night. I was waiting for you."

"You didn't message me."

"Neither did you." I give him back the same accusatory tone.

"Seth suggested that I give you space. Carter agreed with him. I thought I could use some as well, given that you made plans to leave."

"You scared me--"

"I apologized." His words cut me off and I steady myself, pulling my hand back to my lap.

"Do you want me to apologize? I'm sorry. I'm sorry I made you think I'd run." Transparency is what I'm aiming for, so I let the words spill out. Every bit honest. "I could've handled it differently. I didn't trust you'd let me go."

"You're damn right, I wouldn't have and I won't now." Anger simmers inside of me until vulnerability stretches his next words. "You knew before."

My heart does a silly thing. It beats out of rhythm, making sure I'm listening to it. "Knew what?"

"You knew who I was."

"I still know. I'm still here, aren't I?"

He finally glances at me as the expensive car drives over gravel for a short moment, jostling the smooth ride.

"I would do anything for you. Name it, I'll do it. Whatever you need to make you want to stay."

"What?" I say and the word is as exasperated as I am. "What are you talking about?"

"If you want to leave, you come straight to me. In exchange," he says as he taps his thumb rapidly on the leather steering wheel. "Name it. Whatever you need in exchange for *me* being the person you run to."

I don't hesitate to take away the card he's been playing to keep me under his thumb as I say, "Drop the debt."

"It's dropped."

He says it too easily, too quickly. The words were waiting to be spoken. It didn't matter what I said. The long drive is winding as we approach the Cross estate. The dent in the fence is already fixed, but my mind replays the images of when I sped away as we drive by it.

"I don't believe you. The moment I do something you don't like or the second I make you think I'm leaving you, you'll say I owe you."

"I'll write it down in fucking blood, Bethany." There's no menace in his words, only desperation and he adds, "I'm trying," while staring into my eyes. I can feel it deep inside of me, his need to hold me.

I barely whisper, "Why do you want me?"

"Because you make it okay. You make it all right."

"I don't know what I'm making okay, Jase. Can't you understand how *that's* my problem?"

The car comes to a halt on the paved driveway and he lets out a long exhale, staring at the bricked exterior rather than at me before he tells me again, "I'm trying."

"I'll try too," I answer quickly, remembering the tit for tat our relationship started as and may always be. "Let's go back to the beginning. There's no debt this time, but I still have questions. I don't want to forget what happened to my sister. I want to know who. I want to know why."

Jase merely stares at his front door as he turns off the car. Not speaking, not acknowledging what I've said for so long that I eventually move closer to him and almost repeat my suggestions until he takes my hand in his and squeezes lightly.

Hope moves between us, drawing us closer.

"Can you give me a name?" I ask him, praying he'll trust me this time. It's a futile prayer.

"I'd rather not."

"Do you have anything new?"

"No."

I have to swallow to keep from telling him that there's no point if all he'll ever be is a sea of dark secrets to me. I nearly breathe out, *what's the point?* and storm off. I can already hear the car door slamming. Instead, I stay in the parked car with him, letting him hold my hand.

Our relationship is uneven; it may always be. Jase needs this. I think he needs it more than I do.

That's the point. This is for him. I can take what's mine another time. "I don't know that I can live with all the secrets," I admit quietly.

"Ask me something else," Jase says, the slow stroke of his rough thumb pausing on my knuckles as the crisp chill enters the car in place of the heat.

"Whose blood was it?" I dare to ask. There's a pitter-patter in my chest that keeps me from inhaling when he hesitates.

Clearing his throat, he answers, "A man's. Someone who hurt a lot of people."

I push for more, staring at him, willing him to look at me, but he still doesn't.

"Name," I demand. "I deserve to know whose blood was on me."

"Hal."

Settling back into my seat, I note that he doesn't give me more, but he's given me something. "I don't think I like that name anymore."

My off-handed comment is rewarded with a slight huff of a laugh from Jase before he looks at me, really looks at me. The kind of look I'll remember forever. Not at all like the way he was in the bathroom this past weekend.

"Are you okay?" he asks me, and I don't know what prompted it.

"You really do scare me... sometimes."

"I don't want to."

I squeeze his hand when he stops squeezing mine and say, "I know you don't."

"Ask me something else," he says, looking out of the window.

"Are you okay?" It's all I can think to ask.

He nods once but doesn't say anything else and I get the feeling he's keeping something from me. Enough so that I open the car door and head inside. It takes a moment for him to follow. The wind is unkind, ushering us inside as quickly as possible.

It seems like this is temporary. That we're pretending it's okay when it's not. There's something unsettling in the air between us as we walk to the bedroom quietly, our steps even and echoing in the empty hall.

"Do you have a 'something?'" I ask him as his hand grips the doorknob. He twists and pulls it before looking down at me questioningly. "Something other than work?" I ask him and his answer strikes me hard. "Family. I have my brothers."

The pain of loss is a horrid thing. It comes and goes; it sneaks up on you but it also punches you in the face at times.

It feels like it's done all of those things to me in this moment. All at once.

Leaving Jase standing in the doorway, I drop my purse on the bed while kicking my shoes off without looking at him and try not to let it eat at me, but it is. Obviously so. Jase's keys clink on the dresser, then his watch before he takes off his jacket.

"I shouldn't have said that," he admits with his back to me before facing me. "I wasn't thinking."

The comfort of regret is what lifts my eyes to his.

"Yes, you should have. It's what I needed to hear."

Maybe he's my something.

There's no other logical explanation for why I'm so drawn to him. He's talking as he walks to me, saying something but I don't hear a word. Just the soothing cadence of his voice as I stare at his lips, his broad chest.

Just love me.

Pushing myself off the bed, I press my body to his, surprising him as I kiss him. It's needy, it's raw. His response is just as primitive. He tears the clothes from my body, but I don't move to remove his; I don't trust myself to loosen my hold on him. My fingers are braced at the back of his neck, keeping his lips to mine and urging him to devour me. To take from me, to use me. To make me feel alive and worthy of life.

I love you. The words are trapped inside of me. Maybe he can feel them when I kiss him. Maybe his lungs are filled with the knowledge when he breaks our kiss for only a moment to suck in air before tossing me onto the bed and then covering my body with his.

His fingers press on my inner thigh as his tongue delves into my mouth. Each stroke against my clit is sensual but demanding, just as Jase is. Every second I feel hotter. And with his palm pressing against my most sensitive area, a sweat breaks out along my skin so suddenly, I moan into the air and throw my head back to breathe.

He rocks his palm against my heat, and presses his hardened cock into my thigh. His stubble scratches along my neck and the sensation pushes me closer and closer until the all-consuming need throws me off the edge of my release.

"Spread your legs wider," he commands, pulling my thighs farther apart and I obey.

Breathless still with the waves of pleasure rocking through me, my nails dig into the bedsheets as I wait for him to settle between my hips.

There isn't an ounce of hesitation at having him between my legs after touching me like that.

The warmth of the high is still wrapped around me, making the small touches he gives me trace pleasure on my skin. "Are you expecting your period?" His question quickly changes that.

My lungs lurch and I'm quick to push him off of me.

"Fuck." Embarrassment rages in my heated cheeks and I climb off the bed as I snag my clothes, keeping my legs closed tight.

I can't look at him as I scatter to the bathroom, flicking on the light and digging through the basket in the cabinet under the sink. *Damn it. Damn it, damn it, damn it.*

I haven't had many sexual partners and it's been years since I've had a boyfriend, but the last time something like this happened, I stained the sofa cushion of my high school fling. The hollowness that comes with a dry throat and embarrassing memories takes over as I find a thin liner that will have to do for this moment.

I'm sitting there taking care of it all, feeling foolish and wondering if my period is why I've been so emotional and tired and down and unable to think right.

"Are you all right?" Jase's voice comes from outside the bathroom and I prepare to face him.

Opening the door to see him standing there, a small trail of hair leading down and drawing my eyes to the edge of the boxer briefs he slipped on, makes me that much more self-conscious. "I'm sorry."

"It's fine." His expression is easy, but the way he bites the edge of his lip and lets his gaze linger makes me feel anything but. "It's good you got it. We've been reckless."

I hesitate to respond when I look over his shoulder and see he's changed the sheets.

"Thank you for…" Closing my eyes and swallowing tightly, I fail to say the rest out loud.

"It's fine. Do you need anything?"

He leans against the doorjamb, not taking his eyes off of me. When he crosses his arms, his muscles become taut and I find myself feeling hot all over again.

I need my something. I need it more than anything.

A hint of worry crosses his expression when I don't answer him.

"I don't want to lose what we're building, Bethany. I don't want to lose you."

"Then don't."

Jase

I couldn't give two shits about her period.

I couldn't give two shits about her wanting to leave yesterday.

All I care about right now is pressing my body against hers, ravaging her, hearing those soft sounds slip from her lips. I'm still hard for her, still needing to feel her, to remind her how good it is.

"Strip down... all the way." With the simple command she stares up at me, her chest rising and falling heavily. Her hair is a messy halo and her hazel eyes are in disarray.

Leaning forward and bending down enough to whisper at the shell of her ear I say, "Don't make me tell you twice, my fiery girl."

Her eyes close and her head falls back instinctively. Like the good girl she is, her hands move to the button on her pants just as I unhook her bra through her shirt.

"You make me weak," she whispers.

"You do the same to me." No confession has ever felt so sinful to be spoken.

"You want to know why I want you?" I ask her, watching her undress and then stepping out of my boxer briefs to stroke my cock. "I can't get those little sounds you make out of my mind. They're addictive."

Her pale skin turns a bright red, flushing from her chest up to the temples of her hairline.

"You're beautiful, you're innocent in ways I find challenging, and a fighter in ways I respect." I've never thought about it like this before. I've never considered the specifics, and the statement forms itself as I take her nipple between my fingers and pull gently to direct her to the shower.

With a twist of the faucet and then the splash of hot water, steam billows toward us.

"You want to know why I want you?" she questions me as I grip her ass, one cheek in each hand and pull her up to me before stepping into the shower with her.

She gasps from the contrast of the hot water and the cold tile as I press her against the wall, but still keep us under the stream.

The warm water flows over my skin and it feels like heaven. Being cleansed and still having her in my grasp must be what heaven is like.

"Why?" I groan the word in the crook of her neck and then let my teeth drag down her skin, just to feel her squirm.

"Because you make me feel alive. You make me feel like everything matters and yet, nothing but you does."

I have to pull away to look down at her. Her hair's darker and wet, slick against her flushed skin.

Looking up at me through her thick lashes, I bring my lips just millimeters from hers and tell her, "You're damn right, nothing but us matters." Then I slam myself inside of her, letting her scream in pleasure in the hot stream. Her nails dig into my skin as I thrust inside of her, loving the feel of her tightening around my cock as she gets closer and closer.

Steadying her in my grasp, I keep my pace ruthless and deep as she bites into my shoulder to muffle her screams. I'd admonish her, forcing her to let me hear all the sweet noises she makes, but the hint of pain makes the pleasure that much more intense.

So I fuck her harder, silently begging her to bring me more of both the pleasure and the pain.

chapter eight

Bethany

"ANYTHING YOU WANT, IS YOURS."

"You make big promises," I tell Jase as I follow him down the end of the hall. He keeps calling it a "wing" though. He says it's his wing of the estate.

Makeup sex is a real thing. There must be something special that happens to your brain when you have makeup sex. I'm convinced of it. I bet a decade of research could prove a thing or two to support that thought.

The kind of makeup sex that leaves you sore the day after. The kind of sore I am now.

"Anything within reason. Does that make you feel better?" he asks with a grin growing on his face. I can't help but to reach up and brush my thumb against his jaw.

He tells me lowly, "I need to shave," before I can sneak a small kiss that makes me rise up onto my tiptoes. A deep groan of satisfaction comes from his chest when I kiss him again.

"I like the stubble," I comment softly as we stop at the entrance to what looks like a library, one that's worthy of a museum. The antique weapons housed on a bookshelf full of creased leather spines and unique coverings draw me in.

Wow doesn't do it justice.

"The fireplace is real. It's from a castle in Ireland," he says as he walks to it on the other side of the room while my fingers trail down a set of old books with red covers. "Not like the glass one in the other room."

"Fireplaces seem to be your thing," I speak without really thinking about the words as my gaze drifts from one shelf to the next. "You like to read?" He nods. "And collect weapons?" I tilt my head at the knives on display. The bottoms of the blades have rust that extends to the handles.

"Yes," he answers and reaches out to gently caress my hip as I lean against him. The more I touch him, the more he touches me. Tit for tat, like all things with us.

"Where's your desk?" I ask, noting how it looks like a combination of a sitting room and office. "There should be a desk in here." The room has a primitive air to it, dark and cavernous with a large rug on the floor and walls covered with shelves.

"My office is at the bar. Not here. This is just for me." I lift my fingers from the books at his last comment until he adds, "And you, if you like it. You can come in here whenever you'd like."

I can imagine listening to the crackles of the fire as I turn the pages of The Coverless Book. "I think I'd enjoy that."

"Good, let me show you the rest."

Today is apparently the day Jase forces me to go on a tour. Between the gym, the cigar room and the billiard room, all three of which look entirely unused and are outfitted with as much dark polished wood as they are wealth, I'm not sure what Jase does as a hobby.

The only room he truly seems to enjoy is the office that's not an office… and the fire room. Which I've already explored with him.

"I love that you call it a fire room," I comment as we pass it, feeling my cheeks heat.

"What would you call it?" he questions and I change the subject before I find myself wanting to go inside of it—the wooden bench room—rather than hear him tell me more stories. It's the intellectual side of him I need to feel safe. Although his touch is just as addictive.

"You said you didn't used to use this gym," I comment, nodding my head toward the last door we passed on the left. The equipment looks virtually brand new.

"I didn't, but lately the other gym has… The women seem to like the main gym."

"The women?" My eyebrow raises on its own.

"Chloe, Addison, Aria, they live in the estate with us. You'll meet them soon, I think."

I don't anticipate the pressure that overwhelms me at the thought. As we walk down the hall toward the foyer which leads to the door separating this wing from the rest of the estate, I drag my fingertips along the wall. All the while thinking how close he must be to his brothers since they live together. Only a hall away.

"So they… they get how it is?" I ask him, watching my feet and wondering if they feel the same way as I do. "Chloe, Addison and…"

"And Aria. Yes. They grew up in this life. They aren't like you." I can't explain why it hurts so much to hear him say it like that. *Not like me.*

"They're your brothers' girlfriends?" I'm quick to keep up the conversation and not let on how I'm feeling.

"No. Declan is single. He's happy being on his own."

"No one's really happy being on their own." I didn't mean to say that out loud.

"You were alone for a long time," he notes.

"I had my work."

"That's still alone."

"I didn't say I was happy." My rebuttal is quick and unfortunate. I'd rather talk about his brothers.

"So one of the three women is…"

It only takes two more steps and a side-eye for Jase to tell me that Chloe is Sebastian's wife and remind me that I met him in the kitchen the other day.

"Right." I nod and try to picture his face again, but I can't. It seems like most of Jase's family has their own little family. I like that. I don't know why I do, but it makes me feel safer still. "What about Seth?"

"He doesn't have a girl… that I know of. I think he has other things in mind," he answers cryptically.

"What do you mean?"

"He's been off."

With a cocked brow, I motion for him to continue.

"He's seeing someone, that's obvious enough. I just don't know who."

"You could ask him."

"That's not the way I go about things."

"Aren't you friends?" Of everyone I've met, Seth's the only person I had mentally filed as a friend of Jase.

"I trust him to the point where it would be hard to think…" He doesn't finish his thought but before I can pry he speaks again. "I don't really have friends, but I'm friendly with him."

"How did you guys meet?"

"Push came to shove a few years back, and he was there, in a spot where he could have done a lot of things. Seth could have ended us—me and my brothers—before we really got started… all because I fucked up." He scratches the back of his neck and even though he's speaking so casually, his expression is hard and unforgiving.

"What did you do?"

"It was at The Red Room. We'd just opened and I let someone in who I shouldn't have. I showed him something that no one's supposed to see." An ominous tone tinges his last statement.

I whisper, "Are you going to tell me what?"

"A basement where I bring people to…"

"To kill." I finish the sentence so he doesn't have to.

"Yes, let's go with kill."

"And what happened?"

"The doors were open, the man saw and took off. None of us were armed as a show of faith, which was fucking stupid. Seth was out there in the parking lot, and he saw us running after him."

"Seth just happened to be there?" I question, not understanding.

"He'd stopped by The Red Room that night, wanting to work with us. We told him no. He came back at just the right time."

"Why couldn't you work with him?"

"He was too… he was too big, too set in his ways. He came from a town where he was the person everyone went to. I don't need someone looking over my shoulder, someone wanting to take command."

"Too many chefs, so to speak."

"Something like that. Anyway, that night he saw, and he could have let the fucker take off. He didn't."

I've been to The Red Room enough to imagine someone bolting from the doors. The forest is close; the highway is even closer. It wouldn't take much to get away if only you got past the parking lot.

"After helping us take care of the body, he told me, *'If you change your mind, I'm good at taking direction,'* or something like that."

"And that convinced you?" I ask him.

"We would have been done if that asshole had gotten out and told the feds what he saw; it turned out that he was undercover. We didn't have the police back then on our payroll. We didn't have much protection. Things were harder then and we needed the help. That's really what it comes down to."

"So you aren't friends then. Simply coworkers who rely on each other?"

"He's more of a friend to Declan. They're closer than we are."

It's quiet as we come to the stairwell and he tells me the upstairs is mostly unfinished. He's never had a reason to complete it.

Taking my hand, he lets his middle finger trail down the lines in my palm. There's a hint of charm and flirtation I'm not expecting. One that breaks the tension, scattering it in any and all directions until it's gone.

"I like touching you," he says faintly.

Something about the ease he feels around me makes me want to stay by him forever. I'm so aware of it in this moment.

So aware, that it's frightening. With every breadcrumb of information Jase gives me, I fall deeper in love with him. Even if the pieces are perverse and disturbing… maybe more so because of it. Even if I wake up tonight like I have the past few nights, breathless and covered with a cold sweat, dreaming about the darkness I know is inside of him…

even then. The fear is still there, but love is stronger. Which is why I'd fall back asleep next to him, willing my eyelids to shut and show me something sweeter.

"Ask me something," Jase offers.

The memories of everything that's happened flicker through my mind as I search for a question, and one is most apparent. A detail I've yet to tell him.

"Do you know anyone who wears white sneakers with a red stripe down the sides?"

His brow pulls together as he turns to look at me. "Why?" he asks.

I have to pull my hand away, feeling too hot, yet cold at the same time to tell him.

"When my house was broken into, that's all I saw from where I was hiding in the cabinet."

"White sneakers with a red stripe?" he clarifies.

"Right down the center, from front to back on the sides."

"Why haven't you told me this sooner? Is it all you saw? You're sure?" The questions hold an edge to them. Not anger, not resentment, more like an edge of failure and I hate it.

"I'm sorry… I just didn't know."

"You didn't know if you could trust me." He completes the statement for me and I nod. "I'm sorry," is all I can say, feeling like I've failed him.

With his hand brushing against my jaw, I lean into his touch and close my eyes, reveling in it.

"If I could start our story over and start it differently, I would. I want you to know that."

There's so much I'd change if I could. But then I wonder what our story would look like if it hadn't started so intensely.

"How many women have you done this to?"

"Done what?" he asks.

"Brought back here. Showed off this place to… told your deepest, darkest secrets?"

"None. You're the only one, cailín tine." His nickname for me still makes my stomach do little flips in a way that excites me.

"You've never called anyone else that?" I tease him and he nips my neck in admonishment while wrapping his hands around my waist and letting them slip lower.

"Never. You're my only fiery girl."

He's so consumed with lust in the moment, but there's something nagging at me, something that feels off.

"Why don't I believe you?" My question pulls him out of the moment.

"Because you see my sins, however many of them, and you've judged me guilty of them all." The honesty of it stares back at me from the depths of his dark eyes. "If you'll lie, you'll cheat… if you'll cheat…" He doesn't continue and I bring my lips to his even though pain etches its way between us. "Even a saint has to start somewhere… I'll never be a saint though. If I could change for you, change this life, this world, our pasts, I would. But it's not going to happen. I can't start our story over."

I kiss him again, feeling the heat between us, feeling his hard lips soften as I press mine against his. I finally answer him, "I know." And then remind him, "I'm not asking you to."

When Jase tries to take me back to his bedroom, I tell him no. Instead I lead him to the plush rug in his office that's not an office. I ask him to light the fire and I slowly undress, watching both hunger and flames in his eyes once the fire's ignited.

I pick the knife I want him to use on me and I lie down without a weighted blanket at my feet, without cuffs, without rope this time, although I tell him I miss the rough feeling when it's all over.

We're both moths to each other's flames, ignited by our touch. We're drawn together, destroyed together. It used to scare me, but there's no fighting it. *Isn't that what love is?*

You can say chemistry was never our problem. Take away the drugs, his brothers, the feeling of loss and betrayal, and all that's left is the simple truth that's he's mine and I'm his. In the most primitive way, we make perfect sense. We're drawn to one another in a way where nothing else matters. It all fades to a blur when I stare into his eyes.

But that's where the problem truly lies. He wasn't meant for my world and I wasn't meant for his. Everything else matters with him in a world where every step is dangerous, and we should have accounted for that. I'll never be able to escape Jase Cross or his merciless world.

This attraction will never allow it.

Jase

The light of the fire dances across her skin in the darkness, and the shadows from the flame beckon me to touch her. The sight of the dip in her waist is an image that would start wars. Her breathing is steady in her deep sleep and part of me wants to leave her here, resting on her side on the luxurious rug with the only covers being the warmth of the raging fire. The other part wants to have her again in my bed.

The low hum of a vibration steals my attention. My muscles stretch with a beautiful pain as I pull myself away from Bethany and get my phone. Still naked and still hungry for more of her and the promise of keeping her here, I check my messages.

It's a text from Seth, just the person I need to speak with.

Anger has a way of destroying the calm, even when Bethany stirs with a feminine sigh in her sleep. Her hand reaches right where I just was and it seals her fate.

I text Seth back. *Meet me first thing tomorrow. We have things to discuss.*

chapter nine

Bethany

It only takes one deep breath in the massive kitchen and a long stretch of my back to release the tension from last night. Things are better. It feels like a huge step forward, but something's still holding me back. The nightmares haven't stopped; they've only changed.

Last night, my mother reminded me that everyone I loved would die before me and that it was okay. It's not the first time I've dreamed about being back at the home, with my mother looking me directly in the eyes and telling me what felt like a message from death. The terror gripped me the same way she did all those years ago. It was like I was back there, but not really. We were on my porch and I couldn't move. I couldn't speak either. My sister came to help me, ripping our mother away and yelling at her, screaming at her. It was so unlike her, but somehow I believed it.

When they were done fighting with each other, my sister turned to me and looked me in the eyes. She said my mother was right. They would all die before me.

That's when I woke up. At 5:00 a.m. in the morning, in an empty bed that held the faint, masculine scent of Jase Cross.

I can walk around pretending I'm not uneasy, but I've never been good with pretending.

As my gaze falls to the slick counters and I hear the thump of footsteps getting louder, cuing someone's incoming arrival, I put away my thoughts of my family, or what used to be family.

Carter's deep voice reverberates in the expansive space. "Bethany."

His gaze is narrowed and even harsh. Even the air around him warns me not to mess with the man. Some men are just like that; the feel of danger comes with their strong posture and chiseled jaw.

"Cross," I answer him tersely with a cocked brow.

I find myself comparing him to Jase, but even though they look alike, Jase is nothing like him. He's charming and approachable in a way I don't think I'll ever find Carter to be.

An asymmetric grin pulls at his lips. "Funny you should call me Cross when you're with my brother and he's also a Cross."

"Suits you though."

He huffs a short chuckle and lets the smile grow as I pull the fridge door open, searching for a can of Coke or something with caffeine in it. "Something funny?" I ask him.

There's a case of Dr. Pepper and the hint of a smile appears on my face too. It's been a while since I've had one of these and they're in glass bottles… that makes it even better.

"You aren't the only one who thinks that."

"Thinks what?" I ask him genuinely, already forgetting what I'd said before as I'm too distracted by my beverage.

"Nothing." He shrugs it off and goes to the cabinet, pulling out a box of tea bags and a pretty mug with owls on it. I nearly tease him, taunt him for the girly mug, even though I know it must be for his wife. I bite my tongue and stifle the playful thoughts as I prepare to go somewhere else and stay out of Carter's way. This isn't my house and he isn't my family. I'm more than aware of that.

I only get one step away though before Carter speaks with his back to me, putting a mug of water in the microwave. "Spring will be here soon," he tells me.

Stopping in my tracks, I turn rather than look over my shoulder and wait for him to turn as well. He does slowly, awkwardly even with his broad shoulders.

"Why does your face look like that?" he asks me when he takes in what must be a confused expression.

"Is that your attempt at small talk?"

"People like to talk about the weather, Miss Fawn."

It's my turn to let out a huff of a laugh, small and insignificant, but it breaks the tension, one chisel at a time.

"Spring's my favorite season."

"It's Aria's too. Well," he continues talking as he retrieves the mug from the now beeping microwave and sets a bag of tea into the cup. "Spring and fall. She said she can't pick just one."

It doesn't pass my notice that his expression softens when he talks about Aria. The recollection softens something inside of me too.

"How long have you and Aria been together?"

"Just a little while." His answer is… less than informative. Maybe it's a Cross brothers thing.

"I heard she's expecting?"

"That's right." His grin turns cocky and I half expect him to brag about how it happened on the first try or how his swimmers are so strong. Some macho bullshit like that, but it doesn't come.

"Congratulations."

"Thank you."

"Well, I'll let you get to it," I tell him, but he doesn't let the conversation end.

"Jase really likes you." The statement surprises me, holding me where I am.

Warmth flows through me, from my chest all the way to my cheeks. I don't know what to say other than, "I really like him too."

"He's turning back to his emotional… hotheaded younger self."

"Hotheaded?" I pry. Carter doesn't seem to take the bait though.

"When we were younger, he used to be a real troublemaker," Carter says as he leans against the counter, staring into the cup of tea and lifting the bag of leaves. We both watch the steam billow into a swirl of dissipating clouds although I'm across the room.

"Really?" The shock is evident.

"Not because he was… like me. Not that kind of trouble."

If Carter's going to talk, I'm damn well going to listen. Taking a step closer to the counter, I ask him, "What kind of trouble?"

He peers at me, but not for long. "He just couldn't keep his mouth shut. It should have gotten him into more trouble than it did really. I know if I'd done it… My father never hit Jase. I can't remember a single time. He liked the belt and took it out on us mostly, me and Daniel."

A sadness creeps inside of me at the ease with which Carter speaks of his father beating him and his brother. He was the oldest. I'm the youngest, but I remember the way my mother used to yell at my sister for things that I didn't even think were wrong. With parted lips, I grip the edge of the counter, cold and unmoving as he continues. "I remember so many times my father would say to Jase, *your mouth is going to get you in trouble.*"

"Parents sometimes take it out on the eldest."

"If I'd talked like Jase did when we were younger, I'd have been punched in the mouth." Carter's statement doesn't come with emotion. It's merely the way things were for them back then.

"He used to say it like it was. He never had a filter, and couldn't just be quiet. There were so many times he said shit to my father that made my back arch expecting to be hit there. He had the balls to call everyone out on their shit and never stopped for a moment to question what he was saying."

"Honesty without compassion is brutality." I say the quote and then add when Carter looks back at me, "I don't know who said it. It's just a saying."

Standing up straighter, he holds the tea with both hands and tells me, "He was compassionate, too much. That's why he never let a moment pass him where he thought he could change what was happening if he only made people aware of how wrong it was."

It's hard to keep my expression straight. I can only imagine Jase as a young boy, watching everything that happened and speaking up, expecting it to help, when there was never any help coming.

"He used to have hope." My first statement is quiet and I think it goes unheard so I raise my voice. "It sounds like he was a good kid," I comment and Carter's forehead wrinkles with amusement.

"Sure, as good as the Cross boys could ever be."

"You know," I start to say, and that stops him from walking off while I tap the glass base of my Dr. Pepper on the counter. "My sister was like that. When I was growing up and she was in high school and even part of college, she was a lot like that."

"Is that right?" he asks, leaning against one of the stools and listening to my story.

"When our mom got sick, she had Alzheimer's." I have to take a quick sip as the visions of my sister, a younger, healthier version, flood into my mind. Jenny would stand outside the university before every football game and every council meeting with flyers she'd printed from the library. "My sister wanted to educate people. She said it might help them because if you can diagnose it early, it can lessen the symptoms."

I'll never forget how often Jenny stood there after mom was diagnosed. I met her outside the stadium one chilly October night. She had a handful of flyers and tearstained cheeks. She'd been there every night that week, and I wanted her to come home. I needed help. *Mom* needed help.

When I told her to come home, she broke down and cried. She didn't want to go home to a mother who didn't know who she was. She said she blamed herself, because she knew something was wrong and she hadn't said anything. She did nothing when she could have at least spoken up like she would have before she was busy with classes.

All the while she spent her nights standing there, I did what was practical. I listened to Nurse Judy, I figured out the bills and how to pay them all with what we had. I took care of the house and learned how to help any way I could.

My sister looked backward, while I tried to look forward. I think that's where the difference really lay.

"That doesn't sound like mouthing off," Carter comments.

"Maybe that wasn't the best example," I answer under my breath, not seeing the similarity so clearly like I did a moment ago. I find myself lacking, not unlike the way I felt back then. The visions of her that night she cried on the broken sidewalk don't leave me.

"She blames herself then?" Carter asks and I have to blink away the memories.

"Yeah, she did. Blamed," I correct him. "She passed away this past month."

Something strange happens then. The air in the room turns cold and distant as Carter looks away from me.

Some people deal with death differently, but it's odd the way he reacts. He doesn't look back at me. He stares off down the hall and past the kitchen toward his wing of the estate, avoiding my prying gaze.

"I'm sorry," he finally speaks, although he pays close attention to the mug in his hand. His lips part but only to inhale slightly; I think he's going to say more but he doesn't. And then it's silent again.

I don't like it. The little hairs on the back of my neck stand to attention and the uneasiness I felt when I walked into the kitchen greets me again.

"When she died, I inherited her debt and met your brother, so if nothing else..." My voice trails off. *What the fuck am I even saying?*

It's hard to swallow, but I force down a sip of the cold drink and let the taste settle on the back of my tongue where the words all hide. *At least her death led me to Jase.*

Was I really thinking that?

Was I really drawing a positive out of my sister's murder?

"A debt? Did Jase help you out of something?" Carter's dark eyes seek mine and I reach them instantly. Suddenly he's interested.

"The debt my sister owed," I state, feeling a line draw across my forehead as I read his expression. No memory is worn there of the money she owed the Cross brothers. Money Jenny owed to Carter.

Jase blamed Carter, didn't he? He said Carter wouldn't let it go even if Jase wanted to.

"Who did she owe money to?" Carter asks and the wind leaves my lungs in a heavy pull. Drawn from me so violently, that I drop the bottle to the counter with a hard clink.

Jase lied. Staring into Carter's clueless eyes, I see it so clearly now.

He lied to me about the debt.

About my sister owing it.

I thought so poorly of her. That she would owe so much money to men like him.

And he put that on her.

With a sudden twist, my gut wrenches with sickness and I have to focus on breathing just to keep from losing it.

He lied to me. It was all a lie.

How can I believe anything that comes out of his mouth? How many lies has he told me? How many things has he kept from me?

"Where are you going?" Carter's voice carries down the hall, chasing after me and I ignore him. I don't trust myself to speak.

Every step hurts more and more. I've fallen for him. That's the only explanation for the way my face crumples as I storm off. The way my eyes feel hot although there's no fucking way I'll cry. I won't cry for a man who lies to my face over and over again.

I let him touch me. I let him use me. Because he lied about a debt.

I'm foolish. I'm a stupid little girl in his man's world.

"I hate him." The words tumble out in a single breath as my hands form fists. I hate that I believed him. That I fell for him.

No... no I don't. My throat dries at the realization.

I hate that I wanted him to treat me like he loves me. I hate that I believed he did.

You don't lie to the ones you care for. You don't use them.

You don't coerce them and blackmail them.

I thought he loved me though.

Maybe he still does... the small voice whispers. The voice that's gotten me deeper and deeper into bed with a man who tells me lies. A voice I wish would speak louder, because I desperately want it to be speaking the truth. But the rest of me knows it's a childish wish, that I need to grow the fuck up and slap the shit out of Jase's lying mouth.

chapter ten

Jase

"What did he say specifically?" I question Seth, comparing notes.

"To meet... to come alone... and that he has evidence he doesn't want to use against us."

Our pace is even as I walk with him from the foyer to the office. I waited for him outside after taking Bethany to bed last night. Watching the late dusk turn to fog in the early morning and preparing for what has to happen today.

I respond, "Officer Walsh is my new favorite person to hate."

"Do you think it has to do with Jenny?" he asks.

"I doubt it. If he has something on us and if he's going to use it to blackmail us..." My teeth clench hard as I release an agitated exhale.

"Do you think you should tell Bethany? In case this leads to something?"

"No." Shaking my head, I think about the way Bethany's going to react when she finds out about her sister being alive and the fact that I knew this whole time. "I want to know I'll be able to bring her back before I tell her anything."

"Marcus will know when we find her. I don't see how he won't know when we approach. Unless it's only a few of us, but that would be suicide."

"We'll all go. He can know. I would think he already knows we've been watching."

He stops walking and the sound of two men walking down a long hall turns to one and then none as I turn to him, waiting for him to speak.

"You think Marcus would go against us?"

"I don't know," I answer him honestly and feel a chill run up my spine. The silver glimmer of the scar on my knuckles shines in the dim hall lighting. "We've never openly been against him, but he's never taken from us either. He has her. He knows we want her back. It was his call to decide that and ours to decide the consequence."

"We don't know that. We don't know how it happened and what she's doing with him."

"There's too much we don't know, but we don't have time to wait. If we find their lookout point or storage centers, or anything at all, we go in." My words are final and Seth's slight nod is in agreement.

With a tilt of his chin, we continue back to the office. Every step I take grows heavier, and the anxiousness of getting down to what we have to discuss stifles the air and coils every muscle in my body.

I force myself to stay calm with my hand on the doorknob to my office, careful not to say anything until he walks in first.

"Did you get it?" I ask him as I flick on the light. It's still early morning and the sky's a dark gray. Pulling back the curtains, the harsh sound of them opening is the only thing to be heard as Seth walks to the row of books on the other side of the room.

Clouds cover the sky, hanging thick and with varied shades of gray. Rain's coming and with it, a darkness that will cover the day.

"I did," he tells me, leaving a book he's eyeing to come to stand where I am and hand me the box.

"What do you think?" I ask him.

"I agree with you," he says simply. "It's why I like working for you."

As I'm inspecting it, he delivers news I didn't think would come so soon. "There may be a room, or tunnel, or shelter of some kind."

He leans his back against the leather chaise, crossing his arms in front of his chest. "The blueprints for the bridge don't show anything. So what's under the bridge is... we don't know."

"You're sure of it?"

He bows his head in acknowledgment. "We've kept an eye on the people associated with Jenny being taken. They're out there, making these rounds and going to the same spots. Last night, one disappeared. Nik was watching him, and then he was gone. There has to be some hideout there we haven't yet found."

Slipping the box into my pocket, I ask him, "Did he do surveillance?"

"Not yet." Uncrossing his arms, he slips his hands into his pants pockets and glances at the unlit fireplace before turning back to me. "I wasn't sure how you wanted to proceed."

"You seem distracted," I tell him, rather than giving orders. It could be a setup. It could be suicide. Carter should know before we decide anything.

"Me?" he questions.

"You didn't think I'd noticed?"

His answer is to tilt his head. With a cluck of his tongue, he pushes off the chaise and walks to the bookshelf before confiding in me. "We're distracted for the same reasons, I think."

Every hair stands on end at the thought of him being distracted by Bethany. The skin across my knuckles stretches and turns white as I crack them with my thumb, one by one and consciously resist forming a fist.

"What reason is that?" I ask and my voice is low.

"A girl."

"Bethany?" I question and now my tone is threatening.

"She's yours and I have mine."

"So you are seeing someone?" I ask him and the edge of jealousy seeps away, although not as easily as it came.

Instead of answering, he suggests, "You should take Bethany to the graveyard. I think it'd be good for you two."

"You're good at distraction," I comment as I eye him moving down the rows of books he's seen before.

"You go there often..." he pauses before continuing, seeming to struggle with how he wants to say what's on his mind. Choosing a new book, one I recognize by the distinctive spine, he tells me, "I almost took her there when I picked her up a few days ago. Thought you could meet her there, but then I got your message."

"Why would she want to go there?"

"She's empathetic. She reacts to emotion. If she saw the end result of what you've been through... it makes things more real. To see loss."

"She knows what a graveyard looks like. She's been there herself a time or two."

"She hasn't though. She didn't go to her sister's funeral. I don't know about her mother's either. She was working a lot back then."

The fact that Seth knows this and I don't makes me feel a certain way; I hate him for it, but I'm grateful for the message. We work differently, we see things differently. I could have never imagined it'd work so well for so long.

"I have to tell you something before I forget." Tapping my fingers along the hard walnut shelves, I let my gaze stray down the shelves. "You need to get rid of your shoes."

"What?" His surprise is met with a huff of humor. "Now you're going with the distraction method," he jokes although he's still waiting for me to explain what the hell I'm talking about.

"The ones you wore when you went to check on Bethany. When she thought there was a break-in."

"I don't even know what shoes they were."

"White with red stripes on the sides," I answer him and finally make my way to take a seat. "She saw them, so it's best to get rid of them." As I sit down, I focus on the box, thinking about it rather than Seth and the fact that Bethany saw his shoes.

"Fuck." Seth closes the book in his hand with a thwack, lowering his head and shaking it. "That could have ended badly."

"If she didn't tell me, I imagine it would have if she'd seen you in them."

"Are you going to tell her it was Marcus or Romano or some random burglars or what?"

"She's too smart to think it was random." Leaning my head back, I close my eyes and hate the way all this started. "I don't know," I answer him. "One fucking lie after the next with her."

A creaking sound snaps my eyes to the open door of the office. The dim light behind her places a shadow of contempt across her hurt gaze and pouty lips. Her small hands are balled into fists gripping the hem of her gray sweater. Even enraged, she's in pain. It's etched into every detail of her. *Fuck.*

"Bethany." Her name tumbles from my mouth as I stand up, feeling the thrum of disaster in my blood.

chapter eleven

Bethany

"I CAN EXPLAIN," JASE REPEATS AS HE ROUNDS THE WORN LEATHER CHAIR. THROUGH MY blurry vision I can barely make out Seth backing away from both of us as I stalk into the room.

I'm shaking, trembling, on the verge of a rage I didn't know was possible.

"I hate you," I sneer and how my words come out so clearly, I'll never know. They strike him, visibly, across the face as he stops with both hands up a foot away from me.

"What did you hear?" he asks me calmly and I want to spit at him. I can already see him spinning a new lie in his head, just waiting to know what I heard so he can manipulate it. Betrayal is a nasty thing, twisting a knife deeper into my rib cage.

All I can remember is how I felt standing in the threshold of my kitchen, too afraid to speak or move, and knowing I had nowhere to run. "It was Seth? It was your men all along?"

My vision blurs with the present and the past.

"I sent him to check on you. I was with Carter and Aria; I couldn't come so I sent Seth."

"Seth crept into my house. It was Seth." I repeat it and I still can't believe it. I can't believe it's true.

"He was only going to stay with you because I thought someone was threatening you--"

"Someone?" I question, feeling raging tremors run through me. Even now, he hides from me.

"It doesn't matter--"

"The fuck it doesn't!" I scream out of nowhere, shocking both of us.

"It's all right." I can hear Seth but I don't dare rip my eyes away from Jase.

"Get out," Jase gives his partner in crime the command and I listen to his heavy footsteps as he leaves. I can't even look him in the face. He didn't come just to stay with me, that's bullshit. It's all bullshit.

"Who?" I demand.

"Marcus." Jase's chest rises higher and falls deeper, moving slower as he tries to stay calm and collected. I take a step to my right, and he takes a step to his left.

"So you sent your men?"

"Seth said you weren't there, that you took off or something happened. So I sent every man I had."

"He didn't knock. He didn't try calling me or saying my name when he walked in." Shaking my head, I deny the innocence that he's trying to portray.

"He thought he may have frightened you into hiding."

I complete the series of events for him. "You thought that would be good. Scare me into your arms." My glare lifts to the specks of gold in his dark eyes. "You thought it would be easier to convince me, didn't you?"

I can hear the deep inhale he takes as he sucks in a breath. "I made a mistake."

"One fucking lie after the next with her." I repeat the words he used before he knew I was outside the door with a taunting flourish. "How many lies, Jase?"

He doesn't answer me; he merely steps closer. "Can you even remember how many you told?" My voice gets louder with each question. Still, he doesn't answer.

"How about the debt? I just found out Carter never knew about it."

Jase doesn't react, he doesn't falter, still hiding behind a hard façade.

"Are you going to say there was truth to that? That my sister did what? What do you want to say she did, what did she do to rack up that debt? Tell me all the horrible things she did."

I can't explain how the pain flows; the best way to describe it is to say it's like a river flowing over jagged rocks. "You'll never know how much it hurt me to think she'd done something horrible to have a debt like that." I can't even speak the sentence clearly as I brace myself on the furniture.

"I'm sorry."

"So it was a lie too?"

"Yes."

"And the break-in? It was all you all along?"

"Yes."

With heated cheeks and a prick at the back of my eyes, I remember how I fell out of the cabinet that night and called for him. I remember how awful I felt the next day for ever thinking poorly of him.

How stupid I was. All I am with him is a step behind and foolish.

"You held me after. You *knew* and you held me after." I feel sick. My body leans to the left as my head spins and the bastard dares to reach for me.

"Get the fuck off," I say as I shove him away with every ounce of strength I have. It does nothing but push me backward, hitting the chaise and brushing my elbow against the leather. "Stay the fuck away from me," I grit out with disdain, pointing a finger at his chest.

He walks right into it. My finger is now touching his chest.

It's the lack of respect for my boundaries. This is the last fucking time I let him disrespect me.

His chest is like a brick wall, hard and unmoving, even after I slam my fist into it. My throat feels raw as I scream and the sides of my hands spasm with agony as I beat them against his chest over and over. "Get away from me!" Tears stream down my face in an oh-so-familiar path.

I hate it. I hate it all.

I hate the way it hurts. I hate that he did it.

I hate that I know he'd do it again, no matter how much he insists that he'd start the story over if he could. He'd do it the same way each and every time, because he doesn't trust me to love him.

"I hate you," I scream at him and his idiocy. "Stay away from me!"

Jase doesn't try to hold me back or stop me. He simply watches me lose it. The look on his face is one I recognize and it only makes my heart hurt more.

When our patients don't want to admit they're not okay but they're struggling to do anything at all we tell them, sometimes you have to break. You have to let it out, you have to feel it, you have to move through it even if you're a sobbing mess the entire time.

Sometimes a good cry or screaming session to let the anger and sorrow out is unavoidable.

Sometimes you have to break, even if you know you won't be put back together when you get to the other side of it all.

My body feels heavy as I drop to the floor on my knees. Struggling with the weight of it all. I can feel his hands on me, his grip to stay close to him, but I ignore it.

How many times have I held on to someone just as Jase is and told them to do it, to let it all out? To break apart. Not because you want to, not even to make anything better. Simply because you have to.

"You're a monster." The statement swells as it leaves me, strangling me as it goes.

Still, Jase holds on to my wrists.

The smooth wood is cold and I just want to lay my heated face against it. To let it all out, but Jase is there, not leaving me alone.

"I had to," he says and the statement is stretched with desperation.

I can barely swallow at this point, let alone speak.

There's no use fighting his grip on me; he's stronger. There's no use trying to wipe my eyes, since the tears keep coming.

"I didn't mean to hurt you," he whispers once I've stopped altogether, just feeling every piece of me shatter.

He didn't mean to, but he did it anyway.

"I didn't want to lie to you," he says and his voice is calming as he brings me into his lap.

He didn't want to, yet he did.

A heave of sorrow erupts from inside of me as I realize I didn't want to love him, but I did. I didn't want to trust him, but I did.

"There are very few things that a person has to do," I whisper against his shirt, staring at the crack of light under the door. "You *chose* to do that to me. You *chose* to lie and scare me to get me to do what you wanted. You *chose* to manipulate me."

The gentle rocking is paused and it's then that I realize how hot I am, leaning against him and I try to pull away. This time he lets me.

The irony is that all he had to do was ask or even tell me. I was so desperate for someone and something. Him scaring me had nothing to do with it. "You didn't have to do it."

"I told you, I told you if I could start it over, I would." His voice is low, but has an edge of anguish.

"You didn't tell me why though," I say and lift my head to look him in the eyes, finding my own reflection staring back at me. Crumpled and weak, just how he sees me. "You didn't tell me it's because you lied to me every step of the way."

"There are reasons."

"There's no reason good enough."

"I couldn't let you go."

"It's not your decision to make." Every response from me turns colder and more absolute. Inside I'm on fire, the blaze of hate destroying everything that made me feel alive with Jase Cross. It rages in my mind, changing the memories, making me feel like they weren't real.

It was all a lie.

"You wanted me to marry you and weeks ago you fed me one lie after another so I'd do what you want."

"Bethany," he pleads with me.

"I told you I loved you and you made me feel like you loved me too." My brow pinches together as I wipe violently under my eyes. "How could you when you knew it was all a lie?"

"Bethany, don't. It's not like that--"

"But it is! That's exactly what it's like!"

Placing both of his hands on my shoulder, he tries to console me as if he's the man who should be doing that. "It's over with now, it's better now."

"I never want to see you again." As I speak the words, my heart splits in two. I feel it slice cleanly, seemingly fine, then bleeding out in a single beat. "I have to protect myself and you keep hurting me. You won't stop." I hate that my bottom lip wobbles. I hate that I believe what I'm saying. I hate that it's the truth. "If you need me to behave some type of way, you'll lie to me. You'll pull strings and make me do what you say."

My head shakes at the idea, hating what he's done and wanting to deny it; Jase's shakes on its own, but for different reasons I imagine, because he knows I'm telling the truth. I'm not the one who's lied. Feeling my resolve, I push myself up off the floor, ready to leave him. Preparing to piece myself back together and lick my wounds, but he stops me with one statement.

"Marcus has Jenny." Jase's voice is low, the words coming from deep in his chest.

Jenny?

"How dare you." I have no air in my lungs. No will to do anything but slap him. Hard and fast, leaving a red mark and forcing his head to whip to the side. "You don't get to use her against me. You don't get to manipulate me with her *ever again!*" I scream in his face and then clench my teeth together when he grabs my wrists as he pins me to him, restraining my elbows so I can't hit him, so I can't move. All I can do is look in his eyes.

"She's still alive, Bethany," he whispers and it's so compelling.

I want nothing more than to believe him. To believe the liar who's already brought shame to her memory.

"She's dead." A fresh flood of tears threatens to fall, but I won't let him see them. He doesn't get to be there for me. Not again. I pull away from his grasp, ripping my arm away so I can free myself.

The bright red handprint against his cheek is still there. "She's alive. We have a video of her with a man after the funeral. After the trunk was discovered."

"With Marcus?" I can barely remain upright. She's alive. I'm so cold. A freezing wave flows over my skin. *She's alive.*

Hope makes my body tremble.

"A different man. He's dead, but we have an idea where he's keeping her."

"Where who is keeping her?"

"Marcus."

I'm so confused, so consumed by questions, but one begs to be answered. "How long have you known?"

Silence. The silence is my answer.

"I have never hated you more," I speak when he doesn't. Swallowing thickly and feeling a spiked ball form in my throat, I continue. "You saw what that did to me. How could you watch me mourn her death..." I have to stop and breathe in deep.

"Because I love you... I didn't want to tell you if I couldn't save her."

"So you can save her now?" I question him, focused on my sister before realizing what he said.

I love you.

"You're telling me all this now because we've fallen apart." I speak the unforgiving truth. "Not because you can save her." *And not because you truly love me.* I keep that bit to myself.

"I'm trying. We have a plan. I didn't want to tell you until I knew for sure."

"You're sure she's alive?" Jenny. My sister's face plays in my mind and I have to cover my own. *Please, God. Let her be alive.*

"As of two weeks ago, yes."

Two weeks. Two weeks is so long. Too long. Please, God.

"Will you save her for me?" I beg him, looking up at him and praying for him to do just that. Even if he doesn't love me. Even if he lies to me a million times more until the day I can see her again. "I'll do anything," I confess and my voice cracks.

"I'm doing my best. It's the first time we've ever tracked anything that has to do with Marcus."

I have never felt more at his mercy and more alone than in this moment. I don't know what to believe or what to do. It's too much.

"I'm breaking, Jase. I can feel myself slowly breaking down and I can't stop it. Don't take advantage of me. Don't do this to me. I'm not okay."

"I'm not taking advantage of you."

"Then don't say you love me if you really don't. It's not fair. Because I do love you. I hate you right now and we're not okay, but I love you." I don't know how I'm even able to speak, since the sudden rush of emotions are warring with each other at the back of my throat.

Jase struggles to hide his as well. "I don't love you, is that what you want to hear?"

"Don't do that. Don't use what we used to have." My finger raises as I yell at him, my voice cracking. *He loves me.*

Heaving in a breath with the intensity growing in his eyes his own voice trembles as he says, "Whether you believe it or not, I love you and you're staying here."

With an exhale and then another, a calmer one, his expression softens as he waits for me. He's waiting for me to say it again and I know he is. "Everything I've done is for you. I love you, cailín tine."

"I don't want you to call me that right now." I stop him with the statement, not knowing what to believe. Adrenaline is coursing through my body. Fight or flight taking over. He won't let me leave and he's the only one left to fight. "Of everything I learned today, the only thing that I can focus on right now is that my sister is still alive."

"I know. And I'm here for you." He tries again to appeal to the side of me that's still holding on to hope for us. I'm ashamed to admit that side still exists.

"How could you watch me cry for her and accept her death when you knew she was alive? I can't even stomach the thought."

"I'm sorry."

"Do you expect to say you're sorry and I simply forgive you?" I throw his own words back in his face. "Words are meaningless."

"You can't leave me when we fight." He says the words like they're a truth that's undeniable. Like nothing else matters.

"Lying to me isn't the same as fighting. And what you lied about… I'm not okay." Pulling away from him, I feel the chill in the air. "Nothing about this is okay."

My legs feel weak when I stand and he tries to right me, but I do it myself.

"I'm going to the guest room." I give him my final words. The only ones I have for him in this moment. "Don't lock me in and don't trap me. But leave me the hell alone for right now."

Loneliness is a horrible companion, but it's the one I need right now. I think about messaging Laura, but I'm still pissed at her. Instead, I sit on the bed and look out of the window. Just to think. Just to break down again. All alone.

Does he know the nightmares he's given me? The hate I feel for myself knowing I'd said goodbye to my sister, even though I still felt her presence. I knew I shouldn't have, that it was too soon.

Shame is what comes for me when the loneliness no longer matters.

I don't hear the door open and I don't hear Seth walk in until he speaks from across the room. "Are you all right?"

Lifting my head from my folded arms, I glance over my shoulder. I'm certain I look like a wreck, with my knees pulled into my chest so I'm merely a ball of limbs staring out a window.

"What do you think?" I ask him.

"I know you hate me--"

"I don't hate you."

"Well, I know you're mad at me, and I'm sorry."

"Okay." The petty answer leaves me instantly. I'll be damned if I'm simply going to forgive him in this moment.

The bed dips and I turn back to Seth, warning him to get the hell out. "I'd like to be alone."

"Just one thing." Although it's a statement, he says it like it's a question.

With a nod, I agree to hear him out.

"He lied to you, he does that," Seth tells me easily, like there's nothing wrong at all with it. "He made mistakes he's not used to. He decided to do things he shouldn't have." There's a rhythm to his voice that's calming. I fall for it, listening to every word he says. "He's not the only person I've ever met that lies to make other people feel better."

"He could say he's sorry," I counter as if a simple "sorry" would make much of a difference. Then I remember... he did. He said he was sorry. I don't remember for which part. Maybe all of it. He was right though, words are meaningless.

"He's not. He'd do it again if he had to." I'd be pissed off if Seth wasn't so matter of fact and if I wasn't so convinced already that what he's saying is the absolute truth.

"Then why should I ever trust him again?" That's really what it comes down to. I don't know that I can believe him or trust him ever again.

"Because he's trying to be a better man... for you. He's done all of this, *for you.*"

I try to respond, to disagree. But I can't. Intention matters and behind all of this, he wanted to keep me safe. He tells me one last thing as he makes his way out.

"You know he loves you." Seth sounds so sure of it. "Just love him back." With that he shuts the door, not waiting for a response.

chapter twelve

Jase

"I'D SAY SHE'S PISSED," I COMMENT IN THE DARK NIGHT AS I SHUT MY CAR DOOR. I FUCKING hate that I'm not there now, just in case she wants to talk or yell... even if she wants to hit me again.

"I'd say she has a right to be." Glaring at Seth's profile, I note that he doesn't look back at me until he adds, "She loves you, though." When his eyes reach mine, I look ahead instead.

He changes the subject to ask, "You ready for this?"

It's bitter cold as the clear, glassy surface of the puddle beneath my boot is shattered. I don't hesitate to take another step and another. Moving quickly through the harsh wind to the warehouse.

"No one's ever ready for this shit."

"I don't like not knowing what to expect," Seth comments, and it's only then that I notice how tense he seems.

"Whatever happens in there, we'll figure it out," I assure him. "Follow my lead."

"I'm not sure I'm the best at that, Boss."

"You've always been the best."

"Not at following... I like lists and control and knowing what to do. If you're telling me that you don't know, I'm telling you I might not follow."

There's always been direction. Always been a sense of right and wrong and a certain way to do things. Recently though, everything has been like walking through fog.

"Whatever you do," I finally answer him, "don't point your gun at me. Aim it at the prick who brought us here."

With a huff of a laugh he tells me, "I'll try to remember that."

Pushing open the double doors, I feel every muscle in my body coil, ready to act. Bright light greets us instantly, blinding me momentarily. It only makes the adrenaline in my blood pump harder and faster.

"We've been waiting for you." Officer Cody Walsh's voice reverberates in the large empty space. Blood rushes in my ears as I take in the man who's been like a dog with a bone ever since he arrived in town.

There's no back room or secret entrances in the empty warehouse. The ceilings have to be twenty feet high and the room itself is vacant, all 1200 square feet of it. With the exception of a steel shelf on the back wall and several stacks of old metal chairs behind Officer Walsh and another man I've never seen before, there's nothing here. Nowhere for anyone else to hide. That doesn't mean there aren't cameras.

"Good to see you again, Officer," I speak and other than my voice, the only sounds are the large fans spinning above us as we walk to them, slowly closing the distance. Seth stays back slightly, letting me lead the way.

Officer Walsh is in jeans and a black leather jacket, nothing like his typical attire, save the expression on his face.

"Undercover tonight?" Seth mutters beneath his breath, although it's a joke—there's a serious hint of a smirk there—and I share a quick glance with him. All of the

FBI cases we could find on Walsh are sealed, except for one case. The one that has information on Marcus as well. His files were squeaky clean, with numerous medals and honors, referrals. But not a damn thing about undercover work. Anyone could spot him as a cop. He'd die in a week out here if he pulled that shit.

Our boots smack off the cement floor as my eyes adjust to the fluorescent lighting and we get closer to the two of them.

The other man is younger. Maybe in his thirties, or late twenties. In dark gray sweats and a long-sleeve black Henley, he would come off as relaxed if he didn't keep looking between Cody Walsh and the two of us.

"I don't think we've met," I address the other man, and the moment he opens his mouth to greet me, Officer Walsh whips up his gun to the side of the man's head and fires.

The racing of my heart isn't quite as fast as I am to pull my gun from its holster. With both hands on the steel in my hands, I stare at Walsh pointing the barrel at the unsuspecting man beside him. If Walsh sees my gun and Seth's aimed at him, he doesn't react, he only watches the man to his left. The dead man falls to his knees, his eyes dead and vacant with a rough bullet hole leaking blood down his face. Walsh continues to focus on him until finally, the man falls face-first onto the floor with a dull thud.

"I was wondering when you were going to get here so I could kill him," Walsh admits, his eyes watching the bright red blood pool around the nameless man's face.

Our pistols are still on him and he only seems to notice now.

"I wouldn't if I were you. If I don't make it back to the office and pull the tapes out of the mail room, all the evidence will be dispersed."

Seth's gaze sears into me. I can hear the soles of his shoes scrape against the ground as he shuffles his feet although his gun is still up.

Keeping myself calm, I lower the gun and shrug as if I'm unaffected. "I didn't take you for a man who liked the dramatic."

Officer Walsh is a man who's strictly by the book. That's everything we found on him. Clean record and a man who believes in black and white with no grays in between. This… this is to throw us off. It can't be his normal.

"I didn't take you for a man who liked being late."

"You killed him because we were late?" Seth questions. He lets a hint of humor ease into his tone, but his gun still sits at his side.

It's only then that Officer Walsh takes his gaze from me and focuses on Seth.

"No. I shot him because I don't need him and he knows too much."

"Good to know that's how you do business." Seth's criticism is rewarded with a tilt of Walsh's head.

"What's his name?" I question.

"It doesn't matter." Walsh looks between the two of us, making me second-guess his plan of action.

"It does to us," Seth speaks for me, and I don't mind in the least, since the same words were going to come out of my mouth. I want to know everything about the dead man lying on the floor. What he did, who he worked for, and most importantly: why he was standing beside Walsh in the first place?

"Joey Esposito."

"Anything else we should know about him?" Seth asks and Walsh simply stares at him. I didn't come here for a pissing contest.

"What do you want?" I speak loud and clearly, breaking up whatever's starting between the two of them.

"To share two things with you. Both of them are pieces of information I think you'll find valuable," he says and then nudges the leg of the dead man on the floor. It's a dull prod with no emotion behind it, just enough to be noticed. "He worked for Romano."

Just hearing the name *Romano* raises the small hairs on the back of my neck. I feel my eyes narrow but other than that, I keep my composure. Seth does the same. Remaining still, unmoving. Unbothered.

That's more like him.

"I'll hand over the whereabouts of Romano freely. I'd prefer for you…" he pauses to glance at Seth before adding, "the two of you, to know that I'm willing to negotiate."

"Handing something over for free isn't a part of negotiations. Negotiations require something in return." Seth corrects him and I have to fight the grin that plays at my lips.

The irritation in Walsh's demeanor is something I didn't know I'd enjoy so much. Maybe because it's obvious he wanted the upper hand by killing this poor fuck the second we got here. Maybe it's because Seth isn't making it easy for Walsh. Either way, I make a mental note to tell him I like his style when he's not following.

Before Walsh can respond, I comment, "How'd you get the information regarding Romano's whereabouts? Esposito just gave it to you? Or did he think you had a deal?" I let the implication hang in the air, that his deals aren't to be trusted as I take a step forward.

"He came to me, wanting something I couldn't offer. He decided to rat, I decided to skip the judicial system and deliver his sentence to save some financial burdens. How's that sound? Reasonable, *Mr. Cross*? Besides, I already knew where Romano was. That's not the information Joey was giving me. Romano's in protective custody."

The way he says my name makes my skin crawl. He ignores the silent snarl and continues talking, grabbing the back of a simple metal chair, letting it drag across the floor with a shrill sound.

"What's more important is that the indictment was dropped." He leaves the chair in front of Seth, then grabs another. There's a stack of them, and he delivers one to each of us before taking a seat himself.

Seth hesitates, so I sit down first. Both of us, across from Walsh. All of us holding our guns, but settled in our laps.

"Dropped?" I question, feeling my curiosity, my disbelief even, show on my face.

"It's confidential."

"So he gave something up?" Seth surmises and Walsh shrugs but wears a slight grin. "Fucking rat."

"Jail or death. He didn't have many options, did he?" Walsh comments.

"He made a mistake coming back," Seth responds and then sits back in his seat when I give him a look.

"What's the other thing?" I ask Walsh, squaring my shoulders and moving away from the subject of Romano. "You said you had two things to say. The first is that you have Romano's whereabouts. What's the second? I'm guessing it's these recordings you say you have? Negotiation and blackmail in the same conversation?"

Walsh tosses a small notebook into my lap. It's small and something easily tucked away, like something that would fit inside of a wallet. "The hotel Romano's been placed in and his room number. He's got three police offers posted next door. If they hear banging around and screaming, they've been told to let it happen."

"And you're fine with that?" I question, feeling my shoulders tighten. "It's got 'setup' written all over it."

"I'm not letting Romano walk away. He's the reason Marcus came back here."

Walsh leans forward, his elbows resting on his knees so he's closer to me as he tells us, "I want him dead but it can't be on our hands. Too many people are involved. Take him. I've read the files on Aria Talvery. I saw what happened with your brother."

"You saw what happened to Tyler?" I question him, not understanding how he knew.

"Tyler?" he responds with a shake of his head. "Carter. Carter is with Aria, unless I'm mistaken." It's silent for a long moment.

"What happened with Tyler?" he asks when the quiet air lingers for too long.

"Nothing of your concern." I shift my weight in my chair as Walsh leans back further. "I want Romano for an entirely different reason."

"Then take him. I'm giving him to you, both to start off with a good rapport."

"Seconds before blackmailing us?" Seth interrupts him and Officer Walsh shrugs. "Both to have a good rapport. And to show Marcus I'm here and I'm not going anywhere."

"Marcus came back... here? For Romano?" I question, thinking back nearly a decade ago when I first learned about the bogeyman that is Marcus. "How long have you been after him?"

"Six years now," Officer Walsh tells me and it doesn't add up. Marcus never left. Marcus couldn't have been in New York fucking with Walsh while keeping up his reputation down here and pulling strings. The cogs turn slowly as I assess Walsh, wondering where it went wrong, needing to know what piece is missing.

The reality of what Walsh is willing to do in order to get to Marcus coming into focus.

Seth readjusts in the seat, shifting his gun from hand to hand and then he stands, pushing the metal chair back as he does and stating, "I'd rather stand if you two don't mind."

I don't move my gaze from Walsh, who merely watches.

His pale blue eyes raise to mine and then to Seth's as he says, "My only request is that you don't kill him at the hotel. Make it look like he took off and skipped town. Do that and he's yours."

"In exchange for?" I wait for the other shoe to drop. Seth stands still to my left. His wrists are crossed in front of him and one hand still holds the gun.

"What do you think I want?" he asks lowly.

He's slow to pull a recorder out of his pocket, and with the click of a button, Seth's voice is heard and then the sound of something creaking. I recognize it immediately.

"Who's this fuck?" he asks and I answer, "Hal. The second he wakes up, bring him to the cellar."

"You have questions for him?" Seth asks.

"No. No questions."

Officer Walsh stops the recording, although the visual memory of opening the trunk and showing Seth in the parking lot behind The Red Room continues playing out in my mind.

"What was bugged?" I ask Walsh, running my thumb along the rim of the barrel. Motherfucker. Anger courses through me uncontained inside, although I don't let it show.

"I'm guessing a gift from Marcus?" Walsh speculates with a glimmer in his eye. "The recording has enough evidence for me to piece together how you got hold of Mr. Hal Brooks, that he was alive when you took him... and what you did to him after."

"What exactly are you implying?" A trace of anger can be heard in the hiss of my question.

"That you're fucked... unless you've got information for me. It was in his clothes and found on Mr. Brooks body."

It sinks in slowly. Marcus bugged Hal. He set me up. Between Marcus, Walsh and Romano, the list of men to kill keeps getting longer.

"What information are you looking for?" I ask, looking him dead in the eyes.

Walsh merely stands, glancing at the dead man on the floor and the dark pool of red that's staining his face as he looks off to the front double doors in the distance.

"I'll contact you when I have specifics." With that he stands, leaving me to calculate every possible way we can kill him. He's a man hell-bent on vengeance and willing to burn everything that lies between him and it.

As the two of us stand up slowly, watching his hands and how he places the gun back in his holster, Walsh adds, "Go tonight for Romano. Tomorrow the teams change. I mean it when I say I intend to have a good rapport with you two."

Turning his back to us, he places the chair he'd taken on top of the stack. "Unless you want to help me clean up, I think you'd better getting going."

The metal of the gun is warm when I slip it behind my back in the holster, taking in everything I can about Officer Cody Walsh. It's silent, save for the, "Until next time," Walsh gives us on our way out.

Neither of us speaks until we're far enough out in the distance.

Still seething, we both climb into the car and listen to the *thunk* of the doors closing as the sound of crickets off in the distance fades to silence.

"We're screwed if he mails the recordings or hands them out to the fucking FBI." Seth says the fucking obvious, tapping his foot in the car.

We should have incinerated him. That dead fuck and all the evidence along with it. Instead, I had to freak the fuck out over shit that happened years ago.

Seth keeps up with the tapping. Tap, tap, tapping as my frustration grows.

"Knock it the fuck off."

"I'm thinking," he retorts and then lets out a "fuck" and punches the side of the door.

"Feel better?" I ask him when he lifts his fist to examine his hand.

"Much," he answers dryly.

The keys jingle in the ignition as the engine turns over, humming to life. Seth rolls his window down, breathing in the cold air until he comes up with a solution

"I'll find out where the info is and get rid of it then get rid of him," he speaks.

"That easy?"

"If we put him in the cellar, yeah. That easy."

"You think he'll tell us where it is?" I glance at him and let out an uneasy exhale, shaking my head as the wind blows by. "I don't think he will. I think he'd die before quitting."

"Then how?"

"Declan has to find something."

"Declan's looking into something?"

"I asked him to look into something before I know whether or not it's a dead end. I don't know yet; it may be useless."

He's reluctant to nod, but he does. "And what about Romano?"

"Go tonight and take three men with you. Two for lookouts." The order comes out as easy as the plan should be. "If he's in their custody, he's unarmed and it should be in and out."

"We'll hit him with chloroform. Keep it quiet."

"Just make sure you take out any cameras first. And stay silent, wear masks. Don't trust it not to be recorded."

"Got it. Want me to send a report to Carter first?" he asks and I stare off to the right side as the car comes to a stop. Just happens to be the graveyard. "No, I can do it. I'll tell him."

I'll tell my brother just how badly I've fucked up. With all of this.

Then I'll deal with Bethany.

And then Romano.

chapter thirteen

Bethany

My eyes feel so dry but I can't keep them closed. Every time they shut, I see Jenny, in the hands of a villain. She's out there and I'm lying in a comfortable bed, protected and doing nothing.

The thin slit of light from the hallway that lays across the bedroom floor and hits the dresser widens as a soft creak fills the quiet room. Jase's footsteps are cautious and muted.

"You don't have to be quiet," I let him know although I have to clear my throat after. It's raw and in need of a hot cup of tea. A luxury I can afford, as I'm not *missing and presumed dead*.

"You're not sleeping?"

"How could I?" I answer Jase with the question as he walks to the bed and lowers himself to sit by my side, making the mattress dip where my legs lay.

He tells me, "I didn't expect you in here."

For a moment, I reconsider every thought that brought me back to his bedroom and ask, "Do you want me to leave?" If he does, I will. If he doesn't, I'll stay. Simply because I want to be here. I still want to be next to him when I do fall asleep. I want him to hold me, but I'm too prideful to ask. More than that, I'm ashamed that after all the lies, I still feel like I need him.

His answer is quick. "Never."

"I don't want to give you an ultimatum." I spit out the words that I've been saying over and over in my head the last hour or so. "I hate them and I think they're awful."

Jase is deadly silent, listening to what I have to say. I can feel his eyes on me although I don't look up at him. Resting his head on my thigh that's covered by the blanket, he waits for me to continue.

"It hurts to even say it. I can't deal with lies. I don't want to be a woman who lets a man lie to her."

"I won't."

"I don't know that I believe you." Finally looking into his eyes, I suck in a deep inhale to calm my words. "I can't stay if I find out you've lied to me about something. I can't be with you if that's all there is between us."

"There's nothing else and there will never be anything else."

My mother used to warn us about 'always' and 'nevers.' Especially about the people who speak them with certainty.

With the window cracked, a gust of cool air blows in trailing along my skin and with it, the ends of my hair tickle down my bare arm as I prop myself up. "You sound so sure."

"I am." His hard jaw seems sharper in the faint light with the shadows from the moon. There's an intensity that swirls in his eyes, but it seems different now. Not so much riddled with fear as it is with loss and regret.

Or maybe it's a reflection of myself, maybe it's just what I want to see. He may be certain, but I'm not so sure of anything anymore.

I can only nod, and lie back down. Back to his bed although I'm on my side and I intend to sleep all night with my back to him. I'll do it every night until the hurt goes away. That deep pain that's settled into my chest like fucking cancer.

"Is there anything else I can..." Jase pauses and I hear him readjust as the bed jostles.

"Anything else you can say or do?" I finish the question for him, my eyes open and staring straight ahead at nothing in particular.

"Is there?" he asks when I don't answer the question I raised.

"We just move on, don't we?" I tell him, feeling that pain spread like a web, tiny and sticking to everything inside of me as it spins. "That's what happens."

"Why do you sound so defeated?"

"Because it hurts, it all hurts and I don't know how to fix it other than to believe you. Even that hurts right now."

The mattress groans as he leans forward, rubbing my back as I lie there, refusing to give in to anger. "What matters is that Jenny's alive." My bottom lip trembles and my throat goes tight as I ask, "You're going to save her, right? You're going to bring her home?"

"I'm doing everything I can," Jase whispers as he lies down next to me although he's not under the covers. He pulls me in closer to him and as much as I'd love to shove him away for everything he's done, I need to be held by this man for the very same reasons.

"When we were little, she was my hero," I admit to Jase, still staring ahead at the blank wall that's been a photo album to me all night, flicking through memory after memory. "I was thinking about the time when I'd just reached high school and how she helped me with my English homework. She loved poetry. She was so good at it."

It sounds like Jase is going to say something, but instead he stays quiet. He kisses me on my shoulder though, through the sleepshirt and then on my jaw by my ear. The kind of kiss where I'm forced to close my eyes. When he lays my arm in the dip at my side and then rests his forearm in front of me, I twine my fingers with his.

His touch means more to me right now than I think he'll ever know.

The second I part my lips to thank him, he speaks first. "Tell me more about her."

"I don't know what to tell you. She was my big sister, the one who looked out for me, helping me with everything... until it all went wrong."

"What went wrong?"

"Our mom did. That's when everything changed." The hollowness in my chest seems to grow thinking about it all, so I stay quiet. The silence doesn't stretch for long.

"Do you still hate me?"

For lying about my sister while I was mourning her?
For lying about scaring me into staying with you?
For lying about the debt and taking advantage of me?

The questions line themselves up in my head, but stay unspoken.

"No," I answer him. "I hate what you did, but I don't hate you."

"Why do I feel like things aren't okay?" he questions and that gets a reaction from me. Fighting the covers with my legs, I turn around to face him, propping myself up with my elbow and feeling the comforter fall down my shoulder.

"Because I'm still upset," I say and frustration comes out in my tone. "What would you have me do, Jase?" The exasperated question escapes easily from my lips. "I don't know if you've lied about something else... or if you will."

"There are no other lies." Anger colors his statement and reflects in his gaze.

"I don't believe you." There's no emotion in my words, only facts. "There are only so many times you can lie to a person. Only so many. But what am I really going to do? That's why I'm hurt. I don't want to leave you." Fuck, saying the words makes me feel weak, down to my core. I don't want to leave him. Not just for my sister's sake, either. "I feel *pathetic*." I practically spit the word out.

"Do you forgive me?"

"You said you were sorry." That's all I can say.

"That doesn't answer my question."

"It doesn't matter," I tell him.

"It does."

"I forgave you without you even apologizing. It's about trusting you and trusting myself after falling for you. The trust isn't there anymore," I admit.

"I can give you reasons to trust me--"

"Time will," I cut him off. "Even when I hate you, you're still what I need. You don't understand how much I feel that I need you."

"I do. I know what that's like," he confides in me and I feel like it's the truth. Why else would he want me here? Why else would a man like him deal with me, in this state, right now?

When I don't respond, he asks me, "How can I make it right?"

"You can start with finding Jenny and bringing her home."

"I can't guarantee--" he starts to say, but I don't want to hear it.

"I finally let go... I let go and she was still out there." My voice cracks. If I had kept looking, if I'd kept asking around and demanding answers... Maybe she would be home now.

"I can't make that promise to you, Bethany."

Letting go of the regret, I focus on what we can do now when I tell him, "I know you can't promise, but I wish you could."

Instead of lying down like I think he's going to do, he sits up and walks his way around the bed to stand in front of me. "I have to go," he tells me and I nod into the pillow, keeping my hands down on the bed, although I question if I should reach up and wrap them around his neck to pull him down for a kiss. Is it so bad that I want to be kissed when I'm hurting? Even if it's by the one who caused the pain?

"Where are you going?" I ask him, not hiding the surprise or the slight worry in my cadence as I glance at the clock. "It's late." I say the excuse as I sit up and wrap my arms around myself.

I expect him to hesitate, to lie or to give some vague response. "I'm going to kill the man who murdered my brother," he answers and my heart lurches inside of me. All the pain I've been going through and turmoil, he may have had a hand in it, but I forgot he suffers through it too.

"Jase, are you okay?" I don't think I've ever pushed myself up quicker in bed as I get onto my knees and move toward him.

"I'm fine, anxious though," he answers me as I sit in front of him, neither of us touching each other in the dark night. It's all shadows and cool gusts of air between us and I wish it would go away; I wish I could change everything.

"I'm sorry," I whisper, and do exactly what I wanted to do a moment ago for myself, but right now it's for him. Sitting up taller, I press my lips to his for a tender kiss, my fingers brushing against his stubble and then laying across the back of his neck. Jase tilts his head down and cupping the back of my head, keeps me there for a second longer. Just one more beat.

"Are you going to be all right?" I ask him in a whisper, my lips close to his, not wanting to let go.

"I'll be fine," he answers me and I don't think he's lying. I think that *he* thinks he really will be fine, in a situation where nothing at all is fine.

"Do you care that I'm going to kill him?" He doesn't let me go as he asks the question.

"Only in the sense that I care about what it does to you." The answer is immediate and true to the core. Maybe it's wrong, but there's so much that's not right that I simply don't care about being wrong anymore.

"I want you with me. You can know, or you can guess, you can ignore it all. I don't care so long as you're with me."

"I want to know," I tell him even though a tremor of fear runs through me.

"All I care about is you being here when I get back. Tell me you'll be here."

"I'll be here."

I wish I'd told him I loved him, but he kisses me and then leaves me breathless on the bed. I can feel it in his kiss and when he leaves, when the door is closed and he's long gone, I ask as though he's still here with me, *why won't you tell me you love me?*

I refuse to believe it's not love. It's fucked up a million ways and then some, but this is love.

chapter fourteen

Jase

"IN SOME CULTURES, PEOPLE BURY THE MEN THEY MURDER FACE DOWN SO THEY CAN'T come back to haunt them."

Four stories up in the vacant and grand estate, the large windows are open and the rooms are all bare. The empty old office is bigger than the entire house I grew up in. The ceilings are tall; the light wood floors shine with polish. When Romano left his place weeks ago, he took off and got rid of everything. One day he was here, the next he was gone. The worst decision he made was coming back.

"Face down? Like in their grave?" Seth asks from across the large room. There aren't any lights in the room; the full moon and the streetlights give us everything we need. He's still dressed in jeans and a shirt, both black. His men are downstairs sweeping the place and preparing for what's to come, while we're up here with our guest of honor.

I nod, listening to the muffled noises that come from behind the balled-up rag in Romano's mouth. Hysteria is setting in for the old man as his face turns red and Carter, Declan and Daniel join us. He's never looked so old to me. So close to a fucking heart attack and then death. Wouldn't that be ironic? If the fucker had a heart attack while tied down in that desk chair and we didn't even get a chance to kill him.

"They thought if they buried the men they killed face down, when their spirits woke up, they'd be disoriented," I explain to Seth and to whoever else is listening.

Seth lets out a rough chuckle, playing with a knife as he sits in a wingback chair in the corner. The leather is old and cracked. I guess that's why Romano left it behind. Everything left in the room was meant to be thrown away. Now Romano's been added to that category.

"I've heard of feeding the dead to pigs. They'll eat anything," Seth answers.

"Can't bury a man if he dies with dynamite in his lap, can you? Or feed what's left of him to the pigs?" Carter questions and then pats my shoulder as he enters the room. He only glances at Romano, not paying him much mind as he walks around the room. This estate has to be a hundred years old. It was a family legacy. One that's ending tonight.

Although the conversation borders on lighthearted in tone, tension is thick in the room.

"This used to be your office?" Carter asks Romano as he leans forward, placing a hand on the soon-to-be dead man's shoulder. From behind the rag comes nothing but rage and the muted sounds of what I assume are curse words.

I wonder what it's like to be him right now. I'd rather have a heart attack than to be him right now.

Carter only smirks at him, standing up and pushing off of his shoulder, sending Romano rolling away in the wheeled desk chair. Gagged and tied down, this is how he'll die. In the room where he made all of his decisions. Decisions to murder and decisions that require consequences.

"Any situations tonight?" Carter asks Seth who shakes his head. "In and out, he was sleeping so the chloroform was easy. Overall it was," he says as he looks Carter in the eyes, "uneventful."

"And the detail in the next room? Did they try to interfere?"

Seth answers, "Didn't see them, didn't hear them. It was all over in under ten minutes. Even if it was filmed, we were masked and didn't talk. There's no way to ID us."

"Good work," I chime in and my brother agrees.

"Explosives are planted everywhere but the main room where we hid the cash in the safe. It'll look like he came back to hide evidence, but mistakenly set it off too soon," Carter explains.

"What a tragedy." Daniel's comment drips with sarcasm. Out of all of us he's been the most quiet, the most still. Leaning against the back wall and staring at Romano all night.

Romano says something. It could be his last words for all I care, they won't be heard.

Declan adds, "It keeps the feds off our back, they go away. I want them the fuck out of here. And we take over the upper east side."

"All our problems solved." Triumph comes darkly from Carter's voice.

Almost all. Marcus and Walsh are becoming more difficult problems by the day, but I keep that opinion to myself.

"I wish they all knew," Daniel speaks up. As he kicks off the wall and walks closer to the far edge of the room to look down at the tied-up man, the light sends shadows over the harsh expression on his face. "It's too quick and not public enough for what you deserve," he tells Romano. His voice is hoarse, and anger and mourning both linger there.

The memory of Tyler dead in the street plays tricks on my mind as I look out the large window feeling the cool breeze against my face. The cast iron fence separates the estate from the road and it's just beneath us. The road ahead is a backroad; many don't travel on it and it's not the road Tyler where died, but any black road slick with rain will carry that memory forever.

"Justice is a funny thing, isn't it?" I murmur as I tap my blunt nails along the windowsill, opening the window even more, as much as I can to feel the cold air blow in. "It never feels like enough."

"What?" Daniel asks from behind me, so I turn around to face him.

"It's never going to feel like enough… because it's never going to be all right." With the singular truth exposed, a raw pain grows from my empty lungs and radiates upward.

"I'm grateful he didn't get away and the feds didn't fuck this up for us. We'll spread it around, that we didn't like him talking to the cops," Carter says and looks pointedly at Seth, who nods. Rumors travel fast in this town and everyone needs to know it was us. Romano fucked with us. Now he's dead. That'll make a lot of other pricks question whether or not they're willing to do the same.

"What about Tyler?" Daniel asks. His forehead creases as he continues, "They should know Romano killed him and that's what gave him a death sentence."

"We'd be admitting we didn't know the truth until recently," Carter speaks up, shaking his head. "It's easier to keep it a secret."

A lie, hisses in my ear, and I have to turn away from my brothers, once again looking out into the empty street only to see the ghost of memories there.

"I don't like it." Daniel disagrees with Carter. Seth and Declan are quiet, simply observing the two of them.

"Tyler deserves justice," I speak up before being conscious of it. "It shouldn't be kept a secret."

"Romano dies tonight." Carter's harsh words whip through the air. "What more do you want?"

I'm surprised by Daniel's words as he says, "Humiliation, pain... I want it to be a spectacle." He's still filled with hate over Tyler's death. He's still angry. He's still grieving. I'm convinced the five stages of grieving aren't like steps where you take one after the other. I think they're waves that constantly crash onto the shore and you never know which one will hit you.

"That's not going to help our FBI situation," Declan answers, peeking up from the corner of the room where he's standing behind Seth. I can feel all their eyes on me, but I don't look back yet. All I can look at are the spikes that line the top of his iron fence. All I can think about is how awful it would be to die like that, to fall onto the spiked fence beneath us and be impaled next to an asphalt road. It'd be the last thing he ever looked at.

"We decided this was how it would be... now you want to wait?" Carter questions, his voice tight with incredulity.

"No, we don't have to wait." I turn to finish my thought, looking at Daniel as I suggest, "We can throw him out this window. That would be a *spectacle*, as you called it."

Daniel smirks while Declan lets out a chuckle and then asks, "Wait, are you serious?"

"He can die committing suicide by jumping onto a spiked fence," Daniel says and smiles over Romano's muffled pleas. The man's fighting in his chair now, causing it to roll slightly across the floor. I kick the back of it gently, just to push him away from me and torture him some more.

"Who would kill themselves that way?" Declan asks. "Who commits suicide by spearing himself onto a fence?"

"No one," I answer him and Daniel adds, "That's the point."

"That would send a message," Seth comments although it's not meant to agree or disagree. He stays neutral in all of this.

Carter's voice is low as he says, "It would send a message to the feds too. That we don't care they're here and that we're still running this town. Is that the message you want to send?"

"That's the message we *need* to send," Daniel presses. "What are they going to do? We don't leave evidence. They'll know, but they can't do anything about it."

"Just like they can't do anything about Tyler," I say and my statement is the nail in the coffin for me. Romano murdered our brother and left him on the street to die. "This is justice."

He'll do the same.

"No one knew about Tyler; how could they have done anything?" That's the problem, isn't it? With so many lies and secrets, no one could do anything for Tyler. It was just a tragedy.

Just like Jenny. I think about how many times Bethany went to the cops and filed a missing persons report for her sister. How they told her they were sorry, and they didn't know what happened when the trunk was found.

"We need to do this, Carter," I say and look him dead in the eyes, feeling a numbing prick flow over my skin. "No accident, no dynamite. We give him the death he earned."

Time ticks slowly, with Seth shifting behind me and Declan staring at Daniel, who's waiting for Carter's final decision. *Tick, tick, tick.* It's too slow.

"Take the cash, leave the safe empty and open. Wipe for prints." Carter gives the order and I walk from the open window to Daniel, feeling the cold gust of wind at my back carrying Romano's muffled screams.

"You all right?" I ask him lowly so it's just between the two of us, and he nods although he can't look me in the eyes, he can't look away from Romano.

"Who gets to do it?" he asks me although his voice is coarse and he has to clear it. "Who gets to do the honors?"

"You can if you want." I give it to him. I'll suffer the rest of my life, hating that Tyler died in my place. Whether Romano breathes again, whether I kill him, none of it will change that. But at least now everyone will know. And that's something.

"It was supposed to be you," he reminds me, as if there's any way I could forget.

"I know, but doing this isn't going to bring Tyler back." Daniel's expression wavers, the hardness falls for a moment and he nods again. I watch as the cords in his neck tense.

"If we're doing this, it has to be done clean," Declan speaks up. I'm not sure if he disagrees and thinks we should go the safe route, or if he's simply covering our bases.

"We're always clean," Seth answers him.

"Let the feds see," I tell Declan. "Let everyone know." I pat Daniel on the back and then look Carter in the eyes as I say, "No one takes from us and gets away with it."

"It's settled then," Carter agrees. "And the men that came back with him? What about them?"

"Make it clean," Declan repeats to Carter, the undertone of his voice harsh. Romano's cries can still be heard and I kick the chair just slightly, sending him rolling backward again.

"There's no deal to offer any of Romano's men, no loose ends," Seth says and nods.

I wait until Seth lifts his eyes to mine. "Go through every part of this town. Every asshole who ever got a paycheck from him. Find them in their homes, at the bar. I don't care if they're balls deep in the back room of a strip joint. Find them, kill them."

"They die tonight," Carter talks as he walks to where I was, no doubt judging what it'll take to make sure Romano's impaled. It won't take much at all. It's just outside the window. "There aren't many left. We already have locations on most of them."

"They'll scatter like roaches if we wait until tomorrow and the FBI doesn't know yet, but the moment they find Romano, they'll be everywhere. So we end it tonight," Daniel agrees, walking to Romano and turning the chair. He has to crouch down to be at his eye level. "Wipe them all out."

"Start with him," I speak to Daniel, and he looks over his shoulder at me. His lips are pressed in a straight line, with a grim look covering his face.

"End it," I tell him. Carter steps to the side, and we all wait.

Pushing the gagged, screaming man with a bright red face to the window, Daniel looks out onto the road—a backroad that will be empty until the morning.

The gag comes off first, bringing a stream of Italian profanity from the dried throat of this dead fuck. Romano pulls on the ropes, fighting as best he can against them. It's foolish really, he should wait until we untie him for his best chance, but he doesn't, knowing his end is coming.

Seth's the one to cut the rope at his feet; one quick swipe and the nylon threads are released. Romano attempts to run, still bound to the back of the heavy leather chair and he falls hard on his side, seething in pain. The crack of his skull hitting the floor ricochets in the room.

With Carter holding his left side and me holding his right, Seth cuts the binds and helps us hold him up, holding him steady and restraining him as he tries to run and fight. I can't breathe. My muscles are too coiled as Romano struggles with the last bit of strength he has left in him.

Backing him up to the window, I stare at Daniel's face. I expect anger, I expect hate, but agony is all that's on his face. It's still not enough; being the one to end Romano... it's not enough. It won't bring Tyler back.

We release our hold as Romano falls backward from the force of the shove Daniel gives him in his chest. Romano's arms whip out to grab onto whatever he can, but there's nothing there, nothing that can keep him upright. His scream dulls as he falls the four stories and then it's silenced.

Staring down at him and the scene, I no longer see Tyler. The street's empty. All I see is a man who killed all his life, a man impaled with the life draining from him slowly.

Turning to Seth, I tell him, "Check that he's dead, then find the rest."

chapter fifteen

Bethany

It's been quiet the last few days. Too quiet.

The ominous feeling that settles in when you know things won't last... that's in the air. I've been breathing it in and suffocating from it. Jase is being careful with me and both of us are feeling bad for the other one.

It's easy to give someone sympathy, it's easy to love them. Accepting their love though, accepting it in the way they're able to give... that's the difficult part, because that's where you get hurt.

I forgive him, but I'm waiting for the next bad thing to happen.

Jase is just waiting, on edge and waiting for something... I don't know what.

The other end of the line goes to voicemail. So I dial the number again, stretching at the end of the sofa. Jase's non-office is now my hideaway. The smell of old books and leather is too much to resist.

Ring. Ring.

On the second ring, it picks up and I recognize the voice instantly.

"Laura," I say and my gut falls. I wasn't expecting her to answer. "I didn't know you were working day shifts this week."

Animosity and betrayal stir in my stomach. More than that though, I miss her.

"Bethany?" She sounds surprised to hear my voice.

"I just wanted to call about Michelle, the pregnant patient with pica on floor two, and maybe talk to Aiden..." I trail off, waiting for Laura to tell me she'll get him. After a few seconds of silence and then the way she says my name, I know that's not going to happen.

"Bethany," she says but I can already tell there's too much sympathy in her tone. "Michelle died two days ago. I'm sorry. I thought Aiden called."

The leather turns hot under my tight grip. I can barely breathe. When I worked in pediatrics before this for my internship, death was common. It was so common I'd check the paper for the obituaries before coming into work so I'd be prepared. It's also why I left. At the center, it rarely happens, but now it feels like death's following me everywhere.

"Beth? Are you there?"

"I'm here," I answer her although my body's still tense and it hurts to swallow.

"You weren't answering my texts and I know you're mad, but I thought you knew. I swear. I'm so sorry."

"How did it happen?"

"Magnets. They obstructed her bowels," Laura answers.

"If I'd been working--"

"Don't think like that."

"I had a rapport with her." I can't even say her name as tears prick my eyes. She was young and beautiful. Before getting pregnant, she was healthy. If only, if only. I think it too much now. Every day I wonder 'what if' in all aspects of my life. It's not a healthy way to live.

"She wasn't well and..." Laura stops when she hears my quick inhale. I'm not crying, but I'm damn close to it.

"There was nothing any of us could have done. The behavioral approach was working and she was released. Her husband checked her out… it happened in her home."

With a hand over my heated face, I focus on calming down, but it takes a long moment. Struggling not to lose it, I debate on simply hanging up.

"I'm sorry," Laura tells me again and I don't know what to reply. It's not okay, but that's the answer we're supposed to give, isn't it? That or thank you, but there's nothing to be thankful for right now.

"You need to come back to work," Laura tells me when the silence stretches.

"Everything's changed."

My voice is tight when I answer her. "I want to come back." Focusing on breathing, I try to calm down. "I can't believe she's dead. It feels like I was just with her."

"Tragedy happens." Seconds pass as I try to accept it, staring at the unlit fireplace.

"You should come back." I'm grateful for Laura's distraction as she adds, "Aiden's gone for three days and he told me to schedule you for next week. So you're on."

My eyes lift to the bookshelves, feeling wider, more alert. "I can come back to work?"

"We need you. There's so much that's happened."

The way she says it makes my heart still and I can feel a deep crease settle between my brow as I ask, "What? What happened?"

"I can't tell you over the phone; just start back on Monday."

A cold prick flows over my skin, knowing something's wrong, but not knowing what. "Okay." I take a moment, which feels awkward and tense, but I make sure Laura knows I'm genuine when I tell her, "Thank you."

"Are we okay?" she asks me softly. I can practically see her nervously wrapping her finger around the phone cord in the office like she does. It's a habit I picked up from her.

I answer her honestly, "I don't understand why you did it. Why you called him and didn't tell me."

"There's a lot you don't know."

"You could tell me," I offer her. "Really, if you'd told me no, or if you told me you called him before he showed up…"

"I… I can't tell you right now, but soon? I can tell you soon, if you want."

"I want to know. I do."

"And then we'll be okay?" she asks me as if that's all she wants.

"Yeah," I answer her even though I don't know if it's truthful. I don't know why so many people are hiding secrets. Or why each one hurts more than the last.

When I hang up the phone with her, I hear the front door close from all the way down the long hall. Jase is home and it surprises me how much I want to go to him, how much I want him to hold me like he does every time he gets back and just before he leaves.

I wait for him, holding my breath at first, but I can't hear where he's going or what he's doing. Leaving my phone on the glass table, I pick my book back up, although my gaze flicks to the open door.

chapter sixteen

Bethany

He's been quiet, but there's a look in his eyes that's anything but. I can feel the tension crackle and it promises that if I follow him, I'll be given everything I could possibly want in this moment. And so I do. The second he looks at me, I close my book and leave it there to go to him.

"Come on," he commands but it's soft and low, pleading almost. My heart yearns to follow him quickly; to show him I accept his demands.

"I don't want this distance between us anymore." Jase's voice is calming and deep.

"I don't either," I admit to him and reach out to take his hand when he offers it. There's something about the roughness along his knuckles and the warmth of his skin that's soothing. His touch consoles a part of me that's desperate to heal.

"Trust works both ways," Jase tells me as I gauge the changes in the fire room. Everything's been moved out, most notably the chaise and the wooden bench. In place of the plush white rug is a black blanket, large and heavy. The room's barren, but still beautiful, with the crystal fireplace and lit chandeliers.

"Both ways," I repeat, registering his words and wondering what he has planned.

He said he found a solution to our problem. Funny how a man's solution involves sex… or so I assume. To be honest though, I need this.

I need *him* like this. I close my eyes knowing *we* need this.

"Strip here." He gives me orders as he places a handful of things in the middle of the blanket.

A candle, a lighter, a bottle of ethanol, some sort of white cloth, and the weighted blanket. Tremors of pleasure send a warmth flowing through me, meeting at my core and heating instantly.

By the time I've stripped to nothing, he's done the same. The light from the fire emphasizes every etched muscle in his taut skin. His cock is already rigid and my bottom lip drops at the thought of being at this man's mercy.

A deep, rough chuckle whips my eyes from his length to his gaze. "Ever needy and greedy, aren't you?" he teases me and that's when I see the glimmer of light that reflects off the blade. The tension rises, stifling me, wrapping its way around me… and I love it. I crave it. It does nothing but ignite a fire inside of me.

My feet patter on the slick black blanket beneath us as I make my way to him, tucking my hair behind my ear as I prepare to drop to my knees in front of him. I want to please him, to prove to him that I still desire him, that there's still a roaring fire between us. I don't get a chance to though.

Catching my elbow, Jase stops me and instead puts his hand on mine, pulling my fingers back and making me hold my hand out flat. He's silent as he gives me the knife.

"It's heavy," I comment weakly as he sits cross-legged and I do the same in front of him. The heat from the fire is the only thing that keeps the chills of the cool air away. My heart races as I glance at the small silvery scar still on his chest.

"I want us both to play," he tells me, wrapping my hand around the handle of the blade and then bringing it to his chest. "First you need to shave me."

The command is simple although my gaze shifts from the small smattering of hair on his chest to his eyes. Scooting closer to him, I watch the way his throat dips, the way the cords tighten as I prepare for the first stroke.

Before I can press the blade to his skin, he lays a hand on each of my hips, holding me steady. The warmth of the fire is nothing compared to his touch. With every small exhale, I drag the blade down carefully, feeling it nick each hair along his chest. Breathing in, I then drag the blade over his skin, blowing softly across it as I go and gently bring the back of my fingers across his body to check on the smoothness of it.

"Don't leave any behind," he tells me, sitting upright and still not moving.

"Does it hurt at all?" I ask him, running my fingers over what I've just done and then moving the blade to a patch of fuzz on his upper pec by his shoulder.

"You're only shaving me," he answers with a handsome grin, mocking me.

"I mean the scar. Where I cut you before," I whisper, not looking into his eyes and then grabbing the cloth next to Jase to wipe the blade clean.

"No," he answers and then takes the knife from me. "It feels like a memory that fate made happen."

He does the same to me, shaving away the little bits of hair, making sure there's nothing between us that the fire would catch.

"You first," he tells me and he tips the bottle of ethanol, the cloth pressed against the opening. The smell of alcohol hits me as he wets the rag. "Where you put it, the fire will catch, but do it quickly." Before relaxing his shoulders and sitting back, he lights the candle. "Use this for the flame but hold it upright to keep the wax from dripping."

I've paid attention and I've seen what he does. Nodding, I know exactly what he's said and why it works, but still I hesitate, holding the rag in my hand and staring at his chest.

"What if I hurt you?"

"The blanket's fireproof and I can lie down, Bethany. I'm here, and you're more than capable."

I remember what it's like, the memory of the fire tickling then blazing. Heating my skin before vanishing and leaving me breathless and hungry for more. I can give that to him. The very idea of it makes me eager to do it.

Reaching out, I wipe the damp cloth against his skin in a small motion, not covering much area at all. My pulse is fast and my hand trembles slightly. I can't help it; the only thing that keeps me composed is the intimacy of the moment and his touch steadying me.

"A cross?" he questions and I let my lips kick up as I pick up the candle. "Over your heart," I answer him in a whisper as I lift the flame. It catches quicker than I anticipate, blazing in a short burst and vanishing as my heart races.

Releasing my shock in a single breath I look to Jase whose eyes are wide with desire as his chest rises higher. "Again," he commands in a deep groan. This time when I get closer to him, he grips my wrist holding the cloth out and tells me, "Use more and in a different spot. When it lights, press your body against mine and feel the aftershocks of the fire."

He takes his time, moving my hair behind me and telling me to braid it and be careful. Playing with fire is something we've always been warned not to do, and maybe that's why it's so exciting.

I do as he says, wondering what type of pleasure or pain it'll bring. I'm too slow the first time, too slow to feel anything but the heat of his chest where the reddened skin felt the kiss of fire. Still, with my body pressed against his and feeling the rumble of desire against his chest, it's erotic, it's forbidden and I want more of it.

"Fire needs fuel to stay alive. It has to breathe, but you can smother it. It needs to move, but you can deny it." His words are mesmerizing, and the feel of dulled flames extinguished as I press my body against his is unlike anything I've felt before. It's gone too fast.

Taking my hand, he runs the rag over my breasts before I can run it down his body. I light him first and as I lean, the fire catches against my skin. As my head falls back, Jase presses his body to mine, gripping the hair at the base of my skull and pulling it back as his teeth scrape against my neck.

He takes control then, laying me down and playing with me, toying with the fire between us.

It's a dangerous game to play with fire, but I feel like he's made the rules. I feel invincible with him, like nothing matters except for what he tells me in that moment.

The light flicks between us, burning hot and roaring until it extinguishes. It happens so fast, but each moment seems more and more intense. Hotter, heavier and upping the stakes of how much of our skin is sensitized.

Until the lights have gone out and the heat dissipates, leaving me yearning for more.

More than the fire this time. I need *him*. The pieces of him that fire can't give me. I breathe into Jase's kiss, "I want you."

He devours me, pushing me to the floor and bracing himself above me, settling between my spread legs before tilting my hips how he wants them. Jase isn't gentle when he enters me. He teases me at first, pressing the head of his cock against my folds and sliding it up to my clit, rubbing me and taunting me before slamming inside of me to the hilt and making me scream. I watch him hold his breath as he does it, and he watches me just the same.

I'm lost in the lust of his gaze, lost in the gentle touches of his hands on my breasts where the fire just was as he pistons his hips, deliberately and with a steady pace that drives me to near insanity. He's controlled and measured, even through the intense pleasure. I feel him hit my back wall, the ridges of his cock pressing against every sensitive bundle of nerves as he fucks me like this. Deep and ruthlessly, but making every thrust push me higher.

I barely notice when he raises his body from mine. The heat from the fireplace blazes, but it doesn't compare to what it feels like to have his body on top of mine. I lift my shoulders off the ground, reaching up to hold on to his, but he shoves himself deep inside of me, making my back bow. Throwing my head back with pleasure, I see the lit candle, I see him tilt it to its side where it rolls away, the flame still lit, the fire growing, catching in a crevice of the hard wood floors.

Lighting ablaze.

"Jase!" I scream, pausing my body, but he doesn't stop, he crashes his lips to mine, hushing me as the fire roars behind us. Pressing my palms against him, I try to push him away so he can see, but he resists.

He ignores me to the point where I feel as though I've imagined it.

"Fire." I breathe out the word in a ragged whisper as he fucks me while the pleasure mounts and stirs in my belly; it overrides the fear. Jase tells me at the shell of my ear, "I know."

My heart races chaotically as I look into his eyes and he speaks with his lips close to mine, "Trust me." The fire behind us echoes in his eyes.

It takes me a moment to realize he's still. He's stopped. And the fire is real.

With the flames reflecting in his dark gaze, I reach up and pull him toward me, urging him on before kissing him.

The flames grow brighter and I can't stop watching them. Even as he ruts between my legs, bringing my pleasure higher and higher, my body getting hotter and the intensity of everything mixing with the fear and pain and utter rapture.

"It's on fire," I say and the fear creeps into my voice. "The room's on fire." Even so, Jase doesn't stop. He's savage as he fucks me into the ground, kissing his way down my neck. My nails dig into his skin as I hear and feel the fire grow. My heart pounds against his. "Trust me," he whispers.

The flames rise higher and higher, igniting against everything around us, even though it doesn't travel across the black blanket. "Kiss me," Jase commands, gripping my chin and pulling me back to him.

"Jase," I gasp his name, the fear and heat of the fire stealing me from him. His lips crash against mine and with a hand on my back and another on my ass, he moves me to the floor, pinning me there with his weight.

Thrusting himself inside of me, my back arches, my head falls back and I stare at the flickers of red and yellow flames as they engulf the room surrounding us.

And then, just in the moment when I'm breathless with fear, water rains down upon us. It comes down heavily. No sirens, no noises at all. Only water, leaving a chill from the cold droplets to bring goosebumps along my heated skin.

"There's always something to calm the fire," he groans in the crook of my neck and then drags his teeth along my throat as the deluge descends around us, extinguishing the flames. Every thrust is that much deeper as I lift my hips and dig my heels into his ass.

Even knowing it's safe, knowing the fire's gone, my heart still pounds with a primal instinct to run. I can't though, pinned beneath Jase and wanting more of him.

The light goes out around us, the flames diminished to nothing. The warmth of the room vanishes as the water washes us of the fear from being consumed by the fire.

Lifting his head up to look down at me, I stare into Jase's eyes as he presses himself deeper inside of me and then pulls out slowly, just to do it all again. Every agonizingly slow movement draws out my pleasure, raising the threshold and I whimper each time.

That's how I fall. Staring into his eyes longingly, praying for mercy to end it just as I whimper and beg him for more. Clinging to him as he hovers over me and loving this man. Loving him for all he is and knowing what I do. Knowing I never want to stop.

chapter seventeen

Jase

"I LOVE THE SMELL AFTERWARD," I COMMENT, LISTENING TO THE CRACKLING OF THE flames in the fireplace. I lit it for the heat and the light both as Bethany lays against me, still on the floor.

Although I used the thick blanket to dry her off, her hair's still damp and the light from the fire casts shadows against her features, making me want to kiss along every vulnerable curve she has.

"The char?" she asks weakly, sleep pulling her in. The adrenaline should be waning now. Sleep will come for her soon and I hope it comes for me too.

"The water. It has a smell to it, when it puts out the fire."

"It does," she agrees and then lifts her head, placing a small hand on my chest as I stay on my back. "Will you tell me something?"

"What?"

"Anything," she requests in a single breath and lies against my chest. Spearing my fingers through her hair, I think of the worst of times in this room. I think of the fire, the way it feels like everything will end, the intensity and the simplicity of it all being washed away.

"Do you know how many men I've killed?" I ask her as the question rocks in my mind. "Because I don't."

Although I keep running my fingers along her back and then up to her neck, noting the way the fire warms her skin with a gorgeous glow, her own hand has stilled, and her breathing has stopped.

"Are you scared?" I ask her and she shakes her head, letting her hair tickle up my side. "I just don't want to do anything to stop you from saying more. I want to know."

"I used to keep count and memorize their names," I admit to her and remember when I first built this room. Its purpose was different then and the memory causes my throat to tighten.

"I'd sit here, and let the fire go. I'd let it burn whatever I'd brought, I'd let it spread and surround me. All the while, spouting off each person's name. Every person I murdered with intent or for survival. Every one of them. And there were many.

"At first, I'd give both first and last names. Then it became only first names because I'd run out of time otherwise. I thought if I could say them all before the fire went out, it'd be some kind of redemption. In the beginning I could do it. I could say them all before the water would come down. It never made me feel any better, but I did it anyway.

"Then I started forgetting," I confess. "Too many to remember, and the names all ran together. Some names I didn't want to say out loud. Names of men who I'll see in hell and smile knowing I put them there."

"Don't talk like that," Bethany admonishes me. She whispers, "I don't like you talking like that."

"Like what?"

"Like you're going to die and go to hell. Don't say that." The seriousness of her tone makes me smirk at her with disbelief.

"Of everything I've done and said, that's why you're scolding me?"

"I'm serious. I don't like it." She settles herself back down and nestles into me, seeming more awake now than before and with tears in her eyes.

"Why are you crying?"

"I'm not," she tells me. "And you're not a bad man. You just do bad things and there's a difference. God knows there's a difference, and I do too."

"Don't cry for me." I offer her a weak smile and brush under her eyes. Her soft skin begs me to keep touching her, to keep soothing her and never stop.

"I'm not," she repeats although she wipes her eyes and tries to hide it. "Don't talk about you dying... and we have a deal."

She doesn't look me in the eyes until I tilt her chin up, lifting my shoulders off the ground to kiss her gently and whisper, "deal," against her lips. I can feel her heart beat against mine. This is the moment I want to keep forever. If ever given a choice, I'll choose this one.

"Tell me something else." She states it like it's a command, but I can hear the plea in her voice.

"Something nicer to hear?" I let a chuckle leave me with the question in an attempt to ease her.

"No, doesn't have to be nice. Just something more about you." The fire sparks beside us as I look down at her. Her bare chest presses against mine and I drink her in. The goodness of her, the softness of her expression.

"Hal, the man I killed... he hurt Angie. You heard me mention her before."

The mention of another woman's name makes her pause and I remind her, "She wasn't mine and I didn't want her like that, but I've always felt responsible for what happened."

"What happened to her?" She doesn't blink as she whispers her question staring into the fire.

"She came and went when we first... opened the club... she was one of our regulars on the weekends. Buying whatever she wanted to party with her friends."

"Drugs?" Bethany asks and I nod, waiting for judgment but none comes.

"One day she came to the bar on a weekday. I thought it was odd. She was dressed all in black and her makeup was smudged around her eyes. She wanted something hard. That's what she asked for, 'something hard.'" The memory plays itself in the fire and brings with it a hollowness in my chest.

"I told her to get a drink, but she demanded something else. So I told her no. I sent her away."

"Why?"

"I thought she would have regretted it. She'd just come from her father's funeral. There was nothing I had that would take that pain away and I knew she'd chase it with something stronger when it didn't work. She went to someone else. And I regret sending her away. I wish I could take it back. I wish I could take a lot of it back. By the time I saw her again, she'd changed and done things she didn't want to live with anymore. She was so far gone... and I'm the one who watched her walk away and sent her to someone else. Someone who didn't care and didn't mind if she became a shell of a person who regretted everything."

"You tried to help her. You can't be sorry about that." Bethany's adamant although sorrow lingers in her cadence.

"I can still be sorry about it, cailín tine," I whisper the truth as I brush her hair back.

"And I am. I'm sorry about a lot of things. Mistakes in this world are costly. I've made more than my share of them."

"That doesn't make you a bad man," she whispers against my skin, rubbing soothing strokes down my arm, desperate to console me.

"You remind me a little of her in a way," I admit to her. "She was a good person. Angie was good, what I knew of her. She was good but sometimes dabbled in the bad and was able to walk away. I needed her to be able to walk away. To go back to everything and be just fine. To still be good. It made me feel like it was fine. I thought what we were doing was fine; that it was a necessary evil. It's simply something that's inevitable and something we'd rather control than give to someone else. But it's not fine and it never will be."

Bethany asks, "You think I'm a good person, dabbling in the bad?" Her voice chokes and she refuses to look at me even when I cup her chin.

"It's the same with you. I'm not comparing you to her. She's nothing compared to you but the good. You have so much good in you. Even if you cuss up a storm when you're mad and try to shoot strangers."

The small joke at least makes her laugh a small feminine sound between her sniffling.

"I'm not willing to let you go though—I'm afraid you'll never come back to me. Or worse, that you won't be able to go back to the good."

"You are not bad," she says and her words come out hard which is at odds with the tears in her eyes.

"I'm not good, Bethany. We both know it."

"And I'm not all good either. In fact, there are a lot of people out there who would tell you I'm a bitter bitch and they hate me," she attempts to joke, but it comes out with too much emotion. "You don't have to know if I'll still be good if I walk away, Jase. I don't want to walk away. And we can be each other's goods and bads. People are supposed to be a mix of both, I think. You need that in the world, don't you? You are needed," she emphasizes, not waiting for my answer. "And I need you," she whispers with desperation.

"I'm right here," I comfort her and she lets me hold her, clinging to me as if I'm going to leave her.

It's quiet as she calms herself down and I think she's gone to sleep after a while, but then she asks, "Is this... is this cards or bricks for you?"

"I don't understand."

"I'm insecure and I need to know. It's one of the bad parts of me. I'm insecure."

"You need to know... cards or bricks?" I ask, still not understanding.

"There are two kinds of relationships. The first is like a house built of cards; it's fun, but you know it's going to fall down eventually. Or you can have a house made of bricks. Bricks don't fall. Sometimes they're a little rough and it takes time to get them right, but they don't fall down. They're not supposed to anyway--"

"Bricks." I stop her rambling with the single word. "I'm not interested in cards. I don't have time for games."

"Then why lie to me?" She whispers the question with a pained expression. With her hand on my chest, she looks into my eyes. "I don't want to fight; I just want to understand."

"I kept you a few steps behind me. That's how I saw it. Not because I didn't trust you—I didn't trust that the information I had wouldn't hurt you. I didn't want to give you false hope."

She's quiet, and I don't know if she believes me. "Please. Trust me."

"I do. I trust you." At the same time she answers me, my phone pings from where I left it in the pile of clothes.

Bethany doesn't object to me leaving her to answer it. Although she watches intently, waiting for me to come back to her.

Reading the message Carter sent, I try to keep my expression neutral and tell her, "I have to go."

"You do that a lot," she comments before I bend down to give her a goodbye kiss.

"I'm sorry."

"Don't be. I'm right here. I'll always be here." A warmth settles through me with her whispered words.

"Is it going to be okay?" she asks, not hiding her worry.

"As okay as it ever is," I answer her truthfully. "We may know where Jenny is," I tell her and watch as she braces herself from the statement. "We're going to find her tonight."

"Jase, I love you," she whispers. "Make sure you come back to me. I'm not done fighting with you yet." A sad smile attempts to show, masking her worry, although it only makes her look that much more beautiful.

"I look forward to coming back here so you can yell at me some more," I say to play along with her, leaving a gentle kiss against her lips. When I pull back her eyes are still closed, her fist gripping my shirt like she doesn't want to let go.

"I'll come back." I swallow thickly and promise her, "I'll come back."

chapter eighteen

Jase

THERE'S A BRIDGE THAT LOOKS OVER THE FERRY. IT LEADS TO THE DOCKS WHERE OUR SHIPMENTS come in. With my brothers behind me and Seth next to me, we stare at the worn door that lies beneath the bridge.

It's made of steel and looks like it's been here as long as the bridge has; the shrubbery simply obscured it.

"We still don't know what's inside," Sebastian comments.

"Jenny," I answer. "I know she's in there." I can feel it in my bones that we're closer to where we're supposed to be. Even in the pitch-black night, with the cold settling into every crevice, we're close. I know we are.

"Let's hope so." Carter's deep voice is spoken lowly as he steps next to me, facing the bridge and considering the possibilities.

"Ten men?" I ask Carter, looking over my shoulder at the rows of black SUVs parked in a line. "Do they know?"

"They know we need them here and that's all. They're waiting for orders."

"Ten of them?" Seth repeats my question.

"Do you think that's overkill?" Carter questions in return. It's just the four of us, me and Seth and him and Sebastian, along with our ten men. Daniel and Declan are home with guards of their own. Just in case anyone sees us leaving as an opening to hit us where it hurts. In this life, there is never a moment for weakness and having someone you love at home is exactly that, a weakness waiting to be exploited.

"I don't know if it'll be enough," Sebastian answers. His hand hasn't left his gun since we got out of the car. He's ready for war and prepared for the worst. He knows what it's like to be given an order by Marcus better than any of us. By the way he's acting it looks like he expects each of our names to be on a hit list given to Marcus's army.

"It wasn't supposed to turn into this. It should have been low key." Seth looks concerned as he searches the edge of the bridge for signs of anyone watching or waiting. "He has eyes everywhere."

"If Marcus wants to kill us, I imagine he could do it with no men," I tell the group who have gathered around us.

"We're walking underground with no concept of what's there."

"Explosives would do it," I say, completing the thought that lingers in the back of my mind.

"You think he knows?" Carter asks.

"I think we should assume he does," Seth answers.

"If he didn't before we got here, he does now." The realization hits me hard. "All of us can't go in there. This was a mistake."

"What the hell are you talking about?" Carter snaps.

"There are too many questions unanswered. If we all go in, he could see it as either us declaring war or an opportunity... We can't give him the opportunity. He can know war is coming though."

"We go in together," Carter insists as I grip my gun tighter, feeling my palm get hot with the need to do something.

"Think about Aria." I try to persuade him to go back home.

"I am. I'm thinking about my family and about bringing them home. Open up the fucking door."

"Don't leave her a widow," I warn him. "Not for me."

"She knows what I'm doing. She knows the risk." I can only nod, thinking that Bethany knows the same. Carter adds, "She told me not to come home without Bethany's sister. She knows and she wants Jenny home too. Open it." With the command and the four of us moving forward, the men gather behind us, all of us walking to the small door.

With a gun trained on the lock, Sebastian fires and a flash of light and red sparks from the gun being shot leads to the groan of the heavy door being opened. Sebastian steps aside and only nods as we move forward. His eyes are focused straight ahead as he orders the men around us, keeping a lookout and moving forward to clear the way.

"I'll go in first," I tell him, stepping in front and preparing myself for what we'll find.

The steel floors grate as I step forward, letting my eyes adjust and not daring to breathe. The musk of the water's edge is heavier when the door opens. A steel rail keeps me from stepping forward and it's then I notice the door leads to a spiral staircase down. It reminds me of the shed at The Red Room. The place men go to die but unlike them, we're walking down there willingly. A cold prick flows down my skin like needles.

"We don't have a choice." Carter pushes the words through clenched teeth before I can urge him to turn around.

"This is my fight," I tell him one last time.

"We fight together." The weight against me feels more significant than it ever has before. "Bastian," I call before taking another step forward. "Don't let a single man here die."

He tells me simply and then motioning with his chin for me to continue, "I wasn't planning on it. In and out. No casualties."

With a nod and a look back at Carter and Seth, I take the stairs one at a time, noting how many there are and how far down it goes. Maybe two stories, if that. It's got to be twenty feet down and the steady drip from leaking pipes is all that makes a noise down here.

Four men stay at the top and just outside the door as lookouts. The rest join us, making it ten men in a tight space, eight of them waiting on the stairs for the door at the bottom to be opened.

Bang!

It takes a second shot to shatter the lock and I toss it to the floor before slowly pushing open the door. Seth's behind me, his gun raised and ready. Steadying my breathing, focusing on my racing pulse, I take in every inch that I can see.

There's no sign of anyone. No sign of anything at all down here. Anxiousness makes me doubt myself. Maybe she's not here at all. With that thought, unexpectedly the lights turn on, one after the next, quickly illuminating the place.

The sound of guns cocking and raising fills the tight space, but no one fires. The lights are newer than everything else. They're placed into sconces bracketed against the walls which are a mix of thin plaster and tightly packed dirt.

"Electric," Seth notes. "Someone was hired to install these," he says and I can already see the wheels spinning.

"Look for a paper trail when we get back," I tell him, leading the way further into the unknown territory. "If Marcus hired someone, they may have seen him or someone who has."

"Already noted."

I have to stop before I get more than five feet in; there are so many rooms, so many branching paths. "It's almost like a mine the way it's built with a maze of halls."

"Where do we start?" Seth asks. His expression appears overwhelmed as he moves his gaze from one hall to the next. All open doors, and all could lead to armed men or worse.

My brother comes up behind us, considering everything carefully. All the while I hear the tick of a clock in my head.

"It could take hours." The second the words slip out of my mouth, I hear a skittering in the dirt.

A scraggly boy, thin but tall with lean muscle watches from the shadows to the left. The second I spot him, he takes off. My gun lifts first, instinctively ready, but he's unarmed and I can hear his footsteps getting farther away.

"Left," I yell out and chase after him. He's the build of the kid who left the note on Carter's windshield. "He works for Marcus." My lungs scream as I chase after the kid, rounding a hall and barely spotting him through another. Seth's right at my heels and the men behind him spread out, watching each door. Careful and meticulous, not reckless like the man in front has to be.

The need to find this kid, to stop him rages hard inside as I race through the underground, chasing after the sound of him running. He may know where she is. He'll know what this place is at least.

I can hear them all behind me as Seth and I take the hall carefully, checking doors as we go.

My lungs squeeze and I struggle to breathe in the damp air as I lose the sound of him first. Then I lose sight of him with the sconces slowly flickering off and on.

It's my worst nightmare. Trapped in a small space with everything riding on this moment and yet I have no answers and it's all slipping away.

I don't stop running, searching every corner with Seth and listening intently, only to run into a sign. A sign that stops both of us in our tracks. The sign the kid led us to.

Four lines are written on a board blocking the hall. The boy is nowhere to be seen although the click of a door sounds in the far-off distance.

Leave the boy.
All those who made a deal with Walsh can enter.
Everyone else leave now.
Or the girl dies.

"What happened?" Carter questions in a hushed demand as he comes up behind me. My heart's racing, my palms are sweaty. He knew. Marcus knew and let us come.

"You have to go," I answer him as I take in a deep inhale, feeling my pulse pump harder. I can't lift my eyes from the sign. "Or the girl dies."

She can't die. Bethany needs her.

"He knew we were coming," I speak loud enough for all of them to hear as they make their way into the space. "Get them out," I tell Sebastian. "Get everyone out!" I have to raise my voice so Sebastian can hear.

"He wants us to know he knows and to admit it," Seth speaks out loud, referring to the deal with Walsh.

"Admit it in front of our men," Carter adds, looking behind him at the men lined up and ready to fight beside us. Ready to die for us.

"I couldn't give two shits who knows." My hiss of a mutter grabs his attention and

I look him in the eyes and tell my brother, "I promised Bethany I'd bring her sister back." The thumping in my chest rages. "Even if I have to go in alone."

"I'm here, Jase," Seth speaks up, reminding me I'm not alone.

Carter speaks before I can answer, "Then do it." He doesn't let go of me, he grips my arm and forces me to stand there a second longer. "Don't get yourself killed." He says it like it's a demand, but it's drenched with emotion.

"And to think, I was expecting you to tell me you love me," I joke back in a deadpan voice even though dread consumes me. It's just to ease the tension and hurt that riddle every muscle inside of me at the thought of Jenny being dead already and Marcus being one step ahead as usual. Merely toying with us.

"That too," Carter adds.

With a farewell grip on his shoulder, I look him in the eyes and tell him, "I'll try not to be stupid."

"Go," he tells me and shares a glance with Sebastian. With a nod of his head, Sebastian starts to lead the men back.

"I'll see you when it's through," I answer Carter as he walks off without looking back.

"You should go too," I tell Seth as the place empties. "Go with them."

"What are you talking about?" His voice is low with disbelief.

"You stay back. In case it's a setup." I can feel chills flowing down my skin at the thought of Marcus being more prepared than we are. He's the one who made the rules to this game. He knows it better than anyone. He sets himself up to win.

"I'm the one who needs to go in. I'm the one who brought us all here." A cold sweat breaks out across my shoulders and down my back before taking over my entire body as I stare down the barren hall. It feels like my death sentence. I'm a fool to think otherwise, but I have to go in. I can't leave her here. I can't and I won't.

"It says 'all,'" Seth says as he looks me in the eyes, defying me and referring to the sign that blocks the path. "I'm not letting you go in there alone." Disregarding my orders he takes a step forward, pushing the sign to the side, into the dimly lit hall and I yank him back, fisting the thin white cotton of his shirt.

Time passes with both of us waiting for the other, knowing what we're walking into and looking it in the eyes anyway.

"Are you sure?" I ask him.

"We're in this together. I have to admit, I didn't really care for Marcus before, but now I hate the fucker." He offers me a hint of a smirk and a huff of humor leaves me. Patting his back, I grip my gun with both hands. He readies his and I nod.

"We get her and we get out."

"Got it," he says then nods and we go in together.

The thumping in my chest gets harder listening to Seth's pace picking up to match mine as we move down the dark hall, the smell of soil and rust filling my lungs as we move.

"You have a strong family," Seth comments with something that sounds like longing.

"We're close," I answer him and he glances at me, but doesn't say another word.

"Let's not die today. I'd like to go back to them."

chapter nineteen

Bethany

I CAN'T GET THIS FEELING OUT OF THE PIT OF MY STOMACH.
Sitting and waiting. Sitting and waiting. I don't like sitting and fucking waiting around.

Everyone you love will die before you. My mother's voice has kept me company for more hours than I can count. Warning me. I let myself fall and it feels like I've been delivered a death sentence. Why did I let myself fall? Why did he have to keep me from running?

The thump of the book falling from my hand down to the floor scares the shit out of me. My nerves are messier than ever; they're worse than a necklace tangled at the bottom of a luggage case on a bumpy road trip.

I force myself to read The Coverless Book. I read every page in it. I read about Emmy feeling better and the two of them getting married in secret. I read about them falling in love and sharing their first time together.

Then a new sentence started as he watched her lie down, but I don't know how it ends. I stared at the last page for the longest time, not understanding. It's half a sentence, mid-thought from Jacob about how he'd do anything for her. Someone cut the pages out. Lots of them. It looks like there's at least twenty missing that I can spot. So much for reading to distract me.

I know there's more to the story. It can't be cut short like that. The moment the thought hits me, I'm drenched in the nightmare of my sister crying on the floor. Telling me she just wanted them to have a happy ending.

"Jenny," I breathe her name, staring at the clock and wanting Jase to come back with her.

I can't sit here and do nothing.

With nothing to distract me, my mind goes to the worst of places. Pacing and staring into the fire as the smell of leather envelops me.

Dropping my hands to my knees, I feel the flames as my hair hits my face. It's the waiting that kills me. I can't sleep without seeing my mother remind me that *everyone I love will die before me*. I can't think without wondering if Jase has found Jenny and all the things she may have had to endure. I don't know who she'll be when he finds her. *If* he finds her.

This isn't a way to live, waiting and in fear.

Are you there? I text Laura and wait. I'm exhausted from barely sleeping, but there's no way I can sleep now.

I'm scared, I message her again, needing to tell someone. She doesn't text me back though. She could be working; she could be sleeping. I don't know. I don't know anything anymore.

"Fuck this," I say then toss the book down on the table and make my way out of the room. The hall seems longer than it has before as I head for the grand staircase and the hidden door beneath it.

My pulse pounds in my temples as I place my hand on the scanner to open it. It takes a long moment. "Please open," I whisper as the jitters flow through me.

It does, the large door slides aside seamlessly, presenting me with a dark kitchen until I turn the lights on.

It's empty and quiet. The whole world is sleeping while mine crumbles around me. A sudden chill overwhelms me and a split second later the click of the heater makes me jump.

"Carter," I call out as I walk deeper into the kitchen. My feet pad on the floor and that's the only sound other than my racing heart. Something's wrong. I can feel it in my bones.

Wrapping my arms around myself I make my way to the other hall that the kitchen leads to. It's quiet and dark.

"Anyone," I call out and my voice strays from me, receiving no answer. "I don't want to be alone right now." It's a hard feeling to accept, when you open yourself up to love and then feel fate toying with taking them from you. "I don't want to be alone anymore."

"Bethany?" a voice calls out just as I turn on my heel to walk away.

"Daniel?" I question, fairly sure it's him and not Jase's other brother. Someone's here at least. "Were you sleeping? I'm sorry, I hope I didn't wake you up." The sentences tumble from my mouth as he makes his way into the kitchen, also in bare feet and gray pajama bottoms with a white t-shirt tight over his chest. He has to pull it the rest of the way down as he stops at the counter.

"No, you're fine, I was just lying down with Addison but not sleeping." There are bags under his eyes, so I know he's tired. "You okay?"

"Are you?" I ask him, feeling the anxiousness grip my throat.

His expression softens to a knowing look. "It's hard. Moments like this can be difficult," he admits and just to hear someone else say what I feel is a slight relief.

"I don't know how to be okay right now." Gripping the tips of my fingers to have something to hold, I watch as he pulls out a wine glass and then heads to the cellar.

"Do you like white or red?" he asks and I swallow a small laugh at the implication that the answer is to drink. "Red."

It's quiet as he opens the bottle, the dim light from outside glinting off the torn metal wrapper.

"I don't know what I can do to help." I emphasize the last word as he gently pushes the glass toward me and then pours one for himself.

He doesn't answer me; instead he takes a drink and so I do the same, sipping on the decadent wine and feeling guilty that I can.

"I just have a bad feeling," I finally confess. "It won't leave me alone and I'm afraid."

Daniel's still quiet, but he nods in understanding. I start to wonder if he'll speak at all until he says, "Let him do what he knows how to do, what he's good at."

"That doesn't--"

"Yes it does. You want to be involved," he says then looks me in the eyes and that's when I see the remorse in his. "You want to be there in case something happens." His voice drops as he tells me, "I know that feeling."

"I'm sorry."

"Don't be. I get to be here with Addison. Don't be sorry for me. There's nothing in this situation to be guilty or sorry or resentful over." He leans forward on the bar before looking over his shoulder down the empty hall. "We do what we're needed to do," he says with resolve.

"I don't know what I'm needed to do," I admit to him, feeling the weight lift, knowing that's the core of my problem in so many ways.

"When he brings your sister back, you take care of her. You're good at that, aren't you?"

The thought of Jenny being here soon forces me to brace myself on the counter.

"I heard that's what you do," Daniel prods, waiting for me to look back at him and I nod.

"Take care of her when she comes back, because that's something no one else can do. Let Jase do what he does and you do what you do."

"Even if I'm scared?" I question him in a whisper.

"Can I tell you a secret?" he asks and again I nod.

"We all are. Anyone who tells you they're not is lying. We live in a world where there's plenty to be afraid of. It's okay to be scared sometimes, but have hope. Have faith. Jase knows what he's doing."

chapter twenty

Jase

With single bulbs swinging slightly and creaking as they do from the high ceilings, the hall is dim. The rocking of the water can be felt in the aged corridors.

"How old is this place?" Seth murmurs his question as he gently kicks the first steel door open. Without a light in the small ten-by-ten room, it's hard to look in every corner. The rustling of Seth's shirt as he pulls out a small flashlight and clicks it on gets my attention. The heat of worry, of restlessness, is dulled by my conditioned response to chaos, *stay calm*. Always calm and alert. Or else death is sure to come for you.

He brings the light to his gun, both hands holding the pair steady and revealing an empty room inside. There's only a mattress on the floor and nothing else.

The same with the next room and the next.

Rows of doors, mostly open, line each side of the hall and we go through each one. Every door we open that reveals nothing but rumpled blankets and makeshift beds leaves me with the dreadful thought that we're too late… that when we push the next door open wider, it'll reveal a girl on the floor, no longer breathing.

"We can't be too late." The fear disguises itself as a hushed request.

"She's here," Seth reassures me beneath his breath as he turns the knob of the next door, and lets it creak open, revealing another barren room. "Why else would he do this?"

My gaze moves instinctively to him. "Why does Marcus do anything?"

"If you want to beat him, you have to think like him. Why this place? Why the boy? Why the sign?" He pauses to make sure I've heard.

"Why her in the first place?" I add to the pile of questions.

I count the remaining rooms, four of them, two on each side. Three open, one closed.

My mind travels to deceit. Wondering if he already took her away. Wondering if Marcus locked the two of us in here in her place. "If his intention was so easily known, he wouldn't be who he is."

With the slow creak of the next steel door, rusted on the bottom edge, I hear Marcus's rough laugh in my memory and an icy sensation flows over my skin. Unforgiving, cruel.

We betrayed him first. I can already hear his excuse. We came onto his territory; we stole from him. The only question is: what are the consequences?

"Empty too," Seth whispers. The next room and the next prove the same.

Prepared to be left with nothing but more questions and curses hissed beneath our breath, I place my hand on the final closed door and turn the knob, but it doesn't move.

Seth and I share a glance in the silence as I try again and then quietly shake my head. *Locked.*

Hope thrums in my chest as my pulse races and I take one step back and then another.

"On the count of three?" Seth asks, backing up with me. Nodding, I tell him, "Kick it in."

One.
Two.
Three.

My muscles scream as I slam my boot against the door as hard as I can along with Seth, the two of us putting everything we have against the steel lock with the last hope of seeing Jennifer behind it.

The door slams open to reveal darkness and then a shriek. My eyes can't adjust fast enough, although I think I see her small form just before I hear the *bang!*

The heat of a gun going off, the metal against my skin, singeing my shirt and filling the air with the smell of metallic powder is disorienting but familiar. Adrenaline surges in my veins and I'm quick to push forward, not knowing if the bullet hit me, grazed me, or if I was spared from the shot. Anger, fear, and the need to survive all war inside of me to come out on top as I shove myself forward, closer to the gun and whoever's holding it.

Bang! It goes off again, the shot hitting the ceiling with a pop of steel breaking that joins the crackling of the plaster that falls from above my head.

My body hurtles forward, landing on top of the small woman who's desperate to cling to the gun. She fires it again as I grip the barrel, forcing it away from me just in time to send the shot wide and feeling the burning hot metal as I rip it from her hands and toss it away. It thuds on the floor as she turns under me, desperate to get it back.

"Jennifer!" I scream out her name and hear Seth cuss behind me.

She screams and kicks wildly, fighting like her life depends on it.

"Stop!" The command is torn from me with equal parts demand and desperation. Seth moves to the side, kicking the gun farther out of reach. "Stop fighting," I grit out as her heel hits my ribs and she scrambles on the dirt floor.

The impact to my ribs leaves me seething, the pain rocketing through me as I clench my teeth and hold on to her.

"I don't want to hurt you."

"Calm down," Seth demands lowly, and it comes with the faint sound of a gun being cocked. That gives her pause. "I don't want to hurt you either," he says calmly.

Jenny stops moving, stops fighting and her gaze moves to Seth in the darkness. I can barely see him, but I can see the glint of the gun.

Time moves slowly as I back away from her to stand and while I do, Seth lifts his gun the second she looks at him. He uncocks it. "I didn't want to do that," he admits to her, swallowing thickly. "Just calm down. We're here to help you."

It's only then that I can take a good look at her.

What's most alarming is how disoriented Jennifer is. She's not skin and bones like I thought she'd be. Even through the grime that covers her skin, she has weight to her that lets me know she's been eating. Her eyes though are dark with lack of sleep and fear drives every half step she takes as she backs away, trying to get away from us, but knowing the wall is behind her.

With her gaze darting from me, to the gun, to Seth, she crouches down and stares up at us, ready to scream and fight.

"We're here to help you." I keep my voice low as I speak. The ringing in my ears from the gun she just fired has dulled. All I can hear now is her ragged breathing.

Seth tells her calmly, lowering himself down with both hands in the air, "We're here to save you."

I do the same, raising my hands and letting her know, "We're not here to hurt you."

With wild eyes full of disbelief, she shakes her head, letting us know she doesn't believe us.

"I'm not leaving without you," I tell her and the thin girl shoves her weight against me and her ragged nails scratch down my neck. Seething in the slight pain and more pissed than anything, I snatch her wrists and hold her close. "Calm down."

"You're not taking me," she screams out. Even held close, she doesn't stop fighting. It's useless though. She has to know it, but she doesn't stop. Kicking out and wriggling to get away, she never lets up. Pressing her against the wall, I'm careful not to hurt her, just to keep her as still as I can until she can calm down.

"We're taking you to your sister." Seth has the common sense to bring up Bethany.

"Bethany asked us to save you," I tell her and add, "I told her I'd bring you back."

For the second time she stills, but I don't trust it. "To save me? Bethany?"

The mere mention of Bethany paralyzes her. With a gasp and then harsh intakes, Jennifer trembles and her body wracks with sobs. She tries to fight it, writhing in my embrace in an effort to cover her cries, but she breaks down instead. No longer fighting us, instead she wars with herself.

"It's okay," I say and rock her, but my eyes move to the gun on the floor and Seth's quick to take it.

"Where is she?"

Keeping my voice soft and soothing, I answer her. "We'll take you to her."

"Right now, okay?" Seth adds sympathetically, the way someone speaks to a lost child. I pull back slightly, giving Jennifer more space and taking my time to release her, still ready to pin her down again if I need to so she doesn't attack either of us or hurt herself in the process.

"We're going now; we'll take you right to her." The second I release her fully, her arms wrap around herself. Her sweater, once a light cream color judging by its appearance, is dirtied with brown.

"The note said it was time," she murmurs and looks away from us, rocking back and forth.

"Time for what?" Seth questions and I watch her. Her wide eyes are corrupted with fear and regret.

"It just said it was time and there was the gun. I thought…" she trails off as the tears come back and the poor girl's body wracks with a dry heave. She braces herself with both palms on the ground.

"It's okay," I comfort her, rubbing her back and wondering how Bethany is going to react. How she'll be after seeing her after so long.

"What happened?" I have to ask. It's the first time I'm able to look around and the room is the same as the rest. My stomach drops low when she tells me she doesn't remember everything, but she's been in this room for as long as she can remember since she's left.

"This is where he kept you? Marcus put you in here?"

"I asked him to," she admits and her voice cracks. "I just don't remember why or what happened."

"We'll have a doctor come," I tell her, petting her hair and noting that it's clean. It's been washed recently.

"Did he touch you?" I ask her, needing to know what Marcus did. It's the only thought that comes to mind as I stare at the mattress on the floor.

With her disheveled blonde hair a matted mess down her back, she stares down at herself as if seeing her appearance for the first time. She shakes her head and answers in a tight voice, "He didn't." She's quick to add with a hint of desperation, "I want to see a doctor." "I need to know that I'm better."

"Better?"

Her dull eyes lift to meet mine and a chill threatens to linger on my skin, the room getting colder every second we stay here. "He said he'd help me get better if I helped him."

"What did you have to do?" Seth asks, but I cut her off before she can reply.

"We need to get out of here. Come with us," I urge her, feeling a need to get out as quickly as we can. The longer we stay here, the more we talk in Marcus's territory, the more tangled this problem will get.

I usher her to the door, reaching out for her, but she's quick to jump back, smacking her body against the cinder block wall although she doesn't seem to notice. She yells in the way a child does when they're scared and they need an excuse to keep them from having to walk down a dark hallway. "Wait."

Tears leak from the corners of her eyes and their path leaves a clean line down her mucky skin. "Is Bethany okay?" Her voice cracks and her expression crumbles as she holds herself tighter, but her eyes plead with me, wanting to know that everything's all right. "Tell me Bethany's okay… please?"

chapter twenty-one

Bethany

To know something is one thing. It's a piece of a thought, a fact, a quote. It stays in your head and that's all it will ever be. A nonphysical moment in your mind.

But to *see* it—or to see someone—to feel them, smell them, hear them call out your name… There is no replacement for what it does to you. How it changes you. It's not a piece of knowledge. That's life. Making new memories and sharing them with others. There is no way to feel more alive than to do just that.

Than to hold your crying sister, collapsed in your arms as tightly as you can hold her as she cries your name over and over again.

As I breathe in her hair, the faint smell of dirt clings to her, but so do childhood memories and a desperate need to hold on to her. To never let her go again. In any sense of the word.

"I'm so sorry," she murmurs, her breath warm in the crook of my neck as I hug her tighter to me, shaking my head. As if there's no room for apologies.

I don't want to tell her I'd given up. I don't want to tell her what's happened. I want to go back. Back to the very beginning and fight for her and never stop. If only time and memories worked like that.

"Are you okay?" I barely speak the question before a rustling behind her, toward the doorway to the guest bedroom catches my attention.

Jase is hovering, watching us and I wish he'd come in closer to hear. Jenny needs all the help she can get.

Jase clears his throat and speaks before Jenny can. "The doctor is on his way. She's having some minor--"

"I can't remember," my sister cuts Jase off. My gaze moves from his to hers although she won't look me in the eyes.

"I know I left, I know where I was, but the days… I don't remember, Bethy." Her shoulders hunch as her breathing becomes chaotic. The damage has been done. Whatever that damage may be.

"Hey, hey." Keeping my voice as soft and even as I can, I grip her hand and wait for her eyes to meet mine. "It's okay." The words are whispered, but they're true.

"You're here now. You're safe." Jase's voice is stronger, more confident and I thank the Lord for that.

"You remember me, and that's all that matters," I say without thinking. Instantly, I regret it.

"Mom didn't remember us." Jenny's words are lifeless on her tongue.

Digging my teeth into my lower lip, I watch Jase stalk to the corner of the room and take a seat on the edge of the guest bed. The room is still devoid of anything but simple furniture and curtains. It's exactly the same as it was when I was first here, only weeks ago.

It's only been short of a month, and yet so much has changed in the strongest of ways.

"You'll remember the days, or you won't. But it's because of what happened to you. Not because of you," I speak carefully, keeping in mind that Jenny's scared, and that I need to be strong for her.

Even though I feel like crumbling beside her.

Her eyes turn glossy as she sobs, "I'm so sorry I left. I'm sorry I ever left."

"I'm here," is all I can say. Over and over, I pet her hair to calm her and shush her all the while.

Jase is quiet, but there. If I need him, he's there. Gratitude is something I've never felt to this degree before. My life will be dedicated to making him feel the same.

A shower calms my sister. Maybe it's the comfort of the heat, or maybe it's washing away what she does remember. With both of us in the bathroom, her drying off and getting dressed and me staring at the door so as not to watch, I ask her, "What did Marcus do to you?"

The fear creeps up and then consumes me. Imagination is an awful thing and I wish I could stop it.

"I don't remember everything," she confesses. "I know I feel..." she trails off to swallow thickly and I prepare for the worst. Picking under my nails and steeling my composure, I ready myself with what to say back, putting all the right words in order to make her feel like she's all right now, as if there were ever such a combination.

"I feel healthier. More with it. I haven't had a... a need to."

"To what?"

"To take a hit." Her answer comes out tight and I turn to see her staring at me as strength and sorrowful memories are worn on her expression. "I feel better."

She breaks our gaze, maybe from the shame of what used to be, I don't know. I return to looking ahead as she dresses in a pair of my pajama pants and a t-shirt.

Better.

My bottom lip wobbles and I can't help it. I can't help how tense I feel. *Better.*

Of all the things, that's a word I would never have known would come from her.

"I don't know at what cost. The idea of him scares me, even if I don't remember. I know I changed my mind. I changed the deal."

"Even if you don't remember what someone said or what they did to you, you always remember how they made you feel."

The towel drops to the floor as she blurts out, "Marcus scares me, Bethany. He scares the hell out of me."

"Do you remember anything that he did?" I ask her again, this time beneath my breath. All she gives me is a shake of her head.

"I don't know. I don't think he's going to let me walk away though."

The conviction in my voice is enough to break the fixation of her fear. "Then he'll have to fight me to get to you."

With her glancing at the knob, I open the door and cool air greets us. It feels colder without her answering me. She heads out first and after looking at Jase, still in the chair, his phone in his hand she apologizes to him.

"What did you do?" I ask her as Jase tells her it's all right.

"I shot him," she tells me, and I can't help the huff of a laugh that leaves me, although it's short and doesn't carry much humor.

"What's so funny?" She stares at me as if I'm crazy.

"She shot me when she first saw me too," Jase answers for me.

Jenny doesn't answer; she doesn't respond although she nods in recognition. The bed creaks in protest as she sits on the end of it.

"Can we have a minute?" I ask Jase. "I just need to talk to her," I reason with him, but it's unneeded.

With a single nod, he moves to leave and I'm quick to close the distance between us and hug him from behind. He's so much taller and it's awkward at first, but he turns to face me and I rest my cheek against his chest, breathing in his scent and hugging him tighter. "Thank you," I whisper and feel the warmth of my air mix with his body heat.

There's something about the way he holds me back, his strong hand running soothing circles on my skin while his other arm braces and supports me. I could stand here forever, just holding him. But Jenny needs me.

I kiss his chest and he kisses my hair before we say goodbye.

I don't know what Jenny's seen or what she thinks as she's staring out of the window.

The bed dips as I sit down cross-legged behind her, watching Jenny intently and telling her that I'm here for her.

"I miss Mom," is all she says for the longest time. Other than her constant apologies. Sorry for letting me think she was missing and then that she was dead. She didn't think it would happen like this.

After every apology, I tell her it's all right, because truly it is. I only ever wanted her back. This doesn't happen in real life. You don't get to wish for your loved ones to come back and then they do.

"I'm just happy you're here." This time when I tell her, I reach my hand forward, palm upturned and she takes it.

"Me too," she tries to say, but her words are choked.

I struggle to find something else to talk about. Something to distract her, to make her feel better. Life has slowed down since she's left. Slowed down and sped up, a whirlwind of nothing but Jase Cross for me. And I'm not ready to share that story with her yet. It's too closely tied to me mourning her.

"Did you read the book?" she asks in the quiet air. Nothing else can be heard but the owls from outside the windows and far off in the forest. They're relentless as the sky turns dark and the end of winter makes its exit known.

"I did," I answer her and before I can tell her what I thought, she speaks.

"I hated the ending. I'm sorry, I ripped it out." I almost tell her I know. I almost say the words as she does. "I wanted them to have a happily ever after."

My blood turns to ice as the memory of her sobbing on the floor while she ripped out the pages comes back to me. *It was only a dream*, I remind myself. Only a dream. It didn't really happen. But yet, the question, the question asking her if she did that is right there, waiting to be spoken.

A different one creeps out in its place. There was a line I could never forget. "Why did you cross out 'I hate you for giving me hope?'"

"It wasn't me," she answers me and the chill seeps deeper into my bones. "It was Mom. Mom left it for you. I don't know why she pulled off the cover, but I hated the ending, so I ripped out the pages."

Goosebumps don't appear then vanish, instead they come and stay as I remember the dream. My sister and Mom did always look so alike.

"When she died there was that stack of books. This one had a post-it on it instead of a cover. She left it for you, but I took it."

"Why?" I don't know how I can speak when as we sit here, all I can see is the woman in my terrors.

"She said, 'Only you would understand, Bethany.' It pissed me off," my sister admits. "I took it and wanted to read it. I had to know why… why it was always you."

The eerie feeling that's been coming and going comes over me again, clawing for attention and I can barely stand not to react to it.

Bringing my knees into my chest, I try to avoid it, to shake it off. "What was the ending?" I ask her although I already know. It was some kind of tragedy.

"She died," Jenny says and her voice is choked. "That night, their first and only night, she died because she was really sick and there was no way to save her." My sister's shoulders heave as she sobs.

"It's okay." I try to reassure her that it's only a book, but both of us know it's so much more. It's the last words our mother left us.

"Her mother killed herself. The last ten pages is the mother facing Miss Caroline and telling her she hated her for giving her any hope and making her wait longer to end it all."

"That's awful," I comment.

Jenny sucks in a deep steadying breath and says, "The book is awful. It's all about how the ones you love aren't supposed to die before you."

Chills play down my shoulders, like a gentle touch. "What?"

I hear my mother's voice. *Everyone you love will die before you.*

"That was the point, that the greatest tragedy is watching everyone you love die before you do," my sister tells me with disgust. "I hate the book. I hate that Mom left it. I hate even more that she said you'd understand. You don't, do you?" Her eyes beg me to agree with her and I do.

"I hate it too. Mom wasn't well." I use the excuse, but her words keep coming back to me. She thought my life was a tragedy. She hadn't met Jase though. She couldn't have known my life would take this turn. "She's wrong," I say more to myself than to Jenny, but she nods in agreement.

"Even if they die," she whispers before staring out of the window, "you still got to love them."

"Do you ever feel like she's with us?" I ask my sister, feeling the eyes of someone watching us, but not daring to look to my left, toward the bathroom. No one's there, I already know that. But still, something inside of me doesn't want me to look.

"All the time. I can't sleep because of it."

The cold evaporates, the uneasiness settles. It's only me and Jenny and I'll be strong for her.

"We'll get you on a good sleep schedule. I promise everything will be all right." I would give her all the promises in the world right now to keep her safe. Safe from Marcus and the world beyond these doors. Safe from herself and the memories that haunt her.

"I think I know why," Jenny says offhandedly as if she didn't hear me, still staring out of the window.

"Why what?"

"Why she crossed it out…" She doesn't give me the answer until she realizes I'm staring at her, desperate for a reason. "It didn't belong there. Hope is the best thing you can give someone, second to love. If it wasn't there… the mom wouldn't have killed herself."

It's quiet for a long time. The memories of my sister hurting herself stare me in the face, daring me to mention them and beg Jenny to realize there's so much hope.

I cower at the thoughts, mostly because she squeezes my hand, and I'd like to think it's because she already knows.

"If I had known it was a tragedy, I wouldn't have read it," I admit to her and then question why my mother would think I'd understand this book better than my sister. Why she would leave that book just for me? She wasn't well though so there's no reasoning there.

"That's what you have when there's no hope… tragedy." Jenny's comment doesn't go unheard and I let the statement sit before speaking out loud.

Not really to her, more to myself.

"Hope is the opposite of tragedy. It's a glimmer of light in utter darkness. It isn't a long way of saying goodbye. It's knowing you never have to say it, because whoever's gone, is still with you. Always. That's what hope is."

"They really are. They're always with us," she remarks.

"That's what makes it hard to say goodbye."

"You don't have to say goodbye," she says softly, as if she's considered this a million times over.

"Then how can you ever get over it?" I ask her genuinely, thoughts of her disappearance, of Mom being laid to rest playing in my mind. "How do you get over the loneliness and the way you miss them all the time?"

"Get over it?" she asks with near shock—as if she's never thought of it that way—and I nod without conscious reason.

"How?"

"You can never get over it. Whether you say goodbye or not. Loss isn't something you get over." My sister isn't indignant, or hurt. She's simply matter of fact and the truth of it, I've never dared to consider. She looks me dead in the eyes and asks with nothing but compassion, "So why say goodbye? Why do it, when they're still here and you'll never get over it? Never."

chapter twenty-two

Jase

"I JUST NEED TO KNOW..." BETHANY'S VOICE IS DESPERATE, A SOUND I'M NOT USED TO hearing from her unless she's under me. She hasn't laid down since I told her it's time to go to bed. I don't know how long it's been since she's slept. Instead, she sits wrapped in the covers, staring at the door.

"She's all right." My words intertwine with the sound of the comforter rustling as I lean closer to her and wrap my arm around her waist. I pull her closer to me, making her lean slightly so I can kiss her hair, but I don't move her. She'll move when she's ready. I can wait for that.

I'll wait for her.

"Tell me you'll protect her." She swallows hard after blurting out the words. Her eyes are wide and glossy. "Please. I'll do anything." As she speaks her last word cracks and the only thing I can hear is her thumping heart, running like mad in her chest.

"Of course I will. She's family now."

"Family?" she questions me as if it's a foreign word.

"Bricks, cailín tine. I was serious when I said it, and serious about marrying you... even if you aren't ready."

"You really are bringing bricks and not just to fence me in, huh?" I have to laugh at her playful response. More than that, I love that she smiles. Even if it's gentle and small, it's there.

It falls quickly, though, as her gaze moves behind me to the door.

With one arm resting over her midsection and her other hand cradling her elbow, Jenny looks lost and uncertain as she clears her throat.

"Are you okay?" Bethany's quick to question and rise from the bed.

"Sorry," she answers and almost turns to leave, but Bethany stops her. "Wait. What's wrong?"

I stay where I am. Observing and waiting. Waiting for Bethany to tell me what's needed. Whatever it is, I'll be ready.

"I didn't mean to intrude."

"You weren't," Bethany assures her. I have forever with Bethany, so forever can wait a moment.

"Can... can we talk?" Jenny asks Bethany, although she looks hesitantly at me.

"Of course." If Bethany is aware of Jenny's objection toward me listening, she doesn't show it. Instead she drags the bench at the end of the bed closer to the chair by the dresser and pats it, welcoming her to sit.

"If you want me to go," I speak up, "I can grab you something to eat while you two talk?"

Jenny's gaze flicks between the two of us before she shakes her head. "You've already given me dinner, and a place to sleep... and clothes." She goes on and the baggy long-sleeve shirt pools around her thin wrist. "I don't need anything else."

As I stand to go the bathroom and busy myself so they have some semblance of privacy, Jenny adds, "Thank you." A tight smile and a nod is given to Jenny, but Bethany reaches for my hand and squeezes it before I can walk away.

I nearly think she wants me to stay, but she releases me with a *thank you*.

My hand is still warm from her touch when I turn on the faucet. Even over the sound of the water splashing in the sink, I can hear Jenny asks her questions about me.

Does she trust me?

What is she doing with me?

And finally, does she love me?

All of which are answered with many words, but the first of them each time is yes.

"You led him to me," Bethany informs her sister and I remember the first time I saw her. Across the bar, my fiery girl, picking a fight with whoever she could because she was hurting and needed help. Fighting is all either of us knew.

I scrub my face, feeling the roughness along my jaw and listen intently even though I hadn't planned on eavesdropping.

"The only clues you gave me before you left were The Red Room and the Cross brothers. So I went there, searching for you."

Opening the cabinet to get my razor and shaving cream, I grab the bottle of pills and stare at them until they fall from my hand into the bottom of the trashcan beneath the sink. The inhale I take is deep and cathartic, but it doesn't stop the twisted hurt that will always come when I think about that time in my life. I don't need the constant reminder though.

Gripping my razor, I use the back of my hand to close the cabinet door. Jenny's reflection is clear in the mirror. A disturbed look plays on her face when she tells Bethany, "Marcus told me to. He said to make sure you heard me say it."

Staring down at the rippling water, I listen to her explain that she's sorry. She's sorry for everything.

I don't shave. I don't move, other than bracing one hand on each side of the sink and staring down, wondering what Marcus planned, how he thought ahead and what he thought would happen.

It's not until Jenny says good night and I feel Bethany's hand on my back that I bring myself to look at Bethany in the mirror.

"You okay?" she whispers against my back and I almost tell her that I'm fine. Instead I answer, "I hate hearing his name."

"Marcus?" she asks and I nod.

"Seth will find him," she answers me and plants a small kiss on my back through my white t-shirt when I turn off the faucet.

She watches me as I dry my face and thanks me for giving her sister space.

The smile on my lips falters until she reaches out, grabbing my hand and kissing it.

"Isn't that what a man is supposed to do?" I toy with her. "Kneel and kiss the back of a lady's hand."

A glimmer of surprise filters in her eyes as she says, "I thought it's what ladies did to the knights? I thought they kissed the back of their hands when they saved them."

Even though I'm still, she moves, pushing herself between me and the sink and reaching up to kiss me. It's always the same with her. The first is quick and teasing and then she gives me what I need, deep and slow. As I groan into her mouth, she lets out a soft sigh of affection and balls my shirt in her fist, bringing me closer to her.

"So needy," I tell her, my voice low and playful before tugging her bottom lip between my teeth and then letting her go.

I move my hands from her hips to her ass and pick her up, loving the gasp and then the squeal she gives me when I toss her on our bed.

The air heats as I kick off my pants and watch her right herself on the bed, her gaze wandering down my body until I climb on the bed to join her.

With both of her hands in my hair and mine bracing me on the bed as I lean over her, forcing her to lie down, she kisses me with soft, quick kisses all over my lips. I smile as she does it, short pecks moving in a clockwise motion.

I lift my head to look down at her, to joke about what she's done. I stop myself though; there's nothing but seriousness in her gaze.

"Thank you for saving me, Jase."

"You saved me too, you know," I tell her as I pull my shirt off, knowing damn well she has.

She stares at me for an awkward moment and then looks down with a huff. "I don't know what to say."

Confusion takes over. "What do you mean?"

"I don't know what would mean more right now. That I love you. Or that I don't love you."

The short huff of a laugh leaves me with relief. *Thank fuck.*

"Let's stick with I love you from now on."

"Then I love you, Jase Cross. I love you with everything in me."

chapter twenty-three

Bethany

GOOD THINGS DON'T COME OFTEN. NOT FOR ME. NOT FOR MOST PEOPLE. I'M AWARE OF that. I get it. Life isn't meant to be a garden of roses.

I'm used to the thorns. I would even say I like them. They're predictable, when nothing else is.

The sound of the printer in Jase's office that isn't an office makes me jump. It's louder than I anticipated, and I anxiously look to the doorway.

He should be here soon.

Jenny's tucked away in her room. Some days are better than others, but overall she's better. She's better than she has been in a very long time. If only she could remember what happened over the past few months, I think she'd be like my old sister again. Or at least who that girl was supposed to be.

Before the paper can fall to the tray, I catch it and lift it up to look at the certificate. It's so simple and not as expensive as I thought it would be.

It's merely a sheet of paper with ink on it. But then again so are books, and they can be wielded like weapons. They can destroy people; they can give them hope too.

"There you are." Jase's deep voice greets me with a sensual need. I can already feel his warmth before he wraps his arms around my waist and pulls me into his chest. The paper clings to my front as I keep it from his prying eyes.

"What are you hiding from me?" he questions.

"No hiding anything anymore. Isn't that the deal?" I remind him, peeking around to not just see him, but to steal a quick kiss as well. I love it when he smirks at me.

With a lift of his chin he tells me, "Then show it."

I do so willingly, listening to the paper crinkle and watching his dark eyes as he reads each line.

"Marriage certificate?" It's a sin that he looks so handsome, even when he's confused.

"It's a certificate to get a marriage certificate. Like a gift card. I didn't know you could get one of these. You have to be there for it to actually be done and all," I explain to him. I thought this would be the best way to tell him that I want to marry him.

As he steps back, snagging the paper from me and then looking between it and me, nerves flow through every part of me.

"My answer is yes." In my mind, when I decided I'd do this, I said it confidently, playfully even, but the way the words came out now was hurried and with an anxiousness to hear his response.

Which he still hasn't given me.

"At least I answered you quickly," I tell him and pretend like my hands aren't trembling.

"You want to do this?" he asks me, his shoulders squared as he lowers the paper to the leather sofa and closes the space between us.

Reaching up to adjust the collar of his pressed white shirt, I tell him easily, as if he's said yes, "I don't want a big wedding."

"Are you proposing to me?" he finally says with a grin and the playfulness and the charm are obvious. This is the man I love.

Nodding, I fight back the prick at the back of my eyes and tell him, "I am. Are you saying yes?"

"I already asked you, though. You don't get to ask me now." He walks circles around me, making me spin slowly.

"You aren't exactly good at it, so I figured I should give it a shot." I'm just as playful with him as he is me, nipping his bottom lip and then kissing him. He deepens it, stopping where he is and splaying his hands against my lower back and shoulder.

When he breaks the kiss, he stares down at me. "Why?" he asks me, toying with me and my emotions instead of just ending it quickly.

"You have no mercy," I joke with him. "Are you not saying yes?" I can't even voice the word no right now.

He only stares down at me, waiting for a response with a smug look on his face.

"When I'm sad, I want you to be there because then I feel less sad. When I'm happy, I want you there because I want you happy with me. I just want you there... and I want to be there for you. If you'll let me." Tears form but I blink them away.

"I'll let you," he whispers ruggedly as he lowers his lips to the dip in my throat, giving me a chance to breathe easy. And to breathe him in.

"That's not how you say 'yes,' Jase. Or how you make a girl feel secure," I tease him although my words are still a bit unsteady. He pulls back to look at me, both of his hands still on me as I add, "When she prints out a marriage certificate, you're supposed to say yes."

"What if I gave her something else instead?" he asks, reaching into his pocket. "What if it was a tit for tat and I asked her a question to answer her question." My eyes turn watery as he gets down on his knee and pulls out a small black velvet box.

"I have something for you."

I can barely speak. "Jase."

"I love the way you say my name," he tells me, holding the box in one hand and my left hand in his other.

"I realized when I asked you to marry me, I probably should have done it better. I thought you'd be more willing to say 'yes' if there was something in it for you. I didn't think about a ring or feel like a ring would be enough."

Tears are warm as they fall down my face and I sniffle before telling Jase, "You are enough, Jase. It baffles me how you don't see that." I have to sniffle again before I can tell him that I'll remind him of it every day for as long as he lives if that's what it takes.

"Will you marry me?" he finally asks, opening the box. I don't have time to even look at what's inside. I need to touch him more than look at his surprise. I need to hold him and for him to hold me.

"I love you, Jase." I breathe against his shoulder, letting my tears fall to the thin white fabric.

"Say yes, first," he answers in what should be a playful voice, but feels nervous.

"A million times yes. It's always been yes."

Sometimes you meet someone, although maybe *meet* isn't quite the right word. You don't even have to say hello for this to happen. You simply pass by them and everything in your world changes forever. Chills flow from where you imagine he'd kiss you in the crook of your neck, moving all the way down with only a single glance.

I know you know what I'm referring to. The moment when something inside of you ignites to life, recognizing the other half that's been gone for far too long.

It burns hot, destroying any hope that it's only a coincidence, and that life will go back to what it was. These moments are never forgotten.

That's only with a single glance.

I can tell you what a single touch will do. It will consume you and everything you thought you knew.

I felt all of this with Jase Cross, with every flicker of the flames that roared inside of me. I knew he'd be my downfall, and I was determined to be his just the same.

He deserves as much. To have every brick in his guarded walls brought to the ground and be left to turn into something more. I want nothing between us. Nothing but us. Even if that means this world will collapse around us and become a chaos I never imagined.

So long as I'm with him, so long as his touch is within reach, I would give everything else up.

That's the part that scared me in that first moment.

Somewhere deep inside of me I knew I would be his.

And I'll do it again and again. In this life and the next.

chapter twenty-four

Jase

You're welcome for your gift.
It was mine to give all along.

Marcus's handwriting stares back at me until I crumple the small parchment into my hand.

He's had a hand in the details, but he's slipping. More of his intention is showing. It's contradictory and changes on a whim, but he's falling. I can feel it.

One small token won't save him from the consequences of his actions. Our enemies will fall one by one, as they should. Their names will be carved in stone long before I allow anyone I love to meet the same fate.

He's the one who chose to be our enemy. A gift won't change that.

Balling up the note, I think back on everything that's happened. Not just to me, but also to my brothers and to Sebastian. It all comes down to the simple fact that we found irresistible attractions. And all the while, Marcus knew. He used them against us. Each and every one of us.

Sometimes when people are in pain they push love away. Tossing the paper into the metal trashcan outside the old brick building, I think of Sebastian and how much he tried to resist.

Pain makes people go to extremes they know are wrong. Carter is proof of that. Sometimes all life will give you is only a tragedy, but if you have someone to love, someone to hold on to, like Daniel and Addison had each other, then life will go on.

We are only men. Not invincible heroes.

And Marcus is just the same.

He's in pain like all of us. In fear like we've all been in. The answer to finding him, to bringing him to his knees lies in the one thing we've given into that he hasn't.

The girl Officer Walsh can't get over. The girl who ties him and Marcus together...

That girl will make Marcus fall. I know she will.

Seth will find her. *He must.*

"What's wrong?" Bethany's voice carries through the warmth of the April sunshine as her heels click on the sidewalk. Slipping her hand into the pocket of her jacket, she looks up at me and I can't resist brushing the hair from her face to cup her chin in my hand.

Before I can lean down to kiss her, she grips my dress shirt at the buttons, fisting the fabric in her hands and bringing her lips to mine. Desire ignites and the burn from it diminishes any other thought, any other need.

That's how it happens. It's how love conquers. Boldly, without fear, and with a ruling flame that nothing can tame.

Her lips soften the second they meet mine. Her body presses against my own as well. With a hand on the small dip at her waist I pull her closer to me, leaving nothing between us.

It's only when she pulls back that I even dare to breathe.

"I want to kiss you like that forever," she whispers against my lips with her eyes still closed. When they open, she peeks up at me through her lashes and adds, "I want to take my kisses from you every damn day."

A low groan of approval rumbles up my chest as she twines her fingers through mine.

"Now tell me what's wrong."

"A little demanding, aren't you, cailín tine?" A pang of nervousness worms its way between us. Before it can do any damage, I tell her, "I'm considering Marcus's next move." I resist telling her the second piece, but only for a split second. With her lips parted to answer me, I cut her off with, "And ours."

She doesn't let go of my hands, but she takes a half step back, letting her head nod. Intensity, curiosity, even fear swirl in her gaze. All the while, I wait for what she'll say, what she'll do.

"If you need me I'm here," she finally answers.

"All I need is for you to follow me," I tell her and lower my lips to hers. Nipping her bottom lip, the small bit of tension wanes. She may not be involved in what I do, but she'll stay with me.

I know she will. Because she loves me and she knows how deeply I love her.

Moving my hand around her waist, I'll make sure she never forgets, never questions what I feel for her.

She won't go a day without knowing. Her head rests against my arm as we walk, her one hand holding mine, the other on top of our clasped hands.

"It's all going to be all right," she tells me, although she stares ahead, noting the *Rare Books* sign in the window which causes her brow to furrow.

The smell of old books is unique, and it engulfs us as we walk deeper into the aisle. The full shelves of worn and previously read books make rows, but the one shelf at the very back is the one she needs to see.

"What are we doing here?" she questions and lifts her gaze to mine, but I only squeeze her hand in response.

"Jase," Bethany pushes for more, practically hissing my name although her steps have picked up with a giddiness she can't hide, making me chuckle at her impatience.

When I come to a stop in front of the shelves, she brushes against me and steps forward. I watch her reaction to seeing the wall of thin cream pages.

"They don't have covers?" she whispers and reaches out, her fingers trailing down the fronts of them.

I watch as she swallows, her throat tensing and her lips turning down.

"These are the books with no covers. No titles. They're only stories."

Her eyes glaze over, as I'm sure the Coverless Book comes back to her, a gift from her mother and so much more. We may forget words or details, but the way we feel never leaves our memories. I know that book scarred her in a way I can't imagine although I'm not sure why.

"I wanted to get you another one. A different story to take its place."

"We drove hours and hours to get a book?" she questions silently, her eyes beseeching me to explain why.

"This is the only place I found on the East Coast that carried unknown books-"

"I don't want to read another tragedy," she says and cuts me off. "I don't want to risk it."

"You're going to want to though, cailín tine."

A second passes and I swear I can hear her heart beating, waiting in limbo for more.

"These books all came from one person's home years ago. She collected stories that made her feel loved."

Bethany turns her attention back to the books, back to the stories I want her to read.

"I brought you here because they call this the aisle of hope."

chapter twenty-five

Seth

With her legs crossed like that, her red skirt rides up higher. It draws my eye and as she clears her throat, noticing my wandering gaze, I let the smirk appear on my lips before carelessly covering it with my hand.

It's been too long since I've been this close to her, face to face. Too many years since she's sought me out.

My stubble is rough beneath my fingertips; it'll leave small scratches against her soft skin when I ravage her with the hunger I've had for so long.

"Did you hear what I said?" Laura asks. When she got into my car with Bethany, I could feel the waves of apprehension hidden in the silence, the lust that roared back to life when Bethany left us. And we made a deal.

"You said you wanted an exchange. You want to change the details of our deal."

Her doe eyes beg me to consider, and they hold a vulnerability that her tense curves fail to deliver. She grips both arms of the chair across from me as her chest rises and falls with a quickened pace. She can't hide the fear of coming back to this life. *Of coming back to me.*

As her bottom lip slips between her teeth, I note that she can't hide the desire either.

"I've wanted this for too long to consider your proposal," I tell her, spreading my legs wider and leaning forward in my office chair in the back room of the bar. My elbows rest on my knees as I lean closer to her, only inches away as I whisper, "You know what I want."

"I can give you something you want more," she speaks clearly, although her last words waver when her gaze drifts to my lips.

Lies. There's nothing I want more.

I would have told her that and meant it with every bone in my body, but then she tells me, "I can give you Marcus."

about the author

Thank you so much for reading my romances. I'm just a stay at home mom and avid reader turned author and I couldn't be happier.

I hope you love my books as much as I do!

More by Willow Winters
www.willowwinterswrites.com/books

books by
WILLOW WINTERS

www.willowwinterswrites.com/books

Merciless World Standalone Novels:
Possessive
A Kiss to Tell

Start Carter & Aria's saga with Merciless, today for 99c!
Merciless
Heartless
Breathless
Endless

Jase & Bethany - Irresistible Attraction Trilogy
A Single Glance
A Single Kiss
A Single Touch

Seth & Laura - Hard to Love Series
Hard to Love
Desperate to Touch
Tempted to Kiss
Easy to Fall

Standalone Novels:
It's Our Secret
Broken
Forget Me Not

Sins and Secrets Duets:
Imperfect (Imperfect Duet book 1)
Unforgiven (Imperfect Duet book 2)

Damaged (Damaged Duet book 1)
Scarred (Damaged Duet book 2)

Willow Winters
Standalone Novels:

Tell Me to Stay
Second Chance
Knocking Boots
Promise Me
Burned Promises
Forsaken, cowritten with B. B. Hamel

Collections
Don't Let Go
Deepen The Kiss
Kisses and Wishes (A Holiday Collection)

Valetti Crime Family Series:
Dirty Dom
His Hostage
Rough Touch
Cuffed Kiss
Bad Boy

**Highest Bidder Series,
cowritten with Lauren Landish:**
Bought
Sold
Owned
Given

**Bad Boy Standalones,
cowritten with Lauren Landish:**
Inked
Tempted
Mr. CEO

Happy reading and best wishes,
W Winters xx

king of wall street

LOUISE BAY

chapter one

Harper

TEN. WHOLE. MINUTES. IT DIDN'T SOUND LIKE A LONG TIME, BUT AS I SAT ACROSS FROM MAX King, the so-called King of Wall Street, while he silently read through the first draft of a report I'd produced on the textile industry in Bangladesh, it felt like a lifetime.

Resisting the urge to revert to my fourteen-year-old self and ask him what he was thinking, I glanced around, trying to find something else to fixate on.

Max's office suited him perfectly—the A/C was set to the average temperature of an igloo; the walls, ceilings, and floors were all blinding white, adding to the arctic ambience. His desk was glass and chrome, and the New York sun bled through the opaque blinds, trying without success to thaw the frost that penetrated the room. I hated it. Every time I entered the place I had the urge to flash my bra or graffiti the walls in bright red lipstick. It was the place fun came to die.

Max's sigh pulled my attention back to his long index finger that he trailed down the page of my research. He shook his head. My stomach somersaulted. I knew impressing him would be an impossible task but that didn't mean I hadn't secretly hoped I'd nailed it. I'd worked so hard on this report, my first research for *the* Max King. I'd barely slept, working double so I didn't neglect my other duties in the office. I'd printed off and examined everything that had been written on the industry in the last decade. I'd pored over the statistics, trying to find patterns and draw conclusions. And I'd scoured the King & Associates archives trying to find any historical research that we'd produced so we could explain any inconsistencies. I'd covered every base, hadn't I? When I'd printed it out earlier that morning, long before anyone else had arrived, I'd been happy—proud even. I'd done a good job.

"You spoke to Marvin about the latest data?" he asked.

I nodded, though he didn't look up, so I said, "Yes. All the graphs are based on the latest figures." Did they look wrong? Had he expected something else?

I just wanted him to say, "Good job."

I'd been desperate to work for Max King since before I enrolled at business school. He was the power behind the throne of many of the Wall Street success stories in the last few years. King & Associates provided investment banks with critical research that helped their investment decisions. I liked the idea that there were a ton of flashy suits from investment banks shouting about how rich they were and the man who had made it happen was happy to go quietly about his business, just being amazing at what he did. Understated, determined, supremely successful—he was everything I wanted to be. When I got the offer during my final semester to be a junior researcher at King & Associates, I was thrilled, but I also felt an odd sense that the universe was simply unravelling how it should, as though it was simply the next step in my destiny.

Destiny could kiss my ass. My first six weeks in my new position had been nothing I'd expected. I'd assumed I'd be surrounded by ambitious, intelligent, well-dressed twenty and thirty somethings and I'd been right about that. And the clients we worked for—almost every investment bank in Manhattan—were phenomenal and lived up to every expectation I'd had. Max King, however, had turned out to be a huge letdown. The fact was, despite being crazy smart, respected by everyone on Wall Street, and looking as if he should have been on a poster on teenage me's bedroom wall, he was . . .

Cold.

Blunt.

Uncompromising.

A total asshole.

He was as handsome in real life as he was in his picture on the cover of Forbes or any of the other publicity shots I'd clicked through as I stalked him during my MBA at Berkeley. One morning, I'd arrived super early, seen him in his running gear—sweaty, panting, Lycra clad. Thighs so strong they looked as if they might be made of marble. Broad shoulders; a strong Roman nose; dark-brown, glossy hair—the kind wasted on a man—and a year-round tan that screamed, *I vacation four times a year.* In the office he wore custom suits. Handmade suits fell a particular way on the shoulders that I recognized from the few meetings I'd had with my father. His face and body lived up to every expectation I'd had. Working with him, not so much.

I hadn't expected him to be such a tyrant.

Each morning, as he swooped through the throng of open-plan desks to his office, he never so much as greeted any of us with a good morning. He regularly yelled into his phone so loud he could be heard from the elevator lobby. And last Tuesday? When I'd passed him in the office and smiled at him, the veins in his neck began to bulge and he looked as if he was going to reach out and choke me.

I smoothed my palms down the fabric of my Zara skirt. Perhaps I irritated him because I wasn't as sleek as the other women in the office. I didn't dress in the regulation Prada. Did I look as though I didn't care? I just couldn't afford anything better at the moment.

As the most junior member of the team, I was at the bottom of the pecking order. Which meant I knew Mr. King's sandwich order, how to untangle the photocopier, and I had every courier company on speed dial. But that was to be expected and I was just happy because I got to work with the guy I'd looked up to and admired for years.

And here he was, shaking his head and wielding a pen with the reddest ink I'd ever seen. With each circle, crisscross, and exaggerated question mark he made, I seemed to shrink.

"Where are your references?" he asked without looking up.

References? When I looked at the other reports we produced, they never had the sources in the report. "I have them back at my desk—"

"Did you speak to Donny?"

"I'm waiting to hear back from him." He looked up and I tried not to wince. I'd put in two calls to Max's contact at the World Trade Organization, but I couldn't *make* the guy talk to me.

He shook his head and grabbed his phone and dialed. "Hey, hotshot," he said. "I need to understand the position on Everything But Arms. I heard your guys are putting pressure on the EU?" Max didn't put the phone on speaker, so I watched as he scribbled notes over my paper. "It would really help for this thing I'm doing about Bangladesh." Max grinned, looked up briefly, caught my eye, and looked away as if just the sight of me irritated him. *Great.*

Max hung up.

"I put in two calls—"

"Results, not effort, get rewarded," he said in a clipped tone.

So he gave no credit for trying? What could I have done other than turn up at the guy's place of business? I wasn't Max King. Why would someone at the WTO take a call from a barely paid researcher?

Jesus, couldn't he give a girl a break?

Before I had a chance to respond, his cell vibrated on his desk.

"Amanda?" he barked into the phone. Jesus. This was a small office, so I knew Amanda didn't work at King & Associates. I got an odd sense of satisfaction he wasn't just sharp with me. I didn't see him interact much with others, but somehow his attitude toward me felt personal. But it sounded as if Amanda got the same brusque treatment I did. "We're not having this discussion again. I said no." Girlfriend? Page Six had never had any reports of Max dating. But he had to be. A man built like that, asshole or not, wasn't going without. It sounded as though Amanda had the honor of putting up with him outside office hours.

Hanging up, he slung his phone against the desk, watching as it skidded across the glass and came to rest against his laptop. Continuing to read, he rubbed his long, tan fingers over his forehead as if Amanda had given him a headache. I didn't think my report was helping much.

"Typos are not acceptable, Ms. Jayne. There's no excuse for being anything less than exceptional when it comes to something that *only* requires effort." He closed my report, sat back in his chair, and fixed his stare on me. "Attention to detail doesn't require ingenuity, creativity, or lateral thinking. If you can't get the basics right, why should I trust you with anything more complicated?"

Typos? I'd read through that report a thousand times.

He steepled his fingers in front of him. "Revise in accordance with my notes and don't bring it back to me until it's typo free. I'll fine you for every mistake I find."

Fine me? I wanted to fire back that if I could fine him every time he was a penis, I'd retire inside of three months. Asshole.

Slowly, I reached for my report, wondering if he had anything else to add, any words of encouragement or thanks.

But no. I took the stack of papers and headed to the door.

"Oh, and Ms. Jayne?"

This is it. He's going to leave me some morsel of dignity. I turned to him, holding my breath.

"Pastrami on rye, no pickle."

I stood glued to the spot, breathing through the sucker punch to the gut.

What. A. Douche.

"For my lunch," he added, clearly not understanding why I hadn't left already.

I nodded and opened the door. If I didn't leave right now, I might just throw myself across his desk and pull out all his perfect hair.

As I closed the door, Donna, Max's assistant, asked, "How did it go?"

I rolled my eyes. "I don't know how you do it, working for him. He's so . . ." I started to flick through the report, looking for the typos he'd referred to.

Donna rolled her chair away from her desk and stood. "His bark is worse than his bite. Are you off to the deli?"

"Yeah. Pastrami today."

Donna pulled on her jacket. "I'll walk with you. I need a break." She grabbed her wallet and we made our way out into downtown New York. Of course, Max didn't like any of the sandwich shops near the office. Instead we had to head five blocks northeast to

Joey's Café. At least it was sunny, and too early in the year for the humidity to make a trip to the deli feel like a midday hike along the streets of Calcutta.

"Hey, Donna. Hey, Harper," Joey, the owner, called as we entered through the glass door. The deli was exactly the opposite of the type of place where I'd expect Max to order his lunch. It was very clearly a family-owned place that hadn't seen a remodeling since the Beatles were together. In here there was nothing of the slick, modern, ruthless persona that made up Max King.

"How's the bossman?" Joey asked.

"Oh, you know," Donna said. "Working too hard, as usual. What was his order, Harper?"

"Pastrami on rye. Extra pickle." Nothing like passive-aggressive revenge.

Joey raised his eyebrows. "Extra pickle?" Jesus, of course Joey knew Max's preferences.

"Okay." I winced. "No pickle."

Donna elbowed me. "And I'll have a turkey salad on sourdough," she said, then turned to me. "Let's eat in and we can talk."

"Make that two," I said to Joey.

The deli had a few tables, all with mismatched chairs. Most customers took their orders to go, but today I was grateful for a few extra minutes out of the office. I followed Donna as she led us to one of the back tables.

"Extra pickle?" she asked, grinning.

"I know." I sighed. "That was childish. I'm sorry. I just wish he wasn't such a . . ."

"Tell me what happened."

I gave her the rundown on our meeting—his irritation that I hadn't spoken to his contact at the WTO, the lecture about typos, his lack of appreciation for any of my hard work.

"Tell Max the Yankees deserved all they got this weekend," Joey said as he placed our order in front of us, sliding two cans of soda onto the melamine surface, even though we'd not ordered any drinks. Did Joey talk baseball with Max? Had they even met?

"I'll tell him," Donna said, smiling, "but he might move his business elsewhere if I do. You know how touchy he is when the Mets do well."

"He's going to have to get used to it this season. And I'm not worried about losing him. He's been coming here for over a decade."

Over a decade?

"You know what he'd say to that?" Donna asked, unwrapping the waxed-paper parcel in front of her.

"Yeah, yeah, never take your customers for granted." Joey headed back behind the counter. "You know what always shuts him up?" he asked over his shoulder.

Donna laughed. "When you tell him to come back after his business has lasted three generations and is still going?"

Joey pointed at Donna. "You got it."

"So Max has been coming here a long time, huh?" I asked as Joey turned back to the counter to tend to the line of people that had built up since we'd arrived.

"Since I've been working for him. And that's nearly seven years."

"A creature of habit. I get that." There wasn't much spontaneous about Max from what I'd seen.

Donna cocked her head. "More a huge sense of loyalty. As this area built up and lunch places opened up on every corner, Joey's business took a bit of a hit. Max has never gone anywhere else. He's even brought clients here."

Donna's description jarred with the cold egomaniac I encountered in the office. I bit into my sandwich.

"He can be challenging and demanding and a pain in the ass, but that's a big part of what's made him successful."

I wanted to be successful but still a decent human being. Was I naïve to think that was possible on Wall Street?

Donna pressed the top layer of bread down onto the turkey with her fingertips, pushing the layers together. "He's not as bad as you think he is. I mean, if he'd said your report was good to go, what would you have learned?" She picked up her sandwich. "You can't expect to get it all right your first time. And the stuff about the typos—was he wrong?" She took a bite, and waited for me to answer.

"No." I bit the inside of my lip. "But you have to admit, his delivery sucks." I pulled out a piece of my turkey from under the sourdough and put it in my mouth. I'd worked so hard; I'd expected some kind of recognition for that.

"Sometimes. Until you've proved yourself. But once you have, he'll back you completely. He gave me this job knowing I was a single mother, and he's made sure I've never missed a game, event, or PTA meeting." She cracked open a can of soda. "When my daughter got chicken pox just after I started working here, I came into the office anyway. I've never seen him so mad. When he spotted me, he marched me out of the building and sent me home. I mean, my mom was looking after her, she was fine, but he insisted I stay home until she was back in school."

I swallowed. That didn't sound like the Max I knew.

"He's a really good guy. He's just focused and driven. And he takes his responsibility to his employees seriously—especially if they have potential."

"I don't see him taking his responsibility to not be a condescending asshole very seriously."

Donna chuckled. "You're there to learn, to get better. And he's going to teach you, but just saying you did a good job isn't going to help you."

I grabbed a napkin from the old-fashioned dispenser at the edge of the table and wiped the corner of my mouth. How had today helped me other than wrecking my confidence completely?

"If you had known how today's meeting would play out, what would you have done differently?" Donna asked.

I shrugged. I'd done good work, but he'd refused to acknowledge it.

"Come on. You can't tell me you'd do things exactly the same."

"Okay, no. I would have printed out the sources and brought them into the meeting."

Donna nodded. "Good. What else?" She took another bite of her sandwich.

"I would have probably tried Max's contact at the WTO a few more times—maybe emailed him. I could have tried harder to pin him down. And I could have sent the whole thing to proofreading." We had an overnight service, but because I'd worked late on it, I'd missed the deadline to send it. I should have made sure it was ready in time.

I glanced up from picking apart my sandwich. "I'm not saying I didn't learn anything. I just thought he'd be nicer. I've wanted to work with him a long time. I just didn't imagine I'd fantasize about punching him in the face quite so often."

Donna laughed. "That, Harper, is what having a boss means."

Okay, I could accept that Max was nice to Donna, and Joey, by the looks of things. But he wasn't nice to me. Which only made everything worse. What had I ever done to him? Was I being singled out for special treatment? Yes, my report could be improved, but despite what Donna said, I hadn't deserved the reaction I got. He could have thrown me a bone.

Now that my expectations of working with Max were well and truly shattered, I had to concentrate on getting what I could from the experience and moving on. I'd go through my report and make it perfect. I'd take everything I could from working for King & Associates, make a ton of contacts, and then after two years I'd be well placed to set up on my own, or go and work directly for a bank.

<hr />

How I'd talked my best friend, Grace, into moving me into my new apartment, I had no idea. Growing up on Park Avenue, she wasn't raised for manual labor.

"What's in here, a dead body?" she asked, a sheen of sweat on her forehead catching the light in the elevator.

"Yeah, my last best friend." I tipped my head toward the old pine blanket box at our feet and the last thing in the truck. "There's room for another." I laughed.

"There'd better be wine in the refrigerator." Grace fanned her face. "I'm not used to being this physical with my clothes on."

"You see, then you should be grateful. I'm expanding your horizons," I replied with a grin. "Showing you how us ordinary gals live."

I'd been staying with Grace since I got to New York from Berkeley almost three months ago. She'd been fantastically understanding when my mother shipped all my things to her apartment in Brooklyn, but now that I was making her help me move everything into my new place, her patience was running out. "And I'm too poor for a refrigerator. And wine." The rent on my studio was horrific. But it was in Manhattan and that was all I cared about. I wasn't about to be a New Yorker who lived in Brooklyn. I wanted to milk this experience for everything it was worth, so I'd sacrificed space for location—a small Victorian building on the corner of Rivington and Clinton in Lower Manhattan. The buildings on either side were covered with graffiti, but this place had been recently refurbished and I'd been assured it was full of young professionals, being so close to Wall Street. Professional what? Hitmen?

"It's going to be . . . cozy," Grace said. "Are you sure you don't want me to ask about the one bedroom across the hall from me?"

My apartment at Berkeley had been at least twice the size of my new place. Grace's place in Brooklyn was a palace in comparison, but I was okay with small. "I'm sure. It's all part of the New York experience, isn't it?"

"So are roaches, but you don't have to seek them out. The idea is to avoid them." Grace was the person who tried to make everyone else's lives a little bit better, and that was one of the reasons I loved her.

"Yeah, but I want to be in the center of things. Besides, there's a gym in the basement, so I'm saving money there. And on the commute. I can walk to work from here. Hell, I can practically see the office from my bedroom window."

"I thought you hated work. Wouldn't it be better to be further away?" she asked as the elevator pinged open at my floor.

I reached for the bottom of the wooden box. "I don't hate work. I hate my boss."

"The hot one?" Grace asked.

"Can you pick up your end?" I asked. I didn't want to be reminded about my boss's score on the hot-o-meter. I stuck out my leg to try to stop the closing elevator doors. "Crap. Have you got it?" We lurched forward, turning left toward my apartment door.

"We need a man for this shit," Grace said as I struggled with my keys.

"We need men for sex and foot rubs," I replied. "We can carry our own furniture."

"In the future, *you* can carry *your* furniture. I'll find a man."

I opened the door and we slid the box into the living space. "Just leave it here until I decide whether or not it should go at the end of the bed."

"Where's that wine you promised me?" Grace pushed past me and collapsed on my small two-seater couch.

Despite my protestations, the only things my refrigerator *did* contain were two bottles of wine and a slab of parmesan cheese.

"What were you saying about your hot boss? I thought you'd changed religion to the Church of King while you were at Berkeley. What's changed?"

I handed Grace a glass of wine, sat down, and kicked off my sneakers. I didn't want to think about Max or the way he made me feel so inadequate, so out of place and uncomfortable. "I think I need to update my work wardrobe." The more I thought about what I'd worn for my meeting with Max, the more I realized I must stick out like a sore thumb against all the Max Mara and Prada of Wall Street.

"You look fine. You're always super polished. Are you trying to impress your hot boss?"

I rolled my eyes. "That would be impossible. He's the most arrogant man you'll ever meet. Nothing's ever good enough."

My conversation with Donna at lunch yesterday had temporarily dampened my fury at Max, but it was back in full swing today. He might be the best at what he did and look so hot you'd get a tan if you stood too close, but that didn't excuse his assholyness. But I wasn't about to let him beat me. I hated him. Determined to show him he had me wrong, I'd brought home the Bangladesh report to work on over the weekend. A lot of the comments he'd made indicated he knew much more about the textile industry in Bangladesh than I did, even after my research. Had this whole project just been a test? Whether it was or not, I was going to spend the rest of the weekend making my work the best thing he'd ever seen.

"Nothing's ever good enough?" Grace asked. "Sounds familiar."

"I might be a bit of a perfectionist, but I've got nothing on this guy. Believe me. I worked my heart out on a piece of work he gave me, and then he just ripped it to shreds. He had nothing good to say about it at all."

"Why are you letting it bother you? Shrug it off."

Why *wouldn't* I let it bother me? I wanted to be good at my job. I wanted Max to see I was good at my job.

"But I worked really hard on it and it was a good piece of work. He's an asshole."

"So? If he's a total wanker then why does his opinion count for anything?" Grace had lived in the US since she was five, but she still retained some key Britishisms from her family. Her use of wanker was one of my favorites. Especially as it suited Max King perfectly.

"I'm not saying it matters. Just that I'm pissed about it." Except that it did matter, however much I denied it.

"What did you expect? A man that rich and good looking is bound to have a downside." She shrugged and took a sip of wine. "You can't let it affect you so much. Your expectations of men are way too high. You're going to spend your whole life disappointed."

My cell began to ring. "Speaking of being disappointed." I showed the screen to Grace. It was my father's lawyer.

"Harper speaking," I answered.

"Ms. Jayne. It's Kenneth Bray." Why was he calling me at the weekend?

"Yes, Mr. Bray. How can I help?" I rolled my eyes at Grace.

Apparently my father had set me up a trust fund. The letters I'd received about it were stuffed into the chest that we'd just lugged up from the truck. I hadn't answered any of them. I didn't want my father's money. I started accepting his money in college. I figured he owed me that much but after a year, I took a job and stopped cashing his checks. I couldn't accept money from a stranger, even if he was genetically related to me.

"I want to arrange for you to come into the office so I can talk you through the details of the money your father has set aside for you."

"I appreciate your persistence, but I'm not interested in my father's money." All I'd ever wanted was a guy who showed up for birthdays and school plays or for anything as far as I was concerned. Grace was wrong; my expectations of men were at rock bottom. My father's absence from my childhood had ensured that. I didn't expect anything from men except disappointment.

Mr. Bray tried to convince me to meet with him and I resisted. In the end I told him I'd read the paperwork and get back to him.

I hung up and took a deep breath.

"Are you okay?" Grace asked.

I wiped the edge of my glass with my thumb. "Yeah," I said. It was easier when I could pretend my father didn't exist. When I heard from him, or even his lawyer, I felt like Sisyphus watching my boulder tumble back down the hill. It put me back at square one, and all the thoughts of how I should have had a different father, a different life, a different family that I normally managed to bury came rushing to the surface.

My father had gotten my mother pregnant and then refused to do the right thing and marry her. He'd abandoned us both. He'd sent us money—so we were financially taken care of. But what I'd really wanted was a father. Eventually all the broken promises built up into a mountain I couldn't see over. The birthday parties where I watched the door, hoping he'd show up, took their toll. There were one too many Christmases where the only thing I asked Santa for was my dad. It was his absence from my life that had been the real problem because it felt as if there was always someone else that came first, somewhere else he'd rather be. It left me with the feeling that I wasn't worth anyone's time.

"You want to talk about it?" Grace asked.

I smiled. "Absolutely not. I wanna get a little drunk in my new apartment with my best friend. Maybe gossip and eat some ice cream."

"That *is* our speciality," Grace replied. "Can we talk about boys?"

"We can talk about boys but I'm warning you, if you try to set me up I'm kicking your ass back to Brooklyn."

"But you haven't even heard who it's with yet."

I laughed. She was so easy to read. "I'm not interested in dating. I'm focusing on my career. That way I can't be disappointed." Max King's words, *results, not effort, get rewarded*, rang in my ears. I would just have to do better, work harder. There wasn't any time for dating or setups.

"You're so cynical. Not every man is like your father."

"I didn't say they were. Don't play amateur shrink on me. I just want to get established here in New York. Dating isn't my priority. That's all." I took a sip of my wine and tucked my legs under me.

I would win Max King around if it killed me. I'd followed his career so carefully it'd felt as if I knew him. But I'd imagined myself as his protégée. I'd start working for him and he'd tell me he'd never met anyone so talented. I'd assumed within a few days we'd be able to finish each other's sentences and we'd high five each other after meetings. And I admit it, I may have had a sex dream about him. Or two.

That had all been before I'd met him. I'd been an idiot.

"Sex," I blurted. "That's what men are good for. Maybe I'll take a lover."

"That's all?" Grace asked.

I traced the rim of my glass with my finger. "What else do we need them for?"

"Friendship?"

"I have you," I replied.

"Emotional support?"

"Again, that's your job. You share it with ice cream, wine, and the occasional retail overspend."

"And it's a job the four of us take very seriously. But what about when you want babies?" Grace asked.

Kids were the last thing on my mind. My mother had changed careers from working in finance to becoming a teacher so she could spend more time with me. I was sure I wouldn't be able to make such a sacrifice. "If and when I ever get around to thinking about that stuff, I'll go to a sperm bank. Worked for my mother."

"Your mom didn't go to a sperm bank."

I took a gulp from my glass. "Might as well have." I didn't have a father as far as I was concerned.

"Hand me your iPad. I want to see this hot boss of yours again."

I groaned. "Don't." I reached for the tablet on the table beside the couch and handed it over despite myself.

"Max King, right?"

I didn't respond.

"He really is ridiculously good looking." Grace swiped and flicked at the screen. I deliberately didn't look. He didn't deserve my attention.

"Put it away. It's enough that I have to deal with him Monday through Friday. Let me enjoy my weekend without having to look at his arrogant face." I glanced at the Forbes cover image Grace had brought up. Crossed arms, stern expression, full pouty lips.

Asshole.

A crash above me caught my attention and I looked up at my ceiling. The pretty glass light swayed from side to side. "Was that a bomb that just went off?" I asked.

"Sounds like your upstairs neighbor just dropped an anvil on the roadrunner."

I placed my finger over my lips and listened intently. Grace's eyes grew wide as what had started as incoherent mumbling morphed into the unmistakable sound of a woman having sex.

Panting. Moaning. Begging.

Then another crash. What the fuck was going on up there? Were there more than two people involved?

Skin slapped against skin followed by the sound of a woman crying out. Heat crept up my neck and spread across my cheeks. Someone was having much more fun on a Saturday afternoon than we were.

An unmistakably male voice shouted "fuck" and the woman's cries tumbled out fast and desperate. The knock of a headboard against drywall thudded louder and louder. The woman's breathless moaning almost sounded panicked. My chandelier started to sway more furiously, and I swear the vibrations from whatever furniture was knocking against whatever wall travelled down from the ceiling and straight to my groin. I squeezed my thighs together just as the man yelled out to God and she gave a final, sharp scream that echoed through my box-filled apartment.

In the silence that followed, my heart thudded through my sweater. I was half exhilarated by what I'd heard; half embarrassed I'd consciously eavesdropped on something so personal.

Someone less than three yards away from me had just come for America.

"That might be a guy I have to get to know," Grace said when it was clear the sexcapades had stopped. "He certainly sounded like he knew what he was doing."

"They seemed very . . . compatible." Had I ever sounded that desperate during sex, that hungry for my orgasm? I knew the sounds of a woman who *exaggerated* in the bedroom. The woman upstairs hadn't been faking. Like jumping at the scary bits of a horror movie, the sounds from her had been involuntary.

"They sound like they have excellent sex. Maybe you should knock on their door and suggest a threesome."

I rolled my eyes. "Yeah, along with a cup of sugar."

Footsteps clipped along the ceiling. "She kept her heels on," Grace said. "Nice."

The tapping wandered across my ceiling toward my blanket box. The upstairs front door creaked, then slammed. The sound of footsteps disappeared.

"Well, she got what she wanted and split. You're not going to need a TV in this place. You can just tune into the soap opera that is your neighbor."

"You think she was a prostitute?" I asked. A woman leaving less than five minutes after an orgasm like that wasn't normal. Surely she'd stick around for oxygen or round two? Hell, I wasn't sure I'd have made it to a vertical position, let alone in heels, within an hour of what she'd experienced.

"A prostitute? She's a lucky one if she is." Grace giggled. "But I don't think so. A guy who can make a woman sound like that doesn't need to pay for it." She leaned forward and placed her empty glass on one of the dozens of boxes littered about the apartment. "Right, I'm going to get home to my vibrator."

"That's really way too much information."

"But keep me posted on your neighbors. And if you run into them, try to get a picture."

"Yes, because if you're going to masturbate over my neighbors, it would go better with pictures." I nodded sarcastically. "You're a pervert. You know that, right?"

Grace shrugged and stood. "It was better than porn."

She was right. I just hoped it wasn't a regular show I was going to get. If nothing else, I felt plenty inadequate at work. I didn't need to have the same feeling at home.

chapter two

Max

HARPER JAYNE WAS *REALLY* PISSING ME OFF. She'd irritated me from the moment she'd started work almost two months ago. Up until now I'd managed to keep my distance.

She was smart. That wasn't a problem.

And she got on with her co-workers well enough. I couldn't complain.

She didn't seem to mind helping Donna with the photocopier. There were no delusions of grandeur for me to moan about.

She was eager to learn. That had been one of the first things that grated on me. She was *too* eager. The way she looked at me with those big brown eyes as if she'd be willing to do just about anything I suggested was maddening. Every time I glanced at her, even if it was a glimpse of her in the kitchen as I came into the office, I imagined her sliding to her knees in my office, opening her red, wet mouth, and begging for my cock.

And *that* was a problem.

I always had a strict divide between my business life and my personal life, and there'd never been any exception. I was the boss, with a reputation to protect. I didn't want my personal life to ever be more interesting that my business life.

I tapped my pen against my desk. I needed to figure this out. Either fire her or forget about her. But I needed to do something.

I found myself spending more and more time in my office with the door closed in an attempt to create some distance between Harper and me. Ordinarily, I'd spend time out on the floor with people, checking in on how things were going. But the open-plan area felt like contaminated land. When I had to interact with her, I addressed her as *Ms. Jayne* as a way of keeping her at arm's length. It wasn't working. I pushed my hands into my hair. I needed a plan. I couldn't have some junior researcher changing the way I did business, because the way I did business had meant King & Associates was the best at what they did, and the whole of Wall Street knew it.

Distractions were the last thing I needed right now. My focus was split enough as it was. Living with Amanda full time was more challenging than I'd expected and it meant a lot more time out of the office as I spent more time in Connecticut. I was also trying to land a new account with an investment bank King & Associates hadn't worked for before, and I had a key meeting with an insider coming up.

"Come in," I called to the knock at the door, hoping it wasn't Harper with her revised report.

"Good morning, Max," Donna said as she entered my office, closing the door behind her.

"Thanks." I took the tall cup of coffee she offered to me, trying to read her face. "How are you?"

"I'm good. We have a lot to get through." We had a daily lunchtime briefing.

I reached for my collar. "Is it me, or is it hotter in here than normal?"

Donna shook her head. "No, and I'm not turning up the A/C, either. It's ridiculously cold in here."

I sighed. It wasn't worth arguing with Donna about. Most things weren't. That was what I'd learned from the women in my life—pick your battles.

"So," Donna said as she slipped into the seat in front of my desk. The same chair Harper had sat in on Friday. Harper had sat with her legs crossed and her arms fixed to the arms of the chair, almost as if she were bracing herself for a bumpy landing. But it had given me a perfect view of her high tight breasts and her long brown hair sitting gently on her shoulders.

"What's going on?" Donna asked.

"Huh?" I asked, glancing up to look at her.

"Are you okay? You seem distracted."

I shook my head and leaned back in my chair. I needed to focus. "I'm fine. I just have a million things going on in my head. It's going to be a busy week."

"Okay then, let's get started. You have a lunch tomorrow with Wilson at D&G Consulting. It's fixed for twelve at Tribeca Grill."

"I suppose we can't cancel?" Wilson was a competitor and such an egomaniac that canceling would be a problem. And because he couldn't help but be a braggart, I usually got some useful information from our lunches.

"Yes, it's too late. You've canceled the last three times."

"And we can't go to Joey's?"

Donna just raised her eyebrows. I sighed as I reminded myself this was another battle not worth fighting.

"And Harper wanted some time this afternoon as she's revised her report."

I started to click at my calendar. I'd seen Harper on Friday. I needed to be seeing less of her not more.

"What are you doing? I have your calendar right here." She pointed to her tablet. "You have time this afternoon at four."

"I don't think we need a meeting. She should just leave what she's done with you, and I'll look at it when I can." I stared down at my notepad, writing down *Lunch with Wilson* for no particular reason.

"You usually like a follow-up meeting."

"I'm busy and haven't got time to go through work that's probably not good enough." That was unfair. Harper's work hadn't been bad. It had some mistakes in it, but nothing I wouldn't expect of someone who'd never worked with me before—the quality I was used to from new junior researchers was far sloppier and I was demanding, I knew that. She hadn't managed to get hold of Donny, but he was a hierarchical son of a bitch. Asking her to speak to him was asking an almost impossible task.

Turns out she was good at her job—she'd even had some really creative insights—so it didn't look as though she was going to give me a reason to fire her any time soon.

That could be a problem.

"Was the report really that bad?" Donna asked.

"No, but I don't need her sitting there watching me read it through, either." I'd found it utterly distracting on Friday, having her just a couple of yards away. I could barely concentrate because I'd been trying to place her scent—a kind of musky, sexy smell. The way her hands had gripped and then loosened around the arms of the chair—I found myself getting hard at the thought of those hands sliding down my chest and around my cock.

Fuck, she was a problem.

"Especially if you're going to make me have lunch with Wilson," I added when I glanced at Donna and she was looking at me with narrowed eyes. I didn't want her asking any more questions about Harper, even if it was about the quality of her work.

She took a deep breath. "Look, I don't want to speak out of turn—"

"Then don't," I snapped. What was she going to say? Could she tell I was treating Harper differently? That I was attracted to her?

Attracted. Shit. I needed to back up. She was just a pretty face with fantastic tits and a great ass. I knew plenty of women like that. My phone had plenty of women like that on speed dial who would come over and help me get Harper out of my system tonight if I thought it would help. She was nothing special.

"You're being pretty harsh with her, and I don't think it's about her performance in the office."

Pins and needles crackled through me as if my hand had been caught in the cookie jar. I froze, not wanting to react in a way that would confirm any suspicion she had.

"Has this got anything to do with Amanda?" she asked, her head cocked to one side.

My shoulders sagged. She'd not read anything into my interactions with Harper after all.

"It must be an adjustment for both of you. How long since Pandora left?" she asked.

"About six weeks. Yes, it's an adjustment." I raised my eyebrows. Amanda's mother, Pandora, and her husband, Jason, had flown to Zurich because Jason had a new job. "I've always been so involved in her life; I didn't realize how much would change." I'd always shared custody of my fourteen-year-old daughter, but for me that had meant weekends and holidays. I was quickly realizing that for the past fourteen years, I'd gotten the easy bit, the fun times with Amanda. I hadn't had to concern myself with homework, hair dye, or makeup.

"We're getting used to each other. And the commute is a challenge."

I was used to staying in Connecticut for the weekends only, but Pandora and I'd agreed Amanda should stay in her current school. So now I was in Manhattan just two nights a week, when Amanda stayed with her grandparents. I worked on the train and after Amanda went to bed, but it wasn't what I was used to.

Neither was the attitude I was getting from my daughter. "She wants to dye her hair. I've said no a million times, but she won't drop it." I sighed. I wasn't used to having to repeat myself. "I swear I'm going to get home one day to find she's done it anyway."

Donna laughed. "Teenage girls are a challenge. I'm happy I'm still a few years away from that. I mean, I know what used to go through my head at fourteen. It's not pretty."

I had no idea what went on in Amanda's head most of the time. "I'm not sure I want to know," I replied, scrubbing my hands over my face.

Donna grinned. "Believe me, you're better off in the dark. Try to say yes sometimes, that way everything isn't a fight. What does Pandora say?"

"That she'd cut my balls off if I let her dye her hair."

"Well at least you're on the same page."

Pandora and I agreed about most things when it came to our daughter. Because we'd both been so young when Pandora had gotten pregnant, we'd started with a fresh slate. There was no baggage between us. No ill feelings. We'd both just done the best we could. We'd briefly flirted with the idea of trying to make things work between us, but neither of us tried that hard. It'd been a pre-college fling and nothing more.

I wasn't sure whether or not it was a conscious decision, but from the moment Amanda was born, I knew my life was all about my daughter. Yes, my business was important, but it was needing to support Amanda, wanting her to have every advantage, that had driven me. I was determined that even though Pandora and I had made a mistake in getting pregnant, having a daughter never would be. She was the only important thing in my life and the reason there'd never been room for anyone else.

Support from our parents meant we'd both finished college. Pandora had met Jason in her sophomore year and they'd married shortly after graduation. I'd been an usher and Amanda had sat on my lap during the ceremony. It was a weird setup but it worked all these years. But looking back, Pandora had shouldered the day-to-day of bringing Amanda up. Now her baton had been passed to me.

"Yeah. It's more of a change than I expected, though. Before if she'd asked to dye her hair I'd have either told her to ask her mother, or said no and dropped her off at home, leaving Pandora with the fallout. Now it's all on me."

"Remember, Amanda's probably missing her mother, too."

"It was her idea for them to go without her. Jason was ready to turn down the job in Zurich."

"I know, but she's at the age when sometimes she can see an adult's point of view, and yet sometimes still be a kid."

I nodded and my heart tugged in that way only Amanda could elicit. She was only fourteen. Christ, you couldn't pay me enough to go back to that time. Everything was just so awkward. "They Skype all the time. I think I have more to do with Pandora now than I ever did before. We literally Skyped all through dinner last night." I laughed. "It was nice actually. I think Pandora's worried she hasn't done the right thing leaving her with me."

"I'm sure it'll be fine. You just need to get used to each other."

I nodded. "Yes, I hope if she—" My FaceTime chimed. "Here she is now." I picked up my phone. "Hey, Donna's here, say hi."

"Hey, Donna," my daughter replied.

"Hi, Amanda. You look so pretty."

"But I'd look better with blond hair, right?"

Donna chuckled and stood. "I'm so not getting into that. I'll give you guys a few minutes."

"Hey, peanut. What's up?" I asked as Donna closed the door behind her.

"Was just wondering when you were coming home."

I checked the clock on my laptop. It was only noon. "Probably not until eight. Marion's there, right?"

My housekeeper had known Amanda since she was a baby so was the perfect after-school and holiday sitter. This week Amanda was on break.

"Yeah, she's here. I just thought maybe you'd be back early today."

My heart squeezed again. Ninety percent of the time she drove me nuts, but it was moments like these that I lived for. She might be fourteen, but sometimes she still needed her dad.

"How was your morning?"

"Ugh. I don't want to talk about it."

"Are you still fighting with Samantha? You know you'll feel better if you get it out. Problems are like shit—"

"Daaad."

I chuckled. She didn't like any talk that involved bowels or farting, so I teased her with it every chance I got.

"Samantha got asked to the dance already," she mumbled.

That caught my attention. "What do you mean asked? Like a boy asked her? On a date?" My throat started to constrict and I coughed. "You're in middle school, for Christ's sake—you can't be dating." Amanda's eighth grade dance was occupying an awful lot of space in my daughter's head. I'd have preferred math or geography got her focus.

"I'm fourteen, not twelve."

Was there a difference?

"But you're going with Patti and all your friends, aren't you?" I tried to keep the rising panic I felt from reflecting in my tone.

"Sure but—"

"You want a boy to ask you and he hasn't?" I desperately wanted her to say no, to deny my worst nightmare wasn't about to come true.

"No. Not yet. Thanks for reminding me. I'm going to call Mom. I'll talk to you later."

"Amanda, don't go. What—"

She hung up. Jesus, what had I done now? I wasn't getting anything right at the moment. Things were so much easier when she lived with her mother. Up until the move, I could do no wrong. All I had to do was tickle her, crack a joke, read her a bedtime story and she thought I was amazing. Now everything I did led to an eye roll or a *Daaad*.

Fuck. I needed to call to Pandora. Maybe I could send Amanda over to Zurich the weekend of the dance? That way, there would be no boys, no dating and I wouldn't have to worry about going to jail for murder. My daughter was fourteen—she wasn't ready for the reality of the male species.

"Come in," I barked at the loud rap on the door. Harper entered the room. I groaned. Being in the same room as her was the very last thing I needed.

"What?" I asked as she strode toward me.

"The revised Bangladesh report." She held up some papers.

"You could have left it with Donna."

She placed the report down on my desk with a bang. "I'm sure if I'd left it with Donna, you'd have told me I should have handed it to you directly."

Oh. Sass. I hadn't been expecting that. I had to bite down a grin. She was right; I was giving her a hard time. But it wasn't personal. Okay, it was a little bit personal. She just irritated me. I prided myself on being unemotional at work. I'd always been able to separate the different areas of my life, to shut one world down while I was in another. Harper blurred the lines. During our meetings I fixated on the curve of her neck, or the pull of her sweater across her breasts. I'd be left trying to figure out her scent or imagine how her skin would feel under my fingers. I tried to shut that part of my imagination down. Over and over.

I stared at the screen of my laptop. "Well now you're here, just leave it on my desk and I'll try to get to it later."

"I'll leave your sandwich with Donna then," she said as she turned on her heel. Was she wearing a new dress? It looked good on her, showing off her ass and the sway of her hips while being high necked and demure.

I didn't have time to answer as she headed out and slammed the door.

Jesus, I was getting attitude everywhere I turned today. Was there a full moon? I picked up my cell and dialed Amanda. No answer.

I had a pile of papers to get through, but I wanted to get to the bottom of the situation with Amanda. If she was hoping to go to her dance with a date, we had a lot to talk about. I pulled all my things together. I'd work on the train. Leaving the office would be a double bonus—I could be with my daughter and put some distance between me and Harper. But it wasn't a long-term solution. I couldn't just stop coming into the office to avoid Harper. I needed a plan to keep her away from me. A way of making sure she didn't want anything to do with me.

The journey back to Connecticut had unwound me, and I was able to focus better with every mile put between me and Harper.

"Pancakes?" Amanda asked as she skulked into the kitchen. The French doors were open and a light breeze circled around us. Despite us being anything but a traditional family, I'd always liked that this house had a traditional family feel. It had none of the sleek lines, gloss, and glamour of my New York apartment but I liked both of them, felt at home either way.

I nodded, cracking an egg into a bowl. Since she'd transitioned to solid food, Amanda and I had shared pancakes on Sunday mornings and talked. Pancakes were our thing.

"You're home early," she said. She'd hinted that she wanted me home on the phone, but she'd never expect it. It was nice to be able to surprise her. She understood work was important but that she always came first. In so many ways she was mature, but every now and then I'd get a reminder she was still fourteen.

I nodded again.

"Like half a day early," she added.

"Thought I'd spend some time with my favorite lady. I sent Marion home, so we're having pancakes." Marion cooked for both of us on the nights I was home. Two nights a week Amanda's two sets of grandparents fought over her. Because she'd spent so much time with them when she was little, it was almost as if she had three sets of parents, and my two sisters provided the aunt input.

Amanda hopped up onto one of the barstools at the breakfast bar, watching as I whisked up the batter.

"Speak to your mom today?" I asked. I'd learned I couldn't just launch in and ask Amanda who she was hoping to ask her to the dance and on what basis. No, I had to wait for her to talk. Lucky for me, Amanda was a talker.

"Nope. Not yet."

I stayed silent, trying to encourage her to speak.

"Bobby Clapham invited Samantha to the dance."

I gripped the whisk harder but kept my mouth shut. I had to hear her out.

"And I thought that Callum Ryder would ask me, but he hasn't said anything."

Fourteen. No one told me dating was going to start this early. Could I call Pandora and agree we would lock Amanda in her room until she turned twenty-one? I could give up work and home school her for a few years, then she could do a college correspondence course. It was an option.

"Callum Ryder, he's in your class?" I'd never heard her talk about him. Or maybe I had and I'd just taken no notice. Because Amanda liked to talk, I tuned out large chunks of what she said. It was just too much to take in—all the friends, the squabbling, the concerns that would last five seconds. I couldn't keep up. The stuff I did take in passed through my brain quickly, and I retained almost nothing about her friendships at school. I was beginning to realize such an approach may have been a mistake.

"Oh my God. Don't you listen to anything I say?" she whined. "Callum moved here from San Francisco last semester. Don't you remember me telling you?"

"Oh, right." I nodded, trying to cover up the fact I had no idea what she was talking about. Why hadn't we sent her to an all-girls school? "And you want him to ask you to the dance?"

A blush crept up her face and a piercing pain shot through my chest. She was too young for all this. "Maybe," she said. "But only because he's funny, and I saw him dance once during lunch and he seemed to be able to move in time to the music."

"So everyone is going as couples?" I tried not to shudder as I spoke. My baby girl.

"What do you mean?" she asked, plucking a grape from the bowl of fruit on the counter.

"If Callum asked you to the dance, he'd pick you up and—"

"No, Samantha and I are going together. You said you'd drive us. You don't remember?" She splayed her hands in front of her as if I was possibly the stupidest man ever to have lived.

"Yeah, I remember," I lied. "But I thought you and Samantha were no longer friends?"

"Last week, Dad. Keep up."

"Okay, explain it to me because I don't know how these things work. So you'll see Callum there?"

She shrugged. "I guess."

The thudding of my pulse slowed. Maybe labelling this whole thing dating was over-dramatic. I poured the batter onto the griddle as I tried to cover my relief. "So do you have your costume yet for this dance?" I asked.

"Costume? You mean a dress? It's not a costume party."

I sighed. "Give me a break. Do you have a dress?"

She grinned. "I wondered if you wanted some company in the city this week? You know, we could go shopping maybe?"

"In Manhattan?" I wasn't sure I was qualified to take her shopping for a dance. I had no idea what would be appropriate. I didn't like Amanda in the city, and I tried to discourage her attempts to visit me when I was at the Manhattan apartment. New York was no place for a kid. There were far too many bad influences.

"Yes," she replied.

"Don't you like the shops around here?"

"I want something no one else will have." Something in my expression must have caught her eye. "Just because I'm fourteen doesn't mean finding the perfect dress isn't important, if that's what you're thinking. Perhaps if you ever dated, you'd get it."

Here we go. One crisis situation always overlapped with another. Amanda was always nagging me about getting a girlfriend. Or a wife. Women were exhausting. Work was easier. Or it was before Harper started.

"I want you to look pretty. Of course I understand that. I have plenty of women in my life." With two sisters, a daughter, and Pandora, there was no lack of estrogen in my world.

"You always think about it in such a selfish way." Amanda sighed and slipped off the stool. She began to gather plates and cutlery. Helping out in the kitchen without being asked—that was new. I was getting constant reminders about how much she was growing up, and although I was proud, it felt as if we were hurtling downhill with the brakes off. I wanted to pause for a second, enjoy the here and now for a couple of years.

"I'm being selfish by not dating?" I asked, flipping the pancakes over.

"Totally. You know how much I've always wanted a sister. Mom's been married to

Jason for forever and they've completely ignored me, so it's up to you. I don't understand what you're waiting for. Don't you want to get married?"

"Hey, wait. A minute ago you were talking about you dating and now, not only do I have to date, but I have to marry a woman and get her pregnant?" She must have been talking to my sisters. They were always pestering me to date, trying to set me up with their friends. The fact was I didn't need help getting women. But neither Amanda nor my sisters had to hear about my sex life.

She laughed. "Don't you ever think about it? We're here in the big house, just the two of us, and I'll be in college soon."

"Are you trying to kill me today? You have a couple of years before you leave for college." She was right; college was really just around the corner. Of course I wanted her to go, but maybe she could still live at home. I wasn't ready to give her up entirely.

"I think it would be nice for you to have someone. And if I got a baby sister out of it? Well, then that would be even better." She placed the plates on the breakfast bar and set the cutlery on either side.

"What's brought this on? I haven't had this particular lecture from you for a while, peanut." Had this just been my sisters' influence, or did she miss Pandora? I dished up pancakes and turned off the stove. Was I not enough for her?

She shrugged. "Dunno. Samantha's mom was asking whether or not you were dating, and it just got me wondering."

Samantha's mom? Why did I think there was more behind Samantha's recently divorced mom's question than neighborly interest? Since Amanda had been living with me, a number of her friends' moms seemed to find an excuse to come by. I'd never given any one of them a reason to think I was available.

"I think it would be nice if you found someone is all. *And* I want a baby sister."

I *dated*—and by that I meant had sex, plenty of sex. But it always happened in New York. I'd never brought anyone home to Connecticut. I kept my two worlds separate. Never anything more. I had the best of both worlds—my family in Connecticut and King & Associates and my career on Wall Street. I'd never needed anything more. There were no holes in my life as far as I was concerned. Apparently Amanda disagreed.

"You wouldn't miss our father-daughter time together? Eating pancakes, watching the game?"

"Why would we have to stop doing that? The three of us could do it together, and when Chelsea was old enough, she could have pancakes, too."

"Chelsea?" I was confused.

"My baby sister. Or maybe Amy would be better. I like that our names would both begin with an A."

Of course. I chuckled as Amanda grinned at me. "You're crazy, but I love you."

"I could find you a date if you wanted."

"Stop it and eat your pancakes."

"If you agree to go on a date, I won't tell Mom you're feeding me pancakes on a Monday night. You know she'd have a cow." Wow, maybe a few of my negotiation skills had been passed through the genetic line.

"Tell me you're not trying to blackmail me." I ruffled her hair as I sat beside her at the bar. "I'll take my chances with your mother. She knows how sometimes sugar is the only solution."

"You're no fun."

"I'm your dad. I'm not supposed to be fun."

"Please just think about taking a woman to dinner. Tinder is meant to be the place to find someone."

Tinder? "Promise me you're not on Tinder, or I'm taking your phone and you're not getting it back until you hit thirty-five."

"Dad, of course I'm not on Tinder. Are you crazy? I'm fourteen." At last she was making sense. "Tinder's for old people. Like you." Amanda held the syrup high above her plate and amber stickiness trickled out.

Was Harper on Tinder? Perhaps I should try to find out. Fuck, no. Why was I thinking like that?

"Check it out, Dad. Promise me."

"I'm promising nothing," I replied, but I wasn't sure how convincing I sounded.

chapter three

Harper

I'D BEEN WAITING TO HEAR FROM MAX ABOUT THE BANGLADESH REPORT FOR THREE DAYS. I'd worked my ass off all weekend so he could have it on Monday. I shouldn't have bothered. It was Wednesday evening and he'd canceled our follow-up meeting twice. I kicked off my shoes and slumped onto my sofa. I could hear Ben, or maybe it was Jerry, calling from the freezer.

"Knock it off, guys," I yelled. I couldn't spend the evening eating. No. I'd be productive—take advantage of the gym in the basement. That would take my mind off the asshole who was my boss. He'd strode past me in the corridor earlier in the day and totally ignored me. Okay, maybe my report could have been better, but giving me the silent treatment didn't seem like the professional thing to do. I had to keep reminding myself he wasn't the man I'd thought he would be and that still didn't mean I couldn't get a lot out of working for King & Associates.

I changed into my workout gear, grabbed a bottle of water, and headed downstairs. A gym in the building was more than I could have hoped for when I started looking for somewhere in Manhattan, and I'd not had a chance to visit yet. Work might not be good, but home was a cocoon from anything bad. I could relax—focus on the big picture.

Thirty minutes on the elliptical would clear my head and stop me trying to think up ways to physically hurt Max King.

As I entered the gym, I noticed there were three men already there—one using the free weights, one on a bike, the other on a rower. And apart from the muted sounds of CNN coming from a TV fixed on the wall in the corner, it was quiet. I checked out the rest of the space. No mirrors, so I didn't have to look at any part of me wobbling while I moved. Perfect. It was as if I'd invented the place myself.

Moving toward an empty elliptical, I avoided the blatant stare of the guy using the weights. I dropped my water bottle into the holder on the machine just behind the man on the bike—he had an amazing ass—hopped on, and tried to find a program that wouldn't kill me. Just what I needed to stop me from thinking about the office—a hard workout and a nice view.

I found a program on the machine that I knew would be tough, but I wanted to be focused on something other than what a disappointment King & Associates was turning out to be. I needed to be able to tune out when I wasn't in the office or I'd send myself crazy. My first day on the job, my jaw ached from smiling so much. I'd finally achieved my dream, and I'd done it all on my own. It felt as though I'd arrived on the first step of a bright future—where the beginning of all my plans converged. I'd been beside myself with excitement. But the sheen had worn off pretty quickly, sometime in the first week when I was introduced to Max and he'd barely looked up from his desk to say hello.

The guy on the bike gasped and sat up, circling his shoulders, then tilting his head one way and the other as he continued to peddle. He had a nice broad back, and jet-black hair drenched in sweat. He was going to need a serious shower. If he was the guy I'd heard having sex in the penthouse, I'd be happy to keep him company.

"You live in the building?"

I jumped when the guy who'd been using the free weights draped his arm over my machine. I hadn't seen him head over. He was short, overbuilt, and so tan I wanted to ask him whether or not he'd lost a bet. He looked as if he belonged on the Jersey shore rather than downtown Manhattan. I nodded, hoping the fact I didn't speak would put him off.

"You have a nice ass, if you don't mind me saying."

Really? He held up his hands when I shot him a look to kill. "No need to be snotty. I just like a nice ass."

I fixed my stare to my machine's panel, wanting to punch the guy.

"I think you better move on," a man said from behind Jersey Shore.

"Hey," Jersey Shore replied. "I was giving the girl a compliment."

I kept my head down, not wanting to attract any more attention.

"Her loss, right?" my rescuer replied. I recognized that voice. My brain tried to work out if it was a famous person.

Jersey Shore moved away, and I glanced up with a smile. "Thank—"

It was like someone was trying to take a dump over my entire life.

Max-fucking-King stood right in front of me.

Kill. Me. Now.

The guy I'd come down here to escape was standing right in the middle of *my* gym in *my* apartment building. I glanced around. Jersey Shore had left, and the rower was still going. Max King was Nice Ass Guy. Life was just not fair.

My limbs stopped working and I half tripped, half stepped off the elliptical, stumbling into the wall behind the machines. *Really?* The hits just kept on coming.

"Are you okay?"

I peeled myself off the drywall as he moved toward me.

I nodded, unsure what I'd say if I actually managed to form words. How was this possible? My apartment was supposed to be my sanctuary from this man's assholey behavior in the office. Now I had to worry about running into him in the corridors of my apartment building while I was drunk or not wearing makeup. Not that it mattered if he saw me without makeup or in my sweats; it would just be another reason for him to think less of me.

"Okay, well. I guess you live in the building," he said, then clenched his jaw and flicked his eyes to the door as if he wanted to escape.

Fine by me.

"Yeah, I just moved in."

He looked past me and pressed his fingers to his forehead as he had when reviewing my Bangladesh report. "Right."

And that was it. Before I could think of anything else to say, he sped out the door as if his balls were on fire.

He had no more manners outside the office than in. He was still cold and rude.

Despite his nice ass.

I leaned against the wall, trying to make sense of it all. A year ago I would have thought my life had peaked at just being within a five-yard radius of Max King. Now he was not only torturing me at the office, but he'd just made my building gym a no-go area. I grabbed my water bottle and headed back to my apartment. Could my day get any worse?

After my near aneurism at running into Max in the gym, I'd taken the hottest shower possible without landing in the emergency room, blow-dried my hair, and then wrapped myself in my white silk robe, which I'd bought on sale at Barney's. It always made me feel better. As if I had my shit together. I needed a BFF download, and I'd be back on track.

"Hey, Grace," I replied as she answered my call.

"You sound like you're about to put your head in the oven," she said through the sound of her chewing on something.

I wanted to ask her if I could come over and spend the night. For the rest of my lease. "Just a bad day at work." If I told her about Max being in the building, she'd have me moved back to Brooklyn before she could say the words sublet. I'd have to settle for a general gripe session, so I explained I'd still not heard back on the Bangladesh report.

"Have you ever thought about quitting your job? It really can't be worth it."

"I can't quit. This is my dream position. It's what I've worked so hard for. I just need two years on my resume, and then I'm golden." And who knew. I might have won him over with the revised Bangladesh report. I could get into the office tomorrow to find he'd turned over a new leaf.

And I might be the next Beyoncé.

"Two years is a long time to be miserable. You could always talk to your dad."

Was she serious? "Why would you even say something like that?" Grace knew I was the only one of his kids not working at JD Stanley, his investment bank. My three half brothers had all started on the graduate course the September after college. I'd thought I'd get the satisfaction of turning him down, but he never asked. Why would Grace think I would call him? I didn't want anything from him.

"You do the kind of work his firm needs, right? Don't you have like a perfect skill set for him?"

"It doesn't matter." Ben and Jerry's cries from the kitchen were growing louder. "I wouldn't work for him if he was the last man on Earth. And if you remember, he never offered me a job. I didn't have the correct reproductive equipment."

"He probably didn't think you wanted it." It didn't mean he couldn't have asked. "He doesn't know you, doesn't get how brilliant and ambitious you are. He's like a hundred years old. He's probably just old-fashioned." Was he just from a different generation who thought women should stay at home and look after the kids? If he'd ever gotten to know me, he would know I wasn't like that.

"I really can't believe we're having this conversation. I'm not about to quit my dream job, and I'm not about to ask my father for anything." I swung my legs up onto the couch and lay on my back staring at the ceiling. "It's really starting to upset me that you're defending him."

"I'm really not. I'm just trying to offer you a way out."

Grace was always trying to solve my problems. And the problems of all the guys she dated. There just wasn't anything Grace could do to fix this situation.

Footsteps thudded across the ceiling, causing my light fixture to rock gently back and forth. Jesus, the last thing I needed was my neighbors going at it again. I didn't want to be reminded of my lack of sex life.

"Thank you, but I don't need a way out. I'm exactly where I want to be." I wasn't a quitter.

"But you're miserable."

"I'm not." I should complain less. I was just frustrated to find Max in my building.

"My standards are just too high." The thudding upstairs sounded like someone pacing back and forth. "I'm going to readjust, reset, and everything's going to be just fine."

Classical music, Bach maybe, blared from upstairs. It was so loud my apartment started to vibrate. Metalheads or coked-up dance music addicts were supposed to play their music loud and annoy their neighbors, not classical music buffs.

"Do you have classical music on? Jesus, less than a week in Manhattan and we're already growing apart."

I chuckled. "No, it's not me. It's upstairs."

"The shaggers?"

"Yes. Although they're not shagging. One of them put their concrete boots on and is dancing like an elephant across my ceiling." The music hadn't drowned out the consistent pound of footsteps. "I can't tell if there are two people up there."

"Brooklyn looking a little more attractive?" Grace couldn't hide the smug tinge to her voice.

"I'm sure the music will die down in a little bit. Maybe they've had a bad day and they're trying to drown it out, like I do with—"

"Taylor Swift?"

I shrugged, unembarrassed by my Swift predilection. "I was going to say Stevie Wonder, but Taylor will do."

"You're not pissed off by the noise?"

Any other day I would be furious, but if I allowed myself to get irritated with my penthouse neighbors, I'd have nothing left. Work was so disappointing it left me hollow inside. All my excitement about the job had dissolved, and it had become just like my college bartending job—a means to an end. And now with Max in the building, the only place I felt safe was behind my front door. Surely my neighbors would stop pacing and turn down their music soon.

"Tell me about your date?" I asked. "That's why I called."

Grace had a thing for penniless musicians, artists, or really anyone who didn't have their shit together. It meant there was always drama in her life, always someone to fix.

"Ahhh," she sighed. "He's so talented. He just needs to find the right patron, catch a break, you know?" I'd forgotten what this one did. They all seemed to morph into one guy whose middle name was loser.

"You think he's got what it takes?" Grace liked the idea of finding a guy before they made it and being the one who was there from the beginning. Problem was they never made it. She just jumped from one loser to another.

"I really do. This guy is the next Damien Hirst or Jeff Koons, I swear."

Oh, right. This one was an artist. I glanced up at the ceiling as the light fixture swayed even more violently.

"He's putting together an installation in New Jersey next week. You should come. You'll love it."

I wasn't sure New Jersey was the place to showcase the next Jeff Koons, but hey, it would get me out. "Sure. But when you say 'installation', what do you mean?"

"It's an interactive piece he's working on. He won't show me, but I'm sure it's amazing."

Grace was so sensible and practical in every way but wanted to believe the absolute best of everything. It was kinda endearing, kinda annoying.

"And he has a friend I want to introduce you to."

I groaned. "Grace."

"No, you'll like this guy. He's a suit."

Upstairs cranked up the volume. I didn't know classical music, though my mom had a thing for Johann's cello suites. Nice, but did it really have to be this loud?

"I can dress my dog in a suit. It doesn't mean I want to date him."

It wasn't wealth that attracted me; it was drive. It didn't matter if they wore a suit—although there was nothing like a man who could fill out custom-cut, navy wool as though he owned it. I might hate Max King, but Jesus, did he know how to wear a suit. And gym clothes, apparently. Seeing him in the gym hadn't changed my mind that he'd clearly been in the front of the line when they were dealing out hot.

"You don't have a dog," Grace said.

"Not really my point." I didn't want to date anyone, didn't want love to distract me. I'd seen a number of my friends doing so well in their careers and suddenly becoming less ambitious because they'd fallen for some guy, and then when they'd taken their foot off the pedal, the guy would predictably dump them. It had even happened to my mother. And I wasn't going to make the same mistake.

"This guy is successful. He does something in finance, or maybe it was architecture."

"Yeah, I can see how you'd get the two mixed up." The very last thing I wanted was a man in finance. The industry bred men like my father and they were the worst kinds.

Grace laughed. "You know what I mean. Will you come?"

"If you promise not to set me up with anyone. I'm not interested."

"I'm not setting you up. But what can I say? He'll be there; you'll be there."

"I'm hanging up. I have to get my beauty sleep." I pressed cancel on the phone and tossed it on the table. It was just after ten, but an early night would be impossible until my Bach-loving neighbors shut the hell up.

Warm milk and a Benadryl would help me sleep, but I only had wine, and I was out of Benadryl.

I poured myself a glass of Pinot Noir, climbed into bed, and turned on the TV.

After forty-five minutes I could barely hear my TV through the music, and the thudding footsteps hadn't lessened. What, was someone training to climb Kilimanjaro up there? My limbs began to twitch with irritation. Whoever was up there didn't sound as if they were changing things up anytime soon, and I wanted to sleep. I'd been *more* than patient. Could I call the police? Wasn't there something in the lease about not making noise after a certain time? Where had I put my lease?

I threw my covers off and stomped out of bed, then flung open the blanket box Grace and I had lugged up here when I moved in. The box of denial—it was where all my life admin went. Eventually I found the papers I'd signed just over a week ago, and I started to flip through the pages, almost ripping one in half. How could anyone be so selfish? Loud sex was one thing, but music and marching practice was another. I ran my fingers down the pages as I became increasingly impatient. Yes. It said I wasn't allowed to disturb any other neighbor after ten in the evening. The people upstairs were breaching their lease. Clasping my papers, I scrambled toward the front door, grabbed my keys, and took the stairs one flight up. I glanced around. There was just one apartment door. Well at least I didn't have to worry about disturbing the wrong person.

I knocked on the metal, trying to swallow down the anger bubbling at the surface. It was all too much. First I found the perfect job for it to be ruined by the reality of Max King, then I couldn't escape him in my building. Now my noisy neighbors were stopping me from sleeping. Everything seemed so unfair.

I knocked again, louder this time. Did they not know how loud they were being?

Who was I kidding? I was pretty sure I could hear these guys from the Hamptons.

The stomping continued to go up and down, up and down. There was no one coming toward the door.

I slammed my fists against the cold metal and screamed, "Open the fucking door."

Almost immediately the footsteps stopped, then changed direction. My heart began beating out of my chest. Had I gone too far? I might be knocking on the door of a serial killer or drug dealer with penchant for Bach.

Locks began to clunk and I folded my arms, ready to give my loud neighbor a piece of my mind. I should have pulled a sweater on over my silk robe.

The door opened wide and for the second time, I came face to face with Max King where I least expected to find him.

And of course, he had to be shirtless.

"Are you kidding me?" I bellowed, flinging my arms in the air in exasperation.

His eyes were wide and trailed down my body. I followed his eye line; shit, my robe had begun to part. I grabbed the silk and pulled it together, trying to ignore the fact I was almost naked in front of my boss.

His eyebrows nearly hit the ceiling and he reached out. "Get in here," he said as he pulled me by the elbows. "You're not dressed."

I tried to stand firm, but he gripped me with such force I went crashing into him, and we stumbled backward into his apartment.

"Jesus, Harper," he growled, and he pushed me away but didn't let go of my arms. I realized it was the first time I'd heard him call me by my first name. He normally called me Ms. Jayne. He closed his eyes and with gritted teeth, he asked, "What are you doing here?"

chapter four

Max

Being close to her like this made me crazy. Because I'd done such wicked things to her in my head, I was always concerned I'd be over familiar with her in the flesh. And now I had hold of her, I didn't know what to do. I just knew I didn't want to let her go.

"What are you doing up here?" She tried to hold up some papers, but I held her arms firmly by her sides, pushing her up against the wall. "My ceiling is caving in from all the thumping."

My brain wasn't able to function. Why was she in my apartment? Why was she shouting?

Seeing that mafia boss lookalike at the gym hit on Harper had taken away the shock of realizing she was a resident of *my* building. I'd wanted to lift him up and kick him out on his ass. Then when he left I noticed her workout clothes stretched over her body so tight she might as well have been naked, and I'd bolted out of the gym, running away from the twitching across my skin that told me I had to leave before I embarrassed myself.

And now she was against my apartment wall. Enraged. And only partially dressed.

I was speechless.

She was always so cool and in control at work. It was odd to see her so . . . agitated. I clearly didn't know her well, probably because I barely gave her the time of day, too desperate to keep as much distance between us as possible. I'd hate for her to guess what was going on in my perverted little brain, for her to know all the things I imagined doing with her.

"And the music. Anyone would think you had the New York Philharmonic up here. What the hell is going on?"

My hands burned from being wrapped around her arms. I loosened my grip, but couldn't let her go entirely.

"Answer me!" she yelled. "I have to put up with you ignoring me in the office, but you don't sign my paychecks here. You're breaching your lease."

I'd had an inkling there was more under her professional exterior than I normally saw. She'd hinted a couple of times that she thought I was an asshole. It was a relief, because if she hated me it made things easier. It made the distance wider.

But nothing was easy now, not with her right here, almost naked in front of me. Her smooth skin, hot under my fingers, wasn't helping. The scent of musk and sex seeping through my body and going straight to my dick. The way her nipples poked at the silk of her robe. None of it helped. I closed my eyes, trying to claw back some kind of control over what I was feeling.

"Are you listening to me?"

I wasn't. I could hear she was upset, but I couldn't process what she was saying. My senses were too overloaded.

She tipped her head back, exposing her long, creamy neck, and sighed, exasperated. Before I could stop myself, I released her arm and stroked my index finger across her jaw and down her neck. She gasped, but I couldn't hold back. I trailed my finger lower, into the dip at the base of her throat. She was like a drug. Every hit I took of her made me want more. I was chasing the high—her high.

"What are you doing, you asshole?"

Her words brought me up short. Asshole? I froze and looked up. Shit, I did things like that to her in my imagination, not in person.

"I . . . I'm sorry." I let her go and stepped back, pushing my hands through my hair. What was I thinking? I was a father. A businessman. Nothing else mattered.

She paused and frowned at me. "You're vile to me in the office," she said, her voice quiet and questioning.

I nodded. "I know." It was deliberate.

I fixed my stare on her full, pouty lips. All the things I'd imagined those lips doing . . . She was right. I was an asshole.

"And you think I'm stupid," she said.

"Stupid?" If that were true she wouldn't be quite so alluring. Yes, she'd still be beautiful, but there were plenty of beautiful women on this planet. "I don't think you're stupid."

"Then why do you treat me like shit?" She pointed at me; her voice got louder. "You act as if I don't exist." She jabbed her finger into my chest. It was as if she'd pressed a button with the word "cock" on it. My dick pulsed in response to every touch from her.

I grabbed her finger, forcing her to stop pressing her skin against mine, and froze, not wanting to let go, and she didn't pull her hand away from me. Instead we just looked at each other, not knowing what happened next, needing answers from the other. Was she done yelling? Could I keep my hands to myself a second longer?

To my surprise, she dropped her papers, took a step forward, wrapped her free hand around my neck, and pressed her lips to mine. Relief rolled through my body, and instead of pushing her away, I snaked my greedy tongue into her mouth. She groaned, the sound reverberating throughout my body. She touched me as if it were practiced, as if she'd been thinking of it as much as I had.

I pulled back for a second and a look of confusion passed over her face. It was just the encouragement I needed. I pushed her against the wall and dropped my lips to her collarbone.

"I hate you," she whispered.

She wasn't acting as if she hated me, wasn't trying to get away. Had I read her wrong? I glanced up and she frowned.

"Don't stop," she said.

I grinned and bowed my head. She wanted this. "Don't stop?" I asked against her neck. She threaded her fingers into my hair with one hand and smoothed the other over my shoulder. It was my turn to groan. A single touch from her and all my worst fears were confirmed—I wanted this woman. No, it was more than that. I'd found women attractive before, but I'd never had an overwhelming desire to be close to them, all the time. Not when I barely knew anything about them. Never found myself thinking about a woman when I was meant to be concentrating on a conference call or presentation. Never wanted to make them smile, find out all their secrets. I kneed her legs apart, and she ground her hips against my leg.

This girl could end me.

I'd suspected it the moment I saw her. Known it the moment I'd seen her work.

Talented. Beautiful. Sharp. Sexy.

I wanted it all.

There were so many reasons this couldn't happen. She worked for me. I only had sex with women; I didn't do relationships. I'd recited them silently again and again.

I pulled back and she looked up at me, mouth open. I placed my hands against the wall on either side of her head.

"What?" she asked.

"I'm your boss."

"Don't worry. Whatever happens, I'll be filing my sexual harassment claim in the morning." She reached into my pants and wrapped her fingers around my hardening cock. "You might as well make this count."

I smirked. She was going to keep me on my toes.

As I pulled open the tie of her robe, the silk slipped from her shoulders. Sweeping my hands across her skin, I avoided her breasts, then trailed down her stomach to her neatly trimmed pussy. I paused.

She arched her back, pushing her body toward me, wanting more.

"But you hate me," I teased.

"Let's see what you can do to change my mind." She pressed her hand against mine, pushing my fingers into her dampness.

She had no idea what I had planned for her and how long I'd been planning it.

An almost transient afterthought, I slid my lips against hers. And despite my fantasies, I found myself sliding to *my* knees. I needed to know I could make her as crazy as she did me. I tried to pull her leg over my shoulder but she resisted, encouraging me to stand up.

"Did you forget who's the boss?" I asked.

"In the office, maybe."

Forcefully, I pushed her back against the wall and lifted her leg. I knew once she felt my tongue she'd relent. And I was right. I always was. She thrust her hips forward and slid her leg down my back as my tongue flicked over her clit, once, then twice. If she thought I wasn't the boss in the bedroom, she was sorely mistaken.

I curled a hand around one hip and with the other pressed my palm against her flat stomach as I licked from her clit down to the source of her wetness, enjoying her sweet taste. There was so much of it. As if she'd been wet for me since we first met. Her nails dug into my scalp as her pussy pulsed against me. I couldn't remember the last time I went down on a woman, and right at that moment, I couldn't remember it ever tasting this good, this warm, this wet.

Despite my holding her, she seemed to be having a hard time standing up straight.

"I can't," she cried out.

I got the feeling there was nothing Harper couldn't do if she put her mind to it, but I wasn't about to argue with her. I stood and she looked at me, half dazed, half disappointed. Before she had a chance to tell me again how much she hated me, I hoisted her over my shoulder and carried her into my bedroom.

I tipped her onto the bed, her chestnut hair splaying out around her. I grabbed her by the legs and parted her firm thighs, pushing my fingers into her while my tongue circled her clit. She cried out, lifting her hips off the bed. I grabbed her waist and pulled her toward me. She wasn't going anywhere without an orgasm to remember me by. Jesus, just a few minutes ago I'd been coming up with strategies to spend less time with her and now here she was naked on my bed, coating my hand and tongue with her juices.

She let out small whimpers and incoherent sounds about noise and neighbors and chandeliers. I couldn't follow what she was saying. All I cared about was her sweet, hot pussy around my tongue. Her breaths grew sharper and her whole body began to shudder, her movements becoming wild before she cried out, "Max!" Hearing my name on her lips while she climaxed pierced a hole in armor I didn't realize I wore, and suddenly I didn't care that I was her boss or that I had a reputation to protect, a family to focus on. I was so overwhelmingly attracted to her and right then it was the only thing that mattered. I nearly came right with her.

Her panting slowed and she reached out. I should ask her to leave, stop this before it was too late, but instead I took her hand and climbed up next to her.

I rolled to my back, needing to focus on something other than the swell of her tight breasts, the way her body sank against *my* bedsheets, on *my* bed, in *my* apartment.

She was here. Exactly where she shouldn't be.

"Oh my God." Her arm flopped onto my chest. "Forbes was right when they said you were talented."

I couldn't stop the chuckle that rose from my throat. I turned to see her rolling to her side, apparently oblivious of how bizarre this scenario was. She kissed my jaw, and I tried not to look at her, afraid I'd never be able to look away.

Her fingers wrapped around my still rock-hard cock. Jesus. So much for me telling her to leave. She dragged her hand up over the crown. There was little hope of me getting rid of her, not while she was so expertly squeezing and pulling. I gave in and glanced over to find her staring back at me, studying me as if she was trying to work out a crossword clue.

"Got a condom?"

This was a bad idea. "Yes," I said as I reached across to my night table.

She straddled me and took the latex from me. "This is Vegas, right?" she asked.

"Vegas?" I asked as she sheathed my cock, squeezing tightly as she reached the bottom.

"This room. It's Vegas. What happens here, stays here." She positioned my cock at her entrance. "You agree? Maybe if we do this, I can stop hating you. You can just be my boss."

At the moment I'd have agreed to cut off both my legs with a blunt knife, but I liked what she was saying. That after whatever it was we were doing, everything would go back to normal or better than normal—how things should be.

"Vegas," I replied and she sank onto my dick, inch by inch. I squeezed my hands into fists to stop myself from grabbing her hips and slamming her onto me. My jaw tightened as Harper threw her head back and steadied herself. Using her hands on my chest, she sank down a little more.

"So good," she whispered. "So, so deep."

Jesus, how was I supposed to just lie here and take this? It was too much. I needed to be the one who set the pace, or I'd be coming in less than ten seconds.

Her hair fell around her shoulders, and I reached up, pushing it behind her back, wanting nothing to interrupt my view of her high, tight breasts or her pink, swollen nipples jutting out, begging for attention. I pulled at them, one then the other, and she quivered before crashing down on me as far as she would go. She was perfect, far better than I'd imagined and I'd thought about her plenty, wondered what she'd look like above me, naked, legs open, eyes hazy with lust. She was so tight around me that instinct took over, and before I gave her a chance to ride me I flipped her over onto her back and pushed in farther.

"No more," I said. "I've had enough of your constant daily teasing." I didn't know if she meant to be provocative. She wasn't obvious about it in the way a lot of women were. Her clothes weren't flashy or particularly tight; she didn't flirt or even try to make conversation with me. I pulled out and started to fuck her now that I finally had her under me, naked. Each time I thought pushing in would get easier, that she wouldn't be quite so tight, so delicious, but every time I was wrong. She was exceeding each one of the fantasies I'd had about her.

Her hands wrapped around my upper arms, her fingers so tiny they were fascinating. I wanted to pause for a second to ensure they were real, but my headboard smashing against the wall pulled my focus back to wanting to make her come. She looked so perfect, so completely beautiful and if we only had tonight, I was going to have to make it count.

I wanted to go farther, deeper, faster.

I needed to mark her, own her, climb inside her.

It was as if every inappropriate image I'd buried deep in my brain had escaped and come to life.

I lifted one of her legs higher, desperate to be closer. I could tell by the way she opened her mouth slightly wider that the change in angle ratcheted up the pleasure for us both. I dipped my head down to kiss her, and she greedily took my tongue. Despite giving me no sign in the office, she touched me as though I'd lived in her fantasies just as she'd lived in mine. There was a knowingness between us, a familiarity that was unnerving but at the same time I wanted to savor it.

She reached between us and squeezed the base of my cock. I almost exploded. I had to pause.

"You're such an asshole." She grinned and wiped sweat from my brow with her fingertips.

"You seem obsessed with that concept. Perhaps we should try your asshole out next and see if it cures you."

"You wouldn't dare." She pushed her hips up to meet mine, and I raised my eyebrow.

"Wouldn't I?" I asked. "This is Vegas. Anything goes."

"Shut up and concentrate on fucking me."

I loved that mouth, the way it called me names, the way it called *my* name.

She needed to be taught a lesson.

"I'm thinking about nothing else." I pushed into her and her eyes half shut. I started thrusting deeper and deeper, nailing her to the mattress, wanting to make it good, needing to feel her around me. I sat back on my knees, pulling her up onto my thighs, taking the opportunity to watch her breasts bounce with every thrust.

"You think I hate you now?" I asked. Didn't she feel the chemistry between us and understand I had to keep my distance otherwise something like this would happen?

"I don't care. I'm too . . ."

She trailed off and squeezed me harder, creating friction between us that heated the blood in my veins. She gave me a small smile and I wanted her closer. I pulled her up, bringing us face to face, her legs around my waist, and lifted her up and down on my cock. She wrapped her arms around my neck and pressed her lips to mine. It was such an intimate gesture, so normal, so right, as if we'd been lovers for some time, as if we'd known each other for years.

Harper increased the rhythm, her hips lifting easily in my hands and slamming down on my cock.

"Careful," I warned. I wouldn't last long like that.

"I can't stop," she whispered, her fingers running across my shoulders. "I can't stop, don't want to." Her movements grew bigger, wilder, and I used my hands over her hips to keep our rhythm steady and her pussy full of me. Her fingernails dug into my shoulders as she pulled back to look at me and screamed, "Max. Yes, Max." Her pulsating muscles drew me in and in two sharp stabs of my hips I was pouring into her, watching her orgasm seep away as mine took over.

                                      ∽

I woke to traffic noise and the sun pouring into my window. Was it Saturday? No, Thursday.

Fuck. Harper.

I must have blacked out.

I bolted upright, but I was alone. Had I dreamt what had happened last night? The ache in my muscles, the bedsheets crumpled at the bottom of the bed, the tug in my stomach—no, it had happened. "Harper," I called out. She'd gone. I scrubbed my face with my hands then glanced at the clock. Fuck. It was eight thirty. I was usually knee deep in paperwork at my desk by now. I bounded out of bed for the shower.

It was only a few minutes' walk to the office and I went through the sliding doors to the King & Associates office at two minutes to nine. My hair was still wet from my shower.

I had no idea how I was going to handle Harper in the office today. I had a hundred and one things to do and no spare brain space. But the gathering gloom in my head said last night had been a bad idea—the worst idea. I couldn't have casual sex with an employee. It blurred too many lines. Having sex with women I'd see outside of the bedroom had never been an option for me. There were enough women in my life. And Amanda deserved my full attention when I wasn't in the office—it was the deal I'd struck with myself as soon as she was born. Just because I was a young father didn't mean I'd be a bad one. She would always be my priority.

As much as the night with Harper had been everything I'd fantasized about, it had been a stupid idea.

I kept my head down as I strode to my office, but I couldn't resist glancing over to Harper's desk. She'd made it in on time. Her hair was up, folded somehow against her head, revealing her long neck.

"There you are," Donna called. "I've been trying your cell."

Harper turned toward me just as I looked at Donna. Harper hadn't left a note this morning. Had she stayed the night? Did she regret what had happened?

"Did you come in from Connecticut?" Donna asked as she followed me into my office.

"No, I just had some things to sort out." Like washing the smell of sex and Harper off my body. I needed to get my head on straight.

"Okay, well Amanda called. And don't forget your lunch." I nodded and Donna left.

I put my phone on speaker and dialed the house while I took off my jacket and hung it on the back of the door.

"Hey, peanut. Donna said you called. Are you not at gymnastics today?" I took a seat at my desk and turned on my laptop.

"Um, no. It got canceled."

Odd. I was pretty sure Marion would have told me. "It was?" I asked as I scanned my emails.

"Yeah, so I thought maybe I could come into the city tonight and we could go dress shopping tomorrow?" Her tone was bright and matter of fact. She knew I couldn't say no to her I'm-such-a-good-girl voice. "I thought you might help me shop?"

"Did Marion say she'd bring you on the train?" I hoped she didn't think she was coming on her own.

"Aunt Scarlett said she'd bring me, then I could come home with you tomorrow."

"Did Scarlett say she was staying over?" The last thing I wanted was my sister in my apartment meddling.

"No, she has a date."

Dating? She hadn't shared that with me. I'd thought she was still sworn off men after her divorce.

"You should take a leaf out of her book, Dad."

Harper's satisfied smile ran across my brain. Maybe dating would help get her out of my system.

"You keep me plenty busy," I replied. "What time are you planning to arrive tonight with Scarlett?"

"I can come?"

I could hear Amanda's smile, and I couldn't help but grin. I was a sucker for that smile.

"I'm not going to let my little girl go shopping for her eighth grade dance on her own, now am I?"

She shrieked and I turned down the volume on my phone, wincing. "You've got a key, so just let yourself in if I'm not there."

"Can we get takeout?"

I rolled my eyes. "Maybe."

"And watch a mob movie like we did last time?"

I chuckled. Because Amanda didn't have a lot of her stuff in the apartment, when she visited we usually ended up hanging out, eating takeout and watching movies. I loved it.

"No promises. I want you to swear you'll do your piano practice before you leave. If you don't pass the exam, your mother will move you to Zurich."

"It's a deal." The piano began to chime in the background. "You hear that? I've started already."

I shook my head. "See you later, peanut."

"Love you, Dad."

The three best words on the planet.

"Love you, Amanda."

As I hung up, Donna walked in.

"If you're leaving early tomorrow to go shopping, let's do a quick walk-through of your schedule for today and tomorrow."

I leaned back in my chair. "I see the women in my life know what I'm doing before I do."

"Did you ever have any doubt?"

I sighed. "I guess not." It was days like this when I felt as though my life didn't belong to me. Having my own business was tough and took up almost all my energy, but usually the rewards of working for myself outweighed the disadvantages. Today the scales were tipping in the wrong direction. I just wanted to shrug off the constant demands on my time, to check out for a day—fuck around on the internet, go ride my bike, speak to Harper. Though I had no idea what I'd say. Apologize, maybe.

"Do we need to cancel anything?" I asked.

"No, but the meeting with Andrew and his contact at JD Stanley is at ten, and I'm guessing you won't want to miss that?"

She was right. I didn't want to miss it. I was hoping for a little inside knowledge about JD Stanley, the only major investment bank King & Associates didn't work with.

"No, Amanda can hang out at the apartment until after lunch tomorrow. Do we have anything in the afternoon?"

"A meeting with Harper at three, but I can push it to next week." As Donna said her name my face heated and the blood in my veins seemed to speed up.

I ran a finger around my collar. How was I going to approach her? Should I say sorry? She'd been just as up for things as I had, but I was her boss. I didn't want her to think it could happen again. Maybe I should be upfront with her, tell her she was great, but it was a one-time deal. Or should I just pretend it hadn't happened? I had no idea.

"Yeah, that's fine." I was the last person she probably wanted to see. After all, she thought I was an asshole.

∽

I'd been glued to my iPhone, taking my office mobile while Amanda was in the changing room in the small Midtown boutique we were in. My fingers hovered over my emails. Should I drop Harper a note? But I had no idea what I'd say. This was why the rules of casual sex should be established before anyone got naked. But *she'd* been the one to talk about Vegas. Perhaps we didn't need to have an awkward follow-up conversation to reestablish what had already been said. I stuffed the phone back in my pocket and tried to avoid eye contact with the sales assistants.

"What do you think?" Amanda asked, stepping out of a dressing room.

"Are you fucking kidding me?" I asked, recoiling in shock. Shopping was not my favorite activity to do—Pandora usually bought Amanda's clothes—but I was going to have to be involved in every shopping trip from now to eternity if she thought she was going to wear *that*.

Amanda rolled her eyes. "Dad, don't swear."

Don't swear? She was lucky I didn't kill someone. Someone like the designer of the dress she had on. "Take that off, right now. You're fourteen not twenty-five." It showed way too much skin—there seemed to be nothing holding it up and it was about three feet too short. It was as if she was wearing a towel.

"I'm not a child."

I didn't need a reminder she was growing up far too fast. "Yes, you are. That's what fourteen is. And a child doesn't get to wear dresses that don't have arms."

"It's called strapless."

"I don't care what it's called—it barely covers your butt. You're not wearing it." It seemed like yesterday that she'd refused to wear anything but a tutu. That particular obsession had lasted three months. She used to sleep in the thing. I'd laughed when Pandora had asked me to try to coax her out of it. I'd loved it. She'd looked adorable and it made her so happy—what more could I wish for? A tutu would be good right about now. Amanda glared at me. "I mean it, go change."

"I don't work for you. You can't just order me around."

I stared right back, raising my eyebrows. There was no way I was backing down on this. "If you want to go to the dance, you'll go back in there and change." I nodded toward the curtain behind her. "I'll be out here trying to find something appropriate for you to wear."

"Thanks, Coco Chanel."

I wanted to laugh, but she needed to understand that under no circumstances would she be wearing something made for a twenty-five-year-old trying to get laid. Apart from anything else, Pandora would cut off my balls. I was going to have to get proactive.

"Excuse me," I said to the shop assistant. "Can you show me some age-appropriate dresses for my fourteen-year-old daughter?" I'd left Amanda to pick her own outfit. That had been a mistake. I could have headed off this problem before she'd changed into anything.

"Certainly, sir," the tall, blonde woman said. "It's so nice to see a father taking his daughter shopping." She smiled as if she wanted me to respond, but I wasn't in the mood for chitchat. I wanted to find a dress and take Amanda to Serendipity, where we could catch up over ice-cream sundaes and forget she was growing up.

"What about this?" The assistant held up a very short, baby-blue dress.

"Something longer," I said.

"Dad," Amanda called. I turned to see her in a skin-tight dress that looked like it was made of strips of horizontal material sewn together.

I strode toward her. "Get that off. Right now."

"It has sleeves," she said, holding out her arms.

True, but it left nothing to the imagination, clinging to her teenage body and barely covering her bottom. There was no way she was going out in public in that.

"Get it off," I snapped.

She let out a grunt of frustration and stomped back into the changing room.

"This," the assistant said, holding up a pink-lace dress, "is a very popular dress this season."

It looked as though it would hit the floor when Amanda tried it on, so that was a plus. It also had long sleeves. I stepped closer. "Is that see-through?" I asked, staring at the dress. For a second, I imagined Harper in the dress. The color would suit her.

"It's sheer, but the lace covers all the important bits, so it looks more revealing than it is," the assistant said, dissolving my thoughts of Harper.

What was the matter with people? "My daughter is fourteen. She doesn't do revealing, not even fake revealing." I turned toward the dressing room. "Amanda," I shouted. "Get dressed. We're going somewhere else." Clearly this store was in the market to dress up little girls like hookers, so we wouldn't find anything here.

Amanda didn't speak as she emerged from the changing rooms, walked straight past me and out the door into the heat. I followed her as she headed east.

"Where do you want to go now?" I asked.

"Home."

"I thought you wanted a dress?"

"Not if you're going to growl at the clerks and tell me I look slutty in everything."

I sighed. "I don't growl."

She raised her eyebrows at me.

"And you could never look slutty."

She shook her head. "I'm growing up, Dad. You've got to get your head around it."

I preferred it when Amanda screamed and cried to when she was resigned and disappointed in me. All I wanted was for her to be happy. Dressed in a burka, but happy.

"You know I love you, right?" I asked. "And I just want what's best for you."

She shrugged. "It's just you totally go off the deep end. You can have a conversation with me, you know? Use logic rather than just have a meltdown."

I tuned into the thump of my footsteps compared to the light patter of hers. "Yeah, you're right. I could have approached things a different way." I'd just been so stunned, but I didn't want a relationship where we were just fighting from now until she went to college. "I just don't want you growing up too fast, that's all."

"I know, Dad. But it's happening."

She was turning into my shrink slash daughter. "Okay, well you be patient with me and I'll try not to have a meltdown. How about that for the terms of a peace treaty?"

"We can try that," she said, shrugging.

We paused at the corner of Fifty-Sixth and Park. "Serendipity?" I asked.

She nodded. At least that was one thing she hadn't grown out of. Yet.

"You going to put bricks on my head?" she asked.

I'd teased her when she was younger about stunting her growth. Back then she'd seemed to sprout a foot a month. It was like seeing time pass right in front of my eyes.

"If you had a girlfriend, this would be easier."

I chuckled, trying to ignore the flashes of Harper's smile as Amanda said the word *girlfriend*. "How do you figure?" I asked as Amanda linked her arm through mine.

"She'd tell you that those dresses looked pretty on me," she said as we crossed the street, trying to dodge the mix of office workers and tourists coming at us from the opposite direction.

"Amanda, you'd look pretty in anything. That's not the point. A girlfriend wouldn't change my mind about you wearing clothes meant for women much older than you." I liked her dressed as she was now, in jeans and a T-shirt.

"But another girl, an adult, might be able to convince you."

"Honestly, no one would be able to change my mind, and anyway, you have your aunts, and Grandma King and Granny. And your mom. They're girls."

"Mom doesn't count because she's not here. And you've never listened to anything your sisters told you."

"I listen to Violet." I couldn't exactly pinpoint the last time I'd taken her advice, but I was sure there was an example. "And I don't have time for a girlfriend." I hadn't even had a chance to speak to Harper or to think what to say when we did speak.

"Grandpa always said you can always find time to do the things you want to do."

My dad was a very wise man, but I didn't appreciate his advice in this instance. Maybe because it cut a little too close to the bone.

"You could just agree to go to dinner with Scarlett's friend."

"What friend?" I asked as my cell buzzed in my pocket.

"You know, the one Scarlett mentioned earlier?"

I'd clearly tuned out when my sister was speaking. I didn't remember her mentioning anyone. "I don't remember."

"You do. Her friend from college who used to live in LA." She tugged on my jacket. "Please, Dad?"

"Why is this so important to you?" I didn't understand why she was so set on me dating. Was she trying to distract me, hoping if I was dating I'd suddenly have a change of heart about the hair dye and appropriate clothing?

She shrugged. "It's one night out of your life."

God, she sounded like my mother.

"And I'll do piano practice for a week without you having to ask. Think of it as the bill of rights to our treaty."

Maybe having dinner with a woman would get Harper out of my system. She wasn't the only smart, ballsy, beautiful woman in New York City after all. "I shouldn't have to force you to do piano."

"It's up to you." She shrugged. "Seems like a sweet deal to me."

"A month. And you have to drop the whining about the hair dye."

She grinned up at me. "Deal."

Anything to keep my daughter happy—well, anything but a short, tight, or low-cut dress for her eighth grade dance.

chapter five

Harper

MAX. FUCKING. KING.

I thought I'd hated him before but his assholyness had reached dizzying new heights. I stomped into my bedroom, threw the lid off my laundry basket, and started pulling out things to take to wash. I needed to channel my energy into something productive.

Okay, I had to take responsibility. I'd fucked him. I'd *wanted* to fuck him. And it had been great—a release, no more than that. It had been amazing, as if he'd known what I needed before I did. And he'd had all the right equipment and he'd known how to use it. But he hadn't spoken to me since that night two days ago. Hadn't even looked at me. We'd agreed on Vegas; I'd suggested it. But he didn't have to ignore me.

Arrogant men should be illegal. Or sent to an island without any women on it to die of sexual frustration.

Coming to my rescue in the gym suggested he wasn't quite the asshole I thought he was. Then seeing him shirtless, and the way he'd growled at me, like an animal? Well, I don't know what had come over me, but any willpower I'd had just dissolved, and I'd wanted him.

But what had I been thinking? Fucking my boss was a bad idea for so many reasons. I desperately wanted him to think I was good at my job, not just know my depilatory habits. I'd worked hard for this position, and I didn't just want him to see me as a piece of ass. I certainly didn't want it getting out and people to start gossiping about how I was sleeping my way to the top or an easy lay.

Thank God it was Friday and I wouldn't have to see him for two whole days. Not that I had to worry about that—he'd canceled three meetings with me just to avoid me. Which was the behavior of a fifteen-year-old boy.

It wasn't as if I'd expected a ring, or dinner. But, hell, a "Hello, how are you, thanks for the hot sex" was surely only polite.

I grabbed my clothes, piled them into a huge Ikea bag, and dumped it by the door, ready to head down to the laundry room. I just had to find the bra I'd taken off in front of the TV earlier that week. As I entered the sitting area, the ceiling rattled with the clip of heels. Jesus, it had only been two days since Max's dick had been in me, and now he was banging some other girl. I pitied any girl dumb enough to fuck Max King. Which, apparently, included me.

I let out a yell of frustration, then covered my mouth. Had he heard that? I didn't want him to think I cared if he had another girl in the apartment.

I didn't give a shit.

But the last thing I wanted to do was sit here listening to my boss fuck someone else. Maybe it wasn't another woman. Maybe Max liked to dress up. Nothing about that man would surprise me anymore. I smiled, happy with that particular constructed reality.

Feeling under the couch cushions, I grasped a bra strap, then pulled it free and threw it over to join the rest of my laundry. I grabbed my keys from the side table, a report from work, and the detergent I'd bought on my way home from the office. I had at least three loads to do and if I stayed down there, I'd avoid the sexcapades of Max King. As I headed for the elevator, dragging the bag of clothes behind me, the clitter-clatter of heels seemed to follow me out of the door.

The elevator didn't take as long as usual, and I realized it had come straight from the penthouse. When the doors pinged open I came face to face with the knowledge it hadn't been Max wearing the high heels after all. There was only one apartment above me, so the woman Max King had just fucked would be standing before me.

I wanted the kind of superpower where I could stop time and rearrange things. Then I could hide and ensure that when the elevator stopped on my floor, the beauty in front of me would wonder why it had stopped at all. Instead, I had to step into the elevator in my sweats, forced to look up to smile when the gorgeous woman said, "Good evening."

"Hi," I replied as I discreetly studied her. I'd always wanted to be blonde. I'd tried to dye my hair once, but it just turned out a little like orange cotton candy. At least three inches taller than me, she made me feel like a hobbit standing next to her Arwen. Any moment now she'd ruffle my hair and say, "You're a dear little thing."

Max King might be an asshole, but he had great taste in women, even if I did say so myself.

It wasn't as if I'd expected anything from Max, but it stung a little to run into his latest conquest when he hadn't even given me the time of day. Asshole.

"Another glamourous Friday night in New York City?" she asked, smiling as she gestured toward my bag of laundry.

What a bitch. She didn't know I wasn't going out later with a hot guy or a hotter girl. "Something like that," I replied. "But better that than waste my time on men who don't deserve me."

She laughed. "Yes, doing laundry is preferable to spending time with most of the men I've dated."

Okay, maybe she was being funny rather than bitchy. Did she realize what an asshole Max was? Should I warn her?

"Let's hope my date tonight raises the bar," she said. "He seems nice so far, and every now and then you have to take a chance on someone, right?"

I couldn't reply but smiled manically. She thought Max was nice? Oh yeah, a nice kind of *asshole*.

The elevator doors opened and she stepped out.

"Enjoy your evening," she said with a little wave.

Max King was notoriously guarded about his private life. He never mentioned anyone in the articles I'd read about him. It had led to some speculation he was gay. If he was, he certainly did a great impression of a straight man. And he didn't owe me anything, but just because we'd gone to Vegas, didn't mean I wanted him making the trip with someone else quite so soon.

When the elevator got to the basement I got out, dragging my laundry behind me. Maybe I should think about trying to sublet my place and move to Brooklyn after all.

I'd dumped my Ikea bag on the floor, muttering to myself, when I realized I wasn't the only one in the laundry room. A young teen sitting on the long table opposite the washers and dryers caught my eye. I looked up.

"Hi," I said.

"Hey," she replied with a smile. Papers on her lap, she looked like she was doing homework.

"Are you hiding?" I asked. I'd loved escaping from real life at her age. There was never any peace in my house growing up, and I'd longed for quiet.

She furrowed her brow as if thinking hard about my question. "Not really. I'm doing laundry and homework at the same time."

"You do your own laundry?" I flipped open the washer and began to fish out my towels from the bag.

She shrugged. "Only certain times of the month. When I'm at my dad's place there are some things . . ."

"I get it. Boys have it easy, huh?"

She rolled her eyes and I wanted to chuckle. She was a pretty girl with olive skin and long dark hair that fell around her shoulders.

"*So* easy. I mean, no periods? How did God decide that was fair?"

I shut the first washer and flipped open a second. "Well, you've got to assume God is a man, right?" I pulled out my colored items and loaded up the machine. "And I guess he understood that men are such babies they wouldn't be able to cope."

"Babies is right. They squeal when they don't get their way, just like infants."

I laughed. "You're totally right."

"And they always think they're right about *everything*. My dad went ballistic yesterday because I picked out a dress for my eighth grade dance he didn't like." She leaned forward, making circles in the air with her hands. "I told him I'm growing up and that wearing a strapless dress doesn't make me a slut."

"No, it doesn't. But I guess dads have a different view. I can't say because I didn't have a father growing up." I'd always wanted an overprotective father. Someone who would tell my boyfriends to treat me well and keep their hands to themselves. My dad hadn't known when my eighth grade dance was, let alone had an opinion regarding my dress.

"You didn't? Did he die?" she asked, seemingly unaware of how personal her question was.

I smiled. "No. He just wasn't interested in me."

The girl paused and then said, "Well my dad is entirely too interested. I thought my mom was strict."

"What does your mom say about the dress?"

She shrugged. "Dad has the final say. Before she used to be able to talk him around, but now?" She shook her head. "I keep telling him he needs a girlfriend. He needs an adult to tell him I'm right sometimes."

"You want your dad to have a girlfriend?" Didn't kids want divorced parents to get back together rather than move on?

"Sure. He's been on his own for so long and I want him to be happy. I don't ever remember him having a girlfriend, and my mom has Jason. They've been married *forever*. I don't want my dad to be on his own."

Maybe her dad was still in love with her mom? "Does your father get along with your stepdad?"

"Yeah. They used to play basketball every week."

Okay maybe her dad wasn't hung up on her mom. "Wow, that sounds like a friendly divorce," I said.

She frowned. "My mom and dad were never married."

That sounded familiar. Poor girl. Loser dad not wanting to take responsibility—I knew how that one went. I stayed quiet, not wanting to make her feel bad.

"Dad just works too hard, and we have fun but I think he needs fun with a girlfriend.

You know. Plus, I'd like to have someone to hang out with, go shopping with. And most of all, I'd like a baby sister. I've always been the only kid around, amongst a bunch of adults. I'm always the youngest and it sucks."

I laughed. "You're trying to get him to have another baby? You have to go easy on him." I began to load a third washer with my whites. "He'd probably be just the same if he were married. Sounds like he cares about you. And because he is a man, your dad knows what goes on in boys' heads." They thought about sex a *lot*. I could understand her father's concerns. She was sweet and beautiful.

"Do you have a boyfriend?" she asked.

I shook my head. "Nope. I'm concentrating on my work for now." Which was true. I wasn't interested in the distraction a man would bring to my life at the moment. Max King had been just about sex, which was exactly what I wanted. I needed to find someone to fuck who wasn't my boss and wasn't an asshole.

"That's always my dad's answer."

"I'm not good at picking guys." I wasn't sure if I wasn't good at picking them or I wasn't looking for the right thing. I knew what I didn't want. I knew someone who put family first was important to me, and most of the men I came across were driven and ambitious. I didn't want a man who didn't understand what should be a priority. I didn't want a man like my father.

"I figure I'll work hard, make my own money, have fun, and see if Prince Charming shows up unexpectedly." Seemed unlikely but I hadn't entirely given up hope. "The thing about boys is that you can think they're going to be one thing and they turn out to be entirely another." Max King was a perfect example of that. I still didn't really know who he was. Was he an asshole? Someone who cared about a downtown deli-owner's business? Or just a man who knew how to fuck? Maybe all of the above.

"Really?" she asked, her eyes wide.

"Sure. Be careful to avoid the guys who tell you how great they are. I'm looking for a man who *shows* me what a great guy he is." By ignoring me, Max had proved he was an asshole. "Judge people by their actions, not their words."

"Everyone keeps telling me that Callum Ryder likes me, but he hasn't asked me to the dance."

"Does that happen in the eighth grade? You go as boy-girl couples?"

She tucked her hair around her ear. "You don't go together. I guess it just means you'll dance with them when you're there."

That made more sense. "Right. And you want Callum Ryder to ask you?"

"Well, if he likes me, I thought he would."

"But do you like him? Don't be satisfied with a boy just because he likes you." I poured detergent into the machines.

"He's popular, and good at sports."

"Do you get butterflies in your stomach when you see him?" I asked. I might not like him, but Max was hot. And an excellent lay. And I had to admit to a couple of tiny butterflies whenever our eyes met.

"I'm not sure. I don't think so," she replied.

"If he doesn't give you butterflies, he's not worth going toe-to-toe with your dad for. He sounds protective."

I finished loading the final washer and pressed start on all three machines.

"Don't get me wrong, I love my dad. He's just not good with women."

I laughed. "None of them are. It's a good lesson to learn early in life."

"And he wants me to stay a baby. I don't want go to my eighth grade dance wearing a frilly dress that a three-year-old would wear."

"You got a picture of the strapless one?"

She pulled out her phone, scrolled through photos, then held up her handset. The dress *was* a little revealing. "It's pretty, but I think you can do better by leaving a little more to the imagination," I replied. "Can I?" I held out my hand for her phone.

I hopped up next to her and began to scroll through websites. "Have you thought about one of those dresses with a long sheer skirt over a shorter skirt? That might make him happy."

She grinned at me. "What's your name?" she asked.

"Harper. Finder of eighth-grade-dance dresses."

"I'm Amanda. Needer of an eighth-grade-dance dress."

"It's fate," I said, tapping the phone.

"Do you think I could do strapless if it's long?"

Amanda's father didn't sound like a man who wanted his daughter to show any skin. "I don't think strapless is the most flattering style. I think you can still show off some skin here," I said, sweeping my hand below my neck, "without upsetting your dad. We need to find something off the shoulder. Suits all women, young and old."

Amanda grinned at me. "That sounds like it could work."

"And then maybe something long but with a slit up the leg?" I glanced up from the phone to see Amanda fidgeting excitedly.

We spent the next hour looking at different styles, working out what would be demure enough to please her father, but pretty enough to please her.

Eventually Amanda's laundry was ready. "I better go back. He'll be home from work and wondering where I am. I left a note, but he won't read it." She rolled her eyes. Her phone started to vibrate, *Dad* flashing on the screen. "Speak of the devil."

"Hi, Dad." She rolled her eyes. "Yes, I'm coming up now."

"He has dinner ready," she said. "I better go."

Wow. A man so devoted to his daughter he didn't date, and on top of that he cooked. Sounded like a keeper. "Never say no to a man who can cook. And remember, be nice to him. That's the way to get what you want. Men get taken in so easily by a few compliments." I winked at her.

"Thank you so much." She flung her arms around my neck and I froze, her gesture taking me by surprise.

"I'm going shopping again next week," she said as I squeezed her back. "Yesterday was a total bust, but at least now I won't just try the same things again and have the same argument."

"Exactly. Men have to think they've won. Never let on that really, you've gotten your own way."

Amanda laughed. "I need boy lessons from you."

"Single girl," I said, pointing to myself. "I don't know anything."

"That's not true. I'm not going to listen to a word boys say from now on. I'm only going to watch what they do."

"You'll go far if you remember that. It was so nice to meet you, Amanda. Have fun at your dance."

She took her pile of clean, folded laundry and left me to my three washers, my report, and thoughts of my father. Was it because Amanda's father was of a younger generation that he was so involved with her growing up? When I was younger, every now and then my dad had tried to get involved in my life. I even remembered him coming to a couple of my school plays. But it had never lasted long and then we wouldn't see him for months. He'd just disappear as soon as I started to expect anything of him. I grew out of any expectation eventually.

Or maybe not. I still wanted him to ask me to go work for him, even knowing all the times he'd let me down. I guess I still wanted him to prove with his actions that he loved me. It would be like he'd turned up for every birthday and school play. My mother always told me he loved me but I never saw any evidence. So when I graduated and he didn't offer me a job, I stopped answering his intermittent calls. And now my only communications with him happened through his lawyer.

"Is that a penis?" I asked Grace matter-of-factly as we stood in front of a canvas at the exhibition in New Jersey she'd convinced me to attend. The space wasn't a pretty, shiny gallery in Chelsea, but a huge warehouse in the middle of some industrial area. I was pretty sure if we looked hard enough, we'd find a dead body.

"No, it's not a penis. Why would my boyfriend paint a gigantic knob?"

"Men are weird. And obsessed with their penis," I replied. I thought that was obvious. I was always surprised when male artists *didn't* paint their junk. I was sure Van Gogh had plenty of penis drawings hidden away in his attic.

"Many of the great artists painted beautiful women," Grace said.

"Exactly. Because they were obsessed with their penis. Case closed."

"How're things with your asshole boss?" Grace asked as we walked over to a plinth with an empty Perspex case on it.

I hadn't told Grace I'd wound up naked with Max. How could I explain it to her when I didn't understand it myself? She'd think I'd totally lost it. "Still an asshole." Which was true, even more so now that he was ignoring me after the nakedness.

"What are you going to do?" she asked.

I shrugged and took a sip of my warm white wine. "What can I do? I'm just going to grow a thick skin and stick it out." And try not to fuck him again. Scratch that—definitively not fuck him again. I hadn't mentioned to Grace that he lived in the same building. There wasn't any reason to hide that piece of information, but for some reason I didn't feel like sharing.

"Great. So I have to listen to you moan about him for the next two years?"

"You brought it up, and anyway, I have to put up with things like this for you." I twirled my finger in the air, then peered closer at the box in front of us. It was as if someone had stolen the artwork we were meant to be looking at. "Did they forget to put something in here?" I asked.

"No, it's supposed to be some kind of commentary on reality TV and how the public will watch anything the networks commission." Grace pulled her eyebrows together. "I think that's it. Or they might have just forgotten the art."

We giggled before being interrupted by Grace's new boyfriend, Damien, and his very tall friend.

Grace's eyes gleamed as she said, "Harper, this is George."

George had one of those faces people describe as friendly. Five-foot-ten, with brown hair cut short and in a blue, button-down shirt and jeans, he was quite attractive. There was nothing about him that would immediately have me pressing my red emergency button and running for the door, which had happened more often than not when Grace had introduced me to men.

"George, this is Harper, my best friend in the world. Keep her company? Damien's taking me to look at his etchings." Grace pulled Damien's arm, leaving George and I alone and embarrassed.

The word *setup* echoed around the space.

Couldn't we all have just stayed and talked?

"Excuse Grace. She was dropped on her head a lot," I said.

"As a baby?" George asked.

I shook my head. "No, by me, every time she tries to set me up."

He chuckled. "Yeah, she's a force of nature." A half-second of uncomfortable silence followed before George said, "Are you enjoying the art?"

"Honestly, no. I don't get it." I winced as I looked him in the eye.

"Thank God I'm not the only one," he replied, smiling back at me. "Don't tell Damien I said so, but what the fuck? Have you been into the black room?" He pointed across the space to a sectioned-off part of the warehouse. "It's full of women holding their heads and screaming."

"Really?" I asked, intrigued. "Women sick of bad dates? Sorry, present company excepted, of course."

He laughed again. "Maybe. I didn't recognize anyone, so I'm hopeful none of my exes are in there." He winked and for the first time in my life, instead of getting an urge to put a spoon through a guy's eye, I thought the gesture was cute. "Another drink?"

"The bar I like." We walked toward the biggest crowd of people who all seemed to have similar taste in art—the kind that smelled like wine. "So, tell me about yourself. Was your mother a Wham! fan?"

"No, I'm named after my grandfather, not George Michael. Although I *am* a fan, particularly of his day-glow period."

There weren't many men who made me laugh. Maybe this wouldn't turn out to be the worst setup in the world. We got fresh drinks and found a free spot, away from the crowd and the art.

"I'm an architect, I'm from Ohio, and I don't like cats. You?"

"I'm from Sacramento," I replied. "I don't like cats either and I'm a researcher at a consulting firm."

"Grace said you were new to the city. Did you move for the job?"

"Partly." My move had been totally about King & Associates. I'd have moved anywhere to work with Max King. "And to live in New York."

"And now that you're doing it, is it all you thought it would be?"

"I don't get along with my boss."

"Oh," he said, nodding. "But does anyone? I mean, isn't it like the rule that you hate your boss? Isn't he just there to stand between you and your internet surfing habit?"

I tilted my head. "I don't resent him because he interrupts my online shopping experience. I enjoy what I do. My boss is just rude." And gorgeous. "And arrogant." And great in bed. "And ungrateful." And kisses as if it was his major in college. Max King was a man who had every right to be obsessed with his penis.

George had a dimple that appeared on the left of his face when he smiled. "I have my own firm. I wonder if one of the guys working for me is standing at a party having the exact same conversation about me."

I winced. "God, I'm sorry. I'm sure that's not happening—"

"Don't sweat it. Like I said, I think it's part of the job—some people aren't ever going to like you."

"And you're okay with that?" I asked, genuinely interested.

"I'm not sure I've thought about it. Whether or not I'm okay with it, it's still going to happen, right? Not everyone likes you, do they?"

I laughed. "Hey, you've only known me a few minutes and already you think people must hate me?"

"It's not personal. And when you're signing someone's paycheck, things just get magnified. Normally, if you don't get along with people, you don't have chemistry with someone, you can just avoid them. But at work, you're forced to spend time with them, so you're just more aware that you don't like the person."

Generally, he made sense, but he hadn't met the specific asshat that was Max King. "I guess."

"How about I distract you from work one night this week, take you to dinner and prove not all bosses are evil?"

I bit the edge of my plastic cup. "This week?" I asked.

"Yeah, unless you're booked up already."

"No. Not booked up." Did I want to go to dinner with George? The memory of Max's hips pinning me to the wall of his apartment flashed through my head. I touched my neck, as if I could still feel his breath whispering against my skin. "Dinner sounds good."

I needed new memories to replace the ones of Max King.

༄

Monday at King & Associates was busier than I'd expected. I'd gotten pulled in on a new, high profile research project on luxury goods in China. I'd been so excited I'd almost forgotten Max King was my boss. For the first time in forever, I left work with a smile on my face, despite it being past eight.

"Hi, Barry." I waved at the doorman as I passed his desk and pressed the elevator button. I wanted a warm bath, my bed, and maybe a smidgen of *Game of Thrones*.

As the doors slid open, Max stood in front of me in his workout clothes, tall, handsome, and staring at his phone.

God-damn you, Lycra.

I froze, unsure what to do. Was he coming out or going down to the basement? At that moment he glanced up and for the first time since he'd made me come a bazillion times, he looked me in the eye.

"Harper," he said, a note of surprise in his voice.

Had he thought he'd never see me again? I worked for him, lived in his building, for Christ's sake. Maybe he wasn't as smart as people said he was.

"Going up?" I asked.

"No, yes." He sounded confused. "Get in. I've been wanting to speak to you."

"Well you know where I live, and you know where I work, so I'm not sure you gave yourself the most impossible task there." I tapped my forehead. "You just had to set your mind to it."

He grabbed my elbow with his large hand and immediately warmth flooded my body. He pulled me into the elevator just as he had when I'd turned up at his apartment door to complain about the noise, and just like that I was surrounded by him, his smell, the nearness of his breath, his tongue, and his cock.

chapter six

Max

"GET YOUR HANDS OFF ME," SHE SPAT, TWISTING HER ARM AND FORCING ME TO RELEASE HER. "I thought we'd have a chance to speak at work—"

"Funny thing is, when you cancel meetings with people, it means that you don't see them."

Had I canceled meetings? "Last week was difficult. And Donna controls my schedule. I didn't deliberately—"

"Save your breath."

The elevator stopped at the basement and its doors opened. I'd been heading to the gym.

"We live in the same building. You could have knocked on my door." She folded her arms.

I had to try very hard not to smile. She was so pretty, despite her mood. Maybe even because of her mood.

"Are you getting out?" she asked.

I shook my head and she started jabbing at the seventh-floor button. "I couldn't knock on your door. I know you live on the seventh floor because you complained about the stomping on your ceiling, but there are five apartments down there. Trust me." I pulled her chin up with my index finger. "I counted them on Thursday evening."

Her stare was blank. "It's Monday, Max."

It was strange, hearing my name on her lips again. Last time I heard it she'd been about to climax.

I reached out and smoothed her hair over her shoulders. "I'm sorry." It was true; I was. Since the day Amanda was born, I'd sworn I wouldn't be the guy who messed around with women. If I didn't want anyone to do it to my daughter, I couldn't very well do it to someone else's. I might only have casual relationships, but I didn't ever pretend it was anything more. "I wasn't ignoring you. Frankly, I hadn't expected you to have gone when I woke up. I thought we'd talk before work."

"Yeah, well I wanted to be at work on time." She shrugged and I'd taken a half step toward her when the doors opened. I liked her sass. The employees at King & Associates came packaged earnest and compliant. Other than Donna, everyone just nodded their heads and said yes to me. At home, the world tipped on its head, and it was a miracle if I ever got anyone to say yes to anything. Harper continued to blur the boundaries between my work and personal life.

"You made me late," I said, not ready for our conversation to be over.

"What are you doing?" Harper asked as I followed her out of the elevator. "This isn't your floor."

"I want to talk to you." I wasn't sure what I was doing. What could I say to her? "I want to apologize," I said decisively. "For the other night. I shouldn't have taken advantage in the way I did." It was just that all the fantasies that had been filling my brain since she started at King & Associates had come rushing back when she'd stood semi-naked in front of me.

She opened her front door, stepped into her apartment, and spun to face me. "Take advantage? Jesus, you're such a fucking asshole." She tried to slam the door shut but I stuck my foot in the way.

"Get the fuck out," she yelled.

"I think you're beautiful," I said and pushed the door open and stepped inside. "Beautiful, but supremely fucking irritating."

She stared at me, her mouth open as if I'd just stolen all her words. Then she turned, threw her purse down, and stomped over to her bed. I glanced around. Her apartment was tiny and full of things everywhere including piles of books stacked on the floor and shoes wherever I looked. The bed was over to one side, where the floor was slightly raised. She kicked off her shoes and started to undo her blouse. I hardened immediately. She was undressing?

"Harper," I said as I followed her.

"I'm irritating?" she asked.

I didn't know how to react. I wanted to pin her down and make her listen to me. Kiss her. Fuck her.

"I'm irritating?" She shook her head in disbelief and turned to face me. "*I'm* fucking irritating?"

How could I make her see what I meant? I grabbed one of her hands, pulled her toward me, and kissed her. She broke free and pushed at my chest, but I snaked my arms around her so she couldn't escape. Eventually, she stopped trying to move away from me, accepted she was trapped, and stilled. "Kiss me, Harper," I said. "Do as I say."

"You're an asshole," she said as she punched me in the shoulder.

I brought my hands to her face and her lips to mine. She didn't resist. I snaked my tongue into her mouth and found hers hot and ready. I groaned against her lips and slid my hand down to her ass, to pull her against me so she could feel my erection. Her fingers slid into my hair and our kisses became frantic, biting and greedy.

She ended our kiss and moved away. "Max?"

I wasn't sure what came next. Why had she pulled out of my arms? Was she going to ask me to leave? "Yes?" I replied.

"Get your clothes off and fuck me," she said.

I grinned as she began to undo the rest of the buttons on her shirt, her fingers fumbling over each one.

"Come here," I said as I knocked her hands out of the way.

"Be careful with that. This blouse is new and I can't afford to replace it."

I'd undone the buttons before she'd finished her sentence and slid the silk over her shoulders. Her skin looked so smooth that I bent to kiss the exposed, bronzed flesh, desperate to feel her under my lips. She tipped her head back and I grinned against her skin.

"Asshole, huh?" I pulled off my running top and stepped out of my shorts.

"Do you want me to change my mind?" She cocked her hip, the bra straps falling from her shoulders.

"You're not going to change your mind," I said, leaning toward her, pushing her skirt up around her waist, and thrusting my hand into her underwear.

"Don't," she said, her voice breathy. "I can't ruin this skirt. I just bought it." My fingers pressed into her folds and though she wasn't fighting me off, I could tell she was concerned about her clothes. Why?

"Lie down," I said, guiding her to the bed, where I quickly slid off her skirt and panties.

"Max . . ."

I wanted to sink into the way she called my name.

"Yes?" I kissed up the inside of her thigh, along her soft, tight skin, reaching her pussy. I gave her one long lick over her slit but continued to work my way up over her belly and between her breasts. The pace was slower than last week. Her anger had ebbed away and just existed in the way every now and then she scored her fingernails up my arms or whispered, "You're an asshole," as I continued to kiss and lick and suck her entire body.

She reached above her head, pointing at her nightstand. "Condom," she said. She might think I was an asshole, but she didn't mind my dick. I grabbed a condom and as quickly as I could, rolled it on. As I lay on my back, Harper rose off the bed and began to straddle me.

"I don't think so," I said, pushing her to her back. "I'm fucking you. You're not fucking me." I nudged her knees wide with my legs and pushed into her. Her eyebrows pulled together as she concentrated on not making the sound of pleasure I could tell was rippling below the surface. I pulled out and thrust in, wanting to set that moan free.

"If you're going to fuck me, you'd better make it good," she said.

Highly. Fucking. Irritating.

She knew this was so fucking good. I grabbed her leg and lifted it, going deeper, showing how good it was.

She bit down on her lip, still swallowing her reactions.

"Really? You're not going to tell me how good this is?" I asked, panting, pushing into her, feeling her pulse beneath me. "You're not going to say how this is the best you've ever had?" I slammed into her, pushing her up the bed, my jaw tightening.

"Fuck you," she bit out.

"You know it is. You love my dick inside you, making you come. You can't get enough."

A deep moan ripped from her chest. *Finally.*

"There, you see? You just need to give in and realize how good I make you feel."

She tightened around me, lifting her hips to meet my thrusts. A rumble vibrated up my throat at the dizzying sensation. "So. Fucking. Good."

She scratched her nails so hard down my back it interrupted my rhythm. When I glanced at her, she grinned. I pulled her arms down and slid my palms against hers, pinning her to the mattress, and began to push into her again. "Watch your manners, Ms. Jayne. If you're not careful, I won't let you come."

She raised an eyebrow. "As if you could stop me."

She had no idea.

I stilled. "Wanna test that theory?" She squirmed underneath me, desperate for more of my cock. "Yeah, I didn't think so."

"You're an arrogant pig," she spat out and turned her head to the side.

"I think what you meant to say is 'thank you for fucking me.'" I moved on top of her, grinding into her. I might be baiting her, but really I wanted to scream at how perfect she was, how good she made me feel. All these months of denying I wanted her burst out. Harper Jayne was every bit as sexy, passionate, and greedy as I'd imagined.

Her breaths were short and needy and her sounds louder and less and less controlled.

"You're beautiful. And sexy and—" I paused a second. I had to be careful I didn't come first. "And you drive me crazy at work." I thrust again. "Because I want to bend you over my desk and drive my cock into you. Just. Like. That."

She screamed as she came, rippling around me, pulling my come from my cock, milking it, owning it. I couldn't resist her and came, roaring her name.

I collapsed on top of her and savored the feel of my hot skin covering hers.

Rolling onto my back, I reached out and slid her into my arms.

"You looking for a high five?" she asked and I chuckled.

"Stop being annoying for five seconds and come here," I said. She moved a few inches closer and settled into me. "So irritating." I kissed the top of her head.

After a few minutes she pushed herself up on her elbow. "Do you really think about fucking me over your desk?"

I groaned. "You can't question me on stuff I say while I'm fucking."

"Why?" she asked. "Is this some rule I don't know about?"

"Yes, it's a rule. The first rule of dirty talk is that after you come, you don't discuss what was said in the heat of the moment."

I expected abuse in response, but she was quiet for a few moments before saying, "Oh. I didn't know." It was such an uncharacteristic reply. I wanted to ask her what she was thinking but despite the fact that three minutes ago I'd been fucking her, it seemed like prying.

I pulled her closer.

"Did you look at my revised Bangladesh report?"

Did she really just ask me that? "No."

"No?" she asked. "You've had it nearly a week." She ran her fingertips over my chest.

"No, we're not talking about it now. Fucking hell, Harper, I just came like five seconds ago. I don't want to be reminded of the fact that fucking you is totally inappropriate."

"Inappropriate?" she yelled. Were we back to the shouting already? "Get the fuck out of my bed." She tried to push me off the mattress.

Jesus. I couldn't do anything right with this girl. Except make her come, apparently.

I gripped her wrists and she started to kick me, so I rolled her to her back and pinned her thighs to the bed to stop her thrashing. "Jesus, woman, you go from zero to sixty in a millisecond." She closed her eyes and turned her head to the side.

"Get off me."

"Not until you tell me what's wrong and why you're freaking out."

"Unbelievable."

At least she turned and looked at me.

"What?" I asked.

"You just told me fucking me is inappropriate. Like your body acted without your consent. And you expect me not to have a reaction to that? You're an—"

"Asshole," I said, finishing her sentence. "Yes, I heard you the first fifteen thousand times you said it." I released her and rolled off the bed, pissed she was giving me such a hard time every second of every minute of every day. I was her boss; of course it was inappropriate for me to fuck her. I grabbed my shorts and T-shirt and dressed quickly.

"And now you're just going to go?" she asked, propped up on her elbows, her perfectly round tits begging me to come back to bed.

"Did you forget that you ordered me out of your apartment?"

"Whatever." She leapt out of bed and barged into the bathroom, slamming the door shut behind her.

Fucking hell. She was a total pain in the ass. Beautiful. Talented. Sexy. Perfectly infuriating.

Had I been an asshole? She was irritating, but maybe I shouldn't have told her fucking her was inappropriate right after we had sex. I wasn't used to having to mind what I said with the women I was fucking.

I sat on the edge of her bed, waiting for twenty minutes for her to emerge.

"Hi," she said when she finally came out wearing a towel. Her eyes kept flickering from me to the floor.

"Hi," I replied. "I didn't mean to upset you." I never meant to upset the women in my life but it happened far too often.

"Mean it or not, you did." She shook her head. "I don't know what it is. Maybe you don't realize how you come off."

I scrubbed my hands over my face. "I'm not good with . . ." How did I say I wasn't used to having to interact with the women I was fucking outside the bedroom?

"Women?" She finished my sentence for me, arching her eyebrow.

"I don't want to piss you off, Harper." Yes it would be awkward at work, but I actually liked the girl. "I'm the person who signs your paychecks. That's all I was trying to say."

"You need to think about what you say before you say it."

I nodded. "I'll do better in the future."

She stepped toward me. "Okay. The future starts now, right?"

I pulled her onto my lap. I cupped her neck and pressed my lips against hers. Immediately I wanted her again. It wasn't as if we were in the office anyway. Here we were neighbors, not colleagues. I tugged at her towel and it fell away from her body.

"Yeah. The future starts right now."

The next morning I got into the office extra early. I was trying to finish going through Harper's Bangladesh report. I didn't want any other reason for Harper to think I was an asshole.

"I said no calls, Donna," I barked into my speakerphone, then hung up.

My door burst open and I slammed my hand on my desk as I looked up.

"Max, you're going to want to take this call," Donna said. I seriously doubted it. Other than something happening to Amanda—shit. "Press line one."

Instead of leaving me to take the call, she shut the door and leaned against it, a huge grin on her face. Amanda must be okay if Donna was smiling. In fact, this probably was Amanda telling me she'd been asked to her eighth grade dance.

Just as I picked up the receiver and punched line one, Donna said, "Charles Jayne."

Fuck.

Charles Jayne was the founder and senior partner of JD Stanley. His investment bank didn't use outside firms, but I wanted them to make an exception for King & Associates. I'd been hounding them for years. They didn't use outside firms, but I wanted them to make an exception for King & Associates.

"Max King," I answered, trying to keep my voice level as my foot tapped against the desk leg.

"I hear you've been making quite a nuisance of yourself with my director of global research," a man with a deep voice said on the other end of the phone.

Shit, had I pushed things too far? My contact had given me the inside track on Harold Barker. Apparently he liked tennis, so I'd suggested he join me in my box at the US Open later in the summer. I'd invited him to the Met once when I'd run into him at a cocktail reception, but he'd politely declined. I was hoping tennis would hit the spot.

"It's a pleasure to speak to you, sir. I'm not sure I'd describe myself as a nuisance. I just think that we could do a lot for JD Stanley, and I'd like an opportunity to show you what's possible."

"Yes, well, that much you've made clear," he replied. "Which is why I'm calling. Come in on the twenty-fourth and tell us a little about what you do at King & Associates."

Holy crap.

"Yes, sir. What—"

"Ten sharp. You better live up to your hype."

Before I could ask him how long we had, who would be in the room, what he wanted to know, the line went dead. I guess when you were Charles Jayne, you didn't want to waste a second.

I hung up and stared at the phone.

Donna bounded across the room. "Well? What did he want?"

"To give me the opportunity of my career." Had that really just happened? Just like that, Charles Jayne had called and invited me in for a meeting.

"He's going to hire you?"

I shrugged. "He wants me to go in for a meeting on the twenty-fourth."

"I can't believe it," Donna said. "Looks like Harper was a smart hire."

What? I stared at her, expecting her to explain.

"I'm sure your networking helped, but hiring Harper was genius."

"Why does that matter?"

"Well, she's his daughter, right?"

"Harper?" Harper *Jayne*. I'd never made the connection.

"You didn't know?" Donna asked. "That wasn't the reason you hired her?"

"Jesus, you must think I'm a real prick. I wouldn't hire someone just because they had a connection to Charles Jayne. And since when do I get involved with hiring junior researchers?"

Is that what Harper thought? But how could she? She didn't know about my obsession with JD Stanley. "Are you sure that Charles Jayne is Harper's father?" I asked. "I mean, has she acknowledged it? Have you spoken about it?"

Donna blinked. "No, I just assumed, with her name and all. I've never mentioned it."

"Could be a coincidence," I said, thinking out loud.

"Do you want me to ask her?"

Did I? I wanted to know if there was a connection. Had she arranged the meeting?

My mind was a mess. Was Harper just here to spy on things before Charles Jayne decided to invite me to pitch?

"No, I'll ask her. Can you call her in?"

I slid my palms down the front of my pants. I wasn't sure if I was on edge from speaking to Charles Jayne or because I was about to speak to Harper.

A few minutes later, Harper walked into my office, Donna trailing behind her. "Donna, can you close the door, please?" She gave me a pleading look, clearly desperate to know the answer.

Harper watched as Donna shut the door, then turned back to me, glancing at me from under her lashes. Shit, my dick began to stir. I needed to focus.

"Have a seat, Harper." I gestured toward one of the chairs opposite my desk. She took the one I wasn't indicating. Of course.

"We need to talk," I said.

She grimaced. She thought I meant about us. "Regarding a phone call I just had."

"Oh," she said, and she smiled.

I was going to have to just come out and ask her. "Are you related to Charles Jayne?"

Her eyebrows pulled together and she clasped her hands together. "I'm not sure what my last name has to do with anything."

I sat back in my chair and exhaled. I had my answer. She was Charles Jayne's daughter. Donna had been right.

"You're his daughter?" I asked.

She stood up. "I'm not here to talk about my father."

"He just called me," I said, ignoring her glare. "He wants me to meet him and I've wanted to add him as a client for so long—"

"Is that why you hired me?"

Her voice got higher as she spoke. I was handling this all wrong.

"Is that why you fucked me?"

I winced. Christ, I could see how it might look that way. I walked around my desk and leaned against the other side, not wanting to get too close, despite her pull. I had to stop myself from reaching out and touching her.

"You haven't answered my question," she said.

"I didn't know."

She rolled her eyes.

"I'm serious. Donna told me this morning. And anyway, I don't recruit . . ." How did I say her position was too junior for me to have anything to do with? "I don't get involved with human resources stuff."

She wrapped her arms around herself. "Be honest. How long have you been wanting JD Stanley's work?"

"Harper, JD Stanley's one of the most successful investment banks on Wall Street, of course I want to work for them. And you know better than anyone that they protect their research like it's gold bullion. That's why they do almost all of it in house. Any person in my position would want to work with them." I could really do with her inside knowledge.

She stared at me as if I were toxic.

I tapped my fingers on my desk. This could be a win-win situation. "I need your help," I said. Now that she was here, I may as well use it to my advantage. "I want you to work on the pitch with me. Help me land this thing."

"Wow. You don't waste any time, do you? We fucked last night and now you think I'll help you get ahead."

That's not how it was at all. I thought she'd welcome the opportunity to work on such a high-profile account. "No, I just thought you'd want to—"

"Want to get used by a man who wanted to land a new client bad enough to sleep with someone?"

She turned and headed out of my office before I could respond. Once again I'd managed to say the wrong thing. It was becoming a habit as far as Harper was concerned.

chapter seven

Harper

I'D CALLED GRACE RIGHT AFTER MY FIGHT WITH MAX, AND WE'D MET AT A BAR ON MURRAY Street in Tribeca. I waved to the bartender. "Can we get more cocktails and a snack? Something with cheese as a major component." The bartender nodded and I turned back to Grace.

"Okay, I'm totally confused now. You've been banging Max King, the person you hate most in the world?"

"You're totally focusing on the wrong thing."

"Rewind and tell me what the fuck has been going on."

She was looking at me as if I'd just told her I'd decided to move to Alaska.

"I think I got hired by King & Associates because of my sperm donor." I should have changed my last name. We'd never had any sort of connection, so it didn't feel like his name to me.

"The sperm donor being your dad?" Grace asked and I nodded. "How do you know?"

"And he slept with me, like some kind of whore." I shivered. "Well, little does Max know that my father and I only communicate through lawyers these days." How could he have been so cold? I should have trusted my instincts about him.

"We'll get to the sex later. You didn't answer my question." Grace tapped me on the arm, trying to get me to focus. "Who told you that you'd been hired because of who your father is?"

"Max. In his office." I took a sip of my mojito.

She tilted her head to the side. "He said, 'I hired you because of who your father is'?"

"Of course not. He claimed he didn't know. But he was clearly lying." He'd said himself that he really wanted to work for JD Stanley.

"Okay." Grace paused, her eyebrows drawn together. "And you were sleeping with Max? How did *that* happen?" She wiggled her eyebrows. "Late night in the office?"

"He lives in my building. He's penthouse man."

Grace's eyes went wide. "The couple who fucked like bunnies? You banged *that* guy? Jesus, I'm jealous." She took out the cocktail stick from her martini glass and bit off one of the olives.

I tried hard not to smile. She *should* be jealous. Max knew what he was doing with his cock, that was for certain. He probably should have hooked up with Grace in the first place. After all, her family's connections were far more impressive than mine.

"So what are you going to do?" she asked. "Is he boyfriend material?"

"I have no idea. And of course not." I placed my elbows on the bar and pushed my hands through my hair. "What was I thinking, fucking my boss? Now I have to quit."

"He said he didn't know who your father was. Wouldn't he have said something already if he did? Is he the liar-y type?"

"Liar-y?" I glanced at her out of the corner of my eye.

"It's in the Dictionary of Grace. Look it up."

I hadn't thought Max *was* the sort to lie; he was too direct. But it was perfectly possible I'd just been taken in by his hard body and beautiful green eyes. Had I been seduced by his genius brain and passion for what he did? "Does it matter? He knows now. My father invited him to pitch."

"And he said your father told him?"

I waved my hands. "No, he said he put two and two together, and then he asked for my help with the pitch."

"And you don't want to work for your father?"

"Not because of my last name."

Grace nodded vigorously, alcohol clearly loosening her body parts. "I get that, but you are where you are. Max is saying he didn't know. Are you going to cut your face off to spite your nose by quitting?"

"I definitely won't be cutting my face off, or even my nose, but I do think I have to quit. It's all too humiliating. Everyone's going to know who my father is and why I got the job, and I can't work with the man who fucked me to get ahead."

"You're thinking like a woman. You need to think like you have a penis." She slapped her hand on the bar and the bartender jumped before setting down a cheese plate on the counter. "However you got this job, you need to prove you deserve it because you're good at what you do, not because of your last name and not because you're banging the boss." She took a sip of her cocktail. "Men have been getting ahead using the old boy's network for years. You have to take opportunities when you can get them. So not only can't you quit, you need to go in there and tell Max that you should be working on your father's pitch *because* of your name."

She made no sense. "How would that help? That would only make everything worse."

Grace set her glass down, her drink sloshing over the sides. "This, as they say,"—she threw her hands in the air—"is a win, win, win."

I shook my head and checked the time on my phone. I should be getting home, job or no job to go to in the morning.

"Are you listening?" Grace asked.

I wasn't, because she wasn't making any sense, but I put my phone down and gave her my full attention.

"King & Associates does the kind of work you want to do, right?"

"Correct." I nodded.

"And they're good at it, right?"

Why were we recapping this?

"Correct again. Another and you'll win a set of steak knives."

"So, why would you leave a company like that?"

She interrupted me before I could speak. "You just need to shift." She grabbed my barstool and pulled it toward her. "You need to shift your focus. King & Associates is the best place for underpinning capitalism, feeding corporate greed, and all the geeky stuff you do. Am I right?"

I rolled my eyes and took another sip of my drink.

"So stay there. And demand to work on the project. Because your dad is the best at what he does, so the person who lands that account is going to get huge kudos, right?"

"You get the steak knives, yes."

"So play this smart by sticking around. And, while you're at it, prove to your dad why he should have offered you a position in his company over his children who have penises."

I set my empty glass down as I took in what she was saying. Was she on to something? "You're saying I keep working at King & Associates?" Could I bear to keep working with Max?

"Yes, because however you got the job, you're there. So make the most of your opportunity."

"And demand to work on my father's account?"

"As you'll be a star if you land it, right? And you're flipping the bird to your father at the same time. Like I said, it's all win for you." Grace indicated to the bartender that we wanted the check.

"Unless we lose the account." That would be even more humiliating.

"When have you ever lost at anything you wanted?" she asked as she slipped off her stool and handed her black American Express card to the bartender.

"You didn't need to pay," I said.

"*I* didn't. That was courtesy of *my* daddy."

"Thank you, Mr. and Mrs. Park Avenue," I called out. "You might be on to something about not quitting. This could be my opportunity to prove to my father that I can do more than stay at home and lunch for the rest of my life. I'll show him that I'm worth more, and that he should have been begging for me to work for him and his stupid investment bank."

I jumped off my chair. "Yes. That's exactly what I'm going to do." I grabbed Grace's face in my hands and gave her a smack on the lips. "You're a genius."

Somehow between leaving the bar and getting back to my apartment building, all my patience had disappeared and the cocktails I'd consumed over the evening had convinced me it was a great idea to tell Max I would work on the JD Stanley account immediately.

"I'll do it," I said as Max opened his front door.

"Harper, hi." He rubbed the heel of his hand over his eyes and yawned. "I wanted to speak to you earlier, but you ran off."

What was I doing? Standing at my boss's front door in the middle of the night, clearly a little drunk. Did I want to get fired? I stepped back until I hit the wall, but let my eyes trail down Max's hard, naked torso and follow a trail of hair gathering at his belly button before disappearing beneath his pajama bottoms.

"I think you'd better come in," he said, his voice gravelly and deep.

I shook my head in an exaggerated way and slipped my hands behind my back. He stepped toward me and pulled at my elbow. "I said come in."

I lost my balance and toppled toward him. Reaching out to save myself, I pressed my palms on the hot, tight skin of Max's chest. I pushed away, but he pulled me closer, spun us around, and walked us back into his apartment.

"You're drunk," he said as he pressed me up against the wall in his entry and kicked the door shut with his foot. His face was just an inch from mine. I wanted him closer.

"A little," I confessed.

"Why did you run off? You're not quitting, if that's what you think," he said as he dragged his nose against my jaw.

"Tell me when you knew," I said, placing my hands on his bare shoulders.

"Knew?" he asked as he began to kiss my neck.

"Who my father was."

He pulled back and braced himself against the wall, his hands on either side of my head. "I swear to you, I found out today. I think Donna assumed there was a connection but she didn't mention it to me until I got the phone call." He paused and his eyes flickered over my face, as if he were trying to figure out whether I believed him. "Why didn't you say anything?"

I dipped under his arms and walked across the entry. "I don't speak to my father. I don't have anything to do with him." I fiddled with my thumbnail.

"Okay. Well you don't have to work on the pitch. I just thought . . . JD Stanley is the only investment bank on Wall Street I've never done business with."

"So," I replied, and I glanced up.

"Well I can't turn down the opportunity."

"I don't want you to turn it down."

He raised his eyebrows.

"I want you to win that fucking account—and I'm going to help you."

"What changed your mind?"

My eyes hit the floor. "It doesn't matter. You got what you want."

He took a step forward. "Tell me, Harper." I knew I shouldn't say anything more, but there was something in his tone that made it impossible not to comply.

I huffed out a breath. "He has a lot of kids, right?"

His eyes drifted over my face.

"I'm the only girl . . . and the only one he didn't offer a job right out of college."

"Because you're a girl? Or because you don't speak to each other?"

I let his questions drip into my brain. Did he have good relationships with his other children?

Max held out his hand. "Come with me."

All too easily, I slipped my palm into his, his fingers holding me tightly as he led me further down the corridor, deeper into his apartment. What was I doing? I didn't like this man. I should go downstairs to my own apartment. "I'm sorry. It's late. I shouldn't be here."

"Shhh. Let's get you hydrated."

He guided me to a barstool opposite a kitchen island in a huge room I hadn't seen before. The other night I'd only caught the dusky outline of his bedroom and the entryway. I hadn't appreciated the size of the place or how glamorous it was. Max either had incredible taste or he'd hired a great interior designer.

"Drink," he said, setting a glass of water on the white marble counter in front of me.

I took a sip, suddenly much more sober than I'd been when I knocked on his door.

"More," he growled. Jesus, he was so bossy. But I complied and gulped down a couple mouthfuls of water.

He rounded the counter and stood beside me, leaning on the marble. "Tell me about your dad. You think he didn't hire you because—"

"Because I have boobs."

He raised his eyebrows. "Really?"

"He offered me a big chunk of money." I set my glass down. "It's not that he denies my existence—he periodically asks me to dinner."

"So you do speak to him?"

I really needed to leave. "Not since my youngest half brother started his job at JD Stanley the day of his twenty-second birthday. Three weeks after I graduated business school. But not really much before that either."

Max pursed his lips.

"I thought maybe he was waiting for me to finish grad school, and of course I would have said no, but . . ." Max's fingers stroking my arm scattered my thoughts. "He gave us money, me and my mom, but what I wanted was a family."

Max withdrew his hand.

"Sorry, I should stop talking."

"I like to listen. You have a lot to say." His voice was quiet and even, as if he were being sincere, as if he wasn't talking to a drunk woman who thought he was an asshole.

I raised my eyebrows. "I've been drinking. I have more to say in the office, but you're not so interested there."

He cupped my face. "How wrong you are."

His kisses were soft at first, and I closed my eyes, savoring each one.

"We can't do this." My mouth protested, but my hands slipped up his naked back, his warm muscles bunching under my touch. "I can't—"

"I know," he said. "If I'm going to go for the JD Stanley account, I can't exactly be fucking the boss's daughter." As if his body hadn't caught up with his brain, he pulled up my skirt. "But this ass, these legs. They've got me under some kind of spell." He smoothed his hands over my hips and under my ass, slipping inside my panties, then pulled me off the stool and tight to his body.

"We're going to be working together." I wrapped my hands around his neck. "I don't need my head full . . ." . . . *of thoughts of you.* I couldn't say that. I didn't want Max to think I wouldn't be able to concentrate if we were in the office together, but frankly, it was going to be a big ask. "We should focus on the pitch."

He nodded and captured my bottom lip between his teeth. Without thinking, I twisted my hips against his growing erection.

"If my dad suspected . . . I need to show him I'm excellent at my job, not that I got to work at King & Associates because I'm fucking the boss."

"Focused," he repeated. "No boss fucking."

"I'm serious." I pushed against his chest. "Stop thinking with your dick."

"I'm serious, too, but you're encouraging me." He grinned. It was a shock because it happened so rarely. Just for a moment my heart stopped.

"Don't grin at me, you asshole." I tried to twist out of his arms, but he just held me closer.

"Just tonight. This is Vegas. We start with a fresh slate tomorrow morning. No fucking after tonight."

"Vegas? Just for tonight?" I stared into his eyes, trying to see if he was telling the truth. Wondering if I wanted him to be. Yes. Tonight would be my last with Max King. Working on this account and showing my father what he had been missing wasn't worth risking. Not even for the King of Wall Street.

He smoothed a hand over my pussy, then pushed his fingers into my folds. "Just tonight," he whispered.

I lost strength in my knees and stumbled.

"See what a single touch does to you? See the power I have over your body?" He removed his fingers and disappointment caught my breath. I didn't have to answer. "You came here to get fucked, and I'm not going to disappoint you." He bent and lifted me over his shoulder.

"I came to tell you I'd work on the account!" I yelled at his back as I kicked my legs.

"You came to get fucked."

Well, maybe he was right about that. Except sober I'd never have risked colliding with one of his other lovers.

"Vegas," he muttered again. "Just for one more night."

He tipped me onto his bed, my ass bouncing on the mattress, and he grabbed my leg and pulled me toward him. "If I only get to have you for one more night, I need a memory of that pretty mouth of yours wrapped around my cock."

I sat up, my feet dangling over the edge of the bed, and he stepped between my legs, cupping my head in his hand.

"You can't just demand a blow job."

He raised one eyebrow as if to disagree.

I shook my head and pulled down the sides of his pajamas until they hit his ankles. His cock sprang out, hard and thick.

"It seems to be working."

I wanted to have him in my mouth, could feel myself grow wet between my thighs at the thought of his cock between my lips. But I'd clearly made it too easy for him, and I couldn't have that.

I leaned back onto the mattress, opening my legs so my skirt bunched around my hips, then reached into my underwear. Wanting him in no doubt as to what I was doing, I hitched one leg up onto the bed to improve his view and pushed my hands deeper, finding my opening.

"Really?" he asked as he fisted his cock, dragging his hand upward.

"Ask me nicely."

He chuckled, shook his head, and let go of his erection. His energy shifted and he leaned over, stripping me of my clothes. First my skirt, then my panties. Next he fiddled with the buttons of my blouse. He glanced at me, and it was my time to raise my eyebrow at him. "Finding that difficult?" I asked.

Without taking his eyes off me, he ripped my shirt apart. Fuck, that was silk and I'd only worn it three times. "You asshole!"

"Whatever," he replied, reaching behind me and unhooking my bra. "If I only have tonight, I need to see these," he said, staring at my chest as he palmed my skin and pulled at my nipples. My back arched into his touch. He was so forceful, so single-minded about sex—just as he was about everything else. To have that focus concentrated on my body was almost too much to bear.

His hands left my breasts and he dragged his palm down across my stomach until his fingers found my clit. I groaned as his thumb circled and pressed, pulling out my pleasure, inch by inch. His fingers stroked at my folds, and I threw my hands over my head, needing him to send me over the edge.

"Max," I whispered, opening my legs wider, inviting more of him.

"You're desperate for me. My hand is covered in you."

I groaned at his dirty mouth. But he was right. I *was* desperate for him.

"Look at me," he growled.

I opened my eyes. He wore the same look when he was concentrating at work—as if nothing was going to stop him from getting what he wanted.

He stilled and removed his hand, standing up straight. "I want my cock in your mouth. *Please.*" His voice was thick with lust.

He'd been getting me worked up to get his dick sucked? He played dirty.

"Now," he added.

I paused while I thought about my next move. Was I going to give in to him? The thing was, it wasn't giving in if it was what I wanted. And I *did* want to have him in my mouth, to make him feel even half of what he made me feel.

I moved to sit on the edge of the bed. Opening my thighs, I tapped the mattress just in front of my pussy. I cocked my head. "You trust me not to bite?"

He chuckled. "Nope. But that just adds to the fun."

I trailed my nails up his outer thigh, and he tipped his head back on a muffled gasp.

His cock was thick and stood to attention against his stomach. I flickered my gaze from his erection to his eyes, wondering how I was going to handle him. He brushed his thumb over my cheekbone, and I gave him a small smile as I leaned forward, the flat of my tongue connecting with the base of his dick. I dragged it up his shaft.

"Jesus," he called out.

I swirled my tongue around his head and took just the tip of him in my mouth. I wouldn't be able to take him deep—he was too big. I circled my hand around his base, gripping him tight. I couldn't stop myself from letting out a moan from the memory of him inside me, filling me. My nipples pebbled, and he must have been watching because he caught them between his thumbs and forefingers and squeezed and pulled, setting off sharp circuits of pleasure from my breasts to my belly button and then lower to my clit.

I took him deeper, my jaw as wide as it would go.

"Yes, like that. That's how I've imagined you."

I circled again, then took him deeper this time. He groaned, whispering about my mouth and my tongue. His fingers threaded into my hair. Not pushing, not directing, it was as if he just wanted to touch me, to be further connected to me. I pulled back, allowing my teeth to graze his shaft just slightly.

"You're wicked," he growled and I pumped his cock with both hands while sucking on his crown. "But it's not enough." He lifted my chin and I released my hands. I was more than certain I was giving him a great blow job. What was his problem?

"Open your legs," he said. Reaching across to his nightstand, he grabbed a condom, sheathing his cock in seconds. "Wider," he barked, pushing apart my thighs. "I'm going so deep, you're going to forget what day of the week it is."

Before I had a chance to argue, he pushed into me. The sheer force of his body, his cock, stole my breath, despite being ready for him and wet with longing. I looked into his eyes, wanting him to understand it was almost too much.

"You're okay, Harper. I have you."

At just the right time, he knew how to be gentle.

"Relax and feel me." I couldn't do anything else. It was as if I'd lost the fight. My body went limp and I took a deep breath. He circled his hands around my waist and pulled me onto him as he thrust his hips forward. If this was Vegas, I wasn't sure I ever wanted to leave.

Smoothing my hands up his arms, I tugged gently at his biceps. I wanted him over me, touching me, his body pressed against mine. I didn't have to say a word. Disconnecting from me for just a second, he reached under me, pulled me farther up the bed, then braced his body over me and drove back in deep.

Ordinarily, I liked to be on top, to control the rhythm so I could ensure things were just right, but Max left no room for that. Somehow, I didn't need it. Things were more than right. I didn't have space to think; it was all feeling, all sensation. "Oh God, Max," I screamed.

"Again." He pushed in deeper still. "Scream my name again."

It was as if he had his finger on a button deep inside me and kept pressing until everything was at capacity and I exploded. "Max, Max. Oh Jesus, Max."

The bed tilted and the room lit up in pinks and blues as he pushed into me three more times, my name echoing around the room.

Vegas was my new favorite place in America.

chapter eight

Max

I PRESSED MY THUMBS HARD AGAINST THE WOOD, ENSURING THE TAPE ON THE BACK OF MY SIGN stuck to the meeting room door.

"War room?" Donna asked, standing with her arms folded in front of Harper. They were both staring at my sign. I resisted the smile that threated the corners of my mouth as I fixated on Harper's reddened lips and the blush in her cheeks. God she was such a distraction. Perhaps inviting her to work on this pitch wasn't such a good idea after all. I would just have to control myself—she would be a useful resource.

I turned back to the door. "Yes, this is war. We need to get ready."

"Okay." Donna handed me a coffee, leaving me with Harper.

"First thing we need to do is information gather," I said. Harper nodded. Last night had been Vegas. Walking away from anything personal between us was the right thing to do, but it took every drop of self-control I had not to reach out and touch her. "Jim, Marvin," I yelled. I needed to distract myself, find the off switch in my body that would turn off the desire to kiss her, touch her, own her.

Jim and Marvin dutifully left their desks and strode toward us. "Donna."

"I'm here," Donna said from behind me, almost making me jump.

"Stop creeping up on me."

She rolled her eyes and took the tray of water and fruit she was holding past me straight into the meeting room. Or war room.

The team took their seats and I shrugged off my jacket, placing it on the back of the chair.

"We have less than three weeks. You guys know how much working with JD Stanley would mean to King & Associates, and to me personally. Now that we finally have our shot, we're going to throw everything at it." I didn't want to raise expectations. I knew our chances of landing this account were slim to none. We could be being brought in just because I'd been making a nuisance of myself. We might get told to back off. Or JD Stanley could just be using it as an opportunity to gather additional information—key geopolitical insights—without giving anything away, without hiring us. And of course, there was the possibility Harper's father wanted an opportunity to play games, get his daughter's attention. Who knew?

All I cared about was we were being given an opportunity. I was going to make the most out of it. Whatever Jayne's intentions were, I was going to make it difficult if not impossible to say no to me.

"We need to divide our time carefully. First we work out what we know about JD Stanley, Jayne, and the other executives in the business. I want to know everything from what they fed their dogs for breakfast to their mistresses middle names." I shot a glance at Harper. That had been insensitive. Fuck. But this was war and we weren't in Vegas anymore. I wasn't used to having to second-guess what I said at work because I had a single focus and I had to keep that and pretend Harper was just another employee.

Her face was blank, which was a relief. "Then we look at their trading history. I want to understand what they react to, why they invest where they do, why they prefer certain products over others. Look for patterns."

Marvin stuck his hand up. "I've started some of the stuff on their investment history and product preference. Just in my spare time. I knew we'd have this moment at some point." Marvin's capacity for research and modelling was the best I'd ever seen, and it didn't surprise me he had a jump start. He was a hard worker.

"Good. Jim and Harper, you work together on the more personal stuff. Use the agency if you need to." I'd gotten Harper's okay to tell the team about her personal connection, but I wanted to make sure I told them in a way that they understood she was here for her skills. It was obviously a sensitive issue for her. But unless it came up, I wasn't going to raise it.

"I may have some useful insights about their investment decisions," Harper said. She reached down to her laptop case and brought out a thick folio, placing it on the desk in front of her. "But I've also been tracking their investments for the last five years and noticed some interesting choices. I'd be happy to share these."

Jesus, it looked as if she'd skipped business school and dedicated the last five years to researching JD Stanley.

"I'd like to work with Marvin on that, too, if that's okay?"

"Marvin, work with Harper," I said.

Marvin was practically salivating at the sight of her papers. "Sure," he said, blushing when she smiled at him. I knew the feeling. There was something unaffected in her approach in the office that was totally disarming. She didn't have the hard veneer of so many of New York's Wall Street workers. *Focus.*

"Let's meet at seven thirty each morning to update the team. I want us to start thinking propositions, looking for angles. This isn't research for research's sake. We don't want analysis paralysis here." Heads nodded around the table.

"We also need to determine our method of presentation. Do we do PowerPoint? Is it likely to be in an auditorium or boardroom? Talk to your contacts. We need more information than we have, people."

"You should request a preliminary lunch meeting," Harper said, looking directly at me. "Call his assistant personally. Tell her you want to take him to La Grenouille. It's his favorite."

The memory of the smooth skin of her breasts under my hands paralyzed my tongue for a second, and I had to look away before I could answer. "You don't think that's too pushy?"

She shook her head. "He doesn't understand the concept of too pushy. He'll be testing your mettle. He didn't give you much information about your meeting, right?"

"Nothing," I replied.

"He's trying to send you on a wild-goose chase. Don't waste time. Take control. Ask him what he wants."

I nodded. Of course, she was right. "Donna, put some time in my calendar for me to do that." Harper looked glum, but I was grateful for her insight, despite the fact I hated the restaurant she'd suggested. I'd never been because it seemed so stuffy.

"And then in terms of who's presenting, that will be me and Harper. We'll need plenty of time to rehearse."

I glanced at Harper. Her eyes were wide, as if she hadn't expected me to take her. "Do you think that's a good idea?" she asked. "Of course I want to, but—I've never pitched before."

I took a deep breath and tapped my fingers on the back of the chairs. She could be useful, like a carrot we could dangle in front of Charles Jayne. "Donna, what pitches do we have coming up?"

"We have the Asia-Pac for Goldman's," she said. "A week from Wednesday."

"Good. Harper, get read into that. You can be my second chair in that meeting. Give you some experience. I can make a final decision after that."

"Goldman Sachs?" she asked.

"Yes. They're looking for someone to help them with a project in Asia."

"Okay." The slight quiver in her voice was the only thing betraying her lack of confidence. I doubt anyone else noticed. "I'll speak to—"

"Jean," Donna interrupted. "She'll get you read in."

"Good. I'm looking for your best work everyone. We're going to nail this." I smacked my fist on the table. "See you here tomorrow morning at seven thirty."

Silently, people filed out of the room and I crossed my arms. Working with Harper would hopefully help my brain redefine her as a colleague, rather than someone I wanted to fuck—someone from whom it was my job to extract their best work. I needed those barriers between my worlds repaired and restored. Leaving Vegas Harper as part of my history with women would be the first step toward maintaining my distance.

First meeting down.

It would get easier to stop focusing on her neck, her legs, her ass, right? My dick would stop twitching at the thought of her hands spread against the glass of my office door while I fucked her from behind. Soon I'd no longer worry if her frown hid something I could ease or resolve. We were all business and that worked. It would have to.

～

Beginning the prep for the JD Stanley pitch had fired up the competitor in me, but the evening with my daughter and sister put things back into perspective.

"You can't just ban me from wearing makeup," Amanda whined as she twisted on the stool in front of the counter. Scarlett had brought Amanda to town so the three of us could spend Saturday shopping for Amanda's dress. Hopefully it would be the last shopping trip for this dance, and Scarlett would back me up on the whole age-appropriate thing.

"I'm sure he's not saying no makeup at all," Scarlett said.

I ignored them both and continued to stir the spaghetti sauce. The Manhattan apartment had been something of a sanctuary to me over the years—everything was how *I* wanted it. My place in Connecticut was always overrun with my parents, Pandora's parents, my sisters, and various friends of Amanda's. I had no complaints. I loved that side of my life, but it was all the sweeter because I got to escape it every week and come to my quiet, modern New York apartment where I got to watch the game uninterrupted and fuck one of the women who seemed to drift in and out of my life.

"Are you saying that I can't wear any makeup, Dad?"

"Of course he's not." Scarlett interrupted again and I took another opportunity to stay quiet. The less I said, the less of a chance there was to have an argument.

I loved my daughter and my sister, and it wasn't as if there wasn't room for everyone here in Manhattan. But it did mean I didn't have any mental space—a beat after my working day. The edges of my separated worlds were softening, growing fuzzy.

Everything was changing.

"I'll speak to your mother," I said, grabbing the oregano from the counter.

"We're not having pasta, are we?" Scarlett asked.

"You just watched me make the sauce."

"I wasn't watching. I was talking. You know I'm not eating wheat at the moment."

I shut my eyes, took a deep breath, then looked at Scarlett. "Why would I know that you're not eating wheat?"

"Because I've been whining about it non-stop for the last month."

"Come on, Dad. You know she's not eating wheat," Amanda said.

Why did the women in my life have the ability to make me feel so hopeless? In my day job I was respected, some would even say admired. With my family, I was just some guy who forgot that my sister wasn't eating wheat.

Jesus.

"So don't eat it," I snapped. "I have some popsicles in the freezer."

Scarlett rolled her eyes in the exact same way Amanda always did. "I'm not five. I can't have popsicles for dinner."

"Good. So you'll eat spaghetti," I replied.

Scarlett hopped off her stool. "We'll go out," she announced.

"You've just watched me make spaghetti sauce."

She shrugged. "It'll freeze. Come on, Amanda. Get your shoes on. We can go to that place on the corner. I like the sea bass there."

Unbelievable.

In the office if I shouted "jump," a cacophony of voices would ask how high. At home I got an eye roll and a shrug, if anyone heard me at all.

But, as was becoming my mantra, some battles weren't worth fighting. I turned off the stove and grabbed my wallet and my keys and followed them out to the elevators.

Amanda linked her arm into mine and instantly I felt better. She was fourteen going on twenty-seven most of the time, but every now and then she was happy just to be my daughter.

We stepped into the elevator. "Tomorrow, can we go back to the store we tried last time?" Amanda asked.

"The one where I hated everything you tried on?" I wasn't going to change my mind. Surely we weren't going to have the exact same fight in front of Scarlett this time?

"I met a lady in the laundry room the other day. She gave me an idea about a dress I think you'd like, and I think I saw some that might be similar at that store," Amanda said.

"The laundry room?" I asked. Why had Amanda been in the laundry room? I had a housekeeper to do the laundry.

"Yeah. The other day."

"Why were you doing laundry?" I asked, glancing at Scarlett, who was staring at herself in the mirrored wall of the elevator and applying lip gloss.

"Sometimes girls just need to do laundry," Amanda answered as if it were obvious.

I glanced at Scarlett, then back at Amanda, expecting one of them to provide a more detailed explanation.

The elevator stopped prematurely. The doors opened and Harper appeared. I watched in slow motion as she began to grin at my daughter. Her mouth froze when her eyes lifted to mine and then behind me to Scarlett.

I should have seen this coming.

In the same way there was a time lag between the impact of a bullet and the pain being recognized by the brain, I savored the few tenths of a second before I knew things would get messy. Harper looked beautiful. Her shiny chestnut hair was swept up into a ponytail that highlighted her long neck. Seeing her dressed in her workout clothes, I found it difficult to avoid touching her.

"Harper!" Amanda said.

I couldn't comprehend what was happening. How did Amanda know—

"Dad, this is who I was telling you about." She stared up at me, then clearly registering utter confusion on my face, she said, "In the laundry room." She waved at Harper.

I glanced at Harper, who had yet to step inside the car. "There's plenty of room," Scarlett said as she pulled Amanda back, leaving more space next to me. "Hey, we met the other day," Scarlett said.

What the fuck was going on? My separated worlds were literally and figuratively crashing into each other.

"Harper, this is my dad," Amanda said. "Dad, this is Harper."

I cleared my throat, hoping it would help my words come out in a normal pitch when I replied. "Yes, I know Harper. She works for me."

Amanda's eyes widened. "She does? Well that makes sense. She's smart. I told you she had some good ideas about dresses."

The doors shut.

"You're right. She is smart," I replied, glancing at Harper, trying to catch her reaction. It wasn't as if we had a personal relationship, but given what had happened between us, the fact I'd not told her about Amanda seemed wrong all of a sudden. Harper wore the same expression she had in the war room when I'd given people tasks for the JD Stanley research—blank and cold.

"This is perfect," Amanda said. "Like Scarlett says, it's fate."

"You shouldn't listen to everything your aunt says. Use the eighty-twenty rule. I've told you about this before."

Scarlett punched me in the arm and I caught a reaction in Harper's face that I couldn't quite place. "Harper, this is my sister, Scarlett."

Harper's beautiful brown eyes softened slightly as she smiled. "Nice to see you," she said.

"You poor thing, having to work with my brother. I expect he's a total tyrant, isn't he?"

Harper shrugged and Scarlett said, "She's got you pegged, brother."

"He's not a tyrant. He lets me have anything I want," Amanda said.

"I may not be a tyrant, Amanda, but neither am I an idiot who can be easily manipulated by flattery. I do not, and will not, let you go to your eighth grade dance dressed like a twenty-five-year-old."

Amanda ignored me. "That's why this is perfect." She smiled and turned to Harper. "Are you busy tomorrow?"

Harper squinted, trying as hard as I was to keep up with my daughter's train of thought.

"You don't make her work on a Saturday, right, Dad?" She didn't wait for my response before releasing my elbow and putting her hands together in a prayer position. "Pretty please, will you come shopping with us tomorrow? We can find one of those dresses we saw online. And I haven't even begun to find shoes. Please? If I'm on my own with dad, he'll have me go in sneakers—"

What was she asking? I needed to spend *less* time with Harper, keep my worlds *more* separate.

"Amanda, you can't just impose on people like that," I interrupted. "Harper doesn't want to spend her free time schlepping around New York trying to find *you* a dress. And Scarlett's coming with us." Spending the day trying not to touch Harper was the last thing I had on my agenda for the weekend.

"I told you I can't come tomorrow, didn't I?" Scarlett asked. "I have to get the first train back because I'm taking Pablo to the vet."

"Seriously?"

Scarlett just shrugged. Why hadn't she told me she wasn't coming? In fact, why was she in Manhattan at all?

"Sorry," Scarlett said. "I thought I told you. The vet called me this morning. He hasn't had one of the injections he was meant to have."

Amanda slouched against the wall of the elevator just as the doors opened into the lobby. "There's no point in going tomorrow if Scarlett's not there and I can't ask Harper. We'll just end up fighting," she said.

"It will be fine," Scarlett said.

I ruffled Amanda's hair. "Come on. We'll find something, I promise." I stepped off the elevator after Scarlett, holding out my elbow for Amanda, glancing at Harper who was staring at my daughter, her eyebrows pulled together.

"Please, Harper? Come with us? I promise I'll take no more than an hour. Just two stores, maximum."

Harper inhaled and the elevator doors started to close with Amanda still slumped against the mirror.

"Come on, Amanda," I said as I held the doors open. "I'm sure Harper's busy." I turned to Harper. "I'm sorry."

She shook her head. "It's fine . . . I . . . want you to have a great dress and I have a couple of hours tomorrow morning."

"You do?" Amanda clasped her hands together. "You'll come?"

My palms started to get sweaty. It was the last response I'd expected. Working with her this week had been difficult enough. I'd been haunted by flashes of her bent over the conference room table, me pushing her skirt up to reveal her high, tight ass.

"Amanda," I barked. "You can't expect people to just drop everything and do whatever you want."

"Why not?" she replied. "You do."

I caught Harper trying to stifle a giggle. "I don't mind. Honestly. We'll have fun." She grinned at Amanda. "But now I have to go to the gym."

Amanda shot out of the elevator. "And you won't change your mind?"

"If she does, then—"

Harper cut me off. "I won't change my mind. I promise. Have a good night."

Harper glanced up at me as the elevator doors closed, and I had to fight the urge to peel them open, push her against the wall, and press my lips against hers.

I pinched the bridge of my nose. The thought of spending time with Harper on a Saturday with Amanda had given me a headache. What would I say to her? I didn't want my employees to know any other side of me other than the one in the office. And although Harper and I had fucked, it wasn't as if we'd had dinner and I'd confessed all my secrets. Despite being gorgeous, sexy, ballsy with a hint of sweetness to add to her sour, she was my employee. And Vegas was behind us—we were in Manhattan full time now.

chapter nine

Harper

I SLUMPED ON MY COUCH, MY PHONE CLAMPED TO MY EAR. DRESSED AND READY TO GO EIGHTH grade dress shopping with Amanda and my boss, I was just waiting for the knock on my door. "I'm cured. I've been dreaming about his penis and just like that, it's gone. Any attraction I had to him has just disappeared because I never knew him."

"Just like that?" Grace asked, her voice suspicious.

"I'm serious. I can't find someone attractive who had a daughter who wasn't important enough to tell me about, who wasn't man enough to marry the woman he knocked up. I've lived my entire life with the consequences of that kind of selfish behavior." Running into Max in the elevator last night had been a shock. When I'd seen the woman with him, I'd assumed I'd run into him and his wife and child and I'd almost exorcist vomited all over the place. Relief she was his sister had only lasted for as long as it took to register he had a kid.

He was a father and hadn't told me. What else was he hiding?

It wasn't like we were dating; he didn't owe me anything, but the fact he was so secretive about it? It seemed dishonest. He never mentioned his daughter in interviews or around the office, there weren't even any photographs on his desk. It was as if he was hiding her. Ashamed. It made me sick to my stomach. Had that been how my father had felt about me? Embarrassed or ashamed I existed? Poor Amanda.

"But Max isn't your dad. I mean, when did Charles Jayne ever take you dress shopping?"

I dropped my head back on the cushion and stared up at my ceiling. "So he has his daughter on the weekend occasionally—doesn't mean he wants his kid around. Looked like his sister was the one who was looking after her anyway." I sighed. "But this is a good thing. It wasn't as if I enjoyed being attracted to Max—I hated the fact that I'd slept with my boss. Now I'm cured."

Being a controlling asshole was one thing. Turning your back on your family was quite another. Max being a tyrant in the office seemed inextricably linked to his success on Wall Street, so maybe I'd been able to forgive him that on a professional level. Maybe I even enjoyed it. A little. But his hiding the existence of his daughter changed my view of him completely.

I checked my watch. Amanda said she'd swing by at ten. She was a sweet kid, and I couldn't begin to fathom what it would be like to try to pick out a dress with a man who resented my existence. She deserved more, so despite wanting to spend the day in bed recovering from my grueling work week, I'd agreed to go shopping.

"I still don't get why you just stopped wanting to jump his bones because you found out he was a father. Most women would find that a turn on," Grace said.

"Yeah, well, I'm not most women. And I doubt he's winning father of the year anytime soon."

Max wasn't about to win decent human being of the year anytime soon either. He'd seemed to leave Vegas without looking back. He wasn't affected by me at all in the office. Even that first morning after I'd turned up drunk at his door. He'd set up the war room and we'd had our first meeting about JD Stanley. There'd been no compassion in his voice, just cold calculation. He'd seen an opportunity to make money from my connections and nothing more. Well, I'd make it work in my favor, too. I'd ace the Goldman presentation so he couldn't say no to me doing the JD Stanley pitch. If I could go in front of my father as an adult, a business woman—show him what I'd become without any help from him—maybe he'd just wither in my mind and I'd never think of him again. I'd be free.

"So no more sleeping with the boss?" Grace asked.

"Definitely no more sleeping with the boss. I'm not having my father find out and assume that the only reason I got the job was because I looked good on my back." That was the only thing he thought women were good for.

"I thought you said you didn't find Max attractive anymore."

"I don't."

"So if you still found him attractive, you'd still be sleeping with him?"

"Why are you giving me such a hard time, Anderson Cooper? I have more than one reason not to sleep with him."

"Does that mean you're going to call George?"

My brain had to rifle through its filing cabinet to place the name. Oh, the art gallery guy. "Maybe."

"He said you took his number." I had. I'd liked him.

So why hadn't I called him?

I jumped at the loud bang at my door.

"Harper," Amanda called from the corridor.

Shit, this was it. I took a deep breath. "Gotta go," I said into the phone and hung up. I glanced in the mirror by the door, removed a clump of mascara from the corner of my eye, and smoothed down my hair. I could handle a couple of hours with a guy who was my boss and his daughter. Especially now Vegas was over and any attraction I'd had to him had disappeared. This would be a piece of cake.

○∽○

Being in a cab with my boss and his daughter after we'd agreed to stop having sex was beyond weird. I'd let my sympathy for Amanda override my logic when I'd agreed to go shopping today. I'd underestimated how awkward spending time with Max would be. I thought it would be a simple case of saving a fourteen-year-old from her uncompromising, uncaring father. The problem was I'd forgotten the father in question was my boss and had seen me naked.

"Do you agree?" Amanda asked, looking at her dad.

We'd taken a cab uptown and Amanda had been chattering away about the kind of dress she wanted to buy. Max seemed to have little interest in her as he stared out of the window.

"I think it's going to rain," he said.

"Dad." She punched him on the leg and he caught her hand and wrapped it in his. "Do you agree about the dress?"

"I'm not committing to anything until I see it."

"Well, if we don't find something today, I'm going naked."

Max chuckled. "If you were a couple of years older, I might worry. Right now, I think your teenage angst is my insurance policy against that happening."

"I don't understand what you just said," she said.

"And so that's a double win for me, peanut." As he scooped his arm around her shoulder to pull her close, he caught my jacket sleeve. "Sorry," he said and I smiled, staring at my hands in my lap. Unclear whether I was imagining things, I wanted to stare at the two of them. They seemed comfortable with each other, happy to be in each other's company. A pang of jealousy ran through me.

"Here we are," Amanda announced as the cab pulled up.

The humidity hit me as I got out of the car.

"It's definitely going to rain," Max mumbled, staring up at the sky.

He held the door open, gesturing for me to go before him as Amanda led the way into a boutique. I hoped this would be a one-stop shop and I'd be back home by lunchtime.

As we started looking around, Max found a chair outside the dressing rooms and concentrated on his phone rather than his daughter. Typical. Why had he come at all?

"What about this?" Amanda asked, holding a long purple gown against herself as she turned toward me.

I grinned. "We should definitely try it."

We picked out six dresses in total, and Amanda managed to sneak a couple of strapless ones in that I was sure wouldn't go down well with her father.

"We can do shoes and a bag once we get the dress," I said as Amanda stopped on the way to the dressing room, transfixed by a table of sparkly evening bags.

I hung up the dresses I was carrying, then shut the curtain on Amanda.

"Harper, will you stay there while I change so you can see it before my dad? I want to surprise him with the perfect choice."

"Of course," I replied and leaned on the wall opposite Amanda's room. "Which one are you going to try on first?"

"The purple one. Uh-oh," she said. "My dad isn't going to like this one."

The moment she opened the curtain, I knew she was right. Max would never go for the dress. And I couldn't blame him. A twenty-five-year-old would have to make an effort not to look slutty in it. The neckline dipped very low in a big swath of fabric, but it was so low her bra was showing.

"I don't think it suits you," I said, not wanting to hurt her feelings or for her to feel as if her dad's opinion was the only one that counted. "People say that you should wear the dress, the dress shouldn't wear you. Now I'm not sure what that means, but I think we're in dangerous territory. What about the shorter one?"

Next she appeared in a beautiful yellow dress with spaghetti straps, diamanté beading across the bodice, and a netted skirt that fell just above the knee.

"What do you think?" I asked, grinning.

"I think my dad would like it," she replied, but the look on her face said even though she thought her dad would approve, she wasn't in love with it. "But I think I want to look more . . . grown-up."

I nodded. The dress was beautiful on her, though it was a lot like a bigger version of something an eight-year-old might wear. And if Max would like it and she didn't, then we wouldn't even show it to him. "Try the royal blue one. I think it would look great against your black hair, and silver accessories would go beautifully with it. It's more sophisticated."

She turned and swept up her hair and I realized she was asking me to unzip her. "Would you wear it?" she asked as I helped her out of her dress.

I nodded. "Yes. It's beautiful. Not that I would have anywhere to wear a dress like that." I closed the curtain so she could dress in private.

"On a date?" she asked. "Do you have a boyfriend yet?"

My stomach flipped over as I remembered our conversation in the laundry room. Had she told Max anything I'd said? I glanced at the exit to the changing rooms. Could Max hear our interaction? "No, not at the moment."

"You're super pretty. When I'm older, I want to love my job, but I want someone to love me, too." I'd not ruled out love. It had just never found me. Maybe Grace was right and I was looking for perfection. "My dad's like you. Always busy with work. He always says that between work and me, he has more than enough for any man."

I couldn't help but smile at that. She clearly wanted her dad's approval, and I was getting the impression the two of them actually talked. Maybe they were closer than I thought. "Do you hang out a lot?" I asked, lowering my voice.

"Me and my dad? Yeah. Like all the time," she replied.

Before I got a chance to ask Amanda more questions about her and Max's relationship, she opened the curtain, grinning. "I really like this one," she said, stepping out in a long skirt of pleated crepe, which had a slit up the side.

"It's really pretty." I leaned forward to even out the skirt. "I love it. This looks beautiful." The shoulders were a contrasting silver material that came down and crisscrossed around her bust, in a Greek-like style. There was no cleavage, but at the same time it was dramatic. "And it looks gorgeous against your hair. Let me grab some shoes. Stay there."

As I walked out of the dressing rooms, my eyes met Max's as he looked up from his phone.

"Everything all right?" he asked.

I nodded. "Just getting some shoes."

As I passed, he grabbed my wrist. I froze. Almost immediately he dropped my hand. "Sorry. I just wanted to say thank you. This means a lot to Amanda."

I nodded but didn't look at him. My brain was misfiring. One minute Max was thanking me for making his daughter happy, the next he was yelling at me if I didn't get his sandwich order right. And then there were those kisses.

And I couldn't quite work out the dynamic between Max and Amanda. He seemed quite involved in Amanda's life. More than I'd thought. But if he'd never been married to her mother, how had that worked? It had never worked with my father.

I grabbed a pair of silver sandals with a small heel and rushed back to Amanda.

"Will he like it? Can we convince him?" she asked, taking the shoes and strapping them up. "This is the one, right?"

"You know him better than I do, but I think you look beautiful in it."

"Daaad," she called out. "I'm coming out. And I really like this one. It's perfect, so you can't be mean."

Her smile was so wide, I couldn't help but smile back. I really hoped he approved. Amanda deserved to wear this dress. It was age appropriate and really elegant.

She stepped out onto the shop floor and I peeked around the corner at Max's face. His eyebrows were halfway up his forehead as she twirled around three hundred sixty degrees for him. "What do you think?" she asked.

He gave a small shake of his head as he stood and took a deep breath. "I think you look far too grown-up." Amanda's shoulders slumped. "And completely beautiful." He pulled her into a hug. "You found your dress, peanut." He lowered his voice and spoke into her ear as they continued to hug. "You're growing up so fast; you have to forgive me for wanting to keep you mine for longer than I should."

Tears welled in my eyes. He sounded so genuine. So completely besotted with his daughter.

"I'll always be yours, Dad," she said as she smiled. He kissed her on the cheek and released her.

Max seemed to regain his composure. "Twirl for me again," he said, lifting her hand in his and pulling his daughter into a spin.

The skirt of the dress lifted as she turned faster and faster. Max grinned and Amanda giggled. My heart squeezed. It felt as if I were encroaching on what should be a private moment. I should have my own memories like this, not have to steal other people's.

"You know what this means?" Amanda asked as we stepped out onto the sidewalk, the heat swallowing us up immediately. She carried two white boutique bags, one with the dress and one with the shoes and a bag we'd spotted on the way to the cash register.

"We let poor Harper get on with her weekend?" Max replied.

My stomach jolted. Had I overstayed my welcome? I'd just been trying to help. Max didn't need to be so ungrateful. I opened my mouth to excuse myself, but Amanda took her father's hand and tried to pull him along the street. "No silly. It means we have something to celebrate."

Max rolled his eyes. "As if you need any excuse."

"I'll leave you guys to it. Your dress is beautiful, Amanda."

Amanda's eyes narrowed. "No. You have to come," she said. "You have to celebrate with us." She beckoned to me to follow them.

"You celebrate with your dad," I replied, glancing in the other direction. Shopping hadn't really involved much interaction with Max. Most of my time had been spent with Amanda. Other than the cab ride, things hadn't been too uncomfortable. And seeing Max with Amanda suggested they had a better relationship than I'd ever had with my father. If I left now, I would be ahead. I'd survived without calling my boss an asshole and without getting naked with him. Perhaps there was middle ground. And hopefully the constant comparisons I'd been making between Max and Amanda's relationship and my father's and mine would stop.

"I want you to come," Amanda said.

I smiled but before I could think up an excuse, Max intervened. "Amanda, Harper has things to do. We have imposed on her free time enough."

He clearly wanted to be rid of me. And I got it. Just days after agreeing to keep things strictly professional, I was standing on a sidewalk with him and his daughter. And even though I wanted to leave, it hurt just a little that he was so keen for me to go.

Amanda's face fell. "I don't want to celebrate without her. If it hadn't been for Harper, I wouldn't have found my dress. Are you sure you can't come? We're going to my favorite place."

I glanced at Max, whose gaze travelled between me and his daughter. The corners of his mouth twitched, as if he was trying to suppress a smile.

"I'm sure your dad wants to switch off from work and spend time with you—"

"Daaad," Amanda said. "You want Harper to come, don't you?"

Max ruffled his daughter's hair and she quickly moved out of reach. He turned to me and gave me the biggest panty-melting smile I'd ever seen, his green eyes dancing against the New York sun, framed by almost too long lashes. "Harper, we'd love for you to come if you can spare the time. But don't feel you have to give into my daughter's whining. She's far too used to getting her own way."

Before the sensible side of me—the part enjoying this new middle ground—could run back downtown, I agreed.

"I suppose I should have asked before I said yes, but where are we celebrating?" I asked as we walked east.

"Serendipity," Amanda replied. "It's our place. We always come in on the train at the end of summer and celebrate going back to school."

"From your mom's?" I asked.

"From Connecticut. Sometimes my mom and Jason come, but sometimes we come in together. Do you remember that year Aunt Scarlett came as well?" she asked her dad. "She wanted to order one of everything because she couldn't decide."

"She *did* order one of everything," Max said. "Which is pretty typical of my sister."

"My mom and Jason moved to Europe so it's just me and Dad now." She turned back to her dad. "You love having me living with you all the time, don't you?"

Max chuckled and glanced at me. "She's driving me crazy."

They lived together?

"I didn't realize you lived in Connecticut," I said. I was fascinated at how the King of Wall Street had a secret life away from Manhattan. I felt like an investigative journalist, putting little scraps of information together.

"Yeah, near Mom and Jason's place. And Grandma and Grandpa King and Grand-Bob and Grand-Mary. And Scarlett."

"Jesus. It makes us sound like we're living in some kind of commune." Max slung his arms around his daughter's shoulder. "We just all live close. Amanda's mother, Pandora, and I were in high school together, and it made sense after college to make sure we lived near each other. That way," he said, turning to Amanda, "when your mother got sick of you, she could get a break and dump you with me."

Amanda grinned and rolled her eyes, the explanation clearly something she was used to hearing.

"So the apartment is just a pied-à-terre?" I asked.

He nodded. "Yeah. I used to stay in Manhattan all week and go back to the country on weekends, but now I'm only in town two nights a week."

Amanda came to an abrupt halt on the sidewalk. "Oh my God. You'll have to come out, Harper. The night of the dance. Will you help me get ready?"

I didn't know what to say. I concentrated on trying not to look too shocked. I really liked Amanda and at every turn, Max kept surprising me. I wanted to encroach on their world a little longer, but I knew it was entirely inappropriate.

Max cocked his head, indicating she needed to keep walking. "Amanda. That's enough. You can't just assume people want to be monopolized by you."

We resumed walking north towards Sixtieth. "Why not? Grandma says that I get all my charm from her and that God skipped a generation with you."

I laughed and Max rolled his eyes.

Thankfully, Amanda's attention had been diverted away from me. "Oh, I meant to say that I've decided I want to enter that piano competition next semester," she said.

"I thought we checked a few months ago and you have gymnastics the night of the practice, or will the schedule change next semester?" Max asked.

He seemed to have an intricate knowledge of his daughter's schedule, which if someone had told me yesterday, I would have thought it impossible. But as the day wore on, it was clear he was more involved in his daughter's life than I'd given him credit for.

"Well, gymnastics is at six and then piano is at eight. So I think I can do both if we can get Marion to drive me."

This was such a different version of Max King—warm, open, and relaxed. So far removed from the impatient, ruthless man who'd founded King & Associates, to the demanding, sexy man who worked my body as if it belonged to him. *This* Max King was a father and a family man.

Thunder cracked above us. "I told you it was going to rain," Max said. "Come on." He held his hand out for me and then, as if he remembered who we were to each other, withdrew it and nodded up Third Avenue as if we were nearly there instead of two blocks away.

We weren't going to make it. Generous dots of rain began to color the ground.

"Come on, Harper," Amanda called as she and Max started to run.

Amanda pointed at a flash of light above us and began to count, "One banana, two banana, three banana, four banana." Thunder ended her countdown and Amanda squealed. "Quick, it's nearly here."

I ran behind them as we wove in between tourists and underneath umbrellas. As we arrived at Serendipity, the lightning flashed again and the rain began to fall more heavily. "Let's get inside," I said, and we piled into an already crowded entrance and waited to be seated.

"Do I look like a drowned rat, Dad?" Amanda asked, beaming up at her father. She was a beautiful girl who had inherited the large green eyes, olive skin, and near-black hair from her father.

Max chuckled. "A little bit."

I wiped my under eyes, trying to remove the inevitable mascara leak. "I'm sure I look like Alice Cooper," I said.

"You look very pretty, like from a movie or something," Amanda said. "Doesn't she, Dad?"

I shook my head and a soaked strand of hair plastered itself against my cheek. To my surprise, Max reached out and tucked it around my ear. Heat coursed through me and I wanted to reach for his hand, push my fingers through his. But instead I concentrated on the waitress behind Max, worried I'd lose control if I looked at him, maybe pull him into a kiss as I did that first night we were together.

He quickly turned back to Amanda and took her face in her hands. "Not as pretty as my drowned rat," he replied.

"Gah. That's why I'm never going to get a baby sister." She twisted away from him. "You need to learn to give ladies compliments, or you'll never get married."

Married? I kept my eyes firmly on the restaurant, hoping my makeup hid the red in my cheeks. For the first time since leaving the dress store, I felt as if I shouldn't be here. Our conversation in the laundry room came back to me. She wanted her dad to find someone. Was Amanda trying to set us up? She had to know that Max and I were . . . We weren't involved like that, weren't ever going to be involved like that.

chapter ten

Max

THE DAY WITH HARPER AND AMANDA HAD BEEN FAR . . . EASIER THAN I EXPECTED. AFTER finally getting on the train back to Connecticut, Amanda couldn't stop talking about her dress and Harper and how much she liked her. And I hadn't stopped her.

"We could invite Harper to dinner," Amanda said as she set out the knives and forks on the counter in the kitchen.

"Maybe . . . at some point." Would she like it here? Would she like *me* here? I wasn't sure.

"Well it will be the dance soon anyway. Harper will come then for sure."

I wasn't sure Harper had actually accepted that invitation. But Amanda was happy and that was all I could wish for. The fact Harper had picked out a perfect dress didn't hurt. I'd wondered if she'd secretly try something trashy, just to mess with me, get her own back for me being an asshole. I wouldn't have blamed her but she hadn't. She'd been bright and beautiful and all about Amanda. And I'd found myself wanting to extend our time together, keep her for a little bit longer.

"Who's Harper," my sister, Violet, asked. I smelled an interrogation brewing, and my instinct was to press pause on this situation and escape.

"I told you, the girl that works with dad who helped me pick out the dress."

"I thought a friend of yours had gone shopping with you," Violet said to Amanda, trying to catch my eye, but I deliberately busied myself with the salad.

"She *is* a friend of mine," Amanda replied. "She lives in the same building in the city as dad."

"*And* she works with your father?" Violet asked as she reached over the counter and took a chunk of cucumber and popped it in her mouth. I glanced at Amanda, who was nodding. "That seems like a strange coincidence." She lowered her voice. "You see a pretty girl in the corridor of your building and offer her a job sharpening your pencils?"

"Don't be ridiculous," I replied and handed her the salad to put on the counter.

A bang on the door caused Amanda to squeal. "Scarlett!" My sisters were determined to overrun me tonight. Violet lived in Brooklyn, so we didn't see her as often as Scarlett, but she still made an effort to come over once a month. I liked my sisters, but the fewer there were of them in a room at any one time, the better. I grabbed a bottle of Pinot Noir from the counter and uncorked it.

"Hey, asshole," Scarlett said as she entered the family room.

"Nice to see you, too." I handed her a glass of wine and kissed her on the cheek.

"I'm serious. Why didn't you call me back?" Scarlett asked.

"When?" I asked. I didn't remember getting a message.

"I left you a voicemail telling you about my friend April," Scarlett said as she dropped her purse on the counter and took a stool. "She asked me to fix you two up, although God knows why."

"I didn't get the message." Or maybe I'd only listened halfway through and deleted it before she could get to the bit about April. "Sorry."

"So?" she asked.

"So what?" I asked, wanting her to change the subject. I turned back to the oven, taking out the lasagna the housekeeper had left. I never wanted to date my sisters' friends. I was surprised they were still trying. My life was full to the brim.

"So will you take her out?" she asked as if I were stupid. To be fair, I was being deliberately obstructive. I just didn't need my sisters interfering with my dating life. I was happy with things as they were.

"Looks like April may have competition," Violet said. Scarlett shot her a look and Violet shrugged. "We've been talking a lot about Harper this evening. She'd definitely get Amanda's seal of approval."

I'd never had to concern myself with whether Amanda would like any of the women I'd been with. She'd never met any of them and that's the way I liked it. It was simply coincidence Amanda had gotten to meet Harper.

Scarlett continued to chat on about April, which I could easily drown out. Harper was a little more difficult to bury. "April comes from a lovely family. She's blonde, which I know you like."

Did I like blondes? I wasn't sure hair color was a deciding factor for me. Harper's hair was chestnut brown, but had looked almost black in the rain. Images of her standing in the line for Serendipity flashed into my head. She'd looked gorgeous. Her cheeks pinked from running, her eyes bright blue. At one point she'd licked raindrops from her upper lip. It had only been Amanda's presence that had stopped me from pushing her wet hair from her face, relishing her soft skin under my thumbs, and pressing my lips to hers. If it had been just the two of us, I would have dragged her back to the apartment and spent the afternoon naked and indulging myself in her instead of ice cream.

"What are you smiling about?" Violet asked me.

"I'm not smiling about anything." I needed to shake these thoughts about Harper off. A taste of Harper was supposed to cure me. That had been my justification for fucking her the first time, the second time, *and* the third time. But seeing her today, relaxed, warm, and so focused on making sure Amanda was happy, had grown this buzz in my gut I had when she was around or when I thought about her. They laughed and talked together like old friends and listening to them in the changing rooms while I'd pretended to stay focused on my emails made me smile, made me feel good.

"Can I show them my dress?" Amanda asked.

"After dinner you can try it on."

"Daddy bought me the most beautiful shoes to go with it. I'm not sure he would have, but Harper said she'd buy them if he didn't."

"I was always going to buy the shoes. Give me some credit. I know you can't wear your sneakers." Harper's face had lit up when she'd seen the shoes. I'd wanted to ask for a pair in her size as well. Maybe I'd try to find her something similar. After all, I'd ruined her blouse.

"So I want to hear more about Harper," Scarlett said. "How old is she? Is she pretty?"

Amanda took a spoonful of salad and stopped, thinking about the question.

"Come on, Amanda," I said, trying to distract them away from this question. "Don't get it all over the table."

"My age?" Violet asked.

She nodded and dropped some salad on her plate. "I guess. Like, grown-up age. And she's really pretty."

They were right about that. She was very attractive.

"I'd say about twenty-five," Scarlett said. "Gorgeous, too, and she just happens to work with Max." I avoided Scarlett's glances. But she was right, Harper was gorgeous. And smart. And great in bed.

"She's one of my *employees* who happens to live in the building. Amanda begged her to go shopping with her. I'm sure it's the last thing she wanted to do."

"She enjoyed it," Amanda said with total confidence. Because why wouldn't a twenty-something enjoy going shopping with her boss and his kid? Harper had been exceptionally good about it. It had been nice to watch them together.

"Would she go out on a date with your dad, or is she too pretty for him?"

Amanda grinned. "Oh my God, that would be so awesome. And I know she doesn't have a boyfriend."

I pretended I wasn't listening and took the salad spoons from Amanda and finished distributing the salad for everyone. Normally I'd have put an end to the conversation by now. I'd become good at deflecting around my dating life but this was slightly different. I found I liked the conversation about Harper—enjoyed Amanda's reaction to her. And I didn't mind them considering us as some kind of couple. Not that it would ever happen—we'd agreed it wouldn't. It was just I didn't mind it being a possibility in my family's mind.

⁂

Monday I'd gotten into the office late. I'd been shopping for shoes for Harper. It had taken me too long to make the purchase, not knowing what I was doing and why. Now I was behind and grouchy and I still wasn't decided on whether or not I'd actually give her the shoes. Next on my schedule was to follow up on the lunch invitation to Charles Jayne as Harper had suggested.

"Max, I have Margaret Hooper, Charles Jayne's assistant, on the line for you," Donna squawked from my speakerphone.

"Thank you." I cleared my throat and pulled back my shoulders. Assistants had much more power than people realized, and I was sure Margaret held considerable sway with Charles Jayne.

I picked up the receiver. "Ms. Hooper, Max King of King & Associates here." I could tell from her response, which was soft and helpful, that she was pleased I'd called her and not just asked Donna to call on my behalf. Harper had made a good suggestion. So now that Margaret was on our side, I needed to convince her to let me take Charles to lunch.

"As you know, Mr. Jayne has asked me to come in to see him on the twenty-fourth. I don't want to waste his time."

"You're right, he doesn't have much time to do anything, so how can I help?" she asked.

"I want to make the presentation as focused and helpful as possible. Now of course this benefits me because I provide Mr. Jayne with what he most needs."

"Indeed, Mr. King," she replied, skepticism rising in her voice.

"Please, call me Max."

I could hear her smile across Wall Street. "Okay, Max, what is it you want?"

"I want to create a win-win situation. If I understand what it is that Mr. Jayne is looking for then our presentation won't be a waste of anyone's time. He's happy. I'm happy. If I can get lunch with Mr. Jayne—"

"The problem is he doesn't have any lunch availability between now and the twenty-fourth. His schedule books up very quickly, unfortunately." Her tone transitioned from friendly and open to clipped and concise. I wasn't sure if she was being honest, or if I was being given the brush-off.

"I'd be very happy to come to the JD Stanley offices and bring lunch to Mr. Jayne, if that would help?" I suggested. "Alternatively, I'll get a table booked at La Grenouille if that would suit him."

"I'm sorry. If it were up to me, I'd love to find space. But I'm afraid it's not." That sounded like a brush-off. Otherwise she'd have said she'd let me know and checked with Charles Jayne.

"That's such a shame." I paused a second, considering my options. Was it worth trying to press a little more or did I risk backlash?

Maybe I should mention Harper's name. I still wasn't clear what the bad blood was between Harper and her father. It couldn't just be about the fact she didn't get offered a job when she graduated. She'd indicated things went bad between them before that.

Harper knew the reason we were going to give her a slot on the presenting team was because she was Charles Jayne's daughter, right? So she understood to a certain extent she was being used. There's no way I'd ordinarily have a junior researcher second chair a meeting like that. But at the same time, I'd discussed that with her, sought her approval before making any decisions.

I had to decide my next move quickly or Margaret would hang up. Fuck it, this was war. "I'd hoped he'd enjoy seeing his daughter in a professional environment," I said. Silence at the other end of the line nudged me to continue. "I was assuming Harper Jayne would join us for lunch. But I understand that Mr. Jayne is very busy."

"Please hold the line, Mr. King," she replied and her voice was quickly replaced with Vivaldi.

Had I just been the asshole Harper accused me of being? Was using her to get a lunch with Charles Jayne any worse than taking advantage of the fact Charles Jayne's offer of a meeting was probably linked to her working here? The problem was none of us were sure whether or not I got the phone call from Charles Jayne because of Harper. Regardless, I hadn't been the one to play that card—I hadn't even known they were related. All I'd done was take advantage of a business opportunity. Fuck.

Lunch required interaction that went beyond the professional. I had no idea whether or not Harper would think lunch was no big deal, after all she'd agreed to pitch, or if she'd knee me in the balls and hand her notice in if I even suggested it.

I should have thought this whole call through more carefully in advance, maybe had Harper in the room when I spoke to Margaret. It wasn't like me. I couldn't tell if Harper had thrown me off my game or if it was the thought of landing JD Stanley as a client.

Maybe Margaret would come back and still say that Charles Jayne's schedule was full. I reached inside my collar and ran my finger around the starched material. I shouldn't have acted so rashly.

"Mr. King, I can make some time for you on Wednesday. Mr. Jayne will see you and Harper at twelve thirty at La Grenouille."

Shit. That was the answer I wanted and the one that made me feel uncomfortable.

I hoped I'd done the right thing.

After thanking Margaret, I hung up the phone.

Maybe I didn't have to tell Harper. Maybe I could just turn up to lunch on my own and say Harper had been caught up in the office or was sick.

But then Charles Jayne hadn't founded a leading investment bank without the ability to smell bullshit a mile away. No. I'd have to confess to Harper what I'd done, and if she didn't want to come to lunch, I'd have to cancel.

Jesus, why was this so fucking complicated? I'd done what I needed in order to win. If Harper and I hadn't banged, would I be second guessing myself?

"Did you get it?" Donna asked as she burst through the door.

I nodded and leaned back in my chair. "Wednesday," I said.

"Well, why don't you look happier about it? Things are coming together just as you'd planned."

I scrubbed my face with my hands. "Yeah, maybe."

"What's the matter with you? This is great news." She closed the door.

Donna was right; this was what I'd been hoping for. What had been my ultimate goal just three weeks ago was now tarnished with the knowledge I'd gotten there by using Harper.

People said I was ruthless in business and that may be true, but I'd never been underhanded and I always tried to do the right thing. I wanted to be someone my daughter could admire and respect and emulate in some ways. I wanted her to be ambitious and driven. But my greatest wish was for her to grow up knowing what was important, that she became someone who understood integrity and hard work was the way to go. I didn't want to raise a daughter who would sell her soul for a piece of corporate pie. And I'd worked hard not to be that guy. Had I just thrown that all away?

I'd always found the ethical boundaries were drawn quite distinctly on Wall Street, but today that line had become fuzzier and I wasn't sure on which side of it I stood.

Instead of calling for an elevator when I got home after work, I took the stairs. Was I about to make a dick move by giving these shoes to Harper?

Quite possibly.

My shoes made clunking sounds against the metal steps, as if they were trying to call attention to my climb, which was the last thing I wanted. The white Jimmy Choo bag swung against my side. I'd spent about an hour in the Bleaker Street store before committing to the purchase that had made me late to work. I'd never a bought a woman outside of my family anything, ever. But since I'd seen the look of pure joy lighting up Harper's face when she picked out Amanda's shoes, I'd wanted to see that expression again. She'd been excited and bright and full of enthusiasm. And as the daughter of one of the richest men in New York, it was nice to see. She should have been used to luxury, but somehow she'd managed to make Amanda feel special.

I wanted her to feel the same way again.

The assistant at the store had been very patient with me. But I'd seen the pair I wanted as soon as I walked in. They were like an adult version of the pair I'd bought Amanda. The heel was higher and thinner and straps more intricate but they were covered in that glittery finish she and Amanda had gone wild over on Saturday.

I'd torn the buttons from her blouse so I owed her, didn't I? Memories of revealing her full breasts when I'd ripped her blouse drifted into my head, and I tried to shake them off.

But I had more than one reason to buy her shoes. She'd found a dress for my daughter that reduced the chances of me going to jail for the murder of every fourteen-year-old boy who so much as looked at her. I had to thank her, and shoes were an appropriate gift.

As I reached her floor, I paused before opening the fire door. I could just leave them on her doorstep. I wanted her to have them more than I wanted to be the one to give them to her, to see that look of pleasure on her face. At least I hoped it would be pleasure.

Buying an employee shoes wasn't the actions of a boss—they had a touch of Vegas about them and I wasn't sure how she'd react to that.

I needed to stop being such a pussy.

I knocked three times on her door and stretched out my hands, trying to resist the buzz in my fingers I knew would start when she appeared. It was as if I were pre-programmed to reach for her whenever I saw her.

She appeared seconds later, dressed in a Berkeley T-shirt and leggings, her hair in a high ponytail—a style I'd never seen her wear to work. She looked breathtaking.

"Hi," she said, her mouth slightly open.

"Hi." I held out the bag.

Her eyebrows knitted together. "What's that?" she asked, though she didn't take it.

"A thank you. For Saturday and . . . You know, for giving up your time last weekend."

Her eyebrows raised and a smile twinged at the corners of her mouth. "Really?" she asked. "It was fine. You don't need to buy me a gift." And then she frowned.

I hadn't expected this reaction. I'd wanted to make her smile, maybe smooth her hands through my hair and kiss me. "Okay." I should tell her about lunch, get it out of the way. "And I have something to tell you."

She opened the door and I followed her into her apartment, leaving the Jimmy Choos underneath her coat rack. She wasn't even going to look at them? The door clicked shut behind us and instantly I knew I made a mistake. Suddenly I was back in Vegas. I couldn't stop staring at her ass, wondering whether she was wearing a bra under her shirt. The buzz in my fingers grew stronger, and I had to take a deep breath to calm my rising pulse.

"You want a drink?" she asked.

"Sure, thanks." Holding a glass would occupy my hands, stop them from wandering to the hem of her T-shirt, and skirting the smooth skin underneath.

She set two glasses on the small counter as I watched. She seemed unbothered by my presence, as if I was something other than wildly attracted to her.

She handed me a glass of lemonade and leaned against the cabinet. "So," she said.

Her small, delicate fingers wrapped around her glass and I couldn't help imagining how they'd feel, cooled by her drink, trailing down my chest.

"Max," she said and I snapped my head up to look at her. "What did you have to tell me?"

Shit. I shifted my weight from one foot to both, trying to regain control. "I took your advice and called your father's assistant."

"I'd prefer it if you didn't call him my father."

I nodded. I wanted to know why she so clearly didn't like the man. Didn't speak to him, but kept a dossier on his business investments. Didn't want anything to do with him except to show him just how worthy of his attention she was. "Should we talk about this? I don't really understand your history. And I'd like to."

"Is talking about parents something you normally do with employees?" she asked, a frown creasing her forehead. She pushed off the counter and came toward me, clearly wanting me to move out of the way so she could leave the kitchen. Our bodies were close, the heat of her breath puffing against my shirt. I didn't move. I *liked* having her close. I wanted more.

I ran my finger up her exposed neck and her lips parted, but as her eyes met mine, she pushed past me.

I turned to find her loitering by the door. "You should go," she said, her eyes on the floor.

"I should," I agreed. But I didn't want to. I wanted to stay and peel off her T-shirt, bend her over the sofa, and slide into her. I stepped toward her and rested my hand on her hip.

"What did you have to tell me?"

Oh yes, lunch. Her presence, like some kind of fog, clouded my brain *and* my judgement.

She placed her hand on my arm and it drifted up to my shoulder. I had to consciously breathe.

"Max?"

Her clipped tone brought me to attention. "I called his assistant. She found a spot in his schedule." Taking a half step closer, I smoothed my hand from her hip to the small of her back.

She raised her eyebrows as she tilted her head up to look at me. "That's good, right?"

I nodded. "Except he seemed to be busy until I told her you'd be joining us."

Dropping her hand from my shoulder, she took two steps to the side.

"And so you're here. With gifts. And wandering hands."

I took a step back, removing my hand from her warm body. "What? No." Was that what this looked like? As if I were trying to bribe her? Seduce her into agreeing to lunch?

"Jesus, I know you think I'm an asshole. But, no."

She shrugged. Didn't she believe me? Fuck. This was why lines were better when they were clearly drawn—when business was business and fucking was fucking. I shouldn't have come here.

"Don't come to lunch." I reached for the door. "The shoes weren't anything to do with work. I bought them before my call with your father." And my desire for her was nothing to do with Charles Jayne. She conjured that up all by herself.

Jesus, I should never have bought the shoes. Should never have come here. I stepped out of her apartment

"Max," she said and I didn't respond, letting the door shut behind me.

chapter eleven

Harper

I STOOD BY DONNA'S DESK, SHOULDERS BACK, READY FOR WAR.
It was eleven fifty. We needed to leave now if we were sure to be in Midtown on time for lunch with my father, but Max wasn't in his office.

I hadn't spoken to Max since he left my apartment. I'd expected Donna to send me a meeting request or to be summoned into Max's office and told that me going to lunch with my father and Max was for the good of the team. The thing was I was happy to do it. Okay, not happy, but I was *prepared* to lunch with my father. I wanted to be seen on the winning team. Lunch could only help my goal if it meant we were more likely to be successful in our pitch.

I wore a navy dress, just above the knee with a scoop neck, and a matching, collarless jacket I'd had tailored to nip in at the waist. It was my lucky interview suit—and as close to Prada as I could afford.

"Donna, I need to leave," Max said as he swept past me and into his office. Donna followed him and set the file she was carrying down on her desk.

Max appeared in his doorway. "Harper," he said, fiddling with the collar on his navy jacket. I wanted to step forward and smooth my fingers over the fabric. He looked good. He *always* looked good.

"Are you ready?" I asked.

He just nodded and we headed to the elevators.

"Good luck," Donna called after us.

We stood, silently waiting for the elevators, surrounded by employees of King & Associates.

I should also thank him for the shoes. He probably thought I'd been ungrateful but that wasn't it. The present had taken me off guard and brought back memories of the extravagant gifts my father used to send me as a child to try to make up for the fact he'd forgotten my birthday or hadn't turned up to visit me when he said he would.

Perhaps it was unwrapping the beautiful Jimmy Choo's that changed my mind but as I thought about it, it occurred to me perhaps Max just didn't get how his timing had sucked. The gift had been a thank you rather than a bribe. He probably hadn't realized he'd looked as if he was trying to manipulate me with gifts and come-ons. With that realization came an understanding of some of his odd behavior on Saturday. I realized that for whatever reason, he was a little bit awkward with me. That clearly didn't stop him trying to seduce me or fucking me as though it was his job. But outside of the seduction and the sex, he wasn't so confident, so practiced.

As Max and I settled into the cab, which sped off uptown, we started to speak at the same time.

"I wanted to say sorry," I said.

"Thank you for coming," he said.

We turned toward each other and he gave a small smile.

"The shoes were beautiful," I said.

He looked away. "It was inappropriate. I shouldn't have." He dragged his hand through his hair and I gazed at his long fingers, knowing just how they felt all over my body.

"It was a really nice thing to do."

"You just seemed to like the ones Amanda got on Saturday."

I grinned. They were a higher, sparklier, sexier take on his daughter's.

"And I know I take up too much of your time already. Giving up your weekend was—"

"No big deal." I couldn't exactly admit I'd assumed he was disinterested in his daughter and had wanted to save her from his apathy. I couldn't have been more wrong. He clearly loved Amanda and she him. The King of Wall Street had a secret identity in Connecticut as a single father and family man.

We'd first touched, kissed, fucked when I'd only known him as a career driven, ruthless, arrogant egomaniac. And somehow, his life outside work made him all the more attractive. And I knew I had to fight it.

"And thank you for coming today. I assumed you weren't going to join me," he said.

I'd kind of admired the fact he hadn't asked me to come to lunch again, hadn't tried to pressure me. But he didn't need to. I wanted to be here. "I told you. I want this as much as you. Just for different reasons."

"Have you never gotten along with your father—sorry, Charles Jayne?"

I took a breath. I didn't want to talk about this. Not now. Not ever.

I shrugged, and he didn't push me to say anything more. We just sat, the windows rolled down, the hoots and hollers of New York sucking away the silence between us. It should have been awkward. I was sure if we hadn't fucked, I would have tried to make polite conversation, maybe even tried to impress the boss. Somehow all that seemed redundant now. Ridiculous even.

The restaurant was busy with chatter and I slid into the red velvet seat. We were the first to arrive at the booth, which was a relief. I had some time to compose myself. I'd not been to La Grenouille in years, not since the last time I'd seen my father. This place hadn't changed at all.

"This is very . . ." Max looked around the restaurant, his forehead crumpled and his lips tight. I was pretty sure Max was a Four Seasons guy, the type to appreciate and prefer cool and modern. The décor at La Grenouille was old-fashioned. The wallpaper was gold and cream and the crystal chandeliers gave out a yellow light that descended like a heavy blanket. The rest of New York was celebrating twenty-first century America while we were here, pretending we were in nineteenth century France.

I had to stifle a giggle. "Have you never been here before?" I asked.

"No." He frowned. "And now I know why." He shook out his napkin and put it in his lap. "Everyone is so old. And everything is so very—" Before Max could finish his thought, the host approached with my father, who had arrived right on time.

Max stood up but my father greeted me first. "Harper, how are you?" he asked as I leaned forward, accepting his kiss on my cheek. No doubt the order of greeting was more about him trying to make sure Max felt as unimportant as possible, though I couldn't imagine Max giving a shit. In fact, having seen him with his daughter, he probably thought it would be odd any other way.

"And you must be Max King," my father said, stepping back and holding out his hand, which Max took.

He'd aged since I'd last seen him. He was still handsome, but his hair had more salt mixed with the pepper, and the dark shadows beneath his eyes were new. He was still handsome though, and I wondered whether it had been his looks that had seduced my mother and all those other women, or the money, or the power?

"So, Harper," my father said, taking a menu from the waiter. "You're working at King & Associates."

I glanced across at Max, then back to my father. "Yes. For about three months now."

He nodded and set his menu down but he didn't reply. The silence felt awkward, but I didn't know what to say. I didn't want to know anything about him, so what was the point in asking a question? I was pretty sure if I said anything it would come out pointed and a little bitchy because that's how I felt.

"We're delighted to have her on board." Max filled the silence.

My father raised his eyebrows. "Why didn't you tell me?"

What, had he forgotten we didn't speak? He occasionally tried to give me money through his lawyers, and I routinely refused. That was the extent of our relationship.

"She's produced some of the best work I've ever seen from a junior researcher," Max said, leaning back. It was clearly an exaggeration, given all the red pen he'd splashed across my Bangladesh report, but I suppose he thought it would soften up my father.

My father didn't respond. I tried not to turn my head because I didn't want it to be obvious I was looking at Max but wanted to see the expression on his face. Was he as awkward as I was?

"You've been after my work for years, Mr. King," my father said, straightening his tie. "Is that why you hired my daughter?"

Max paused before he answered. "I was lucky to recruit someone so talented. She's smart and works hard." Max grinned. "I'm just grateful you weren't successful in convincing her to work for JD Stanley," he said as if he hadn't just given him the biggest backhanded compliment in the history of backhanded compliments, and I wanted to smile at him, touch him, give him some indication I appreciated his support. "But to answer your question, I had no idea she was your daughter until after our telephone conversation. It's not something she's ever mentioned."

"Really?" he asked.

"One thing you should know about me up front," Max said as he leaned forward. "I don't lie."

"But you've wanted to work for JD Stanley for a long time," my father said.

"You're right. I have. As have the rest of my competitors."

The waiter filled our water glasses and I pulled mine toward me, fiddling with the stem.

"You seem a little more tenacious than most. A little more willing to do whatever it takes," my father commented.

"I'm glad you've noticed my tenacity," Max replied. "It's what's helped make King & Associates the most successful geopolitical research firm in America." My father looked at me and I stared into my lap. "That and the quality of work we do."

Max clearly didn't lack confidence and rightly so. He should be proud and in that moment I was proud to know him.

"Did you know Harper was working with us when you called me?" Max asked, turning the tables on my father. It was a question I was desperate for the answer to. In my experience, my father's actions were almost always selfish, and if he called Max because he knew I was working at King & Associates, I didn't know why.

"Will my answer change anything?" my father asked.

"Absolutely not. I know that when you see our work, understand what we can do for you, then the reason you called won't matter anymore."

My father put a fist to his mouth and coughed. "People do say you're the best at what you do." He paused. "Which was the reason I called. I didn't know Harper worked for you until you called Margaret."

I took a swig of my water. I was pretty sure my father was telling the truth. Why would he have known? He'd taken little to no interest in my life up until this point; why would that change now?

"Are you enjoying your work, Harper?" he asked.

I nodded. "I am. I chose to work at King & Associates because they're the best. I didn't apply anywhere else." I felt Max's gaze on me. I'd bordered on obsessed and had been completely single-minded in getting a job working with Max. I'd tailored my projects at business school to things I thought would catch King & Associates' attention on my resume, and even visited the lobby of our building when I'd flown to New York to see Grace over the Fourth of July weekend last year. I'd always known King & Associates was where I was meant to be.

"You know that you can do anything you like with your trust fund now you're twenty-five. You don't have to do anything you don't want to do," my father said, stroking down the front of his tie.

Was he really talking about my trust fund in front of my boss? The trust fund I didn't want anything to do with? Was he deliberately trying to embarrass me? Make Max feel awkward? I'd thought we'd come here to talk about business.

"I want to work at King & Associates. I worked hard for my opportunity. And I don't need your money." Was it so difficult for him to believe I was good enough, that I would want this? This lunch should be about business and beginning to prove to my father I didn't need a trust fund. "May I ask why you're thinking about outsourcing some of your research at this point? Has something changed at your end?" I asked.

My eyes flickered to Max, who was nodding, encouraging my question and I allowed myself to relax a little bit.

My father sighed. "Well, I think it's good to keep the people who work for you on their toes, and I've been following what you do and I thought I'd like to hear a little more about it."

I kept quiet for most of the rest of lunch, concentrating on the answers my father gave to Max's questions, committing them to memory. I tried to forget the man sitting kitty-corner to me was genetically linked to me and focused on him as a client.

It was the first time I'd seen Max with a client. And it was easy to understand why he was so successful. He had an easy charm that had my father revealing things I wasn't sure he'd planned to. And Max did it all without giving anything of himself. He let my father dominate the conversation in terms of number of words spoken, but the way Max nudged him toward certain topics meant Max was the one pulling the strings.

He was as brilliant as they said he was.

I'd known he was smart, but I hadn't expected the rest of it—the charisma, the control. It was like watching a wizard at work, casting spells over people so they'd tell him their secrets.

"And of course Harper will work on the presentation," Max said, catching my eye as I stared at him. I glanced back at my father, giving him a tight smile.

"She will?" he asked, sounding surprised. "With so little experience?"

Great. Another put-down in front of my boss. I wondered if he knew he didn't have to verbalize every thought he had.

The worst part of it all was I was pretty sure he hadn't said it to try to put me down. I think he just had so little regard for my feelings it didn't occur to him he was being hurtful.

"Yes sir. I want to put my best people on it," Max said.

"Well, if you're as good as you say you are, I should just trust your judgment," my father replied and smiled tightly.

Memories of waiting for his car to pull up on my birthday or that call at Christmas kept interrupting my concentration. The expensive gift that would sometimes follow to apologize for not making it would trick me into liking him again until the next time he disappointed me. The tight knot that sat inside my stomach when my mother apologized for his absence at dance class or school plays nudged at my belly. The humiliation I'd felt when I realized my youngest half brother had been offered a job at JD Stanley straight after graduation heated my skin.

I thought I'd feel nothing if we came to lunch after all the time that had passed, that we could be all business.

But his abandonment was too painful to forget.

I shouldn't have come today. It was like slicing open an old scar. He didn't deserve my time or attention. He didn't deserve me to bleed for him. Not anymore.

※

Standing in my kitchen, I poured Patron into the Golden Gate Bridge shot glass I'd placed on the counter and set the bottle beside it. Tequila would make today ebb away and help me sleep.

Max had gone on to another Midtown meeting after lunch, leaving me to go back to Wall Street on my own. I'd been grateful for the space, the time to compose myself before getting back to the office. I'd been unproductive for the rest of the afternoon, going through the motions, watching the clock, willing it to speed up. I left as soon as I could so I could come home and drink.

And so tequila. Booze would lift me out of my sense of loss, of abandonment, of shame at him still having the power to wound me.

As I reached for the glass, there was a knock at my door. It could be Grace, but it was unlikely because she would have called to make sure I was in. No, it would be Max.

The thought of Max's hard body over mine, pushing into me, filling me with nothing but him, sounded better than tequila.

I opened the door wide, inviting him in. He stepped over the threshold and I let the door slam shut.

"Hi. I just wanted to check—"

"Do you want a shot?" I asked.

He squinted at me and shook his head and I turned and headed back into the kitchen.

I picked up the full glass and before I could lift it to my lips, Max grabbed it out of my hand.

I expected him to throw back the shot, but instead he slung the glass and its contents into the sink. The sound of splintering glass hitting metal echoed into the silence between us.

Pretending he hadn't just done that, I reached into the cabinet and pulled out a shot glass featuring the space needle. I filled it with tequila, then gripped the glass so Max couldn't take it from me. He plucked it from my hand as though it was nothing. As he went to throw it into the sink, I said, "Don't break that one. I like it."

"Liquor won't help," he said, pouring it into the sink and setting the glass down. He grabbed the bottle and screwed on the cap.

I folded my arms. "You're so boring." I sounded like a teenager, but he was used to that.

He put the bottle on top of my refrigerator and stepped toward me. "I know." He lifted my chin and looked at me. "How much have you had to drink?"

I shrugged, unwilling to tell him he'd put a stop to my fun before it started.

"Tell me, Harper." He dragged his thumb along my jaw, rough and intimate. My body relaxed as if *he* were tequila, and I closed my eyes in a long blink.

I uncrossed my arms. "Nothing,"

He nodded and pulled me into a hug, wrapping his long arms around me, enveloping me in the scent I now associated with sex and comfort and peace. I let him hold me, pressing my face against his chest and tightening my arms around his waist.

"I'm not psychic, but I think that maybe today brought some issues to the surface for you." He squeezed me a little bit tighter when I didn't answer. "You want to talk about it rather than drink them away?"

"Definitely not," I replied. Him just being here, holding me, made everything feel so much better. "And I'm sorry about the shoes. They're beautiful and I love them. Sometimes I don't accept gifts well."

He chuckled. "Can I ask why?"

I shrugged and he didn't ask me anything else.

We stood in my kitchen for what seemed like hours, just holding each other until I managed to say, "I'm okay." His chest muffled my words.

He sighed, his ribcage rising and lowering against my breasts. "I should go," he said, but didn't release me.

"Don't," I whispered.

"I don't want to." He sounded tired. As if by hugging him, I'd sapped him of his energy. "And that's why I should. We said no more trips to Vegas."

We had, and it had been the right thing to do. The problem was the more time I spent with him, the more I wanted.

"Then let's go somewhere else," I said, smoothing my hands up his back, shifting my hips just a fraction.

"Harper," he whispered.

"Aruba," I suggested. "Or Paris."

He dipped his head and kissed my neck. My knees weakened in relief. It was what I'd been waiting for since he arrived, since lunch, since the last time he'd touched me.

"Or just here," I said, trailing my fingers up his sides and around his neck. "Kiss me," I whispered. "Just be here with me."

He grabbed my ass and brushed my lips with his, first left then right. I wanted more. I wanted him. I didn't know if he was trying to torment me or still weighing the advantages and disadvantages of being with me again.

I slid my hands down his chest and he caught my wrists before I could convince him to stay.

"You want me, huh?" he asked, placing my hands on the counter behind me.

I wanted to drown out the day. "Kiss me."

"You think this is about making you feel better about today. But it's not," he said, his eyes not leaving my face. "It's about this." His hands swept up my arms and cupped my face. "About the way you feel when I touch you." He bent and placed a kiss on the corner of my lips, teasing me, making me wait. "About how you need me to fuck you more than you need your next breath." He knocked my legs apart with his knee.

I couldn't argue with him. Nothing he was saying was untrue.

I wanted him. Every second. Since before I'd met him.

Even when I thought he was an asshole, I wanted him.

But I wasn't about to admit it.

I squirmed when he reached into the waistband of my leggings, his insistent hand pushing into my panties. "You see?" he asked. "You're wet for me."

He ran two fingers up and down from my clit to my entrance, giving neither relief. I twisted my hips in an effort to feel him deeper, harder.

"Admit it," he said. "Admit how much you want me."

I shifted my hands from the counter where he'd placed them and grabbed his shirt, fumbling with the buttons.

"No," he said, removing his hands from my underwear and batting my hands away.

I groaned in frustration.

"Admit it," he said.

"I want to get fucked." It was true.

"You are the most infuriating woman I know. And that's a mighty high bar given the women in my life." He pulled up my T-shirt, making me shiver as he grazed my skin with his palms. "Fuck," he said when he realized I wasn't wearing a bra. "Tell me. Tell me now."

"You want to feel special?" I asked, taunting him. "You need to know that women desire you over anyone else?"

He shook his head slowly. "Just you. I need to hear it from *you*."

"Why?" I asked as he bent and took a nipple in his mouth, his tongue circling and sucking, his fingers tugging at the other.

"Because it's the truth," he said and he kissed me again on the lips. "Because it's what I feel whenever I think of you, whenever you're near."

Heat ran into my limbs and I put my arms around his neck, gazing into his eyes. He stared back and lifted me onto the kitchen counter.

I nodded. "It's true. I want you." The words sounded soft as they came out. Did he notice?

"I know," he said, his gaze flickering to my mouth just before he pressed his lips to mine. I sighed with relief. A layer of calm engulfed us as if our mutual admissions bound us together. My tongue found his and instead of being urgent and possessive, I allowed myself to go at his pace. I encouraged his seduction of me.

He leaned back and placed a kiss on my nose. "If you're still wearing clothes, I'm not doing something correctly," he said as he pulled at my waistband.

What had I just admitted to him? Had I said I wanted more? I wasn't sure, but all I could focus on were his fingers pulling down my leggings, the glazed look in his eyes as he examined every inch of my skin as if he couldn't quite believe what he was seeing. Nothing else seemed to matter.

As my clothes hit the floor, he scooped me off the counter and walked me out of the kitchen and over to my bed. When we'd been together before, we'd both acted as if we were against the clock. Tugging at each other, desperate to make each other feel good as soon as possible in case someone rang the bell and told us our time was up. This was different. Our kisses were lazy, our movements languid. He ran his palms down my body and brought his hand to my inner thigh as he lay next to me.

"You're wearing a tie," I whispered.

"Like I said, one of the brightest junior researchers I've ever worked with."

I smiled and reached out, pulled the silk material clear of his neck, opened the top couple of buttons of his shirt, and slipped my hand against the skin just below his neck. I sighed. He would make today go away.

Quickly, he stood, stripping completely naked in seconds, throwing his three-thousand-dollar suit on the back of my couch. Then without asking, he opened the drawer to my nightstand and took out a condom.

"Are you dating?" he asked as he joined me on the bed. "No. Don't answer that."

I stroked his cheek and he looked up at me. "Are you dating?" I asked.

"No," he responded. "I'm—"

I stroked my thumb over his lips. He didn't need to explain himself. I didn't really care, because whatever else was going on in his world, or my world, I wanted this to happen. I didn't want to think about tomorrow, to consider consequences. I wanted to drink in the way his eyes, tongue, and hands all seemed to worship me.

He leaned forward and kissed me, taking my bottom lip between his teeth before biting down until it stung, then pushed his tongue against mine. I could kiss him forever. If his penis fell off, I could be happy for the rest of my life with just his tongue. Without stopping kissing me, he put on a condom.

"I love your kisses," I said before I had time to think maybe that wasn't something I should say.

He groaned against my mouth. "And what else?" he asked, his fingers skimming the juncture of my inner thigh.

"Your fingers, your face, your cock." The words tripped out of my mouth, and before I had time to take any of them back, he was over me, pushing into me, slowly but so deep. I brought my knees up as far as they would go, opening myself as wide as I could for him.

"Like that?" he asked as he paused deep inside me.

I nodded, my fingers digging into his shoulders.

"Relax," he said. "It's just you and me."

I exhaled. It was just him and me. Nothing else mattered.

His eyes opened wider, as if he were asking me if I was ready, and I slid my hands over his ass in response. He pulled out almost as slowly as he'd filled me up and I whimpered, overcome with sensation.

"Harper," he whispered. "Look at me."

I watched as his erection entered me. I glanced up and he slammed in while I clung to him. "You love my cock. You said it, baby, and now you're going to get it. I'm going to give you everything you need."

He plunged into me, this time giving me no time to recover before pulling out and then pushing back in. He groaned through a clenched jaw.

I do that to you, was all I could think.

This man, who looked like Gucci made suits just because he existed, groaned because of *me.*

This man, whose beautiful green eyes told everyone who met him he was the boss, was fucking *me.*

This man, who ruled Wall Street, the power behind the performance of leading investment banks in Manhattan, was having to concentrate so he didn't come too quickly because of *me.*

I brought the King of Wall Street to his knees.

"Jesus, Harper."

I pushed against his chest and shifted so he stopped. We were both going to come within seconds if we stayed like that. I moved under him.

"What? That was perfect," he said.

"Too perfect," I replied and flipped over onto my stomach. Seeing him so undone would push me over the edge too soon.

He slid his hands under my thighs and pulled me toward him and straight onto his dick. My back arched as pleasure shot through my legs and ricocheted left and right then up my body. I pushed myself up onto my hands, trying to participate in some way, but I couldn't.

I clenched as he ran the heel of his hand up my spine then clasped my shoulder. "So tight. So good," he groaned.

In seconds I was right on the edge, the change of position having done nothing to dampen my desire for him, to ward off my orgasm. His touch made sure everything was just as intense.

"Max," I cried out.

He thrust in, harder this time. "Again," he choked out.

"Max. Please. God. Max." I couldn't hold it off any longer.

As I spiraled down from my climax, Max bellowed out my name and collapsed on top of me, his front to my back, then rolled to the side, pulling me with him.

chapter twelve

Max

I CAME OUT OF THE BATHROOM TO FIND HARPER HADN'T MOVED A MUSCLE. I COULDN'T BLAME her; we'd spent most of the night fucking and I was exhausted.

"From what I saw today, your father still has quite the hold on you."

Harper pulled the sheet up over her face. "Really? You're standing there with your dick out looking at me while I still have your come between my legs, and we're going to talk about my father?"

"You don't have my come between your legs. I just threw out the condom."

She popped out from under the sheet to scowl at me. "I meant it figuratively."

She was so completely breathtaking when she was mad with me, and I quickly forgot what we were talking about. "You look beautiful." I crawled onto the mattress. I wanted to pull her into me, but she swiped me on the arm and headed to the bathroom.

"You don't take any money from him, do you?" I called after her. Her apartment, her clothes. She wasn't taking any handouts from what I could see. I liked that about her. She was independent. Unable to be bought.

"Why do you ask?" She appeared in the bathroom doorway, one hand on the frame, totally unconcerned by her nakedness. I *really* liked that about her. I liked the way her hips flared, emphasizing her small waist. Liked the way her tits jutted out as if they wanted to join in the conversation. My dick hardened.

"Max?" she prompted, and I pulled my gaze back up to meet hers. "You're a pervert."

"You're naked. What am I going to do other than look at you?"

"I don't know, answer me?"

Even her sarcasm got me hard.

She pulled her hair back as if she were going to tie it up, which lifted up her breasts and lengthened her stomach. "Get the fuck over here before I start jerking myself off."

She released her hair and stepped toward the bed. I grabbed her, pulling her down and against me, wrapping my legs around hers, clasping her to my chest. I couldn't get close enough to quench my thirst for her.

"You're right. I don't take money from him. I started to take some money when I went to college. I figured he owed me that. But it didn't feel right. I didn't know that man."

I pulled her closer. They seemed like strangers at lunch; he was asking her the most basic questions any father should already have known the answer to. There was no affection on Harper's side. He was the man I'd never wanted to be for Amanda.

"Did he and your mother divorce?" I asked.

"No." She exhaled sharply. "He didn't have the decency to marry her in the first place."

Oh. "Pandora and I didn't marry," I replied.

"Yeah, you said. Did you not want to marry her?" she asked. After seeing her with her father today, I wondered if she'd wanted to ask me that question for a while.

I tucked one arm behind my head. "Neither of us wanted to get married."

"But you wanted Amanda. I mean you stayed in contact with her."

My thumb skirted over her hip. "Sure. Pandora and I talked about getting married, and I can't say I know why we didn't go through with it. We were both about to go off to college and maybe we knew we'd be compounding one mistake with another." It had been the right decision. "Not that Amanda was a mistake. Just the pregnancy wasn't planned. Clearly." Harper glanced up at me and I smiled at her. "Pandora and I were good friends, and just before graduation one thing led to another . . . It was never meant to be anything more than a good-bye." I sighed. "It bound us together forever."

Harper pressed her lips against my chest. "She never wanted to get married, not even after Amanda was born?"

I kissed the top of her forehead. "I don't think so. She met Jason when Amanda was about a year old."

"Did that bother you?" she asked.

"No, not at all." It genuinely never had. I liked Jason. He was good to Pandora and my daughter. "I think her parents were worried, but I always wanted Pandora to be happy. We'd been friends a long time. And it didn't stop me from wanting to be the best dad I could be."

Harper didn't respond but I could tell she had more to say. I was content to stay wrapped around her in silence.

Eventually she sighed and said, "I agreed to come shopping because I assumed Amanda would be miserable going shopping with you. I assumed you took as much interest in Amanda as my father did in me."

I pulled back slightly to look at her. "Really?" I said. "She loves shopping. Doesn't mind who she's with but I like to take her. I think since Pandora left, she misses. . ." I almost said *her mother* but I didn't want Harper to misunderstand what I was saying. "You know, the girl thing. And Scarlett is dating like a dozen men and Violet is—"

"Violet?" she asked.

"My other sister," I explained. "And both grandmas want Amanda to stay a little girl for as long as possible. So, we have mutual aims and objectives there." I pulled her close and she pressed her cheek against my chest. "She loved having you there. Didn't stop going on about you when we got home—it certainly raised some eyebrows."

"It did?" she asked. "What kind of eyebrows?"

"The busybody kind. I guess because we work together and live in the same building. I think my sisters believed . . ." What had they thought? That we were dating?

"Is Violet younger than you?" she asked and I was grateful she had gone in a different direction.

"Yes, and a complete pain in the ass. Always interfering in everyone's business. She's a meddler." I chuckled as I realized it might be a genetic thing. "She's a lot like Amanda in that way." Amanda dressed her constant whining about wanting a baby sister as self-interest but I was pretty sure she wanted me happy. "They have a lot in common."

"Sounds like you have your hands full. Even without King & Associates."

I sighed. "They occupy two different spaces in my brain."

"Maybe," she said. She wiggled her body against mine, and I rolled us over until she was on her back and I was looking down at her.

"You're the exception," I said. "You seem to have taken up residence in both spaces." I brushed my nose against hers and pulled back to look at her. "I realized it in the cab today. I liked that we could just be together, near each other. No talking, no touching."

She nodded very slightly.

"This is new to me," I said. I wasn't sure what *this* was. If I was just having a personal relationship with someone I worked with, or having sex with someone I knew more about than just their last name. Or was it the fact that whenever I saw her, whenever I thought about her, whenever I touched her, I wanted more. It was all new.

I dipped my head to kiss her nose as she wrapped her legs around me, pulling me close until my cock pushed against her.

I'd fucked a lot of attractive women with nice, firm asses; long, lean legs; and huge tits. Harper was attractive, gorgeous even, but with her, the stuff that made me hard, that had me moaning, was more than just the physical. I liked the way the silences were comfortable, the way she could make me laugh, the way she seemed to open up as I drove into her.

"You want some of this?" I asked, rocking against her. She grinned and I shook my head. "Insatiable," I said as I lowered myself onto my forearms and licked along her collarbone. She threaded her hands through the back of my hair, setting goosebumps off across my skin. I took her breasts in my hands, grazed her nipples with my tongue and then again with my teeth. She arched against me as my nips became careless and harder. My dick throbbed at her reaction, but it wouldn't find relief any time soon. Winding up her lust got me hard, her desire towing me along.

"I want to see you in those shoes I bought you," I said, my voice hoarse. Her naked in those shoes had been an image front and center of my thoughts since I made the purchase.

She grinned up at me and ducked under my arm, heading across to her closet. I shifted to my back, waiting for her. She stepped out into the door frame, her hands above her, bracing on either side of the wood, one high shoe stroking up the side of long, tan leg. I couldn't stop the groan that ripped out of my chest. I reached for her but instead she turned around, swaying her hips one way and then another. "How do they look from the back?" she asked. I didn't know where to focus—her thick, soft hair sweeping down her back, down to her small waist, or her high, tight ass as it jutted out to get my attention, or between her thighs where I knew it was so soft and wet. The shoes magnified every inch of her perfect body.

"Get over here and let me show you what I think about you in those shoes."

She took small steps toward the bed, her perfectly neat pussy mesmerizing me as she got closer. Fuck, I couldn't get enough.

She grasped her breasts, kneading them together as she approached the bed. I rose onto my knees to meet her, wanting the space between us to disappear. Reaching between her thighs with one hand, I grabbed her ass and pulled her onto my fingers. "You are perfect," I whispered. She gave me a small smile and her head tipped back as my fingers drove deeper.

Blood rushed to my dick and I wanted it in my fist, in her pussy, but I didn't want to let go of her. She stumbled slightly, which made it worse, she was so affected by just my fingers she couldn't stand. "I want you on your back, your feet in the air," I said and pulled her onto the bed.

I kissed my way down to her belly button. She shifted, getting more and more restless, twisting and squirming beneath me. I moved farther down and gripped her thighs, pushing them open, her heels high in the air either side of me.

She cried out when I blew across her sex. Her sounds urged me on. I spread the lips of her sex, exposing her clitoris. She tensed. I wasn't sure if it was in anticipation or embarrassment. I leaned forward and circled the bundle of nerves with my tongue. Her breaths came louder and deeper as I suckled before licking down to her entrance.

Like nothing I'd ever tasted before. Like springtime—warm, fresh, and inviting. I couldn't get enough as I delved into her, lapping up the wetness that hadn't already coated my chin.

I could stay like this, my face buried in her, for the rest of my days. I reached for my rock-hard cock, which was desperate to taste the sweetness coating my tongue. I dragged my fist up and forced myself to let go; I wasn't ready to come yet. As soon as I pushed into her I'd be lost—my body would crash through every urge I had to please her in an effort to get to my orgasm.

I elbowed her thighs open wider still, my tongue connecting with her clitoris as my thumbs delved into her, pulling at her entrance, twisting then circling back. Her body began to shudder and I heard the whisper of my name on her lips. I wanted it louder. I increased the pressure of my tongue and her hands flew into my hair as she called, "Max, my God, Max."

Her orgasm spread through her like an electricity bolt, her pussy contracting, pushing against my thumbs. I removed my hands and slid my tongue back to soothe her, feeling her pulse just below the surface of her skin.

I glanced up at her, her arms overhead as her back began to lower back into the mattress. It was the first time I'd ever had the urge to film a woman before. I'd never need to date again if I had a recording of Harper coming on my tongue like that.

God, she was perfect when she was undone.

I moved to her side as she opened her eyes and smiled at me. "You're good at that," she said.

"What am I supposed to say?" I chuckled.

"Learn how to accept a compliment," she replied as she pushed herself up then straddled me. "Just say 'thank you'."

I shook my head, my hands going to her hips. Her wetness coated my cock as she shifted back and forward.

I groaned, her heat seeping into my veins. I wasn't going to last long. Desperate, I reached for the nightstand. I fumbled with the drawer, had to stretch to reach inside. The wood dug into my wrist and I scrambled for a condom.

Grinning, she took the square packet before I had a chance to argue and rolled the condom on, tantalizingly slowly, both of us staring at my jutting cock in her hands.

"It's not been long, but do you remember how good it feels?" she asked as she squeezed the base of me. "How tight I am?"

I groaned, needing her to remind me.

She lifted herself up and positioned the tip at her opening. "How you slide in so deep?"

"Fuck, Harper. Are you trying to kill me?"

She scooped up her hair, then let it tumble back down, smoothing her hands over her breasts as she twisted her hips and took me a little deeper. "You remember how you fit so good? You're almost too big." She took me in a little more. "*Almost.*" A little more. "I always think it's going to be painful, but no." She placed her hands on my torso, steadying herself, which squeezed her tits together, pushing them nearer me. Her head snapped back and I almost came right there. "It feels too good to be painful," she continued, twisting her hips, teasing me, knowing I wanted to be in deep. "Do you remember how good it feels?"

I gripped her hips, trying to do anything I could to prevent myself from jabbing my cock so deep she'd never walk again.

She let herself sink all the way down, her eyes widening with every movement, then stilled. "I never remember," she whispered. "I always forget just how good it feels."

Patience deserting me, I growled and sat up, spinning her onto her back and pushing back into her. "I'm going to make sure you never forget again."

I wanted to fuck her forever.

~

After spending the night with Harper, I had taken longer than usual to get through everything I needed to do, so I got a later train.

"I'm home," I shouted. I could hear the television from the family room. Usually I came back to Connecticut in the week to find Marion clearing up the kitchen, but her car wasn't in the drive. Was she here alone? "Amanda," I shouted. I supposed she didn't need to be babysat anymore but I didn't like the idea of her being alone, waiting for me to come back.

"In here," she yelled over the noise of music and shouting. I took off my jacket and put it on the back of one of the barstools and dropped my cell on the counter. A nice glass of Pinot Noir was what I needed. It had been a tough week. I placed a glass on the counter and pulled out a bottle from the wine fridge.

"Can I have one of those?" Scarlett asked from behind me.

"Hey." I grabbed another glass. "What are you doing here?"

She slid onto the middle barstool. "I didn't want to be on my own tonight. Can I stay over?"

I nodded. She clearly wanted to talk. I poured the wine into her glass as she held the stem.

"I'm thinking of moving into the city," she said, tilting her head as she watched her glass fill up. "Sometimes it feels like Connecticut is where I should be in ten years rather than now. Does that make sense?" she asked.

"It's good to change things up, I guess. You've never lived in Manhattan. What would you do about work?" She worked at an investment bank just outside Westhaven.

She shrugged.

Fuck, I hoped she wasn't going to ask me for a job.

"I thought I'd apply for a transfer. There's a treasury position in Manhattan at the moment. It's a level up, but I have the experience."

I nodded, relieved we weren't about to have a difficult conversation. My phone vibrated on the counter with a message, Harper's name flashing up on the screen. I watched as Scarlett saw the message, then met my gaze.

She didn't say anything, so I grabbed my phone and opened the message. *Manhattan's no fun when the King's not in residence.*

I grinned and glanced up at Scarlett, whose eyebrows were so high they nearly disappeared into her hairline. "Anything you care to share?"

I swallowed my smile and picked up my glass. "Just work." I took a sip.

"Yeah, that looked like work."

Thoughts of trying to keep my feelings for Harper professional had long since disappeared. Harper had been clear she didn't want to be seen as the girl fucking the boss, and I didn't want to muddy waters between professional and personal any more than I already had. In the office we'd agreed to just avoid each other. Easily done as the morning meetings about JD Stanley were the only times we really saw each other. Some distance in the office was a good thing.

But all the distance disappeared as soon as we were back in her apartment—for some reason she refused to come up to my place, even though it was bigger.

"Hey, Dad," Amanda said, interrupting the silence.

"Hey, beautiful," I replied, bending to kiss my daughter hello. I wondered how soon she'd no longer want to kiss me. Parents kept warning me about the teenage years, assuring me our disagreement over her dress was only the tip of a very large iceberg.

"You going to text Harper back?" Scarlett asked, grinning at me. If the Pinot Noir hadn't been so good, I'd have tipped the rest of the bottle over her head. My daughter wouldn't miss the reference and Scarlett knew it.

"Harper texted?" Amanda asked predictably. "Can you ask her if she'll come help me get ready for the dance? I want her to do my eyeliner just like hers."

I put my phone back on the counter. "No, I'm not asking Harper to come out to Connecticut to help you get ready. She's not your personal stylist."

"She's too busy attending to someone else's needs in this family, isn't she?" Scarlett joked and I shot her a dirty look.

"What?" Amanda asked.

"Let's talk about your dating life, shall we, Scarlett?" I asked.

She tilted her head. "Oh, so you admit Harper's part of your dating life then?"

Shit. I was usually better at avoiding Scarlett's interrogations. I turned toward the refrigerator. "Have you eaten?" I asked Amanda, trying to ignore my sister.

"Tell me more about Harper, Amanda."

Inwardly I groaned.

"I want to be just like her when I'm older. You've seen her, right?" Amanda babbled on about how great Harper was, how wise she was about boys and what a great fashion sense she had. It sounded like Amanda'd known her for years rather than only spent time with her twice.

"So, dinner?" I asked, hoping to get them to change the subject.

"Can I have the cold lasagna in there?" Amanda asked, gesturing to the fridge.

Sounded like a great idea. Marion had even left a salad, too.

"Harper's great, isn't she?" Amanda asked.

I glanced at my sister, who held my gaze and asked Amanda, "Do you think she likes your dad?"

"Scarlett," I warned.

"Does she have a boyfriend?" Scarlett asked, which was a question I had a little more interest in. Had Harper talked to Amanda about anyone?

"No, she says she's too focused on work," Amanda replied. "When I talked to her, she pretty much agreed boys were douchebags who should be avoided at all costs."

I couldn't hold back a chuckle, which won me a suspicious glance from my sister. "She's a very sensible woman."

I put the salad on the counter. "Can you get plates?" I asked Amanda. She hopped off her stool and began to set things out as I dished up the lasagna.

"You know we just want you to be happy," my sister said, lowering her voice. "And from what I can remember, Harper is beautiful." She clinked her glass against mine before taking another sip. "Amanda clearly likes her."

I handed her a plate of food, pretending I wasn't listening.

"Have you thought about asking her out?"

Ignoring Scarlett, I spooned pasta onto mine and Amanda's plates, then placed the dish back in the refrigerator. My sister bugged me about getting a girlfriend almost as much as Amanda did, but why were they fixating on Harper? That was my job. When I turned back to the counter, Amanda and Scarlett were both staring at me as if waiting for me to say something.

"What?" I asked, grabbing the seat next to them and taking a forkful of food.

"Have you thought about asking Harper out on a date, Dad?" Amanda asked, as if I were the most ludicrous person she'd ever had to deal with.

I swallowed and put some salad on my plate. "What is with you two? I've told you, Harper works for me. What is your obsession with her?"

"I like her." Amanda shrugged.

Scarlett grinned. "And that should be reason enough. Why don't you take her to dinner? What could one evening hurt?"

Little did they know trying to keep time spent with Harper limited to just one evening would be impossible. Whatever boundaries I set with her got torn down and overrun. We'd never really been in Vegas. Well, I hadn't managed it anyway. Even here, with my sister and daughter, a situation that had only ever been completely consuming, I was wondering what Harper was doing, who she was spending time with. Did she feel the same? And if she did, then what? Would she come out here to Connecticut? Meet my family?

Did I want her to?

"You think I should date, huh?" I asked. Scarlett was right; it was good that Amanda seemed to like Harper. If my daughter was open to it, maybe I should ask Harper out. Officially.

Amanda tapped on my head with her fist. "Come on, Dad, duh. I've only been saying this my whole life."

"Okay," I said.

"What does okay mean?" Amanda said.

"It means please don't speak with your mouth full," I said, glaring at my daughter.

She giggled and swallowed. "Sorry. But what does 'okay' mean?"

"It means, okay, I'll think about asking her out." The situation with Harper felt like a jigsaw puzzle with too many pieces. Harper working for me complicated things, and her father was the founder of JD Stanley. We also lived in the same building. I'd never really dated before—I was bound to fuck things up. There were a lot of downsides. One of Scarlett's friends would probably be less complicated to date. There would be fewer aftershocks if it didn't work out.

But she wouldn't be Harper.

"You will?" Amanda squealed. "Does that mean she can come help me get ready for the dance? Can I call her now to ask?"

"I said I'd think about asking her to dinner, not employ her to do your makeup. Jeez."

Amanda paused, which meant she was thinking, which could only be bad. "You could make her dinner, here. After I leave for the dance."

I could. It would be nice to see Harper in Connecticut. It wasn't the worst idea Amanda had ever had.

"I'll think about it," I said and Amanda squealed again.

I glanced across at Scarlett, who beamed at me. "What?" I asked her.

She shrugged. "Nothing."

Amanda abandoned her plate of food and headed toward the den, no doubt to find her phone. "Can I call her now? Check if she's free? This is going to be so much fun. It will be like, the best night ever!"

"You need to lower your expectations," I told my daughter. "And prepare yourself for the fact that she might say no."

She paused and spun around to face me. "So what if she does? You've always told me that you don't take no for an answer."

I couldn't argue with that. I was used to getting what I wanted. And right now, I wanted Harper.

chapter thirteen

Harper

I COULDN'T EVER REMEMBER BEING SO NERVOUS. I'D REHEARSED AND PREPARED FOR THE Goldman's pitch and thirty minutes ago I was feeling pretty confident. But as the appointment grew closer, my heartrate had started to speed as if I were sprinting across hot coals.

"So, you'll handle any questions about the process?" Max asked.

I nodded, picking at the hem of my skirt as we sat in the back of the cab to Midtown. I wished I'd brought some water. My throat was dry and tight. They'd have water when we arrived, wouldn't they?

It was the questions I was most worried about. I'd been practicing my ass off for this presentation. It might be a warm-up to the JD Stanley pitch, but it was still important. There was six figures in profit to be lost if I fucked this up. That might be a drop in Wall Street's ocean, but it seemed like a lot of money to me.

My parts of the presentation? Those I'd own. Unlike Max, who appeared to speak off the cuff, I'd written myself a script and memorized it. I'd practiced out loud at home over and over. I knew exactly when to pause, when to ask people to turn the pages in their slide deck, and when to draw emphasis. As long as I hadn't forgotten the printouts, I'd be fine. I scrambled at my feet, reaching into my business carryall to make sure the papers were all there. They were. Just like the last thirty-six times I'd checked.

"Don't be nervous," Max said, smoothing down his tie. "It will be fine. The rehearsal was good."

How would he know if this was going to be fine? Sure, he'd seen the rehearsal, but when the pressure was on, no one knew how things would turn out. I overcame nerves and pressure by being over-prepared—but I couldn't prepare for questions, at least not all of them.

"Easy for you to say," I replied.

"I mean it," he said, placing his hand on my knee.

I pushed it off. The last thing I needed was to be thinking about him naked. "Sorry, I need to . . ." I wasn't sure what I needed.

He glanced out the window. "Okay, I get it. What if I was to ask you a favor? Would that help take your mind off things?" he asked.

I didn't respond, unsure of everything other than my script.

"Amanda wants you to help her get ready for the dance. I said I'd ask."

That wasn't what I'd expected at all. "In Connecticut?" I asked.

He nodded. "You don't have to come, but I know Amanda would like you to. She suggested you and I have dinner together when she left."

"Is she trying to set us up?" I laughed.

"I think so. She's a big fan of yours." Max smiled. "Runs in the family, apparently."

I grinned. Max and I hadn't talked about how we felt about each other, so his comment was unexpected. I wanted to reach for him, kiss him, but I didn't. I needed to keep my head in the game.

"I'd like you to come," he said.

I liked Amanda, but I didn't know how I felt about her setting me and Max up on a date. "Is that weird, having your daughter set you up?"

Max tilted his head. "It should be, I guess. But she goes on and on about me getting marrie—dating. I'm used to it."

"Have you told her that we're . . ."

"Fucking like bunnies? Funnily enough, no," he said, chuckling.

Was that what we were doing? Just fucking? I wasn't sure. I liked the guy, really liked him, but he was my boss and he had a daughter and this whole secret life in Connecticut I'd never seen.

"I think maybe she's picked up on the fact that I like you," he said. Butterflies in my stomach took my mind off my quickening pulse. "I know my sister has."

Liked me? Did that mean it wasn't just fucking for him? I wasn't sure it was for me anymore either.

"Scarlett?" I asked.

"Yeah, she's made a few comments when your name's come up." He slung his arm across the back of the seat. "Look, don't feel any pressure, but I'd like it if you came up, even if it isn't for the dance—it's only three weeks away. You might have plans."

"I don't."

He raised an eyebrow at me. "You don't have plans?" he asked. I shook my head.

"So? Does that mean you'll come?"

"Sure." I grinned and the corner of his mouth turned up. I could tell we both wanted to touch each other, lean in for a kiss, but there was some kind of imaginary force field that existed when we were in work clothes.

The cab pulled to a halt on Fifth Avenue. Shit, we were here.

"Max King for Peter Jones," he said when we reached the receptionist.

As we made our way up in the elevators, he said, "I've done this a million times, Harper. I'll step in if it gets too much."

He meant to be reassuring, but I didn't want him to step in. I wanted to nail this so the presentation to JD Stanley would be easy. Or easier. I really wanted my father to see what I'd been able to do despite him. Maybe then he'd wonder if he'd missed out, realize just throwing money at a situation didn't mean you knew a person, influenced or inspired them.

"I'm good," I said with an open, professional smile. "Everything's fine."

As we entered the conference room, three men stood from their chairs across the oval mahogany table to greet us. All white, all balding, all slightly overweight. In fact, I could have interchanged any parts of them and I was pretty sure no one would notice.

After the introductions, we took our seats across the table.

"Gentlemen, we have some slides we'd like to pass around," Max said as I slid three copies of our presentation across the table.

Not one of them made a move to take the papers.

The man in a gray suit steepled his fingers in front of him. "Why don't you just talk to us about the experience you have in Asia. Most of your competitors have local offices, and I'd like to understand a little more about how you'll be able to provide any real value from your desks here in Manhattan.

Shit. Shit. Shit. Shit. Shit.

This wasn't going as planned. The presentation was where I felt safe.

I glanced across at Max, who looked as relaxed as if he'd just been asked his mother's maiden name. He sat back in his chair and nodded. "Sure. I'm very happy to talk about our strategic choices in terms of international reach."

He went on to explain how his low overheads meant he could spend money employing experts on the ground, which could be different project to project, where his competitors had to use the people they'd employed in their local office regardless of whether or not they were qualified. "You see someone at their desk in Kuala Lumpur is still at their desk—they're not out meeting people, finding out what's happening on the ground. My network of contacts are the people living the day-to-day reality of the geopolitical situations across many industries." Max sat forward as he spoke, looking at his audience as if they were the most important people in the world and he had precious information to share with them. They seemed to find him as compelling as I did.

Max batted away each of the questions as if he were Nadal returning serve, and as the meeting progressed, the suits visibly relaxed, even chuckling at a few of Max's wry comments.

"Do you think the actual process produces anything we've not seen before?" The middle man tapped his fingers against the arm of his chair. "You clearly see it as part of your competitive advantage."

Max turned to me. This was the part of the presentation I'd prepared. "Harper, did you want to add anything here?"

I lifted the corner of my mouth, trying to fake a smile, wanting to cover the fact my mind had gone blank. Completely blank.

"Yes, well." I flicked through my copy of the presentation that had gone unopened. "As you said, we see this is as a key competitive advantage over others in the marketplace . . ." I glanced up and scanned the three sets of eyes all staring at me. I reached for my glass of water and took a sip. My mind was blank. I'd been over this hundreds of times, but I needed a prompt. "We like to conclude things," I blurted. That was one of my key points, wasn't it? I didn't know what I was saying. I started flicking through my presentation manically. "I . . . If I could just . . ."

Max placed his hand on my forearm. "Harper's quite right. One of the key things that differentiates us from others in the marketplace is the conclusions we are able to draw." Several times Max paused and turned to me, which would have allowed me to step in and say something if only I could have thought of a single thing to say.

Eventually I tuned out and slumped back in my seat.

I'd been given this huge opportunity and I'd totally bombed. What the hell was the matter with me? I'd been well prepared for today. I couldn't have done more. Did I subconsciously not think I deserved to be here? Had my father's comments at lunch last week burrowed deeper than I realized? I was trying so hard to prove to my father I was worthy of this job, but I wasn't sure I really believed it.

⁓

I tried to wash away the awful meeting at Goldman Sachs but my bath wasn't helping. Nor was the Jo Malone bath oil or the so-called soothing music filtering through from my bedroom. I was trying to relax, calm down. Nothing was working. All I could do was replay the disastrous meeting earlier in the day over and over again.

I slid under the water, submerging my entire head in the vain hope it would cleanse away the embarrassment.

I came up for air. Nope, I still wanted to die.

Max must think I'm an idiot.

My breath caught at the sharp knock at the door. Perfect timing. Here he was to tell me so. Well, I didn't have to answer the door. I ignored him.

"Harper, I know you're in there. Answer the door."

I shouldn't have put that music on. I stood up and wrapped a towel around me.

Max started pounding on the door.

"I'm coming," I shouted. I threw it open, then immediately turned around and headed back to the bathroom.

"Nice to see you, too," he mumbled. I dropped my towel and slid back into the bath.

I expected him to follow me, but instead I heard cabinet doors opening in the kitchen. What was he doing?

He appeared, barefoot, his jacket and tie gone, holding two glasses of wine. Right then he might just have been the perfect man.

"You have a nice, tight ass," I said. He grinned. "And I'm really sorry I fucked up."

He handed me a glass, which I took gratefully. He'd definitely brought the bottle with him—I didn't own anything this good. It tasted like it cost a month's salary.

He sighed, closed the bathroom door, and began unbuttoning his shirt. When he undid the last one, he took a swig of his wine and placed it on the side of the bath and stripped off the rest of his clothes.

"What are you doing?" I asked as he stepped into the bath.

He didn't respond, just sat down at the opposite end, pulling my legs over his.

"You choked today," he said, taking a sip of his wine.

"Yeah, thanks, Captain Obvious. If you're here to make me feel worse, you can leave right now."

He acted as if he hadn't heard me, stroking up the leg I had resting on his thigh. "You know Michael Jordan?"

Now he's going to talk about sports? Great. Just what I needed.

I nodded.

"Greatest basketball player of all time, right? A consummate winner."

"Er . . . yes." Where the hell was he going with this?

"Well something he said was the best business advice I've ever received. It went like this, 'I've missed more than nine-thousand shots in my career and I've lost almost three-hundred games.'" He smoothed his hands up and down my legs "'Twenty-six times I've been trusted to take the game-winning shot and missed. 'I've failed over and over and over again in my life. And that is why I succeed.'"

He paused and we stared at each other.

"We all fuck up, Harper. We all choke. It's how we get better."

I sighed and skimmed the top of the water with my palms. "Yeah, well, I'm not a basketball player," I muttered.

"Of course you are. We all are. You didn't come out of the womb ready. How many times did you fall over before you learned to walk? You can't give up when you fail the first time." He took my foot, pressing his thumbs into my sole. "The problem is there comes a point in life when you haven't fucked up in a while. You get good at passing exams, you graduate, you get a job. Everything is great. But it's a false sense of security because if you're going to learn and grow, fucking up is inevitable."

"So if you're saying my choking was always going to happen, why did you take me to the presentation?" I tried to pull my leg away but he held on tight.

"I might be good but I'm not a fucking psychic. No one knows *when* they're going to fail, just that they will at some point."

The pressure in my chest started to lift. He was right. Of course he was. "But I hate it."

"I'm sure Michael Jordan hated missing game-winning shots."

I didn't say anything. I was new and inexperienced and I'd let it show.

"Harper, it's why I wanted you to present to Goldman's. I didn't want you to choke in front of your father."

Had he really been trying to protect me? Warmth for him spread through my body. I wasn't used to someone having my back in such an obvious way. Not a man anyway. And I liked it. More than liked it.

I pulled my foot from his hands and moved to straddle him. "You always say exactly the right thing."

He chuckled. "I think my daughter would disagree."

I wrapped my arms around his neck and kissed him briefly on his jaw. "You look sexy wet," I said.

"You look sexy all the time," he replied.

"Exactly the right thing," I whispered and I pressed my lips to his. His tongue reached for mine.

He shifted, pushing me away. "Come on. Let's get out. I want to fuck you without being interrupted by neighbors complaining about water coming through their ceiling."

Well, I couldn't argue with that logic, either.

He held me tight as he walked me out of the bathroom and pushed me onto the bed, collapsing beside me. He opened my towel as if inspecting me for clues, his eyes raking over my naked body. "You're beautiful," he said, squinting as he said it, as if he couldn't quite believe it.

A rush of panic hit me in the chest as I pushed my fingers through his hair. I couldn't imagine not having this, not having him, to talk to, to kiss, to fuck. What would I do when this was all over?

"I can't wait for you to come to Connecticut," he said. "I want to have you in my bed for a change." He dipped his head and circled one of my nipples with his tongue.

The pulling sensation in my stomach chased away the panic and I shifted my hips sideways, tangling my legs with his. His towel had fallen open and I reached for his hard, heavy cock. I shivered as I began to pump my fist up and down. He hissed through his teeth, throwing his head back.

"I've been thinking about having your hands wrapped around my dick all day," he said. "You're so utterly distracting."

"And infuriating, remember?"

He reached for my pussy, and I flicked my hips up to meet his fingers, always eager for his touch. "That's part of the distraction, part of the attraction." His fingers dipped inside me, his thumb pressing against my clitoris, the frustration and embarrassment of the day dissolving under his touch.

"Do you think about me?" he asked, slowly thrusting into my hands. "You think about this?" He grazed my shoulder with his teeth, then bit down, causing me to moan.

"All the time." It was true. The only way I survived in the office was by avoiding him, but that was like trying to avoid gravity. My pull toward him was inevitable.

I released his dick and he began to slide it over my sex, teasing, promising. I reached behind me for the nightstand, but he took over my search for a condom.

"I've got to be inside you right now," he whispered. "I've been wanting you all day." He paused in his rhythm and I whimpered. "I know, Harper, I need it, too."

I'd never been so sexually vulnerable with a man, never offered up so much of myself. But with him it wasn't a choice; it was mandatory. There was no other way I could be.

He slipped his palms under my ass and pulled me toward him as he sat back onto his knees, the warmth of his eyes replacing his body heat.

His gaze bore into me as he thrust. He didn't take his time, but he didn't rush, either, just moved into me with a strong, confident force that nearly had me climaxing—the feeling of being totally consumed by him mentally and physically pushing me to the brink, threatening to tip me over the edge.

"Max," I called out.

"I'm here. I'm fucking you, needing you, owning you."

He was right. He *did* own me.

I lifted my knees and he growled, "I'm going to fuck you over my desk one day while you look out over Manhattan, your skirt around your waist, your ass in the air." He thrust again. "I want you in my bed in Connecticut, on the stairs, against the lobby wall of this apartment. I want you in every cab we ever share together. I've never wanted anyone like this."

His words drifted over me like sunshine, heating my skin, ridding my brain of shadows.

I wanted him so badly it was almost terrifying. Before fear could take hold, pleasure pushed out from my belly and down my limbs. "Max," I whispered, my fingernails digging into his skin.

"I know. I know. I know." He knew me, understood *everything*.

In that moment we were joined; we were connected; we were inseparable.

chapter fourteen

Max

"Good morning," I said as I passed Donna's desk. She looked at me suspiciously, probably because I was grinning.

"You okay?" she asked from the doorway as I shrugged off my jacket.

I looked up at her, still smiling. "I'm excellent, how are you?" Last night with Harper had been great. Sex had always been an important part of my routine, of my life, but with Harper there was a level of connection I'd never had with anyone else. Perhaps it was the reason my family continually bugged me about finding a girlfriend. Maybe they realized relationships could be this good, this easy with someone. Harper made me laugh, got me hot, and drove me crazy all within a ten-second window. I couldn't get enough of her.

"I'm okay, thanks. A little concerned the body snatchers have taken over my boss, but hey, we're in Manhattan, so it's to be expected."

"You're too young to be so cynical, Donna," I replied.

"Okay, now you're really starting to freak me out. Can I get you a coffee? Maybe that will kick you back into a normal gear," she said as her phone rang. "Be right back," she said, then closed the door.

I sat down and spun my chair around, facing out into the city. I was about to land JD Stanley, my personal Everest. Amanda was happy and healthy. I was fucking the most beautiful girl I'd ever laid eyes on. No, we were doing more than fucking. Were we dating? I turned back to my desk. Maybe when she came up to Connecticut we should have a conversation about what we were doing. I wanted her to meet Scarlett and Violet properly—they could come over for drinks that evening, but I wanted her to myself when Amanda left for the dance. Maybe brunch the next morning would be better. I hoped Harper planned to stay over. Once I had her in my house, I knew I'd find it hard to let her leave.

I pressed the speaker button when Donna buzzed my phone. "Charles Jayne on line one."

Puzzled, I picked up the receiver. Lunch had gone well. I had everything I needed and we were on track to nail our pitch next week. I hoped he wasn't going to try to cancel on me.

"Max King. How can I help?"

"I want to talk to you about the presentation next week."

Shit, he was going to cancel. I sat back in my chair. I wouldn't let him hear I was rattled. "Yes, sir, we're looking forward to it. Harper's been doing some excellent work. I'm sure you'll be impressed."

"It's Harper's involvement that I want to talk to you about."

I gripped the phone tighter. "I'm listening," I replied, my tone a little more terse than before.

"I like to keep my work life and my personal life separate," Charles began. That had been my policy before Harper smudged the lines between the two. I still believed it was a good policy. Harper was just someone I couldn't resist. But Charles had employed his sons in the business, so what he was saying didn't make much sense.

"Okay," I replied.

"I don't think it's a good idea for Harper to work on the JD Stanley account. You understand?"

I pushed my chair away from my desk. "I'm not sure I do," I replied.

"I don't want anyone to think that a decision I make on King & Associates has anything to do with Harper. Business is business."

"But I want to give you our best people and—"

"It's entirely up to you," he said. "I'm not forcing you to do anything. But if you're going to pitch next week, I don't want Harper on the team."

Shit. I mean, I got it. And I thought I'd feel the same way. I wasn't sure Harper would be so understanding. But he was a potential client, one I was desperate to land. "Of course, sir, it's entirely up to you what team you want to work with."

"I'm pleased you understand. I'm looking forward to what you have to say."

I hung up and slumped back in my chair. Should I have said no? How would I tell Harper? I guess I could pull out? But this was the opportunity I'd been waiting for and Harper knew that. She'd understand, wouldn't she? This wasn't personal. It was business.

Crap. I stood and grabbed my jacket. I needed some fresh air and common sense. "I'm going to Joey's for a coffee," I told Donna as I headed toward the elevators.

"Everything okay?" she called after me. I couldn't reply.

Harper would understand. In fact, she might be relieved. She could take some time, build up her confidence after the way she'd choked at Goldman's.

But something told me she wasn't going to think like that. This might be business to me, but it was very personal to Harper.

It was as if Charles Jayne had thrown a grenade, and I was left bracing myself for the explosion but hoping it was a dud.

Three . . . two . . . one.

༄

"Can you get Harper?" I asked Donna through the speakerphone, wiping the screen with my thumb.

"Sure thing."

I stood, took off my jacket, and rolled up my sleeves. Coffee and a conversation with Joey about baseball had helped me make up my mind to tell Harper she was dropped from the JD Stanley team and to do it as soon as possible. As it was a work-related matter, I should tell her at the office. Part of me wanted to take a bottle of wine over to her apartment, run a bath, and tell her when we were both a glass down. That way I could hold her if she got upset. But Harper had been clear she wanted no special treatment at work.

"Hi," Harper said as she appeared in my doorway.

"Hi," I croaked, then cleared my throat. "Close the door and take a seat."

She frowned and did as I asked.

I took a deep breath. "I want to talk to you about the JD Stanley account." Her hands curled around the arm of the chair. "I'm going to make a change and get Marvin to be my second chair on the JD Stanley pitch."

I waited for the explosion.

Her gaze fell to her lap, then came back up to meet mine. "Is this because I choked at the Goldman meeting?" she asked.

Of course that was what she'd think. This was my out. I could tell her we needed a more experienced speaker. I didn't have to tell her what her father had said. I didn't have to hurt her.

"How am I supposed to learn from my mistakes if you don't give me another shot?" She leaned forward a little. "I'm ready this time. I really know the material—even your sections."

She *was* ready. I could tell by the way she spoke in our morning meetings that instead of the failure at Goldman's sapping her confidence, it had fed it.

I brought my hands together on my desk. Should I lie to her? Could I?

I liked to get what I wanted. And I *wanted* to do the JD Stanley pitch without Harper *and* have Harper okay about it. But I couldn't be dishonest to make that happen. It wasn't the man I was.

"I know you're ready. It's not that."

"I mean it, Max. I can show you. Seriously. I can give the presentation to the whole company, bring people in off the street even. I can do this."

Fuck, this was going to be harder than I expected. She was so committed to this pitch. Even if her reasons weren't all business, her attitude was. I nodded. "I know there isn't a better person for the job."

"Then why?" she asked, slamming her hands on the arms of her chair.

"Your father called me this morning." She shifted forward in her seat and I took a deep breath. "He said he didn't want you at the presentation."

She flopped back in her chair, staring at my desk, her eyes glazed. I'd never experienced anything like this. In the office everything was so clear to me. It was at home that everything was gray and I always questioned my decisions. Telling Harper this brought out a different side of me. I wanted to go over to her and comfort her.

"Did he say why?" she asked.

"Just that he didn't want to mix personal and professional. Which I can understand."

She rose to her feet. "He employs his three male children. That's not mixing business and personal?"

I scrubbed my hands over my face. How could I make this okay? "I understand this is frustrating."

"Frustrating?" she yelled. "Are you kidding me? The guy's an asshole. He's trying to ruin my career."

I hadn't gotten the impression he was doing anything but being selfish. "Maybe he felt a little uncomfortable because the two of you are estranged." I thought I'd feel the same. "I'm sure he wasn't trying to make you look bad."

Harper laid her hands on my desk, and leaned toward me. "And so what, you just said, 'yes, sir, thank you, sir? Who cares if I fuck over the girl I've been screwing the last few weeks. Who gives a shit about her feelings? As long as I'm still in line for your business, I'll do anything you say.' Is that how it went?"

There was real venom in her tone and she was out of line. I'd acted in the best interests of King & Associates and if she was being rational she'd see it. "No, I said that I thought that you were the best person for the job." Had she expected me to argue with him? Ultimately he was the client. He got to choose his team.

She shook her head. "But you still told him you'd swap me out?"

"Harper, he's the client. He can choose who he wants working for him."

She shifted, putting her hand on her hip. "Guess what, asshole? *You* can choose who you work for, too. Don't you see? He was testing you. Seeing if he asked you to jump, if you'd ask how high. He's a piece of shit who's determined to make me miserable." She covered her face with her hands and my heart squeezed. Fuck, I hated that she did that to me. I hadn't done anything wrong. The last thing I wanted to do was upset her. I desperately wanted to go to comfort her, but this was business.

She smoothed down her skirt and pulled back her shoulders. "He asked you to choose between him and me," she said, her voice quiet. "And you made your decision. So good luck." She turned and headed to the exit.

I wanted to run after her, make her understand, but she was out of my door before I'd stood up. The last thing I wanted to do was make a scene, escalate the situation. I'd leave early, but instead of going back to Connecticut tonight, I'd go to her place and we could talk.

chapter fifteen

Harper

I ARRIVED AT GRACE'S APARTMENT STRAIGHT FROM WORK, TEARSTAINED. ON THE SUBWAY RIDE over, I'd tried to figure out why I was upset, who I was most upset with—my father or Max. I hadn't come to any conclusions.

"Do you think he knew?" Grace asked.

I sat on her gray five-thousand-dollar couch in Brooklyn, stroking the velvet arm, which was providing me with some small comfort. Grace handed me a huge glass of red wine and sat.

"What? That my father was testing him?" I asked. Was that what it was? A test? Or a show of power?

I'd left Max's office, gone straight back to my desk, printed out my resignation, put it into an envelope, and given it to Donna to deliver to Max. I didn't have a lot of personal items in the office and I'd managed to get them all into my work carryall.

I'd cried all the way to Brooklyn.

"No, do you think your father knew Max King was fucking his daughter?"

I lifted my head. "How could he? And anyway, why would he care?"

She shrugged. "I don't know. Fathers are protective over their daughters."

I snorted. "Yeah well, sperm donors aren't." I was pretty sure Charles Jayne hadn't had a parental instinct in his life.

"I just think it's a little strange that he accepted the lunch invitation and then didn't want you working on the account."

A lot of what Charles Jayne did didn't add up. He must have known JD Stanley was a big account and if he requested I was dropped from the team it would look bad on me. "He just doesn't want me anywhere near him." I dug my fingernail into the pile of the velvet.

Grace took a sip of her wine. "Maybe."

"Maybe?" I asked.

"It just feels like we're not seeing the whole picture."

Jesus, since when did Grace give my father the benefit of the doubt? She knew what an asshole he'd been over the years. "Are you taking his side?"

She twisted the stem of her glass between her fingers. "No, not at all. There is no side for me except yours. I'm just saying things don't add up."

I glugged down some wine, desperate for the liquid relaxation to do its magic.

"Okay, so your father's an asshole. Let's just take that as read. And, for whatever reason, he didn't want you working on his account." She rolled her lips together as if she was trying to stop herself from saying what came next. "I'm worried about how bothered you are by it. And that you resigned from a job you worked so hard for. Aren't you just letting your father control you?"

When the JD Stanley pitch had come up, I thought it would be an opportunity for me to finally be free of my father. "I just thought I had the upper hand this time. I was going to get my chance to press his nose up against the glass and show him what he'd been missing." I should have known better. I never had the upper hand as far as my father was concerned.

"I'm guessing he knew that and didn't want to see. Most assholes don't want to be reminded of their assholishness. They either reinvent reality so they're not assholes, or they avoid any situation where they could be reminded." Grace was talking from experience and suddenly I felt bad for being here and dumping all this on her. Her father had cheated on her mother more than once, and she always said afterward it was as if he'd used an imaginary chisel and gone through people's memories, re-carving history. "Your father's a powerful man and powerful men don't like to be wrong."

"But he was okay to go to lunch." I wiped a nonexistent drop of wine from the outside of my glass. Why had he agreed to lunch knowing I would be there and then had a problem with me working on the account?

Grace nodded. "He was probably curious, wanted to see if you'd forgiven him."

Lunch had been fine. Polite and professional. Had he really expected anything else?

"And he probably didn't give any thought to how you'd feel about it," Grace continued. "I'm sure he's like most men—too focused on themselves to worry about anyone else."

Selfish was exactly what my father was. When I was little and he didn't turn up when he said he would, I would pretend to my mom it was no big deal. I remember understanding he made her cry, a lot, and that she'd cry more if I was disappointed. So I learned early to mask my hurt and upset. But it was soon replaced by anger and frustration I wasn't so good at covering up.

I looked up from my glass to find Grace poised with a top up. "I'd be surprised if he was trying to sabotage your career," she said as the wine glugged into my glass. "I'm sure he could have stopped you from getting a job on Wall Street very easily if that's what he'd wanted to do. Did he tell Max to fire you?"

I shook my head. "I don't think so. Just said he didn't want me working on the account because he wanted to keep the personal and professional separate."

Maybe Grace was right and it had been less about my father trying to ruin me and more about him protecting himself. Tears welled in my eyes. I covered my face with my free hand in some kind of futile effort to stop them from falling.

If I wasn't so embarrassed by the fact my father hadn't wanted me working on the account just like he hadn't wanted me when I was born, things might be different. A regular client requesting a team change would have been bruising but I'd have gotten over it. My father requesting I didn't work on his account if we were on good terms may have been bearable, but it was the Max element that made it so humiliating. Somehow, having told him about my father, having confided in him, I found his decision to accept my father's wishes without question rusted the knife, made the cut deeper.

I'd wanted to work for Max King for as long as I could remember and I'd ruined it by sleeping with him.

"It's such a betrayal," I managed to choke out.

The cushions beside me dipped and I moved my hand as Grace took my wine from me. She grinned. "I'm sorry. I can't have you spill red wine over this beautiful couch. Let it out, have a good cry, but don't hold red wine while you're doing it."

I laughed, her concern over her couch breaking me out of my misery. "You're right. This couch is too good to spoil for a man. You pretend you don't like the finer things in life, my friend, but you can't help generations of breeding."

She took a sip of the wine she'd just taken from me. "I know. However hard I try, I can't help reverting back to type. I have such good taste."

I laughed. "You do. However much you fight it, you're always going to be a Park Avenue princess."

"There, you see? At least I can make you laugh with my ridiculous life choices." Grace shifted, sitting cross-legged on the couch facing me, giving me her full attention. "Speaking of ridiculous choices, tell me about the resigning thing."

"Max had a decision to make. He knew how I felt about my father and he didn't hesitate to pick him over me." I shook my head. "If he'd just been my boss, if I hadn't told him how my father had abandoned me, I might have been able to swallow getting kicked off the JD Stanley account. But the way he so easily chose business over me was just too much." It was as if he'd drawn a line in the sand and said my feelings would never be more important than his job.

"I didn't realize it was that serious between you two," she said.

"It's not serious." Perhaps it had become more serious than I'd realized.

"But serious enough that you want him to pick you over his job," Grace said. I didn't reply. I didn't know what to say. "What did he give as an excuse?" Grace asked.

"He just said that the client can pick the team."

Grace winced.

"Don't you dare say he's right." He wasn't right, was he? "It would be different if Max and I weren't fucking, but we are. Were. I'm not just his employee." I wasn't sure what we were to each other and I supposed it didn't matter anymore. But he'd owed me something. Some kind of loyalty. Hadn't he?

"I'm not sure you'd be quite this upset—so upset you handed in your notice—if it were just 'fucking'. You say it's not serious but it sounds like it is from your perspective. Do you have feelings for him?"

I scraped my hair back from my face as if it would help me see more clearly. Did I have feelings for him? "I feel like I want to punch him in the face; does that count?" I asked as Grace rubbed my back.

But I didn't want to punch Max, not really. I wasn't angry. I felt broken, as if I'd taken a right hook to my stomach. Somewhere along the road, I'd let him in, enjoyed being with him—I'd been happy, and not just when we had sex. I couldn't remember a time when that had been true of any of my other relationships. My father had ensured I grew up heartbroken, the scars of our relationship creating a barrier between me and other men. No one had ever broken through. No one except Max. It had just been sex—amazing sex—and then somewhere along the line, as he'd revealed himself to me, I'd been forced to do the same. He'd opened me up and I'd let myself care.

"I think maybe you feel more for him than you're admitting to yourself," Grace said.

Of course I had feelings for him.

Max was the only experience I'd had of being with a man where I'd not worked out how or when we would end before anything started. I knew I would leave my college boyfriend when we graduated. I knew the guy I saw occasionally at Berkeley would never leave Northern California and I'd never stay. I always saw the end before anything began. And that suited me. It meant I didn't get attached, didn't have any false expectations. With Max, I'd never seen the end and so I felt cheated of all the time we could have had together in the future. My expectations of him, of us, had been too high because they hadn't had limits.

I wanted so desperately for Max to have told my father if he didn't want me working on the account, Max didn't want his business. Finally, I wanted a man to put me first. Ahead of money, ahead of business. I wanted Max to stand up and claim me as my father never had.

I understood now my heart was closed to any happy futures. Shut down. Every man who came after this would always have limits.

I stood in Grace's closet, surrounded by her designer wardrobe I'd been pilfering since I arrived a little over a week ago. She might not wear them often, but she sure had a lot of beautiful clothes. I couldn't avoid going back to Manhattan any longer. I figured there was no running into Max if I went back on a Saturday. I needed to go back to my apartment.

"This is Gucci," I yelled from her bedroom, pulling out a black pencil skirt.

"Jesus, your voice carries three blocks. I think I prefer you mute."

I hadn't had much to say for the first few days of my stay at Grace's. It was as if the pain of walking away from my life had stolen my words. But after my third day in bed Grace had literally pulled me into the sitting room and forced me to watch TV and join in commentary on episode after episode of Real Housewives. Things got a little better after that and I was able to contain my gloom. But it was still there, lurking, waiting for me to be on my own so it could take over.

"Yeah, that skirt looks great with the YSL gray silk cami."

"I can't wear Gucci anything when I'm just packing up a few things and dragging a suitcase around on the subway." I wasn't sure how I was going to pay my rent, but something had stopped me giving notice on my apartment. I'd waited a long time to live in Manhattan and work at King & Associates—I just wasn't ready to let it all go yet. Reluctantly, I put the skirt back in the closet.

Grace appeared at the door to her closet and rested against the door frame. "You love me, right?"

I snapped my head around at her. When Grace started a sentence with that preface, I knew the follow-up wasn't something I wanted to hear.

I turned back to the racks of clothes. "I don't know, it depends what you're going to say next," I replied.

"Well, I was thinking that while you're in Manhattan, maybe you'd want to call your father."

I turned to look at her, completely confused. "And why would I want to do that?"

"To get some answers. Hear what he has to say."

"Why would I give him any of my time or energy?" Just because Grace seemed to be reconsidering her relationship with her parents and their money, didn't mean I had to.

"Honestly?" she asked. "Because I think you spend far too much of your time and energy on him. Everything you do seems to be a reaction to your father."

I looked up from the stack of T-shirts I was examining. "How can you say that? I haven't taken anything from him since college."

"You think ending up at King & Associates, working for the only place in town that didn't work for your father, had nothing to do with him? You walked out of a job you supposedly loved because of him."

"That wasn't about him, it was about Max," I replied. "You've got this all wrong."

She pushed off the door frame and stood in front of me, placing her hands on my shoulders. "It was about a business decision Max made regarding JD Stanley—your father's business. Despite your desire to avoid him, he's everywhere in your life, pushing you down one path or another, whether it's to avoid him or show him his mistakes." She released her hands and splayed out her fingers. "Aren't you exhausted with it?"

I was stunned. Was that what she thought? I sank to my knees, cross-legged. "You think I have some kind of warped obsession with my dad?"

Grace followed me to the floor. "Look, you're not Kathy Bates Misery obsessed, but yes, I think you let him consume too much of your life, your energy . . ." Grace paused. "Your happiness."

I looked up at her. I wanted to see doubt in her eyes but there was none. And I knew she did love me and I knew she wanted the best for me. "But he abandoned me and my mother. Fucked every woman in the tristate area. And all his sons work—"

"Look, I'm not saying you're wrong. I'm saying get some kind of closure so you can let it go. Don't let it rule your life. You're an adult."

"Just like that, let it go?" He was always going to be my father, and he was always going to be an asshole. I didn't see that changing.

"Well, clearly it's not that easy—we're not in a Disney musical—but maybe have a conversation with him. Tell him how you feel. I don't see how you've got anything to lose. This is ruining your life."

I snorted. "That's a little dramatic, isn't it?"

She shrugged. "Maybe I've got it wrong, but you're talking to me from the floor of my closet." She put her hands on her hips. "You're convinced your father is trying to ruin you. Well, you're letting him."

I lay back on the floor, needing to think. Was I letting my father run my life? By not taking his money I thought I was doing the opposite. And I'd done well in my career without him. I'd resigned because Max had put business before me. My father wasn't the issue there . . . Except it was JD Stanley's business we were talking about.

"I'm not saying your father isn't an asshole. He's not going to win father of the year anytime soon. And I understand that when you were little he let you down again and again." He had let me down. "And I'm not saying you have to have some kind of idyllic relationship. Just accept the reality of the situation and get on with your own life. I think a conversation with him might help."

She was right. Since I'd moved to New York, my thoughts of my father had gathered like waves heading for shore. Turns out they'd just hit the beach.

My obsession with King & Associates had genuinely been all about Max King. It had nothing to do with my father or the fact Max didn't work with JD Stanley. But part of me had always known going to business school had been about proving to him he was missing out on knowing me, and I was just as good as my half brothers. And Grace was right, part of the reason I'd resigned had been about my father not wanting me—the bruises he'd formed being pressed by someone else this time.

My disappointment at my father wasn't going anywhere. It floated around me like a bad smell, influencing me so subtly I didn't realize his hold over me. Grace was right; he had far too much power over my here and now.

"You have to deal with the root of the issue," Grace said. "My grandma always said, 'If you just chop the heads off of weeds, they come back.' So far, she's never been wrong."

Maybe if I just got it all out—raged at him—it would be like expelling poison and I'd be free. I had nothing to lose by confronting him, telling him how I was feeling—how he'd made me feel.

I jumped to my feet and scanned her racks of clothing. "Which one is the YSL vest?"

Even though I had no money, no job, and the fare would be something approaching the amount of a small car, I'd taken Grace's suggestion and grabbed a cab into Manhattan. I stepped onto the sidewalk, the heat almost unbearable, next to my father's Upper East Side brownstone.

I had no idea whether my father was in. Even if he was, he might have company or be busy. I probably should have called first, but I couldn't bear the idea he'd tell me no, and I was sure to chicken out if he suggested another time.

I walked up the stoop and rang the bell. Immediately footsteps scuffled behind the door.

"Hello?" My father's housekeeper squinted at me.

"Hi, Miriam, is my father home?"

"Harper? Good God, child, I've not seen you in years." She bundled me into the hallway. "You're looking too thin. Can I get you something to eat? The soup I'm making won't be ready for a few hours, but I roasted a chicken yesterday. I could make you a sandwich."

"Thank you, but I'm fine." I hadn't expected the warmth, the welcome, to be treated as if I were family. "It's nice to see you looking so well."

"Old, dear, that's how I look, but that's what I am." She began to make her way down the hall, beckoning me with her. "Let me call upstairs to his study."

I couldn't hear my father's reaction to my arrival, but the conversation was short and didn't seem to involve any cajoling to see me.

"You can go up, lovely. It's the second floor, first door on your right."

I smiled and took a deep breath. I was really doing this.

Climbing the stairs, I looked toward the top. My father stood there, looking down.

"Harper. How lovely to see you."

He acted as if it wasn't completely ridiculous for me to be here. I'd been to this house three, maybe four times in my entire life, and not once in the last five years. "Thanks for seeing me," I replied. I didn't quite know how to handle the welcome.

"Of course. I'm delighted." As I reached the top of the stairs he grasped me by my upper arms and kissed my cheek. "Did Miriam offer you something to eat or drink?"

I chuckled despite myself. "An entire roast dinner if I'd wanted, I think."

"Good, good. Come in."

We went into his office, a room in all pale blues and whites that reminded me of the ocean. It had been given a makeover since I'd been here last. I took a seat in the chair opposite his desk. He sat, then stood again. "Sorry, we shouldn't be across a desk like this. We can go downstairs. Or out in the garden. I didn't think."

He was nervous. I wasn't. I rarely saw him ruffled—he always acted as if everything was playing out exactly as he'd planned.

"I'm fine," I said, shaking my head. "Here's good."

He sat back down. "If you're sure. Miriam sent you up here because I'm not as good with the stairs since I injured my knee playing tennis last summer."

I couldn't ever remember my father being so open, sharing anything so personal with me before. "Are you okay?" I asked.

"Yes, yes, but I'm getting older and my body doesn't bounce back in the way it used to." He leaned back in his chair. "Anyway, it's very nice to see you." He nodded as if he were trying to convince himself. "We didn't really get to speak as much as I'd hoped at lunch. How are you? Are you enjoying being in New York?"

I felt as if I'd gone to the theater and during the intermission come back to my seat to find I was watching a completely different play. My father was talking to me as if I'd been away for the summer rather than absent from his life.

"Everything's good." I twisted my hands in my lap. "I imagine you're wondering why I'm here—"

"I don't blame you for King & Associates canceling our meeting, if that's what you think. I should never have asked for you to be replaced. I just thought it would be easier if . . ."

"What?" Easier? Easier for him maybe.

"But all's well that ends well. You're here."

The conversation wasn't going as I'd planned. I'd expected to ask him questions, for him to answer in half-truths and lies and I would call him on it. I had no idea what was going on. "I'm not following you. King & Associates canceled their meeting with you?"

"Yes, which is fine. We have excellent in-house resources."

Why would Max do that? JD Stanley could have made him considerably richer than he already was.

"Yesterday." His eyebrows pinched together. "You didn't know?"

Thoughts of Max canceling the pitch created a swirl of guilt in my stomach. Wasn't that what I'd wanted? I shook my head. I needed to focus on the here and now, not get distracted by thoughts of Max. "Can I ask you a question?"

My father looked a little uncomfortable but nodded.

"Why didn't you offer me a job at JD Stanley?"

There. It was out. And even if I didn't get an answer, I still felt a sense of relief from finally asking the question.

My father's mouth opened, but he didn't speak. He sighed and his head fell back on the chair. For a few awkward seconds we sat in silence before he finally said, "Look, I know I haven't been a very good father."

I'd never expected to hear those words. My stomach swooped and instinctively I glanced around for a trashcan, looking for something to throw up in. I'd opened a door and there was no closing it now—I'd lost control of this situation and felt as if I were tumbling down a rabbit hole.

"I never got it right with my kids when they were young. I didn't have much of a relationship with any of your mothers, and I always felt like a fraud whenever I spent time with any of you. It was easier to throw money at a situation and go about my day."

"A fraud?" I asked. Wasn't that really him simply saying he felt uncomfortable and so took the easy way out?

He raised an eyebrow. "No one could ever describe me as a family man, and your mother was a good person."

"I know." I didn't want him talking about my mother. "She did the best she could."

"Which was pretty damn good given the way you turned out. You're a beautiful, bright, accomplished woman. And I can take none of the credit."

We could both agree on that, but it was uncomfortable to hear it. I'd expected an argument, for him to justify what he'd done. Instead I was getting a mea culpa. I didn't know what to do with that.

Was he just telling me what I wanted to hear?

"It's a shitty excuse, but I guess I didn't feel I could do anything but make the situation worse. The best way I knew how to contribute was through money."

Did he know he'd also contributed to my insecurity, my pain, my lack of trust? He focused on what he gave rather than what he'd taken away.

"And I was young and I was working twenty hours a day and . . ." His eyes went wide. "You know. I liked the women. So I guess I felt like a hypocrite then, trying to play the family man."

"I guess the first time you got a girl pregnant that would make sense." My mother had been the first woman he got pregnant, but he should have learned his lesson.

He nodded. "You're right. I haven't just made mistakes in my life, I've repeated them. But I have to answer to my other children about their situation. I'm describing my reasons for acting the way I did with you."

"You haven't answered my question."

He sighed. "Why would I offer you a job when you so clearly held me in contempt? It was different with your brothers—they allowed me to make amends."

I laughed. "Right. So this is my fault." Typical. I'd expected him to shift the blame so I shouldn't be surprised.

"I'm not blaming you, but somehow I built a relationship with your brothers."

Jealousy tugged at me. Why had they ended up with a father?

"I'd hoped we would do the same, but while you were at college, you cut off all contact."

"And you threw money at the situation by setting up the trust?" I asked.

"I guess. I thought that at least if you were okay financially for the rest of your life then I didn't have that guilt to live with."

"So it wasn't because I'm a girl? Woman."

"What?" He chuckled, a look of surprise on his face. "Of course not. You made it clear you didn't want a relationship, and if I'm going to be completely honest, I didn't want a constant reminder of how I'd failed with you. It's hard knowing your kid hates you, sees you as some kind of monster. Even harder to know it's in some ways justified."

I couldn't speak. Had I let the lack of job offer fuel my resentment? Or had those feelings been there all along? "Is that why you told Max to drop me from the team?"

He took a deep breath. "Partly. But also because I couldn't engage a company for a large amount of money when my daughter was involved in the account." He held up his hand, indicating he hadn't finished. "I know I employ my sons, but I don't manage them, and their salaries are considerably less than what I would have spent with King & Associates." He swept his hand through his hair. "I should have mentioned something at lunch, or called you afterward. It was just that things were civil between us and I didn't want to ruin that."

He laughed and put his head in his hands. "It's like I lose all sense of judgment when it comes to you. I get things wrong however hard I try."

Everything he said made sense, but instead of feeling relieved or happy, I felt cheated. As if someone had stolen my justification for hating him. He'd fucked up, gotten it wrong. But the way he explained it, his actions no longer sounded malicious. He was either the best liar I'd ever come across, or he was just a flawed human being. Maybe there was a bit of both there. It was as if I'd been suffering a chronic pain for years and, now it had just disappeared, I'd forgotten who I was without it. My hatred had become such a part of me that without it, I didn't quite know what to do. Still, Grace was right; I felt lighter from talking to him.

"I never wanted to hurt you, but I just didn't know how to avoid it," he said.

I squinted, trying to rid my eyes of the forming tears. He had hurt me. Over and over. But I didn't think he was lying when he said it hadn't been intentional. I nodded. "I believe you."

He pinched the bridge of his nose. "I can't tell you—" He paused and just nodded. "I'd like a chance to do better, if that's something you'd be interested in? Maybe we could spend some time together, have dinner or something."

He was asking for a chance to make amends. Even now when I'd not spoken to him for years. He didn't blame me, didn't express any resentment—he was just sad and regretful and it neutralized my anger toward him.

I took a deep breath and stood. "I need a chance to digest this."

He stood, stuffed his hands in his pockets, and walked around his desk toward me, his gaze trailing the floor. "I understand." He thought I was giving him the brush-off, when really I was fighting against years of rejecting him before he could reject me.

"Maybe I can stay for a drink and a sandwich next time." My words pushed out of my dry throat but I was determined to speak them. I couldn't say it but I was sorry. I'd held on to the feelings I'd had as a child and given them adult importance and justification. And although those feelings hadn't just disappeared, I saw them for what they were—pointless and unhelpful. He'd been right when he said I'd seen him as a monster. I was old enough now to know that fear of monsters was as much about imagination as reality.

He lifted his head. "I would love that. You just decide when."

I turned and we headed out of his office.

"Maybe next weekend," I said.

"I would like that very much," he said, his voice cracking at the end.

As we got to the top of the stairs, I turned to him and smiled. "Save your knee—I'll see you on Saturday."

∽

"Oh, yes and one final thing," I said as I gave Grace a rundown on the conversation with my father. Good friend that she was, she'd handed me a glass of wine within ninety seconds of me walking through the door. "He said Max canceled his appointment."

Had Max done that for me? I tried to think of other possible motivations. I knew how much he wanted JD Stanley as a client.

"Wow." Grace's eyebrows disappeared into her bangs. "So now you can make up with Max."

I almost choked on my wine. "What are you talking about? Max is history," I said when I recovered. "I need to move on." The truth was, Max was never far from my mind. I wondered constantly about who he was with, what he was working on. I felt like an open wound, constantly being doused in vinegar. I did my best to not let it show. We hadn't known each other that long, and I felt stupid for taking it so hard.

Grace sighed. "I've known you a long time, Harper. You can't fool me."

"I don't know what you mean."

"If Max was history, you wouldn't have moved out of your apartment."

"I'm avoiding him because it's over." Part of the reason I hadn't turned on my phone was because I didn't want to find Max *hadn't* called or texted.

"No, you're avoiding him because you don't want it to be. First, you quit your job because he didn't choose you over a business deal," she said, holding up a finger. "Then you were practically catatonic for the first few days after you split and although you're moving around now, your neutral gear is still set to mope." She held up a second finger. "You won't turn your phone on because you're avoiding his messages." She held up a third finger. "My point is, he's the more handsome version of the best-looking man on the planet, and you are in love with him."

"In love with him?" I snorted. "Don't be ridiculous." This wasn't what love felt like. This was hurt, betrayal, anger. Wasn't it?

"And the fact that he pulled out of the JD Stanley pitch, well that's—"

"That's what? He should have done that to start with."

"Are you crazy? Max was right; the client gets to choose their team. If you two were just banging, he would have told you to suck it up. He clearly cares about you."

Had I expected too much from him? I'd felt so strongly for him; I'd just wanted him to feel the same.

"You were waiting for him to fail, to live down to who you thought your father was," Grace said.

I'd started off thinking Max King was an asshole but discovered someone very different was just below the surface, someone caring and generous and special. My heart squeezed as if it were stretching after a nap.

I missed him.

"He's not my father." But had I expected him to fail? Even looked for it?

"So turn on your phone. Actually, no, I'll do it." Grace scrambled to the kitchen. I'd left my phone on top of the refrigerator. I knew if I had it in my room at night, I'd be tempted to switch it on.

Grace wouldn't dare turn it on without my say so, would she?

Of course she would, and I didn't have the energy to argue. I was sick of missing him. I longed for Max's arms around me, his wise words telling me everything was going to be okay, for the way he didn't have to do anything but hold me to make me feel better. My stomach churned.

She tossed my beeping phone at me. "I guarantee you'll have a hundred messages and voicemails from him. Not many men can break through that invisible force field you have around your heart, my beautiful friend. Don't take it for granted. Make it right before it's too late."

chapter sixteen

Max

"You seem off," Scarlett said as she popped an olive into her mouth. She was supposed to be helping me prepare dinner, while Amanda and Violet hung out in the living room. Instead, Scarlett sat at the breakfast bar, drinking and watching me cook. "What's the matter with you?"

"You always think I'm off," I replied, but she was right. I hadn't slept well since Harper walked out of King & Associates ten days ago. She'd just disappeared. Our doorman hadn't seen her; she wasn't answering her phone. She could be in a ditch, or just ignoring me.

"True, but this is different. Tell your sister all about it. Is it work?" She gasped. "Have you become addicted to gambling? Lost all your money? Did you find out you have a horrible disease of the penis?"

I sighed. "Stop it. I'm just busy at the office." I started to slice the tomatoes, ignoring Scarlett. I was usually so good at hiding what I was feeling. Was my worry for Harper beginning to show?

"That's bullshit. I know busy-at-work off."

I glanced up. "It's nothing. A girl at work disappeared and I'm just a little concerned. That's all."

"What do you mean disappeared? Like kidnapped?"

I rolled my eyes. "You always assume the most dramatic scenario possible, don't you?"

She slipped off her stool and grabbed the wine from the refrigerator. "Well, if it's got you all somber and mopey with dark circles under your eyes, I'm assuming something really bad happened."

"I'm not somber and mopey," I snapped. "Harper resigned and I can't get ahold of her."

"Harper?" she asked.

I could tell from the tone in her voice and the smile she wore that I'd just let open the gates of Troy. Fuck. I should have kept my mouth shut.

"What's up?" Violet asked as she set her glass on the counter. "Are we eating soon? I'm famished."

"Harper resigned and Max can't get hold of her," Scarlett said, slowing her words, trying to convey meaning to Violet. She was an idiot if she didn't think I knew what she was doing.

"It's no big deal," I said. "Do you want a refill?" I asked Violet.

"Always. Where do you think she's gone?" Violet asked.

Her matter-of-fact tone flicked a switch. I was sick of keeping all this in.

I released the knife onto the chopping board. "I have no idea." I pushed the heels of my hands over my eyes. "I've called her a million times but she's just not answering. I can only hope she's mad and not, you know, hurting." I found it hard to even think she'd be in pain because of anything I'd done. What was worse was I couldn't do anything to make it right. That loss of power wasn't something I was used to or comfortable with. Since

Amanda, I'd worked hard to be the guy who had a solution—to everything. It was part of the reason I was so focused at work—I knew money solved a lot of problems.

I ignored the glance that passed between my sisters. I was too frustrated to care. I hadn't met any of Harper's friends, didn't know any of her hangouts. We'd existed in a perfect bubble together, and I was happy with that. Or had been. Now I just wish I'd known her better. Partly because I might know where she was, and partly because I realized now there was so much more to get to know. And I hated myself for fucking things up and missing out on it all.

"What did you do?" Scarlett asked.

"I fucked everything up. That's what I did. I tossed her off a big pitch and she quit." I explained everything that had happened with JD Stanley and that Charles Jayne was Harper's father. I barely paused for breath—it felt good to get it out. How I hadn't taken Harper's feelings into account when I told her she was off the team. Whenever clients made team change requests, I'd never had to concern myself with the feelings of the person receiving the news. It was just business. But Charles Jayne's decision to cut Harper was personal. And I should have realized that. The fact I'd accepted his ultimatum so easily made me feel uneasy—a little dirty. I was sure I didn't want to do business with a man who made such cold decisions in relation to his daughter. To me, Amanda would come ahead of business, my pride. Everything. I'd never not put her first. Charles Jayne wasn't a man to be trusted.

"I feel like you're missing an important part of the story," Scarlett said. "I'm not sure, but you kicking an employee off the team and her quitting wouldn't normally get you this ruffled."

I didn't know what to say. I'd never discussed women with my sisters. Never talked about heartache or discussed a fight with a girlfriend—because I'd never experienced any of those things. I picked up the bottle of Pinot Noir Violet had left sitting on the counter and topped up my wine, impatient to get the glass as full as possible.

"You like her?" Violet asked.

I nodded.

"Finally," Scarlett said, almost to herself.

"And was it reciprocated?" Violet asked.

I took a deep breath. Was it? Things had been good between us, I thought. "How could I tell?"

Violet's smile lit up her face as if she'd been waiting for this conversation her whole life. "Well, does she maintain eye contact with you? Does she—"

"Jesus, Violet, do you know our brother at all? The man's not a monk; he knows when women want him. He's asking how does he know if she has feelings. Am I right?" Scarlett asked.

I nodded. "Yes." This was excruciating. I was rarely in a position where Scarlett had more of a handle on the conversation than I did.

"So you were sleeping together?" Violet asked.

Scarlett slapped her hand on the counter. "Try to keep up."

"What?" Violet shrieked. "No one told me he was sleeping with her. You knew?"

"I suspected."

"You did not," I said. "You say that now, but you knew nothing."

"I could tell when I met her in the elevator that there was something between you two." Scarlett shrugged. "I have a sixth sense for these things. Anyway, let's get back to the fact that our brother has feelings for someone. I mean, this has never happened before. We need to stay focused. How long has the sex been going on?"

There was no point in suggesting I didn't want to talk about it now—that ship had sailed. And anyway, I did want to talk about it. I needed to know if there was anything I could do. I wanted a chance to tell Harper how I felt, that I wanted her back.

"It was casual; we didn't go out." Did she think it had been just sex? "I should have taken her on a date or something. I was planning to talk to her about what she wanted when she came up for Amanda's dance."

"What, so it was a series of booty calls?" Violet asked.

Is that what it had been? Not for me, but looking at it maybe that was all it had been for her. "I've never really done the dating thing," I admitted. "We live in the same building and I'm here so much of the time . . ." From the outside it did look like convenient sex. But for me, since she'd started at King & Associates, she'd had my attention like no other woman.

"Did you do things together? Cook? Hang out without the sex?" Violet asked.

I winced. "We got takeout, does that count?"

Apparently not, if my sisters' faces were anything to go by.

"We'd spend the evening together. Talk." Take a bath, although I wasn't admitting that to my sisters. I loved hearing her take on the world. She was ballsy mixed with a little bit of idealistic. It was a perfect combination.

"Well, that's good. And it was early days, right?"

"Yeah," I replied, but it had felt so good between us. When we were together it was as if I didn't want to rush forward to the next part because the space we were in was so good and I wanted to squeeze out every last drop.

"And she quit because you kicked her off the team pitching to her father?" Violet asked.

"Yes. Her father called and said he didn't want her involved in the account because he wanted to keep business and personal separate."

"And you thought that was fine because it's how you like to operate too?" Scarlett asked.

"Yeah. I saw him as a potential client asking for a simple team change, rather than a father who was not putting his daughter first."

"Honestly," Violet said, "that doesn't sound like anything you can't come back from."

"I pulled out of the pitch," I said.

"You did?" Scarlett asked. "Wow. Does she know?"

I shook my head. "No, I did it after I saw how upset she was and I realized how he just hadn't given a shit about her. If he was prepared to do that to his daughter, what would he do to a business partner?" It wasn't the first time I'd turned down a client because I didn't like their approach to business. I just wished I could explain to her that I understood I'd made the wrong call. "Now she's gone, just disappeared."

"You must really love this girl." Scarlett grinned. "I've never seen you like this."

"Quit the dramatics. I'm not saying I love her, I . . ." I was lost. In new territory with no map. "But if she won't speak to me, won't answer the phone or the door, what do I do?"

Scarlett tilted her head to the side. "Amanda!" she yelled.

"Don't say anything to her," I whispered.

"Just trust me" she said.

Amanda wandered in, her stare fixed on her phone. How she didn't break bones on a regular basis I had no idea. She never looked where she was going. "Put your phone down while you're walking. One day you're going to step out in front of a bus because you're fixating over Snapchat."

Amanda rolled her eyes but slipped her phone into her jeans pocket. "Is dinner ready? I'm hungry."

"Are you looking forward to the dance tomorrow?" Scarlett asked. I wasn't sure what she was up to, but I could tell she had a plan.

Amanda's eyes lit up. "Yes, it's going to be perfect. Callum finally asked me yesterday. I told him I was going stag. I don't need a man."

The King women shared a chorus of good for yous, absolutelys, and high fives. I could only hope it was the first step in a lifetime of celibacy for my daughter.

"And your dress is all set?" Scarlett asked.

Amanda slipped onto the barstool facing me. "Yes, you saw it right? The one Harper helped me pick out."

"Harper's the girl your dad works with who you like to hang out with?" Violet asked. Christ, they were playing tag team.

Amanda nodded, her eyes flickering from me to her two aunts. "You met her, right, Scarlett? She's so cool and pretty. Isn't she, Dad?"

The sound of Harper's name sped up my pulse. I smiled sadly. "Yes, she's very pretty."

"You'll get to meet her too, Violet. You're coming to help me get ready for the dance, right?"

Shit, how could I break it to my daughter that Harper wasn't going to make it?

"Of course. Wouldn't miss it for the world." My daughter was the only person who could get my sisters to do anything.

"I need to talk to you about Harper, sweetheart," I said.

"What? She doesn't need a ride from the station because she's driving."

What? I'd never talked to Harper about how she was getting to Connecticut.

"I'm not sure if she's still going to make it, peanut. But you'll have your aunts. And we can put your mother on Skype the entire time you're getting ready."

Amanda looked at me, her lips pursed. "What are you talking about? Of course Harper's going to make it. She said this morning that she'd be here by four. She's bringing her makeup."

My heart started to pound. Had I heard her right? Had Amanda been talking to Harper? I gripped the counter, trying to make sense of what she was saying.

"You spoke to her?" Scarlett asked.

"Of course I did. She's my friend." Amanda looked around at the three of us. "What's the matter with you guys? You're all acting weird."

Harper was coming here. I would get a chance to explain, tell her she was important to me. More than important. I wouldn't let her go until she'd heard my arguments, understood I was sorry. I wouldn't let her push me away. I was used to getting what I wanted and Harper Jayne would be no exception.

※

"Just because she's agreed to come and help Amanda doesn't mean she wants anything to do with me," I reminded my sister a little after three thirty in the afternoon. "You don't think this is a little bit much?" I looked around at the dining room, the table set with the china and glassware my mother had forced me to buy when I hit thirty and she decided I was finally an adult, despite having been a father for over a decade at that point.

"No, it's not too much," Scarlett said. "And anyway, what have you got to lose? Worst case scenario you're no worse off than you were before she walked in."

I had to keep reminding myself I knew how to go after what I wanted. I did it for a living. Winning Harper back had to be a possibility, didn't it?

"I polished all the silverware, just how Grandma King showed me," Amanda said, joining Scarlett and I at the table. She patted me on the back. "It looks good. She won't be able to resist your lasagna, Dad. It's the best."

I didn't have the heart to tell her I had no idea whether Harper would even hear me out.

I had to admit, the table looked nice, but something was missing. "We forgot the flowers," I said.

Amanda had helped me pick some from the garden that we could use as a centerpiece. I couldn't find a vase, so we'd improvised and used a water glass. Amanda disappeared to retrieve them

"So what, you guys are going to take Amanda and then I just turn around and ask Harper if she's hungry?" I asked Scarlett.

"Jesus, did you lose your balls somewhere along the line?" Scarlett asked. "You ask her if you can talk for a few minutes. Then you apologize and admit you're an idiot. See how she reacts—if you need to apologize again, do it and then tell her how you feel. Jesus, man, you run a multimillion-dollar company; it's not that hard."

This was much harder than anything I'd ever done, but she was right; I needed to find my balls. I'd tell Harper how I felt. Tell her we shouldn't let business get in the way.

It was going to be easy, right?

"You're not wearing that, are you?" Violet asked as she wandered in.

"Good point," Scarlett said. "Go put on your best jeans and a blue button down. The slogan T-shirt isn't working for you."

"Hey, this is vintage," I said.

"Go change," Violet said.

Did I have time for a shower? I looked at my watch and my stomach churned. Only twenty minutes until she'd be here. In my house. In the place I'd fantasied about fucking her. Harper was the only woman I'd ever wanted to bring here, into my home, into my life.

I bounded upstairs, taking the steps two at a time. I needed to run through what I wanted to say and I didn't want anyone disturbing me.

It was the most important pitch of my life and I hadn't rehearsed.

chapter seventeen

Harper

"WHAT DID YOU MAKE ME DO?" I YELLED INTO THE SPEAKER OF MY PHONE AS I pulled off the I-95. The GPS told me I was six minutes away. I hated driving, especially on routes I didn't know, and this was my first time in Connecticut. "This is a terrible idea."

"It's a great idea," Grace said. "And anyway, whatever happens, you've done the right thing by Amanda."

I'd promised Amanda I'd help her get ready for her dance and I wasn't about to let a fourteen-year-old girl down. I knew what it felt like to be disappointed by an adult, and I'd never knowingly inflict that feeling on someone else.

"What did you end up wearing?" Grace said. "Please tell me you put a skirt on. Men like skirts."

"I'm wearing shorts."

"That hot combination you do with the buttoned-up blouse and the casual, bordering on slutty shorts?"

I grinned, secretly pleased with the endorsement. "They're not slutty. Just short." Okay, they were a *little* bit slutty.

Amanda was only part of the reason I'd borrowed Grace's new car to drive to Connecticut. I wanted to see Max. To figure out whether the ache in my bones would ease when I saw him. To work out whether it was love or just regret that tugged at my heart.

Men before Max had always been a stop on the way to something else. I'd always seen the way out, never had both feet in. With Max I wasn't constantly seeking the exit. I'd been happy to be in the moment with him, share things, talk, enjoy just being together. My feelings for him had snuck up from behind me and only screamed *boo* when Max had already gone.

"Okay, well, you won't need it, but good luck."

How could she say that? There was a real possibility Max would be furious with me. I'd walked out of my job without giving any notice. I'd screamed at him in his office, then turned off my phone and ignored every one of his messages.

Worst of all, Max hadn't really done anything wrong when he'd agreed to take me off the team. Maybe he'd been a little insensitive, but my relationship with my father wasn't Max's battle to fight. It wasn't as if the only reason King & Associates had landed the pitch was because I worked there.

My stomach churned at the thought of no longer being an employee at King & Associates. I'd worked so hard to get there. But I wouldn't have any regrets. I'd met Max and whatever happened between us, I'd always be grateful for that. It had forced me to deal with my father. I'd thought King & Associates would help build my career, but really it had helped patch up my soul.

As I pulled up in front of the gray clapboard, two-story house, my nerves took hold. I didn't know the man who lived here. The place looked so . . . domestic. There was a field to one side, and what looked like a barn on the other. I counted four cars in the gravel driveway. Wow. Were they having a party?

I reached into the backseat and pulled out the sparkling cider I'd brought along with my makeup.

"Hey, Harper."

I climbed out and saw Amanda waving at me from the doorway. I smiled, unable to wave back because I had my hands full.

"Hey, how are you?" I called, looking up over the roof of the car. "Are you nervous?"

"Not nervous at all," she said as I locked the car. "Especially not now that you're here."

Voices grew louder as Amanda and I crossed the slate-floored entry. The home had a completely different feel from Max's office. Photographs of Amanda dotted the walls. The doors, frames, and ceiling beams were stained a warm honey and the space was large and airy with open doors leading out onto a pool area. As we headed toward the kitchen, Max came into view.

My ache for him disappeared, my body sagging with relief as if it had been starved of water and had finally found an oasis.

Aware of everyone around us, I avoided eye contact. If he was angry with me, I wasn't sure how I'd react.

"Harper," he said. "Come in. You're kind to come all this way. I'm sure I don't know what Amanda did to deserve it." He didn't sound in the least bit angry, so I looked up to find him grinning at me. I tried to cover my delight, nodding as I glanced behind him at two women looking at us.

His sister Scarlett I'd met before. Who was the other one? I knew Amanda's mother couldn't make it back from Europe. Was I too late? Had Max moved on? No, it must be Violet. She looked like Max and Amanda.

"Come on upstairs. We don't have long," Amanda said.

"You have two hours, which is plenty long enough to introduce Harper to your aunts," Max said.

I was sure my relief showed in my sharp exhale. Yes, aunts. "Hi," I said, offering a half wave. They both slipped off their barstools to greet me.

"I'm Scarlett—we met in the elevator," the blonde said as she pulled me into a hug as if I'd known her my whole life.

"I'm Violet, the youngest." Violet's hug was slightly less effusive but a little more familiar than I'd expected.

I got the distinct impression I'd been the subject of a discussion between the two of them.

"Can I get you something to drink?" Max asked.

I held up the cider. "I brought something." I glanced between Max and his daughter.

"You should know what to do when someone brings you a gift," Max said.

Amanda covered her mouth with both hands, then said, "I'm so sorry. That's really kind of you and you didn't have to."

She was such a sweet girl. "It's my total pleasure," I replied.

"Why don't you get into the shower? Violet can bring you some cider when she comes to do your hair."

Amanda raced upstairs, leaving me in the kitchen with Max and his two sisters. I'd expected to have Amanda as a buffer while I was here. And I didn't know whether Max's friendly veil would drop once she'd left the room. I took a breath. I could do this. Max deserved the humble pie I was about to dish up.

"I have the grown-up alternative to sparkling cider if you're interested?" he asked.

"What's that?" I couldn't help but smile. Not seeing him for so long, I'd forgotten the pull. Forgotten how every time I was around him, I wanted to touch him. And now that I was here I wanted to talk to him, apologize, ask him if it was too late to go back to how things had been between us.

"Champagne," he said with a grin. He didn't seem mad, but I'd seen him at the lunch with my father; he was great at making people feel comfortable. Was he just putting on an act?

"Did someone drop you on your head?" Scarlett asked. "I'm always asking for a glass of champagne."

Max shrugged. "What can I say, I'm not wasting champagne on my sister." He shot me a glance as he pulled out three glasses and set them on the counter.

Was he trying to impress me? I rolled my lips together, trying to hold back a grin at just the thought he might be.

"It's so nice of you to come out all the way from the city," Violet said, leaving the sentence a little unfinished. Did I look ridiculous coming all this way for a fourteen-year-old girl I barely knew? Did she know that although I genuinely wanted to make tonight special for Amanda, I wanted to see Max? I needed to apologize.

I glanced around, wanting to tell Max I'd come for him as much as I had for his daughter. "Amanda's a lovely girl and . . ." I shrugged, unable to get the words out quite yet.

"Well, I know that my brother is pleased you came."

My heart squeezed. Was Max pleased I was here? Because of Amanda or because he wanted to see me?

Max handed me a glass and as I took it from him our fingers brushed. I glanced up at him and he grinned. Should I pull him to one side and apologize now?

"Violet, Harper," Amanda called from upstairs. "I need my glam squad. I'm out of the shower."

I giggled. "Glam squad? She's fourteen, right?"

Max rolled his eyes. "Going on twenty-seven."

"Coming," I yelled, bending to pick up my bag. I hated to see overly made up teenagers, and I knew Max didn't want his daughter to look like the twenty-seven-year-old she thought she was, so alongside some bits of my makeup, I'd brought a tinted moisturizer and a glittery lip gloss. Add in a bit of mascara and I didn't think she'd need much else.

"I'll follow with the drinks," Max said pulling out a tray as Violet and I made our way upstairs. As we passed a table on the landing, I bent to look more closely at a wedding picture.

"Beautiful," I said to myself. Amanda, dressed as a flower girl, stood alongside a bride and groom I didn't recognize.

"Pandora and Jason's wedding," Max said from behind me.

He had his ex's wedding photo up in his house? "Wow, that's . . ." I wanted to say weird because it was, but it was also sweet and open hearted and all the things I knew Max to be.

"Pandora's beautiful," I said, turning to look over my shoulder at Max. He nodded as if it were just a statement of fact.

Amanda's room was everything I'd expected of a normal fourteen-year-old girl. A Pitch Perfect poster over her bed, a blue-and-white-striped bedspread, and full bookshelves running across the length of one wall. Despite the house being large, it was all about family. There were no airs or graces.

"How about a face mask while Violet dries your hair?" I suggested.

Amanda grinned. "That would be awesome."

Max set the tray down.

"Thanks, Dad. Make sure you put the oven on for the lasagna." She took a champagne glass from her father, who obviously wanted to make her feel special. "You'll love it, Harper. My dad's a great chef and pasta is his specialty."

It was sweet that she thought I was staying for dinner. I didn't need to set her straight. I'd pull Max to the side before he left to take Amanda and then when he'd had a chance to consider what I had to say, maybe he'd call. Hopefully he'd forgive me.

"Thank you, peanut, but I think I can handle the stove." He continued to speak but held my gaze and I couldn't look away. "And anyway, Harper hasn't agreed to stay for dinner yet."

My heart fluttered, suddenly beating twice as fast. He *wanted* me to stay for dinner. But I hadn't apologized yet.

"But she will, won't you, Harper? Keep my dad company while I'm at the dance?"

"Amanda," Max warned.

"Dad, ask her. She can't say yes until you do. Tell him, Violet."

"It may sound like my daughter is strong-arming me into this, which is the last thing I want you to think." He sighed, shaking his head at his sister and daughter. "And I really appreciate getting the opportunity to ask you in front of the two most interfering women on this planet." Max turned to look at me. "But I'd really like you to stay to dinner so we can talk and hopefully set things straight between us." He pushed his hands through his hair.

I tried to hide my grin. I wasn't sure what set things straight meant. I hoped at the very least it would mean we wouldn't hate each other. But a huge part of me really wanted more, more than I deserved. I wanted Max. I had to believe I wasn't too late.

"Lasagna's my favorite," I replied.

~

"Oh my God, I remember when she was born," Violet said as we came down the stairs after primping Amanda for as long as we could stretch out. "It seems like yesterday. And now . . ."

Max slung his phone on the counter and raised his eyebrows, instantly in the moment with his family despite whatever corporate emergency was bound to be causing him stress. "Is she ready?" he asked. He'd left us to primp and prime his daughter, but was clearly as invested in the event as the rest of us were.

I nodded. "She's coming."

Violet had put some waves in Amanda's hair, so it looked very natural falling over her shoulders. And although I'd spent a lot of time on her makeup, it could have been done in two minutes—it was just a little mascara and a touch of lip gloss. Hopefully Max would approve.

I watched Max as he gazed at his daughter coming down the stairs in the blue and silver dress we'd picked out. His eyes went glassy and he tilted his head. "Peanut, you look completely beautiful."

My heart squeezed. I wanted to reach out for him.

He walked toward her and she stepped back, putting her hands up to stop him from coming closer.

"You can't touch me; you'll ruin my hair or smudge my makeup."

He chuckled, bent down, and kissed the top of her head. "You're getting so tall. Are you going to FaceTime your mom?"

She shook her head. "She'll just get emotional. We took some photos. I'll send them tomorrow."

She might only be fourteen but worrying about her mother's feelings in a situation that was really all about her showed a great deal about her character. A personality that had been shaped in part by the man I'd so foolishly let go.

I hung back as Scarlett and Violet gathered their things and ushered Amanda out the door. Max followed, then stopped to lean against the doorway.

Before she got in the car, Amanda turned and waved. "Bye, Dad. Bye, Harper. Enjoy your date."

I got the impression Amanda would be very happy to see our dinner become something more than apology and air clearing and that gave me some hope she knew something of Max's intentions.

We watched them drive off until their taillights had completely disappeared.

"She's beautiful, Max," I said.

"She is. Thank you for being here, for helping her. I wanted this to be special; she's been so excited."

"It's been a total pleasure. You didn't want to go with them?" I asked as Max closed the door.

"Amanda wouldn't let me. I think she was concerned I'd kick Callum Ryder's ass given half a chance. And anyway, we have things to talk about," he replied. He held my gaze and my breathing hitched.

I had things to apologize for. "Max, I don't know what to say. I'm so sorry. I've been an idiot and selfish and I lost all judgment when it came to JD Stanley. You did nothing wrong . . ." My words were running together; I wanted to get them all out before he had a chance to say anything that would make it harder to get them out, wanted to make him see how I understood he'd done nothing wrong. I covered my face with my hands.

"I'm the one who's sorry." He removed my hands from my face and threaded his fingers through mine. "We were involved and I didn't think through the consequences of accepting your father's ultimatum. I have no experience mixing the personal and the professional, so I didn't think about you or your feelings. I should have."

"It wasn't as if we were serious, but if we had been . . ."

He squeezed my hands and heat travelled up my body. "Maybe I gave you the impression that it was just sex, but I'm not sure it was ever that for me. I want to take you out on dates, to have you here with me and Amanda. I want to talk and laugh and wake up together." He sighed and shook his head. "I thought we had time. I missed the bit where I told you how important you were to me. I told you I've had zero practice at this stuff."

My stomach twisted. "I *was* important?" Did that mean he'd moved on?

"Was and *are*," he said. "I'm just so sorry I screwed it up."

How was he making this so easy for me? I'd expected to have to try to convince him, talk him round.

It wasn't too late. I closed my eyes, trying to compose myself. "You didn't. We'd made no promises to each other, and my issues with my father aren't your battles to fight."

"I want your battles to be my battles," he replied.

The corners of my lips twitched. "You do?"

He nodded. "And I'm ready to make any promises you want. I want to be the man who deserves you. The man who will do anything for the woman he loves."

I swallowed. "Loves?" I stepped toward him until our bodies were almost touching.

He shrugged. "Yeah. I love you and I need you to know. And I want you to give me a chance. I'm going to get this wrong. A lot. I haven't had much practice—I'll need you to stick with me."

"Max, I've never trusted a man. I don't know how to be that woman." I'd never expected a relationship to work before, never needed it to. "You're going to have to be patient with me, but I promise I will do my best if you give me another chance."

"You can have a lifetime of chances," he said. "I can't think of anything I wouldn't forgive you for." His eyes were soft and I reached out and stroked his jaw. He was still breathtakingly handsome but somehow the photographs I'd seen of him before I knew him had never done him justice. They'd not seen what a beautiful soul he had, what a wonderful father he was.

I tilted my head to one side. "You know someone told me about this thing Michael Jordan once said." I released his hands and smoothed my palms up his chest, staring up at him. "He said, 'I've missed more than nine-thousand shots in my career and I've lost almost three-hundred games.'"

Max lifted an eyebrow.

I continued. "He said, 'I've failed over and over and over again in my life. And that is why I succeed.'"

I lifted my shoulder in a half shrug as he slid his hands around my waist. "Some guy I'm in love with told me about it. I think he'd say that we should keep trying until we win."

Max's grin made my stomach swoop. "Sounds like a smart guy." He paused, then said, "Sounds like a lucky guy." He pulled me closer and pressed his lips against mine. "I've missed you so much."

His tongue trailed along my lips before pushing in to find my tongue. I'd forgotten how urgent his mouth was, how passionate his kisses could be. With every second, my knees got weaker, my breaths got shorter, but I wanted more.

We separated, panting, our foreheads resting against each other. "I've missed you, too." I slid my arms around his neck. As he lifted me, I wrapped my legs around his waist.

"Lasagna will have to wait," he said as he carried me toward the stairs. "I've fantasized about having you in this house a million times. I've dreamt about bending you over on the kitchen counter and fucking you from behind, thought about laying you out on the dining table and making your pussy quiver with my tongue. But right now I'm going to make love to you in my bed."

When we got to the bedroom, I unwrapped myself from Max's body and pulled his shirt from his jeans, undoing the buttons keeping his skin from mine. I wanted time to take in where I was, to get to know more about Max, to hear stories of the black-and-white photographs that lined his bedroom walls and to understand why he'd chosen the huge mahogany four-poster bed. But his touch temporarily wiped all my questions from my head.

"These have been driving me crazy," he said, reaching under my shorts and cupping my ass.

"They had the desired effect then," I replied.

"Harper, you could turn up in a trash bag and it would work magic on me."

"I know that feeling," I said.

When we were both naked, we stood, staring into each other's eyes, Max cupping my face. "It's so good to have you here," he whispered. "I've missed your beautiful, soft skin." He smoothed his hands over my breasts, around my waist, and across my ass, "Your perfectly wet pussy." He dipped his hand between my legs and groaned. "I've missed this. Your sounds, your wetness."

My skin tightened and I shivered.

"I've got to be inside you. I'll take my time with you later, but I need to feel you around me. I need to be close."

It was what I needed, too.

He spun us around, then pushed me against the wall. Lifting my leg, he rubbed his tip along the length of my sex.

"Max, condom," I said, breathless and desperate.

He shook his head. "I just had my annual checks. I'm all good."

Oh. I hadn't slept with anyone but him since I'd last been tested. "Me too, and I'm on the pill."

I moaned as he pushed into me and stilled. "Good," he said.

"Max." I tightened my fingers around his arms. I needed him to wait a few seconds for me to adjust to him. After not having him for so long, in this position, he seemed to fill me more than usual.

He increased his rhythm. "I'm not going to be able to last long, and after I'm done, I'm going to have you on the bed, then in the shower. I'm going to be inside you for *hours*."

The thought of the relentless drive of his dick in and out of me chased my breath from my lungs.

"Once is never enough with you. I need you all the time, forever."

I felt as if I were cycling toward the top of a mountain, panting and moaning, desperate to get to the top. As Max thrust into me again, his dick reaching deep inside me, I found myself at the summit. I arched my back as I began to freewheel down the other side.

"I love you," I whispered into the wind.

Max was right behind me, grunting my name in my ear as he jabbed his hips into me so sharply it would have hurt if it weren't for the insulating effect of my orgasm. "I love you," he shouted out.

His skin was hot and sticky with exertion when I put my arms around him, pressing my breasts to his chest, hoping I could attach myself to him permanently. He lifted my ass and I wrapped my legs around him as he walked us toward the bed, still joined, him still inside me. He sat on the edge of the bed, my knees coming to rest on either side of him.

"Lie back," I said. His eyes looked dazed as he did what I said. "I wasn't too late," I mumbled as I began to move my hips, just slightly, enjoying the feel of him still inside me.

He reached toward my breasts, rubbing my nipples with his thumbs as he looked up. His touch melted me around my edges. I contracted my muscles, trying to stem the wetness his touch released.

He groaned, and slipped one hand down to my clit. "Too late?"

I wasn't sure I could get the words out to clarify. Already I wanted him again, wanted to make the climb up the mountain, even though I was still out of breath from my first trip.

"I was worried you'd be . . ." I gasped as he increased the pressure on my clit. "I was . . ." I couldn't speak or move while ribbons of pleasure unraveled over and through me. My brain didn't have capacity.

As if he understood, Max lifted his hips off the bed and I stilled, happy to sit on him, to be taken by him.

"Tell me what you were worried about," Max said, the muscles in his neck straining.

I pressed my palms against his chest. "That it was too late for us," I said.

He grabbed my hips and rolled me to my back. "Never," he said as he pushed into me. "Not ever."

It was just what I needed to hear. I reached up and traced my fingers over his eyebrows. "I love you." I couldn't stop repeating those words. I'd never said them to any man before. No one before Max had ever deserved them.

My orgasm crept up on me, pushing through my body like a tremor: silent, intense, and powerful.

"Oh God, your face when you come." Max growled and thrust again, erupting into me.

He rolled off me, then pulled me toward him.

"When I get my breath back I'm going to kiss every inch of your skin, then make you come with my tongue."

"We may run out of time." I fingered his hair. "I have to make my way back to the city."

He squeezed me tighter. "Stay. Don't ever leave."

I chuckled. "You're ridiculous."

"Maybe."

"Things feel a little different," I said. Perhaps because we were away from the city. Perhaps because I knew how painful losing him had been and knew I'd work hard never to make that mistake again. "I don't know why, I just—"

"I think it feels like the beginning of forever," he replied simply.

epilogue

Three months later
Max

"Come in," I barked without looking away from my laptop. I thought I was the last one in the office. I was keen to get this piece of work finished and get back to the apartment and get my girl naked, and I didn't really want any interruptions.

"I'm looking for the King of Wall Street," Harper said as she opened my door.

I pushed my chair back from my desk. "Hey, I thought I was meeting you back at the apartment."

She walked toward me, rounding my desk, trailing her hands over the papers stacked up on it. "I couldn't wait," she replied, placing her purse on the table by the window.

I swiveled my chair so I was facing her. "How was dinner with your father?" Harper and her dad had seen each other a couple of times in the last few months.

"It was good." At times I wondered whether or not it was worth the tears that often followed one of their meetings, but she assured me she was crying over their history not their future. If she wanted to try to build a relationship with her father, I was happy to support her in anything she did. "Nice actually. We're getting to know each other a bit better now." She leaned forward and unknotted my tie. "And I thought I'd come back here and make sure you were keeping focused." Gently, she pulled my tie from my neck and sat on my desk. "I remember how you used to tell me how you *weren't* so focused when I worked here," she said, pulling up her skirt a little, revealing more of her long, brown thighs.

"Yeah," I said, a little dazed by the woman in front of me. "It's better for the bottom line that you don't work here anymore."

"I agree," she said, pushing my chair around with her foot so I was facing her.

"I like your shoes," I said. They were the first pair I'd bought her from Jimmy Choo. I was becoming quite the regular customer. I'd never seen her wear them outside of the bedroom and they seemed a little much for dinner with her father.

She began unbuttoning her blouse. "I remember you saying you used to think about me . . ." She opened the cream silk, revealing her high, tight breasts. ". . . here." She leaned back. "On your desk."

Jesus. Blood rushed to my cock. I'd thought about little else while Harper worked at King & Associates. And despite us being together as a couple, I couldn't persuade Harper to come back to work for me. Perhaps it was better all round.

"Tell me what you used to think about." Her back arched and she slid her feet over my thighs.

I grabbed her legs and pushed them apart, her skirt riding up around her waist. Yes, this was just how I'd imagined her.

"Christ, Harper, you're not wearing underwear."

She tilted her head. "Is that what you imagined?"

I lifted her legs, putting them over my shoulders, and dipped my head. "Yeah, you making my desk all wet." I breathed over her pussy. She moaned, her pitch getting higher as I licked over her slit before slipping a thumb into her entrance. "I fantasized about making you come on this desk." I circled her clit with my tongue and she slid down onto her back as if admitting defeat, her fingers snaking through my hair. She'd come to get fucked in the office and she was about to get her wish.

Her moans got louder and louder as her pussy got wetter and wetter. For a brief moment I worried we'd be overheard, but fuck it, I was the boss and I could do what I wanted with the woman who I was going to be with for the rest of my life.

I fumbled with my fly, my erection straining almost painfully against my zipper. It sprung free and I fisted it in my hand. Eating her out here, making her crazy with my tongue, the lights of the city behind me, the wealth of Manhattan around us, made me feel like a king.

"I have to fuck you," I said, peeling her legs from around my neck and standing. I dropped my pants and plunged into her. Jesus, she was always so fucking tight. Her hands reached behind her for the edge of the desk as she tried to resist my thrusts pushing her off the other side. She was perfect. I circled my hands around her waist and pulled her onto me harder as she began to twist her hips. She was too close, too soon.

"I think you fantasized about this too," I said, slamming into her again and again.

She cried out. "Max." Her calling my name was always the starting pistol for my orgasm. I thrust harder and she screamed louder, "Max, Max, oh Jesus."

Just before I came I pulled out of her and pulled her up. "Lean over, I want to see that beautiful ass bent over my desk." If she wanted to give me my fantasy, I wanted the whole thing.

She grinned and spun around, her heels thrusting her firm, tight ass in the air. Her arms spread across the desk, my papers flying off the edges. "You want me like this?" she asked.

I responded by parting her legs slightly and thrusting into her again. My force pushed her further onto the desk and she curled her fingers around the edge as if hanging on for her life.

"Yes," I groaned. "This is how I wanted you, that first day you stepped into my office." She shuddered underneath me, the start of her orgasm stirring across her skin. "And how I've thought about you every day since."

"Max," she whimpered, lifting up her head with what energy she had left. "Please, God, Max." And she tightened and stilled and I allowed myself a final thrust before pouring into her and collapsing over her back.

We stayed there for a minute or so, panting, our clothes half hanging off us, sweaty and rumpled.

"Well, that was a nice surprise," I said as I stood up, fastening my pants.

Harper was still wobbly on her feet as she got up from the desk and I reached out to steady her. "I thought it was weird we'd never fucked here, given this was where it all began," she said and glanced around my office while doing up her blouse.

Bending forward, I gave her a kiss on the lips. "It doesn't have to be a one-time deal," I said. "I'm all for working late if this is the reward I get." I didn't work late in the office very often. I still only spent two nights a week in Manhattan and both those nights were always spent with Harper.

"You get plenty of rewards, my friend," she said, smoothing her hand over my chest.

I grabbed her wrist. "I want more."

She opened her mouth slightly and I could tell she had some sarcastic comeback and then changed her mind about sharing it with me. "More?" she asked.

I nodded. "For us, for you and me. I want us to be fucking on my desk when we're ninety and have been married sixty years and have four kids."

Harper took a step back. "What are you talking about?" She shook her head. "I'm not going anywhere."

"Do you promise?" I asked.

"Do I promise to fuck you on your desk when you're ninety?" she asked, laughing.

"Marry me, Harper." This wasn't what I had planned. I assumed we'd be together forever and I'd thought about proposing but I hadn't expected those words would leave my lips today.

My eyes flickered between hers and I circled my hands around her waist. "Marry me," I said again. "I can do the big proposal thing, another time, with a ring and a string quartet but just tell me now you'll say yes. I don't want to go another day without knowing you're going to be my wife."

She tilted her head and gave me a small smile. "Okay, but I get two proposals, right? This one and one with a ring?"

"Jesus, always so demanding."

She shrugged. "I'm just confirming what the offer was."

"Yeah, two proposals. And you agree to be my wife, have ten kids with me, and fuck me on my desk when I'm ninety."

"Sounds like a deal," she said and she wound her hand around my neck, pulling my mouth down to meet hers.

One Year Later
Harper

"**Holy crap,**" I shouted from the downstairs bathroom.

"I told you," Max yelled back.

I wandered back into the kitchen, clutching the pregnancy test. "We're going to need a bigger boat," I said.

Max grinned. He'd gotten me pregnant with Amy just over a year ago, the night we'd first fucked on his desk. It had happened several times since then. Pregnancy had made me hornier than usual.

"What are you talking about?" Amanda said as she lifted her little sister out of her bouncer and put her on her hip. "We don't have a boat."

As I reached Max, he put his arm around my neck and pulled me toward him, kissing me on the head. "Congratulations."

"What did you do to me?" I asked, shaking my head.

"What I do best," he said. "No doubt it's another girl, because I don't have enough women in my life."

"What are you talking about?" Amanda repeated, her eyes narrowed as she glanced between us.

"Harper's pregnant," Max announced.

"Again?" Amanda asked.

I grinned. "Again."

Amanda handed me Amy and hugged us both. "This is amazing. I wanted a sister for so long and now I'm going to lose count."

"You're going to *have* to marry me now," Max said.

"I don't see why. I told you there's no rush, and anyway, if you were serious, you'd propose properly. Like on one knee, with a ring. That was the deal. Remember, effort gets rewarded, Mr. King." I stood with my hands on my hips.

"Do you ever do as you're told?" he asked, rolling his eyes.

"Apparently, I get pregnant on demand. Does that count?"

"I do all the hard work as far as that's concerned." He grinned at me.

I rolled my eyes. "Oh really?"

"Now's the time, Harper."

"Max, I'm pregnant. Did you miss that? I'm not walking down the aisle knocked up."

"I really want to be bridesmaid," Amanda said. "In fact, I might just buy a dress and wear it around the house if you two don't get your act together."

"Mr. King." One of the guys from the catering company came from the pool area into the dining room. Thank God we had help today. We lived in a state of perpetual chaos on the best of days. Today we'd added to the fray, throwing a welcome home barbeque for Pandora and Jason. "We're set up and ready for whenever your guests arrive. I'm just going to start pouring some drinks."

I turned to Max. "Holy crap. That's another eighteen months without booze."

"Well, you'll be in good company," Max said, hugging me close, Amy grabbing at his hair.

Pandora and Jason were pregnant as well. It was the reason they were coming back to America. That and they missed Amanda.

"I'm not sure everyone at this party's going to fit," I mumbled. The party was just a family occasion but that list was growing by the day. Along with my mom, we were expecting Max's parents, Pandora's parents, Scarlett and her new boyfriend, Violet, Grace, and Jason's brother.

"I spoke to an architect last week," Max said, taking Amy. Max King was never short of female attention of any kind, so of course Amy was a daddy's girl.

"An architect?" I asked, opening the refrigerator. Now I had an explanation for that cheese craving; I was going to give in to it.

"You're right; we need a bigger space. I thought maybe we'd add a pool house, too, because we need live-in help." Max wandered out of the kitchen mid-conversation before I could tell him I was sure we could manage without anyone living in.

It was as if life was set to fast forward—Max and I living together, Amy, a second baby.

"Girls," Max called from the study.

I knocked the fridge door shut with my hip "What does he want?" I asked Amanda.

"I don't know, but let's go," she replied, bundling me toward the study.

"Do you smell that?" I asked. "And where's that music coming from?"

I opened the door to the study to find the room empty but the doors leading out onto the patio open, the white curtains lifting in the breeze.

"What's going on, Amanda?" I asked. She shrugged, nudging me toward the patio doors. As I stepped outside I saw Max right in front of me, on one knee, surrounded by every colored rose ever to exist. I glanced around. Flowers covered the ground and huge vases were scattered across the lawn, adding color wherever I looked. To my left was a cello player, and I instantly recognized the music as Bach's suites, the same piece Max had turned up to full volume the night we'd first slept together.

Amy was on her mat next to Max, looking up at me, grinning, her eyes a beautiful green, just like her father.

"What are you doing?" I asked. "How . . . when—" I turned to Amanda, whose grin told me she was clearly in on the whole setup.

"Well, wheffort's required, there's no excuse not to make things perfect," he said. "And I thought, the four of us here, together and now with number five on the way . . ." He took a deep breath. "I can't imagine anything more perfect than that."

He opened the red box he held, revealing a huge princess-cut diamond. "Harper, I've loved you from the very moment I laid eyes on you. You are already my heart, my soul, my family—and now I want the world to know. As the King of Wall Street, I need you to be my queen. Marry me."

I smiled. How could a girl say no to a proposal like that?

books by LOUISE BAY

Mr. Mayfair
International Player
Hollywood Scandal
Love Unexpected
Hopeful
The Empire State Series

Gentleman Series (each book is standalone with different main characters)
The Wrong Gentleman
The Ruthless Gentleman

The Royals Series (each book is standalone with different main characters)
The Earl of London
The British Knight
Duke of Manhattan
Park Avenue Prince
King of Wall Street

Nights Series (each book is standalone with different main characters)
Indigo Nights
Promised Nights
Parisian Nights

Faithful

Read more at www.louisebay.com